Arsène Lupin Complete Collection:

5 Books in 1:

Arsène Lupin, Gentleman-Burglar,
Arsène Lupin Vs Herlock Sholmes,
The Hollow Needle,
The Confessions Of Arsène Lupin,
The Golden Triangle.

Maurice Leblanc

TRANSLATED BY ALEXANDER TEXEIRA DA MATOS

CONTENTS

- CONTENTS 2
- BOOK ONE. Arsène Lupin, Gentleman-Burglar 1
  - I. THE ARREST OF ARSÈNE LUPIN 1
  - II. ARSÈNE LUPIN IN PRISON 6
  - III. THE ESCAPE OF ARSÈNE LUPIN 16
  - IV. THE MYSTERIOUS TRAVELLER 25
  - V. THE QUEEN'S NECKLACE 32
  - VI. THE SEVEN OF HEARTS 39
  - VII. MADAME IMBERT'S SAFE 55
  - VIII. THE BLACK PEARL 60
  - IX. HERLOCK SHOLMES ARRIVES TOO LATE 66
- BOOK TWO. ARSÈNE LUPIN VERSUS HERLOCK SHOLMES 78
  - I. LOTTERY TICKET NO. 514. 78
  - II. THE BLUE DIAMOND. 90
  - III. HERLOCK SHOLMES OPENS HOSTILITIES. 101
  - IV. LIGHT IN THE DARKNESS. 111
  - V. AN ABDUCTION. 121
  - VI. SECOND ARREST OF ARSÈNE LUPIN. 132
  - VII. THE SHIPWRECK. 157
- BOOK THREE. THE HOLLOW NEEDLE. FURTHER ADVENTURES OF ARSENE LUPIN 171
  - I. THE SHOT 171
  - II. ISIDORE BEAUTRELET, SIXTH-FORM SCHOOLBOY 182
  - III. THE CORPSE 193
  - IV. FACE TO FACE 203
  - V. ON THE TRACK 213
  - VI. AN HISTORIC SECRET 221
  - VII. THE TREATISE OF THE NEEDLE 229
  - VIII. FROM CAESAR TO LUPIN 239
  - IX. OPEN, SESAME! 245
  - X. THE TREASURES OF THE KINGS OF FRANCE 252
- BOOK FOUR. 265
- 813 265
  - I. THE TRAGEDY AT THE PALACE HOTEL 265
  - II. THE BLUE-EDGED LABEL 276
  - III. M. LENORMAND OPENS HIS CAMPAIGN 285
  - IV. PRINCE SERNINE AT WORK 293
  - V. M. LENORMAND AT WORK 309

   VI. M. LENORMAND SUCCUMBS 318

   VII. PARBURY-RIBEIRA-ALTENHEIM 329

   VIII. THE OLIVE-GREEN FROCK-COAT 341

   IX. "SANTÉ PALACE" 352

   X. LUPIN'S GREAT SCHEME 366

   XI. CHARLEMAGNE 372

   XII. THE EMPEROR'S LETTERS 380

   XIII. THE SEVEN SCOUNDRELS 394

   XIV. THE MAN IN BLACK 406

   XV. THE MAP OF EUROPE 416

   XVI. ARSÈNE LUPIN'S THREE MURDERS 426

   EPILOGUE: THE SUICIDE 437

BOOK FIVE. THE CRYSTAL STOPPER 441

   I. THE ARRESTS 441

   II. EIGHT FROM NINE LEAVES ONE 449

   III. THE HOME LIFE OF ALEXIS DAUBRECQ 458

   IV. THE CHIEF OF THE ENEMIES 466

   V. THE TWENTY-SEVEN 473

   VI. THE DEATH-SENTENCE 483

   VII. THE PROFILE OF NAPOLEON 493

   VIII. THE LOVERS' TOWER 501

   IX. IN THE DARK 508

   X. EXTRA-DRY? 517

   XI. THE CROSS OF LORRAINE 523

   XII. THE SCAFFOLD 533

   XIII. THE LAST BATTLE 539

[Handwritten note at top: Mingled Feeling of Pleasure & Fear — the perfect Combination of any Seduction]

BOOK ONE.
ARSÈNE LUPIN, GENTLEMAN-BURGLAR

I. THE ARREST OF ARSÈNE LUPIN

It was a strange ending to a voyage that had commenced in a most auspicious manner. The transatlantic steamship `La Provence' was a swift and comfortable vessel, under the command of a most affable man. The passengers constituted a select and delightful society. The charm of new acquaintances and improvised amusements served to make the time pass agreeably. We enjoyed the pleasant sensation of being separated from the world, living, as it were, upon an unknown island, and consequently obliged to be sociable with each other.

Have you ever stopped to consider how much originality and spontaneity emanate from these various individuals who, on the preceding evening, did not even know each other, and who are now, for several days, condemned to lead a life of extreme intimacy, jointly defying the anger of the ocean, the terrible onslaught of the waves, the violence of the tempest and the agonizing monotony of the calm and sleepy water? Such a life becomes a sort of tragic existence, with its storms and its grandeurs, its monotony and its diversity; and that is why, perhaps, we embark upon that short voyage with mingled feelings of pleasure and fear.

But, during the past few years, a new sensation had been added to the life of the transatlantic traveler. The little floating island is now attached to the world from which it was once quite free. A bond united them, even in the very heart of the watery wastes of the Atlantic. That bond is the wireless telegraph, by means of which we receive news in the most mysterious manner. We know full well that the message is not transported by the medium of a hollow wire. No, the mystery is even more inexplicable, more romantic, and we must have recourse to the wings of the air in order to explain this new miracle. During the first day of the voyage, we felt that we were being followed, escorted, preceded even, by that distant voice, which, from time to time, whispered to one of us a few words from the receding world. Two friends spoke to me. Ten, twenty others sent gay or somber words of parting to other passengers.

On the second day, at a distance of five hundred miles from the French coast, in the midst of a violent storm, we received the following message by means of the wireless telegraph:

"Arsène Lupin is on your vessel, first cabin, blonde hair, wound right fore-arm, traveling alone under name of R........"

At that moment, a terrible flash of lightning rent the stormy skies. The electric waves were interrupted. The remainder of the dispatch never reached us. Of the name under which Arsène Lupin was concealing himself, we knew only the initial.

If the news had been of some other character, I have no doubt that the secret would have been carefully guarded by the telegraphic operator as well as by the officers of the vessel. But it was one of those events calculated to escape from the most rigorous discretion. The same day, no one knew how, the incident became a matter of current gossip and every passenger was aware that the famous Arsène Lupin was hiding in our midst.

Arsène Lupin in our midst! the irresponsible burglar whose exploits had been narrated in all the newspapers during the past few months! the mysterious individual with whom Ganimard, our shrewdest detective, had been engaged in an implacable conflict amidst interesting and picturesque surroundings. Arsène Lupin, the eccentric gentleman who operates only in the chateaux and salons, and who, one night, entered the residence of Baron Schormann, but emerged empty-handed, leaving, however, his card on which he had scribbled these words: "Arsène Lupin, gentleman-burglar, will return when the furniture is genuine." Arsène Lupin, the man of a thousand disguises: in turn a chauffer, detective, bookmaker, Russian physician, Spanish bull-fighter, commercial traveler, robust youth, or decrepit old man.

Then consider this startling situation: Arsène Lupin was wandering about within the limited bounds of a transatlantic steamer; in that very small corner of the world, in that dining saloon, in that smoking room, in

1

that music room! Arsène Lupin was, perhaps, this gentleman.... or that one.... my neighbor at the table.... the sharer of my stateroom....

"And this condition of affairs will last for five days!" exclaimed Miss Nelly Underdown, next morning. "It is unbearable! I hope he will be arrested."

Then, addressing me, she added:

"And you, Monsieur d'Andrézy, you are on intimate terms with the captain; surely you know something?"

I should have been delighted had I possessed any information that would interest Miss Nelly. She was one of those magnificent creatures who inevitably attract attention in every assembly. Wealth and beauty form an irresistible combination, and Nelly possessed both.

Educated in Paris under the care of a French mother, she was now going to visit her father, the millionaire Underdown of Chicago. She was accompanied by one of her friends, Lady Jerland.

At first, I had decided to open a flirtation with her; but, in the rapidly growing intimacy of the voyage, I was soon impressed by her charming manner and my feelings became too deep and reverential for a mere flirtation. Moreover, she accepted my attentions with a certain degree of favor. She condescended to laugh at my witticisms and display an interest in my stories. Yet I felt that I had a rival in the person of a young man with quiet and refined tastes; and it struck me, at times, that she preferred his taciturn humor to my Parisian frivolity. He formed one in the circle of admirers that surrounded Miss Nelly at the time she addressed to me the foregoing question. We were all comfortably seated in our deck-chairs. The storm of the preceding evening had cleared the sky. The weather was now delightful.

"I have no definite knowledge, mademoiselle," I replied, "but can not we, ourselves, investigate the mystery quite as well as the detective Ganimard, the personal enemy of Arsène Lupin?"

"Oh! oh! you are progressing very fast, monsieur."

"Not at all, mademoiselle. In the first place, let me ask, do you find the problem a complicated one?"

"Very complicated."

"Have you forgotten the key we hold for the solution to the problem?"

"What key?"

"In the first place, Lupin calls himself Monsieur R————-."

"Rather vague information," she replied.

"Secondly, he is traveling alone."

"Does that help you?" she asked.

"Thirdly, he is blonde."

"Well?"

"Then we have only to peruse the passenger-list, and proceed by process of elimination."

I had that list in my pocket. I took it out and glanced through it. Then I remarked:

"I find that there are only thirteen men on the passenger-list whose names begin with the letter R."

"Only thirteen?"

"Yes, in the first cabin. And of those thirteen, I find that nine of them are accompanied by women, children or servants. That leaves only four who are traveling alone. First, the Marquis de Raverdan————"

"Secretary to the American Ambassador," interrupted Miss Nelly. "I know him."

"Major Rawson," I continued.

"He is my uncle," some one said.

"Mon. Rivolta."

"Here!" exclaimed an Italian, whose face was concealed beneath a heavy black beard.

Miss Nelly burst into laughter, and exclaimed: "That gentleman can scarcely be called a blonde."

"Very well, then," I said, "we are forced to the conclusion that the guilty party is the last one on the list."

"What is his name?"

"Mon. Rozaine. Does anyone know him?"

No one answered. But Miss Nelly turned to the taciturn young man, whose attentions to her had annoyed me, and said:

"Well, Monsieur Rozaine, why do you not answer?"

All eyes were now turned upon him. He was a blonde. I must confess that I myself felt a shock of surprise, and the profound silence that followed her question indicated that the others present also viewed the situation with a feeling of sudden alarm. However, the idea was an absurd one, because the gentleman in question presented an air of the most perfect innocence.

"Why do I not answer?" he said. "Because, considering my name, my position as a solitary traveler and the color of my hair, I have already reached the same conclusion, and now think that I should be arrested."

He presented a strange appearance as he uttered these words. His thin lips were drawn closer than usual and his face was ghastly pale, whilst his eyes were streaked with blood. Of course, he was joking, yet his appearance and attitude impressed us strangely.

"But you have not the wound?" said Miss Nelly, naively.

"That is true," he replied, "I lack the wound."

Then he pulled up his sleeve, removing his cuff, and showed us his arm. But that action did not deceive me. He had shown us his left arm, and I was on the point of calling his attention to the fact, when another incident diverted our attention. Lady Jerland, Miss Nelly's friend, came running towards us in a state of great excitement, exclaiming:

"My jewels, my pearls! Some one has stolen them all!"

No, they were not all gone, as we soon found out. The thief had taken only part of them; a very curious thing. Of the diamond sunbursts, jeweled pendants, bracelets and necklaces, the thief had taken, not the largest but the finest and most valuable stones. The mountings were lying upon the table. I saw them there, despoiled of their jewels, like flowers from which the beautiful colored petals had been ruthlessly plucked. And this theft must have been committed at the time Lady Jerland was taking her tea; in broad daylight, in a stateroom opening on a much frequented corridor; moreover, the thief had been obliged to force open the door of the stateroom, search for the jewel-case, which was hidden at the bottom of a hat-box, open it, select his booty and remove it from the mountings.

Of course, all the passengers instantly reached the same conclusion; it was the work of Arsène Lupin.

That day, at the dinner table, the seats to the right and left of Rozaine remained vacant; and, during the evening, it was rumored that the captain had placed him under arrest, which information produced a feeling of safety and relief. We breathed once more. That evening, we resumed our games and dances. Miss Nelly, especially, displayed a spirit of thoughtless gayety which convinced me that if Rozaine's attentions had been agreeable to her in the beginning, she had already forgotten them. Her charm and good-humor completed my conquest. At midnight, under a bright moon, I declared my devotion with an ardor that did not seem to displease her.

But, next day, to our general amazement, Rozaine was at liberty. We learned that the evidence against him was not sufficient. He had produced documents that were perfectly regular, which showed that he was the son of a wealthy merchant of Bordeaux. Besides, his arms did not bear the slightest trace of a wound.

"Documents! Certificates of birth!" exclaimed the enemies of Rozaine, "of course, Arsène Lupin will furnish you as many as you desire. And as to the wound, he never had it, or he has removed it."

Then it was proven that, at the time of the theft, Rozaine was promenading on the deck. To which fact, his enemies replied that a man like Arsène Lupin could commit a crime without being actually present. And then, apart from all other circumstances, there remained one point which even the most skeptical could not answer: Who except Rozaine, was traveling alone, was a blonde, and bore a name beginning with R? To whom did the telegram point, if it were not Rozaine?

And when Rozaine, a few minutes before breakfast, came boldly toward our group, Miss Nelly and Lady Jerland arose and walked away.

An hour later, a manuscript circular was passed from hand to hand amongst the sailors, the stewards, and the passengers of all classes. It announced that Mon. Louis Rozaine offered a reward of ten thousand francs for the discovery of Arsène Lupin or other person in possession of the stolen jewels.

"And if no one assists me, I will unmask the scoundrel myself," declared Rozaine.

Rozaine against Arsène Lupin, or rather, according to current opinion, Arsène Lupin himself against Arsène Lupin; the contest promised to be interesting.

Nothing developed during the next two days. We saw Rozaine wandering about, day and night, searching, questioning, investigating. The captain, also, displayed commendable activity. He caused the vessel to be searched from stern to stern; ransacked every stateroom under the plausible theory that the jewels might be concealed anywhere, except in the thief's own room.

"I suppose they will find out something soon," remarked Miss Nelly to me. "He may be a wizard, but he cannot make diamonds and pearls become invisible."

"Certainly not," I replied, "but he should examine the lining of our hats and vests and everything we carry with us."

Then, exhibiting my Kodak, a 9x12 with which I had been photographing her in various poses, I added: "In an apparatus no larger than that, a person could hide all of Lady Jerland's jewels. He could pretend to take pictures and no one would suspect the game."

"But I have heard it said that every thief leaves some clue behind him."

"That may be generally true," I replied, "but there is one exception: Arsène Lupin."

"Why?"

"Because he concentrates his thoughts not only on the theft, but on all the circumstances connected with it that could serve as a clue to his identity."

"A few days ago, you were more confident."

"Yes, but since I have seen him at work."

"And what do you think about it now?" she asked.

"Well, in my opinion, we are wasting our time."

And, as a matter of fact, the investigation had produced no result. But, in the meantime, the captain's watch had been stolen. He was furious. He quickened his efforts and watched Rozaine more closely than before. But, on the following day, the watch was found in the second officer's collar box.

This incident caused considerable astonishment, and displayed the humorous side of Arsène Lupin, burglar though he was, but dilettante as well. He combined business with pleasure. He reminded us of the author who almost died in a fit of laughter provoked by his own play. Certainly, he was an artist in his particular line of work, and whenever I saw Rozaine, gloomy and reserved, and thought of the double role that he was playing, I accorded him a certain measure of admiration.

On the following evening, the officer on deck duty heard groans emanating from the darkest corner of the ship. He approached and found a man lying there, his head enveloped in a thick gray scarf and his hands tied together with a heavy cord. It was Rozaine. He had been assaulted, thrown down and robbed. A card, pinned to his coat, bore these words: "Arsène Lupin accepts with pleasure the ten thousand francs offered by Mon. Rozaine." As a matter of fact, the stolen pocket-book contained twenty thousand francs.

Of course, some accused the unfortunate man of having simulated this attack on himself. But, apart from the fact that he could not have bound himself in that manner, it was established that the writing on the card was entirely different from that of Rozaine, but, on the contrary, resembled the handwriting of Arsène Lupin as it was reproduced in an old newspaper found on board.

Thus it appeared that Rozaine was not Arsène Lupin; but was Rozaine, the son of a Bordeaux merchant. And the presence of Arsène Lupin was once more affirmed, and that in a most alarming manner.

Such was the state of terror amongst the passengers that none would remain alone in a stateroom or wander singly in unfrequented parts of the vessel. We clung together as a matter of safety. And yet the most intimate acquaintances were estranged by a mutual feeling of distrust. Arsène Lupin was, now, anybody and everybody. Our excited imaginations attributed to him miraculous and unlimited power. We supposed him capable of assuming the most unexpected disguises; of being, by turns, the highly respectable Major Rawson or the noble Marquis de Raverdan, or even—for we no longer stopped with the accusing letter of R—or even such or such a person well known to all of us, and having wife, children and servants.

The first wireless dispatches from America brought no news; at least, the captain did not communicate any to us. The silence was not reassuring.

Our last day on the steamer seemed interminable. We lived in constant fear of some disaster. This time, it would not be a simple theft or a comparatively harmless assault; it would be a crime, a murder. No one imagined that Arsène Lupin would confine himself to those two trifling offenses. Absolute master of the ship, the authorities powerless, he could do whatever he pleased; our property and lives were at his mercy.

Yet those were delightful hours for me, since they secured to me the confidence of Miss Nelly. Deeply moved by those startling events and being of a highly nervous nature, she spontaneously sought at my side a protection and security that I was pleased to give her. Inwardly, I blessed Arsène Lupin. Had he not been the means of bringing me and Miss Nelly closer to each other? Thanks to him, I could now indulge in delicious dreams of love and happiness—dreams that, I felt, were not unwelcome to Miss Nelly. Her smiling eyes authorized me to make them; the softness of her voice bade me hope.

As we approached the American shore, the active search for the thief was apparently abandoned, and we were anxiously awaiting the supreme moment in which the mysterious enigma would be explained. Who was Arsène Lupin? Under what name, under what disguise was the famous Arsène Lupin concealing himself? And, at last, that supreme moment arrived. If I live one hundred years, I shall not forget the slightest details of it.

"How pale you are, Miss Nelly," I said to my companion, as she leaned upon my arm, almost fainting.

"And you!" she replied, "ah! you are so changed."

"Just think! this is a most exciting moment, and I am delighted to spend it with you, Miss Nelly. I hope that your memory will sometimes revert——"

But she was not listening. She was nervous and excited. The gangway was placed in position, but, before we could use it, the uniformed customs officers came on board. Miss Nelly murmured:

"I shouldn't be surprised to hear that Arsène Lupin escaped from the vessel during the voyage."

"Perhaps he preferred death to dishonor, and plunged into the Atlantic rather than be arrested."

"Oh, do not laugh," she said.

Suddenly I started, and, in answer to her question, I said:

"Do you see that little old man standing at the bottom of the gangway?"

"With an umbrella and an olive-green coat?"

"It is Ganimard."

"Ganimard?"

"Yes, the celebrated detective who has sworn to capture Arsène Lupin. Ah! I can understand now why we did not receive any news from this side of the Atlantic. Ganimard was here! and he always keeps his business secret."

"Then you think he will arrest Arsène Lupin?"

"Who can tell? The unexpected always happens when Arsène Lupin is concerned in the affair."

"Oh!" she exclaimed, with that morbid curiosity peculiar to women, "I should like to see him arrested."

"You will have to be patient. No doubt, Arsène Lupin has already seen his enemy and will not be in a hurry to leave the steamer."

The passengers were now leaving the steamer. Leaning on his umbrella, with an air of careless indifference, Ganimard appeared to be paying no attention to the crowd that was hurrying down the gangway. The Marquis de Raverdan, Major Rawson, the Italian Rivolta, and many others had already left the vessel before Rozaine appeared. Poor Rozaine!

"Perhaps it is he, after all," said Miss Nelly to me. "What do you think?"

"I think it would be very interesting to have Ganimard and Rozaine in the same picture. You take the camera. I am loaded down."

I gave her the camera, but too late for her to use it. Rozaine was already passing the detective. An American officer, standing behind Ganimard, leaned forward and whispered in his ear. The French detective shrugged his shoulders and Rozaine passed on. Then, my God, who was Arsène Lupin?

"Yes," said Miss Nelly, aloud, "who can it be?"

Not more than twenty people now remained on board. She scrutinized them one by one, fearful that Arsène Lupin was not amongst them.

"We cannot wait much longer," I said to her.

She started toward the gangway. I followed. But we had not taken ten steps when Ganimard barred our passage.

"Well, what is it?" I exclaimed.

"One moment, monsieur. What's your hurry?"

"I am escorting mademoiselle."

"One moment," he repeated, in a tone of authority. Then, gazing into my eyes, he said:

"Arsène Lupin, is it not?"

I laughed, and replied: "No, simply Bernard d'Andrézy."

"Bernard d'Andrézy died in Macedonia three years ago."

"If Bernard d'Andrézy were dead, I should not be here. But you are mistaken. Here are my papers."

"They are his; and I can tell you exactly how they came into your possession."

"You are a fool!" I exclaimed. "Arsène Lupin sailed under the name of R——-"

"Yes, another of your tricks; a false scent that deceived them at Havre. You play a good game, my boy, but this time luck is against you."

I hesitated a moment. Then he hit me a sharp blow on the right arm, which caused me to utter a cry of pain. He had struck the wound, yet unhealed, referred to in the telegram.

I was obliged to surrender. There was no alternative. I turned to Miss Nelly, who had heard everything. Our eyes met; then she glanced at the Kodak I had placed in her hands, and made a gesture that conveyed to me the impression that she understood everything. Yes, there, between the narrow folds of black leather, in the hollow centre of the small object that I had taken the precaution to place in her hands before Ganimard arrested me, it was there I had deposited Rozaine's twenty thousand francs and Lady Jerland's pearls and diamonds.

Oh! I pledge my oath that, at that solemn moment, when I was in the grasp of Ganimard and his two assistants, I was perfectly indifferent to everything, to my arrest, the hostility of the people, everything except this one question: what will Miss Nelly do with the things I had confided to her?

In the absence of that material and conclusive proof, I had nothing to fear; but would Miss Nelly decide to furnish that proof? Would she betray me? Would she act the part of an enemy who cannot forgive, or that of a woman whose scorn is softened by feelings of indulgence and involuntary sympathy?

She passed in front of me. I said nothing, but bowed very low. Mingled with the other passengers, she advanced to the gangway with my Kodak in her hand. It occurred to me that she would not dare to expose me publicly, but she might do so when she reached a more private place. However, when she had passed only a few feet down the gangway, with a movement of simulated awkwardness, she let the camera fall into the water between the vessel and the pier. Then she walked down the gangway, and was quickly lost to sight in the crowd. She had passed out of my life forever.

For a moment, I stood motionless. Then, to Ganimard's great astonishment, I muttered:

"What a pity that I am not an honest man!"

Such was the story of his arrest as narrated to me by Arsène Lupin himself. The various incidents, which I shall record in writing at a later day, have established between us certain ties.... shall I say of friendship? Yes, I venture to believe that Arsène Lupin honors me with his friendship, and that it is through friendship that he occasionally calls on me, and brings, into the silence of my library, his youthful exuberance of spirits, the contagion of his enthusiasm, and the mirth of a man for whom destiny has naught but favors and smiles.

His portrait? How can I describe him? I have seen him twenty times and each time he was a different person; even he himself said to me on one occasion: "I no longer know who I am. I cannot recognize myself in the mirror." Certainly, he was a great actor, and possessed a marvelous faculty for disguising himself. Without the slightest effort, he could adopt the voice, gestures and mannerisms of another person.

"Why," said he, "why should I retain a definite form and feature? Why not avoid the danger of a personality that is ever the same? My actions will serve to identify me."

Then he added, with a touch of pride:

"So much the better if no one can ever say with absolute certainty: There is Arsène Lupin! The essential point is that the public may be able to refer to my work and say, without fear of mistake: Arsène Lupin did that!"

II. ARSÈNE LUPIN IN PRISON

There is no tourist worthy of the name who does not know the banks of the Seine, and has not noticed, in passing, the little feudal castle of the Malaquis, built upon a rock in the centre of the river. An arched bridge connects it with the shore. All around it, the calm waters of the great river play peacefully amongst the reeds, and the wagtails flutter over the moist crests of the stones.

The history of the Malaquis castle is stormy like its name, harsh like its outlines. It has passed through a long series of combats, sieges, assaults, rapines and massacres. A recital of the crimes that have been committed there would cause the stoutest heart to tremble. There are many mysterious legends connected with the castle, and they tell us of a famous subterranean tunnel that formerly led to the abbey of Jumieges and to the manor of Agnes Sorel, mistress of Charles VII.

In that ancient habitation of heroes and brigands, the Baron Nathan Cahorn now lived; or Baron Satan as he was formerly called on the Bourse, where he had acquired a fortune with incredible rapidity. The lords of Malaquis, absolutely ruined, had been obliged to sell the ancient castle at a great sacrifice. It contained an admirable collection of furniture, pictures, wood carvings, and faience. The Baron lived there alone, attended by three old servants. No one ever enters the place. No one had ever beheld the three Rubens that he possessed, his two Watteau, his Jean Goujon pulpit, and the many other treasures that he had acquired by a vast expenditure of money at public sales.

Baron Satan lived in constant fear, not for himself, but for the treasures that he had accumulated with such an earnest devotion and with so much perspicacity that the shrewdest merchant could not say that the Baron had ever erred in his taste or judgment. He loved them—his bibelots. He loved them intensely, like a miser; jealously, like a lover. Every day, at sunset, the iron gates at either end of the bridge and at the entrance to the court of honor are closed and barred. At the least touch on these gates, electric bells will ring throughout the castle.

One Thursday in September, a letter-carrier presented himself at the gate at the head of the bridge, and, as usual, it was the Baron himself who partially opened the heavy portal. He scrutinized the man as minutely as if he were a stranger, although the honest face and twinkling eyes of the postman had been familiar to the Baron for many years. The man laughed, as he said:

"It is only I, Monsieur le Baron. It is not another man wearing my cap and blouse."

"One can never tell," muttered the Baron.

The man handed him a number of newspapers, and then said:

"And now, Monsieur le Baron, here is something new."

"Something new?"

"Yes, a letter. A registered letter."

Living as a recluse, without friends or business relations, the baron never received any letters, and the one now presented to him immediately aroused within him a feeling of suspicion and distrust. It was like an evil omen. Who was this mysterious correspondent that dared to disturb the tranquility of his retreat?

"You must sign for it, Monsieur le Baron."

He signed; then took the letter, waited until the postman had disappeared beyond the bend in the road, and, after walking nervously to and fro for a few minutes, he leaned against the parapet of the bridge and opened the envelope. It contained a sheet of paper, bearing this heading: Prison de la Santé, Paris. He looked at the signature: Arsène Lupin. Then he read:

"Monsieur le Baron: "There is, in the gallery in your castle, a picture of Philippe de Champaigne, of exquisite finish, which pleases me beyond measure.

Your Rubens are also to my taste, as well as your smallest Watteau.

In the salon to the right, I have noticed the Louis XIII cadence-table, the tapestries of Beauvais, the Empire gueridon signed `Jacob,' and the Renaissance chest. In the salon to the left, all the cabinet full of jewels and miniatures.

"For the present, I will content myself with those articles that can be conveniently removed. I will therefore ask you to pack them carefully and ship them to me, charges prepaid, to the station at Batignolles, within eight days, otherwise I shall be obliged to remove them myself during the night of 27 September; but, under those circumstances, I shall not content myself with the articles above mentioned. "Accept my apologies for any inconvenience I may cause you, and believe me to be your humble servant, "Arsène Lupin." "

P. S.—Please do not send the largest Watteau. Although you paid thirty thousand francs for it, it is only a copy, the original having been burned, under the Directoire by Barras, during a night of debauchery. Consult the memoirs of Garat. "I do not care for the Louis XV chatelaine, as I doubt its authenticity."

That letter completely upset the baron. Had it borne any other signature, he would have been greatly alarmed—but signed by Arsène Lupin!

As an habitual reader of the newspapers, he was versed in the history of recent crimes, and was therefore well acquainted with the exploits of the mysterious burglar. Of course, he knew that Lupin had been arrested in America by his enemy Ganimard and was at present incarcerated in the Prison de la Santé. But he knew also that any miracle might be expected from Arsène Lupin. Moreover, that exact knowledge of the castle, the location of the pictures and furniture, gave the affair an alarming aspect. How could he have acquired that information concerning things that no one had ever seen?

The baron raised his eyes and contemplated the stern outlines of the castle, its steep rocky pedestal, the depth of the surrounding water, and shrugged his shoulders. Certainly, there was no danger. No one in the world could force an entrance to the sanctuary that contained his priceless treasures.

No one, perhaps, but Arsène Lupin! For him, gates, walls and drawbridges did not exist. What use were the most formidable obstacles or the most careful precautions, if Arsène Lupin had decided to effect an entrance?

That evening, he wrote to the Procurer of the Republique at Rouen. He enclosed the threatening letter and solicited aid and protection.

The reply came at once to the effect that Arsène Lupin was in custody in the Prison de la Santé, under close surveillance, with no opportunity to write such a letter, which was, no doubt, the work of some imposter. But, as an act of precaution, the Procurer had submitted the letter to an expert in handwriting, who declared that, in spite of certain resemblances, the writing was not that of the prisoner.

But the words "in spite of certain resemblances" caught the attention of the baron; in them, he read the possibility of a doubt which appeared to him quite sufficient to warrant the intervention of the law. His fears increased. He read Lupin's letter over and over again. "I shall be obliged to remove them myself." And then there was the fixed date: the night of 27 September.

To confide in his servants was a proceeding repugnant to his nature; but now, for the first time in many years, he experienced the necessity of seeking counsel with some one. Abandoned by the legal official of his own district, and feeling unable to defend himself with his own resources, he was on the point of going to Paris to engage the services of a detective.

Two days passed; on the third day, he was filled with hope and joy as he read the following item in the `Reveil de Caudebec', a newspaper published in a neighboring town:

"We have the pleasure of entertaining in our city, at the present time, the veteran detective Mon. Ganimard who acquired a world-wide reputation by his clever capture of Arsène Lupin. He has come here for rest and recreation, and, being an enthusiastic fisherman, he threatens to capture all the fish in our river."

Ganimard! Ah, here is the assistance desired by Baron Cahorn! Who could baffle the schemes of Arsène Lupin better than Ganimard, the patient and astute detective? He was the man for the place.

The baron did not hesitate. The town of Caudebec was only six kilometers from the castle, a short distance to a man whose step was accelerated by the hope of safety.

After several fruitless attempts to ascertain the detective's address, the baron visited the office of the `Reveil,' situated on the quai. There he found the writer of the article who, approaching the window, exclaimed:

"Ganimard? Why, you are sure to see him somewhere on the quai with his fishing-pole. I met him there and chanced to read his name engraved on his rod. Ah, there he is now, under the trees."

"That little man, wearing a straw hat?"

"Exactly. He is a gruff fellow, with little to say."

Five minutes later, the baron approached the celebrated Ganimard, introduced himself, and sought to commence a conversation, but that was a failure. Then he broached the real object of his interview, and briefly stated his case. The other listened, motionless, with his attention riveted on his fishing-rod. When the baron had finished his story, the fisherman turned, with an air of profound pity, and said:

"Monsieur, it is not customary for thieves to warn people they are about to rob. Arsène Lupin, especially, would not commit such a folly."

"But——"

"Monsieur, if I had the least doubt, believe me, the pleasure of again capturing Arsène Lupin would place me at your disposal. But, unfortunately, that young man is already under lock and key."

"He may have escaped."

"No one ever escaped from the Santé."

"But, he——"

"He, no more than any other."

"Yet——"

"Well, if he escapes, so much the better. I will catch him again. Meanwhile, you go home and sleep soundly. That will do for the present. You frighten the fish."

The conversation was ended. The baron returned to the castle, reassured to some extent by Ganimard's indifference. He examined the bolts, watched the servants, and, during the next forty-eight hours, he became almost persuaded that his fears were groundless. Certainly, as Ganimard had said, thieves do not warn people they are about to rob.

The fateful day was close at hand. It was now the twenty-sixth of September and nothing had happened. But at three o'clock the bell rang. A boy brought this telegram:

"No goods at Batignolles station. Prepare everything for tomorrow night. Arsène."

This telegram threw the baron into such a state of excitement that he even considered the advisability of yielding to Lupin's demands.

However, he hastened to Caudebec. Ganimard was fishing at the same place, seated on a campstool. Without a word, he handed him the telegram.

"Well, what of it?" said the detective.

"What of it? But it is tomorrow."

"What is tomorrow?"

"The robbery! The pillage of my collections!"

Ganimard laid down his fishing-rod, turned to the baron, and exclaimed, in a tone of impatience:

"Ah! Do you think I am going to bother myself about such a silly story as that!"

"How much do you ask to pass tomorrow night in the castle?"

"Not a sou. Now, leave me alone."

"Name your own price. I am rich and can pay it."

This offer disconcerted Ganimard, who replied, calmly:

"I am here on a vacation. I have no right to undertake such work."

"No one will know. I promise to keep it secret."

"Oh! nothing will happen."

"Come! three thousand francs. Will that be enough?"

The detective, after a moment's reflection, said:

"Very well. But I must warn you that you are throwing your money out of the window."

"I do not care."

"In that case... but, after all, what do we know about this devil Lupin! He may have quite a numerous band of robbers with him. Are you sure of your servants?"

"My faith——"

"Better not count on them. I will telegraph for two of my men to help me. And now, go! It is better for us not to be seen together. Tomorrow evening about nine o'clock."

The following day—the date fixed by Arsène Lupin—Baron Cahorn arranged all his panoply of war, furbished his weapons, and, like a sentinel, paced to and fro in front of the castle. He saw nothing, heard nothing. At half-past eight o'clock in the evening, he dismissed his servants. They occupied rooms in a wing of the building, in a retired spot, well removed from the main portion of the castle. Shortly thereafter, the baron heard the sound of approaching footsteps. It was Ganimard and his two assistants—great, powerful fellows with immense hands, and necks like bulls. After asking a few questions relating to the location of the various entrances and rooms, Ganimard carefully closed and barricaded all the doors and windows through which one could gain access to the threatened rooms. He inspected the walls, raised the tapestries, and finally installed his assistants in the central gallery which was located between the two salons.

"No nonsense! We are not here to sleep. At the slightest sound, open the windows of the court and call me. Pay attention also to the water-side. Ten metres of perpendicular rock is no obstacle to those devils."

Ganimard locked his assistants in the gallery, carried away the keys, and said to the baron:

"And now, to our post."

He had chosen for himself a small room located in the thick outer wall, between the two principal doors, and which, in former years, had been the watchman's quarters. A peep-hole opened upon the bridge; another on the court. In one corner, there was an opening to a tunnel.

"I believe you told me, Monsieur le Baron, that this tunnel is the only subterranean entrance to the castle and that it has been closed up for time immemorial?"

9

"Yes."

"Then, unless there is some other entrance, known only to Arsène Lupin, we are quite safe."

He placed three chairs together, stretched himself upon them, lighted his pipe and sighed:

"Really, Monsieur le Baron, I feel ashamed to accept your money for such a sinecure as this. I will tell the story to my friend Lupin. He will enjoy it immensely."

The baron did not laugh. He was anxiously listening, but heard nothing save the beating of his own heart. From time to time, he leaned over the tunnel and cast a fearful eye into its depths. He heard the clock strike eleven, twelve, one.

Suddenly, he seized Ganimard's arm. The latter leaped up, awakened from his sleep.

"Do you hear?" asked the baron, in a whisper.

"Yes."

"What is it?"

"I was snoring, I suppose."

"No, no, listen."

"Ah! yes, it is the horn of an automobile."

"Well?"

"Well! it is very improbable that Lupin would use an automobile like a battering-ram to demolish your castle. Come, Monsieur le Baron, return to your post. I am going to sleep. Good-night."

That was the only alarm. Ganimard resumed his interrupted slumbers, and the baron heard nothing except the regular snoring of his companion. At break of day, they left the room. The castle was enveloped in a profound calm; it was a peaceful dawn on the bosom of a tranquil river. They mounted the stairs, Cahorn radiant with joy, Ganimard calm as usual. They heard no sound; they saw nothing to arouse suspicion.

"What did I tell you, Monsieur le Baron? Really, I should not have accepted your offer. I am ashamed."

He unlocked the door and entered the gallery. Upon two chairs, with drooping heads and pendent arms, the detective's two assistants were asleep.

"Tonnerre de nom d'un chien!" exclaimed Ganimard. At the same moment, the baron cried out:

"The pictures! The credence!"

He stammered, choked, with arms outstretched toward the empty places, toward the denuded walls where naught remained but the useless nails and cords. The Watteau, disappeared! The Rubens, carried away! The tapestries taken down! The cabinets, despoiled of their jewels!

"And my Louis XVI candelabra! And the Regent chandelier!...And my twelfth-century Virgin!"

He ran from one spot to another in wildest despair. He recalled the purchase price of each article, added up the figures, counted his losses, pell-mell, in confused words and unfinished phrases. He stamped with rage; he groaned with grief. He acted like a ruined man whose only hope is suicide.

If anything could have consoled him, it would have been the stupefaction displayed by Ganimard. The famous detective did not move. He appeared to be petrified; he examined the room in a listless manner. The windows?.... closed. The locks on the doors?.... intact. Not a break in the ceiling; not a hole in the floor. Everything was in perfect order. The theft had been carried out methodically, according to a logical and inexorable plan.

"Arsène Lupin....Arsène Lupin," he muttered.

Suddenly, as if moved by anger, he rushed upon his two assistants and shook them violently. They did not awaken.

"The devil!" he cried. "Can it be possible?"

He leaned over them and, in turn, examined them closely. They were asleep; but their response was unnatural.

"They have been drugged," he said to the baron.

"By whom?"

"By him, of course, or his men under his discretion. That work bears his stamp."

"In that case, I am lost—nothing can be done."

"Nothing," assented Ganimard.

"It is dreadful; it is monstrous."

"Lodge a complaint."

"What good will that do?"

"Oh; it is well to try it. The law has some resources."

"The law! Bah! it is useless. You represent the law, and, at this moment, when you should be looking for a clue and trying to discover something, you do not even stir."

"Discover something with Arsène Lupin! Why, my dear monsieur, Arsène Lupin never leaves any clue behind him. He leaves nothing to chance. Sometimes I think he put himself in my way and simply allowed me to arrest him in America."

"Then, I must renounce my pictures! He has taken the gems of my collection. I would give a fortune to recover them. If there is no other way, let him name his own price."

Ganimard regarded the baron attentively, as he said:

"Now, that is sensible. Will you stick to it?"

"Yes, yes. But why?"

"An idea that I have."

"What is it?"

"We will discuss it later—if the official examination does not succeed. But, not one word about me, if you wish my assistance."

He added, between his teeth:

"It is true I have nothing to boast of in this affair."

The assistants were gradually regaining consciousness with the bewildered air of people who come out of an hypnotic sleep. They opened their eyes and looked about them in astonishment. Ganimard questioned them; they remembered nothing.

"But you must have seen some one?"

"No."

"Can't you remember?"

"No, no."

"Did you drink anything?"

They considered a moment, and then one of them replied:

"Yes, I drank a little water."

"Out of that carafe?"

"Yes."

"So did I," declared the other.

Ganimard smelled and tasted it. It had no particular taste and no odor.

"Come," he said, "we are wasting our time here. One can't decide an Arsène Lupin problem in five minutes. But, morbleau! I swear I will catch him again."

The same day, a charge of burglary was duly performed by Baron Cahorn against Arsène Lupin, a prisoner in the Prison de la Santé.

The baron afterwards regretted making the charge against Lupin when he saw his castle delivered over to the gendarmes, the procureur, the judge d'instruction, the newspaper reporters and photographers, and a throng of idle curiosity-seekers.

The affair soon became a topic of general discussion, and the name of Arsène Lupin excited the public imagination to such an extent that the newspapers filled their columns with the most fantastic stories of his exploits which found ready credence amongst their readers.

But the letter of Arsène Lupin that was published in the `Echo de France' (no one ever knew how the newspaper obtained it), that letter in which Baron Cahorn was impudently warned of the coming theft, caused considerable excitement. The most fabulous theories were advanced. Some recalled the existence of the famous subterranean tunnels, and that was the line of research pursued by the officers of the law, who searched the house from top to bottom, questioned every stone, studied the wainscoting and the chimneys, the window-frames and the girders in the ceilings. By the light of torches, they examined the immense cellars where the lords of Malaquis were wont to store their munitions and provisions. They sounded the rocky foundation to its very centre. But it was all in vain. They discovered no trace of a subterranean tunnel. No secret passage existed.

But the eager public declared that the pictures and furniture could not vanish like so many ghosts. They are substantial, material things and require doors and windows for their exits and their entrances, and so do the people that remove them. Who were those people? How did they gain access to the castle? And how did they leave it?

The police officers of Rouen, convinced of their own impotence, solicited the assistance of the Parisian detective force. Mon. Dudouis, chief of the Sûreté, sent the best sleuths of the iron brigade. He himself spent forty-eight hours at the castle, but met with no success. Then he sent for Ganimard, whose past services had proved so useful when all else failed.

Ganimard listened, in silence, to the instructions of his superior; then, shaking his head, he said:

"In my opinion, it is useless to ransack the castle. The solution of the problem lies elsewhere."

"Where, then?"

"With Arsène Lupin."

"With Arsène Lupin! To support that theory, we must admit his intervention."

"I do admit it. In fact, I consider it quite certain."

"Come, Ganimard, that is absurd. Arsène Lupin is in prison."

"I grant you that Arsène Lupin is in prison, closely guarded; but he must have fetters on his feet, manacles on his wrists, and gag in his mouth before I change my opinion."

"Why so obstinate, Ganimard?"

"Because Arsène Lupin is the only man in France of sufficient calibre to invent and carry out a scheme of that magnitude."

"Mere words, Ganimard."

"But true ones. Look! What are they doing? Searching for subterranean passages, stones swinging on pivots, and other nonsense of that kind. But Lupin doesn't employ such old-fashioned methods. He is a modern cracksman, right up to date."

"And how would you proceed?"

"I should ask your permission to spend an hour with him."

"In his cell?"

"Yes. During the return trip from America we became very friendly, and I venture to say that if he can give me any information without compromising himself he will not hesitate to save me from incurring useless trouble."

It was shortly after noon when Ganimard entered the cell of Arsène Lupin. The latter, who was lying on his bed, raised his head and uttered a cry of apparent joy.

"Ah! This is a real surprise. My dear Ganimard, here!"

"Ganimard himself."

"In my chosen retreat, I have felt a desire for many things, but my fondest wish was to receive you here."

"Very kind of you, I am sure."

"Not at all. You know I hold you in the highest regard."

"I am proud of it."

"I have always said: Ganimard is our best detective. He is almost,—you see how candid I am!—he is almost as clever as Herlock Sholmes. But I am sorry that I cannot offer you anything better than this hard stool. And no refreshments! Not even a glass of beer! Of course, you will excuse me, as I am here only temporarily."

Ganimard smiled, and accepted the proffered seat. Then the prisoner continued:

"Mon Dieu, how pleased I am to see the face of an honest man. I am so tired of those devils of spies who come here ten times a day to ransack my pockets and my cell to satisfy themselves that I am not preparing to escape. The government is very solicitous on my account."

"It is quite right."

"Why so? I should be quite contented if they would allow me to live in my own quiet way."

"On other people's money."

"Quite so. That would be so simple. But here, I am joking, and you are, no doubt, in a hurry. So let us come to business, Ganimard. To what do I owe the honor of this visit?

"The Cahorn affair," declared Ganimard, frankly.

"Ah! Wait, one moment. You see I have had so many affairs! First, let me fix in my mind the circumstances of this particular case....Ah! yes, now I have it. The Cahorn affair, Malaquis castle, Seine-Inférieure....Two Rubens, a Watteau, and a few trifling articles."

"Trifling!"

"Oh! ma foi, all that is of slight importance. But it suffices to know that the affair interests you. How can I serve you, Ganimard?"

"Must I explain to you what steps the authorities have taken in the matter?"

"Not at all. I have read the newspapers and I will frankly state that you have made very little progress."

"And that is the reason I have come to see you."

"I am entirely at your service."

"In the first place, the Cahorn affair was managed by you?"

"From A to Z."

"The letter of warning? the telegram?"

"All mine. I ought to have the receipts somewhere."

Arsène opened the drawer of a small table of plain white wood which, with the bed and stool, constituted all the furniture in his cell, and took therefrom two scraps of paper which he handed to Ganimard.

"Ah!" exclaimed the detective, in surprise, "I though you were closely guarded and searched, and I find that you read the newspapers and collect postal receipts."

"Bah! these people are so stupid! They open the lining of my vest, they examine the soles of my shoes, they sound the walls of my cell, but they never imagine that Arsène Lupin would be foolish enough to choose such a simple hiding place."

Ganimard laughed, as he said:

"What a droll fellow you are! Really, you bewilder me. But, come now, tell me about the Cahorn affair."

"Oh! oh! not quite so fast! You would rob me of all my secrets; expose all my little tricks. That is a very serious matter."

"Was I wrong to count on your complaisance?"

"No, Ganimard, and since you insist—-"

Arsène Lupin paced his cell two or three times, then, stopping before Ganimard, he asked:

"What do you think of my letter to the baron?"

"I think you were amusing yourself by playing to the gallery."

"Ah! playing to the gallery! Come, Ganimard, I thought you knew me better. Do I, Arsène Lupin, ever waste my time on such puerilities? Would I have written that letter if I could have robbed the baron without writing to him? I want you to understand that the letter was indispensable; it was the motor that set the whole machine in motion. Now, let us discuss together a scheme for the robbery of the Malaquis castle. Are you willing?"

"Yes, proceed."

"Well, let us suppose a castle carefully closed and barricaded like that of the Baron Cahorn. Am I to abandon my scheme and renounce the treasures that I covet, upon the pretext that the castle which holds them is inaccessible?"

"Evidently not."

"Should I make an assault upon the castle at the head of a band of adventurers as they did in ancient times?"

"That would be foolish."

"Can I gain admittance by stealth or cunning?"

"Impossible."

"Then there is only one way open to me. I must have the owner of the castle invite me to it."

"That is surely an original method."

"And how easy! Let us suppose that one day the owner receives a letter warning him that a notorious burglar known as Arsène Lupin is plotting to rob him. What will he do?"

"Send a letter to the Procureur."

"Who will laugh at him, *because the said Arsène Lupin is actually in prison.* Then, in his anxiety and fear, the simple man will ask the assistance of the first-comer, will he not?"

"Very likely."

"And if he happens to read in a country newspaper that a celebrated detective is spending his vacation in a neighboring town—-"

"He will seek that detective."

"Of course. But, on the other hand, let us presume that, having foreseen that state of affairs, the said Arsène Lupin has requested one of his friends to visit Caudebec, make the acquaintance of the editor of the `Réveil,' a newspaper to which the baron is a subscriber, and let said editor understand that such person is the celebrated detective—then, what will happen?"

"The editor will announce in the `Réveil' the presence in Caudebec of said detective."

"Exactly; and one of two things will happen: either the fish—I mean Cahorn—will not bite, and nothing will happen; or, what is more likely, he will run and greedily swallow the bait. Thus, behold my Baron Cahorn imploring the assistance of one of my friends against me."

"Original, indeed!"

"Of course, the pseudo-detective at first refuses to give any assistance. On top of that comes the telegram from Arsène Lupin. The frightened baron rushes once more to my friend and offers him a definite sum of money for his services. My friend accepts and summons two members of our band, who, during the night, whilst Cahorn is under the watchful eye of his protector, removes certain articles by way of the window and lowers them with ropes into a nice little launch chartered for the occasion. Simple, isn't it?"

"Marvelous! Marvelous!" exclaimed Ganimard. "The boldness of the scheme and the ingenuity of all its details are beyond criticism. But who is the detective whose name and fame served as a magnet to attract the baron and draw him into your net?"

"There is only one name could do it—only one."

"And that is?"

"Arsène Lupin's personal enemy—the most illustrious Ganimard."

"I?"

"Yourself, Ganimard. And, really, it is very funny. If you go there, and the baron decides to talk, you will find that it will be your duty to arrest yourself, just as you arrested me in America. Hein! the revenge is really amusing: I cause Ganimard to arrest Ganimard."

Arsène Lupin laughed heartily. The detective, greatly vexed, bit his lips; to him the joke was quite devoid of humor. The arrival of a prison guard gave Ganimard an opportunity to recover himself. The man brought Arsène Lupin's luncheon, furnished by a neighboring restaurant. After depositing the tray upon the table, the guard retired. Lupin broke his bread, ate a few morsels, and continued:

"But, rest easy, my dear Ganimard, you will not go to Malaquis. I can tell you something that will astonish you: the Cahorn affair is on the point of being settled."

"Excuse me; I have just seen the Chief of the Sureté."

"What of that? Does Mon. Dudouis know my business better than I do myself? You will learn that Ganimard—excuse me—that the pseudo-Ganimard still remains on very good terms with the baron. The latter has authorized him to negotiate a very delicate transaction with me, and, at the present moment, in consideration of a certain sum, it is probable that the baron has recovered possession of his pictures and other treasures. And on their return, he will withdraw his complaint. Thus, there is no longer any theft, and the law must abandon the case."

Ganimard regarded the prisoner with a bewildered air.

"And how do you know all that?"

"I have just received the telegram I was expecting."

"You have just received a telegram?"

"This very moment, my dear friend. Out of politeness, I did not wish to read it in your presence. But if you will permit me—-"

"You are joking, Lupin."

"My dear friend, if you will be so kind as to break that egg, you will learn for yourself that I am not joking."

Mechanically, Ganimard obeyed, and cracked the egg-shell with the blade of a knife. He uttered a cry of surprise. The shell contained nothing but a small piece of blue paper. At the request of Arsène he unfolded it. It was a telegram, or rather a portion of a telegram from which the post-marks had been removed. It read as follows:

"Contract closed. Hundred thousand balls delivered. All well."

"One hundred thousand balls?" said Ganimard.

"Yes, one hundred thousand francs. Very little, but then, you know, these are hard times....And I have some heavy bills to meet. If you only knew my budget.... living in the city comes very high."

Ganimard arose. His ill humor had disappeared. He reflected for a moment, glancing over the whole affair in an effort to discover a weak point; then, in a tone and manner that betrayed his admiration of the prisoner, he said:

"Fortunately, we do not have a dozen such as you to deal with; if we did, we would have to close up shop."

Arsène Lupin assumed a modest air, as he replied:

"Bah! a person must have some diversion to occupy his leisure hours, especially when he is in prison."

"What!" exclaimed Ganimard, "your trial, your defense, the examination—isn't that sufficient to occupy your mind?"

"No, because I have decided not to be present at my trial."

"Oh! oh!"

Arsène Lupin repeated, positively:

"I shall not be present at my trial."

"Really!"

"Ah! my dear monsieur, do you suppose I am going to rot upon the wet straw? You insult me. Arsène Lupin remains in prison just as long as it pleases him, and not one minute more."

"Perhaps it would have been more prudent if you had avoided getting there," said the detective, ironically.

"Ah! monsieur jests? Monsieur must remember that he had the honor to effect my arrest. Know then, my worthy friend, that no one, not even you, could have placed a hand upon me if a much more important event had not occupied my attention at that critical moment."

"You astonish me."

"A woman was looking at me, Ganimard, and I loved her. Do you fully understand what that means: to be under the eyes of a woman that one loves? I cared for nothing in the world but that. And that is why I am here."

"Permit me to say: you have been here a long time."

"In the first place, I wished to forget. Do not laugh; it was a delightful adventure and it is still a tender memory. Besides, I have been suffering from neurasthenia. Life is so feverish these days that it is necessary to take the `rest cure' occasionally, and I find this spot a sovereign remedy for my tired nerves."

"Arsène Lupin, you are not a bad fellow, after all."

"Thank you," said Lupin. "Ganimard, this is Friday. On Wednesday next, at four o'clock in the afternoon, I will smoke my cigar at your house in the rue Pergolese."

"Arsène Lupin, I will expect you."

They shook hands like two old friends who valued each other at their true worth; then the detective stepped to the door.

"Ganimard!"

"What is it?" asked Ganimard, as he turned back.

"You have forgotten your watch."

"My watch?"

"Yes, it strayed into my pocket."

He returned the watch, excusing himself.

"Pardon me.... a bad habit. Because they have taken mine is no reason why I should take yours. Besides, I have a chronometer here that satisfies me fairly well."

He took from the drawer a large gold watch and heavy chain.

"From whose pocket did that come?" asked Ganimard.

Arsène Lupin gave a hasty glance at the initials engraved on the watch.

"J.B.....Who the devil can that be?....Ah! yes, I remember. Jules Bouvier, the judge who conducted my examination. A charming fellow!...."

III. THE ESCAPE OF ARSÈNE LUPIN

Arsène Lupin had just finished his repast and taken from his pocket an excellent cigar, with a gold band, which he was examining with unusual care, when the door of his cell was opened. He had barely time to throw the cigar into the drawer and move away from the table. The guard entered. It was the hour for exercise.

"I was waiting for you, my dear boy," exclaimed Lupin, in his accustomed good humor.

They went out together. As soon as they had disappeared at a turn in the corridor, two men entered the cell and commenced a minute examination of it. One was Inspector Dieuzy; the other was Inspector Folenfant. They wished to verify their suspicion that Arsène Lupin was in communication with his accomplices outside of the prison. On the preceding evening, the `Grand Journal' had published these lines addressed to its court reporter:

"Monsieur:

"In a recent article you referred to me in most unjustifiable terms. Some days before the opening of my trial I will call you to account. Arsène Lupin."

The handwriting was certainly that of Arsène Lupin. Consequently, he sent letters; and, no doubt, received letters. It was certain that he was preparing for that escape thus arrogantly announced by him.

The situation had become intolerable. Acting in conjunction with the examining judge, the chief of the Sûreté, Mon. Dudouis, had visited the prison and instructed the gaoler in regard to the precautions necessary to insure Lupin's safety. At the same time, he sent the two men to examine the prisoner's cell. They raised every stone, ransacked the bed, did everything customary in such a case, but they discovered nothing, and were about to abandon their investigation when the guard entered hastily and said:

"The drawer.... look in the table-drawer. When I entered just now he was closing it."

They opened the drawer, and Dieuzy exclaimed:

"Ah! we have him this time."

Folenfant stopped him.

"Wait a moment. The chief will want to make an inventory."

"This is a very choice cigar."

"Leave it there, and notify the chief."

Two minutes later Mon. Dudouis examined the contents of the drawer. First he discovered a bundle of newspaper clippings relating to Arsène Lupin taken from the `Argus de la Presse,' then a tobacco-box, a pipe, some paper called "onion-peel," and two books. He read the titles of the books. One was an English edition of Carlyle's "Hero-worship"; the other was a charming elzevir, in modern binding, the "Manual of Epictetus," a German translation published at Leyden in 1634. On examining the books, he found that all the pages were underlined and annotated. Were they prepared as a code for correspondence, or did they simply express the studious character of the reader? Then he examined the tobacco-box and the pipe. Finally, he took up the famous cigar with its gold band.

"Fichtre!" he exclaimed. "Our friend smokes a good cigar. It's a Henry Clay."

With the mechanical action of an habitual smoker, he placed the cigar close to his ear and squeezed it to make it crack. Immediately he uttered a cry of surprise. The cigar had yielded under the pressure of his fingers. He examined it more closely, and quickly discovered something white between the leaves of tobacco. Delicately, with the aid of a pin, he withdrew a roll of very thin paper, scarcely larger than a toothpick. It was a letter. He unrolled it, and found these words, written in a feminine handwriting:

"The basket has taken the place of the others. Eight out of ten are ready. On pressing the outer foot the plate goes downward. From twelve to sixteen every day, H-P will wait. But where? Reply at once. Rest easy; your friend is watching over you."

Mon. Dudouis reflected a moment, then said:

"It is quite clear.... the basket.... the eight compartments.... From twelve to sixteen means from twelve to four o'clock."

"But this H-P, that will wait?"

"H-P must mean automobile. H-P, horsepower, is the way they indicate strength of the motor. A twenty-four H-P is an automobile of twenty-four horsepower."

Then he rose, and asked:

"Had the prisoner finished his breakfast?"

"Yes."

"And as he has not yet read the message, which is proved by the condition of the cigar, it is probable that he had just received it."

"How?"

"In his food. Concealed in his bread or in a potato, perhaps."

"Impossible. His food was allowed to be brought in simply to trap him, but we have never found anything in it."

"We will look for Lupin's reply this evening. Detain him outside for a few minutes. I shall take this to the examining judge, and, if he agrees with me, we will have the letter photographed at once, and in an hour you can replace the letter in the drawer in a cigar similar to this. The prisoner must have no cause for suspicion."

It was not without a certain curiosity that Mon. Dudouis returned to the prison in the evening, accompanied by Inspector Dieuzy. Three empty plates were sitting on the stove in the corner.

"He has eaten?"

"Yes," replied the guard.

"Dieuzy, please cut that macaroni into very small pieces, and open that bread-roll....Nothing?"

"No, chief."

Mon. Dudouis examined the plates, the fork, the spoon, and the knife—an ordinary knife with a rounded blade. He turned the handle to the left; then to the right. It yielded and unscrewed. The knife was hollow, and served as a hiding-place for a sheet of paper.

"Peuh!" he said, "that is not very clever for a man like Arsène. But we mustn't lose any time. You, Dieuzy, go and search the restaurant."

Then he read the note:

"I trust to you, H-P will follow at a distance every day. I will go ahead. Au revoir, dear friend."

"At last," cried Mon. Dudouis, rubbing his hands gleefully, "I think we have the affair in our own hands. A little strategy on our part, and the escape will be a success in so far as the arrest of his confederates are concerned."

"But if Arsène Lupin slips through your fingers?" suggested the guard.

"We will have a sufficient number of men to prevent that. If, however, he displays too much cleverness, ma foi, so much the worse for him! As to his band of robbers, since the chief refuses to speak, the others must."

And, as a matter of fact, Arsène Lupin had very little to say. For several months, Mon. Jules Bouvier, the examining judge, had exerted himself in vain. The investigation had been reduced to a few uninteresting arguments between the judge and the advocate, Maître Danval, one of the leaders of the bar. From time to time, through courtesy, Arsène Lupin would speak. One day he said:

"Yes, monsieur, le judge, I quite agree with you: the robbery of the Crédit Lyonnais, the theft in the rue de Babylone, the issue of the counterfeit bank-notes, the burglaries at the various châteaux, Armesnil, Gouret, Imblevain, Groseillers, Malaquis, all my work, monsieur, I did it all."

"Then will you explain to me—"

"It is useless. I confess everything in a lump, everything and even ten times more than you know nothing about."

Wearied by his fruitless task, the judge had suspended his examinations, but he resumed them after the two intercepted messages were brought to his attention; and regularly, at mid-day, Arsène Lupin was taken from the prison to the Dépôt in the prison-van with a certain number of other prisoners. They returned about three or four o'clock.

Now, one afternoon, this return trip was made under unusual conditions. The other prisoners not having been examined, it was decided to take back Arsène Lupin first, thus he found himself alone in the vehicle.

These prison-vans, vulgarly called "panniers à salade"—or salad-baskets—are divided lengthwise by a central corridor from which open ten compartments, five on either side. Each compartment is so arranged that the occupant must assume and retain a sitting posture, and, consequently, the five prisoners are seated one upon the other, and yet separated one from the other by partitions. A municipal guard, standing at one end, watches over the corridor.

Arsène was placed in the third cell on the right, and the heavy vehicle started. He carefully calculated when they left the quai de l'Horloge, and when they passed the Palais de Justice. Then, about the centre of the bridge Saint Michel, with his outer foot, that is to say, his right foot, he pressed upon the metal plate that closed his cell. Immediately something clicked, and the metal plate moved. He was able to ascertain that he was located between the two wheels.

He waited, keeping a sharp look-out. The vehicle was proceeding slowly along the boulevard Saint Michel. At the corner of Saint Germain it stopped. A truck horse had fallen. The traffic having been interrupted, a vast throng of fiacres and omnibuses had gathered there. Arsène Lupin looked out. Another prison-van had stopped close to the one he occupied. He moved the plate still farther, put his foot on one of the spokes of the wheel and leaped to the ground. A coachman saw him, roared with laughter, then tried to raise an outcry, but his voice was lost in the noise of the traffic that had commenced to move again. Moreover, Arsène Lupin was already far away.

He had run for a few steps; but, once upon the sidewalk, he turned and looked around; he seemed to scent the wind like a person who is uncertain which direction to take. Then, having decided, he put his hands in his pockets, and, with the careless air of an idle stroller, he proceeded up the boulevard. It was a warm, bright autumn day, and the cafés were full. He took a seat on the terrace of one of them. He ordered a bock and a package of cigarettes. He emptied his glass slowly, smoked one cigarette and lighted a second. Then he asked the waiter to send the proprietor to him. When the proprietor came, Arsène spoke to him in a voice loud enough to be heard by everyone:

"I regret to say, monsieur, I have forgotten my pocketbook. Perhaps, on the strength of my name, you will be pleased to give me credit for a few days. I am Arsène Lupin."

The proprietor looked at him, thinking he was joking. But Arsène repeated:

"Lupin, prisoner at the Santé, but now a fugitive. I venture to assume that the name inspires you with perfect confidence in me."

And he walked away, amidst shouts of laughter, whilst the proprietor stood amazed.

Lupin strolled along the rue Soufflot, and turned into the rue Saint Jacques. He pursued his way slowly, smoking his cigarettes and looking into the shop-windows. At the Boulevard de Port Royal he took his bearings, discovered where he was, and then walked in the direction of the rue de la Santé. The high forbidding walls of the prison were now before him. He pulled his hat forward to shade his face; then, approaching the sentinel, he asked:

"It this the prison de la Santé?"

"Yes."

"I wish to regain my cell. The van left me on the way, and I would not abuse—"

"Now, young man, move along—quick!" growled the sentinel.

"Pardon me, but I must pass through that gate. And if you prevent Arsène Lupin from entering the prison it will cost you dear, my friend."

"Arsène Lupin! What are you talking about!"

"I am sorry I haven't a card with me," said Arsène, fumbling in his pockets.

The sentinel eyed him from head to foot, in astonishment. Then, without a word, he rang a bell. The iron gate was partly opened, and Arsène stepped inside. Almost immediately he encountered the keeper of the prison, gesticulating and feigning a violent anger. Arsène smiled and said:

"Come, monsieur, don't play that game with me. What! they take the precaution to carry me alone in the van, prepare a nice little obstruction, and imagine I am going to take to my heels and rejoin my friends. Well, and what about the twenty agents of the Sûreté who accompanied us on foot, in fiacres and on bicycles? No, the arrangement did not please me. I should not have got away alive. Tell me, monsieur, did they count on that?"

He shrugged his shoulders, and added:

"I beg of you, monsieur, not to worry about me. When I wish to escape I shall not require any assistance."

On the second day thereafter, the `Echo de France,' which had apparently become the official reporter of the exploits of Arsène Lupin,—it was said that he was one of its principal shareholders—published a most complete account of this attempted escape. The exact wording of the messages exchanged between the prisoner and his mysterious friend, the means by which correspondence was constructed, the complicity of the police, the promenade on the Boulevard Saint Michel, the incident at the café Soufflot, everything was disclosed. It was known that the search of the restaurant and its waiters by Inspector Dieuzy had been fruitless. And the public also learned an extraordinary thing which demonstrated the infinite variety of resources that Lupin possessed: the prison-van, in which he was being carried, was prepared for the occasion and substituted by his accomplices for one of the six vans which did service at the prison.

The next escape of Arsène Lupin was not doubted by anyone. He announced it himself, in categorical terms, in a reply to Mon. Bouvier on the day following his attempted escape. The judge having made a jest about the affair, Arsène was annoyed, and, firmly eyeing the judge, he said, emphatically:

"Listen to me, monsieur! I give you my word of honor that this attempted flight was simply preliminary to my general plan of escape."

"I do not understand," said the judge.

"It is not necessary that you should understand."

And when the judge, in the course of that examination which was reported at length in the columns of the `Echo de France,' when the judge sought to resume his investigation, Arsène Lupin exclaimed, with an assumed air of lassitude:

"Mon Dieu, Mon Dieu, what's the use! All these questions are of no importance!"

"What! No importance?" cried the judge.

"No; because I shall not be present at the trial."

"You will not be present?"

"No; I have fully decided on that, and nothing will change my mind."

Such assurance combined with the inexplicable indiscretions that Arsène committed every day served to annoy and mystify the officers of the law. There were secrets known only to Arsène Lupin; secrets that he alone could divulge. But for what purpose did he reveal them? And how?

Arsène Lupin was changed to another cell. The judge closed his preliminary investigation. No further proceedings were taken in his case for a period of two months, during which time Arsène was seen almost constantly lying on his bed with his face turned toward the wall. The changing of his cell seemed to discourage him. He refused to see his advocate. He exchanged only a few necessary words with his keepers.

During the fortnight preceding his trial, he resumed his vigorous life. He complained of want of air. Consequently, early every morning he was allowed to exercise in the courtyard, guarded by two men.

Public curiosity had not died out; every day it expected to be regaled with news of his escape; and, it is true, he had gained a considerable amount of public sympathy by reason of his verve, his gayety, his diversity, his inventive genius and the mystery of his life. Arsène Lupin must escape. It was his inevitable fate. The public expected it, and was surprised that the event had been delayed so long. Every morning the Préfect of Police asked his secretary:

"Well, has he escaped yet?"

"No, Monsieur le Préfect."

"To-morrow, probably."

And, on the day before the trial, a gentleman called at the office of the `Grand Journal,' asked to see the court reporter, threw his card in the reporter's face, and walked rapidly away. These words were written on the card: "Arsène Lupin always keeps his promises."

It was under these conditions that the trial commenced. An enormous crowd gathered at the court. Everybody wished to see the famous Arsène Lupin. They had a gleeful anticipation that the prisoner would play some audacious pranks upon the judge. Advocates and magistrates, reporters and men of the world, actresses and society women were crowded together on the benches provided for the public.

It was a dark, sombre day, with a steady downpour of rain. Only a dim light pervaded the courtroom, and the spectators caught a very indistinct view of the prisoner when the guards brought him in. But his heavy, shambling walk, the manner in which he dropped into his seat, and his passive, stupid appearance were not at all prepossessing. Several times his advocate—one of Mon. Danval's assistants—spoke to him, but he simply shook his head and said nothing.

The clerk read the indictment, then the judge spoke:

"Prisoner at the bar, stand up. Your name, age, and occupation?"

Not receiving any reply, the judge repeated:

"Your name? I ask you your name?"

A thick, slow voice muttered:

"Baudru, Désiré."

A murmur of surprise pervaded the courtroom. But the judge proceeded:

"Baudru, Désiré? Ah! a new alias! Well, as you have already assumed a dozen different names and this one is, no doubt, as imaginary as the others, we will adhere to the name of Arsène Lupin, by which you are more generally known."

The judge referred to his notes, and continued:

"For, despite the most diligent search, your past history remains unknown. Your case is unique in the annals of crime. We know not whom you are, whence you came, your birth and breeding—all is a mystery to us. Three years ago you appeared in our midst as Arsène Lupin, presenting to us a strange combination of intelligence and perversion, immorality and generosity. Our knowledge of your life prior to that date is vague and problematical. It may be that the man called Rostat who, eight years ago, worked with Dickson, the prestidigitator, was none other than Arsène Lupin. It is probable that the Russian student who, six years ago, attended the laboratory of Doctor Altier at the Saint Louis Hospital, and who often astonished the doctor by the ingenuity of his hypotheses on subjects of bacteriology and the boldness of his experiments in diseases of the skin, was none other than Arsène Lupin. It is probable, also, that Arsène Lupin was the professor who introduced the Japanese art of jiu-jitsu to the Parisian public. We have some reason to believe that Arsène Lupin was the bicyclist who won the Grand Prix de l'Exposition, received his ten thousand francs, and was never heard of again. Arsène Lupin may have been, also, the person who saved so many lives through the little dormer-window at the Charity Bazaar; and, at the same time, picked their pockets."

The judge paused for a moment, then continued:

"Such is that epoch which seems to have been utilized by you in a thorough preparation for the warfare you have since waged against society; a methodical apprenticeship in which you developed your strength, energy and skill to the highest point possible. Do you acknowledge the accuracy of these facts?"

During this discourse the prisoner had stood balancing himself, first on one foot, then on the other, with shoulders stooped and arms inert. Under the strongest light one could observe his extreme thinness, his hollow cheeks, his projecting cheek-bones, his earthen-colored face dotted with small red spots and framed in a rough, straggling beard. Prison life had caused him to age and wither. He had lost the youthful face and elegant figure we had seen portrayed so often in the newspapers.

It appeared as if he had not heard the question propounded by the judge. Twice it was repeated to him. Then he raised his eyes, seemed to reflect, then, making a desperate effort, he murmured:

"Baudru, Désiré."

The judge smiled, as he said:

"I do not understand the theory of your defense, Arsène Lupin. If you are seeking to avoid responsibility for your crimes on the ground of imbecility, such a line of defense is open to you. But I shall proceed with the trial and pay no heed to your vagaries."

He then narrated at length the various thefts, swindles and forgeries charged against Lupin. Sometimes he questioned the prisoner, but the latter simply grunted or remained silent. The examination of witnesses commenced. Some of the evidence given was immaterial; other portions of it seemed more important, but through all of it there ran a vein of contradictions and inconsistencies. A wearisome obscurity enveloped the proceedings, until Detective Ganimard was called as a witness; then interest was revived.

From the beginning the actions of the veteran detective appeared strange and unaccountable. He was nervous and ill at ease. Several times he looked at the prisoner, with obvious doubt and anxiety. Then, with his hands resting on the rail in front of him, he recounted the events in which he had participated, including his pursuit of the prisoner across Europe and his arrival in America. He was listened to with great avidity, as his capture of Arsène Lupin was well known to everyone through the medium of the press. Toward the close of his testimony, after referring to his conversations with Arsène Lupin, he stopped, twice, embarrassed and undecided. It was apparent that he was possessed of some thought which he feared to utter. The judge said to him, sympathetically:

"If you are ill, you may retire for the present."

"No, no, but——"

He stopped, looked sharply at the prisoner, and said:

"I ask permission to scrutinize the prisoner at closer range. There is some mystery about him that I must solve."

He approached the accused man, examined him attentively for several minutes, then returned to the witness-stand, and, in an almost solemn voice, he said:

"I declare, on oath, that the prisoner now before me is not Arsène Lupin."

A profound silence followed the statement. The judge, nonplused for a moment, exclaimed:

"Ah! What do you mean? That is absurd!"

The detective continued:

"At first sight there is a certain resemblance, but if you carefully consider the nose, the mouth, the hair, the color of skin, you will see that it is not Arsène Lupin. And the eyes! Did he ever have those alcoholic eyes!"

"Come, come, witness! What do you mean? Do you pretend to say that we are trying the wrong man?"

"In my opinion, yes. Arsène Lupin has, in some manner, contrived to put this poor devil in his place, unless this man is a willing accomplice."

This dramatic dénouement caused much laughter and excitement amongst the spectators. The judge adjourned the trial, and sent for Mon. Bouvier, the gaoler, and guards employed in the prison.

When the trial was resumed, Mon. Bouvier and the gaoler examined the accused and declared that there was only a very slight resemblance between the prisoner and Arsène Lupin.

"Well, then!" exclaimed the judge, "who is this man? Where does he come from? What is he in prison for?"

Two of the prison-guards were called and both of them declared that the prisoner was Arsène Lupin. The judged breathed once more.

But one of the guards then said:

"Yes, yes, I think it is he."

"What!" cried the judge, impatiently, "you *think* it is he! What do you mean by that?"

"Well, I saw very little of the prisoner. He was placed in my charge in the evening and, for two months, he seldom stirred, but laid on his bed with his face to the wall."

"What about the time prior to those two months?"

"Before that he occupied a cell in another part of the prison. He was not in cell 24."

Here the head gaoler interrupted, and said:

"We changed him to another cell after his attempted escape."

"But you, monsieur, you have seen him during those two months?"

"I had no occasion to see him. He was always quiet and orderly."

"And this prisoner is not Arsène Lupin?"

"No."

"Then who is he?" demanded the judge.

"I do not know."

"Then we have before us a man who was substituted for Arsène Lupin, two months ago. How do you explain that?"

"I cannot."

In absolute despair, the judge turned to the accused and addressed him in a conciliatory tone:

"Prisoner, can you tell me how, and since when, you became an inmate of the Prison de la Santé?"

The engaging manner of the judge was calculated to disarm the mistrust and awaken the understanding of the accused man. He tried to reply. Finally, under clever and gentle questioning, he succeeded in framing a few phrases from which the following story was gleaned: Two months ago he had been taken to the Dépôt, examined and released. As he was leaving the building, a free man, he was seized by two guards and placed in the prison-van. Since then he had occupied cell 24. He was contented there, plenty to eat, and he slept well—so he did not complain.

All that seemed probable; and, amidst the mirth and excitement of the spectators, the judge adjourned the trial until the story could be investigated and verified.

The following facts were at once established by an examination of the prison records: Eight weeks before a man named Baudru Désiré had slept at the Dépôt. He was released the next day, and left the Dépôt at two o'clock in the afternoon. On the same day at two o'clock, having been examined for the last time, Arsène Lupin left the Dépôt in a prison-van.

Had the guards made a mistake? Had they been deceived by the resemblance and carelessly substituted this man for their prisoner?

Another question suggested itself: Had the substitution been arranged in advance? In that event Baudru must have been an accomplice and must have caused his own arrest for the express purpose of taking Lupin's place. But then, by what miracle had such a plan, based on a series of improbable chances, been carried to success?

Baudru Désiré was turned over to the anthropological service; they had never seen anything like him. However, they easily traced his past history. He was known at Courbevois, at Asnières and at Levallois. He lived on alms and slept in one of those rag-picker's huts near the barrier de Ternes. He had disappeared from there a year ago.

Had he been enticed away by Arsène Lupin? There was no evidence to that effect. And even if that was so, it did not explain the flight of the prisoner. That still remained a mystery. Amongst twenty theories which sought to explain it, not one was satisfactory. Of the escape itself, there was no doubt; an escape that was incomprehensible, sensational, in which the public, as well as the officers of the law, could detect a carefully prepared plan, a combination of circumstances marvelously dove-tailed, whereof the dénouement fully justified the confident prediction of Arsène Lupin: "I shall not be present at my trial."

After a month of patient investigation, the problem remained unsolved. The poor devil of a Baudru could not be kept in prison indefinitely, and to place him on trial would be ridiculous. There was no charge against him. Consequently, he was released; but the chief of the Sûreté resolved to keep him under surveillance. This idea originated with Ganimard. From his point of view there was neither complicity nor chance. Baudru was an instrument upon which Arsène Lupin had played with his extraordinary skill. Baudru, when set at liberty, would lead them to Arsène Lupin or, at least, to some of his accomplices. The two inspectors, Folenfant and Dieuzy, were assigned to assist Ganimard.

One foggy morning in January the prison gates opened and Baudru Désiré stepped forth—a free man. At first he appeared to be quite embarrassed, and walked like a person who has no precise idea whither he is going. He followed the rue de la Santé and the rue Saint Jacques. He stopped in front of an old-clothes shop, removed his jacket and his vest, sold his vest on which he realized a few sous; then, replacing his jacket, he proceeded on his way. He crossed the Seine. At the Châtelet an omnibus passed him. He wished to enter it, but there was no place. The controller advised him to secure a number, so he entered the waiting-room.

Ganimard called to his two assistants, and, without removing his eyes from the waiting room, he said to them:

"Stop a carriage.... no, two. That will be better. I will go with one of you, and we will follow him."

The men obeyed. Yet Baudru did not appear. Ganimard entered the waiting-room. It was empty.

"Idiot that I am!" he muttered, "I forgot there was another exit."

There was an interior corridor extending from the waiting-room to the rue Saint Martin. Ganimard rushed through it and arrived just in time to observe Baudru upon the top of the Batignolles-Jardin de Plates omnibus as it was turning the corner of the rue de Rivoli. He ran and caught the omnibus. But he had lost his two assistants. He must continue the pursuit alone. In his anger he was inclined to seize the man by the collar without ceremony. Was it not with premeditation and by means of an ingenious ruse that his pretended imbecile had separated him from his assistants?

He looked at Baudru. The latter was asleep on the bench, his head rolling from side to side, his mouth half-opened, and an incredible expression of stupidity on his blotched face. No, such an adversary was incapable of deceiving old Ganimard. It was a stroke of luck—nothing more.

At the Galleries-Lafayette, the man leaped from the omnibus and took the La Muette tramway, following the boulevard Haussmann and the avenue Victor Hugo. Baudru alighted at La Muette station; and, with a nonchalant air, strolled into the Bois de Boulogne.

He wandered through one path after another, and sometimes retraced his steps. What was he seeking? Had he any definite object? At the end of an hour, he appeared to be faint from fatigue, and, noticing a bench, he sat down. The spot, not far from Auteuil, on the edge of a pond hidden amongst the trees, was absolutely deserted. After the lapse of another half-hour, Ganimard became impatient and resolved to speak to the man. He approached and took a seat beside Baudru, lighted a cigarette, traced some figures in the sand with the end of his cane, and said:

"It's a pleasant day."

No response. But, suddenly the man burst into laughter, a happy, mirthful laugh, spontaneous and irresistible. Ganimard felt his hair stand on end in horror and surprise. It was that laugh, that infernal laugh he knew so well!

With a sudden movement, he seized the man by the collar and looked at him with a keen, penetrating gaze; and found that he no longer saw the man Baudru. To be sure, he saw Baudru; but, at the same time, he saw the other, the real man, Lupin. He discovered the intense life in the eyes, he filled up the shrunken features, he perceived the real flesh beneath the flabby skin, the real mouth through the grimaces that deformed it. Those were the eyes and mouth of the other, and especially his keen, alert, mocking expression, so clear and youthful!

"Arsène Lupin, Arsène Lupin," he stammered.

Then, in a sudden fit of rage, he seized Lupin by the throat and tried to hold him down. In spite of his fifty years, he still possessed unusual strength, whilst his adversary was apparently in a weak condition. But the struggle was a brief one. Arsène Lupin made only a slight movement, and, as suddenly as he had made the attack, Ganimard released his hold. His right arm fell inert, useless.

"If you had taken lessons in jiu-jitsu at the quai des Orfèvres," said Lupin, "you would know that that blow is called udi-shi-ghi in Japanese. A second more, and I would have broken your arm and that would have been just what you deserve. I am surprised that you, an old friend whom I respect and before whom I voluntarily expose my incognito, should abuse my confidence in that violent manner. It is unworthy—Ah! What's the matter?"

Ganimard did not reply. That escape for which he deemed himself responsible—was it not he, Ganimard, who, by his sensational evidence, had led the court into serious error? That escape appeared to him like a dark cloud on his professional career. A tear rolled down his cheek to his gray moustache.

"Oh! mon Dieu, Ganimard, don't take it to heart. If you had not spoken, I would have arranged for some one else to do it. I couldn't allow poor Baudru Désiré to be convicted."

"Then," murmured Ganimard, "it was you that was there? And now you are here?"

"It is I, always I, only I."

"Can it be possible?"

"Oh, it is not the work of a sorcerer. Simply, as the judge remarked at the trial, the apprenticeship of a dozen years that equips a man to cope successfully with all the obstacles in life."

"But your face? Your eyes?"

"You can understand that if I worked eighteen months with Doctor Altier at the Saint-Louis hospital, it was not out of love for the work. I considered that he, who would one day have the honor of calling himself Arsène Lupin, ought to be exempt from the ordinary laws governing appearance and identity. Appearance? That can be modified at will. For instance, a hypodermic injection of paraffine will puff up the skin at the desired spot. Pyrogallic acid will change your skin to that of an Indian. The juice of the greater celandine will adorn you with the most beautiful eruptions and tumors. Another chemical affects the growth of your beard and hair; another changes the tone of your voice. Add to that two months of dieting in cell 24; exercises repeated a thousand times to enable me to hold my features in a certain grimace, to carry my head at a certain inclination, and adapt my back and shoulders to a stooping posture. Then five drops of atropine in the eyes to make them haggard and wild, and the trick is done."

"I do not understand how you deceived the guards."

"The change was progressive. The evolution was so gradual that they failed to notice it."

"But Baudru Désiré?" "Baudru exists. He is a poor, harmless fellow whom I met last year; and, really, he bears a certain resemblance to me. Considering my arrest as a possible event, I took charge of Baudru and studied the points wherein we differed in appearance with a view to correct them in my own person. My friends caused him to remain at the Dépôt overnight, and to leave there next day about the same hour as I did—a coincidence easily arranged. Of course, it was necessary to have a record of his detention at the Dépôt in order to establish the fact that such a person was a reality; otherwise, the police would have sought elsewhere to find out my identity. But, in offering to them this excellent Baudru, it was inevitable, you understand, inevitable that they would seize upon him, and, despite the insurmountable difficulties of a substitution, they would prefer to believe in a substitution than confess their ignorance."

"Yes, yes, of course," said Ganimard.

"And then," exclaimed Arsène Lupin, "I held in my hands a trump-card: an anxious public watching and waiting for my escape. And that is the fatal error into which you fell, you and the others, in the course of that fascinating game pending between me and the officers of the law wherein the stake was my liberty. And you supposed that I was playing to the gallery; that I was intoxicated with my success. I, Arsène Lupin, guilty of such weakness! Oh, no! And, no longer ago than the Cahorn affair, you said: "When Arsène Lupin cries from the housetops that he will escape, he has some object in view." But, sapristi, you must understand that in order to escape I must create, in advance, a public belief in that escape, a belief amounting to an article of faith, an absolute conviction, a reality as glittering as the sun. And I did create that belief that Arsène Lupin would escape, that Arsène Lupin would not be present at his trial. And when you gave your evidence and said: "That man is not Arsène Lupin," everybody was prepared to believe you. Had one person doubted it, had any one uttered this simple restriction: Suppose it is Arsène Lupin?—from that moment, I was lost. If anyone had scrutinized my face, not imbued with the idea that I was not Arsène Lupin, as you and the others did at my trial, but with the idea that I might be Arsène Lupin; then, despite all my precautions, I should have been recognized. But I had no fear. Logically, psychologically, no once could entertain the idea that I was Arsène Lupin."

He grasped Ganimard's hand.

"Come, Ganimard, confess that on the Wednesday after our conversation in the prison de la Santé, you expected me at your house at four o'clock, exactly as I said I would go."

"And your prison-van?" said Ganimard, evading the question.

"A bluff! Some of my friends secured that old unused van and wished to make the attempt. But I considered it impractical without the concurrence of a number of unusual circumstances. However, I found it useful to carry out that attempted escape and give it the widest publicity. An audaciously planned escape, though not completed, gave to the succeeding one the character of reality simply by anticipation."

"So that the cigar...."

"Hollowed by myself, as well as the knife."

"And the letters?"

"Written by me."

"And the mysterious correspondent?"

"Did not exist."

Ganimard reflected a moment, then said:

"When the anthropological service had Baudru's case under consideration, why did they not perceive that his measurements coincided with those of Arsène Lupin?"

"My measurements are not in existence."

"Indeed!"

"At least, they are false. I have given considerable attention to that question. In the first place, the Bertillon system of records the visible marks of identification—and you have seen that they are not infallible—and, after that, the measurements of the head, the fingers, the ears, etc. Of course, such measurements are more or less infallible."

"Absolutely."

"No; but it costs money to get around them. Before we left America, one of the employees of the service there accepted so much money to insert false figures in my measurements. Consequently, Baudru's measurements should not agree with those of Arsène Lupin."

After a short silence, Ganimard asked:

"What are you going to do now?"

"Now," replied Lupin, "I am going to take a rest, enjoy the best of food and drink and gradually recover my former healthy condition. It is all very well to become Baudru or some other person, on occasion, and to change your personality as you do your shirt, but you soon grow weary of the change. I feel exactly as I imagine the man who lost his shadow must have felt, and I shall be glad to be Arsène Lupin once more."

He walked to and fro for a few minutes, then, stopping in front of Ganimard, he said:

"You have nothing more to say, I suppose?"

"Yes. I should like to know if you intend to reveal the true state of facts connected with your escape. The mistake that I made——"

"Oh! no one will ever know that it was Arsène Lupin who was discharged. It is to my own interest to surround myself with mystery, and therefore I shall permit my escape to retain its almost miraculous character. So, have no fear on that score, my dear friend. I shall say nothing. And now, good-bye. I am going out to dinner this evening, and have only sufficient time to dress."

"I though you wanted a rest."

"Ah! there are duties to society that one cannot avoid. To-morrow, I shall rest."

"Where do you dine to-night?"

"With the British Ambassador!"

IV. THE MYSTERIOUS TRAVELLER

The evening before, I had sent my automobile to Rouen by the highway. I was to travel to Rouen by rail, on my way to visit some friends that live on the banks of the Seine.

At Paris, a few minutes before the train started, seven gentlemen entered my compartment; five of them were smoking. No matter that the journey was a short one, the thought of traveling with such a company was not agreeable to me, especially as the car was built on the old model, without a corridor. I picked up my overcoat, my newspapers and my time-table, and sought refuge in a neighboring compartment.

It was occupied by a lady, who, at sight of me, made a gesture of annoyance that did not escape my notice, and she leaned toward a gentleman who was standing on the step and was, no doubt, her husband. The gentleman scrutinized me closely, and, apparently, my appearance did not displease him, for he smiled as he spoke to his wife with the air of one who reassures a frightened child. She smiled also, and gave me a friendly glance as if she now understood that I was one of those gallant men with whom a woman can remain shut up for two hours in a little box, six feet square, and have nothing to fear.

Her husband said to her:

"I have an important appointment, my dear, and cannot wait any longer. Adieu."

He kissed her affectionately and went away. His wife threw him a few kisses and waved her handkerchief. The whistle sounded, and the train started.

At that precise moment, and despite the protests of the guards, the door was opened, and a man rushed into our compartment. My companion, who was standing and arranging her luggage, uttered a cry of terror and fell upon the seat. I am not a coward—far from it—but I confess that such intrusions at the last minute are always disconcerting. They have a suspicious, unnatural aspect.

However, the appearance of the new arrival greatly modified the unfavorable impression produced by his precipitant action. He was correctly and elegantly dressed, wore a tasteful cravat, correct gloves, and his face was refined and intelligent. But, where the devil had I seen that face before? Because, beyond all possible doubt, I had seen it. And yet the memory of it was so vague and indistinct that I felt it would be useless to try to recall it at that time.

Then, directing my attention to the lady, I was amazed at the pallor and anxiety I saw in her face. She was looking at her neighbor—they occupied seats on the same side of the compartment—with an expression of intense alarm, and I perceived that one of her trembling hands was slowly gliding toward a little traveling bag that was lying on the seat about twenty inches from her. She finished by seizing it and nervously drawing it to her. Our eyes met, and I read in hers so much anxiety and fear that I could not refrain from speaking to her:

"Are you ill, madame? Shall I open the window?"

Her only reply was a gesture indicating that she was afraid of our companion. I smiled, as her husband had done, shrugged my shoulders, and explained to her, in pantomime, that she had nothing to fear, that I was there, and, besides, the gentleman appeared to be a very harmless individual. At that moment, he turned toward us, scrutinized both of us from head to foot, then settled down in his corner and paid us no more attention.

After a short silence, the lady, as if she had mustered all her energy to perform a desperate act, said to me, in an almost inaudible voice:

"Do you know who is on our train?"

"Who?"

"He.... he....I assure you...."

"Who is he?"

"Arsène Lupin!"

She had not taken her eyes off our companion, and it was to him rather than to me that she uttered the syllables of that disquieting name. He drew his hat over his face. Was that to conceal his agitation or, simply, to arrange himself for sleep? Then I said to her:

"Yesterday, through contumacy, Arsène Lupin was sentenced to twenty years' imprisonment at hard labor. Therefore it is improbable that he would be so imprudent, to-day, as to show himself in public. Moreover, the newspapers have announced his appearance in Turkey since his escape from the Santé."

"But he is on this train at the present moment," the lady proclaimed, with the obvious intention of being heard by our companion; "my husband is one of the directors in the penitentiary service, and it was the stationmaster himself who told us that a search was being made for Arsène Lupin."

"They may have been mistaken—-"

"No; he was seen in the waiting-room. He bought a first-class ticket for Rouen."

"He has disappeared. The guard at the waiting-room door did not see him pass, and it is supposed that he had got into the express that leaves ten minutes after us."

"In that case, they will be sure to catch him."

"Unless, at the last moment, he leaped from that train to come here, into our train.... which is quite probable.... which is almost certain."

"If so, he will be arrested just the same; for the employees and guards would no doubt observe his passage from one train to the other, and, when we arrive at Rouen, they will arrest him there."

"Him—never! He will find some means of escape."

"In that case, I wish him 'bon voyage.'"

"But, in the meantime, think what he may do!"

"What?"

"I don't know. He may do anything."

She was greatly agitated, and, truly, the situation justified, to some extent, her nervous excitement. I was impelled to say to her:

"Of course, there are many strange coincidences, but you need have no fear. Admitting that Arsène Lupin is on this train, he will not commit any indiscretion; he will be only too happy to escape the peril that already threatens him."

My words did not reassure her, but she remained silent for a time. I unfolded my newspapers and read reports of Arsène Lupin's trial, but, as they contained nothing that was new to me, I was not greatly interested. Moreover, I was tired and sleepy. I felt my eyelids close and my head drop.

"But, monsieur, you are not going to sleep!"

She seized my newspaper, and looked at me with indignation.

"Certainly not," I said.

"That would be very imprudent."

"Of course," I assented.

I struggled to keep awake. I looked through the window at the landscape and the fleeting clouds, but in a short time all that became confused and indistinct; the image of the nervous lady and the drowsy gentleman were effaced from my memory, and I was buried in the soothing depths of a profound sleep. The tranquility of my response was soon disturbed by disquieting dreams, wherein a creature that had played the part and bore the name of Arsène Lupin held an important place. He appeared to me with his back laden with articles of value; he leaped over walls, and plundered castles. But the outlines of that creature, who was no longer

Arsène Lupin, assumed a more definite form. He came toward me, growing larger and larger, leaped into the compartment with incredible agility, and landed squarely on my chest. With a cry of fright and pain, I awoke. The man, the traveller, our companion, with his knee on my breast, held me by the throat.

My sight was very indistinct, for my eyes were suffused with blood. I could see the lady, in a corner of the compartment, convulsed with fright. I tried even not to resist. Besides, I did not have the strength. My temples throbbed; I was almost strangled. One minute more, and I would have breathed my last. The man must have realized it, for he relaxed his grip, but did not remove his hand. Then he took a cord, in which he had prepared a slip-knot, and tied my wrists together. In an instant, I was bound, gagged, and helpless.

Certainly, he accomplished the trick with an ease and skill that revealed the hand of a master; he was, no doubt, a professional thief. Not a word, not a nervous movement; only coolness and audacity. And I was there, lying on the bench, bound like a mummy, I—Arsène Lupin!

It was anything but a laughing matter, and yet, despite the gravity of the situation, I keenly appreciated the humor and irony that it involved. Arsène Lupin seized and bound like a novice! robbed as if I were an unsophisticated rustic—for, you must understand, the scoundrel had deprived me of my purse and wallet! Arsène Lupin, a victim, duped, vanquished....What an adventure!

The lady did not move. He did not even notice her. He contented himself with picking up her traveling-bag that had fallen to the floor and taking from it the jewels, purse, and gold and silver trinkets that it contained. The lady opened her eyes, trembled with fear, drew the rings from her fingers and handed them to the man as if she wished to spare him unnecessary trouble. He took the rings and looked at her. She swooned.

Then, quite unruffled, he resumed his seat, lighted a cigarette, and proceeded to examine the treasure that he had acquired. The examination appeared to give him perfect satisfaction.

But I was not so well satisfied. I do not speak of the twelve thousand francs of which I had been unduly deprived: that was only a temporary loss, because I was certain that I would recover possession of that money after a very brief delay, together with the important papers contained in my wallet: plans, specifications, addresses, lists of correspondents, and compromising letters. But, for the moment, a more immediate and more serious question troubled me: How would this affair end? What would be the outcome of this adventure?

As you can imagine, the disturbance created by my passage through the Saint-Lazare station has not escaped my notice. Going to visit friends who knew me under the name of Guillaume Berlat, and amongst whom my resemblance to Arsène Lupin was a subject of many innocent jests, I could not assume a disguise, and my presence had been remarked. So, beyond question, the commissary of police at Rouen, notified by telegraph, and assisted by numerous agents, would be awaiting the train, would question all suspicious passengers, and proceed to search the cars.

Of course, I had foreseen all that, but it had not disturbed me, as I was certain that the police of Rouen would not be any shrewder than the police of Paris and that I could escape recognition; would it not be sufficient for me to carelessly display my card as "député," thanks to which I had inspired complete confidence in the gate-keeper at Saint-Lazare?—But the situation was greatly changed. I was no longer free. It was impossible to attempt one of my usual tricks. In one of the compartments, the commissary of police would find Mon. Arsène Lupin, bound hand and foot, as docile as a lamb, packed up, all ready to be dumped into a prison-van. He would have simply to accept delivery of the parcel, the same as if it were so much merchandise or a basket of fruit and vegetables. Yet, to avoid that shameful dénouement, what could I do?—bound and gagged, as I was? And the train was rushing on toward Rouen, the next and only station.

Another problem was presented, in which I was less interested, but the solution of which aroused my professional curiosity. What were the intentions of my rascally companion? Of course, if I had been alone, he could, on our arrival at Rouen, leave the car slowly and fearlessly. But the lady? As soon as the door of the compartment should be opened, the lady, now so quiet and humble, would scream and call for help. That was the dilemma that perplexed me! Why had he not reduced her to a helpless condition similar to mine? That would have given him ample time to disappear before his double crime was discovered.

He was still smoking, with his eyes fixed upon the window that was now being streaked with drops of rain. Once he turned, picked up my time-table, and consulted it.

The lady had to feign a continued lack of consciousness in order to deceive the enemy. But fits of coughing, provoked by the smoke, exposed her true condition. As to me, I was very uncomfortable, and very tired. And I meditated; I plotted.

The train was rushing on, joyously, intoxicated with its own speed.

Saint Etienne!....At that moment, the man arose and took two steps toward us, which caused the lady to utter a cry of alarm and fall into a genuine swoon. What was the man about to do? He lowered the window on our side. A heavy rain was now falling, and, by a gesture, the man expressed his annoyance at his not having an umbrella or an overcoat. He glanced at the rack. The lady's umbrella was there. He took it. He also took my overcoat and put it on.

We were now crossing the Seine. He turned up the bottoms of his trousers, then leaned over and raised the exterior latch of the door. Was he going to throw himself upon the track? At that speed, it would have been instant death. We now entered a tunnel. The man opened the door half-way and stood on the upper step. What folly! The darkness, the smoke, the noise, all gave a fantastic appearance to his actions. But suddenly, the train diminished its speed. A moment later it increased its speed, then slowed up again. Probably, some repairs were being made in that part of the tunnel which obliged the trains to diminish their speed, and the man was aware of the fact. He immediately stepped down to the lower step, closed the door behind him, and leaped to the ground. He was gone.

The lady immediately recovered her wits, and her first act was to lament the loss of her jewels. I gave her an imploring look. She understood, and quickly removed the gag that stifled me. She wished to untie the cords that bound me, but I prevented her.

"No, no, the police must see everything exactly as it stands. I want them to see what the rascal did to us."

"Suppose I pull the alarm-bell?"

"Too late. You should have done that when he made the attack on me."

"But he would have killed me. Ah! monsieur, didn't I tell you that he was on this train. I recognized him from his portrait. And now he has gone off with my jewels."

"Don't worry. The police will catch him."

"Catch Arsène Lupin! Never."

"That depends on you, madame. Listen. When we arrive at Rouen, be at the door and call. Make a noise. The police and the railway employees will come. Tell what you have seen: the assault made on me and the flight of Arsène Lupin. Give a description of him—soft hat, umbrella—yours—gray overcoat...."

"Yours," said she.

"What! mine? Not at all. It was his. I didn't have any."

"It seems to me he didn't have one when he came in."

"Yes, yes.... unless the coat was one that some one had forgotten and left in the rack. At all events, he had it when he went away, and that is the essential point. A gray overcoat—remember!....Ah! I forgot. You must tell your name, first thing you do. Your husband's official position will stimulate the zeal of the police."

We arrived at the station. I gave her some further instructions in a rather imperious tone:

"Tell them my name—Guillaume Berlat. If necessary, say that you know me. That will save time. We must expedite the preliminary investigation. The important thing is the pursuit of Arsène Lupin. Your jewels, remember! Let there be no mistake. Guillaume Berlat, a friend of your husband."

"I understand....Guillaume Berlat."

She was already calling and gesticulating. As soon as the train stopped, several men entered the compartment. The critical moment had come.

Panting for breath, the lady exclaimed:

"Arsène Lupin.... he attacked us.... he stole my jewels....I am Madame Renaud.... my husband is a director of the penitentiary service....Ah! here is my brother, Georges Ardelle, director of the Crédit Rouennais.... you must know...."

She embraced a young man who had just joined us, and whom the commissary saluted. Then she continued, weeping:

"Yes, Arsène Lupin.... while monsieur was sleeping, he seized him by the throat....Mon. Berlat, a friend of my husband."

The commissary asked:

"But where is Arsène Lupin?"

"He leaped from the train, when passing through the tunnel."

"Are you sure that it was he?"

"Am I sure! I recognized him perfectly. Besides, he was seen at the Saint-Lazare station. He wore a soft hat—-"

"No, a hard felt, like that," said the commissary, pointing to my hat.

"He had a soft hat, I am sure," repeated Madame Renaud, "and a gray overcoat."

"Yes, that is right," replied the commissary, "the telegram says he wore a gray overcoat with a black velvet collar."

"Exactly, a black velvet collar," exclaimed Madame Renaud, triumphantly.

I breathed freely. Ah! the excellent friend I had in that little woman.

The police agents had now released me. I bit my lips until they ran blood. Stooping over, with my handkerchief over my mouth, an attitude quite natural in a person who has remained for a long time in an uncomfortable position, and whose mouth shows the bloody marks of the gag, I addressed the commissary, in a weak voice:

"Monsieur, it was Arsène Lupin. There is no doubt about that. If we make haste, he can be caught yet. I think I may be of some service to you."

The railway car, in which the crime occurred, was detached from the train to serve as a mute witness at the official investigation. The train continued on its way to Havre. We were then conducted to the station-master's office through a crowd of curious spectators.

Then, I had a sudden access of doubt and discretion. Under some pretext or other, I must gain my automobile, and escape. To remain there was dangerous. Something might happen; for instance, a telegram from Paris, and I would be lost.

Yes, but what about my thief? Abandoned to my own resources, in an unfamiliar country, I could not hope to catch him.

"Bah! I must make the attempt," I said to myself. "It may be a difficult game, but an amusing one, and the stake is well worth the trouble."

And when the commissary asked us to repeat the story of the robbery, I exclaimed:

"Monsieur, really, Arsène Lupin is getting the start of us. My automobile is waiting in the courtyard. If you will be so kind as to use it, we can try...."

The commissary smiled, and replied:

"The idea is a good one; so good, indeed, that it is already being carried out. Two of my men have set out on bicycles. They have been gone for some time."

"Where did they go?"

"To the entrance of the tunnel. There, they will gather evidence, secure witnesses, and follow on the track of Arsène Lupin."

I could not refrain from shrugging my shoulders, as I replied:

"Your men will not secure any evidence or any witnesses."

"Really!"

"Arsène Lupin will not allow anyone to see him emerge from the tunnel. He will take the first road——"

"To Rouen, where we will arrest him."

"He will not go to Rouen."

"Then he will remain in the vicinity, where his capture will be even more certain."

"He will not remain in the vicinity."

"Oh! oh! And where will he hide?"

I looked at my watch, and said:

"At the present moment, Arsène Lupin is prowling around the station at Darnétal. At ten fifty, that is, in twenty-two minutes from now, he will take the train that goes from Rouen to Amiens."

"Do you think so? How do you know it?"

"Oh! it is quite simple. While we were in the car, Arsène Lupin consulted my railway guide. Why did he do it? Was there, not far from the spot where he disappeared, another line of railway, a station upon that line, and a train stopping at that station? On consulting my railway guide, I found such to be the case."

"Really, monsieur," said the commissary, "that is a marvelous deduction. I congratulate you on your skill."

I was now convinced that I had made a mistake in displaying so much cleverness. The commissary regarded me with astonishment, and I thought a slight suspicion entered his official mind....Oh! scarcely that, for the photographs distributed broadcast by the police department were too imperfect; they presented an

Arsène Lupin so different from the one he had before him, that he could not possibly recognize me by it. But, all the same, he was troubled, confused and ill-at-ease.

"Mon Dieu! nothing stimulates the comprehension so much as the loss of a pocketbook and the desire to recover it. And it seems to me that if you will give me two of your men, we may be able...."

"Oh! I beg of you, monsieur le commissaire," cried Madame Renaud, "listen to Mon. Berlat."

The intervention of my excellent friend was decisive. Pronounced by her, the wife of an influential official, the name of Berlat became really my own, and gave me an identity that no mere suspicion could affect. The commissary arose, and said:

"Believe me, Monsieur Berlat, I shall be delighted to see you succeed. I am as much interested as you are in the arrest of Arsène Lupin."

He accompanied me to the automobile, and introduced two of his men, Honoré Massol and Gaston Delivet, who were assigned to assist me. My chauffer cranked up the car and I took my place at the wheel. A few seconds later, we left the station. I was saved.

Ah! I must confess that in rolling over the boulevards that surrounded the old Norman city, in my swift thirty-five horse-power Moreau-Lepton, I experienced a deep feeling of pride, and the motor responded, sympathetically to my desires. At right and left, the trees flew past us with startling rapidity, and I, free, out of danger, had simply to arrange my little personal affairs with the two honest representatives of the Rouen police who were sitting behind me. Arsène Lupin was going in search of Arsène Lupin!

Modest guardians of social order—Gaston Delivet and Honoré Massol—how valuable was your assistance! What would I have done without you? Without you, many times, at the cross-roads, I might have taken the wrong route! Without you, Arsène Lupin would have made a mistake, and the other would have escaped!

But the end was not yet. Far from it. I had yet to capture the thief and recover the stolen papers. Under no circumstances must my two acolytes be permitted to see those papers, much less to seize them. That was a point that might give me some difficulty.

We arrived at Darnétal three minutes after the departure of the train. True, I had the consolation of learning that a man wearing a gray overcoat with a black velvet collar had taken the train at the station. He had bought a second-class ticket for Amiens. Certainly, my début as detective was a promising one.

Delivet said to me:

"The train is express, and the next stop is Montérolier-Buchy in nineteen minutes. If we do not reach there before Arsène Lupin, he can proceed to Amiens, or change for the train going to Clères, and, from that point, reach Dieppe or Paris."

"How far to Montérolier?"

"Twenty-three kilometres."

"Twenty-three kilometres in nineteen minutes....We will be there ahead of him."

We were off again! Never had my faithful Moreau-Repton responded to my impatience with such ardor and regularity. It participated in my anxiety. It indorsed my determination. It comprehended my animosity against that rascally Arsène Lupin. The knave! The traitor!

"Turn to the right," cried Delivet, "then to the left."

We fairly flew, scarcely touching the ground. The mile-stones looked like little timid beasts that vanished at our approach. Suddenly, at a turn of the road, we saw a vortex of smoke. It was the Northern Express. For a kilometre, it was a struggle, side by side, but an unequal struggle in which the issue was certain. We won the race by twenty lengths.

In three seconds we were on the platform standing before the second-class carriages. The doors were opened, and some passengers alighted, but not my thief. We made a search through the compartments. No sign of Arsène Lupin.

"Sapristi!" I cried, "he must have recognized me in the automobile as we were racing, side by side, and he leaped from the train."

"Ah! there he is now! crossing the track."

I started in pursuit of the man, followed by my two acolytes, or rather followed by one of them, for the other, Massol, proved himself to be a runner of exceptional speed and endurance. In a few moments, he had made an appreciable gain upon the fugitive. The man noticed it, leaped over a hedge, scampered across a meadow, and entered a thick grove. When we reached this grove, Massol was waiting for us. He went no farther, for fear of losing us.

"Quite right, my dear friend," I said. "After such a run, our victim must be out of wind. We will catch him now."

I examined the surroundings with the idea of proceeding alone in the arrest of the fugitive, in order to recover my papers, concerning which the authorities would doubtless ask many disagreeable questions. Then I returned to my companions, and said:

"It is all quite easy. You, Massol, take your place at the left; you, Delivet, at the right. From there, you can observe the entire posterior line of the bush, and he cannot escape without you seeing him, except by that ravine, and I shall watch it. If he does not come out voluntarily, I will enter and drive him out toward one or the other of you. You have simply to wait. Ah! I forgot: in case I need you, a pistol shot."

Massol and Delivet walked away to their respective posts. As soon as they had disappeared, I entered the grove with the greatest precaution so as to be neither seen nor heard. I encountered dense thickets, through which narrow paths had been cut, but the overhanging boughs compelled me to adopt a stooping posture. One of these paths led to a clearing in which I found footsteps upon the wet grass. I followed them; they led me to the foot of a mound which was surmounted by a deserted, dilapidated hovel.

"He must be there," I said to myself. "It is a well-chosen retreat."

I crept cautiously to the side of the building. A slight noise informed me that he was there; and, then, through an opening, I saw him. His back was turned toward me. In two bounds, I was upon him. He tried to fire a revolver that he held in his hand. But he had no time. I threw him to the ground, in such a manner that his arms were beneath him, twisted and helpless, whilst I held him down with my knee on his breast.

"Listen, my boy," I whispered in his ear. "I am Arsène Lupin. You are to deliver over to me, immediately and gracefully, my pocketbook and the lady's jewels, and, in return therefore, I will save you from the police and enroll you amongst my friends. One word: yes or no?"

"Yes," he murmured.

"Very good. Your escape, this morning, was well planned. I congratulate you."

I arose. He fumbled in his pocket, drew out a large knife and tried to strike me with it.

"Imbecile!" I exclaimed.

With one hand, I parried the attack; with the other, I gave him a sharp blow on the carotid artery. He fell—stunned!

In my pocketbook, I recovered my papers and bank-notes. Out of curiosity, I took his. Upon an envelope, addressed to him, I read his name: Pierre Onfrey. It startled me. Pierre Onfrey, the assassin of the rue Lafontaine at Auteuil! Pierre Onfrey, he who had cut the throats of Madame Delbois and her two daughters. I leaned over him. Yes, those were the features which, in the compartment, had evoked in me the memory of a face I could not then recall.

But time was passing. I placed in an envelope two bank-notes of one hundred francs each, with a card bearing these words: "Arsène Lupin to his worthy colleagues Honoré Massol and Gaston Delivet, as a slight token of his gratitude." I placed it in a prominent spot in the room, where they would be sure to find it. Beside it, I placed Madame Renaud's handbag. Why could I not return it to the lady who had befriended me? I must confess that I had taken from it everything that possessed any interest or value, leaving there only a shell comb, a stick of rouge Dorin for the lips, and an empty purse. But, you know, business is business. And then, really, her husband is engaged in such a dishonorable vocation!

The man was becoming conscious. What was I to do? I was unable to save him or condemn him. So I took his revolver and fired a shot in the air.

"My two acolytes will come and attend to his case," I said to myself, as I hastened away by the road through the ravine. Twenty minutes later, I was seated in my automobile.

At four o'clock, I telegraphed to my friends at Rouen that an unexpected event would prevent me from making my promised visit. Between ourselves, considering what my friends must now know, my visit is postponed indefinitely. A cruel disillusion for them!

At six o'clock I was in Paris. The evening newspapers informed me that Pierre Onfrey had been captured at last.

Next day,—let us not despise the advantages of judicious advertising,—the `Echo de France' published this sensational item:

"Yesterday, near Buchy, after numerous exciting incidents, Arsène Lupin effected the arrest of Pierre Onfrey. The assassin of the rue Lafontaine had robbed Madame Renaud, wife of the director in the penitentiary service, in a railway carriage on the Paris-Havre line. Arsène Lupin restored to Madame Renaud the hand-bag that contained her jewels, and gave a generous recompense to the two detectives who had assisted him in making that dramatic arrest."

V. THE QUEEN'S NECKLACE

Two or three times each year, on occasions of unusual importance, such as the balls at the Austrian Embassy or the soirées of Lady Billingstone, the Countess de Dreux-Soubise wore upon her white shoulders "The Queen's Necklace."

It was, indeed, the famous necklace, the legendary necklace that Bohmer and Bassenge, court jewelers, had made for Madame Du Barry; the veritable necklace that the Cardinal de Rohan-Soubise intended to give to Marie-Antoinette, Queen of France; and the same that the adventuress Jeanne de Valois, Countess de la Motte, had pulled to pieces one evening in February, 1785, with the aid of her husband and their accomplice, Rétaux de Villette.

To tell the truth, the mounting alone was genuine. Rétaux de Villette had kept it, whilst the Count de la Motte and his wife scattered to the four winds of heaven the beautiful stones so carefully chosen by Bohmer. Later, he sold the mounting to Gaston de Dreux-Soubise, nephew and heir of the Cardinal, who re-purchased the few diamonds that remained in the possession of the English jeweler, Jeffreys; supplemented them with other stones of the same size but of much inferior quality, and thus restored the marvelous necklace to the form in which it had come from the hands of Bohmer and Bassenge.

For nearly a century, the house of Dreux-Soubise had prided itself upon the possession of this historic jewel. Although adverse circumstances had greatly reduced their fortune, they preferred to curtail their household expenses rather than part with this relic of royalty. More particularly, the present count clung to it as a man clings to the home of his ancestors. As a matter of prudence, he had rented a safety-deposit box at the Crédit Lyonnais in which to keep it. He went for it himself on the afternoon of the day on which his wife wished to wear it, and he, himself, carried it back next morning.

On this particular evening, at the reception given at the Palais de Castille, the Countess achieved a remarkable success; and King Christian, in whose honor the fête was given, commented on her grace and beauty. The thousand facets of the diamond sparkled and shone like flames of fire about her shapely neck and shoulders, and it is safe to say that none but she could have borne the weight of such an ornament with so much ease and grace.

This was a double triumph, and the Count de Dreux was highly elated when they returned to their chamber in the old house of the faubourg Saint-Germain. He was proud of his wife, and quite as proud, perhaps, of the necklace that had conferred added luster to his noble house for generations. His wife, also, regarded the necklace with an almost childish vanity, and it was not without regret that she removed it from her shoulders and handed it to her husband who admired it as passionately as if he had never seen it before. Then, having placed it in its case of red leather, stamped with the Cardinal's arms, he passed into an adjoining room which was simply an alcove or cabinet that had been cut off from their chamber, and which could be entered only by means of a door at the foot of their bed. As he had done on previous occasions, he hid it on a high shelf amongst hat-boxes and piles of linen. He closed the door, and retired.

Next morning, he arose about nine o'clock, intending to go to the Crédit Lyonnais before breakfast. He dressed, drank a cup of coffee, and went to the stables to give his orders. The condition of one of the horses worried him. He caused it to be exercised in his presence. Then he returned to his wife, who had not yet left the chamber. Her maid was dressing her hair. When her husband entered, she asked:

"Are you going out?"

"Yes, as far as the bank."

"Of course. That is wise."

He entered the cabinet; but, after a few seconds, and without any sign of astonishment, he asked:

"Did you take it, my dear?"

"What?....No, I have not taken anything."

"You must have moved it."

"Not at all. I have not even opened that door."

He appeared at the door, disconcerted, and stammered, in a scarcely intelligible voice:

"You haven't....It wasn't you?....Then...."

She hastened to his assistance, and, together, they made a thorough search, throwing the boxes to the floor and overturning the piles of linen. Then the count said, quite discouraged:

"It is useless to look any more. I put it here, on this shelf."

"You must be mistaken."

"No, no, it was on this shelf—nowhere else."

They lighted a candle, as the room was quite dark, and then carried out all the linen and other articles that the room contained. And, when the room was emptied, they confessed, in despair, that the famous necklace had disappeared. Without losing time in vain lamentations, the countess notified the commissary of police, Mon. Valorbe, who came at once, and, after hearing their story, inquired of the count:

"Are you sure that no one passed through your chamber during the night?"

"Absolutely sure, as I am a very light sleeper. Besides, the chamber door was bolted, and I remember unbolting it this morning when my wife rang for her maid."

"And there is no other entrance to the cabinet?"

"None."

"No windows?"

"Yes, but it is closed up."

"I will look at it."

Candles were lighted, and Mon. Valorbe observed at once that the lower half of the window was covered by a large press which was, however, so narrow that it did not touch the casement on either side.

"On what does this window open?"

"A small inner court."

"And you have a floor above this?"

"Two; but, on a level with the servant's floor, there is a close grating over the court. That is why this room is so dark."

When the press was moved, they found that the window was fastened, which would not have been the case if anyone had entered that way.

"Unless," said the count, "they went out through our chamber."

"In that case, you would have found the door unbolted."

The commissary considered the situation for a moment, then asked the countess:

"Did any of your servants know that you wore the necklace last evening?"

"Certainly; I didn't conceal the fact. But nobody knew that it was hidden in that cabinet."

"No one?"

"No one.... unless...."

"Be quite sure, madam, as it is a very important point."

She turned to her husband, and said:

"I was thinking of Henriette."

"Henriette? She didn't know where we kept it."

"Are you sure?"

"Who is this woman Henriette?" asked Mon. Valorbe.

"A school-mate, who was disowned by her family for marrying beneath her. After her husband's death, I furnished an apartment in this house for her and her son. She is clever with her needle and has done some work for me."

"What floor is she on?"

"Same as ours.... at the end of the corridor.... and I think.... the window of her kitchen...."

"Opens on this little court, does it not?"

"Yes, just opposite ours."

Mon. Valorbe then asked to see Henriette. They went to her apartment; she was sewing, whilst her son Raoul, about six years old, was sitting beside her, reading. The commissary was surprised to see the wretched apartment that had been provided for the woman. It consisted of one room without a fireplace, and a very small room that served as a kitchen. The commissary proceeded to question her. She appeared to be overwhelmed on learning of the theft. Last evening she had herself dressed the countess and placed the necklace upon her shoulders.

"Good God!" she exclaimed, "it can't be possible!"

"And you have no idea? Not the least suspicion? Is it possible that the thief may have passed through your room?"

She laughed heartily, never supposing that she could be an object of suspicion.

"But I have not left my room. I never go out. And, perhaps, you have not seen?"

She opened the kitchen window, and said:

"See, it is at least three metres to the ledge of the opposite window."

"Who told you that we supposed the theft might have been committed in that way?"

"But.... the necklace was in the cabinet, wasn't it?"

"How do you know that?"

"Why, I have always known that it was kept there at night. It had been mentioned in my presence."

Her face, though still young, bore unmistakable traces of sorrow and resignation. And it now assumed an expression of anxiety as if some danger threatened her. She drew her son toward her. The child took her hand, and kissed it affectionately.

When they were alone again, the count said to the commissary:

"I do not suppose you suspect Henriette. I can answer for her. She is honesty itself."

"I quite agree with you," replied Mon. Valorbe. "At most, I thought there might have been an unconscious complicity. But I confess that even that theory must be abandoned, as it does not help solve the problem now before us."

The commissary of police abandoned the investigation, which was now taken up and completed by the examining judge. He questioned the servants, examined the condition of the bolt, experimented with the opening and closing of the cabinet window, and explored the little court from top to bottom. All was in vain. The bolt was intact. The window could not be opened or closed from the outside.

The inquiries especially concerned Henriette, for, in spite of everything, they always turned in her direction. They made a thorough investigation of her past life, and ascertained that, during the last three years, she had left the house only four times, and her business, on those occasions, was satisfactorily explained. As a matter of fact, she acted as chambermaid and seamstress to the countess, who treated her with great strictness and even severity.

At the end of a week, the examining judge had secured no more definite information than the commissary of police. The judge said:

"Admitting that we know the guilty party, which we do not, we are confronted by the fact that we do not know how the theft was committed. We are brought face to face with two obstacles: a door and a window—both closed and fastened. It is thus a double mystery. How could anyone enter, and, moreover, how could any one escape, leaving behind him a bolted door and a fastened window?"

At the end of four months, the secret opinion of the judge was that the count and countess, being hard pressed for money, which was their normal condition, had sold the Queen's Necklace. He closed the investigation.

The loss of the famous jewel was a severe blow to the Dreux-Soubise. Their credit being no longer propped up by the reserve fund that such a treasure constituted, they found themselves confronted by more exacting creditors and money-lenders. They were obliged to cut down to the quick, to sell or mortgage every article that possessed any commercial value. In brief, it would have been their ruin, if two large legacies from some distant relatives had not saved them.

Their pride also suffered a downfall, as if they had lost a quartering from their escutcheon. And, strange to relate, it was upon her former schoolmate, Henriette, that the countess vented her spleen. Toward her, the countess displayed the most spiteful feelings, and even openly accused her. First, Henriette was relegated to the servants' quarters, and, next day, discharged.

For some time, the count and countess passed an uneventful life. They traveled a great deal. Only one incident of record occurred during that period. Some months after the departure of Henriette, the countess was surprised when she received and read the following letter, signed by Henriette:

"Madame," "I do not know how to thank you; for it was you, was it not, who sent me that? It could not have been anyone else. No one but you knows where I live. If I am wrong, excuse me, and accept my sincere thanks for your past favors...."

What did the letter mean? The present or past favors of the countess consisted principally of injustice and neglect. Why, then, this letter of thanks?

When asked for an explanation, Henriette replied that she had received a letter, through the mails, enclosing two bank-notes of one thousand francs each. The envelope, which she enclosed with her reply, bore the Paris post-mark, and was addressed in a handwriting that was obviously disguised. Now, whence came those two thousand francs? Who had sent them? And why had they sent them?

Henriette received a similar letter and a like sum of money twelve months later. And a third time; and a fourth; and each year for a period of six years, with this difference, that in the fifth and sixth years the sum was doubled. There was another difference: the post-office authorities having seized one of the letters under the pretext that it was not registered, the last two letters were duly sent according to the postal regulations, the first dated from Saint-Germain, the other from Suresnes. The writer signed the first one, "Anquety"; and the other, "Péchard." The addresses that he gave were false.

At the end of six years, Henriette died, and the mystery remained unsolved.

All these events are known to the public. The case was one of those which excite public interest, and it was a strange coincidence that this necklace, which had caused such a great commotion in France at the close of the eighteenth century, should create a similar commotion a century later. But what I am about to relate is known only to the parties directly interested and a few others from whom the count exacted a promise of secrecy. As it is probable that some day or other that promise will be broken, I have no hesitation in rending the veil and thus disclosing the key to the mystery, the explanation of the letter published in the morning papers two days ago; an extraordinary letter which increased, if possible, the mists and shadows that envelope this inscrutable drama.

Five days ago, a number of guests were dining with the Count de Dreux-Soubise. There were several ladies present, including his two nieces and his cousin, and the following gentlemen: the president of Essaville, the deputy Bochas, the chevalier Floriani, whom the count had known in Sicily, and General Marquis de Rouzières, and old club friend.

After the repast, coffee was served by the ladies, who gave the gentlemen permission to smoke their cigarettes, provided they would not desert the salon. The conversation was general, and finally one of the guests chanced to speak of celebrated crimes. And that gave the Marquis de Rouzières, who delighted to tease the count, an opportunity to mention the affair of the Queen's Necklace, a subject that the count detested.

Each one expressed his own opinion of the affair; and, of course, their various theories were not only contradictory but impossible.

"And you, monsieur," said the countess to the chevalier Floriani, "what is your opinion?"

"Oh! I—I have no opinion, madame."

All the guests protested; for the chevalier had just related in an entertaining manner various adventures in which he had participated with his father, a magistrate at Palermo, and which established his judgment and taste in such manners.

"I confess," said he, "I have sometimes succeeded in unraveling mysteries that the cleverest detectives have renounced; yet I do not claim to be Herlock Sholmes. Moreover, I know very little about the affair of the Queen's Necklace."

Everybody now turned to the count, who was thus obliged, quite unwillingly, to narrate all the circumstances connected with the theft. The chevalier listened, reflected, asked a few questions, and said:

"It is very strange.... at first sight, the problem appears to be a very simple one."

The count shrugged his shoulders. The others drew closer to the chevalier, who continued, in a dogmatic tone:

"As a general rule, in order to find the author of a crime or a theft, it is necessary to determine how that crime or theft was committed, or, at least, how it could have been committed. In the present case, nothing is more simple, because we are face to face, not with several theories, but with one positive fact, that is to say: the thief could only enter by the chamber door or the window of the cabinet. Now, a person cannot open a bolted door from the outside. Therefore, he must have entered through the window."

"But it was closed and fastened, and we found it fastened afterward," declared the count.

"In order to do that," continued Floriani, without heeding the interruption, "he had simply to construct a bridge, a plank or a ladder, between the balcony of the kitchen and the ledge of the window, and as the jewel-case——"

"But I repeat that the window was fastened," exclaimed the count, impatiently.

This time, Floriani was obliged to reply. He did so with the greatest tranquility, as if the objection was the most insignificant affair in the world.

"I will admit that it was; but is there not a transom in the upper part of the window?"

"How do you know that?"

"In the first place, that was customary in houses of that date; and, in the second place, without such a transom, the theft cannot be explained."

"Yes, there is one, but it was closed, the same as the window. Consequently, we did not pay attention to it."

"That was a mistake; for, if you had examined it, you would have found that it had been opened."

"But how?"

"I presume that, like all others, it opens by means of a wire with a ring on the lower end."

"Yes, but I do not see——"

"Now, through a hole in the window, a person could, by the aid of some instrument, let us say a poker with a hook at the end, grip the ring, pull down, and open the transom."

The count laughed and said:

"Excellent! excellent! Your scheme is very cleverly constructed, but you overlook one thing, monsieur, there is no hole in the window."

"There was a hole."

"Nonsense, we would have seen it."

"In order to see it, you must look for it, and no one has looked. The hole is there; it must be there, at the side of the window, in the putty. In a vertical direction, of course."

The count arose. He was greatly excited. He paced up and down the room, two or three times, in a nervous manner; then, approaching Floriani, said:

"Nobody has been in that room since; nothing has been changed."

"Very well, monsieur, you can easily satisfy yourself that my explanation is correct."

"It does not agree with the facts established by the examining judge. You have seen nothing, and yet you contradict all that we have seen and all that we know."

Floriani paid no attention to the count's petulance. He simply smiled and said:

"Mon Dieu, monsieur, I submit my theory; that is all. If I am mistaken, you can easily prove it."

"I will do so at once....I confess that your assurance——"

The count muttered a few more words; then suddenly rushed to the door and passed out. Not a word was uttered in his absence; and this profound silence gave the situation an air of almost tragic importance. Finally, the count returned. He was pale and nervous. He said to his friends, in a trembling voice:

"I beg your pardon.... the revelations of the chevalier were so unexpected....I should never have thought...."

His wife questioned him, eagerly:

"Speak.... what is it?"

He stammered: "The hole is there, at the very spot, at the side of the window——"

He seized the chevalier's arm, and said to him in an imperious tone:

"Now, monsieur, proceed. I admit that you are right so far, but now.... that is not all.... go on.... tell us the rest of it."

Floriani disengaged his arm gently, and, after a moment, continued:

"Well, in my opinion, this is what happened. The thief, knowing that the countess was going to wear the necklace that evening, had prepared his gangway or bridge during your absence. He watched you through the window and saw you hide the necklace. Afterward, he cut the glass and pulled the ring."

"Ah! but the distance was so great that it would be impossible for him to reach the window-fastening through the transom."

"Well, then, if he could not open the window by reaching through the transom, he must have crawled through the transom."

"Impossible; it is too small. No man could crawl through it."

"Then it was not a man," declared Floriani.

"What!"

"If the transom is too small to admit a man, it must have been a child."

"A child!"

"Did you not say that your friend Henriette had a son?"

"Yes; a son named Raoul."

"Then, in all probability, it was Raoul who committed the theft."

"What proof have you of that?"

"What proof! Plenty of it....For instance——"

He stopped, and reflected for a moment, then continued:

"For instance, that gangway or bridge. It is improbable that the child could have brought it in from outside the house and carried it away again without being observed. He must have used something close at hand. In the little room used by Henriette as a kitchen, were there not some shelves against the wall on which she placed her pans and dishes?"

"Two shelves, to the best of my memory."

"Are you sure that those shelves are really fastened to the wooden brackets that support them? For, if they are not, we could be justified in presuming that the child removed them, fastened them together, and thus formed his bridge. Perhaps, also, since there was a stove, we might find the bent poker that he used to open the transom."

Without saying a word, the count left the room; and, this time, those present did not feel the nervous anxiety they had experienced the first time. They were confident that Floriani was right, and no one was surprised when the count returned and declared:

"It was the child. Everything proves it."

"You have seen the shelves and the poker?"

"Yes. The shelves have been unnailed, and the poker is there yet."

But the countess exclaimed:

"You had better say it was his mother. Henriette is the guilty party. She must have compelled her son—-"

"No," declared the chevalier, "the mother had nothing to do with it."

"Nonsense! they occupied the same room. The child could not have done it without the mother's knowledge."

"True, they lived in the same room, but all this happened in the adjoining room, during the night, while the mother was asleep."

"And the necklace?" said the count. "It would have been found amongst the child's things."

"Pardon me! He had been out. That morning, on which you found him reading, he had just come from school, and perhaps the commissary of police, instead of wasting his time on the innocent mother, would have been better employed in searching the child's desk amongst his school-books."

"But how do you explain those two thousand francs that Henriette received each year? Are they not evidence of her complicity?"

"If she had been an accomplice, would she have thanked you for that money? And then, was she not closely watched? But the child, being free, could easily go to a neighboring city, negotiate with some dealer and sell him one diamond or two diamonds, as he might wish, upon condition that the money should be sent from Paris, and that proceeding could be repeated from year to year."

An indescribable anxiety oppressed the Dreux-Soubise and their guests. There was something in the tone and attitude of Floriani—something more than the chevalier's assurance which, from the beginning, had so annoyed the count. There was a touch of irony, that seemed rather hostile than sympathetic. But the count affected to laugh, as he said:

"All that is very ingenious and interesting, and I congratulate you upon your vivid imagination."

"No, not at all," replied Floriani, with the utmost gravity, "I imagine nothing. I simply describe the events as they must have occurred."

"But what do you know about them?"

"What you yourself have told me. I picture to myself the life of the mother and child down there in the country; the illness of the mother, the schemes of and inventions of the child sell the precious stones in order to save his mother's life, or, at least, soothe her dying moments. Her illness overcomes her. She dies. Years roll on. The child becomes a man; and then—and now I will give my imagination a free rein—let us suppose that the man feels a desire to return to the home of his childhood, that he does so, and that he meets there certain people who suspect and accuse his mother.... do you realize the sorrow and anguish of such an interview in the very house wherein the original drama was played?"

His words seemed to echo for a few seconds in the ensuing silence, and one could read upon the faces of the Count and Countess de Dreux a bewildered effort to comprehend his meaning and, at the same time, the fear and anguish of such a comprehension. The count spoke at last, and said:

"Who are you, monsieur?"

"I? The chevalier Floriani, whom you met at Palermo, and whom you have been gracious enough to invite to your house on several occasions."

"Then what does this story mean?"

"Oh! nothing at all! It is simply a pastime, so far as I am concerned. I endeavor to depict the pleasure that Henriette's son, if he still lives, would have in telling you that he was the guilty party, and that he did it because his mother was unhappy, as she was on the point of losing the place of a.... servant, by which she lived, and because the child suffered at sight of his mother's sorrow."

He spoke with suppressed emotion, rose partially and inclined toward the countess. There could be no doubt that the chevalier Floriani was Henriette's son. His attitude and words proclaimed it. Besides, was it not his obvious intention and desire to be recognized as such?

The count hesitated. What action would he take against the audacious guest? Ring? Provoke a scandal? Unmask the man who had once robbed him? But that was a long time ago! And who would believe that absurd story about the guilty child? No; better far to accept the situation, and pretend not to comprehend the true meaning of it. So the count, turning to Floriani, exclaimed:

"Your story is very curious, very entertaining; I enjoyed it much. But what do you think has become of this young man, this model son? I hope he has not abandoned the career in which he made such a brilliant début."

"Oh! certainly not."

"After such a début! To steal the Queen's Necklace at six years of age; the celebrated necklace that was coveted by Marie-Antoinette!"

"And to steal it," remarked Floriani, falling in with the count's mood, "without costing him the slightest trouble, without anyone thinking to examine the condition of the window, or to observe that the window-sill was too clean—that window-sill which he had wiped in order to efface the marks he had made in the thick dust. We must admit that it was sufficient to turn the head of a boy at that age. It was all so easy. He had simply to desire the thing, and reach out his hand to get it."

"And he reached out his hand."

"Both hands," replied the chevalier, laughing.

His companions received a shock. What mystery surrounded the life of the so-called Floriani? How wonderful must have been the life of that adventurer, a thief at six years of age, and who, to-day, in search of excitement or, at most, to gratify a feeling of resentment, had come to brave his victim in her own house, audaciously, foolishly, and yet with all the grace and delicacy of a courteous guest!

He arose and approached the countess to bid her adieu. She recoiled, unconsciously. He smiled.

"Oh! Madame, you are afraid of me! Did I pursue my role of parlor-magician a step too far?"

She controlled herself, and replied, with her accustomed ease:

"Not at all, monsieur. The legend of that dutiful son interested me very much, and I am pleased to know that my necklace had such a brilliant destiny. But do you not think that the son of that woman, that Henriette, was the victim of hereditary influence in the choice of his vocation?"

He shuddered, feeling the point, and replied:

"I am sure of it; and, moreover, his natural tendency to crime must have been very strong or he would have been discouraged."

"Why so?"

"Because, as you must know, the majority of the diamonds were false. The only genuine stones were the few purchased from the English jeweler, the others having been sold, one by one, to meet the cruel necessities of life."

"It was still the Queen's Necklace, monsieur," replied the countess, haughtily, "and that is something that he, Henriette's son, could not appreciate."

"He was able to appreciate, madame, that, whether true or false, the necklace was nothing more that an object of parade, an emblem of senseless pride."

The count made a threatening gesture, but his wife stopped him.

"Monsieur," she said, "if the man to whom you allude has the slightest sense of honor——"

She stopped, intimidated by Floriani's cool manner.

"If that man has the slightest sense of honor," he repeated.

She felt that she would not gain anything by speaking to him in that manner, and in spite of her anger and indignation, trembling as she was from humiliated pride, she said to him, almost politely:

"Monsieur, the legend says that Rétaux de Villette, when in possession of the Queen's Necklace, did not disfigure the mounting. He understood that the diamonds were simply the ornament, the accessory, and that the mounting was the essential work, the creation of the artist, and he respected it accordingly. Do you think that this man had the same feeling?"

"I have no doubt that the mounting still exists. The child respected it."

"Well, monsieur, if you should happen to meet him, will you tell him that he unjustly keeps possession of a relic that is the property and pride of a certain family, and that, although the stones have been removed, the Queen's necklace still belongs to the house of Dreux-Soubise. It belongs to us as much as our name or our honor."

The chevalier replied, simply:

"I shall tell him, madame."

He bowed to her, saluted the count and the other guests, and departed.

Four days later, the countess de Dreux found upon the table in her chamber a red leather case bearing the cardinal's arms. She opened it, and found the Queen's Necklace.

But as all things must, in the life of a man who strives for unity and logic, converge toward the same goal—and as a little advertising never does any harm—on the following day, the `Echo de France' published these sensational lines:

"The Queen's Necklace, the famous historical jewelry stolen from the family of Dreux-Soubise, has been recovered by Arsène Lupin, who hastened to restore it to its rightful owner. We cannot too highly commend such a delicate and chivalrous act."

VI. THE SEVEN OF HEARTS

I am frequently asked this question: "How did you make the acquaintance of Arsène Lupin?"

My connection with Arsène Lupin was well known. The details that I gather concerning that mysterious man, the irrefutable facts that I present, the new evidence that I produce, the interpretation that I place on certain acts of which the public has seen only the exterior manifestations without being able to discover the secret reasons or the invisible mechanism, all establish, if not an intimacy, at least amicable relations and regular confidences.

But how did I make his acquaintance? Why was I selected to be his historiographer? Why I, and not some one else?

The answer is simple: chance alone presided over my choice; my merit was not considered. It was chance that put me in his way. It was by chance that I was participant in one of his strangest and most mysterious adventures; and by chance that I was an actor in a drama of which he was the marvelous stage director; an obscure and intricate drama, bristling with such thrilling events that I feel a certain embarrassment in undertaking to describe it.

The first act takes place during that memorable night of 22 June, of which so much has already been said. And, for my part, I attribute the anomalous conduct of which I was guilty on that occasion to the unusual frame of mind in which I found myself on my return home. I had dined with some friends at the Cascade restaurant, and, the entire evening, whilst we smoked and the orchestra played melancholy waltzes, we talked only of crimes and thefts, and dark and frightful intrigues. That is always a poor overture to a night's sleep.

The Saint-Martins went away in an automobile. Jean Daspry—that delightful, heedless Daspry who, six months later, was killed in such a tragic manner on the frontier of Morocco—Jean Daspry and I returned on foot through the dark, warm night. When we arrived in front of the little house in which I had lived for a year at Neuilly, on the boulevard Maillot, he said to me:

"Are you afraid?"

"What an idea!"

"But this house is so isolated.... no neighbors.... vacant lots....Really, I am not a coward, and yet——-"

"Well, you are very cheering, I must say."

"Oh! I say that as I would say anything else. The Saint-Martins have impressed me with their stories of brigands and thieves."

We shook hands and said good-night. I took out my key and opened the door.

"Well, that is good," I murmured, "Antoine has forgotten to light a candle."

Then I recalled the fact that Antoine was away; I had given him a short leave of absence. Forthwith, I was disagreeably oppressed by the darkness and silence of the night. I ascended the stairs on tiptoe, and reached my room as quickly as possible; then, contrary to my usual habit, I turned the key and pushed the bolt.

The light of my candle restored my courage. Yet I was careful to take my revolver from its case—a large, powerful weapon—and place it beside my bed. That precaution completed my reassurance. I laid down and, as usual, took a book from my night-table to read myself to sleep. Then I received a great surprise. Instead of the paper-knife with which I had marked my place on the preceding, I found an envelope, closed with five seals of red wax. I seized it eagerly. It was addressed to me, and marked: "Urgent."

A letter! A letter addressed to me! Who could have put it in that place? Nervously, I tore open the envelope, and read:

"From the moment you open this letter, whatever happens, whatever you may hear, do not move, do not utter one cry. Otherwise you are doomed."

I am not a coward, and, quite as well as another, I can face real danger, or smile at the visionary perils of imagination. But, let me repeat, I was in an anomalous condition of mind, with my nerves set on edge by the events of the evening. Besides, was there not, in my present situation, something startling and mysterious, calculated to disturb the most courageous spirit?

My feverish fingers clutched the sheet of paper, and I read and re-read those threatening words: "Do not move, do not utter one cry. Otherwise, you are doomed."

"Nonsense!" I thought. "It is a joke; the work of some cheerful idiot."

I was about to laugh—a good loud laugh. Who prevented me? What haunting fear compressed my throat?

At least, I would blow out the candle. No, I could not do it. "Do not move, or you are doomed," were the words he had written.

These auto-suggestions are frequently more imperious than the most positive realities; but why should I struggle against them? I had simply to close my eyes. I did so.

At that moment, I heard a slight noise, followed by crackling sounds, proceeding from a large room used by me as a library. A small room or antechamber was situated between the library and my bedchamber.

The approach of an actual danger greatly excited me, and I felt a desire to get up, seize my revolver, and rush into the library. I did not rise; I saw one of the curtains of the left window move. There was no doubt about it: the curtain had moved. It was still moving. And I saw—oh! I saw quite distinctly—in the narrow space between the curtains and the window, a human form; a bulky mass that prevented the curtains from hanging straight. And it is equally certain that the man saw me through the large meshes of the curtain. Then, I understood the situation. His mission was to guard me while the others carried away their booty. Should I rise and seize my revolver? Impossible! He was there! At the least movement, at the least cry, I was doomed.

Then came a terrific noise that shook the house; this was followed by lighter sounds, two or three together, like those of a hammer that rebounded. At least, that was the impression formed in my confused brain. These were mingled with other sounds, thus creating a veritable uproar which proved that the intruders were not only bold, but felt themselves secure from interruption.

They were right. I did not move. Was it cowardice? No, rather weakness, a total inability to move any portion of my body, combined with discretion; for why should I struggle? Behind that man, there were ten others who would come to his assistance. Should I risk my life to save a few tapestries and bibelots?

Throughout the night, my torture endured. Insufferable torture, terrible anguish! The noises had stopped, but I was in constant fear of their renewal. And the man! The man who was guarding me, weapon in hand. My fearful eyes remained cast in his direction. And my heart beat! And a profuse perspiration oozed from every pore of my body!

Suddenly, I experienced an immense relief; a milk-wagon, whose sound was familiar to me, passed along the boulevard; and, at the same time, I had an impression that the light of a new day was trying to steal through the closed window-blinds.

At last, daylight penetrated the room; other vehicles passed along the boulevard; and all the phantoms of the night vanished. Then I put one arm out of the bed, slowly and cautiously. My eyes were fixed upon the curtain, locating the exact spot at which I must fire; I made an exact calculation of the movements I must make; then, quickly, I seized my revolver and fired.

I leaped from my bed with a cry of deliverance, and rushed to the window. The bullet had passed through the curtain and the window-glass, but it had not touched the man—for the very good reason that there was none there. Nobody! Thus, during the entire night, I had been hypnotized by a fold of the curtain. And, during that time, the malefactors....Furiously, with an enthusiasm that nothing could have stopped, I turned the key, opened the door, crossed the antechamber, opened another door, and rushed into the library. But amazement stopped me on the threshold, panting, astounded, more astonished than I had been by the absence of the man. All the things that I supposed had been stolen, furniture, books, pictures, old tapestries, everything was in its proper place.

It was incredible. I could not believe my eyes. Notwithstanding that uproar, those noises of removal....I made a tour, I inspected the walls, I made a mental inventory of all the familiar objects. Nothing was missing. And, what was more disconcerting, there was no clue to the intruders, not a sign, not a chair disturbed, not the trace of a footstep.

"Well! Well!" I said to myself, pressing my hands on my bewildered head, "surely I am not crazy! I hear something!"

Inch by inch, I made a careful examination of the room. It was in vain. Unless I could consider this as a discovery: Under a small Persian rug, I found a card—an ordinary playing card. It was the seven of hearts; it was like any other seven of hearts in French playing-cards, with this slight but curious exception: The extreme point of each of the seven red spots or hearts was pierced by a hole, round and regular as if made with the point of an awl.

Nothing more. A card and a letter found in a book. But was not that sufficient to affirm that I had not been the plaything of a dream?

Throughout the day, I continued my searches in the library. It was a large room, much too large for the requirements of such a house, and the decoration of which attested the bizarre taste of its founder. The floor was a mosaic of multicolored stones, formed into large symmetrical designs. The walls were covered with a similar mosaic, arranged in panels, Pompeiian allegories, Byzantine compositions, frescoes of the Middle Ages. A Bacchus bestriding a cask. An emperor wearing a gold crown, a flowing beard, and holding a sword in his right hand.

Quite high, after the style of an artist's studio, there was a large window—the only one in the room. That window being always open at night, it was probable that the men had entered through it, by the aid of a ladder. But, again, there was no evidence. The bottom of the ladder would have left some marks in the soft earth beneath the window; but there were none. Nor were there any traces of footsteps in any part of the yard.

I had no idea of informing the police, because the facts I had before me were so absurd and inconsistent. They would laugh at me. However, as I was then a reporter on the staff of the `Gil Blas,' I wrote a lengthy account of my adventure and it was published in the paper on the second day thereafter. The article attracted some attention, but no one took it seriously. They regarded it as a work of fiction rather than a story of real life. The Saint-Martins rallied me. But Daspry, who took an interest in such matters, came to see me, made a study of the affair, but reached no conclusion.

A few mornings later, the door-bell rang, and Antoine came to inform me that a gentleman desired to see me. He would not give his name. I directed Antoine to show him up. He was a man of about forty years of age with a very dark complexion, lively features, and whose correct dress, slightly frayed, proclaimed a taste that contrasted strangely with his rather vulgar manners. Without any preamble, he said to me—in a rough voice that confirmed my suspicion as to his social position:

"Monsieur, whilst in a café, I picked up a copy of the `Gil Blas,' and read your article. It interested me very much.

"Thank you."

"And here I am."

"Ah!"

"Yes, to talk to you. Are all the facts related by you quite correct?"

"Absolutely so."

"Well, in that case, I can, perhaps, give you some information."

"Very well; proceed."

"No, not yet. First, I must be sure that the facts are exactly as you have related them."

"I have given you my word. What further proof do you want?"

"I must remain alone in this room."

"I do not understand," I said, with surprise.

"It's an idea that occurred to me when reading your article. Certain details established an extraordinary coincidence with another case that came under my notice. If I am mistaken, I shall say nothing more. And the only means of ascertaining the truth is by my remaining in the room alone."

What was at the bottom of this proposition? Later, I recalled that the man was exceedingly nervous; but, at the same time, although somewhat astonished, I found nothing particularly abnormal about the man or the request he had made. Moreover, my curiosity was aroused; so I replied:

"Very well. How much time do you require?"

"Oh! three minutes—not longer. Three minutes from now, I will rejoin you."

I left the room, and went downstairs. I took out my watch. One minute passed. Two minutes. Why did I feel so depressed? Why did those moments seem so solemn and weird? Two minutes and a half....Two minutes and three quarters. Then I heard a pistol shot.

I bounded up the stairs and entered the room. A cry of horror escaped me. In the middle of the room, the man was lying on his left side, motionless. Blood was flowing from a wound in his forehead. Near his hand was a revolver, still smoking.

But, in addition to this frightful spectacle, my attention was attracted by another object. At two feet from the body, upon the floor, I saw a playing-card. It was the seven of hearts. I picked it up. The lower extremity of each of the seven spots was pierced with a small round hole.

A half-hour later, the commissary of police arrived, then the coroner and the chief of the Sûreté, Mon. Dudouis. I had been careful not to touch the corpse. The preliminary inquiry was very brief, and disclosed nothing. There were no papers in the pockets of the deceased; no name upon his clothes; no initial upon his linen; nothing to give any clue to his identity. The room was in the same perfect order as before. The furniture had not been disturbed. Yet this man had not come to my house solely for the purpose of killing himself, or because he considered my place the most convenient one for his suicide! There must have been a motive for his act of despair, and that motive was, no doubt, the result of some new fact ascertained by him during the three minutes he was alone.

What was that fact? What had he seen? What frightful secret had been revealed to him? There was no answer to these questions. But, at the last moment, an incident occurred that appeared to us of considerable importance. As two policemen were raising the body to place it on a stretcher, the left hand thus being disturbed, a crumpled card fell from it. The card bore these words: "Georges Andermatt, 37 Rue de Berry."

What did that mean? Georges Andermatt was a rich banker in Paris, the founder and president of the Metal Exchange which had given such an impulse to the metallic industries in France. He lived in princely style; was the possessor of numerous automobiles, coaches, and an expensive racing-stable. His social affairs were very select, and Madame Andermatt was noted for her grace and beauty.

"Can that be the man's name?" I asked.

The chief of the Sûreté leaned over him.

"It is not he. Mon. Andermatt is a thin man, and slightly grey."

"But why this card?"

"Have you a telephone, monsieur?"

"Yes, in the vestibule. Come with me."

He looked in the directory, and then asked for number 415.21.

"Is Mon. Andermatt at home?....Please tell him that Mon. Dudouis wished him to come at once to 102 Boulevard Maillot. Very important."

Twenty minutes later, Mon. Andermatt arrived in his automobile. After the circumstances had been explained to him, he was taken in to see the corpse. He displayed considerable emotion, and spoke, in a low tone, and apparently unwillingly:

"Etienne Varin," he said.

"You know him?"

"No.... or, at least, yes.... by sight only. His brother...."

"Ah! he has a brother?"

"Yes, Alfred Varin. He came to see me once on some matter of business....I forget what it was."

"Where does he live?"

"The two brothers live together—rue de Provence, I think."

"Do you know any reason why he should commit suicide?"

"None."

"He held a card in his hand. It was your card with your address."

"I do not understand that. It must have been there by some chance that will be disclosed by the investigation."

A very strange chance, I thought; and I felt that the others entertained the same impression.

I discovered the same impression in the papers next day, and amongst all my friends with whom I discussed the affair. Amid the mysteries that enveloped it, after the double discovery of the seven of hearts pierced with seven holes, after the two inscrutable events that had happened in my house, that visiting card promised to throw some light on the affair. Through it, the truth may be revealed. But, contrary to our expectations, Mon. Andermatt furnished no explanation. He said:

"I have told you all I know. What more can I do? I am greatly surprised that my card should be found in such a place, and I sincerely hope the point will be cleared up."

It was not. The official investigation established that the Varin brothers were of Swiss origin, had led a shifting life under various names, frequenting gambling resorts, associating with a band of foreigners who had been dispersed by the police after a series of robberies in which their participation was established only by their flight. At number 24 rue de Provence, where the Varin brothers had lived six years before, no one knew what had become of them.

I confess that, for my part, the case seemed to me so complicated and so mysterious that I did not think the problem would ever be solved, so I concluded to waste no more time upon it. But Jean Daspry, whom I frequently met at that period, became more and more interested in it each day. It was he who pointed out to me that item from a foreign newspaper which was reproduced and commented upon by the entire press. It was as follows:

"The first trial of a new model of submarine boat, which is expected to revolutionize naval warfare, will be given in presence of the former Emperor at a place that will be kept secret until the last minute. An indiscretion has revealed its name; it is called `The Seven-of-Hearts.'"

The Seven-of-Hearts! That presented a new problem. Could a connection be established between the name of the sub-marine and the incidents which we have related? But a connection of what nature? What had happened here could have no possible relation with the sub-marine.

"What do you know about it?" said Daspry to me. "The most diverse effects often proceed from the same cause."

Two days later, the following foreign news item was received and published:

"It is said that the plans of the new sub-marine `Seven-of-Hearts' were prepared by French engineers, who, having sought, in vain, the support of their compatriots, subsequently entered into negotiations with the British Admiralty, without success."

I do not wish to give undue publicity to certain delicate matters which once provoked considerable excitement. Yet, since all danger of injury therefrom has now come to an end, I must speak of the article that appeared in the `Echo de France,' which aroused so much comment at that time, and which threw considerable light upon the mystery of the Seven-of-Hearts. This is the article as it was published over the signature of Salvator:

"THE AFFAIR OF THE SEVEN-OF-HEARTS. "A CORNER OF THE VEIL RAISED.

"We will be brief. Ten years ago, a young mining engineer, Louis Lacombe, wishing to devote his time and fortune to certain studies, resigned his position he then held, and rented number 102 boulevard Maillot, a small house that had been recently built and decorated for an Italian count. Through the agency of the Varin brothers of Lausanne, one of whom assisted in the preliminary experiments and the other acted as financial agent, the young engineer was introduced to Georges Andermatt, the founder of the Metal Exchange.

"After several interviews, he succeeded in interesting the banker in a sub-marine boat on which he was working, and it was agreed that as soon as the invention was perfected, Mon. Andermatt would use his influence with the Minister of Marine to obtain a series of trials under the direction of the government. For two years, Louis Lacombe was a frequent visitor at Andermatt's house, and he submitted to the banker the various improvements he made upon his original plans, until one day, being satisfied with the perfection of his work, he asked Mon. Andermatt to communicate with the Minister of Marine.

That day, Louis Lacombe dined at Mon. Andermatt's house. He left there about half-past eleven at night. He has not been seen since. "A perusal of the newspapers of that date will show that the young man's family caused every possible inquiry to be made, but without success; and it was the general opinion that Louis Lacombe— who was known as an original and visionary youth—had quietly left for parts unknown. "Let us accept that theory—improbable, though it be,—and let us consider another question, which is a most important one for our country: What has become of the plans of the sub-marine? Did Louis Lacombe carry them away? Are they destroyed? "After making a thorough investigation, we are able to assert, positively, that the plans are in existence, and are now in the possession of the two brothers Varin.

How did they acquire such a possession? That is a question not yet determined; nor do we know why they have not tried to sell them at an earlier date. Did they fear that their title to them would be called in question? If so, they have lost that fear, and we can announce definitely, that the plans of Louis Lacombe are now the property of foreign power, and we are in a position to publish the correspondence that passed between the Varin brothers and the representative of that power. The `Seven-of-Hearts' invented by Louis Lacombe has been actually constructed by our neighbor. "Will the invention fulfill the optimistic expectations of those who were concerned in that treacherous act?"

And a post-script adds:

"Later.—Our special correspondent informs us that the preliminary trial of the `Seven-of-Hearts' has not been satisfactory. It is quite likely that the plans sold and delivered by the Varin brothers did not include the final document carried by Louis Lacombe to Mon. Andermatt on the day of his disappearance, a document that was indispensable to a thorough understanding of the invention. It contained a summary of the final conclusions of the inventor, and estimates and figures not contained in the other papers.

Without this document, the plans are incomplete; on the other hand, without the plans, the document is worthless. "Now is the time to act and recover what belongs to us. It may be a difficult matter, but we rely upon the assistance of Mon. Andermatt.

It will be to his interest to explain his conduct which has hitherto been so strange and inscrutable. He will explain not only why he concealed these facts at the time of the suicide of Etienne Varin, but also why he has never revealed the disappearance of the paper—a fact well known to him.

He will tell why, during the last six years, he paid spies to watch the movements of the Varin brothers. We expect from him, not only words, but acts. And at once. Otherwise—-"

The threat was plainly expressed. But of what did it consist? What whip was Salvator, the anonymous writer of the article, holding over the head of Mon. Andermatt?

An army of reporters attacked the banker, and ten interviewers announced the scornful manner in which they were treated. Thereupon, the `Echo de France' announced its position in these words:

"Whether Mon. Andermatt is willing or not, he will be, henceforth, our collaborator in the work we have undertaken."

Daspry and I were dining together on the day on which that announcement appeared. That evening, with the newspapers spread over my table, we discussed the affair and examined it from every point of view with that exasperation that a person feels when walking in the dark and finding himself constantly falling over the same obstacles. Suddenly, without any warning whatsoever, the door opened and a lady entered. Her face was hidden behind a thick veil. I rose at once and approached her.

"Is it you, monsieur, who lives here?" she asked.

"Yes, madame, but I do not understand——"

"The gate was not locked," she explained.

"But the vestibule door?"

She did not reply, and it occurred to me that she had used the servants' entrance. How did she know the way? Then there was a silence that was quite embarrassing. She looked at Daspry, and I was obliged to introduce him. I asked her to be seated and explain the object of her visit. She raised her veil, and I saw that she was a brunette with regular features and, though not handsome, she was attractive—principally, on account of her sad, dark eyes.

"I am Madame Andermatt," she said.

"Madame Andermatt!" I repeated, with astonishment.

After a brief pause, she continued with a voice and manner that were quite easy and natural:

"I have come to see you about that affair—you know. I thought I might be able to obtain some information——"

"Mon Dieu, madame, I know nothing but what has already appeared in the papers. But if you will point out in what way I can help you...."

"I do not know....I do not know."

Not until then did I suspect that her calm demeanor was assumed, and that some poignant grief was concealed beneath that air of tranquility. For a moment, we were silent and embarrassed. Then Daspry stepped forward, and said:

"Will you permit me to ask you a few questions?"

"Yes, yes," she cried. "I will answer."

"You will answer.... whatever those questions may be?"

"Yes."

"Did you know Louis Lacombe?" he asked.

"Yes, through my husband."

"When did you see him for the last time?"

"The evening he dined with us."

"At that time, was there anything to lead you to believe that you would never see him again?"

"No. But he had spoken of a trip to Russia—in a vague way."

"Then you expected to see him again?"

"Yes. He was to dine with us, two days later."

"How do you explain his disappearance?"

"I cannot explain it."

"And Mon. Andermatt?"

"I do not know."

"Yet the article published in the `Echo de France' indicates——"

"Yes, that the Varin brothers had something to do with his disappearance."

"Is that your opinion?"

"Yes."

"On what do you base your opinion?"

"When he left our house, Louis Lacombe carried a satchel containing all the papers relating to his invention. Two days later, my husband, in a conversation with one of the Varin brothers, learned that the papers were in their possession."

"And he did not denounce them?"

"No."

"Why not?"

"Because there was something else in the satchel—something besides the papers of Louis Lacombe."

"What was it?"

She hesitated; was on the point of speaking, but, finally, remained silent. Daspry continued:

"I presume that is why your husband has kept a close watch over their movements instead of informing the police. He hoped to recover the papers and, at the same time, that compromising article which has enabled the two brothers to hold over him threats of exposure and blackmail."

"Over him, and over me."

"Ah! over you, also?"

"Over me, in particular."

She uttered the last words in a hollow voice. Daspry observed it; he paced to and fro for a moment, then, turning to her, asked:

"Had you written to Louis Lacombe?"

"Of course. My husband had business with him—"

"Apart from those business letters, had you written to Louis Lacombe.... other letters? Excuse my insistence, but it is absolutely necessary that I should know the truth. Did you write other letters?"

"Yes," she replied, blushing.

"And those letters came into the possession of the Varin brothers?"

"Yes."

"Does Mon. Andermatt know it?"

"He has not seen them, but Alfred Varin has told him of their existence and threatened to publish them if my husband should take any steps against him. My husband was afraid.... of a scandal."

"But he has tried to recover the letters?"

"I think so; but I do not know. You see, after that last interview with Alfred Varin, and after some harsh words between me and my husband in which he called me to account—we live as strangers."

"In that case, as you have nothing to lose, what do you fear?"

"I may be indifferent to him now, but I am the woman that he has loved, the one he would still love—oh! I am quite sure of that," she murmured, in a fervent voice, "he would still love me if he had not got hold of those cursed letters——"

"What! Did he succeed?....But the two brothers still defied him?"

"Yes, and they boasted of having a secure hiding-place."

"Well?"

"I believe my husband discovered that hiding-place."

"Well?"

"I believe my husband has discovered that hiding-place."

"Ah! where was it?"

"Here."

"Here!" I cried in alarm.

"Yes. I always had that suspicion. Louis Lacombe was very ingenious and amused himself in his leisure hours, by making safes and locks. No doubt, the Varin brothers were aware of that fact and utilized one of Lacombe's safes in which to conceal the letters.... and other things, perhaps."

"But they did not live here," I said.

"Before you came, four months ago, the house had been vacant for some time. And they may have thought that your presence here would not interfere with them when they wanted to get the papers. But they did not count on my husband, who came here on the night of 22 June, forced the safe, took what he was seeking, and left his card to inform the two brothers that he feared them no more, and that their positions were now reversed. Two days later, after reading the article in the `Gil Blas,' Etienne Varin came here, remained alone in this room, found the safe empty, and.... killed himself."

After a moment, Daspry said:

"A very simple theory....Has Mon. Andermatt spoken to you since then?"

"No."

"Has his attitude toward you changed in any way? Does he appear more gloomy, more anxious?"

"No, I haven't noticed any change."

"And yet you think he has secured the letters. Now, in my opinion, he has not got those letters, and it was not he who came here on the night of 22 June."

"Who was it, then?"

"The mysterious individual who is managing this affair, who holds all the threads in his hands, and whose invisible but far-reaching power we have felt from the beginning. It was he and his friends who entered this house on 22 June; it was he who discovered the hiding-place of the papers; it was he who left Mon. Andermatt's card; it is he who now holds the correspondence and the evidence of the treachery of the Varin brothers."

"Who is he?" I asked, impatiently.

"The man who writes letters to the `Echo de France'.... Salvator! Have we not convincing evidence of that fact? Does he not mention in his letters certain details that no one could know, except the man who had thus discovered the secrets of the two brothers?"

"Well, then," stammered Madame Andermatt, in great alarm, "he has my letters also, and it is he who now threatens my husband. Mon Dieu! What am I to do?"

"Write to him," declared Daspry. "Confide in him without reserve. Tell him all you know and all you may hereafter learn. Your interest and his interest are the same. He is not working against Mon. Andermatt, but against Alfred Varin. Help him."

"How?"

"Has your husband the document that completes the plans of Louis Lacombe?"

"Yes."

"Tell that to Salvator, and, if possible, procure the document for him. Write to him at once. You risk nothing."

The advice was bold, dangerous even at first sight, but Madame Andermatt had no choice. Besides, as Daspry had said, she ran no risk. If the unknown writer were an enemy, that step would not aggravate the situation. If he were a stranger seeking to accomplish a particular purpose, he would attach to those letters only a secondary importance. Whatever might happen, it was the only solution offered to her, and she, in her anxiety, was only too glad to act on it. She thanked us effusively, and promised to keep us informed.

In fact, two days later, she sent us the following letter that she had received from Salvator:

"Have not found the letters, but I will get them. Rest easy. I am watching everything. S."

I looked at the letter. It was in the same handwriting as the note I found in my book on the night of 22 June.

Daspry was right. Salvator was, indeed, the originator of that affair.

We were beginning to see a little light coming out of the darkness that surrounded us, and an unexpected light was thrown on certain points; but other points yet remained obscure—for instance, the finding of the two seven-of-hearts. Perhaps I was unnecessarily concerned about those two cards whose seven punctured spots had appeared to me under such startling circumstances! Yet I could not refrain from asking myself: What role will they play in the drama? What importance do they bear? What conclusion must be drawn from the fact that the submarine constructed from the plans of Louis Lacombe bore the name of `Seven-of-Hearts'?

Daspry gave little thought to the other two cards; he devoted all his attention to another problem which he considered more urgent; he was seeking the famous hiding-place.

"And who knows," said he, "I may find the letters that Salvator did not find—by inadvertence, perhaps. It is improbable that the Varin brothers would have removed from a spot, which they deemed inaccessible, the weapon which was so valuable to them."

And he continued to search. In a short time, the large room held no more secrets for him, so he extended his investigations to the other rooms. He examined the interior and the exterior, the stones of the foundation, the bricks in the walls; he raised the slates of the roof.

One day, he came with a pickaxe and a spade, gave me the spade, kept the pickaxe, pointed to the adjacent vacant lots, and said: "Come."

I followed him, but I lacked his enthusiasm. He divided the vacant land into several sections which he examined in turn. At last, in a corner, at the angle formed by the walls of two neighboring proprietors, a small pile of earth and gravel, covered with briers and grass, attracted his attention. He attacked it. I was obliged to help him. For an hour, under a hot sun, we labored without success. I was discouraged, but Daspry urged me on. His ardor was as strong as ever.

At last, Daspry's pickaxe unearthed some bones—the remains of a skeleton to which some scraps of clothing still hung. Suddenly, I turned pale. I had discovered, sticking in the earth, a small piece of iron cut in the form of a rectangle, on which I thought I could see red spots. I stooped and picked it up. That little iron plate was the exact size of a playing-card, and the red spots, made with red lead, were arranged upon it in a manner similar to the seven-of-hearts, and each spot was pierced with a round hole similar to the perforations in the two playing cards.

"Listen, Daspry, I have had enough of this. You can stay if it interests you. But I am going."

Was that simply the expression of my excited nerves? Or was it the result of a laborious task executed under a burning sun? I know that I trembled as I walked away, and that I went to bed, where I remained forty-eight hours, restless and feverish, haunted by skeletons that danced around me and threw their bleeding hearts at my head.

Daspry was faithful to me. He came to my house every day, and remained three or four hours, which he spent in the large room, ferreting, thumping, tapping.

"The letters are here, in this room," he said, from time to time, "they are here. I will stake my life on it."

On the morning of the third day I arose—feeble yet, but cured. A substantial breakfast cheered me up. But a letter that I received that afternoon contributed, more than anything else, to my complete recovery, and aroused in me a lively curiosity. This was the letter:

"Monsieur,

"The drama, the first act of which transpired on the night of 22 June, is now drawing to a close.

Force of circumstances compel me to bring the two principal actors in that drama face to face, and I wish that meeting to take place in your house, if you will be so kind as to give me the use of it for this evening from nine o'clock to eleven. It will be advisable to give your servant leave of absence for the evening, and, perhaps, you will be so kind as to leave the field open to the two adversaries.

You will remember that when I visited your house on the night of 22 June, I took excellent care of your property. I feel that I would do you an injustice if I should doubt, for one moment, your absolute discretion in this affair.

Your devoted,

"SALVATOR."

I was amused at the facetious tone of his letter and also at the whimsical nature of his request. There was a charming display of confidence and candor in his language, and nothing in the world could have induced me to deceive him or repay his confidence with ingratitude.

I gave my servant a theatre ticket, and he left the house at eight o'clock. A few minutes later, Daspry arrived. I showed him the letter.

"Well?" said he.

"Well, I have left the garden gate unlocked, so anyone can enter."

"And you—are you going away?"

"Not at all. I intend to stay right here."

"But he asks you to go——"

"But I am not going. I will be discreet, but I am resolved to see what takes place."

"Ma foi!" exclaimed Daspry, laughing, "you are right, and I shall stay with you. I shouldn't like to miss it."

We were interrupted by the sound of the door-bell.

"Here already?" said Daspry, "twenty minutes ahead of time! Incredible!"

I went to the door and ushered in the visitor. It was Madame Andermatt. She was faint and nervous, and in a stammering voice, she ejaculated:

"My husband.... is coming.... he has an appointment.... they intend to give him the letters...."

"How do you know?" I asked.

"By chance. A message came for my husband while we were at dinner. The servant gave it to me by mistake. My husband grabbed it quickly, but he was too late. I had read it."

"You read it?"

"Yes. It was something like this: `At nine o'clock this evening, be at Boulevard Maillot with the papers connected with the affair. In exchange, the letters.' So, after dinner, I hastened here."

"Unknown to your husband?"

"Yes."

"What do you think about it?" asked Daspry, turning to me.

"I think as you do, that Mon. Andermatt is one of the invited guests."

"Yes, but for what purpose?"

"That is what we are going to find out."

I led the men to a large room. The three of us could hide comfortably behind the velvet chimney-mantle, and observe all that should happen in the room. We seated ourselves there, with Madame Andermatt in the centre.

The clock struck nine. A few minutes later, the garden gate creaked upon its hinges. I confess that I was greatly agitated. I was about to learn the key to the mystery. The startling events of the last few weeks were about to be explained, and, under my eyes, the last battle was going to be fought. Daspry seized the hand of Madame Andermatt, and said to her:

"Not a word, not a movement! Whatever you may see or hear, keep quiet!"

Some one entered. It was Alfred Varin. I recognized him at once, owing to the close resemblance he bore to his brother Etienne. There was the same slouching gait; the same cadaverous face covered with a black beard.

He entered with the nervous air of a man who is accustomed to fear the presence of traps and ambushes; who scents and avoids them. He glanced about the room, and I had the impression that the chimney, masked with a velvet portiere, did not please him. He took three steps in our direction, when something caused him to turn and walk toward the old mosaic king, with the flowing beard and flamboyant sword, which he examined minutely, mounting on a chair and following with his fingers the outlines of the shoulders and head and feeling certain parts of the face. Suddenly, he leaped from the chair and walked away from it. He had heard the sound of approaching footsteps. Mon. Andermatt appeared at the door.

"You! You!" exclaimed the banker. "Was it you who brought me here?"

"I? By no means," protested Varin, in a rough, jerky voice that reminded me of his brother, "on the contrary, it was your letter that brought me here."

"My letter?"

"A letter signed by you, in which you offered——"

"I never wrote to you," declared Mon. Andermatt.

"You did not write to me!"

Instinctively, Varin was put on his guard, not against the banker, but against the unknown enemy who had drawn him into this trap. A second time, he looked in our direction, then walked toward the door. But Mon. Andermatt barred his passage.

"Well, where are you going, Varin?"

"There is something about this affair I don't like. I am going home. Good evening."

"One moment!"

"No need of that, Mon. Andermatt. I have nothing to say to you."

"But I have something to say to you, and this is a good time to say it."

"Let me pass."

"No, you will not pass."

Varin recoiled before the resolute attitude of the banker, as he muttered:

"Well, then, be quick about it."

One thing astonished me; and I have no doubt my two companions experienced a similar feeling. Why was Salvator not there? Was he not a necessary party at this conference? Or was he satisfied to let these two adversaries fight it out between themselves? At all events, his absence was a great disappointment, although it did not detract from the dramatic strength of the situation.

After a moment, Mon. Andermatt approached Varin and, face to face, eye to eye, said:

"Now, after all these years and when you have nothing more to fear, you can answer me candidly: What have you done with Louis Lacombe?"

"What a question! As if I knew anything about him!"

"You do know! You and your brother were his constant companions, almost lived with him in this very house. You knew all about his plans and his work. And the last night I ever saw Louis Lacombe, when I parted with him at my door, I saw two men slinking away in the shadows of the trees. That, I am ready to swear to."

"Well, what has that to do with me?"

"The two men were you and your brother."

"Prove it."

"The best proof is that, two days later, you yourself showed me the papers and the plans that belonged to Lacombe and offered to sell them. How did these papers come into your possession?"

"I have already told you, Mon. Andermatt, that we found them on Louis Lacombe's table, the morning after his disappearance."

"That is a lie!"

"Prove it."

"The law will prove it."

"Why did you not appeal to the law?"

"Why? Ah! Why——," stammered the banker, with a slight display of emotion.

"You know very well, Mon. Andermatt, if you had the least certainty of our guilt, our little threat would not have stopped you."

"What threat? Those letters? Do you suppose I ever gave those letters a moment's thought?"

"If you did not care for the letters, why did you offer me thousands of francs for their return? And why did you have my brother and me tracked like wild beasts?"

"To recover the plans."

"Nonsense! You wanted the letters. You knew that as soon as you had the letters in your possession, you could denounce us. Oh! no, I couldn't part with them!"

He laughed heartily, but stopped suddenly, and said:

"But, enough of this! We are merely going over old ground. We make no headway. We had better let things stand as they are."

"We will not let them stand as they are," said the banker, "and since you have referred to the letters, let me tell you that you will not leave this house until you deliver up those letters."

"I shall go when I please."

"You will not."

"Be careful, Mon. Andermatt. I warn you——"

"I say, you shall not go."

"We will see about that," cried Varin, in such a rage that Madame Andermatt could not suppress a cry of fear. Varin must have heard it, for he now tried to force his way out. Mon. Andermatt pushed him back. Then I saw him put his hand into his coat pocket.

"For the last time, let me pass," he cried.

"The letters, first!"

Varin drew a revolver and, pointing it at Mon. Andermatt, said:

"Yes or no?"

The banker stooped quickly. There was the sound of a pistol-shot. The weapon fell from Varin's hand. I was amazed. The shot was fired close to me. It was Daspry who had fired it at Varin, causing him to drop the revolver. In a moment, Daspry was standing between the two men, facing Varin; he said to him, with a sneer:

"You were lucky, my friend, very lucky. I fired at your hand and struck only the revolver."

Both of them looked at him, surprised. Then he turned to the banker, and said:

"I beg your pardon, monsieur, for meddling in your business; but, really, you play a very poor game. Let me hold the cards."

Turning again to Varin, Daspry said:

"It's between us two, comrade, and play fair, if you please. Hearts are trumps, and I play the seven."

Then Daspry held up, before Varin's bewildered eyes, the little iron plate, marked with the seven red spots. It was a terrible shock to Varin. With livid features, staring eyes, and an air of intense agony, the man seemed to be hypnotized at the sight of it.

"Who are you?" he gasped.

"One who meddles in other people's business, down to the very bottom."

"What do you want?"

"What you brought here tonight."

"I brought nothing."

"Yes, you did, or you wouldn't have come. This morning, you received an invitation to come here at nine o'clock, and bring with you all the papers held by you. You are here. Where are the papers?"

There was in Daspry's voice and manner a tone of authority that I did not understand; his manner was usually quite mild and conciliatory. Absolutely conquered, Varin placed his hand on one of his pockets, and said:

"The papers are here."

"All of them?"

"Yes."

"All that you took from Louis Lacombe and afterwards sold to Major von Lieben?"

"Yes."

"Are these the copies or the originals?"

"I have the originals."

"How much do you want for them?"

"One hundred thousand francs."

"You are crazy," said Daspry. "Why, the major gave you only twenty thousand, and that was like money thrown into the sea, as the boat was a failure at the preliminary trials."

"They didn't understand the plans."

"The plans are not complete."

"Then, why do you ask me for them?"

"Because I want them. I offer you five thousand francs—not a sou more."

"Ten thousand. Not a sou less."

"Agreed," said Daspry, who now turned to Mon. Andermatt, and said:

"Monsieur will kindly sign a check for the amount."

"But....I haven't got——"

"Your check-book? Here it is."

Astounded, Mon. Andermatt examined the check-book that Daspry handed to him.

"It is mine," he gasped. "How does that happen?"

"No idle words, monsieur, if you please. You have merely to sign."

The banker took out his fountain pen, filled out the check and signed it. Varin held out his hand for it.

"Put down your hand," said Daspry, "there is something more." Then, to the banker, he said: "You asked for some letters, did you not?"

"Yes, a package of letters."

"Where are they, Varin?"

"I haven't got them."

"Where are they, Varin?"

"I don't know. My brother had charge of them."

"They are hidden in this room."

"In that case, you know where they are."

"How should I know?"

"Was it not you who found the hiding-place? You appear to be as well informed.... as Salvator."

"The letters are not in the hiding-place."

"They are."

"Open it."

Varin looked at him, defiantly. Were not Daspry and Salvator the same person? Everything pointed to that conclusion. If so, Varin risked nothing in disclosing a hiding-place already known.

"Open it," repeated Daspry.

"I have not got the seven of hearts."

"Yes, here it is," said Daspry, handing him the iron plate. Varin recoiled in terror, and cried:

"No, no, I will not."

"Never mind," replied Daspry, as he walked toward the bearded king, climbed on a chair and applied the seven of hearts to the lower part of the sword in such a manner that the edges of the iron plate coincided exactly with the two edges of the sword. Then, with the assistance of an awl which he introduced alternately into each of the seven holes, he pressed upon seven of the little mosaic stones. As he pressed upon the seventh one, a clicking sound was heard, and the entire bust of the King turned upon a pivot, disclosing a large opening lined with steel. It was really a fire-proof safe.

"You can see, Varin, the safe is empty."

"So I see. Then, my brother has taken out the letters."

Daspry stepped down from the chair, approached Varin, and said:

"Now, no more nonsense with me. There is another hiding-place. Where is it?"

"There is none."

"Is it money you want? How much?"

"Ten thousand."

"Monsieur Andermatt, are those letters worth then thousand francs to you?"

"Yes," said the banker, firmly.

Varin closed the safe, took the seven of hearts and placed it again on the sword at the same spot. He thrust the awl into each of the seven holes. There was the same clicking sound, but this time, strange to relate, it was only a portion of the safe that revolved on the pivot, disclosing quite a small safe that was built within the door of the larger one. The packet of letters was here, tied with a tape, and sealed. Varin handed the packet to Daspry. The latter turned to the banker, and asked:

"Is the check ready, Monsieur Andermatt?"

"Yes."

"And you have also the last document that you received from Louis Lacombe—the one that completes the plans of the sub-marine?"

"Yes."

The exchange was made. Daspry pocketed the document and the checks, and offered the packet of letters to Mon. Andermatt.

"This is what you wanted, Monsieur."

The banker hesitated a moment, as if he were afraid to touch those cursed letters that he had sought so eagerly. Then, with a nervous movement, he took them. Close to me, I heard a moan. I grasped Madame Andermatt's hand. It was cold.

"I believe, monsieur," said Daspry to the banker, "that our business is ended. Oh! no thanks. It was only by a mere chance that I have been able to do you a good turn. Good-night."

Mon. Andermatt retired. He carried with him the letters written by his wife to Louis Lacombe.

"Marvelous!" exclaimed Daspry, delighted. "Everything is coming our way. Now, we have only to close our little affair, comrade. You have the papers?"

"Here they are—all of them."

Daspry examined them carefully, and then placed them in his pocket.

"Quite right. You have kept your word," he said.

"But—"

"But what?"

"The two checks? The money?" said Varin, eagerly.

"Well, you have a great deal of assurance, my man. How dare you ask such a thing?"

"I ask only what is due to me."

"Can you ask pay for returning papers that you stole? Well, I think not!"

Varin was beside himself. He trembled with rage; his eyes were bloodshot.

"The money.... the twenty thousand...." he stammered.

"Impossible! I need it myself."

"The money!"

"Come, be reasonable, and don't get excited. It won't do you any good."

Daspry seized his arm so forcibly, that Varin uttered a cry of pain. Daspry continued:

"Now, you can go. The air will do you good. Perhaps you want me to show you the way. Ah! yes, we will go together to the vacant lot near here, and I will show you a little mound of earth and stones and under it——"

"That is false! That is false!"

"Oh! no, it is true. That little iron plate with the seven spots on it came from there. Louis Lacombe always carried it, and you buried it with the body—and with some other things that will prove very interesting to a judge and jury."

Varin covered his face with his hands, and muttered:

"All right, I am beaten. Say no more. But I want to ask you one question. I should like to know——"

"What is it?"

"Was there a little casket in the large safe?"

"Yes."

"Was it there on the night of 22 June?"

"Yes."

"What did it contain?"

"Everything that the Varin brothers had put in it—a very pretty collection of diamonds and pearls picked up here and there by the said brothers."

"And did you take it?"

"Of course I did. Do you blame me?"

"I understand.... it was the disappearance of that casket that caused my brother to kill himself."

"Probably. The disappearance of your correspondence was not a sufficient motive. But the disappearance of the casket....Is that all you wish to ask me?"

"One thing more: your name?"

"You ask that with an idea of seeking revenge."

"Parbleu! The tables may be turned. Today, you are on top. To-morrow——"

"It will be you."

"I hope so. Your name?"

"Arsène Lupin."

"Arsène Lupin!"

The man staggered, as though stunned by a heavy blow. Those two words had deprived him of all hope.

Daspry laughed, and said:

"Ah! did you imagine that a Monsieur Durand or Dupont could manage an affair like this? No, it required the skill and cunning of Arsène Lupin. And now that you have my name, go and prepare your revenge. Arsène Lupin will wait for you."

Then he pushed the bewildered Varin through the door.

"Daspry! Daspry!" I cried, pushing aside the curtain. He ran to me.

"What? What's the matter?"

"Madame Andermatt is ill."

He hastened to her, caused her to inhale some salts, and, while caring for her, questioned me:

"Well, what did it?"

"The letters of Louis Lacombe that you gave to her husband."

He struck his forehead and said:

"Did she think that I could do such a thing!...But, of course she would. Imbecile that I am!"

Madame Andermatt was now revived. Daspry took from his pocket a small package exactly similar to the one that Mon. Andermatt had carried away.

"Here are your letters, Madame. These are the genuine letters."

"But.... the others?"

"The others are the same, rewritten by me and carefully worded. Your husband will not find anything objectionable in them, and will never suspect the substitution since they were taken from the safe in his presence."

"But the handwriting—-"

"There is no handwriting that cannot be imitated."

She thanked him in the same words she might have used to a man in her own social circle, so I concluded that she had not witnessed the final scene between Varin and Arsène Lupin. But the surprising revelation caused me considerable embarrassment. Lupin! My club companion was none other than Arsène Lupin. I could not realize it. But he said, quite at his ease:

"You can say farewell to Jean Daspry."

"Ah!"

"Yes, Jean Daspry is going on a long journey. I shall send him to Morocco. There, he may find a death worthy of him. I may say that that is his expectation."

"But Arsène Lupin will remain?"

"Oh! Decidedly. Arsène Lupin is simply at the threshold of his career, and he expects—-"

I was impelled by curiosity to interrupt him, and, leading him away from the hearing of Madame Andermatt, I asked:

"Did you discover the smaller safe yourself—the one that held the letters?"

"Yes, after a great deal of trouble. I found it yesterday afternoon while you were asleep. And yet, God knows it was simple enough! But the simplest things are the ones that usually escape our notice." Then, showing me the seven-of-hearts, he added: "Of course I had guessed that, in order to open the larger safe, this card must be placed on the sword of the mosaic king."

"How did you guess that?"

"Quite easily. Through private information, I knew that fact when I came here on the evening of 22 June—-"

"After you left me—-"

"Yes, after turning the subject of our conversation to stories of crime and robbery which were sure to reduce you to such a nervous condition that you would not leave your bed, but would allow me to complete my search uninterrupted."

"The scheme worked perfectly."

"Well, I knew when I came here that there was a casket concealed in a safe with a secret lock, and that the seven-of-hearts was the key to that lock. I had merely to place the card upon the spot that was obviously intended for it. An hour's examination showed me where the spot was."

"One hour!"

"Observe the fellow in mosaic."

"The old emperor?"

"That old emperor is an exact representation of the king of hearts on all playing cards."

"That's right. But how does the seven of hearts open the larger safe at one time and the smaller safe at another time? And why did you open only the larger safe in the first instance? I mean on the night of 22 June."

"Why? Because I always placed the seven of hearts in the same way. I never changed the position. But, yesterday, I observed that by reversing the card, by turning it upside down, the arrangement of the seven spots on the mosaic was changed."

"Parbleu!"

"Of course, parbleu! But a person has to think of those things."

"There is something else: you did not know the history of those letters until Madame Andermatt—-"

"Spoke of them before me? No. Because I found in the safe, besides the casket, nothing but the correspondence of the two brothers which disclosed their treachery in regard to the plans."

"Then it was by chance that you were led, first, to investigate the history of the two brothers, and then to search for the plans and documents relating to the sub-marine?"

"Simply by chance."

"For what purpose did you make the search?"

"Mon Dieu!" exclaimed Daspry, laughing, "how deeply interested you are!"

"The subject fascinates me."

"Very well, presently, after I have escorted Madame Andermatt to a carriage, and dispatched a short story to the `Echo de France,' I will return and tell you all about it."

He sat down and wrote one of those short, clear-cut articles which served to amuse and mystify the public. Who does not recall the sensation that followed that article produced throughout the entire world?

"Arsène Lupin has solved the problem recently submitted by Salvator. Having acquired possession of all the documents and original plans of the engineer Louis Lacombe, he has placed them in the hands of the Minister of Marine, and he has headed a subscription list for the purpose of presenting to the nation the first submarine constructed from those plans. His subscription is twenty thousand francs."

"Twenty thousand francs! The checks of Mon. Andermatt?" I exclaimed, when he had given me the paper to read.

"Exactly. It was quite right that Varin should redeem his treachery."

And that is how I made the acquaintance of Arsène Lupin. That is how I learned that Jean Daspry, a member of my club, was none other than Arsène Lupin, gentleman-thief. That is how I formed very agreeable ties of friendship with that famous man, and, thanks to the confidence with which he honored me, how I became his very humble and faithful historiographer.

VII. MADAME IMBERT'S SAFE

At three o'clock in the morning, there were still half a dozen carriages in front of one of those small houses which form only the side of the boulevard Berthier. The door of that house opened, and a number of guests, male and female, emerged. The majority of them entered their carriages and were quickly driven away, leaving behind only two men who walked down Courcelles, where they parted, as one of them lived in that street. The other decided to return on foot as far as the Porte-Maillot. It was a beautiful winter's night, clear and cold; a night on which a brisk walk is agreeable and refreshing.

But, at the end of a few minutes, he had the disagreeable impression that he was being followed. Turning around, he saw a man sulking amongst the trees. He was not a coward; yet he felt it advisable to increase his speed. Then his pursuer commenced to run; and he deemed it prudent to draw his revolver and face him. But he had no time. The man rushed at him and attacked him violently. Immediately, they were engaged in a desperate struggle, wherein he felt that his unknown assailant had the advantage. He called for help, struggled, and was thrown down on a pile of gravel, seized by the throat, and gagged with a handkerchief that his assailant forced into his mouth. His eyes closed, and the man who was smothering him with his weight arose to defend himself against an unexpected attack. A blow from a cane and a kick from a boot; the man uttered two cries of pain, and fled, limping and cursing. Without deigning to pursue the fugitive, the new arrival stooped over the prostrate man and inquired:

"Are you hurt, monsieur?"

He was not injured, but he was dazed and unable to stand. His rescuer procured a carriage, placed him in it, and accompanied him to his house on the avenue de la Grande-Armée. On his arrival there, quite recovered, he overwhelmed his saviour with thanks.

"I owe you my life, monsieur, and I shall not forget it. I do not wish to alarm my wife at this time of night, but, to-morrow, she will be pleased to thank you personally. Come and breakfast with us. My name is Ludovic Imbert. May I ask yours?"

"Certainly, monsieur."

And he handed Mon. Imbert a card bearing the name: "Arsène Lupin."

At that time, Arsène Lupin did not enjoy the celebrity which the Cahorn affair, his escape from the Prison de la Santé, and other brilliant exploits, afterwards gained for him. He had not even used the name of Arsène Lupin. The name was specially invented to designate the rescuer of Mon. Imbert; that is to say, it was in that affair that Arsène Lupin was baptized. Fully armed and ready for the fray, it is true, but lacking the resources and authority which command success, Arsène Lupin was then merely an apprentice in a profession wherein he soon became a master.

With what a thrill of joy he recalled the invitation he received that night! At last, he had reached his goal! At last, he had undertaken a task worthy of his strength and skill! The Imbert millions! What a magnificent feast for an appetite like his!

He prepared a special toilet for the occasion; a shabby frock-coat, baggy trousers, a frayed silk hat, well-worn collar and cuffs, all quite correct in form, but bearing the unmistakable stamp of poverty. His cravat was a black ribbon pinned with a false diamond. Thus accoutred, he descended the stairs of the house in which he lived at Montmartre. At the third floor, without stopping, he rapped on a closed door with the head of his cane. He walked to the exterior boulevards. A tram-car was passing. He boarded it, and some one who had been following him took a seat beside him. It was the lodger who occupied the room on the third floor. A moment later, this man said to Lupin:

"Well, governor?"

"Well, it is all fixed."

"How?"

"I am going there to breakfast."

"You breakfast—there!"

"Certainly. Why not? I rescued Mon. Ludovic Imbert from certain death at your hands. Mon. Imbert is not devoid of gratitude. He invited me to breakfast."

There was a brief silence. Then the other said:

"But you are not going to throw up the scheme?"

"My dear boy," said Lupin, "When I arranged that little case of assault and battery, when I took the trouble at three o'clock in the morning, to rap you with my cane and tap you with my boot at the risk of injuring my only friend, it was not my intention to forego the advantages to be gained from a rescue so well arranged and executed. Oh! no, not at all."

"But the strange rumors we hear about their fortune?"

"Never mind about that. For six months, I have worked on this affair, investigated it, studied it, questioned the servants, the money-lenders and men of straw; for six months, I have shadowed the husband and wife. Consequently, I know what I am talking about. Whether the fortune came to them from old Brawford, as they pretend, or from some other source, I do not care. I know that it is a reality; that it exists. And some day it will be mine."

"Bigre! One hundred millions!"

"Let us say ten, or even five—that is enough! They have a safe full of bonds, and there will be the devil to pay if I can't get my hands on them."

The tram-car stopped at the Place de l'Etoile. The man whispered to Lupin:

"What am I to do now?"

"Nothing, at present. You will hear from me. There is no hurry."

Five minutes later, Arsène Lupin was ascending the magnificent flight of stairs in the Imbert mansion, and Mon. Imbert introduced him to his wife. Madame Gervaise Imbert was a short plump woman, and very talkative. She gave Lupin a cordial welcome.

"I desired that we should be alone to entertain our saviour," she said.

From the outset, they treated "our saviour" as an old and valued friend. By the time dessert was served, their friendship was well cemented, and private confidences were being exchanged. Arsène related the story of his life, the life of his father as a magistrate, the sorrows of his childhood, and his present difficulties. Gervaise, in turn, spoke of her youth, her marriage, the kindness of the aged Brawford, the hundred millions that she had inherited, the obstacles that prevented her from obtaining the enjoyment of her inheritance, the moneys she had been obliged to borrow at an exorbitant rate of interest, her endless contentions with Brawford's nephews, and the litigation! the injunctions! in fact, everything!

"Just think of it, Monsieur Lupin, the bonds are there, in my husband's office, and if we detach a single coupon, we lose everything! They are there, in our safe, and we dare not touch them."

Monsieur Lupin shivered at the bare idea of his proximity to so much wealth. Yet he felt quite certain that Monsieur Lupin would never suffer from the same difficulty as his fair hostess who declared she dare not touch the money.

"Ah! they are there!" he repeated, to himself; "they are there!"

A friendship formed under such circumstances soon led to closer relations. When discreetly questioned, Arsène Lupin confessed his poverty and distress. Immediately, the unfortunate young man was appointed private secretary to the Imberts, husband and wife, at a salary of one hundred francs a month. He was to come to the house every day and receive orders for his work, and a room on the second floor was set apart as his office. This room was directly over Mon. Imbert's office.

Arsène soon realized that his position as secretary was essentially a sinecure. During the first two months, he had only four important letters to recopy, and was called only once to Mon. Imbert's office; consequently, he had only one opportunity to contemplate, officially, the Imbert safe. Moreover, he noticed that the secretary was not invited to the social functions of the employer. But he did not complain, as he preferred to remain, modestly, in the shade and maintain his peace and freedom.

However, he was not wasting any time. From the beginning, he made clandestine visits to Mon. Imbert's office, and paid his respects to the safe, which was hermetically closed. It was an immense block of iron and steel, cold and stern in appearance, which could not be forced open by the ordinary tools of the burglar's trade. But Arsène Lupin was not discouraged.

"Where force fails, cunning prevails," he said to himself. "The essential thing is to be on the spot when the opportunity occurs. In the meantime, I must watch and wait."

He made immediately some preliminary preparations. After careful soundings made upon the floor of his room, he introduced a lead pipe which penetrated the ceiling of Mon. Imbert's office at a point between the two screeds of the cornice. By means of this pipe, he hoped to see and hear what transpired in the room below.

Henceforth, he passed his days stretched at full length upon the floor. He frequently saw the Imberts holding a consultation in front of the safe, investigating books and papers. When they turned the combination lock, he tried to learn the figures and the number of turns they made to the right and left. He watched their movements; he sought to catch their words. There was also a key necessary to complete the opening of the safe. What did they do with it? Did they hide it?

One day, he saw them leave the room without locking the safe. He descended the stairs quickly, and boldly entered the room. But they had returned.

"Oh! excuse me," said, "I made a mistake in the door."

"Come in, Monsieur Lupin, come in," cried Madame Imbert, "are you not at home here? We want your advice. What bonds should we sell? The foreign securities or the government annuities?"

"But the injunction?" said Lupin, with surprise.

"Oh! it doesn't cover all the bonds."

She opened the door of the safe and withdrew a package of bonds. But her husband protested.

"No, no, Gervaise, it would be foolish to sell the foreign bonds. They are going up, whilst the annuities are as high as they ever will be. What do you think, my dear friend?"

The dear friend had no opinion; yet he advised the sacrifice of the annuities. Then she withdrew another package and, from it, she took a paper at random. It proved to be a three-per-cent annuity worth two thousand francs. Ludovic placed the package of bonds in his pocket. That afternoon, accompanied by his secretary, he sold the annuities to a stock-broker and realized forty-six thousand francs.

Whatever Madame Imbert might have said about it, Arsène Lupin did not feel at home in the Imbert house. On the contrary, his position there was a peculiar one. He learned that the servants did not even know his name. They called him "monsieur." Ludovic always spoke of him in the same way: "You will tell monsieur. Has monsieur arrived?" Why that mysterious appellation?

Moreover, after their first outburst of enthusiasm, the Imberts seldom spoke to him, and, although treating him with the consideration due to a benefactor, they gave him little or no attention. They appeared to regard him as an eccentric character who did not like to be disturbed, and they respected his isolation as if it were a stringent rule on his part. On one occasion, while passing through the vestibule, he heard Madame Imbert say to the two gentlemen:

"He is such a barbarian!"

"Very well," he said to himself, "I am a barbarian."

And, without seeking to solve the question of their strange conduct, he proceeded with the execution of his own plans. He had decided that he could not depend on chance, nor on the negligence of Madame Imbert, who carried the key of the safe, and who, on locking the safe, invariably scattered the letters forming the combination of the lock. Consequently, he must act for himself.

Finally, an incident precipitated matters; it was the vehement campaign instituted against the Imberts by certain newspapers that accused the Imberts of swindling. Arsène Lupin was present at certain family conferences when this new vicissitude was discussed. He decided that if he waited much longer, he would lose everything. During the next five days, instead of leaving the house about six o'clock, according to his usual habit, he locked himself in his room. It was supposed that he had gone out. But he was lying on the floor surveying the office of Mon. Imbert. During those five evenings, the favorable opportunity that he awaited did not take place. He left the house about midnight by a side door to which he held the key.

But on the sixth day, he learned that the Imberts, actuated by the malevolent insinuations of their enemies, proposed to make an inventory of the contents of the safe.

"They will do it to-night," thought Lupin.

And truly, after dinner, Imbert and his wife retired to the office and commenced to examine the books of account and the securities contained in the safe. Thus, one hour after another passed away. He heard the servants go upstairs to their rooms. No one now remained on the first floor. Midnight! The Imberts were still at work.

"I must get to work," murmured Lupin.

He opened his window. It opened on a court. Outside, everything was dark and quiet. He took from his desk a knotted rope, fastened it to the balcony in front of his window, and quietly descended as far as the window below, which was that of the of Imbert's office. He stood upon the balcony for a moment, motionless, with attentive ear and watchful eye, but the heavy curtains effectually concealed the interior of the room. He cautiously pushed on the double window. If no one had examined it, it ought to yield to the slightest pressure, for, during the afternoon, he had so fixed the bolt that it would not enter the staple.

The window yielded to his touch. Then, with infinite care, he pushed it open sufficiently to admit his head. He parted the curtains a few inches, looked in, and saw Mon. Imbert and his wife sitting in front of the safe, deeply absorbed in their work and speaking softly to each other at rare intervals.

He calculated the distance between him and them, considered the exact movements he would require to make in order to overcome them, one after the other, before they could call for help, and he was about to rush upon them, when Madame Imbert said:

"Ah! the room is getting quite cold. I am going to bed. And you, my dear?"

"I shall stay and finish."

"Finish! Why, that will take you all night."

"Not at all. An hour, at the most."

She retired. Twenty minutes, thirty minutes passed. Arsène pushed the window a little farther open. The curtains shook. He pushed once more. Mon. Imbert turned, and, seeing the curtains blown by the wind, he rose to close the window.

There was not a cry, not the trace of struggle. With a few precise moments, and without causing him the least injury, Arsène stunned him, wrapped the curtain about his head, bound him hand and foot, and did it all in such a manner that Mon. Imbert had no opportunity to recognize his assailant.

Quickly, he approached the safe, seized two packages that he placed under his arm, left the office, and opened the servants' gate. A carriage was stationed in the street.

"Take that, first—and follow me," he said to the coachman. He returned to the office, and, in two trips, they emptied the safe. Then Arsène went to his own room, removed the rope, and all other traces of his clandestine work.

A few hours later, Arsène Lupin and his assistant examined the stolen goods. Lupin was not disappointed, as he had foreseen that the wealth of the Imberts had been greatly exaggerated. It did not consist of hundreds of millions, nor even tens of millions. Yet it amounted to a very respectable sum, and Lupin expressed his satisfaction.

"Of course," he said, "there will be a considerable loss when we come to sell the bonds, as we will have to dispose of them surreptitiously at reduced prices. In the meantime, they will rest quietly in my desk awaiting a propitious moment."

Arsène saw no reason why he should not go to the Imbert house the next day. But a perusal of the morning papers revealed this startling fact: Ludovic and Gervaise Imbert had disappeared.

When the officers of the law seized the safe and opened it, they found there what Arsène Lupin had left—nothing.

Such are the facts; and I learned the sequel to them, one day, when Arsène Lupin was in a confidential mood. He was pacing to and fro in my room, with a nervous step and a feverish eye that were unusual to him.

"After all," I said to him, "it was your most successful venture."

Without making a direct reply, he said:

"There are some impenetrable secrets connected with that affair; some obscure points that escape my comprehension. For instance: What caused their flight? Why did they not take advantage of the help I unconsciously gave them? It would have been so simple to say: `The hundred millions were in the safe. They are no longer there, because they have been stolen.'"

"They lost their nerve."

"Yes, that is it—they lost their nerve...On the other hand, it is true—-"

"What is true?"

"Oh! nothing."

What was the meaning of Lupin's reticence? It was quite obvious that he had not told me everything; there was something he was loath to tell. His conduct puzzled me. It must indeed be a very serious matter to cause such a man as Arsène Lupin even a momentary hesitation. I threw out a few questions at random.

"Have you seen them since?"

"No."

"And have you never experienced the slightest degree of pity for those unfortunate people?"

"I!" he exclaimed, with a start.

His sudden excitement astonished me. Had I touched him on a sore spot? I continued:

"Of course. If you had not left them alone, they might have been able to face the danger, or, at least, made their escape with full pockets."

"What do you mean?" he said, indignantly. "I suppose you have an idea that my soul should be filled with remorse?"

"Call it remorse or regrets—anything you like—-"

"They are not worth it."

"Have you no regrets or remorse for having stolen their fortune?"

"What fortune?"

"The packages of bonds you took from their safe."

"Oh! I stole their bonds, did I? I deprived them of a portion of their wealth? Is that my crime? Ah! my dear boy, you do not know the truth. You never imagined that those bonds were not worth the paper they were written on. Those bonds were false—they were counterfeit—every one of them—do you understand? THEY WERE COUNTERFEIT!"

I looked at him, astounded.

"Counterfeit! The four or five millions?"

"Yes, counterfeit!" he exclaimed, in a fit of rage. "Only so many scraps of paper! I couldn't raise a sou on the whole of them! And you ask me if I have any remorse. THEY are the ones who should have remorse and pity. They played me for a simpleton; and I fell into their trap. I was their latest victim, their most stupid gull!"

He was affected by genuine anger—the result of malice and wounded pride. He continued:

"From start to finish, I got the worst of it. Do you know the part I played in that affair, or rather the part they made me play? That of André Brawford! Yes, my boy, that is the truth, and I never suspected it. It was not until afterwards, on reading the newspapers, that the light finally dawned in my stupid brain. Whilst I was posing as his "saviour," as the gentleman who had risked his life to rescue Mon. Imbert from the clutches of an assassin, they were passing me off as Brawford. Wasn't that splendid? That eccentric individual who had a room on the second floor, that barbarian that was exhibited only at a distance, was Brawford, and

Brawford was I! Thanks to me, and to the confidence that I inspired under the name of Brawford, they were enabled to borrow money from the bankers and other money-lenders. Ha! what an experience for a novice! And I swear to you that I shall profit by the lesson!"

He stopped, seized my arm, and said to me, in a tone of exasperation:

"My dear fellow, at this very moment, Gervaise Imbert owes me fifteen hundred francs."

I could not refrain from laughter, his rage was so grotesque. He was making a mountain out of a molehill. In a moment, he laughed himself, and said:

"Yes, my boy, fifteen hundred francs. You must know that I had not received one sou of my promised salary, and, more than that, she had borrowed from me the sum of fifteen hundred francs. All my youthful savings! And do you know why? To devote the money to charity! I am giving you a straight story. She wanted it for some poor people she was assisting—unknown to her husband. And my hard-earned money was wormed out of me by that silly pretense! Isn't it amusing, hein? Arsène Lupin done out of fifteen hundred francs by the fair lady from whom he stole four millions in counterfeit bonds! And what a vast amount of time and patience and cunning I expended to achieve that result! It was the first time in my life that I was played for a fool, and I frankly confess that I was fooled that time to the queen's taste!"

VIII. THE BLACK PEARL

A violent ringing of the bell awakened the concierge of number nine, avenue Hoche. She pulled the doorstring, grumbling:

"I thought everybody was in. It must be three o'clock!"

"Perhaps it is some one for the doctor," muttered her husband.

"Third floor, left. But the doctor won't go out at night."

"He must go to-night."

The visitor entered the vestibule, ascended to the first floor, the second, the third, and, without stopping at the doctor's door, he continued to the fifth floor. There, he tried two keys. One of them fitted the lock.

"Ah! good!" he murmured, "that simplifies the business wonderfully. But before I commence work I had better arrange for my retreat. Let me see.... have I had sufficient time to rouse the doctor and be dismissed by him? Not yet.... a few minutes more."

At the end of ten minutes, he descended the stairs, grumbling noisily about the doctor. The concierge opened the door for him and heard it click behind him. But the door did not lock, as the man had quickly inserted a piece of iron in the lock in such a manner that the bolt could not enter. Then, quietly, he entered the house again, unknown to the concierge. In case of alarm, his retreat was assured. Noiselessly, he ascended to the fifth floor once more. In the antechamber, by the light of his electric lantern, he placed his hat and overcoat on one of the chairs, took a seat on another, and covered his heavy shoes with felt slippers.

"Ouf! Here I am—and how simple it was! I wonder why more people do not adopt the profitable and pleasant occupation of burglar. With a little care and reflection, it becomes a most delightful profession. Not too quiet and monotonous, of course, as it would then become wearisome."

He unfolded a detailed plan of the apartment.

"Let me commence by locating myself. Here, I see the vestibule in which I am sitting. On the street front, the drawing-room, the boudoir and dining-room. Useless to waste any time there, as it appears that the countess has a deplorable taste.... not a bibelot of any value!...Now, let's get down to business!... Ah! here is a corridor; it must lead to the bed chambers. At a distance of three metres, I should come to the door of the wardrobe-closet which connects with the chamber of the countess." He folded his plan, extinguished his lantern, and proceeded down the corridor, counting his distance, thus:

"One metre.... two metres.... three metres....Here is the door....Mon Dieu, how easy it is! Only a small, simple bolt now separates me from the chamber, and I know that the bolt is located exactly one metre, forty-three centimeters, from the floor. So that, thanks to a small incision I am about to make, I can soon get rid of the bolt."

He drew from his pocket the necessary instruments. Then the following idea occurred to him:

"Suppose, by chance, the door is not bolted. I will try it first."

He turned the knob, and the door opened.

"My brave Lupin, surely fortune favors you....What's to be done now? You know the situation of the rooms; you know the place in which the countess hides the black pearl. Therefore, in order to secure the black pearl, you have simply to be more silent than silence, more invisible than darkness itself."

Arsène Lupin was employed fully a half-hour in opening the second door—a glass door that led to the countess' bedchamber. But he accomplished it with so much skill and precaution, that even had had the countess been awake, she would not have heard the slightest sound. According to the plan of the rooms, that he holds, he has merely to pass around a reclining chair and, beyond that, a small table close to the bed. On the table, there was a box of letter-paper, and the black pearl was concealed in that box. He stooped and crept cautiously over the carpet, following the outlines of the reclining-chair. When he reached the extremity of it, he stopped in order to repress the throbbing of his heart. Although he was not moved by any sense of fear, he found it impossible to overcome the nervous anxiety that one usually feels in the midst of profound silence. That circumstance astonished him, because he had passed through many more solemn moments without the slightest trace of emotion. No danger threatened him. Then why did his heart throb like an alarm-bell? Was it that sleeping woman who affected him? Was it the proximity of another pulsating heart?

He listened, and thought he could discern the rhythmical breathing of a person asleep. It gave him confidence, like the presence of a friend. He sought and found the armchair; then, by slow, cautious movements, advanced toward the table, feeling ahead of him with outstretched arm. His right had touched one of the feet of the table. Ah! now, he had simply to rise, take the pearl, and escape. That was fortunate, as his heart was leaping in his breast like a wild beast, and made so much noise that he feared it would waken the countess. By a powerful effort of the will, he subdued the wild throbbing of his heart, and was about to rise from the floor when his left hand encountered, lying on the floor, an object which he recognized as a candlestick—an overturned candlestick. A moment later, his hand encountered another object: a clock—one of those small traveling clocks, covered with leather. ———-

Well! What had happened? He could not understand. That candlestick, that clock; why were those articles not in their accustomed places? Ah! what had happened in the dread silence of the night?

Suddenly a cry escaped him. He had touched—oh! some strange, unutterable thing! "No! no!" he thought, "it cannot be. It is some fantasy of my excited brain." For twenty seconds, thirty seconds, he remained motionless, terrified, his forehead bathed with perspiration, and his fingers still retained the sensation of that dreadful contact.

Making a desperate effort, he ventured to extend his arm again. Once more, his hand encountered that strange, unutterable thing. He felt it. He must feel it and find out what it is. He found that it was hair, human hair, and a human face; and that face was cold, almost icy.

However frightful the circumstances may be, a man like Arsène Lupin controls himself and commands the situation as soon as he learns what it is. So, Arsène Lupin quickly brought his lantern into use. A woman was lying before him, covered with blood. Her neck and shoulders were covered with gaping wounds. He leaned over her and made a closer examination. She was dead.

"Dead! Dead!" he repeated, with a bewildered air.

He stared at those fixed eyes, that grim mouth, that livid flesh, and that blood—all that blood which had flowed over the carpet and congealed there in thick, black spots. He arose and turned on the electric lights. Then he beheld all the marks of a desperate struggle. The bed was in a state of great disorder. On the floor, the candlestick, and the clock, with the hands pointing to twenty minutes after eleven; then, further away, an overturned chair; and, everywhere, there was blood, spots of blood and pools of blood.

"And the black pearl?" he murmured.

The box of letter-paper was in its place. He opened it, eagerly. The jewel-case was there, but it was empty.

"Fichtre!" he muttered. "You boasted of your good fortune much too soon, my friend Lupin. With the countess lying cold and dead, and the black pearl vanished, the situation is anything but pleasant. Get out of here as soon as you can, or you may get into serious trouble."

Yet, he did not move.

"Get out of here? Yes, of course. Any person would, except Arsène Lupin. He has something better to do. Now, to proceed in an orderly way. At all events, you have a clear conscience. Let us suppose that you are the commissary of police and that you are proceeding to make an inquiry concerning this affair——Yes, but in order to do that, I require a clearer brain. Mine is muddled like a ragout."

He tumbled into an armchair, with his clenched hands pressed against his burning forehead.

The murder of the avenue Hoche is one of those which have recently surprised and puzzled the Parisian public, and, certainly, I should never have mentioned the affair if the veil of mystery had not been removed by Arsène Lupin himself. No one knew the exact truth of the case.

Who did not know—from having met her in the Bois—the fair Léotine Zalti, the once-famous cantatrice, wife and widow of the Count d'Andillot; the Zalti, whose luxury dazzled all Paris some twenty years ago; the Zalti who acquired an European reputation for the magnificence of her diamonds and pearls? It was said that she wore upon her shoulders the capital of several banking houses and the gold mines of numerous Australian companies. Skilful jewelers worked for Zalti as they had formerly wrought for kings and queens. And who does not remember the catastrophe in which all that wealth was swallowed up? Of all that marvelous collection, nothing remained except the famous black pearl. The black pearl! That is to say a fortune, if she had wished to part with it.

But she preferred to keep it, to live in a commonplace apartment with her companion, her cook, and a man-servant, rather than sell that inestimable jewel. There was a reason for it; a reason she was not afraid to disclose: the black pearl was the gift of an emperor! Almost ruined, and reduced to the most mediocre existence, she remained faithful to the companion of her happy and brilliant youth. The black pearl never left her possession. She wore it during the day, and, at night, concealed it in a place known to her alone.

All these facts, being republished in the columns of the public press, served to stimulate curiosity; and, strange to say, but quite obvious to those who have the key to the mystery, the arrest of the presumed assassin only complicated the question and prolonged the excitement. Two days later, the newspapers published the following item:

"Information has reached us of the arrest of Victor Danègre, the servant of the Countess d'Andillot. The evidence against him is clear and convincing. On the silken sleeve of his liveried waistcoat, which chief detective Dudouis found in his garret between the mattresses of his bed, several spots of blood were discovered. In addition, a cloth-covered button was missing from that garment, and this button was found beneath the bed of the victim.

"It is supposed that, after dinner, in place of going to his own room, Danègre slipped into the wardrobe-closet, and, through the glass door, had seen the countess hide the precious black pearl. This is simply a theory, as yet unverified by any evidence. There is, also, another obscure point. At seven o'clock in the morning, Danègre went to the tobacco-shop on the Boulevard de Courcelles; the concierge and the shop-keeper both affirm this fact. On the other hand, the countess' companion and cook, who sleep at the end of the hall, both declare that, when they arose at eight o'clock, the door of the antechamber and the door of the kitchen were locked. These two persons have been in the service of the countess for twenty years, and are above suspicion. The question is: How did Danègre leave the apartment? Did he have another key? These are matters that the police will investigate."

As a matter of fact, the police investigation threw no light on the mystery. It was learned that Victor Danègre was a dangerous criminal, a drunkard and a debauchee. But, as they proceeded with the investigation, the mystery deepened and new complications arose. In the first place, a young woman, Mlle. De Sinclèves, the cousin and sole heiress of the countess, declared that the countess, a month before her death, had written a letter to her and in it described the manner in which the black pearl was concealed. The letter disappeared the day after she received it. Who had stolen it?

Again, the concierge related how she had opened the door for a person who had inquired for Doctor Harel. On being questioned, the doctor testified that no one had rung his bell. Then who was that person? An accomplice?

The theory of an accomplice was thereupon adopted by the press and public, and also by Ganimard, the famous detective.

"Lupin is at the bottom of this affair," he said to the judge.

"Bah!" exclaimed the judge, "you have Lupin on the brain. You see him everywhere."

"I see him everywhere, because he is everywhere."

"Say rather that you see him every time you encounter something you cannot explain. Besides, you overlook the fact that the crime was committed at twenty minutes past eleven in the evening, as is shown by the clock, while the nocturnal visit, mentioned by the concierge, occurred at three o'clock in the morning."

Officers of the law frequently form a hasty conviction as to the guilt of a suspected person, and then distort all subsequent discoveries to conform to their established theory. The deplorable antecedents of Victor Danègre, habitual criminal, drunkard and rake, influenced the judge, and despite the fact that nothing new was discovered in corroboration of the early clues, his official opinion remained firm and unshaken. He closed his investigation, and, a few weeks later, the trial commenced. It proved to be slow and tedious. The judge was listless, and the public prosecutor presented the case in a careless manner. Under those circumstances, Danègre's counsel had an easy task. He pointed out the defects and inconsistencies of the case for the prosecution, and argued that the evidence was quite insufficient to convict the accused. Who had made the key, the indispensable key without which Danègre, on leaving the apartment, could not have locked the door behind him? Who had ever seen such a key, and what had become of it? Who had seen the assassin's knife, and where is it now?

"In any event," argued the prisoner's counsel, "the prosecution must prove, beyond any reasonable doubt, that the prisoner committed the murder. The prosecution must show that the mysterious individual who entered the house at three o'clock in the morning is not the guilty party. To be sure, the clock indicated eleven o'clock. But what of that? I contend, that proves nothing. The assassin could turn the hands of the clock to any hour he pleased, and thus deceive us in regard to the exact hour of the crime."

Victor Danègre was acquitted.

He left the prison on Friday about dusk in the evening, weak and depressed by his six months' imprisonment. The inquisition, the solitude, the trial, the deliberations of the jury, combined to fill him with a nervous fear. At night, he had been afflicted with terrible nightmares and haunted by weird visions of the scaffold. He was a mental and physical wreck.

Under the assumed name of Anatole Dufour, he rented a small room on the heights of Montmartre, and lived by doing odd jobs wherever he could find them. He led a pitiful existence. Three times, he obtained regular employment, only to be recognized and then discharged. Sometimes, he had an idea that men were following him—detectives, no doubt, who were seeking to trap and denounce him. He could almost feel the strong hand of the law clutching him by the collar.

One evening, as he was eating his dinner at a neighboring restaurant, a man entered and took a seat at the same table. He was a person about forty years of age, and wore a frock-coat of doubtful cleanliness. He ordered soup, vegetables, and a bottle of wine. After he had finished his soup, he turned his eyes on Danègre, and gazed at him intently. Danègre winced. He was certain that this was one of the men who had been following him for several weeks. What did he want? Danègre tried to rise, but failed. His limbs refused to support him. The man poured himself a glass of wine, and then filled Danègre's glass. The man raised his glass, and said:

"To your health, Victor Danègre."

Victor started in alarm, and stammered:

"I!....I!.... no, no....I swear to you...."

"You will swear what? That you are not yourself? The servant of the countess?"

"What servant? My name is Dufour. Ask the proprietor."

"Yes, Anatole Dufour to the proprietor of this restaurant, but Victor Danègre to the officers of the law."

"That's not true! Some one has lied to you."

The new-comer took a card from his pocket and handed it to Victor, who read on it: "Grimaudan, ex-inspector of the detective force. Private business transacted." Victor shuddered as he said:

"You are connected with the police?"

"No, not now, but I have a liking for the business and I continue to work at it in a manner more—profitable. From time to time I strike upon a golden opportunity—such as your case presents."

"My case?"

"Yes, yours. I assure you it is a most promising affair, provided you are inclined to be reasonable."

"But if I am not reasonable?"

"Oh! my good fellow, you are not in a position to refuse me anything I may ask."

"What is it.... you want?" stammered Victor, fearfully.

"Well, I will inform you in a few words. I am sent by Mademoiselle de Sinclèves, the heiress of the Countess d'Andillot."

"What for?"

"To recover the black pearl."

"Black pearl?"

"That you stole."

"But I haven't got it."

"You have it."

"If I had, then I would be the assassin."

"You are the assassin."

Danègre showed a forced smile.

"Fortunately for me, monsieur, the Assizecourt was not of your opinion. The jury returned an unanimous verdict of acquittal. And when a man has a clear conscience and twelve good men in his favor—"

The ex-inspector seized him by the arm and said:

"No fine phrases, my boy. Now, listen to me and weigh my words carefully. You will find they are worthy of your consideration. Now, Danègre, three weeks before the murder, you abstracted the cook's key to the servants' door, and had a duplicate key made by a locksmith named Outard, 244 rue Oberkampf."

"It's a lie—it's a lie!" growled Victor. "No person has seen that key. There is no such key."

"Here it is."

After a silence, Grimaudan continued:

"You killed the countess with a knife purchased by you at the Bazar de la Republique on the same day as you ordered the duplicate key. It has a triangular blade with a groove running from end to end."

"That is all nonsense. You are simply guessing at something you don't know. No one ever saw the knife."

"Here it is."

Victor Danègre recoiled. The ex-inspector continued:

"There are some spots of rust upon it. Shall I tell you how they came there?"

"Well!.... you have a key and a knife. Who can prove that they belong to me?"

"The locksmith, and the clerk from whom you bought the knife. I have already refreshed their memories, and, when you confront them, they cannot fail to recognize you."

His speech was dry and hard, with a tone of firmness and precision. Danègre was trembling with fear, and yet he struggled desperately to maintain an air of indifference.

"Is that all the evidence you have?"

"Oh! no, not at all. I have plenty more. For instance, after the crime, you went out the same way you had entered. But, in the centre of the wardrobe-room, being seized by some sudden fear, you leaned against the wall for support."

"How do you know that? No one could know such a thing," argued the desperate man.

"The police know nothing about it, of course. They never think of lighting a candle and examining the walls. But if they had done so, they would have found on the white plaster a faint red spot, quite distinct, however, to trace in it the imprint of your thumb which you had pressed against the wall while it was wet with blood. Now, as you are well aware, under the Bertillon system, thumb-marks are one of the principal means of identification."

Victor Danègre was livid; great drops of perspiration rolled down his face and fell upon the table. He gazed, with a wild look, at the strange man who had narrated the story of his crime as faithfully as if he had been an invisible witness to it. Overcome and powerless, Victor bowed his head. He felt that it was useless to struggle against this marvelous man. So he said:

"How much will you give me, if I give you the pearl?"

"Nothing."

"Oh! you are joking! Or do you mean that I should give you an article worth thousands and hundreds of thousands and get nothing in return?"

"You will get your life. Is that nothing?"

The unfortunate man shuddered. Then Grimaudan added, in a milder tone:

"Come, Danègre, that pearl has no value in your hands. It is quite impossible for you to sell it; so what is the use of your keeping it?"

"There are pawnbrokers.... and, some day, I will be able to get something for it."

"But that day may be too late."

"Why?"

"Because by that time you may be in the hands of the police, and, with the evidence that I can furnish—the knife, the key, the thumb-mark—what will become of you?"

Victor rested his head on his hands and reflected. He felt that he was lost, irremediably lost, and, at the same time, a sense of weariness and depression overcame him. He murmured, faintly:

"When must I give it to you?"

"To-night——within an hour."

"If I refuse?"

"If you refuse, I shall post this letter to the Procureur of the Republic; in which letter Mademoiselle de Sinclèves denounces you as the assassin."

Danègre poured out two glasses of wine which he drank in rapid succession, then, rising, said:

"Pay the bill, and let us go. I have had enough of the cursed affair."

Night had fallen. The two men walked down the rue Lepic and followed the exterior boulevards in the direction of the Place de l'Etoile. They pursued their way in silence; Victor had a stooping carriage and a dejected face. When they reached the Parc Monceau, he said:

"We are near the house."

"Parbleu! You only left the house once, before your arrest, and that was to go to the tobacco-shop."

"Here it is," said Danègre, in a dull voice.

They passed along the garden wall of the countess' house, and crossed a street on a corner of which stood the tobacco-shop. A few steps further on, Danègre stopped; his limbs shook beneath him, and he sank to a bench.

"Well! what now?" demanded his companion.

"It is there."

"Where? Come, now, no nonsense!"

"There—in front of us."

"Where?"

"Between two paving-stones."

"Which?"

"Look for it."

"Which stones?"

Victor made no reply.

"Ah; I see!" exclaimed Grimaudan, "you want me to pay for the information."

"No.... but....I am afraid I will starve to death."

"So! that is why you hesitate. Well, I'll not be hard on you. How much do you want?"

"Enough to buy a steerage pass to America."

"All right."

"And a hundred francs to keep me until I get work there."

"You shall have two hundred. Now, speak."

"Count the paving-stones to the right from the sewer-hole. The pearl is between the twelfth and thirteenth."

"In the gutter?"

"Yes, close to the sidewalk."

Grimaudan glanced around to see if anyone were looking. Some tram-cars and pedestrians were passing. But, bah, they will not suspect anything. He opened his pocketknife and thrust it between the twelfth and thirteenth stones.

"And if it is not there?" he said to Victor.

"It must be there, unless someone saw me stoop down and hide it."

Could it be possible that the back pearl had been cast into the mud and filth of the gutter to be picked up by the first comer? The black pearl—a fortune!

"How far down?" he asked.

"About ten centimetres."

He dug up the wet earth. The point of his knife struck something. He enlarged the hole with his finger. Then he abstracted the black pearl from its filthy hiding-place.

"Good! Here are your two hundred francs. I will send you the ticket for America."

On the following day, this article was published in the `Echo de France,' and was copied by the leading newspapers throughout the world:

> *"Yesterday, the famous black pearl came into the possession of Arsène Lupin, who recovered it from the murderer of the Countess d'Andillot. In a short time, facsimiles of that precious jewel will be exhibited in London, St. Petersburg, Calcutta, Buenos Ayres and New York.*
>
> *"Arsène Lupin will be pleased to consider all propositions submitted to him through his agents."*

"And that is how crime is always punished and virtue rewarded," said Arsène Lupin, after he had told me the foregoing history of the black pearl.

"And that is how you, under the assumed name of Grimaudan, ex-inspector of detectives, were chosen by fate to deprive the criminal of the benefit of his crime."

"Exactly. And I confess that the affair gives me infinite satisfaction and pride. The forty minutes that I passed in the apartment of the Countess d'Andillot, after learning of her death, were the most thrilling and absorbing moments of my life. In those forty minutes, involved as I was in a most dangerous plight, I calmly studied the scene of the murder and reached the conclusion that the crime must have been committed by one of the house servants. I also decided that, in order to get the pearl, that servant must be arrested, and so I left the wainscoat button; it was necessary, also, for me to hold some convincing evidence of his guilt, so I carried away the knife which I found upon the floor, and the key which I found in the lock. I closed and locked the door, and erased the finger-marks from the plaster in the wardrobe-closet. In my opinion, that was one of those flashes—"

"Of genius," I said, interrupting.

"Of genius, if you wish. But, I flatter myself, it would not have occurred to the average mortal. To frame, instantly, the two elements of the problem—an arrest and an acquittal; to make use of the formidable machinery of the law to crush and humble my victim, and reduce him to a condition in which, when free, he would be certain to fall into the trap I was laying for him!"

"Poor devil—"

"Poor devil, do you say? Victor Danègre, the assassin! He might have descended to the lowest depths of vice and crime, if he had retained the black pearl. Now, he lives! Think of that: Victor Danègre is alive!"

"And you have the black pearl."

He took it out of one of the secret pockets of his wallet, examined it, gazed at it tenderly, and caressed it with loving fingers, and sighed, as he said:

"What cold Russian prince, what vain and foolish rajah may some day possess this priceless treasure! Or, perhaps, some American millionaire is destined to become the owner of this morsel of exquisite beauty that once adorned the fair bosom of Leontine Zalti, the Countess d'Andillot."

IX. HERLOCK SHOLMES ARRIVES TOO LATE

"It is really remarkable, Velmont, what a close resemblance you bear to Arsène Lupin!"

"How do you know?"

"Oh! like everyone else, from photographs, no two of which are alike, but each of them leaves the impression of a face.... something like yours."

Horace Velmont displayed some vexation.

"Quite so, my dear Devanne. And, believe me, you are not the first one who has noticed it."

"It is so striking," persisted Devanne, "that if you had not been recommended to me by my cousin d'Estevan, and if you were not the celebrated artist whose beautiful marine views I so admire, I have no doubt I should have warned the police of your presence in Dieppe."

This sally was greeted with an outburst of laughter. The large dining-hall of the Château de Thibermesnil contained on this occasion, besides Velmont, the following guests: Father Gélis, the parish priest, and a dozen officers whose regiments were quartered in the vicinity and who had accepted the invitation of the banker Georges Devanne and his mother. One of the officers then remarked:

"I understand that an exact description of Arsène Lupin has been furnished to all the police along this coast since his daring exploit on the Paris-Havre express."

"I suppose so," said Devanne. "That was three months ago; and a week later, I made the acquaintance of our friend Velmont at the casino, and, since then, he has honored me with several visits—an agreeable preamble to a more serious visit that he will pay me one of these days—or, rather, one of these nights."

This speech evoked another round of laughter, and the guests then passed into the ancient "Hall of the Guards," a vast room with a high ceiling, which occupied the entire lower part of the Tour Guillaume—William's Tower—and wherein Georges Devanne had collected the incomparable treasures which the lords of Thibermesnil had accumulated through many centuries. It contained ancient chests, credences, andirons and chandeliers. The stone walls were overhung with magnificent tapestries. The deep embrasures of the four windows were furnished with benches, and the Gothic windows were composed of small panes of colored glass set in a leaden frame. Between the door and the window to the left stood an immense bookcase of Renaissance style, on the pediment of which, in letters of gold, was the world "Thibermesnil," and, below it, the proud family device: "Fais ce que veulx" (Do what thou wishest). When the guests had lighted their cigars, Devanne resumed the conversation.

"And remember, Velmont, you have no time to lose; in fact, to-night is the last chance you will have."

"How so?" asked the painter, who appeared to regard the affair as a joke. Devanne was about to reply, when his mother mentioned to him to keep silent, but the excitement of the occasion and a desire to interest his guests urged him to speak.

"Bah!" he murmured. "I can tell it now. It won't do any harm."

The guests drew closer, and he commenced to speak with the satisfied air of a man who has an important announcement to make.

"To-morrow afternoon at four o'clock, Herlock Sholmes, the famous English detective, for whom such a thing as mystery does not exist; Herlock Sholmes, the most remarkable solver of enigmas the world has ever known, that marvelous man who would seem to be the creation of a romantic novelist—Herlock Sholmes will be my guest!"

Immediately, Devanne was the target of numerous eager questions. "Is Herlock Sholmes really coming?" "Is it so serious as that?" "Is Arsène Lupin really in this neighborhood?"

"Arsène Lupin and his band are not far away. Besides the robbery of the Baron Cahorn, he is credited with the thefts at Montigny, Gruchet and Crasville."

"Has he sent you a warning, as he did to Baron Cahorn?"

"No," replied Devanne, "he can't work the same trick twice."

"What then?"

"I will show you."

He rose, and pointing to a small empty space between the two enormous folios on one of the shelves of the bookcase, he said:

"There used to be a book there—a book of the sixteenth century entitled `Chronique de Thibermesnil,' which contained the history of the castle since its construction by Duke Rollo on the site of a former feudal fortress. There were three engraved plates in the book; one of which was a general view of the whole estate; another, the plan of the buildings; and the third—I call your attention to it, particularly—the third was the sketch of a subterranean passage, an entrance to which is outside the first line of ramparts, while the other end of the passage is here, in this very room. Well, that book disappeared a month ago."

"The deuce!" said Velmont, "that looks bad. But it doesn't seem to be a sufficient reason for sending for Herlock Sholmes."

"Certainly, that was not sufficient in itself, but another incident happened that gives the disappearance of the book a special significance. There was another copy of this book in the National Library at Paris, and the two books differed in certain details relating to the subterranean passage; for instance, each of them contained drawings and annotations, not printed, but written in ink and more or less effaced. I knew those facts, and I knew that the exact location of the passage could be determined only by a comparison of the two books. Now, the day after my book disappeared, the book was called for in the National Library by a reader who carried it away, and no one knows how the theft was effected."

The guests uttered many exclamations of surprise.

"Certainly, the affair looks serious," said one.

"Well, the police investigated the matter, and, as usual, discovered no clue whatever."

"They never do, when Arsène Lupin is concerned in it."

"Exactly; and so I decided to ask the assistance of Herlock Sholmes, who replied that he was ready and anxious to enter the lists with Arsène Lupin."

"What glory for Arsène Lupin!" said Velmont. "But if our national thief, as they call him, has no evil designs on your castle, Herlock Sholmes will have his trip in vain."

"There are other things that will interest him, such as the discovery of the subterranean passage."

"But you told us that one end of the passage was outside the ramparts and the other was in this very room!"

"Yes, but in what part of the room? The line which represents the passage on the charts ends here, with a small circle marked with the letters `T.G.,' which no doubt stand for `Tour Guillaume.' But the tower is round, and who can tell the exact spot at which the passage touches the tower?"

Devanne lighted a second cigar and poured himself a glass of Benedictine. His guests pressed him with questions and he was pleased to observe the interest that his remarks had created. The he continued:

"The secret is lost. No one knows it. The legend is to the effect that the former lords of the castle transmitted the secret from father to son on their deathbeds, until Geoffroy, the last of the race, was beheaded during the Revolution in his nineteenth year."

"That is over a century ago. Surely, someone has looked for it since that time?"

"Yes, but they failed to find it. After I purchased the castle, I made a diligent search for it, but without success. You must remember that this tower is surrounded by water and connected with the castle only by a bridge; consequently, the passage must be underneath the old moat. The plan that was in the book in the National Library showed a series of stairs with a total of forty-eight steps, which indicates a depth of more than ten meters. You see, the mystery lies within the walls of this room, and yet I dislike to tear them down."

"Is there nothing to show where it is?"

"Nothing."

"Mon. Devanne, we should turn our attention to the two quotations," suggested Father Gélis.

"Oh!" exclaimed Mon. Devanne, laughing, "our worthy father is fond of reading memoirs and delving into the musty archives of the castle. Everything relating to Thibermesnil interests him greatly. But the quotations that he mentions only serve to complicate the mystery. He has read somewhere that two kings of France have known the key to the puzzle."

"Two kings of France! Who were they?"

"Henry the Fourth and Louis the Sixteenth. And the legend runs like this: On the eve of the battle of Arques, Henry the Fourth spent the night in this castle. At eleven o'clock in the evening, Louise de Tancarville, the prettiest woman in Normandy, was brought into the castle through the subterranean passage by Duke Edgard, who, at the same time, informed the king of the secret passage. Afterward, the king confided the secret to his minister Sully, who, in turn, relates the story in his book, "Royales Economies d'Etat," without making any comment upon it, but linking with it this incomprehensible sentence: `Turn one eye on the bee that shakes, the other eye will lead to God!'"

After a brief silence, Velmont laughed and said:

"Certainly, it doesn't throw a dazzling light upon the subject."

"No; but Father Gélis claims that Sully concealed the key to the mystery in this strange sentence in order to keep the secret from the secretaries to whom he dictated his memoirs."

"That is an ingenious theory," said Velmont.

"Yes, and it may be nothing more; I cannot see that it throws any light on the mysterious riddle."

"And was it also to receive the visit of a lady that Louis the Sixteenth caused the passage to be opened?"

"I don't know," said Mon. Devanne. "All I can say is that the king stopped here one night in 1784, and that the famous Iron Casket found in the Louvre contained a paper bearing these words in the king's own writing: `Thibermesnil 3-4-11.'"

Horace Velmont laughed heartily, and exclaimed:

"At last! And now that we have the magic key, where is the man who can fit it to the invisible lock?"

"Laugh as much as you please, monsieur," said Father Gèlis, "but I am confident the solution is contained in those two sentences, and some day we will find a man able to interpret them."

"Herlock Sholmes is the man," said Mon. Devanne, "unless Arsène Lupin gets ahead of him. What is your opinion, Velmont?"

Velmont arose, placed his hand on Devanne's shoulder, and declared:

"I think that the information furnished by your book and the book of the National Library was deficient in a very important detail which you have now supplied. I thank you for it."

"What is it?"

"The missing key. Now that I have it, I can go to work at once," said Velmont.

"Of course; without losing a minute," said Devanne, smiling.

"Not even a second!" replied Velmont. "To-night, before the arrival of Herlock Sholmes, I must plunder your castle."

"You have no time to lose. Oh! by the way, I can drive you over this evening."

"To Dieppe?"

"Yes. I am going to meet Monsieur and Madame d'Androl and a young lady of their acquaintance who are to arrive by the midnight train."

Then addressing the officers, Devanne added:

"Gentlemen, I shall expect to see all of you at breakfast to-morrow."

The invitation was accepted. The company dispersed, and a few moments later Devanne and Velmont were speeding toward Dieppe in an automobile. Devanne dropped the artist in front of the Casino, and proceeded to the railway station. At twelve o'clock his friends alighted from the train. A half hour later the automobile was at the entrance to the castle. At one o'clock, after a light supper, they retired. The lights were extinguished, and the castle was enveloped in the darkness and silence of the night.

The moon appeared through a rift in the clouds, and filled the drawing-room with its bright white light. But only for a moment. Then the moon again retired behind its ethereal draperies, and darkness and silence reigned supreme. No sound could be heard, save the monotonous ticking of the clock. It struck two, and then continued its endless repetitions of the seconds. Then, three o'clock.

Suddenly, something clicked, like the opening and closing of a signal-disc that warns the passing train. A thin stream of light flashed to every corner of the room, like an arrow that leaves behind it a trail of light. It shot forth from the central fluting of a column that supported the pediment of the bookcase. It rested for a moment on the panel opposite like a glittering circle of burnished silver, then flashed in all directions like a guilty eye that scrutinizes every shadow. It disappeared for a short time, but burst forth again as a whole section of the bookcase revolved on a picot and disclosed a large opening like a vault.

A man entered, carrying an electric lantern. He was followed by a second man, who carried a coil of rope and various tools. The leader inspected the room, listened a moment, and said:

"Call the others."

Then eight men, stout fellows with resolute faces, entered the room, and immediately commenced to remove the furnishings. Arsène Lupin passed quickly from one piece of furniture to another, examined each, and, according to its size or artistic value, he directed his men to take it or leave it. If ordered to be taken, it was carried to the gaping mouth of the tunnel, and ruthlessly thrust into the bowels of the earth. Such was the fate of six armchairs, six small Louis XV chairs, a quantity of Aubusson tapestries, some candelabra, paintings by Fragonard and Nattier, a bust by Houdon, and some statuettes. Sometimes, Lupin would linger before a beautiful chest or a superb picture, and sigh:

"That is too heavy.... too large.... what a pity!"

In forty minutes the room was dismantled; and it had been accomplished in such an orderly manner and with as little noise as if the various articles had been packed and wadded for the occasion.

Lupin said to the last man who departed by way of the tunnel:

"You need not come back. You understand, that as soon as the auto-van is loaded, you are to proceed to the grange at Roquefort."

"But you, patron?"

"Leave me the motor-cycle."

When the man had disappeared, Arsène Lupin pushed the section of the bookcase back into its place, carefully effaced the traces of the men's footsteps, raised a portiere, and entered a gallery, which was the only means of communication between the tower and the castle. In the center of this gallery there was a glass cabinet which had attracted Lupin's attentions. It contained a valuable collection of watches, snuff-boxes, rings, chatelaines and miniatures of rare and beautiful workmanship. He forced the lock with a small jimmy, and experienced a great pleasure in handling those gold and silver ornaments, those exquisite and delicate works of art.

He carried a large linen bag, specially prepared for the removal of such knick-knacks. He filled it. Then he filled the pockets of his coat, waistcoat and trousers. And he was just placing over his left arm a number of pearl reticules when he heard a slight sound. He listened. No, he was not deceived. The noise continued. Then he remembered that, at one end of the gallery, there was a stairway leading to an unoccupied apartment, but which was probably occupied that night by the young lady whom Mon. Devanne had brought from Dieppe with his other visitors.

Immediately he extinguished his lantern, and had scarcely gained the friendly shelter of a window-embrasure, when the door at the top of the stairway was opened and a feeble light illuminated the gallery. He could feel—for, concealed by a curtain, he could not see—that a woman was cautiously descending the upper steps of the stairs. He hoped she would come no closer. Yet, she continued to descend, and even advanced some distance into the room. Then she uttered a faint cry. No doubt she had discovered the broken and dismantled cabinet.

She advanced again. Now he could smell the perfume, and hear the throbbing of her heart as she drew closer to the window where he was concealed. She passed so close that her skirt brushed against the window-curtain, and Lupin felt that she suspected the presence of another, behind her, in the shadow, within reach of her hand. He thought: "She is afraid. She will go away." But she did not go. The candle, that she carried in her trembling hand, grew brighter. She turned, hesitated a moment, appeared to listen, then suddenly drew aside the curtain.

They stood face to face. Arsène was astounded. He murmured, involuntarily:

"You—you—mademoiselle."

It was Miss Nelly. Miss Nelly! his fellow passenger on the transatlantic steamer, who had been the subject of his dreams on that memorable voyage, who had been a witness to his arrest, and who, rather than betray him, had dropped into the water the Kodak in which he had concealed the bank-notes and diamonds. Miss Nelly! that charming creature, the memory of whose face had sometimes sheered, sometimes saddened the long hours of imprisonment.

It was such an unexpected encounter that brought them face to face in that castle at that hour of the night, that they could not move, nor utter a word; they were amazed, hypnotized, each at the sudden apparition of the other. Trembling with emotion, Miss Nelly staggered to a seat. He remained standing in front of her.

Gradually, he realized the situation and conceived the impression he must have produced at that moment with his arms laden with knick-knacks, and his pockets and a linen sack overflowing with plunder. He was overcome with confusion, and he actually blushed to find himself in the position of a thief caught in the act. To her, henceforth, he was a thief, a man who puts his hand in another's pocket, who steals into houses and robs people while they sleep.

A watch fell upon the floor; then another. These were followed by other articles which slipped from his grasp one by one. Then, actuated by a sudden decision, he dropped the other articles into an armchair, emptied his pockets and unpacked his sack. He felt very uncomfortable in Nelly's presence, and stepped toward her with the intention of speaking to her, but she shuddered, rose quickly and fled toward the salon. The portiere closed behind her. He followed her. She was standing trembling and amazed at the sight of the devastated room. He said to her, at once:

"To-morrow, at three o'clock, everything will be returned. The furniture will be brought back."

She made no reply, so he repeated:

"I promise it. To-morrow, at three o'clock. Nothing in the world could induce me to break that promise....To-morrow, at three o'clock."

Then followed a long silence that he dared not break, whilst the agitation of the young girl caused him a feeling of genuine regret. Quietly, without a word, he turned away, thinking: "I hope she will go away. I can't endure her presence." But the young girl suddenly spoke, and stammered:

"Listen.... footsteps....I hear someone...."

He looked at her with astonishment. She seemed to be overwhelmed by the thought of approaching peril.

"I don't hear anything," he said.

"But you must go—you must escape!"

"Why should I go?"

"Because—you must. Oh! do not remain here another minute. Go!"

She ran, quickly, to the door leading to the gallery and listened. No, there was no one there. Perhaps the noise was outside. She waited a moment, then returned reassured.

But Arsène Lupin had disappeared.

As soon as Mon. Devanne was informed of the pillage of his castle, he said to himself: It was Velmont who did it, and Velmont is Arsène Lupin. That theory explained everything, and there was no other plausible explanation. And yet the idea seemed preposterous. It was ridiculous to suppose that Velmont was anyone else than Velmont, the famous artist, and club-fellow of his cousin d'Estevan. So, when the captain of the gendarmes arrived to investigate the affair, Devanne did not even think of mentioning his absurd theory.

Throughout the forenoon there was a lively commotion at the castle. The gendarmes, the local police, the chief of police from Dieppe, the villagers, all circulated to and fro in the halls, examining every nook and corner that was open to their inspection. The approach of the maneuvering troops, the rattling fire of the musketry, added to the picturesque character of the scene.

The preliminary search furnished no clue. Neither the doors nor windows showed any signs of having been disturbed. Consequently, the removal of the goods must have been effected by means of the secret passage. Yet, there were no indications of footsteps on the floor, nor any unusual marks upon the walls.

Their investigations revealed, however, one curious fact that denoted the whimsical character of Arsène Lupin: the famous Chronique of the sixteenth century had been restored to its accustomed place in the library and, beside it, there was a similar book, which was none other than the volume stolen from the National Library.

At eleven o'clock the military officers arrived. Devanne welcomed them with his usual gayety; for, no matter how much chagrin he might suffer from the loss of his artistic treasures, his great wealth enabled him to bear his loss philosophically. His guests, Monsieur and Madame d'Androl and Miss Nelly, were introduced; and it was then noticed that one of the expected guests had not arrived. It was Horace Velmont. Would he come? His absence had awakened the suspicions of Mon. Devanne. But at twelve o'clock he arrived. Devanne exclaimed:

"Ah! here you are!"

"Why, am I not punctual?" asked Velmont.

"Yes, and I am surprised that you are.... after such a busy night! I suppose you know the news?"

"What news?"

"You have robbed the castle."

"Nonsense!" exclaimed Velmont, smiling.

"Exactly as I predicted. But, first escort Miss Underdown to the dining-room. Mademoiselle, allow me—"

He stopped, as he remarked the extreme agitation of the young girl. Then, recalling the incident, he said:

"Ah! of course, you met Arsène Lupin on the steamer, before his arrest, and you are astonished at the resemblance. Is that it?"

She did not reply. Velmont stood before her, smiling. He bowed. She took his proffered arm. He escorted her to her place, and took his seat opposite her. During the breakfast, the conversation related exclusively to Arsène Lupin, the stolen goods, the secret passage, and Herlock Sholmes. It was only at the close of the repast, when the conversation had drifted to other subjects, that Velmont took any part in it. Then he was, by turns, amusing and grave, talkative and pensive. And all his remarks seemed to be directed to the young girl. But she, quite absorbed, did not appear to hear them.

Coffee was served on the terrace overlooking the court of honor and the flower garden in front of the principal façade. The regimental band played on the lawn, and scores of soldiers and peasants wandered through the park.

Miss Nelly had not forgotten, for one moment, Lupin's solemn promise: "To-morrow, at three o'clock, everything will be returned."

At three o'clock! And the hands of the great clock in the right wing of the castle now marked twenty minutes to three. In spite of herself, her eyes wandered to the clock every minute. She also watched Velmont, who was calmly swinging to and fro in a comfortable rocking chair.

Ten minutes to three!....Five minutes to three!....Nelly was impatient and anxious. Was it possible that Arsène Lupin would carry out his promise at the appointed hour, when the castle, the courtyard, and the park were filled with people, and at the very moment when the officers of the law were pursuing their investigations? And yet....Arsène Lupin had given her his solemn promise. "It will be exactly as he said," thought she, so deeply was she impressed with the authority, energy and assurance of that remarkable man. To her, it no longer assumed the form of a miracle, but, on the contrary, a natural incident that must occur in the ordinary course of events. She blushed, and turned her head.

Three o'clock! The great clock struck slowly: one.... two.... three....Horace Velmont took out his watch, glanced at the clock, then returned the watch to his pocket. A few seconds passed in silence; and then the crowd in the courtyard parted to give passage to two wagons, that had just entered the park-gate, each drawn by two horses. They were army-wagons, such as are used for the transportation of provisions, tents, and other necessary military stores. They stopped in front of the main entrance, and a commissary-sergeant leaped from one of the wagons and inquired for Mon. Devanne. A moment later, that gentleman emerged from the house, descended the steps, and, under the canvas covers of the wagons, beheld his furniture, pictures and ornaments carefully packaged and arranged.

When questioned, the sergeant produced an order that he had received from the officer of the day. By that order, the second company of the fourth battalion were commanded to proceed to the crossroads of Halleux in the forest of Arques, gather up the furniture and other articles deposited there, and deliver same to Monsieur Georges Devanne, owner of the Thibermesnil castle, at three o'clock. Signed: Col. Beauvel.

"At the crossroads," explained the sergeant, "we found everything ready, lying on the grass, guarded by some passers-by. It seemed very strange, but the order was imperative."

One of the officers examined the signature. He declared it a forgery; but a clever imitation. The wagons were unloaded, and the goods restored to their proper places in the castle.

During this commotion, Nelly had remained alone at the extreme end of the terrace, absorbed by confused and distracted thoughts. Suddenly, she observed Velmont approaching her. She would have avoided him, but the balustrade that surrounded the terrace cut off her retreat. She was cornered. She could not move. A gleam of sunshine, passing through the scant foliage of a bamboo, lighted up her beautiful golden hair. Some one spoke to her in a low voice:

"Have I not kept my promise?"

Arsène Lupin stood close to her. No one else was near. He repeated, in a calm, soft voice:

"Have I not kept my promise?"

He expected a word of thanks, or at least some slight movement that would betray her interest in the fulfillment of his promise. But she remained silent.

Her scornful attitude annoyed Arsène Lupin; and he realized the vast distance that separated him from Miss Nelly, now that she had learned the truth. He would gladly have justified himself in her eyes, or at least pleaded extenuating circumstances, but he perceived the absurdity and futility of such an attempt. Finally, dominated by a surging flood of memories, he murmured:

"Ah! how long ago that was! You remember the long hours on the deck of the `Provence.' Then, you carried a rose in your hand, a white rose like the one you carry to-day. I asked you for it. You pretended you did not hear me. After you had gone away, I found the rose—forgotten, no doubt—and I kept it."

She made no reply. She seemed to be far away. He continued:

"In memory of those happy hours, forget what you have learned since. Separate the past from the present. Do not regard me as the man you saw last night, but look at me, if only for a moment, as you did in those far-off days when I was Bernard d'Andrezy, for a short time. Will you, please?"

She raised her eyes and looked at him as he had requested. Then, without saying a word, she pointed to a ring he was wearing on his forefinger. Only the ring was visible; but the setting, which was turned toward the palm of his hand, consisted of a magnificent ruby. Arsène Lupin blushed. The ring belonged to Georges Devanne. He smiled bitterly, and said:

"You are right. Nothing can be changed. Arsène Lupin is now and always will be Arsène Lupin. To you, he cannot be even so much as a memory. Pardon me....I should have known that any attention I may now offer you is simply an insult. Forgive me."

He stepped aside, hat in hand. Nelly passed before him. He was inclined to detain her and beseech her forgiveness. But his courage failed, and he contented himself by following her with his eyes, as he had done when she descended the gangway to the pier at New York. She mounted the steps leading to the door, and disappeared within the house. He saw her no more.

A cloud obscured the sun. Arsène Lupin stood watching the imprints of her tiny feet in the sand. Suddenly, he gave a start. Upon the box which contained the bamboo, beside which Nelly had been standing, he saw the rose, the white rose which he had desired but dared not ask for. Forgotten, no doubt—it, also! But how—designedly or through distraction? He seized it eagerly. Some of its petals fell to the ground. He picked them up, one by one, like precious relics.

"Come!" he said to himself, "I have nothing more to do here. I must think of my safety, before Herlock Sholmes arrives."

The park was deserted, but some gendarmes were stationed at the park-gate. He entered a grove of pine trees, leaped over the wall, and, as a short cut to the railroad station, followed a path across the fields. After walking about ten minutes, he arrived at a spot where the road grew narrower and ran between two steep banks. In this ravine, he met a man traveling in the opposite direction. It was a man about fifty years of age, tall, smooth-shaven, and wearing clothes of a foreign cut. He carried a heavy cane, and a small satchel was strapped across his shoulder. When they met, the stranger spoke, with a slight English accent:

"Excuse me, monsieur, is this the way to the castle?"

"Yes, monsieur, straight ahead, and turn to the left when you come to the wall. They are expecting you."

"Ah!"

"Yes, my friend Devanne told us last night that you were coming, and I am delighted to be the first to welcome you. Herlock Sholmes has no more ardent admirer than.... myself."

There was a touch of irony in his voice that he quickly regretted, for Herlock Sholmes scrutinized him from head to foot with such a keen, penetrating eye that Arsène Lupin experienced the sensation of being seized, imprisoned and registered by that look more thoroughly and precisely than he had ever been by a camera.

"My negative is taken now," he thought, "and it will be useless to use a disguise with that man. He would look right through it. But, I wonder, has he recognized me?"

They bowed to each other as if about to part. But, at that moment, they heard a sound of horses' feet, accompanied by a clinking of steel. It was the gendarmes. The two men were obliged to draw back against the embankment, amongst the brushes, to avoid the horses. The gendarmes passed by, but, as they followed each other at a considerable distance, they were several minutes in doing so. And Lupin was thinking:

"It all depends on that question: has he recognized me? If so, he will probably take advantage of the opportunity. It is a trying situation."

When the last horseman had passed, Herlock Sholmes stepped forth and brushed the dust from his clothes. Then, for a moment, he and Arsène Lupin gazed at each other; and, if a person could have seen them at that moment, it would have been an interesting sight, and memorable as the first meeting of two remarkable men, so strange, so powerfully equipped, both of superior quality, and destined by fate, through their peculiar attributes, to hurl themselves one at the other like two equal forces that nature opposes, one against the other, in the realms of space.

Then the Englishman said: "Thank you, monsieur."

They parted. Lupin went toward the railway station, and Herlock Sholmes continued on his way to the castle.

The local officers had given up the investigation after several hours of fruitless efforts, and the people at the castle were awaiting the arrival of the English detective with a lively curiosity. At first sight, they were a little disappointed on account of his commonplace appearance, which differed so greatly from the pictures they had formed of him in their own minds. He did not in any way resemble the romantic hero, the mysterious and diabolical personage that the name of Herlock Sholmes had evoked in their imaginations. However, Mon. Devanne exclaimed with much gusto:

"Ah! monsieur, you are here! I am delighted to see you. It is a long-deferred pleasure. Really, I scarcely regret what has happened, since it affords me the opportunity to meet you. But, how did you come?"

"By the train."

"But I sent my automobile to meet you at the station."

"An official reception, eh? with music and fireworks! Oh! no, not for me. That is not the way I do business," grumbled the Englishman.

This speech disconcerted Devanne, who replied, with a forced smile:

"Fortunately, the business has been greatly simplified since I wrote to you."

"In what way?"

"The robbery took place last night."

"If you had not announced my intended visit, it is probable the robbery would not have been committed last night."

"When, then?"

"To-morrow, or some other day."

"And in that case?"

"Lupin would have been trapped," said the detective.

"And my furniture?"

"Would not have been carried away."

"Ah! but my goods are here. They were brought back at three o'clock."

"By Lupin."

"By two army-wagons."

Herlock Sholmes put on his cap and adjusted his satchel. Devanne exclaimed, anxiously:

"But, monsieur, what are you going to do?"

"I am going home."

"Why?"

"Your goods have been returned; Arsène Lupin is far away—there is nothing for me to do."

"Yes, there is. I need your assistance. What happened yesterday, may happen again to-morrow, as we do not know how he entered, or how he escaped, or why, a few hours later, he returned the goods."

"Ah! you don't know—"

The idea of a problem to be solved quickened the interest of Herlock Sholmes.

"Very well, let us make a search—at once—and alone, if possible."

Devanne understood, and conducted the Englishman to the salon. In a dry, crisp voice, in sentences that seemed to have been prepared in advance, Holmes asked a number of questions about the events of the preceding evening, and enquired also concerning the guests and the members of the household. Then he examined the two volumes of the "Chronique," compared the plans of the subterranean passage, requested a repetition of the sentences discovered by Father Gélis, and then asked:

"Was yesterday the first time you have spoken hose two sentences to any one?"

"Yes."

"You had never communicated then to Horace Velmont?"

"No."

"Well, order the automobile. I must leave in an hour."

"In an hour?"

"Yes; within that time, Arsène Lupin solved the problem that you placed before him."

"I.... placed before him—"

"Yes, Arsène Lupin or Horace Velmont—same thing."

"I thought so. Ah! the scoundrel!"

"Now, let us see," said Holmes, "last night at ten o'clock, you furnished Lupin with the information that he lacked, and that he had been seeking for many weeks. During the night, he found time to solve the problem, collect his men, and rob the castle. I shall be quite as expeditious."

He walked from end to end of the room, in deep thought, then sat down, crossed his long legs and closed his eyes.

Devanne waited, quite embarrassed. Thought he: "Is the man asleep? Or is he only meditating?" However, he left the room to give some orders, and when he returned he found the detective on his knees scrutinizing the carpet at the foot of the stairs in the gallery.

"What is it?" he enquired.

"Look.... there.... spots from a candle."

"You are right—and quite fresh."

"And you will also find them at the top of the stairs, and around the cabinet that Arsène Lupin broke into, and from which he took the bibelots that he afterward placed in this armchair."

"What do you conclude from that?"

"Nothing. These facts would doubtless explain the cause for the restitution, but that is a side issue that I cannot wait to investigate. The main question is the secret passage. First, tell me, is there a chapel some two or three hundred metres from the castle?"

"Yes, a ruined chapel, containing the tomb of Duke Rollo."

"Tell your chauffer to wait for us near that chapel."

"My chauffer hasn't returned. If he had, they would have informed me. Do you think the secret passage runs to the chapel? What reason have—"

"I would ask you, monsieur," interrupted the detective, "to furnish me with a ladder and a lantern."

"What! do you require a ladder and a lantern?"

"Certainly, or I shouldn't have asked for them."

Devanne, somewhat disconcerted by this crude logic, rang the bell. The two articles were given with the sternness and precision of military commands.

"Place the ladder against the bookcase, to the left of the word Thibermesnil."

Devanne placed the ladder as directed, and the Englishman continued:

"More to the left.... to the right....There!....Now, climb up.... All the letters are in relief, aren't they?"

"Yes."

"First, turn the letter I one way or the other."

"Which one? There are two of them."

"The first one."

Devanne took hold of the letter, and exclaimed:

"Ah! yes, it turns toward the right. Who told you that?"

Herlock Sholmes did not reply to the question, but continued his directions:

"Now, take the letter B. Move it back and forth as you would a bolt."

Devanne did so, and, to his great surprise, it produced a clicking sound.

"Quite right," said Holmes. "Now, we will go to the other end of the word Thibermesnil, try the letter I, and see if it will open like a wicket."

With a certain degree of solemnity, Devanne seized the letter. It opened, but Devanne fell from the ladder, for the entire section of the bookcase, lying between the first and last letters of the words, turned on a picot and disclosed the subterranean passage.

Herlock Sholmes said, coolly:

"You are not hurt?"

"No, no," said Devanne, as he rose to his feet, "not hurt, only bewildered. I can't understand now.... those letters turn.... the secret passage opens...."

"Certainly. Doesn't that agree exactly with the formula given by Sully? Turn one eye on the bee that shakes, the other eye will lead to God."

"But Louis the sixteenth?" asked Devanne.

"Louis the sixteenth was a clever locksmith. I have read a book he wrote about combination locks. It was a good idea on the part of the owner of Thibermesnil to show His Majesty a clever bit of mechanism. As an aid to his memory, the king wrote: 3-4-11, that is to say, the third, fourth and eleventh letters of the word."

"Exactly. I understand that. It explains how Lupin got out of the room, but it does not explain how he entered. And it is certain he came from the outside."

Herlock Sholmes lighted his lantern, and stepped into the passage.

"Look! All the mechanism is exposed here, like the works of a clock, and the reverse side of the letters can be reached. Lupin worked the combination from this side—that is all."

"What proof is there of that?"

"Proof? Why, look at that puddle of oil. Lupin foresaw that the wheels would require oiling."

"Did he know about the other entrance?"

"As well as I know it," said Holmes. "Follow me."

"Into that dark passage?"

"Are you afraid?"

"No, but are you sure you can find the way out?"

"With my eyes closed."

At first, they descended twelve steps, then twelve more, and, farther on, two other flights of twelve steps each. Then they walked through a long passageway, the brick walls of which showed the marks of successive restorations, and, in spots, were dripping with water. The earth, also, was very damp.

"We are passing under the pond," said Devanne, somewhat nervously.

At last, they came to a stairway of twelve steps, followed by three others of twelve steps each, which they mounted with difficulty, and then found themselves in a small cavity cut in the rock. They could go no further.

"The deuce!" muttered Holmes, "nothing but bare walls. This is provoking."

"Let us go back," said Devanne. "I have seen enough to satisfy me."

But the Englishman raised his eye and uttered a sigh of relief. There, he saw the same mechanism and the same word as before. He had merely to work the three letters. He did so, and a block of granite swung out of place. On the other side, this granite block formed the tombstone of Duke Rollo, and the word "Thibermesnil" was engraved on it in relief. Now, they were in the little ruined chapel, and the detective said:

"The other eye leads to God; that means, to the chapel."

"It is marvelous!" exclaimed Devanne, amazed at the clairvoyance and vivacity of the Englishman. "Can it be possible that those few words were sufficient for you?"

"Bah!" declared Holmes, "they weren't even necessary. In the chart in the book of the National Library, the drawing terminates at the left, as you know, in a circle, and at the right, as you do not know, in a cross. Now, that cross must refer to the chapel in which we now stand."

Poor Devanne could not believe his ears. It was all so new, so novel to him. He exclaimed:

"It is incredible, miraculous, and yet of a childish simplicity! How is it that no one has ever solved the mystery?"

"Because no one has ever united the essential elements, that is to say, the two books and the two sentences. No one, but Arsène Lupin and myself."

"But, Father Gélis and I knew all about those things, and, likewise—"

Holmes smiled, and said:

"Monsieur Devanne, everybody cannot solve riddles."

"I have been trying for ten years to accomplish what you did in ten minutes."

"Bah! I am used to it."

They emerged from the chapel, and found an automobile.

"Ah! there's an auto waiting for us."

"Yes, it is mine," said Devanne.

"Yours? You said your chauffeur hadn't returned."

They approached the machine, and Mon. Devanne questioned the chauffer:

"Edouard, who gave you orders to come here?"

"Why, it was Monsieur Velmont."

"Mon. Velmont? Did you meet him?"

"Near the railway station, and he told me to come to the chapel."

"To come to the chapel! What for?"

"To wait for you, monsieur, and your friend."

Devanne and Holmes exchanged looks, and Mon. Devanne said:

"He knew the mystery would be a simple one for you. It is a delicate compliment."

A smile of satisfaction lighted up the detective's serious features for a moment. The compliment pleased him. He shook his head, as he said:

"A clever man! I knew that when I saw him."

"Have you seen him?"

"I met him a short time ago—on my way from the station."

"And you knew it was Horace Velmont—I mean, Arsène Lupin?"

"That is right. I wonder how it came—"

"No, but I supposed it was—from a certain ironical speech he made."

"And you allowed him to escape?"

"Of course I did. And yet I had everything on my side, such as five gendarmes who passed us."

"Sacrableu!" cried Devanne. "You should have taken advantage of the opportunity."

"Really, monsieur," said the Englishman, haughtily, "when I encounter an adversary like Arsène Lupin, I do not take advantage of chance opportunities, I create them."

But time pressed, and since Lupin had been so kind as to send the automobile, they resolved to profit by it. They seated themselves in the comfortable limousine; Edouard took his place at the wheel, and away they went toward the railway station. Suddenly, Devanne's eyes fell upon a small package in one of the pockets of the carriage.

"Ah! what is that? A package! Whose is it? Why, it is for you."

"For me?"

"Yes, it is addressed: Herlock Sholmes, from Arsène Lupin."

The Englishman took the package, opened it, and found that it contained a watch.

"Ah!" he exclaimed, with an angry gesture.

"A watch," said Devanne. "How did it come there?"

The detective did not reply.

"Oh! it is your watch! Arsène Lupin returns your watch! But, in order to return it, he must have taken it. Ah! I see! He took your watch! That is a good one! Herlock Sholmes' watch stolen by Arsène Lupin! Mon Dieu! that is funny! Really.... you must excuse me....I can't help it."

He roared with laughter, unable to control himself. After which, he said, in a tone of earnest conviction:

"A clever man, indeed!"

The Englishman never moved a muscle. On the way to Dieppe, he never spoke a word, but fixed his gaze on the flying landscape. His silence was terrible, unfathomable, more violent than the wildest rage. At the railway station, he spoke calmly, but in a voice that impressed one with the vast energy and will power of that famous man. He said:

"Yes, he is a clever man, but some day I shall have the pleasure of placing on his shoulder the hand I now offer to you, Monsieur Devanne. And I believe that Arsène Lupin and Herlock Sholmes will meet again some day. Yes, the world is too small—we will meet—we must meet—and then—"

THE END

BOOK TWO.
ARSÈNE LUPIN
VERSUS HERLOCK SHOLMES

I. LOTTERY TICKET NO. 514.

On the eighth day of last December, Mon. Gerbois, professor of mathematics at the College of Versailles, while rummaging in an old curiosity-shop, unearthed a small mahogany writing-desk which pleased him very much on account of the multiplicity of its drawers.

"Just the thing for Suzanne's birthday present," thought he. And as he always tried to furnish some simple pleasures for his daughter, consistent with his modest income, he enquired the price, and, after some keen bargaining, purchased it for sixty-five francs. As he was giving his address to the shopkeeper, a young man, dressed with elegance and taste, who had been exploring the stock of antiques, caught sight of the writing-desk, and immediately enquired its price.

"It is sold," replied the shopkeeper.

"Ah! to this gentleman, I presume?"

Monsieur Gerbois bowed, and left the store, quite proud to be the possessor of an article which had attracted the attention of a gentleman of quality. But he had not taken a dozen steps in the street, when he was overtaken by the young man who, hat in hand and in a tone of perfect courtesy, thus addressed him:

"I beg your pardon, monsieur; I am going to ask you a question that you may deem impertinent. It is this: Did you have any special object in view when you bought that writing-desk?"

"No, I came across it by chance and it struck my fancy."

"But you do not care for it particularly?"

"Oh! I shall keep it—that is all."

"Because it is an antique, perhaps?"

"No; because it is convenient," declared Mon. Gerbois.

"In that case, you would consent to exchange it for another desk that would be quite as convenient and in better condition?"

"Oh! this one is in good condition, and I see no object in making an exchange."

"But——"

Mon. Gerbois is a man of irritable disposition and hasty temper. So he replied, testily:

"I beg of you, monsieur, do not insist."

But the young man firmly held his ground.

"I don't know how much you paid for it, monsieur, but I offer you double."

"No."

"Three times the amount."

"Oh! that will do," exclaimed the professor, impatiently; "I don't wish to sell it."

The young man stared at him for a moment in a manner that Mon. Gerbois would not readily forget, then turned and walked rapidly away.

An hour later, the desk was delivered at the professor's house on the Viroflay road. He called his daughter, and said:

"Here is something for you, Suzanne, provided you like it."

Suzanne was a pretty girl, with a gay and affectionate nature. She threw her arms around her father's neck and kissed him rapturously. To her, the desk had all the semblance of a royal gift. That evening, assisted by Hortense, the servant, she placed the desk in her room; then she dusted it, cleaned the drawers and pigeon-holes, and carefully arranged within it her papers, writing material, correspondence, a collection of post-cards, and some souvenirs of her cousin Philippe that she kept in secret.

Next morning, at half past seven, Mon. Gerbois went to the college. At ten o'clock, in pursuance of her usual custom, Suzanne went to meet him, and it was a great pleasure for him to see her slender figure and childish smile waiting for him at the college gate. They returned home together.

"And your writing desk—how is it this morning!"

"Marvellous! Hortense and I have polished the brass mountings until they look like gold."

"So you are pleased with it?"

"Pleased with it! Why, I don't see how I managed to get on without it for such a long time."

As they were walking up the pathway to the house, Mon. Gerbois said:

"Shall we go and take a look at it before breakfast?"

"Oh! yes, that's a splendid idea!"

She ascended the stairs ahead of her father, but, on arriving at the door of her room, she uttered a cry of surprise and dismay.

"What's the matter?" stammered Mon. Gerbois.

"The writing-desk is gone!"

When the police were called in, they were astonished at the admirable simplicity of the means employed by the thief. During Suzanne's absence, the servant had gone to market, and while the house was thus left unguarded, a drayman, wearing a badge—some of the neighbors saw it—stopped his cart in front of the house and rang twice. Not knowing that Hortense was absent, the neighbors were not suspicious; consequently, the man carried on his work in peace and tranquility.

Apart from the desk, not a thing in the house had been disturbed. Even Suzanne's purse, which she had left upon the writing-desk, was found upon an adjacent table with its contents untouched. It was obvious that the thief had come with a set purpose, which rendered the crime even more mysterious; because, why did he assume so great a risk for such a trifling object?

The only clue the professor could furnish was the strange incident of the preceding evening. He declared:

"The young man was greatly provoked at my refusal, and I had an idea that he threatened me as he went away."

But the clue was a vague one. The shopkeeper could not throw any light on the affair. He did not know either of the gentlemen. As to the desk itself, he had purchased it for forty francs at an executor's sale at Chevreuse, and believed he had resold it at its fair value. The police investigation disclosed nothing more.

But Mon. Gerbois entertained the idea that he had suffered an enormous loss. There must have been a fortune concealed in a secret drawer, and that was the reason the young man had resorted to crime.

"My poor father, what would we have done with that fortune?" asked Suzanne.

"My child! with such a fortune, you could make a most advantageous marriage."

Suzanne sighed bitterly. Her aspirations soared no higher than her cousin Philippe, who was indeed a most deplorable object. And life, in the little house at Versailles, was not so happy and contented as of yore.

Two months passed away. Then came a succession of startling events, a strange blending of good luck and dire misfortune!

On the first day of February, at half-past five, Mon. Gerbois entered the house, carrying an evening paper, took a seat, put on his spectacles, and commenced to read. As politics did not interest him, he turned to the inside of the paper. Immediately his attention was attracted by an article entitled:

"Third Drawing of the Press Association Lottery.

"No. 514, series 23, draws a million."

The newspaper slipped from his fingers. The walls swam before his eyes, and his heart ceased to beat. He held No. 514, series 23. He had purchased it from a friend, to oblige him, without any thought of success, and behold, it was the lucky number!

Quickly, he took out his memorandum-book. Yes, he was quite right. The No. 514, series 23, was written there, on the inside of the cover. But the ticket?

He rushed to his desk to find the envelope-box in which he had placed the precious ticket; but the box was not there, and it suddenly occurred to him that it had not been there for several weeks. He heard footsteps on the gravel walk leading from the street.

He called:

"Suzanne! Suzanne!"

She was returning from a walk. She entered hastily. He stammered, in a choking voice:

"Suzanne ... the box ... the box of envelopes?"

"What box?"

"The one I bought at the Louvre ... one Saturday ... it was at the end of that table."

"Don't you remember, father, we put all those things away together."

"When?"

"The evening ... you know ... the same evening...."

"But where?... Tell me, quick!... Where?"

"Where? Why, in the writing-desk."

"In the writing-desk that was stolen?"

"Yes."

"Oh, mon Dieu!... In the stolen desk!"

He uttered the last sentence in a low voice, in a sort of stupor. Then he seized her hand, and in a still lower voice, he said:

"It contained a million, my child."

"Ah! father, why didn't you tell me?" she murmured, naively.

"A million!" he repeated. "It contained the ticket that drew the grand prize in the Press Lottery."

The colossal proportions of the disaster overwhelmed them, and for a long time they maintained a silence that they feared to break. At last, Suzanne said:

"But, father, they will pay you just the same."

"How? On what proof?"

"Must you have proof?"

"Of course."

"And you haven't any?"

"It was in the box."

"In the box that has disappeared."

"Yes; and now the thief will get the money."

"Oh! that would be terrible, father. You must prevent it."

For a moment he was silent; then, in an outburst of energy, he leaped up, stamped on the floor, and exclaimed:

"No, no, he shall not have that million; he shall not have it! Why should he have it? Ah! clever as he is, he can do nothing. If he goes to claim the money, they will arrest him. Ah! now, we will see, my fine fellow!"

"What will you do, father?"

"Defend our just rights, whatever happens! And we will succeed. The million francs belong to me, and I intend to have them."

A few minutes later, he sent this telegram:

"Governor Crédit Foncier

"rue Capucines, Paris.

"Am holder of No. 514, series 23. Oppose by all legal means any other claimant.

"GERBOIS."

Almost at the same moment, the Crédit Foncier received the following telegram:

"No. 514, series 23, is in my possession.

"ARSÈNE LUPIN."

Every time I undertake to relate one of the many extraordinary adventures that mark the life of Arsène Lupin, I experience a feeling of embarrassment, as it seems to me that the most commonplace of those adventures is already well known to my readers. In fact, there is not a movement of our "national thief," as he has been so aptly described, that has not been given the widest publicity, not an exploit that has not been studied in all its phases, not an action that has not been discussed with that particularity usually reserved for the recital of heroic deeds.

For instance, who does not know the strange history of "The Blonde Lady," with those curious episodes which were proclaimed by the newspapers with heavy black headlines, as follows: "Lottery Ticket No. 514!" ... "The Crime on the Avenue Henri-Martin!" ... "The Blue Diamond!" ... The interest created by the intervention of the celebrated English detective, Herlock Sholmes! The excitement aroused by the various vicissitudes which marked the struggle between those famous artists! And what a commotion on the boulevards, the day on which the newsboys announced: "Arrest of Arsène Lupin!"

My excuse for repeating these stories at this time is the fact that I produce the key to the enigma. Those adventures have always been enveloped in a certain degree of obscurity, which I now remove. I reproduce old newspaper articles, I relate old-time interviews, I present ancient letters; but I have arranged and classified all that material and reduced it to the exact truth. My collaborators in this work have been Arsène Lupin himself, and also the ineffable Wilson, the friend and confidant of Herlock Sholmes.

Every one will recall the tremendous burst of laughter which greeted the publication of those two telegrams. The name "Arsène Lupin" was in itself a stimulus to curiosity, a promise of amusement for the gallery. And, in this case, the gallery means the entire world.

An investigation was immediately commenced by the Crédit Foncier, which established these facts: That ticket No. 514, series 23, had been sold by the Versailles branch office of the Lottery to an artillery officer named Bessy, who was afterward killed by a fall from his horse. Some time before his death, he informed some of his comrades that he had transferred his ticket to a friend.

"And I am that friend," affirmed Mon. Gerbois.

"Prove it," replied the governor of the Crédit Foncier.

"Of course I can prove it. Twenty people can tell you that I was an intimate friend of Monsieur Bessy, and that we frequently met at the Café de la Place-d'Armes. It was there, one day, I purchased the ticket from him for twenty francs—simply as an accommodation to him.

"Have you any witnesses to that transaction?"

"No."

"Well, how do you expect to prove it?"

"By a letter he wrote to me."

"What letter?"

"A letter that was pinned to the ticket."

"Produce it."

"It was stolen at the same time as the ticket."

"Well, you must find it."

It was soon learned that Arsène Lupin had the letter. A short paragraph appeared in the *Echo de France*—which has the honor to be his official organ, and of which, it is said, he is one of the principal shareholders—the paragraph announced that Arsène Lupin had placed in the hands of Monsieur Detinan, his advocate and legal adviser, the letter that Monsieur Bessy had written to him—to him personally.

This announcement provoked an outburst of laughter. Arsène Lupin had engaged a lawyer! Arsène Lupin, conforming to the rules and customs of modern society, had appointed a legal representative in the person of a well-known member of the Parisian bar!

Mon. Detinan had never enjoyed the pleasure of meeting Arsène Lupin—a fact he deeply regretted—but he had actually been retained by that mysterious gentleman and felt greatly honored by the choice. He was prepared to defend the interests of his client to the best of his ability. He was pleased, even proud, to exhibit the letter of Mon. Bessy, but, although it proved the transfer of the ticket, it did not mention the name of the purchaser. It was simply addressed to "My Dear Friend."

"My Dear Friend! that is I," added Arsène Lupin, in a note attached to Mon. Bessy's letter. "And the best proof of that fact is that I hold the letter."

The swarm of reporters immediately rushed to see Mon. Gerbois, who could only repeat:

"My Dear Friend! that is I.... Arsène Lupin stole the letter with the lottery ticket."

"Let him prove it!" retorted Lupin to the reporters.

"He must have done it, because he stole the writing-desk!" exclaimed Mon. Gerbois before the same reporters.

"Let him prove it!" replied Lupin.

Such was the entertaining comedy enacted by the two claimants of ticket No. 514; and the calm demeanor of Arsène Lupin contrasted strangely with the nervous perturbation of poor Mon. Gerbois. The newspapers were filled with the lamentations of that unhappy man. He announced his misfortune with pathetic candor.

"Understand, gentlemen, it was Suzanne's dowry that the rascal stole! Personally, I don't care a straw for it,... but for Suzanne! Just think of it, a whole million! Ten times one hundred thousand francs! Ah! I knew very well that the desk contained a treasure!"

It was in vain to tell him that his adversary, when stealing the desk, was unaware that the lottery ticket was in it, and that, in any event, he could not foresee that the ticket would draw the grand prize. He would reply;

"Nonsense! of course, he knew it ... else why would he take the trouble to steal a poor, miserable desk?"

"For some unknown reason; but certainly not for a small scrap of paper which was then worth only twenty francs."

"A million francs! He knew it;... he knows everything! Ah! you do not know him—the scoundrel!... He hasn't robbed you of a million francs!"

The controversy would have lasted for a much longer time, but, on the twelfth day, Mon. Gerbois received from Arsène Lupin a letter, marked "confidential," which read as follows:

"Monsieur, the gallery is being amused at our expense. Do you not think it is time for us to be serious? The situation is this: I possess a ticket to which I have no legal right, and you have the legal right to a ticket you do not possess. Neither of us can do anything. You will not relinquish your rights to me; I will not deliver the ticket to you. Now, what is to be done?

"I see only one way out of the difficulty: Let us divide the spoils. A half-million for you; a half-million for me. Is not that a fair division? In my opinion, it is an equitable solution, and an immediate one. I will give you three days' time to consider the proposition. On Thursday morning I shall expect to read in the personal column of the Echo de France a discreet message addressed to *M. Ars. Lup*, expressing in veiled terms your consent to my offer. By so doing you will recover immediate possession of the ticket; then you can collect the money and send me half a million in a manner that I will describe to you later.

"In case of your refusal, I shall resort to other measures to accomplish the same result. But, apart from the very serious annoyances that such obstinacy on your part will cause you, it will cost you twenty-five thousand francs for supplementary expenses.

"Believe me, monsieur, I remain your devoted servant, ARSÈNE LUPIN."

In a fit of exasperation Mon. Gerbois committed the grave mistake of showing that letter and allowing a copy of it to be taken. His indignation overcame his discretion.

"Nothing! He shall have nothing!" he exclaimed, before a crowd of reporters. "To divide my property with him? Never! Let him tear up the ticket if he wishes!"

"Yet five hundred thousand francs is better than nothing."

"That is not the question. It is a question of my just right, and that right I will establish before the courts."

"What! attack Arsène Lupin? That would be amusing."

"No; but the Crédit Foncier. They must pay me the million francs."

"Without producing the ticket, or, at least, without proving that you bought it?"

"That proof exists, since Arsène Lupin admits that he stole the writing-desk."

"But would the word of Arsène Lupin carry any weight with the court?"

"No matter; I will fight it out."

The gallery shouted with glee; and wagers were freely made upon the result with the odds in favor of Lupin. On the following Thursday the personal column in the *Echo de France* was eagerly perused by the expectant public, but it contained nothing addressed to *M. Ars. Lup*. Mon. Gerbois had not replied to Arsène Lupin's letter. That was the declaration of war.

That evening the newspapers announced the abduction of Mlle. Suzanne Gerbois.

The most entertaining feature in what might be called the Arsène Lupin dramas is the comic attitude displayed by the Parisian police. Arsène Lupin talks, plans, writes, commands, threatens and executes as if the police did not exist. They never figure in his calculations.

And yet the police do their utmost. But what can they do against such a foe—a foe that scorns and ignores them?

Suzanne had left the house at twenty minutes to ten; such was the testimony of the servant. On leaving the college, at five minutes past ten, her father did not find her at the place she was accustomed to wait for him. Consequently, whatever had happened must have occurred during the course of Suzanne's walk from the house to the college. Two neighbors had met her about three hundred yards from the house. A lady had seen, on the avenue, a young girl corresponding to Suzanne's description. No one else had seen her.

Inquiries were made in all directions; the employees of the railways and street-car lines were questioned, but none of them had seen anything of the missing girl. However, at Ville-d'Avray, they found a shopkeeper who had furnished gasoline to an automobile that had come from Paris on the day of the abduction. It was occupied by a blonde woman—extremely blonde, said the witness. An hour later, the automobile again passed through Ville-d'Avray on its way from Versailles to Paris. The shopkeeper declared that the automobile now contained a second woman who was heavily veiled. No doubt, it was Suzanne Gerbois.

The abduction must have taken place in broad daylight, on a frequented street, in the very heart of the town. How? And at what spot? Not a cry was heard; not a suspicious action had been seen. The shopkeeper described the automobile as a royal-blue limousine of twenty-four horse-power made by the firm of Peugeon & Co. Inquiries were then made at the Grand-Garage, managed by Madame Bob-Walthour, who made a specialty of abductions by automobile. It was learned that she had rented a Peugeon limousine on that day to a blonde woman whom she had never seen before nor since.

"Who was the chauffeur?"

"A young man named Ernest, whom I had engaged only the day before. He came well recommended."

"Is he here now?"

"No. He brought back the machine, but I haven't seen him since," said Madame Bob-Walthour.

"Do you know where we can find him?"

"You might see the people who recommended him to me. Here are the names."

Upon inquiry, it was learned that none of these people knew the man called Ernest. The recommendations were forged.

Such was the fate of every clue followed by the police. It ended nowhere. The mystery remained unsolved.

Mon. Gerbois had not the strength or courage to wage such an unequal battle. The disappearance of his daughter crushed him;, he capitulated to the enemy. A short an announcement in the *Echo de France* proclaimed his unconditional surrender.

Two days later, Mon. Gerbois visited the office of the Crédit Foncier and handed lottery ticket number 514, series 23, to the governor, who exclaimed, with surprise:

"Ah! you have it! He has returned it to you!"

"It was mislaid. That was all," replied Mon. Gerbois.

"But you pretended that it had been stolen."

"At first, I thought it had ... but here it is."

"We will require some evidence to establish your right to the ticket."

"Will the letter of the purchaser, Monsieur Bessy, be sufficient!"

"Yes, that will do."

"Here it is," said Mon. Gerbois, producing the letter.

"Very well. Leave these papers with us. The rules of the lottery allow us fifteen days' time to investigate your claim. I will let you know when to call for your money. I presume you desire, as much as I do, that this affair should be closed without further publicity."

"Quite so."

Mon. Gerbois and the governor henceforth maintained a discreet silence. But the secret was revealed in some way, for it was soon commonly known that Arsène Lupin had returned the lottery ticket to Mon. Gerbois. The public received the news with astonishment and admiration. Certainly, he was a bold gamester who thus threw upon the table a trump card of such importance as the precious ticket. But, it was true, he still retained a trump card of equal importance. However, if the young girl should escape? If the hostage held by Arsène Lupin should be rescued?

The police thought they had discovered the weak spot of the enemy, and now redoubled their efforts. Arsène Lupin disarmed by his own act, crushed by the wheels of his own machination, deprived of every sou of the coveted million ... public interest now centered in the camp of his adversary.

But it was necessary to find Suzanne. And they did not find her, nor did she escape. Consequently, it must be admitted, Arsène Lupin had won the first hand. But the game was not yet decided. The most difficult point remained. Mlle. Gerbois is in his possession, and he will hold her until he receives five hundred thousand francs. But how and where will such an exchange be made? For that purpose, a meeting must be arranged, and then what will prevent Mon. Gerbois from warning the police and, in that way, effecting the rescue of his daughter and, at the same time, keeping his money? The professor was interviewed, but he was extremely reticent. His answer was:

"I have nothing to say."

"And Mlle. Gerbois?"

"The search is being continued."

"But Arsène Lupin has written to you?"

"No."

"Do you swear to that?"

"No."

"Then it is true. What are his instructions?"

"I have nothing to say."

Then the interviewers attacked Mon. Detinan, and found him equally discreet.

"Monsieur Lupin is my client, and I cannot discuss his affairs," he replied, with an affected air of gravity.

These mysteries served to irritate the gallery. Obviously, some secret negotiations were in progress. Arsène Lupin had arranged and tightened the meshes of his net, while the police maintained a close watch, day and night, over Mon. Gerbois. And the three and only possible dénouements—the arrest, the triumph, or the ridiculous and pitiful abortion—were freely discussed; but the curiosity of the public was only partially satisfied, and it was reserved for these pages to reveal the exact truth of the affair.

On Monday, March 12th, Mon. Gerbois received a notice from the Crédit Foncier. On Wednesday, he took the one o'clock train for Paris. At two o'clock, a thousand bank-notes of one thousand francs each were delivered to him. Whilst he was counting them, one by one, in a state of nervous agitation—that money, which represented Suzanne's ransom—a carriage containing two men stopped at the curb a short distance from the bank. One of the men had grey hair and an unusually shrewd expression which formed a striking contrast to his shabby make-up. It was Detective Ganimard, the relentless enemy of Arsène Lupin. Ganimard said to his companion, Folenfant:

"In five minutes, we will see our clever friend Lupin. Is everything ready?"

"Yes."

"How many men have we?"

"Eight—two of them on bicycles."

"Enough, but not too many. On no account, must Gerbois escape us; if he does, it is all up. He will meet Lupin at the appointed place, give half a million in exchange for the girl, and the game will be over."

"But why doesn't Gerbois work with us? That would be the better way, and he could keep all the money himself."

"Yes, but he is afraid that if he deceives the other, he will not get his daughter."

"What other?"

"Lupin."

Ganimard pronounced the word in a solemn tone, somewhat timidly, as if he were speaking of some supernatural creature whose claws he already felt.

"It is very strange," remarked Folenfant, judiciously, "that we are obliged to protect this gentleman contrary to his own wishes."

"Yes, but Lupin always turns the world upside down," said Ganimard, mournfully.

A moment later, Mon. Gerbois appeared, and started up the street. At the end of the rue des Capucines, he turned into the boulevards, walking slowly, and stopping frequently to gaze at the shop-windows.

"Much too calm, too self-possessed," said Ganimard. "A man with a million in his pocket would not have that air of tranquillity."

"What is he doing?"

"Oh! nothing, evidently.... But I have a suspicion that it is Lupin—yes, Lupin!"

At that moment, Mon. Gerbois stopped at a news-stand, purchased a paper, unfolded it and commenced to read it as he walked slowly away. A moment later, he gave a sudden bound into an automobile that was standing at the curb. Apparently, the machine had been waiting for him, as it started away rapidly, turned at the Madeleine and disappeared.

"Nom de nom!" cried Ganimard, "that's one of his old tricks!"

Ganimard hastened after the automobile around the Madeleine. Then, he burst into laughter. At the entrance to the Boulevard Malesherbes, the automobile had stopped and Mon. Gerbois had alighted.

"Quick, Folenfant, the chauffeur! It may be the man Ernest."

Folenfant interviewed the chauffeur. His name was Gaston; he was an employee of the automobile cab company; ten minutes ago, a gentleman had engaged him and told him to wait near the news-stand for another gentleman.

"And the second man—what address did he give?" asked Folenfant.

"No address. 'Boulevard Malesherbes ... avenue de Messine ... double pourboire.' That is all."

But, during this time, Mon. Gerbois had leaped into the first passing carriage.

"To the Concorde station, Metropolitan," he said to the driver.

He left the underground at the Place du Palais-Royal, ran to another carriage and ordered it to go to the Place de la Bourse. Then a second journey by the underground to the Avenue de Villiers, followed by a third carriage drive to number 25 rue Clapeyron.

Number 25 rue Clapeyron is separated from the Boulevard des Batignolles by the house which occupies the angle formed by the two streets. He ascended to the first floor and rang. A gentleman opened the door.

"Does Monsieur Detinan live here?"

"Yes, that is my name. Are you Monsieur Gerbois?"

"Yes."

"I was expecting you. Step in."

As Mon. Gerbois entered the lawyer's office, the clock struck three. He said:

"I am prompt to the minute. Is he here?"

"Not yet."

Mon. Gerbois took a seat, wiped his forehead, looked at his watch as if he did not know the time, and inquired, anxiously:

"Will he come?"

"Well, monsieur," replied the lawyer, "that I do not know, but I am quite as anxious and impatient as you are to find out. If he comes, he will run a great risk, as this house has been closely watched for the last two weeks. They distrust me."

"They suspect me, too. I am not sure whether the detectives lost sight of me or not on my way here."

"But you were—"

"It wouldn't be my fault," cried the professor, quickly. "You cannot reproach me. I promised to obey his orders, and I followed them to the very letter. I drew the money at the time fixed by him, and I came here in the manner directed by him. I have faithfully performed my part of the agreement—let him do his!"

After a short silence, he asked, anxiously:

"He will bring my daughter, won't he?"

"I expect so."

"But ... you have seen him?"

"I? No, not yet. He made the appointment by letter, saying both of you would be here, and asking me to dismiss my servants before three o'clock and admit no one while you were here. If I would not consent to that arrangement, I was to notify him by a few words in *the Echo de France*. But I am only too happy to oblige Mon. Lupin, and so I consented."

"Ah! how will this end?" moaned Mon. Gerbois.

He took the bank-notes from his pocket, placed them on the table and divided them into two equal parts. Then the two men sat there in silence. From time to time, Mon. Gerbois would listen. Did someone ring?... His nervousness increased every minute, and Monsieur Detinan also displayed considerable anxiety. At last, the lawyer lost his patience. He rose abruptly, and said:

"He will not come.... We shouldn't expect it. It would be folly on his part. He would run too great a risk."

And Mon. Gerbois, despondent, his hands resting on the bank-notes, stammered:

"Oh! Mon Dieu! I hope he will come. I would give the whole of that money to see my daughter again."

The door opened.

"Half of it will be sufficient, Monsieur Gerbois."

These words were spoken by a well-dressed young man who now entered the room and was immediately recognized by Mon. Gerbois as the person who had wished to buy the desk from him at Versailles. He rushed toward him.

"Where is my daughter—my Suzanne?"

Arsène Lupin carefully closed the door, and, while slowly removing his gloves, said to the lawyer:

"My dear maître, I am indebted to you very much for your kindness in consenting to defend my interests. I shall not forget it."

Mon. Detinan murmured:

"But you did not ring. I did not hear the door—"

"Doors and bells are things that should work without being heard. I am here, and that is the important point."

"My daughter! Suzanne! Where is she!" repeated the professor.

"Mon Dieu, monsieur," said Lupin, "what's your hurry? Your daughter will be here in a moment."

Lupin walked to and fro for a minute, then, with the pompous air of an orator, he said:

"Monsieur Gerbois, I congratulate you on the clever way in which you made the journey to this place."

Then, perceiving the two piles of bank-notes, he exclaimed:

"Ah! I see! the million is here. We will not lose any time. Permit me."

"One moment," said the lawyer, placing himself before the table. "Mlle. Gerbois has not yet arrived."

"Well?"

"Is not her presence indispensable?"

"I understand! I understand! Arsène Lupin inspires only a limited confidence. He might pocket the half-million and not restore the hostage. Ah! monsieur, people do not understand me. Because I have been obliged, by force of circumstances, to commit certain actions a little ... out of the ordinary, my good faith is impugned ... I, who have always observed the utmost scrupulosity and delicacy in business affairs. Besides, my dear monsieur if you have any fear, open the window and call. There are at least a dozen detectives in the street."

"Do you think so?"

Arsène Lupin raised the curtain.

"I think that Monsieur Gerbois could not throw Ganimard off the scent.... What did I tell you? There he is now."

"Is it possible!" exclaimed the professor. "But I swear to you—"

"That you have not betrayed me?... I do not doubt you, but those fellows are clever—sometimes. Ah! I can see Folenfant, and Greaume, and Dieuzy—all good friends of mine!"

Mon. Detinan looked at Lupin in amazement. What assurance! He laughed as merrily as if engaged in some childish sport, as if no danger threatened him. This unconcern reassured the lawyer more than the presence of the detectives. He left the table on which the bank-notes were lying. Arsène Lupin picked up one pile of bills after the other, took from each of them twenty-five bank-notes which he offered to Mon. Detinan, saying:

"The reward of your services to Monsieur Gerbois and Arsène Lupin. You well deserve it."

"You owe me nothing," replied the lawyer.

"What! After all the trouble we have caused you!"

"And all the pleasure you have given me!"

"That means, my dear monsieur, that you do not wish to accept anything from Arsène Lupin. See what it is to have a bad reputation."

He then offered the fifty thousand francs to Mon. Gerbois, saying:

"Monsieur, in memory of our pleasant interview, permit me to return you this as a wedding-gift to Mlle. Gerbois."

Mon. Gerbois took the money, but said:

"My daughter will not marry."

"She will not marry if you refuse your consent; but she wishes to marry."

"What do you know about it!"

"I know that young girls often dream of such things unknown to their parents. Fortunately, there are sometimes good genii like Arsène Lupin who discover their little secrets in the drawers of their writing desks."

"Did you find anything else?" asked the lawyer. "I confess I am curious to know why you took so much trouble to get possession of that desk."

"On account of its historic interest, my friend. Although despite the opinion of Monsieur Gerbois, the desk contained no treasure except the lottery ticket—and that was unknown to me—I had been seeking it for a long time. That writing-desk of yew and mahogany was discovered in the little house in which Marie Walêwska once lived in Boulogne, and, on one of the drawers there is this inscription: '*Dedicated to Napoleon I, Emperor of the French, by his very faithful servant, Mancion.*' And above it, these words, engraved with the point of a knife: 'To you, Marie.' Afterwards, Napoleon had a similar desk made for the Empress Josephine; so that the secretary that was so much admired at the Malmaison was only an imperfect copy of the one that will henceforth form part of my collection."

"Ah! if I had known, when in the shop, I would gladly have given it up to you," said the professor.

Arsène Lupin smiled, as he replied:

"And you would have had the advantage of keeping for your own use lottery ticket number 514."

"And you would not have found it necessary to abduct my daughter."

"Abduct your daughter?"

"Yes."

"My dear monsieur, you are mistaken. Mlle. Gerbois was not abducted."

"No?"

"Certainly not. Abduction means force or violence. And I assure you that she served as hostage of her own free will."

"Of her own free will!" repeated Mon. Gerbois, in amazement.

"In fact, she almost asked to be taken. Why, do you suppose that an intelligent young girl like Mlle. Gerbois, and who, moreover, nourishes an unacknowledged passion, would hesitate to do what was necessary to secure her dowry. Ah! I swear to you it was not difficult to make her understand that it was the only way to overcome your obstinacy."

Mon. Detinan was greatly amused. He replied to Lupin:

"But I should think it was more difficult to get her to listen to you. How did you approach her?"

"Oh! I didn't approach her myself. I have not the honor of her acquaintance. A friend of mine, a lady, carried on the negotiations."

"The blonde woman in the automobile, no doubt."

"Precisely. All arrangements were made at the first interview near the college. Since then, Mlle. Gerbois and her new friend have been travelling in Belgium and Holland in a manner that should prove most pleasing and instructive to a young girl. She will tell you all about it herself—"

The bell of the vestibule door rang, three rings in quick succession, followed by two isolated rings.

"It is she," said Lupin. "Monsieur Detinan, if you will be so kind—"

The lawyer hastened to the door.

Two young women entered. One of them threw herself into the arms of Mon. Gerbois. The other approached Lupin. The latter was a tall woman of a good figure, very pale complexion, and with blond hair, parted over her forehead in undulating waves, that glistened and shone like the setting sun. She was dressed in black, with no display of jewelled ornaments; but, on the contrary, her appearance indicated good taste and refined elegance. Arsène Lupin spoke a few words to her; then, bowing to Mlle. Gerbois, he said:

"I owe you an apology, mademoiselle, for all your troubles, but I hope you have not been too unhappy—"

"Unhappy! Why, I should have been very happy, indeed, if it hadn't been for leaving my poor father."

"Then all is for the best. Kiss him again, and take advantage of the opportunity—it is an excellent one—to speak to him about your cousin."

"My cousin! What do you mean? I don't understand."

"Of course, you understand. Your cousin Philippe. The young man whose letters you kept so carefully."

Suzanne blushed; but, following Lupin's advice, she again threw herself into her father's arms. Lupin gazed upon them with a tender look.

"Ah! Such is my reward for a virtuous act! What a touching picture! A happy father and a happy daughter! And to know that their joy is your work, Lupin! Hereafter these people will bless you, and reverently transmit your name unto their descendants, even unto the fourth generation. What a glorious reward, Lupin, for one act of kindness!"

He walked to the window.

"Is dear old Ganimard still waiting?... He would like very much to be present at this charming domestic scene!... Ah! he is not there.... Nor any of the others.... I don't see anyone. The deuce! The situation is becoming serious. I dare say they are already under the porte-cochère ... talking to the concierge, perhaps ... or, even, ascending the stairs!"

Mon. Gerbois made a sudden movement. Now, that his daughter had been restored to him, he saw the situation in a different light. To him, the arrest of his adversary meant half-a-million francs. Instinctively, he made a step forward. As if by chance, Lupin stood in his way.

"Where are you going, Monsieur Gerbois! To defend me against them! That is very kind of you, but I assure you it is not necessary. They are more worried than I."

Then he continued to speak, with calm deliberation:

"But, really, what do they know! That you are here, and, perhaps, that Mlle. Gerbois is here, for they may have seen her arrive with an unknown lady. But they do not imagine that I am here. How is it possible that I could be in a house that they ran-sacked from cellar to garret this morning! They suppose that the unknown lady was sent by me to make the exchange, and they will be ready to arrest her when she goes out—"

At that moment, the bell rang. With a brusque movement, Lupin seized Mon. Gerbois, and said to him, in an imperious tone:

"Do not move! Remember your daughter, and be prudent—otherwise—As to you, Monsieur Detinan, I have your promise."

Mon. Gerbois was rooted to the spot. The lawyer did not stir. Without the least sign of haste, Lupin picked up his hat and brushed the dust from off it with his sleeve.

"My dear Monsieur Detinan, if I can ever be of service to you.... My best wishes, Mademoiselle Suzanne, and my kind regards to Monsieur Philippe."

He drew a heavy gold watch from his pocket.

"Monsieur Gerbois, it is now forty-two minutes past three. At forty-six minutes past three, I give you permission to leave this room. Not one minute sooner than forty-six minutes past three."

"But they will force an entrance," suggested Mon. Detinan.

"You forget the law, my dear monsieur! Ganimard would never venture to violate the privacy of a French citizen. But, pardon me, time flies, and you are all slightly nervous."

He placed his watch on the table, opened the door of the room and addressing the blonde lady he said:

"Are you ready my dear?"

He drew back to let her pass, bowed respectfully to Mlle. Gerbois, and went out, closing the door behind him. Then they heard him in the vestibule, speaking, in a loud voice: "Good-day, Ganimard, how goes it? Remember me to Madame Ganimard. One of these days, I shall invite her to breakfast. Au revoir, Ganimard."

The bell rang violently, followed by repeated rings, and voices on the landing.

"Forty-five minutes," muttered Mon. Gerbois.

After a few seconds, he left the room and stepped into the vestibule. Arsène Lupin and the blonde lady had gone.

"Papa!... you mustn't! Wait!" cried Suzanne.

"Wait! you are foolish!... No quarter for that rascal!... And the half-million?"

He opened the outer door. Ganimard rushed in.

"That woman—where is she? And Lupin?"

"He was here ... he is here."

Ganimard uttered a cry of triumph.

"We have him. The house is surrounded."

"But the servant's stairway?" suggested Mon. Detinan.

"It leads to the court," said Ganimard. "There is only one exit—the street-door. Ten men are guarding it."

"But he didn't come in by the street-door, and he will not go out that way."

"What way, then?" asked Ganimard. "Through the air?"

He drew aside a curtain and exposed a long corridor leading to the kitchen. Ganimard ran along it and tried the door of the servants' stairway. It was locked. From the window he called to one of his assistants:

"Seen anyone?"

"No."

"Then they are still in the house!" he exclaimed. "They are hiding in one of the rooms! They cannot have escaped. Ah! Lupin, you fooled me before, but, this time, I get my revenge."

At seven o'clock in the evening, Mon. Dudonis, chief of the detective service, astonished at not receiving any news, visited the rue Clapeyron. He questioned the detectives who were guarding the house, then ascended to Mon. Detinan's apartment. The lawyer led him into his room. There, Mon. Dudonis beheld a man, or rather two legs kicking in the air, while the body to which they belonged was hidden in the depths of the chimney.

"Ohé!... Ohé!" gasped a stifled voice. And a more distant voice, from on high, replied:

"Ohé!... Ohé!"

Mon. Dudonis laughed, and exclaimed:

"Here! Ganimard, have you turned chimney-sweep?"

The detective crawled out of the chimney. With his blackened face, his sooty clothes, and his feverish eyes, he was quite unrecognizable.

"I am looking for *him*," he growled.

"Who?"

"Arsène Lupin ... and his friend."

"Well, do you suppose they are hiding in the chimney?"

Ganimard arose, laid his sooty hand on the sleeve of his superior officer's coat, and exclaimed, angrily:

"Where do you think they are, chief? They must be somewhere! They are flesh and blood like you and me, and can't fade away like smoke."

"No, but they have faded away just the same."

"But how? How? The house is surrounded by our men—even on the roof."

"What about the adjoining house?"

"There's no communication with it."

"And the apartments on the other floors?"

"I know all the tenants. They have not seen anyone."

"Are you sure you know all of them?"

"Yes. The concierge answers for them. Besides, as an extra precaution, I have placed a man in each apartment. They can't escape. If I don't get them to-night, I will get them to-morrow. I shall sleep here."

He slept there that night and the two following nights. Three days and nights passed away without the discovery of the irrepressible Lupin or his female companion; more than that, Ganimard did not unearth the slightest clue on which to base a theory to explain their escape. For that reason, he adhered to his first opinion.

"There is no trace of their escape; therefore, they are here."

It may be that, at the bottom of his heart, his conviction was less firmly established, but he would not confess it. No, a thousand times, no! A man and a woman could not vanish like the evil spirits in a fairy tale. And, without losing his courage, he continued his searches, as if he expected to find the fugitives concealed in some impenetrable retreat, or embodied in the stone walls of the house.

II. THE BLUE DIAMOND.

On the evening of March 27, at number 134 avenue Henri-Martin, in the house that he had inherited from his brother six months before, the old general Baron d'Hautrec, ambassador at Berlin under the second Empire, was asleep in a comfortable armchair, while his secretary was reading to him, and the Sister Auguste was warming his bed and preparing the night-lamp. At eleven o'clock, the Sister, who was obliged to return to the convent of her order at that hour, said to the secretary:

"Mademoiselle Antoinette, my work is finished; I am going."

"Very well, Sister."

"Do not forget that the cook is away, and that you are alone in the house with the servant."

"Have no fear for the Baron. I sleep in the adjoining room and always leave the door open."

The Sister left the house. A few moments later, Charles, the servant, came to receive his orders. The Baron was now awake, and spoke for himself.

"The usual orders, Charles: see that the electric bell rings in your room, and, at the first alarm, run for the doctor. Now, Mademoiselle Antoinette, how far did we get in our reading?"

"Is Monsieur not going to bed now?"

"No, no, I will go later. Besides, I don't need anyone."

Twenty minutes later, he was sleeping again, and Antoinette crept away on tiptoe. At that moment, Charles was closing the shutters on the lower floor. In the kitchen, he bolted the door leading to the garden, and, in the vestibule, he not only locked the door but hooked the chain as well. Then he ascended to his room on the third floor, went to bed, and was soon asleep.

Probably an hour had passed, when he leaped from his bed in alarm. The bell was ringing. It rang for some time, seven or eight seconds perhaps, without intermission.

"Well!" muttered Charles, recovering his wits, "another of the Baron's whims."

He dressed himself quickly, descended the stairs, stopped in front of the door, and rapped, according to his custom. He received no reply. He opened the door and entered.

"Ah! no light," he murmured. "What is that for?"

Then, in a low voice, he called:

"Mademoiselle?"

No reply.

"Are you there, mademoiselle? What's the matter? Is Monsieur le Baron ill?"

No reply. Nothing but a profound silence that soon became depressing. He took two steps forward; his foot struck a chair, and, having touched it, he noticed that it was overturned. Then, with his hand, he discovered other objects on the floor—a small table and a screen. Anxiously, he approached the wall, felt for the electric button, and turned on the light.

In the centre of the room, between the table and dressing-case, lay the body of his master, the Baron d'Hautrec.

"What!... It can't be possible!" he stammered.

He could not move. He stood there, with bulging eyes, gazing stupidly at the terrible disorder, the overturned chairs, a large crystal candelabra shattered in a thousand pieces, the clock lying on the marble hearthstone, all evidence of a fearful and desperate struggle. The handle of a stiletto glittered, not far from the corpse; the blade was stained with blood. A handkerchief, marked with red spots, was lying on the edge of the bed.

Charles recoiled with horror: the body lying at his feet extended itself for a moment, then shrunk up again; two or three tremors, and that was the end.

He stooped over the body. There was a clean-cut wound on the neck from which the blood was flowing and then congealing in a black pool on the carpet. The face retained an expression of extreme terror.

"Some one has killed him!" he muttered, "some one has killed him!"

Then he shuddered at the thought that there might be another dreadful crime. Did not the baron's secretary sleep in the adjoining room! Had not the assassin killed her also! He opened the door; the room was empty. He concluded that Antoinette had been abducted, or else she had gone away before the crime. He returned to the baron's chamber, his glance falling on the secretary, he noticed that that article of furniture remained intact. Then, he saw upon a table, beside a bunch of keys and a pocketbook that the baron placed there every night, a handful of golden louis. Charles seized the pocketbook, opened it, and found some bank-notes. He counted them; there were thirteen notes of one hundred francs each.

Instinctively, mechanically, he put the bank-notes in his pocket, rushed down the stairs, drew the bolt, unhooked the chain, closed the door behind him, and fled to the street.

Charles was an honest man. He had scarcely left the gate, when, cooled by the night air and the rain, he came to a sudden halt. Now, he saw his action in its true light, and it filled him with horror. He hailed a passing cab, and said to the driver:

"Go to the police-office, and bring the commissary. Hurry! There has been a murder in that house."

The cab-driver whipped his horse. Charles wished to return to the house, but found the gate locked. He had closed it himself when he came out, and it could not be opened from the outside. On the other hand, it was useless to ring, as there was no one in the house.

It was almost an hour before the arrival of the police. When they came, Charles told his story and handed the bank-notes to the commissary. A locksmith was summoned, and, after considerable difficulty, he succeeded in forcing open the garden gate and the vestibule door. The commissary of police entered the room first, but, immediately, turned to Charles and said:

"You told me that the room was in the greatest disorder."

Charles stood at the door, amazed, bewildered; all the furniture had been restored to its accustomed place. The small table was standing between the two windows, the chairs were upright, and the clock was on the centre of the mantel. The debris of the candelabra had been removed.

"Where is.... Monsieur le Baron?" stammered Charles.

"That's so!" exclaimed the officer, "where is the victim?"

He approached the bed, and drew aside a large sheet, under which reposed the Baron d'Hautrec, formerly French Ambassador at Berlin. Over him, lay his military coat, adorned with the Cross of Honor. His features were calm. His eyes were closed.

"Some one has been here," said Charles.

"How did they get in?"

"I don't know, but some one has been here during my absence. There was a stiletto on the floor—there! And a handkerchief, stained with blood, on the bed. They are not here now. They have been carried away. And some one has put the room in order."

"Who would do that?"

"The assassin."

"But we found all the doors locked."

"He must have remained in the house."

"Then he must be here yet, as you were in front of the house all the time."

Charles reflected a moment, then said, slowly:

"Yes ... of course.... I didn't go away from the gate."

"Who was the last person you saw with the baron?"

"Mademoiselle Antoinette, his secretary."

"What has become of her?"

"I don't know. Her bed wasn't occupied, so she must have gone out. I am not surprised at that, as she is young and pretty."

"But how could she leave the house?"

"By the door," said Charles.

"But you had bolted and chained it."

"Yes, but she must have left before that."

"And the crime was committed after her departure?"

"Of course," said the servant.

The house was searched from cellar to garret, but the assassin had fled. How? And when? Was it he or an accomplice who had returned to the scene of the crime and removed everything that might furnish a clue to his identity? Such were the questions the police were called upon to solve.

The coroner came at seven o'clock; and, at eight o'clock, Mon. Dudouis, the head of the detective service, arrived on the scene. They were followed by the Procureur of the Republic and the investigating magistrate. In addition to these officials, the house was overrun with policemen, detectives, newspaper reporters, photographers, and relatives and acquaintances of the murdered man.

A thorough search was made; they studied out the position of the corpse according to the information furnished by Charles; they questioned Sister Auguste when she arrived; but they discovered nothing new. Sister Auguste was astonished to learn of the disappearance of Antoinette Bréhat. She had engaged the young girl twelve days before, on excellent recommendations, and refused to believe that she would neglect her duty by leaving the house during the night.

"But, you see, she hasn't returned yet," said the magistrate, "and we are still confronted with the question: What has become of her?"

"I think she was abducted by the assassin," said Charles.

The theory was plausible, and was borne out by certain facts. Mon. Dudouis agreed with it. He said:

"Abducted? ma foi! that is not improbable."

"Not only improbable," said a voice, "but absolutely opposed to the facts. There is not a particle of evidence to support such a theory."

The voice was harsh, the accent sharp, and no one was surprised to learn that the speaker was Ganimard. In no one else, would they tolerate such a domineering tone.

"Ah! it is you, Ganimard!" exclaimed Mon. Dudouis. "I had not seen you before."

"I have been here since two o'clock."

"So you are interested in some things outside of lottery ticket number 514, the affair of the rue Clapeyron, the blonde lady and Arsène Lupin?"

"Ha-ha!" laughed the veteran detective. "I would not say that Lupin is a stranger to the present case. But let us forget the affair of the lottery ticket for a few moments, and try to unravel this new mystery."

Ganimard is not one of those celebrated detectives whose methods will create a school, or whose name will be immortalized in the criminal annals of his country. He is devoid of those flashes of genius which characterize the work of Dupin, Lecoq and Sherlock Holmes. Yet, it must be admitted, he possesses superior qualities of observation, sagacity, perseverance and even intuition. His merit lies in his absolute independence. Nothing troubles or influences him, except, perhaps, a sort of fascination that Arsène Lupin holds over him. However that may be, there is no doubt that his position on that morning, in the house of the late Baron d'Hautrec, was one of undoubted superiority, and his collaboration in the case was appreciated and desired by the investigating magistrate.

"In the first place," said Ganimard, "I will ask Monsieur Charles to be very particular on one point: He says that, on the occasion of his first visit to the room, various articles of furniture were overturned and strewn about the place; now, I ask him whether, on his second visit to the room, he found all those articles restored to their accustomed places—I mean, of course, correctly placed."

"Yes, all in their proper places," replied Charles.

"It is obvious, then, that the person who replaced them must have been familiar with the location of those articles."

The logic of this remark was apparent to his hearers. Ganimard continued:

"One more question, Monsieur Charles. You were awakened by the ringing of your bell. Now, who, do you think, rang it?"

"Monsieur le baron, of course."

"When could he ring it!"

"After the struggle ... when he was dying."

"Impossible; because you found him lying, unconscious, at a point more than four metres from the bell-button."

"Then he must have rung during the struggle."

"Impossible," declared Ganimard, "since the ringing, as you have said, was continuous and uninterrupted, and lasted seven or eight seconds. Do you think his antagonist would have permitted him to ring the bell in that leisurely manner?"

"Well, then, it was before the attack."

"Also, quite impossible, since you have told us that the lapse of time between the ringing of the bell and your entrance to the room was not more than three minutes. Therefore, if the baron rang before the attack, we are forced to the conclusion that the struggle, the murder and the flight of the assassin, all occurred within the short space of three minutes. I repeat: that is impossible."

"And yet," said the magistrate, "some one rang. If it were not the baron, who was it?"

"The murderer."

"For what purpose?"

"I do not know. But the fact that he did ring proves that he knew that the bell communicated with the servant's room. Now, who would know that, except an inmate of the house?"

Ganimard was drawing the meshes of his net closer and tighter. In a few clear and logical sentences, he had unfolded and defined his theory of the crime, so that it seemed quite natural when the magistrate said:

"As I understand it, Ganimard, you suspect the girl Antoinette Bréhat?"

"I do not suspect her; I accuse her."

"You accuse her of being an accomplice?"

"I accuse her of having killed Baron d'Hautrec."

"Nonsense! What proof have you?"

"The handful of hair I found in the right hand of the victim."

He produced the hair; it was of a beautiful blond color, and glittered like threads of gold. Charles looked at it, and said:

"That is Mademoiselle Antoinette's hair. There can be no doubt of it. And, then, there is another thing. I believe that the knife, which I saw on my first visit to the room, belonged to her. She used it to cut the leaves of books."

A long, dreadful silence followed, as if the crime had acquired an additional horror by reason of having been committed by a woman. At last, the magistrate said:

"Let us assume, until we are better informed, that the baron was killed by Antoinette Bréhat. We have yet to learn where she concealed herself after the crime, how she managed to return after Charles left the house, and how she made her escape after the arrival of the police. Have you formed any opinion on those points Ganimard?"

"None."

"Well, then, where do we stand?"

Ganimard was embarrassed. Finally, with a visible effort, he said:

"All I can say is that I find in this case the same method of procedure as we found in the affair of the lottery ticket number 514; the same phenomena, which might be termed the faculty of disappearing. Antoinette Bréhat has appeared and disappeared in this house as mysteriously as Arsène Lupin entered the house of Monsieur Detinan and escaped therefrom in the company of the blonde lady.

"Does that signify anything?"

"It does to me. I can see a probable connection between those two strange incidents. Antoinette Bréhat was hired by Sister Auguste twelve days ago, that is to say, on the day after the blonde Lady so cleverly slipped through my fingers. In the second place, the hair of the blonde Lady was exactly of the same brilliant golden hue as the hair found in this case."

"So that, in your opinion, Antoinette Bréhat—"

"Is the blonde Lady—precisely."

"And that Lupin had a hand in both cases!"

"Yes, that is my opinion."

This statement was greeted with an outburst of laughter. It came from Mon. Dudouis.

"Lupin! always Lupin! Lupin is into everything; Lupin is everywhere!"

"Yes, Lupin is into everything of any consequence," replied Ganimard, vexed at the ridicule of his superior.

"Well, so far as I see," observed Mon. Dudouis, "you have not discovered any motive for this crime. The secretary was not broken into, nor the pocketbook carried away. Even, a pile of gold was left upon the table."

"Yes, that is so," exclaimed Ganimard, "but the famous diamond?"

"What diamond?"

"The blue diamond! The celebrated diamond which formed part of the royal crown of France, and which was given by the Duke d'Aumale to Leonide Lebrun, and, at the death of Leonide Lebrun, was purchased by the Baron d'Hautrec as a souvenir of the charming comedienne that he had loved so well. That is one of those things that an old Parisian, like I, does not forget."

"It is obvious that if the blue diamond is not found, the motive for the crime is disclosed," said the magistrate. "But where should we search for it?"

"On the baron's finger," replied Charles. "He always wore the blue diamond on his left hand."

"I saw that hand, and there was only a plain gold ring on it," said Ganimard, as he approached the corpse.

"Look in the palm of the hand," replied the servant.

Ganimard opened the stiffened hand. The bezel was turned inward, and, in the centre of that bezel, the blue diamond shone with all its glorious splendor.

"The deuce!" muttered Ganimard, absolutely amazed, "I don't understand it."

"You will now apologize to Lupin for having suspected him, eh?" said Mon. Dudouis, laughing.

Ganimard paused for a moment's reflection, and then replied, sententiously:

"It is only when I do not understand things that I suspect Arsène Lupin."

Such were the facts established by the police on the day after the commission of that mysterious crime. Facts that were vague and incoherent in themselves, and which were not explained by any subsequent discoveries. The movements of Antoinette Bréhat remained as inexplicable as those of the blonde Lady, and the police discovered no trace of that mysterious creature with the golden hair who had killed Baron d'Hautrec and had failed to take from his finger the famous diamond that had once shone in the royal crown of France.

The heirs of the Baron d'Hautrec could not fail to benefit by such notoriety. They established in the house an exhibition of the furniture and other objects which were to be sold at the auction rooms of Drouot & Co. Modern furniture of indifferent taste, various objects of no artistic value ... but, in the centre of the room, in a case of purple velvet, protected by a glass globe, and guarded by two officers, was the famous blue diamond ring.

A large magnificent diamond of incomparable purity, and of that indefinite blue which the clear water receives from an unclouded sky, of that blue which can be detected in the whiteness of linen. Some admired, some enthused ... and some looked with horror on the chamber of the victim, on the spot where the corpse had lain, on the floor divested of its blood-stained carpet, and especially the walls, the unsurmountable walls over which the criminal must have passed. Some assured themselves that the marble mantel did not move, others imagined gaping holes, mouths of tunnels, secret connections with the sewers, and the catacombs—

The sale of the blue diamond took place at the salesroom of Drouot & Co. The place was crowded to suffocation, and the bidding was carried to the verge of folly. The sale was attended by all those who usually appear at similar events in Paris; those who buy, and those who make a pretense of being able to buy; bankers, brokers, artists, women of all classes, two cabinet ministers, an Italian tenor, an exiled king who, in order to maintain his credit, bid, with much ostentation, and in a loud voice, as high as one hundred thousand francs. One hundred thousand francs! He could offer that sum without any danger of his bid being accepted. The Italian tenor risked one hundred and fifty thousand, and a member of the Comédie-Française bid one hundred and seventy-five thousand francs.

When the bidding reached two hundred thousand francs, the smaller competitors fell out of the race. At two hundred and fifty thousand, only two bidders remained in the field: Herschmann, the well-known capitalist, the king of gold mines; and the Countess de Crozon, the wealthy American, whose collection of diamonds and precious stones is famed throughout the world.

"Two hundred and sixty thousand ... two hundred and seventy thousand ... seventy-five ... eighty...." exclaimed the auctioneer, as he glanced at the two competitors in succession. "Two hundred and eighty thousand for madame.... Do I hear any more?"

"Three hundred thousand," said Herschmann.

There was a short silence. The countess was standing, smiling, but pale from excitement. She was leaning against the back of the chair in front of her. She knew, and so did everyone present, that the issue of the duel was certain; logically, inevitably, it must terminate to the advantage of the capitalist, who had untold millions with which to indulge his caprices. However, the countess made another bid:

"Three hundred and five thousand."

Another silence. All eyes were now directed to the capitalist in the expectation that he would raise the bidding. But Herschmann was not paying any attention to the sale; his eyes were fixed on a sheet of paper which he held in his right hand, while the other hand held a torn envelope.

"Three hundred and five thousand," repeated the auctioneer. "Once!... Twice!... For the last time.... Do I hear any more?... Once!... Twice!... Am I offered any more? Last chance!..."

Herschmann did not move.

"Third and last time!... Sold!" exclaimed the auctioneer, as his hammer fell.

"Four hundred thousand," cried Herschman, starting up, as if the sound of the hammer had roused him from his stupor.

Too late; the auctioneer's decision was irrevocable. Some of Herschmann's acquaintances pressed around him. What was the matter? Why did he not speak sooner? He laughed, and said:

"Ma foi! I simply forgot—in a moment of abstraction."

"That is strange."

"You see, I just received a letter."

"And that letter was sufficient—"

"To distract my attention? Yes, for a moment."

Ganimard was there. He had come to witness the sale of the ring. He stopped one of the attendants of the auction room, and said:

"Was it you who carried the letter to Monsieur Herschmann?"

"Yes."

"Who gave it to you?"

"A lady."

"Where is she?"

"Where is she?... She was sitting down there ... the lady who wore a thick veil."

"She has gone?"

"Yes, just this moment."

Ganimard hastened to the door, and saw the lady descending the stairs. He ran after her. A crush of people delayed him at the entrance. When he reached the sidewalk, she had disappeared. He returned to the auction room, accosted Herschmann, introduced himself, and enquired about the letter. Herschmann handed it to him. It was carelessly scribbled in pencil, in a handwriting unknown to the capitalist, and contained these few words:

"The blue diamond brings misfortune. Remember the Baron d'Hautrec."

The vicissitudes of the blue diamond were not yet at an end. Although it had become well-known through the murder of the Baron d'Hautrec and the incidents at the auction-rooms, it was six months later that it attained even greater celebrity. During the following summer, the Countess de Crozon was robbed of the famous jewel she had taken so much trouble to acquire.

Let me recall that strange affair, of which the exciting and dramatic incidents sent a thrill through all of us, and over which I am now permitted to throw some light.

On the evening of August 10, the guests of the Count and Countess de Crozon were assembled in the drawing-room of the magnificent château which overlooks the Bay de Somme. To entertain her friends, the countess seated herself at the piano to play for them, after first placing her jewels on a small table near the piano, and, amongst them, was the ring of the Baron d'Hautrec.

An hour later, the count and the majority of the guests retired, including his two cousins and Madame de Réal, an intimate friend of the countess. The latter remained in the drawing-room with Herr Bleichen, the Austrian consul, and his wife.

They conversed for a time, and then the countess extinguished the large lamp that stood on a table in the centre of the room. At the same moment, Herr Bleichen extinguished the two piano lamps. There was a momentary darkness; then the consul lighted a candle, and the three of them retired to their rooms. But, as soon as she reached her apartment, the countess remembered her jewels and sent her maid to get them. When the maid returned with the jewels, she placed them on the mantel without the countess looking at them. Next day, Madame de Crozon found that one of her rings was missing; it was the blue diamond ring.

She informed her husband, and, after talking it over, they reached the conclusion that the maid was above suspicion, and that the guilty party must be Herr Bleichen.

The count notified the commissary of police at Amiens, who commenced an investigation and, discreetly, exercised a strict surveillance over the Austrian consul to prevent his disposing of the ring.

The château was surrounded by detectives day and night. Two weeks passed without incident. Then Herr Bleichen announced his intended departure. That day, a formal complaint was entered against him. The police made an official examination of his luggage. In a small satchel, the key to which was always carried by the consul himself, they found a bottle of dentifrice, and in that bottle they found the ring.

Madame Bleichen fainted. Her husband was placed under arrest.

Everyone will remember the line of defense adopted by the accused man. He declared that the ring must have been placed there by the Count de Crozen as an act of revenge. He said:

"The count is brutal and makes his wife very unhappy. She consulted me, and I advised her to get a divorce. The count heard of it in some way, and, to be revenged on me, he took the ring and placed it in my satchel."

The count and countess persisted in pressing the charge. Between the explanation which they gave and that of the consul, both equally possible and equally probable, the public had to choose. No new fact was discovered to turn the scale in either direction. A month of gossip, conjectures and investigations failed to produce a single ray of light.

Wearied of the excitement and notoriety, and incapable of securing the evidence necessary to sustain their charge against the consul, the count and countess at last sent to Paris for a detective competent to unravel the tangled threads of this mysterious skein. This brought Ganimard into the case.

For four days, the veteran detective searched the house from top to bottom, examined every foot of the ground, had long conferences with the maid, the chauffeur, the gardeners, the employees in the neighboring post-offices, visited the rooms that had been occupied by the various guests. Then, one morning, he disappeared without taking leave of his host or hostess. But a week later, they received this telegram:

"Please come to the Japanese Tea-room, rue Boissy d'Anglas, to-morrow, Friday, evening at five o'clock. Ganimard."

At five o'clock, Friday evening, their automobile stopped in front of number nine rue Boissy-d'Anglas. The old detective was standing on the sidewalk, waiting for them. Without a word, he conducted them to the first floor of the Japanese Tea-room. In one of the rooms, they met two men, whom Ganimard introduced in these words:

"Monsieur Gerbois, professor in the College of Versailles, from whom, you will remember, Arsène Lupin stole half a million; Monsieur Léonce d'Hautrec, nephew and sole legatee of the Baron d'Hautrec."

A few minutes later, another man arrived. It was Mon. Dudouis, head of the detective service, and he appeared to be in a particularly bad temper. He bowed, and then said:

"What's the trouble now, Ganimard! I received your telephone message asking me to come here. Is it anything of consequence?"

"Yes, chief, it is a very important matter. Within an hour, the last two cases to which I was assigned will have their dénouement here. It seemed to me that your presence was indispensable."

"And also the presence of Dieuzy and Folenfant, whom I noticed standing near the door as I came in?"

"Yes, chief."

"For what? Are you going to make an arrest, and you wish to do it with a flourish? Come, Ganimard, I am anxious to hear about it."

Ganimard hesitated a moment, then spoke with the obvious intention of making an impression on his hearers:

"In the first place, I wish to state that Herr Bleichen had nothing to do with the theft of the ring."

"Oh! oh!" exclaimed Mon. Dudouis, "that is a bold statement and a very serious one."

"And is that all you have discovered?" asked the Count de Crozon.

"Not at all. On the second day after the theft, three of your guests went on an automobile trip as far as Crécy. Two of them visited the famous battlefield; and, while they were there, the third party paid a hasty visit to the post-office, and mailed a small box, tied and sealed according to the regulations, and declared its value to be one hundred francs."

"I see nothing strange in that," said the count.

"Perhaps you will see something strange in it when I tell you that this person, in place of giving her true name, sent the box under the name of Rousseau, and the person to whom it was addressed, a certain Monsieur Beloux of Paris, moved his place of residence immediately after receiving the box, in other words, the ring."

"I presume you refer to one of my cousins d'Andelle?"

"No," replied Ganimard.

"Madame de Réal, then?"

"Yes."

"You accuse my friend, Madam de Réal?" cried the countess, shocked and amazed.

"I wish to ask you one question, madame," said Ganimard. "Was Madam de Réal present when you purchased the ring?"

"Yes, but we did not go there together."

"Did she advise you to buy the ring?"

The countess considered for a moment, then said:

"Yes, I think she mentioned it first—"

"Thank you, madame. Your answer establishes the fact that it was Madame de Réal who was the first to mention the ring, and it was she who advised you to buy it."

"But, I consider my friend is quite incapable—"

"Pardon me, countess, when I remind you that Madame de Réal is only a casual acquaintance and not your intimate friend, as the newspapers have announced. It was only last winter that you met her for the first time. Now, I can prove that everything she has told you about herself, her past life, and her relatives, is absolutely false; that Madame Blanche de Réal had no actual existence before she met you, and she has now ceased to exist."

"Well?"

"Well?" replied Ganimard.

"Your story is a very strange one," said the countess, "but it has no application to our case. If Madame de Réal had taken the ring, how do you explain the fact that it was found in Herr Bleichen's tooth-powder? Anyone who would take the risk and trouble of stealing the blue diamond would certainly keep it. What do you say to that?"

"I—nothing—but Madame de Réal will answer it."

"Oh! she does exist, then?"

"She does—and does not. I will explain in a few words. Three days ago, while reading a newspaper, I glanced over the list of hotel arrivals at Trouville, and there I read: 'Hôtel Beaurivage—Madame de Réal, etc.'

"I went to Trouville immediately, and interviewed the proprietor of the hotel. From the description and other information I received from him, I concluded that she was the very Madame de Réal that I was seeking; but she had left the hotel, giving her address in Paris as number three rue de Colisée. The day before yesterday I went to that address, and learned that there was no person there called Madame de Réal, but there was a Madame Réal, living on the second floor, who acted as a diamond broker and was frequently away from home. She had returned from a journey on the preceding evening. Yesterday, I called on her and, under an assumed name, I offered to act as an intermedium in the sale of some diamonds to certain wealthy friends of mine. She is to meet me here to-day to carry out that arrangement."

"What! You expect her to come here?"

"Yes, at half-past five."

"Are you sure it is she?"

"Madame de Réal of the Château de Crozon? Certainly. I have convincing evidence of that fact. But ... listen!... I hear Folenfant's signal."

It was a whistle. Ganimard arose quickly.

"There is no time to lose. Monsieur and Madame de Crozon, will you be kind enough to go into the next room. You also, Monsieur d'Hautrec, and you, Monsieur Gerbois. The door will remain open, and when I give the signal, you will come out. Of course, Chief, you will remain here."

"We may be disturbed by other people," said Mon. Dudouis.

"No. This is a new establishment, and the proprietor is one of my friends. He will not let anyone disturb us—except the blonde Lady."

"The blonde Lady! What do you mean?"

"Yes, the blonde Lady herself, chief; the friend and accomplice of Arsène Lupin, the mysterious blonde Lady against whom I hold convincing evidence; but, in addition to that, I wish to confront her with all the people she has robbed."

He looked through the window.

"I see her. She is coming in the door now. She can't escape: Folenfant and Dieuzy are guarding the door.... The blonde Lady is captured at last, Chief!"

A moment later a woman appeared at the door; she was tall and slender, with a very pale complexion and bright golden hair. Ganimard trembled with excitement; he could not move, nor utter a word. She was there, in front of him, at his mercy! What a victory over Arsène Lupin! And what a revenge! And, at the same time, the victory was such an easy one that he asked himself if the blonde Lady would not yet slip through his fingers by one of those miracles that usually terminated the exploits of Arsène Lupin. She remained standing near the door, surprised at the silence, and looked about her without any display of suspicion or fear.

"She will get away! She will disappear!" thought Ganimard.

Then he managed to get between her and the door. She turned to go out.

"No, no!" he said. "Why are you going away?"

"Really, monsieur, I do not understand what this means. Allow me—"

"There is no reason why you should go, madame, and very good reasons why you should remain."

"But—"

"It is useless, madame. You cannot go."

Trembling, she sat on a chair, and stammered:

"What is it you want?"

Ganimard had won the battle and captured the blonde Lady. He said to her:

"Allow me to present the friend I mentioned, who desires to purchase some diamonds. Have you procured the stones you promised to bring?"

"No—no—I don't know. I don't remember."

"Come! Jog your memory! A person of your acquaintance intended to send you a tinted stone.... 'Something like the blue diamond,' I said, laughing; and you replied: 'Exactly, I expect to have just what you want.' Do you remember!"

She made no reply. A small satchel fell from her hand. She picked it up quickly, and held it securely. Her hands trembled slightly.

"Come!" said Ganimard, "I see you have no confidence in us, Madame de Réal. I shall set you a good example by showing you what I have."

He took from his pocketbook a paper which he unfolded, and disclosed a lock of hair.

"These are a few hairs torn from the head of Antoinette Bréhat by the Baron d'Hautrec, which I found clasped in his dead hand. I have shown them to Mlle. Gerbois, who declares they are of the exact color of the hair of the blonde Lady. Besides, they are exactly the color of your hair—the identical color."

Madame Réal looked at him in bewilderment, as if she did not understand his meaning. He continued:

"And here are two perfume bottles, without labels, it is true, and empty, but still sufficiently impregnated with their odor to enable Mlle. Gerbois to recognize in them the perfume used by that blonde Lady who was her traveling companion for two weeks. Now, one of these bottles was found in the room that Madame de Réal occupied at the Château de Crozon, and the other in the room that you occupied at the Hôtel Beaurivage."

"What do you say?... The blonde Lady ... the Château de Crozon...."

The detective did not reply. He took from his pocket and placed on the table, side by side, four small sheets of paper. Then he said:

"I have, on these four pieces of paper, various specimens of handwriting; the first is the writing of Antoinette Bréhat; the second was written by the woman who sent the note to Baron Herschmann at the auction sale of the blue diamond; the third is that of Madame de Réal, written while she was stopping at the

Château de Crozon; and the fourth is your handwriting, madame ... it is your name and address, which you gave to the porter of the Hôtel Beaurivage at Trouville. Now, compare the four handwritings. They are identical."

"What absurdity is this! really, monsieur, I do not understand. What does it mean?"

"It means, madame," exclaimed Ganimard, "that the blonde Lady, the friend and accomplice of Arsène Lupin, is none other than you, Madame Réal."

Ganimard went to the adjoining room and returned with Mon. Gerbois, whom he placed in front of Madame Réal, as he said:

"Monsieur Gerbois, is this the person who abducted your daughter, the woman you saw at the house of Monsieur Detinan?"

"No."

Ganimard was so surprised that he could not speak for a moment; finally, he said: "No?... You must be mistaken...."

"I am not mistaken. Madame is blonde, it is true, and in that respect resembles the blonde Lady; but, in all other respects, she is totally different."

"I can't believe it. You must be mistaken."

Ganimard called in his other witnesses.

"Monsieur d'Hautrec," he said, "do you recognize Antoinette Bréhat?"

"No, this is not the person I saw at my uncle's house."

"This woman is not Madame de Réal," declared the Count de Crozon.

That was the finishing touch. Ganimard was crushed. He was buried beneath the ruins of the structure he had erected with so much care and assurance. His pride was humbled, his spirit was broken, by the force of this unexpected blow.

Mon. Dudouis arose, and said:

"We owe you an apology, madame, for this unfortunate mistake. But, since your arrival here, I have noticed your nervous agitation. Something troubles you; may I ask what it is?"

"Mon Dieu, monsieur, I was afraid. My satchel contains diamonds to the value of a hundred thousand francs, and the conduct of your friend was rather suspicious."

"But you were frequently absent from Paris. How do you explain that?"

"I make frequent journeys to other cities in the course of my business. That is all."

Mon. Dudouis had nothing more to ask. He turned to his subordinate, and said:

"Your investigation has been very superficial, Ganimard, and your conduct toward this lady is really deplorable. You will come to my office to-morrow and explain it."

The interview was at an end, and Mon. Dudouis was about to leave the room when a most annoying incident occurred. Madame Réal turned to Ganimard, and said:

"I understand that you are Monsieur Ganimard. Am I right?"

"Yes."

"Then, this letter must be for you. I received it this morning. It was addressed to 'Mon. Justin Ganimard, care of Madame Réal.' I thought it was a joke, because I did not know you under that name, but it appears that your unknown correspondent knew of our rendezvous."

Ganimard was inclined to put the letter in his pocket unread, but he dared not do so in the presence of his superior, so he opened the envelope and read the letter aloud, in an almost inaudible tone:

"Once upon a time, there were a blonde Lady, a Lupin, and a Ganimard. Now, the wicked Ganimard had evil designs on the pretty blonde Lady, and the good Lupin was her friend and protector. When the good Lupin wished the blonde Lady to become the friend of the Countess de Crozon, he caused her to assume the name of Madame de Réal, which is a close resemblance to the name of a certain diamond broker, a woman with a pale complexion and golden hair. And the good Lupin said to himself: If ever the wicked Ganimard gets upon the track of the blonde Lady, how useful it will be to me if he should be diverted to the track of the honest diamond broker. A wise precaution that has borne good fruit. A little note sent to the newspaper read by the wicked Ganimard, a perfume bottle intentionally forgotten by the genuine blonde Lady at the Hôtel Beaurivage, the name and address of Madame Réal written on the hotel register by the genuine blonde Lady, and the trick is played. What do you think of it, Ganimard! I wished to tell you the true story of this affair, knowing that you would be the first to laugh over it. Really, it is quite amusing, and I have enjoyed it very much.

"Accept my best wishes, dear friend, and give my kind regards to the worthy Mon. Dudouis.

"ARSÈNE LUPIN."

"He knows everything," muttered Ganimard, but he did not see the humor of the situation as Lupin had predicted. "He knows some things I have never mentioned to any one. How could he find out that I was going to invite you here, chief? How could he know that I had found the first perfume bottle? How could he find out those things?"

He stamped his feet and tore his hair—a prey to the most tragic despair. Mon. Dudouis felt sorry for him, and said:

"Come, Ganimard, never mind; try to do better next time."

And Mon. Dudouis left the room, accompanied by Madame Réal.

During the next ten minutes, Ganimard read and re-read the letter of Arsène Lupin. Monsieur and Madame de Crozon, Monsieur d'Hautrec and Monsieur Gerbois were holding an animated discussion in a corner of the room. At last, the count approached the detective, and said:

"My dear monsieur, after your investigation, we are no nearer the truth than we were before."

"Pardon me, but my investigation has established these facts: that the blonde Lady is the mysterious heroine of these exploits, and that Arsène Lupin directed them."

"Those facts do not solve the mystery; in fact, they render it more obscure. The blonde Lady commits a murder in order to steal the blue diamond, and yet she does not steal it. Afterward she steals it and gets rid of it by secretly giving it to another person. How do you explain her strange conduct?"

"I cannot explain it."

"Of course; but, perhaps, someone else can."

"Who?"

The Count hesitated, so the Countess replied, frankly:

"There is only one man besides yourself who is competent to enter the arena with Arsène Lupin and overcome him. Have you any objection to our engaging the services of Herlock Sholmes in this case?"

Ganimard was vexed at the question, but stammered a reply:

"No ... but ... I do not understand what——"

"Let me explain. All this mystery annoys me. I wish to have it cleared up. Monsieur Gerbois and Monsieur d'Hautrec have the same desire, and we have agreed to send for the celebrated English detective."

"You are right, madame," replied the detective, with a loyalty that did him credit, "you are right. Old Ganimard is not able to overcome Arsène Lupin. But will Herlock Sholmes succeed? I hope so, as I have the greatest admiration for him. But ... it is improbable."

"Do you mean to say that he will not succeed?"

"That is my opinion. I can foresee the result of a duel between Herlock Sholmes and Arsène Lupin. The Englishman will be defeated."

"But, in any event, can we count on your assistance?"

"Quite so, madame. I shall be pleased to render Monsieur Sholmes all possible assistance."

"Do you know his address?"

"Yes; 219 Parker street."

That evening Monsieur and Madame de Crozon withdrew the charge they had made against Herr Bleichen, and a joint letter was addressed to Herlock Sholmes.

III. HERLOCK SHOLMES OPENS HOSTILITIES.

"What does monsieur wish?"

"Anything," replied Arsène Lupin, like a man who never worries over the details of a meal; "anything you like, but no meat or alcohol."

The waiter walked away, disdainfully.

"What! still a vegetarian?" I exclaimed.

"More so than ever," replied Lupin.

"Through taste, faith, or habit?"

"Hygiene."

"And do you never fall from grace?"

"Oh! yes ... when I am dining out ... and wish to avoid being considered eccentric."

We were dining near the Northern Railway station, in a little restaurant to which Arsène Lupin had invited me. Frequently he would send me a telegram asking me to meet him in some obscure restaurant, where we could enjoy a quiet dinner, well served, and which was always made interesting to me by his recital of some startling adventure theretofore unknown to me.

On that particular evening he appeared to be in a more lively mood than usual. He laughed and joked with careless animation, and with that delicate sarcasm that was habitual with him—a light and spontaneous sarcasm that was quite free from any tinge of malice. It was a pleasure to find him in that jovial mood, and I could not resist the desire to tell him so.

"Ah! yes," he exclaimed, "there are days in which I find life as bright and gay as a spring morning; then life seems to be an infinite treasure which I can never exhaust. And yet God knows I lead a careless existence!"

"Too much so, perhaps."

"Ah! but I tell you, the treasure is infinite. I can spend it with a lavish hand. I can cast my youth and strength to the four winds of Heaven, and it is replaced by a still younger and greater force. Besides, my life is so pleasant!... If I wished to do so, I might become—what shall I say?... An orator, a manufacturer, a politician.... But, I assure you, I shall never have such a desire. Arsène Lupin, I am; Arsène Lupin, I shall remain. I have made a vain search in history to find a career comparable to mine; a life better filled or more intense.... Napoleon? Yes, perhaps.... But Napoleon, toward the close of his career, when all Europe was trying to crush him, asked himself on the eve of each battle if it would not be his last."

Was he serious? Or was he joking? He became more animated as he proceeded:

"That is everything, do you understand, the danger! The continuous feeling of danger! To breathe it as you breathe the air, to scent it in every breath of wind, to detect it in every unusual sound.... And, in the midst of the tempest, to remain calm ... and not to stumble! Otherwise, you are lost. There is only one sensation equal to it: that of the chauffeur in an automobile race. But that race lasts only a few hours; my race continues until death!"

"What fantasy!" I exclaimed. "And you wish me to believe that you have no particular motive for your adoption of that exciting life?"

"Come," he said, with a smile, "you are a clever psychologist. Work it out for yourself."

He poured himself a glass of water, drank it, and said:

"Did you read *'Le Temps'* to-day?"

"No."

"Herlock Sholmes crossed the Channel this afternoon, and arrived in Paris about six o'clock."

"The deuce! What is he coming for?"

"A little journey he has undertaken at the request of the Count and Countess of Crozon, Monsieur Gerbois, and the nephew of Baron d'Hautrec. They met him at the Northern Railway station, took him to meet Ganimard, and, at this moment, the six of them are holding a consultation."

Despite a strong temptation to do so, I had never ventured to question Arsène Lupin concerning any action of his private life, unless he had first mentioned the subject to me. Up to that moment his name had not been mentioned, at least officially, in connection with the blue diamond. Consequently, I consumed my curiosity in patience. He continued:

"There is also in 'Le Temps' an interview with my old friend Ganimard, according to whom a certain blonde lady, who should be my friend, must have murdered the Baron d'Hautrec and tried to rob Madame de Crozon of her famous ring. And—what do you think?—he accuses me of being the instigator of those crimes."

I could not suppress a slight shudder. Was this true? Must I believe that his career of theft, his mode of existence, the logical result of such a life, had drawn that man into more serious crimes, including murder? I looked at him. He was so calm, and his eyes had such a frank expression! I observed his hands: they had been formed from a model of exceeding delicacy, long and slender; inoffensive, truly; and the hands of an artist....

"Ganimard has pipe-dreams," I said.

"No, no!" protested Lupin. "Ganimard has some cleverness; and, at times, almost inspiration."

"Inspiration!"

"Yes. For instance, that interview is a master-stroke. In the first place, he announces the coming of his English rival in order to put me on my guard, and make his task more difficult. In the second place, he indicates the exact point to which he has conducted the affair in order that Sholmes will not get credit for the work already done by Ganimard. That is good warfare."

"Whatever it may be, you have two adversaries to deal with, and such adversaries!"

"Oh! one of them doesn't count."

"And the other?"

"Sholmes? Oh! I confess he is a worthy foe; and that explains my present good humor. In the first place, it is a question of self-esteem; I am pleased to know that they consider me a subject worthy the attention of the celebrated English detective. In the next place, just imagine the pleasure a man, such as I, must experience in the thought of a duel with Herlock Sholmes. But I shall be obliged to strain every muscle; he is a clever fellow, and will contest every inch of the ground."

"Then you consider him a strong opponent?"

"I do. As a detective, I believe, he has never had an equal. But I have one advantage over him; he is making the attack and I am simply defending myself. My rôle is the easier one. Besides, I am familiar with his method of warfare, and he does not know mine. I am prepared to show him a few new tricks that will give him something to think about."

He tapped the table with his fingers as he uttered the following sentences, with an air of keen delight:

"Arsène Lupin against Herlock Sholmes.... France against England.... Trafalgar will be revenged at last.... Ah! the rascal ... he doesn't suspect that I am prepared ... and a Lupin warned—"

He stopped suddenly, seized with a fit of coughing, and hid his face in his napkin, as if something had stuck in his throat.

"A bit of bread?" I inquired. "Drink some water."

"No, it isn't that," he replied, in a stifled voice.

"Then, what is it?"

"The want of air."

"Do you wish a window opened?"

"No, I shall go out. Give me my hat and overcoat, quick! I must go."

"What's the matter?"

"The two gentlemen who came in just now.... Look at the taller one ... now, when we go out, keep to my left, so he will not see me."

"The one who is sitting behind you?"

"Yes. I will explain it to you, outside."

"Who is it?"

"Herlock Sholmes."

He made a desperate effort to control himself, as if he were ashamed of his emotion, replaced his napkin, drank a glass of water, and, quite recovered, said to me, smiling:

"It is strange, hein, that I should be affected so easily, but that unexpected sight—"

"What have you to fear, since no one can recognize you, on account of your many transformations? Every time I see you it seems to me your face is changed; it's not at all familiar. I don't know why."

"But *he* would recognize me," said Lupin. "He has seen me only once; but, at that time, he made a mental photograph of me—not of my external appearance but of my very soul—not what I appear to be but just what I am. Do you understand? And then ... and then.... I did not expect to meet him here.... Such a strange encounter!... in this little restaurant...."

"Well, shall we go out?"

"No, not now," said Lupin.

"What are you going to do?"

"The better way is to act frankly ... to have confidence in him—trust him...."

"You will not speak to him?"

"Why not! It will be to my advantage to do so, and find out what he knows, and, perhaps, what he thinks. At present I have the feeling that his gaze is on my neck and shoulders, and that he is trying to remember where he has seen them before."

He reflected a moment. I observed a malicious smile at the corner of his mouth; then, obedient, I think, to a whim of his impulsive nature, and not to the necessities of the situation, he arose, turned around, and, with a bow and a joyous air, he said:

"By what lucky chance? Ah! I am delighted to see you. Permit me to introduce a friend of mine."

For a moment the Englishman was disconcerted; then he made a movement as if he would seize Arsène Lupin. The latter shook his head, and said:

"That would not be fair; besides, the movement would be an awkward one and ... quite useless."

The Englishman looked about him, as if in search of assistance.

"No use," said Lupin. "Besides, are you quite sure you can place your hand on me? Come, now, show me that you are a real Englishman and, therefore, a good sport."

This advice seemed to commend itself to the detective, for he partially rose and said, very formally:

"Monsieur Wilson, my friend and assistant—Monsieur Arsène Lupin."

Wilson's amazement evoked a laugh. With bulging eyes and gaping mouth, he looked from one to the other, as if unable to comprehend the situation. Herlock Sholmes laughed and said:

"Wilson, you should conceal your astonishment at an incident which is one of the most natural in the world."

"Why do you not arrest him?" stammered Wilson.

"Have you not observed, Wilson, that the gentleman is between me and the door, and only a few steps from the door. By the time I could move my little finger he would be outside."

"Don't let that make any difference," said Lupin, who now walked around the table and seated himself so that the Englishman was between him and the door—thus placing himself at the mercy of the foreigner.

Wilson looked at Sholmes to find out if he had the right to admire this act of wanton courage. The Englishman's face was impenetrable; but, a moment later, he called:

"Waiter!"

When the waiter came he ordered soda, beer and whisky. The treaty of peace was signed—until further orders. In a few moments the four men were conversing in an apparently friendly manner.

Herlock Sholmes is a man such as you might meet every day in the business world. He is about fifty years of age, and looks as if he might have passed his life in an office, adding up columns of dull figures or writing out formal statements of business accounts. There was nothing to distinguish him from the average citizen of London, except the appearance of his eyes, his terribly keen and penetrating eyes.

But then he is Herlock Sholmes—which means that he is a wonderful combination of intuition, observation, clairvoyance and ingenuity. One could readily believe that nature had been pleased to take the two most extraordinary detectives that the imagination of man has hitherto conceived, the Dupin of Edgar Allen Poe and the Lecoq of Emile Gaboriau, and, out of that material, constructed a new detective, more extraordinary and supernatural than either of them. And when a person reads the history of his exploits, which have made him famous throughout the entire world, he asks himself whether Herlock Sholmes is not a mythical personage, a fictitious hero born in the brain of a great novelist—Conan Doyle, for instance.

When Arsène Lupin questioned him in regard to the length of his sojourn in France he turned the conversation into its proper channel by saying:

"That depends on you, monsieur."

"Oh!" exclaimed Lupin, laughing, "if it depends on me you can return to England to-night."

"That is a little too soon, but I expect to return in the course of eight or nine days—ten at the outside."

"Are you in such a hurry?"

"I have many cases to attend to; such as the robbery of the Anglo-Chinese Bank, the abduction of Lady Eccleston.... But, don't you think, Monsieur Lupin, that I can finish my business in Paris within a week?"

"Certainly, if you confine your efforts to the case of the blue diamond. It is, moreover, the length of time that I require to make preparations for my safety in case the solution of that affair should give you certain dangerous advantages over me."

"And yet," said the Englishman, "I expect to close the business in eight or ten days."

"And arrest me on the eleventh, perhaps?"

"No, the tenth is my limit."

Lupin shook his head thoughtfully, as he said:

"That will be difficult—very difficult."

"Difficult, perhaps, but possible, therefore certain—"

"Absolutely certain," said Wilson, as if he had clearly worked out the long series of operations which would conduct his collaborator to the desired result.

"Of course," said Herlock Sholmes, "I do not hold all the trump cards, as these cases are already several months old, and I lack certain information and clues upon which I am accustomed to base my investigations."

"Such as spots of mud and cigarette ashes," said Wilson, with an air of importance.

"In addition to the remarkable conclusions formed by Monsieur Ganimard, I have obtained all the articles written on the subject, and have formed a few deductions of my own."

"Some ideas which were suggested to us by analysis or hypothesis," added Wilson, sententiously.

"I wish to enquire," said Arsène Lupin, in that deferential tone which he employed in speaking to Sholmes, "would I be indiscreet if I were to ask you what opinion you have formed about the case?"

Really, it was a most exciting situation to see those two men facing each other across the table, engaged in an earnest discussion as if they were obliged to solve some abstruse problem or come to an agreement upon some controverted fact. Wilson was in the seventh heaven of delight. Herlock Sholmes filled his pipe slowly, lighted it, and said:

"This affair is much simpler than it appeared to be at first sight."

"Much simpler," said Wilson, as a faithful echo.

"I say 'this affair,' for, in my opinion, there is only one," said Sholmes. "The death of the Baron d'Hautrec, the story of the ring, and, let us not forget, the mystery of lottery ticket number 514, are only different phases of what one might call the mystery of the blonde Lady. Now, according to my view, it is simply a question of discovering the bond that unites those three episodes in the same story—the fact which proves the unity of the three events. Ganimard, whose judgment is rather superficial, finds that unity in the faculty of disappearance; that is, in the power of coming and going unseen and unheard. That theory does not satisfy me."

"Well, what is your idea?" asked Lupin.

"In my opinion," said Sholmes, "the characteristic feature of the three episodes is your design and purpose of leading the affair into a certain channel previously chosen by you. It is, on your part, more than a plan; it is a necessity, an indispensable condition of success."

"Can you furnish any details of your theory?"

"Certainly. For example, from the beginning of your conflict with Monsieur Gerbois, is it not evident that the apartment of Monsieur Detinan is the place selected by you, the inevitable spot where all the parties must meet? In your opinion, it was the only safe place, and you arranged a rendezvous there, publicly, one might say, for the blonde Lady and Mademoiselle Gerbois."

"The professor's daughter," added Wilson. "Now, let us consider the case of the blue diamond. Did you try to appropriate it while the Baron d'Hautrec possessed it! No. But the baron takes his brother's house. Six months later we have the intervention of Antoinette Bréhat and the first attempt. The diamond escapes you, and the sale is widely advertised to take place at the Drouot auction-rooms. Will it be a free and open sale? Is the richest amateur sure to carry off the jewel! No. Just as the banker Herschmann is on the point of buying the ring, a lady sends him a letter of warning, and it is the Countess de Crozon, prepared and influenced by the same lady, who becomes the purchaser of the diamond. Will the ring disappear at once?

No; you lack the opportunity. Therefore, you must wait. At last the Countess goes to her château. That is what you were waiting for. The ring disappears."

"To reappear again in the tooth-powder of Herr Bleichen," remarked Lupin.

"Oh! such nonsense!" exclaimed Sholmes, striking the table with his fist, "don't tell me such a fairy tale. I am too old a fox to be led away by a false scent."

"What do you mean?"

"What do I mean?" said Sholmes, then paused a moment as if he wished to arrange his effect. At last he said:

"The blue diamond that was found in the tooth-powder was false. You kept the genuine stone."

Arsène Lupin remained silent for a moment; then, with his eyes fixed on the Englishman, he replied, calmly:

"You are impertinent, monsieur."

"Impertinent, indeed!" repeated Wilson, beaming with admiration.

"Yes," said Lupin, "and, yet, to do you credit, you have thrown a strong light on a very mysterious subject. Not a magistrate, not a special reporter, who has been engaged on this case, has come so near the truth. It is a marvellous display of intuition and logic."

"Oh! a person has simply to use his brains," said Herlock Sholmes, nattered at the homage of the expert criminal.

"And so few have any brains to use," replied Lupin. "And, now, that the field of conjectures has been narrowed down, and the rubbish cleared away——"

"Well, now, I have simply to discover why the three episodes were enacted at 25 rue Clapeyron, 134 avenue Henri-Martin, and within the walls of the Château de Crozon and my work will be finished. What remains will be child's play. Don't you think so?"

"Yes, I think you are right."

"In that case, Monsieur Lupin, am I wrong in saying that my business will be finished in ten days?"

"In ten days you will know the whole truth," said Lupin.

"And you will be arrested."

"No."

"No?"

"In order that I may be arrested there must occur such a series of improbable and unexpected misfortunes that I cannot admit the possibility of such an event."

"We have a saying in England that 'the unexpected always happens.'"

They looked at each other for a moment calmly and fearlessly, without any display of bravado or malice. They met as equals in a contest of wit and skill. And this meeting was the formal crossing of swords, preliminary to the duel.

"Ah!" exclaimed Lupin, "at last I shall have an adversary worthy of the name—one whose defeat will be the proudest achievement in my career."

"Are you not afraid!" asked Wilson.

"Almost, Monsieur Wilson," replied Lupin, rising from his chair, "and the proof is that I am about to make a hasty retreat. Then, we will say ten days, Monsieur Sholmes?"

"Yes, ten days. This is Sunday. A week from next Wednesday, at eight o'clock in the evening, it will be all over."

"And I shall be in prison?"

"No doubt of it."

"Ha! not a pleasant outlook for a man who gets so much enjoyment out of life as I do. No cares, a lively interest in the affairs of the world, a justifiable contempt for the police, and the consoling sympathy of numerous friends and admirers. And now, behold, all that is about to be changed! It is the reverse side of the medal. After sunshine comes the rain. It is no longer a laughing matter. Adieu!"

"Hurry up!" said Wilson, full of solicitude for a person in whom Herlock Sholmes had inspired so much respect, "do not lose a minute."

"Not a minute, Monsieur Wilson; but I wish to express my pleasure at having met you, and to tell you how much I envy the master in having such a valuable assistant as you seem to be."

Then, after they had courteously saluted each other, like adversaries in a duel who entertain no feeling of malice but are obliged to fight by force of circumstances, Lupin seized me by the arm and drew me outside.

"What do you think of it, dear boy? The strange events of this evening will form an interesting chapter in the memoirs you are now preparing for me."

He closed the door of the restaurant behind us, and, after taking a few steps, he stopped and said:

"Do you smoke?"

"No. Nor do you, it seems to me."

"You are right, I don't."

He lighted a cigarette with a wax-match, which he shook several times in an effort to extinguish it. But he threw away the cigarette immediately, ran across the street, and joined two men who emerged from the shadows as if called by a signal. He conversed with them for a few minutes on the opposite sidewalk, and then returned to me.

"I beg your pardon, but I fear that cursed Sholmes is going to give me trouble. But, I assure you, he is not yet through with Arsène Lupin. He will find out what kind of fuel I use to warm my blood. And now—au revoir! The genial Wilson is right; there is not a moment to lose."

He walked away rapidly.

Thus ended the events of that exciting evening, or, at least, that part of them in which I was a participant. Subsequently, during the course of the evening, other stirring incidents occurred which have come to my knowledge through the courtesy of other members of that unique dinner-party.

At the very moment in which Lupin left me, Herlock Sholmes rose from the table, and looked at his watch.

"Twenty minutes to nine. At nine o'clock I am to meet the Count and Countess at the railway station."

"Then, we must be off!" exclaimed Wilson, between two drinks of whisky.

They left the restaurant.

"Wilson, don't look behind. We may be followed, and, in that case, let us act as if we did not care. Wilson, I want your opinion: why was Lupin in that restaurant?"

"To get something to eat," replied Wilson, quickly.

"Wilson, I must congratulate you on the accuracy of your deduction. I couldn't have done better myself."

Wilson blushed with pleasure, and Sholmes continued:

"To get something to eat. Very well, and, after that, probably, to assure himself whether I am going to the Château de Crozon, as announced by Ganimard in his interview. I must go in order not to disappoint him. But, in order to gain time on him, I shall not go."

"Ah!" said Wilson, nonplused.

"You, my friend, will walk down this street, take a carriage, two, three carriages. Return later and get the valises that we left at the station, and make for the Elysée-Palace at a galop."

"And when I reach the Elysée-Palace?"

"Engage a room, go to sleep, and await my orders."

Quite proud of the important rôle assigned to him, Wilson set out to perform his task. Herlock Sholmes proceeded to the railway station, bought a ticket, and repaired to the Amiens' express in which the Count and Countess de Crozon were already installed. He bowed to them, lighted his pipe, and had a quiet smoke in the corridor. The train started. Ten minutes later he took a seat beside the Countess, and said to her:

"Have you the ring here, madame?"

"Yes."

"Will you kindly let me see it?"

He took it, and examined it closely.

"Just as I suspected: it is a manufactured diamond."

"A manufactured diamond?"

"Yes; a new process which consists in submitting diamond dust to a tremendous heat until it melts and is then molded into a single stone."

"But my diamond is genuine."

"Yes, *your* diamond is; but this is not yours."

"Where is mine?"

"It is held by Arsène Lupin."

"And this stone?"

"Was substituted for yours, and slipped into Herr Bleichen's tooth-powder, where it was afterwards found."

"Then you think this is false?"

"Absolutely false."

The Countess was overwhelmed with surprise and grief, while her husband scrutinized the diamond with an incredulous air. Finally she stammered:

"Is it possible? And why did they not merely steal it and be done with it? And how did they steal it?"

"That is exactly what I am going to find out."

"At the Château de Crozon?"

"No. I shall leave the train at Creil and return to Paris. It is there the game between me and Arsène Lupin must be played. In fact, the game has commenced already, and Lupin thinks I am on my way to the château."

"But—"

"What does it matter to you, madame? The essential thing is your diamond, is it not?"

"Yes."

"Well, don't worry. I have just undertaken a much more difficult task than that. You have my promise that I will restore the true diamond to you within ten days."

The train slackened its speed. He put the false diamond in his pocket and opened the door. The Count cried out:

"That is the wrong side of the train. You are getting out on the tracks."

"That is my intention. If Lupin has anyone on my track, he will lose sight of me now. Adieu."

An employee protested in vain. After the departure of the train, the Englishman sought the station-master's office. Forty minutes later he leaped into a train that landed him in Paris shortly before midnight. He ran across the platform, entered the lunch-room, made his exit at another door, and jumped into a cab.

"Driver—rue Clapeyron."

Having reached the conclusion that he was not followed, he stopped the carriage at the end of the street, and proceeded to make a careful examination of Monsieur Detinan's house and the two adjoining houses. He made measurements of certain distances and entered the figures in his notebook.

"Driver—avenue Henri-Martin."

At the corner of the avenue and the rue de la Pompe, he dismissed the carriage, walked down the street to number 134, and performed the same operations in front of the house of the late Baron d'Hautrec and the two adjoining houses, measuring the width of the respective façades and calculating the depth of the little gardens that stood in front of them.

The avenue was deserted, and was very dark under its four rows of trees, between which, at considerable intervals, a few gas-lamps struggled in vain to light the deep shadows. One of them threw a dim light over a portion of the house, and Sholmes perceived the "To-let" sign posted on the gate, the neglected walks which encircled the small lawn, and the large bare windows of the vacant house.

"I suppose," he said to himself, "the house has been unoccupied since the death of the baron.... Ah! if I could only get in and view the scene of the murder!"

No sooner did the idea occur to him than he sought to put it in execution. But how could he manage it? He could not climb over the gate; it was too high. So he took from his pocket an electric lantern and a skeleton key which he always carried. Then, to his great surprise, he discovered that the gate was not locked; in fact, it was open about three or four inches. He entered the garden, and was careful to leave the gate as he had found it—partly open. But he had not taken many steps from the gate when he stopped. He had seen a light pass one of the windows on the second floor.

He saw the light pass a second window and a third, but he saw nothing else, except a silhouette outlined on the walls of the rooms. The light descended to the first floor, and, for a long time, wandered from room to room.

"Who the deuce is walking, at one o'clock in the morning, through the house in which the Baron d'Hautrec was killed?" Herlock Sholmes asked himself, deeply interested.

There was only one way to find out, and that was to enter the house himself. He did not hesitate, but started for the door of the house. However, at the moment when he crossed the streak of gaslight that came from the street-lamp, the man must have seen him, for the light in the house was suddenly extinguished and Herlock Sholmes did not see it again. Softly, he tried the door. It was open, also. Hearing no sound, he advanced through the hallway, encountered the foot of the stairs, and ascended to the first floor. Here there was the same silence, the same darkness.

He entered, one of the rooms and approached a window through which came a feeble light from the outside. On looking through the window he saw the man, who had no doubt descended by another stairway and escaped by another door. The man was threading his way through the shrubbery which bordered the wall that separated the two gardens.

"The deuce!" exclaimed Sholmes, "he is going to escape."

He hastened down the stairs and leaped over the steps in his eagerness to cut off the man's retreat. But he did not see anyone, and, owing to the darkness, it was several seconds before he was able to distinguish a bulky form moving through the shrubbery. This gave the Englishman food for reflection. Why had the man not made his escape, which he could have done so easily! Had he remained in order to watch the movements of the intruder who had disturbed him in his mysterious work!

"At all events," concluded Sholmes, "it is not Lupin; he would be more adroit. It may be one of his men."

For several minutes Herlock Sholmes remained motionless, with his gaze fixed on the adversary who, in his turn was watching the detective. But as that adversary had become passive, and as the Englishman was not one to consume his time in idle waiting, he examined his revolver to see if it was in good working order, remove his knife from its sheath, and walked toward the enemy with that cool effrontery and scorn of danger for which he had become famous.

He heard a clicking sound; it was his adversary preparing his revolver. Herlock Sholmes dashed boldly into the thicket, and grappled with his foe. There was a sharp, desperate struggle, in the course of which Sholmes suspected that the man was trying to draw a knife. But the Englishman, believing his antagonist to be an accomplice of Arsène Lupin and anxious to win the first trick in the game with that redoubtable foe, fought with unusual strength and determination. He hurled his adversary to the ground, held him there with the weight of his body, and, gripping him by the throat with one hand, he used his free hand to take out his electric lantern, press the button, and throw the light over the face of his prisoner.

"Wilson!" he exclaimed, in amazement.

"Herlock Sholmes!" stammered a weak, stifled voice.

For a long time they remained silent, astounded, foolish. The shriek of an automobile rent the air. A slight breeze stirred the leaves. Suddenly, Herlock Sholmes seized his friend by the shoulders and shook him violently, as he cried:

"What are you doing here? Tell me.... What?... Did I tell you to hide in the bushes and spy on me!"

"Spy on you!" muttered Wilson, "why, I didn't know it was you."

"But what are you doing here? You ought to be in bed."

"I was in bed."

"You ought to be asleep."

"I was asleep."

"Well, what brought you here?" asked Sholmes.

"Your letter."

"My letter? I don't understand."

"Yes, a messenger brought it to me at the hotel."

"From me? Are you crazy?"

"It is true—I swear it."

"Where is the letter?"

Wilson handed him a sheet of paper, which he read by the light of his lantern. It was as follows:

"Wilson, come at once to avenue Henri-Martin. The house is empty. Inspect the whole place and make an exact plan. Then return to hotel.—Herlock Sholmes."

"I was measuring the rooms," said Wilson, "when I saw a shadow in the garden. I had only one idea——"

"That was to seize the shadow.... The idea was excellent.... But remember this, Wilson, whenever you receive a letter from me, be sure it is my handwriting and not a forgery."

"Ah!" exclaimed Wilson, as the truth dawned on him, "then the letter wasn't from you?"

"No."

"Who sent it, then?"

"Arsène Lupin."

"Why? For what purpose?" asked Wilson.

"I don't know, and that's what worries me. I don't understand why he took the trouble to disturb you. Of course, if he had sent me on such a foolish errand I wouldn't be surprised; but what was his object in disturbing you?"

"I must hurry back to the hotel."

"So must I, Wilson."

They arrived at the gate. Wilson, who was ahead, took hold of it and pulled.

"Ah! you closed it?" he said.

"No, I left it partly open."

Sholmes tried the gate; then, alarmed, he examined the lock. An oath escaped him:

"Good God! it is locked! locked with a key!"

He shook the gate with all his strength; then, realizing the futility of his efforts, he dropped his arms, discouraged, and muttered, in a jerky manner:

"I can see it all now—it is Lupin. He fore-saw that I would leave the train at Creil, and he prepared this neat little trap for me in case I should commence my investigation this evening. Moreover, he was kind enough to send me a companion to share my captivity. All done to make me lose a day, and, perhaps, also, to teach me to mind my own business."

"Do you mean to say we are prisoners?"

"Exactly. Herlock Sholmes and Wilson are the prisoners of Arsène Lupin. It's a bad beginning; but he laughs best who laughs last."

Wilson seized Sholmes' arm, and exclaimed:

"Look!... Look up there!... A light...."

A light shone through one of the windows of the first floor. Both of them ran to the house, and each ascended by the stairs he had used on coming out a short time before, and they met again at the entrance to the lighted chamber. A small piece of a candle was burning in the center of the room. Beside it there was a basket containing a bottle, a roasted chicken, and a loaf of bread.

Sholmes was greatly amused, and laughed heartily.

"Wonderful! we are invited to supper. It is really an enchanted place, a genuine fairy-land. Come, Wilson, cheer up! this is not a funeral. It's all very funny."

"Are you quite sure it is so very funny?" asked Wilson, in a lugubrious tone.

"Am I sure?" exclaimed Sholmes, with a gaiety that was too boisterous to be natural, "why, to tell the truth, it's the funniest thing I ever saw. It's a jolly good comedy! What a master of sarcasm this Arsène Lupin is! He makes a fool of you with the utmost grace and delicacy. I wouldn't miss this feast for all the money in the Bank of England. Come, Wilson, you grieve me. You should display that nobility of character which rises superior to misfortune. I don't see that you have any cause for complaint, really, I don't."

After a time, by dint of good humor and sarcasm, he managed to restore Wilson to his normal mood, and make him swallow a morsel of chicken and a glass of wine. But when the candle went out and they prepared to spend the night there, with the bare floor for a mattress and the hard wall for a pillow, the harsh and ridiculous side of the situation was impressed upon them. That particular incident will not form a pleasant page in the memoirs of the famous detective.

Next morning Wilson awoke, stiff and cold. A slight noise attracted his attention: Herlock Sholmes was kneeling on the floor, critically examining some grains of sand and studying some chalk-marks, now almost effaced, which formed certain figures and numbers, which figures he entered in his notebook.

Accompanied by Wilson, who was deeply interested in the work, he examined each room, and found similar chalk-marks in two other apartments. He noticed, also, two circles on the oaken panels, an arrow on a wainscot, and four figures on four steps of the stairs. At the end of an hour Wilson said:

"The figures are correct, aren't they!"

"I don't know; but, at all events, they mean something," replied Sholmes, who had forgotten the discomforts of the night in the joy created by his new discoveries.

"It is quite obvious," said Wilson, "they represent the number of pieces in the floor."

"Ah!"

"Yes. And the two circles indicate that the panels are false, as you can readily ascertain, and the arrow points in the direction in which the panels move."

Herlock Sholmes looked at Wilson, in astonishment.

"Ah! my dear friend, how do you know all that? Your clairvoyance makes my poor ability in that direction look quite insignificant."

"Oh! it is very simple," said Wilson, inflated with pride; "I examined those marks last night, according to your instructions, or, rather, according to the instructions of Arsène Lupin, since he wrote the letter you sent to me."

At that moment Wilson faced a greater danger than he had during his struggle in the garden with Herlock Sholmes. The latter now felt a furious desire to strangle him. But, dominating his feelings, Sholmes made a grimace which was intended for a smile, and said:

"Quite so, Wilson, you have done well, and your work shows commendable progress. But, tell me, have you exercised your powers of observation and analysis on any other points? I might profit by your deductions."

"Oh! no, I went no farther."

"That's a pity. Your début was such a promising one. But, since that is all, we may as well go."

"Go! but how can we get out?"

"The way all honest people go out: through the gate."

"But it is locked."

"It will be opened."

"By whom?"

"Please call the two policemen who are strolling down the avenue."

"But——"

"But what?"

"It is very humiliating. What will be said when it becomes known that Herlock Sholmes and Wilson were the prisoners of Arsène Lupin?"

"Of course, I understand they will roar with laughter," replied Herlock Sholmes, in a dry voice and with frowning features, "but we can't set up housekeeping in this place."

"And you will not try to find another way out?"

"No."

"But the man who brought us the basket of provisions did not cross the garden, coming or going. There is some other way out. Let us look for it, and not bother with the police."

"Your argument is sound, but you forget that all the detectives in Paris have been trying to find it for the last six months, and that I searched the house from top to bottom while you were asleep. Ah! my dear Wilson, we have not been accustomed to pursue such game as Arsène Lupin. He leaves no trail behind him."

At eleven o'clock, Herlock Sholmes and Wilson were liberated, and conducted to the nearest police station, where the commissary, after subjecting them to a severe examination, released them with an affectation of good-will that was quite exasperating.

"I am very sorry, messieurs, that this unfortunate incident has occurred. You will have a very poor opinion of French hospitality. Mon Dieu! what a night you must have passed! Ah! that rascally Lupin is no respecter of persons."

They took a carriage to their hotel. At the office Wilson asked for the key of his room.

After some search the clerk replied, much astonished:

"But, monsieur, you have given up the room."

"I gave it up? When?"

"This morning, by the letter your friend brought here."

"What friend?"

"The gentleman who brought your letter.... Ah! your card is still attached to the letter. Here they are."

Wilson looked at them. Certainly, it was one of his cards, and the letter was in his handwriting.

"Good Lord!" he muttered, "this is another of his tricks," and he added, aloud: "Where is my luggage?"

"Your friend took it."

"Ah!... and you gave it to him?"

"Certainly; on the strength of your letter and card."

"Of course ... of course."

They left the hotel and walked, slowly and thoughtfully, through the Champs-Elysées. The avenue was bright and cheerful beneath a clear autumn sun; the air was mild and pleasant.

At Rond-Point, Herlock Sholmes lighted his pipe. Then Wilson spoke:

"I can't understand you, Sholmes. You are so calm and unruffled. They play with you as a cat plays with a mouse, and yet you do not say a word."

Sholmes stopped, as he replied:

"Wilson, I was thinking of your card."

"Well!"

"The point is this: here is a man who, in view of a possible struggle with us, procures specimens of our handwriting, and who holds, in his possession, one or more of your cards. Now, have you considered how much precaution and skill those facts represent?"

"Well!"

"Well, Wilson, to overcome an enemy so well prepared and so thoroughly equipped requires the infinite shrewdness of ... of a Herlock Sholmes. And yet, as you have seen, Wilson, I have lost the first round."

At six o'clock the *Echo de France* published the following article in its evening edition:

"This morning Mon. Thenard, commissary of police in the sixteenth district, released Herlock Sholmes and his friend Wilson, both of whom had been locked in the house of the late Baron d'Hautrec, where they spent a very pleasant night—thanks to the thoughtful care and attention of Arsène Lupin."

"In addition to their other troubles, these gentlemen have been robbed of their valises, and, in consequence thereof, they have entered a formal complaint against Arsène Lupin."

"Arsène Lupin, satisfied that he has given them a mild reproof, hopes these gentlemen will not force him to resort to more stringent measures."

"Bah!" exclaimed Herlock Sholmes, crushing the paper in his hands, "that is only child's play! And that is the only criticism I have to make of Arsène Lupin: he plays to the gallery. There is that much of the fakir in him."

"Ah! Sholmes, you are a wonderful man! You have such a command over your temper. Nothing ever disturbs you."

"No, nothing disturbs me," replied Sholmes, in a voice that trembled from rage; "besides, what's the use of losing my temper?... I am quite confident of the final result; I shall have the last word."

IV. LIGHT IN THE DARKNESS.

However well-tempered a man's character may be—and Herlock Sholmes is one of those men over whom ill-fortune has little or no hold—there are circumstances wherein the most courageous combatant feels the necessity of marshaling his forces before risking the chances of a battle.

"I shall take a vacation to-day," said Sholmes.

"And what shall I do?" asked Wilson.

"You, Wilson—let me see! You can buy some underwear and linen to replenish our wardrobe, while I take a rest."

"Very well, Sholmes, I will watch while you sleep."

Wilson uttered these words with all the importance of a sentinel on guard at the outpost, and therefore exposed to the greatest danger. His chest was expanded; his muscles were tense. Assuming a shrewd look, he scrutinized, officially, the little room in which they had fixed their abode.

"Very well, Wilson, you can watch. I shall occupy myself in the preparation of a line of attack more appropriate to the methods of the enemy we are called upon to meet. Do you see, Wilson, we have been deceived in this fellow Lupin. My opinion is that we must commence at the very beginning of this affair."

"And even before that, if possible. But have we sufficient time?"

"Nine days, dear boy. That is five too many."

The Englishman spent the entire afternoon in smoking and sleeping. He did not enter upon his new plan of attack until the following day. Then he said:

"Wilson, I am ready. Let us attack the enemy."

"Lead on, Macduff!" exclaimed Wilson, full of martial ardor. "I wish to fight in the front rank. Oh! have no fear. I shall do credit to my King and country, for I am an Englishman."

In the first place, Sholmes had three long and important interviews: With Monsieur Detinan, whose rooms he examined with the greatest care and precision; with Suzanne Gerbois, whom he questioned in regard to the blonde Lady; and with Sister Auguste, who had retired to the convent of the Visitandines since the murder of Baron d'Hautrec.

At each of these interviews Wilson had remained outside; and each time he asked:

"Satisfactory?"

"Quite so."

"I was sure we were on the right track."

They paid a visit to the two houses adjoining that of the late Baron d'Hautrec in the avenue Henri-Martin; then they visited the rue Clapeyron, and, while he was examining the front of number 25, Sholmes said:

"All these houses must be connected by secret passages, but I can't find them."

For the first time in his life, Wilson doubted the omnipotence of his famous associate. Why did he now talk so much and accomplish so little?

"Why?" exclaimed Sholmes, in answer to Wilson's secret thought, "because, with this fellow Lupin, a person has to work in the dark, and, instead of deducting the truth from established facts, a man must extract it from his own brain, and afterward learn if it is supported by the facts in the case."

"But what about the secret passages?"

"They must exist. But even though I should discover them, and thus learn how Arsène Lupin made his entrance to the lawyer's house and how the blonde Lady escaped from the house of Baron d'Hautrec after the murder, what good would it do? How would it help me? Would it furnish me with a weapon of attack?"

"Let us attack him just the same," exclaimed Wilson, who had scarcely uttered these words when he jumped back with a cry of alarm. Something had fallen at their feet; it was a bag filled with sand which might have caused them serious injury if it had struck them.

Sholmes looked up. Some men were working on a scaffolding attached to the balcony at the fifth floor of the house. He said:

"We were lucky; one step more, and that heavy bag would have fallen on our heads. I wonder if—"

Moved by a sudden impulse, he rushed into the house, up the five flights of stairs, rang the bell, pushed his way into the apartment to the great surprise and alarm of the servant who came to the door, and made his way to the balcony in front of the house. But there was no one there.

"Where are the workmen who were here a moment ago?" he asked the servant.

"They have just gone."

"Which way did they go?"

"By the servants' stairs."

Sholmes leaned out of the window. He saw two men leaving the house, carrying bicycles. They mounted them and quickly disappeared around the corner.

"How long have they been working on this scaffolding!"

"Those men!... only since this morning. It's their first day."

Sholmes returned to the street, and joined Wilson. Together they returned to the hotel, and thus the second day ended in a mournful silence.

On the following day their programme was almost similar. They sat together on a bench in the avenue Henri-Martin, much to Wilson's disgust, who did not find it amusing to spend long hours watching the house in which the tragedy had occurred.

"What do you expect, Sholmes! That Arsène Lupin will walk out of the house!"

"No."

"That the blonde Lady will make her appearance!"

"No."

"What then!"

"I am looking for something to occur; some slight incident that will furnish me with a clue to work on."

"And if it does not occur!"

"Then I must, myself, create the spark that will set fire to the powder."

A solitary incident—and that of a disagreeable nature—broke the monotony of the forenoon.

A gentleman was riding along the avenue when his horse suddenly turned aside in such a manner that it ran against the bench on which they were sitting, and struck Sholmes a slight blow on the shoulder.

"Ha!" exclaimed Sholmes, "a little more and I would have had a broken shoulder."

The gentleman struggled with his horse. The Englishman drew his revolver and pointed it; but Wilson seized his arm, and said:

"Don't be foolish! What are you going to do! Kill the man!"

"Leave me alone, Wilson! Let go!"

During the brief struggle between Sholmes and Wilson the stranger rode away.

"Now, you can shoot," said Wilson, triumphantly, when the horseman was at some distance.

"Wilson, you're an idiot! Don't you understand that the man is an accomplice of Arsène Lupin?"

Sholmes was trembling from rage. Wilson stammered pitifully:

"What!... that man ... an accomplice?"

"Yes, the same as the workmen who tried to drop the bag of sand on us yesterday."

"It can't be possible!"

"Possible or not, there was only one way to prove it."

"By killing the man?"

"No—by killing the horse. If you hadn't grabbed my arm, I should have captured one of Lupin's accomplices. Now, do you understand the folly of your act?"

Throughout the afternoon both men were morose. They did not speak a word to each other. At five o'clock they visited the rue Clapeyron, but were careful to keep at a safe distance from the houses. However, three young men who were passing through the street, arm in arm, singing, ran against Sholmes and Wilson and refused to let them pass. Sholmes, who was in an ill humor, contested the right of way with them. After a brief struggle, Sholmes resorted to his fists. He struck one of the men a hard blow on the chest, another a blow in the face, and thus subdued two of his adversaries. Thereupon the three of them took to their heels and disappeared.

"Ah!" exclaimed Sholmes, "that does me good. I needed a little exercise."

But Wilson was leaning against the wall. Sholmes said:

"What's the matter, old chap? You're quite pale."

Wilson pointed to his left arm, which hung inert, and stammered:

"I don't know what it is. My arm pains me."

"Very much?... Is it serious?"

"Yes, I am afraid so."

He tried to raise his arm, but it was helpless. Sholmes felt it, gently at first, then in a rougher way, "to see how badly it was hurt," he said. He concluded that Wilson was really hurt, so he led him to a neighboring pharmacy, where a closer examination revealed the fact that the arm was broken and that Wilson was a candidate for the hospital. In the meantime they bared his arm and applied some remedies to ease his suffering.

"Come, come, old chap, cheer up!" said Sholmes, who was holding Wilson's arm, "in five or six weeks you will be all right again. But I will pay them back ... the rascals! Especially Lupin, for this is his work ... no doubt of that. I swear to you if ever——"

He stopped suddenly, dropped the arm—which caused Wilson such an access of pain that he almost fainted—and, striking his forehead, Sholmes said:

"Wilson, I have an idea. You know, I have one occasionally."

He stood for a moment, silent, with staring eyes, and then muttered, in short, sharp phrases:

"Yes, that's it ... that will explain all ... right at my feet ... and I didn't see it ... ah, parbleu! I should have thought of it before.... Wilson, I shall have good news for you."

Abruptly leaving his old friend, Sholmes ran into the street and went directly to the house known as number 25. On one of the stones, to the right of the door, he read this inscription: "Destange, architect, 1875."

There was a similar inscription on the house numbered 23.

Of course, there was nothing unusual in that. But what might be read on the houses in the avenue Henri-Martin?

A carriage was passing. He engaged it and directed the driver to take him to No. 134 avenue Henri-Martin. He was roused to a high pitch of excitement. He stood up in the carriage and urged the horse to greater speed. He offered extra pourboires to the driver. Quicker! Quicker!

How great was his anxiety as they turned from the rue de la Pompe! Had he caught a glimpse of the truth at last?

On one of the stones of the late Baron's house he read the words: "Destange, architect, 1874." And a similar inscription appeared on the two adjoining houses.

The reaction was such that he settled down in the seat of the carriage, trembling from joy. At last, a tiny ray of light had penetrated the dark shadows which encompassed these mysterious crimes! In the vast sombre forest wherein a thousand pathways crossed and re-crossed, he had discovered the first clue to the track followed by the enemy!

He entered a branch postoffice and obtained telephonic connection with the château de Crozon. The Countess answered the telephone call.

"Hello!... Is that you, madame?"

"Monsieur Sholmes, isn't it? Everything going all right?"

"Quite well, but I wish to ask you one question.... Hello!"

"Yes, I hear you."

"Tell me, when was the château de Crozon built?"

"It was destroyed by fire and rebuilt about thirty years ago."

"Who built it, and in what year?"

"There is an inscription on the front of the house which reads: 'Lucien Destange, architect, 1877.'"

"Thank you, madame, that is all. Good-bye."

He went away, murmuring: "Destange ... Lucien Destange ... that name has a familiar sound."

He noticed a public reading-room, entered, consulted a dictionary of modern biography, and copied the following information: "Lucien Destange, born 1840, Grand-Prix de Rome, officer of the Legion of Honor, author of several valuable books on architecture, etc...."

Then he returned to the pharmacy and found that Wilson had been taken to the hospital. There Sholmes found him with his arm in splints, and shivering with fever.

"Victory! Victory!" cried Sholmes. "I hold one end of the thread."

"Of what thread?"

"The one that leads to victory. I shall now be walking on solid ground, where there will be footprints, clues...."

"Cigarette ashes?" asked Wilson, whose curiosity had overcome his pain.

"And many other things! Just think, Wilson, I have found the mysterious link which unites the different adventures in which the blonde Lady played a part. Why did Lupin select those three houses for the scenes of his exploits?"

"Yes, why?"

"Because those three houses were built by the same architect. That was an easy problem, eh? Of course ... but who would have thought of it?"

"No one but you."

"And who, except I, knows that the same architect, by the use of analogous plans, has rendered it possible for a person to execute three distinct acts which, though miraculous in appearance, are, in reality, quite simple and easy?"

"That was a stroke of good luck."

"And it was time, dear boy, as I was becoming very impatient. You know, this is our fourth day."

"Out of ten."

"Oh! after this——"

Sholmes was excited, delighted, and gayer than usual.

"And when I think that these rascals might have attacked me in the street and broken my arm just as they did yours! Isn't that so, Wilson?"

Wilson simply shivered at the horrible thought. Sholmes continued:

"We must profit by the lesson. I can see, Wilson, that we were wrong to try and fight Lupin in the open, and leave ourselves exposed to his attacks."

"I can see it, and feel it, too, in my broken arm," said Wilson.

"You have one consolation, Wilson; that is, that I escaped. Now, I must be doubly cautious. In an open fight he will defeat me; but if I can work in the dark, unseen by him, I have the advantage, no matter how strong his forces may be."

"Ganimard might be of some assistance."

"Never! On the day that I can truly say: Arsène Lupin is there; I show you the quarry, and how to catch it; I shall go and see Ganimard at one of the two addresses that he gave me—his residence in the rue Pergolese, or at the Suisse tavern in the Place du Châtelet. But, until that time, I shall work alone."

He approached the bed, placed his hand on Wilson's shoulder—on the sore one, of course—and said to him:

"Take care of yourself, old fellow. Henceforth your rôle will be to keep two or three of Arsène Lupin's men busy watching here in vain for my return to enquire about your health. It is a secret mission for you, eh!"

"Yes, and I shall do my best to fulfil it conscientiously. Then you do not expect to come here any more?"

"What for?" asked Sholmes.

"I don't know ... of course.... I am getting on as well as possible. But, Herlock, do me a last service: give me a drink."

"A drink?"

"Yes, I am dying of thirst; and with my fever——"

"To be sure—directly——"

He made a pretense of getting some water, perceived a package of tobacco, lighted his pipe, and then, as if he had not heard his friend's request, he went away, whilst Wilson uttered a mute prayer for the inaccessible water.

"Monsieur Destange!"

The servant eyed from head to foot the person to whom he had opened the door of the house—the magnificent house that stood at the corner of the Place Malesherbes and the rue Montchanin—and at the sight of the man with gray hairs, badly shaved, dressed in a shabby black coat, with a body as ill-formed and ungracious as his face, he replied with the disdain which he thought the occasion warranted:

"Monsieur Destange may or may not be at home. That depends. Has monsieur a card?"

Monsieur did not have a card, but he had a letter of introduction and, after the servant had taken the letter to Mon. Destange, he was conducted into the presence of that gentleman who was sitting in a large circular room or rotunda which occupied one of the wings of the house. It was a library, and contained a profusion of books and architectural drawings. When the stranger entered, the architect said to him:

"You are Monsieur Stickmann?"

"Yes, monsieur."

"My secretary tells me that he is ill, and has sent you to continue the general catalogue of the books which he commenced under my direction, and, more particularly, the catalogue of German books. Are you familiar with that kind of work?"

"Yes, monsieur, quite so," he replied, with a strong German accent.

Under those circumstances the bargain was soon concluded, and Mon. Destange commenced work with his new secretary.

Herlock Sholmes had gained access to the house.

In order to escape the vigilance of Arsène Lupin and gain admittance to the house occupied by Lucien Destange and his daughter Clotilde, the famous detective had been compelled to resort to a number of stratagems, and, under a variety of names, to ingratiate himself into the good graces and confidence of a number of persons—in short, to live, during forty-eight hours, a most complicated life. During that time he had acquired the following information: Mon. Destange, having retired from active business on account of his failing health, now lived amongst the many books he had accumulated on the subject of architecture. He derived infinite pleasure in viewing and handling those dusty old volumes.

His daughter Clotilde was considered eccentric. She passed her time in another part of the house, and never went out.

"Of course," Sholmes said to himself, as he wrote in a register the titles of the books which Mon. Destange dictated to him, "all that is vague and incomplete, but it is quite a long step in advance. I shall surely solve one of these absorbing problems: Is Mon. Destange associated with Arsène Lupin? Does he continue to see him? Are the papers relating to the construction of the three houses still in existence? Will those papers not furnish me with the location of other houses of similar construction which Arsène Lupin and his associates will plunder in the future?

"Monsieur Destange, an accomplice of Arsène Lupin! That venerable man, an officer of the Legion of Honor, working in league with a burglar—such an idea was absurd! Besides, if we concede that such a complicity exists, how could Mon. Destange, thirty years ago, have possibly foreseen the thefts of Arsène Lupin, who was then an infant?"

No matter! The Englishman was implacable. With his marvellous scent, and that instinct which never fails him, he felt that he was in the heart of some strange mystery. Ever since he first entered the house, he had been under the influence of that impression, and yet he could not define the grounds on which he based his suspicions.

Up to the morning of the second day he had not made any significant discovery. At two o'clock of that day he saw Clotilde Destange for the first time; she came to the library in search of a book. She was about thirty years of age, a brunette, slow and silent in her movements, with features imbued with that expression of indifference which is characteristic of people who live a secluded life. She exchanged a few words with her father, and then retired, without even looking at Sholmes.

The afternoon dragged along monotonously. At five o'clock Mon. Destange announced his intention to go out. Sholmes was alone on the circular gallery that was constructed about ten feet above the floor of the rotunda. It was almost dark. He was on the point of going out, when he heard a slight sound and, at the same time, experienced the feeling that there was someone in the room. Several minutes passed before he saw or heard anything more. Then he shuddered; a shadowy form emerged from the gloom, quite close to him, upon the balcony. It seemed incredible. How long had this mysterious visitor been there? Whence did he come?

The strange man descended the steps and went directly to a large oaken cupboard. Sholmes was a keen observer of the man's movements. He watched him searching amongst the papers with which the cupboard was filled. What was he looking for?

Then the door opened and Mlle. Destange entered, speaking to someone who was following her:

"So you have decided not to go out, father?... Then I will make a light ... one second ... do not move...."

The strange man closed the cupboard and hid in the embrasure of a large window, drawing the curtains together. Did Mlle. Destange not see him? Did she not hear him? Calmly she turned on the electric lights; she and her father sat down close to each other. She opened a book she had brought with her, and commenced to read. After the lapse of a few minutes she said:

"Your secretary has gone."

"Yes, I don't see him."

"Do you like him as well as you did at first?" she asked, as if she were not aware of the illness of the real secretary and his replacement by Stickmann.

"Oh! yes."

Monsieur Destange's head bobbed from one side to the other. He was asleep. The girl resumed her reading. A moment later one of the window curtains was pushed back, and the strange man emerged and glided along the wall toward the door, which obliged him to pass behind Mon. Destange but in front of Clotilde, and brought him into the light so that Herlock Sholmes obtained a good view of the man's face. It was Arsène Lupin.

The Englishman was delighted. His forecast was verified; he had penetrated to the very heart of the mystery, and found Arsène Lupin to be the moving spirit in it.

Clotilde had not yet displayed any knowledge of his presence, although it was quite improbable that any movement of the intruder had escaped her notice. Lupin had almost reached the door and, in fact, his hand was already seeking the door-knob, when his coat brushed against a small table and knocked something to the floor. Monsieur Destange awoke with a start. Arsène Lupin was already standing in front of him, hat in hand, smiling.

"Maxime Bermond," exclaimed Mon. Destange, joyfully. "My dear Maxime, what lucky chance brings you here?"

"The wish to see you and Mademoiselle Destange."

"When did you return from your journey?"

"Yesterday."

"You must stay to dinner."

"No, thank you, I am sorry, but I have an appointment to dine with some friends at a restaurant."

"Come, to-morrow, then, Clotilde, you must urge him to come to-morrow. Ah! my dear Maxime.... I thought of you many times during your absence."

"Really?"

"Yes, I went through all my old papers in that cupboard, and found our last statement of account."

"What account?"

"Relating to the avenue Henri-Martin."

"Ah! do you keep such papers? What for?"

Then the three of them left the room, and continued their conversation in a small parlor which adjoined the library.

"Is it Lupin?" Sholmes asked himself, in a sudden access of doubt. Certainly, from all appearances, it was he; and yet it was also someone else who resembled Arsène Lupin in certain respects, and who still maintained his own individuality, features, and color of hair. Sholmes could hear Lupin's voice in the adjoining room. He was relating some stories at which Mon. Destange laughed heartily, and which even brought a smile to the lips of the melancholy Clotilde. And each of those smiles appeared to be the reward which Arsène Lupin was seeking, and which he was delighted to have secured. His success caused him to redouble his efforts and, insensibly, at the sound of that clear and happy voice, Clotilde's face brightened and lost that cold and listless expression which usually pervaded it.

"They love each other," thought Sholmes, "but what the deuce can there be in common between Clotilde Destange and Maxime Bermond? Does she know that Maxime is none other than Arsène Lupin?"

Until seven o'clock Sholmes was an anxious listener, seeking to profit by the conversation. Then, with infinite precaution, he descended from the gallery, crept along the side of the room to the door in such a manner that the people in the adjoining room did not see him.

When he reached the street Sholmes satisfied himself that there was neither an automobile nor a cab waiting there; then he slowly limped along the boulevard Malesherbes. He turned into an adjacent street, donned the overcoat which he had carried on his arm, altered the shape of his hat, assumed an upright carriage, and, thus transformed, returned to a place whence he could watch the door of Mon. Destange's house.

In a few minutes Arsène Lupin came out, and proceeded to walk toward the center of Paris by way of the rues de Constantinople and London. Herlock Sholmes followed at a distance of a hundred paces.

Exciting moments for the Englishman! He sniffed the air, eagerly, like a hound following a fresh scent. It seemed to him a delightful thing thus to follow his adversary. It was no longer Herlock Sholmes who was being watched, but Arsène Lupin, the invisible Arsène Lupin. He held him, so to speak, within the grasp of his eye, by an imperceptible bond that nothing could break. And he was pleased to think that the quarry belonged to him.

But he soon observed a suspicious circumstance. In the intervening space between him and Arsène Lupin he noticed several people traveling in the same direction, particularly two husky fellows in slouch hats on the left side of the street, and two others on the right wearing caps and smoking cigarettes. Of course, their presence in that vicinity may have been the result of chance, but Sholmes was more astonished when he observed that the four men stopped when Lupin entered a tobacco shop; and still more surprised when the four men started again after Lupin emerged from the shop, each keeping to his own side of the street.

"Curse it!" muttered Sholmes; "he is being followed."

He was annoyed at the idea that others were on the trail of Arsène Lupin; that someone might deprive him, not of the glory—he cared little for that—but of the immense pleasure of capturing, single-handed, the most formidable enemy he had ever met. And he felt that he was not mistaken; the men presented to Sholmes' experienced eye the appearance and manner of those who, while regulating their gait to that of another, wish to present a careless and natural air.

"Is this some of Ganimard's work?" muttered Sholmes. "Is he playing me false?"

He felt inclined to speak to one of the men with a view of acting in concert with him; but as they were now approaching the boulevard the crowd was becoming denser, and he was afraid he might lose sight of Lupin. So he quickened his pace and turned into the boulevard just in time to see Lupin ascending the steps of the Hungarian restaurant at the corner of the rue du Helder. The door of the restaurant was open, so that Sholmes, while sitting on a bench on the other side of the boulevard, could see Lupin take a seat at a table, luxuriously appointed and decorated with flowers, at which three gentlemen and two ladies of elegant appearance were already seated and who extended to Lupin a hearty greeting.

Sholmes now looked about for the four men and perceived them amongst a crowd of people who were listening to a gipsy orchestra that was playing in a neighboring café. It was a curious thing that they were paying no attention to Arsène Lupin, but seemed to be friendly with the people around them. One of them took a cigarette from his pocket and approached a gentleman who wore a frock coat and silk hat. The gentleman offered the other his cigar for a light, and Sholmes had the impression that they talked to each other much longer than the occasion demanded. Finally the gentleman approached the Hungarian restaurant, entered and looked around. When he caught sight of Lupin he advanced and spoke to him for a moment, then took a seat at an adjoining table. Sholmes now recognized this gentleman as the horseman who had tried to run him down in the avenue Henri-Martin.

Then Sholmes understood that these men were not tracking Arsène Lupin; they were a part of his band. They were watching over his safety. They were his bodyguard, his satellites, his vigilant escort. Wherever danger threatened Lupin, these confederates were at hand to avert it, ready to defend him. The four men were accomplices. The gentleman in the frock coat was an accomplice. These facts furnished the Englishman with food for reflection. Would he ever succeed in capturing that inaccessible individual? What unlimited power was possessed by such an organization, directed by such a chief!

He tore a leaf from his notebook, wrote a few lines in pencil, which he placed in an envelope, and said to a boy about fifteen years of age who was sitting on the bench beside him:

"Here, my boy; take a carriage and deliver this letter to the cashier of the Suisse tavern, Place du Châtelet. Be quick!"

He gave him a five-franc piece. The boy disappeared.

A half hour passed away. The crowd had grown larger, and Sholmes perceived only at intervals the accomplices of Arsène Lupin. Then someone brushed against him and whispered in his ear:

"Well! what is it, Monsieur Sholmes?"

"Ah! it is you, Ganimard?"

"Yes; I received your note at the tavern. What's the matter?"

"He is there."

"What do you mean?"

"There ... in the restaurant. Lean to the right.... Do you see him now?"

"No."

"He is pouring a glass of champagne for the lady."

"That is not Lupin."

"Yes, it is."

"But I tell you.... Ah! yet, it may be. It looks a great deal like him," said Ganimard, naively. "And the others—accomplices?"

"No; the lady sitting beside him is Lady Cliveden; the other is the Duchess de Cleath. The gentleman sitting opposite Lupin is the Spanish Ambassador to London."

Ganimard took a step forward. Sholmes retained him.

"Be prudent. You are alone."

"So is he."

"No, he has a number of men on the boulevard mounting guard. And inside the restaurant that gentleman——"

"And I, when I take Arsène Lupin by the collar and announce his name, I shall have the entire room on my side and all the waiters."

"I should prefer to have a few policemen."

"But, Monsieur Sholmes, we have no choice. We must catch him when we can."

He was right; Sholmes knew it. It was better to take advantage of the opportunity and make the attempt. Sholmes simply gave this advice to Ganimard:

"Conceal your identity as long as possible."

Sholmes glided behind a newspaper kiosk, whence he could still watch Lupin, who was leaning toward Lady Cliveden, talking and smiling.

Ganimard crossed the street, hands in his pockets, as if he were going down the boulevard, but when he reached the opposite sidewalk he turned quickly and bounded up the steps of the restaurant. There was a shrill whistle. Ganimard ran against the head waiter, who had suddenly planted himself in the doorway and now pushed Ganimard back with a show of indignation, as if he were an intruder whose presence would bring disgrace upon the restaurant. Ganimard was surprised. At the same moment the gentleman in the frock coat came out. He took the part of the detective and entered into an exciting argument with the waiter; both of them hung on to Ganimard, one pushing him in, the other pushing him out in such a manner that, despite all his efforts and despite his furious protestations, the unfortunate detective soon found himself on the sidewalk.

The struggling men were surrounded by a crowd. Two policemen, attracted by the noise, tried to force their way through the crowd, but encountered a mysterious resistance and could make no headway through the opposing backs and pressing shoulders of the mob.

But suddenly, as if by magic, the crowd parted and the passage to the restaurant was clear. The head waiter, recognizing his mistake, was profuse in his apologies; the gentleman in the frock coat ceased his efforts on behalf of the detective, the crowd dispersed, the policemen passed on, and Ganimard hastened to the table at which the six guests were sitting. But now there were only five! He looked around.... The only exit was the door.

"The person who was sitting here!" he cried to the five astonished guests. "Where is he?"

"Monsieur Destro?"

"No; Arsène Lupin!"

A waiter approached and said:

"The gentleman went upstairs."

Ganimard rushed up in the hope of finding him. The upper floor of the restaurant contained private dining-rooms and had a private stairway leading to the boulevard.

"No use looking for him now," muttered Ganimard. "He is far away by this time."

He was not far away—two hundred yards at most—in the Madeleine-Bastille omnibus, which was rolling along very peacefully with its three horses across the Place de l'Opéra toward the Boulevard des Capucines. Two sturdy fellows were talking together on the platform. On the roof of the omnibus near the stairs an old fellow was sleeping; it was Herlock Sholmes.

With bobbing head, rocked by the movement of the vehicle, the Englishman said to himself:

"If Wilson could see me now, how proud he would be of his collaborator!... Bah! It was easy to foresee that the game was lost, as soon as the man whistled; nothing could be done but watch the exits and see that our man did not escape. Really, Lupin makes life exciting and interesting."

At the terminal point Herlock Sholmes, by leaning over, saw Arsène Lupin leaving the omnibus, and as he passed in front of the men who formed his bodyguard Sholmes heard him say: "A l'Etoile."

"A l'Etoile, exactly, a rendezvous. I shall be there," thought Sholmes. "I will follow the two men."

Lupin took an automobile; but the men walked the entire distance, followed by Sholmes. They stopped at a narrow house, No. 40 rue Chalgrin, and rang the bell. Sholmes took his position in the shadow of a doorway, whence he could watch the house in question. A man opened one of the windows of the ground floor and closed the shutters. But the shutters did not reach to the top of the window. The impost was clear.

At the end of ten minutes a gentleman rang at the same door and a few minutes later another man came. A short time afterward an automobile stopped in front of the house, bringing two passengers: Arsène Lupin and a lady concealed beneath a large cloak and a thick veil.

"The blonde Lady, no doubt," said Sholmes to himself, as the automobile drove away.

Herlock Sholmes now approached the house, climbed to the window-ledge and, by standing on tiptoe, he was able to see through the window above the shutters. What did he see?

Arsène Lupin, leaning against the mantel, was speaking with considerable animation. The others were grouped around him, listening to him attentively. Amongst them Sholmes easily recognized the gentleman in the frock coat and he thought one of the other men resembled the head-waiter of the restaurant. As to the blonde Lady, she was seated in an armchair with her back to the window.

"They are holding a consultation," thought Sholmes. "They are worried over the incident at the restaurant and are holding a council of war. Ah! what a master stroke it would be to capture all of them at one fell stroke!"

One of them, having moved toward the door, Sholmes leaped to the ground and concealed himself in the shadow. The gentleman in the frock coat and the head-waiter left the house. A moment later a light appeared at the windows of the first floor, but the shutters were closed immediately and the upper part of the house was dark as well as the lower.

"Lupin and the woman are on the ground floor; the two confederates live on the upper floor," said Sholmes.

Sholmes remained there the greater part of the night, fearing that if he went away Arsène Lupin might leave during his absence. At four o'clock, seeing two policemen at the end of the street, he approached them, explained the situation and left them to watch the house. He went to Ganimard's residence in the rue Pergolese and wakened him.

"I have him yet," said Sholmes.

"Arsène Lupin?"

"Yes."

"If you haven't got any better hold on him than you had a while ago, I might as well go back to bed. But we may as well go to the station-house."

They went to the police station in the rue Mesnil and from there to the residence of the commissary, Mon. Decointre. Then, accompanied by half a dozen policemen, they went to the rue Chalgrin.

"Anything new?" asked Sholmes, addressing the two policemen.

"Nothing."

It was just breaking day when, after taking necessary measures to prevent escape, the commissary rang the bell and commenced to question the concierge. The woman was greatly frightened at this early morning invasion, and she trembled as she replied that there were no tenants on the ground floor.

"What! not a tenant?" exclaimed Ganimard.

"No; but on the first floor there are two men named Leroux. They have furnished the apartment on the ground floor for some country relations."

"A gentleman and lady."

"Yes."

"Who came here last night."

"Perhaps ... but I don't know ... I was asleep. But I don't think so, for the key is here. They did not ask for it."

With that key the commissary opened the door of the ground-floor apartment. It comprised only two rooms and they were empty.

"Impossible!" exclaimed Sholmes. "I saw both of them in this room."

"I don't doubt your word," said the commissary; "but they are not here now."

"Let us go to the first floor. They must be there."

"The first floor is occupied by two men named Leroux."

"We will examine the Messieurs Leroux."

They all ascended the stairs and the commissary rang. At the second ring a man opened the door; he was in his shirt-sleeves. Sholmes recognized him as one of Lupin's bodyguard. The man assumed a furious air:

"What do you mean by making such a row at this hour of the morning ... waking people up...."

But he stopped suddenly, astounded.

"God forgive me!... really, gentlemen, I didn't notice who it was. Why, it is Monsieur Decointre!... and you, Monsieur Ganimard. What can I do for you!"

Ganimard burst into an uncontrollable fit of laughter, which caused him to bend double and turn black in the face.

"Ah! it is you, Leroux," he stammered. "Oh! this is too funny! Leroux, an accomplice of Arsène Lupin! Oh, I shall die! and your brother, Leroux, where is he?"

"Edmond!" called the man. "It is Ganimard, who has come to visit us."

Another man appeared and at sight of him Ganimard's mirth redoubled.

"Oh! oh! we had no idea of this! Ah! my friends, you are in a bad fix now. Who would have ever suspected it?"

Turning to Sholmes, Ganimard introduced the man:

"Victor Leroux, a detective from our office, one of the best men in the iron brigade ... Edmond Leroux, chief clerk in the anthropometric service."

V. AN ABDUCTION.

Herlock Sholmes said nothing. To protest? To accuse the two men? That would be useless. In the absence of evidence which he did not possess and had no time to seek, no one would believe him. Moreover, he was stifled with rage, but would not display his feelings before the triumphant Ganimard. So he bowed respectfully to the brothers Leroux, guardians of society, and retired.

In the vestibule he turned toward a low door which looked like the entrance to a cellar, and picked up a small red stone; it was a garnet. When he reached the street he turned and read on the front of the house this inscription: "Lucien Destange, architect, 1877."

The adjoining house, No. 42, bore the same inscription.

"Always the double passage—numbers 40 and 42 have a secret means of communication. Why didn't I think of that? I should have remained with the two policemen."

He met the policemen near the corner and said to them:

"Two people came out of house No. 42 during my absence, didn't they?"

"Yes; a gentleman and lady."

Ganimard approached. Sholmes took his arm, and as they walked down the street he said:

"Monsieur Ganimard, you have had a good laugh and will no doubt forgive me for the trouble I have caused you."

"Oh! there's no harm done; but it was a good joke."

"I admit that; but the best jokes have only a short life, and this one can't last much longer."

"I hope not."

"This is now the seventh day, and I can remain only three days more. Then I must return to London."

"Oh!"

"I wish to ask you to be in readiness, as I may call on you at any hour on Tuesday or Wednesday night."

"For an expedition of the same kind as we had to-night?"

"Yes, monsieur, the very same."

"With what result?"

"The capture of Arsène Lupin," replied Sholmes.

"Do you think so!"

"I swear it, on my honor, monsieur."

Sholmes bade Ganimard good-bye and went to the nearest hotel for a few hours' sleep; after which, refreshed and with renewed confidence in himself, he returned to the rue Chalgrin, slipped two louis into the hand of the concierge, assured himself that the brothers Leroux had gone out, learned that the house belonged to a Monsieur Harmingeat, and, provided with a candle, descended to the cellar through the low door near which he had found the garnet. At the bottom of the stairs he found another exactly like it.

"I am not mistaken," he thought; "this is the means of communication. Let me see if my skeleton-key will open the cellar reserved for the tenant of the ground floor. Yes; it will. Now, I will examine those cases of wine... oh! oh! here are some places where the dust has been cleared away ... and some footprints on the ground...."

A slight noise caused him to listen attentively. Quickly he pushed the door shut, blew out his candle and hid behind a pile of empty wine cases. After a few seconds he noticed that a portion of the wall swung on a pivot, the light of a lantern was thrown into the cellar, an arm appeared, then a man entered.

He was bent over, as if he were searching for something. He felt in the dust with his fingers and several times he threw something into a cardboard box that he carried in his left hand. Afterward he obliterated the traces of his footsteps, as well as the footprints left by Lupin and the blonde lady, and he was about to leave the cellar by the same way as he had entered, when he uttered a harsh cry and fell to the ground. Sholmes had leaped upon him. It was the work of a moment, and in the simplest manner in the world the man found himself stretched on the ground, bound and handcuffed. The Englishman leaned over him and said:

"Have you anything to say?... To tell what you know?"

The man replied by such an ironical smile that Sholmes realized the futility of questioning him. So he contented himself by exploring the pockets of his captive, but he found only a bunch of keys, a handkerchief and the small cardboard box which contained a dozen garnets similar to those which Sholmes had found.

Then what was he to do with the man? Wait until his friends came to his help and deliver all of them to the police? What good would that do? What advantage would that give him over Lupin?

He hesitated; but an examination of the box decided the question. The box bore this name and address: "Leonard, jeweler, rue de la Paix."

He resolved to abandon the man to his fate. He locked the cellar and left the house. At a branch postoffice he sent a telegram to Monsieur Destange, saying that he could not come that day. Then he went to see the jeweler and, handing him the garnets, said:

"Madame sent me with these stones. She wishes to have them reset."

Sholmes had struck the right key. The jeweler replied:

"Certainly; the lady telephoned to me. She said she would be here to-day."

Sholmes established himself on the sidewalk to wait for the lady, but it was five o'clock when he saw a heavily-veiled lady approach and enter the store. Through the window he saw her place on the counter a piece of antique jewelry set with garnets.

She went away almost immediately, walking quickly and passed through streets that were unknown to the Englishman. As it was now almost dark, he walked close behind her and followed her into a five-story house of double flats and, therefore, occupied by numerous tenants. At the second floor she stopped and entered. Two minutes later the Englishman commenced to try the keys on the bunch he had taken from the man in the rue Chalgrin. The fourth key fitted the lock.

Notwithstanding the darkness of the rooms, he perceived that they were absolutely empty, as if unoccupied, and the various doors were standing open so that he could see all the apartments. At the end of a corridor he perceived a ray of light and, by approaching on tiptoe and looking through the glass door, he saw the veiled lady who had removed her hat and dress and was now wearing a velvet dressing-gown. The discarded garments were lying on the only chair in the room and a lighted lamp stood on the mantel.

Then he saw her approach the fireplace and press what appeared to be the button of an electric bell. Immediately the panel to the right of the fireplace moved and slowly glided behind the adjoining panel, thus disclosing an opening large enough for a person to pass through. The lady disappeared through this opening, taking the lamp with her.

The operation was a very simple one. Sholmes adopted it and followed the lady. He found himself in total darkness and immediately he felt his face brushed by some soft articles. He lighted a match and found that he was in a very small room completely filled with cloaks and dresses suspended on hangers. He picked his way through until he reached a door that was draped with a portiere. He peeped through and, behold, the blonde lady was there, under his eyes, and almost within reach of his hand.

She extinguished the lamp and turned on the electric lights. Then for the first time Herlock Sholmes obtained a good look at her face. He was amazed. The woman, whom he had overtaken after so much trouble and after so many tricks and manoeuvres, was none other than Clotilde Destange.

Clotilde Destange, the assassin of the Baron d'Hautrec and the thief who stole the blue diamond! Clotilde Destange, the mysterious friend of Arsène Lupin! And the blonde lady!

"Yes, I am only a stupid ass," thought Herlock Sholmes at that moment. "Because Lupin's friend was a blonde and Clotilde is a brunette, I never dreamed that they were the same person. But how could the blonde lady remain a blonde after the murder of the baron and the theft of the diamond?"

Sholmes could see a portion of the room; it was a boudoir, furnished with the most delightful luxury and exquisite taste, and adorned with beautiful tapestries and costly ornaments. A mahogany couch, upholstered in silk, was located on the side of the room opposite the door at which Sholmes was standing. Clotilde was sitting on this couch, motionless, her face covered by her hands. Then he perceived that she was weeping. Great tears rolled down her pale cheeks and fell, drop by drop, on the velvet corsage. The tears came thick and fast, as if their source were inexhaustible.

A door silently opened behind her and Arsène Lupin entered. He looked at her for a long time without making his presence known; then he approached her, knelt at her feet, pressed her head to his breast, folded her in his arms, and his actions indicated an infinite measure of love and sympathy. For a time not a word was uttered, but her tears became less abundant.

"I was so anxious to make you happy," he murmured.

"I am happy."

"No; you are crying.... Your tears break my heart, Clotilde."

The caressing and sympathetic tone of his voice soothed her, and she listened to him with an eager desire for hope and happiness. Her features were softened by a smile, and yet how sad a smile! He continued to speak in a tone of tender entreaty:

"You should not be unhappy, Clotilde; you have no cause to be."

She displayed her delicate white hands and said, solemnly:

"Yes, Maxime; so long as I see those hands I shall be sad."

"Why?"

"They are stained with blood."

"Hush! Do not think of that!" exclaimed Lupin. "The dead is past and gone. Do not resurrect it."

And he kissed the long, delicate hand, while she regarded him with a brighter smile as if each kiss effaced a portion of that dreadful memory.

"You must love me, Maxime; you must—because no woman will ever love you as I do. For your sake, I have done many things, not at your order or request, but in obedience to your secret desires. I have done things at which my will and conscience revolted, but there was some unknown power that I could not resist. What I did I did involuntarily, mechanically, because it helped you, because you wished it ... and I am ready to do it again to-morrow ... and always."

"Ah, Clotilde," he said, bitterly, "why did I draw you into my adventurous life? I should have remained the Maxime Bermond that you loved five years ago, and not have let you know the ... other man that I am."

She replied in a low voice:

"I love the other man, also, and I have nothing to regret."

"Yes, you regret your past life—the free and happy life you once enjoyed."

"I have no regrets when you are here," she said, passionately. "All faults and crimes disappear when I see you. When you are away I may suffer, and weep, and be horrified at what I have done; but when you come it is all forgotten. Your love wipes it all away. And I am happy again.... But you must love me!"

"I do not love you on compulsion, Clotilde. I love you simply because ... I love you."

"Are you sure of it?"

"I am just as sure of my own love as I am of yours. Only my life is a very active and exciting one, and I cannot spend as much time with you as I would like—just now."

"What is it? Some new danger? Tell me!"

"Oh! nothing serious. Only...."

"Only what?" she asked.

"Well, he is on our track."

"Who? Herlock Sholmes?"

"Yes; it was he who dragged Ganimard into that affair at the Hungarian restaurant. It was he who instructed the two policemen to watch the house in the rue Chalgrin. I have proof of it. Ganimard searched the house this morning and Sholmes was with him. Besides——"

"Besides? What?"

"Well, there is another thing. One of our men is missing."

"Who?"

"Jeanniot."

"The concierge?"

"Yes."

"Why, I sent him to the rue Chalgrin this morning to pick up the garnets that fell out of my brooch."

"There is no doubt, then, that Sholmes caught him."

"No; the garnets were delivered to the jeweler in the rue de la Paix."

"Then, what has become of him!"

"Oh! Maxime, I am afraid."

"There is nothing to be afraid of, but I confess the situation is very serious. What does he know? Where does he hide himself? His isolation is his strong card. I cannot reach him."

"What are you going to do?"

"Act with extreme prudence, Clotilde. Some time ago I decided to change my residence to a safer place, and Sholmes' appearance on the scene has prompted me to do so at once. When a man like that is on your track, you must be prepared for the worst. Well, I am making my preparations. Day after to-morrow, Wednesday, I shall move. At noon it will be finished. At two o'clock I shall leave the place, after removing the last trace of our residence there, which will be no small matter. Until then——"

"Well?"

"Until then we must not see each other and no one must see you, Clotilde. Do not go out. I have no fear for myself, but I have for you."

"That Englishman cannot possibly reach me."

"I am not so sure of that. He is a dangerous man. Yesterday I came here to search the cupboard that contains all of Monsieur Destange's old papers and records. There is danger there. There is danger everywhere. I feel that he is watching us—that he is drawing his net around us closer and closer. It is one of those intuitions which never deceive me."

"In that case, Maxime, go, and think no more of my tears. I shall be brave, and wait patiently until the danger is past. Adieu, Maxime."

They held one another for some time in a last fond embrace. And it was she that gently pushed him outside. Sholmes could hear the sound of their voices in the distance.

Emboldened by the necessities of the situation and the urgent need of bringing his investigation to a speedy termination, Sholmes proceeded to make an examination of the house in which he now found himself. He passed through Clotilde's boudoir into a corridor, at the end of which there was a stairway leading to the lower floor; he was about to descend this stairway when he heard voices below, which caused him to change his route. He followed the corridor, which was a circular one, and discovered another stairway, which he descended and found himself amidst surroundings that bore a familiar appearance. He passed through a door that stood partly open and entered a large circular room. It was Monsieur Destange's library.

"Ah! splendid!" he exclaimed. "Now I understand everything. The boudoir of Mademoiselle Clotilde—the blonde Lady—communicates with a room in the adjoining house, and that house does not front on the Place Malesherbes, but upon an adjacent street, the rue Montchanin, if I remember the name correctly.... And I now understand how Clotilde Destange can meet her lover and at the same time create the impression that she never leaves the house; and I understand also how Arsène Lupin was enabled to make his mysterious entrance to the gallery last night. Ah! there must be another connection between the library and the adjoining room. One more house full of ways that are dark! And no doubt Lucien Destange was the architect, as usual!... I should take advantage of this opportunity to examine the contents of the cupboard and perhaps learn the location of other houses with secret passages constructed by Monsieur Destange."

Sholmes ascended to the gallery and concealed himself behind some draperies, where he remained until late in the evening. At last a servant came and turned off the electric lights. An hour later the Englishman, by the light of his lantern, made his way to the cupboard. As he had surmised, it contained the architect's old papers, plans, specifications and books of account. It also contained a series of registers, arranged according to date, and Sholmes, having selected those of the most recent dates, searched in the indexes for the name "Harmingeat." He found it in one of the registers with a reference to page 63. Turning to that page, he read:

"Harmingeat, 40 rue Chalgrin."

This was followed by a detailed account of the work done in and about the installation of a furnace in the house. And in the margin of the book someone had written these words: "See account M.B."

"Ah! I thought so!" said Sholmes; "the account M.B. is the one I want. I shall learn from it the actual residence of Monsieur Lupin."

It was morning before he found that important account. It comprised sixteen pages, one of which was a copy of the page on which was described the work done for Mon. Harmingeat of the rue Chalgrin. Another page described the work performed for Mon. Vatinel as owner of the house at No. 25 rue Clapeyron. Another page was reserved for the Baron d'Hautrec, 134 avenue Henri-Martin; another was devoted to the Château de Crozon, and the eleven other pages to various owners of houses in Paris.

Sholmes made a list of those eleven names and addresses; after which he returned the books to their proper places, opened a window, jumped out onto the deserted street and closed the shutters behind him.

When he reached his room at the hotel he lighted his pipe with all the solemnity with which he was wont to characterize that act, and amidst clouds of smoke he studied the deductions that might be drawn from the account of M.B., or rather, from the account of Maxime Bermond alias Arsène Lupin.

At eight o'clock he sent the following message to Ganimard:

"I expect to pass through the rue Pergolese this forenoon and will inform you of a person whose arrest is of the highest importance. In any event, be at home to-night and to-morrow until noon and have at least thirty men at your service."

Then he engaged an automobile at the stand on the boulevard, choosing one whose chauffeur looked good-natured but dull-witted, and instructed him to drive to the Place Malesherbes, where he stopped him about one hundred feet from Monsieur Destange's house.

"My boy, close your carriage," he said to the chauffeur; "turn up the collar of your coat, for the wind is cold, and wait patiently. At the end of an hour and a half, crank up your machine. When I return we will go to the rue Pergolese."

As he was ascending the steps leading to the door a doubt entered his mind. Was it not a mistake on his part to be spending his time on the affairs of the blonde Lady, while Arsène Lupin was preparing to move? Would he not be better engaged in trying to find the abode of his adversary amongst the eleven houses on his list?

"Ah!" he exclaimed, "when the blonde Lady becomes my prisoner, I shall be master of the situation."

And he rang the bell.

Monsieur Destange was already in the library. They had been working only a few minutes, when Clotilde entered, bade her father good morning, entered the adjoining parlor and sat down to write. From his place Sholmes could see her leaning over the table and from time to time absorbed in deep meditation. After a short time he picked up a book and said to Monsieur Destange:

"Here is a book that Mademoiselle Destange asked me to bring to her when I found it."

He went into the little parlor, stood before Clotilde in such a manner that her father could not see her, and said:

"I am Monsieur Stickmann, your father's new secretary."

"Ah!" said Clotilde, without moving, "my father has changed his secretary? I didn't know it."

"Yes, mademoiselle, and I desire to speak with you."

"Kindly take a seat, monsieur; I have finished."

She added a few words to her letter, signed it, enclosed it in the envelope, sealed it, pushed her writing material away, rang the telephone, got in communication with her dressmaker, asked the latter to hasten the completion of a traveling dress, as she required it at once, and then, turning to Sholmes, she said:

"I am at your service, monsieur. But do you wish to speak before my father? Would not that be better?"

"No, mademoiselle; and I beg of you, do not raise your voice. It is better that Monsieur Destange should not hear us."

"For whose sake is it better?"

"Yours, mademoiselle."

"I cannot agree to hold any conversation with you that my father may not hear."

"But you must agree to this. It is imperative."

Both of them arose, eye to eye. She said:

"Speak, monsieur."

Still standing, he commenced:

"You will be so good as to pardon me if I am mistaken on certain points of secondary importance. I will guarantee, however, the general accuracy of my statements."

"Can we not dispense with these preliminaries, monsieur? Or are they necessary?"

Sholmes felt the young woman was on her guard, so he replied:

"Very well; I will come to the point. Five years ago your father made the acquaintance of a certain young man called Maxime Bermond, who was introduced as a contractor or an architect, I am not sure which it was; but it was one or the other. Monsieur Destange took a liking to the young man, and as the state of his health compelled him to retire from active business, he entrusted to Monsieur Bermond the execution of certain orders he had received from some of his old customers and which seemed to come within the scope of Monsieur Bermond's ability."

Herlock Sholmes stopped. It seemed to him that the girl's pallor had increased. Yet there was not the slightest tremor in her voice when she said:

"I know nothing about the circumstances to which you refer, monsieur, and I do not see in what way they can interest me."

"In this way, mademoiselle: You know, as well as I, that Maxime Bermond is also known by the name of Arsène Lupin."

She laughed, and said:

"Nonsense! Arsène Lupin? Maxime Bermond is Arsène Lupin? Oh! no! It isn't possible!"

"I have the honor to inform you of that fact, and since you refuse to understand my meaning, I will add that Arsène Lupin has found in this house a friend—more than a friend—and accomplice, blindly and passionately devoted to him."

Without emotion, or at least with so little emotion that Sholmes was astonished at her self-control, she declared:

"I do not understand your object, monsieur, and I do not care to; but I command you to say no more and leave this house."

"I have no intention of forcing my presence on you," replied Sholmes, with equal sang-froid, "but I shall not leave this house alone."

"And who will accompany you, monsieur?"

"You will."

"I?"

"Yes, mademoiselle, we will leave this house together, and you will follow me without one word of protest."

The strange feature of the foregoing interview was the absolute coolness of the two adversaries. It bore no resemblance to an implacable duel between two powerful wills; but, judging solely from their attitude and the tone of their voices, an onlooker would have supposed their conversation to be nothing more serious than a courteous argument over some impersonal subject.

Clotilde resumed her seat without deigning to reply to the last remark of Herlock Sholmes, except by a shrug of her shoulders. Sholmes looked at his watch and said:

"It is half-past ten. We will leave here in five minutes."

"Perhaps."

"If not, I shall go to Monsieur Destange, and tell him——"

"What?"

"The truth. I will tell him of the vicious life of Maxime Bermond, and I will tell him of the double life of his accomplice."

"Of his accomplice?"

"Yes, of the woman known as the blonde Lady, of the woman who was blonde."

"What proofs will you give him?"

"I will take him to the rue Chalgrin, and show him the secret passage made by Arsène Lupin's workmen,—while doing the work of which he had the control—between the houses numbered 40 and 42; the passage which you and he used two nights ago."

"Well?"

"I will then take Monsieur Destange to the house of Monsieur Detinan; we will descend the servant's stairway which was used by you and Arsène Lupin when you escaped from Ganimard, and we will search together the means of communication with the adjoining house, which fronts on the Boulevard des Batignolles, and not upon the rue Clapeyron."

"Well?"

"I will take Monsieur Destange to the château de Crozon, and it will be easy for him, who knows the nature of the work performed by Arsène Lupin in the restoration of the Château, to discover the secret passages constructed there by his workmen. It will thus be established that those passages allowed the blonde Lady to make a nocturnal visit to the Countess' room and take the blue diamond from the mantel; and, two weeks later, by similar means, to enter the room of Herr Bleichen and conceal the blue diamond in his tooth-powder—a strange action, I confess; a woman's revenge, perhaps; but I don't know, and I don't care."

"Well?"

"After that," said Herlock Sholmes, in a more serious tone, "I will take Monsieur Destange to 134 avenue Henri-Martin, and we will learn how the Baron d'Hautrec———"

"No, no, keep quiet," stammered the girl, struck with a sudden terror, "I forbid you!... you dare to say that it was I ... you accuse me?..."

"I accuse you of having killed the Baron d'Hautrec."

"No, no, it is a lie."

"You killed the Baron d'Hautrec, mademoiselle. You entered his service under the name of Antoinette Bréhat, for the purpose of stealing the blue diamond and you killed him."

"Keep quiet, monsieur," she implored him. "Since you know so much, you must know that I did not murder the baron."

"I did not say that you murdered him, mademoiselle. Baron d'Hautrec was subject to fits of insanity that only Sister Auguste could control. She told me so herself. In her absence, he must have attacked you, and in the course of the struggle you struck him in order to save your own life. Frightened at your awful situation, you rang the bell, and fled without even taking the blue diamond from the finger of your victim. A few minutes later you returned with one of Arsène Lupin's accomplices, who was a servant in the adjoining house, you placed the baron on the bed, you put the room in order, but you were afraid to take the blue diamond. Now, I have told you what happened on that night. I repeat, you did not murder the baron, and yet it was your hand that struck the blow."

She had crossed them over her forehead—those long delicate white hands—and kept them thus for a long time. At last, loosening her fingers, she said, in a voice rent by anguish:

"And do you intend to tell all that to my father?"

"Yes; and I will tell him that I have secured as witnesses: Mademoiselle Gerbois, who will recognize the blonde Lady; Sister Auguste, who will recognize Antoinette Bréhat; and the Countess de Crozon, who will recognize Madame de Réal. That is what I shall tell him."

"You will not dare," she said, recovering her self-possession in the face of an immediate peril.

He arose, and made a step toward the library. Clotilde stopped him:

"One moment, monsieur."

She paused, reflected a moment, and then, perfect mistress of herself, said:

"You are Herlock Sholmes?"

"Yes."

"What do you want of me?"

"What do I want? I am fighting a duel with Arsène Lupin, and I must win. The contest is now drawing to a climax, and I have an idea that a hostage as precious as you will give me an important advantage over my adversary. Therefore, you will follow me, mademoiselle; I will entrust you to one of my friends. As soon as the duel is ended, you will be set at liberty."

"Is that all?"

"That is all. I do not belong to the police service of this country, and, consequently, I do not consider that I am under any obligation ... to cause your arrest."

She appeared to have come to a decision ... yet she required a momentary respite. She closed her eyes, the better to concentrate her thoughts. Sholmes looked at her in surprise; she was now so tranquil and, apparently, indifferent to the dangers which threatened her. Sholmes thought: Does she believe that she is in danger? Probably not—since Lupin protects her. She has confidence in him. She believes that Lupin is omnipotent, and infallible.

"Mademoiselle," he said, "I told you that we would leave here in five minutes. That time has almost expired."

"Will you permit me to go to my room, monsieur, to get some necessary articles?"

"Certainly, mademoiselle; and I will wait for you in the rue Montchanin. Jeanniot, the concierge, is a friend of mine."

"Ah! you know...." she said, visibly alarmed.

"I know many things."

"Very well. I will ring for the maid."

The maid brought her hat and jacket. Then Sholmes said:

"You must give Monsieur Destange some reason for our departure, and, if possible, let your excuse serve for an absence of several days."

"That shall not be necessary. I shall be back very soon."

"They exchanged defiant glances and an ironic smile.

"What faith you have in him!" said Sholmes.

"Absolute."

"He does everything well, doesn't he? He succeeds in everything he undertakes. And whatever he does receives your approval and cooperation."

"I love him," she said, with a touch of passion in her voice.

"And you think that he will save you?"

She shrugged her shoulders, and, approaching her father, she said:

"I am going to deprive you of Monsieur Stickmann. We are going to the National Library."

"You will return for luncheon?"

"Perhaps ... no, I think not ... but don't be uneasy."

Then she said to Sholmes, in a firm voice:

"I am at your service, monsieur."

"Absolutely?"

"Quite so."

"I warn you that if you attempt to escape, I shall call the police and have you arrested. Do not forget that the blonde Lady is on parole."

"I give you my word of honor that I shall not attempt to escape."

"I believe you. Now, let us go."

They left the house together, as he had predicted.

The automobile was standing where Sholmes had left it. As they approached it, Sholmes could hear the rumbling of the motor. He opened the door, asked Clotilde to enter, and took a seat beside her. The machine started at once, gained the exterior boulevards, the avenue Hoche and the avenue de la Grande-Armée. Sholmes was considering his plans. He thought:

"Ganimard is at home. I will leave the girl in his care. Shall I tell him who she is? No, he would take her to prison at once, and that would spoil everything. When I am alone, I can consult my list of addresses taken from the 'account M.B.,' and run them down. To-night, or to-morrow morning at the latest, I shall go to Ganimard, as I agreed, and deliver into his hands Arsène Lupin and all his band."

He rubbed his hand, gleefully, at the thought that his duel with Lupin was drawing to a close, and he could not see any serious obstacle in the way of his success. And, yielding to an irrepressible desire to give vent to his feelings—an unusual desire on his part—he exclaimed:

"Excuse me, mademoiselle, if I am unable to conceal my satisfaction and delight. The battle has been a difficult one, and my success is, therefore, more enjoyable."

"A legitimate success, monsieur, of which you have a just right to be proud."

"Thank you. But where are we going? The chauffeur must have misunderstood my directions."

At that moment they were leaving Paris by the gate de Neuilly. That was strange, as the rue Pergolese is not outside the fortifications. Sholmes lowered the glass, and said:

"Chauffeur, you have made a mistake.... Rue Pergolese!"

The man made no reply. Sholmes repeated, in a louder voice:

"I told you to go to the rue Pergolese."

Still the man did not reply.

"Ah! but you are deaf, my friend. Or is he doing it on purpose? We are very much out of our way.... Rue Pergolese!... Turn back at once!... Rue Pergolese!"

The chauffeur made no sign of having heard the order. The Englishman fretted with impatience. He looked at Clotilde; a mysterious smile played upon her lips.

"Why do you laugh?" he said. "It is an awkward mistake, but it won't help you."

"Of course not," she replied.

Then an idea occurred to him. He rose and made a careful scrutiny of the chauffeur. His shoulders were not so broad; his bearing was not so stiff and mechanical. A cold perspiration covered his forehead and his hands clenched with sudden fear, as his mind was seized with the conviction that the chauffeur was Arsène Lupin.

"Well, Monsieur Sholmes, what do you think of our little ride?"

"Delightful, monsieur, really delightful," replied Sholmes.

Never in his life had he experienced so much difficulty in uttering a few simple words without a tremor, or without betraying his feelings in his voice. But quickly, by a sort of reaction, a flood of hatred and rage burst its bounds, overcame his self-control, and, brusquely drawing his revolver, he pointed it at Mademoiselle Destange.

"Lupin, stop, this minute, this second, or I fire at mademoiselle."

"I advise you to aim at the cheek if you wish to hit the temple," replied Lupin, without turning his head.

"Maxime, don't go so fast," said Clotilde, "the pavement is slippery and I am very timid."

She was smiling; her eyes were fixed on the pavement, over which the carriage was traveling at enormous speed.

"Let him stop! Let him stop!" said Sholmes to her, wild with rage, "I warn you that I am desperate."

The barrel of the revolver brushed the waving locks of her hair. She replied, calmly:

"Maxime is so imprudent. He is going so fast, I am really afraid of some accident."

Sholmes returned the weapon to his pocket and seized the handle of the door, as if to alight, despite the absurdity of such an act. Clotilde said to him:

"Be careful, monsieur, there is an automobile behind us."

He leaned over. There was an automobile close behind; a large machine of formidable aspect with its sharp prow and blood-red body, and holding four men clad in fur coats.

"Ah! I am well guarded," thought Sholmes. "I may as well be patient."

He folded his arms across his chest with that proud air of submission so frequently assumed by heroes when fate has turned against them. And while they crossed the river Seine and rushed through Suresnes, Rueil and Chatou, motionless and resigned, controlling his actions and his passions, he tried to explain to his own satisfaction by what miracle Arsène Lupin had substituted himself for the chauffeur. It was quite improbable that the honest-looking fellow he had selected on the boulevard that morning was an accomplice placed there in advance. And yet Arsène Lupin had received a warning in some way, and it must have been after he, Sholmes, had approached Clotilde in the house, because no one could have suspected his project prior to that time. Since then, Sholmes had not allowed Clotilde out of his sight.

Then an idea struck him: the telephone communication desired by Clotilde and her conversation with the dressmaker. Now, it was all quite clear to him. Even before he had spoken to her, simply upon his request to speak to her as the new secretary of Monsieur Destange, she had scented the danger, surmised the name and purpose of the visitor, and, calmly, naturally, as if she were performing a commonplace action of her every-day life, she had called Arsène Lupin to her assistance by some preconcerted signal.

How Arsène Lupin had come and caused himself to be substituted for the chauffeur were matters of trifling importance. That which affected Sholmes, even to the point of appeasing his fury, was the recollection of that incident whereby an ordinary woman, a sweetheart it is true, mastering her nerves, controlling her features, and subjugating the expression of her eyes, had completely deceived the astute detective Herlock Sholmes. How difficult to overcome an adversary who is aided by such confederates, and who, by the mere force of his authority, inspires in a woman so much courage and strength!

They crossed the Seine and climbed the hill at Saint-Germain; but, some five hundred metres beyond that town, the automobile slackened its speed. The other automobile advanced, and the two stopped, side by side. There was no one else in the neighborhood.

"Monsieur Sholmes," said Lupin, "kindly exchange to the other machine. Ours is really a very slow one."

"Indeed!" said Sholmes, calmly, convinced that he had no choice.

"Also, permit me to loan you a fur coat, as we will travel quite fast and the air is cool. And accept a couple of sandwiches, as we cannot tell when we will dine."

The four men alighted from the other automobile. One of them approached, and, as he raised his goggles, Sholmes recognized in him the gentleman in the frock coat that he had seen at the Hungarian restaurant. Lupin said to him:

"You will return this machine to the chauffeur from whom I hired it. He is waiting in the first wine-shop to the right as you go up the rue Legendre. You will give him the balance of the thousand francs I promised him.... Ah! yes, kindly give your goggles to Monsieur Sholmes."

He talked to Mlle. Destange for a moment, then took his place at the wheel and started, with Sholmes at his side and one of his men behind him. Lupin had not exaggerated when he said "we will travel quite fast." From the beginning he set a breakneck pace. The horizon rushed to meet them, as if attracted by some mysterious force, and disappeared instantly as though swallowed up in an abyss, into which many other things, such as trees, houses, fields and forests, were hurled with the tumultuous fury and haste of a torrent as it approached the cataract.

Sholmes and Lupin did not exchange a word. Above their heads the leaves of the poplars made a great noise like the waves of the sea, rhythmically arranged by the regular spacing of the trees. And the towns swept by like spectres: Manteo, Vernon, Gaillon. From one hill to the other, from Bon-Secours to Canteleu, Rouen, its suburbs, its harbor, its miles of wharves, Rouen seemed like the straggling street of a country village. And this was Duclair, Caudebec, the country of Caux which they skimmed over in their terrific flight, and Lillebonne, and Quillebeuf. Then, suddenly, they found themselves on the banks of the Seine, at the extremity of a little wharf, beside which lay a staunch sea-going yacht that emitted great volumes of black smoke from its funnel.

The automobile stopped. In two hours they had traveled over forty leagues.

A man, wearing a blue uniform and a goldlaced cap, came forward and saluted. Lupin said to him:

"All ready, captain? Did you receive my telegram?"

"Yes, I got it."

"Is *The Swallow* ready?"

"Yes, monsieur."

"Come, Monsieur Sholmes."

The Englishman looked around, saw a group of people on the terrace in front of a café, hesitated a moment, then, realizing that before he could secure any assistance he would be seized, carried aboard and placed in the bottom of the hold, he crossed the gang-plank and followed Lupin into the captain's cabin. It was quite a large room, scrupulously clean, and presented a cheerful appearance with its varnished woodwork and polished brass. Lupin closed the door and addressed Sholmes abruptly, and almost rudely, as he said:

"Well, what do you know?"

"Everything."

"Everything? Come, be precise."

His voice contained no longer that polite, if ironical, tone, which he had affected when speaking to the Englishman. Now, his voice had the imperious tone of a master accustomed to command and accustomed to be obeyed—even by a Herlock Sholmes. They measured each other by their looks, enemies now—open and implacable foes. Lupin spoke again, but in a milder tone:

"I have grown weary of your pursuit, and do not intend to waste any more time in avoiding the traps you lay for me. I warn you that my treatment of you will depend on your reply. Now, what do you know?"

"Everything, monsieur."

Arsène Lupin controlled his temper and said, in a jerky manner:

"I will tell you what you know. You know that, under the name of Maxime Bermond, I have ... *improved* fifteen houses that were originally constructed by Monsieur Destange."

"Yes."

"Of those fifteen houses, you have seen four."

"Yes."

"And you have a list of the other eleven."

"Yes."

"You made that list at Monsieur Destange's house on that night, no doubt."

"Yes."

"And you have an idea that, amongst those eleven houses, there is one that I have kept for the use of myself and my friends, and you have intrusted to Ganimard the task of finding my retreat."

"No."

"What does that signify?"

"It signifies that I choose to act alone, and do not want his help."

"Then I have nothing to fear, since you are in my hands."

"You have nothing to fear as long as I remain in your hands."

"You mean that you will not remain?"

"Yes."

Arsène Lupin approached the Englishman and, placing his hand on the latter's shoulder, said:

"Listen, monsieur; I am not in a humor to argue with you, and, unfortunately for you, you are not in a position to choose. So let us finish our business."

"Very well."

"You are going to give me your word of honor that you will not try to escape from this boat until you arrive in English waters."

"I give you my word of honor that I shall escape if I have an opportunity," replied the indomitable Sholmes.

"But, sapristi! you know quite well that at a word from me you would soon be rendered helpless. All these men will obey me blindly. At a sign from me they would place you in irons———"

"Irons can be broken."

"And throw you overboard ten miles from shore."

"I can swim."

"I hadn't thought of that," said Lupin, with a laugh. "Excuse me, master ... and let us finish. You will agree that I must take the measures necessary to protect myself and my friends."

"Certainly; but they will be useless."

"And yet you do not wish me to take them."

"It is your duty."

"Very well, then."

Lupin opened the door and called the captain and two sailors. The latter seized the Englishman, bound him hand and foot, and tied him to the captain's bunk.

"That will do," said Lupin. "It was only on account of your obstinacy and the unusual gravity of the situation, that I ventured to offer you this indignity."

The sailors retired. Lupin said to the captain:

"Let one of the crew remain here to look after Monsieur Sholmes, and you can give him as much of your own company as possible. Treat him with all due respect and consideration. He is not a prisoner, but a guest. What time have you, captain?"

"Five minutes after two."

Lupin consulted his watch, then looked at the clock that was attached to the wall of the cabin.

"Five minutes past two is right. How long will it take you to reach Southampton?"

"Nine hours, easy going."

"Make it eleven. You must not land there until after the departure of the midnight boat, which reaches Havre at eight o'clock in the morning. Do you understand, captain? Let me repeat: As it would be very dangerous for all of us to permit Monsieur to return to France by that boat, you must not reach Southampton before one o'clock in the morning."

"I understand."

"Au revoir, master; next year, in this world or in the next."

"Until to-morrow," replied Sholmes.

A few minutes later Sholmes heard the automobile going away, and at the same time the steam puffed violently in the depths of *The Swallow*. The boat had started for England. About three o'clock the vessel left the mouth of the river and plunged into the open sea. At that moment Sholmes was lying on the captain's bunk, sound asleep.

Next morning—it being the tenth and last day of the duel between Sholmes and Lupin—the *Echo de France* published this interesting bit of news:

"Yesterday a judgment of ejectment was entered in the case of Arsène Lupin against Herlock Sholmes, the English detective. Although signed at noon, the judgment was executed the same day. At one o'clock this morning Sholmes was landed at Southampton."

VI. SECOND ARREST OF ARSÈNE LUPIN.

Since eight o'clock a dozen moving-vans had encumbered the rue Crevaux between the avenue du Bois-de-Boulogne and the avenue Bugeaud. Mon. Felix Davey was leaving the apartment in which he lived on the fourth floor of No. 8; and Mon. Dubreuil, who had united into a single apartment the fifth floor of the same house and the fifth floor of the two adjoining houses, was moving on the same day—a mere coincidence, since the gentlemen were unknown to each other—the vast collection of furniture regarding which so many foreign agents visited him every day.

A circumstance which had been noticed by some of the neighbors, but was not spoken of until later, was this: None of the twelve vans bore the name and address of the owner, and none of the men accompanying them visited the neighboring wine shops. They worked so diligently that the furniture was all out by eleven o'clock. Nothing remained but those scraps of papers and rags that are always left behind in the corners of the empty rooms.

Mon. Felix Davey, an elegant young man, dressed in the latest fashion, carried in his hand a walking-stick, the weight of which indicated that its owner possessed extraordinary biceps—Mon. Felix Davey walked calmly away and took a seat on a bench in the avenue du Bois-de-Boulogne facing the rue Pergolese. Close to him a woman, dressed in a neat but inexpensive costume, was reading a newspaper, whilst a child was playing with a shovel in a heap of sand.

After a few minutes Felix Davey spoke to the woman, without turning his head:

"Ganimard!"

"Went out at nine o'clock this morning."

"Where?"

"To police headquarters."

"Alone?"

"Yes."

"No telegram during the night?"

"No."

"Do they suspect you in the house?"

"No; I do some little things for Madame Ganimard, and she tells me everything her husband does. I have been with her all morning."

"Very well. Until further orders come here every day at eleven o'clock."

He rose and walked away in the direction of the Dauphine gate, stopping at the Chinese pavilion, where he partook of a frugal repast consisting of two eggs, with some fruit and vegetables. Then he returned to the rue Crevaux and said to the concierge:

"I will just glance through the rooms and then give you the keys."

He finished his inspection of the room that he had used as a library; then he seized the end of a gas-pipe, which hung down the side of the chimney. The pipe was bent and a hole made in the elbow. To this hole he fitted a small instrument in the form of an ear-trumpet and blew into it. A slight whistling sound came by way of reply. Placing the trumpet to his mouth, he said:

"Anyone around, Dubreuil?"

"No."

"May I come up!"

"Yes."

He returned the pipe to its place, saying to himself:

"How progressive we are! Our century abounds with little inventions which render life really charming and picturesque. And so amusing!... especially when a person knows how to enjoy life as I do."

He turned one of the marble mouldings of the mantel, and the entire half of the mantel moved, and the mirror above it glided in invisible grooves, disclosing an opening and the lower steps of a stairs built in the very body of the chimney; all very clean and complete—the stairs were constructed of polished metal and the walls of white tiles. He ascended the steps, and at the fifth floor there was the same opening in the chimney. Mon. Dubreuil was waiting for him.

"Have you finished in your rooms?"

"Yes."

"Everything cleared out?"

"Yes."

"And the people?"

"Only the three men on guard."

"Very well; come on."

They ascended to the upper floor by the same means, one after the other, and there found three men, one of whom was looking through the window.

"Anything new?"

"Nothing, governor."

"All quiet in the street?"

"Yes."

"In ten minutes I will be ready to leave. You will go also. But in the meantime if you see the least suspicious movement in the street, warn me."

"I have my finger on the alarm-bell all the time."

"Dubreuil, did you tell the moving men not to touch the wire of that bell?"

"Certainly; it is working all right."

"That is all I want to know."

The two gentlemen then descended to the apartment of Felix Davey and the latter, after adjusting the marble mantel, exclaimed, joyfully:

"Dubreuil, I should like to see the man who is able to discover all the ingenious devices, warning bells, net-works of electric wires and acoustic tubes, invisible passages, moving floors and hidden stairways. A real fairy-land!"

"What fame for Arsène Lupin!"

"Fame I could well dispense with. It's a pity to be compelled to leave a place so well equipped, and commence all over again, Dubreuil ... and on a new model, of course, for it would never do to duplicate this. Curse Herlock Sholmes!"

"Has he returned to Paris?"

"How could he? There has been only one boat come from Southampton and it left there at midnight; only one train from Havre, leaving there at eight o'clock this morning and due in Paris at eleven fifteen. As he could not catch the midnight boat at Southampton—and the instructions to the captain on that point were explicit—he cannot reach France until this evening via Newhaven and Dieppe."

"Do you think he will come back?"

"Yes; he never gives up. He will return to Paris; but it will be too late. We will be far away."

"And Mademoiselle Destange?"

"I am to see her in an hour."

"At her house?"

"Oh! no; she will not return there for several days. But you, Dubreuil, you must hurry. The loading of our goods will take a long time and you should be there to look after them."

"Are you sure that we are not being watched?"

"By whom? I am not afraid of anyone but Sholmes."

Dubreuil retired. Felix Davey made a last tour of the apartment, picked up two or three torn letters, then, noticing a piece of chalk, he took it and, on the dark paper of the drawing-room, drew a large frame and wrote within it the following:

"*Arsène Lupin, gentleman-burglar, lived here for five years at the beginning of the twentieth century.*"

This little pleasantry seemed to please him very much. He looked at it for a moment, whistling a lively air, then said to himself:

"Now that I have placed myself in touch with the historians of future generations, I can go. You must hurry, Herlock Sholmes, as I shall leave my present abode in three minutes, and your defeat will be an accomplished fact.... Two minutes more! you are keeping me waiting, Monsieur Sholmes.... One minute more! Are you not coming? Well, then, I proclaim your downfall and my apotheosis. And now I make my escape. Farewell, kingdom of Arsène Lupin! I shall never see you again. Farewell to the fifty-five rooms of the six apartments over which I reigned! Farewell, my own royal bed chamber!"

His outburst of joy was interrupted by the sharp ringing of a bell, which stopped twice, started again and then ceased. It was the alarm bell.

What was wrong? What unforeseen danger? Ganimard? No; that wasn't possible!

He was on the point of returning to his library and making his escape. But, first, he went to the window. There was no one in the street. Was the enemy already in the house? He listened and thought he could discern certain confused sounds. He hesitated no longer. He ran to his library, and as he crossed the threshold he heard the noise of a key being inserted in the lock of the vestibule door.

"The deuce!" he murmured; "I have no time to lose. The house may be surrounded. The servants' stairway—impossible! Fortunately, there is the chimney."

He pushed the moulding; it did not move. He made a greater effort—still it refused to move. At the same time he had the impression that the door below opened and that he could hear footsteps.

"Good God!" he cried; "I am lost if this cursed mechanism—"

He pushed with all his strength. Nothing moved—nothing! By some incredible accident, by some evil stroke of fortune, the mechanism, which had worked only a few moments ago, would not work now.

He was furious. The block of marble remained immovable. He uttered frightful imprecations on the senseless stone. Was his escape to be prevented by that stupid obstacle? He struck the marble wildly, madly; he hammered it, he cursed it.

"Ah! what's the matter, Monsieur Lupin? You seem to be displeased about something."

Lupin turned around. Herlock Sholmes stood before him!

Herlock Sholmes!... Lupin gazed at him with squinting eyes as if his sight were defective and misleading. Herlock Sholmes in Paris! Herlock Sholmes, whom he had shipped to England only the day before as a dangerous person, now stood before him free and victorious!... Ah! such a thing was nothing less than a miracle; it was contrary to all natural laws; it was the culmination of all that is illogical and abnormal.... Herlock Sholmes here—before his face!

And when the Englishman spoke his words were tinged with that keen sarcasm and mocking politeness with which his adversary had so often lashed him. He said:

"Monsieur Lupin, in, the first place I have the honor to inform you that at this time and place I blot from my memory forever all thoughts of the miserable night that you forced me to endure in the house of Baron d'Hautrec, of the injury done to my friend Wilson, of my abduction in the automobile, and of the voyage I took yesterday under your orders, bound to a very uncomfortable couch. But the joy of this moment effaces all those bitter memories. I forgive everything. I forget everything—I wipe out the debt. I am paid—and royally paid."

Lupin made no reply. So the Englishman continued:

"Don't you think so yourself?"

He appeared to insist as if demanding an acquiescence, as a sort of receipt in regard to the part.

After a moment's reflection, during which the Englishman felt that he was scrutinized to the very depth of his soul, Lupin declared:

"I presume, monsieur, that your conduct is based upon serious motives?"

"Very serious."

"The fact that you have escaped from my captain and his crew is only a secondary incident of our struggle. But the fact that you are here before me alone—understand, alone—face to face with Arsène Lupin, leads me to think that your revenge is as complete as possible."

"As complete as possible."

"This house?"

"Surrounded."

"The two adjoining houses?"

"Surrounded."

"The apartment above this?"

"The *three* apartments on the fifth floor that were formerly occupied by Monsieur Dubreuil are surrounded."

"So that——"

"So that you are captured, Monsieur Lupin—absolutely captured."

The feelings that Sholmes had experienced during his trip in the automobile were now suffered by Lupin, the same concentrated fury, the same revolt, and also, let us admit, the same loyalty of submission to force of circumstances. Equally brave in victory or defeat.

"Our accounts are squared, monsieur," said Lupin, frankly.

The Englishman was pleased with that confession. After a short silence Lupin, now quite self-possessed, said smiling:

"And I am not sorry! It becomes monotonous to win all the time. Yesterday I had only to stretch out my hand to finish you forever. Today I belong to you. The game is yours." Lupin laughed heartily and then continued: "At last the gallery will be entertained! Lupin in prison! How will he get out? In prison!... What an adventure!... Ah! Sholmes, life is just one damn thing after another!"

He pressed his closed hands to his temples as if to suppress the tumultuous joy that surged within him, and his actions indicated that he was moved by an uncontrollable mirth. At last, when he had recovered his self-possession, he approached the detective and said:

"And now what are you waiting for?"

"What am I waiting for?"

"Yes; Ganimard is here with his men—why don't they come in?"

"I asked him not to."

"And he consented?"

"I accepted his services on condition that he would be guided by me. Besides, he thinks that Felix Davey is only an accomplice of Arsène Lupin."

"Then I will repeat my question in another form. Why did you come in alone?"

"Because I wished to speak to you alone."

"Ah! ah! you have something to say to me."

That idea seemed to please Lupin immensely. There are certain circumstances in which words are preferable to deeds.

"Monsieur Sholmes, I am sorry I cannot offer you an easy chair. How would you like that broken box? Or perhaps you would prefer the window ledge? I am sure a glass of beer would be welcome ... light or dark?... But sit down, please."

"Thank you; we can talk as well standing up."

"Very well—proceed."

"I will be brief. The object of my sojourn in France was not to accomplish your arrest. If I have been led to pursue you, it was because I saw no other way to achieve my real object."

"Which was?"

"To recover the blue diamond."

"The blue diamond!"

"Certainly; since the one found in Herr Bleichen's tooth-powder was only an imitation."

"Quite right; the genuine diamond was taken by the blonde Lady. I made an exact duplicate of it and then, as I had designs on other jewels belonging to the Countess and as the Consul Herr Bleichen was already under suspicion, the aforesaid blonde Lady, in order to avert suspicion, slipped the false stone into the aforesaid Consul's luggage."

"While you kept the genuine diamond?"

"Of course."

"That diamond—I want it."

"I am very sorry, but it is impossible."

"I have promised it to the Countess de Crozon. I must have it."

"How will you get it, since it is in my possession?"

"That is precisely the reason—because it is in your possession."

"Oh! I am to give it to you?"

"Yes."

"Voluntarily?"

"I will buy it."

"Ah!" exclaimed Lupin, in an access of mirth, "you are certainly an Englishman. You treat this as a matter of business."

"It is a matter of business."

"Well! what is your offer?"

"The liberty of Mademoiselle Destange."

"Her liberty?... I didn't know she was under arrest."

"I will give Monsieur Ganimard the necessary information. When deprived of your protection, she can readily be taken."

Lupin laughed again, and said:

"My dear monsieur, you are offering me something you do not possess. Mademoiselle Destange is in a place of safety, and has nothing to fear. You must make me another offer."

The Englishman hesitated, visibly embarrassed and vexed. Then, placing his hand on the shoulder of his adversary, he said:

"And if I should propose to you-"

"My liberty?"

"No ... but I can leave the room to consult with Ganimard."

"And leave me alone!"

"Yes."

"Ah! mon dieu, what good would that be? The cursed mechanism will not work," said Lupin, at the same time savagely pushing the moulding of the mantel. He stifled a cry of surprise; this time fortune favored him—the block of marble moved. It was his salvation; his hope of escape. In that event, why submit to the conditions imposed by Sholmes? He paced up and down the room, as if he were considering his reply. Then, in his turn, he placed his hand on the shoulder of his adversary, and said:

"All things considered, Monsieur Sholmes, I prefer to do my own business in my own way."

"But—"

"No, I don't require anyone's assistance."

"When Ganimard gets his hand on you, it will be all over. You can't escape from them."

"Who knows?"

"Come, that is foolish. Every door and window is guarded."

"Except one."

"Which?"

"*The one I will choose*."

"Mere words! Your arrest is as good as made."

"Oh! no—not at all."

"Well?"

"I shall keep the blue diamond."

Sholmes looked at his watch, and said:

"It is now ten minutes to three. At three o'clock I shall call Ganimard."

"Well, then, we have ten minutes to chat. And to satisfy my curiosity, Monsieur Sholmes, I should like to know how you procured my address and my name of Felix Davey?"

Although his adversary's easy manner caused Sholmes some anxiety, he was willing to give Lupin the desired information since it reflected credit on his professional astuteness; so he replied:

"Your address? I got it from the blonde Lady."

"Clotilde!"

"Herself. Do you remember, yesterday morning, when I wished to take her away in the automobile, she telephoned to her dressmaker."

"Well?"

"Well, I understood, later, that you were the dressmaker. And last night, on the boat, by exercising my memory—and my memory is something I have good reason to be proud of—I was able to recollect the last two figures of your telephone number—73. Then, as I possessed a list of the houses you had 'improved,' it was an easy matter, on my arrival in Paris at eleven o'clock this morning, to search in the telephone directory and find there the name and address of Felix Davey. Having obtained that information, I asked the aid of Monsieur Ganimard."

"Admirable! I congratulate you. But bow did you manage to catch the eight o'clock train at Havre! How did you escape from *The Swallow*?"

"I did not escape."

"But——"

"You ordered the captain not to reach Southampton before one o'clock. He landed me there at midnight. I was able to catch the twelve o'clock boat for Havre."

"Did the captain betray me? I can't believe it."

"No, he did not betray you."

"Well, what then?"

"It was his watch."

"His watch?"

"Yes, I put it ahead one hour."

"How?"

"In the usual way, by turning the hands. We were sitting side by side, talking, and I was telling him some funny stories.... Why! he never saw me do it."

"Bravo! a very clever trick. I shall not forget it. But the clock that was hanging on the wall of the cabin?"

"Ah! the clock was a more difficult matter, as my feet were tied, but the sailor, who guarded me during the captain's absence, was kind enough to turn the hands for me."

"He? Nonsense! He wouldn't do it."

"Oh! but he didn't know the importance of his act. I told him I must catch the first train for London, at any price, and ... he allowed himself to be persuaded——"

"By means of——"

"By means of a slight gift, which the excellent fellow, loyal and true to his master, intends to send to you."

"What was it!"

"A mere trifle."

"But what?"

"The blue diamond."

"The blue diamond!"

"Yes, the false stone that you substituted for the Countess' diamond. She gave it to me."

There was a sudden explosion of violent laughter. Lupin laughed until the tears started in his eyes.

"Mon dieu, but it is funny! My false diamond palmed off on my innocent sailor! And the captain's watch! And the hands of the clock!"

Sholmes felt that the duel between him and Lupin was keener than ever. His marvellous instinct warned him that, behind his adversary's display of mirth, there was a shrewd intellect debating the ways and means to escape. Gradually Lupin approached the Englishman, who recoiled, and, unconsciously, slipped his hand into his watch-pocket.

"It is three o'clock, Monsieur Lupin."

"Three o'clock, already! What a pity! We were enjoying our chat so much."

"I am waiting for your answer."

"My answer? Mon dieu! but you are particular!... And so this is the last move in our little game—and the stake is my liberty!"

"Or the blue diamond."

"Very well. It's your play. What are you going to do!"

"I play the king," said Sholmes, as he fired his revolver.

"And I the ace," replied Lupin, as he struck at Sholmes with his fist.

Sholmes had fired into the air, as a signal to Ganimard, whose assistance he required. But Lupin's fist had caught Sholmes in the stomach, and caused him to double up with pain. Lupin rushed to the fireplace and set the marble slab in motion.... Too late! The door opened.

"Surrender, Lupin, or I fire!"

Ganimard, doubtless stationed closer than Lupin had thought, Ganimard was there, with his revolver turned on Lupin. And behind Ganimard there were twenty men, strong and ruthless fellows, who would beat him like a dog at the least sign of resistance.

"Hands down! I surrender!" said Lupin, calmly; and he folded his arms across his breast.

Everyone was amazed. In the room, divested of its furniture and hangings, Arsène Lupin's words sounded like an echo.... "I surrender!" ... It seemed incredible. No one would have been astonished if he had suddenly vanished through a trap, or if a section of the wall had rolled away and allowed him to escape. But he surrendered!

Ganimard advanced, nervously, and with all the gravity that the importance of the occasion demanded, he placed his hand on the shoulder of his adversary, and had the infinite pleasure of saying:

"I arrest you, Arsène Lupin."

"Brrr!" said Lupin, "you make me shiver, my dear Ganimard. What a lugubrious face! One would imagine you were speaking over the grave of a friend. For Heaven's sake, don't assume such a funereal air."

"I arrest you."

"Don't let that worry you! In the name of the law, of which he is a well-deserving pillar, Ganimard, the celebrated Parisian detective, arrests the wicked Arsène Lupin. An historic event, of which you will appreciate the true importance.... And it is the second time that it has happened. Bravo, Ganimard, you are sure of advancement in your chosen profession!"

And he held out his wrists for the hand-cuffs. Ganimard adjusted them in a most solemn manner. The numerous policemen, despite their customary presumption and the bitterness of their feelings toward Lupin, conducted themselves with becoming modesty, astonished at being permitted to gaze upon that mysterious and intangible creature.

"My poor Lupin," sighed our hero, "what would your aristocratic friends say if they should see you in this humiliating position?"

He pulled his wrists apart with all his strength. The veins in his forehead expanded. The links of the chain cut into his flesh. The chain fell off—broken.

"Another, comrades, that one was useless."

They placed two on him this time.

"Quite right," he said. "You cannot be too careful."

Then, counting the detectives and policemen, he said:

"How many are you, my friends? Twenty-five? Thirty? That's too many. I can't do anything. Ah! if there had been only fifteen!"

There was something fascinating about Lupin; it was the fascination of the great actor who plays his rôle with spirit and understanding, combined with assurance and ease. Sholmes regarded him as one might regard a beautiful painting with a due appreciation of all its perfection in coloring and technique. And he really thought that it was an equal struggle between those thirty men on one side, armed as they were with all the strength and majesty of the law, and, on the other side, that solitary individual, unarmed and handcuffed. Yes, the two sides were well-matched.

"Well, master," said Lupin to the Englishman, "this is your work. Thanks to you, Lupin is going to rot on the damp straw of a dungeon. Confess that your conscience pricks you a little, and that your soul is filled with remorse."

In spite of himself, Sholmes shrugged his shoulders, as if to say: "It's your own fault."

"Never! never!" exclaimed Lupin. "Give you the blue diamond? Oh! no, it has cost me too much trouble. I intend to keep it. On my occasion of my first visit to you in London—which will probably be next month—I will tell you my reasons. But will you be in London next month! Or do you prefer Vienna! Or Saint Petersburg?"

Then Lupin received a surprise. A bell commenced to ring. It was not the alarm-bell, but the bell of the telephone which was located between the two windows of the room and had not yet been removed.

The telephone! Ah! Who could it be? Who was about to fall into this unfortunate trap? Arsène Lupin exhibited an access of rage against the unlucky instrument as if he would like to break it into a thousand pieces and thus stifle the mysterious voice that was calling for him. But it was Ganimard who took down the receiver, and said:

"Hello!... Hello!... number 648.73 ... yes, this is it."

Then Sholmes stepped up, and, with an air of authority, pushed Ganimard aside, took the receiver, and covered the transmitter with his handkerchief in order to obscure the tone of his voice. At that moment he glanced toward Lupin, and the look which they exchanged indicated that the same idea had occurred to each of them, and that they fore-saw the ultimate result of that theory: it was the blonde Lady who was telephoning. She wished to telephone to Felix Davey, or rather to Maxime Bermond, and it was to Sholmes she was about to speak. The Englishman said:

"Hello ... Hello!"

Then, after a silence, he said:

"Yes, it is I, Maxime."

The drama had commenced and was progressing with tragic precision. Lupin, the irrepressible and nonchalant Lupin, did not attempt to conceal his anxiety, and he strained every nerve in a desire to hear or, at least, to divine the purport of the conversation. And Sholmes continued, in reply to the mysterious voice:

"Hello!... Hello!... Yes, everything has been moved, and I am just ready to leave here and meet you as we agreed.... Where?... Where you are now.... Don't believe that he is here yet!..."

Sholmes stopped, seeking for words. It was clear that he was trying to question the girl without betraying himself, and that he was ignorant of her whereabouts. Moreover, Ganimard's presence seemed to embarrass him.... Ah! if some miracle would only interrupt that cursed conversation! Lupin prayed for it with all his strength, with all the intensity of his incited nerves! After a momentary pause, Sholmes continued:

"Hello!... Hello!... Do you hear me?... I can't hear you very well.... Can scarcely make out what you say.... Are you listening? Well, I think you had better return home.... No danger now.... But he is in England! I have received a telegram from Southampton announcing his arrival."

The sarcasm of those words! Sholmes uttered them with an inexpressible comfort. And he added:

"Very well, don't lose any time. I will meet you there."

He hung up the receiver.

"Monsieur Ganimard, can you furnish me with three men?"

"For the blonde Lady, eh?"

"Yes."

"You know who she is, and where she is?"

"Yes."

"Good! That settles Monsieur Lupin.... Folenfant, take two men, and go with Monsieur Sholmes."

The Englishman departed, accompanied by the three men.

The game was ended. The blonde Lady was, also, about to fall into the hands of the Englishman. Thanks to his commendable persistence and to a combination of fortuitous circumstances, the battle had resulted in a victory for the detective, and in irreparable disaster for Lupin.

"Monsieur Sholmes!"

The Englishman stopped.

"Monsieur Lupin?"

Lupin was clearly shattered by this final blow. His forehead was marked by deep wrinkles. He was sullen and dejected. However, he pulled himself together, and, notwithstanding his defeat, he exclaimed, in a cheerful tone:

"You will concede that fate has been against me. A few minutes ago, it prevented my escape through that chimney, and delivered me into your hands. Now, by means of the telephone, it presents you with the blonde Lady. I submit to its decrees."

"What do you mean?"

"I mean that I am ready to re-open our negotiation."

Sholmes took Ganimard aside and asked, in a manner that did not permit a reply, the authority to exchange a few words with the prisoner. Then he approached Lupin, and said, in a sharp, nervous tone:

"What do you want?"

"Mademoiselle Destange's liberty."

"You know the price."

"Yes."

"And you accept?"

"Yes; I accept your terms."

"Ah!" said the Englishman, in surprise, "but ... you refused ... for yourself——"

"Yes, I can look out for myself, Monsieur Sholmes, but now the question concerns a young woman ... and a woman I love. In France, understand, we have very decided ideas about such things. And Lupin has the same feelings as other people."

He spoke with simplicity and candor. Sholmes replied by an almost imperceptible inclination of his head, and murmured:

"Very well, the blue diamond."

"Take my cane, there, at the end of the mantel. Press on the head of the cane with one hand, and, with the other, turn the iron ferrule at the bottom."

Holmes took the cane and followed the directions. As he did so, the head of the cane divided and disclosed a cavity which contained a small ball of wax which, in turn, enclosed a diamond. He examined it. It was the blue diamond.

"Monsieur Lupin, Mademoiselle Destange is free."

"Is her future safety assured? Has she nothing to fear from you?"

"Neither from me, nor anyone else."

"How can you manage it?"

"Quite easily. I have forgotten her name and address."

"Thank you. And au revoir—for I will see you again, sometime, Monsieur Sholmes?"

"I have no doubt of it."

Then followed an animated conversation between Sholmes and Ganimard, which was abruptly terminated by the Englishman, who said:

"I am very sorry, Monsieur Ganimard, that we cannot agree on that point, but I have no time to waste trying to convince you. I leave for England within an hour."

"But ... the blonde Lady?"

"I do not know such a person."

"And yet, a moment ago——"

"You must take the affair as it stands. I have delivered Arsène Lupin into your hands. Here is the blue diamond, which you will have the pleasure of returning to the Countess de Crozon. What more do you want?"

"The blonde Lady."

"Find her."

Sholmes pulled his cap down over his forehead and walked rapidly away, like a man who is accustomed to go as soon as his business is finished.

"Bon voyage, monsieur," cried Lupin, "and, believe me, I shall never forget the friendly way in which our little business affairs have been arranged. My regards to Monsieur Wilson."

Not receiving any reply, Lupin added, sneeringly:

"That is what is called 'taking British leave.' Ah! their insular dignity lacks the flower of courtesy by which we are distinguished. Consider for a moment, Ganimard, what a charming exit a Frenchman would have made under similar circumstances! With what exquisite courtesy he would have masked his triumph!... But, God bless me, Ganimard, what are you doing? Making a search? Come, what's the use? There is nothing left—not even a scrap of paper. I assure you my archives are in a safe place."

"I am not so sure of that," replied Ganimard. "I must search everything."

Lupin submitted to the operation. Held by two detectives and surrounded by the others, he patiently endured the proceedings for twenty minutes, then he said:

"Hurry up, Ganimard, and finish!"

"You are in a hurry."

"Of course I am. An important appointment."

"At the police station?"

"No; in the city."

"Ah! at what time?"

"Two o'clock."

"It is three o'clock now."

"Just so; I will be late. And punctuality is one of my virtues."

"Well, give me five minutes."

"Not a second more," said Lupin.

"I am doing my best to expedite——"

"Oh! don't talk so much.... Still searching that cupboard? It is empty."

"Here are some letters."

"Old invoices, I presume!"

"No; a packet tied with a ribbon."

"A red ribbon? Oh! Ganimard, for God's sake, don't untie it!"

"From a woman?"

"Yes."

"A woman of the world?"

"The best in the world."

"Her name?"

"Madame Ganimard."

"Very funny! very funny!" exclaimed the detective.

At that moment the men, who had been sent to search the other rooms, returned and announced their failure to find anything. Lupin laughed and said:

"Parbleu! Did you expect to find my visiting list, or evidence of my business relations with the Emperor of Germany? But I can tell you what you should investigate, Ganimard: All the little mysteries of this apartment. For instance, that gas-pipe is a speaking tube. That chimney contains a stairway. That wall is hollow. And the marvellous system of bells! Ah! Ganimard, just press that button!"

Ganimard obeyed.

"Did you hear anything?" asked Lupin.

"No."

"Neither did I. And yet you notified my aeronaut to prepare the dirigible balloon which will soon carry us into the clouds.

"Come!" said Ganimard, who had completed his search; "we've had enough nonsense—let's be off."

He started away, followed by his men. Lupin did not move. His guardians pushed him in vain.

"Well," said Ganimard, "do you refuse to go?"

"Not at all. But it depends."

"On what?"

"Where you want to take me."

"To the station-house, of course."

"Then I refuse to go. I have no business there."

"Are you crazy?"

"Did I not tell you that I had an important appointment?"

"Lupin!"

"Why, Ganimard, I have an appointment with the blonde Lady, and do you suppose I would be so discourteous as to cause her a moment's anxiety? That would be very ungentlemanly."

"Listen, Lupin," said the detective, who was becoming annoyed by this persiflage; "I have been very patient with you, but I will endure no more. Follow me."

"Impossible; I have an appointment and I shall keep it."

"For the last time—follow me!"

"Im-pos-sible!"

At a sign from Ganimard two men seized Lupin by the arms; but they released him at once, uttering cries of pain. Lupin had thrust two long needles into them. The other men now rushed at Lupin with cries of rage and hatred, eager to avenge their comrades and to avenge themselves for the many affronts he had heaped upon them; and now they struck and beat him to their heart's desire. A violent blow on the temple felled Lupin to the floor.

"If you hurt him you will answer to me," growled Ganimard, in a rage.

He leaned over Lupin to ascertain his condition. Then, learning that he was breathing freely, Ganimard ordered his men to carry the prisoner by the head and feet, while he himself supported the body.

"Go gently, now!... Don't jolt him. Ah! the brutes would have killed him.... Well, Lupin, how goes it!"

"None too well, Ganimard ... you let them knock me out."

"It was your own fault; you were so obstinate," replied Ganimard. "But I hope they didn't hurt you."

They had left the apartment and were now on the landing. Lupin groaned and stammered:

"Ganimard ... the elevator ... they are breaking my bones."

"A good idea, an excellent idea," replied Ganimard. "Besides, the stairway is too narrow."

He summoned the elevator. They placed Lupin on the seat with the greatest care. Ganimard took his place beside him and said to his men:

"Go down the stairs and wait for me below. Understand?"

Ganimard closed the door of the elevator. Suddenly the elevator shot upward like a balloon released from its cable. Lupin burst into a fit of sardonic laughter.

"Good God!" cried Ganimard, as he made a frantic search in the dark for the button of descent. Having found it, he cried:

"The fifth floor! Watch the door of the fifth floor."

His assistants clambered up the stairs, two and three steps at a time. But this strange circumstance happened: The elevator seemed to break through the ceiling of the last floor, disappeared from the sight of Ganimard's assistants, suddenly made its appearance on the upper floor—the servants' floor—and stopped.

Three men were there waiting for it. They opened the door. Two of them seized Ganimard, who, astonished at the sudden attack, scarcely made any defence. The other man carried off Lupin.

"I warned you, Ganimard ... about the dirigible balloon. Another time, don't be so tender-hearted. And, moreover, remember that Arsène Lupin doesn't allow himself to be struck and knocked down without sufficient reason. Adieu."

The door of the elevator was already closed on Ganimard, and the machine began to descend; and it all happened so quickly that the old detective reached the ground floor as soon as his assistants. Without exchanging a word they crossed the court and ascended the servants' stairway, which was the only way to reach the servants' floor through which the escape had been made.

A long corridor with several turns and bordered with little numbered rooms led to a door that was not locked. On the other side of this door and, therefore, in another house there was another corridor with similar turns and similar rooms, and at the end of it a servants' stairway. Ganimard descended it, crossed a court and a vestibule and found himself in the rue Picot. Then he understood the situation: the two houses, built the entire depth of the lots, touched at the rear, while the fronts of the houses faced upon two streets that ran parallel to each other at a distance of more than sixty metres apart.

He found the concierge and, showing his card, enquired:

"Did four men pass here just now?"

"Yes; the two servants from the fourth and fifth floors, with two friends."

"Who lives on the fourth and fifth floors?"

"Two men named Fauvel and their cousins, whose name is Provost. They moved to-day, leaving the two servants, who went away just now."

"Ah!" thought Ganimard; "what a grand opportunity we have missed! The entire band lived in these houses."

And he sank down on a chair in despair.

Forty minutes later two gentlemen were driven up to the station of the Northern Railway and hurried to the Calais express, followed by a porter who carried their valises. One of them had his arm in a sling, and the pallor of his face denoted some illness. The other man was in a jovial mood.

"We must hurry, Wilson, or we will miss the train.... Ah! Wilson, I shall never forget these ten days."

"Neither will I."

"Ah! it was a great struggle!"

"Superb!"

"A few repulses, here and there—"

"Of no consequence."

"And, at last, victory all along the line. Lupin arrested! The blue diamond recovered!"

"My arm broken!"

"What does a broken arm count for in such a victory as that?"

"Especially when it is my arm."

"Ah! yes, don't you remember, Wilson, that it was at the very time you were in the pharmacy, suffering like a hero, that I discovered the clue to the whole mystery!"

"How lucky!"

The doors of the carriages were being closed.

"All aboard. Hurry up, gentlemen!"

The porter climbed into an empty compartment and placed their valises in the rack, whilst Sholmes assisted the unfortunate Wilson.

"What's the matter, Wilson? You're not done up, are you? Come, pull your nerves together."

"My nerves are all right."

"Well, what is it, then?"

"I have only one hand."

"What of it?" exclaimed Sholmes, cheerfully. "You are not the only one who has had a broken arm. Cheer up!"

Sholmes handed the porter a piece of fifty centimes.

"Thank you, Monsieur Sholmes," said the porter.

The Englishman looked at him; it was Arsène Lupin.

"You!... you!" he stammered, absolutely astounded.

And Wilson brandished his sound arm in the manner of a man who demonstrates a fact as he said:

"You! you! but you were arrested! Sholmes told me so. When he left you Ganimard and thirty men had you in charge."

Lupin folded his arms and said, with an air of indignation:

"Did you suppose I would let you go away without bidding you adieu? After the very friendly relations that have always existed between us! That would be discourteous and ungrateful on my part."

The train whistled. Lupin continued:

"I beg your pardon, but have you everything you need? Tobacco and matches ... yes ... and the evening papers? You will find in them an account of my arrest—your last exploit, Monsieur Sholmes. And now, au revoir. Am delighted to have made your acquaintance. And if ever I can be of any service to you, I shall be only too happy...." He leaped to the platform and closed the door.

"Adieu," he repeated, waving his handkerchief. "Adieu.... I shall write to you.... You will write also, eh? And your arm broken, Wilson.... I am truly sorry.... I shall expect to hear from both of you. A postal card, now and then, simply address: Lupin, Paris. That is sufficient.... Adieu.... See you soon."

VII. THE JEWISH LAMP.

Herlock Sholmes and Wilson were sitting in front of the fireplace, in comfortable armchairs, with the feet extended toward the grateful warmth of a glowing coke fire.

Sholmes' pipe, a short brier with a silver band, had gone out. He knocked out the ashes, filled it, lighted it, pulled the skirts of his dressing-gown over his knees, and drew from his pipe great puffs of smoke, which ascended toward the ceiling in scores of shadow rings.

Wilson gazed at him, as a dog lying curled up on a rug before the fire might look at his master, with great round eyes which have no hope other than to obey the least gesture of his owner. Was the master going to break the silence? Would he reveal to Wilson the subject of his reverie and admit his satellite into the charmed realm of his thoughts? When Sholmes had maintained his silent attitude for some time. Wilson ventured to speak:

"Everything seems quiet now. Not the shadow of a case to occupy our leisure moments."

Sholmes did not reply, but the rings of smoke emitted by Sholmes were better formed, and Wilson observed that his companion drew considerable pleasure from that trifling fact—an indication that the great man was not absorbed in any serious meditation. Wilson, discouraged, arose and went to the window.

The lonely street extended between the gloomy façades of grimy houses, unusually gloomy this morning by reason of a heavy downfall of rain. A cab passed; then another. Wilson made an entry of their numbers in his memorandum-book. One never knows!

"Ah!" he exclaimed, "the postman."

The man entered, shown in by the servant.

"Two registered letters, sir ... if you will sign, please?"

Sholmes signed the receipts, accompanied the man to the door, and was opening one of the letters as he returned.

"It seems to please you," remarked Wilson, after a moment's silence.

"This letter contains a very interesting proposition. You are anxious for a case—here's one. Read——"

Wilson read:

"Monsieur,

"I desire the benefit of your services and experience. I have been the victim of a serious theft, and the investigation has as yet been unsuccessful. I am sending to you by this mail a number of newspapers which will inform you of the affair, and if you will undertake the case, I will place my house at your disposal and ask you to fill in the enclosed check, signed by me, for whatever sum you require for your expenses.

"Kindly reply by telegraph, and much oblige,

"Your humble servant,

"Baron Victor d'Imblevalle,

"18 rue Murillo, Paris."

"Ah!" exclaimed Sholmes, "that sounds good ... a little trip to Paris ... and why not, Wilson? Since my famous duel with Arsène Lupin, I have not had an excuse to go there. I should be pleased to visit the capital of the world under less strenuous conditions."

He tore the check into four pieces and, while Wilson, whose arm had not yet regained its former strength, uttered bitter words against Paris and the Parisians, Sholmes opened the second envelope. Immediately, he made a gesture of annoyance, and a wrinkle appeared on his forehead during the reading of the letter; then, crushing the paper into a ball, he threw it, angrily, on the floor.

"Well! What's the matter?" asked Wilson, anxiously.

He picked up the ball of paper, unfolded it, and read, with increasing amazement:

"My Dear Monsieur:

"You know full well the admiration I have for you and the interest I take in your renown. Well, believe me, when I warn you to have nothing whatever to do with the case on which you have just now been called to Paris. Your intervention will cause much harm; your efforts will produce a most lamentable result; and you will be obliged to make a public confession of your defeat.

"Having a sincere desire to spare you such humiliation, I implore you, in the name of the friendship that unites us, to remain peacefully reposing at your own fireside.

"My best wishes to Monsieur Wilson, and, for yourself, the sincere regards of your devoted ARSÈNE LUPIN."

"Arsène Lupin!" repeated Wilson, astounded.

Sholmes struck the table with his fist, and exclaimed:

"Ah! he is pestering me already, the fool! He laughs at me as if I were a schoolboy! The public confession of my defeat! Didn't I force him to disgorge the blue diamond?"

"I tell you—he's afraid," suggested Wilson.

"Nonsense! Arsène Lupin is not afraid, and this taunting letter proves it."

"But how did he know that the Baron d'Imblevalle had written to you?"

"What do I know about it? You do ask some stupid questions, my boy."

"I thought ... I supposed——"

"What? That I am a clairvoyant? Or a sorcerer?"

"No, but I have seen you do some marvellous things."

"No person can perform *marvellous* things. I no more than you. I reflect, I deduct, I conclude—that is all; but I do not divine. Only fools divine."

Wilson assumed the attitude of a whipped cur, and resolved not to make a fool of himself by trying to divine why Sholmes paced the room with quick, nervous strides. But when Sholmes rang for the servant and ordered his valise, Wilson thought that he was in possession of a material fact which gave him the right to reflect, deduct and conclude that his associate was about to take a journey. The same mental operation permitted him to assert, with almost mathematical exactness:

"Sholmes, you are going to Paris."

"Possibly."

"And Lupin's affront impels you to go, rather than the desire to assist the Baron d'Imblevalle."

"Possibly."

"Sholmes, I shall go with you."

"Ah; ah! my old friend," exclaimed Sholmes, interrupting his walking, "you are not afraid that your right arm will meet the same fate as your left?"

"What can happen to me? You will be there."

"That's the way to talk, Wilson. We will show that clever Frenchman that he made a mistake when he threw his glove in our faces. Be quick, Wilson, we must catch the first train."

"Without waiting for the papers the baron has sent you?"

"What good are they?"

"I will send a telegram."

"No; if you do that, Arsène Lupin will know of my arrival. I wish to avoid that. This time, Wilson, we must fight under cover."

That afternoon, the two friends embarked at Dover. The passage was a delightful one. In the train from Calais to Paris, Sholmes had three hours sound sleep, while Wilson guarded the door of the compartment.

Sholmes awoke in good spirits. He was delighted at the idea of another duel with Arsène Lupin, and he rubbed his hands with the satisfied air of a man who looks forward to a pleasant vacation.

"At last!" exclaimed Wilson, "we are getting to work again."

And he rubbed his hands with the same satisfied air.

At the station, Sholmes took the wraps and, followed by Wilson, who carried the valises, he gave up his tickets and started off briskly.

"Fine weather, Wilson.... Blue sky and sunshine! Paris is giving us a royal reception."

"Yes, but what a crowd!"

"So much the better, Wilson, we will pass unnoticed. No one will recognize us in such a crowd."

"Is this Monsieur Sholmes?"

He stopped, somewhat puzzled. Who the deuce could thus address him by his name? A woman stood beside him; a young girl whose simple dress outlined her slender form and whose pretty face had a sad and anxious expression. She repeated her enquiry:

"You are Monsieur Sholmes?"

As he still remained silent, as much from confusion as from a habit of prudence, the girl asked a third time:

"Have I the honor of addressing Monsieur Sholmes?"

"What do you want?" he replied, testily, considering the incident a suspicious one.

"You must listen to me, Monsieur Sholmes, as it is a serious matter. I know that you are going to the rue Murillo."

"What do you say?"

"I know ... I know ... rue Murillo ... number 18. Well, you must not go ... no, you must not. I assure you that you will regret it. Do not think that I have any interest in the matter. I do it because it is right ... because my conscience tells me to do it."

Sholmes tried to get away, but she persisted:

"Oh! I beg of you, don't neglect my advice.... Ah! if I only knew how to convince you! Look at me! Look into my eyes! They are sincere ... they speak the truth."

She gazed at Sholmes, fearlessly but innocently, with those beautiful eyes, serious and clear, in which her very soul seemed to be reflected.

Wilson nodded his head, as he said:

"Mademoiselle looks honest."

"Yes," she implored, "and you must have confidence——"

"I have confidence in you, mademoiselle," replied Wilson.

"Oh, how happy you make me! And so has your friend? I feel it ... I am sure of it! What happiness! Everything will be all right now!... What a good idea of mine!... Ah! yes, there is a train for Calais in twenty minutes. You will take it.... Quick, follow me ... you must come this way ... there is just time."

She tried to drag them along. Sholmes seized her arm, and in as gentle a voice as he could assume, said to her:

"Excuse me, mademoiselle, if I cannot yield to your wishes, but I never abandon a task that I have once undertaken."

"I beseech you ... I implore you.... Ah if you could only understand!"

Sholmes passed outside and walked away at a quick pace. Wilson said to the girl:

"Have no fear ... he will be in at the finish. He never failed yet."

And he ran to overtake Sholmes.

HERLOCK SHOLMES—ARSÈNE LUPIN.

These words, in great black letters, met their gaze as soon as they left the railway station. A number of sandwich-men were parading through the street, one behind the other, carrying heavy canes with iron ferrules with which they struck the pavement in harmony, and, on their backs, they carried large posters, on which one could read the following notice:

THE MATCH BETWEEN HERLOCK SHOLMES

AND ARSÈNE LUPIN. ARRIVAL OF THE ENGLISH
CHAMPION. THE GREAT DETECTIVE ATTACKS
THE MYSTERY OF THE RUE MURILLO. READ THE
DETAILS IN THE "ECHO DE FRANCE".

Wilson shook his head, and said:

"Look at that, Sholmes, and we thought we were traveling incognito! I shouldn't be surprised to find the republican guard waiting for us at the rue Murillo to give us an official reception with toasts and champagne."

"Wilson, when you get funny, you get beastly funny," growled Sholmes.

Then he approached one of the sandwich-men with the obvious intention of seizing him in his powerful grip and crushing him, together with his infernal sign-board. There was quite a crowd gathered about the men, reading the notices, and joking and laughing.

Repressing a furious access of rage, Sholmes said to the man:

"When did they hire you?"

"This morning."

"How long have you been parading?"

"About an hour."

"But the boards were ready before that?"

"Oh, yes, they were ready when we went to the agency this morning."

So then it appears that Arsène Lupin had foreseen that he, Sholmes, would accept the challenge. More than that, the letter written by Lupin showed that he was eager for the fray and that he was prepared to measure swords once more with his formidable rival. Why! What motive could Arsène Lupin have in renewing the struggle!

Sholmes hesitated for a moment. Lupin must be very confident of his success to show so much insolence in advance; and was not he, Sholmes, falling into a trap by rushing into the battle at the first call for help?

However, he called a carriage.

"Come, Wilson!... Driver, 18 rue Murillo!" he exclaimed, with an outburst of his accustomed energy. With distended veins and clenched fists, as if he were about to engage in a boxing bout, he jumped into the carriage.

The rue Murillo is bordered with magnificent private residences, the rear of which overlook the Parc Monceau. One of the most pretentious of these houses is number 18, owned and occupied by the Baron d'Imblevalle and furnished in a luxurious manner consistent with the owner's taste and wealth. There was a courtyard in front of the house, and, in the rear, a garden well filled with trees whose branches mingle with those of the park.

After ringing the bell, the two Englishmen were admitted, crossed the courtyard, and were received at the door by a footman who showed them into a small parlor facing the garden in the rear of the house. They sat down and, glancing about, made a rapid inspection of the many valuable objects with which the room was filled.

"Everything very choice," murmured Wilson, "and in the best of taste. It is a safe deduction to make that those who had the leisure to collect these articles must now be at least fifty years of age."

The door opened, and the Baron d'Imblevalle entered, followed by his wife. Contrary to the deduction made by Wilson, they were both quite young, of elegant appearance, and vivacious in speech and action. They were profuse in their expressions of gratitude.

"So kind of you to come! Sorry to have caused you so much trouble! The theft now seems of little consequence, since it has procured us this pleasure."

"How charming these French people are!" thought Wilson, evolving one of his commonplace deductions.

"But time is money," exclaimed the baron, "especially your time, Monsieur Sholmes. So I will come to the point. Now, what do you think of the affair? Do you think you can succeed in it?"

"Before I can answer that I must know what it is about."

"I thought you knew."

"No; so I must ask you for full particulars, even to the smallest detail. First, what is the nature of the case?"

"A theft."

"When did it take place?"

"Last Saturday," replied the baron, "or, at least, some time during Saturday night or Sunday morning."

"That was six days ago. Now, you can tell me all about it."

"In the first place, monsieur, I must tell you that my wife and I, conforming to the manner of life that our position demands, go out very little. The education of our children, a few receptions, and the care and decoration of our house—such constitutes our life; and nearly all our evenings are spent in this little room, which is my wife's boudoir, and in which we have gathered a few artistic objects. Last Saturday night, about eleven o'clock, I turned off the electric lights, and my wife and I retired, as usual, to our room."

"Where is your room?"

"It adjoins this. That is the door. Next morning, that is to say, Sunday morning, I arose quite early. As Suzanne, my wife, was still asleep, I passed into the boudoir as quietly as possible so as not to wake her. What was my astonishment when I found that window open—as we had left it closed the evening before!"

"A servant——"

"No one enters here in the morning until we ring. Besides, I always take the precaution to bolt the second door which communicates with the ante-chamber. Therefore, the window must have been opened from the outside. Besides, I have some evidence of that: the second pane of glass from the right—close to the fastening—had been cut."

"And what does that window overlook?"

"As you can see for yourself, it opens on a little balcony, surrounded by a stone railing. Here, we are on the first floor, and you can see the garden behind the house and the iron fence which separates it from the Parc Monceau. It is quite certain that the thief came through the park, climbed the fence by the aid of a ladder, and thus reached the terrace below the window."

"That is quite certain, you say!"

"Well, in the soft earth on either side of the fence, they found the two holes made by the bottom of the ladder, and two similar holes can be seen below the window. And the stone railing of the balcony shows two scratches which were doubtless made by the contact of the ladder."

"Is the Parc Monceau closed at night?"

"No; but if it were, there is a house in course of erection at number 14, and a person could enter that way."

Herlock Sholmes reflected for a few minutes, and then said:

"Let us come down to the theft. It must have been committed in this room?"

"Yes; there was here, between that twelfth century Virgin and that tabernacle of chased silver, a small Jewish lamp. It has disappeared."

"And is that all?"

"That is all."

"Ah!... And what is a Jewish lamp!"

"One of those copper lamps used by the ancient Jews, consisting of a standard which supported a bowl containing the oil, and from this bowl projected several burners intended for the wicks."

"Upon the whole, an object of small value."

"No great value, of course. But this one contained a secret hiding-place in which we were accustomed to place a magnificent jewel, a chimera in gold, set with rubies and emeralds, which was of great value."

"Why did you hide it there?"

"Oh! I can't give any reason, monsieur, unless it was an odd fancy to utilize a hiding-place of that kind."

"Did anyone know it?"

"No."

"No one—except the thief," said Sholmes. "Otherwise he would not have taken the trouble to steal the lamp."

"Of course. But how could he know it, as it was only by accident that the secret mechanism of the lamp was revealed to us."

"A similar accident has revealed it to some one else ... a servant ... or an acquaintance. But let us proceed: I suppose the police have been notified?"

"Yes. The examining magistrate has completed his investigation. The reporter-detectives attached to the leading newspapers have also made their investigations. But, as I wrote to you, it seems to me the mystery will never be solved."

Sholmes arose, went to the window, examined the casement, the balcony, the terrace, studied the scratches on the stone railing with his magnifying-glass, and then requested Mon. d'Imblevalle to show him the garden.

Outside, Sholmes sat down in a rattan chair and gazed at the roof of the house in a dreamy way. Then he walked over to the two little wooden boxes with which they had covered the holes made in the ground by the bottom of the ladder with a view of preserving them intact. He raised the boxes, kneeled on the ground, scrutinized the holes and made some measurements. After making a similar examination of the holes near the fence, he and the baron returned to the boudoir where Madame d'Imblevalle was waiting for them. After a short silence Sholmes said:

"At the very outset of your story, baron, I was surprised at the very simple methods employed by the thief. To raise a ladder, cut a window-pane, select a valuable article, and walk out again—no, that is not the way such things are done. All that is too plain, too simple."

"Well, what do you think!"

"That the Jewish lamp was stolen under the direction of Arsène Lupin."

"Arsène Lupin!" exclaimed the baron.

"Yes, but he did not do it himself, as no one came from the outside. Perhaps a servant descended from the upper floor by means of a waterspout that I noticed when I was in the garden."

"What makes you think so!"

"Arsène Lupin would not leave this room empty-handed."

"Empty-handed! But he had the lamp."

"But that would not have prevented his taking that snuff-box, set with diamonds, or that opal necklace. When he leaves anything, it is because he can't carry it away."

"But the marks of the ladder outside!"

"A false scent. Placed there simply to avert suspicion."

"And the scratches on the balustrade?"

"A farce! They were made with a piece of sandpaper. See, here are scraps of the paper that I picked up in the garden."

"And what about the marks made by the bottom of the ladder?"

"Counterfeit! Examine the two rectangular holes below the window, and the two holes near the fence. They are of a similar form, but I find that the two holes near the house are closer to each other than the two holes near the fence. What does that fact suggest? To me, it suggested that the four holes were made by a piece of wood prepared for the purpose."

"The better proof would be the piece of wood itself."

"Here it is," said Sholmes, "I found it in the garden, under the box of a laurel tree."

The baron bowed to Sholmes in recognition of his skill. Only forty minutes had elapsed since the Englishman had entered the house, and he had already exploded all the theories theretofore formed, and which had been based on what appeared to be obvious and undeniable facts. But what now appeared to be the real facts of the case rested upon a more solid foundation, to-wit, the astute reasoning of a Herlock Sholmes.

"The accusation which you make against one of our household is a very serious matter," said the baroness. "Our servants have been with us a long time and none of them would betray our trust."

"If none of them has betrayed you, how can you explain the fact that I received this letter on the same day and by the same mail as the letter you wrote to me?"

He handed to the baroness the letter that he had received from Arsène Lupin. She exclaimed, in amazement:

"Arsène Lupin! How could he know?"

"Did you tell anyone that you had written to me?"

"No one," replied the baron. "The idea occurred to us the other evening at the dinner-table."

"Before the servants?"

"No, only our two children. Oh, no ... Sophie and Henriette had left the table, hadn't they, Suzanne?"

Madame d'Imblevalle, after a moment's reflection, replied:

"Yes, they had gone to Mademoiselle."

"Mademoiselle?" queried Sholmes.

"The governess, Mademoiselle Alice Demun."

"Does she take her meals with you?"

"No. Her meals are served in her room."

Wilson had an idea. He said:

"The letter written to my friend Herlock Sholmes was posted?"

"Of course."

"Who posted it?"

"Dominique, who has been my valet for twenty years," replied the baron. "Any search in that direction would be a waste of time."

"One never wastes his time when engaged in a search," said Wilson, sententiously.

This preliminary investigation now ended, and Sholmes asked permission to retire.

At dinner, an hour later, he saw Sophie and Henriette, the two children of the family, one was six and the other eight years of age. There was very little conversation at the table. Sholmes responded to the friendly advances of his hosts in such a curt manner that they were soon reduced to silence. When the coffee was served, Sholmes swallowed the contents of his cup, and rose to take his leave.

At that moment, a servant entered with a telephone message addressed to Sholmes. He opened it, and read:

"You have my enthusiastic admiration. The results attained by you in so short a time are simply marvellous. I am dismayed.

"ARSÈNE LUPIN."

Sholmes made a gesture of indignation and handed the message to the baron, saying:

"What do you think now, monsieur? Are the walls of your house furnished with eyes and ears?"

"I don't understand it," said the baron, in amazement.

"Nor do I; but I do understand that Lupin has knowledge of everything that occurs in this house. He knows every movement, every word. There is no doubt of it. But how does he get his information? That is the first mystery I have to solve, and when I know that I will know everything."

That night, Wilson retired with the clear conscience of a man who has performed his whole duty and thus acquired an undoubted right to sleep and repose. So he fell asleep very quickly, and was soon enjoying the most delightful dreams in which he pursued Lupin and captured him single-handed; and the sensation was so vivid and exciting that it woke him from his sleep. Someone was standing at his bedside. He seized his revolver, and cried:

"Don't move, Lupin, or I'll fire."

"The deuce! Wilson, what do you mean?"

"Oh! it is you, Sholmes. Do you want me!"

"I want to show you something. Get up."

Sholmes led him to the window, and said:

"Look!... on the other side of the fence...."

"In the park?"

"Yes. What do you see?"

"I don't see anything."

"Yes, you do see something."

"Ah! of course, a shadow ... two of them."

"Yes, close to the fence. See, they are moving. Come, quick!"

Quickly they descended the stairs, and reached a room which opened into the garden. Through the glass door they could see the two shadowy forms in the same place.

"It is very strange," said Sholmes, "but it seems to me I can hear a noise inside the house."

"Inside the house? Impossible! Everybody is asleep."

"Well, listen——"

At that moment a low whistle came from the other side of the fence, and they perceived a dim light which appeared to come from the house.

"The baron must have turned on the light in his room. It is just above us."

"That must have been the noise you heard," said Wilson. "Perhaps they are watching the fence also."

Then there was a second whistle, softer than before.

"I don't understand it; I don't understand," said Sholmes, irritably.

"No more do I," confessed Wilson.

Sholmes turned the key, drew the bolt, and quietly opened the door. A third whistle, louder than before, and modulated to another form. And the noise above their heads became more pronounced. Sholmes said:

"It seems to be on the balcony outside the boudoir window."

He put his head through the half-opened door, but immediately recoiled, with a stifled oath. Then Wilson looked. Quite close to them there was a ladder, the upper end of which was resting on the balcony.

"The deuce!" said Sholmes, "there is someone in the boudoir. That is what we heard. Quick, let us remove the ladder."

But at that instant a man slid down the ladder and ran toward the spot where his accomplices were waiting for him outside the fence. He carried the ladder with him. Sholmes and Wilson pursued the man and overtook him just as he was placing the ladder against the fence. From the other side of the fence two shots were fired.

"Wounded?" cried Sholmes.

"No," replied Wilson.

Wilson seized the man by the body and tried to hold him, but the man turned and plunged a knife into Wilson's breast. He uttered a groan, staggered and fell.

"Damnation!" muttered Sholmes, "if they have killed him I will kill them."

He laid Wilson on the grass and rushed toward the ladder. Too late—the man had climbed the fence and, accompanied by his confederates, had fled through the bushes.

"Wilson, Wilson, it is not serious, hein? Merely a scratch."

The house door opened, and Monsieur d'Imblevalle appeared, followed by the servants, carrying candles.

"What's the matter?" asked the baron. "Is Monsieur Wilson wounded?"

"Oh! it's nothing—a mere scratch," repeated Sholmes, trying to deceive himself.

The blood was flowing profusely, and Wilson's face was livid. Twenty minutes later the doctor ascertained that the point of the knife had penetrated to within an inch and a half of the heart.

"An inch and a half of the heart! Wilson always was lucky!" said Sholmes, in an envious tone.

"Lucky ... lucky...." muttered the doctor.

"Of course! Why, with his robust constitution he will soon be out again."

"Six weeks in bed and two months of convalescence."

"Not more?"

"No, unless complications set in."

"Oh! the devil! what does he want complications for?"

Fully reassured, Sholmes joined the baron in the boudoir. This time the mysterious visitor had not exercised the same restraint. Ruthlessly, he had laid his vicious hand upon the diamond snuff-box, upon the opal necklace, and, in a general way, upon everything that could find a place in the greedy pockets of an enterprising burglar.

The window was still open; one of the window-panes had been neatly cut; and, in the morning, a summary investigation showed that the ladder belonged to the house then in course of construction.

"Now, you can see," said Mon. d'Imblevalle, with a touch of irony, "it is an exact repetition of the affair of the Jewish lamp."

"Yes, if we accept the first theory adopted by the police."

"Haven't you adopted it yet? Doesn't this second theft shatter your theory in regard to the first?"

"It only confirms it, monsieur."

"That is incredible! You have positive evidence that last night's theft was committed by an outsider, and yet you adhere to your theory that the Jewish lamp was stolen by someone in the house."

"Yes, I am sure of it."

"How do you explain it?"

"I do not explain anything, monsieur; I have established two facts which do not appear to have any relation to each other, and yet I am seeking the missing link that connects them."

His conviction seemed to be so earnest and positive that the baron submitted to it, and said:

"Very well, we will notify the police———"

"Not at all!" exclaimed the Englishman, quickly, "not at all! I intend to ask for their assistance when I need it—but not before."

"But the attack on your friend?"

"That's of no consequence. He is only wounded. Secure the license of the doctor. I shall be responsible for the legal side of the affair."

The next two days proved uneventful. Yet Sholmes was investigating the case with a minute care, and with a sense of wounded pride resulting from that audacious theft, committed under his nose, in spite of his presence and beyond his power to prevent it. He made a thorough investigation of the house and garden, interviewed the servants, and paid lengthy visits to the kitchen and stables. And, although his efforts were fruitless, he did not despair.

"I will succeed," he thought, "and the solution must be sought within the walls of this house. This affair is quite different from that of the blonde Lady, where I had to work in the dark, on unknown ground. This time I am on the battlefield itself. The enemy is not the elusive and invisible Lupin, but the accomplice, in flesh and blood, who lives and moves within the confines of this house. Let me secure the slightest clue and the game is mine!"

That clue was furnished to him by accident.

On the afternoon of the third day, when he entered a room located above the boudoir, which served as a study for the children, he found Henriette, the younger of the two sisters. She was looking for her scissors.

"You know," she said to Sholmes, "I make papers like that you received the other evening."

"The other evening?"

"Yes, just as dinner was over, you received a paper with marks on it ... you know, a telegram.... Well, I make them, too."

She left the room. To anyone else these words would seem to be nothing more than the insignificant remark of a child, and Sholmes himself listened to them with a distracted air and continued his investigation. But, suddenly, he ran after the child, and overtook her at the head of the stairs. He said to her:

"So you paste stamps and marks on papers?"

Henriette, very proudly, replied:

"Yes, I cut them out and paste them on."

"Who taught you that little game?"

"Mademoiselle ... my governess ... I have seen her do it often. She takes words out of the newspapers and pastes them———"

"What does she make out of them?"

"Telegrams and letters that she sends away."

Herlock Sholmes returned to the study, greatly puzzled by the information and seeking to draw from it a logical deduction. There was a pile of newspapers on the mantel. He opened them and found that many words and, in some places, entire lines had been cut out. But, after reading a few of the word's which preceded or followed, he decided that the missing words had been cut out at random—probably by the child. It was possible that one of the newspapers had been cut by mademoiselle; but how could he assure himself that such was the case?

Mechanically, Sholmes turned over the school-books on the table; then others which were lying on the shelf of a bookcase. Suddenly he uttered a cry of joy. In a corner of the bookcase, under a pile of old exercise books, he found a child's alphabet-book, in which the letters were ornamented with pictures, and on one of the pages of that book he discovered a place where a word had been removed. He examined it. It was a list of the days of the week. Monday, Tuesday, Wednesday, etc. The word "Saturday" was missing. Now, the theft of the Jewish lamp had occurred on a Saturday night.

Sholmes experienced that slight fluttering of the heart which always announced to him, in the clearest manner, that he had discovered the road which leads to victory. That ray of truth, that feeling of certainty, never deceived him.

With nervous fingers he hastened to examine the balance of the book. Very soon he made another discovery. It was a page composed of capital letters, followed by a line of figures. Nine of those letters and three of those figures had been carefully cut out. Sholmes made a list of the missing letters and figures in his memorandum book, in alphabetical and numerical order, and obtained the following result:

CDEHNOPEZ—237.

"Well! at first sight, it is a rather formidable puzzle," he murmured, "but, by transposing the letters and using all of them, is it possible to form one, two or three complete words?"

Sholmes tried it, in vain.

Only one solution seemed possible; it constantly appeared before him, no matter which way he tried to juggle the letters, until, at length, he was satisfied it was the true solution, since it harmonized with the logic of the facts and the general circumstances of the case.

As that page of the book did not contain any duplicate letters it was probable, in fact quite certain, that the words he could form from those letters would be incomplete, and that the original words had been completed with letters taken from other pages. Under those conditions he obtained the following solution, errors and omissions excepted:

REPOND Z—CH—237.

The first word was quite clear: répondez [reply], a letter E is missing because it occurs twice in the word, and the book furnished only one letter of each kind.

As to the second incomplete word, no doubt it formed, with the aid of the number 237, an address to which the reply was to be sent. They appointed Saturday as the time, and requested a reply to be sent to the address CH. 237.

Or, perhaps, CH. 237 was an address for a letter to be sent to the "general delivery" of some postoffice, or, again, they might form a part of some incomplete word. Sholmes searched the book once more, but did not discover that any other letters had been removed. Therefore, until further orders, he decided to adhere to the foregoing interpretation.

Henriette returned and observed what he was doing.

"Amusing, isn't it?"

"Yes, very amusing," he replied. "But, have you any other papers?... Or, rather, words already cut out that I can paste?"

"Papers?... No.... And Mademoiselle wouldn't like it."

"Mademoiselle?"

"Yes, she has scolded me already."

"Why?"

"Because I have told you some things ... and she says that a person should never tell things about those they love."

"You are quite right."

Henriette was delighted to receive his approbation, in fact so highly pleased that she took from a little silk bag that was pinned to her dress some scraps of cloth, three buttons, two cubes of sugar and, lastly, a piece of paper which she handed to Sholmes.

"See, I give it to you just the same."

It was the number of a cab—8,279.

"Where did this number come from?"

"It fell out of her pocketbook."

"When?"

"Sunday, at mass, when she was taking out some sous for the collection."

"Exactly! And now I shall tell you how to keep from being scolded again. Do not tell Mademoiselle that you saw me."

Sholmes then went to Mon. d'Imblevalle and questioned him in regard to Mademoiselle. The baron replied, indignantly:

"Alice Demun! How can you imagine such a thing? It is utterly impossible!"

"How long has she been in your service?"

"Only a year, but there is no one in the house in whom I have greater confidence."

"Why have I not seen her yet?"

"She has been away for a few days."

"But she is here now."

"Yes; since her return she has been watching at the bedside of your friend. She has all the qualities of a nurse ... gentle ... thoughtful ... Monsieur Wilson seems much pleased...."

"Ah!" said Sholmes, who had completely neglected to inquire about his friend. After a moment's reflection he asked:

"Did she go out on Sunday morning?"

"The day after the theft?"

"Yes."

The baron called his wife and asked her. She replied:

"Mademoiselle went to the eleven o'clock mass with the children, as usual."

"But before that?"

"Before that? No.... Let me see!... I was so upset by the theft ... but I remember now that, on the evening before, she asked permission to go out on Sunday morning ... to see a cousin who was passing through Paris, I think. But, surely, you don't suspect her?"

"Of course not ... but I would like to see her."

He went to Wilson's room. A woman dressed in a gray cloth dress, as in the hospitals, was bending over the invalid, giving him a drink. When she turned her face Sholmes recognized her as the young girl who had accosted him at the railway station.

Alice Demun smiled sweetly; her great serious, innocent eyes showed no sign of embarrassment. The Englishman tried to speak, muttered a few syllables, and stopped. Then she resumed her work, acting quite naturally under Sholmes' astonished gaze, moved the bottles, unrolled and rolled cotton bandages, and again regarded Sholmes with her charming smile of pure innocence.

He turned on his heels, descended the stairs, noticed Mon. d'Imblevalle's automobile in the courtyard, jumped into it, and went to Levallois, to the office of the cab company whose address was printed on the paper he had received from Henriette. The man who had driven carriage number 8,279 on Sunday morning not being there, Sholmes dismissed the automobile and waited for the man's return. He told Sholmes that he had picked up a woman in the vicinity of the Parc Monceau, a young woman dressed in black, wearing a heavy veil, and, apparently, quite nervous.

"Did she have a package?"

"Yes, quite a long package."

"Where did you take her?"

"Avenue des Ternes, corner of the Place Saint-Ferdinand. She remained there about ten minutes, and then returned to the Parc Monceau."

"Could you recognize the house in the avenue des Ternes?"

"Parbleu! Shall I take you there?"

"Presently. First take me to 36 quai des Orfèvres."

At the police office he saw Detective Ganimard.

"Monsieur Ganimard, are you at liberty?"

"If it has anything to do with Lupin—no!"

"It has something to do with Lupin."

"Then I do not go."

"What! you surrender——"

"I bow to the inevitable. I am tired of the unequal struggle, in which we are sure to be defeated. Lupin is stronger than I am—stronger than the two of us; therefore, we must surrender."

"I will not surrender."

"He will make you, as he has all others."

"And you would be pleased to see it—eh, Ganimard?"

"At all events, it is true," said Ganimard, frankly. "And since you are determined to pursue the game, I will go with you."

Together they entered the carriage and were driven to the avenue des Ternes. Upon their order the carriage stopped on the other side of the street, at some distance from the house, in front of a little café, on the terrace of which the two men took seats amongst the shrubbery. It was commencing to grow dark.

"Waiter," said Sholmes, "some writing material."

He wrote a note, recalled the waiter and gave him the letter with instructions to deliver it to the concierge of the house which he pointed out.

In a few minutes the concierge stood before them. Sholmes asked him if, on the Sunday morning, he had seen a young woman dressed in black.

"In black! Yes, about nine o'clock. She went to the second floor."

"Have you seen her often?"

"No, but for some time—well, during the last few weeks, I have seen her almost every day."

"And since Sunday?"

"Only once ... until to-day."

"What! Did she come to-day?"

"She is here now."

"Here now?"

"Yes, she came about ten minutes ago. Her carriage is standing in the Place Saint-Ferdinand, as usual. I met her at the door."

"Who is the occupant of the second floor?"

"There are two: a modiste, Mademoiselle Langeais, and a gentleman who rented two furnished rooms a month ago under the name of Bresson."

"Why do you say 'under the name'?"

"Because I have an idea that it is an assumed name. My wife takes care of his rooms, and ... well, there are not two shirts there with the same initials."

"Is he there much of the time?"

"No; he is nearly always out. He has not been here for three days."

"Was he here on Saturday night?"

"Saturday night?... Let me think.... Yes, Saturday night, he came in and stayed all night."

"What sort of a man is he?"

"Well, I can scarcely answer that. He is so changeable. He is, by turns, big, little, fat, thin ... dark and light. I do not always recognize him."

Ganimard and Sholmes exchanged looks.

"That is he, all right," said Ganimard.

"Ah!" said the concierge, "there is the girl now."

Mademoiselle had just emerged from the house and was walking toward her carriage in the Place Saint-Ferdinand.

"And there is Monsieur Bresson."

"Monsieur Bresson? Which is he?"

"The man with the parcel under his arm."

"But he is not looking after the girl. She is going to her carriage alone."

"Yes, I have never seen them together."

The two detectives had arisen. By the light of the street-lamps they recognized the form of Arsène Lupin, who had started off in a direction opposite to that taken by the girl.

"Which will you follow?" asked Ganimard.

"I will follow him, of course. He's the biggest game."

"Then I will follow the girl," proposed Ganimard.

"No, no," said Sholmes, quickly, who did not wish to disclose the girl's identity to Ganimard, "I know where to find her. Come with me."

They followed Lupin at a safe distance, taking care to conceal themselves as well as possible amongst the moving throng and behind the newspaper kiosks. They found the pursuit an easy one, as he walked steadily forward without turning to the right or left, but with a slight limp in the right leg, so slight as to require the keen eye of a professional observer to detect it. Ganimard observed it, and said:

"He is pretending to be lame. Ah! if we could only collect two or three policemen and pounce on our man! We run a chance to lose him."

But they did not meet any policemen before they reached the Porte des Ternes, and, having passed the fortifications, there was no prospect of receiving any assistance.

"We had better separate," said Sholmes, "as there are so few people on the street."

They were now on the Boulevard Victor-Hugo. They walked one on each side of the street, and kept well in the shadow of the trees. They continued thus for twenty minutes, when Lupin turned to the left and followed the Seine. Very soon they saw him descend to the edge of the river. He remained there only a few seconds, but they could not observe his movements. Then Lupin retraced his steps. His pursuers concealed themselves in the shadow of a gateway. Lupin passed in front of them. His parcel had disappeared. And as he walked away another man emerged from the shelter of a house and glided amongst the trees.

"He seems to be following him also," said Sholmes, in a low voice.

The pursuit continued, but was now embarrassed by the presence of the third man. Lupin returned the same way, passed through the Porte des Ternes, and re-entered the house in the avenue des Ternes.

The concierge was closing the house for the night when Ganimard presented himself.

"Did you see him?"

"Yes," replied the concierge, "I was putting out the gas on the landing when he closed and bolted his door."

"Is there any person with him?"

"No; he has no servant. He never eats here."

"Is there a servants' stairway?"

"No."

Ganimard said to Sholmes:

"I had better stand at the door of his room while you go for the commissary of police in the rue Demours."

"And if he should escape during that time?" said Sholmes.

"While I am here! He can't escape."

"One to one, with Lupin, is not an even chance for you."

"Well, I can't force the door. I have no right to do that, especially at night."

Sholmes shrugged his shoulders and said:

"When you arrest Lupin no one will question the methods by which you made the arrest. However, let us go up and ring, and see what happens then."

They ascended to the second floor. There was a double door at the left of the landing. Ganimard rang the bell. No reply. He rang again. Still no reply.

"Let us go in," said Sholmes.

"All right, come on," replied Ganimard.

Yet, they stood still, irresolute. Like people who hesitate when they ought to accomplish a decisive action they feared to move, and it seemed to them impossible that Arsène Lupin was there, so close to them, on the other side of that fragile door that could be broken down by one blow of the fist. But they knew Lupin too well to suppose that he would allow himself to be trapped in that stupid manner. No, no—a thousand times, no—Lupin was no longer there. Through the adjoining houses, over the roofs, by some conveniently prepared exit, he must have already made his escape, and, once more, it would only be Lupin's shadow that they would seize.

They shuddered as a slight noise, coming from the other side of the door, reached their ears. Then they had the impression, amounting almost to a certainty, that he was there, separated from them by that frail wooden door, and that he was listening to them, that he could hear them.

What was to be done? The situation was a serious one. In spite of their vast experience as detectives, they were so nervous and excited that they thought they could hear the beating of their own hearts. Ganimard questioned Sholmes by a look. Then he struck the door a violent blow with his fist. Immediately they heard the sound of footsteps, concerning which there was no attempt at concealment.

Ganimard shook the door. Then he and Sholmes, uniting their efforts, rushed at the door, and burst it open with their shoulders. Then they stood still, in surprise. A shot had been fired in the adjoining room. Another shot, and the sound of a falling body.

When they entered they saw the man lying on the floor with his face toward the marble mantel. His revolver had fallen from his hand. Ganimard stooped and turned the man's head. The face was covered with blood, which was flowing from two wounds, one in the cheek, the other in the temple.

"You can't recognize him for blood."

"No matter!" said Sholmes. "It is not Lupin."

"How do you know? You haven't even looked at him."

"Do you think that Arsène Lupin is the kind of a man that would kill himself?" asked Sholmes, with a sneer.

"But we thought we recognized him outside."

"We thought so, because the wish was father to the thought. That man has us bewitched."

"Then it must be one of his accomplices."

"The accomplices of Arsène Lupin do not kill themselves."

"Well, then, who is it?"

They searched the corpse. In one pocket Herlock Sholmes found an empty pocketbook; in another Ganimard found several louis. There were no marks of identification on any part of his clothing. In a trunk and two valises they found nothing but wearing apparel. On the mantel there was a pile of newspapers. Ganimard opened them. All of them contained articles referring to the theft of the Jewish lamp.

An hour later, when Ganimard and Sholmes left the house, they had acquired no further knowledge of the strange individual who had been driven to suicide by their untimely visit.

Who was he! Why had he killed himself? What was his connection with the affair of the Jewish lamp? Who had followed him on his return from the river? The situation involved many complex questions—many mysteries—

Herlock Sholmes went to bed in a very bad humor. Early next morning he received the following telephonic message: "Arsène Lupin has the honor to inform you of his tragic death in the person of Monsieur Bresson, and requests the honor of your presence at the funeral service and burial, which will be held at the public expense on Thursday, 25 June."

VII. THE SHIPWRECK.

"That's what I don't like, Wilson," said Herlock Sholmes, after he had read Arsène Lupin's message; "that is what exasperates me in this affair—to feel that the cunning, mocking eye of that fellow follows me everywhere. He sees everything; he knows everything; he reads my inmost thoughts; he even foresees my slightest movement. Ah! he is possessed of a marvellous intuition, far surpassing that of the most instinctive woman, yes, surpassing even that of Herlock Sholmes himself. Nothing escapes him. I resemble an actor whose every step and movement are directed by a stage-manager; who says this and does that in obedience to a superior will. That is my position. Do you understand, Wilson?"

Certainly Wilson would have understood if his faculties had not been deadened by the profound slumber of a man whose temperature varies between one hundred and one hundred and three degrees. But whether he heard or not was a matter of no consequence to Herlock Sholmes, who continued:

"I have to concentrate all my energy and bring all my resources into action in order to make the slightest progress. And, fortunately for me, those petty annoyances are like so many pricks from a needle and serve only to stimulate me. As soon as the heat of the wound is appeased and the shock to my vanity has subsided I say to myself: 'Amuse yourself, my dear fellow, but remember that he who laughs last laughs best. Sooner or later you will betray yourself.' For you know, Wilson, it was Lupin himself, who, by his first dispatch and the observation that it suggested to little Henriette, disclosed to me the secret of his correspondence with Alice Hemun. Have you forgotten that circumstance, dear boy?"

But Wilson was asleep; and Sholmes, pacing to and fro, resumed his speech:

"And, now, things are not in a bad shape; a little obscure, perhaps, but the light is creeping in. In the first place, I must learn all about Monsieur Bresson. Ganimard and I will visit the bank of the river, at the spot where Bresson threw away the package, and the particular rôle of that gentleman will be known to me. After that the game will be played between me and Alice Demun. Rather a light-weight opponent, hein, Wilson? And do you not think that I will soon know the phrase represented by the letters clipped from the alphabet-book, and what the isolated letters—the 'C' and the 'H'—mean? That is all I want to know, Wilson."

Mademoiselle entered at that moment, and, observing Sholmes gesticulating, she said, in her sweetest manner:

"Monsieur Sholmes, I must scold you if you waken my patient. It isn't nice of you to disturb him. The doctor has ordered absolute rest."

He looked at her in silence, astonished, as on their first meeting, at her wonderful self-possession.

"Why do you look at me so, Monsieur Sholmes?... You seem to be trying to read my thoughts.... No?... Then what is it?"

She questioned him with the most innocent expression on her pretty face and in her frank blue eyes. A smile played upon her lips; and she displayed so much unaffected candor that the Englishman almost lost his temper. He approached her and said, in a low voice:

"Bresson killed himself last night."

She affected not to understand him; so he repeated:

"Bresson killed himself yesterday...."

She did not show the slightest emotion; she acted as if the matter did not concern or interest her in any way.

"You have been informed," said Sholmes, displaying his annoyance. "Otherwise, the news would have caused you to start, at least. Ah! you are stronger than I expected. But what's the use of your trying to conceal anything from me?"

He picked up the alphabet-book, which he had placed on a convenient table, and, opening it at the mutilated page, said:

"Will you tell me the order in which the missing letters should be arranged in order to express the exact wording of the message you sent to Bresson four days before the theft of the Jewish lamp?"

"The order?... Bresson?... the theft of the Jewish lamp?"

She repeated the words slowly, as if trying to grasp their meaning. He continued:

"Yes. Here are the letters employed ... on this bit of paper.... What did you say to Bresson?"

"The letters employed ... what did I say...."

Suddenly she burst into laughter:

"Ah! that is it! I understand! I am an accomplice in the crime! There is a Monsieur Bresson who stole the Jewish lamp and who has now committed suicide. And I am the friend of that gentleman. Oh! how absurd you are!"

"Whom did you go to see last night on the second floor of a house in the avenue des Ternes?"

"Who? My modiste, Mademoiselle Langeais. Do you suppose that my modiste and my friend Monsieur Bresson are the same person?"

Despite all he knew, Sholmes was now in doubt. A person can feign terror, joy, anxiety, in fact all emotions; but a person cannot feign absolute indifference or light, careless laughter. Yet he continued to question her:

"Why did you accost me the other evening at the Northern Railway station? And why did you entreat me to leave Paris immediately without investigating this theft?"

"Ah! you are too inquisitive, Monsieur Sholmes," she replied, still laughing in the most natural manner. "To punish you I will tell you nothing, and, besides, you must watch the patient while I go to the pharmacy on an urgent message. Au revoir."

She left the room.

"I am beaten ... by a girl," muttered Sholmes. "Not only did I get nothing out of her but I exposed my hand and put her on her guard."

And he recalled the affair of the blue diamond and his first interview with Clotilde Destange. Had not the blonde Lady met his question with the same unruffled serenity, and was he not once more face to face with one of those creatures who, under the protection and influence of Arsène Lupin, maintain the utmost coolness in the face of a terrible danger?

"Sholmes ... Sholmes...."

It was Wilson who called him. Sholmes approached the bed, and, leaning over, said:

"What's the matter, Wilson? Does your wound pain you?"

Wilson's lips moved, but he could not speak. At last, with a great effort, he stammered:

"No ... Sholmes ... it is not she ... that is impossible——"

"Come, Wilson, what do you know about it? I tell you that it is she! It is only when I meet one of Lupin's creatures, prepared and instructed by him, that I lose my head and make a fool of myself.... I bet you that within an hour Lupin will know all about our interview. Within an hour? What am I saying?... Why, he may know already. The visit to the pharmacy ... urgent message. All nonsense!... She has gone to telephone to Lupin."

Sholmes left the house hurriedly, went down the avenue de Messine, and was just in time to see Mademoiselle enter a pharmacy. Ten minutes later she emerged from the shop carrying some small packages and a bottle wrapped in white paper. But she had not proceeded far, when she was accosted by a man who, with hat in hand and an obsequious air, appeared to be asking for charity. She stopped, gave him something, and proceeded on her way.

"She spoke to him," said the Englishman to himself.

If not a certainty, it was at least an intuition, and quite sufficient to cause him to change his tactics. Leaving the girl to pursue her own course, he followed the suspected mendicant, who walked slowly to the avenue des Ternes and lingered for a long time around the house in which Bresson had lived, sometimes raising his eyes to the windows of the second floor and watching the people who entered the house.

At the end of an hour he climbed to the top of a tramcar going in the direction of Neuilly. Sholmes followed and took a seat behind the man, and beside a gentleman who was concealed behind the pages of a newspaper. At the fortifications the gentleman lowered the paper, and Sholmes recognized Ganimard, who thereupon whispered, as he pointed to the man in front:

"It is the man who followed Bresson last night. He has been watching the house for an hour."

"Anything new in regard to Bresson?" asked Sholmes.

"Yes, a letter came to his address this morning."

"This morning? Then it was posted yesterday before the sender could know of Bresson's death."

"Exactly. It is now in the possession of the examining magistrate. But I read it. It says: *He will not accept any compromise. He wants everything—the first thing as well as those of the second affair. Otherwise he will proceed.*"

"There is no signature," added Ganimard. "It seems to me those few lines won't help us much."

"I don't agree with you, Monsieur Ganimard. To me those few lines are very interesting."

"Why so? I can't see it."

"For reasons that are personal to me," replied Sholmes, with the indifference that he frequently displayed toward his colleague.

The tramcar stopped at the rue de Château, which was the terminus. The man descended and walked away quietly. Sholmes followed at so short a distance that Ganimard protested, saying:

"If he should turn around he will suspect us."

"He will not turn around."

"How do you know?"

"He is an accomplice of Arsène Lupin, and the fact that he walks in that manner, with his hands in his pockets, proves, in the first place, that he knows he is being followed and, in the second place, that he is not afraid."

"But I think we are keeping too close to him."

"Not too close to prevent his slipping through our fingers. He is too sure of himself."

"Ah! Look there! In front of that café there are two of the bicycle police. If I summon them to our assistance, how can the man slip through our fingers?"

"Well, our friend doesn't seem to be worried about it. In fact, he is asking for their assistance himself."

"Mon Dieu!" exclaimed Ganimard, "he has a nerve."

The man approached the two policemen just as they were mounting their bicycles. After a few words with them he leaped on a third bicycle, which was leaning against the wall of the café, and rode away at a fast pace, accompanied by the two policemen.

"Hein! one, two, three and away!" growled Sholmes. "And through, whose agency, Monsieur Ganimard? Two of your colleagues.... Ah! but Arsène Lupin has a wonderful organization! Bicycle policemen in his service!... I told you our man was too calm, too sure of himself."

"Well, then," said Ganimard, quite vexed, "what are we to do now? It is easy enough to laugh! Anyone can do that."

"Come, come, don't lose your temper! We will get our revenge. But, in the meantime, we need reinforcements."

"Folenfant is waiting for me at the end of the avenue de Neuilly."

"Well, go and get him and join me later. I will follow our fugitive."

Sholmes followed the bicycle tracks, which were plainly visible in the dust of the road as two of the machines were furnished with striated tires. Very soon he ascertained that the tracks were leading him to the edge of the Seine, and that the three men had turned in the direction taken by Bresson on the preceding evening. Thus he arrived at the gateway where he and Ganimard had concealed themselves, and, a little farther on, he discovered a mingling of the bicycle tracks which showed that the men had halted at that spot. Directly opposite there was a little point of land which projected into the river and, at the extremity thereof, an old boat was moored.

It was there that Bresson had thrown away the package, or, rather, had dropped it. Sholmes descended the bank and saw that the declivity was not steep and the water quite shallow, so it would be quite easy to recover the package, provided the three men had not forestalled him.

"No, that can't be," he thought, "they have not had time. A quarter of an hour at the most. And yet, why did they come this way?"

A fisherman was seated on the old boat. Sholmes asked him:

"Did you see three men on bicycles a few minutes ago?"

The fisherman made a negative gesture. But Sholmes insisted:

"Three men who stopped on the road just on top of the bank?"

The fisherman rested his pole under his arm, took a memorandum book from his pocket, wrote on one of the pages, tore it out, and handed it to Sholmes. The Englishman gave a start of surprise. In the middle of the paper which he held in his hand he saw the series of letters cut from the alphabet-book:

CDEHNOPRZEO—237.

The man resumed his fishing, sheltered from the sun by a large straw hat, with his coat and vest lying beside him. He was intently watching the cork attached to his line as it floated on the surface of the water.

There was a moment of silence—solemn and terrible.

"Is it he?" conjectured Sholmes, with an anxiety that was almost pitiful. Then the truth burst upon him:

"It is he! It is he! No one else could remain there so calmly, without the slightest display of anxiety, without the least fear of what might happen. And who else would know the story of those mysterious letters? Alice had warned him by means of her messenger."

Suddenly the Englishman felt that his hand—that his own hand had involuntarily seized the handle of his revolver, and that his eyes were fixed on the man's back, a little below the neck. One movement, and the drama would be finished; the life of the strange adventurer would come to a miserable end.

The fisherman did not stir.

Sholmes nervously toyed with his revolver, and experienced a wild desire to fire it and end everything; but the horror of such an act was repugnant to his nature. Death would be certain and would end all.

"Ah!" he thought, "let him get up and defend himself. If he doesn't, so much the worse for him. One second more ... and I fire...."

But a sound of footsteps behind him caused him to turn his head. It was Ganimard coming with some assistants.

Then, quickly changing his plans, Sholmes leaped into the boat, which was broken from its moorings by his sudden action; he pounced upon the man and seized him around the body. They rolled to the bottom of the boat together.

"Well, now!" exclaimed Lupin, struggling to free himself, "what does this mean? When one of us has conquered the other, what good will it do? You will not know what to do with me, nor I with you. We will remain here like two idiots."

The two oars slipped into the water. The boat drifted into the stream.

"Good Lord, what a fuss you make! A man of your age ought to know better! You act like a child."

Lupin succeeded in freeing himself from the grasp of the detective, who, thoroughly exasperated and ready to kill, put his hand in his pocket. He uttered an oath: Lupin had taken his revolver. Then he knelt down and tried to capture one of the lost oars in order to regain the shore, while Lupin was trying to capture the other oar in order to drive the boat down the river.

"It's gone! I can't reach it," said Lupin. "But it's of no consequence. If you get your oar I can prevent your using it. And you could do the same to me. But, you see, that is the way in this world, we act without any purpose or reason, as our efforts are in vain since Fate decides everything. Now, don't you see, Fate is on the side of his friend Lupin. The game is mine! The current favors me!"

The boat was slowly drifting down the river.

"Look out!" cried Lupin, quickly.

Someone on the bank was pointing a revolver. Lupin stooped, a shot was fired; it struck the water beyond the boat. Lupin burst into laughter.

"God bless me! It's my friend Ganimard! But it was very wrong of you to do that, Ganimard. You have no right to shoot except in self-defense. Does poor Lupin worry you so much that you forget yourself?... Now, be good, and don't shoot again!... If you do you will hit our English friend."

He stood behind Sholmes, facing Ganimard, and said:

"Now, Ganimard, I am ready! Aim for his heart!... Higher!... A little to the left.... Ah! you missed that time ... deuced bad shot.... Try again.... Your hand shakes, Ganimard.... Now, once more ... one, two, three, fire!... Missed!... Parbleu! the authorities furnish you with toy-pistols."

Lupin drew a long revolver and fired without taking aim. Ganimard put his hand to his hat: the bullet had passed through it.

"What do you think of that, Ganimard! Ah! that's a real revolver! A genuine English bulldog. It belongs to my friend, Herlock Sholmes."

And, with a laugh, he threw the revolver to the shore, where it landed at Ganimard's feet.

Sholmes could not withhold a smile of admiration. What a torrent of youthful spirits! And how he seemed to enjoy himself! It appeared as if the sensation of peril caused him a physical pleasure; and this extraordinary man had no other purpose in life than to seek for dangers simply for the amusement it afforded him in avoiding them.

Many people had now gathered on the banks of the river, and Ganimard and his men followed the boat as it slowly floated down the stream. Lupin's capture was a mathematical certainty.

"Confess, old fellow," said Lupin, turning to the Englishman, "that you would not exchange your present position for all the gold in the Transvaal! You are now in the first row of the orchestra chairs! But, in the first place, we must have the prologue ... after which we can leap, at one bound, to the fifth act of the drama, which will represent the capture or escape of Arsène Lupin. Therefore, I am going to ask you a plain question, to which I request a plain answer—a simple yes or no. Will you renounce this affair? At present I can repair the damage you have done; later it will be beyond my power. Is it a bargain?"

"No."

Lupin's face showed his disappointment and annoyance. He continued:

"I insist. More for your sake than my own, I insist, because I am certain you will be the first to regret your intervention. For the last time, yes or no?"

"No."

Lupin stooped down, removed one of the boards in the bottom of the boat, and, for some minutes, was engaged in a work the nature of which Sholmes could not discern. Then he arose, seated himself beside the Englishman, and said:

"I believe, monsieur, that we came to the river to-day for the same purpose: to recover the object which Bresson threw away. For my part I had invited a few friends to join me here, and I was on the point of making an examination of the bed of the river when my friends announced your approach. I confess that the news did not surprise me, as I have been notified every hour concerning the progress of your investigation. That was an easy matter. Whenever anything occurred in the rue Murillo that might interest me, simply a ring on the telephone and I was informed."

He stopped. The board that he had displaced in the bottom of the boat was rising and water was working into the boat all around it.

"The deuce! I didn't know how to fix it. I was afraid this old boat would leak. You are not afraid, monsieur?"

Sholmes shrugged his shoulders. Lupin continued:

"You will understand then, in those circumstances, and knowing in advance that you would be more eager to seek a battle than I would be to avoid it, I assure you I was not entirely displeased to enter into a contest of which the issue is quite certain, since I hold all the trump cards in my hand. And I desired that our meeting should be given the widest publicity in order that your defeat may be universally known, so that another Countess de Crozon or another Baron d'Imblevalle may not be tempted to solicit your aid against me. Besides, my dear monsieur—"

He stopped again and, using his half-closed hands as a lorgnette, he scanned the banks of the river.

"Mon Dieu! they have chartered a superb boat, a real war-vessel, and see how they are rowing. In five minutes they will be along-side, and I am lost. Monsieur Sholmes, a word of advice; you seize me, bind me and deliver me to the officers of the law. Does that programme please you?... Unless, in the meantime, we are shipwrecked, in which event we can do nothing but prepare our wills. What do you think?"

They exchanged looks. Sholmes now understood Lupin's scheme: he had scuttled the boat. And the water was rising. It had reached the soles of their boots. Then it covered their feet; but they did not move. It was half-way to their knees. The Englishman took out his tobacco, rolled a cigarette, and lighted it. Lupin continued to talk:

"But do not regard that offer as a confession of my weakness. I surrender to you in a battle in which I can achieve a victory in order to avoid a struggle upon a field not of my own choosing. In so doing I recognize the fact that Sholmes is the only enemy I fear, and announce my anxiety that Sholmes will not be diverted from my track. I take this opportunity to tell you these things since fate has accorded me the honor of a conversation with you. I have only one regret; it is that our conversation should have occurred while we are taking a foot-bath ... a situation that is lacking in dignity, I must confess.... What did I say? A foot-bath? It is worse than that."

The water had reached the board on which they were sitting, and the boat was gradually sinking.

Sholmes, smoking his cigarette, appeared to be calmly admiring the scenery. For nothing in the world, while face to face with that man who, while threatened by dangers, surrounded by a crowd, followed by a posse of police, maintained his equanimity and good humor, for nothing in the world would he, Sholmes, display the slightest sign of nervousness.

Each of them looked as if he might say: Should a person be disturbed by such trifles? Are not people drowned in a river every day? Is it such an unusual event as to deserve special attention? One chatted, whilst the other dreamed; both concealing their wounded pride beneath a mask of indifference.

One minute more and the boat will sink. Lupin continued his chatter:

"The important thing to know is whether we will sink before or after the arrival of the champions of the law. That is the main question. As to our shipwreck, that is a fore-gone conclusion. Now, monsieur, the hour has come in which we must make our wills. I give, devise and bequeath all my property to Herlock Sholmes, a citizen of England, for his own use and benefit. But, mon Dieu, how quickly the champions of the law are approaching! Ah! the brave fellows! It is a pleasure to watch them. Observe the precision of the oars! Ah! is it you, Brigadier Folenfant? Bravo! The idea of a war-vessel is an excellent one. I commend you to your superiors, Brigadier Folenfant.... Do you wish a medal? You shall have it. And your comrade Dieuzy, where is he?... Ah! yes, I think I see him on the left bank of the river at the head of a hundred natives. So that, if I escape shipwreck, I shall be captured on the left by Dieuzy and his natives, or, on the right, by Ganimard and the populace of Neuilly. An embarrassing dilemma!"

The boat entered an eddy; it swung around and Sholmes caught hold of the oarlocks. Lupin said to him:

"Monsieur, you should remove your coat. You will find it easier to swim without a coat. No? You refuse? Then I shall put on my own."

He donned his coat, buttoned it closely, the same as Sholmes, and said:

"What a discourteous man you are! And what a pity that you should be so stubborn in this affair, in which, of course, you display your strength, but, oh! so vainly! really, you mar your genius——"

"Monsieur Lupin," interrupted Sholmes, emerging from his silence, "you talk too much, and you frequently err through excess of confidence and through your frivolity."

"That is a severe reproach."

"Thus, without knowing it, you furnished me, only a moment ago, with the information I required."

"What! you required some information and you didn't tell me?"

"I had no occasion to ask you for it—you volunteered it. Within three hours I can deliver the key of the mystery to Monsieur d'Imblevalle. That is the only reply———"

He did not finish the sentence. The boat suddenly sank, taking both of the men down with it. It emerged immediately, with its keel in the air. Shouts were heard on either bank, succeeded by an anxious moment of silence. Then the shouts were renewed: one of the shipwrecked party had come to the surface.

It was Herlock Sholmes. He was an excellent swimmer, and struck out, with powerful strokes, for Folenfant's boat.

"Courage, Monsieur Sholmes," shouted Folenfant; "we are here. Keep it up ... we will get you ... a little more, Monsieur Sholmes ... catch the rope."

The Englishman seized the rope they had thrown to him. But, while they were hauling him into the boat, he heard a voice behind him, saying:

"The key of the mystery, monsieur, yes, you shall have it. I am astonished that you haven't got it already. What then? What good will it do you? By that time you will have lost the battle...."

Now comfortably installed astride the keel of the boat, Lupin continued his speech with solemn gestures, as if he hoped to convince his adversary.

"You must understand, my dear Sholmes, there is nothing to be done, absolutely nothing. You find yourself in the deplorable position of a gentleman———"

"Surrender, Lupin!" shouted Folenfant.

"You are an ill-bred fellow, Folenfant, to interrupt me in the middle of a sentence. I was saying———"

"Surrender, Lupin!"

"Oh! parbleu! Brigadier Folenfant, a man surrenders only when he is in danger. Surely, you do not pretend to say that I am in any danger."

"For the last time, Lupin, I call on you to surrender."

"Brigadier Folenfant, you have no intention of killing me; you may wish to wound me since you are afraid I may escape. But if by chance the wound prove mortal! Just think of your remorse! It would embitter your old age."

The shot was fired.

Lupin staggered, clutched at the keel of the boat for a moment, then let go and disappeared.

It was exactly three o'clock when the foregoing events transpired. Precisely at six o'clock, as he had foretold, Herlock Sholmes, dressed in trousers that were too short and a coat that was too small, which he had borrowed from an innkeeper at Neuilly, wearing a cap and a flannel shirt, entered the boudoir in the Rue Murillo, after having sent word to Monsieur and Madame d'Imblevalle that he desired an interview.

They found him walking up and down the room. And he looked so ludicrous in his strange costume that they could scarcely suppress their mirth. With pensive air and stooped shoulders, he walked like an automaton from the window to the door and from the door to the window, taking each time the same number of steps, and turning each time in the same manner.

He stopped, picked up a small ornament, examined it mechanically, and resumed his walk. At last, planting himself before them, he asked:

"Is Mademoiselle here?"

"Yes, she is in the garden with the children.'"

"I wish Mademoiselle to be present at this interview."

"Is it necessary———"

"Have a little patience, monsieur. From the facts I am going to present to you, you will see the necessity for her presence here."

"Very well. Suzanne, will you call her?"

Madame d'Imblevalle arose, went out, and returned almost immediately, accompanied by Alice Demun. Mademoiselle, who was a trifle paler than usual, remained standing, leaning against a table, and without even asking why she had been called. Sholmes did not look at her, but, suddenly turning toward Monsieur d'Imblevalle, he said, in a tone which did not admit of a reply:

"After several days' investigation, monsieur, I must repeat what I told you when I first came here: the Jewish lamp was stolen by some one living in the house."

"The name of the guilty party?"

"I know it."

"Your proof?"

"I have sufficient to establish that fact."

"But we require more than that. We desire the restoration of the stolen goods."

"The Jewish lamp? It is in my possession."

"The opal necklace? The snuff-box?"

"The opal necklace, the snuff-box, and all the goods stolen on the second occasion are in my possession."

Sholmes delighted in these dramatic dialogues, and it pleased him to announce his victories in that curt manner. The baron and his wife were amazed, and looked at Sholmes with a silent curiosity, which was the highest praise.

He related to them, very minutely, what he had done during those three days. He told of his discovery of the alphabet book, wrote upon a sheet of paper the sentence formed by the missing letters, then related the journey of Bresson to the bank of the river and the suicide of the adventurer, and, finally, his struggle with Lupin, the shipwreck, and the disappearance of Lupin. When he had finished, the baron said, in a low voice:

"Now, you have told us everything except the name of the guilty party. Whom do you accuse?"

"I accuse the person who cut the letters from the alphabet book, and communicated with Arsène Lupin by means of those letters."

"How do you know that such correspondence was carried on with Arsène Lupin?"

"My information comes from Lupin himself."

He produced a piece of paper that was wet and crumpled. It was the page which Lupin had torn from his memorandum-book, and upon which he had written the phrase.

"And you will notice," said Sholmes, with satisfaction, "that he was not obliged to give me that sheet of paper, and, in that way, disclose his identity. Simple childishness on his part, and yet it gave me exactly the information I desired."

"What was it?" asked the baron. "I don't understand."

Sholmes took a pencil and made a fresh copy of the letters and figures.

"CDEHNOPRZEO—237."

"Well?" said the baron; "it is the formula you showed me yourself."

"No. If you had turned and returned that formula in every way, as I have done, you would have seen at first glance that this formula is not like the first one."

"In what respect do they differ?"

"This one has two more letters—an E and an O."

"Really; I hadn't noticed that."

"Join those two letters to the C and the H which remained after forming the word 'respondez,' and you will agree with me that the only possible word is ECHO."

"What does that mean?"

"It refers to the *Echo de France*, Lupin's newspaper, his official organ, the one in which he publishes his communications. Reply in the *Echo de France*, in the personal advertisements, under number 237. That is the key to the mystery, and Arsène Lupin was kind enough to furnish it to me. I went to the newspaper office."

"What did you find there?"

"I found the entire story of the relations between Arsène Lupin and his accomplice."

Sholmes produced seven newspapers which he opened at the fourth page and pointed to the following lines:

1. Ars. Lup. Lady implores protection. 540.

2. 540. Awaiting particulars. A.L.

3. A.L. Under domin. enemy. Lost.

4. 540. Write address. Will make investigation.

5. A.L. Murillo.

6. 540. Park three o'clock. Violets.

7. 237. Understand. Sat. Will be Sun. morn. park.

"And you call that the whole story!" exclaimed the baron.

"Yes, and if you will listen to me for a few minutes, I think I can convince you. In the first place, a lady who signs herself 540 implores the protection of Arsène Lupin, who replies by asking for particulars. The lady replies that she is under the domination of an enemy—who is Bresson, no doubt—and that she is lost if some one does not come to her assistance. Lupin is suspicious and does not yet venture to appoint an interview with the unknown woman, demands the address and proposes to make an investigation. The lady hesitates for four days—look at the dates—finally, under stress of circumstances and influenced by Bresson's threats, she gives the name of the street—Murillo. Next day, Arsène Lupin announces that he will be in the Park Monceau at three o'clock, and asks his unknown correspondent to wear a bouquet of violets as a means of identification. Then there is a lapse of eight days in the correspondence. Arsène Lupin and the lady do not require to correspond through the newspaper now, as they see each other or write directly. The scheme is arranged in this way: in order to satisfy Bresson's demands, the lady is to carry off the Jewish lamp. The date is not yet fixed. The lady who, as a matter of prudence, corresponds by means of letters cut out of a book, decides on Saturday and adds: *Reply Echo 237*. Lupin replies that it is understood and that he will be in the park on Sunday morning. Sunday morning, the theft takes place."

"Really, that is an excellent chain of circumstantial evidence and every link is complete," said the baron.

"The theft has taken place," continued Sholmes. "The lady goes out on Sunday morning, tells Lupin what she has done, and carries the Jewish lamp to Bresson. Everything occurs then exactly as Lupin had foreseen. The officers of the law, deceived by an open window, four holes in the ground and two scratches on the balcony railing, immediately advance the theory that the theft was committed by a burglar. The lady is safe."

"Yes, I confess the theory was a logical one," said the baron. "But the second theft—"

"The second theft was provoked by the first. The newspapers having related how the Jewish lamp had disappeared, some one conceived the idea of repeating the crime and carrying away what had been left. This time, it was not a simulated theft, but a real one, a genuine burglary, with ladders and other paraphernalia—"

"Lupin, of course—"

"No. Lupin does not act so stupidly. He doesn't fire at people for trifling reasons."

"Then, who was it?"

"Bresson, no doubt, and unknown to the lady whom he had menaced. It was Bresson who entered here; it was Bresson that I pursued; it was Bresson who wounded poor Wilson."

"Are you sure of it?"

"Absolutely. One of Bresson's accomplices wrote to him yesterday, before his suicide, a letter which proves that negotiations were pending between this accomplice and Lupin for the restitution of all the articles stolen from your house. Lupin demanded everything, '*the first thing* (that is, the Jewish lamp) *as well as those of the second affair.*' Moreover, he was watching Bresson. When the latter returned from the river last night, one of Lupin's men followed him as well as we."

"What was Bresson doing at the river?"

"Having been warned of the progress of my investigations——"

"Warned! by whom?"

"By the same lady, who justly feared that the discovery of the Jewish lamp would lead to the discovery of her own adventure. Thereupon, Bresson, having been warned, made into a package all the things that could compromise him and threw them into a place where he thought he could get them again when the danger was past. It was after his return, tracked by Ganimard and myself, having, no doubt, other sins on his conscience, that he lost his head and killed himself."

"But what did the package contain?"

"The Jewish lamp and your other ornaments."

"Then, they are not in your possession?"

"Immediately after Lupin's disappearance, I profited by the bath he had forced upon me, went to the spot selected by Bresson, where I found the stolen articles wrapped in some soiled linen. They are there, on the table."

Without a word, the baron cut the cord, tore open the wet linen, picked out the lamp, turned a screw in the foot, then divided the bowl of the lamp which opened in two equal parts and there he found the golden chimera, set with rubies and emeralds.

It was intact.

There was in that scene, so natural in appearance and which consisted of a simple exposition of facts, something which rendered it frightfully tragic—it was the formal, direct, irrefutable accusation that Sholmes launched in each of his words against Mademoiselle. And it was also the impressive silence of Alice Demun.

During that long, cruel accumulation of accusing circumstances heaped one upon another, not a muscle of her face had moved, not a trace of revolt or fear had marred the serenity of her limpid eyes. What were her thoughts. And, especially, what was she going to say at the solemn moment when it would become necessary for her to speak and defend herself in order to break the chain of evidence that Herlock Sholmes had so cleverly woven around her?

That moment had come, but the girl was silent.

"Speak! Speak!" cried Mon. d'Imblevalle.

She did not speak. So he insisted:

"One word will clear you. One word of denial, and I will believe you."

That word, she would not utter.

The baron paced to and fro in his excitement; then, addressing Sholmes, he said:

"No, monsieur, I cannot believe it, I do not believe it. There are impossible crimes! and this is opposed to all I know and to all that I have seen during the past year. No, I cannot believe it."

He placed his hand on the Englishman's shoulder, and said:

"But you yourself, monsieur, are you absolutely certain that you are right?"

Sholmes hesitated, like a man on whom a sudden demand is made and cannot frame an immediate reply. Then he smiled, and said:

"Only the person whom I accuse, by reason of her situation in your house, could know that the Jewish lamp contained that magnificent jewel."

"I cannot believe it," repeated the baron.

"Ask her."

It was, really, the very thing he would not have done, blinded by the confidence the girl had inspired in him. But he could no longer refrain from doing it. He approached her and, looking into her eyes, said:

"Was it you, mademoiselle? Was it you who took the jewel? Was it you who corresponded with Arsène Lupin and committed the theft?"

"It was I, monsieur," she replied.

She did not drop her head. Her face displayed no sign of shame or fear.

"Is it possible?" murmured Mon. d'Imblevalle. "I would never have believed it…. You are the last person in the world that I would have suspected. How did you do it?"

"I did it exactly as Monsieur Sholmes has told it. On Saturday night I came to the boudoir, took the lamp, and, in the morning I carried it … to that man."

"No," said the baron; "what you pretend to have done is impossible."

"Impossible—why?"

"Because, in the morning I found the door of the boudoir bolted."

She blushed, and looked at Sholmes as if seeking his counsel. Sholmes was astonished at her embarrassment. Had she nothing to say? Did the confessions, which had corroborated the report that he, Sholmes, had made concerning the theft of the Jewish lamp, merely serve to mask a lie? Was she misleading them by a false confession?

The baron continued:

"That door was locked. I found the door exactly as I had left it the night before. If you entered by that door, as you pretend, some one must have opened it from the interior—that is to say, from the boudoir or from our chamber. Now, there was no one inside these two rooms … there was no one except my wife and myself."

Sholmes bowed his head and covered his face with his hands in order to conceal his emotion. A sudden light had entered his mind, that startled him and made him exceedingly uncomfortable. Everything was revealed to him, like the sudden lifting of a fog from the morning landscape. He was annoyed as well as ashamed, because his deductions were fallacious and his entire theory was wrong.

Alice Demun was innocent!

Alice Demun was innocent. That proposition explained the embarrassment he had experienced from the beginning in directing the terrible accusation against that young girl. Now, he saw the truth; he knew it. After a few seconds, he raised his head, and looked at Madame d'Imblevalle as naturally as he could. She was pale—with that unusual pallor which invades us in the relentless moments of our lives. Her hands, which she endeavored to conceal, were trembling as if stricken with palsy.

"One minute more," thought Sholmes, "and she will betray herself."

He placed himself between her and her husband in the desire to avert the awful danger which, *through his fault*, now threatened that man and woman. But, at sight of the baron, he was shocked to the very centre of his soul. The same dreadful idea had entered the mind of Monsieur d'Imblevalle. The same thought was at work in the brain of the husband. He understood, also! He saw the truth!

In desperation, Alice Demun hurled herself against the implacable truth, saying:

"You are right, monsieur. I made a mistake. I did not enter by this door. I came through the garden and the vestibule ... by aid of a ladder—"

It was a supreme effort of true devotion. But a useless effort! The words rang false. The voice did not carry conviction, and the poor girl no longer displayed those clear, fearless eyes and that natural air of innocence which had served her so well. Now, she bowed her head—vanquished.

The silence became painful. Madame d'Imblevalle was waiting for her husband's next move, overwhelmed with anxiety and fear. The baron appeared to be struggling against the dreadful suspicion, as if he would not submit to the overthrow of his happiness. Finally, he said to his wife:

"Speak! Explain!"

"I have nothing to tell you," she replied, in a very low voice, and with features drawn by anguish.

"So, then ... Mademoiselle...."

"Mademoiselle saved me ... through devotion ... through affection ... and accused herself...."

"Saved you from what? From whom?"

"From that man."

"Bresson?"

"Yes; it was I whom he held in fear by threats.... I met him at one of my friends'.... and I was foolish enough to listen to him. Oh! there was nothing that you cannot pardon. But I wrote him two letters ... letters which you will see.... I had to buy them back ... you know how.... Oh! have pity on me!... I have suffered so much!"

"You! You! Suzanne!"

He raised his clenched fists, ready to strike her, ready to kill her. But he dropped his arms, and murmured:

"You, Suzanne.... You!... Is it possible?"

By short detached sentences, she related the heartrending story, her dreadful awakening to the infamy of the man, her remorse, her fear, and she also told of Alice's devotion; how the young girl divined the sorrow of her mistress, wormed a confession out of her, wrote to Lupin, and devised the scheme of the theft in order to save her from Bresson.

"You, Suzanne, you," repeated Monsieur d'Imblevalle, bowed with grief and shame.... "How could you?"

On the same evening, the steamer "City of London," which plies between Calais and Dover, was gliding slowly over the smooth sea. The night was dark; the wind was fainter than a zephyr. The majority of the passengers had retired to their cabins; but a few, more intrepid, were promenading on the deck or sleeping in large rocking-chairs, wrapped in their travelling-rugs. One could see, here and there, the light of a cigar, and one could hear, mingled with the soft murmur of the breeze, the faint sound of voices which were carefully subdued to harmonize with the deep silence of the night.

One of the passengers, who had been pacing to and fro upon the deck, stopped before a woman who was lying on a bench, scrutinized her, and, when she moved a little, he said:

"I thought you were asleep, Mademoiselle Alice."

"No, Monsieur Sholmes, I am not sleepy. I was thinking."

"Of what? If I may be so bold as to inquire?"

"I was thinking of Madame d'Imblevalle. She must be very unhappy. Her life is ruined."

"Oh! no, no," he replied quickly. "Her mistake was not a serious one. Monsieur d'Imblevalle will forgive and forget it. Why, even before we left, his manner toward her had softened."

"Perhaps ... but he will remember it for a long time ... and she will suffer a great deal."

"You love her?"

"Very much. It was my love for her that gave me strength to smile when I was trembling from fear, that gave me courage to look in your face when I desired to hide from your sight."

"And you are sorry to leave her?"

"Yes, very sorry. I have no relatives, no friends—but her."

"You will have friends," said the Englishman, who was affected by her sorrow. "I have promised that. I have relatives ... and some influence. I assure you that you will have no cause to regret coming to England."

"That may be, monsieur, but Madame d'Imblevalle will not be there."

Herlock Sholmes resumed his promenade upon the deck. After a few minutes, he took a seat near his travelling companion, filled his pipe, and struck four matches in a vain effort to light it. Then, as he had no more matches, he arose and said to a gentleman who was sitting near him:

"May I trouble you for a match?"

The gentleman opened a box of matches and struck one. The flame lighted up his face. Sholmes recognized him—it was Arsène Lupin.

If the Englishman had not given an almost imperceptible movement of surprise, Lupin would have supposed that his presence on board had been known to Sholmes, so well did he control his feelings and so natural was the easy manner in which he extended his hand to his adversary.

"How's the good health, Monsieur Lupin?"

"Bravo!" exclaimed Lupin, who could not repress a cry of admiration at the Englishman's sang-froid.

"Bravo? and why?"

"Why? Because I appear before you like a ghost, only a few hours after you saw me drowned in the Seine; and through pride—a quality that is essentially English—you evince not the slightest surprise. You greet me as a matter of course. Ah! I repeat: Bravo! Admirable!"

"There is nothing remarkable about it. From the manner in which you fell from the boat, I knew very well that you fell voluntarily, and that the bullet had not touched you."

"And you went away without knowing what had become of me?"

"What had become of you? Why, I knew that. There were at least five hundred people on the two banks of the river within a space of half-a-mile. If you escaped death, your capture was certain."

"And yet I am here."

"Monsieur Lupin, there are two men in the world at whom I am never astonished: in the first place, myself—and then, Arsène Lupin."

The treaty of peace was concluded.

If Sholmes had not been successful in his contests with Arsène Lupin; if Lupin remained the only enemy whose capture he must never hope to accomplish; if, in the course of their struggles, he had not always displayed a superiority, the Englishman had, none the less, by means of his extraordinary intuition and tenacity, succeeded in recovering the Jewish lamp as well as the blue diamond.

This time, perhaps, the finish had not been so brilliant, especially from the stand-point of the public spectators, since Sholmes was obliged to maintain a discreet silence in regard to the circumstances in which the Jewish lamp had been recovered, and to announce that he did not know the name of the thief. But as man to man, Arsène Lupin against Herlock Sholmes, detective against burglar, there was neither victor nor vanquished. Each of them had won corresponding victories.

Therefore they could now converse as courteous adversaries who had lain down their arms and held each other in high regard.

At Sholmes' request, Arsène Lupin related the strange story of his escape.

"If I may dignify it by calling it an escape," he said. "It was so simple! My friends were watching for me, as I had asked them to meet me there to recover the Jewish lamp. So, after remaining a good half-hour under the overturned boat, I took advantage of an occasion when Folenfant and his men were searching for my dead body along the bank of the river, to climb on top of the boat. Then my friends simply picked me up as they passed by in their motor-boat, and we sailed away under the staring eyes of an astonished multitude, including Ganimard and Folenfant."

"Very good," exclaimed Sholmes, "very neatly played. And now you have some business in England?"

"Yes, some accounts to square up.... But I forgot ... what about Monsieur d'Imblevalle?"

"He knows everything."

"Ah! my dear Sholmes, what did I tell you? The wrong is now irreparable. Would it not have been better to have allowed me to carry out the affair in my own way? In a day or two more, I should have recovered the stolen goods from Bresson, restored them to Monsieur d'Imblevalle, and those two honest citizens would have lived together in peace and happiness ever after. Instead of that—"

"Instead of that," said Sholmes, sneeringly, "I have mixed the cards and sown the seeds of discord in the bosom of a family that was under your protection."

"Mon Dieu! of course, I was protecting them. Must a person steal, cheat and wrong all the time?"

"Then you do good, also?"

"When I have the time. Besides, I find it amusing. Now, for instance, in our last adventure, I found it extremely diverting that I should be the good genius seeking to help and save unfortunate mortals, while you were the evil genius who dispensed only despair and tears."

"Tears! Tears!" protested Sholmes.

"Certainly! The d'Imblevalle household is demolished, and Alice Demun weeps."

"She could not remain any longer. Ganimard would have discovered her some day, and, through her, reached Madame d'Imblevalle."

"Quite right, monsieur; but whose fault is it?"

Two men passed by. Sholmes said to Lupin, in a friendly tone:

"Do you know those gentlemen?"

"I thought I recognized one of them as the captain of the steamer."

"And the other?"

"I don't know."

"It is Austin Gilett, who occupies in London a position similar to that of Monsieur Dudouis in Paris."

"Ah! how fortunate! Will you be so kind as to introduce me? Monsieur Dudouis is one of my best friends, and I shall be delighted to say as much of Monsieur Austin Gilett."

The two gentlemen passed again.

"And if I should take you at your word, Monsieur Lupin?" said Sholmes, rising, and seizing Lupin's wrist with a hand of iron.

"Why do you grasp me so tightly, monsieur? I am quite willing to follow you."

In fact, he allowed himself to be dragged along without the least resistance. The two gentlemen were disappearing from sight. Sholmes quickened his pace. His finger-nails even sank into Lupin's flesh.

"Come! Come!" he exclaimed, with a sort of feverish haste, in harmony with his action. "Come! quicker than that."

But he stopped suddenly. Alice Demun was following them.

"What are you doing, Mademoiselle? You need not come. You must not come!"

It was Lupin who replied:

"You will notice, monsieur, that she is not coming of her own free will. I am holding her wrist in the same tight grasp that you have on mine."

"Why!"

"Because I wish to present her also. Her part in the affair of the Jewish lamp is much more important than mine. Accomplice of Arsène Lupin, accomplice of Bresson, she has a right to tell her adventure with the Baroness d'Imblevalle—which will deeply interest Monsieur Gilett as an officer of the law. And by introducing her also, you will have carried your gracious intervention to the very limit, my dear Sholmes."

The Englishman released his hold on his prisoner's wrist. Lupin liberated Mademoiselle.

They stood looking at each other for a few seconds, silently and motionless. Then Sholmes returned to the bench and sat down, followed by Lupin and the girl. After a long silence, Lupin said: "You see, monsieur, whatever we may do, we will never be on the same side. You are on one side of the fence; I am on the other.

We can exchange greetings, shake hands, converse a moment, but the fence is always there. You will remain Herlock Sholmes, detective, and I, Arsène Lupin, gentleman-burglar. And Herlock Sholmes will ever obey, more or less spontaneously, with more or less propriety, his instinct as a detective, which is to pursue the burglar and run him down, if possible. And Arsène Lupin, in obedience to his burglarious instinct, will always be occupied in avoiding the reach of the detective, and making sport of the detective, if he can do it. And, this time, he can do it. Ha-ha-ha!"

He burst into a loud laugh, cunning, cruel and odious.

Then, suddenly becoming serious, he addressed Alice Demun:

"You may be sure, mademoiselle, even when reduced to the last extremity, I shall not betray you. Arsène Lupin never betrays anyone—especially those whom he loves and admires. And, may I be permitted to say, I love and admire the brave, dear woman you have proved yourself to be."

He took from his pocket a visiting card, tore it in two, gave one-half of it to the girl, as he said, in a voice shaken with emotion:

"If Monsieur Sholmes' plans for you do not succeed, mademoiselle, go to Lady Strongborough—you can easily find her address—and give her that half of the card, and, at the same time, say to her: *Faithful friend*. Lady Strongborough will show you the true devotion of a sister."

"Thank you," said the girl; "I shall see her to-morrow."

"And now, Monsieur Sholmes," exclaimed Lupin, with the satisfied air of a gentleman who has fulfilled his duty, "I will say good-night. We will not land for an hour yet, so I will get that much rest."

He lay down on the bench, with his hands beneath his head.

In a short time the high cliffs of the English coast loomed up in the increasing light of a new-born day. The passengers emerged from the cabins and crowded the deck, eagerly gazing on the approaching shore. Austin Gilette passed by, accompanied by two men whom Sholmes recognized as sleuths from Scotland Yard.

Lupin was asleep, on his bench.

THE END.

BOOK THREE.
THE HOLLOW NEEDLE.
FURTHER ADVENTURES OF ARSENE LUPIN

I. THE SHOT

Raymonde listened. The noise was repeated twice over, clearly enough to be distinguished from the medley of vague sounds that formed the great silence of the night and yet too faintly to enable her to tell whether it was near or far, within the walls of the big country-house, or outside, among the murky recesses of the park.

She rose softly. Her window was half open: she flung it back wide. The moonlight lay over a peaceful landscape of lawns and thickets, against which the straggling ruins of the old abbey stood out in tragic outlines, truncated columns, mutilated arches, fragments of porches and shreds of flying buttresses. A light breeze hovered over the face of things, gliding noiselessly through the bare motionless branches of the trees, but shaking the tiny budding leaves of the shrubs.

And, suddenly, she heard the same sound again. It was on the left and on the floor below her, in the living rooms, therefore, that occupied the left wing of the house. Brave and plucky though she was, the girl felt afraid. She slipped on her dressing gown and took the matches.

"Raymonde—Raymonde!"

A voice as low as a breath was calling to her from the next room, the door of which had not been closed. She was feeling her way there, when Suzanne, her cousin, came out of the room and fell into her arms:

"Raymonde—is that you? Did you hear—?"

"Yes. So you're not asleep?"

"I suppose the dog woke me—some time ago. But he's not barking now. What time is it?"

"About four."

"Listen! Surely, some one's walking in the drawing room!"

"There's no danger, your father is down there, Suzanne."

"But there is danger for him. His room is next to the boudoir."

"M. Daval is there too—"

"At the other end of the house. He could never hear."

They hesitated, not knowing what course to decide upon. Should they call out? Cry for help? They dared not; they were frightened of the sound of their own voices. But Suzanne, who had gone to the window, suppressed a scream:

"Look!—A man!—Near the fountain!"

A man was walking away at a rapid pace. He carried under his arm a fairly large load, the nature of which they were unable to distinguish: it knocked against his leg and impeded his progress. They saw him pass near the old chapel and turn toward a little door in the wall. The door must have been open, for the man disappeared suddenly from view and they failed to hear the usual grating of the hinges.

"He came from the drawing room," whispered Suzanne.

"No, the stairs and the hall would have brought him out more to the left—Unless—"

The same idea struck them both. They leant out. Below them, a ladder stood against the front of the house, resting on the first floor. A glimmer lit up the stone balcony. And another man, who was also carrying something, bestrode the baluster, slid down the ladder and ran away by the same road as the first.

Suzanne, scared to the verge of swooning, fell on her knees, stammering:

"Let us call out—let us call for help—"

"Who would come? Your father—and if there are more of them left—and they throw themselves upon him—?"

"Then—then—we might call the servants—Your bell rings on their floor."

"Yes—yes—perhaps, that's better. If only they come in time!"

Raymonde felt for the electric push near her bed and pressed it with her finger. They heard the bell ring upstairs and had an impression that its shrill sound must also reach any one below.

They waited. The silence became terrifying and the very breeze no longer shook the leaves of the shrubs.

"I'm frightened—frightened," said Suzanne.

And, suddenly, from the profound darkness below them, came the sound of a struggle, a crash of furniture overturned, words, exclamations and then, horrible and ominous, a hoarse groan, the gurgle of a man who is being murdered—

Raymonde leapt toward the door. Suzanne clung desperately to her arm:

"No—no—don't leave me—I'm frightened—"

Raymonde pushed her aside and darted down the corridor, followed by Suzanne, who staggered from wall to wall, screaming as she went. Raymonde reached the staircase, flew down the stairs, flung herself upon the door of the big drawing room and stopped short, rooted to the threshold, while Suzanne sank in a heap by her side. Facing them, at three steps' distance, stood a man, with a lantern in his hand. He turned it upon the two girls, blinding them with the light, stared long at their pale faces, and then, without hurrying, with the calmest movements in the world, took his cap, picked up a scrap of paper and two bits of straw, removed some footmarks from the carpet, went to the balcony, turned to the girls, made them a deep bow and disappeared.

Suzanne was the first to run to the little boudoir which separated the big drawing-room from her father's bedroom. But, at the entrance, a hideous sight appalled her. By the slanting rays of the moon, she saw two apparently lifeless bodies lying close to each other on the floor. She leaned over one of them:

"Father!—Father!—Is it you? What has happened to you?" she cried, distractedly.

After a moment, the Comte de Gesvres moved. In a broken voice, he said:

"Don't be afraid—I am not wounded—Daval?—Is he alive?—The knife?—The knife?—"

Two men-servants now arrived with candles. Raymonde flung herself down before the other body and recognized Jean Daval, the count's private secretary. A little stream of blood trickled from his neck. His face already wore the pallor of death.

Then she rose, returned to the drawing room, took a gun that hung in a trophy of arms on the wall and went out on the balcony. Not more than fifty or sixty seconds had elapsed since the man had set his foot on the top rung of the ladder. He could not, therefore, be very far away, the more so as he had taken the precaution to remove the ladder, in order to prevent the inmates of the house from using it. And soon she saw him skirting the remains of the old cloister. She put the gun to her shoulder, calmly took aim and fired. The man fell.

"That's done it! That's done it!" said one of the servants. "We've got this one. I'll run down."

"No, Victor, he's getting up.... You had better go down by the staircase and make straight for the little door in the wall. That's the only way he can escape."

Victor hurried off, but, before he reached the park, the man fell down again. Raymonde called the other servant:

"Albert, do you see him down there? Near the main cloister?—"

"Yes, he's crawling in the grass. He's done for—"

"Watch him from here."

"There's no way of escape for him. On the right of the ruins is the open lawn—"

"And, Victor, do you guard the door, on the left," she said, taking up her gun.

"But, surely, you are not going down, miss?"

"Yes, yes," she said, with a resolute accent and abrupt movements; "let me be—I have a cartridge left—If he stirs—"

She went out. A moment later, Albert saw her going toward the ruins. He called to her from the window:

"He's dragged himself behind the cloister. I can't see him. Be careful, miss—"

Raymonde went round the old cloisters, to cut off the man's retreat, and Albert soon lost sight of her. After a few minutes, as he did not see her return, he became uneasy and, keeping his eye on the ruins, instead of going down by the stairs he made an effort to reach the ladder. When he had succeeded, he scrambled down and ran straight to the cloisters near which he had seen the man last. Thirty paces farther, he found Raymonde, who was searching with Victor.

"Well?" he asked.

"There's no laying one's hands on him," replied Victor.

"The little door?"

"I've been there; here's the key."

"Still—he must—"

"Oh, we've got him safe enough, the scoundrel—He'll be ours in ten minutes."

The farmer and his son, awakened by the shot, now came from the farm buildings, which were at some distance on the right, but within the circuit of the walls. They had met no one.

"Of course not," said Albert. "The ruffian can't have left the ruins—We'll dig him out of some hole or other."

They organized a methodical search, beating every bush, pulling aside the heavy masses of ivy rolled round the shafts of the columns. They made sure that the chapel was properly locked and that none of the panes were broken. They went round the cloisters and examined every nook and corner. The search was fruitless.

There was but one discovery: at the place where the man had fallen under Raymonde's gun, they picked up a chauffeur's cap, in very soft buff leather; besides that, nothing.

The gendarmerie of Ouville-la-Riviere were informed at six o'clock in the morning and at once proceeded to the spot, after sending an express to the authorities at Dieppe with a note describing the circumstances of the crime, the imminent capture of the chief criminal and "the discovery of his headgear and of the dagger with which the crime had been committed."

At ten o'clock, two hired conveyances came down the gentle slope that led to the house. One of them, an old-fashioned calash, contained the deputy public prosecutor and the examining magistrate, accompanied by his clerk. In the other, a humble fly, were seated two reporters, representing the Journal de Rouen and a great Paris paper.

The old chateau came into view—once the abbey residence of the priors of Ambrumesy, mutilated under the Revolution, both restored by the Comte de Gesvres, who had now owned it for some twenty years. It consists of a main building, surmounted by a pinnacled clock-tower, and two wings, each of which is surrounded by a flight of steps with a stone balustrade. Looking across the walls of the park and beyond the upland supported by the high Norman cliffs, you catch a glimpse of the blue line of the Channel between the villages of Sainte-Marguerite and Varengeville.

Here the Comte de Gesvres lived with his daughter Suzanne, a delicate, fair-haired, pretty creature, and his niece Raymonde de Saint-Veran, whom he had taken to live with him two years before, when the simultaneous death of her father and mother left Raymonde an orphan. Life at the chateau was peaceful and regular. A few neighbors paid an occasional visit. In the summer, the count took the two girls almost every day to Dieppe. He was a tall man, with a handsome, serious face and hair that was turning gray. He was very rich, managed his fortune himself and looked after his extensive estates with the assistance of his secretary, Jean Daval.

Immediately upon his arrival, the examining magistrate took down the first observations of Sergeant Quevillon of the gendarmes. The capture of the criminal, imminent though it might be, had not yet been effected, but every outlet of the park was held. Escape was impossible.

The little company next crossed the chapter-hall and the refectory, both of which are on the ground floor, and went up to the first story. They at once remarked the perfect order that prevailed in the drawing room. Not a piece of furniture, not an ornament but appeared to occupy its usual place; nor was there any gap among the ornaments or furniture. On the right and left walls hung magnificent Flemish tapestries with figures. On the panels of the wall facing the windows were four fine canvases, in contemporary frames, representing mythological scenes. These were the famous pictures by Rubens which had been left to the Comte de Gesvres, together with the Flemish tapestries, by his maternal uncle, the Marques de Bobadilla, a Spanish grandee.

M. Filleul remarked:

"If the motive of the crime was theft, this drawing room, at any rate, was not the object of it."

"You can't tell!" said the deputy, who spoke little, but who, when he did, invariably opposed the magistrate's views.

"Why, my dear sir, the first thought of a burglar would be to carry off those pictures and tapestries, which are universally renowned."

"Perhaps there was no time."

"We shall see."

At that moment, the Comte de Gesvres entered, accompanied by the doctor. The count, who did not seem to feel the effects of the attack to which he had been subjected, welcomed the two officials. Then he opened the door of the boudoir.

This room, which no one had been allowed to enter since the discovery of the crime, differed from the drawing room inasmuch as it presented a scene of the greatest disorder. Two chairs were overturned, one of the tables smashed to pieces and several objects—a traveling-clock, a portfolio, a box of stationery—lay on the floor. And there was blood on some of the scattered pieces of note-paper.

The doctor turned back the sheet that covered the corpse. Jean Daval, dressed in his usual velvet suit, with a pair of nailed boots on his feet, lay stretched on his back, with one arm folded beneath him. His collar and tie had been removed and his shirt opened, revealing a large wound in the chest.

"Death must have been instantaneous," declared the doctor. "One blow of the knife was enough."

"It was, no doubt, the knife which I saw on the drawing-room mantelpiece, next to a leather cap?" said the examining magistrate.

"Yes," said the Comte de Gesvres, "the knife was picked up here. It comes from the same trophy in the drawing room from which my niece, Mlle. de Saint-Veran, snatched the gun. As for the chauffeur's cap, that evidently belongs to the murderer."

M. Filleul examined certain further details in the room, put a few questions to the doctor and then asked M. de Gesvres to tell him what he had seen and heard. The count worded his story as follows:

"Jean Daval woke me up. I had been sleeping badly, for that matter, with gleams of consciousness in which I seemed to hear noises, when, suddenly opening my eyes, I saw Daval standing at the foot of my bed, with his candle in his hand and fully dressed—as he is now, for he often worked late into the night. He seemed greatly excited and said, in a low voice: 'There's some one in the drawing room.' I heard a noise myself. I got up and softly pushed the door leading to this boudoir. At the same moment, the door over there, which opens into the big drawing room, was thrown back and a man appeared who leaped at me and stunned me with a blow on the temple. I am telling you this without any details, Monsieur le Juge d'Instruction, for the simple reason that I remember only the principal facts, and that these facts followed upon one another with extraordinary swiftness."

"And after that?—"

"After that, I don't know—I fainted. When I came to, Daval lay stretched by my side, mortally wounded."

"At first sight, do you suspect no one?"

"No one."

"You have no enemy?"

"I know of none."

"Nor M. Daval either?"

"Daval! An enemy? He was the best creature that ever lived. M. Daval was my secretary for twenty years and, I may say, my confidant; and I have never seen him surrounded with anything but love and friendship."

"Still, there has been a burglary and there has been a murder: there must be a motive for all that."

"The motive? Why, it was robbery pure and simple."

"Robbery? Have you been robbed of something, then?"

"No, nothing."

"In that case—?"

"In that case, if they have stolen nothing and if nothing is missing, they at least took something away."

"What?"

"I don't know. But my daughter and my niece will tell you, with absolute certainty, that they saw two men in succession cross the park and that those two men were carrying fairly heavy loads."

"The young ladies—"

"The young ladies may have been dreaming, you think? I should be tempted to believe it, for I have been exhausting myself in inquiries and suppositions ever since this morning. However, it is easy enough to question them."

The two cousins were sent for to the big drawing room. Suzanne, still quite pale and trembling, could hardly speak. Raymonde, who was more energetic, more of a man, better looking, too, with the golden glint in her brown eyes, described the events of the night and the part which she had played in them.

"So I may take it, mademoiselle, that your evidence is positive?"

"Absolutely. The men who went across the park were carrying things away with them."

"And the third man?"

"He went from here empty-handed."

"Could you describe him to us?"

"He kept on dazzling us with the light of his lantern. All that I could say is that he is tall and heavily built."

"Is that how he appeared to you, mademoiselle?" asked the magistrate, turning to Suzanne de Gesvres.

"Yes—or, rather, no," said Suzanne, reflecting. "I thought he was about the middle height and slender."

M. Filleul smiled; he was accustomed to differences of opinion and sight in witnesses to one and the same fact:

"So we have to do, on the one hand, with a man, the one in the drawing room, who is, at the same time, tall and short, stout and thin, and, on the other, with two men, those in the park, who are accused of removing from that drawing room objects—which are still here!"

M. Filleul was a magistrate of the ironic school, as he himself would say. He was also a very ambitious magistrate and one who did not object to an audience nor to an occasion to display his tactful resource in public, as was shown by the increasing number of persons who now crowded into the room. The journalists had been joined by the farmer and his son, the gardener and his wife, the indoor servants of the chateau and the two cabmen who had driven the flies from Dieppe.

M. Filleul continued:

"There is also the question of agreeing upon the way in which the third person disappeared. Was this the gun you fired, mademoiselle, and from this window?"

"Yes. The man reached the tombstone which is almost buried under the brambles, to the left of the cloisters."

"But he got up again?"

"Only half. Victor ran down at once to guard the little door and I followed him, leaving the second footman, Albert, to keep watch here."

Albert now gave his evidence and the magistrate concluded:

"So, according to you, the wounded man was not able to escape on the left, because your fellow-servant was watching the door, nor on the right, because you would have seen him cross the lawn. Logically, therefore, he is, at the present moment, in the comparatively restricted space that lies before our eyes."

"I am sure of it."

"And you, mademoiselle?"

"Yes."

"And I, too," said Victor.

The deputy prosecutor exclaimed, with a leer:

"The field of inquiry is quite narrow. We have only to continue the search commenced four hours ago."

"We may be more fortunate."

M. Filleul took the leather cap from the mantel, examined it and, beckoning to the sergeant of gendarmes, whispered:

"Sergeant, send one of your men to Dieppe at once. Tell him to go to Maigret, the hatter, in the Rue de la Barre, and ask M. Maigret to tell him, if possible, to whom this cap was sold."

The "field of inquiry," in the deputy's phrase, was limited to the space contained between the house, the lawn on the right and the angle formed by the left wall and the wall opposite the house, that is to say, a quadrilateral of about a hundred yards each way, in which the ruins of Ambrumesy, the famous mediaeval monastery, stood out at intervals.

They at once noticed the traces left by the fugitive in the trampled grass. In two places, marks of blackened blood, now almost dried up, were observed. After the turn at the end of the cloisters, there was nothing more to be seen, as the nature of the ground, here covered with pine-needles, did not lend itself to the imprint of a body. But, in that case, how had the wounded man succeeded in escaping the eyes of Raymonde, Victor and Albert? There was nothing but a few brakes, which the servants and the gendarmes had beaten over and over again, and a number of tombstones, under which they had explored. The examining magistrate made the gardener, who had the key, open the chapel, a real gem of carving, a shrine in stone which had been respected by time and the revolutionaries, and which, with the delicate sculpture work of its porch and its miniature population of statuettes, was always looked upon as a marvelous specimen of the Norman-Gothic style. The chapel, which was very simple in the interior, with no other ornament than its marble altar, offered no hiding-place. Besides, the fugitive would have had to obtain admission. And by what means?

The inspection brought them to the little door in the wall that served as an entrance for the visitors to the ruins. It opened on a sunk road running between the park wall and a copsewood containing some abandoned quarries. M. Filleul stooped forward: the dust of the road bore marks of anti-skid pneumatic tires. Raymonde and Victor remembered that, after the shot, they had seemed to hear the throb of a motor-car.

The magistrate suggested:

"The man must have joined his confederates."

"Impossible!" cried Victor. "I was here while mademoiselle and Albert still had him in view."

"Nonsense, he must be somewhere! Outside or inside: we have no choice!"

"He is here," the servants insisted, obstinately.

The magistrate shrugged his shoulders and went back to the house in a more or less sullen mood. There was no doubt that it was an unpromising case. A theft in which nothing had been stolen; an invisible prisoner: what could be less satisfactory?

It was late. M. de Gesvres asked the officials and the two journalists to stay to lunch. They ate in silence and then M. Filleul returned to the drawing room, where he questioned the servants. But the sound of a horse's hoofs came from the courtyard and, a moment after, the gendarme who had been sent to Dieppe entered.

"Well, did you see the hatter?" exclaimed the magistrate, eager at last to obtain some positive information.

"I saw M. Maigret. The cap was sold to a cab-driver."

"A cab-driver!"

"Yes, a driver who stopped his fly before the shop and asked to be supplied with a yellow-leather chauffeur's cap for one of his customers. This was the only one left. He paid for it, without troubling about the size, and drove off. He was in a great hurry."

"What sort of fly was it?"

"A calash."

"And on what day did this happen?"

"On what day? Why, to-day, at eight o'clock this morning."

"This morning? What are you talking about?"

"The cap was bought this morning."

"But that's impossible, because it was found last night in the park. If it was found there, it must have been there; and, consequently, it must have been bought before."

"The hatter told me it was bought this morning."

There was a moment of general bewilderment. The nonplussed magistrate strove to understand. Suddenly, he started, as though struck with a gleam of light:

"Fetch the cabman who brought us here this morning! The man who drove the calash! Fetch him at once!"

The sergeant of gendarmes and his subordinate ran off to the stables. In a few minutes, the sergeant returned alone.

"Where's the cabman?"

"He asked for food in the kitchen, ate his lunch and then—"

"And then—?"

"He went off."

"With his fly?"

"No. Pretending that he wanted to go and see a relation at Ouville, he borrowed the groom's bicycle. Here are his hat and greatcoat."

"But did he leave bare-headed?"

"No, he took a cap from his pocket and put it on."

"A cap?"

"Yes, a yellow leather cap, it seems."

"A yellow leather cap? Why, no, we've got it here!"

"That's true, Monsieur le Juge d'Instruction, but his is just like it."

The deputy sniggered:

"Very funny! Most amusing! There are two caps—One, the real one, which constituted our only piece of evidence, has gone off on the head of the sham flyman! The other, the false one, is in your hands. Oh, the fellow has had us nicely!"

"Catch him! Fetch him back!" cried M. Filleul. "Two of your men on horseback, Sergeant Quevillon, and at full speed!"

"He is far away by this time," said the deputy.

"He can be as far as he pleases, but still we must lay hold of him."

"I hope so; but I think, Monsieur le Juge d'Instruction, that your efforts should be concentrated here above all. Would you mind reading this scrap of paper, which I have just found in the pocket of the coat?"

"Which coat?"

"The driver's."

And the deputy prosecutor handed M. Filleul a piece of paper, folded in four, containing these few words written in pencil, in a more or less common hand:

"Woe betide the young lady, if she has killed the governor!"

The incident caused a certain stir.

"A word to the wise!" muttered the deputy. "We are now forewarned."

"Monsieur le Comte," said the examining magistrate, "I beg you not to be alarmed. Nor you either, mademoiselle. This threat is of no importance, as the police are on the spot. We shall take every precaution and I will answer for your safety. As for you, gentlemen. I rely on your discretion. You have been present at this inquiry, thanks to my excessive kindness toward the Press, and it would be making me an ill return—"

He interrupted himself, as though an idea had struck him, looked at the two young men, one after the other, and, going up to the first, asked:

"What paper do you represent, sir?"

"The Journal de Rouen."

"Have you your credentials?"

"Here."

The card was in order. There was no more to be said. M. Filleul turned to the other reporter:

"And you, sir?"

"I?"

"Yes, you: what paper do you belong to?"

"Why, Monsieur le Juge d'Instruction, I write for a number of papers—all over the place—"

"Your credentials?"

"I haven't any."

"Oh! How is that?"

"For a newspaper to give you a card, you have to be on its regular staff."

"Well?"

"Well, I am only an occasional contributor, a free-lance. I send articles to this newspaper and that. They are published or declined according to circumstances."

"In that case, what is your name? Where are your papers?"

"My name would tell you nothing. As for papers, I have none."

"You have no paper of any kind to prove your profession!"

"I have no profession."

"But look here, sir," cried the magistrate, with a certain asperity, "you can't expect to preserve your incognito after introducing yourself here by a trick and surprising the secrets of the police!"

"I beg to remark, Monsieur le Juge d'Instruction, that you asked me nothing when I came in, and that therefore I had nothing to say. Besides, it never struck me that your inquiry was secret, when everybody was admitted—including even one of the criminals!"

He spoke softly, in a tone of infinite politeness. He was quite a young man, very tall, very slender and dressed without the least attempt at fashion, in a jacket and trousers both too small for him. He had a pink face like a girl's, a broad forehead topped with close-cropped hair, and a scrubby and ill-trimmed fair beard. His bright eyes gleamed with intelligence. He seemed not in the least embarrassed and wore a pleasant smile, free from any shade of banter.

M. Filleul looked at him with an aggressive air of distrust. The two gendarmes came forward. The young man exclaimed, gaily:

"Monsieur le Juge d'Instruction, you clearly suspect me of being an accomplice. But, if that were so, would I not have slipped away at the right moment, following the example of my fellow-criminal?"

"You might have hoped—"

"Any hope would have been absurd. A moment's reflection, Monsieur le Juge d'Instruction, will make you agree with me that, logically speaking—"

M. Filleul looked him straight in the eyes and said, sharply:

"No more jokes! Your name?"

"Isidore Beautrelet."

"Your occupation?"

"Sixth-form pupil at the Lycee Janson-de-Sailly."

M. Filleul opened a pair of startled eyes.

"What are you talking about? Sixth-form pupil—"

"At the Lycee Janson, Rue de la Pompe, number—"

"Oh, look here," exclaimed M. Filleul, "you're trying to take me in! This won't do, you know; a joke can go too far!"

"I must say, Monsieur le Juge d'Instruction, that your astonishment surprises me. What is there to prevent my being a sixth-form pupil at the Lycee Janson? My beard, perhaps? Set your mind at ease: my beard is false!"

Isidore Beautrelet pulled off the few curls that adorned his chin, and his beardless face appeared still younger and pinker, a genuine schoolboy's face. And, with a laugh like a child's, revealing his white teeth:

"Are you convinced now?" he asked. "Do you want more proofs? Here, you can read the address on these letters from my father: 'To Monsieur Isidore Beautrelet, Indoor Pupil, Lycee Janson-de-Sailly.'"

Convinced or not, M. Filleul did not look as if he liked the story. He asked, gruffly:

"What are you doing here?"

"Why—I'm—I'm improving my mind."

"There are schools for that: yours, for instance."

"You forget, Monsieur le Juge d'Instruction, that this is the twenty-third of April and that we are in the middle of the Easter holidays."

"Well?"

"Well, I have every right to spend my holidays as I please."

"Your father—"

"My father lives at the other end of the country, in Savoy, and he himself advised me to take a little trip on the North Coast."

"With a false beard?"

"Oh, no! That's my own idea. At school, we talk a great deal about mysterious adventures; we read detective stories, in which people disguise themselves; we imagine any amount of terrible and intricate cases. So I thought I would amuse myself; and I put on this false beard. Besides, I enjoyed the advantage of being taken seriously and I pretended to be a Paris reporter. That is how, last night, after an uneventful period of more than a week, I had the pleasure of making the acquaintance of my Rouen colleague; and, this morning, when he heard of the Ambrumesy murder, he very kindly suggested that I should come with him and that we should share the cost of a fly."

Isidore Beautrelet said all this with a frank and artless simplicity of which it was impossible not to feel the charm. M. Filleul himself, though maintaining a distrustful reserve, took a certain pleasure in listening to him. He asked him, in a less peevish tone:

"And are you satisfied with your expedition?"

"Delighted! All the more as I had never been present at a case of the sort and I find that this one is not lacking in interest."

"Nor in that mysterious intricacy which you prize so highly—"

"And which is so stimulating, Monsieur le Juge d'Instruction! I know nothing more exciting than to see all the facts coming up out of the shadow, clustering together, so to speak, and gradually forming the probable truth."

"The probable truth! You go pretty fast, young man! Do you suggest that you have your little solution of the riddle ready?"

"Oh, no!" replied Beautrelet, with a laugh.

"Only—it seems to me that there are certain points on which it is not impossible to form an opinion; and others, even, are so precise as to warrant—a conclusion."

"Oh, but this is becoming very curious and I shall get to know something at last! For I confess, to my great confusion, that I know nothing."

"That is because you have not had time to reflect, Monsieur le Juge d'Instruction. The great thing is to reflect. Facts very seldom fail to carry their own explanation!"

"And, according to you, the facts which we have just ascertained carry their own explanation?"

"Don't you think so yourself? In any case, I have ascertained none besides those which are set down in the official report."

"Good! So that, if I were to ask you which were the objects stolen from this room—"

"I should answer that I know."

"Bravo! My gentleman knows more about it than the owner himself. M. de Gesvres has everything accounted for: M. Isidore Beautrelet has not. He misses a bookcase in three sections and a life-size statue which nobody ever noticed. And, if I asked you the name of the murderer?"

"I should again answer that I know it."

All present gave a start. The deputy and the journalist drew nearer. M. de Gesvres and the two girls, impressed by Beautrelet's tranquil assurance, listened attentively.

"You know the murderer's name?"

"Yes."

"And the place where he is concealed, perhaps?"

"Yes."

M. Filleul rubbed his hands.

"What a piece of luck! This capture will do honor to my career. And can you make me these startling revelations now?"

"Yes, now—or rather, if you do not mind, in an hour or two, when I shall have assisted at your inquiry to the end."

"No, no, young man, here and now, please." At that moment Raymonde de Saint-Veran, who had not taken her eyes from Isidore Beautrelet since the beginning of this scene, came up to M. Filleul:

"Monsieur le Juge d'Instruction—"

"Yes, mademoiselle?"

She hesitated for two or three seconds, with her eyes fixed on Beautrelet, and then, addressing M. Filleul:

"I should like you to ask monsieur the reason why he was walking yesterday in the sunk road which leads up to the little door."

It was an unexpected and dramatic stroke. Isidore Beautrelet appeared nonplussed:

"I, mademoiselle? I? You saw me yesterday?"

Raymonde remained thoughtful, with her eyes upon Beautrelet, as though she were trying to settle her own conviction, and then said, in a steady voice:

"At four o'clock in the afternoon, as I was crossing the wood, I met in the sunk road a young man of monsieur's height, dressed like him and wearing a beard cut in the same way—and I received a very clear impression that he was trying to hide."

"And it was I?"

"I could not say that as an absolute certainty, for my recollection is a little vague. Still—still, I think so—if not, it would be an unusual resemblance—"

M. Filleul was perplexed. Already taken in by one of the confederates, was he now going to let himself be tricked by this self-styled schoolboy? Certainly, the young man's manner spoke in his favor; but one can never tell!

"What have you to say, sir?"

"That mademoiselle is mistaken, as I can easily show you with one word. Yesterday, at the time stated, I was at Veules."

"You will have to prove it, you will have to. In any case, the position is not what it was. Sergeant, one of your men will keep monsieur company."

Isidore Beautrelet's face denoted a keen vexation.

"Will it be for long?"

"Long enough to collect the necessary information."

"Monsieur le Juge d'Instruction, I beseech you to collect it with all possible speed and discretion."

"Why?"

"My father is an old man. We are very much attached to each other—and I would not have him suffer on my account."

The more or less pathetic note in his voice made a bad impression on M. Filleul. It suggested a scene in a melodrama. Nevertheless, he promised:

"This evening—or to-morrow at latest, I shall know what to think."

The afternoon was wearing on. The examining magistrate returned to the ruins of the cloisters, after giving orders that no unauthorized persons were to be admitted, and patiently, methodically, dividing the ground into lots which were successively explored, himself directed the search. But at the end of the day he was no farther than at the start; and he declared, before an army of reporters who, during that time, had invaded the chateau:

"Gentlemen, everything leads us to suppose that the wounded man is here, within our reach; everything, that is, except the reality, the fact. Therefore, in our humble opinion, he must have escaped and we shall find him outside."

By way of precaution, however, he arranged, with the sergeant of gendarmes, for a complete watch to be kept over the park and, after making a fresh examination of the two drawing rooms, visiting the whole of the chateau and surrounding himself with all the necessary information, he took the road back to Dieppe, accompanied by the deputy prosecutor.

Night fell. As the boudoir was to remain locked, Jean Daval's body had been moved to another room. Two women from the neighborhood sat up with it, assisted by Suzanne and Raymonde. Downstairs, young Isidore Beautrelet slept on the bench in the old oratory, under the watchful eye of the village policeman, who had been attached to his person. Outside, the gendarmes, the farmer and a dozen peasants had taken up their position among the ruins and along the walls.

All was still until eleven o'clock; but, at ten minutes past eleven, a shot echoed from the other side of the house.

"Attention!" roared the sergeant. "Two men remain here: you, Fossier—and you, Lecanu—The others at the double!"

They all rushed forward and ran round the house on the left. A figure was seen to make away in the dark. Then, suddenly, a second shot drew them farther on, almost to the borders of the farm. And, all at once, as they arrived, in a band, at the hedge which lines the orchard, a flame burst out, to the right of the farmhouse, and other names also rose in a thick column. It was a barn burning, stuffed to the ridge with straw.

"The scoundrels!" shouted the sergeant. "They've set fire to it. Have at them, lads! They can't be far away!"

But the wind was turning the flames toward the main building; and it became necessary, before all things, to ward off the danger. They all exerted themselves with the greater ardor inasmuch as M. de Gesvres, hurrying to the scene of the disaster, encouraged them with the promise of a reward. By the time that they had mastered the flames, it was two o'clock in the morning. All pursuit would have been vain.

"We'll look into it by daylight," said the sergeant. "They are sure to have left traces: we shall find them."

"And I shall not be sorry," added M. de Gesvres, "to learn the reason of this attack. To set fire to trusses of straw strikes me as a very useless proceeding."

"Come with me, Monsieur le Comte: I may be able to tell you the reason."

Together they reached the ruins of the cloisters. The sergeant called out:

"Lecanu!—Fossier!"

The other gendarmes were already hunting for their comrades whom they had left standing sentry. They ended by finding them at a few paces from the little door. The two men were lying full length on the ground, bound and gagged, with bandages over their eyes.

"Monsieur le Comte," muttered the sergeant, while his men were being released; "Monsieur le Comte, we have been tricked like children."

"How so?"

"The shots—the attack on the barn—the fire—all so much humbug to get us down there—a diversion. During that time they were tying up our two men and the business was done."

"What business?"

"Carrying off the wounded man, of course!"

"You don't mean to say you think—?"

"Think? Why, it's as plain as a pikestaff! The idea came to me ten minutes ago—but I'm a fool not to have thought of it earlier. We should have nabbed them all." Quevillon stamped his foot on the ground, with a sudden attack of rage. "But where, confound it, where did they go through? Which way did they carry him off? For, dash it all, we beat the ground all day; and a man can't hide in a tuft of grass, especially when he's wounded! It's witchcraft, that's what it is!—"

Nor was this the last surprise awaiting Sergeant Quevillon. At dawn, when they entered the oratory which had been used as a cell for young Isidore Beautrelet, they realized that young Isidore Beautrelet had vanished.

On a chair slept the village policeman, bent in two. By his side stood a water-bottle and two tumblers. At the bottom of one of those tumblers a few grains of white powder.

On examination, it was proved, first, that young Isidore Beautrelet had administered a sleeping draught to the village policeman; secondly, that he could only have escaped by a window situated at a height of seven or eight feet in the wall; and lastly—a charming detail, this—that he could only have reached this window by using the back of his warder as a footstool.

II. ISIDORE BEAUTRELET, SIXTH-FORM SCHOOLBOY

From the Grand Journal.

LATEST NEWS

DOCTOR DELATTRE KIDNAPPED A MAD PIECE OF CRIMINAL DARING

At the moment of going to press, we have received an item of news which we dare not guarantee as authentic, because of its very improbable character. We print it, therefore, with all reserve.

Yesterday evening, Dr. Delattre, the well-known surgeon, was present, with his wife and daughter, at the performance of Hernani at the Comedie Francaise. At the commencement of the third act, that is to say, at about ten o'clock, the door of his box opened and a gentleman, accompanied by two others, leaned over to the doctor and said to him, in a low voice, but loud enough for Mme. Delattre to hear:

"Doctor, I have a very painful task to fulfil and I shall be very grateful to you if you will make it as easy for me as you can."

"Who are you, sir?"

"M. Thezard, commissary of police of the first district; and my instructions are to take you to M. Dudouis, at the prefecture."

"But—"

"Not a word, doctor, I entreat you, not a movement—There is some regrettable mistake; and that is why we must act in silence and not attract anybody's attention. You will be back, I have no doubt, before the end of the performance."

The doctor rose and went with the commissary. At the end of the performance, he had not returned. Mme. Delattre, greatly alarmed, drove to the office of the commissary of police. There she found the real M. Thezard and discovered, to her great terror, that the individual who had carried off her husband was an impostor.

Inquiries made so far have revealed the fact that the doctor stepped into a motor car and that the car drove off in the direction of the Concorde.

Readers will find further details of this incredible adventure in our second edition.

Incredible though it might be, the adventure was perfectly true. Besides, the issue was not long delayed and the Grand Journal, while confirming the story in its midday edition, described in a few lines the dramatic ending with which it concluded:

THE STORY ENDS

AND

GUESS-WORK BEGINS

Dr. Delattre was brought back to 78, Rue Duret, at nine o'clock this morning, in a motor car which drove away immediately at full speed.

No. 78, Rue Duret, is the address of Dr. Delattre's clinical surgery, at which he arrives every morning at the same hour. When we sent in our card, the doctor, though closeted with the chief of the detective service, was good enough to consent to receive us.

"All that I can tell you," he said, in reply to our questions, "is that I was treated with the greatest consideration. My three companions were the most charming people I have ever met, exquisitely well-mannered and bright and witty talkers: a quality not to be despised, in view of the length of the journey."

"How long did it take?"

"About four hours and as long returning."

"And what was the object of the journey?"

"I was taken to see a patient whose condition rendered an immediate operation necessary."

"And was the operation successful?"

"Yes, but the consequences may be dangerous. I would answer for the patient here. Down there—under his present conditions—"

"Bad conditions?"

"Execrable!—A room in an inn—and the practically absolute impossibility of being attended to."

"Then what can save him?"

"A miracle—and his constitution, which is an exceptionally strong one."

"And can you say nothing more about this strange patient?"

"No. In the first place, I have taken an oath; and, secondly, I have received a present of ten thousand francs for my free surgery. If I do not keep silence, this sum will be taken from me."

"You are joking! Do you believe that?"

"Indeed I do. The men all struck me as being very much in earnest."

This is the statement made to us by Dr. Delattre. And we know, on the other hand, that the head of the detective service, in spite of all his insisting, has not yet succeeded in extracting any more precise particulars from him as to the operation which he performed, the patient whom he attended or the district traversed by the car. It is difficult, therefore, to arrive at the truth.

This truth, which the writer of the interview confessed himself unable to discover, was guessed by the more or less clear-sighted minds that perceived a connection with the facts which had occurred the day before at the Chateau d'Ambrumesy, and which were reported, down to the smallest detail, in all the newspapers of that day. There was evidently a coincidence to be reckoned with in the disappearance of a wounded burglar and the kidnapping of a famous surgeon.

The judicial inquiry, moreover, proved the correctness of the hypothesis. By following the track of the sham flyman, who had fled on a bicycle, they were able to show that he had reached the forest of Arques, at some ten miles' distance, and that from there, after throwing his bicycle into a ditch, he had gone to the village of Saint-Nicolas, whence he had dispatched the following telegram:

A. L. N., Post-office 45, Paris.

Situation desperate. Operation urgently necessary.

Send celebrity by national road fourteen.

The evidence was undeniable. Once apprised the accomplices in Paris hastened to make their arrangements. At ten o'clock in the evening they sent their celebrity by National Road No. 14, which skirts the forest of Arques and ends at Dieppe. During this time, under cover of the fire which they themselves had caused, the gang of burglars carried off their leader and moved him to an inn, where the operation took place on the arrival of the surgeon, at two o'clock in the morning.

About that there was no doubt. At Pontoise, at Gournay, at Forges, Chief-inspector Ganimard, who was sent specially from Paris, with Inspector Folenfant, as his assistant, ascertained that a motor car had passed in the course of the previous night. The same on the road from Dieppe to Ambrumesy. And, though the traces of the car were lost at about a mile and a half from the chateau, at least a number of footmarks were seen between the little door in the park wall and the abbey ruins. Besides, Ganimard remarked that the lock of the little door had been forced.

So all was explained. It remained to decide which inn the doctor had spoken of: an easy piece of work for a Ganimard, a professional ferret, a patient old stager of the police. The number of inns is limited and this one, given the condition of the wounded man, could only be one quite close to Ambrumesy. Ganimard and Sergeant Quevillon set to work. Within a circle of five hundred yards, of a thousand yards, of fifteen hundred yards, they visited and ransacked everything that could pass for an inn. But, against all expectation, the dying man persisted in remaining invisible.

Ganimard became more resolved than ever. He came back to sleep at the chateau, on the Saturday night, with the intention of making his personal inquiry on the Sunday. On Sunday morning, he learned that, during the night, a posse of gendarmes had seen a figure gliding along the sunk road, outside the wall. Was it an accomplice who had come back to investigate? Were they to suppose that the leader of the gang had not left the cloisters or the neighborhood of the cloisters?

That night, Ganimard openly sent the squad of gendarmes to the farm and posted himself and Folenfant outside the walls, near the little door.

A little before midnight, a person passed out of the wood, slipped between them, went through the door and entered the park. For three hours, they saw him wander from side to side across the ruins, stooping, climbing up the old pillars, sometimes remaining for long minutes without moving. Then he went back to the door and again passed between the two inspectors.

Ganimard caught him by the collar, while Folenfant seized him round the body. He made no resistance of any kind and, with the greatest docility, allowed them to bind his wrists and take him to the house. But, when they attempted to question him, he replied simply that he owed them no account of his doings and that he would wait for the arrival of the examining magistrate. Thereupon, they fastened him firmly to the foot of a bed, in one of the two adjoining rooms which they occupied.

At nine o'clock on Monday morning, as soon as M. Filleul had arrived, Ganimard announced the capture which he had made. The prisoner was brought downstairs. It was Isidore Beautrelet.

"M. Isidore Beautrelet!" exclaimed M. Filleul with an air of rapture, holding out both his hands to the newcomer. "What a delightful surprise! Our excellent amateur detective here! And at our disposal too! Why, it's a windfall!—M. Chief-inspector, allow me to introduce to you M. Isidore Beautrelet, a sixth-form pupil at the Lycee Janson-de-Sailly."

Ganimard seemed a little nonplussed. Isidore made him a very low bow, as though he were greeting a colleague whom he knew how to esteem at his true value, and, turning to M. Filleul:

"It appears, Monsieur le Juge d'Instruction, that you have received a satisfactory account of me?"

"Perfectly satisfactory! To begin with, you were really at Veules-les-Roses at the time when Mlle. de Saint-Veran thought she saw you in the sunk road. I dare say we shall discover the identity of your double. In the second place, you are in very deed Isidore Beautrelet, a sixth-form pupil and, what is more, an excellent pupil, industrious at your work and of exemplary behavior. As your father lives in the country, you go out once a month to his correspondent, M. Bernod, who is lavish in his praises of you."

"So that—"

"So that you are free, M. Isidore Beautrelet."

"Absolutely free?"

"Absolutely. Oh, I must make just one little condition, all the same. You can understand that I can't release a gentleman who administers sleeping-draughts, who escapes by the window and who is afterward caught in the act of trespassing upon private property. I can't release him without a compensation of some kind."

"I await your pleasure."

"Well, we will resume our interrupted conversation and you shall tell me how far you have advanced with your investigations. In two days of liberty, you must have carried them pretty far?" And, as Ganimard was preparing to go, with an affectation of contempt for that sort of practice, the magistrate cried, "Not at all, M. Inspector, your place is here—I assure you that M. Isidore Beautrelet is worth listening to. M. Isidore Beautrelet, according to my information, has made a great reputation at the Lycee Janson-de-Sailly as an observer whom nothing escapes; and his schoolfellows, I hear, look upon him as your competitor and a rival of Holmlock Shears!"

"Indeed!" said Ganimard, ironically.

"Just so. One of them wrote to me, 'If Beautrelet declares that he knows, you must believe him; and, whatever he says, you may be sure that it is the exact expression of the truth.' M. Isidore Beautrelet, now or never is the time to vindicate the confidence of your friends. I beseech you, give us the exact expression of the truth."

Isidore listened with a smile and replied:

"Monsieur le Juge d'Instruction, you are very cruel. You make fun of poor schoolboys who amuse themselves as best they can. You are quite right, however, and I will give you no further reason to laugh at me."

"The fact is that you know nothing, M. Isidore Beautrelet."

"Yes, I confess in all humility that I know nothing. For I do not call it 'knowing anything' that I happen to have hit upon two or three more precise points which, I am sure, cannot have escaped you."

"For instance?"

"For instance, the object of the theft."

"Ah, of course, you know the object of the theft?"

"As you do, I have no doubt. In fact, it was the first thing I studied, because the task struck me as easier."

"Easier, really?"

"Why, of course. At the most, it's a question of reasoning."

"Nothing more than that?"

"Nothing more."

"And what is your reasoning?"

"It is just this, stripped of all extraneous comment: on the one hand, THERE HAS BEEN A THEFT, because the two young ladies are agreed and because they really saw two men running away and carrying things with them."

"There has been a theft."

"On the other hand, NOTHING HAS DISAPPEARED, because M. de Gesvres says so and he is in a better position than anybody to know."

"Nothing has disappeared."

"From those two premises I arrive at this inevitable result: granted that there has been a theft and that nothing has disappeared, it is because the object carried off has been replaced by an exactly similar object. Let me hasten to add that possibly my argument may not be confirmed by the facts. But I maintain that it is the first argument that ought to occur to us and that we are not entitled to waive it until we have made a serious examination."

"That's true—that's true," muttered the magistrate, who was obviously interested.

"Now," continued Isidore, "what was there in this room that could arouse the covetousness of the burglars? Two things. The tapestry first. It can't have been that. Old tapestry cannot be imitated: the fraud would have been palpable at once. There remain the four Rubens pictures."

"What's that you say?"

"I say that the four Rubenses on that wall are false."

"Impossible!"

"They are false a priori, inevitably and without a doubt."

"I tell you, it's impossible."

"It is very nearly a year ago, Monsieur le Juge d'Instruction, since a young man, who gave his name as Charpenais, came to the Chateau d'Ambrumesy and asked permission to copy the Rubens pictures. M. de Gesvres gave him permission. Every day for five months Charpenais worked in this room from morning till dusk. The copies which he made, canvases and frames, have taken the place of the four original pictures bequeathed to M. de Gesvres by his uncle, the Marques de Bobadilla."

"Prove it!"

"I have no proof to give. A picture is false because it is false; and I consider that it is not even necessary to examine these four."

M. Filleul and Ganimard exchanged glances of unconcealed astonishment. The inspector no longer thought of withdrawing. At last, the magistrate muttered:

"We must have M. de Gesvres's opinion."

And Ganimard agreed:

"Yes, we must have his opinion."

And they sent to beg the count to come to the drawing room.

The young sixth-form pupil had won a real victory. To compel two experts, two professionals like M. Filleul and Ganimard to take account of his surmises implied a testimony of respect of which any other would have been proud. But Beautrelet seemed not to feel those little satisfactions of self-conceit and, still smiling without the least trace of irony, he placidly waited.

M. de Gesvres entered the room.

"Monsieur le Comte," said the magistrate, "the result of our inquiry has brought us face to face with an utterly unexpected contingency, which we submit to you with all reserve. It is possible—I say that it is possible—that the burglars, when breaking into the house, had it as their object to steal your four pictures by Rubens—or, at least, to replace them by four copies—copies which are said to have been made last year by a painter called Charpenais. Would you be so good as to examine the pictures and to tell us if you recognize them as genuine?"

The count appeared to suppress a movement of annoyance, looked at Isidore Beautrelet and at M. Filleul and replied, without even troubling to go near the pictures:

"I hoped, Monsieur le Juge d'Instruction, that the truth might have remained unknown. As this is not so, I have no hesitation in declaring that the four pictures are false."

"You knew it, then?"

"From the beginning."

"Why didn't you say so?"

"The owner of a work is never in a hurry to declare that that work is not—or, rather, is no longer genuine."

"Still, it was the only means of recovering them."

"I consider that there was another and a better."

"Which was that?"

"Not to make the secret known, not to frighten my burglars and to offer to buy back the pictures, which they must find more or less difficult to dispose of."

"How would you communicate with them?"

As the count did not reply, Isidore answered for him:

"By means of an advertisement in the papers. The paragraph inserted in the agony column of the Journal, the Echo de Paris and the Matin runs, 'Am prepared to buy back the pictures.'"

The count agreed with a nod. Once again, the young man was teaching his elders. M. Filleul showed himself a good sportsman.

"There's no doubt about it, my dear sir," he exclaimed. "I'm beginning to think your school-fellows were not quite wrong. By Jove, what an eye! What intuition! If this goes on, there will be nothing left for M. Ganimard and me to do."

"Oh, none of this part was so very complicated!"

"You mean to say that the rest was more so I remember, in fact, that, when we first met you seemed to know all about it. Let me see, a far as I recollect, you said that you knew the name of the murderer."

"So I do."

"Well, then, who killed Jean Daval? Is the man alive? Where is he hiding?"

"There is a misunderstanding between us, Monsieur le Juge d'Instruction, or, rather, you have misunderstood the facts from the beginning The murderer and the runaway are two distinct persons."

"What's that?" exclaimed M. Filleul. "The man whom M. de Gesvres saw in the boudoir and struggled with, the man whom the young ladies saw in the drawing-room and whom Mlle. de Saint-Veran shot at, the man who fell in the park and whom we are looking for: do you suggest that he is not the man who killed Jean Daval?"

"I do."

"Have you discovered the traces of a third accomplice who disappeared before the arrival of the young ladies?"

"I have not."

"In that case, I don't understand.—Well, who is the murderer of Jean Daval?"

"Jean Daval was killed by—"

Beautrelet interrupted himself, thought for a moment and continued:

"But I must first show you the road which I followed to arrive at the certainty and the very reasons of the murder—without which my accusation would seem monstrous to you.—And it is not—no, it is not monstrous at all.—There is one detail which has passed unobserved and which, nevertheless, is of the greatest importance; and that is that Jean Daval, at the moment when he was stabbed, had all his clothes on, including his walking boots, was dressed, in short, as a man is dressed in the middle of the day, with a waistcoat, collar, tie and braces. Now the crime was committed at four o'clock in the morning."

"I reflected on that strange fact," said the magistrate, "and M. de Gesvres replied that Jean Daval spent a part of his nights in working."

"The servants say, on the contrary, that he went to bed regularly at a very early hour. But, admitting that he was up, why did he disarrange his bedclothes, to make believe that he had gone to bed? And, if he was in bed, why, when he heard a noise, did he take the trouble to dress himself from head to foot, instead of slipping on anything that came to hand? I went to his room on the first day, while you were at lunch: his slippers were at the foot of the bed. What prevented him from putting them on rather than his heavy nailed boots?"

"So far, I do not see—"

"So far, in fact, you cannot see anything, except anomalies. They appeared much more suspicious to me, however, when I learned that Charpenais the painter, the man who copied the Rubens pictures, had been introduced and recommended to the Comte de Gesvres by Jean Daval himself."

"Well?"

"Well, from that to the conclusion that Jean Daval and Charpenais were accomplices required but a step. I took that step at the time of our conversation."

"A little quickly, I think."

"As a matter of fact, a material proof was wanted. Now I had discovered in Daval's room, on one of the sheets of the blotting-pad on which he used to write, this address: 'Monsieur A.L.N., Post-office 45, Paris.' You will find it there still, traced the reverse way on the blotting-paper. The next day, it was discovered that the telegram sent by the sham flyman from Saint-Nicolas bore the same address: 'A.L.N., Post-office 45.' The material proof existed: Jean Daval was in correspondence with the gang which arranged the robbery of the pictures."

M. Filleul raised no objection.

"Agreed. The complicity is established. And what conclusion do you draw?"

"This, first of all, that it was not the runaway who killed Jean Daval, because Jean Daval was his accomplice."

"And after that?"

"Monsieur le Juge d'Instruction, I will ask you to remember the first sentence uttered by Monsieur le Comte when he recovered from fainting. The sentence forms part of Mlle. de Gesvres' evidence and is in the official report: 'I am not wounded.—Daval?—Is he alive?—The knife?' And I will ask you to compare it with that part of his story, also in the report, in which Monsieur le Comte describes the assault: 'The man leaped at me and felled me with a blow on the temple!' How could M. de Gesvres, who had fainted, know, on waking, that Daval had been stabbed with a knife?"

Isidore Beautrelet did not wait for an answer to his question. It seemed as though he were in a hurry to give the answer himself and to avoid all comment. He continued straightway:

"Therefore it was Jean Daval who brought the three burglars to the drawing room. While he was there with the one whom they call their chief, a noise was heard in the boudoir. Daval opened the door. Recognizing M. de Gesvres, he rushed at him, armed with the knife. M. de Gesvres succeeded in snatching the knife from him, struck him with it and himself fell, on receiving a blow from the man whom the two girls were to see a few minutes after."

Once again, M. Filleul and the inspector exchanged glances. Ganimard tossed his head in a disconcerted way. The magistrate said:

"Monsieur le Comte, am I to believe that this version is correct?"

M. de Gesvres made no answer.

"Come, Monsieur le Comte, your silence would us to suppose—I beg you to speak."

Replying in a very clear voice, M. de Gesvres said:

"The version is correct in every particular."

The magistrate gave a start.

"Then I cannot understand why you misled the police. Why conceal an act which you were lawfully entitled to commit in defense of your life?"

"For twenty years," said M. de Gesvres, "Daval worked by my side. I trusted him. If he betrayed me, as the result of some temptation or other, I was, at least, unwilling, for the sake of the past, that his treachery should become known."

"You were unwilling, I agree, but you had no right to be."

"I am not of your opinion, Monsieur le Juge d'Instruction. As long as no innocent person was accused of the crime, I was absolutely entitled to refrain from accusing the man who was at the same time the culprit and the victim. He is dead. I consider death a sufficient punishment."

"But now, Monsieur le Comte, now that the truth is known, you can speak."

"Yes. Here are two rough drafts of letters written by him to his accomplices. I took them from his pocket-book, a few minutes after his death."

"And the motive of his theft?"

"Go to 18, Rue de la Barre, at Dieppe, which is the address of a certain Mme. Verdier. It was for this woman, whom he got to know two years ago, and to supply her constant need of money that Daval turned thief."

So everything was cleared up. The tragedy rose out of the darkness and gradually appeared in its true light.

"Let us go on," said M. Filluel after the count had withdrawn.

"Upon my word," said Beautrelet, gaily, "I have said almost all that I had to say."

"But the runaway, the wounded man?"

"As to that, Monsieur le Juge d'Instruction, you know as much as I do. You have followed his tracks in the grass by the cloisters—you have—"

"Yes, yes, I know. But, since then, his friends have removed him and what I want is a clue or two as regards that inn—"

Isidore Beautrelet burst out laughing:

"The inn! The inn does not exist! It's an invention, a trick to put the police on the wrong scent, an ingenious trick, too, for it seems to have succeeded."

"But Dr. Delattre declares—"

"Ah, that's just it!" cried Beautrelet, in a tone of conviction. "It is just because Dr. Delattre declares that we mustn't believe him. Why, Dr. Delattre refused to give any but the vaguest details concerning his adventure! He refused to say anything that might compromise his patient's safety!—And suddenly he calls attention to an inn!—You may be sure that he talked about that inn because he was told to. You may be sure that the whole story which he dished up to us was dictated to him under the threat of terrible reprisals. The doctor has a wife. The doctor has a daughter. He is too fond of them to disobey people of whose formidable power he has seen proofs. And that is why he has assisted your efforts by supplying the most precise clues."

"So precise that the inn is nowhere to be found."

"So precise that you have never ceased looking for it, in the face of all probability, and that your eyes have been turned away from the only spot where the man can be, the mysterious spot which he has not left, which he has been unable to leave ever since the moment when, wounded by Mlle. de Saint-Veran, he succeeded in dragging himself to it, like a beast to its lair."

"But where, confound it all?—In what corner of Hades—?"

"In the ruins of the old abbey."

"But there are no ruins left!—A few bits of wall!—A few broken columns!"

"That's where he's gone to earth. Monsieur le Juge d'Instruction!" shouted Beautrelet. "That's where you will have to look for him! It's there and nowhere else that you will find Arsene Lupin!"

"Arsene Lupin!" yelled M. Filleul, springing to his feet.

There was a rather solemn pause, amid which the syllables of the famous name seemed to prolong their sound. Was it possible that the vanquished and yet invisible adversary, whom they had been hunting in vain for several days, could really be Arsene Lupin? Arsene Lupin, caught in a trap, arrested, meant immediate promotion, fortune, glory to any examining magistrate!

Ganimard had not moved a limb. Isidore said to him:

"You agree with me, do you not, M. Inspector?"

"Of course I do!"

"You have not doubted either, for a moment have you, that he managed this business?"

"Not for a second! The thing bears his signature. A move of Arsene Lupin's is as different from a move made by another man as one face is from another. You have only to open your eyes."

"Do you think so? Do you think so?" said M. Filleul.

"Think so!" cried the young man. "Look, here's one little fact: what are the initials under which those men correspond among themselves? 'A. L. N.,' that is to say, the first letter of the name Arsene and the first and last letters of the name Lupin."

"Ah," said Ganimard, "nothing escapes you! Upon my word, you're a fine fellow and old Ganimard lays down his arms before you!"

Beautrelet flushed with pleasure and pressed the hand which the chief-inspector held out to him. The three men had drawn near the balcony and their eyes now took in the extent of the ruins. M. Filleul muttered:

"So he ought to be there."

"HE IS THERE," said Beautrelet, in a hollow voice. "He has been there ever since the moment when he fell. Logically and practically, he could not escape without being seen by Mlle. de Saint-Veran and the two servants."

"What proof have you?"

"His accomplices have furnished the proof. On the very morning, one of them disguised himself as a flyman and drove you here—"

"To recover the cap, which would serve to identify him."

"Very well, but also and more particularly to examine the spot, find out and see for himself what had become of the 'governor.'"

"And did he find out?"

"I presume so, as he knew the hiding-place. And I presume that he became aware of the desperate condition of his chief, because, under the impulse of his alarm, he committed the imprudence to write that threat: 'Woe betide the young lady, if she has killed the governor!'"

"But his friends were able to take him away afterward?"

"When? Your men have never left the ruins. And where could they have moved him to? At most, a few hundred yards away, for one doesn't let a dying man travel—and then you would have found him. No, I tell you, he is there. His friends would never have removed him from the safest of hiding-places. It was there that they brought the doctor, while the gendarmes were running to the fire like children."

"But how is he living? How will he keep alive? To keep alive you need food and drink."

"I can't say. I don't know. But he is there, I will swear it. He is there, because he can't help being there. I am as sure of it as if I saw as if I touched him. He is there."

With his finger outstretched toward the ruins, he traced in the air a little circle which became smaller and smaller until it was only a point. And that point his two companions sought desperately, both leaning into space, both moved by the same faith in Beautrelet and quivering with the ardent conviction which he had forced upon them. Yes, Arsene Lupin was there. In theory and in fact, he was there: neither of them was now able to doubt it.

And there was something impressive and tragic in knowing that the famous adventurer was lying in some dark shelter, below the ground, helpless, feverish and exhausted.

"And if he dies?" asked M. Filleul, in a low voice.

"If he dies," said Beautrelet, "and if his accomplices are sure of it, then see to the safety of Mlle. de Saint-Veran. Monsieur le Juge d'Instruction, for the vengeance will be terrible."

A few minutes later and in spite of the entreaties of M. Filleul, who would gladly have made further use of this fascinating auxiliary, Isidore Beautrelet, whose holidays ended that day, went off by the Dieppe Road. He stepped from the train in Paris at five o'clock and, at eight o'clock, returned to the Lycee Janson together with his schoolfellows.

Ganimard, after a minute, but utterly useless exploration of the ruins of Ambrumesy, returned to Paris by the fast night-train. On reaching his apartment in the Rue Pergolese, he found an express letter awaiting him:

Monsieur l'Inspecteur Principal:

Finding that I had a little time to spare at the end of the day, I have succeeded in collecting a few additional particulars which are sure to interest you.

Arsene Lupin has been living in Paris for twelve months under the name of Etienne de Vaudreix. It is a name which you will often come across in the society notes or the sporting columns of the newspapers. He is a great traveler and is absent for long periods, during which, by his own account, he goes hunting tigers in Bengal or blue foxes in Siberia. He is supposed to be in business of some kind, although nobody is able to say for certain what his business is.

His present address is 38, Rue Marbeuf; and I will call your attention to the fact that the Rue Marbeuf is close to Post-office Number 45. Since Thursday the twenty-third of April, the day before the burglary at Ambrumesy, there has been no news at all of Etienne de Vaudreix.

With very many thanks for the kindness which you have shown me, believe me to be,

Monsieur l'Inspecteur Principal,

Yours sincerely,

ISIDORE BEAUTRELET.

P.S.—Please on no account think that it cost me any great trouble to obtain this information. On the very morning of the crime, while M. Filleul was pursuing his examination before a few privileged persons, I had the fortunate inspiration to glance at the runaway's cap, before the sham flyman came to change it. The hatter's name was enough, as you may imagine, to enable me to find the clue that led to the identification of the purchaser and his address.

The next morning, Ganimard called at 36, Rue Marbeuf. After questioning the concierge, he made him open the door of the ground-floor flat on the right, a very comfortable apartment, elegantly furnished, in which, however, he discovered nothing beyond some cinders in the fireplace. Two friends had come, four days earlier, to burn all compromising papers.

But, just as he was leaving, Ganimard passed the postman, who was bringing a letter for M. de Vaudreix. That afternoon, the public prosecutor was informed of the case and ordered the letter to be given up. It bore an American postmark and contained the following lines, in English:

DEAR SIR:

I write to confirm the answer which I gave your representative. As soon as you have M. de Gesvres's four pictures in your possession, you can forward them as arranged.

You may add the rest, if you are able to succeed, which I doubt.

An unexpected business requires my presence in Europe and I shall reach Paris at the same time as this letter. You will find me at the Grand Hotel.

Yours faithfully,

EPHRAIM B. HARLINGTON.

That same day, Ganimard applied for a warrant and took Mr. E. B. Harlington, an American citizen, to the police-station, on a charge of receiving and conspiracy.

Thus, within the space of twenty-four hours, all the threads of the plot had been unraveled, thanks to the really unforeseen clues supplied by a schoolboy of seventeen. In twenty-four hours, what had seemed inexplicable became simple and clear. In twenty-four hours, the scheme devised by the accomplices to save their leader was baffled; the capture of Arsene Lupin, wounded and dying, was no longer in doubt, his gang was disorganized, the address of his establishment in Paris and the name which he assumed were known and, for the first time, one of his cleverest and most carefully elaborated feats was seen through before he had been able to ensure its complete execution.

An immense clamor of astonishment, admiration and curiosity arose among the public. Already, the Rouen journalist, in a very able article, had described the first examination of the sixth-form pupil, laying stress upon his personal charm, his simplicity of manner and his quiet assurance. The indiscretions of Ganimard and M. Filleul, indiscretions to which they yielded in spite of themselves, under an impulse that proved stronger than their professional pride, suddenly enlightened the public as to the part played by Isidore Beautrelet in recent events. He alone had done everything. To him alone the merit of the victory was due.

The excitement was intense. Isidore Beautrelet awoke to find himself a hero; and the crowd, suddenly infatuated, insisted upon the fullest information regarding its new favorite. The reporters were there to supply it. They rushed to the assault of the Lycee Janson-de-Sailly, waited for the day-boarders to come out after schoolhours and picked up all that related, however remotely, to Beautrelet. It was in this way that they learned the reputation which he enjoyed among his schoolfellows, who called him the rival of Holmlock

Shears. Thanks to his powers of logical reasoning, with no further data than those which he was able to gather from the papers, he had, time after time, proclaimed the solution of very complicated cases long before they were cleared up by the police.

It had become a game at the Lycee Janson to put difficult questions and intricate problems to Beautrelet; and it was astonishing to see with what unhesitating and analytical power and by means of what ingenious deductions he made his way through the thickest darkness. Ten days before the arrest of Jorisse, the grocer, he showed what could be done with the famous umbrella. In the same way, he declared from the beginning, in the matter of the Saint-Cloud mystery, that the concierge was the only possible murderer.

But most curious of all was the pamphlet which was found circulating among the boys at the school, a typewritten pamphlet signed by Beautrelet and manifolded to the number of ten copies. It was entitled, ARSENE LUPIN AND HIS METHOD, SHOWING IN HOW FAR THE LATTER IS BASED UPON TRADITION AND IN HOW FAR ORIGINAL. FOLLOWED BY A COMPARISON BETWEEN ENGLISH HUMOR AND FRENCH IRONY.

It contained a profound study of each of the exploits of Arsene Lupin, throwing the illustrious burglar's operations into extraordinary relief, showing the very mechanism of his way of setting to work, his special tactics, his letters to the press, his threats, the announcement of his thefts, in short, the whole bag of tricks which he employed to bamboozle his selected victim and throw him into such a state of mind that the victim almost offered himself to the plot contrived against him and that everything took place, as it were, with his own consent.

And the work was so just, regarded as a piece of criticism, so penetrating, so lively and marked by a wit so clever and, at the same time, so cruel that the lawyers at once passed over to his side, that the sympathy of the crowd was summarily transferred from Lupin to Beautrelet and that, in the struggle engaged upon between the two, the schoolboy's victory was loudly proclaimed in advance.

Be this as it may, both M. Filleul and the Paris public prosecutor seemed jealously to reserve the possibility of this victory for him. On the one hand, they failed to establish Mr. Harlington's identity or to furnish a definite proof of his connection with Lupin's gang. Confederate or not, he preserved an obstinate silence. Nay, more, after examining his handwriting, it was impossible to declare that he was the author of the intercepted letter. A Mr. Harlington, carrying a small portmanteau and a pocket-book stuffed with banknotes, had taken up his abode at the Grand Hotel: that was all that could be stated with certainty.

On the other hand, at Dieppe, M. Filleul lay down on the positions which Beautrelet had won for him. He did not move a step forward. Around the individual whom Mlle. de Saint-Veran had taken for Beautrelet, on the eve of the crime, the same mystery reigned as heretofore. The same obscurity also surrounded everything connected with the removal of the four Rubens pictures. What had become of them? And what road had been taken by the motor car in which they were carried off during the night?

Evidence of its passing was obtained at Luneray at Yerville, at Yvetot and at Caudebec-en-Caux, where it must have crossed the Seine at daybreak in the steam-ferry. But, when the matter came to be inquired into more thoroughly, it was stated that the motor car was an uncovered one and that it would have been impossible to pack four large pictures into it unobserved by the ferryman.

It was very probably the same car; but then the question cropped up again: what had become of the four Rubenses?

These were so many problems which M. Filleul unanswered. Every day, his subordinates searched the quadrilateral of the ruins. Almost every day, he came to direct the explorations. But between that and discovering the refuge in which Lupin lay dying—if it were true that Beautrelet's opinion was correct—there was a gulf fixed which the worthy magistrate did not seem likely to cross.

And so it was natural that they should turn once more to Isidore Beautrelet, as he alone had succeeded in dispelling shadows which, in his absence, gathered thicker and more impenetrable than ever. Why did he not go on with the case? Seeing how far he had carried it, he required but an effort to succeed.

The question was put to him by a member of the staff of the Grand Journal, who had obtained admission to the Lycee Janson by assuming the name of Bernod, the friend of Beautrelet's father. And Isidore very sensibly replied:

"My dear sir, there are other things besides Lupin in this world, other things besides stories about burglars and detectives. There is, for instance, the thing which is known as taking one's degree. Now I am going up for my examination in July. This is May. And I don't want to be plucked. What would my worthy parent say?"

"But what would he say if you delivered Arsene Lupin into the hands of the police?"

"Tut! There's a time for everything. In the next holidays—"

"Whitsuntide?"

"Yes—I shall go down on Saturday the sixth of June by the first train."

"And, on the evening of that Saturday, Lupin will be taken."

"Will you give me until the Sunday?" asked Beautrelet, laughing.

"Why delay?" replied the journalist, quite seriously.

This inexplicable confidence, born of yesterday and already so strong, was felt with regard to the young man by one and all, even though, in reality, events had justified it only up to a certain point. No matter, people believed in him! Nothing seemed difficult to him. They expected from him what they were entitled to expect at most from some phenomenon of penetration and intuition, of experience and skill. That day of the sixth of June was made to sprawl over all the papers. On the sixth of June, Isidore Beautrelet would take the fast train to Dieppe: and Lupin would be arrested on the same evening.

"Unless he escapes between this and then," objected the last remaining partisans of the adventurer.

"Impossible! Every outlet is watched."

"Unless he has succumbed to his wounds, then," said the partisans, who would have preferred their hero's death to his capture.

And the retort was immediate:

"Nonsense! If Lupin were dead, his confederates would know it by now, and Lupin would be revenged. Beautrelet said so!"

And the sixth of June came. Half a dozen journalists were looking out for Isidore at the Gare Saint-Lazare. Two of them wanted to accompany him on his journey. He begged them to refrain.

He started alone, therefore, in a compartment to himself. He was tired, thanks to a series of nights devoted to study, and soon fell asleep. He slept heavily. In his dreams, he had an impression that the train stopped at different stations and that people got in and out. When he awoke, within sight of Rouen, he was still alone. But, on the back of the opposite seat, was a large sheet of paper, fastened with a pin to the gray cloth. It bore these words:

"Every man should mind his own business. Do you mind yours. If not, you must take the consequences."

"Capital!" he exclaimed, rubbing his hands with delight. "Things are going badly in the adversary's camp. That threat is as stupid and vulgar as the sham flyman's. What a style! One can see that it wasn't composed by Lupin."

The train threaded the tunnel that precedes the old Norman city. On reaching the station, Isidore took a few turns on the platform to stretch his legs. He was about to re-enter his compartment, when a cry escaped him. As he passed the bookstall, he had read, in an absent-minded way, the following lines on the front page of a special edition of the Journal de Rouen; and their alarming sense suddenly burst upon him:

STOP-PRESS NEWS

We hear by telephone from Dieppe that the Chateau d'Ambrumesy was broken into last night by criminals, who bound and gagged Mlle. de Gesvres and carried off Mlle. de Saint-Veran. Traces of blood have been seen at a distance of five hundred yards from the house and a scarf has been found close by, which is also stained with blood. There is every reason to fear that the poor young girl has been murdered.

Isidore Beautrelet completed his journey to Dieppe without moving a limb. Bent in two, with his elbows on his knees and his hands plastered against his face, he sat thinking.

At Dieppe, he took a fly. At the door of Ambrumesy, he met the examining magistrate, who confirmed the horrible news.

"You know nothing more?" asked Beautrelet.

"Nothing. I have only just arrived."

At that moment, the sergeant of gendarmes came up to M. Filleul and handed him a crumpled, torn and discolored piece of paper, which he had picked up not far from the place where the scarf was found. M. Filleul looked at it and gave it to Beautrelet, saying:

"I don't suppose this will help us much in our investigations."

Isidore turned the paper over and over. It was covered with figures, dots and signs and presented the exact appearance reproduced below:

2.1.1..2..2.1..1..
1...2.2. 2.43.2..2.
.45..2.4...2..2.4..2
D DF square 19F+44triangle357triangle
13.53..2 ..25.2

III. THE CORPSE

At six o'clock in the evening, having finished all he had to do, M. Filluel, accompanied by M. Bredoux, his clerk, stood waiting for the carriage which was to take him back to Dieppe. He seemed restless, nervous. Twice over, he asked:

"You haven't seen anything of young Beautrelet, I suppose?"

"No, Monsieur le Juge d'Instruction, I can't say I have."

"Where on earth can he be? I haven't set eyes on him all day!"

Suddenly, he had an idea, handed his portfolio to Bredoux, ran round the chateau and made for the ruins. Isidore Beautrelet was lying near the cloisters, flat on his face, with one arm folded under his head, on the ground carpeted with pine-needles. He seemed drowsing.

"Hullo, young man, what are you doing here? Are you asleep?"

"I'm not asleep. I've been thinking."

"Ever since this morning?"

"Ever since this morning."

"It's not a question of thinking! One must see into things first, study facts, look for clues, establish connecting links. The time for thinking comes after, when one pieces all that together and discovers the truth."

"Yes, I know.—That's the usual way, the right one, I dare say.—Mine is different.—I think first, I try, above all, to get the general hang of the case, if I may so express myself. Then I imagine a reasonable and logical hypothesis, which fits in with the general idea. And then, and not before, I examine the facts to see if they agree with my hypothesis."

"That's a funny method and a terribly complicated one!"

"It's a sure method, M. Filleul, which is more than can be said of yours."

"Come, come! Facts are facts."

"With your ordinary sort of adversary, yes. But, given an enemy endowed with a certain amount of cunning, the facts are those which he happens to have selected. Take the famous clues upon which you base your inquiry: why, he was at liberty to arrange them as he liked. And you see where that can lead you, into what mistakes and absurdities, when you are dealing with a man like Arsene Lupin. Holmlock Shears himself fell into the trap."

"Arsene Lupin is dead."

"No matter. His gang remains and the pupils of such a master are masters themselves."

M. Filleul took Isidore by the arm and, leading him away:

"Words, young man, words. Here is something of more importance. Listen to me. Ganimard is otherwise engaged at this moment and will not be here for a few days. On the other hand, the Comte de Gesvres has telegraphed to Holmlock Shears, who has promised his assistance next week. Now don't you think, young man, that it would be a feather in our cap if we were able to say to those two celebrities, on the day of their arrival, 'Awfully sorry, gentlemen, but we couldn't wait. The business is done'?"

It was impossible for M. Filleul to confess helplessness with greater candor. Beautrelet suppressed a smile and, pretending not to see through the worthy magistrate, replied:

"I confess. Monsieur le Juge d'Instruction, that, if I was not present at your inquiry just now, it was because I hoped that you would consent to tell me the results. May I ask what you have learned?"

"Well, last night, at eleven o'clock, the three gendarmes whom Sergeant Quevillon had left on guard at the chateau received a note from the sergeant telling them to hasten with all speed to Ouville, where they are stationed. They at once rode off, and when they arrived at Ouville—"

"They discovered that they had been tricked, that the order was a forgery and that there was nothing for them to do but return to Ambrumesy."

"This they did, accompanied by Sergeant Quevillon. But they were away for an hour and a half and, during this time, the crime was committed."

"In what circumstances?"

"Very simple circumstances, indeed. A ladder was removed from the farm buildings and placed against the second story of the chateau. A pane of glass was cut out and a window opened. Two men, carrying a dark lantern, entered Mlle. de Gesvres's room and gagged her before she could cry out. Then, after binding her with cords, they softly opened the door of the room in which Mlle. de Saint-Veran was sleeping. Mlle. de Gesvres heard a stifled moan, followed by the sound of a person struggling. A moment later, she saw two men carrying her cousin, who was also bound and gagged. They passed in front of her and went out through the window. Then Mlle. de Gesvres, terrified and exhausted, fainted."

"But what about the dogs? I thought M. de Gesvres had bought two almost wild sheep-dogs, which were let loose at night?"

"They were found dead, poisoned."

"By whom? Nobody could get near them."

"It's a mystery. The fact remains that the two men crossed the ruins without let or hindrance and went out by the little door which we have heard so much about. They passed through the copsewood, following the line of the disused quarries. It was not until they were nearly half a mile from the chateau, at the foot of the tree known as the Great Oak, that they stopped—and executed their purpose."

"If they came with the intention of killing Mlle. de Saint-Veran, why didn't they murder her in her room?"

"I don't know. Perhaps the incident that settled their determination only occurred after they had left the house. Perhaps the girl succeeded in releasing herself from her bonds. In my opinion, the scarf which was picked up was used to fasten her wrists. In any case, the blow was struck at the foot of the Great Oak. I have collected indisputable proofs—"

"But the body?"

"The body has not been found, but there is nothing excessively surprising in that. As a matter of fact, the trail which I followed brought me to the church at Varengeville and the old cemetery perched on the top of the cliff. From there it is a sheer precipice, a fall of over three hundred feet to the rocks and the sea below. In a day or two, a stronger tide than usual will cast up the body on the beach."

"Obviously. This is all very simple."

"Yes, it is all very simple and doesn't trouble me in the least. Lupin is dead, his accomplices heard of it and, to revenge themselves, have killed Mlle. de Saint-Veran. These are facts which did not even require checking. But Lupin?"

"What about him?"

"What has become of him? In all probability, his confederates removed his corpse at the same time that they carried away the girl; but what proof have we? None at all. Any more than of his staying in the ruins, or of his death, or of his life. And that is the real mystery, M. Beautrelet. The murder of Mlle. Raymonde solves nothing. On the contrary, it only complicates matters. What has been happening during the past two months at the Chateau d'Ambrumesy? If we don't clear up the riddle, young man, others will give us the go-by."

"On what day are those others coming?"

"Wednesday—Tuesday perhaps—"

Beautrelet seemed to be making an inward calculation and then declared:

"Monsieur le Juge d'Instruction, this is Saturday. I have to be back at school on Monday evening. Well, if you will have the goodness to be here at ten o'clock exactly on Monday morning, I will try to give you the key to the riddle."

"Really, M. Beautrelet—do you think so? Are you sure?"

"I hope so, at any rate."

"And where are you going now?"

"I am going to see if the facts consent to fit in with the general theory which I am beginning to perceive."

"And if they don't fit in?"

"Well, Monsieur le Juge d'Instruction," said Beautrelet, with a laugh, "then it will be their fault and I must look for others which, will prove more tractable. Till Monday, then?"

"Till Monday."

A few minutes later, M. Filleul was driving toward Dieppe, while Isidore mounted a bicycle which he had borrowed from the Comte de Gesvres and rode off along the road to Yerville and Caudebec-en-Caux.

There was one point in particular on which the young man was anxious to form a clear opinion, because this just appeared to him to be the enemy's weakest point. Objects of the size of the four Rubens pictures cannot be juggled away. They were bound to be somewhere. Granting that it was impossible to find them for the moment, might one not discover the road by which they had disappeared?

What Beautrelet surmised was that the four pictures had undoubtedly been carried off in the motor car, but that, before reaching Caudebec, they were transferred to another car, which had crossed the Seine either above Caudebec or below it. Now the first horse-boat down the stream was at Quillebeuf, a greatly frequented ferry and, consequently, dangerous. Up stream, there was the ferry-boat at La Mailleraie, a large, but lonely market-town, lying well off the main road.

By midnight, Isidore had covered the thirty-five or forty miles to La Mailleraie and was knocking at the door of an inn by the waterside. He slept there and, in the morning, questioned the ferrymen.

They consulted the counterfoils in the traffic-book. No motor-car had crossed on Thursday the 23rd of April.

"A horse-drawn vehicle, then?" suggested Beautrelet. "A cart? A van?"

"No, not either."

Isidore continued his inquiries all through the morning. He was on the point of leaving for Quillebeuf, when the waiter of the inn at which he had spent the night said:

"I came back from my thirteen days' training on the morning of which you are speaking and I saw a cart, but it did not go across."

"Really?"

"No, they unloaded it onto a flat boat, a barge of sorts, which was moored to the wharf."

"And where did the cart come from?"

"Oh, I knew it at once. It belonged to Master Vatinel, the carter."

"And where does he live?"

"At Louvetot."

Beautrelet consulted his military map. The hamlet of Louvetot lay where the highroad between Yvetot and Caudebec was crossed by a little winding road that ran through the woods to La Mailleraie.

Not until six o'clock in the evening did Isidore succeed in discovering Master Vatinel, in a pothouse. Master Vatinel was one of those artful old Normans who are always on their guard, who distrust strangers, but who are unable to resist the lure of a gold coin or the influence of a glass or two:

"Well, yes, sir, the men in the motor car that morning had told me to meet them at five o'clock at the crossroads. They gave me four great, big things, as high as that. One of them went with me and we carted the things to the barge."

"You speak of them as if you knew them before."

"I should think I did know them! It was the sixth time they were employing me."

Isidore gave a start:

"The sixth time, you say? And since when?"

"Why every day before that one, to be sure! But it was other things then—great blocks of stone—or else smaller, longish ones, wrapped up in newspapers, which they carried as if they were worth I don't know what. Oh, I mustn't touch those on any account!—But what's the matter? You've turned quite white."

"Nothing—the heat of the room—"

Beautrelet staggered out into the air. The joy, the surprise of the discovery made him feel giddy. He went back very quietly to Varengeville, slept in the village, spent an hour at the mayor's offices with the schoolmaster and returned to the chateau. There he found a letter awaiting him "care of M. le Comte de Gesvres." It consisted of a single line:

"Second warning. Hold your tongue. If not—"

"Come," he muttered. "I shall have to make up my mind and take a few precautions for my personal safety. If not, as they say—"

It was nine o'clock. He strolled about among the ruins and then lay down near the cloisters and closed his eyes.

"Well, young man, are you satisfied with the results of your campaign?"

It was M. Filleul.

"Delighted, Monsieur le Juge d'Instruction."

"By which you mean to say—?"

"By which I mean to say that I am prepared to keep my promise—in spite of this very uninviting letter."

He showed the letter to M. Filleul.

"Pooh! Stuff and nonsense!" cried the magistrate. "I hope you won't let that prevent you—"

"From telling you what I know? No, Monsieur le Juge d'Instruction. I have given my word and I shall keep it. In less than ten minutes, you shall know—a part of the truth."

"A part?"

"Yes, in my opinion, Lupin's hiding-place does not constitute the whole of the problem. Far from it. But we shall see later on."

"M. Beautrelet, nothing that you do could astonish me now. But how were you able to discover—?"

"Oh, in a very natural way! In the letter from old man Harlington to M. Etienne de Vaudreix, or rather to Lupin—"

"The intercepted letter?"

"Yes. There is a phrase which always puzzled me. After saying that the pictures are to be forwarded as arranged, he goes on to say, 'You may add THE REST, if you are able to succeed, which I doubt.'"

"Yes, I remember."

"What was this 'rest'? A work of art, a curiosity? The chateau contains nothing of any value besides the Rubenses and the tapestries. Jewelry? There is very little and what there is of it is not worth much. In that case, what could it be?—On the other hand, was it conceivable that people so prodigiously clever as Lupin should not have succeeded in adding 'the rest,' which they themselves had evidently suggested? A difficult undertaking, very likely; exceptional, surprising, I dare say; but possible and therefore certain, since Lupin wished it."

"And yet he failed: nothing has disappeared."

"He did not fail: something has disappeared."

"Yes, the Rubenses—but—"

"The Rubenses and something besides—something which has been replaced by a similar thing, as in the case of the Rubenses; something much more uncommon, much rarer, much more valuable than the Rubenses."

"Well, what? You're killing me with this procrastination!"

While talking, the two men had crossed the ruins, turned toward the little door and were now walking beside the chapel. Beautrelet stopped:

"Do you really want to know, Monsieur le Juge d'Instruction?"

"Of course, I do."

Beautrelet was carrying a walking-stick, a strong, knotted stick. Suddenly, with a back stroke of this stick, he smashed one of the little statues that adorned the front of the chapel.

"Why, you're mad!" shouted M. Filleul, beside himself, rushing at the broken pieces of the statue. "You're mad! That old saint was an admirable bit of work—"

"An admirable bit of work!" echoed Isidore, giving a whirl which brought down the Virgin Mary.

M. Filleul took hold of him round the body:

"Young man, I won't allow you to commit—"

A wise man of the East came toppling to the ground, followed by a manger containing the Mother and Child. . . .

"If you stir another limb, I fire!"

The Comte de Gesvres had appeared upon the scene and was cocking his revolver. Beautrelet burst out laughing:

"That's right, Monsieur le Comte, blaze away!—Take a shot at them, as if you were at a fair!—Wait a bit—this chap carrying his head in his hands—"

St. John the Baptist fell, shattered to pieces.

"Oh!" shouted the count, pointing his revolver. "You young vandal!—Those masterpieces!"

"Sham, Monsieur le Comte!"

"What? What's that?" roared M. Filleul, wresting the Comte de Gesvres's weapon from him.

"Sham!" repeated Beautrelet. "Paper-pulp and plaster!"

"Oh, nonsense! It can't be true!"

"Hollow plaster, I tell you! Nothing at all!"

The count stooped and picked up a sliver of a statuette.

"Look at it, Monsieur le Comte, and see for yourself: it's plaster! Rusty, musty, mildewed plaster, made to look like old stone—but plaster for all that, plaster casts!—That's all that remains of your perfect masterpiece!—That's what they've done in just a few days!-That's what the Sieur Charpenais who copied the Rubenses, prepared a year ago." He seized M. Filleul's arm in his turn. "What do you think of it, Monsieur le Juge d'Instruction? Isn't it fine? Isn't it grand? Isn't it gorgeous? The chapel has been removed! A whole Gothic chapel collected stone by stone! A whole population of statues captured and replaced by these chaps in stucco! One of the most magnificent specimens of an incomparable artistic period confiscated! The chapel, in short, stolen! Isn't it immense? Ah, Monsieur le Juge d'Instruction, what a genius the man is!"

"You're allowing yourself to be carried away, M. Beautrelet."

"One can't be carried away too much, monsieur, when one has to do with people like that. Everything above the average deserves our admiration. And this man soars above everything. There is in his flight a wealth of imagination, a force and power, a skill and freedom that send a thrill through me!"

"Pity he's dead," said M. Filleul, with a grin. "He'd have ended by stealing the towers of Notre-Dame."

Isidore shrugged his shoulders:

"Don't laugh, monsieur. He upsets you, dead though he may be."

"I don't say not, I don't say not, M. Beautrelet, I confess that I feel a certain excitement now that I am about to set eyes on him—unless, indeed, his friends have taken away the body."

"And always admitting," observed the Comte de Gesvres, "that it was really he who was wounded by my poor niece."

"It was he, beyond a doubt, Monsieur le Comte," declared Beautrelet; "it was he, believe me, who fell in the ruins under the shot fired by Mlle. de Saint-Veran; it was he whom she saw rise and who fell again and dragged himself toward the cloisters to rise again for the last time—this by a miracle which I will explain to you presently—to rise again for the last time and reach this stone shelter—which was to be his tomb."

And Beautrelet struck the threshold of the chapel with his stick.

"Eh? What?" cried M. Filleul, taken aback. "His tomb?—Do you think that that impenetrable hiding-place—"

"It was here—there," he repeated.

"But we searched it."

"Badly."

"There is no hiding-place here," protested M. de Gesvres. "I know the chapel."

"Yes, there is, Monsieur le Comte. Go to the mayor's office at Varengeville, where they have collected all the papers that used to be in the old parish of Ambrumesy, and you will learn from those papers, which belong to the eighteenth century, that there is a crypt below the chapel. This crypt doubtless dates back to the Roman chapel, upon the site of which the present one was built."

"But how can Lupin have known this detail?" asked M. Filleul.

"In a very simple manner: because of the works which he had to execute to take away the chapel."

"Come, come, M. Beautrelet, you're exaggerating. He has not taken away the whole chapel. Look, not one of the stones of this top course has been touched."

"Obviously, he cast and took away only what had a financial value: the wrought stones, the sculptures, the statuettes, the whole treasure of little columns and carved arches. He did not trouble about the groundwork of the building itself. The foundations remain."

"Therefore, M. Beautrelet, Lupin was not able to make his way into the crypt."

At that moment, M. de Gesvres, who had been to call a servant, returned with the key of the chapel. He opened the door. The three men entered. After a short examination Beautrelet said:

"The flag-stones on the ground have been respected, as one might expect. But it is easy to perceive that the high altar is nothing more than a cast. Now, generally, the staircase leading to the crypt opens in front of the high altar and passes under it."

"What do you conclude?"

"I conclude that Lupin discovered the crypt when working at the altar."

The count sent for a pickaxe and Beautrelet attacked the altar. The plaster flew to right and left. He pushed the pieces aside as he went on.

"By Jove!" muttered M. Filleul, "I am eager to know—"

"So am I," said Beautrelet, whose face was pale with anguish.

He hurried his blows. And, suddenly, his pickaxe, which, until then, had encountered no resistance, struck against a harder material and rebounded. There was a sound of something falling in; and all that remained of the altar went tumbling into the gap after the block of stone which had been struck by the pickaxe. Beautrelet bent forward. A puff of cold air rose to his face. He lit a match and moved it from side to side over the gap:

"The staircase begins farther forward than I expected, under the entrance-flags, almost. I can see the last steps, there, right at the bottom."

"Is it deep?"

"Three or four yards. The steps are very high—and there are some missing."

"It is hardly likely," said M. Filleul, "that the accomplices can have had time to remove the body from the cellar, when they were engaged in carrying off Mlle. de Saint-Veran—during the short absence of the gendarmes. Besides, why should they?—No, in my opinion, the body is here."

A servant brought them a ladder. Beautrelet let it down through the opening and fixed it, after groping among the fallen fragments. Holding the two uprights firmly:

"Will you go down, M. Filleul?" he asked.

The magistrate, holding a candle in his hand, ventured down the ladder. The Comte de Gesvres followed him and Beautrelet, in his turn, placed his foot on the first rung.

Mechanically, he counted eighteen rungs, while his eyes examined the crypt, where the glimmer of the candle struggled against the heavy darkness. But, at the bottom, his nostrils were assailed by one of those foul and violent smells which linger in the memory for many a long day. And, suddenly, a trembling hand seized him by the shoulder.

"Well, what is it?"

"B-beautrelet," stammered M. Filleul. "B-beau-trelet—"

He could not get a word out for terror.

"Come, Monsieur le Juge d'Instruction, compose yourself!"

"Beautrelet—he is there—"

"Eh?"

"Yes—there was something under the big stone that broke off the altar—I pushed the stone—and I touched—I shall never—shall never forget.—"

"Where is it?"

"On this side.—Don't you notice the smell?—And then look—see."

He took the candle and held it towards a motionless form stretched upon the ground.

"Oh!" exclaimed Beautrelet, in a horror-stricken tone.

The three men bent down quickly. The corpse lay half-naked, lean, frightful. The flesh, which had the greenish hue of soft wax, appeared in places through the torn clothes. But the most hideous thing, the thing that had drawn a cry of terror from the young man's lips, was the head, the head which had just been crushed by the block of stone, the shapeless head, a repulsive mass in which not one feature could be distinguished.

Beautrelet took four strides up the ladder and fled into the daylight and the open air.

M. Filleul found him again lying flat on the around, with his hands glued to his face:

"I congratulate you, Beautrelet," he said. "In addition to the discovery of the hiding-place, there are two points on which I have been able to verify the correctness of your assertions. First of all, the man on whom Mlle. de Saint-Veran fired was indeed Arsene Lupin, as you said from the start. Also, he lived in Paris under the name of Etienne de Vaudreix. His linen is marked with the initials E. V. That ought to be sufficient proof, I think: don't you?"

Isidore did not stir.

"Monsieur le Comte has gone to have a horse put to. They're sending for Dr. Jouet, who will make the usual examination. In my opinion, death must have taken place a week ago, at least. The state of decomposition of the corpse—but you don't seem to be listening—"

"Yes, yes."

"What I say is based upon absolute reasons. Thus, for instance—"

M. Filleul continued his demonstrations, without, however, obtaining any more manifest marks of attention. But M. de Gesvres's return interrupted his monologue. The comte brought two letters. One was to tell him that Holmlock Shears would arrive next morning.

"Capital!" cried M. Filleul, joyfully. "Inspector Ganimard will be here too. It will be delightful."

"The other letter is for you, Monsieur le Juge d'Instruction," said the comte.

"Better and better," said M. Filleul, after reading it. "There will certainly not be much for those two gentlemen to do. M. Beautrelet, I hear from Dieppe that the body of a young woman was found by some shrimpers, this morning, on the rocks."

Beautrelet gave a start:

"What's that? The body—"

"Of a young woman.—The body is horribly mutilated, they say, and it would be impossible to establish the identity, but for a very narrow little gold curb-bracelet on the right arm which has become encrusted in the swollen skin. Now Mlle. de Saint-Veran used to wear a gold curb-bracelet on her right arm. Evidently, therefore, Monsieur le Comte, this is the body of your poor niece, which the sea must have washed to that distance. What do you think, Beautrelet?"

"Nothing—nothing—or, rather, yes—everything is connected, as you see—and there is no link missing in my argument. All the facts, one after the other, however contradictory, however disconcerting they may appear, end by supporting the supposition which I imagined from the first."

"I don't understand."

"You soon will. Remember, I promised you the whole truth."

"But it seems to me—"

"A little patience, Monsieur le Juge d'Instruction. So far, you have had no cause to complain of me. It is a fine day. Go for a walk, lunch at the chateau, smoke your pipe. I shall be back by four o'clock. As for my school, well, I don't care: I shall take the night train."

They had reached the out-houses at the back of the chateau. Beautrelet jumped on his bicycle and rode away.

At Dieppe, he stopped at the office of the local paper, the Vigie, and examined the file for the last fortnight. Then he went on to the market-town of Envermeu, six or seven miles farther. At Envermeu, he talked to the mayor, the rector and the local policeman. The church-clock struck three. His inquiry was finished.

He returned singing for joy. He pressed upon the two pedals turn by turn, with an equal and powerful rhythm; his chest opened wide to take in the keen air that blew from the sea. And, from time to time, he forgot himself to the extent of uttering shouts of triumph to the sky, when he thought of the aim which he was pursuing and of the success that was crowning his efforts.

Ambrumesy appeared in sight. He coasted at full speed down the slope leading to the chateau. The top rows of venerable trees that line the road seemed to run to meet him and to vanish behind him forthwith. And, all at once, he uttered a cry. In a sudden vision, he had seen a rope stretched from one tree to another, across the road.

His machine gave a jolt and stopped short. Beautrelet was flung three yards forward, with immense violence, and it seemed to him that only chance, a miraculous chance, caused him to escape a heap of pebbles on which, logically, he ought to have broken his head.

He lay for a few seconds stunned. Then, all covered with bruises, with the skin flayed from his knees, he examined the spot. On the right lay a small wood, by which his aggressor had no doubt fled. Beautrelet untied the rope. To the tree on the left around which it was fastened a small piece of paper was fixed with string. Beautrelet unfolded it and read:

"The third and last warning."

He went on to the chateau, put a few questions to the servants and joined the examining magistrate in a room on the ground floor, at the end of the right wing, where M. Filleul used to sit in the course of his operations. M. Filleul was writing, with his clerk seated opposite to him. At a sign from him, the clerk left the room; and the magistrate exclaimed:

"Why, what have you been doing to yourself, M. Beautrelet? Your hands are covered with blood."

"It's nothing, it's nothing," said the young man. "Just a fall occasioned by this rope, which was stretched in front of my bicycle. I will only ask you to observe that the rope comes from the chateau. Not longer than twenty minutes ago, it was being used to dry linen on, outside the laundry."

"You don't mean to say so!"

"Monsieur le Juge d'Instruction, I am being watched here, by some one in the very heart of the place, who can see me, who can hear me and who, minute by minute, observes my actions and knows my intentions."

"Do you think so?"

"I am sure of it. It is for you to discover him and you will have no difficulty in that. As for myself, I want to have finished and to give you the promised explanations. I have made faster progress than our adversaries expected and I am convinced that they mean to take vigorous measures on their side. The circle is closing around me. The danger is approaching. I feel it."

"Nonsense, Beautrelet—"

"You wait and see! For the moment, let us lose no time. And, first, a question on a point which I want to have done with at once. Have you spoken to anybody of that document which Sergeant Quevillon picked up and handed you in my presence?"

"No, indeed; not to a soul. But do you attach any value—?"

"The greatest value. It's an idea of mine, an idea, I confess, which does not rest upon a proof of any kind—for, up to the present, I have not succeeded in deciphering the document. And therefore I am mentioning it—so that we need not come back to it."

Beautrelet pressed his hand on M. Filleul's and whispered:

"Don't speak—there's some one listening—outside—"

The gravel creaked. Beautrelet ran to the window and leaned out:

"There's no one there—but the border has been trodden down—we can easily identify the footprints—"

He closed the window and sat down again:

"You see, Monsieur le Juge d'Instruction, the enemy has even ceased to take the most ordinary precautions—he has not time left—he too feels that the hour is urgent. Let us be quick, therefore, and speak, since they do not wish us to speak."

He laid the document on the table and held it in position, unfolded:

"One observation, Monsieur le Juge d'Instruction, to begin with. The paper consists almost entirely of dots and figures. And in the first three lines and the fifth—the only ones with which we have to do at present, for the fourth seems to present an entirely different character—not one of those figures is higher than the figure 5. There is, therefore, a great chance that each of these figures represents one of the five vowels, taken in alphabetical order. Let us put down the result."

He wrote on a separate piece of paper:

E.A.A..E..E.A..A..
A...E.E..E OI.E..E.
.OU..E.O...E..E.O..E
AI.UI..E..EU.E

Then he continued:

"As you see, this does not give us much to go upon. The key is, at the same time, very easy, because the inventor has contented himself with replacing the vowels by figures and the consonants by dots, and very difficult, if not impossible, because he has taken no further trouble to complicate the problem."

"It is certainly pretty obscure."

"Let us try to throw some light upon it. The second line is divided into two parts; and the second part appears in such a way that it probably forms one word. If we now seek to replace the intermediary dots by consonants, we arrive at the conclusion, after searching and casting about, that the only consonants which are logically able to support the vowels are also logically able to produce only one word, the word DEMOISELLES."

"That would refer to Mlle. de Gesvres and Mlle. de Saint-Veran."

"Undoubtedly."

"And do you see nothing more?"

"Yes. I also note an hiatus in the middle of the last line; and, if I apply a similar operation to the beginning of the line, I at once see that the only consonant able to take the place of the dot between the diphthongs FAI and UI is the letter G and that, when I have thus formed the first five letters of the word, AIGUI, it is natural and inevitable that, with the two next dots and the final E, I should arrive at the word AIGUILLE."

"Yes, the word AIGUILLE forces itself upon us."

"Finally, for the last word, I have three vowels and three consonants. I cast about again, I try all the letters, one after the other, and, starting with the principle that the two first letters are necessary consonants, I find that three words apply: F*EUVE, PREUVE and CREUSE. I eliminate the words F*EUVE and PREUVE, as possessing no possible relation to a needle, and I keep the word CREUSE."

"Making 'hollow needle'! By jove! I admit that your solution is correct, because it needs must be; but how does it help us?"

"Not at all," said Beautrelet, in a thoughtful tone. "Not at all, for the moment.—Later on, we shall see.—I have an idea that a number of things are included in the puzzling conjunction of those two words, AIGUILLE CREUSE. What is troubling me at present is rather the material on which the document is written, the paper employed.—Do they still manufacture this sort of rather coarse-grained parchment? And then this ivory color.—And those folds—the wear of those folds—and, lastly, look, those marks of red sealing-wax, on the back—"

At that moment Beautrelet, was interrupted by Bredoux, the magistrate's clerk, who opened the door and announced the unexpected arrival of the chief public prosecutor. M. Filleul rose:

"Anything new? Is Monsieur le Procureur General downstairs?"

"No, Monsieur le Juge d'Instruction. Monsieur le Procureur General has not left his carriage. He is only passing through Ambrumesy and begs you to be good enough to go down to him at the gate. He only has a word to say to you."

"That's curious," muttered M. Filleul. "However—we shall see. Excuse me, Beautrelet, I shan't be long."

He went away. His footsteps sounded outside. Then the clerk closed the door, turned the key and put it in his pocket.

"Hullo!" exclaimed Beautrelet, greatly surprised. "What are you locking us in for?"

"We shall be able to talk so much better," retorted Bredoux.

Beautrelet rushed toward another door, which led to the next room. He had understood: the accomplice was Bredoux, the clerk of the examining magistrate himself. Bredoux grinned:

"Don't hurt your fingers, my young friend. I have the key of that door, too."

"There's the window!" cried Beautrelet.

"Too late," said Bredoux, planting himself in front of the casement, revolver in hand.

Every chance of retreat was cut off. There was nothing more for Isidore to do, nothing except to defend himself against the enemy who was revealing himself with such brutal daring. He crossed his arms.

"Good," mumbled the clerk. "And now let us waste no time." He took out his watch. "Our worthy M. Filleul will walk down to the gate. At the gate, he will find nobody, of course: no more public prosecutor than my eye. Then he will come back. That gives us about four minutes. It will take me one minute to escape by this window, clear through the little door by the ruins and jump on the motor cycle waiting for me. That leaves three minutes, which is just enough."

Bredoux was a queer sort of misshapen creature, who balanced on a pair of very long spindle-legs a huge trunk, as round as the body of a spider and furnished with immense arms. A bony face and a low, small stubborn forehead pointed to the man's narrow obstinacy.

Beautrelet felt a weakness in the legs and staggered. He had to sit down:

"Speak," he said. "What do you want?"

"The paper. I've been looking for it for three days."

"I haven't got it."

"You're lying. I saw you put it back in your pocket-book when I came in."

"Next?"

"Next, you must undertake to keep quite quiet. You're annoying us. Leave us alone and mind your own business. Our patience is at an end."

He had come nearer, with the revolver still aimed at the young man's head, and spoke in a hollow voice, with a powerful stress on each syllable that he uttered. His eyes were hard, his smile cruel.

Beautrelet gave a shudder. It was the first time that he was experiencing the sense of danger. And such danger! He felt himself in the presence of an implacable enemy, endowed with blind and irresistible strength.

"And next?" he asked, with less assurance in his voice.

"Next? Nothing.—You will be free.—We will forget—"

There was a pause. Then Bredoux resumed:

"There is only a minute left. You must make up your mind. Come, old chap, don't be a fool.—We are the stronger, you know, always and everywhere.—Quick, the paper—"

Isidore did not flinch. With a livid and terrified face, he remained master of himself, nevertheless, and his brain remained clear amid the breakdown of his nerves. The little black hole of the revolver was pointing at six inches from his eyes. The finger was bent and obviously pressing on the trigger. It only wanted a moment—

"The paper," repeated Bredoux. "If not—"

"Here it is," said Beautrelet.

He took out his pocket-book and handed it to the clerk, who seized it eagerly.

"Capital! We've come to our senses. I've no doubt there's something to be done with you.—You're troublesome, but full of common sense. I'll talk about it to my pals. And now I'm off. Good-bye!"

He pocketed his revolver and turned back the fastening of the window. There was a noise in the passage.

"Good-bye," he said again. "I'm only just in time."

But the idea stopped him. With a quick movement, he examined the pocket-book:

"Damn and blast it!" He grated through his teeth. "The paper's not there.—You've done me—"

He leaped into the room. Two shots rang out. Isidore, in his turn, had seized his pistol and fired.

"Missed, old chap!" shouted Bredoux. "Your hand's shaking.—You're afraid—"

They caught each other round the body and came down to the floor together. There was a violent and incessant knocking at the door. Isidore's strength gave way and he was at once over come by his adversary. It was the end. A hand was lifted over him, armed with a knife, and fell. A fierce pain burst into his shoulder. He let go.

He had an impression of some one fumbling in the inside pocket of his jacket and taking the paper from it. Then, through the lowered veil of his eyelids, he half saw the man stepping over the window-sill.

The same newspapers which, on the following morning, related the last episodes that had occurred at the Chateau d'Ambrumesy—the trickery at the chapel, the discovery of Arsene Lupin's body and of Raymonde's body and, lastly, the murderous attempt made upon Beautrelet by the clerk to the examining magistrate—also announced two further pieces of news: the disappearance of Ganimard, and the kidnapping of Holmlock Shears, in broad daylight, in the heart of London, at the moment when he was about to take the train for Dover.

Lupin's gang, therefore, which had been disorganized for a moment by the extraordinary ingenuity of a seventeen-year-old schoolboy, was now resuming the offensive and was winning all along the line from the first. Lupin's two great adversaries, Shears and Ganimard, were put away. Isidore Beautrelet was disabled. The police were powerless. For the moment there was no one left capable of struggling against such enemies.

IV. FACE TO FACE

One evening, five weeks later, I had given my man leave to go out. It was the day before the 14th of July. The night was hot, a storm threatened and I felt no inclination to leave the flat. I opened wide the glass doors leading to my balcony, lit my reading lamp and sat down in an easy-chair to look through the papers, which I had not yet seen.

It goes without saying that there was something about Arsene Lupin in all of them. Since the attempt at murder of which poor Isidore Beautrelet had been the victim, not a day had passed without some mention of the Ambrumesy mystery. It had a permanent headline devoted to it. Never had public opinion been excited to that extent, thanks to the extraordinary series of hurried events, of unexpected and disconcerting surprises. M. Filleul, who was certainly accepting the secondary part allotted to him with a good faith worthy of all praise, had let the interviewers into the secret of his young advisor's exploits during the memorable three days, so that the public was able to indulge in the rashest suppositions. And the public gave itself free scope. Specialists and experts in crime, novelists and playwrights, retired magistrates and chief-detectives, erstwhile Lecocqs and budding Holmlock Shearses, each had his theory and expounded it in lengthy contributions to the press. Everybody corrected and supplemented the inquiry of the examining magistrate; and all on the word of a child, on the word of Isidore Beautrelet, a sixth-form schoolboy at the Lycee Janson-de-Sailly!

For really, it had to be admitted, the complete elements of the truth were now in everybody's possession. What did the mystery consist of? They knew the hiding-place where Arsene Lupin had taken refuge and lain a-dying; there was no doubt about it: Dr. Delattre, who continued to plead professional secrecy and refused to give evidence, nevertheless confessed to his intimate friends—who lost no time in blabbing—that he really had been taken to a crypt to attend a wounded man whom his confederates introduced to him by the name of Arsene Lupin. And, as the corpse of Etienne de Vaudreix was found in that same crypt and as the said Etienne de Vaudreix was none other than Arsene Lupin—as the official examination went to show—all this provided an additional proof, if one were needed, of the identity of Arsene Lupin and the wounded man. Therefore, with Lupin dead and Mlle. de Saint-Veran's body recognized by the curb-bracelet on her wrist, the tragedy was finished.

It was not. Nobody thought that it was, because Beautrelet had said the contrary. Nobody knew in what respect it was not finished, but, on the word of the young man, the mystery remained complete. The evidence of the senses did not prevail against the statement of a Beautrelet. There was something which people did not know, and of that something they were convinced that he was in position to supply a triumphant explanation.

It is easy, therefore, to imagine the anxiety with which, at first, people awaited the bulletins issued by the two Dieppe doctors to whose care the Comte de Gesvres entrusted his patient; the distress that prevailed during the first few days, when his life was thought to be in danger; and the enthusiasm of the morning when the newspapers announced that there was no further cause for fear. The least details excited the crowd. People wept at the thought of Beautrelet nursed by his old father, who had been hurriedly summoned by telegram, and they also admired the devotion of Mlle. Suzanne de Gesvres, who spent night after night by the wounded lad's bedside.

Next came a swift and glad convalescence. At last, the public were about to know! They would know what Beautrelet had promised to reveal to M. Filleul and the decisive words which the knife of the would-be assassin had prevented him from uttering! And they would also know everything, outside the tragedy itself, that remained impenetrable or inaccessible to the efforts of the police.

With Beautrelet free and cured of his wound, one could hope for some certainty regarding Harlington, Arsene Lupin's mysterious accomplice, who was still detained at the Sante prison. One would learn what had become, after the crime, of Bredoux the clerk, that other accomplice, whose daring was really terrifying.

With Beautrelet free, one could also form a precise idea concerning the disappearance of Ganimard and the kidnapping of Shears. How was it possible for two attempts of this kind to take place? Neither the English detectives nor their French colleagues possessed the slightest clue on the subject. On Whit-Sunday, Ganimard did not come home, nor on the Monday either, nor during the five weeks that followed. In London, on Whit-Monday, Holmlock Shears took a cab at eight o'clock in the evening to drive to the station. He had hardly stepped in, when he tried to alight, probably feeling a presentiment of danger. But two men jumped into the hansom, one on either side, flung him back on the seat and kept him there between them, or rather under them. All this happened in sight of nine or ten witnesses, who had no time to interfere. The cab drove off at a gallop. And, after that, nothing. Nobody knew anything.

Perhaps, also, Beautrelet would be able to give the complete explanation of the document, the mysterious paper to which. Bredoux, the magistrate's clerk, attached enough importance to recover it, with blows of the knife, from the person in whose possession it was. The problem of the Hollow Needle it was called, by the countless solvers of riddles who, with their eyes bent upon the figures and dots, strove to read a meaning into them. The Hollow Needle! What a bewildering conjunction of two simple words! What an incomprehensible question was set by that scrap of paper, whose very origin and manufacture were unknown! The Hollow Needle! Was it a meaningless expression, the puzzle of a schoolboy scribbling with pen and ink on the corner of a page? Or were they two magic words which could compel the whole great adventure of Lupin the great adventurer to assume its true significance? Nobody knew.

But the public soon would know. For some days, the papers had been announcing the approaching arrival of Beautrelet. The struggle was on the point of recommencing; and, this time, it would be implacable on the part of the young man, who was burning to take his revenge. And, as it happened, my attention, just then, was drawn to his name, printed in capitals. The Grand Journal headed its front page with the following paragraph:

WE HAVE PERSUADED M. ISIDORE BEAUTRELET TO GIVE US THE FIRST RIGHT OF PRINTING HIS REVELATIONS. TO-MORROW, TUESDAY, BEFORE THE POLICE THEMSELVES ARE INFORMED, THE Grand Journal WILL PUBLISH THE WHOLE TRUTH OF THE AMBRUMESY MYSTERY.

"That's interesting, eh? What do you think of it, my dear chap?"

I started from my chair. There was some one sitting beside me, some one I did not know. I cast my eyes round for a weapon. But, as my visitor's attitude appeared quite inoffensive, I restrained myself and went up to him.

He was a young man with strongly-marked features, long, fair hair and a short, tawny beard, divided into two points. His dress suggested the dark clothes of an English clergyman; and his whole person, for that matter, wore an air of austerity and gravity that inspired respect.

"Who are you?" I asked. And, as he did not reply, I repeated, "Who are you? How did you get in? What are you here for?"

He looked at me and said:

"Don't you know me?"

"No—no!"

"Oh, that's really curious! Just search your memory—one of your friends—a friend of a rather special kind—however—"

I caught him smartly by the arm:

"You lie! You lie! No, you're not the man you say you are—it's not true."

"Then why are you thinking of that man rather than another?" he asked, with a laugh.

Oh, that laugh! That bright and clear young laugh, whose amusing irony had so often contributed to my diversion! I shivered. Could it be?

"No, no," I protested, with a sort of terror. "It cannot be."

"It can't be I, because I'm dead, eh?" he retorted. "And because you don't believe in ghosts." He laughed again. "Am I the sort of man who dies? Do you think I would die like that, shot in the back by a girl? Really, you misjudge me! As though I would ever consent to such a death as that!"

"So it is you!" I stammered, still incredulous and yet greatly excited. "So it is you! I can't manage to recognize you."

"In that case," he said, gaily, "I am quite easy. If the only man to whom I have shown myself in my real aspect fails to know me to-day, then everybody who will see me henceforth as I am to-day is bound not to know me either, when he sees me in my real aspect—if, indeed, I have a real aspect—"

I recognized his voice, now that he was no longer changing its tone, and I recognized his eyes also and the expression of his face and his whole attitude and his very being, through the counterfeit appearance in which he had shrouded it:

"Arsene Lupin!" I muttered.

"Yes, Arsene Lupin!" he cried, rising from his chair. "The one and only Arsene Lupin, returned from the realms of darkness, since it appears that I expired and passed away in a crypt! Arsene Lupin, alive and kicking, in the full exercise of his will, happy and free and more than ever resolved to enjoy that happy freedom in a world where hitherto he has received nothing but favors and privileges!"

It was my turn to laugh:

"Well, it's certainly you, and livelier this time than on the day when I had the pleasure of seeing you, last year—I congratulate you."

I was alluding to his last visit, the visit following on the famous adventure of the diadem,[1] his interrupted marriage, his flight with Sonia Kirchnoff and the Russian girl's horrible death. On that day, I had seen an Arsene Lupin whom I did not know, weak, down-hearted, with eyes tired with weeping, seeking for a little sympathy and affection.

"Be quiet," he said. "The past is far away."

"It was a year ago," I observed.

"It was ten years ago," he declared. "Arsene Lupin's years count for ten times as much as another man's."

I did not insist and, changing the conversation:

"How did you get in?"

"Why, how do you think? Through the door, of course. Then, as I saw nobody, I walked across the drawing room and out by the balcony, and here I am."

"Yes, but the key of the door—?"

"There are no doors for me, as you know. I wanted your flat and I came in."

"It is at your disposal. Am I to leave you?"

"Oh, not at all! You won't be in the way. In fact, I can promise you an interesting evening."

"Are you expecting some one?"

"Yes. I have given him an appointment here at ten o'clock." He took out his watch. "It is ten now. If the telegram reached him, he ought to be here soon."

The front-door bell rang.

"What did I tell you? No, don't trouble to get up: I'll go."

---

[1] Arsene Lupin, play in three acts and four scenes, by Maurice Leblanc and Francis de Croisset.

With whom on earth could he have made an appointment? And what sort of scene was I about to assist at: dramatic or comic? For Lupin himself to consider it worthy of interest, the situation must be somewhat exceptional.

He returned in a moment and stood back to make way for a young man, tall and thin and very pale in the face.

Without a word and with a certain solemnity about his movements that made me feel ill at ease. Lupin switched on all the electric lamps, one after the other, till the room was flooded with light. Then the two men looked at each other, exchanged profound and penetrating glances, as if, with all the effort of their gleaming eyes, they were trying to pierce into each other's souls.

It was an impressive sight to see them thus, grave and silent. But who could the newcomer be?

I was on the point of guessing the truth, through his resemblance to a photograph which had recently appeared in the papers, when Lupin turned to me:

"My dear chap, let me introduce M. Isidore Beautrelet." And, addressing the young man, he continued, "I have to thank you, M. Beautrelet, first, for being good enough, on receipt of a letter from me, to postpone your revelations until after this interview and, secondly, for granting me this interview with so good a grace."

Beautrelet smiled:

"Allow me to remark that my good grace consists, above all, in obeying your orders. The threat which you made to me in the letter in question was the more peremptory in being aimed not at me, but at my father."

"My word," said Lupin laughing, "we must do the best we can and make use of the means of action vouchsafed to us. I knew by experience that your own safety was indifferent to you, seeing that you resisted the arguments of Master Bredoux. There remained your father—your father for whom you have a great affection—I played on that string."

"And here I am," said Beautrelet, approvingly.

I motioned them to be seated. They consented and Lupin resumed, in that tone of imperceptible banter which is all his own:

"In any case, M. Beautrelet, if you will not accept my thanks, you will at least not refuse my apologies."

"Apologies! Bless my soul, what for?"

"For the brutality which Master Bredoux showed you."

"I confess that the act surprised me. It was not Lupin's usual way of behaving. A stab—"

"I assure you I had no hand in it. Bredoux is a new recruit. My friends, during the time that they had the management of our affairs, thought that it might be useful to win over to our cause the clerk of the magistrate himself who was conducting the inquiry."

"Your friends were right."

"Bredoux, who was specially attached to your person, was, in fact, most valuable to us. But, with the ardor peculiar to any neophyte who wishes to distinguish himself, he pushed his zeal too far and thwarted my plans by permitting himself, on his own initiative, to strike you a blow."

"Oh, it was a little accident!"

"Not at all, not at all! And I have reprimanded him severely! I am bound, however, to say in his favor that he was taken unawares by the really unexpected rapidity of your investigation. If you had only left us a few hours longer, you would have escaped that unpardonable attempt."

"And I should doubtless have enjoyed the enormous advantage of undergoing the same fate as M. Ganimard and Mr. Holmlock Shears?"

"Exactly," said Lupin, laughing heartily. "And I should not have known the cruel terrors which your wound caused me. I have had an atrocious time because of it, believe me, and, at this moment, your pallor fills me with all the stings of remorse. Can you ever forgive me?"

"The proof of confidence which you have shown me in delivering yourself unconditionally into my hands—it would have been so easy for me to bring a few of Ganimard's friends with me—that proof of confidence wipes out everything."

Was he speaking seriously? I confess frankly that I was greatly perplexed. The struggle between the two men was beginning in a manner which I was simply unable to understand. I had been present at the first meeting between Lupin and Holmlock Shears, in the cafe near the Gare Montparnesse,[2] and I could not help recalling the haughty carriage of the two combatants, the terrific clash of their pride under the politeness of their manners, the hard blows which they dealt each other, their feints, their arrogance.

Here, it was quite different. Lupin, it is true, had not changed; he exhibited the same tactics, the same crafty affability. But what a strange adversary he had come upon! Was it even an adversary? Really, he had neither the tone of one nor the appearance. Very calm, but with a real calmness, not one assumed to cloak the passion of a man endeavoring to restrain himself; very polite, but without exaggeration; smiling, but without chaff, he presented the most perfect contrast to Arsene Lupin, a contrast so perfect even that, to my mind, Lupin appeared as much perplexed as myself.

No, there was no doubt about it: in the presence of that frail stripling, with cheeks smooth as a girl's and candid and charming eyes, Lupin was losing his ordinary self-assurance. Several times over, I observed traces of embarrassment in him. He hesitated, did not attack frankly, wasted time in mawkish and affected phrases.

It also looked as though he wanted something. He seemed to be seeking, waiting. What for? Some aid?

There was a fresh ring of the bell. He himself ran and opened the door. He returned with a letter:

"Will you allow me, gentlemen?" he asked.

He opened the letter. It contained a telegram. He read it—and became as though transformed. His face lit up, his figure righted itself and I saw the veins on his forehead swell. It was the athlete who once more stood before me, the ruler, sure of himself, master of events and master of persons. He spread the telegram on the table and, striking it with his fist, exclaimed:

"Now, M. Beautrelet, it's you and I!"

Beautrelet adopted a listening attitude and Lupin began, in measured, but harsh and masterful tones:

"Let us throw off the mask—what say you?—and have done with hypocritical compliments. We are two enemies, who know exactly what to think of each other; we act toward each other as enemies; and therefore we ought to treat with each other as enemies."

"To treat?" echoed Beautrelet, in a voice of surprise.

"Yes, to treat. I did not use that word at random and I repeat it, in spite of the effort, the great effort, which it costs me. This is the first time I have employed it to an adversary. But also, I may as well tell you at once, it is the last. Make the most of it. I shall not leave this flat without a promise from you. If I do, it means war."

Beautrelet seemed more and more surprised. He said very prettily:

"I was not prepared for this—you speak so funnily! It's so different from what I expected! Yes, I thought you were not a bit like that! Why this display of anger? Why use threats? Are we enemies because circumstances bring us into opposition? Enemies? Why?"

Lupin appeared a little out of countenance, but he snarled and, leaning over the boy:

"Listen to me, youngster," he said. "It's not a question of picking one's words. It's a question of a fact, a positive, indisputable fact; and that fact is this: in all the past ten years, I have not yet knocked up against an adversary of your capacity. With Ganimard and Holmlock Shears I played as if they were children. With you, I am obliged to defend myself, I will say more, to retreat. Yes, at this moment, you and I well know that I must look upon myself as worsted in the fight. Isidore Beautrelet has got the better of Arsene Lupin. My plans are upset. What I tried to leave in the dark you have brought into the full light of day. You annoy me, you stand in my way. Well, I've had enough of it—Bredoux told you so to no purpose. I now tell you so again; and I insist upon it, so that you may take it to heart: I've had enough of it!"

Beautrelet nodded his head:

"Yes, but what do you want?"

"Peace! Each of us minding his own business, keeping to his own side!"

"That is to say, you free to continue your burglaries undisturbed, I free to return to my studies."

"Your studies—anything you please—I don't care. But you must leave me in peace—I want peace."

"How can I trouble it now?"

Lupin seized his hand violently:

---

[2] Arsene Lupin versus Herlock Sholmes (or Holmlock Shears in other versions).

"You know quite well! Don't pretend not to know. You are at this moment in possession of a secret to which I attach the highest importance. This secret you were free to guess, but you have no right to give it to the public."

"Are you sure that I know it?"

"You know it, I am certain: day by day, hour by hour, I have followed your train of thought and the progress of your investigations. At the very moment when Bredoux struck you, you were about to tell all. Subsequently, you delayed your revelations, out of solicitude for your father. But they are now promised to this paper here. The article is written. It will be set up in an hour. It will appear to-morrow."

"Quite right."

Lupin rose, and slashing the air with his hand,

"It shall not appear!" he cried.

"It shall appear!" said Beautrelet, starting up in his turn.

At last, the two men were standing up to each other. I received the impression of a shock, as if they had seized each other round the body. Beautrelet seemed to burn with a sudden energy. It was as though a spark had kindled within him a group of new emotions: pluck, self-respect, the passion of fighting, the intoxication of danger. As for Lupin, I read in the radiance of his glance the joy of the duellist who at length encounters the sword of his hated rival.

"Is the article in the printer's hands?"

"Not yet."

"Have you it there—on you?"

"No fear! I shouldn't have it by now, in that case!"

"Then—"

"One of the assistant editors has it, in a sealed envelope. If I am not at the office by midnight, he will have set it up."

"Oh, the scoundrel!" muttered Lupin. "He has provided for everything!"

His anger was increasing, visibly and frightfully. Beautrelet chuckled, jeering in his turn, carried away by his success.

"Stop that, you brat!" roared Lupin. "You're forgetting who I am—and that, if I wished—upon my word, he's daring to laugh!"

A great silence fell between them. Then Lupin stepped forward and, in muttered tones, with his eyes on Beautrelet's:

"You shall go straight to the Grand Journal."

"No."

"Tear up your article."

"No."

"See the editor."

"No."

"Tell him you made a mistake."

"No."

"And write him another article, in which you will give the official version of the Ambrumesy mystery, the one which every one has accepted."

"No."

Lupin took up a steel ruler that lay on my desk and broke it in two without an effort. His pallor was terrible to see. He wiped away the beads of perspiration that stood on his forehead. He, who had never known his wishes resisted, was being maddened by the obstinacy of this child. He pressed his two hands on Beautrelet's shoulder and, emphasizing every syllable, continued:

"You shall do as I tell you, Beautrelet. You shall say that your latest discoveries have convinced you of my death, that there is not the least doubt about it. You shall say so because I wish it, because it has to be believed that I am dead. You shall say so, above all, because, if you do not say so—"

"Because, if I do not say so—?"

"Your father will be kidnapped to-night, as Ganimard and Holmlock Shears were."

Beautrelet gave a smile.

"Don't laugh—answer!"

"My answer is that I am very sorry to disappoint you, but I have promised to speak and I shall speak."

"Speak in the sense which I have told you."

"I shall speak the truth," cried Beautrelet, eagerly. "It is something which you can't understand, the pleasure, the need, rather, of saying the thing that is and saying it aloud. The truth is here, in this brain which has guessed it and discovered it; and it will come out, all naked and quivering. The article, therefore, will be printed as I wrote it. The world shall know that Lupin is alive and shall know the reason why he wished to be considered dead. The world shall know all." And he added, calmly, "And my father shall not be kidnapped."

Once again, they were both silent, with their eyes still fixed upon each other. They watched each other. Their swords were engaged up to the hilt. And it was like the heavy silence that goes before the mortal blow. Which of the two was to strike it?

Lupin said, between his teeth:

"Failing my instructions to the contrary, two of my friends have orders to enter your father's room to-night, at three o'clock in the morning, to seize him and carry him off to join Ganimard and Holmlock Shears."

A burst of shrill laughter interrupted him:

"Why, you highwayman, don't you understand," cried Beautrelet, "that I have taken my precautions? So you think that I am innocent enough, ass enough, to have sent my father home to his lonely little house in the open country!" Oh, the gay, bantering laughter that lit up the boy's face! It was a new sort of laugh on his lips, a laugh that showed the influence of Lupin himself. And the familiar form of address which he adopted placed him at once on his adversary's level. He continued:

"You see, Lupin, your great fault is to believe your schemes infallible. You proclaim yourself beaten, do you? What humbug! You are convinced that you will always win the day in the end—and you forget that others can have their little schemes, too. Mine is a very simple one, my friend."

It was delightful to hear him talk. He walked up and down, with his hands in his pockets and with the easy swagger of a boy teasing a caged beast. Really, at this moment, he was revenging, with the most terrible revenges, all the victims of the great adventurer. And he concluded:

"Lupin, my father is not in Savoy. He is at the other end of France, in the centre of a big town, guarded by twenty of our friends, who have orders not to lose sight of him until our battle is over. Would you like details? He is at Cherbourg, in the house of one of the keepers of the arsenal. And remember that the arsenal is closed at night and that no one is allowed to enter it by day, unless he carries an authorization and is accompanied by a guide."

He stopped in front of Lupin and defied him, like a child making faces at his playmate:

"What do you say to that, master?"

For some minutes, Lupin had stood motionless. Not a muscle of his face had moved. What were his thoughts? Upon what action was he resolving? To any one knowing the fierce violence of his pride the only possible solution was the total, immediate, final collapse of his adversary. His fingers twitched. For a second, I had a feeling that he was about to throw himself upon the boy and wring his neck.

"What do you say to that, master?" Beautrelet repeated.

Lupin took up the telegram that lay on the table, held it out and said, very calmly:

"Here, baby, read that."

Beautrelet became serious, suddenly, impressed by the gentleness of the movement. He unfolded the paper and, at once, raising his eyes, murmured:

"What does it mean? I don't understand."

"At any rate, you understand the first word," said Lupin, "the first word of the telegram—that is to say, the name of the place from which it was sent—look—'Cherbourg.'"

"Yes—yes," stammered Beautrelet. "Yes—I understand—'Cherbourg'-and then?"

"And then?—I should think the rest is quite plain: 'Removal of luggage finished. Friends left with it and will wait instructions till eight morning. All well.' Is there anything there that seems obscure? The word 'luggage'? Pooh, you wouldn't have them write 'M. Beautrelet, senior'! What then? The way in which the operation was performed? The miracle by which your father was taken out of Cherbourg Arsenal, in spite of his twenty body-guards? Pooh, it's as easy as A B C! And the fact remains that the luggage has been dispatched. What do you say to that, baby?"

With all his tense being, with all his exasperated energy, Isidore tried to preserve a good countenance. But I saw his lips quiver, his jaw shrink, his eyes vainly strive to fix upon a point. He lisped a few words, then was silent and, suddenly, gave way and, with his hands before his face, burst into loud sobs:

"Oh, father! Father!"

An unexpected result, which was certainly the collapse which Lupin's pride demanded, but also something more, something infinitely touching and infinitely artless. Lupin gave a movement of annoyance and took up his hat, as though this unaccustomed display of sentiment were too much for him. But, on reaching the door, he stopped, hesitated and then returned, slowly, step by step.

The soft sound of the sobs rose like the sad wailing of a little child overcome with grief. The lad's shoulders marked the heart-rending rhythm. Tears appeared through the crossed fingers. Lupin leaned forward and, without touching Beautrelet, said, in a voice that had not the least tone of pleasantry, nor even of the offensive pity of the victor:

"Don't cry, youngster. This is one of those blows which a man must expect when he rushes headlong into the fray, as you did. The worst disasters lie in wait for him. The destiny of fighters will have it so. We must suffer it as bravely as we can." Then, with a sort of gentleness, he continued, "You were right, you see: we are not enemies. I have known it for long. From the very first, I felt for you, for the intelligent creature that you are, an involuntary sympathy—and admiration. And that is why I wanted to say this to you—don't be offended, whatever you do: I should be extremely sorry to offend you—but I must say it: well, give up struggling against me. I am not saying this out of vanity—nor because I despise you—but, you see, the struggle is too unequal. You do not know—nobody knows all the resources which I have at my command. Look here, this secret of the Hollow Needle which you are trying so vainly to unravel: suppose, for a moment, that it is a formidable, inexhaustible treasure—or else an invisible, prodigious, fantastic refuge—or both perhaps. Think of the superhuman power which I must derive from it! And you do not know, either, all the resources which I have within myself—all that my will and my imagination enable me to undertake and to undertake successfully. Only think that my whole life—ever since I was born, I might almost say—has tended toward the same aim, that I worked like a convict before becoming what I am and to realize, in its perfection, the type which I wished to create—which I have succeeded in creating. That being so—what can you do? At that very moment when you think that victory lies within your grasp, it will escape you—there will be something of which you have not thought—a trifle—a grain of sand which I shall have put in the right place, unknown to you. I entreat you, give up—I should be obliged to hurt you; and the thought distresses me." And, placing his hand on the boy's forehead, he repeated, "Once more, youngster, give up. I should only hurt you. Who knows if the trap into which you will inevitably fall has not already opened under your footsteps?"

Beautrelet uncovered his face. He was no longer crying. Had he heard Lupin's words? One might have doubted it, judging by his inattentive air.

For two or three minutes, he was silent. He seemed to weigh the decision which he was about to take, to examine the reasons for and against, to count up the favorable and unfavorable chances. At last, he said to Lupin:

"If I change the sense of the article, if I confirm the version of your death and if I undertake never to contradict the false version which I shall have sanctioned, do you swear that my father will be free?"

"I swear it. My friends have taken your father by motor car to another provincial town. At seven o'clock to-morrow morning, if the article in the Grand Journal is what I want it to be, I shall telephone to them and they will restore your father to liberty."

"Very well," said Beautrelet. "I submit to your conditions."

Quickly, as though he saw no object in prolonging the conversation after accepting his defeat, he rose, took his hat, bowed to me, bowed to Lupin and went out. Lupin watched him go, listened to the sound of the door closing and muttered:

"Poor little beggar!"

At eight o'clock the next morning, I sent my man out to buy the Grand Journal. It was twenty minutes before he brought me a copy, most of the kiosks being already sold out.

I unfolded the paper with feverish hands. Beautrelet's article appeared on the front page. I give it as it stood and as it was quoted in the press of the whole world:

THE AMBRUMESY MYSTERY

I do not intend in these few sentences to set out in detail the mental processes and the investigations that have enabled me to reconstruct the tragedy—I should say the twofold tragedy—of Ambrumesy. In my opinion, this sort of work and the judgments which it entails, deductions, inductions, analyses and so on, are only interesting in a minor degree and, in any case, are highly commonplace. No, I shall content myself with setting forth the two leading ideas which I followed; and, if I do that, it will be seen that, in so setting them forth and in solving the two problems which they raise, I shall have told the story just as it happened, in the exact order of the different incidents.

It may be said that some of these incidents are not proved and that I leave too large a field to conjecture. That is quite true. But, in my view, my theory is founded upon a sufficiently large number of proved facts to be able to say that even those facts which are not proved must follow from the strict logic of events. The stream is so often lost under the pebbly bed: it is nevertheless the same stream that reappears at intervals and mirrors back the blue sky.

The first riddle that confronted me, a riddle not in detail, but as a whole, was how came it that Lupin, mortally wounded, one might say, managed to live for five or six weeks without nursing, medicine or food, at the bottom of a dark hole?

Let us start at the beginning. On Thursday the sixteenth of April, at four o'clock in the morning, Arsene Lupin, surprised in the middle of one of his most daring burglaries, runs away by the path leading to the ruins and drops down shot. He drags himself painfully along, falls again and picks himself up in the desperate hope of reaching the chapel. The chapel contains a crypt, the existence of which he has discovered by accident. If he can burrow there, he may be saved. By dint of an effort, he approaches it, he is but a few yards away, when a sound of footsteps approaches. Harassed and lost, he lets himself go. The enemy arrives. It is Mlle. Raymonde de Saint-Veran.

This is the prologue or rather the first scene of the drama.

What happened between them? This is the easier to guess inasmuch as the sequel of the adventure gives us all the necessary clues. At the girl's feet lies a wounded man, exhausted by suffering, who will be captured in two minutes. THIS MAN HAS BEEN WOUNDED BY HERSELF. Will she also give him up?

If he is Jean Daval's murderer, yes, she will let destiny take its course. But, in quick sentences, he tells her the truth about this awful murder committed by her uncle, M. de Gesvres. She believes him. What will she do?

Nobody can see them. The footman Victor is watching the little door. The other, Albert, posted at the drawing-room window, has lost sight of both of them. Will she give up the man she has wounded?

The girl is carried away by a movement of irresistible pity, which any woman will understand. Instructed by Lupin, with a few movements she binds up the wound with his handkerchief, to avoid the marks which the blood would leave. Then, with the aid of the key which he gives her, she opens the door of the chapel. He enters, supported by the girl. She locks the door again and walks away. Albert arrives.

If the chapel had been visited at that moment or at least during the next few minutes, before Lupin had had time to recover his strength, to raise the flagstone and disappear by the stairs leading to the crypt, he would have been taken. But this visit did not take place until six hours later and then only in the most superficial way. As it is, Lupin is saved; and saved by whom? By the girl who very nearly killed him.

Thenceforth, whether she wishes it or no, Mlle. de Saint-Veran is his accomplice. Not only is she no longer able to give him up, but she is obliged to continue her work, else the wounded man will perish in the shelter in which she has helped to conceal him. Therefore she continues.

For that matter, if her feminine instinct makes the task a compulsory one, it also makes it easy. She is full of artifice, she foresees and forestalls everything. It is she who gives the examining magistrate a false description of Arsene Lupin (the reader will remember the difference of opinion on this subject between the cousins). It is she, obviously, who, thanks to certain signs which I do not know of, suspects an accomplice of Lupin's in the driver of the fly. She warns him. She informs him of the urgent need of an operation. It is she, no doubt, who substitutes one cap for the other. It is she who causes the famous letter to be written in which she is personally threatened. How, after that, is it possible to suspect her?

It is she, who at that moment when I was about to confide my first impressions to the examining magistrate, pretends to have seen me, the day before, in the copsewood, alarms M. Filleul on my score and reduces me to silence: a dangerous move, no doubt, because it arouses my attention and directs it against the person who assails me with an accusation which I know to be false; but an efficacious move, because the most important thing of all is to gain time and close my lips.

Lastly, it is she who, during forty days, feeds Lupin, brings him his medicine (the chemist at Ouville will produce the prescriptions which he made up for Mlle. de Saint-Veran), nurses him, dresses his wound, watches over him AND CURES HIM.

Here we have the first of our two problems solved, at the same time that the Ambrumesy mystery is set forth. Arsene Lupin found, close at hand, in the chateau itself, the assistance which was indispensable to him in order, first, not to be discovered and, secondly, to live.

He now lives. And we come to the second problem, corresponding with the second Ambrumesy mystery, the study of which served me as a conducting medium. Why does Lupin, alive, free, at the head of his gang, omnipotent as before, why does Lupin make desperate efforts, efforts with which I am constantly coming into collision, to force the idea of his death upon the police and the public?

We must remember that Mlle. de Saint-Veran was a very pretty girl. The photographs reproduced in the papers after her disappearance give but an imperfect notion of her beauty. That follows which was bound to follow. Lupin, seeing this lovely girl daily for five or six weeks, longing for her presence when she is not there, subjected to her charm and grace when she is there, inhaling the cool perfume of her breath when she bends over him, Lupin becomes enamored of his nurse. Gratitude turns to love, admiration to passion. She is his salvation, but she is also the joy of his eyes, the dream of his lonely hours, his light, his hope, his very life.

He respects her sufficiently not to take advantage of the girl's devotion and not to make use of her to direct his confederates. There is, in fact, a certain lack of decision apparent in the acts of the gang. But he loves her also, his scruples weaken and, as Mlle. de Saint-Veran refuses to be touched by a love that offends her, as she relaxes her visits when they become less necessary, as she ceases them entirely on the day when he is cured—desperate, maddened by grief, he takes a terrible resolve. He leaves his lair, prepares his stroke and, on Saturday the sixth of June, assisted by his accomplices, he carries off the girl.

This is not all. The abduction must not be known. All search, all surmises, all hope, even, must be cut short. Mlle. de Saint-Veran must pass for dead. There is a mock murder: proofs are supplied for the police inquiries. There is doubt about the crime, a crime, for that matter, not unexpected, a crime foretold by the accomplices, a crime perpetrated to revenge the chief's death. And, through this very fact—observe the marvelous ingenuity of the conception—through this very fact, the belief in this death is, so to speak, stimulated.

It is not enough to suggest a belief; it is necessary to compel a certainty. Lupin foresees my interference. I am sure to guess the trickery of the chapel. I am sure to discover the crypt. And, as the crypt will be empty, the whole scaffolding will come to the ground.

THE CRYPT SHALL NOT BE EMPTY.

In the same way, the death of Mlle. de Saint-Veran will not be definite, unless the sea gives up her corpse.

THE SEA SHALL GIVE UP THE CORPSE OF MLLE. DE SAINT-VERAN.

The difficulty is tremendous. The double obstacle seems insurmountable. Yes, to any one but Lupin, but not to Lupin.

As he had foreseen, I guess the trickery of the chapel, I discover the crypt and I go down into the lair where Lupin has taken refuge. His corpse is there!

Any person who had admitted the death of Lupin as possible would have been baffled. But I had not admitted this eventuality for an instant (first, by intuition and, secondly, by reasoning). Pretense thereupon became useless and every scheme vain. I said to myself at once that the block of stone disturbed by the pickaxe had been placed there with a very curious exactness, that the least knock was bound to make it fall and that, in falling, it must inevitably reduce the head of the false Arsene Lupin to pulp, in such a way as to make it utterly irrecognizable.

Another discovery: half an hour later, I hear that the body of Mlle. de Saint-Veran has been found on the rocks at Dieppe—or rather a body which is considered to be Mlle. de Saint-Veran's, for the reason that the arm has a bracelet similar to one of that young lady's bracelets. This, however, is the only mark of identity, for the corpse is irrecognizable.

Thereupon I remember and I understand. A few days earlier, I happened to read in a number of the Vigie de Dieppe that a young American couple staying at Envermeu had committed suicide by taking poison and that their bodies had disappeared on the very night of the death. I hasten to Envermeu. The story is true, I am told, except in so far as concerns the disappearance, because the brothers of the victims came to claim the corpses and took them away after the usual formalities. The name of these brothers, no doubt, was Arsene Lupin & Co.

Consequently, the thing is proved. We know why Lupin shammed the murder of the girl and spread the rumor of his own death. He is in love and does not wish it known. And, to reach his ends, he shrinks from nothing, he even undertakes that incredible theft of the two corpses which he needs in order to impersonate himself and Mlle. de Saint-Veran. In this way, he will be at ease. No one can disturb him. No one will ever suspect the truth which he wishes to suppress.

No one? Yes—three adversaries, at the most, might conceive doubts: Ganimard, whose arrival is hourly expected; Holmlock Shears, who is about to cross the Channel; and I, who am on the spot. This constitutes a threefold danger. He removes it. He kidnaps Ganimard. He kidnaps Holmlock Shears. He has me stabbed by Bredoux.

One point alone remains obscure. Why was Lupin so fiercely bent upon snatching the document about the Hollow Needle from me? He surely did not imagine that, by taking it away, he could wipe out from my memory the text of the five lines of which it consists! Then why? Did he fear that the character of the paper itself, or some other clue, could give me a hint?

Be that as it may, this is the truth of the Ambrumesy mystery. I repeat that conjecture plays a certain part in the explanation which I offer, even as it played a great part in my personal investigation. But, if one waited for proofs and facts to fight Lupin, one would run a great risk either of waiting forever or else of discovering proofs and facts carefully prepared by Lupin, which would lead in a direction immediately opposite to the object in view. I feel confident that the facts, when they are known, will confirm my surmise in every respect.

So Isidore Beautrelet, mastered for a moment by Arsene Lupin, distressed by the abduction of his father and resigned to defeat, Isidore Beautrelet, in the end, was unable to persuade himself to keep silence. The truth was too beautiful and too curious, the proofs which he was able to produce were too logical and too conclusive for him to consent to misrepresent it. The whole world was waiting for his revelations. He spoke.

On the evening of the day on which his article appeared, the newspapers announced the kidnapping of M. Beautrelet, senior. Isidore was informed of it by a telegram from Cherbourg, which reached him at three o'clock.

V. ON THE TRACK

Young Beautrelet was stunned by the violence of the blow. As a matter of fact, although, in publishing his article, he had obeyed one of those irresistible impulses which make a man despise every consideration of prudence, he had never really believed in the possibility of an abduction. His precautions had been too thorough. The friends at Cherbourg not only had instructions to guard and protect Beautrelet the elder: they were also to watch his comings and goings, never to let him walk out alone and not even to hand him a single letter without first opening it. No, there was no danger. Lupin, wishing to gain time, was trying to intimidate his adversary.

The blow, therefore, was almost unexpected; and Isidore, because he was powerless to act, felt the pain of the shock during the whole of the remainder of the day. One idea alone supported him: that of leaving Paris, going down there, seeing for himself what had happened and resuming the offensive.

He telegraphed to Cherbourg. He was at Saint-Lazare a little before nine. A few minutes after, he was steaming out of the station in the Normandy express.

It was not until an hour later, when he mechanically unfolded a newspaper which he had bought on the platform, that he became aware of the letter by which Lupin indirectly replied to his article of that morning:

To the Editor of the Grand Journal.

SIR: I cannot pretend but that my modest personality, which would certainly have passed unnoticed in more heroic times, has acquired a certain prominence in the dull and feeble period in which we live. But there is a limit beyond which the morbid curiosity of the crowd cannot go without becoming indecently indiscreet. If the walls that surround our private lives be not respected, what is to safeguard the rights of the citizen?

Will those who differ plead the higher interest of truth? An empty pretext in so far as I am concerned, because the truth is known and I raise no difficulty about making an official confession of the truth in writing. Yes, Mlle. de Saint-Veran is alive. Yes, I love her. Yes, I have the mortification not to be loved by her. Yes, the results of the boy Beautrelet's inquiry are wonderful in their precision and accuracy. Yes, we agree on every point. There is no riddle left. There is no mystery. Well, then, what?

Injured to the very depths of my soul, bleeding still from cruel wounds, I ask that my more intimate feelings and secret hopes may no longer be delivered to the malevolence of the public. I ask for peace, the peace which I need to conquer the affection of Mlle. de Saint-Veran and to wipe out from her memory the thousand little injuries which she has had to suffer at the hands of her uncle and cousin—this has not been told—because of her position as a poor relation. Mlle. de Saint-Veran will forget this hateful past. All that she can desire, were it the fairest jewel in the world, were it the most unattainable treasure, I shall lay at her feet. She will be happy. She will love me.

But, if I am to succeed, once more, I require peace. That is why I lay down my arms and hold out the olive-branch to my enemies—while warning them, with every magnanimity on my part, that a refusal on theirs might bring down upon them the gravest consequences.

One word more on the subject of Mr. Harlington. This name conceals the identity of an excellent fellow, who is secretary to Cooley, the American millionaire, and instructed by him to lay hands upon every object of ancient art in Europe which it is possible to discover. His evil star brought him into touch with my friend Etienne de Vaudreix, ALIAS Arsene Lupin, ALIAS myself. He learnt, in this way, that a certain M. de Gesvres was willing to part with four pictures by Rubens, ostensibly on the condition that they were replaced by copies and that the bargain to which he was consenting remained unknown. My friend Vaudreix also undertook to persuade M. de Gesvres to sell his chapel. The negotiations were conducted with entire good faith on the side of my friend Vaudreix and with charming ingenuousness on the side of Mr. Harlington, until the day when the Rubenses and the carvings from the chapel were in a safe place and Mr. Harlington in prison. There remains nothing, therefore, to be done but to release the unfortunate American, because he was content to play the modest part of a dupe; to brand the millionaire Cooley, because, for fear of possible unpleasantness, he did not protest against his secretary's arrest; and to congratulate my friend Etienne de Vaudreix, because he is revenging the outraged morality of the public by keeping the hundred thousand francs which he was paid on account by that singularly unattractive person, Cooley.

Pray, pardon the length of this letter and permit me to be, Sir,

Your obedient servant,

ARSENE LUPIN.

Isidore weighed the words of this communication as minutely, perhaps, as he had studied the document concerning the Hollow Needle. He went on the principle, the correctness of which was easily proved, that Lupin had never taken the trouble to send one of his amusing letters to the press without absolute necessity, without some motive which events were sure, sooner or later, to bring to light.

What was the motive for this particular letter? For what hidden reason was Lupin confessing his love and the failure of that love? Was it there that Beautrelet had to seek, or in the explanations regarding Mr. Harlington, or further still, between the lines, behind all those words whose apparent meaning had perhaps no other object than to suggest some wicked, perfidious, misleading little idea?

For hours, the young man, confined to his compartment, remained pensive and anxious. The letter filled him with mistrust, as though it had been written for his benefit and were destined to lead him, personally, into error. For the first time and because he found himself confronted not with a direct attack, but with an ambiguous, indefinable method of fighting, he underwent a distinct sensation of fear. And, when he thought of his good old, easy-going father, kidnapped through his fault, he asked himself, with a pang, whether he was not mad to continue so unequal a contest. Was the result not certain? Had Lupin not won the game in advance?

It was but a short moment of weakness. When he alighted from his compartment, at six o'clock in the morning, refreshed by a few hours' sleep, he had recovered all his confidence.

On the platform, Froberval, the dockyard clerk who had given hospitality to M. Beautrelet, senior, was waiting for him, accompanied by his daughter Charlotte, an imp of twelve or thirteen.

"Well?" cried Isidore.

The worthy man beginning to moan and groan, he interrupted him, dragged him to a neighboring tavern, ordered coffee and began to put plain questions, without permitting the other the slightest digression:

"My father has not been carried off, has he? It was impossible."

"Impossible. Still, he has disappeared."

"Since when?"

"We don't know."

"What!"

"No. Yesterday morning, at six o'clock, as I had not seen him come down as usual, I opened his door. He was gone."

"But was he there on the day before, two days ago?"

"Yes. On the day before yesterday, he did not leave his room. He was a little tired; and Charlotte took his lunch up to him at twelve and his dinner at seven in the evening."

"So it was between seven o'clock in the evening, on the day before yesterday, and six o'clock on yesterday morning that he disappeared?"

"Yes, during the night before last. Only—"

"Only what?"

"Well, it's like this: you can't leave the arsenal at night."

"Do you mean that he has not left it?"

"That's impossible! My friends and I have searched the whole naval harbor."

"Then he has left it!"

"Impossible, every outlet is guarded!"

Beautrelet reflected and then said:

"What next?"

"Next, I hurried to the commandant's and informed the officer in charge."

"Did he come to your house?"

"Yes; and a gentleman from the public prosecutor's also. They searched all through the morning; and, when I saw that they were making no progress and that there was no hope left, I telegraphed to you."

"Was the bed disarranged in his room?"

"No."

"Nor the room disturbed in any way?"

"No. I found his pipe in its usual place, with his tobacco and the book which he was reading. There was even this little photograph of yourself in the middle of the book, marking the page."

"Let me see it."

Froberval passed him the photograph. Beautrelet gave a start of surprise. He had recognized himself in the snapshot, standing, with his two hands in his pockets, on a lawn from which rose trees and ruins.

Froberval added:

"It must be the last portrait of yourself which you sent him. Look, on the back, you will see the date, 3 April, the name of the photographer, R. de Val, and the name of the town, Lion—Lion-sur-Mer, perhaps."

Isidore turned the photograph over and read this little note, in his own handwriting:

"R. de Val.—3.4—Lion."

He was silent for a few minutes and resumed:

"My father hadn't shown you that snapshot yet?"

"No—and that's just what astonished me when I saw it yesterday—for your father used so often to talk to us about you."

There was a fresh pause, greatly prolonged. Froberval muttered:

"I have business at the workshop. We might as well go in—"

He was silent. Isidore had not taken his eyes from the photograph, was examining it from every point of view. At last, the boy asked:

"Is there such a thing as an inn called the Lion d'Or at a short league outside the town?"

"Yes, about a league from here."

"On the Route de Valognes, is it?"

"Yes, on the Route de Valognes."

"Well, I have every reason to believe that this inn was the head-quarters of Lupin's friends. It was from there that they entered into communication with my father."

"What an idea! Your father spoke to nobody. He saw nobody."

"He saw nobody, but they made use of an intermediary."

"What proof have you?"

"This photograph."

"But it's your photograph!"

"It's my photograph, but it was not sent by me. I was not even aware of its existence. It was taken, without my knowledge, in the ruins of Ambrumesy, doubtless by the examining-magistrate's clerk, who, as you know, was an accomplice of Arsene Lupin's."

"And then?"

"Then this photograph became the passport, the talisman, by means of which they obtained my father's confidence."

"But who? Who was able to get into my house?"

"I don't know, but my father fell into the trap. They told him and he believed that I was in the neighborhood, that I was asking to see him and that I was giving him an appointment at the Golden Lion."

"But all this is nonsense! How can you assert—?"

"Very simply. They imitated my writing on the back of the photograph and specified the meeting-place: Valognes Road, 3 kilometres 400, Lion Inn. My father came and they seized him, that's all."

"Very well," muttered Froberval, dumbfounded, "very well. I admit it—things happened as you say—but that does not explain how he was able to leave during the night."

"He left in broad daylight, though he waited until dark to go to the meeting-place."

"But, confound it, he didn't leave his room the whole of the day before yesterday!"

"There is one way of making sure: run down to the dockyard, Froberval, and look for one of the men who were on guard in the afternoon, two days ago.—Only, be quick, if you wish to find me here."

"Are you going?"

"Yes, I shall take the next train back."

"What!—Why, you don't know—your inquiry—"

"My inquiry is finished. I know pretty well all that I wanted to know. I shall have left Cherbourg in an hour."

Froberval rose to go. He looked at Beautrelet with an air of absolute bewilderment, hesitated a moment and then took his cap:

"Are you coming, Charlotte?"

"No," said Beautrelet, "I shall want a few more particulars. Leave her with me. Besides, I want to talk to her. I knew her when she was quite small."

Froberval went away. Beautrelet and the little girl remained alone in the tavern smoking room. A few minutes passed, a waiter entered, cleared away some cups and left the room again. The eyes of the young man and the child met; and Beautrelet placed his hand very gently on the little girl's hand. She looked at him for two or three seconds, distractedly, as though about to choke. Then, suddenly hiding her head between her folded arms, she burst into sobs.

He let her cry and, after a while, said:

"It was you, wasn't it, who did all the mischief, who acted as go-between? It was you who took him the photograph? You admit it, don't you? And, when you said that my father was in his room, two days ago, you knew that it was not true, did you not, because you yourself had helped him to leave it—?"

She made no reply. He asked:

"Why did you do it? They offered you money, I suppose—to buy ribbons with a frock—?"

He uncrossed Charlotte's arms and lifted up her head. He saw a poor little face all streaked with tears, the attractive, disquieting, mobile face of one of those little girls who seem marked out for temptation and weakness.

"Come," said Beautrelet, "it's over, we'll say no more about it. I will not even ask you how it happened. Only you must tell me everything that can be of use to me.—Did you catch anything—any remark made by those men? How did they carry him off?"

She replied at once:

"By motor car. I heard them talking about it—"

"And what road did they take?"

"Ah, I don't know that!"

"Didn't they say anything before you—something that might help us?"

"No—wait, though: there was one who said, 'We shall have no time to lose—the governor is to telephone to us at eight o'clock in the morning—'"

"Where to?"

"I can't say.—I've forgotten—"

"Try—try and remember. It was the name of a town, wasn't it?"

"Yes—a name—like Chateau—"

"Chateaubriant?—Chateau-Thierry?—"

"No-no—"

"Chateauroux?"

"Yes, that was it—Chateauroux—"

Beautrelet did not wait for her to complete her sentence. Already he was on his feet and, without giving a thought to Froberval, without even troubling about the child, who stood gazing at him in stupefaction, he opened the door and ran to the station:

"Chateauroux, madame—a ticket for Chateauroux—"

"Over Mans and Tours?" asked the booking-clerk.

"Of course—the shortest way. Shall I be there for lunch?"

"Oh, no!"

"For dinner? Bedtime—?"

"Oh, no! For that, you would have to go over Paris. The Paris express leaves at nine o'clock. You're too late—"

It was not too late. Beautrelet was just able to catch the train.

"Well," said Beautrelet, rubbing his hands, "I have spent only two hours or so at Cherbourg, but they were well employed."

He did not for a moment think of accusing Charlotte of lying. Weak, unstable, capable of the worst treacheries, those petty natures also obey impulses of sincerity; and Beautrelet had read in her affrighted eyes her shame for the harm which she had done and her delight at repairing it in part. He had no doubt, therefore, that Chateauroux was the other town to which Lupin had referred and where his confederates were to telephone to him.

On his arrival in Paris, Beautrelet took every necessary precaution to avoid being followed. He felt that it was a serious moment. He was on the right road that was leading him to his father: one act of imprudence might ruin all.

He went to the flat of one of his schoolfellows and came out, an hour later, irrecognizable, rigged out as an Englishman of thirty, in a brown check suit, with knickerbockers, woolen stockings and a cap, a high-colored complexion and a red wig. He jumped on a bicycle laden with a complete painter's outfit and rode off to the Gare d'Austerlitz.

He slept that night at Issoudun. The next morning, he mounted his machine at break of day. At seven o'clock, he walked into the Chateauroux post-office and asked to be put on to Paris. As he had to wait, he entered into conversation with the clerk and learnt that, two days before, at the same hour, a man dressed for motoring had also asked for Paris.

The proof was established. He waited no longer.

By the afternoon, he had ascertained, from undeniable evidence, that a limousine car, following the Tours road, had passed through the village of Buzancais and the town of Chateauroux and had stopped beyond the town, on the verge of the forest. At ten o'clock, a hired gig, driven by a man unknown, had stopped beside the car and then gone off south, through the valley of the Bouzanne. There was then another person seated beside the driver. As for the car, it had turned in the opposite direction and gone north, toward Issoudun.

Beautrelet easily discovered the owner of the gig, who, however, had no information to supply. He had hired out his horse and trap to a man who brought them back himself next day.

Lastly, that same evening, Isidore found out that the motor car had only passed through Issoudun, continuing its road toward Orleans, that is to say, toward Paris.

From all this, it resulted, in the most absolute fashion, that M. Beautrelet was somewhere in the neighborhood. If not, how was it conceivable that people should travel nearly three hundred miles across France in order to telephone from Chateauroux and next to return, at an acute angle, by the Paris road?

This immense circuit had a more definite object: to move M. Beautrelet to the place assigned to him.

"And this place is within reach of my hand," said Isidore to himself, quivering with hope and expectation. "My father is waiting for me to rescue him at ten or fifteen leagues from here. He is close by. He is breathing the same air as I."

He set to work at once. Taking a war-office map, he divided it into small squares, which he visited one after the other, entering the farmhouses making the peasants talk, calling on the schoolmasters, the mayors, the parish priests, chatting to the women. It seemed to him that he must attain his end without delay and his dreams grew until it was no longer his father alone whom he hoped to deliver, but all those whom Lupin was holding captive: Raymonde de Saint-Veran, Ganimard, Holmlock Shears, perhaps, and others, many others; and, in reaching them, he would, at the same time, reach Lupin's stronghold, his lair, the impenetrable retreat where he was piling up the treasures of which he had robbed the wide world.

But, after a fortnight's useless searching, his enthusiasm ended by slackening and he very soon lost confidence. Because success was slow in appearing, from one day to the next, almost, he ceased to believe in it; and, though he continued to pursue his plan of investigations, he would have felt a real surprise if his efforts had led to the smallest discovery.

More days still passed by, monotonous days of discouragement. He read in the newspapers that the Comte de Gesvres and his daughter had left Ambrumesy and gone to stay near Nice. He also learnt that Harlington had been released, that gentleman's innocence having become self-obvious, in accordance with the indications supplied by Arsene Lupin.

Isidore changed his head-quarters, established himself for two days at the Chatre, for two days at Argenton. The result was the same.

Just then, he was nearly throwing up the game. Evidently, the gig in which his father had been carried off could only have furnished a stage, which had been followed by another stage, furnished by some other conveyance. And his father was far away.

He was thinking of leaving, when, one Monday morning, he saw, on the envelope of an unstamped letter, sent on to him from Paris, a handwriting that set him trembling with emotion. So great was his excitement that, for some minutes, he dared not open the letter, for fear of a disappointment. His hand shook. Was it possible? Was this not a trap laid for him by his infernal enemy?

He tore open the envelope. It was indeed a letter from his father, written by his father himself. The handwriting presented all the peculiarities, all the oddities of the hand which he knew so well.

He read:

Will these lines ever reach you, my dear son? I dare not believe it.

During the whole night of my abduction, we traveled by motor car; then, in the morning, by carriage. I could see nothing. My eyes were bandaged. The castle in which I am confined should be somewhere in the midlands, to judge by its construction and the vegetation in the park. The room which I occupy is on the second floor: it is a room with two windows, one of which is almost blocked by a screen of climbing glycines. In the afternoon, I am allowed to walk about the park, at certain hours, but I am kept under unrelaxing observation.

I am writing this letter, on the mere chance of its reaching you, and fastening it to a stone. Perhaps, one day, I shall be able to throw it over the wall and some peasant will pick it up.

But do not be distressed about me. I am treated with every consideration.

Your old father, who is very fond of you and very sad to think of the trouble he is giving you,
BEAUTRELET.

Isidore at once looked at the postmarks. They read, "Cuzion, Indre."

The Indre! The department which he had been stubbornly searching for weeks!

He consulted a little pocket-guide which he always carried. Cuzion, in the canton of Eguzon—he had been there too.

For prudence's sake, he discarded his personality as an Englishman, which was becoming too well known in the district, disguised himself as a workman and made for Cuzion. It was an unimportant village. He would easily discover the sender of the letter.

For that matter, chance served him without delay:

"A letter posted on Wednesday last?" exclaimed the mayor, a respectable tradesman in whom he confided and who placed himself at his disposal. "Listen, I think I can give you a valuable clue: on Saturday morning, Gaffer Charel, an old knife-grinder who visits all the fairs in the department, met me at the end of the village and asked, 'Monsieur le maire, does a letter without a stamp on it go all the same?' 'Of course,' said I. 'And does it get there?' 'Certainly. Only there's double postage to pay on it, that's all the difference.'"

"And where does he live?"

"He lives over there, all alone—on the slope—the hovel that comes next after the churchyard.—Shall I go with you?"

It was a hovel standing by itself, in the middle of an orchard surrounded by tall trees. As they entered the orchard, three magpies flew away with a great splutter and they saw that the birds were flying out of the very hole in which the watch-dog was fastened. And the dog neither barked nor stirred as they approached.

Beautrelet went up in great surprise. The brute was lying on its side, with stiff paws, dead.

They ran quickly to the cottage. The door stood open. They entered. At the back of a low, damp room, on a wretched straw mattress, flung on the floor itself, lay a man fully dressed.

"Gaffer Charel!" cried the mayor. "Is he dead, too?"

The old man's hands were cold, his face terribly pale, but his heart was still beating, with a faint, slow throb, and he seemed not to be wounded in any way.

They tried to resuscitate him and, as they failed in their efforts, Beautrelet went to fetch a doctor. The doctor succeeded no better than they had done. The old man did not seem to be suffering. He looked as if he were just asleep, but with an artificial slumber, as though he had been put to sleep by hypnotism or with the aid of a narcotic.

In the middle of the night that followed, however, Isidore, who was watching by his side, observed that the breathing became stronger and that his whole being appeared to be throwing off the invisible bonds that paralyzed it.

At daybreak, he woke up and resumed his normal functions: ate, drank and moved about. But, the whole day long, he was unable to reply to the young man's questions and his brain seemed as though still numbed by an inexplicable torpor.

The next day, he asked Beautrelet:

"What are you doing here, eh?"

It was the first time that he had shown surprise at the presence of a stranger beside him.

Gradually, in this way, he recovered all his faculties. He talked. He made plans. But, when Beautrelet asked him about the events immediately preceding his sleep, he seemed not to understand.

And Beautrelet felt that he really did not understand. He had lost the recollection of all that had happened since the Friday before. It was like a sudden gap in the ordinary flow of his life. He described his morning and afternoon on the Friday, the purchases he had made at the fair, the meals he had taken at the inn. Then—nothing—nothing more. He believed himself to be waking on the morrow of that day.

It was horrible for Beautrelet. The truth lay there, in those eyes which had seen the walls of the park behind which his father was waiting for him, in those hands which had picked up the letter, in that muddled brain which had recorded the whereabouts of that scene, the setting, the little corner of the world in which the play had been enacted. And from those hands, from that brain he was unable to extract the faintest echo of the truth so near at hand!

Oh, that impalpable and formidable obstacle, against which all his efforts hurled themselves in vain, that obstacle built up of silence and oblivion! How clearly it bore the mark of Arsene Lupin! He alone, informed, no doubt, that M. Beautrelet had attempted to give a signal, he alone could have struck with partial death the one man whose evidence could injure him. It was not that Beautrelet felt himself to be discovered or thought that Lupin, hearing of his stealthy attack and knowing that a letter had reached him, was defending himself against him personally. But what an amount of foresight and real intelligence it displayed to suppress any possible accusation on the part of that chance wayfarer! Nobody now knew that within the walls of a park there lay a prisoner asking for help.

Nobody? Yes, Beautrelet. Gaffer Charel was unable to speak. Very well. But, at least, one could find out which fair the old man had visited and which was the logical road that he had taken to return by. And, along this road, perhaps it would at last be possible to find—

Isidore, as it was, had been careful not to visit Gaffer Charel's hovel except with the greatest precautions and in such a way as not to give an alarm. He now decided not to go back to it. He made inquiries and learnt that Friday was market-day at Fresselines, a fair-sized town situated a few leagues off, which could be reached either by the rather winding highroad or by a series of short cuts.

On the Friday, he chose the road and saw nothing that attracted his attention, no high walled enclosure, no semblance of an old castle.

He lunched at an inn at Fresselines and was on the point of leaving when he saw Gaffer Charel arrive and cross the square, wheeling his little knife-grinding barrow before him. He at once followed him at a good distance.

The old man made two interminable waits, during which he ground dozens of knives. Then, at last, he went away by a quite different road, which ran in the direction of Crozant and the market-town of Eguzon.

Beautrelet followed him along this road. But he had not walked five minutes before he received the impression that he was not alone in shadowing the old fellow. A man was walking along between them, stopping at the same time as Charel and starting off again when he did, without, for that matter, taking any great precautions against being seen.

"He is being watched," thought Beautrelet. "Perhaps they want to know if he stops in front of the walls—"

His heart beat violently. The event was at hand.

The three of them, one behind the other, climbed up and down the steep slopes of the country and arrived at Crozant, famed for the colossal ruins of its castle. There Charel made a halt of an hour's duration. Next he went down to the riverside and crossed the bridge.

But then a thing happened that took Beautrelet by surprise. The other man did not cross the river. He watched the old fellow move away and, when he had lost sight of him, turned down a path that took him right across the fields.

Beautrelet hesitated for a few seconds as to what course to take, and then quietly decided. He set off in pursuit of the man.

"He has made sure," he thought, "that Gaffer Charel has gone straight ahead. That is all he wanted to know and so he is going—where? To the castle?"

He was within touch of the goal. He felt it by a sort of agonizing gladness that uplifted his whole being.

The man plunged into a dark wood overhanging the river and then appeared once more in the full light, where the path met the horizon.

When Beautrelet, in his turn, emerged from the wood, he was greatly surprised no longer to see the man. He was seeking him with his eyes when, suddenly, he gave a stifled cry and, with a backward spring, made for the line of trees which he had just left. On his right, he had seen a rampart of high walls, flanked, at regular distances, by massive buttresses.

It was there! It was there! Those walls held his father captive! He had found the secret place where Lupin confined his victim.

He dared not quit the shelter which the thick foliage of the wood afforded him. Slowly, almost on all fours, he bore to the right and in this way reached the top of a hillock that rose to the level of the neighboring trees. The walls were taller still. Nevertheless, he perceived the roof of the castle which they surrounded, an old Louis XIII. roof, surmounted by very slender bell-turrets arranged corbel-wise around a higher steeple which ran to a point.

Beautrelet did no more that day. He felt the need to reflect and to prepare his plan of attack without leaving anything to chance. He held Lupin safe; and it was for Beautrelet now to select the hour and the manner of the combat.

He walked away.

Near the bridge, he met two country-girls carrying pails of milk. He asked:

"What is the name of the castle over there, behind the trees?"

"That's the Chateau de l'Aiguille, sir."

He had put his question without attaching any importance to it. The answer took away his breath:

"The Chateau de l'Aiguille?—Oh!—But in what department are we? The Indre?"

"Certainly not. The Indre is on the other side of the river. This side, it's the Creuse."

Isidore saw it all in a flash. The Chateau de l'Aiguille! The department of the Creuse! L'AIGUILLE CREUSE! The Hollow Needle! The very key to the document! Certain, decisive, absolute victory!

Without another word, he turned his back on the two girls and went his way, tottering like a drunken man.

VI. AN HISTORIC SECRET

Beautrelet's resolve was soon taken: he would act alone. To inform the police was too dangerous. Apart from the fact that he could only offer presumptions, he dreaded the slowness of the police, their inevitable indiscretions, the whole preliminary inquiry, during which Lupin, who was sure to be warned, would have time to effect a retreat in good order.

At eight o'clock the next morning, with his bundle under his arm, he left the inn in which he was staying near Cuzion, made for the nearest thicket, took off his workman's clothes, became once more the young English painter that he had been and went to call on the notary at Eguzon, the largest place in the immediate neighborhood.

He said that he liked the country and that he was thinking of taking up his residence there, with his relations, if he could find a suitable house.

The notary mentioned a number of properties. Beautrelet took note of them and let fall that some one had spoken to him of the Chateau de l'Aiguille, on the bank of the Creuse.

"Oh, yes, but the Chateau de l'Aiguille, which has belonged to one of my clients for the last five years, is not for sale."

"He lives in it, then?"

"He used to live in it, or rather his mother did. But she did not care for it; found the castle rather gloomy. So they left it last year."

"And is no one living there at present?"

"Yes, an Italian, to whom my client let it for the summer season: Baron Anfredi."

"Oh, Baron Anfredi! A man still young, rather grave and solemn-looking—?"

"I'm sure I can't say.—My client dealt with him direct. There was no regular agreement, just a letter—"

"But you know the baron?"

"No, he never leaves the castle.—Sometimes, in his motor, at night, so they say. The marketing is done by an old cook, who talks to nobody. They are queer people—"

"Do you think your client would consent to sell his castle?"

"I don't think so. It's an historic castle, built in the purest Louis XIII. style. My client was very fond of it; and, unless he has changed his mind-"

"Can you give me his name and address?"

"Louis Valmeras, 34, Rue du Mont-Thabor."

Beautrelet took the train for Paris at the nearest station. On the next day but one, after three fruitless calls, he at last found Louis Valmeras at home. He was a man of about thirty, with a frank and pleasing face. Beautrelet saw no need to beat about the bush, stated who he was and described his efforts and the object of the step which he was now taking:

"I have good reason to believe," he concluded, "that my father is imprisoned in the Chateau de l'Aiguille, doubtless in the company of other victims. And I have come to ask you what you know of your tenant, Baron Anfredi."

"Not much. I met Baron Anfredi last winter at Monte Carlo. He had heard by accident that I was the owner of the Chateau de l'Aiguille and, as he wished to spend the summer in France, he made me an offer for it."

"He is still a young man—"

"Yes, with very expressive eyes, fair hair—"

"And a beard?"

"Yes, ending in two points, which fall over a collar fastened at the back, like a clergyman's. In fact, he looks a little like an English parson."

"It's he," murmured Beautrelet, "it's he, as I have seen him: it's his exact description."

"What! Do you think—?"

"I think, I am sure that your tenant is none other than Arsene Lupin."

The story amused Louis Valmeras. He knew all the adventures of Arsene Lupin and the varying fortunes of his struggle with Beautrelet. He rubbed his hands:

"Ha, the Chateau de l'Aiguille will become famous!—I'm sure I don't mind, for, as a matter of fact, now that my mother no longer lives in it, I have always thought that I would get rid of it at the first opportunity. After this, I shall soon find a purchaser. Only—"

"Only what?"

"I will ask you to act with the most extreme prudence and not to inform the police until you are quite sure. Can you picture the situation, supposing my tenant were not Arsene Lupin?"

Beautrelet set forth his plan. He would go alone at night; he would climb the walls; he would sleep in the park— Louis Valmeras stopped him at once:

"You will not climb walls of that height so easily. If you do, you will be received by two huge sheep-dogs which belonged to my mother and which I left behind at the castle."

"Pooh! A dose of poison—"

"Much obliged. But suppose you escaped them. What then? How would you get into the castle? The doors are massive, the windows barred. And, even then, once you were inside, who would guide you? There are eighty rooms."

"Yes, but that room with two windows, on the second story—"

"I know it, we call it the glycine room. But how will you find it? There are three staircases and a labyrinth of passages. I can give you the clue and explain the way to you, but you would get lost just the same."

"Come with me," said Beautrelet, laughing.

"I can't. I have promised to go to my mother in the South."

Beautrelet returned to the friend with whom he was staying and began to make his preparations. But, late in the day, as he was getting ready to go, he received a visit from Valmeras.

"Do you still want me?"

"Rather!"

"Well, I'm coming with you. Yes, the expedition fascinates me. I think it will be very amusing and I like being mixed up in this sort of thing.—Besides, my help will be of use to you. Look, here's something to start with."

He held up a big key, all covered with rust and looking very old.

"What does the key open?" asked Beautrelet.

"A little postern hidden between two buttresses and left unused since centuries ago. I did not even think of pointing it out to my tenant. It opens straight on the country, just at the verge of the wood."

Beautrelet interrupted him quickly:

"They know all about that outlet. It was obviously by this way that the man whom I followed entered the park. Come, it's fine game and we shall win it. But, by Jupiter, we must play our cards carefully!"

Two days later, a half-famished horse dragged a gipsy caravan into Crozant. Its driver obtained leave to stable it at the end of the village, in an old deserted cart-shed. In addition to the driver, who was none other than Valmeras, there were three young men, who occupied themselves in the manufacture of wicker-work chairs: Beautrelet and two of his Janson friends.

They stayed there for three days, waiting for a propitious, moonless night and roaming singly round the outskirts of the park. Once Beautrelet saw the postern. Contrived between two buttresses placed very close together, it was almost merged, behind the screen of brambles that concealed it, in the pattern formed by the stones of the wall.

At last, on the fourth evening, the sky was covered with heavy black clouds and Valmeras decided that they should go reconnoitring, at the risk of having to return again, should circumstances prove unfavorable.

All four crossed the little wood. Then Beautrelet crept through the heather, scratched his hands at the bramble-hedge and, half raising himself, slowly, with restrained movements, put the key into the lock. He turned it gently. Would the door open without an effort? Was there no bolt closing it on the other side? He pushed: the door opened, without a creak or jolt. He was in the park.

"Are you there, Beautrelet?" asked Valmeras. "Wait for me. You two chaps, watch the door and keep our line of retreat open. At the least alarm, whistle."

He took Beautrelet's hand and they plunged into the dense shadow of the thickets. A clearer space was revealed to them when they reached the edge of the central lawn. At the same moment a ray of moonlight pierced the clouds; and they saw the castle, with its pointed turrets arranged around the tapering spire to which, no doubt, it owed its name. There was no light in the windows; not a sound.

Valmeras grasped his companion's arm:

"Keep still!"

"What is it?"

"The dogs, over there—look—"

There was a growl. Valmeras gave a low whistle. Two white forms leapt forward and, in four bounds, came and crouched at their master's feet.

"Gently—lie down—that's it—good dogs—stay there."

And he said to Beautrelet:

"And now let us push on. I feel more comfortable."

"Are you sure of the way?"

"Yes. We are near the terrace."

"And then?"

"I remember that, on the left, at a place where the river terrace rises to the level of the ground-floor windows, there is a shutter which closes badly and which can be opened from the outside."

They found, when they came to it, that the shutter yielded to pressure. Valmeras removed a pane with a diamond which he carried. He turned the window-latch. First one and then the other stepped over the balcony. They were now in the castle, at the end of a passage which divided the left wing into two.

"This room," said Valmeras, "opens at the end of a passage. Then comes an immense hall, lined with statues, and at the end of the hall a staircase which ends near the room occupied by your father."

He took a step forward.

"Are you coming, Beautrelet?"

"Yes, yes."

"But no, you're not coming—What's the matter with you?"

He seized him by the hand. It was icy cold and he perceived that the young man was cowering on the floor.

"What's the matter with you?" he repeated.

"Nothing—it'll pass off—"

"But what is it?"

"I'm afraid—"

"You're afraid?"

"Yes," Beautrelet confessed, frankly, "it's my nerves giving way—I generally manage to control them—but, to-day, the silence—the excitement—And then, since I was stabbed by that magistrate's clerk—But it will pass off—There, it's passing now—"

He succeeded in rising to his feet and Valmeras dragged him out of the room. They groped their way along the passage, so softly that neither could hear a sound made by the other.

A faint glimmer, however, seemed to light the hall for which they were making. Valmeras put his head round the corner. It was a night-light placed at the foot of the stairs, on a little table which showed through the frail branches of a palm tree.

"Halt!" whispered Valmeras.

Near the night-light, a man stood sentry, carrying a gun.

Had he seen them? Perhaps. At least, something must have alarmed him, for he brought the gun to his shoulder.

Beautrelet had fallen on his knees, against a tub containing a plant, and he remained quite still, with his heart thumping against his chest.

Meanwhile, the silence and the absence of all movement reassured the man. He lowered his weapon. But his head was still turned in the direction of the tub.

Terrible minutes passed: ten minutes, fifteen. A moonbeam had glided through a window on the staircase. And, suddenly, Beautrelet became aware that the moonbeam was shifting imperceptibly, and that, before fifteen, before ten more minutes had elapsed, it would be shining full in his face.

Great drops of perspiration fell from his forehead on his trembling hands. His anguish was such that he was on the point of getting up and running away—But, remembering that Valmeras was there, he sought him with his eyes and was astounded to see him, or rather to imagine him, creeping in the dark, under cover of the statues and plants. He was already at the foot of the stairs, within a few steps of the man.

What was he going to do? To pass in spite of all? To go upstairs alone and release the prisoner? But could he pass?

Beautrelet no longer saw him and he had an impression that something was about to take place, something that seemed foreboded also by the silence, which hung heavier, more awful than before.

And, suddenly, a shadow springing upon the man, the night-light extinguished, the sound of a struggle—Beautrelet ran up. The two bodies had rolled over on the flagstones. He tried to stoop and see. But he heard a hoarse moan, a sigh; and one of the adversaries rose to his feet and seized him by the arm:

"Quick!—Come along!"

It was Valmeras.

They went up two storys and came out at the entrance to a corridor, covered by a hanging.

"To the right," whispered Valmeras. "The fourth room on the left."

They soon found the door of the room. As they expected, the captive was locked in. It took them half an hour, half an hour of stifled efforts, of muffled attempts, to force open the lock. The door yielded at last.

Beautrelet groped his way to the bed. His father was asleep.

He woke him gently:

"It's I—Isidore—and a friend—don't be afraid—get up—not a word."

The father dressed himself, but, as they were leaving the room, he whispered:

"I am not alone in the castle—"

"Ah? Who else? Ganimard? Shears?"

"No—at least, I have not seen them."

"Who then?"

"A young girl."

"Mlle. de Saint-Veran, no doubt."

"I don't know—I saw her several times at a distance, in the park—and, when I lean out of my window, I can see hers. She has made signals to me."

"Do you know which is her room?"

"Yes, in this passage, the third on the right."

"The blue room," murmured Valmeras. "It has folding doors: they won't give us so much trouble."

One of the two leaves very soon gave way. Old Beautrelet undertook to tell the girl.

Ten minutes later, he left the room with her and said to his son:

"You were right—Mlle. de Saint-Veran—;"

They all four went down the stairs. When they reached the bottom, Valmeras stopped and bent over the man. Then, leading them to the terrace-room:

"He is not dead," he said. "He will live."

"Ah!" said Beautrelet, with a sigh of relief.

"No, fortunately, the blade of my knife bent: the blow is not fatal. Besides, in any case, those rascals deserve no pity."

Outside, they were met by the dogs, which accompanied them to the postern. Here, Beautrelet found his two friends and the little band left the park. It was three o'clock in the morning.

This first victory was not enough to satisfy Beautrelet. As soon as he had comfortably settled his father and Mlle. de Saint-Veran, he asked them about the people who lived at the castle, and, particularly, about the habits of Arsene Lupin. He thus learnt that Lupin came only every three or four days, arriving at night in his motor car and leaving again in the morning. At each of his visits, he called separately upon his two prisoners, both of whom agreed in praising his courtesy and his extreme civility. For the moment, he was not at the castle.

Apart from him, they had seen no one except an old woman, who ruled over the kitchen and the house, and two men, who kept watch over them by turns and never spoke to them: subordinates, obviously, to judge by their manners and appearance.

"Two accomplices, for all that," said Beautrelet, in conclusion, "or rather three, with the old woman. It is a bag worth having. And, if we lose no time—"

He jumped on his bicycle, rode to Eguzon, woke up the gendarmerie, set them all going, made them sound the boot and saddle and returned to Crozant at eight o'clock, accompanied by the sergeant and eight gendarmes. Two of the men were posted beside the gipsy-van. Two others took up their positions outside the postern-door. The last four, commanded by their chief and accompanied by Beautrelet and Valmeras, marched to the main entrance of the castle.

Too late. The door was wide open. A peasant told them that he had seen a motor car drive out of the castle an hour before.

Indeed, the search led to no result. In all probability, the gang had installed themselves there picnic fashion. A few clothes were found, a little linen, some household implements; and that was all.

What astonished Beautrelet and Valmeras more was the disappearance of the wounded man. They could not see the faintest trace of a struggle, not even a drop of blood on the flagstones of the hall.

All said, there was no material evidence to prove the fleeting presence of Lupin at the Chateau de l'Aiguille; and the authorities would have been entitled to challenge the statements of Beautrelet and his father, of Valmeras and Mlle. de Saint-Veran, had they not ended by discovering, in a room next to that occupied by the young girl, some half-dozen exquisite bouquets with Arsene Lupin's card pinned to them, bouquets scorned by her, faded and forgotten—One of them, in addition to the card, contained a letter which Raymonde had not seen. That afternoon, when opened by the examining magistrate, it was found to contain page upon page of prayers, entreaties, promises, threats, despair, all the madness of a love that has encountered nothing but contempt and repulsion.

And the letter ended: *I shall come on Tuesday evening, Raymonde. Reflect between now and then. As for me, I will wait no longer. I am resolved on all.*

Tuesday evening was the evening of the very day on which Beautrelet had released Mlle. de Saint-Veran from her captivity.

The reader will remember the extraordinary explosion of surprise and enthusiasm that resounded throughout the world at the news of that unexpected issue: Mlle. de Saint-Veran free! The pretty girl whom Lupin coveted, to secure whom he had contrived his most Machiavellian schemes, snatched from his claws! Free also Beautrelet's father, whom Lupin had chosen as a hostage in his extravagant longing for the armistice demanded by the needs of his passion! They were both free, the two prisoners! And the secret of the Hollow Needle was known, published, flung to the four corners of the world!

The crowd amused itself with a will. Ballads were sold and sung about the defeated adventurer: Lupin's Little Love-Affairs!—Arsene's Piteous Sobs!—The Lovesick Burglar! The Pickpocket's Lament!—They were cried on the boulevards and hummed in the artists' studios.

Raymonde, pressed with questions and pursued by interviewers, replied with the most extreme reserve. But there was no denying the letter, or the bouquets of flowers, or any part of the pitiful story! Then and there, Lupin, scoffed and jeered at, toppled from his pedestal.

And Beautrelet became the popular idol. He had foretold everything, thrown light on everything. The evidence which Mlle. de Saint-Veran gave before the examining magistrate confirmed, down to the smallest detail, the hypothesis imagined by Isidore. Reality seemed to submit, in every point, to what he had decreed beforehand. Lupin had found his master.—

Beautrelet insisted that his father, before returning to his mountains in Savoy, should take a few months' rest in the sunshine, and himself escorted him and Mlle. de Saint-Veran to the outskirts of Nice, where the Comte de Gesvres and his daughter Suzanne were already settled for the winter. Two days later, Valmeras brought his mother to see his new friends and they thus composed a little colony grouped around the Villa de Gesvres and watched over day and night by half a dozen men engaged by the comte.

Early in October, Beautrelet, once more the sixth-form pupil, returned to Paris to resume the interrupted course of his studies and to prepare for his examinations. And life began again, calmer, this time, and free from incident. What could happen, for that matter. Was the war not over?

Lupin, on his side, must have felt this very clearly, must have felt that there was nothing left for him but to resign himself to the accomplished fact; for, one fine day, his two other victims, Ganimard and Holmlock Shears, made their reappearance. Their return to the life of this planet, however, was devoid of any sort of glamor or fascination. An itinerant rag-man picked them up on the Quai des Orfevres, opposite the headquarters of police. Both of them were gagged, bound and fast asleep.

After a week of complete bewilderment, they succeeded in recovering the control of their thought and told—or rather Ganimard told, for Shears wrapped himself in a fierce and stubborn silence—how they had made a voyage of circumnavigation round the coast of Africa on board the yacht Hirondelle, a voyage combining amusement with instruction, during which they could look upon themselves as free, save for a few hours which they spent at the bottom of the hold, while the crew went on shore at outlandish ports.

As for their landing on the Quai des Orfevres, they remembered nothing about it and had probably been asleep for many days before.

This liberation of the prisoners was the final confession of defeat. By ceasing to fight, Lupin admitted it without reserve.

One incident, moreover, made it still more glaring, which was the engagement of Louis Valmeras and Mlle. de Saint-Veran. In the intimacy created between them by the new conditions under which they lived, the two young people fell in love with each other. Valmeras loved Raymonde's melancholy charm; and she, wounded by life, greedy for protection, yielded before the strength and energy of the man who had contributed so gallantly to her preservation.

The wedding day was awaited with a certain amount of anxiety. Would Lupin not try to resume the offensive? Would he accept with a good grace the irretrievable loss of the woman he loved? Twice or three times, suspicious-looking people were seen prowling round the villa; and Valmeras even had to defend himself one evening against a so-called drunken man, who fired a pistol at him and sent a bullet through his hat. But, in the end, the ceremony was performed at the appointed hour and day and Raymonde de Saint-Veran became Mme. Louis Valmeras.

It was as though Fate herself had taken sides with Beautrelet and countersigned the news of victory. This was so apparent to the crowd that his admirers now conceived the notion of entertaining him at a banquet to celebrate his triumph and Lupin's overthrow. It was a great idea and aroused general enthusiasm. Three hundred tickets were sold in less than a fortnight. Invitations were issued to the public schools of Paris, to send two sixth-form pupils apiece. The press sang paeans. The banquet was what it could not fail to be, an apotheosis.

But it was a charming and simple apotheosis, because Beautrelet was its hero. His presence was enough to bring things back to their due proportion. He showed himself modest, as usual, a little surprised at the excessive cheering, a little embarrassed by the extravagant panegyrics in which he was pronounced greater than the most illustrious detectives—a little embarrassed, but also not a little touched.

He said as much in a few words that pleased all his hearers and with the shyness of a child that blushes when you look at it. He spoke of his delight, of his pride. And really, reasonable and self-controlled as he was, this was for him a moment of never-to-be-forgotten exultation. He smiled to his friends, to his fellow-Jansonians, to Valmeras, who had come specially to give him a cheer, to M. de Gesvres, to his father.

When he had finished speaking; and while he still held his glass in his hand, a sound of voices came from the other end of the room and some one was gesticulating and waving a newspaper. Silence was restored and the importunate person sat down again: but a thrill of curiosity ran round the table, the newspaper was passed from hand to hand and, each time that one of the guests cast his eyes upon the page at which it was opened, exclamations followed:

"Read it! Read it!" they cried from the opposite side.

The people were leaving their seats at the principal table. M. Beautrelet went and took the paper and handed it to his son.

"Read it out! Read it out!" they cried, louder.

And others said:

"Listen! He's going to read it! Listen!"

Beautrelet stood facing his audience, looked in the evening paper which his father had given him for the article that was causing all this uproar and, suddenly, his eyes encountering a heading underlined in blue pencil, he raised his hand to call for silence and began in a loud voice to read a letter addressed to the editor by M. Massiban, of the Academy of Inscriptions and Belles-Lettres. His voice broke and fell, little by little, as he read those stupefying revelations, which reduced all his efforts to nothing, upset his notions concerning the Hollow Needle and proved the vanity of his struggle with Arsene Lupin:

Sir:
On the 17th of March, 1679, there appeared a little book with the following title: The Mystery of the Hollow Needle. The Whole Truth now first exhibited. One hundred copies printed by myself for the instruction of the Court.

At nine o'clock on the morning of that day, the author, a very young man, well-dressed, whose name has remained unknown, began to leave his book on the principal persons at court. At ten o'clock, when he had fulfilled four of these errands, he was arrested by a captain in the guards, who took him to the king's closet and forthwith set off in search of the four copies distributed.

When the hundred copies were got together, counted, carefully looked through and verified, the king himself threw them into the fire and burnt them, all but one, which he kept for his own purposes.

Then he ordered the captain of the guards to take the author of the book to M. de Saint-Mars, who confined his prisoner first at Pignerol and then in the fortress of the Ile Sainte-Marguerite. This man was obviously no other than the famous Man with the Iron Mask.

The truth would never have been known, or at least a part of the truth, if the captain in the guards had not been present at the interview and if, when the king's back was turned, he had not been tempted to withdraw another of the copies from the chimney, before the fire got to it.

Six months later, the captain was found dead on the highroad between Gaillon and Mantes. His murderers had stripped him of all his apparel, forgetting, however, in his right boot a jewel which was discovered there afterward, a diamond of the first water and of considerable value.

Among his papers was found a sheet in his handwriting, in which he did not speak of the book snatched from the flames, but gave a summary of the earlier chapters. It referred to a secret which was known to the Kings of England, which was lost by them when the crown passed from the poor fool, Henry VI., to the Duke of York, which was revealed to Charles VII., King of France, by Joan of Arc and which, becoming a State secret, was handed down from sovereign to sovereign by means of a letter, sealed anew on each occasion, which was found in the deceased monarch's death-bed with this superscription: "For the King of France."

This secret concerned the existence and described the whereabouts of a tremendous treasure, belonging to the kings, which increased in dimensions from century to century.

One hundred and fourteen years later, Louis XVI., then a prisoner in the Temple, took aside one of the officers whose duty it was to guard the royal family, and asked:

"Monsieur, had you not an ancestor who served as a captain under my predecessor, the Great King?"

"Yes, sire."

"Well, could you be relied upon—could you be relied upon—"

He hesitated. The officer completed the sentence:

"Not to betray your Majesty! Oh, sire!—"

"Then listen to me."

He took from his pocket a little book of which he tore out one of the last pages. But, altering his mind:

"No, I had better copy it—"

He seized a large sheet of paper and tore it in such a way as to leave only a small rectangular space, on which he copied five lines of dots, letters and figures from the printed page. Then, after burning the latter, he folded the manuscript sheet in four, sealed it with red wax, and gave it to the officer.

"Monsieur, after my death, you must hand this to the Queen and say to her, 'From the King, madame—for Your Majesty and for your son.' If she does not understand—"

"If she does not understand, sire—"

"You must add, 'It concerns the secret, the secret of the Needle.' The Queen will understand."

When he had finished speaking, he flung the book into the embers glowing on the hearth.

He ascended the scaffold on the 21st of January.

It took the officer several months, in consequence of the removal of the Queen to the Conciergerie, before he could fulfil the mission with which he was entrusted. At last, by dint of cunning intrigues, he succeeded, one day, in finding himself in the presence of Marie Antoinette.

Speaking so that she could just hear him, he said:

"Madame, from the late King, your husband, for Your Majesty and your son."

And he gave her the sealed letter.

She satisfied herself that the jailers could not see her, broke the seals, appeared surprised at the sight of those undecipherable lines and then, all at once, seemed to understand.

She smiled bitterly and the officer caught the words:

"Why so late?"

She hesitated. Where should she hide this dangerous document? At last, she opened her book of hours and slipped the paper into a sort of secret pocket contrived between the leather of the binding and the parchment that covered it.

"Why so late?" she had asked.

It is, in fact, probable that this document, if it could have saved her, came too late, for, in the month of October next, Queen Marie Antoinette ascended the scaffold in her turn.

Now the officer, when going through his family papers, came upon his ancestor's manuscript. From that moment, he had but one idea, which was to devote his leisure to elucidating this strange problem. He read all the Latin authors, studied all the chronicles of France and those of the neighboring countries, visited the monasteries, deciphered account-books, cartularies, treaties; and, in this way, succeeded in discovering certain references scattered over the ages.

In Book III of Caesar's Commentaries on the Gallic War (MS. edition, Alexandria), it is stated that, after the defeat of Veridovix by G. Titullius Sabinus, the chief of the Caleti was brought before Caesar and that, for his ransom, he revealed the secret of the Needle—

The Treaty of Saint-Clair-sur-Epte, between Charles the Simple and Rollo, the chief of the Norse barbarians, gives Rollo's name followed by all his titles, among which we read that of Master of the Secret of the Needle.

The Saxon Chronicle (Gibson's edition, page 134), speaking of William the Conqueror, says that the staff of his banner ended in a steel point pierced with an eye, like a needle.

In a rather ambiguous phrase in her examination, Joan of Arc admits that she has still a great secret to tell the King of France. To which her judges reply, "Yes, we know of what you speak; and that, Joan, is why you shall die the death."

Philippe de Comines mentions it in connection with Louis XI., and, later, Sully in connection with Henry IV.: "By the virtue of the Needle!" the good king sometimes swears.

Between these two, Francis I., in a speech addressed to the notables of the Havre, in 1520, uttered this phrase, which has been handed down in the diary of a Honfleur burgess; "The Kings of France carry secrets that often decide the conduct of affairs and the fate of towns."

All these quotations, all the stories relating to the Iron Mask, the captain of the guards and his descendant, I have found to-day in a pamphlet written by this same descendant and published in the month of June, 1815, just before or just after the battle of Waterloo, in a period, therefore, of great upheavals, in which the revelations which it contained were likely to pass unperceived.

What is the value of this pamphlet? Nothing, you will tell me, and we must attach no credit to it. And this is the impression which I myself would have carried away, if it had not occurred to me to open Caesar's Commentaries at the chapter given. What was my astonishment when I came upon the phrase quoted in the little book before me! And it was the same thing with the Treaty of Saint-Clair-sur-Epte, with the Saxon Chronicle, with the examination of Joan of Arc, in short, with all that I have been able to verify up to the present.

Lastly, there is an even more precise fact related by the author of the pamphlet of 1815. During the French campaign, he being then an officer under Napoleon, his horse dropped dead, one evening, and he rang at the door of a castle where he was received by an old knight of St. Louis. And, in the course of conversation with the old man, he learnt that this castle, standing on the bank of the Creuse, was called the Chateau de l'Aiguille, that it had been built and christened by Louis XIV., and that, by his express order, it was adorned with turrets and with a spire which represented the Needle. As its date it bore, it must still bear, the figure 1680.

1680! One year after the publication of the book and the imprisonment of the Iron Mask! Everything was now explained: Louis XIV., foreseeing that the secret might be noised abroad, had built and named that castle so as to offer the quidnuncs a natural explanation of the ancient mystery. The Hollow Needle! A castle with pointed bell-turrets standing on the bank of the Creuse and belonging to the King. People would at once think that they had the key to the riddle and all enquiries would cease.

The calculation was just, seeing that, more than two centuries later, M. Beautrelet fell into the trap. And this, Sir, is what I was leading up to in writing this letter. If Lupin, under the name of Anfredi, rented from M. Valmeras the Chateau de l'Aiguille on the bank of the Creuse; if, admitting the success of the inevitable investigations of M. Beautrelet, he lodged his two prisoners there, it was because he admitted the success of the inevitable researches made by M. Beautrelet and because, with the object of obtaining the peace for which he had asked, he laid for M. Beautrelet precisely what we may call the historic trap of Louis XIV.

And hence we come to this undeniable conclusion, that he, Lupin, by his unaided lights, without possessing any other facts than those which we possess, managed by means of the witchcraft of a really extraordinary genius, to decipher the undecipherable document; and that he, Lupin, the last heir of the Kings of France, knows the royal mystery of the Hollow Needle!

Here ended the letter. But, for some minutes, from the passage that referred to the Chateau de l'Aiguille onward, it was not Beautrelet's but another voice that read it aloud. Realizing his defeat, crushed under the weight of his humiliation, Isidore had dropped the newspaper and sunk into his chair, with his face buried in his hands.

Panting, shaken with excitement by this incredible story, the crowd had come gradually nearer and was now pressing round.

With a thrill of anguish, they waited for the words which he would say in reply, the objections which he would raise.

He did not stir.

Valmeras gently uncrossed his hands and raised his head.

Isidore Beautrelet was weeping.

VII. THE TREATISE OF THE NEEDLE

It is four o'clock in the morning. Isidore has not returned to the Lycee Janson. He has no intention of returning before the end of the war of extermination which he has declared against Lupin. This much he swore to himself under his breath, while his friends drove off with him, all faint and bruised, in a cab.

A mad oath! An absurd and illogical war! What can he do, a single, unarmed stripling, against that phenomenon of energy and strength? On which side is he to attack him? He is unassailable. Where to wound him? He is invulnerable. Where to get at him? He is inaccessible.

Four o'clock in the morning. Isidore has again accepted his schoolfellow's hospitality. Standing before the chimney in his bedroom, with his elbows flat on the mantel-shelf and his two fists under his chin, he stares at his image in the looking-glass. He is not crying now, he can shed no more tears, nor fling himself about on his bed, nor give way to despair, as he has been doing for the last two hours and more. He wants to think, to think and understand.

And he does not remove his eyes from those same eyes reflected in the glass, as though he hoped to double his powers of thought by contemplating his pensive image, as though he hoped to find at the back of that mirrored Beautrelet the unsolvable solution of what he does not find within himself.

He stands thus until six o'clock, and, little by little, the question presents itself to his mind with the strictness of an equation, bare and dry and cleared of all the details that complicate and obscure it.

Yes, he has made a mistake. Yes, his reading of the document is all wrong. The word aiguille does not point to the castle on the Creuse. Also, the word demoiselles cannot be applied to Raymonde de Saint-Veran and her cousin, because the text of the document dates back for centuries.

Therefore, all must be done over again, from the beginning.

How?

One piece of evidence alone would be incontestible: the book published under Louis XIV. Now of those hundred copies printed by the person who was presumed to be the Man with the Iron Mask only two escaped the flames. One was purloined by the captain of the guards and lost. The other was kept by Louis XIV., handed down to Louis XV., and burnt by Louis XVI. But a copy of the essential page, the page containing the solution of the problem, or at least a cryptographic solution, was conveyed to Marie Antoinette, who slipped it into the binding of her book of hours. What has become of this paper? Is it the one which Beautrelet has held in his hands and which Lupin recovered from him through Bredoux, the magistrate's clerk? Or is it still in Marie Antoinette's book of hours? And the question resolves itself into this: what has become of the Queen's book of hours?

After taking a short rest, Beautrelet consulted his friend's father, an old and experienced collector, who was often called upon officially to give an expert opinion and who had quite lately been invited to advise the director of one of our museums on the drawing up of the catalogue.

"Marie Antoinette's book of hours?" he exclaimed. "Why, the Queen left it to her waiting-woman, with secret instructions to forward it to Count Fersen. After being piously preserved in the count's family, it has been, for the last five years, in a glass case—"

"A glass case?"

"In the Musee Carnavalet, quite simply."

"When will the museum be open?"

"At twenty minutes from now, as it is every morning."

Isidore and his friend jumped out of a cab at the moment when the doors of Madame de Sevigne's old mansion were opening.

"Hullo! M. Beautrelet!"

A dozen voices greeted his arrival. To his great surprise, he recognized the whole crowd of reporters who were following up "the mystery of the Hollow Needle." And one of them exclaimed:

"Funny, isn't it, that we should all have had the same idea? Take care, Arsene Lupin may be among us!"

They entered the museum together. The director was at once informed, placed himself entirely at their disposal, took them to the glass case and skewed them a poor little volume, devoid of all ornament, which certainly had nothing royal about it. Nevertheless, they were overcome by a certain emotion at the sight of this object which the Queen had touched in those tragic days, which her eyes, red with tears, had looked upon—And they dared not take it and hunt through it: it was as though they feared lest they should be guilty of a sacrilege—

"Come, M. Beautrelet, it's your business!"

He took the book with an anxious gesture. The description corresponded with that given by the author of the pamphlet. Outside was a parchment cover, dirty, stained and worn in places, and under it, the real binding, in stiff leather. With what a thrill Beautrelet felt for the hidden pocket! Was it a fairy tale? Or would he find the document written by Louis XVI. and bequeathed by the queen to her fervent admirer?

At the first page, on the upper side of the book, there was no receptacle.

"Nothing," he muttered.

"Nothing," they echoed, palpitating with excitement.

But, at the last page, forcing back the book a little, he at once saw that the parchment was not stuck to the binding. He slipped his fingers in between—there was something—yes, he felt something—a paper—

"Oh!" he gasped, in an accent almost of pain. "Here—is it possible?"

"Quick, quick!" they cried. "What are you waiting for?"

He drew out a sheet folded in two.

"Well, read it!—There are words in red ink—Look!—it might be blood—pale, faded blood—Read it!—"

He read:

To you, Fersen. For my son.
16 October, 1793. MARIE ANTOINETTE.

And suddenly Beautrelet gave a cry of stupefaction. Under the queen's signature there were—there were two words, in black ink, underlined with a flourish—two words:

ARSENE LUPIN.

All, in turns, took the sheet of paper and the same cry escaped from the lips of all of them:

"Marie Antoinette!—Arsene Lupin!"

A great silence followed. That double signature: those two names coupled together, discovered hidden in the book of hours; that relic in which the poor queen's desperate appeal had slumbered for more than a century: that horrible date of the 16th of October, 1793, the day on which the Royal head fell: all of this was most dismally and disconcertingly tragic.

"Arsene Lupin!" stammered one of the voices, thus emphasizing the scare that underlay the sight of that demoniacal name at the foot of the hallowed page.

"Yes, Arsene Lupin," repeated Beautrelet. "The Queen's friend was unable to understand her desperate dying appeal. He lived with the keepsake in his possession which the woman whom he loved had sent him and he never guessed the reason of that keepsake. Lupin discovered everything, on the other hand—and took it."

"Took what?"

"The document, of course! The document written by Louis XVI.; and it is that which I held in my hands. The same appearance, the same shape, the same red seals. I understand why Lupin would not leave me a document which I could turn to account by merely examining the paper, the seals and so on."

"And then?"

"Well, then, since the document is genuine, since I have, with my own eyes, seen the marks of the red seals, since Marie Antoinette herself assures me, by these few words in her hand, that the whole story of the pamphlet, as printed by M. Massiban, is correct, because a problem of the Hollow Needle really exists, I am now certain to succeed."

"But how? Whether genuine or not, the document is of no use to you if you do not manage to decipher it, because Louis XVI. destroyed the book that gave the explanation."

"Yes, but the other copy, which King Louis XVI.'s captain of the guards snatched from the flames, was not destroyed."

"How do you know?"

"Prove the contrary."

After uttering this defiance, Beautrelet was silent for a time and then, slowly, with his eyes closed, as though trying to fix and sum up his thoughts, he said:

"Possessing the secret, the captain of the guards begins by revealing it bit by bit in the journal found by his descendant. Then comes silence. The answer to the riddle is withheld. Why? Because the temptation to make use of the secret creeps over him little by little and he gives way to it. A proof? His murder. A further proof? The magnificent jewel found upon him, which he must undoubtedly have taken from some royal treasure the hiding-place of which, unknown to all, would just constitute the mystery of the Hollow Needle. Lupin conveyed as much to me; Lupin was not lying."

"Then what conclusion do you draw, Beautrelet?"

"I draw this conclusion, my friends, that it be a good thing to advertise this story as much as possible, so that people may know, through all the papers, that we are looking for a book entitled The Treatise of the Needle. It may be fished out from the back shelves of some provincial library."

The paragraph was drawn up forthwith; and Beautrelet set to work at once, without even waiting for it to produce a result. A first scent suggested itself: the murder was committed near Gaillon. He went there that same day. Certainly, he did not hope to reconstruct a crime perpetrated two hundred years ago. But, all the same, there are crimes that leave traces in the memories, in the traditions of a countryside. They are recorded in the local chronicles. One day, some provincial archaeologist, some lover of old legends, some student of the minor incidents of the life of the past makes them the subject of an article in a newspaper or of a communication to the academy of his departmental town.

Beautreiet saw three or four of these archaeologists. With one of them in particular, an old notary, he examined the prison records, the ledgers of the old bailiwicks and the parish registers. There was no entry referring to the murder of a captain of the guards in the seventeenth century.

He refused to be discouraged and continued his search in Paris, where the magistrate's examination might have taken place. His efforts came to nothing.

But the thought of another track sent him off in a fresh direction. Was there no chance of finding out the name of that captain whose descendant served in the armies of the Republic and was quartered in the Temple during the imprisonment of the Royal family? By dint of patient working, he ended by making out a list in which two names at least presented an almost complete resemblance: M. de Larbeyrie, under Louis XIV., and Citizen Larbrie, under the Terror.

This already was an important point. He stated it with precision in a note which he sent to the papers, asking for any information concerning this Larbeyrie or his descendants.

It was M. Massiban, the Massiban of the pamphlet, the member of the Institute, who replied to him:

SIR:

Allow me to call your attention to the following passage of Voltaire, which I came upon in his manuscript of Le Siecle de Louis XIV. (Chapter XXV: Particularites et anecdotes du regne). The passage has been suppressed in all the printed editions:

"I have heard it said by the late M. de Caumartin, intendant of finance, who was a friend of Chamillard the minister, that the King one day left hurriedly in his carriage at the news that M. de Larbeyrie had been murdered and robbed of some magnificent jewels. He seemed greatly excited and repeated:

"'All is lost—all is lost—'

"In the following year, the son of this Larbeyrie and his daughter, who had married the Marquis de Velines, were banished to their estates in Provence and Brittany. We cannot doubt that there is something peculiar in this."

I, in my turn, will add that we can doubt it all the less inasmuch as M. de Chamillard, according to Voltaire, WAS THE LAST MINISTER WHO POSSESSED THE STRANGE SECRET OF THE IRON MASK.

You will see for yourself, Sir, the profit that can be derived from this passage and the evident link established between the two adventures. As for myself, I will not venture to imagine any very exact surmise as regards the conduct, the suspicions, and the apprehensions of Louis XIV. in these circumstances; but, on the other hand, seeing that M. de Larbeyrie left a son, who was probably the grandfather of Larbrie the citizen-officer, and also a daughter, is it not permissible to suppose that a part of the papers left by Larbeyrie came to the daughter and that among these papers was the famous copy which the captain of the guards saved from the flames?

I have consulted the Country-house Year-book. There is a Baron de Velines living not far from Rennes. Could he be a descendant of the marquis? At any rate, I wrote to him yesterday, on chance, to ask if he had not in his possession a little old book bearing on its title-page the word aiguille; and I am awaiting his reply.

It would give me the greatest pleasure to talk of all these matters with you. If you can spare the time, come and see me.

I am, Sir, etc., etc.

P.S.—Of course, I shall not communicate these little discoveries to the press. Now that you are near the goal, discretion is essential.

Beautrelet absolutely agreed. He even went further: to two journalists who were worrying him that morning he gave the most fanciful particulars as to his plans and his state of mind.

In the afternoon, he hurried round to see Massiban, who lived at 17, Quai Voltaire. To his great surprise, he was told that M. Massiban had gone out of town unexpectedly, leaving a note for him in case he should call. Isidore opened it and read:

I have received a telegram which gives me some hope. So I am leaving town and shall sleep at Rennes. You might take the evening train and, without stopping at Rennes, go on to the little station of Velines. We would meet at the castle, which is two miles and a half from the station.

The programme appealed to Beautrelet, and especially the idea that he would reach the castle at almost the same time as Massiban, for he feared some blunder on the part of that inexperienced man. He went back to his friend and spent the rest of the day with him. In the evening, he took the Brittany express and got out at Velines as six o'clock in the morning.

He did the two and a half miles, between bushy woods, on foot. He could see the castle, perched on a height, from a distance: it was a hybrid edifice, a mixture of the Renascence and Louis Philippe styles, but it bore a stately air, nevertheless, with its four turrets and its ivy-mantled draw-bridge.

Isidore felt his heart beat as he approached. Was he really nearing the end of his race? Did the castle contain the key to the mystery?

He was not without fear. It all seemed too good to be true; and he asked himself if he was not once more acting in obedience to some infernal plan contrived by Lupin, if Massiban was not for instance, a tool in the hands of his enemy. He burst out laughing:

"Tut, tut, I'm becoming absurd! One would really think that Lupin was an infallible person who foresees everything, a sort of divine omnipotence against whom nothing can prevail! Dash it all, Lupin makes his mistakes; Lupin, too, is at the mercy of circumstances; Lupin has an occasional slip! And it is just because of his slip in losing the document that I am beginning to have the advantage of him. Everything starts from that. And his efforts, when all is said, serve only to repair the first blunder."

And blithely, full of confidence, Beautrelet rang the bell.

"Yes, sir?" said the servant who opened the door.

"Can I see the Baron de Velines?"

And he gave the man his card.

"Monsieur le baron is not up yet, but, if monsieur will wait—"

"Has not some one else been asking for him, a gentleman with a white beard and a slight stoop?" asked Beautrelet, who knew Massiban's appearance from the photographs in the newspapers.

"Yes, the gentleman came about ten minutes ago; I showed him into the drawing room. If monsieur will come this way—"

The interview between Massiban and Beautrelet was of the most cordial character. Isidore thanked the old man for the first-rate information which he owed to him and Massiban expressed his admiration for Beautrelet in the warmest terms. Then they exchanged impressions on the document, on their prospects of discovering the book; and Massiban repeated what he had heard at Rennes regarding M. de Velines. The baron was a man of sixty, who had been left a widower many years ago and who led a very retired life with his daughter, Gabrielle de Villemon. This lady had just suffered a cruel blow through the loss of her husband and her eldest son, both of whom had died as the result of a motor-car accident.

"Monsieur le baron begs the gentlemen to be good enough to come upstairs."

The servant led the way to the first floor, to a large, bare-walled room, very simply furnished with desks, pigeon-holes and tables covered with papers and account-books.

The baron received them very affably and with the volubility often displayed by people who live too much alone. They had great difficulty in explaining the object of their visit.

"Oh, yes, I know, you wrote to me about it, M. Massiban. It has something to do with a book about a needle, hasn't it, a book which is supposed to have come down to me from my ancestors?"

"Just so."

"I may as well tell you that my ancestors and I have fallen out. They had funny ideas in those days. I belong to my own time. I have broken with the past."

"Yes," said Beautrelet, impatiently, "but have you no recollection of having seen the book?—"

"Certainly, I said so in my telegram," he exclaimed, addressing M. Massiban, who, in his annoyance, was walking up and down the room and looking out of the tall windows. "Certainly—or, at least, my daughter thought she had seen the title among the thousands of books that lumber up the library, upstairs—for I don't care about reading myself—I don't even read the papers. My daughter does, sometimes, but only when there is nothing the matter with Georges, her remaining son! As for me, as long as my tenants pay their rents and my leases are kept up—! You see my account-books: I live in them, gentlemen; and I confess that I know absolutely nothing whatever about that story of which you wrote to me in your letter, M. Massiban—"

Isidore Beautrelet, nerve-shattered at all this talk, interrupted him bluntly:

"I beg your pardon, monsieur, but the book—"

"My daughter has looked for it. She looked for it all day yesterday."

"Well?"

"Well, she found it; she found it a few hours ago. When you arrived--"

"And where is it?"

"Where is it? Why, she put it on that table—there it is—over there—"

Isidore gave a bound. At one end of the table, on a muddled heap of papers, lay a little book bound in red morocco. He banged his fist down upon it, as though he were forbidding anybody to touch it—and also a little as though he himself dared not take it up.

"Well!" cried Massiban, greatly excited.

"I have it—here it is—we're there at last!"

"But the title—are you sure?—"

"Why, of course: look!"

"Are you convinced? Have we mastered the secret at last?"

"The front page—what does the front page say?"

"Read: The Whole Truth now first exhibited. One hundred copies printed by myself for the instruction of the Court."

"That's it, that's it," muttered Massiban, in a hoarse voice. "It's the copy snatched from the flames! It's the very book which Louis XIV. condemned."

They turned over the pages. The first part set forth the explanations given by Captain de Larbeyrie in his journal.

"Get on, get on!" said Beautrelet, who was in a hurry to come to the solution.

"Get on? What do you mean? Not at all! We know that the Man with the Iron Mask was imprisoned because he knew and wished to divulge the secret of the Royal house of France. But how did he know it? And why did he wish to divulge it? Lastly, who was that strange personage? A half-brother of Louis XIV., as Voltaire maintained, or Mattioli, the Italian minister, as the modern critics declare? Hang it, those are questions of the very first interest!"

"Later, later," protested Beautrelet, feverishly turning the pages, as though he feared that the book would fly out of his hands before he had solved the riddle.

"But—" said Massiban, who doted on historical details.

"We have plenty of time—afterward—let's see the explanation first—"

Suddenly Beautrelet stopped. The document! In the middle of a left-hand page, his eyes saw the five mysterious lines of dots and figures! He made sure, with a glance, that the text was identical with that which he had studied so long; the same arrangement of the signs, the same intervals that permitted of the isolation of the word demoiselles and the separation of the two words aiguille and creuse.

A short note preceded it:

All the necessary indications, it appears, were reduced by King Louis XIII. into a little table which I transcribe below.

Here followed the table of dots and figures.

Then came the explanation of the document itself. Beautrelet read, in a broken voice:

As will be seen, this table, even after we have changed the figures into vowels, affords no light. One might say that, in order to decipher the puzzle, we must first know it. It is, at most, a clue given to those who know the paths of the labyrinth.

Let us take this clue and proceed. I will guide you.

The fourth line first. The fourth line contains measurements and indications. By complying with the indications and noting the measurements set down, we inevitably attain our object, on condition, be it understood, that we know where we are and whither we are going, in a word, that we are enlightened as to the real meaning of the Hollow Needle. This is what we may learn from the first three lines. The first is so conceived to revenge myself on the King; I had warned him, for that matter—

Beautrelet stopped, nonplussed.

"What? What is it?" said Massiban.

"The words don't make sense."

"No more they do," replied Massiban. "'The first is so conceived to revenge myself on the King—' What can that mean?"

"Damn!" yelled Beautrelet.

"Well?"

"Torn! Two pages! The next two pages! Look at the marks!"

He trembled, shaking with rage and disappointment. Massiban bent forward.

"It is true—there are the ends of two pages left, like bookbinders' guards. The marks seem pretty fresh. They've not been cut, but torn out—torn out with violence. Look, all the pages at the end of the book have been rumpled."

"But who can have done it? Who?" moaned Isidore, wringing his hands. "A servant? An accomplice?"

"All the same, it may date back to a few months since," observed Massiban.

"Even so—even so—some one must have hunted out and taken the book—Tell me, monsieur," cried Beautrelet, addressing the baron, "is there no one whom you suspect?"

"We might ask my daughter."

"Yes—yes—that's it—perhaps she will know."

M. de Velines rang for the footman. A few minutes later, Mme. de Villemon entered. She was a young woman, with a sad and resigned face. Beautrelet at once asked her:

"You found this volume upstairs, madame, in the library?"

"Yes, in a parcel of books that had not been uncorded."

"And you read it?"

"Yes, last night."

"When you read it, were those two pages missing? Try and remember: the two pages following this table of figures and dots?"

"No, certainly not," she said, greatly astonished. "There was no page missing at all."

"Still, somebody has torn—"

"But the book did not leave my room last night."

"And this morning?"

"This morning, I brought it down here myself, when M. Massiban's arrival was announced."

"Then—?"

"Well, I don't understand—unless—but no."

"What?"

"Georges—my son—this morning—Georges was playing with the book."

She ran out headlong, accompanied by Beautrelet, Massiban and the baron. The child was not in his room. They hunted in every direction. At last, they found him playing behind the castle. But those three people seemed so excited and called him so peremptorily to account that he began to yell aloud.

Everybody ran about to right and left. The servants were questioned. It was an indescribable tumult. And Beautrelet received the awful impression that the truth was ebbing away from him, like water trickling through his fingers.

He made an effort to recover himself, took Mme. de Villemon's arm, and, followed by the baron and Massiban, led her back to the drawing room and said:

"The book is incomplete. Very well. There are two pages torn out; but you read them, did you not, madame?"

"Yes."

"You know what they contained?"

"Yes."

"Could you repeat it to us?"

"Certainly. I read the book with a great deal of curiosity, but those two pages struck me in particular because the revelations were so very interesting."

"Well, then, speak madame, speak, I implore you! Those revelations are of exceptional importance. Speak, I beg of you: minutes lost are never recovered. The Hollow Needle—"

"Oh, it's quite simple. The Hollow Needle means—"

At that moment, a footman entered the room:

"A letter for madame."

"Oh, but the postman has passed!"

"A boy brought it."

Mme. de Villemon opened the letter, read it, and put her hand to her heart, turning suddenly livid and terrified, ready to faint.

The paper had slipped to the floor. Beautrelet picked it up and, without troubling to apologize, read:

Not a word! If you say a word, your son will never wake again.

"My son—my son!" she stammered, too weak even to go to the assistance of the threatened child.

Beautrelet reassured her:

"It is not serious—it's a joke. Come, who could be interested?"

"Unless," suggested Massiban, "it was Arsene Lupin."

Beautrelet made him a sign to hold his tongue. He knew quite well, of course, that the enemy was there, once more, watchful and determined; and that was just why he wanted to tear from Mme. de Villemon the decisive words, so long awaited, and to tear them from her on the spot, that very moment:

"I beseech you, madame, compose yourself. We are all here. There is not the least danger."

Would she speak? He thought so, he hoped so. She stammered out a few syllables. But the door opened again. This time, the nurse entered. She seemed distraught:

"M. Georges—madame—M. Georges—!"

Suddenly, the mother recovered all her strength. Quicker than any of them, and urged by an unfailing instinct, she rushed down the staircase, across the hall and on to the terrace. There lay little Georges, motionless, on a wicker chair.

"Well, what is it? He's asleep!—"

"He fell asleep suddenly, madame," said the nurse. "I tried to prevent him, to carry him to his room. But he was fast asleep and his hands—his hands were cold."

"Cold!" gasped the mother. "Yes—it's true. Oh dear, oh dear—IF HE ONLY WAKES UP!"

Beautrelet put his hand in his trousers pocket, seized the butt of his revolver, cocked it with his forefinger, then suddenly produced the weapon and fired at Massiban.

Massiban, as though he were watching the boy's movements, had avoided the shot, so to speak, in advance. But already Beautrelet had sprung upon him, shouting to the servants:

"Help! It's Lupin!"

Massiban, under the weight of the impact, fell back into one of the wicker chairs. In a few seconds, he rose, leaving Beautrelet stunned, choking; and, holding the young man's revolver in his hands:

"Good!—that's all right!—don't stir—you'll be like that for two or three minutes—no more. But, upon my word, you took your time to recognize me! Was my make-up as old Massiban so good as all that?"

He was now standing straight up on his legs, his body squared, in a formidable attitude, and he grinned as he looked at the three petrified footmen and the dumbfounded baron:

"Isidore, you've missed the chance of a lifetime. If you hadn't told them I was Lupin, they'd have jumped on me. And, with fellows like that, what would have become of me, by Jove, with four to one against me?"

He walked up to them:

"Come, my lads, don't be afraid—I shan't hurt you. Wouldn't you like a sugar-stick apiece to screw your courage up? Oh, you, by the way, hand me back my hundred-franc note, will you? Yes, yes, I know you! You're the one I bribed just now to give the letter to your mistress. Come hurry, you faithless servant."

He took the blue bank-note which the servant handed him and tore it into tiny shreds:

"The price of treachery! It burns my fingers."

He took off his hat and, bowing very low before Mme. de Villemon:

"Will you forgive me, madame? The accidents of life—of mine especially—often drive one to acts of cruelty for which I am the first to blush. But have no fear for your son: it's a mere prick, a little puncture in the arm which I gave him while we were questioning him. In an hour, at the most, you won't know that it happened. Once more, all my apologies. But I had to make sure of your silence." He bowed again, thanked M. de Velines for his kind hospitality, took his cane, lit a cigarette, offered one to the baron, gave a circular sweep with his hat and, in a patronizing tone, said to Beautrelet:

"Good-bye, baby."

And he walked away quietly, puffing the smoke of his cigarette into the servants' faces.

Beautrelet waited for a few minutes. Mme. de Villemon, now calmer, was watching by her son. He went up to her, with the intention of making one last appeal to her. Their eyes met. He said nothing. He had understood that she would never speak now, whatever happened. There, once more, in that mother's brain, the secret of the Hollow Needle lay buried as deeply as in the night of the past.

Then he gave up and went away.

It was half-past ten. There was a train at eleven-fifty. He slowly followed the avenue in the park and turned into the road that led to the station.

"Well, what do you say to that?"

It was Massiban, or rather Lupin, who appeared out of the wood adjoining the road.

"Was it pretty well contrived, or was it not? Is your old friend great on the tight-rope, or is he not? I'm sure that you haven't got over it, eh, and that you're asking yourself whether the so-called Massiban, member of the Academy of Inscriptions and Belles-Lettres, ever existed. But, of course, he exists. I'll even show him to you, if you're good. But, first, let me give you back your revolver. You're looking to see if it's loaded? Certainly, my lad. There are five charges left, one of which would be enough to send me ad patres.—Well, so you're putting it in your pocket? Quite right. I prefer that to what you did up there.—A nasty little impulse, that, of yours!—Still, you're young, you suddenly see—in a flash!—that you've once more been done by that confounded Lupin and that he is standing there in front of you, at three steps from you—and bang! You fire!—I'm not angry with you, bless your little heart! To prove it, I offer you a seat in my 100 h.p. car. Will that suit you?"

He put his fingers to his mouth and whistled.

The contrast was delicious between the venerable appearance of this elderly Massiban and the schoolboy ways and accent which Lupin was putting on. Beautrelet could not help laughing.

"He's laughed! He's laughed!" cried Lupin, jumping for joy. "You see, baby, what you fall short in is the power of smiling; you're a trifle serious for your age. You're a very likeable boy, you have a charming candor and simplicity—but you have no sense of humor." He placed himself in front of him. "Look here, bet you I make you cry! Do you know how I was able to follow up all your inquiry, how I knew of the letter Massiban wrote you and his appointment to meet you this morning at the Chateau de Velines? Through the prattle of your friend, the one you're staying with. You confide in that idiot and he loses no time, but goes and tells everything to his best girl. And his best girl has no secrets for Lupin.—What did I tell you? I've made you feel, anyhow; your eyes are quite wet!—Friendship betrayed: that upsets you, eh? Upon my word, you're wonderful! I could take you in my arms and hug you! You always wear that look of astonishment which goes straight to my heart.—I shall never forget the other evening at Gaillon, when you consulted me.—Yes, I was the old notary!—But why don't you laugh, youngster? As I said, you have no sense of a joke. Look here, what you want is—what shall I call it?—imagination, imaginative impulse. Now, I'm full of imaginative impulse."

A motor was heard panting not far off. Lupin seized Beautrelet roughly by the arm and in a cold voice, looking him straight in the eyes:

"You're going to keep quiet now, aren't you? You can see there's nothing to be done. Then what's the use of wasting your time and energy? There are plenty of highway robbers in the world. Run after them and let me be—if not!—It's settled, isn't it?"

He shook him as though to enforce his will upon him. Then he grinned:

"Fool that I am! You leave me alone? You're not one of those who let go! Oh, I don't know what restrains me! In half a dozen turns of the wrist, I could have you bound and gagged—and, in two hours, safe under lock and key, for some months to come. And then I could twist my thumbs in all security, withdraw to the peaceful retreat prepared for me by my ancestors, the Kings of France, and enjoy the treasures which they have been good enough to accumulate for me. But no, it is doomed that I must go on blundering to the end. I can't help it, we all have our weaknesses—and I have one for you. Besides, it's not done yet. From now until you put your finger into the hollow of the Needle, a good deal of water will flow under the bridges. Dash it all, it took me ten days! Me! Lupin! You will want ten years, at least! There's that much distance between us, after all!"

The motor arrived, an immense closed car. Lupin opened the door and Beautreiet gave a cry. There was a man inside and that man was Lupin, or rather Massiban. Suddenly understanding, he burst out laughing. Lupin said:

"Don't be afraid, he's sound asleep. I promised that you should see him. Do you grasp the situation now? At midnight, I knew of your appointment at the castle. At seven in the morning, I was there. When Massiban passed, I had only to collect him—give him a tiny prick with a needle—and the thing—was done. Sleep old chap, sleep away. We'll set you down on the slope. That's it—there—capital—right in the sun, then you won't catch cold—good! And our hat in our hand.—Spare a copper, kind gentleman!—Oh. my dear old Massiban, so you were after Arsene Lupin!"

It was really a huge joke to see the two Massibans face to face, one asleep with his head on his chest, the other seriously occupied in paying him every sort of attention and respect:

"Pity a poor blind man! There, Massiban, here's two sous and my visiting-card. And now, my lads, off we go at the fourth speed. Do you hear, driver? You've got to do seventy-five miles an hour. Jump in, Isidore. There's a full sitting of the Institute to-day, and Massiban is to read a little paper, on I don't know what, at half-past three. Well, he'll read them his little paper. I'll dish them up a complete Massiban, more real than the real one, with my own ideas, on the lacustrine inscriptions. I don't have an opportunity of lecturing at the Institute ever day!—Faster, chauffeur: we're only doing seventy-one and a half!—Are you afraid? Remember you're with Lupin!—Ah, Isidore, and then people say that life is monotonous! Why, life's an adorable thing, my boy; only one has to know—and I know—. Wasn't it enough to make a man jump out of his skin for joy, just now, at the castle, when you were chattering with old Velines and I, up against the window, was tearing out the pages of the historic book? And then, when you were questioning the Dame de Villemon about the Hollow Needle! Would she speak? Yes, she would—no, she wouldn't—yes—no. It gave me gooseflesh, I assure you.—If she spoke, I should have to build up my life anew, the whole scaffolding was destroyed.—Would the footman come in time? Yes—no—there he is.—But Beautrelet will unmask me! Never! He's too much of a flat! Yes, though—no—there, he's done it—no, he hasn't—yes—he's eyeing me—that's it—he's feeling for his revolver!—Oh, the delight of it!—Isidore, you're talking too much, you'll hurt yourself!—Let's have a snooze, shall we?—I'm dying of sleep.—Good night."

Beautrelet looked at him. He seemed almost asleep already. He slept.

The motor-car, darting through space, rushed toward a horizon that was constantly reached and as constantly retreated. There was no impression of towns, villages, fields or forests; simply space, space devoured, swallowed up.

Beautrelet looked at his traveling companion, for a long time, with eager curiosity and also with a keen wish to fathom his real character through the mask that covered it. And he thought of the circumstances that confined them, like that, together, in the close contact of that motor car. But, after the excitement and disappointment of the morning, tired in his turn, he too fell asleep.

When he woke, Lupin was reading. Beautrelet leant over to see the title of the book. It was the Epistolae ad Lucilium of Seneca the philosopher.

VIII. FROM CAESAR TO LUPIN

Dash it all, it took me ten days! Me! Lupin!

You will want ten years, at least!—

These words, uttered by Lupin after leaving the Chateau de Velines, had no little influence on Beautrelet's conduct.

Though very calm in the main and invariably master of himself, Lupin, nevertheless, was subject to moments of exaltation, of a more or less romantic expansiveness, at once theatrical and good-humored, when he allowed certain admissions to escape him, certain imprudent speeches which a boy like Beautrelet could easily turn to profit.

Rightly or wrongly, Beautrelet read one of these involuntary admissions into that phrase. He was entitled to conclude that, if Lupin drew a comparison between his own efforts and Beautrelet's in pursuit of the truth about the Hollow Needle, it was because the two of them possessed identical means of attaining their object, because Lupin had no elements of success different from those possessed by his adversary. The chances were alike. Now, with the same chances, the same elements of success, the same means, ten days had been enough for Lupin.

What were those elements, those means, those chances? They were reduced, when all was said, to a knowledge of the pamphlet published in 1815, a pamphlet which Lupin, no doubt, like Massiban, had found by accident and thanks to which he had succeeded in discovering the indispensable document in Marie Antoinette's book of hours.

Therefore, the pamphlet and the document were the only two fundamental facts upon which Lupin had relied. With these he had built up the whole edifice. He had had no extraneous aid. The study of the pamphlet and the study of the document—full stop—that was all.

Well, could not Beautrelet confine himself to the same ground? What was the use of an impossible struggle? What was the use of those vain investigations, in which, even supposing that he avoided the pitfalls that were multiplied under his feet, he was sure, in the end, to achieve the poorest of results?

His decision was clear and immediate; and, in adopting it, he had the happy instinct that he was on the right path. He began by leaving his Janson-de-Sailly schoolfellow, without indulging in useless recriminations, and, taking his portmanteau with him, went and installed himself, after much hunting about, in a small hotel situated in the very heart of Paris. This hotel he did not leave for days. At most, he took his meals at the table d'hote. The rest of the time, locked in his room, with the window-curtains close-drawn, he spent in thinking.

"Ten days," Arsene Lupin had said.

Beautrelet, striving to forget all that he had done and to remember only the elements of the pamphlet and the document, aspired eagerly to keep within the limit of those ten days. However the tenth day passed and the eleventh and the twelfth; but, on the thirteenth day, a gleam lit up his brain and, very soon, with the bewildering rapidity of those ideas which develop in us like miraculous plants, the truth emerged, blossomed, gathered strength. On the evening of the thirteenth day, he certainly did not know the answer to the problem, but he knew, to a certainty, one of the methods which Lupin had, beyond a doubt, employed.

It was a very simple method, hinging on this one question: Is there a link of any sort uniting all the more or less important historic events with which the pamphlet connects the mystery of the Hollow Needle?

The great diversity of these events made the question difficult to answer. Still, the profound examination to which Beautrelet applied himself ended by pointing to one essential characteristic which was common to them all. Each one of them, without exception, had happened within the boundaries of the old kingdom of Neustria, which correspond very nearly with those of our present-day Normandy. All the heroes of the fantastic adventure are Norman, or become Norman, or play their part in the Norman country.

What a fascinating procession through the ages! What a rousing spectacle was that of all those barons, dukes and kings, starting from such widely opposite points to meet in this particular corner of the world! Beautrelet turned the pages of history at haphazard: it was Rolf, or Rou, or Rollo, first Duke of Normandy, who was master of the secret of the Needle, according to the treaty of Saint-Clair-sur-Epte!

It was William the Conqueror, Duke of Normandy and King of England, whose bannerstaff was pierced like a needle!

It was at Rouen that the English burnt Joan of Arc, mistress of the secret!

And right at the beginning of the adventure, who is that chief of the Caleti who pays his ransom to Caesar with the secret of the Needle but the chief of the men of the Caux country, which lies in the very heart of Normandy?

The supposition becomes more definite. The field narrows. Rouen, the banks of the Seine, the Caux country: it really seems as though all roads lead in that direction. Two kings of France are mentioned more particularly, after the secret is lost by the Dukes of Normandy and their heirs, the kings of England, and becomes the royal secret of France; and these two are King Henry IV., who laid siege to Rouen and won the battle of Arques, near Dieppe, and Francis I., who founded the Havre and uttered that suggestive phrase:

"The kings of France carry secrets that often decide the fate of towns!"

Rouen, Dieppe, the Havre: the three angles of the triangle, the three large towns that occupy the three points. In the centre, the Caux country.

The seventeenth century arrives. Louis XIV. burns the book in which a person unknown reveals the truth. Captain de Larbeyrie masters a copy, profits by the secret thus obtained, steals a certain number of jewels and dies by the hand of highway murderers. Now at which spot is the ambush laid? At Gaillon! At Gaillon, a little town on the road leading from Havre, Rouen or Dieppe to Paris!

A year later, Louis XIV. buys a domain and builds the Chateau de l'Aiguille. Where does he select his site? In the Midlands of France, with the result that the curious are thrown off the scent and do not hunt about in Normandy.

Rouen, Dieppe, the Havre—the Cauchois triangle—everything lies there. On one side, the sea; on another, the Seine: on the third, the two valleys that lead from Rouen to Dieppe.

A light flashed across Beautrelet's mind. That extent of ground, that country of the high tablelands which run from the cliffs of the Seine to the cliffs of the Channel almost invariably constituted the field of operations of Arsene Lupin. For ten years, it was just this district which he parcelled out for his purposes, as though he had his haunt in the very centre of the region with which, the legend of the Hollow Needle was most closely connected.

The affair of Baron Cahorn?[3] Or the banks of the Seine, between Rouen and the Havre.

The Thibermenil case?[4] At the other end of the tableland, between Rouen and Dieppe.

The Gruchet, Montigny, Crasville burglaries? In the midst of the Caux country.

Where was Lupin going when he was attacked and bound hand and foot, in his compartment by Pierre Onfrey, the Auteuil murderer?[5] To Rouen.

Where was Holmlock Shears, Lupin's prisoner, put on board ship?[6] Near the Havre.

And what was the scene of the whole of the present tragedy? Ambrumesy, on the road between the Havre and Dieppe.

Rouen, Dieppe, the Havre: always the Cauchois triangle.

And so, a few years earlier, possessing the pamphlet and knowing the hiding-place in which Marie Antoinette had concealed the document, Arsene Lupin had ended by laying his hand on the famous book of hours. Once in possession of the document, he took the field, "found" and settled down as in a conquered country.

Beautrelet took the field.

He set out in genuine excitement, thinking of the same journey which Lupin had taken, of the same hopes with which he must have throbbed when he thus went in search of the tremendous secret which was to arm him with so great a power. Would his, Beautrelet's efforts have the same victorious results?

He left Rouen early in the morning, on foot, with his face very much disguised and his bag at the end of a stick on his shoulder, like an apprentice doing his round of France. He walked straight to Duclair, where he lunched. On leaving this town, he followed the Seine and practically did not lose sight of it again. His instinct, strengthened, moreover, by numerous influences, always brought him back to the sinuous banks of the stately river. When the Chateau du Malaquis was robbed, the objects stolen from Baron Cahorn's collection were sent by way of the Seine. The old carvings removed from the chapel at Ambrumesy were

---

[3] The Seven of Hearts. II; Arsene Lupin in Prison
[4] The Seven of Hearts. IX: Holmlock Shears Arrives Too Late
[5] The Seven of Hearts. IV: The Mysterious Railway-passenger
[6] Arsene Lupin versus Holmlock Shears, Chapter V: Kidnapped

carried to the Seine bank. He pictured the whole fleet of pinnaces performing a regular service between Rouen and the Havre and draining the works of art and treasures from a countryside to dispatch them thence to the land of millionaires.

"I'm burning! I'm burning!" muttered the boy, gasping under the truth, which came to him in a mighty series of shocks and took away his breath.

The checks encountered on the first few days, did not discourage him. He had a firm and profound belief in the correctness of the supposition that was guiding him. It was bold, perhaps, and extravagant; no matter: it was worthy of the adversary pursued. The supposition was on a level with the prodigious reality that bore the name of Lupin. With a man like that, of what good could it be to look elsewhere than in the domain of the enormous, the exaggerated, the superhuman?

Jumieges, the Mailleraye, Saint-Wandrille, Caudebec, Tancarville, Quillebeuf were places filled with his memories. How often he must have contemplated the glory of their Gothic steeples or the splendor of their immense ruins!

But the Havre, the neighborhood of the Havre drew Isidore like a beacon-fire.

"The kings of France carry secrets that often decide the fate of towns!"

Cryptic words which, suddenly, for Beautrelet, shone bright with clearness! Was this not an exact statement of the reasons that determined Francis I. to create a town on this spot and was not the fate of the Havre-de-Grace linked with the very secret of the Needle?

"That's it, that's it," stammered Beautrelet, excitedly. "The old Norman estuary, one of the essential points, one of the original centres around which our French nationality was formed, is completed by those two forces, one in full view, alive, known to all, the new port commanding the ocean and opening on the world; the other dim and obscure, unknown and all the more alarming, inasmuch as it is invisible and impalpable. A whole side of the history of France and of the royal house is explained by the Needle, even as it explains the whole story of Arsene Lupin. The same sources of energy and power supply and renew the fortunes of kings and of the adventurer."

Beautrelet ferreted and snuffed from village to village, from the river to the sea, with his nose in the wind, his ears pricked, trying to compel the inanimate things to surrender their deep meaning. Ought this hill-slope to be questioned? Or that forest? Or the houses of this hamlet? Or was it among the insignificant phrases spoken by that peasant yonder that he might hope to gather the one little illuminating word?

One morning, he was lunching at an inn, within sight of Honfleur, the old city of the estuary. Opposite him was sitting one of those heavy, red-haired Norman horse-dealers who do the fairs of the district, whip in hand and clad in a long smock-frock. After a moment, it seemed to Beautrelet that the man was looking at him with a certain amount of attention, as though he knew him or, at least, was trying to recognize him.

"Pooh," he thought, "there's some mistake: I've never seen that merchant before, nor he me."

As a matter of fact, the man appeared to take no further interest in him. He lit his pipe, called for coffee and brandy, smoked and drank.

When Beautrelet had finished his meal, he paid and rose to go. A group of men entered just as he was about to leave and he had to stand for a few seconds near the table at which the horse-dealer sat. He then heard the man say in a low voice:

"Good-afternoon, M. Beautrelet."

Without hesitation, Isidore sat down beside the man and said:

"Yes, that is my name—but who are you? How did you know me?"

"That's not difficult—and yet I've only seen your portrait in the papers. But you are so badly—what do you call it in French—so badly made-up."

He had a pronounced foreign accent and Beautrelet seemed to perceive, as he looked at him, that he too wore a facial disguise that entirely altered his features.

"Who are you?" he repeated. "Who are you?"

The stranger smiled:

"Don't you recognize me?"

"No, I never saw you before."

"Nor I you. But think. The papers print my portrait also—and pretty often. Well, have you got it?"

"No."

"Holmlock Shears."

It was an amusing and, at the same time, a significant meeting. The boy at once saw the full bearing of it. After an exchange of compliments, he said to Shears:

"I suppose that you are here—because of 'him'?"

"Yes."

"So—so—you think we have a chance—in this direction."

"I'm sure of it."

Beautrelet's delight at finding that Shears's opinion agreed with his own was not unmingled with other feelings. If the Englishman attained his object, it meant that, at the very best, the two would share the victory; and who could tell that Shears would not attain it first?

"Have you any proofs? Any clues?"

"Don't be afraid," grinned the Englishman, who understood his uneasiness. "I am not treading on your heels. With you, it's the document, the pamphlet: things that do not inspire me with any great confidence."

"And with you?"

"With me, it's something different."

"Should I be indiscreet, if—?"

"Not at all. You remember the story of the coronet, the story of the Duc de Charmerac?"[7]

"Yes."

"You remember Victoire, Lupin's old foster-mother, the one whom my good friend Ganimard allowed to escape in a sham prison-van?"

"Yes."

"I have found Victoire's traces. She lives on a farm, not far from National Road No. 25. National Road No. 25 is the road from the Havre to Lille. Through Victoire I shall easily get at Lupin."

"It will take long."

"No matter! I have dropped all my cases. This is the only one I care about. Between Lupin and me, it's a fight—a fight to the death."

He spoke these words with a sort of ferocity that betrayed all his bitterness at the humiliations which he had undergone, all his fierce hatred of the great enemy who had tricked him so cruelly.

"Go away, now," he whispered, "we are observed. It's dangerous. But mark my words: on the day when Lupin and I meet face to face, it will be—it will be tragic."

Beautrelet felt quite reassured on leaving Shears: he need not fear that the Englishman would gain on him. And here was one more proof which this chance interview had brought him: the road from the Havre to Lille passes through Dieppe! It is the great seaside road of the Caux country, the coast road commanding the Channel cliffs! And it was on a farm near this road that Victoire was installed, Victoire, that is to say, Lupin, for one did not move without the other, the master without the blindly devoted servant.

"I'm burning! I'm burning!" he repeated to himself. "Whenever circumstances bring me a new element of information, it confirms my supposition. On the one hand, I have the absolute certainty of the banks of the Seine; on the other, the certainty of the National Road. The two means of communication meet at the Havre, the town of Francis I., the town of the secret. The boundaries are contracting. The Caux country is not large; and, even so, I have only the western portion of the Caux country to search."

He set to work with renewed stubbornness:

"Anything that Lupin has found," he kept on saying to himself, "there is no reason for my not finding."

Certainly, Lupin had some great advantage over him, perhaps a thorough acquaintance with the country, a precise knowledge of the local legends, or less than that, a memory: invaluable advantages these, for he, Beautrelet, knew nothing, was totally ignorant of the country, which he had first visited at the time of the Ambrumesy burglary and then only rapidly, without lingering.

But what did it matter? Though he had to devote ten years of his life to this investigation, he would carry it to a successful issue. Lupin was there. He could see him, he could feel him there. He expected to come

---

[7] Arsene Lupin, play in four acts, by Maurice Leblanc and Francis de Croisset

upon him at the next turn of the road, on the skirt of the next wood, outside the next village. And, though continually disappointed, he seemed to find in each disappointment a fresh reason for persisting.

Often, he would fling himself on the slope by the roadside and plunge into wild examination of the copy of the document which he always carried on him, a copy, that is to say, with vowels taking the place of the figures:

    e.a.a..e..e.a..a..
    a...e.e..e.oi.e..e.
    .ou..e.o...e.e.o..e
    ai.ui..e..eu.e

Often, also, according to his habit, he would lie down flat on his stomach in the tall grass and think for hours. He had time enough. The future belonged to him.

With wonderful patience, he tramped from the Seine to the sea, and from the sea to the Seine, going gradually farther, retracing his steps and never quitting the ground until, theoretically speaking, there was not a chance left of gathering the smallest particle upon it.

He studied and explored Montivilliers and Saint-Romani and Octeville and Gonneville and Criquetot.

At night, he knocked at the peasants' doors and asked for a lodging. After dinner, they smoked together and chatted. He made them tell him the stories which they told one another on the long winter nights. And he never omitted to insinuate, slily:

"What about the Needle? The legend of the Hollow Needle? Don't you know that?"

"Upon my word, I don't—never heard of it—"

"Just think—an old wives' tale—something that has to do with a needle. An enchanted needle, perhaps.—I don't know—"

Nothing. No legend, no recollection. And the next morning he walked blithely away again.

One day, he passed through the pretty village of Saint-Jouin, which overlooks the sea, and descending among the chaos of rocks that have slipped from cliffs, he climbed up to the tableland and went in the direction of the dry valley of Bruneval, Cap d'Antifer and the little creek of Belle-Plage. He was walking gaily and lightly, feeling a little tired, perhaps, but glad to be alive, so glad, even, that he forgot Lupin and the mystery of the Hollow Needle and Victoire and Shears, and interested himself in the sight of nature: the blue sky, the great emerald sea, all glittering in the sunshine.

Some straight slopes and remains of brick walls, in which he seemed to recognize the vestiges of a Roman camp, interested him. Then his eyes fell upon a sort of little castle, built in imitation of an ancient fort, with cracked turrets and Gothic windows. It stood on a jagged, rugged, rising promontory, almost detached from the cliff. A barred gate, flanked by iron hand-rails and bristling spikes, guarded the narrow passage.

Beautrelet succeeded in climbing over, not without some difficulty. Over the pointed door, which was closed with an old rusty lock, he read the words:

FORT DE FREFOSSE

He did not attempt to enter, but, turning to the right, after going down a little slope, he embarked upon a path that ran along a ridge of land furnished with a wooden handrail. Right at the end was a cave of very small dimensions, forming a sort of watch-tower at the point of the rock in which it was hollowed out, a rock falling abruptly into the sea.

There was just room to stand up in the middle of the cave. Multitudes of inscriptions crossed one another on the walls. An almost square hole, cut in the stone, opened like a dormer window on the land side, exactly opposite Fort Frefosse, the crenellated top of which appeared at thirty or forty yards' distance.

Beautrelet threw off his knapsack and sat down. He had had a hard and tiring day. He fell asleep for a little. Then the cool wind that blew inside the cave woke him up. He sat for a few minutes without moving, absent-minded, vague-eyed. He tried to reflect, to recapture his still torpid thoughts. And, as he recovered his consciousness, he was on the point of rising, when he received the impression that his eyes, suddenly fixed, suddenly wide-open, saw—

A thrill shook him from head to foot. His hands clutched convulsively and he felt the beads of perspiration forming at the roots of his hair:

"No, no," he stammered. "It's a dream, an hallucination. Let's look: it's not possible!"

He plunged down on his knees and stooped over. Two huge letters, each perhaps a foot long, appeared cut in relief in the granite of the floor. Those two letters, clumsily, but plainly carved, with their corners rounded and their surface smoothed by the wear and tear of centuries, were a D and an F.

D and F! Oh, bewildering miracle! D and F: just two letters of the document! Oh, Beautrelet had no need to consult it to bring before his mind that group of letters in the fourth line, the line of the measurements and indications! He knew them well! They were inscribed for all time at the back of his pupils, encrusted for good and all in the very substance of his brain!

He rose to his feet, went down the steep road, climbed back along the old fort, hung on to the spikes of the rail again, in order to pass, and walked briskly toward a shepherd whose flock was grazing some way off on a dip in the tableland:

"That cave, over there—that cave—"

His lips trembled and he tried to find the words that would not come. The shepherd looked at him in amazement. At last, Isidore repeated:

"Yes, that cave—over there—to the right of the fort. Has it a name?"

"Yes, I should think so. All the Etretat folk like to call it the Demoiselles."

"What?—What?—What's that you say?"

"Why, of course—it's the Chambre des Demoiselles."

Isidore felt like flying at his throat, as though all the truth lived in that man and he hoped to get it from him at one swoop, to tear it from him.

The Demoiselles! One of the words, one of the only three known words of the document!

A whirlwind of madness shook Beautrelet where he stood. And it rose all around him, blew upon him like a tempestuous squall that came from the sea, that came from the land, that came from every direction and whipped him with great lashes of the truth.

He understood. The document appeared to him in its real sense. The Chambre des Demoiselles—Etretat—

"That's it," he thought, his brain filled with light, "it must be that. But why didn't I guess earlier?"

He said to the shepherd, in a low voice:

"That will do—go away—you can go—thank you."

The man, not knowing what to think, whistled to his dog and went.

Left alone, Beautrelet returned to the fort. He had almost passed it when, suddenly, he dropped to the ground and lay cowering against a piece of wall. And, wringing his hands, he thought:

"I must be mad! If 'he' were to see me! Or his accomplices! I've been moving about for an hour—!"

He did not stir another limb.

The sun went down. Little by little, the night mingled with the day, blurring the outline of things.

Then, with little imperceptible movements, flat on his stomach, gliding, crawling, he crept along one of the points of the promontory to the extreme edge of the cliff.

He reached it. Stretching out his hands, he pushed aside some tufts of grass and his head appeared over the precipice.

Opposite him, almost level with the cliff, in the open sea rose an enormous rock, over eighty yards high, a colossal obelisk, standing straight on its granite base, which showed at the surface of the water, and tapering toward the summit, like the giant tooth of a monster of the deep. White with the dirty gray white of the cliff, the awful monolith was streaked with horizontal lines marked by flint and displaying the slow work of the centuries, which had heaped alternate layers of lime and pebble-stone one atop of the other.

Here and there, a fissure, a break; and, wherever these occurred, a scrap of earth, with grass and leaves.

And all this was mighty and solid and formidable, with the look of an indestructible thing against which the furious assault of the waves and storms could not prevail. And it was definite and permanent and grand, despite the grandeur of the cliffy rampart that commanded it, despite the immensity of the space in which it stood.

Beautrelet's nails dug into the soil like the claws of an animal ready to leap upon its prey. His eyes penetrated the wrinkled texture of the rock, penetrated its skin, so it seemed to him, its very flesh. He touched it, felt it, took cognizance and possession of it, absorbed and assimilated it.

The horizon turned crimson with all the flames of the vanished sun; and long, red clouds, set motionless in the sky, formed glorious landscapes, fantastic lagoons, fiery plains, forests of gold, lakes of blood, a whole glowing and peaceful phantasmagoria.

The blue of the sky grew darker. Venus shone with a marvelous brightness; then other stars lit up, timid as yet.

And Beautrelet suddenly closed his eyes and convulsively pressed his folded arms to his forehead. Over there—oh, he felt as though he would die for joy, so great was the cruel emotion that wrung his heart!—over there, almost at the top of the Needle of Etretat, a little below the extreme point round which the sea-mews fluttered, a thread of smoke came filtering through a crevice, as though from an invisible chimney, a thread of smoke rose in slow spirals in the calm air of the twilight.

IX. OPEN, SESAME!

The Etretat Needle was hollow!

Was it a natural phenomenon, an excavation produced by internal cataclysms or by the imperceptible action of the rushing sea and the soaking rain? Or was it a superhuman work executed by human beings, Gauls, Celts, prehistoric men?

These, no doubt, were insoluble questions; and what did it matter? The essence of the thing was contained in this fact: The Needle was hollow. At forty or fifty yards from that imposing arch which is called the Porte d'Aval and which shoots out from the top of the cliff, like the colossal branch of a tree, to take root in the submerged rocks, stands an immense limestone cone; and this cone is no more than the shell of a pointed cap poised upon the empty waters!

A prodigious revelation! After Lupin, here was Beautrelet discovering the key to the great riddle that had loomed over more than twenty centuries! A key of supreme importance to whoever possessed it in the days of old, in those distant times when hordes of barbarians rode through and overran the old world! A magic key that opens the cyclopean cavern to whole tribes fleeing before the enemy! A mysterious key that guards the door of the most inviolable shelter! An enchanted key that gives power and ensures preponderance!

Because he knows this key, Caesar is able to subdue Gaul. Because they know it, the Normans force their sway upon the country and, from there, later, backed by that support, conquer the neighboring island, conquer Sicily, conquer the East, conquer the new world!

Masters of the secret, the Kings of England lord it over France, humble her, dismember her, have themselves crowned at Paris. They lose the secret; and the rout begins.

Masters of the secret, the Kings of France push back and overstep the narrow limits of their dominion, gradually founding a great nation and radiating with glory and power. They forget it or know not how to use it; and death, exile, ruin follow.

An invisible kingdom, in mid-water and at ten fathoms from land! An unknown fortress, taller than the towers of Notre Dame and built upon a granite foundation larger than a public square! What strength and what security! From Paris to the sea, by the Seine. There, the Havre, the new town, the necessary town. And, sixteen miles thence, the Hollow Needle, the impregnable sanctuary!

It is a sanctuary and also a stupendous hiding-place. All the treasures of the kings, increasing from century to century, all the gold of France, all that they extort from the people, all that they snatch from the clergy, all the booty gathered on the battle-fields of Europe lie heaped up in the royal cave. Old Merovingian gold sous, glittering crown-pieces, doubloons, ducats, florins, guineas; and the precious stones and the diamonds; and all the jewels and all the ornaments: everything is there. Who could discover it? Who could ever learn the impenetrable secret of the Needle? Nobody.

And Lupin becomes that sort of really disproportionate being whom we know, that miracle incapable of explanation so long as the truth remains in the shadow. Infinite though the resources of his genius be, they cannot suffice for the mad struggle which he maintains against society. He needs other, more material resources. He needs a sure place of retreat, he needs the certainty of impunity, the peace that allows of the execution of his plans.

Without the Hollow Needle, Lupin is incomprehensible, a myth, a character in a novel, having no connection with reality.

Master of the secret—and of such a secret!—he becomes simply a man like another, but gifted with the power of wielding in a superior manner the extraordinary weapon with which destiny has endowed him.

So the Needle was hollow.

It remained to discover how one obtained access to it.

From the sea, obviously. There must be, on the side of the offing, some fissure where boats could land at certain hours of the tide.

But on the side of the land?

Beautrelet lay until ten o'clock at night hanging over the precipice, with his eyes riveted on the shadowy mass formed by the pyramid, thinking and pondering with all the concentrated effort of his mind.

Then he went down to Etretat, selected the cheapest hotel, dined, went up to his room and unfolded the document.

It was the merest child's play to him now to establish its exact meaning. He at once saw that the three vowels of the word Etretat occurred in the first line, in their proper order and at the necessary intervals. This first line now read as follows:

e . a . a .. etretat . a ..

What words could come before Etretat? Words, no doubt, that referred to the position of the Needle with regard to the town. Now the Needle stood on the left, on the west—He ransacked his memory and, recollecting that westerly winds are called vents d'aval on the coast and that the nearest porte was known as the Porte d'Aval, he wrote down:

"En aval d'Etretat . a .."

The second line was that containing the word Demoiselles and, at once seeing, in front of that word, the series of all the vowels that form part of the words la chambre des, he noted the two phrases:

"En aval d'Etretat. La Chambre des Demoiselles."

The third line gave him more trouble; and it was not until some groping that, remembering the position, near the Chambre des Demoiselles, of the Fort de Frefosse, he ended by almost completely reconstructing the document:

"En aval d'Etretat. La Chambre des Demoiselles. Sous le Fort de

Frefosse. L'Aiguille creuse."

These were the four great formulas, the essential and general formulas which you had to know. By means of them, you turned en aval, that is to say, below or west of Etretat, entered the Chambre des Demoiselles, in all probability passed under Fort Frefosse and thus arrived at the Needle.

How? By means of the indications and measurements that constituted the fourth line: [a drawing of an outline of paper with writing and drawing on it—numbers, dots, some letters, signs and symbols...]

These were evidently the more special formulas to enable you to find the outlet through which you made your way and the road that led to the Needle.

Beautrelet at once presumed—and his surmise was no more than the logical consequence of the document—that, if there really was a direct communication between the land and the obelisk of the Needle, the underground passage must start from the Chambre des Demoiselles, pass under Fort Frefosse, descend perpendicularly the three hundred feet of cliff and, by means of a tunnel contrived under the rocks of the sea, end at the Hollow Needle.

Which was the entrance to the underground passage? Did not the two letters D and F, so plainly cut, point to it and admit to it, with the aid, perhaps, of some ingenious piece of mechanism?

The whole of the next morning, Isidore strolled about Etretat and chatted with everybody he met, in order to try and pick up useful information. At last, in the afternoon, he went up the cliff. Disguised as a sailor, he had made himself still younger and, in a pair of trousers too short for him and a fishing jersey, he looked a mere scape-grace of twelve or thirteen.

As soon as he entered the cave, he knelt down before the letters. Here a disappointment awaited him. It was no use his striking them, pushing them, manipulating them in every way: they refused to move. And it was not long, in fact, before he became aware that they were really unable to move and that, therefore, they controlled no mechanism.

And yet—and yet they must mean something! Inquiries which he had made in the village went to show that no one had ever been able to explain their existence and that the Abbe Cochet, in his valuable little book on Etretat,[8] had also tried in vain to solve this little puzzle. But Isidore knew what the learned Norman archaeologist did not know, namely, that the same two letters figured in the document, on the line containing the indications. Was it a chance coincidence: Impossible. Well, then—?

An idea suddenly occurred to him, an idea so reasonable, so simple that he did not doubt its correctness for a second. Were not that D and that F the initials of the two most important words in the document, the words that represented—together with the Needle—the essential stations on the road to be followed: the Chambre des Demoiselles and Fort Frefosse: D for Demoiselles, F for Frefosse: the connection was too remarkable to be a mere accidental fact.

In that case, the problem stood thus: the two letters D F represent the relation that exists between the Chambre des Demoiselles and Fort Frefosse, the single letter D, which begins the line, represents the Demoiselles, that is to say, the cave in which you have to begin by taking up your position, and the single letter F, placed in the middle of the line, represents Frefosse, that is to say, the probable entrance to the underground passage.

Between these various signs, are two more: first, a sort of irregular rectangle, marked with a stripe in the left bottom corner, and, next, the figure 19, signs which obviously indicate to those inside the cave the means of penetrating beneath the fort.

The shape of this rectangle puzzled Isidore. Was there around him, on the walls of the cave, or at any rate within reach of his eyes, an inscription, anything whatever, affecting a rectangular shape?

He looked for a long time and was on the point of abandoning that particular scent when his eyes fell upon the little opening, pierced in the rock, that acted as a window to the chamber.

Now the edges of this opening just formed a rectangle: corrugated, uneven, clumsy, but still a rectangle; and Beautrelet at once saw that, by placing his two feet on the D and the F carved in the stone floor—and this explained the stroke that surmounted the two letters in the document—he found himself at the exact height of the window!

He took up his position in this place and gazed out. The window looking landward, as we know, he saw, first, the path that connected the cave with the land, a path hung between two precipices; and, next, he caught sight of the foot of the hillock on which the fort stood. To try and see the fort, Beautrelet leaned over to the left and it was then that he understood the meaning of the curved stripe, the comma that marked the left bottom corner in the document: at the bottom on the left-hand side of the window, a piece of flint projected and the end of it was curved like a claw. It suggested a regular shooter's mark. And, when a man applied his eye to this mark, he saw cut out, on the slope of the mound facing him, a restricted surface of land occupied almost entirely by an old brick wall, a remnant of the original Fort Frefosse or of the old Roman oppidum built on this spot.

Beautrelet ran to this piece of wall, which was, perhaps, ten yards long. It was covered with grass and plants. There was no indication of any kind visible. And yet that figure 19?

He returned to the cave, took from his pocket a ball of string and a tape-measure, tied the string to the flint corner, fastened a pebble at the nineteenth metre and flung it toward the land side. The pebble at most reached the end of the path.

"Idiot that I am!" thought Beautrelet. "Who reckoned by metres in those days? The figure 19 means 19 fathoms[9] or nothing!"

Having made the calculation, he ran out the twine, made a knot and felt about on the piece of wall for the exact and necessarily one point at which the knot, formed at 37 metres from the window of the Demoiselles, should touch the Frefosse wall. In a few moments, the point of contact was established. With his free hand, he moved aside the leaves of mullein that had grown in the interstices. A cry escaped him. The knot, which he held pressed down with his fore-finger, was in the centre of a little cross carved in relief on a brick. And the sign that followed on the figure 19 in the document was a cross!

It needed all his will-power to control the excitement with which he was overcome. Hurriedly, with convulsive fingers, he clutched the cross and, pressing upon it, turned it as he would have turned the spokes of a wheel. The brick heaved. He redoubled his effort; it moved no further. Then, without turning, he pressed harder. He at once felt the brick give way. And, suddenly, there was the click of a bolt that is released, the

---

[8] Les Origines d'Etretat. The Abbe Cochet seems to conclude, in the end, that the two letters are the initials of a passer-by. The revelations now made prove the fallacy of the theory.
[9] The toise, or fathom, measured 1.949 metres.—Translator's Note

sound of a lock opening and, on the right of the brick, to the width of about a yard, the wall swung round on a pivot and revealed the orifice of an underground passage.

Like a madman, Beautrelet seized the iron door in which the bricks were sealed, pulled it back, violently and closed it. Astonishment, delight, the fear of being surprised convulsed his face so as to render it unrecognizable. He beheld the awful vision of all that had happened there, in front of that door, during twenty centuries; of all those people, initiated into the great secret, who had penetrated through that issue: Celts, Gauls, Romans, Normans, Englishmen, Frenchmen, barons, dukes, kings—and, after all of them, Arsene Lupin—and, after Lupin, himself, Beautrelet. He felt that his brain was slipping away from him. His eyelids fluttered. He fell fainting and rolled to the bottom of the slope, to the very edge of the precipice.

His task was done, at least the task which he was able to accomplish alone, with his unaided resources.

That evening, he wrote a long letter to the chief of the detective service, giving a faithful account of the results of his investigations and revealing the secret of the Hollow Needle. He asked for assistance to complete his work and gave his address.

While waiting for the reply, he spent two consecutive nights in the Chambre des Demoiselles. He spent them overcome with fear, his nerves shaken with a terror which was increased by the sounds of the night. At every moment, he thought he saw shadows approach in his direction. People knew of his presence in the cave—they were coming—they were murdering him!

His eyes, however, staring madly before them, sustained by all the power of his will, clung to the piece of wall.

On the first night, nothing stirred; but, on the second, by the light of the stars and a slender crescent-moon, he saw the door open and figures emerge from the darkness: he counted two, three, four, five of them.

It seemed to him that those five men were carrying fairly large loads. He followed them for a little way. They cut straight across the fields to the Havre road; and he heard the sound of a motor car driving away.

He retraced his steps, skirting a big farm. But, at the turn of the road that ran beside it, he had only just time to scramble up a slope and hide behind some trees. More men passed—four, five men—all carrying packages. And, two minutes later, another motor snorted.

This time, he had not the strength to return to his post; and he went back to bed.

When he woke and had finished dressing, the hotel waiter brought him a letter. He opened it. It contained Ganimard's card.

"At last!" cried Beautrelet, who, after so hard a campaign, was really feeling the need of a comrade-in-arms.

He ran downstairs with outstretched hands. Ganimard took them, looked at him for a moment and said:

"You're a fine fellow, my lad!"

"Pooh!" he said. "Luck has served me."

"There's no such thing as luck with 'him,'" declared the inspector, who always spoke of Lupin in a solemn tone and without mentioning his name.

He sat down:

"So we've got him!"

"Just as we've had him twenty times over," said Beautrelet, laughing.

"Yes, but to-day—"

"To-day, of course, the case is different. We know his retreat, his stronghold, which means, when all is said, that Lupin is Lupin. He can escape. The Etretat Needle cannot."

"Why do you suppose that he will escape?" asked Ganimard, anxiously.

"Why do you suppose that he requires to escape?" replied Beautrelet. "There is nothing to prove that he is in the Needle at present. Last night, eleven of his men left it. He may be one of the eleven."

Ganimard reflected:

"You are right. The great thing is the Hollow Needle. For the rest, let us hope that chance will favor us. And now, let us talk."

He resumed his serious voice, his self-important air and said:

"My dear Beautrelet, I have orders to recommend you to observe the most absolute discretion in regard to this matter."

"Orders from whom?" asked Beautrelet, jestingly. "The prefect of police?"

"Higher than that."

"The prime minister?"

"Higher."

"Whew!"

Ganimard lowered his voice:

"Beautrelet, I was at the Elysee last night. They look upon this matter as a state secret of the utmost gravity. There are serious reasons for concealing the existence of this citadel—reasons of military strategy, in particular. It might become a revictualling centre, a magazine for new explosives, for lately-invented projectiles, for anything of that sort: the secret arsenal of France, in fact."

"But how can they hope to keep a secret like this? In the old days, one man alone held it: the king. To-day, already, there are a good few of us who know it, without counting Lupin's gang."

"Still, if we gained only ten years', only five years' silence! Those five years may be—the saving of us."

"But, in order to capture this citadel, this future arsenal, it will have to be attacked, Lupin must be dislodged. And all this cannot be done without noise."

"Of course, people will guess something, but they won't know. Besides, we can but try."

"All right. What's your plan?"

"Here it is, in two words. To begin with, you are not Isidore Beautrelet and there's no question of Arsene Lupin either. You are and you remain a small boy of Etretat, who, while strolling about the place, caught some fellows coming out of an underground passage. This makes you suspect the existence of a flight of steps which cuts through the cliff from top to bottom."

"Yes, there are several of those flights of steps along the coast. For instance, to the right of Etretat, opposite Benouville, they showed me the Devil's Staircase, which every bather knows. And I say nothing of the three or four tunnels used by the fishermen."

"So you will guide me and one-half of my men. I shall enter alone, or accompanied, that remains to be seen. This much is certain, that the attack must be delivered that way. If Lupin is not in the Needle, we shall fix up a trap in which he will be caught sooner or later. If he is there—"

"If he is there, he will escape from the Needle by the other side, the side overlooking the sea."

"In that case, he will at once be arrested by the other half of my men."

"Yes, but if, as I presume, you choose a moment when the sea is at low ebb, leaving the base of the Needle uncovered, the chase will be public, because it will take place before all the men and women fishing for mussels, shrimps and shell-fish who swarm on the rocks round about."

"That is why I just mean to select the time when the sea is full."

"In that case, he will make off in a boat."

"Ah, but I shall have a dozen fishing-smacks, each of which will be commanded by one of my men, and we shall collar him—"

"If he doesn't slip through your dozen smacks, like a fish through the meshes."

"All right, then I'll sink him."

"The devil you will! Shall you have guns?"

"Why, of course! There's a torpedo-boat at the Havre at this moment. A telegram from me will bring her to the Needle at the appointed hour."

"How proud Lupin will be! A torpedo-boat! Well, M. Ganimard, I see that you have provided for everything. We have only to go ahead. When do we deliver the assault?"

"To-morrow."

"At night?"

"No, by daylight, at the flood-tide, as the clock strikes ten in the morning."

"Capital."

Under his show of gaiety, Beautrelet concealed a real anguish of mind. He did not sleep until the morning, but lay pondering over the most impracticable schemes, one after the other.

Ganimard had left him in order to go to Yport, six or seven miles from Etretat, where, for prudence's sake, he had told his men to meet him, and where he chartered twelve fishing smacks, with the ostensible object of taking soundings along the coast.

At a quarter to ten, escorted by a body of twelve stalwart men, he met Isidore at the foot of the road that goes up the cliff.

At ten o'clock exactly, they reached the skirt of wall. It was the decisive moment.

At ten o'clock exactly.

"Why, what's the matter with you, Beautrelet?" jeered Ganimard. "You're quite green in the face!"

"It's as well you can't see yourself, Ganimard," the boy retorted. "One would think your last hour had come!"

They both had to sit down and Ganimard swallowed a few mouthfuls of rum.

"It's not funk," he said, "but, by Jove, this is an exciting business! Each time that I'm on the point of catching him, it takes me like that in the pit of the stomach. A dram of rum?"

"No."

"And if you drop behind?"

"That will mean that I'm dead."

"B-r-r-r! However, we'll see. And now, open, sesame! No danger of our being observed, I suppose?"

"No. The Needle is not so high as the cliff, and, besides, there's a bend in the ground where we are."

Beautrelet went to the wall and pressed upon the brick. The bolt was released and the underground passage came in sight. By the gleam of the lanterns which they lit, they saw that it was cut in the shape of a vault and that both the vaulting and the floor itself were entirely covered with bricks.

They walked for a few seconds and, suddenly, a staircase appeared. Beautrelet counted forty-five brick steps, which the slow action of many footsteps had worn away in the middle.

"Blow!" said Ganimard, holding his head and stopping suddenly, as though he had knocked against something.

"What is it?"

"A door."

"Bother!" muttered Beautrelet, looking at it. "And not an easy one to break down either. It's just a solid block of iron."

"We are done," said Ganimard. "There's not even a lock to it."

"Exactly. That's what gives me hope."

"Why?"

"A door is made to open; and, as this one has no lock, that means that there is a secret way of opening it."

"And, as we don't know the secret—"

"I shall know it in a minute."

"How?"

"By means of the document. The fourth line has no other object but to solve each difficulty as and when it crops up. And the solution is comparatively easy, because it's not written with a view to throwing searchers off the scent, but to assisting them."

"Comparatively easy! I don't agree with you," cried Ganimard, who had unfolded the document. "The number 44 and a triangle with a dot in it: that doesn't tell us much!"

"Yes, yes, it does! Look at the door. You see it's strengthened, at each corner, with a triangular slab of iron; and the slabs are fixed with big nails. Take the left-hand bottom slab and work the nail in the corner: I'll lay ten to one we've hit the mark."

"You've lost your bet," said Ganimard, after trying.

"Then the figure 44 must mean—"

In a low voice, reflecting as he spoke, Beautrelet continued:

"Let me see—Ganimard and I are both standing on the bottom step of the staircase—there are 45. Why 45, when the figure in the document is 44? A coincidence? No. In all this business, there is no such thing as a coincidence, at least not an involuntary one. Ganimard, be so good as to move one step higher up. That's it, don't leave this forty-fourth step. And now I will work the iron nail. And the trick's done, or I'll eat my boots!"

The heavy door turned on its hinges. A fairly spacious cavern appeared before their eyes.

"We must be exactly under Fort Frefosse," said Beautrelet. "We have passed through the different earthy layers by now. There will be no more brick. We are in the heart of the solid limestone."

The room was dimly lit by a shaft of daylight that came from the other end. Going up to it, they saw that it was a fissure in the cliff, contrived in a projecting wall and forming a sort of observatory. In front of them, at a distance of fifty yards, the impressive mass of the Needle loomed from the waves. On the right, quite close, was the arched buttress of the Porte d'Aval and, on the left, very far away, closing the graceful curve of a large inlet, another rocky gateway, more imposing still, was cut out of the cliff; the Manneporte,[* Magna porta] which was so wide and tall that a three-master could have passed through it with all sail set. Behind and everywhere, the sea.

"I don't see our little fleet," said Beautrelet.

"I know," said Ganimard. "The Porte d'Aval hides the whole of the coast of Etretat and Yport. But look, over there, in the offing, that black line, level with the water—"

"Well?"

"That's our fleet of war, Torpedo-boat No. 25. With her there, Lupin is welcome to break loose—if he wants to study the landscape at the bottom of the sea."

A baluster marked the entrance to the staircase, near the fissure. They started on their way down. From time to time, a little window pierced the wall of the cliff; and, each time, they caught sight of the Needle, whose mass seemed to them to grow more and more colossal.

A little before reaching high-water level, the windows ceased and all was dark.

Isidore counted the steps aloud. At the three hundred and fifty-eight, they emerged into a wider passage, which was barred by another iron door strengthened with slabs and nails.

"We know all about this," said Beautrelet. "The document gives us 357 and a triangle dotted on the right. We have only to repeat the performance."

The second door obeyed like the first. A long, a very long tunnel appeared, lit up at intervals by the gleam of a lantern swung from the vault. The walls oozed moisture and drops of water fell to the ground, so that, to make walking easier a regular pavement of planks had been laid from end to end.

"We are passing under the sea," said Beautrelet. "Are you coming, Ganimard?"

Without replying, the inspector ventured into the tunnel, followed the wooden foot-plank and stopped before a lantern, which he took down.

"The utensils may date back to the Middle Ages, but the lighting is modern," he said. "Our friends use incandescent mantles."

He continued his way. The tunnel ended in another and a larger cave, with, on the opposite side, the first steps of a staircase that led upward.

"It's the ascent of the Needle beginning," said Ganimard. "This is more serious."

But one of his men called him:

"There's another flight here, sir, on the left."

And, immediately afterward, they discovered a third, on the right.

"The deuce!" muttered the inspector. "This complicates matters. If we go by this way, they'll make tracks by that."

"Shall we separate?" asked Beautrelet.

"No, no—that would mean weakening ourselves. It would be better for one of us to go ahead and scout."

"I will, if you like—"

"Very well, Beautrelet, you go. I will remain with my men—then there will be no fear of anything. There may be other roads through the cliff than that by which we came and several roads also through the Needle. But it is certain that, between the cliff and the Needle, there is no communication except the tunnel.

Therefore they must pass through this cave. And so I shall stay here till you come back. Go ahead, Beautrelet, and be prudent: at the least alarm, scoot back again."

Isidore disappeared briskly up the middle staircase. At the thirtieth step, a door, an ordinary wooden door, stopped him. He seized the handle turned it. The door was not locked.

He entered a room that seemed to him very low owing to its immense size. Lit by powerful lamps and supported by squat pillars, with long vistas showing between them, it had nearly the same dimensions as the Needle itself. It was crammed with packing cases and miscellaneous objects—pieces of furniture, oak settees, chests, credence-tables, strong-boxes—a whole confused heap of the kind which one sees in the basement of an old curiosity shop.

On his right and left, Beautrelet perceived the wells of two staircases, the same, no doubt, that started from the cave below. He could easily have gone down, therefore, and told Ganimard. But a new flight of stairs led upward in front of him and he had the curiosity to pursue his investigations alone.

Thirty more steps. A door and then a room, not quite so large as the last, Beautrelet thought. And again, opposite him, an ascending flight of stairs.

Thirty steps more. A door. A smaller room.

Beautrelet grasped the plan of the works executed inside the Needle. It was a series or rooms placed one above the other and, therefore, gradually decreasing in size. They all served as store-rooms.

In the fourth, there was no lamp. A little light filtered in through clefts in the walls and Beautrelet saw the sea some thirty feet below him.

At that moment, he felt himself so far from Ganimard that a certain anguish began to take hold of him and he had to master his nerves lest he should take to his heels. No danger threatened him, however, and the silence around him was even so great that he asked himself whether the whole Needle had not been abandoned by Lupin and his confederates.

"I shall not go beyond the next floor," he said to himself.

Thirty stairs again and a door. This door was lighter in construction and modern in appearance. He pushed it open gently, quite prepared for flight. There was no one there. But the room differed from the others in its purpose. There were hangings on the walls, rugs on the floor. Two magnificent sideboards, laden with gold and silver plate, stood facing each other. The little windows contrived in the deep, narrow cleft were furnished with glass panes.

In the middle of the room was a richly-decked table, with a lace-edged cloth, dishes of fruits and cakes, champagne in decanters and flowers, heaps of flowers.

Three places were laid around the table.

Beautrelet walked up. On the napkins were cards with the names of the party. He read first:

"Arsene Lupin."

"Mme. Arsene Lupin."

He took up the third card and started back with surprise. It bore his own name:

"Isidore Beautrelet!"

X. THE TREASURES OF THE KINGS OF FRANCE

A curtain was drawn back.

"Good morning, my dear Beautrelet, you're a little late. Lunch was fixed for twelve. However, it's only a few minutes—but what's the matter? Don't you know me? Have I changed so much?"

In the course of his fight with Lupin, Beautrelet had met with many surprises and he was still prepared, at the moment of the final catastrophe, to experience any number of further emotions; but the shock which he received this time was utterly unexpected. It was not astonishment, but stupefaction, terror. The man who stood before him, the man whom the brutal force of events compelled him to look upon as Arsene Lupin, was—Valmeras! Valmeras, the owner of the Chateau de l'Aiguille! Valmeras, the very man to whom he had applied for assistance against Arsene Lupin! Valmeras, his companion on the expedition to Crozant! Valmeras, the plucky friend who had made Raymonde's escape possible by felling one of Lupin's accomplices, or pretending to fell him, in the dusk of the great hall! And Valmeras was Lupin!

"You—you—So it's you!" he stammered.

"Why not?" exclaimed Lupin. "Did you think that you knew me for good and all because you had seen me in the guise of a clergyman or under the features of M. Massiban? Alas, when a man selects the position in society which I occupy, he must needs make use of his little social gifts! If Lupin were not able to change himself, at will, into a minister of the Church of England or a member of the Academy of Inscriptions and

Belles-Lettres, it would be a bad lookout for Lupin! Now Lupin, the real Lupin, is here before you, Beautrelet! Take a good look at him."

"But then—if it's you—then—Mademoiselle—"

"Yes, Beautrelet, as you say—"

He again drew back the hanging, beckoned and announced:

"Mme. Arsene Lupin."

"Ah," murmured the lad, confounded in spite of everything, "Mlle. de Saint-Veran!"

"No, no," protested Lupin. "Mme. Arsene Lupin, or rather, if you prefer, Mme. Louis Valmeras, my wedded wife, married to me in accordance with the strictest forms of law; and all thanks to you, my dear Beautrelet."

He held out his hand to him.

"All my acknowledgements—and no ill will on your side, I trust?"

Strange to say, Beautrelet felt no ill will at all, no sense of humiliation, no bitterness. He realized so strongly the immense superiority of his adversary that he did not blush at being beaten by him. He pressed the offered hand.

"Luncheon is served, ma'am."

A butler had placed a tray of dishes on the table.

"You must excuse us, Beautrelet: my chef is away and we can only give you a cold lunch."

Beautrelet felt very little inclined to eat. He sat down, however, and was enormously interested in Lupin's attitude. How much exactly did he know? Was he aware of the danger he was running? Was he ignorant of the presence of Ganimard and his men?

And Lupin continued:

"Yes, thanks to you, my dear friend. Certainly, Raymonde and I loved each other from the first. Just so, my boy—Raymonde's abduction, her imprisonment, were mere humbug: we loved each other. But neither she nor I, when we were free to love, would allow a casual bond at the mercy of chance, to be formed between us. The position, therefore, was hopeless for Lupin. Fortunately, it ceased to be so if I resumed my identity as the Louis Valmeras that I had been from a child. It was then that I conceived the idea, as you refused to relinquish your quest and had found the Chateau de l'Aiguille, of profiting by your obstinacy."

"And my silliness."

"Pooh! Any one would have been caught as you were!"

"So you were really able to succeed because I screened you and assisted you?"

"Of course! How could any one suspect Valmeras of being Lupin, when Valmeras was Beautrelet's friend and after Valmeras had snatched from Lupin's clutches the girl whom Lupin loved? And how charming it was! Such delightful memories! The expedition to Crozant! The bouquets we found! My pretended love letter to Raymonde! And, later, the precautions which I, Valmeras, had to take against myself, Lupin, before my marriage! And the night of your great banquet, Beautrelet, when you fainted in my arms! Oh, what memories!"

There was a pause. Beautrelet watched Raymonde. She had listened to Lupin without saying a word and looked at him with eyes in which he read love, passion and something else besides, something which the lad could not define, a sort of anxious embarrassment and a vague sadness. But Lupin turned his eyes upon her and she gave him an affectionate smile. Their hands met over the table.

"What do you say to the way I have arranged my little home, Beautrelet?" cried Lupin. "There's a style about it, isn't there? I don't pretend that it's as comfortable as it might be. And yet, some have been quite satisfied with it; and not the least of mankind, either!—Look at the list of distinguished people who have owned the Needle in their time and who thought it an honor to leave a mark of their sojourn."

On the walls, one below the other, were carved the following names:

JULIUS CAESAR

CHARLEMAGNE ROLLO

WILLIAM THE CONQUEROR

RICHARD COEUR-DE-LEON

LOUIS XI.

FRANCIS I.

HENRY IV.

LOUIS XIV.

ARSENE LUPIN

"Whose name will figure after ours?" he continued. "Alas, the list is closed! From Caesar to Lupin—and there it ends. Soon the nameless mob will come to visit the strange citadel. And to think that, but for Lupin, all this would have remained for ever unknown to men! Ah Beautrelet, what a feeling of pride was mine on the day when I first set foot on this abandoned soil. To have found the lost secret and become its master, its sole master! To inherit such an inheritance! To live in the Needle, after all those kings!—"

He was interrupted by a gesture of his wife's. She seemed greatly agitated.

"There is a noise," she said. "Underneath us.—You can hear it."

"It's the lapping of the water," said Lupin.

"No, indeed it's not. I know the sound of the waves. This is something different."

"What would you have it be, darling?" said Lupin, smiling. "I invited no one to lunch except Beautrelet." And, addressing the servant, "Charolais, did you lock the staircase doors behind the gentleman?"

"Yes, sir, and fastened the bolts."

Lupin rose:

"Come, Raymonde, don't shake like that. Why, you're quite pale!"

He spoke a few words to her in an undertone, as also to the servant, drew back the curtain and sent them both out of the room.

The noise below grew more distinct. It was a series of dull blows, repeated at intervals. Beautrelet thought:

"Ganimard has lost patience and is breaking down the doors."

Lupin resumed the thread of his conversation, speaking very calmly and as though he had really not heard:

"By Jove, the Needle was badly damaged when I succeeded in discovering it! One could see that no one had possessed the secret for more than a century, since Louis XVI. and the Revolution. The tunnel was threatening to fall in. The stairs were in a shocking state. The water was trickling in from the sea. I had to prop up and strengthen and rebuild the whole thing."

Beautrelet could not help asking:

"When you arrived, was it empty?"

"Very nearly. The kings did not use the Needle, as I have done, as a warehouse."

"As a place of refuge, then?"

"Yes, no doubt, in times of invasion and during the civil wars. But its real destination was to be—how shall I put it?—the strong-room or the bank of the kings of France."

The sound of blows increased, more distinctly now. Ganimard must have broken down the first door and was attacking the second. There was a short silence and then more blows, nearer still. It was the third door. Two remained.

Through one of the windows, Beautrelet saw a number of fishing-smacks sailing round the Needle and, not far away, floating on the waters like a great black fish, the torpedo-boat.

"What a row!" exclaimed Lupin. "One can't hear one's self speak! Let's go upstairs, shall we? It may interest you to look over the Needle."

They climbed to the floor above, which was protected, like the others, by a door which Lupin locked behind him.

"My picture gallery," he said.

The walls were covered with canvases on which Beautrelet recognized the most famous signatures. There were Raphael's Madonna of the Agnus Dei, Andrea del Sarto's Portrait of Lucrezia Fede, Titian's Salome, Botticelli's Madonna and Angels and numbers of Tintorettos, Carpaccios, Rembrandts, Velasquez.

"What fine copies!" said Beautrelet, approvingly.

Lupin looked at him with an air of stupefaction:

"What! Copies! You must be mad! The copies are in Madrid, my dear fellow, in Florence, Venice, Munich, Amsterdam."

"Then these—"

"Are the original pictures, my lad, patiently collected in all the museums of Europe, where I have replaced them, like an honest man, with first-rate copies."

"But some day or other—"

"Some day or other, the fraud will be discovered? Well, they will find my signature on each canvas—at the back—and they will know that it was I who have endowed my country with the original masterpieces. After all, I have only done what Napoleon did in Italy.—Oh, look, Beautrelet: here are M. de Gesvres's four Rubenses!—"

The knocking continued within the hollow of the Needle without ceasing.

"I can't stand this!" said Lupin. "Let's go higher."

A fresh staircase. A fresh door.

"The tapestry-room," Lupin announced.

The tapestries were not hung on the walls, but rolled, tied up with cord, ticketed; and, in addition, there were parcels of old fabrics which Lupin unfolded: wonderful brocades, admirable velvets, soft, faded silks, church vestments woven with silver and gold—

They went higher still and Beautrelet saw the room containing the clocks and other time-pieces, the book-room—oh, the splendid bindings, the precious, undiscoverable volumes, the unique copies stolen from the great public libraries—the lace-room, the knicknack-room.

And each time the circumference of the room grew smaller.

And each time, now, the sound of knocking was more distant. Ganimard was losing ground.

"This is the last room," said Lupin. "The treasury."

This one was quite different. It was round also, but very high and conical in shape. It occupied the top of the edifice and its floor must have been fifteen or twenty yards below the extreme point of the Needle.

On the cliff side there was no window. But on the side of the sea, whence there were no indiscreet eyes to fear, two glazed openings admitted plenty of light.

The ground was covered with a parqueted flooring of rare wood, forming concentric patterns. Against the walls stood glass cases and a few pictures.

"The pearls of my collection," said Lupin. "All that you have seen so far is for sale. Things come and things go. That's business. But here, in this sanctuary, everything is sacred. There is nothing here but choice, essential pieces, the best of the best, priceless things. Look at these jewels, Beautrelet: Chaldean amulets, Egyptian necklaces, Celtic bracelets, Arab chains. Look at these statuettes, Beautrelet, at this Greek Venus, this Corinthian Apollo. Look at these Tanagras, Beautrelet: all the real Tanagras are here. Outside this glass case, there is not a single genuine Tanagra statuette in the whole wide world. What a delicious thing to be able to say!—Beautrelet, do you remember Thomas and his gang of church-pillagers in the South—agents of mine, by the way? Well, here is the Ambazac reliquary, the real one, Beautrelet! Do you remember the Louvre scandal, the tiara which was admitted to be false, invented and manufactured by a modern artist? Here is the tiara of Saitapharnes, the real one, Beautrelet! Look, Beautrelet, look with all your eyes: here is the marvel of marvels, the supreme masterpiece, the work of no mortal brain; here is Leonardo's Gioconda, the real one! Kneel, Beautrelet, kneel; all womankind stands before you in this picture."

There was a long silence between them. Below, the sound of blows drew nearer. Two or three doors, no more, separated them from Ganimard. In the offing, they saw the black back of the torpedo-boat and the fishing-smacks cruising to and fro.

The boy asked:

"And the treasure?"

"Ah, my little man, that's what interests you most! None of those masterpieces of human art can compete with the contemplation of the treasure as a matter of curiosity, eh?—And the whole crowd will be like you!—Come, you shall be satisfied."

He stamped his foot, and, in so doing, made one of the discs composing the floor-pattern turn right over. Then, lifting it as though it were the lid of a box, he uncovered a sort of large round bowl, dug in the thickness of the rock. It was empty.

A little farther, he went through the same performance. Another large bowl appeared. It was also empty.

He did this three times over again. The three other bowls were empty.

"Eh," grinned Lupin. "What a disappointment! Under Louis XL, under Henry IV., under Richelieu, the five bowls were full. But think of Louis XIV., the folly of Versailles, the wars, the great disasters of the reign! And think of Louis XV., the spendthrift king, with his Pompadour and his Du Barry! How they must have drawn on the treasure in those days! With what thieving claws they must have scratched at the stone. You see, there's nothing left."

He stopped.

"Yes, Beautrelet, there is something—the sixth hiding-place! This one was intangible. Not one of them dared touch it. It was the very last resource, the nest-egg, the something put by for a rainy day. Look, Beautrelet!"

He stooped and lifted up the lid. An iron box filled the bowl. Lupin took from his pocket a key with a complicated bit and wards and opened the box.

A dazzling sight presented itself. Every sort of precious stone sparkled there, every color gleamed, the blue of the sapphires, the red of the rubies, the green of the emeralds, the yellow of the topazes.

"Look, look, little Beautrelet! They have squandered all the cash, all the gold, all the silver, all the crown pieces and all the ducats and all the doubloons; but the chest with the jewels has remained intact. Look at the settings. They belong to every period, to every century, to every country. The dowries of the queens are here. Each brought her share: Margaret of Scotland and Charlotte of Savoy; duchesses of Austria: Eleonore, Elisabeth, Marie-Therese, Mary of England and Catherine de Medicis; and all the arch—Marie Antoinette. Look at those pearls, Beautrelet! And those diamonds: look at the size of the diamonds! Not one of them but is worthy of an empress! The Pitt Diamond is no finer!"

He rose to his feet and held up his hand as one taking an oath:

"Beautrelet, you shall tell the world that Lupin has not taken a single one of the stones that were in the royal chest, not a single one, I swear it on my honor! I had no right to. They are the fortune of France."

Below them, Ganimard was making all speed. It was easy to judge by the reverberation of the blows that his men were attacking the last door but one, the door that gave access to the knicknack-room.

"Let us leave the chest open," said Lupin, "and all the cavities, too, all those little empty graves."

He went round the room, examined some of the glass cases, gazed at some of the pictures and, as he walked, said, pensively:

"How sad it is to leave all this! What a wrench! The happiest hours of my life have been spent here, alone, in the presence of these objects which I loved. And my eyes will never behold them again and my hands will never touch them again—"

His drawn face bore such an expression of lassitude upon it that Beautrelet felt a vague sort of pity for him. Sorrow in that man must assume larger proportions than in another, even as joy did, or pride, or humiliation. He was now standing by the window, and, with his finger pointing to the horizon, said:

"What is sadder still is that I must abandon that, all that! How beautiful it is! The boundless sea—the sky.—On either side, the cliffs of Etretat with their three natural archways: the Porte d'Armont, the Porte d'Aval, the Manneporte—so many triumphal arches for the master. And the master was I! I was the king of the story, the king of fairyland, the king of the Hollow Needle! A strange and supernatural kingdom! From Caesar to Lupin: what a destiny!" He burst out laughing. "King of fairyland! Why not say King of Yvetot at once? What nonsense! King of the world, yes, that's more like it! From this topmost point of the Needle, I ruled the globe! I held it in my claws like a prey! Lift the tiara of Saitaphernes, Beautrelet.—You see those two telephones? The one on the right communicates with Paris: a private line; the one on the left with London: a private line. Through London, I am in touch with America, Asia, Australia, South Africa. In all those continents, I have my offices, my agents, my jackals, my scouts! I drive an international trade. I hold the great market in art and antiquities, the world's fair! Ah, Beautrelet, there are moments when my power turns my head! I feel intoxicated with strength and authority."

The door gave way below. They heard Ganimard and his men running about and searching.

After a moment, Lupin continued, in a low voice:

"And now it's over. A little girl crossed my path, a girl with soft hair and wistful eyes and an honest, yes, an honest soul—and it's over. I myself am demolishing the mighty edifice.—All the rest seems absurd and childish to me—nothing counts but her hair—and her wistful eyes—and her honest little soul—"

The men came up the staircase. A blow shook the door, the last door—

Lupin seized the boy sharply by the arm:

"Do you understand, Beautrelet, why I let you have things your own way when I could have crushed you, time after time, weeks ago? Do you understand how you succeeded in getting as far as this? Do you understand that I had given each of my men his share of the plunder when you met them the other night on the cliff? You do understand, don't you? The Hollow Needle is the great adventure. As long as it belongs to me, I remain the great adventurer. Once the Needle is recaptured, it means that the past and I are parted and that the future begins, a future of peace and happiness, in which I shall have no occasion to blush when Raymonde's eyes are turned upon me, a future—"

He turned furiously toward the door:

"Stop that noise, Ganimard, will you? I haven't finished my speech!"

The blows came faster. It was like the sound of a beam that was being hurled against the door. Beautrelet, mad with curiosity, stood in front of Lupin and awaited events, without understanding what Lupin was doing or contemplating. To give up the Needle was all very well; but why was he giving up himself? What was his plan? Did he hope to escape from Ganimard? And, on the other hand, where was Raymonde?

Lupin, meantime, was murmuring, dreamily:

"An honest man.—Arsene Lupin an honest man—no more robbery—leading the life of everybody else.—And why not? There is no reason why I should not meet with the same success.—But do stop that now, Ganimard! Don't you know, you ass, that I'm uttering historic words and that Beautrelet is taking them in for the benefit of posterity?" He laughed. "I am wasting my time. Ganimard will never grasp the use of my historic words."

He took a piece of red chalk, put a pair of steps to the wall and wrote, in large letters:

Arsene Lupin gives and bequeaths to France all the treasures contained in the Hollow Needle, on the sole condition that these treasures be housed at the Musee du Louvre in rooms which shall be known as the Arsene Lupin Rooms.

"Now," he said, "my conscience is at ease. France and I are quits."

The attackers were striking with all their might. One of the panels burst in two. A hand was put through and fumbled for the lock.

"Thunder!" said Lupin. "That idiot of a Ganimard is capable of effecting his purpose for once in his life."

He rushed to the lock and removed the key.

"Sold, old chap!—The door's tough.—I have plenty of time—Beautrelet, I must say good-bye. And thank you!—For really you could have complicated the attack—but you're so tactful!"

While speaking, he moved toward a large triptych by Van der Weyden, representing the Wise Men of the East. He shut the right-hand panel and, in so doing, exposed a little door concealed behind it and seized the handle.

"Good luck to your hunting, Ganimard! And kind regards at home!"

A pistol-shot resounded. Lupin jumped back: "Ah, you rascal, full in the heart! Have you been taking lessons? You've done for the Wise Man! Full in the heart! Smashed to smithereens, like a pipe at the fair!—"

"Lupin, surrender!" roared Ganimard, with his eyes glittering and his revolver showing through the broken panel of the door. "Surrender, I say!"

"Did the old guard surrender?"

"If you stir a limb, I'll blow your brains out!"

"Nonsense! You can't get me here!"

As a matter of fact, Lupin had moved away; and, though Ganimard was able to fire straight in front of him through the breach in the door, he could not fire, still less take aim, on the side where Lupin stood. Lupin's position was a terrible one for all that, because the outlet on which he was relying, the little door behind the triptych, opened right in front of Ganimard. To try to escape meant to expose himself to the detective's fire; and there were five bullets left in the revolver.

"By Jove," he said, laughing, "there's a slump in my shares this afternoon! You've done a nice thing. Lupin, old fellow: you wanted a last sensation and you've gone a bit too far. You shouldn't have talked so much."

He flattened himself against the wall. A further portion of the panel had given way under the men's pressure and Ganimard was less hampered in his movements. Three yards, no more, separated the two antagonists. But Lupin was protected by a glass case with a gilt-wood framework.

"Why don't you help, Beautrelet?" cried the old detective, gnashing his teeth with rage. "Why don't you shoot him, instead of staring at him like that?"

Isidore, in fact, had not budged, had remained, till that moment, an eager, but passive spectator. He would have liked to fling himself into the contest with all his strength and to bring down the prey which he held at his mercy. He was prevented by some inexplicable sentiment.

But Ganimard's appeal for assistance shook him. His hand closed on the butt of his revolver:

"If I take part in it," he thought, "Lupin is lost. And I have the right—it's my duty."

Their eyes met. Lupin's were calm, watchful, almost inquisitive, as though, in the awful danger that threatened him, he were interested only in the moral problem that held the young man in its clutches. Would Isidore decide to give the finishing stroke to the defeated enemy?

The door cracked from top to bottom.

"Help, Beautrelet, we've got him!" Ganimard bellowed.

Isidore raised his revolver.

What happened was so quick that he knew of it, so to speak, only by the result. He saw Lupin bob down and run along the wall, skimming the door right under the weapon which Ganimard was vainly brandishing; and he felt himself suddenly flung to the ground, picked up the next moment and lifted by an invincible force.

Lupin held him in the air, like a living shield, behind which he hid himself.

"Ten to one that I escape, Ganimard! Lupin, you see, has never quite exhausted his resources—"

He had taken a couple of brisk steps backward to the triptych. Holding Beautrelet with one hand flat against his chest, with the other he cleared the passage and closed the little door behind them.

A steep staircase appeared before their eyes.

"Come along," said Lupin, pushing Beautrelet before him. "The land forces are beaten—let us turn our attention to the French fleet.—After Waterloo, Trafalgar.—You're having some fun for your money, eh, my lad?—Oh, how good: listen to them knocking at the triptych now!—It's too late, my children.—But hurry along, Beautrelet!"

The staircase, dug out in the wall of the Needle, dug in its very crust, turned round and round the pyramid, encircling it like the spiral of a tobogganslide. Each hurrying the other, they clattered down the treads, taking two or three at a bound. Here and there, a ray of light trickled through a fissure; and Beautrelet carried away the vision of the fishing-smacks hovering a few dozen fathoms off, and of the black torpedo-boat.

They went down and down, Isidore in silence, Lupin still bubbling over with merriment:

"I should like to know what Ganimard is doing? Is he tumbling down the other staircases to bar the entrance to the tunnel against me? No, he's not such a fool as that. He must have left four men there—and four men are sufficient—" He stopped. "Listen—they're shouting up above. That's it, they've opened the window and are calling to their fleet.—Why, look, the men are busy on board the smacks—they're exchanging signals.—The torpedo-boat is moving.—Dear old torpedo-boat! I know you, you're from the Havre.—Guns' crews to the guns!—Hullo, there's the commander!—How are you, Duguay-Trouin?"

He put his arm through a cleft and waved his handkerchief. Then he continued his way downstairs:

"The enemy's fleet have set all sail," he said. "We shall be boarded before we know where we are. Heavens, what fun!"

They heard the sound of voices below them. They were just then approaching the level of the sea and they emerged, almost at once, into a large cave into which two lanterns were moving about in the dark.

A woman's figure appeared and threw itself on Lupin's neck:

"Quick, quick, I was so nervous about you. What have you been doing?—But you're not alone!—"

Lupin reassured her:

"It's our friend Beautrelet.—Just think, Beautrelet had the tact—but I'll talk about that later—there's no time now.—Charolais are you there? That's right!—And the boat?"

"The boat's ready, sir," Charolais replied,

"Fire away," said Lupin.

In a moment, the noise of a motor crackled and Beautrelet, whose eyes were gradually becoming used to the gloom, ended by perceiving that they were on a sort of quay, at the edge of the water, and that a boat was floating before them.

"A motor boat," said Lupin, completing Beautrelet's observations. "This knocks you all of a heap, eh, Isidore, old chap?—You don't understand.—Still, you have only to think.—As the water before your eyes is no other than the water of the sea, which filters into this excavation each high tide, the result is that I have a safe little private roadstead all to myself."

"But it's closed," Beautrelet protested. "No one can get in or out."

"Yes, I can," said Lupin; "and I'm going to prove it to you."

He began by handing Raymonde in. Then he came back to fetch Beautrelet. The lad hesitated.

"Are you afraid?" asked Lupin.

"What of?"

"Of being sunk by the torpedo-boat."

"No."

"Then you're considering whether it's not your duty to stay with Ganimard, law and order, society and morality, instead of going off with Lupin, shame, infamy and disgrace."

"Exactly."

"Unfortunately, my boy, you have no choice. For the moment, they must believe the two of us dead—and leave me the peace to which a prospective honest man is entitled. Later on, when I have given you your liberty, you can talk as much as you please—I shall have nothing more to fear."

By the way in which Lupin clutched his arm, Beautrelet felt that all resistance was useless. Besides, why resist? Had he not discovered and handed over the Hollow Needle? What did he care about the rest? Had he not the right to humor the irresistible sympathy with which, in spite of everything, this man inspired him?

The feeling was so clear in him that he was half inclined to say to Lupin:

"Look here, you're running another, a more serious danger; Holmlock Shears is on your track."

"Come along!" said Lupin, before Isidore had made up his mind to speak.

He obeyed and let Lupin lead him to the boat, the shape of which struck him as peculiar and its appearance quite unexpected.

Once on deck, they went down a little steep staircase, or rather a ladder hooked on to a trap door, which closed above their heads. At the foot of the ladder, brightly lit by a lamp, was a very small saloon, where Raymonde was waiting for them and where the three had just room to sit down.

Lupin took the mouthpiece of a speaking tube from a hook and gave the order:

"Let her go, Charolais!"

Isidore had the unpleasant sensation which one feels when going down in a lift: the sensation of the ground vanishing beneath you, the impression of emptiness, space. This time, it was the water retreating; and space opened out, slowly.

"We're sinking, eh?" grinned Lupin. "Don't be afraid—we've only to pass from the upper cave where we were to another little cave, situated right at the bottom and half open to the sea, which can be entered at low tide. All the shellfish-catchers know it. Ah, ten seconds' wait! We're going through the passage and it's very narrow, just the size of the submarine."

"But," asked Beautrelet, "how is it that the fishermen who enter the lower cave don't know that it's open at the top and that it communicates with another from which a staircase starts and runs through the Needle? The facts are at the disposal of the first-comer."

"Wrong, Beautrelet! The top of the little public cave is closed, at low tide, by a movable platform, painted the color of the rock, which the sea, when it rises, shifts and carries up with it and, when it goes down, fastens firmly over the little cave. That is why I am able to pass at high tide. A clever notion, what? It's an idea of my own. True, neither Caesar nor Louis XIV., nor, in short, any of my distinguished predecessors could have had it, because they did not possess submarines. They were satisfied with the staircase, which then ran all the way down to the little bottom cave. I did away with the last treads of the staircase and invented the trick of the movable ceiling: it's a present I'm making to France—Raymonde, my love, put out the lamp beside you—we shan't want it now—on the contrary—"

A pale light, which seemed to be of the same color as the water, met them as they left the cave and made its way into the cabin through the two portholes and through a thick glass skylight that projected above the planking of the deck and allowed the passengers to inspect the upper layers of the sea. And, suddenly, a shadow glided over their heads.

"The attack is about to take place. The fleet is investing the Needle. But, hollow as the Needle is, I don't see how they propose to enter it."

He took up the speaking tube:

"Don't leave the bottom, Charolais. Where are we going? Why, I told you: to Port-Lupin. And at full speed, do you hear? We want water to land by—there's a lady with us."

They skimmed over the rocky bed. The seaweed stood up on end like a heavy, dark vegetation and the deep currents made it wave gracefully, stretching and billowing like floating hair.

Another shadow, a longer one.

"That's the torpedo-boat," said Lupin. "We shall hear the roar of the guns presently. What will Duguay-Trouin do? Bombard the Needle? Think of what we're missing, Beautrelet, by not being present at the meeting of Duguay-Trouin and Ganimard! The juncture of the land and naval forces! Hi, Charolais, don't go to sleep, my man!"

They were moving very fast, for all that. The rocks had been succeeded by sand-fields and then, almost at once, they saw more rocks, which marked the eastern extremity of Etretat, the Porte d'Amont. Fish fled at their approach. One of them, bolder than the rest, fastened on to a porthole and looked at the occupants of the saloon with its great, fixed, staring eyes.

"That's better," cried Lupin. "We're going now. What do you think of my cockle-shell, Beautrelet? Not so bad, is she? Do you remember the story of the Seven of Hearts,[10] the wretched end of Lacombe, the engineer, and how, after punishing his murderers, I presented the State with his papers and his plans for the construction of a new submarine: one more gift to France? Well, among the plans, I kept those of a submersible motor boat and that is how you come to have the honor of sailing in my company."

He called to Charolais:

"Take us up, Charolais—there's no danger now—"

They shot up to the surface and the glass skylight emerged above the water.

They were a mile from the coast, out of sight, therefore, and Beautrelet was now able to realize more fully at what a headlong pace they were traveling. First Fecamp passed before them, then all the Norman seaside places: Saint-Pierre, the Petits—Dalles, Veulettes, Saint-Valery, Veules, Quiberville. Lupin kept on jesting and Isidore never wearied of watching and listening to him, amazed as he was at the man's spirits, at his gaiety, his mischievous ways, his careless chaff, his delight in life.

He also noticed Raymonde. The young woman sat silent, nestling up against the man she loved. She had taken his hands between her own and kept on raising her eyes to him; and Beautrelet constantly observed that her hands were twitching and that the wistful sadness of her eyes increased. And, each time, it was like a dumb and sorrowful reply to Lupin's sallies. One would have thought that his frivolous words, his sarcastic outlook on life, caused her physical pain.

"Hush!" she whispered. "It's defying destiny to laugh—so many misfortunes can reach us still!"

Opposite Dieppe, they had to dive lest they should be seen by the fishing-craft. And twenty minutes later, they shot at an angle toward the coast and the boat entered a little submarine harbor formed by a regular gap between the rocks, drew up beside a jetty and rose gently to the surface.

Lupin announced:

"Port-Lupin!"

---

[10] The Exploits of Arsene Lupin: VI: The Seven of Hearts.

The spot, situated at sixteen miles from Dieppe and twelve from the Treport and protected, moreover, by the two landslips of cliff, was absolutely deserted. A fine sand carpeted the rounded slope of the tiny beach.

"Jump on shore, Beautrelet—Raymonde, give me your hand. You, Charolais, go back to the Needle, see what happens between Ganimard and Duguay-Trouin and come back and tell me at the end of the day. The thing interests me tremendously."

Beautrelet asked himself with a certain curiosity how they were going to get out of this hemmed-in creek which was called Port-Lupin, when, at the foot of the cliff, he saw the uprights of an iron ladder.

"Isidore," said Lupin, "if you knew your geography and your history, you would know that we are at the bottom of the gorge of Parfonval, in the parish of Biville. More than a century ago, on the night of the twenty-third of August, 1803, Georges Cadoudal and six accomplices, who had landed in France with the intention of kidnapping the first consul, Bonaparte, scrambled up to the top by the road which I will show you. Since then, this road has been demolished by landslips. But Louis Valmeras, better known by the name of Arsene Lupin, had it restored at his own expense and bought the farm of the Neuvillette, where the conspirators spent the first night and where, retired from business and withdrawing from the affairs of this world, he means to lead the life of a respectable country squire with his wife and his mother by his side. The gentleman-burglar is dead! Long live the gentleman-farmer!"

After the ladder came a sort of gully, an abrupt ravine hollowed out, apparently, by the rains, at the end of which they laid hold of a makeshift staircase furnished with a hand-rail. As Lupin explained, this hand-rail had been placed where it was in the stead of the estamperche, a long rope fastened to stakes, by which the people of the country, in the old days, used to help themselves down when going to the beach.

After a painful climb of half an hour, they emerged on the tableland, not far from one of those little cabins, dug out of the soil itself, which serve as shelters for the excisemen. And, as it happened, two minutes later, at a turn in the path, one of these custom-house officials appeared.

He drew himself up and saluted.

Lupin asked:

"Any news, Gomel?"

"No, governor."

"You've met no one at all suspicious-looking?"

"No, governor—only—"

"What?"

"My wife—who does dressmaking at the Neuvillette—"

"Yes, I know—Cesarine—my mother spoke of her. Well?"

"It seems a sailor was prowling about the village this morning."

"What sort of face had he?"

"Not a natural face—a sort of Englishman's face."

"Ah!" said Lupin, in a tone preoccupied. "And you have given Cesarine orders—"

"To keep her eyes open. Yes, governor."

"Very well. Keep a lookout for Charolais's return in two or three hours from now. If there's anything, I shall be at the farm."

He walked on and said to Beautrelet:

"This makes me uneasy—is it Shears? Ah, if it's he, in his present state of exasperation, I have everything to fear!"

He hesitated a moment: "I wonder if we hadn't better turn back. Yes, I have a nasty presentiment of evil."

Gently undulating plains stretched before them as far as the eye could see. A little to the left, a series of handsome avenues of trees led to the farm of the Neuvillette, the buildings of which were now in view. It was the retreat which he had prepared, the haven of rest which he had promised Raymonde. Was he, for the sake of an absurd idea, to renounce happiness at the very moment when it seemed within his reach?

He took Isidore by the arm and, calling his attention to Raymonde, who was walking in front of them:

"Look at her. When she walks, her figure has a little swing at the waist which I cannot see without quivering. But everything in her gives me that thrill of emotion and love: her movements and her repose, her silence and the sound of her voice. I tell you, the mere fact that I am walking in the track of her footsteps makes me feel in the seventh heaven. Ah, Beautrelet, will she ever forget that I was once Lupin? Shall I ever be able to wipe out from her memory the past which she loathes and detests?" He mastered himself and, with obstinate assurance. "She will forget!" he declared. "She will forget, because I have made every sacrifice for her sake. I have sacrificed the inviolable sanctuary of the Hollow Needle, I have sacrificed my treasures, my power, my pride—I will sacrifice everything—I don't want to be anything more—but just a man in love—and an honest man, because she can only love an honest man. After all, why should I not be honest? It is no more degrading than anything else!"

The quip escaped him, so to speak, unawares. His voice remained serious and free of all chaff. And he muttered, with restrained violence:

"Ah, Beautrelet, you see, of all the unbridled joys which I have tasted in my adventurous life, there is not one that equals the joy with which her look fills me when she is pleased with me. I feel quite weak then, and I should like to cry—" Was he crying? Beautrelet had an intuition that his eyes were wet with tears. Tears in Lupin's eyes!—Tears of love!

They were nearing an old gate that served as an entrance to the farm. Lupin stopped for a moment and stammered:

"Why am I afraid?—I feel a sort of weight on my chest. Is the adventure of the Hollow Needle not over? Has destiny not accepted the issue which I selected?"

Raymonde turned round, looking very anxious.

"Here comes Cesarine. She's running."

The exciseman's wife was hurrying from the farm as fast as she could. Lupin rushed up to her:

"What is it? What has happened? Speak!"

Choking, quite out of breath, Cesarine stuttered:

"A man—I saw a man this morning!

"A man—I saw a man in the sitting-room."

"The Englishman of this morning?"

"Yes—but in a different disguise."

"Did he see you?"

"No. He saw your mother. Mme. Valmeras caught him as he was just going away."

"Well?"

"He told her that he was looking for Louis Valmeras, that he was a friend of yours."

"Then?"

"The madame said that her son had gone abroad—for years."

"And he went away?"

"No, he made signs through the window that overlooks the plain—as if he were calling to some one."

Lupin seemed to hesitate. A loud cry tore the air. Raymonde moaned:

"It's your mother—I recognize—"

He flung himself upon her and, dragging her away, in a burst of fierce passion:

"Come—let us fly—you first."

But, suddenly, he stopped, distraught, overcome:

"No, I can't do it—it's too awful. Forgive me—Raymonde—that poor woman down there—Stay here. Beautrelet, don't leave her."

He darted along the slope that surrounds the farm, turned and followed it, at a run, till he came to the gate that opens on the plain.

Raymonde, whom Beautrelet had been unable to hold back, arrived almost as soon as he did; and Beautrelet, hiding behind the trees, saw, in the lonely walk that led from the farm to the gate, three men, of whom one, the tallest, went ahead, while the two others were holding by the arms a woman who tried to resist and who uttered moans of pain.

The daylight was beginning to fade. Nevertheless, Beautrelet recognized Holmlock Shears. The woman seemed of a certain age. Her livid features were set in a frame of white hair.

They all four came up.

They reached the gate. Shears opened one of the folding leaves.

Then Lupin strode forward and stood in front of him.

The encounter appeared all the more terrible inasmuch as it was silent, almost solemn.

For long moments, the two enemies took each other's measure with their eyes. An equal hatred distorted the features of both of them. Neither moved.

Then Lupin spoke, in a voice of terrifying calmness:

"Tell your men to leave that woman alone."

"No."

It was as though both of them feared to engage in the supreme struggle, as though both were collecting all their strength. And there were no words wasted this time, no insults, no bantering challenges. Silence, a deathlike silence.

Mad with anguish, Raymonde awaited the issue of the duel. Beautrelet had caught her arms and was holding her motionless.

After a second, Lupin repeated:

"Order your men to leave that woman alone."

"No."

Lupin said:

"Listen, Shears—"

But he interrupted himself, realizing the silliness of the words. In the face of that colossus of pride and will-power which called itself Holmlock Shears, of what use were threats?

Resolved upon the worst, suddenly he put his hand to his jacket pocket. The Englishman anticipated his movement and, leaping upon his prisoner, thrust the barrel of his revolver within two inches of her temple:

"If you stir a limb, I fire!"

At the same time his two satellites drew their weapons and aimed them at Lupin.

Lupin drew himself up, stifled the rage within him and, coolly, with his hands in his pockets and his breast exposed to the enemy, began once more:

"Shears, for the third time, let that woman be—"

The Englishman sneered:

"I have no right to touch her, I suppose? Come, come, enough of this humbug! Your name isn't Valmeras any more than it's Lupin: you stole the name just as you stole the name of Charmerace. And the woman whom you pass off as your mother is Victoire, your old accomplice, the one who brought you up—" (See *Arsene Lupin, play in four acts*).

Shears made a mistake. Carried away by his longing for revenge, he glanced across at Raymonde, whom these revelations filled with horror. Lupin took advantage of his imprudence. With a sudden movement, he fired.

"Damnation!" bellowed Shears, whose arm, pierced by a bullet, fell to his side. And, addressing his men, "Shoot, you two! Shoot him down!"

But already Lupin was upon them: and not two seconds had elapsed before the one on the right was sprawling on the ground, with his chest smashed, while the other, with his jaw broken, fell back against the gate.

"Hurry up, Victoire. Tie them down. And now, Mr. Englishman, it's you and I."

He ducked with an oath:

"Ah, you scoundrel!"

Shears had picked up his revolver with his left hand and was taking aim at him.

A shot—a cry of distress—Raymonde had flung herself between the two men, facing the Englishman. She staggered back, brought her hand to her neck, drew herself up, spun round on her heels and fell at Lupin's feet.

"Raymonde!—Raymonde!"

He threw himself upon her, took her in his arms and pressed her to him.

"Dead—" he said.

There was a moment of stupefaction. Shears seemed confounded by his own act. Victoire stammered:

"My poor boy—my poor boy—"

Beautrelet went up to the young woman and stooped to examine her. Lupin repeated:

"Dead—dead—"

He said it in a reflective tone, as though he did not yet understand. But his face became hollow, suddenly transformed, ravaged by grief. And then he was seized with a sort of madness, made senseless gestures, wrung his hands, stamped his feet, like a child that suffers more than it is able to bear.

"You villain!" he cried, suddenly, in an access of hatred.

And, flinging Shears back with a formidable blow, he took him by the throat and dug his twitching fingers into his flesh.

The Englishman gasped, without even struggling.

"My boy—my boy—" said Victoire, in a voice of entreaty.

Beautrelet ran up. But Lupin had already let go and stood sobbing beside his enemy stretched upon the ground.

O pitiful sight! Beautrelet never forgot its tragic horror, he who knew all Lupin's love for Raymonde and all that the great adventurer had sacrificed of his own being to bring a smile to the face of his well-beloved.

Night began to cover the field of battle with a shroud of darkness. The three Englishmen lay bound and gagged in the tall grass. Distant songs broke the vast silence of the plain. It was the farm-hands returning from their work.

Lupin drew himself up. He listened to the monotonous voices. Then he glanced at the happy homestead of the Neuvillette, where he had hoped to live peacefully with Raymonde. Then he looked at her, the poor, loving victim, whom love had killed and who, all white, was sleeping her last, eternal sleep.

The men were coming nearer, however.

Then Lupin bent down, took the dead woman in his powerful arms, lifted the corpse with a single effort and, bent in two, stretched it across his back:

"Let us go, Victoire."

"Let us go, dear."

"Good-bye, Beautrelet," he said.

And, bearing his precious and awful burden followed by his old servant, silent and fierce he turned toward the sea and plunged into the darkness of the night.

THE END

BOOK FOUR.

813

I. THE TRAGEDY AT THE PALACE HOTEL

Mr. Kesselbach stopped short on the threshold of the sitting-room, took his secretary's arm and, in an anxious voice, whispered:

"Chapman, some one has been here again."

"Surely not, sir," protested the secretary. "You have just opened the hall-door yourself; and the key never left your pocket while we were lunching in the restaurant."

"Chapman, some one has been here again," Mr. Kesselbach repeated. He pointed to a traveling-bag on the mantelpiece. "Look, I can prove it. That bag was shut. It is now open."

Chapman protested.

"Are you quite sure that you shut it, sir? Besides, the bag contains nothing but odds and ends of no value, articles of dress. . . ."

"It contains nothing else, because I took my pocket-book out before we went down, by way of precaution. . . . But for that. . . . No, Chapman, I tell you, some one has been here while we were at lunch."

There was a telephone on the wall. He took down the receiver:

"Hallo! . . . I'm Mr. Kesselbach. . . . Suite 415 . . . That's right. . . . Mademoiselle, would you please put me on to the Prefecture of Police . . . the detective department. . . . I know the number . . . one second . . . Ah, here it is! Number 822.48. . . . I'll hold the line."

A moment later he continued:

"Are you 822.48? I should like a word with M. Lenormand, the chief of the detective-service. My name's Kesselbach. . . . Hullo! . . . Yes, the chief detective knows what it's about. He has given me leave to ring him up. . . . Oh, he's not there? . . . To whom am I speaking? . . . Detective-sergeant Gourel? . . . You were there yesterday, were you not, when I called on M. Lenormand? Well, the same thing that I told M. Lenormand yesterday has occurred again to-day. . . . Some one has entered the suite which I am occupying. And, if you come at once, you may be able to discover some clues. . . . In an hour or two? All right; thanks. . . . You have only to ask for suite 415. . . . Thank you again."

Rudolf Kesselbach, nicknamed alternatively the King of Diamonds and the Lord of the Cape, possessed a fortune estimated at nearly twenty millions sterling. For the past week, he had occupied suite 415, on the fourth floor of the Palace Hotel, consisting of three rooms, of which the two larger, on the right, the sitting-room and the principal bedroom, faced the avenue; while the other, on the left, in which Chapman, the secretary, slept, looked out on the Rue de Judée.

Adjoining this bedroom, a suite of five rooms had been reserved for Mrs. Kesselbach, who was to leave Monte Carlo, where she was at present staying, and join her husband the moment she heard from him.

Rudolf Kesselbach walked up and down for a few minutes with a thoughtful air. He was a tall man, with a ruddy complexion, and still young; and his dreamy eyes, which showed pale blue through his gold-rimmed spectacles, gave him an expression of gentleness and shyness that contrasted curiously with the strength of the square forehead and the powerfully-developed jaws.

He went to the window: it was fastened. Besides, how could any one have entered that way? The private balcony that ran round the flat broke off on the right and was separated on the left by a stone channel from the balconies in the Rue de Judée.

He went to his bedroom: it had no communication with the neighboring rooms. He went to his secretary's bedroom: the door that led into the five rooms reserved for Mrs. Kesselbach was locked and bolted.

"I can't understand it at all, Chapman. Time after time I have noticed things here . . . funny things, as you must admit. Yesterday, my walking-stick was moved. . . . The day before that, my papers had certainly been touched. . . . And yet how was it possible? . . .

"It is not possible, sir!" cried Chapman, whose honest, placid features displayed no anxiety. "You're imagining things, that's all. . . . You have no proof, nothing but impressions, to go upon. . . . Besides, look here: there is no way into this suite except through the entrance-lobby. Very well. You had a special key made on the day of our arrival: and your own man, Edwards, has the only duplicate. Do you trust him?"

"Of course I do! . . . He's been with me for ten years! . . . But Edwards goes to lunch at the same time that we do; and that's a mistake. He must not go down, in future, until we come back."

Chapman gave a slight shrug of the shoulders. There was no doubt about it, the Lord of the Cape was becoming a trifle eccentric, with those incomprehensible fears of his. What risk can you run in an hotel, especially when you carry no valuables, no important sum of money on you or with you?

They heard the hall-door opening. It was Edwards. Mr. Kesselbach called him:

"Are you dressed, Edwards? Ah, that's right! . . . I am expecting no visitors to-day, Edwards . . . or, rather, one visitor only, M. Gourel. Meantime, remain in the lobby and keep an eye on the door. Mr. Chapman and I have some serious work to do."

The serious work lasted for a few minutes, during which Mr. Kesselbach went through his correspondence, read three or four letters and gave instructions how they were to be answered. But, suddenly, Chapman, waiting with pen poised, saw that Mr. Kesselbach was thinking of something quite different from his correspondence. He was holding between his fingers and attentively examining a pin, a black pin bent like a fish-hook:

"Chapman," he said, "look what I've found on the table. This bent pin obviously means something. It's a proof, a material piece of evidence. You can't pretend now that no one has been in the room. For, after all, this pin did not come here of itself."

"Certainly not," replied the secretary. "It came here through me."

"What do you mean?"

"Why, it's a pin which I used to fasten my tie to my collar. I took it out last night, while you were reading, and I twisted it mechanically."

Mr. Kesselbach rose from his chair, with a great air of vexation, took a few steps and stopped.

"You're laughing at me, Chapman, I feel you are . . . and you're quite right. . . . I won't deny it, I have been rather . . . odd, since my last journey to the Cape. It's because . . . well . . . you don't know the new factor in my life . . . a tremendous plan . . . a huge thing . . . I can only see it, as yet, in the haze of the future . . . but it's taking shape for all that . . . and it will be something colossal. . . . Ah, Chapman, you can't imagine. . . . Money I don't care a fig for: I have money, I have too much money. . . . But this, this means a great deal more; it means power, might, authority. If the reality comes up to my expectations, I shall be not only Lord of the Cape, but lord of other realms as well. . . . Rudolf Kesselbach, the son of the Augsburg ironmonger, will be on a par with many people who till now have looked down upon him. . . . He will even take precedence of them, Chapman; he will, take precedence of them, mark my words . . . and, if ever I . . ."

He interrupted himself, looked at Chapman as though he regretted having said too much and, nevertheless, carried away by his excitement, concluded:

"You now understand the reasons of my anxiety, Chapman. . . . Here, in this brain, is an idea that is worth a great deal . . . and this idea is suspected perhaps . . . and I am being spied upon. . . . I'm convinced of it. . . ."

A bell sounded.

"The telephone," said Chapman.

"Could it," muttered Kesselbach, "by any chance be . . . ?" He took down the instrument. "Hullo! . . . Who? The Colonel? Ah, good! Yes, it's I. . . . Any news? . . . Good! . . . Then I shall expect you. . . . You will come with one of your men? Very well. . . . What? No, we shan't be disturbed. . . . I will give the necessary orders. . . . It's as serious as that, is it? . . . I tell you, my instructions will be positive. . . . my secretary and my man shall keep the door; and no one shall be allowed in. . . . You know the way, don't you? . . . Then don't lose a minute."

He hung up the receiver and said:

"Chapman, there are two gentlemen coming. Edwards will show them in. . . ."

"But M. Gourel . . . the detective-sergeant. . . . ?"

"He will come later . . . in an hour. . . . And, even then, there's no harm in their meeting. So send Edwards down to the office at once, to tell them. I am at home to nobody . . . except two gentlemen, the Colonel and his friend, and M. Gourel. He must make them take down the names."

Chapman did as he was asked. When he returned to the room, he found Mr. Kesselbach holding in his hand an envelope, or, rather, a little pocket-case, in black morocco leather, apparently empty. He seemed to hesitate, as though he did not know what to do with it. Should he put it in his pocket or lay it down elsewhere? At last he went to the mantelpiece and threw the leather envelope into his traveling-bag:

"Let us finish the mail, Chapman. We have ten minutes left. Ah, a letter from Mrs. Kesselbach! Why didn't you tell me of it, Chapman? Didn't you recognize the handwriting?"

He made no attempt to conceal the emotion which he felt in touching and contemplating that paper which his wife had held in her fingers and to which she had added a look of her eyes, an atom of her scent, a suggestion of her secret thoughts. He inhaled its perfume and, unsealing it, read the letter slowly in an undertone, in fragments that reached Chapman's ears:

"Feeling a little tired. . . . Shall keep my room to-day. . . . I feel so bored. . . . When can I come to you? I am longing for your wire. . . ."

"You telegraphed this morning, Chapman? Then Mrs. Kesselbach will be here to-morrow, Wednesday."

He seemed quite gay, as though the weight of his business had been suddenly relieved and he freed from all anxiety. He rubbed his hands and heaved a deep breath, like a strong man certain of success, like a lucky man who possessed happiness and who was big enough to defend himself.

"There's some one ringing, Chapman, some one ringing at the hall door. Go and see who it is."

But Edwards entered and said:

"Two gentlemen asking for you, sir. They are the ones. . . ."

"I know. Are they there, in the lobby?"

"Yes, sir."

"Close the hall-door and don't open it again except to M. Gourel, the detective-sergeant. You go and bring the gentlemen in, Chapman, and tell them that I would like to speak to the Colonel first, to the Colonel alone."

Edwards and Chapman left the room, shutting the door after them. Rudolf Kesselbach went to the window and pressed his forehead against the glass.

Outside, just below his eyes, the carriages and motor-cars rolled along in parallel furrows, marked by the double line of refuges. A bright spring sun made the brass-work and the varnish gleam again. The trees were putting forth their first green shoots; and the buds of the tall chestnuts were beginning to unfold their new-born leaves.

"What on earth is Chapman doing?" muttered Kesselbach. "The time he wastes in palavering! . . ."

He took a cigarette from the table, lit it and drew a few puffs. A faint exclamation escaped him. Close before him stood a man whom he did not know.

He started back:

"Who are you?"

The man—he was a well-dressed individual, rather smart-looking, with dark hair, a dark moustache and hard eyes—the man gave a grin:

"Who am I? Why, the Colonel!"

"No, no. . . . The one I call the Colonel, the one who writes to me under that . . . adopted . . . signature . . . is not you!"

"Yes, yes . . . the other was only . . . But, my dear sir, all this, you know, is not of the smallest importance. The essential thing is that I . . . am myself. And that, I assure you, I *am*!"

"But your name, sir? . . ."

"The Colonel . . . until further orders."

Mr. Kesselbach was seized with a growing fear. Who was this man? What did he want with him?

He called out:

"Chapman!"

"What a funny idea, to call out! Isn't my company enough for you?"

"Chapman!" Mr. Kesselbach cried again. "Chapman! Edwards!"

"Chapman! Edwards!" echoed the stranger, in his turn. "What are you doing? You're wanted!"

"Sir, I ask you, I order you to let me pass."

"But, my dear sir, who's preventing you?"

He politely made way. Mr. Kesselbach walked to the door, opened it and gave a sudden jump backward. Behind the door stood another man, pistol in hand. Kesselbach stammered:

"Edwards . . . Chap . . ."

He did not finish. In a corner of the lobby he saw his secretary and his servant lying side by side on the floor, gagged and bound.

Mr. Kesselbach, notwithstanding his nervous and excitable nature, was not devoid of physical courage; and the sense of a definite danger, instead of depressing him, restored all his elasticity and vigor. Pretending dismay and stupefaction, he moved slowly back to the chimneypiece and leant against the wall. His hand felt for the electric bell. He found it and pressed the button without removing his finger.

"Well?" asked the stranger.

Mr. Kesselbach made no reply and continued to press the button.

"Well? Do you expect they will come, that the whole hotel is in commotion, because you are pressing that bell? Why, my dear sir, look behind you and you will see that the wire is cut!"

Mr. Kesselbach turned round sharply, as though he wanted to make sure; but, instead, with a quick movement, he seized the traveling-bag, thrust his hand into it, grasped a revolver, aimed it at the man and pulled the trigger.

"Whew!" said the stranger. "So you load your weapons with air and silence?"

The cock clicked a second time and a third, but there was no report.

"Three shots more, Lord of the Cape! I shan't be satisfied till you've lodged six bullets in my carcass. What! You give up? That's a pity . . . you were making excellent practice!"

He took hold of a chair by the back, spun it round, sat down a-straddle and, pointing to an arm-chair, said:

"Won't you take a seat, my dear sir, and make yourself at home? A cigarette? Not for me, thanks: I prefer a cigar."

There was a box on the table: he selected an Upmann, light in color and flawless in shape, lit it and, with a bow:

"Thank you! That's a perfect cigar. And now let's have a chat, shall we?"

Rudolf Kesselbach listened to him in amazement. Who could this strange person be? . . . Still, at the sight of his visitor sitting there so quiet and so chatty, he became gradually reassured and began to think that the situation might come to an end without any need to resort to violence or brute force.

He took out a pocket-book, opened it, displayed a respectable bundle of bank-notes and asked:

"How much?"

The other looked at him with an air of bewilderment, as though he found a difficulty in understanding what Kesselbach meant. Then, after a moment, he called:

"Marco!"

The man with the revolver stepped forward.

"Marco, this gentleman is good enough to offer you a few bits of paper for your young woman. Take them, Marco."

Still aiming his revolver with his right hand, Marco put out his left, took the notes and withdrew.

"Now that this question is settled according to your wishes," resumed the stranger, "let us come to the object of my visit. I will be brief and to the point. I want two things. In the first place, a little black morocco pocket-case, shaped like an envelope, which you generally carry on you. Secondly, a small ebony box, which was in that traveling-bag yesterday. Let us proceed in order. The morocco case?"

"Burnt."

The stranger knit his brows. He must have had a vision of the good old days when there were peremptory methods of making the contumacious speak:

"Very well. We shall see about that. And the ebony box?"

"Burnt."

"Ah," he growled, "you're getting at me, my good man!" He twisted the other's arm with a pitiless hand. "Yesterday, Rudolf Kesselbach, you walked into the Crédit Lyonnais, on the Boulevard des Italiens, hiding a parcel under your overcoat. You hired a safe . . . let us be exact: safe No. 16, in recess No. 9. After signing the book and paying your safe-rent, you went down to the basement; and, when you came up again, you no longer had your parcel with you. Is that correct?"

"Quite."

"Then the box and the pocket-case are at the Crédit Lyonnais?"

"No."

"Give me the key of your safe."

"No."

"Marco!"

Marco ran up.

"Look sharp, Marco! The quadruple knot!"

Before he had even time to stand on the defensive, Rudolf Kesselbach was tied up in a network of cords that cut into his flesh at the least attempt which he made to struggle. His arms were fixed behind his back, his body fastened to the chair and his legs tied together like the legs of a mummy.

"Search him, Marco."

Marco searched him. Two minutes after, he handed his chief a little flat, nickel-plated key, bearing the numbers 16 and 9.

"Capital. No morocco pocket-case?"

"No, governor."

"It is in the safe. Mr. Kesselbach, will you tell me the secret cypher that opens the lock?"

"No."

"You refuse?"

"Yes."

"Marco!"

"Yes, governor."

"Place the barrel of your revolver against the gentleman's temple."

"It's there."

"Now put your finger to the trigger."

"Ready."

"Well, Kesselbach, old chap, do you intend to speak?"

"No."

"I'll give you ten seconds, and not one more. Marco!"

"Yes, governor."

"In ten seconds, blow out the gentleman's brains."

"Right you are, governor."

"Kesselbach, I'm counting. One, two, three, four, five, six . . ."

Rudolph Kesselbach made a sign.

"You want to speak?"

"Yes."

"You're just in time. Well, the cypher . . . the word for the lock?"

"Dolor."

"Dolor . . . Dolor . . . Mrs. Kesselbach's name is Dolores, I believe? You dear boy! . . . Marco, go and do as I told you. . . . No mistake, mind! I'll repeat it: meet Jérôme at the omnibus office, give him the key, tell him the word: Dolor. Then, the two of you, go to the Crédit Lyonnais. Jérôme is to walk in alone, sign the name-book, go down to the basement and bring away everything in the safe. Do you quite understand?"

"Yes, governor. But if the safe shouldn't open; if the word Dolor . . ."

"Silence, Marco. When you come out of the Crédit Lyonnais, you must leave Jérôme, go to your own place and telephone the result of the operation to me. Should the word Dolor by any chance fail to open the safe, we (my friend Rudolf Kesselbach and I) will have one . . . *last* . . . interview. Kesselbach, you're quite sure you're not mistaken?"

"Yes."

"That means that you rely upon the futility of the search. We shall see. Be off, Marco!"

"What about you, governor?"

"I shall stay. Oh, I'm not afraid! I've never been in less danger than at this moment. Your orders about the door were positive, Kesselbach, were they not?"

"Yes."

"Dash it all, you seemed very eager to get that said! Can you have been trying to gain time? If so, I should be caught in a trap like a fool. . . ." He stopped to think, looked at his prisoner and concluded, "No . . . it's not possible . . . we shall not be disturbed . . ."

He had not finished speaking, when the door-bell rang. He pressed his hand violently on Rudolf Kesselbach's mouth:

"Oh, you old fox, you were expecting some one!"

The captive's eyes gleamed with hope. He could be heard chuckling under the hand that stifled him.

The stranger shook with rage:

"Hold your tongue, or I'll strangle you! Here, Marco, gag him! Quick! . . . That's it!"

The bell rang again. He shouted, as though he himself were Kesselbach and as though Edwards were still there:

"Why don't you open the door, Edwards?"

Then he went softly into the lobby and, pointing to the secretary and the manservant, whispered:

"Marco, help me shift these two into the bedroom . . . over there . . . so that they can't be seen."

He lifted the secretary. Marco carried the servant.

"Good! Now go back to the sitting-room."

He followed him in and at once returned to the lobby and said, in a loud tone of astonishment:

"Why, your man's not here, Mr. Kesselbach. . . . No, don't move . . . finish your letter. . . . I'll go myself."

And he quietly opened the hall-door.

"Mr. Kesselbach?"

He found himself faced by a sort of jovial, bright-eyed giant, who stood swinging from one foot to the other and twisting the brim of his hat between his fingers. He answered:

"Yes, that's right. Who shall I say . . . ?"

"Mr. Kesselbach telephoned. . . . He expects me. . . ."

"Oh, it's you. . . . I'll tell him. . . . Do you mind waiting a minute? . . . Mr. Kesselbach will speak to you."

He had the audacity to leave the visitor standing on the threshold of the little entrance-hall, at a place from which he could see a portion of the sitting-room through the open door, and, slowly, without so much as turning round, he entered the room, went to his confederate by Mr. Kesselbach's side and whispered:

"We're done! It's Gourel, the detective. . . ."

The other drew his knife. He caught him by the arm:

"No nonsense! I have an idea. But, for God's sake, Marco, understand me and speak in your turn. Speak *as if you were Kesselbach.* . . . You hear, Marco! You *are* Kesselbach."

He expressed himself so coolly, so forcibly and with such authority that Marco understood, without further explanation, that he himself was to play the part of Kesselbach. Marco said, so as to be heard:

"You must apologize for me, my dear fellow. Tell M. Gourel I'm awfully sorry, but I'm over head and ears in work. . . . I will see him to-morrow morning, at nine . . . yes, at nine o'clock punctually."

"Good!" whispered the other. "Don't stir."

He went back to the lobby, found Gourel waiting, and said:

"Mr. Kesselbach begs you to excuse him. He is finishing an important piece of work. Could you possibly come back at nine o'clock to-morrow morning?"

There was a pause. Gourel seemed surprised, more or less bothered and undecided. The other man's hand clutched the handle of a knife at the bottom of his pocket. At the first suspicious movement, he was prepared to strike.

At last, Gourel said:

"Very well. . . . At nine o'clock to-morrow. . . . But, all the same . . . However, I shall be here at nine to-morrow. . . ."

And, putting on his hat, he disappeared down the passage of the hotel.

Marco, in the sitting-room, burst out laughing:

"That was jolly clever of you, governor! Oh, how nicely you spoofed him!"

"Look alive, Marco, and follow him. If he leaves the hotel, let him be, meet Jérôme at the omnibus-office as arranged . . . and telephone."

Marco went away quickly.

Then the man took a water-bottle on the chimneypiece, poured himself out a tumblerful, which he swallowed at a draught, wetted his handkerchief, dabbed his forehead, which was covered with perspiration, and then sat down beside his prisoner and, with an affectation of politeness, said:

"But I must really have the honor, Mr. Kesselbach, of introducing myself to you."

And, taking a card from his pocket, he said: "Allow me. . . . Arsène Lupin, gentleman-burglar."

The name of the famous adventurer seemed to make the best of impressions upon Mr. Kesselbach. Lupin did not fail to observe the fact and exclaimed:

"Aha, my dear sir, you breathe again! Arsène Lupin is a delicate, squeamish burglar. He loathes bloodshed, he has never committed a more serious crime than that of annexing other people's property . . . a mere peccadillo, eh? And what you're saying to yourself is that he is not going to burden his conscience with a useless murder. Quite so. . . . But will your destruction be so useless as all that? Everything depends on the answer. And I assure you that I'm not larking at present. Come on, old chap!"

He drew up his chair beside the arm-chair, removed the prisoner's gag and, speaking very plainly:

"Mr. Kesselbach," he said, "on the day when you arrived in Paris you entered into relations with one Barbareux, the manager of a confidential inquiry agency; and, as you were acting without the knowledge of your secretary, Chapman, it was arranged that the said Barbareux, when communicating with you by letter or telephone, should call himself 'the Colonel.' I hasten to tell you that Barbareux is a perfectly honest man. But I have the good fortune to number one of his clerks among my own particular friends. That is how I discovered the motive of your application to Barbareux and how I came to interest myself in you and to make a search or two here, with the assistance of a set of false keys . . . in the course of which search or two, I may as well tell you, I did not find what I was looking for."

He lowered his voice and, with his eyes fixed on the eyes of his prisoner, watching his expression, searching his secret thoughts, he uttered these words:

"Mr. Kesselbach, your instructions to Barbareux were that he should find a man hidden somewhere in the slums of Paris who bears or used to bear the name of Pierre Leduc. The man answers to this brief description: height, five feet nine inches; hair and complexion, fair; wears a moustache. Special mark: the tip of the little finger of the left hand is missing, as the result of a cut. Also, he has an almost imperceptible scar on the right cheek. You seem to attach enormous importance to this man's discovery, as though it might lead to some great advantage to yourself. Who is the man?"

"I don't know."

The answer was positive, absolute. Did he know or did he not know? It made little difference. The great thing was that he was determined not to speak.

"Very well," said his adversary, "but you have fuller particulars about him than those with which you furnished Barbareux."

"I have not."

"You lie, Mr. Kesselbach. Twice, in Barbareux's presence, you consulted papers contained in the morocco case."

"I did."

"And the case?"

"Burnt."

Lupin quivered with rage. The thought of torture and of the facilities which it used to offer was evidently passing through his mind again.

"Burnt? But the box? . . . Come, own up . . . confess that the box is at the Crédit Lyonnais."

"Yes."

"And what's inside it?"

"The finest two hundred diamonds in my private collection."

This statement did not seem to displease the adventurer.

"Aha, the finest two hundred diamonds! But, I say, that's a fortune! . . . Yes, that makes you smile. . . . It's a trifle to you, no doubt. . . . And your secret is worth more than that. . . . To you, yes . . . but to me? . . ."

He took a cigar, lit a match, which he allowed to go out again mechanically, and sat for some time thinking, motionless.

The minutes passed.

He began to laugh:

"I dare say you're hoping that the expedition will come to nothing and that they won't open the safe? . . . Very likely, old chap! But, in that case, you'll have to pay me for my trouble. I did not come here to see what sort of figure you cut in an arm-chair. . . . The diamonds, since diamonds there appear to be . . . or else the morocco case. . . . There's your dilemma." He looked at his watch. "Half an hour. . . . Hang it all! . . . Fate is moving very slowly. . . . But there's nothing for you to grin at, Mr. Kesselbach. I shall not go back empty-handed, make no mistake about that! . . . At last!"

It was the telephone-bell. Lupin snatched at the receiver and, changing the sound of his voice, imitated the rough accent of his prisoner:

"Yes, Rudolf Kesselbach . . . you're speaking to him. . . . Yes, please, mademoiselle, put me on. . . . Is that you, Marco? . . . Good. . . . Did it go off all right? . . . Excellent! . . . No hitch? . . . My best compliments! . . . Well, what did you pick up? . . . The ebony box? . . . Nothing else? . . . No papers? . . . Tut, tut! . . . And what's in the box? . . . Are they fine diamonds? . . . Capital, capital! . . . One minute, Marco, while I think. . . . You see, all this. . . . If I were to tell you my opinion. . . . Wait, don't go away . . . hold the line. . . ."

He turned round.

"Mr. Kesselbach, are you keen on your diamonds?"

"Yes."

"Would you buy them back of me?"

"Possibly."

"For how much? Five hundred thousand francs?"

"Five hundred thousand . . . yes."

"Only, here's the rub: how are we to make the exchange? A cheque? No, you'd swindle me . . . or else I'd swindle you. . . . Listen. On the day after to-morrow, go to the Crédit Lyonnais in the morning, draw out your five hundred bank-notes of a thousand each and go for a walk in the Bois, on the Auteuil side. . . . I shall have the diamonds in a bag: that's handier. . . . The box shows too much. . . ."

Kesselbach gave a start:

"No, no . . . the box, too. . . . I want everything. . . ."

"Ah," cried Lupin, shouting with laughter, "you've fallen into the trap! . . . The diamonds you don't care about . . . they can be replaced. . . . But you cling to that box as you cling to your skin. . . . Very well, you shall have your box . . . on the word of Arsène . . . you shall have it to-morrow morning, by parcel post!"

He went back to the telephone:

"Marco, have you the box in front of you? . . . Is there anything particular about it? . . . Ebony inlaid with ivory. . . . Yes, I know the sort of thing. . . . Japanese, from the Faubourg Saint-Antoine. . . . No mark? . . . Ah, a little round label, with a blue border and a number! . . . Yes, a shop-mark . . . no importance. And is the bottom of the box thick? . . . Not very thick. . . . Bother! No false bottom, then? . . . Look here, Marco: just examine the ivory inlay on the outside . . . or, rather, no, the lid." He reveled with delight. "The lid! That's it, Marco! Kesselbach blinked his eyes just now. . . . We're burning! . . . Ah, Kesselbach, old chap, didn't you see me squinting at you? You silly fellow!" And, to Marco, "Well, what do you see? . . . A looking-glass inside the lid? . . . Does it slide? . . . Is it on hinges? . . . No! . . . Well, then, break it. . . . Yes, yes, I tell you to break it. . . . That glass serves no purpose there . . . it's been added since!" He lost patience. "Mind your own business, idiot! . . . Do as I say! . . ."

He must have heard the noise which Marco made at the other end of the wire in breaking the glass, for he shouted, in triumph.

"Didn't I tell you, Mr. Kesselbach, that we should find something? . . . Hullo! Have you done it? . . . Well? . . . A letter? Victory! All the diamonds in the Cape and old man Kesselbach's secret into the bargain!"

He took down the second receiver, carefully put the two discs to his ears and continued:

"Read it to me, Marco, read it to me slowly. . . . The envelope first. . . . Good. . . . Now, repeat." He himself repeated, "'Copy of the letter contained in the black morocco case.' And next? Tear the envelope, Marco. . . . Have I your permission, Mr. Kesselbach? It's not very good form, but, however . . . Go on, Marco, Mr. Kesselbach gives you leave. . . . Done it? . . . Well, then, read it out."

He listened and, with a chuckle:

"The deuce! That's not quite as clear as a pikestaff! Listen. I'll repeat: a plain sheet of paper folded in four, the folds apparently quite fresh. . . . Good. . . . At the top of the page, on the right, these words: 'Five feet nine, left little finger cut.' And so on. . . . Yes, that's the description of Master Pierre Leduc. In Kesselbach's handwriting, I suppose? . . . Good. . . . And, in the middle of the page, this word in printed capitals: 'APOON.' Marco, my lad, leave the paper as it is and don't touch the box or the diamonds. I shall have done with our friend here in ten minutes and I shall be with you in twenty. . . . Oh, by the way, did you send back the motor for me? Capital! So long!"

He replaced the instrument, went into the lobby and into the bedroom, made sure that the secretary and the manservant had not unloosed their bonds and, on the other hand, that they were in no danger of being choked by their gags. Then he returned to his chief prisoner.

He wore a determined and relentless look:

"We've finished joking, Kesselbach. If you don't speak, it will be the worse for you. Have you made up your mind?"

"What about?"

"No nonsense, please. Tell me what you know."

"I know nothing."

"You lie. What does this word 'APOON' mean?"

"If I knew, I should not have written it down."

"Very well; but whom or what does it refer to? Where did you copy it? Where did you get it from?"

Mr. Kesselbach made no reply. Lupin, now speaking in nervous, jerky tones, resumed:

"Listen, Kesselbach, I have a proposal to make to you. Rich man, big man though you may be, there is not so much difference between us. The son of the Augsburg ironmonger and Arsène Lupin, prince of burglars, can come to an understanding without shame on either side. I do my thieving indoors; you do yours on the Stock Exchange. It's all much of a muchness. So here we are, Kesselbach. Let's be partners in this business. I have need of you, because I don't know what it's about. You have need of me, because you will never be able to manage it alone. Barbareux is an ass. I am Lupin. Is it a bargain?"

No answer. Lupin persisted, in a voice shaking with intensity:

"Answer, Kesselbach, is it a bargain? If so, I'll find your Pierre Leduc for you in forty-eight hours. For he's the man you're after, eh? Isn't that the business? Come along, answer! Who is the fellow? Why are you looking for him? What do you know about him?"

He calmed himself suddenly, laid his hand on Kesselbach's shoulder and, harshly:

"One word only. Yes or no?"

"No!"

He drew a magnificent gold watch from Kesselbach's fob and placed it on the prisoner's knees. He unbuttoned Kesselbach's waistcoat, opened his shirt, uncovered his chest and, taking a steel dagger, with a gold-crusted handle, that lay on the table beside him, he put the point of it against the place where the pulsations of the heart made the bare flesh throb:

"For the last time?"

"No!"

"Mr. Kesselbach, it is eight minutes to three. If you don't answer within eight minutes from now, you are a dead man!"

The next morning, Sergeant Gourel walked into the Palace Hotel punctually at the appointed hour. Without stopping, scorning to take the lift, he went up the stairs. On the fourth floor he turned to the right, followed the passage and rang at the door of 415.

Hearing no sound, he rang again. After half-a-dozen fruitless attempts, he went to the floor office. He found a head-waiter there:

"Mr. Kesselbach did not sleep here last night. We have not seen him since yesterday afternoon."

"But his servant? His secretary?"

"We have not seen them either."

"Then they also did not sleep in the hotel?"

"I suppose not."

"You suppose not? But you ought to be certain."

"Why? Mr. Kesselbach is not staying in the hotel; he is at home here, in his private flat. He is not waited on by us, but by his own man; and we know nothing of what happens inside."

"That's true. . . . That's true. . . ."

Gourel seemed greatly perplexed. He had come with positive orders, a precise mission, within the limits of which his mind was able to exert itself. Outside those limits he did not quite know how to act:

"If the chief were here," he muttered, "if the chief were here. . . ."

He showed his card and stated his quality. Then he said, on the off-chance:

"So you have not seen them come in?"

"No."

"But you saw them go out?"

"No, I can't say I did."

"In that case, how do you know that they went out?"

"From a gentleman who called yesterday afternoon."

"A gentleman with a dark mustache?"

"Yes. I met him as he was going away, about three o'clock. He said: 'The people in 415 have gone out. Mr. Kesselbach will stay at Versailles to-night, at the Reservoirs; you can send his letters on to him there.'"

"But who was this gentleman? By what right did he speak?"

"I don't know."

Gourel felt uneasy. It all struck him as rather queer.

"Have you the key?"

"No. Mr. Kesselbach had special keys made."

"Let's go and look."

Gourel rang again furiously. Nothing happened. He was about to go when, suddenly, he bent down and clapped his ear to the keyhole:

"Listen. . . . I seem to hear . . . Why, yes . . . it's quite distinct. . . . I hear moans. . . ."

He gave the door a tremendous blow with his fist.

"But, sir, you have not the right . . ."

"Oh, hang the right!"

He struck the door with renewed force, but to so little purpose that he abandoned the attempt forthwith:

"Quick, quick, a locksmith!"

One of the waiters started off at a run. Gourel, blustering and undecided, walked to and fro. The servants from the other floors collected in groups. People from the office, from the manager's department arrived. Gourel cried:

"But why shouldn't we go in though the adjoining rooms? Do they communicate with this suite?"

"Yes; but the communicating doors are always bolted on both sides."

"Then I shall telephone to the detective-office," said Gourel, to whose mind obviously there existed no salvation without his chief.

"And to the commissary of police," observed some one.

"Yes, if you like," he replied, in the tone of a gentleman who took little or no interest in that formality.

When he returned from the telephone, the locksmith had nearly finished trying the keys. The last worked the lock. Gourel walked briskly in.

He at once hastened in the direction from which the moans came and hit against the bodies of Chapman the secretary, and Edwards the manservant. One of them, Chapman, had succeeded, by dint of patience, in loosening his gag a little and was uttering short, stifled moans. The other seemed asleep.

They were released. But Gourel was anxious:

"Where's Mr. Kesselbach?"

He went into the sitting-room. Mr. Kesselbach was sitting strapped to the back of the arm-chair, near the table. His head hung on his chest.

"He has fainted," said Gourel, going up to him. "He must have exerted himself beyond his strength."

Swiftly he cut the cords that fastened the shoulders. The body fell forward in an inert mass. Gourel caught it in his arms and started back with a cry of horror:

"Why, he's dead! Feel . . . his hands are ice-cold! And look at his eyes!"

Some one ventured the opinion:

"An apoplectic stroke, no doubt . . . or else heart-failure."

"True, there's no sign of a wound . . . it's a natural death."

They laid the body on the sofa and unfastened the clothes. But red stains at once appeared on the white shirt; and, when they pushed it back, they saw that, near the heart, the chest bore a little scratch through which had trickled a thin stream of blood.

And on the shirt was pinned a card. Gourel bent forward. It was Arsène Lupin's card, bloodstained like the rest.

Then Gourel drew himself up, authoritatively and sharply:

"Murdered! . . . Arsène Lupin! . . . Leave the flat. . . . Leave the flat, all of you! . . . No one must stay here or in the bedroom. . . . Let the two men be removed and seen to elsewhere! . . . Leave the flat . . . and don't touch a thing . . .

"*The chief is on his way! . . .*"

II. THE BLUE-EDGED LABEL

"Arsène Lupin!"

Gourel repeated these two fateful words with an absolutely petrified air. They rang within him like a knell. Arsène Lupin! The great, the formidable Arsène Lupin. The burglar-king, the mighty adventurer! Was it possible?

"No, no," he muttered, "it's not possible, *because he's dead!*"

Only that was just it . . . was he really dead?

Arsène Lupin!

Standing beside the corpse, he remained dull and stunned, turning the card over and over with a certain dread, as though he had been challenged by a ghost. Arsène Lupin! What ought he to do? Act? Take the field with his resources? No, no . . . better not act . . . . He was bound to make mistakes if he entered the lists with an adversary of that stamp. Besides, the chief was on his way!

The chief was on his way! All Gourel's intellectual philosophy was summed up in that short sentence. An able, persevering officer, full of courage and experience and endowed with Herculean strength, he was one of those who go ahead only when obeying directions and who do good work only when ordered. And this lack of initiative had become still more marked since M. Lenormand had taken the place of M. Dudouis in the detective-service. M. Lenormand was a chief indeed! With him, one was sure of being on the right track. So sure, even, that Gourel stopped the moment that the chief's incentive was no longer behind him.

But the chief was on his way! Gourel took out his watch and calculated the exact time when he would arrive. If only the commissary of police did not get there first, if only the examining-magistrate, who was no doubt already appointed, or the divisional surgeon, did not come to make inopportune discoveries before the chief had time to fix the essential points of the case in his mind!

"Well, Gourel, what are you dreaming about?"

"The chief!"

M. Lenormand was still a young man, if you took stock only of the expression of his face and his eyes gleaming through his spectacles; but he was almost an old man when you saw his bent back, his skin dry and yellow as wax, his grizzled hair and beard, his whole decrepit, hesitating, unhealthy appearance. He had spent his life laboriously in the colonies as government commissary, in the most dangerous posts. He had there acquired a series of fevers; an indomitable energy, notwithstanding his physical weariness; the habit of living alone, of talking little and acting in silence; a certain misanthropy; and, suddenly, at the age of fifty-five, in consequence of the famous case of the three Spaniards at Biskra, a great and well-earned notoriety.

The injustice was then repaired; and he was straightway transferred to Bordeaux, was next appointed deputy in Paris, and lastly, on the death of M. Dudouis, chief of the detective-service. And in each of these posts he displayed such a curious faculty of inventiveness in his proceedings, such resourcefulness, so many new and original qualities; and above all, he achieved such correct results in the conduct of the last four or five cases with which public opinion had been stirred, that his name was quoted in the same breath with those of the most celebrated detectives.

Gourel, for his part, had no hesitation. Himself a favourite of the chief, who liked him for his frankness and his passive obedience, he set the chief above them all. The chief to him was an idol, an infallible god.

M. Lenormand seemed more tired than usual that day. He sat down wearily, parted the tails of his frock-coat—an old frock-coat, famous for its antiquated cut and its olive-green hue—untied his neckerchief—an equally famous maroon-coloured neckerchief, rested his two hands on his stick, and said:

"Speak!"

Gourel told all that he had seen, and all that he had learnt, and told it briefly, according to the habit which the chief had taught him.

But, when he produced Lupin's card, M. Lenormand gave a start:

"Lupin!"

"Yes, Lupin. The brute's bobbed up again."

"That's all right, that's all right," said M. Lenormand, after a moment's thought.

"That's all right, of course," said Gourel, who loved to add a word of his own to the rare speeches of a superior whose only fault in his eyes was an undue reticence. "That's all right, for at last you will measure your strength with an adversary worthy of you. . . . And Lupin will meet his master. . . . Lupin will cease to exist. . . . Lupin . . ."

"Ferret!" said M. Lenormand, cutting him short.

It was like an order given by a sportsman to his dog. And Gourel ferreted after the manner of a good dog, a lively and intelligent animal, working under his master's eyes. M. Lenormand pointed his stick to a corner, to an easy chair, just as one points to a bush or a tuft of grass, and Gourel beat up the bush or the tuft of grass with conscientious thoroughness.

"Nothing," said the sergeant, when he finished.

"Nothing for you!" grunted M. Lenormand.

"That's what I meant to say. . . . I know that, for you, chief, there are things that talk like human beings, real living witnesses. For all that, here is a murder well and duly added to our score against Master Lupin."

"The first," observed M. Lenormand.

"The first, yes. . . . But it was bound to come. You can't lead that sort of life without, sooner or later, being driven by circumstances to serious crime. Mr. Kesselbach must have defended himself. . . ."

"No, because he was bound."

"That's true," owned Gourel, somewhat disconcertedly, "and it's rather curious too. . . . Why kill an adversary who has practically ceased to exist? . . . But, no matter, if I had collared him yesterday, when we were face to face at the hall-door . . ."

M. Lenormand had stepped out on the balcony. Then he went to Mr. Kesselbach's bedroom, on the right, and tried the fastenings of the windows and doors.

"The windows of both rooms were shut when I came in," said Gourel.

"Shut, or just pushed to?"

"No one has touched them since. And they are shut, chief."

A sound of voices brought them back to the sitting-room. Here they found the divisional surgeon, engaged in examining the body, and M. Formerie, the magistrate. M. Formerie exclaimed:

"Arsène Lupin! I am glad that at last a lucky chance has brought me into touch with that scoundrel again! I'll show the fellow the stuff I'm made of! . . . And this time it's a murder! . . . It's a fight between you and me now, Master Lupin!"

M. Formerie had not forgotten the strange adventure of the Princesse de Lamballe's diadem, nor the wonderful way in which Lupin had tricked him a few years before.[11] The thing had remained famous in the annals of the law-courts. People still laughed at it; and in M. Formerie it had left a just feeling of resentment, combined with the longing for a striking revenge.

"The nature of the crime is self-evident," he declared, with a great air of conviction, "and we shall have no difficulty in discovering the motive. So all is well. . . . M. Lenormand, how do you do? . . . I am delighted to see you. . . ."

M. Formerie was not in the least delighted. On the contrary, M. Lenormand's presence did not please him at all, seeing that the chief detective hardly took the trouble to disguise the contempt in which he held him. However, the magistrate drew himself up and, in his most solemn tones:

"So, doctor, you consider that death took place about a dozen hours ago, perhaps more! . . . That, in fact, was my own idea. . . . We are quite agreed. . . . And the instrument of the crime?"

"A knife with a very thin blade, Monsieur le Juge d'Instruction," replied the surgeon. "Look, the blade has been wiped on the dead man's own handkerchief. . . ."

"Just so . . . just so . . . you can see the mark. . . . And now let us go and question Mr. Kesselbach's secretary and man-servant. I have no doubt that their examination will throw some more light on the case."

Chapman, who together with Edwards, had been moved to his own room, on the left of the sitting-room, had already recovered from his experiences. He described in detail the events of the previous day, Mr. Kesselbach's restlessness, the expected visit of the Colonel and, lastly, the attack of which they had been the victims.

---

[11] See *Arsène Lupin, Book three of this collection.*

"Aha!" cried M. Formerie. "So there's an accomplice! And you heard his name! . . . Marco, you say? . . . This is very important. When we've got the accomplice, we shall be a good deal further advanced. . . ."

"Yes, but we've not got him," M. Lenormand ventured to remark.

"We shall see. . . . One thing at a time. . . . And then, Mr. Chapman, this Marco went away immediately after M. Gourel had rung the bell?"

"Yes, we heard him go."

"And after he went, did you hear nothing else?"

"Yes . . . from time to time, but vaguel. . . . The door was shut."

"And what sort of noises did you hear?"

"Bursts of voices. The man . . ."

"Call him by his name, Arsène Lupin."

"Arsène Lupin must have telephoned."

"Capital! We will examine the person of the hotel who has charge of the branch exchange communicating with the outside. And, afterward, did you hear him go out, too?"

"He came in to see if we were still bound; and, a quarter of an hour later, he went away, closing the hall-door after him."

"Yes, as soon as his crime was committed. Good. . . . Good. . . . It all fits in. . . . And, after that?"

"After that, we heard nothing more. . . . The night passed. . . . I fell asleep from exhaustion. . . . So did Edwards. . . . And it was not until this morning . . ."

"Yes, I know. . . . There, it's not going badly . . . it all fits in. . . ."

And, marking off the stages of his investigation, in a tone as though he were enumerating so many victories over the stranger, he muttered thoughtfully:

"The accomplice . . . the telephone . . . the time of the murder . . . the sounds that were heard. . . . Good. . . . Very good. . . . We have still to establish the motive of the crime. . . . In this case, as we have Lupin to deal with, the motive is obvious. M. Lenormand, have you noticed the least sign of anything being broken open?"

"No."

"Then the robbery must have been effected upon the person of the victim himself. Has his pocket-book been found?"

"I left it in the pocket of his jacket," said Gourel.

They all went into the sitting-room, where M. Formerie discovered that the pocket-book contained nothing but visiting-cards and papers establishing the murdered man's identity.

"That's odd. Mr. Chapman, can you tell us if Mr. Kesselbach had any money on him?"

"Yes. On the previous day—that is, on Monday, the day before yesterday—we went to the Crédit Lyonnais, where Mr. Kesselbach hired a safe . . ."

"A safe at the Crédit Lyonnais? Good. . . . We must look into that."

"And, before we left, Mr. Kesselbach opened an account and drew out five or six thousand francs in bank-notes."

"Excellent . . . that tells us just what we want to know."

Chapman continued:

"There is another point, Monsieur le Juge d'Instruction. Mr. Kesselbach, who for some days had been very uneasy in his mind—I have told you the reason: a scheme to which he attached the utmost importance—Mr. Kesselbach seemed particularly anxious about two things. There was, first, a little ebony box, which he put away safely at the Crédit Lyonnais; and, next, a little black morocco note-case, in which he kept a few papers."

"And where is that?"

"Before Lupin's arrival, he put it, in my presence, into that travelling-bag."

M. Formerie took the bag and felt about in it. The note-case was not there. He rubbed his hands:

"Ah, everything fits in! . . . We know the culprit, the conditions and the motive of the crime. This case won't take long. Are we quite agreed upon everything, M. Lenormand?"

"Upon not one single thing."

There was a moment of stupefaction. The commissary of police had arrived: and, behind him, in spite of the constables keeping the door, a troop of journalists, and the hotel staff had forced their way in and were standing in the entrance-lobby.

Notorious though the old fellow was for his bluntness—a bluntness which was not without a certain discourtesy and which had already procured him an occasional reprimand in high quarters—the abruptness of this reply took every one aback. And M. Formerie in particular appeared utterly nonplussed:

"Still," he said, "I can see nothing that isn't quite simple. Lupin is the thief. . . ."

"Why did he commit the murder?" M. Lenormand flung at him.

"In order to commit the theft."

"I beg your pardon; the witnesses' story proves that the theft took place before the murder. Mr. Kesselbach was first bound and gagged, then robbed. Why should Lupin, who has never resorted to murder, choose this time to kill a man whom he had rendered helpless and whom he had already robbed?"

The examining-magistrate stroked his long, fair whiskers, with the gesture customary to him when a question seemed incapable of solution. He replied in a thoughtful tone:

"There are several answers to that. . . ."

"What are they?"

"It depends . . . it depends upon a number of facts as yet unknown. . . . And, moreover, the objection applies only to the nature of the motives. We are agreed as to the remainder."

"No."

This time, again, the denial was flat, blunt, almost impolite; so much so that the magistrate was absolutely nonplussed, dared not even raise a protest, and remained abashed in the presence of this strange collaborator. At last he said:

"We all have our theories. I should like to know yours."

"I have none."

The chief detective rose and, leaning on his stick, took a few steps through the room. All the people around him were silent. . . . And it was rather curious, in a group in which, after all, his position was only that of an auxiliary, a subordinate, to see this ailing, decrepit, elderly man dominate the others by the sheer force of an authority which they had to feel, even though they did not accept it. After a long pause he said:

"I should like to inspect the rooms which adjoin this suite."

The manager showed him the plan of the hotel. The only way out of the right-hand bedroom, which was Mr. Kesselbach's, was through the little entrance-hall of the suite. But the bedroom on the left, the room occupied by the secretary, communicated with another apartment.

"Let us inspect it," said M. Lenormand.

M. Formerie could not help shrugging his shoulders and growling:

"But the communicating door is bolted and the window locked."

"Let us inspect it," repeated M. Lenormand.

He was taken into the apartment, which was the first of the five rooms reserved for Mrs. Kesselbach. Then, at his request, he was taken to the rooms leading out of it. All the communicating doors were bolted on both sides.

"Are not any of these rooms occupied?" he asked.

"No."

"Where are the keys?"

"The keys are always kept in the office."

"Then no one can have got in? . . ."

"No one, except the floor-waiter who airs and dusts the rooms."

"Send for him, please."

The man, whose name was Gustave Beudot, replied that he had closed the windows of five rooms on the previous day in accordance with his general instructions.

"At what time?"

"At six o'clock in the evening."

"And you noticed nothing?"

"No, sir."

"And, this morning . . . ?"

"This morning, I opened the windows at eight o'clock exactly."

"And you found nothing?"

He hesitated. He was pressed with questions and ended by admitting:

"Well, I picked up a cigarette-case near the fireplace in 420. . . . I intended to take it to the office this evening."

"Have you it on you?"

"No, it is in my room. It is a gun-metal case. It has a space for tobacco and cigarette-papers on one side and for matches on the other. There are two initials in gold: an L and an M. . . ."

"What's that?"

Chapman had stepped forward. He seemed greatly surprised and, questioning the servant:

"A gun-metal cigarette-case, you say?"

"Yes."

"With three compartments—for tobacco, cigarette-papers, and matches. . . . Russian tobacco, wasn't it, very fine and light?"

"Yes."

"Go and fetch it. . . . I should like to see it for myself . . . to make sure. . . ."

At a sign from the chief detective, Gustave Beudot left the room.

M. Lenormand sat down and his keen eyes examined the carpet, the furniture and the curtains. He asked:

"This is room 420, is it not?"

"Yes."

The magistrate grinned:

"I should very much like to know what connection you establish between this incident and the tragedy. Five locked doors separate us from the room in which Mr. Kesselbach was murdered."

M. Lenormand did not condescend to reply.

Time passed. Gustave did not return.

"Where does he sleep?" asked the chief detective.

"On the sixth floor," answered the manager. "The room is on the Rue de Judée side: above this, therefore. It's curious that he's not back yet."

"Would you have the kindness to send some one to see?"

The manager went himself, accompanied by Chapman. A few minutes after, he returned alone, running, with every mark of consternation on his face.

"Well?"

"Dead!"

"Murdered?"

"Yes."

"Oh, by thunder, how clever these scoundrels are!" roared M. Lenormand, "Off with you, Gourel, and have the doors of the hotel locked. . . . Watch every outlet. . . . And you, Mr. Manager, please take us to Gustave Beudot's room."

The manager led the way. But as they left the room, M. Lenormand stooped and picked up a tiny little round piece of paper, on which his eyes had already fixed themselves.

It was a label surrounded with a blue border and marked with the number 813. He put it in his pocket, on chance, and joined the others. . . .

A small wound in the back, between the shoulder-blades. . . .

"Exactly the same wound as Mr. Kesselbach's," declared the doctor.

"Yes," said M. Lenormand, "it was the same hand that struck the blow and the same weapon was used."

Judging by the position of the body, the man had been surprised when on his knees before the bed, feeling under the mattress for the cigarette-case which he had hidden there. His arm was still caught between the mattress and the bed, but the cigarette-case was not to be found.

"That cigarette-case must have been devilish compromising!" timidly suggested M. Formerie, who no longer dared put forward any definite opinion.

"Well, of course!" said the chief detective.

"At any rate, we know the initials: an L and an M. And with that, together with what Mr. Chapman appears to know, we shall easily learn...."

M. Lenormand gave a start:

"Chapman! But where is he?"

They looked in the passage among the groups of people crowded together. Chapman was not there.

"Mr. Chapman came with me," said the manager.

"Yes, yes, I know, but he did not come back with you."

"No, I left him with the corpse."

"You left him! ... Alone?"

"I said to him, 'Stay here ... don't move.'"

"And was there no one about? Did you see no one?"

"In the passage? No."

"But in the other attics? ... Or else, look here, round that corner: was there no one hiding there?"

M. Lenormand seemed greatly excited. He walked up and down, he opened the doors of the rooms. And, suddenly, he set off at a run, with an agility of which no one would have thought him capable. He rattled down the six storeys, followed at a distance by the manager and the examining-magistrate. At the bottom, he found Gourel in front of the main door.

"Has no one gone out?"

"No, chief."

"What about the other door, in the Rue Orvieto?"

"I have posted Dieuzy there."

"With firm orders?"

"Yes, chief."

The huge hall of the hotel was crowded with anxious visitors, all commenting on the more or less accurate versions that had reached them of the crime. All the servants had been summoned by telephone and were arriving, one by one. M. Lenormand questioned them without delay. None of them was able to supply the least information. But a fifth-floor chambermaid appeared. Ten minutes earlier, or thereabouts, she had passed two gentlemen who were coming down the servants' staircase between the fifth and the fourth floors.

"They came down very fast. The one in front was holding the other by the hand. I was surprised to see those two gentlemen on the servants' staircase."

"Would you know them again?"

"Not the first one. He had his head turned the other way. He was a thin, fair man. He wore a soft black hat ... and black clothes."

"And the other?"

"Oh, the other was an Englishman, with a big, clean-shaven face and a check suit. He had no hat on."

The description obviously referred to Chapman.

The woman added:

"He looked ... he looked quite funny ... as if he was mad."

Gourel's word was not enough for M. Lenormand. One after the other, he questioned the under-porters standing at the two doors:

"Did you know Mr. Chapman?"

"Yes, sir, he always spoke to us."

"And you have not seen him go out?"

"No, sir. He has not been out this morning."

M. Lenormand turned to the commissary of police: "How many men have you with you, Monsieur le Commissaire?"

"Four."

"That's not sufficient. Telephone to your secretary to send you all the men available. And please be so good as yourself to organize the closest watch at every outlet. The state of siege, Monsieur le Commissaire...."

"But I say," protested the manager, "my customers?"

"I don't care a hang, sir, for your customers! My duty comes before everything; and my duty is at all costs to arrest...."

"So you believe..." the examining-magistrate ventured to interpolate.

"I don't *believe*, monsieur... I am sure that the perpetrator of both the murders is still in the hotel."

"But then Chapman..."

"At this moment, I cannot guarantee that Chapman is still alive. In any case, it is only a question of minutes, of seconds.... Gourel, take two men and search all the rooms on the fourth floor.... Mr. Manager, send one of your clerks with them.... As for the other floors, I shall proceed as soon as we are reënforced. Come, Gourel, off with you, and keep your eyes open.... It's big game you're hunting!"

Gourel and his men hurried away. M. Lenormand himself remained in the hall, near the office. This time, he did not think of sitting down, as his custom was. He walked from the main entrance to the door in the Rue Orvieto and returned to the point from which he had started. At intervals he gave instructions:

"Mr. Manager, see that the kitchens are watched. They may try to escape that way.... Mr. Manager, instruct your young lady at the telephone not to put any of the people in the hotel into communication with outside subscribers. If a call comes from the outside, she can connect the caller with the person asked for, but she must take a note of that person's name.... Mr. Manager, have a list made out of all your visitors whose name begins with an L or an M."

The tension caught the spectators by the throat, as they stood clustered in the middle of the hall, silent and gasping for breath, shaking with fear at the least sound, obsessed by the infernal image of the murderer. Where was he hiding? Would he show himself? Was he not one of themselves: this one, perhaps... or that one?...

And all eyes were turned on the gray-haired gentleman in spectacles, an olive-green frock-coat and a maroon-colored neckerchief, who was walking about, with his bent back, on a pair of shaky legs.

At times, one of the waiters accompanying Sergeant Gourel on his search would come running up.

"Any news?" asked M. Lenormand.

"No, sir, we've found nothing."

The manager made two attempts to induce him to relax his orders regarding the doors. The situation was becoming intolerable. The office was filled with loudly-protesting visitors, who had business outside, or who had arranged to leave Paris.

"I don't care a hang!" said M. Lenormand again.

"But I know them all."

"I congratulate you."

"You are exceeding your powers."

"I know."

"The law will decide against you."

"I'm convinced of that."

"Monsieur le Juge d'Instruction himself...."

"M. Formerie had better not interfere. He can mind his own business, which is to examine the servants, as he is doing now. Besides, it has nothing to do with the examining-magistrate, it has to do with the police. It's my affair."

Just then a squad of police burst into the hotel. The chief detective divided them into several sections which he sent up to the third floor. Then, addressing the commissary of police:

"My dear commissary, I leave the task of watching the doors to you. No weakness, I entreat you. I will take the responsibility for anything that happens."

And, turning to the lift, he had himself conveyed to the second floor.

It was a difficult business and a long one, for they had to open the doors of the sixty bedrooms, to inspect all the bathrooms, all the recesses, all the cupboards, every nook and corner.

And it was also fruitless. An hour later, on the stroke of twelve, M. Lenormand had just done the second floor; the other parties had not yet finished the upper floors; and no discovery had been made.

M. Lenormand hesitated: had the murderer retreated to the attics?

He was deciding, however, to go downstairs, when he was told that Mrs. Kesselbach had just arrived with her lady-companion. Edwards, the old confidential man-servant, had accepted the task of informing her of Mr. Kesselbach's death.

M. Lenormand found her in one of the drawing rooms, overcome by the unexpected shock, dry-eyed, but with her features wrung with grief and her body trembling all over, as though convulsed with fever. She was a rather tall, dark woman; and her black and exceedingly beautiful eyes were filled with gold, with little gold spots, like spangles gleaming in the dark. Her husband had met her in Holland, where Dolores was born of an old family of Spanish origin, the Amontis. He fell in love with her at first sight; and for four years the harmony between them, built up of mutual affection and devotion, had never been interrupted.

M. Lenormand introduced himself. She looked at him without replying; and he was silent, for she did not appear, in her stupor, to understand what he said. Then, suddenly, she began to shed copious tears and asked to be taken to her husband.

In the hall, M. Lenormand found Gourel, who was looking for him and who rushed at him with a hat which he held in his hand:

"I picked this up, chief. . . . There's no doubt whom it belongs to, is there?"

It was a soft, black felt hat and resembled the description given. There was no lining or label inside it.

"Where did you pick it up?"

"On the second-floor landing of the servants' staircase."

"Nothing on the other floors?"

"Nothing. We've searched everywhere. There is only the first floor left. And this hat shows that the man went down so far. We're burning, chief!"

"I think so."

At the foot of the stairs M. Lenormand stopped:

"Go back to the commissary and give him my orders: he must post two men at the foot of each of the four staircases, revolver in hand. And they are to fire, if necessary. Understand this, Gourel: if Chapman is not saved and if the fellow escapes, it means my resignation. I've been wool-gathering for over two hours."

He went up the stairs. On the first floor he met two policemen leaving a bedroom, accompanied by a servant of the hotel.

The passage was deserted. The hotel staff dared not venture into it. Some of the permanent visitors had locked themselves in their rooms; and the police had to knock for a long time and proclaim who they were before they could get the doors opened.

Farther on, M. Lenormand saw another group of policemen searching the maid's pantry and, at the end of a long passage, he saw some more men who were approaching the turning, that is to say, that part of the passage which contained the rooms overlooking the Rue de Judée.

And, suddenly, he heard these men shouting; and they disappeared at a run.

He hurried after them.

The policemen had stopped in the middle of the passage. At their feet, blocking their way, with its face on the carpet, lay a corpse.

M. Lenormand bent down and took the lifeless head in his hands:

"Chapman," he muttered. "He is dead."

He examined the body. A white knitted silk muffler was tied round the neck. He undid it. Red stains appeared; and he saw that the muffler held a thick wad of cotton-wool in position against the nape of the neck. The wad was soaked with blood.

Once again there was the same little wound, clean, frank and pitiless.

M. Formerie and the commissary were at once told and came hastening up.

"No one gone out?" asked the chief detective. "No surprise?"

"No," said the commissary. "There are two men on guard at the foot of each staircase."

"Perhaps he has gone up again?" said M. Formerie.

"No! . . . No! . . ."

"But some one must have met him. . . ."

"No. . . . This all happened quite a long time ago. The hands are cold. . . . The murder must have been committed almost immediately after the other . . . as soon as the two men came here by the servants' staircase."

"But the body would have been seen! Think, fifty people must have passed this spot during the last two hours. . . ."

"The body was not here."

"Then where was it?"

"Why, how can I tell?" snapped the chief detective. "Do as I'm doing, look for yourself! You can't find things by talking."

He furiously patted the knob of his stick with a twitching hand; and he stood there, with his eyes fixed on the body, silent and thoughtful. At last he spoke:

"Monsieur le Commissaire, be so good as to have the victim taken to an empty room. Let them fetch the doctor. Mr. Manager, would you mind opening the doors of all the rooms on this passage for me?"

On the left were three bedrooms and two sitting-rooms, forming an empty suite, which M. Lenormand inspected. On the right were four bedrooms. Two were occupied respectively by a M. Reverdat and an Italian, Baron Giacomini, who were both then out. In the third room they found an elderly English maiden lady still in bed; and, in the fourth, an Englishman who was placidly reading and smoking and who had not been in the least disturbed by the noises in the passage. His name was Major Parbury.

No amount of searching or questioning led to any result. The old maid had heard nothing before the exclamations of the policeman: no noise of a struggle, no cry of pain, no sound of quarreling; and Major Parbury neither.

Moreover, there was no suspicious clue found, no trace of blood, nothing to lead them to suppose that the unfortunate Chapman had been in one of those rooms.

"It's queer," muttered the examining-magistrate, "it's all very queer. . . ." And he confessed, ingenuously, "I feel more and more at sea. . . . There is a whole series of circumstances that are partly beyond me. What do you make of it, M. Lenormand?"

M. Lenormand was on the point of letting off one of those pointed rejoinders in which he was wont to give vent to his chronic ill-temper, when Gourel appeared upon the scene, all out of breath.

"Chief," he panted, "they've found this . . . downstairs . . . in the office . . . on a chair. . . ."

It was a parcel of moderate dimensions, wrapped up in a piece of black serge.

"Did they open it?" asked the chief.

"Yes, but when they saw what the parcel contained, they did it up again exactly as it was . . . fastened very tight, as you can see. . . ."

"Untie it."

Gourel removed the wrapper and disclosed a black diagonal jacket and trousers, which had evidently been packed up in a hurry, as the creases in the cloth showed. In the middle was a towel, covered with blood, which had been dipped in water, in order, no doubt, to destroy the marks of the hands that had been wiped on it. Inside the napkin was a steel dagger, with a handle encrusted with gold. This also was red with blood, the blood of three men stabbed within the space of a few hours by an invisible hand, amid the crowd of three hundred people moving about in the huge hotel.

Edwards, the man-servant, at once identified the dagger as belonging to Mr. Kesselbach. He had seen it on the table on the previous day, before the assault committed by Lupin.

"Mr. Manager," said the chief detective, "the restriction is over. Gourel, go and give orders to leave the doors free."

"So you think that Lupin has succeeded in getting out?" asked M. Formerie.

"No. The perpetrator of the three murders which we have discovered is in one of the rooms of the hotel, or, rather, he is among the visitors in the hall or in the reception-rooms. In my opinion, he was staying in the hotel."

"Impossible! Besides, where would he have changed his clothes? And what clothes would he have on now?"

"I don't know, but I am stating a fact."

"And you are letting him go? Why, he'll just walk out quietly, with his hands in his pockets!"

"The one who walks away like that, without his luggage, and who does not return, will be the criminal. Mr. Manager, please come with me to the office. I should like to make a close inspection of your visitors' book."

In the office, M. Lenormand found a few letters addressed to Mr. Kesselbach. He handed them to the examining-magistrate. There was also a parcel that had just come by the Paris parcel-post. The paper in which it was packed was partly torn; and M. Lenormand saw that it held a small ebony box, engraved with the name of Rudolf Kesselbach. Feeling curious, he opened the parcel. The box contained the fragments of a looking-glass which had evidently been fixed to the inside of the lid. It also contained the card of Arsène Lupin.

But one detail seemed to strike the chief detective. On the outside, at the bottom of the box, was a little blue-edged label, similar to the label which he had picked up in the room on the fourth floor where the cigarette-case was found, and this label bore the same number, 813.

III. M. LENORMAND OPENS HIS CAMPAIGN

"Auguste, show M. Lenormand in."

The messenger went out and, a few seconds later, announced the chief of the detective-service.

There were three men in the prime minister's private room on the Place Beauvau: the famous Valenglay, leader of the radical party for the past thirty years and now president of the council and minister of the interior; the attorney-general, M. Testard; and the prefect of police, Delaume.

The prefect of police and the attorney-general did not rise from the chairs which they had occupied during their long conversation with the prime minister. Valenglay, however, stood up and, pressing the chief detective's hand, said, in the most cordial tones:

"I have no doubt, my dear Lenormand, that you know the reason why I asked you to come."

"The Kesselbach case?"

"Yes."

The Kesselbach case! Not one of us but is able to recall not only the main details of this tragic affair, the tangled skein of which I have set myself to unravel, but even its very smallest incidents, so greatly did the tragedy excite us all during these recent years. Nor is there one of us but remembers the extraordinary stir which it created both in and outside France. And yet there was one thing that upset the public even more than the three murders committed in such mysterious circumstances, more than the detestable atrocity of that butchery, more than anything else; and that was the reappearance—one might almost say the resurrection—of Arsène Lupin.

Arsène Lupin! No one had heard speak of him for over four years, since his incredible, his astounding adventure of the Hollow Needle, since the day when he had slunk away into the darkness before the eyes of Holmlock Shears and Isidore Beautrelet, carrying on his back the dead body of the woman whom he loved, and followed by his old servant, Victoire.

From that day onward he had been generally believed to be dead. This was the version put about by the police, who, finding no trace of their adversary, were content purely and simply to bury him.

Some, however, believing him to be saved, described him as leading a placid, Philistine existence. According to them, he was living with his wife and children, growing his small potatoes; whereas others maintained that, bent down with the weight of sorrow and weary of the vanities of this world, he had sought the seclusion of a Trappist monastery.

And here he was once more looming large in the public view and resuming his relentless struggle against society! Arsène Lupin was Arsène Lupin again, the fanciful, intangible, disconcerting, audacious, genial Arsène Lupin! But, this time, a cry of horror arose. Arsène Lupin had taken human life! And the fierceness, the cruelty, the ruthless cynicism of the crime were so great that, then and there, the legend of the popular hero, of the chivalrous and occasionally sentimental adventurer, made way for a new conception of an inhuman, bloodthirsty, and ferocious monster. The crowd now loathed and feared its former idol with more intensity than it had once shown in admiring him for his easy grace and his diverting good-humor.

And, forthwith, the indignation of that frightened crowd turned against the police. Formerly, people had laughed. They forgave the beaten commissary of police for the comical fashion in which he allowed himself to be beaten. But the joke had lasted too long; and, in a burst of revolt and fury, they now called the authorities to account for the unspeakable crimes which these were powerless to prevent.

In the press, at public meetings, in the streets and even in the tribune of the Chamber of Deputies there was such an explosion of wrath that the government grew alarmed and strove by every possible means to allay the public excitement.

It so happened that Valenglay, the premier, took a great interest in all these police questions and had often amused himself by going closely into different cases with the chief of the detective-service, whose good qualities and independent character he valued highly. He sent for the prefect and the attorney-general to see him in his room, talked to them and then sent for M. Lenormand.

"Yes, my dear Lenormand, it's about the Kesselbach case. But, before we discuss it, I must call your attention to a point which more particularly affects and, I may say, annoys Monsieur le Préfet de Police. M. Delaume, will you explain to M. Lenormand . . . ?

"Oh, M. Lenormand knows quite well how the matter stands," said the prefect, in a tone which showed but little good-will toward his subordinate. "We have talked it over already and I have told him what I thought of his improper conduct at the Palace Hotel. People are generally indignant."

M. Lenormand rose, took a paper from his pocket and laid it on the table.

"What is this?" asked Valenglay.

"My resignation, Monsieur le Président du Conseil."

Valenglay gave a jump:

"What! Your resignation! For a well-meaning remark which Monsieur le Préfet thinks fit to address to you and to which, for that matter, he attaches no importance whatever—do you, Delaume? No importance whatever—and there you go, taking offence! You must confess, my dear Lenormand, that you're devilish touchy! Come, put that bit of paper back in your pocket and let's talk seriously."

The chief detective sat down again, and Valenglay, silencing the prefect, who made no attempt to conceal his dissatisfaction, said:

"In two words, Lenormand, the thing is that Lupin's reappearance upon the scene annoys us. The brute has defied us long enough. It used to be funny, I confess, and I, for my part, was the first to laugh at it. But it's no longer a question of that. It's a question of murder now. We could stand Lupin, as long as he amused the gallery. But, when he takes to killing people, no!"

"Then what is it that you ask, Monsieur le Président?"

"What we ask? Oh, it's quite simple! First, his arrest and then his head!"

"I can promise you his arrest, some day or another, but not his head."

"What! If he's arrested, it means trial for murder, a verdict of guilty, and the scaffold."

"No!"

"And why not?"

"Because Lupin has not committed murder."

"Eh? Why, you're mad, Lenormand! The corpses at the Palace Hotel are so many inventions, I suppose! And the three murders were never committed!"

"Yes, but not by Lupin."

The chief spoke these words very steadily, with impressive calmness and conviction. The attorney and the prefect protested.

"I presume, Lenormand," said Valenglay, "that you do not put forward that theory without serious reasons?"

"It is not a theory."

"What proof have you?"

"There are two, to begin with, two proofs of a moral nature, which I at once placed before Monsieur le Juge d'Instruction and which the newspapers have laid stress upon. First and foremost, Lupin does not kill people. Next, why should he have killed anybody, seeing that the object which he set out to achieve, the theft, was accomplished and that he had nothing to fear from an adversary who was gagged and bound?"

"Very well. But the facts?"

"Facts are worth nothing against reason and logic; and, moreover, the facts also are on my side. What would be the meaning of Lupin's presence in the room in which the cigarette-case was discovered? On the other hand, the black clothes which were found and which evidently belonged to the murderer are not in the least of a size to fit Lupin."

"You know him, then, do you?"

"I? No. But Edwards saw him, Gourel saw him; and the man whom they saw is not the man whom the chambermaid saw, on the servants' staircase, dragging Chapman by the hand."

"Then your idea . . ."

"You mean to say, the truth, M. le Président. Here it is, or, at least, here is the truth as far as I know it. On Tuesday, the 16th of April, a man—-Lupin—broke into Mr. Kesselbach's room at about two o'clock in the afternoon. . . ."

M. Lenormand was interrupted by a burst of laughter. It came from the prefect of police.

"Let me tell you, M. Lenormand, that you are in rather too great a hurry to state your precise facts. It has been shown that, at three o'clock on that day, Mr. Kesselbach walked into the Crédit Lyonnais and went down to the safe deposit. His signature in the register proves it."

M. Lenormand waited respectfully until his superior had finished speaking. Then, without even troubling to reply directly to the attack, he continued:

"At about two o'clock in the afternoon, Lupin, assisted by an accomplice, a man named Marco, bound Mr. Kesselbach hand and foot, robbed him of all the loose cash which he had upon him and compelled him to reveal the cypher of his safe at the Crédit Lyonnais. As soon as the secret was told, Marco left. He joined another accomplice, who, profiting by a certain resemblance to Mr. Kesselbach—a resemblance which he accentuated that day by wearing clothes similar to Mr. Kesselbach's and putting on a pair of gold spectacles—entered the Crédit Lyonnais, imitated Mr. Kesselbach's signature, emptied the safe of its contents and walked off, accompanied by Marco. Marco at once telephoned to Lupin. Lupin, as soon as he was sure that Mr. Kesselbach had not deceived him and that the object of his expedition was attained, went away."

Valenglay seemed to waver in his mind:

"Yes, yes . . . we'll admit that. . . . But what surprises me is that a man like Lupin should have risked so much for such a paltry profit: a few bank-notes and the hypothetical contents of a safe."

"Lupin was after more than that. He wanted either the morocco envelope which was in the traveling-bag, or else the ebony box which was in the safe. He had the ebony box, because he has sent it back empty. Therefore, by this time, he knows, or is in a fair way for knowing, the famous scheme which Mr. Kesselbach was planning, and which he was discussing with his secretary a few minutes before his death."

"What was the scheme?"

"I don't exactly know. The manager of Barbareux's agency, to whom he had opened his mind about it, has told me that Mr. Kesselbach was looking for a man who went by the name of Pierre Leduc, a man who had lost caste, it appears. Why and how the discovery of this person was connected with the success of his scheme, I am unable to say."

"Very well," said Valenglay. "So much for Arsène Lupin. His part is played. Mr. Kesselbach is bound hand and foot, robbed, but alive! . . . What happens up to the time when he is found dead?"

"Nothing, for several hours, nothing until night. But, during the night, some one made his way in."

"How?"

"Through room 420, one of the rooms reserved by Mr. Kesselbach. The person in question evidently possessed a false key."

"But," exclaimed the prefect of police, "all the doors between that room and Mr. Kesselbach's flat were bolted; and there were five of them!"

"There was always the balcony."

"The balcony!"

"Yes; the balcony runs along the whole floor, on the Rue de Judée side."

"And what about the spaces in between?"

"An active man can step across them. Our man did. I have found marks."

"But all the windows of the suite were shut; and it was ascertained, after the crime, that they were still shut."

"All except one, the secretary's window, Chapman's, which was only pushed to. I tried it myself."

This time the prime minister seemed a little shaken, so logical did M. Lenormand's version seem, so precise and supported by such sound facts. He asked, with growing interest:

"But what was the man's object in coming?"

"I don't know."

"Ah, you don't know!"

"Any more than I know his name."

"But why did he kill Mr. Kesselbach?"

"I don't know. This all remains a mystery. The utmost that we have the right to suppose is that he did not come with the intention of killing, but with the intention, he too, of taking the documents contained in the morocco note-case and the ebony box; and that, finding himself by accident in the presence of the enemy reduced to a state of helplessness, he killed him."

Valenglay muttered:

"Yes, strictly speaking, that is possible. . . . And, according to you, did he find the documents?"

"He did not find the box, because it was not there; but he found the black morocco note-case. So that Lupin and . . . the other are in the same position. Each knows as much as the other about the Kesselbach scheme."

"That means," remarked the premier, "that they will fight."

"Exactly. And the fight has already begun. The murderer, finding a card of Arsène Lupin's, pinned it to the corpse. All the appearances would thus be against Arsène Lupin . . . therefore, Arsène Lupin would be the murderer."

"True . . . true," said Valenglay. "The calculation seemed pretty accurate."

"And the stratagem would have succeeded," continued M. Lenormand, "if in consequence of another and a less favorable accident, the murderer had not, either in coming or going, dropped his cigarette-case in room 420, and if the floor-waiter, Gustave Beudot, had not picked it up. From that moment, knowing himself to be discovered, or on the point of being discovered . . ."

"How did he know it?"

"How? Why, through M. Formerie, the examining-magistrate, himself! The investigation took place with open doors. It is certain that the murderer was concealed among the people, members of the hotel staff and journalists, who were present when Gustave Beudot was giving his evidence; and when the magistrate sent Gustave Beudot to his attic to fetch the cigarette-case, the man followed and struck the blow. Second victim!"

No one protested now. The tragedy was being reconstructed before their eyes with a realism and a probable accuracy which were equally striking.

"And the third victim?" asked Valenglay.

"He himself gave the ruffian his opportunity. When Beudot did not return, Chapman, curious to see the cigarette-case for himself, went upstairs with the manager of the hotel. He was surprised by the murderer, dragged away by him, taken to one of the bedrooms and murdered in his turn."

"But why did he allow himself to be dragged away like that and to be led by a man whom he knew to be the murderer of Mr. Kesselbach and of Gustave Beudot?"

"I don't know, any more than I know the room in which the crime was committed, or the really miraculous way in which the criminal escaped."

"Something has been said about two blue labels."

"Yes, one was found on the box which Lupin sent back; and the other was found by me and doubtless came from the morocco note-case stolen by the murderer."

"Well?"

"I don't think that they mean anything. What does mean something is the number 813, which Mr. Kesselbach wrote on each of them. His handwriting has been recognized."

"And that number 813?"

"It's a mystery."

"Then?"

"I can only reply again that I don't know."

"Have you no suspicions?"

"None at all. Two of my men are occupying one of the rooms in the Palace Hotel, on the floor where Chapman's body was found. I have had all the people in the hotel watched by these two men. The criminal is not one of those who have left."

"Did no one telephone while the murders were being committed?"

"Yes, some one telephoned from the outside to Major Parbury, one of the four persons who occupied rooms on the first-floor passage."

"And this Major Parbury?"

"I am having him watched by my men. So far, nothing has been discovered against him."

"And in which direction do you intend to seek?"

"Oh, in a very limited direction. In my opinion, the murderer must be numbered among the friends or connections of Mr. and Mrs. Kesselbach. He followed their scent, knew their habits, the reason of Mr. Kesselbach's presence in Paris; and he at least suspected the importance of Mr. Kesselbach's plans."

"Then he was not a professional criminal?"

"No, no, certainly not! The murder was committed with extraordinary cleverness and daring, but it was due to circumstances. I repeat, we shall have to look among the people forming the immediate circle of Mr. and Mrs. Kesselbach. And the proof is that Mr. Kesselbach's murderer killed Gustave Beudot for the sole reason that the waiter had the cigarette-case in his possession; and Chapman for the sole reason that the secretary knew of its existence. Remember Chapman's excitement: at the mere description of the cigarette-case, Chapman received a sudden insight into the tragedy. If he had seen the cigarette-case, we should have been fully informed. The man, whoever he may be, was well aware of that: and he put an end to Chapman. And we know nothing, nothing but the initials L and M."

He reflected for a moment and said:

"There is another proof, which forms an answer to one of your questions, Monsieur le Président: Do you believe that Chapman would have accompanied that man along the passages and staircases of the hotel if he did not already know him?"

The facts were accumulating. The truth or, at least, the probable truth was gaining strength. Many of the points at issue, the most interesting, perhaps, remained obscure. But what a light had been thrown upon the subject! Short of the motives that inspired them, how clearly Lenormand's hearers now perceived the sequence of acts performed on that tragic morning!

There was a pause. Every one was thinking, seeking for arguments, for objections. At last, Valenglay exclaimed:

"My dear Lenormand, this is all quite excellent. You have convinced me. . . . But, taking one thing with another, we are no further than we were."

"What do you mean?"

"What I say. The object of our meeting is not to clear up a portion of the mystery, which, one day, I am sure, you will clear up altogether, but to satisfy the public demand as fully as we possibly can. Now whether the murderer is Lupin or another; whether there are two criminals, or three, or only one: all this gives us neither the criminal's name nor his arrest. And the public continues under the disastrous impression that the law is powerless."

"What can I do?"

"Give the public the definite satisfaction which it demands."

"But it seems to me that this explanation ought to be enough. . . ."

"Words! The public wants deeds! One thing alone will satisfy it: an arrest."

"Hang it all! Hang it all! We can't arrest the first person that comes along!"

"Even that would be better than arresting nobody," said Valenglay, with a laugh. "Come, have a good look round! Are you sure of Edwards, Kesselbach's servant?"

"Absolutely sure. Besides . . . No, Monsieur le Président, it would be dangerous and ridiculous; and I am sure that Mr. Attorney-General himself . . . There are only two people whom we have the right to arrest: the murderer—I don't know who he is—and Arsène Lupin."

"Well?"

"There is no question of arresting Arsène Lupin, or, at least, it requires time, a whole series of measures, which I have not yet had the leisure to contrive, because I looked upon Lupin as settled down . . . or dead."

Valenglay stamped his foot with the impatience of a man who likes to see his wishes realized on the spot:

"And yet . . . and yet, my dear Lenormand, something must be done . . . if only for your own sake. You know as well as I do that you have powerful enemies . . . and that, if I were not there . . . In short, Lenormand, you can't be allowed to get out of it like this. What are you doing about the accomplices? There are others besides Lupin. There is Marco; and there's the rogue who impersonated Mr. Kesselbach in order to visit the cellars of the Crédit Lyonnais."

"Would you be satisfied if you got him, Monsieur le Président?"

"Would I be satisfied? Heavens alive, I should think I would!"

"Well, give me seven days."

"Seven days! Why, it's not a question of days, my dear Lenormand! It's a question of hours!"

"How many will you give me, Monsieur le Président?"

Valenglay took out his watch and chuckled:

"I will give you ten minutes, my dear Lenormand!"

The chief took out his, and emphasizing each syllable, said calmly:

"That is four minutes more than I want, Monsieur le Président."

Valenglay looked at him in amazement.

"Four minutes more than you want? What do you mean by that?"

"I mean, Monsieur le Président, that the ten minutes which you allow me are superfluous. I want six, and not one minute more."

"Oh, but look here, Lenormand . . . if you imagine that this is the time for joking . . ."

The chief detective went to the window and beckoned to two men who were walking round the courtyard.

Then he returned:

"Mr. Attorney-General, would you have the kindness to sign a warrant for the arrest of Auguste Maximin Philippe Daileron, aged forty-seven? You might leave the profession open."

He went to the door:

"Come in, Gourel. You, too, Dieuzy."

Gourel entered, accompanied by Inspector Dieuzy.

"Have you the handcuffs, Gourel?"

"Yes, chief."

M. Lenormand went up to Valenglay:

"Monsieur le Président, everything is ready. But I entreat you most urgently to forego this arrest. It upsets all my plans; it may render them abortive; and, for the sake of what, after all, is a very trifling satisfaction, it exposes us to the risk of jeopardizing the whole business."

"M. Lenormand, let me remark that you have only eighty seconds left."

The chief suppressed a gesture of annoyance, strode across the room and, leaning on his stick, sat down angrily, as though he had decided not to speak. Then, suddenly making up his mind:

"Monsieur le Président, the first person who enters this room will be the man whose arrest you asked for . . . against my wish, as I insist on pointing out to you."

"Fifteen seconds, Lenormand!"

"Gourel . . . Dieuzy . . . the first person, do you understand? . . . Mr. Attorney, have you signed the warrant?"

"Ten seconds, Lenormand!"

"Monsieur le Président, would you be so good as to ring the bell?"

Valenglay rang.

The messenger appeared in the doorway and waited.

Valenglay turned to the chief:

"Well, Lenormand, he's waiting for your orders. Whom is he to show in?"

"No one."

"But the rogue whose arrest you promised us? The six minutes are more than past."

"Yes, but the rogue is here!"

"Here? I don't understand. No one has entered the room!"

"I beg your pardon."

"Oh, I say. . . . Look here, Lenormand, you're making fun of us. I tell you again that no one has entered the room."

"There were six of us in this room, Monsieur le Président; there are seven now. Consequently, some one has entered the room."

Valenglay started:

"Eh! But this is madness! . . . What! You mean to say . . ."

The two detectives had slipped between the messenger and the door. M. Lenormand walked up to the messenger, clapped his hand on his shoulder and, in a loud voice:

"In the name of the law, Auguste Maximin Philippe Daileron, chief messenger at the Ministry of the Interior, I arrest you."

Valenglay burst out laughing.

"Oh, what a joke! What a joke! That infernal Lenormand! Of all the first-rate notions! Well done, Lenormand! It's long since I enjoyed so good a laugh."

M. Lenormand turned to the attorney-general:

"Mr. Attorney, you won't forget to fill in Master Daileron's profession on the warrant, will you? Chief messenger at the Ministry of the Interior."

"Oh, good! . . . Oh, capital! . . . Chief messenger at the Ministry of the Interior!" spluttered Valenglay, holding his sides. "Oh, this wonderful Lenormand gets hold of ideas that would never occur to anybody else! The public is clamoring for an arrest. . . . Whoosh, he flings at its head my chief messenger . . . Auguste . . . the model servant! Well, Lenormand, my dear fellow, I knew you had a certain gift of imagination, but I never suspected that it would go so far as this! The impertinence of it!"

From the commencement of this scene, Auguste had not stirred a limb and seemed to understand nothing of what was going on around him. His face, the typical face of a good, loyal, faithful serving-man, seemed absolutely bewildered. He looked at the gentlemen turn and turn about, with a visible effort to catch the meaning of their words.

M. Lenormand said a few words to Gourel, who went out. Then, going up to Auguste and speaking with great decision, he said:

"There's no way out of it. You're caught. The best thing to do, when the game is lost, is to throw down your cards. What were you doing on Tuesday?"

"I? Nothing. I was here."

"You lie. You were off duty. You went out for the day."

"Oh, yes . . . I remember . . . I had a friend to see me from the country. . . . We went for a walk in the Bois."

"Your friend's name was Marco. And you went for a walk in the cellars of the Crédit Lyonnais."

"I? What an idea! . . . Marco! . . . I don't know any one by that name."

"And these? Do you know these?" cried the chief, thrusting a pair of gold-rimmed spectacles under his nose.

"No . . . certainly not. . . . I don't wear spectacles. . . ."

"Yes, you do; you wear them when you go to the Crédit Lyonnais and when you pass yourself off as Mr. Kesselbach. These come from your room, the room which you occupy, under the name of M. Jérôme, at No. 50 Rue du Colisee."

"My room? *My* room? I sleep here, at the office."

"But you change your clothes over there, to play your parts in Lupin's gang."

A blow in the chest made him stagger back. Auguste reached the window at a bound, climbed over the balcony and jumped into the courtyard.

"Dash it all!" shouted Valenglay. "The scoundrel!"

He rang the bell, ran to the window, wanted to call out. M. Lenormand, with the greatest calm, said:

"Don't excite yourself, Monsieur le Président . . ."

"But that blackguard of an Auguste . . ."

"One second, please. . . . I foresaw this ending . . . in fact, I allowed for it. . . . It's the best confession we could have. . . ."

Yielding in the presence of this coolness, Valenglay resumed his seat. In a moment, Gourel entered, with his hand on the collar of Master Auguste Maximin Philippe Daileron, *alias* Jérôme, chief messenger at the Ministry of the Interior.

"Bring him, Gourel!" said M. Lenormand, as who should say, "Fetch it! Bring it!" to a good retriever carrying the game in its jaws. "Did he come quietly?"

"He bit me a little, but I held tight," replied the sergeant, showing his huge, sinewy hand.

"Very well, Gourel. And now take this chap off to the Dépôt in a cab. Good-bye for the present, M. Jérôme."

Valenglay was immensely amused. He rubbed his hands and laughed. The idea that his chief messenger was one of Lupin's accomplices struck him as a most delightfully ludicrous thing.

"Well done, my dear Lenormand; this is wonderful! But how on earth did you manage it?"

"Oh, in the simplest possible fashion. I knew that Mr. Kesselbach was employing the Barbareux agency and that Lupin had called on him, pretending to come from the agency. I hunted in that direction and discovered that, when the indiscretion was committed to the prejudice of Mr. Kesselbach and of Barbareux, it could only have been to the advantage of one Jérôme, a friend of one of the clerks at the agency. If you had not ordered me to hustle things, I should have watched the messenger and caught Marco and then Lupin."

"You'll catch them, Lenormand, you'll catch them, I assure you. And we shall be assisting at the most exciting spectacle in the world: the struggle between Lupin and yourself. I shall bet on you."

The next morning the newspapers published the following letter:

"*Open Letter to M. Lenormand, Chief of the Detective-service.*

"All my congratulations, dear sir and dear friend, on your arrest of Jérôme the messenger. It was a smart piece of work, well executed and worthy of you.

"All my compliments, also, on the ingenious manner in which you proved to the prime minister that I was not Mr. Kesselbach's murderer. Your demonstration was clear, logical, irrefutable and, what is more, truthful. As you know, I do not kill people. Thank you for proving it on this occasion. The esteem of my contemporaries and of yourself, dear sir and dear friend, are indispensable to my happiness.

"In return, allow me to assist you in the pursuit of the monstrous assassin and to give you a hand with the Kesselbach case, a very interesting case, believe me: so interesting and so worthy of my attention that I have determined to issue from the retirement in which I have been living for the past four years, between my books and my good dog Sherlock, to beat all my comrades to arms and to throw myself once more into the fray.

"What unexpected turns life sometimes takes! Here am I, your fellow-worker! Let me assure you, dear sir and dear friend, that I congratulate myself upon it, and that I appreciate this favor of destiny at its true value.

"Arsène Lupin.

"P.S.—One word more, of which I feel sure that you will approve. As it is not right and proper that a gentleman who has had the glorious privilege of fighting under my banner should languish on the straw of your prisons, I feel it my duty to give you fair warning that, in five weeks' time, on Friday, the 31st of May, I shall set at liberty Master Jérôme, promoted by me to the rank of chief messenger at the Ministry of the Interior. Don't forget the date: Friday, the 31st of May.

"A. L."

IV. PRINCE SERNINE AT WORK

A ground-floor flat, at the corner of the Boulevard Haussmann and the Rue de Courcelles. Here lived Prince Sernine: Prince Sernine, one of the most brilliant members of the Russian colony in Paris, whose name was constantly recurring in the "Arrivals and Departures" column in the newspapers.

Eleven o'clock in the morning. The prince entered his study. He was a man of thirty-eight or forty years of age, whose chestnut hair was mingled with a few silver threads on the temples. He had a fresh, healthy complexion and wore a large mustache and a pair of whiskers cut extremely short, so as to be hardly noticeable against the fresh skin of his cheeks.

He was smartly dressed in a tight-fitting frock-coat and a white drill waistcoat, which showed above the opening.

"Come on!" he said, in an undertone. "I have a hard day's work before me, I expect."

He opened a door leading into a large room where a few people sat waiting, and said:

"Is Varnier there? Come in, Varnier."

A man looking like a small tradesman, squat, solidly built, firmly set upon his legs, entered at the summons. The prince closed the door behind him:

"Well, Varnier, how far are you?"

"Everything's ready for this evening, governor."

"Good. Tell me in a few words."

"It's like this. After her husband's murder, Mrs. Kesselbach, on the strength of the prospectuses which you ordered to be sent to her, selected as her residence the establishment known as the Retreat for Gentlewomen, at Garches. She occupies the last of the four small houses, at the bottom of the garden, which the management lets to ladies who prefer to live quite apart from the other boarders, the house known as the Pavillon de l'Impératrice."

"What servants has she?"

"Her companion, Gertrude, with whom she arrived a few hours after the crime, and Gertrude's sister Suzanne, whom she sent for to Monte Carlo and who acts as her maid. The two sisters are devoted to her."

"What about Edwards, the valet?"

"She did not keep him. He has gone back to his own country."

"Does she see people?"

"No. She spends her time lying on a sofa. She seems very weak and ill. She cries a great deal. Yesterday the examining-magistrate was with her for two hours."

"Very good. And now about the young girl."

"Mlle. Geneviève Ernemont lives across the way . . . in a lane running toward the open country, the third house on the right in the lane. She keeps a free school for backward children. Her grandmother, Mme. Ernemont, lives with her."

"And, according to what you wrote to me, Geneviève Ernemont and Mrs. Kesselbach have become acquainted?"

"Yes. The girl went to ask Mrs. Kesselbach for a subscription for her school. They must have taken a liking to each other, for, during the past four days, they have been walking together in the Parc de Villeneuve, of which the garden of the Retreat is only a dependency."

"At what time do they go out?"

"From five to six. At six o'clock exactly the young lady goes back to her school."

"So you have arranged the thing?"

"For six o'clock to-day. Everything is ready."

"Will there be no one there?"

"There is never any one in the park at that hour."

"Very well. I shall be there. You can go."

He sent him out through the door leading to the hall, and, returning to the waiting-room, called:

"The brothers Doudeville."

Two young men entered, a little overdressed, keen-eyed and pleasant-looking.

"Good morning, Jean. Good morning, Jacques. Any news at the Prefecture?"

"Nothing much, governor."

"Does M. Lenormand continue to have confidence in you?"

"Yes. Next to Gourel, we are his favorite inspectors. A proof is that he has posted us in the Palace Hotel to watch the people who were living on the first-floor passage at the time of Chapman's murder. Gourel comes every morning, and we make the same report to him that we do to you."

"Capital. It is essential that I should be informed of all that happens and all that is said at the Prefecture of Police. As long as Lenormand looks upon you as his men, I am master of the situation. And have you discovered a trail of any kind in the hotel?"

Jean Doudeville, the elder of the two, replied:

"The Englishwoman who occupied one of the bedrooms has gone."

"That doesn't interest me. I know all about her. But her neighbor, Major Parbury?"

They seemed embarrassed. At last, one of them replied:

"Major Parbury, this morning, ordered his luggage to be taken to the Gare du Nord, for the twelve-fifty train, and himself drove away in a motor. We were there when the train left. The major did not come."

"And the luggage?"

"He had it fetched at the station."

"By whom?"

"By a commissionaire, so we were told."

"Then his tracks are lost?"

"Yes."

"At last!" cried the prince, joyfully.

The others looked at him in surprise.

"Why, of course," he said, "that's a clue!"

"Do you think so?"

"Evidently. The murder of Chapman can only have been committed in one of the rooms on that passage. Mr. Kesselbach's murderer took the secretary there, to an accomplice, killed him there, changed his clothes there; and, once the murderer had got away, the accomplice placed the corpse in the passage. But which accomplice? The manner of Major Parbury's disappearance goes to show that he knows something of the business. Quick, telephone the good news to M. Lenormand or Gourel. The Prefecture must be informed as soon as possible. The people there and I are marching hand in hand."

He gave them a few more injunctions, concerning their double rôle as police-inspectors in the service of Prince Sernine, and dismissed them.

Two visitors remained in the waiting-room. He called one of them in:

"A thousand pardons, Doctor," he said. "I am quite at your orders now. How is Pierre Leduc?"

"He's dead."

"Aha!" said Sernine. "I expected it, after your note of this morning. But, all the same, the poor beggar has not been long. . . ."

"He was wasted to a shadow. A fainting-fit; and it was all over."

"Did he not speak?"

"No."

"Are you sure that, from the day when the two of us picked him up under the table in that low haunt at Belleville, are you sure that nobody in your nursing-home suspected that he was the Pierre Leduc whom the police were looking for, the mysterious Pierre Leduc whom Mr. Kesselbach was trying to find at all costs?"

"Nobody. He had a room to himself. Moreover, I bandaged up his left hand so that the injury to the little finger could not be seen. As for the scar on the cheek, it is hidden by the beard."

"And you looked after him yourself?"

"Myself. And, according to your instructions, I took the opportunity of questioning him whenever he seemed at all clear in his head. But I could never get more than an inarticulate stammering out of him."

The prince muttered thoughtfully:

"Dead! . . . So Pierre Leduc is dead? . . . The whole Kesselbach case obviously turned on him, and now he disappears . . . without a revelation, without a word about himself, about his past. . . . Ought I to embark on this adventure, in which I am still entirely in the dark? It's dangerous. . . . I may come to grief. . . ."

He reflected for a moment and exclaimed:

"Oh, who cares? I shall go on for all that. It's no reason, because Pierre Leduc is dead, that I should throw up the game. On the contrary! And the opportunity is too tempting! Pierre Leduc is dead! Long live Pierre Leduc! . . . Go, Doctor, go home. I shall ring you up before dinner."

The doctor went out.

"Now then, Philippe," said Sernine to his last remaining visitor, a little gray-haired man, dressed like a waiter at a hotel, a very tenth-rate hotel, however.

"You will remember, governor," Philippe began, "that last week, you made me go as boots to the Hôtel des Deux-Empereurs at Versailles, to keep my eye on a young man."

"Yes, I know. . . . Gérard Baupré. How do things stand with him?"

"He's at the end of his resources."

"Still full of gloomy ideas?"

"Yes. He wants to kill himself."

"Is he serious?"

"Quite. I found this little note in pencil among his papers."

"Ah!" said Sernine, reading the note. "He announces his suicide . . . and for this evening too!"

"Yes, governor, he has bought the rope and screwed the hook to the ceiling. Thereupon, acting on your instructions, I talked to him. He told me of his distress, and I advised him to apply to you: 'Prince Sernine is rich,' I said; 'he is generous; perhaps he will help you.'"

"All this is first-rate. So he is coming?"

"He is here."

"How do you know?"

"I followed him. He took the train to Paris, and he is walking up and down the boulevard at this minute. He will make up his mind from one moment to the other."

Just then the servant brought in a card. The prince glanced at it and said to the man:

"Show M. Gérard Baupré in."

Then, turning to Philippe:

"You go into the dressing-room, here; listen and don't stir."

Left alone, the prince muttered:

"Why should I hesitate? It's fate that sends him my way...."

A few minutes later a tall young man entered. He was fair and slender, with an emaciated face and feverish eyes, and he stood on the threshold embarrassed, hesitating, in the attitude of a beggar who would like to put out his hand for alms and dares not.

The conversation was brief:

"Are you M. Gérard Baupré?"

"Yes ... yes ... that is my name."

"I have not the honor ..."

"It's like this, sir.... Some one told me ..."

"Who?"

"A hotel servant ... who said he had been in your service...."

"Please come to the point...."

"Well!..."

The young man stopped, taken aback and frightened by the haughty attitude adopted by the prince, who exclaimed:

"But, sir, there must be some ..."

"Well, sir, the man told me that you were very rich ... and very generous.... And I thought that you might possibly ..."

He broke off short, incapable of uttering the word of prayer and humiliation.

Sernine went up to him.

"M. Gérard Baupré, did you not publish a volume of poetry called *The Smile of Spring*?"

"Yes, yes," cried the young man, his face lighting up. "Have you read it?"

"Yes.... Very pretty, your poems, very pretty.... Only, do you reckon upon being able to live on what they will bring you?"

"Certainly ... sooner or later...."

"Sooner or later? Later rather than sooner, I expect! And, meantime, you have come to ask me for the wherewithal to live?"

"For the wherewithal to buy food, sir."

Sernine put his hand on the young man's shoulder and, coldly:

"Poets do not need food, monsieur. They live on rhymes and dreams. Do as they do. That is better than begging for bread."

The young man quivered under the insult. He turned to the door without a word.

Sernine stopped him:

"One thing more, monsieur. Have you no resources of any kind?"

"None at all."

"And you are not reckoning on anything?"

"I have one hope left: I have written to one of my relations, imploring him to send me something. I shall have his answer to-day. It is my last chance."

"And, if you have no answer, you have doubtless made up your mind, this very evening, to ..."

"Yes, sir."

This was said quite plainly and simply.

Sernine burst out laughing:

"Bless my soul, what a queer young man you are! And full of artless conviction, too! Come and see me again next year, will you? We will talk about all this ... it's so curious, so interesting ... and, above all, so funny!... Ha, ha, ha, ha!"

And, shaking with laughter, with affected bows and gestures, he showed him the door.

"Philippe," he said, admitting the hotel-servant, "did you hear?"

"Yes, governor."

"Gérard Baupré is expecting a telegram this afternoon, a promise of assistance. . . ."

"Yes, it's his last hope."

"He must not receive that telegram. If it comes, intercept it and tear it up."

"Very well, governor."

"Are you alone at your hotel?"

"Yes, with the cook, who does not sleep in. The boss is away."

"Good. So we are the masters. Till this evening, at eleven. Be off."

Prince Sernine went to his room and rang for his servant:

"My hat, gloves, and stick. Is the car there?"

"Yes, sir."

He dressed, went out, and sank into a large, comfortable limousine, which took him to the Bois de Boulogne, to the Marquis and Marquise de Gastyne's, where he was engaged for lunch.

At half-past two he took leave of his hosts, stopped in the Avenue Kléber, picked up two of his friends and a doctor, and at five minutes to three arrived at the Parc des Princes.

At three o'clock he fought a sword duel with the Italian Major Spinelli, cut his adversary's ear in the first bout, and, at a quarter to four, took a bank at the Rue Cambon Club, from which he retired, at twenty minutes past five, after winning forty-seven thousand francs.

And all this without hurrying, with a sort of haughty indifference, as though the feverish activity that sent his life whizzing through a whirl of tempestuous deeds and events were the ordinary rule of his most peaceful days.

"Octave," he said to his chauffeur, "go to Garches."

And at ten minutes to six he alighted outside the old walls of the Parc de Villeneuve.

Although broken up nowadays and spoilt, the Villeneuve estate still retains something of the splendor which it knew at the time when the Empress Eugénie used to stay there. With its old trees, its lake and the leafy horizon of the woods of Saint-Cloud, the landscape has a certain melancholy grace.

An important part of the estate was made over to the Pasteur Institute. A smaller portion, separated from the other by the whole extent of the space reserved for the public, forms a property contained within the walls which is still fairly large, and which comprises the House of Retreat, with four isolated garden-houses standing around it.

"That is where Mrs. Kesselbach lives," said the prince to himself, catching sight of the roofs of the house and the four garden-houses in the distance.

He crossed the park and walked toward the lake.

Suddenly he stopped behind a clump of trees. He had seen two ladies against the parapet of the bridge that crossed the lake:

"Varnier and his men must be somewhere near. But, by Jove, they are keeping jolly well hidden! I can't see them anywhere. . . ."

The two ladies were now strolling across the lawns, under the tall, venerable trees. The blue of the sky appeared between the branches, which swayed in the peaceful breeze, and the scent of spring and of young vegetation was wafted through the air.

On the grassy slopes that ran down to the motionless water, daisies, violets, daffodils, lilies of the valley, all the little flowers of April and May stood grouped, and, here and there, formed constellations of every color. The sun was sinking on the horizon.

And, all at once, three men started from a thicket of bushes and made for the two ladies.

They accosted them. A few words were exchanged. The ladies gave visible signs of dread. One of the men went up to the shorter of the two and tried to snatch the gold purse which she was carrying in her hand. They cried out; and the three men flung themselves upon them.

"Now or never!" said the prince.

And he rushed forward. In ten seconds he had almost reached the brink of the water. At his approach, the three men fled.

"Run away, you vagabonds," he chuckled; "run for all you are worth! Here's the rescuer coming!"

And he set out in pursuit of them. But one of the ladies entreated him:

"Oh, sir, I beg of you . . . my friend is ill."

The shorter lady had fallen on the grass in a dead faint.

He retraced his steps and, anxiously:

"She is not wounded?" he asked. "Did those scoundrels . . ."

"No . . . no . . . it's only the fright . . . the excitement. . . . Besides you will understand . . . the lady is Mrs. Kesselbach. . . ."

"Oh!" he said.

He produced a bottle of smelling-salts, which the younger woman at once applied to her friend's nostrils. And he added:

"Lift the amethyst that serves as a stopper. . . . You will see a little box containing some tabloids. Give madame one of them . . . one, no more . . . they are very strong. . . ."

He watched the young woman helping her friend. She was fair-haired, very simply dressed; and her face was gentle and grave, with a smile that lit up her features even when she was not smiling.

"That is Geneviève," he thought. And he repeated with emotion, "Geneviève . . . Geneviève. . . ."

Meanwhile, Mrs. Kesselbach gradually recovered consciousness. She was astonished at first, seemed not to understand. Then, her memory returning, she thanked her deliverer with a movement of the head.

He made a deep bow and said:

"Allow me to introduce myself. . . . I am Prince Sernine. . . ."

She said, in a faint voice:

"I do not know how to express my gratitude."

"By not expressing it at all, madame. You must thank chance, the chance that turned my steps in this direction. May I offer you my arm?"

A few minutes later, Mrs. Kesselbach rang at the door of the House of Retreat and said to the prince:

"I will ask one more service of you, monsieur. Do not speak of this assault."

"And yet, madame, it would be the only way of finding out . . ."

"Any attempt to find out would mean an inquiry; and that would involve more noise and fuss about me, examinations, fatigue; and I am worn out as it is."

The prince did not insist. Bowing to her, he asked:

"Will you allow me to call and ask how you are?"

"Oh, certainly. . . ."

She kissed Geneviève and went indoors.

Meantime, night was beginning to fall. Sernine would not let Geneviève return alone. But they had hardly entered the path, when a figure, standing out against the shadow, hastened toward them.

"Grandmother!" cried Geneviève.

She threw herself into the arms of an old woman, who covered her with kisses:

"Oh, my darling, my darling, what has happened? How late you are! . . . And you are always so punctual!"

Geneviève introduced the prince:

"Prince Sernine . . . Mme. Ernemont, my grandmother. . . ."

Then she related the incident, and Mme. Ernemont repeated:

"Oh, my darling, how frightened you must have been! . . . I shall never forget your kindness, monsieur, I assure you. . . . But how frightened you must have been, my poor darling!"

"Come, granny, calm yourself, as I am here. . . ."

"Yes, but the fright may have done you harm. . . . One never knows the consequences. . . . Oh, it's horrible! . . ."

They went along a hedge, through which a yard planted with trees, a few shrubs, a playground and a white house were just visible. Behind the house, sheltered by a clump of elder-trees arranged to form a covered walk, was a little gate.

The old lady asked Prince Sernine to come in and led the way to a little drawing-room or parlor. Geneviève asked leave to withdraw for a moment, to go and see her pupils, whose supper-time it was. The prince and Mme. Ernemont remained alone.

The old lady had a sad and a pale face, under her white hair, which ended in two long, loose curls. She was too stout, her walk was heavy and, notwithstanding her appearance and her dress, which was that of a lady, she had something a little vulgar about her; but her eyes were immensely kind.

Prince Sernine went up to her, took her head in his two hands and kissed her on both cheeks:

"Well, old one, and how are you?"

She stood dumfounded, wild-eyed, open-mouthed. The prince kissed her again, laughing.

She spluttered:

"You! It's you! O mother of God! . . . O mother of God! . . . Is it possible! . . . O mother of God! . . ."

"My dear old Victoire!"

"Don't call me that," she cried, shuddering. "Victoire is dead . . . your old servant no longer exists. I belong entirely to Geneviève." And, lowering her voice, "O mother of God! . . . I saw your name in the papers: then it's true that you have taken to your wicked life again?"

"As you see."

"And yet you swore to me that it was finished, that you were going away for good, that you wanted to become an honest man."

"I tried. I have been trying for four years. . . . You can't say that I have got myself talked about during those four years!"

"Well?"

"Well, it bores me."

She gave a sigh and asked:

"Always the same. . . . You haven't changed. . . . Oh, it's settled, you never will change. . . . So you are in the Kesselbach case?"

"Why, of course! But for that, would I have taken the trouble to arrange for an attack on Mrs. Kesselbach at six o'clock, so that I might have the opportunity of delivering her from the clutches of my own men at five minutes past? Looking upon me as her rescuer, she is obliged to receive me. I am now in the heart of the citadel and, while protecting the widow, can keep a lookout all round. Ah, you see, the sort of life which I lead does not permit me to lounge about and waste my time on little questions of politeness and such outside matters. I have to go straight to the point, violently, brutally, dramatically. . . ."

She looked at him in dismay and gasped:

"I see . . . I see . . . it's all lies about the attack. . . . But then . . . Geneviève . . ."

"Why, I'm killing two birds with one stone! It was as easy to rescue two as one. Think of the time it would have taken, the efforts—useless efforts, perhaps—to worm myself into that child's friendship! What was I to her? What should I be now? An unknown person . . . a stranger. Whereas now I am the rescuer. In an hour I shall be . . . the friend."

She began to tremble:

"So . . . so you did not rescue Geneviève. . . . So you are going to mix us up in your affairs. . . ." And, suddenly, in a fit of rebellion, seizing him by the shoulders, "No, I won't have it, do you understand? You brought the child to me one day, saying, 'Here, I entrust her to you . . . her father and mother are dead . . . take her under your protection.' Well, she's under my protection now and I shall know how to defend her against you and all your manœuvers!"

Standing straight upright, in a very determined attitude, Mme. Ernemont seemed ready for all emergencies.

Slowly and deliberately Sernine loosened the two hands, one after the other, that held him, and in his turn, took the old lady by the shoulders, forced her into an arm-chair, stooped over and, in a very calm voice, said:

"Rot!"

She began to cry and, clasping her hands together, implored him:

"I beseech you, leave us in peace. We were so happy! I thought that you had forgotten us and I blessed Heaven every time a day had passed. Why, yes . . . I love you just the same. But, Geneviève . . . you see, there's nothing that I wouldn't do for that child. She has taken your place in my heart."

"So I perceive," said he, laughing. "You would send me to the devil with pleasure. Come, enough of this nonsense! I have no time to waste. I must talk to Geneviève."

"You're going to talk to her?"

"Well, is that a crime?"

"And what have you to tell her?"

"A secret . . . a very grave secret . . . and a very touching one. . . ."

The old lady took fright:

"And one that will cause her sorrow, perhaps? Oh, I fear everything, I fear everything, where she's concerned! . . ."

"She is coming," he said.

"No, not yet."

"Yes, yes, I hear her. . . . Wipe your eyes and be sensible."

"Listen," said she, eagerly, "listen. I don't know what you are going to say, what secret you mean to reveal to this child whom you don't know. But I, who do know her, tell you this: Geneviève has a very plucky, very spirited, but very sensitive nature. Be careful how you choose your words. . . . You might wound feelings . . . the existence of which you cannot even suspect. . . ."

"Lord bless me! And why not?"

"Because she belongs to another race than you, to a different world. . . . I mean, a different moral world. . . . There are things which you are forbidden to understand nowadays. Between you and her, the obstacle is insurmountable. . . . Geneviève has the most unblemished and upright conscience . . . and you . . ."

"And I?"

"And you are not an honest man!"

Geneviève entered, bright and charming:

"All my babies have gone to bed; I have ten minutes to spare. . . . Why, grandmother, what's the matter? You look quite upset. . . . Is it still that business with the . . ."

"No, mademoiselle," said Sernine, "I believe I have had the good fortune to reassure your grandmother. Only, we were talking of you, of your childhood; and that is a subject, it seems, which your grandmother cannot touch upon without emotion."

"Of my childhood?" said Geneviève, reddening. "Oh, grandmother!"

"Don't scold her, mademoiselle. The conversation turned in that direction by accident. It so happens that I have often passed through the little village where you were brought up."

"Aspremont?"

"Yes, Aspremont, near Nice. You used to live in a new house, white all over. . . ."

"Yes," she said, "white all over, with a touch of blue paint round the windows. . . . I was only seven years old when I left Aspremont; but I remember the least things of that period. And I have not forgotten the glare of the sun on the white front of the house, nor the shade of the eucalyptus-tree at the bottom of the garden."

"At the bottom of the garden, mademoiselle, was a field of olive-trees; and under one of those olive-trees stood a table at which your mother used to work on hot days. . . ."

"That's true, that's true," she said, quite excitedly, "I used to play by her side. . . ."

"And it was there," said he, "that I saw your mother several times. . . . I recognized her image the moment I set eyes on you . . . but it was a brighter, happier image."

"Yes, my poor mother was not happy. My father died on the very day of my birth, and nothing was ever able to console her. She used to cry a great deal. I still possess a little handkerchief with which I used to dry her tears at that time."

"A little handkerchief with a pink pattern."

"What!" she exclaimed, seized with surprise. "You know . . ."

"I was there one day when you were comforting her. . . . And you comforted her so prettily that the scene remained impressed on my memory."

She gave him a penetrating glance and murmured, almost to herself:

"Yes, yes. . . . I seem to . . . The expression of your eyes . . . and then the sound of your voice. . . ."

She lowered her eyelids for a moment and reflected as if she were vainly trying to bring back a recollection that escaped her. And she continued:

"Then you knew her?"

"I had some friends living near Aspremont and used to meet her at their house. The last time I saw her, she seemed to me sadder still . . . paler . . . and, when I came back again . . ."

"It was all over, was it not?" said Geneviève. "Yes, she went very quickly . . . in a few weeks . . . and I was left alone with neighbors who sat up with her . . . and one morning they took her away. . . . And, on the evening of that day, some one came, while I was asleep, and lifted me up and wrapped me in blankets. . . ."

"A man?" asked the prince.

"Yes, a man. He talked to me, quite low, very gently . . . his voice did me good . . . and, as he carried me down the road and also in the carriage, during the night, he rocked me in his arms and told me stories . . . in the same voice . . . in the same voice . . ."

She broke off gradually and looked at him again, more sharply than before and with a more obvious effort to seize the fleeting impression that passed over her at moments. He asked:

"And then? Where did he take you?"

"I can't recollect clearly . . . it is just as though I had slept for several days. . . . I can remember nothing before the little town of Montégut, in the Vendée, where I spent the second half of my childhood, with Father and Mother Izereau, a worthy couple who reared me and brought me up and whose love and devotion I shall never forget."

"And did they die, too?"

"Yes," she said, "of an epidemic of typhoid fever in the district . . . but I did not know that until later. . . . As soon as they fell ill, I was carried off as on the first occasion and under the same conditions, at night, by some one who also wrapped me up in blankets. . . . Only, I was bigger, I struggled, I tried to call out . . . and he had to close my mouth with a silk handkerchief."

"How old were you then?"

"Fourteen . . . it was four years ago."

"Then you were able to see what the man was like?"

"No, he hid his face better and he did not speak a single word to me. . . . Nevertheless, I have always believed him to be the same one . . . for I remember the same solicitude, the same attentive, careful movements. . . ."

"And after that?"

"After that, came oblivion, sleep, as before. . . . This time, I was ill, it appears; I was feverish. . . . And I woke in a bright, cheerful room. A white-haired lady was bending over me and smiling. It was grandmother . . . and the room was the one in which I now sleep upstairs."

She had resumed her happy face, her sweet, radiant expression; and she ended, with a smile:

"That was how she became my grandmother and how, after a few trials, the little Aspremont girl now knows the delights of a peaceful life and teaches grammar and arithmetic to little girls who are either naughty or lazy . . . but who are all fond of her."

She spoke cheerfully, in a tone at once thoughtful and gay, and it was obvious that she possessed a reasonable, well-balanced mind. Sernine listened to her with growing surprise and without trying to conceal his agitation:

"Have you never heard speak of that man since?" he asked.

"Never."

"And would you be glad to see him again?"

"Oh, very glad."

"Well, then, mademoiselle . . ."

Geneviève gave a start:

"You know something . . . the truth perhaps . . ."

"No . . . no . . . only . . ."

He rose and walked up and down the room. From time to time, his eyes fell upon Geneviève; and it looked as though he were on the point of giving a more precise answer to the question which she had put to him. Would he speak?

Mme. Ernemont awaited with anguish the revelation of the secret upon which the girl's future peace might depend.

He sat down beside Geneviève, appeared to hesitate, and said at last:

"No . . . no . . . just now . . . an idea occurred to me . . . a recollection . . ."

"A recollection? . . . And . . ."

"I was mistaken. Your story contained certain details that misled me."

"Are you sure?"

He hesitated and then declared:

"Absolutely sure."

"Oh," said she, greatly disappointed. "I had half guessed . . . that that man whom I saw twice . . . that you knew him . . . that . . ."

She did not finish her sentence, but waited for an answer to the question which she had put to him without daring to state it completely.

He was silent. Then, insisting no further, she bent over Mme. Ernemont:

"Good night, grandmother. My children must be in bed by this time, but they could none of them go to sleep before I had kissed them."

She held out her hand to the prince:

"Thank you once more. . . ."

"Are you going?" he asked quickly.

"Yes, if you will excuse me; grandmother will see you out."

He bowed low and kissed her hand. As she opened the door, she turned round and smiled. Then she disappeared. The prince listened to the sound of her footsteps diminishing in the distance and stood stock-still, his face white with emotion.

"Well," said the old lady, "so you did not speak?"

"No. . . ."

"That secret . . ."

"Later. . . . To-day . . . oddly enough . . . I was not able to."

"Was it so difficult? Did not she herself feel that you were the stranger who took her away twice. . . . A word would have been enough. . . ."

"Later, later," he repeated, recovering all his assurance. "You can understand . . . the child hardly knows me. . . . I must first gain the right to her affection, to her love. . . . When I have given her the life which she deserves, a wonderful life, such as one reads of in fairy-tales, then I will speak."

The old lady tossed her head:

"I fear that you are making a great mistake. Geneviève does not want a wonderful life. She has simple tastes."

"She has the tastes of all women; and wealth, luxury and power give joys which not one of them despises."

"Yes, Geneviève does. And you would do much better . . ."

"We shall see. For the moment, let me go my own way. And be quite easy. I have not the least intention, as you say, of mixing her up in any of my manœuvres. She will hardly ever see me. . . . Only, we had to come into contact, you know. . . . That's done. . . . Good-bye."

He left the school and walked to where his motor-car was waiting for him. He was perfectly happy:

"She is charming . . . and so gentle, so grave! Her mother's eyes, eyes that soften you . . . Heavens, how long ago that all is! And what a delightful recollection! A little sad, but so delightful!" And he said, aloud, "Certainly I shall look after her happiness! And that at once! This very evening! That's it, this very evening she shall have a sweetheart! Is not love the essential condition of any young girl's happiness?"

He found his car on the high-road:

"Home," he said to Octave.

When Sernine reached home, he rang up Neuilly and telephoned his instructions to the friend whom he called the doctor. Then he dressed, dined at the Rue Cambon Club, spent an hour at the opera and got into his car again:

"Go to Neuilly, Octave. We are going to fetch the doctor. What's the time?"

"Half-past ten."

"Dash it! Look sharp!"

Ten minutes later, the car stopped at the end of the Boulevard Inkerman, outside a villa standing in its own grounds. The doctor came down at the sound of the hooter. The prince asked:

"Is the fellow ready?"

"Packed up, strung up, sealed up."

"In good condition?"

"Excellent. If everything goes as you telephoned, the police will be utterly at sea."

"That's what they're there for. Let's get him on board."

They carried into the motor a sort of long sack shaped like a human being and apparently rather heavy. And the prince said:

"Go to Versailles, Octave, Rue de la Vilaine. Stop outside the Hôtel des Deux-Empereurs."

"Why, it's a filthy hotel," observed the doctor. "I know it well; a regular hovel."

"You needn't tell me! And it will be a hard piece of work, for me, at least. . . . But, by Jove, I wouldn't sell this moment for a fortune! Who dares pretend that life is monotonous?"

They reached the Hôtel des Deux-Empereurs. A muddy alley; two steps down; and they entered a passage lit by a flickering lamp.

Sernine knocked with his fist against a little door.

A waiter appeared, Philippe, the man to whom Sernine had given orders, that morning, concerning Gérard Baupré.

"Is he here still?" asked the prince.

"Yes."

"The rope?"

"The knot is made."

"He has not received the telegram he was hoping for?"

"I intercepted it: here it is."

Sernine took the blue paper and read it:

"Gad!" he said. "It was high time. This is to promise him a thousand francs for to-morrow. Come, fortune is on my side. A quarter to twelve. . . . In a quarter of an hour, the poor devil will take a leap into eternity. Show me the way, Philippe. You stay here, Doctor."

The waiter took the candle. They climbed to the third floor, and, walking on tip-toe, went along a low and evil-smelling corridor, lined with garrets and ending in a wooden staircase covered with the musty remnants of a carpet.

"Can no one hear me?" asked Sernine.

"No. The two rooms are quite detached. But you must be careful not to make a mistake: he is in the room on the left."

"Very good. Now go downstairs. At twelve o'clock, the doctor, Octave and you are to carry the fellow up here, to where we now stand, and wait till I call you."

The wooden staircase had ten treads, which the prince climbed with definite caution. At the top was a landing with two doors. It took Sernine quite five minutes to open the one of the right without breaking the silence with the least sound of a creaking hinge.

A light gleamed through the darkness of the room. Feeling his way, so as not to knock against one of the chairs, he made for that light. It came from the next room and filtered through a glazed door covered with a tattered hanging.

The prince pulled the threadbare stuff aside. The panes were of ground glass, but scratched in parts, so that, by applying one eye, it was easy to see all that happened in the other room.

Sernine saw a man seated at a table facing him. It was the poet, Gérard Baupré. He was writing by the light of a candle.

Above his head hung a rope, which was fastened to a hook fixed in the ceiling. At the end of the rope was a slip-knot.

A faint stroke sounded from a clock in the street.

"Five minutes to twelve," thought Sernine. "Five minutes more."

The young man was still writing. After a moment, he put down his pen, collected the ten or twelve sheets of paper which he had covered and began to read them over.

What he read did not seem to please him, for an expression of discontent passed across his face. He tore up his manuscript and burnt the pieces in the flame of the candle.

Then, with a fevered hand, he wrote a few words on a clean sheet, signed it savagely and rose from his chair.

But, seeing the rope at ten inches above his head, he sat down again suddenly with a great shudder of alarm.

Sernine distinctly saw his pale features, his lean cheeks, against which he pressed his clenched fists. A tear trickled slowly down his face, a single, disconsolate tear. His eyes gazed into space, eyes terrifying in their unutterable sadness, eyes that already seemed to behold the dread unknown.

And it was so young a face! Cheeks still so smooth, with not a blemish, not a wrinkle! And blue eyes, blue like an eastern sky! . . .

Midnight . . . the twelve tragic strokes of midnight, to which so many a despairing man has hitched the last second of his existence!

At the twelfth stroke, he stood up again and, bravely this time, without trembling, looked at the sinister rope. He even tried to give a smile, a poor smile, the pitiful grimace of the doomed man whom death has already seized for its own.

Swiftly he climbed the chair and took the rope in one hand.

For a moment, he stood there, motionless: not that he was hesitating or lacking in courage. But this was the supreme moment, the one minute of grace which a man allows himself before the fatal deed.

He gazed at the squalid room to which his evil destiny had brought him, the hideous paper on the walls, the wretched bed.

On the table, not a book: all were sold. Not a photograph, not a letter: he had no father, no mother, no relations. What was there to make him cling to life?

With a sudden movement he put his head into the slip-knot and pulled at the rope until the noose gripped his neck.

And, kicking the chair from him with both feet, he leapt into space.

Ten seconds, fifteen seconds passed, twenty formidable, eternal seconds. . . .

The body gave two or three jerks. The feet had instinctively felt for a resting-place. Then nothing moved. . . .

A few seconds more. . . . The little glazed door opened.

Sernine entered.

Without the least haste he took the sheet of paper to which the young man had set his signature, and read:

"Tired of living, ill, penniless, hopeless, I am taking my own life. Let no one be accused of my death.

"GÉRARD BAUPRÉ.

"30 *April.*"

He put back the paper on the table where it could be seen, picked up the chair and placed it under the young man's feet. He himself climbed up on the table and, holding the body close to him, lifted it up, loosened the slip-knot and passed the head through it.

The body sank into his arms. He let it slide along the table and, jumping to the floor, laid it on the bed.

Then, with the same coolness, he opened the door on the passage:

"Are you there, all the three of you?" he whispered.

Some one answered from the foot of the wooden staircase near him:

"We are here. Are we to hoist up our bundle?"

"Yes, come along!"

He took the candle and showed them a light.

The three men trudged up the stairs, carrying the sack in which the "fellow" was tied up.

"Put him here," he said, pointing to the table.

With a pocket-knife, he cut the cords round the sack. A white sheet appeared, which he flung back. In the sheet was a corpse, the corpse of Pierre Leduc.

"Poor Pierre Leduc!" said Sernine. "You will never know what you lost by dying so young! I should have helped you to go far, old chap. However, we must do without your services. . . . Now then, Philippe, get up on the table; and you, Octave, on the chair. Lift up his head and fasten the slip-knot."

Two minutes later, Pierre Leduc's body was swinging at the end of the rope.

"Capital, that was quite simple! Now you can all of you go. You, Doctor, will call back here to-morrow morning; you will hear of the suicide of a certain Gérard Baupré: you understand, Gérard Baupré. Here is his farewell letter. You will send for the divisional surgeon and the commissary; you will arrange that neither of them notices that the deceased has a cut finger or a scar on one cheek. . . ."

"That's easy."

"And you will manage so as to have the report written then and there, to your dictation."

"That's easy."

"Lastly, avoid having the body sent to the Morgue and make them give permission for an immediate burial."

"That's not so easy."

"Try. Have you examined the other one?"

He pointed to the young man lying lifeless on the bed.

"Yes," said the doctor. "The breathing is becoming normal. But it was a big risk to run . . . the carotid artery might have . . ."

"Nothing venture, nothing have. . . . How soon will he recover consciousness?"

"In a few minutes."

"Very well. Oh, by the way, don't go yet, Doctor. Wait for me downstairs. There is more for you to do."

The prince, when he found himself alone, lit a cigarette and puffed at it quietly, sending little blue rings of smoke floating up to the ceiling.

A sigh roused him from his thoughts. He went to the bed. The young man was beginning to move; and his chest rose and fell violently, like that of a sleeper under the influence of a nightmare. He put his hands to his throat, as though he felt a pain there; and this action suddenly made him sit up, terrified, panting. . . .

Then he saw Sernine in front of him:

"You?" he whispered, without understanding. "You? . . ."

He gazed at him stupidly, as though he had seen a ghost.

He again touched his throat, felt round his neck. . . . And suddenly he gave a hoarse cry; a mad terror dilated his eyes, made his hair stand on end, shook him from head to foot like an aspen-leaf! The prince had moved aside; and he saw the man's corpse hanging from the rope.

He flung himself back against the wall. That man, that hanged man, was himself! He was dead and he was looking at his own dead body! Was this a hideous dream that follows upon death? A hallucination that comes to those who are no more and whose distracted brain still quivers with a last flickering gleam of life? . . .

His arms struck at the air. For a moment, he seemed to be defending himself against the squalid vision. Then, exhausted, he fainted away for the second time.

"First-rate," said the prince, with a grin. "A sensitive, impressionable nature. . . . At present, the brain is out of gear. . . . Come, this is a propitious moment. . . . But, if I don't get the business done in twenty minutes . . . he'll escape me. . . ."

He pushed open the door between the two garrets, came back to the bed, lifted the young man and carried him to the bed in the other room. Then he bathed his temples with cold water and made him sniff at some salts.

This time, the swoon did not last long.

Gérard timidly opened his eyes and raised them to the ceiling. The vision was gone. But the arrangement of the furniture, the position of the table and the fireplace, and certain other details all surprised him . . . And then came the remembrance of his act, the pain which he felt at his throat. . . .

He said to the prince:

"I have had a dream, have I not?"

"No."

"How do you mean, no?" And, suddenly recollecting, "Oh, that's true, I remember. . . . I meant to kill myself . . . and I even . . ." Bending forward anxiously, "But the rest, the vision . . ."

"What vision?"

"The man . . . the rope . . . was that a dream? . . ."

"No," said Sernine. "That also was real."

"What are you saying? What are you saying? . . . Oh, no, no! . . . I entreat you! . . . Wake me, if I am asleep . . . or else let me die! . . . But I am dead, am I not? And this is the nightmare of a corpse! . . . Oh, I feel my brain going! . . . I entreat you. . . ."

Sernine placed his hand gently on the young man's head and, bending over him:

"Listen to me . . . listen to me carefully and understand what I say. You are alive. Your matter and your mind are as they were and live. But Gérard Baupré is dead. You understand me, do you not? That member of society who was known as Gérard Baupré has ceased to exist. You have done away with that one. To-morrow, the registrar will write in his books, opposite the name you bore, the word 'Dead,' with the date of your decease."

"It's a lie!" stammered the terrified lad. "It's a lie! Considering that I, Gérard Baupré, am here!"

"You are not Gérard Baupré," declared Sernine. And, pointing to the open door, "Gérard Baupré is there, in the next room. Do you wish to see him? He is hanging from the nail to which you hooked him. On the table is a letter in which you certify his death with your signature. It is all quite regular, it is all final. There is no getting away from the irrevocable, brutal fact: Gérard Baupré has ceased to exist!"

The young man listened in despair. Growing calmer, now that facts were assuming a less tragic significance, he began to understand:

"And then . . ." he muttered.

"And then . . . let us talk."

"Yes, yes . . . let us talk. . . ."

"A cigarette?" asked the prince. "Will you have one? Ah, I see that you are becoming reconciled to life! So much the better: we shall understand each other; and that quickly."

He lit the young man's cigarette and his own and, at once, in a few words uttered in a hard voice, explained himself:

"You, the late Gérard Baupré, were weary of life, ill, penniless, hopeless. . . . Would you like to be well, rich, and powerful?"

"I don't follow you."

"It is quite simple. Accident has placed you on my path. You are young, good-looking, a poet; you are intelligent and—your act of despair shows it—you have a fine sense of conduct. These are qualities which are rarely found united in one person. I value them . . . and I take them for my account."

"They are not for sale."

"Idiot! Who talks of buying or selling? Keep your conscience. It is too precious a jewel for me to relieve you of it."

"Then what do you ask of me?"

"Your life!" And, pointing to the bruises on the young man's throat, "Your life, which you have not known how to employ! Your life, which you have bungled, wasted, destroyed and which, I propose to build up again, in accordance with an ideal of beauty, greatness and dignity that would make you giddy, my lad, if you saw the abyss into which my secret thought plunges. . . ." He had taken Gérard's head between his hands and he continued, eagerly: "You are free! No shackles! You have no longer the weight of your name to bear! You have got rid of that number with which society had stamped you as though branding you on the shoulder. You are free! In this world of slaves where each man bears his label you can either come and go unknown, invisible, as if you owned Gyges' ring . . . or else you can choose your own label, the one you like best! Do you understand the magnificent treasure which you represent to an artist . . . to yourself, if you like? A virgin life, a brand-new life! Your life is the wax which you have the right to fashion as you please, according to the whims of your imagination and the counsels of your reason."

The young man made a gesture expressive of weariness:

"Ah, what would you have me do with that treasure? What have I done with it so far? Nothing!"

"Give it to me."

"What can you do with it?"

"Everything. If you are not an artist, I am; and an enthusiastic artist, inexhaustible, indomitable, exuberant. If you have not the Promethean fire, I have! Where you failed, I shall succeed. Give me your life."

"Words, promises!" cried the young man, whose features began to glow with animation. "Empty dreams! I know my own worthlessness! I know my cowardice, my despondency, my efforts that come to nothing, all my wretchedness. To begin life anew, I should need a will which I do not possess. . . ."

"I possess mine."

"Friends. . . ."

"You shall have them."

"Means. . . ."

"I am providing you with means . . . and such means! You will only have to dip, as one would dip into a magic coffer."

"But who are you?" cried the young man, wildly.

"To others, Prince Sernine. . . . To you . . . what does it matter? I am more than a prince, more than a king, more than an emperor. . . ."

"Who are you? . . . Who are you?" stammered Baupré.

"The Master . . . he who will and who can . . . he who acts. . . . There are no bounds to my will, there is none to my power. I am richer than the richest man alive, for his fortune is mine. . . . I am more powerful than the mightiest, for their might is at my service!"

He took the other's head in his hands again and, looking deep into his eyes:

"Be rich, too . . . be mighty. . . . I offer you happiness . . . and the joy of living . . . and peace for your poet's brain . . . and fame and glory also. . . . Do you accept?"

"Yes . . . yes . . ." whispered Gérard, dazzled and overmastered. "What am I to do?"

"Nothing."

"But . . ."

"Nothing, I say. The whole scaffolding of my plans rests on you, but you do not count. You have no active part to play. You are, for the moment, but a silent actor, or not even that, but just a pawn which I move along the board."

"What shall I do?"

"Nothing. Write poetry. You shall live as you please. You shall have money. You shall enjoy life. I will not even bother my head about you. I repeat, you play no part in my venture."

"And who shall I be?"

Sernine stretched out his arm and pointed to the next room:

"You shall take that man's place. *You are that man!*"

Gérard shuddered with revolt and disgust:

"Oh, no, he is dead! . . . And then . . . it is a crime! . . . No, I want a new life, made for me, thought out for me . . . an unknown name. . . ."

"That man, I tell you!" cried Sernine, irresistible in his energy and authority. "You shall be that man and none other! That man, because his destiny is magnificent, because his name is illustrious, and because he hands down to you a thrice-venerable heritage of ancestral dignity and pride."

"It is a crime!" moaned Baupré, faltering.

"You shall be that man!" spoke Sernine, with unparalleled vehemence. "You shall be that man! If not, you become Baupré again; and over Baupré I own rights of life and death. Choose."

He drew his revolver, cocked it and took aim at the young man:

"Choose," he repeated.

The expression of his face was implacable. Gérard was frightened and sank down on his bed sobbing:

"I wish to live!"

"You wish it firmly, irrevocably?"

"Yes, a thousand times yes! After the terrible thing which I attempted, death appals me. . . . Anything . . . anything rather than death! . . . Anything! . . . Pain . . . hunger . . . illness . . . every torture, every shame . . . crime itself, if need be . . . but not death!"

He shivered with fever and agony, as though the great enemy were still prowling round him and as though he felt himself powerless to escape from its clutches. The prince redoubled his efforts and, in a fervent voice, holding him under him like a prey:

"I will ask nothing impossible of you, nothing wrong. . . . If there is anything, I am responsible. . . . No, no crime . . . a little pain at most. . . . A little of your blood must flow. But what is that, compared with the dread of dying?"

"Pain is indifferent to me."

"Then here and now!" shouted Sernine. "Here and now! Ten seconds of pain and that is all. . . . Ten seconds and the other's life is yours. . . ."

He had seized him round the body and forced him down on a chair; and he now held the young man's left hand flat on the table, with his fingers spread out. He swiftly took a knife from his pocket, pressed the blade against the little finger, between the first and second joints, and commanded:

"Strike! Strike your own blow. One blow of the fist and that is all!"

He had taken Gérard's right hand and was trying to bring it down upon the other like a hammer.

Gérard writhed and twisted, convulsed with horror. He understood:

"Never!" he stuttered. "Never!"

"Strike! One blow and it's done! One blow and you will be like that man: no one will recognize you."

"Tell me his name. . . ."

"Strike first!"

"Never! Oh, what torture! . . . I beseech you . . . presently. . . ."

"Now. . . . I insist . . . you must . . ."

"No . . . no . . . I can't do it. . . ."

"Strike, you fool! It means fortune, fame, love. . . ."

Gérard raised his fist with a sudden movement.

"Love," he said, "yes . . . for that, yes. . . ."

"You will love and be loved," said Sernine. "Your betrothed awaits you. I have chosen her myself. She is the purest of the pure, the fairest of the fair. But you must win her. Strike!"

The lad's arm stiffened for the fatal blow; but the instinct of self-preservation was too strong for him. His body was wrung with a superhuman effort. He suddenly released himself from Sernine's hold and fled.

He rushed like a madman to the other room. A yell of terror escaped him, at the sight of the abominable vision, and he came back and fell on his knees before Sernine, beside the table.

"Strike!" said the prince, again spreading out the lad's fingers and fixing the blade of the knife.

What followed was done mechanically. With an automatic movement, with haggard eyes and a livid face, the young man raised his fist and struck:

"Ah!" he cried, with a moan of pain.

A small piece of flesh was separated from the little finger. Blood flowed. For the third time, Gérard fainted.

Sernine looked at him for a second or two and said, gently:

"Poor little chap! . . . There, I'll reward you for what you've done; and a hundred times over. I always pay generously."

He went downstairs and found the doctor waiting below:

"It's done. Go upstairs, you, and make a little cut in his right cheek, similar to Pierre Leduc's. The two scars must be exactly alike. I shall come back for you in an hour."

"Where are you going?"

"To take the air. My heart feels anyhow."

Outside he drew a long breath and lit another cigarette:

"A good day's work," he muttered. "A little over-crowded, a little tiring, but fruitful, really fruitful. I am Dolores Kesselbach's friend. I am Geneviève's friend. I have manufactured a new Pierre Leduc, a very presentable one and entirely at my disposal. Lastly, I have found Geneviève a husband of the sort that you don't find by the dozen. Now my task is done. I have only to gather the fruit of my efforts. It's your turn to work, M. Lenormand. I, for my part, am ready." And he added, thinking of the poor mutilated lad whom he had dazzled with his promises, "Only—for there is an 'only'—I have not the slightest notion who this Pierre Leduc was, whose place I have magnanimously awarded to that good young man. And that's very annoying. . . . For when all is said, there's nothing to prove to me that Pierre Leduc was not the son of a pork-butcher! . . ."

V. M. LENORMAND AT WORK

On the morning of the 31st of May, all the newspapers reminded their readers that Lupin, in a letter addressed to M. Lenormand, had announced the escape of the messenger Jérôme for that date. And one of them summed up the situation, as it then stood, in very able terms:

"The horrible carnage at the Palace Hotel took place as far back as the 17th of April. What has been discovered since? Nothing.

"There were three clues: the cigarette-case, the initials L and M and the parcel of clothes left behind in the office of the hotel. What advantage has been taken of these clues? None.

"It appears that the police suspect one of the visitors who was staying on the first floor and who disappeared in a doubtful manner. Have they found him? Have they established his identity? No.

"The tragedy, therefore, remains as mysterious as at the beginning, the gloom is impenetrable.

"To complete the picture, we are told that dissension prevails between the prefect of police and his subordinate, M. Lenormand, and that the latter, finding himself less vigorously supported by the prime minister, virtually sent in his resignation several days ago. According to our information, the conduct of the Kesselbach case is now in the hands of the deputy-chief of the detective-service, M. Weber, a personal enemy of M. Lenormand's.

"In short, disorder and confusion reign; and this in the face of Lupin, who stands for method, energy and steadfastness of mind.

"What conclusion do we draw from these facts? Briefly, this: Lupin will release his accomplice to-day, the 31st of May, as he foretold."

This conclusion, which was echoed in all the other newspapers, was also the conclusion at which the general public had arrived. And we must take it that the threat was not considered devoid of importance in high places, for the prefect of police and, in the absence of M. Lenormand, who was said to be unwell, the deputy-chief of the detective-service, M. Weber, had adopted the most stringent measures, both at the Palais de Justice and at the Santé Prison, where the prisoner was confined.

They did not dare, for sheer reasons of shame, to suspend on that particular day the examinations conducted daily by M. Formerie; but, from the prison to the Boulevard du Palais, a regular mobilization of police-forces guarded the streets along the line.

To the intense astonishment of one and all, the 31st of May passed and the threatened escape did not take place.

One thing did happen, an attempt to execute the plan, as was betrayed by a block of tramway-cars, omnibuses and drays along the road taken by the prison-van and the unaccountable breaking of one of the wheels of the van itself. But the attempt assumed no more definite form.

Lupin, therefore, had met with a check. The public felt almost disappointed and the police triumphed loudly.

On the next day, Saturday, an incredible rumour spread through the Palais and the newspaper-offices: Jérôme the messenger had disappeared.

Was it possible? Although the special editions confirmed the news, people refused to believe it. But, at six o'clock, a note published by the *Dépêche du Soir* made it official:

"We have received the following communication signed by Arsène Lupin. The special stamp affixed to it, in accordance with the circular which Lupin recently sent to the press, guarantees the genuineness of the document:

"'*To the Editor of the* Dépêche du Soir.

"'SIR,

"'Pray make my apologies to the public for not keeping my word yesterday. I remembered, at the last moment, that the 31st of May fell on a Friday! Could I set my friend at liberty on a Friday? I did not think it right to assume that responsibility.

"'I must also apologize for not on this occasion explaining, with my customary frankness, how this little event was managed. My process is so ingenious and so simple that I fear lest, if I revealed it, every criminal should be inspired by it. How surprised people will be on the day when I am free to speak! "Is that all?" I shall be asked. That is all; but it had to be thought of.

"'Permit me to be, Sir,

"'Your obedient servant,

"'ARSÈNE LUPIN.'"

An hour later, M. Lenormand was rung up on the telephone and informed that Valenglay, the prime minister, wished to see him at the Ministry of the Interior.

"How well you're looking, my dear Lenormand! And I who thought that you were ill and dared not leave your room!"

"I am not ill, Monsieur le Président."

"So you were sulking in your tent! . . . But you were always a bad-tempered fellow."

"I confess to the bad temper, Monsieur le Président, but not to the sulking."

"But you stay at home! And Lupin takes advantage of it to release his friends. . . ."

"How could I stop him?"

"How? Why, Lupin's trick was of the plainest. In accordance with his usual method, he announced the date of the escape beforehand; everybody believed in it; an apparent attempt was planned; the escape was not made; and, on the next day, when nobody is thinking about it—whoosh!—the bird takes flight."

"Monsieur le Président," said the chief of the detective-service, solemnly, "Lupin disposes of such means that we are not in a position to prevent what he has decided on. The escape was mathematically certain. I preferred to pass the hand . . . and leave the laughter for others to face."

Valenglay chuckled:

"It's a fact that Monsieur le Préfet de Police and M. Weber cannot be enjoying themselves at the present moment. . . . But, when all is said, can you explain to me, M. Lenormand . . ."

"All that we know, Monsieur le Président, is that the escape took place from the Palais de Justice. The prisoner was brought in a prison-van and taken to M. Formerie's room. He left M. Formerie's room, but he did not leave the Palais de Justice. And yet nobody knows what became of him."

"It's most bewildering."

"Most bewildering."

"And has nothing else been discovered?"

"Yes. The inner corridor leading to the examining magistrates' rooms was blocked by an absolutely unprecedented crowd of prisoners, warders, counsel and doorkeepers; and it was discovered that all those people had received forged notices to appear at the same hour. On the other hand, not one of the examining-magistrates who were supposed to have summoned them sat in his room that day; and this because of forged notices from the public prosecutor's office, sending them to every part of Paris . . . and of the outskirts."

"Is that all?"

"No. Two municipal guards and a prisoner were seen to cross the courtyards. A cab was waiting for them outside and all three stepped in.

"And your supposition, Lenormand, your opinion. . . ."

"My supposition, Monsieur le Président, is that the two municipal guards were accomplices who, profiting by the disorder in the corridor, took the place of the three warders. And my opinion is that this escape succeeded only through such special circumstances and so strange a combination of facts that we must look upon the most unlikely cases of complicity as absolutely certain. Lupin, for that matter, has connections at the Palais that balk all our calculations. He has agents in your ministry. He has agents at the Prefecture of Police. He has agents around me. It is a formidable organization, a detective-service a thousand times more clever, more daring, more varied and more supple than that under my own orders."

"And you stand this, Lenormand?"

"No, I do not."

"Then why this slackness on your part since the beginning of the case? What have you done against Lupin?"

"I have prepared for the struggle."

"Ah, capital! And, while you were preparing, he was acting."

"So was I."

"And do you know anything?"

"I know a great deal."

"What? Speak!"

Leaning on his stick, M. Lenormand took a little contemplative walk across the spacious room. Then he sat down opposite Valenglay, brushed the facings of his olive-green coat with his finger-tips, settled his spectacles on his nose and said, plainly:

"M. le Président, I hold three trump-cards in my hand. First, I know the name under which Arsène Lupin is hiding at this moment, the name under which he lived on the Boulevard Haussmann, receiving his assistants daily, reconstructing and directing his gang."

"But then why, in heaven's name, don't you arrest him?"

"I did not receive these particulars until later. The prince—let us call him Prince Dash—has disappeared. He is abroad, on other business."

"And, if he does not return . . ."

"The position which he occupies, the manner in which he has flung himself into the Kesselbach case, necessitate his return and under the same name."

"Nevertheless . . ."

"Monsieur le Président, I come to my second trump. I have at last discovered Pierre Leduc."

"Nonsense!"

"Or rather Lupin discovered him, and before disappearing, settled him in a little villa in the neighborhood of Paris."

"By Jove! But how did you know . . ."

"Oh, easily! Lupin has placed two of his accomplices with Pierre Leduc, to watch him and defend him. Now these accomplices are two of my own detectives, two brothers whom I employ in the greatest secrecy and who will hand him over to me at the first opportunity!"

"Well done you! So that . . ."

"So that, as Pierre Leduc, we may say, is the central point of the efforts of all those who are trying to solve the famous Kesselbach secret, I shall, sooner or later, through Pierre Leduc, catch, first, the author of the treble murder, because that miscreant substituted himself for Mr. Kesselbach in the accomplishment of an immense scheme and because Mr. Kesselbach had to find Pierre Leduc in order to be able to accomplish that scheme; and, secondly, Arsène Lupin, because Arsène Lupin is pursuing the same object."

"Splendid! Pierre Leduc is the bait which you are throwing to the enemy."

"And the fish is biting, Monsieur le Président. I have just had word that a suspicious person was seen, a short time ago, prowling round the little villa where Pierre Leduc is living under the protection of my officers. I shall be on the spot in four hours."

"And the third trump, Lenormand?"

"Monsieur le Président, a letter arrived yesterday, addressed to Mr. Rudolf Kesselbach, which I intercepted. . . ."

"Intercepted, eh? You're getting on!"

"Yes, I intercepted it, opened it and kept it for myself. Here it is. It is dated two months back. It bears the Capetown postmark and contains these words: 'My dear Rudolf, I shall be in Paris on the 1st of June and in just as wretched a plight as when you came to my assistance. But I have great hopes of this Pierre Leduc affair of which I told you. What a strange story it is! Have you found the man I mean? Where do we stand? I am most anxious to know.' The letter is signed, 'Steinweg.' The first of June," continued M. Lenormand, "is to-day. I have ordered one of my inspectors to hunt me out this Steinweg. I have no doubt that he will succeed."

"Nor I, no doubt at all," cried Valenglay, rising from his chair, "and I make you every apology, my dear Lenormand, and my humble confession: I was on the point of letting you slide . . . for good and all! To-morrow I was expecting the prefect of police and M. Weber."

"I knew that, Monsieur le Président."

"Impossible!"

"But for that, should I have put myself out? You now see my plan of campaign. On the one side, I am setting traps in which the murderer will be caught sooner or later. Pierre Leduc or Steinweg will deliver him into my hands. On the other side, I am on Arsène Lupin's heels. Two of his agents are in my pay and he believes them to be his most devoted helpers. In addition to this, he is working for me, because he is pursuing the perpetrator of the threefold crime as I am. Only, he imagines that he is dishing me, whereas it is I who am dishing him. So I shall succeed, but on one condition. . . ."

"What is that?"

"That I am given free scope and allowed to act according to the needs of the moment, without troubling about the public, who are growing impatient, or my superiors, who are intriguing against me."

"I agree."

"In that case, Monsieur le Président, in a few days from this I shall be the victor . . . or I shall be dead."

At Saint-Cloud. A little villa situated on one of the highest points of the upland, in an unfrequented road.

It was eleven o'clock at night. M. Lenormand left his car at Saint-Cloud and walked cautiously along the road. A shadow appeared.

"Is that you, Gourel?"

"Yes, chief."

"Did you tell the brothers Doudeville that I was coming?"

"Yes, your room is ready, you can go to bed and sleep . . . unless they try to carry off Pierre Leduc to-night, which would not surprise me, considering the behavior of the fellow whom the Doudevilles saw."

They walked across the garden, softly entered the house and went up to the first floor. The two brothers, Jean and Jacques Doudeville, were there.

"No news of Prince Sernine?" asked Lenormand.

"No, chief."

"What about Pierre Leduc?"

"He spends the whole day lying flat on his back in his room on the ground-floor, or else in the garden. He never comes up to see us."

"Is he better?"

"Much better. The rest has made a great change in his appearance."

"Is he wholly devoted to Lupin?"

"To Prince Sernine, rather, for he does not suspect that the two are one and the same man. At least, I suppose so. One never knows, with him. He does not speak at all. Oh, he's a queer fish! There's only one person who has the gift of cheering him up, of making him talk and even laugh. That's a young girl from Garches, to whom Prince Sernine introduced him. Geneviève Ernemont her name is. She has been here three times already . . . she was here to-day." He added, jestingly, "I believe there's a little flirting going on. . . . It's like his highness Prince Sernine and Mrs. Kesselbach. . . . It seems he's making eyes at her! . . . That devil of a Lupin!"

M. Lenormand did not reply. But it was obvious that all these details, to which he seemed to attach no importance, were noted in the recesses of his memory, to be used whenever he might need to draw the logical inferences from them. He lit a cigar, chewed it without smoking it, lit it again and dropped it.

He asked two or three more questions and then, dressed as he was, threw himself on his bed:

"If the least thing happens, let me be awakened. . . . If not, I shall sleep through the night. . . . Go to your posts, all of you."

The others left the room.

An hour passed, two hours.

Suddenly, M. Lenormand felt some one touch him and Gourel said to him:

"Get up, chief; they have opened the gate."

"One man or two?"

"I only saw one . . . the moon appeared just then . . . he crouched down against a hedge."

"And the brothers Doudeville?"

"I sent them out by the back. They will cut off his retreat when the time comes."

Gourel took M. Lenormand's hand, led him downstairs and then into a little dark room:

"Don't stir, chief; we are in Pierre Leduc's dressing-room. I am opening the door of the recess in which his bed stands. . . . Don't be afraid . . . he has taken his veronal as he does every evening . . . nothing can wake him. Come this way. . . . It's a good hiding-place, isn't it? . . . These are the curtains of his bed. . . . From here you can see the window and the whole side of the room between the window and the bed."

The casement stood open and admitted a vague light, which became very precise at times, when the moon burst through her veil of clouds. The two men did not take their eyes from the empty window-frame, feeling certain that the event which they were awaiting would come from that side.

A slight, creaking noise . . .

"He is climbing the trellis," whispered Gourel.

"Is it high?"

"Six feet or so."

The creaking became more distinct.

"Go, Gourel," muttered M. Lenormand, "find the Doudevilles, bring them back to the foot of the wall and bar the road to any one who tries to get down this way."

Gourel went. At the same moment, a head appeared at the level of the window. Then a leg was flung over the balcony. M. Lenormand distinguished a slenderly-built man, below the middle height, dressed in dark colours and without a hat.

The man turned and, leaning over the balcony, looked for a few seconds into space, as though to make sure that no danger threatened him. Then he stooped down and lay at full length on the floor. He appeared motionless. But soon M. Lenormand realized that the still blacker shadow which he formed against the surrounding darkness was coming forward, nearer.

It reached the bed.

M. Lenormand had an impression that he could hear the man's breathing and, at the same time, that he could just see his eyes, keen, glittering eyes, which pierced the darkness like shafts of fire and which themselves could see through that same darkness.

Pierre Leduc gave a deep sigh and turned over.

A fresh silence. . . .

The man had glided along the bed with imperceptible movements and his dark outline now stood out against the whiteness of the sheets that hung down to the floor.

M. Lenormand could have touched him by putting out his arm. This time, he clearly distinguished the breathing, which alternated with that of the sleeper, and he had the illusion that he also heard the sound of a heart beating.

Suddenly, a flash of light. . . . The man had pressed the spring of an electric lantern; and Pierre Leduc was lit full in the face, but the man remained in the shade, so that M. Lenormand was unable to see his features.

All that he saw was something that shone in the bright space; and he shuddered. It was the blade of a knife; and that thin, tapering knife, more like a stiletto than a dagger, seemed to him identical with the weapon which he had picked up by the body of Chapman, Mr. Kesselbach's secretary.

He put forth all his will-power to restrain himself from springing upon the man. He wanted first to know what the man had come to do.

The hand was raised. Was he going to strike? M. Lenormand calculated the distance in order to stop the blow. . . . But no, it was not a murderous gesture, but one of caution. The hand would only fall if Pierre Leduc stirred or tried to call out. And the man bent over the sleeper, as though he were examining something.

"The right cheek," thought M. Lenormand, "the scar on the right cheek. . . . He wants to make sure that it is really Pierre Leduc."

The man had turned a little to one side, so that only his shoulders were visible. But his clothes, his overcoat, were so near that they brushed against the curtains behind which M. Lenormand was hiding.

"One movement on his part," thought the chief detective, "a thrill of alarm; and I shall collar him."

But the man, entirely absorbed in his examination, did not stir. At last, after shifting the dagger to the hand that held the lantern, he raised the sheet, at first hardly at all, then a little more, then more still, until the sleeper's left arm was uncovered and the hand laid bare. The flash of the lantern shone upon the hand. The fingers lay outspread. The little finger was cut on the second joint.

Again Pierre Leduc made a movement. The light was immediately put out; and, for an instant, the man remained beside the bed, motionless, standing straight up. Would he make up his mind to strike? M. Lenormand underwent the agony of the crime which he could so easily prevent, but which he did not want to forestall before the very last second.

A long, a very long silence. Suddenly, he saw or rather fancied that he saw an arm uplifted. Instinctively he moved, stretching his hand above the sleeper. In making this gesture, he hit against the man.

A dull cry. The fellow struck out at space, defended himself at random and fled toward the window. But M. Lenormand had leapt upon him and had his two arms around the man's shoulders.

He at once felt him yielding and, as the weaker of the two, powerless in Lenormand's hands, trying to avoid the struggle and to slip from between his arms. Lenormand, exerting all his strength, held him flat against his chest, bent him in two and stretched him on his back on the floor.

"Ah, I've got him, I've got him!" he muttered triumphantly.

And he felt a singular elation at imprisoning that terrifying criminal, that unspeakable monster, in his irresistible grip. He felt him living and quivering, enraged and desperate, their two lives mingled, their breaths blended:

"Who are you?" he asked. "Who are you? . . . You'll have to speak. . . ."

And he clasped the enemy's body with still greater force, for he had an impression that that body was diminishing between his arms, that it was vanishing. He gripped harder . . . and harder. . . .

And suddenly he shuddered from head to foot. He had felt, he still felt a tiny prick in the throat. . . . In his exasperation, he gripped harder yet: the pain increased! And he observed that the man had succeeded in twisting one arm round, slipping his hand to his chest and holding the dagger on end. The arm, it was true, was incapable of motion; but the closer M. Lenormand tightened his grip, the deeper did the point of the dagger enter the proffered flesh.

He flung back his head a little to escape the point: the point followed the movement and the wound widened.

Then he moved no more, remembering the three crimes and all the alarming, atrocious and prophetic things represented by that same little steel needle which was piercing his skin and which, in its turn, was implacably penetrating. . . .

Suddenly, he let go and gave a leap backwards. Then, at once, he tried to resume the offensive. It was too late. The man flung his legs across the window-sill and jumped.

"Look out, Gourel!" he cried, knowing that Gourel was there, ready to catch the fugitive.

He leant out. A crunching of pebbles . . . a shadow between two trees, the slam of the gate. . . . And no other sound . . . no interference. . . .

Without giving a thought to Pierre Leduc, he called:

"Gourel! . . . Doudeville!"

No answer. The great silence of the countryside at night. . . .

In spite of himself, he continued to think of the treble murder, the steel dagger. But no, it was impossible, the man had not had time, had not even had the need to strike, as he had found the road clear.

M. Lenormand jumped out in his turn and, switching on his lantern, recognized Gourel lying on the ground:

"Damn it!" he swore. "If they've killed him, they'll have to pay dearly for it."

But Gourel was not dead, only stunned; and, a few minutes later, he came to himself and growled:

"Only a blow of the fist, chief . . . just a blow of the fist which caught me full in the chest. But what a fellow!"

"There were two of them then?"

"Yes, a little one, who went up, and another, who took me unawares while I was watching."

"And the Doudevilles?"

"Haven't seen them."

One of them, Jacques, was found near the gate, bleeding from a punch in the jaw; the other a little farther, gasping for breath from a blow full on the chest.

"What is it? What happened?" asked M. Lenormand.

Jacques said that his brother and he had knocked up against an individual who had crippled them before they had time to defend themselves.

"Was he alone?"

"No; when he passed near us, he had a pal with him, shorter than himself."

"Did you recognize the man who struck you?"

"Judging by the breadth of his shoulders, I thought he might be the Englishman of the Palace Hotel, the one who left the hotel and whose traces we lost."

"The major?"

"Yes, Major Parbury."

After a moment's reflection, M. Lenormand said:

"There is no doubt possible. There were two of them in the Kesselbach case: the man with the dagger, who committed the murders, and his accomplice, the major."

"That is what Prince Sernine thinks," muttered Jacques Doudeville.

"And to-night," continued the chief detective, "it is they again: the same two." And he added, "So much the better. The chance of catching two criminals is a hundred times greater than the chance of catching one."

M. Lenormand attended to his men, had them put to bed and looked to see if the assailants had dropped anything or left any traces. He found nothing and went back to bed again himself.

In the morning, as Gourel and the Doudevilles felt none the worse for their injuries, he told the two brothers to scour the neighborhood and himself set out with Gourel for Paris, in order to hurry matters on and give his orders.

He lunched in his office. At two o'clock, he heard good news. One of his best detectives, Dieuzy, had picked up Steinweg, Rudolf Kesselbach's correspondent, as the German was stepping out of a train from Marseilles.

"Is Dieuzy there?"

"Yes, chief," said Gourel. "He's here with the German."

"Have them brought in to me."

At that moment, the telephone-bell rang. It was Jean Doudeville, speaking from the post-office at Garches. The conversation did not take long:

"Is that you, Jean? Any news?"

"Yes, chief, Major Parbury. . . ."

"Well?"

"We have found him. He has become a Spaniard and has darkened his skin. We have just seen him. He was entering the Garches free-school. He was received by that young lady . . . you know, the girl who knows Prince Sernine, Geneviève Ernemont."

"Thunder!"

M. Lenormand let go the receiver, made a grab at his hat, flew into the passage, met Dieuzy and the German, shouted to them to meet him in his office at six o'clock, rushed down the stairs, followed by Gourel and two inspectors whom he picked up on the way, and dived into a taxi-cab:

"Quick as you can to Garches . . . ten francs for yourself!"

He stopped the car a little before the Parc de Villeneuve, at the turn of the lane that led to the school. Jean Doudeville was waiting for him and at once exclaimed:

"He slipped away, ten minutes ago, by the other end of the lane."

"Alone?"

"No, with the girl."

M. Lenormand took Doudeville by the collar:

"Wretch! You let him go! But you ought to have . . . you ought to have . . ."

"My brother is on his track."

"A lot of good that will do us! He'll stick your brother. You're no match for him, either of you!"

He himself took the steering-wheel of the taxi, and resolutely drove into the lane, regardless of the cart-ruts and of the bushes on each side. They soon emerged on a parish-road, which took them to a crossway where five roads met. M. Lenormand, without hesitation chose the one on the left, the Saint-Cucufa Road. As a matter of fact, at the top of the slope that runs down to the lake, they met the other Doudeville brother, who shouted:

"They are in a carriage . . . half a mile away."

The chief did not stop. He sent the car flying down the incline, rushed along the bends, drove round the lake and suddenly uttered an exclamation of triumph. Right at the top of a little hill that stood in front of them, he had seen the hood of a carriage.

Unfortunately, he had taken the wrong road and had to back the machine. When he reached the place where the roads branched, the carriage was still there, stationary. And, suddenly, while he was turning, he saw a girl spring from the carriage. A man appeared on the step. The girl stretched out her arm. Two reports rang out.

She had taken bad aim, without a doubt, for a head looked round the other side of the hood and the man, catching sight of the motor-cab, gave his horse a great lash with the whip and it started off at a gallop. The next moment, a turn of the road hid the carriage from sight.

M. Lenormand finished his tacking in a few seconds, darted straight up the incline, passed the girl without stopping and turned round boldly. He found himself on a steep, pebbly forest road, which ran down between dense woods and which could only be followed very slowly and with the greatest caution. But what did he care! Twenty yards in front of him, the carriage, a sort of two-wheeled cabriolet, was dancing over the stones, drawn, or rather held back, by a horse which knew enough only to go very carefully, feeling its way and taking no risks. There was nothing to fear; escape was impossible.

And the two conveyances went shaking and jolting down-hill. At one moment, they were so close together that M. Lenormand thought of alighting and running with his men. But he felt the danger of putting on the brake on so steep a slope; and he went on, pressing the enemy closely, like a prey which one keeps within sight, within touch. . . .

"We've got him, chief, we've got him!" muttered the inspectors, excited by the unexpected nature of the chase.

At the bottom, the way flattened out into a road that ran towards the Seine, towards Bougival. The horse, on reaching level ground, set off at a jog-trot, without hurrying itself and keeping to the middle of the road.

A violent effort shook the taxi. It appeared, instead of rolling, to proceed by bounds, like a darting fawn, and, slipping by the roadside slope, ready to smash any obstacle, it caught up the carriage, came level with it, passed it. . . .

An oath from M. Lenormand . . . shouts of fury. . . . The carriage was empty!

The carriage was empty. The horse was going along peacefully, with the reins on its back, no doubt returning to the stable of some inn in the neighborhood, where it had been hired for the day. . . .

Suppressing his inward rage, the chief detective merely said:

"The major must have jumped out during the few seconds when we lost sight of the carriage, at the top of the descent."

"We have only to beat the woods, chief, and we are sure . . ."

"To return empty-handed. The beggar is far away by this time. He's not one of those who are caught twice in one day. Oh, hang it all, hang it all!"

They went back to the young girl, whom they found in the company of Jacques Doudeville and apparently none the worse for her adventure. M. Lenormand introduced himself, offered to take her back home and at once questioned her about the English major, Parbury.

She expressed astonishment:

"He is neither English nor a major; and his name is not Parbury."

"Then what is his name?"

"Juan Ribeira. He is a Spaniard sent by his government to study the working of the French schools."

"As you please. His name and his nationality are of no importance. He is the man we are looking for. Have you known him long?"

"A fortnight or so. He had heard about a school which I have founded at Garches and he interested himself in experiment to the extent of proposing to make me an annual grant, on the one condition that he might come from time to time to observe the progress of my pupils. I had not the right to refuse. . . ."

"No, of course not; but you should have consulted your acquaintances. Is not Prince Sernine a friend of yours? He is a man of good counsel."

"Oh, I have the greatest confidence in him; but he is abroad at present."

"Did you not know his address?"

"No. And, besides, what could I have said to him? That gentleman behaved very well. It was not until to-day . . . But I don't know if . . ."

"I beg you, mademoiselle, speak frankly. You can have confidence in me also."

"Well, M. Ribeira came just now. He told me that he had been sent by a French lady who was paying a short visit to Bougival, that this lady had a little girl whose education she would like to entrust to me and that she wished me to come and see her without delay. The thing seemed quite natural. And, as this is a holiday and as M. Ribeira had hired a carriage which was waiting for him at the end of the road, I made no difficulty about accepting a seat in it."

"But what was his object, after all?"

She blushed and said:

"To carry me off, quite simply. He confessed it to me after half an hour. . . ."

"Do you know nothing about him?"

"No."

"Does he live in Paris?"

"I suppose so."

"Has he ever written to you? Do you happen to have a few lines in his handwriting, anything which he left behind, that may serve us as a clue?"

"No clue at all. . . . Oh, wait a minute . . . but I don't think that has any importance. . . ."

"Speak, speak . . . please. . . ."

"Well, two days ago, the gentleman asked permission to use my typewriting machine; and he typed out—with difficulty, for he evidently had no practice—a letter of which I saw the address by accident."

"What was the address?"

"He was writing to the *Journal* and he put about twenty stamps into the envelope."

"Yes . . . the agony-column, no doubt," said M. Lenormand.

"I have to-day's number with me, chief," said Gourel.

M. Lenormand unfolded the sheet and looked at the eighth page. Presently, he gave a start. He had read the following sentence, printed with the usual abbreviation:[12]

"To any person knowing Mr. Steinweg. Advertiser wishes to know if he is in Paris and his address. Reply through this column."

"Steinweg!" exclaimed Gourel. "But that's the very man whom Dieuzy is bringing to you!"

"Yes, yes," said M. Lenormand, to himself, "it's the man whose letter to Mr. Kesselbach I intercepted, the man who put Kesselbach on the track of Pierre Leduc. . . . So they, too, want particulars about Pierre Leduc and his past? . . . They, too, are groping in the dark? . . ."

He rubbed his hands: Steinweg was at his disposal. In less than an hour, Steinweg would have spoken. In less than an hour, the murky veil which oppressed him and which made the Kesselbach case the most agonizing and the most impenetrable that he had ever had in hand: that veil would be torn asunder.

VI. M. LENORMAND SUCCUMBS

M. Lenormand was back in his room at the Prefecture of Police at six o'clock in the evening. He at once sent for Dieuzy:

"Is your man here?"

"Yes, chief."

"How far have you got with him?"

"Not very. He won't speak a word. I told him that, by a new regulation, foreigners were 'bliged to make a declaration at the Prefecture as to the object and the probable length of their stay in Paris; and I brought him here, to your secretary's office."

"I will question him."

But, at that moment, an office-messenger appeared:

"There's a lady asking to see you at once, chief."

"Have you her card?"

"Here, chief."

"Mrs. Kesselbach! Show her in."

He walked across the room to receive the young widow at the door and begged her to take a seat. She still wore the same disconsolate look, the same appearance of illness and that air of extreme lassitude which revealed the distress of her life.

She held out a copy of the *Journal* and pointed to the line in the agony-column which mentioned Steinweg:

"Old Steinweg was a friend of my husband's," she said, "and I have no doubt that he knows a good many things."

---

[12]Personal advertisements in the French newspapers are charged by the line, not by the word; and consequently nearly every word is clipped down to two, three or four letters.—*Translator's Note*

"Dieuzy," said M. Lenormand, "bring the person who is waiting. . . . Your visit, madame, will not have been useless. I will only ask you, when this person enters, not to say a word."

The door opened. A man appeared, an old man with white whiskers meeting under his chin and a face furrowed with deep wrinkles, poorly clad and wearing the hunted look of those wretches who roam about the world in search of their daily pittance.

He stood on the threshold, blinking his eyelids, stared at M. Lenormand, seemed confused by the silence that greeted him on his entrance and turned his hat in his hands with embarrassment.

But, suddenly, he appeared stupefied, his eyes opened wide and he stammered:

"Mrs. . . . Mrs. Kesselbach!"

He had seen the young widow. And, recovering his serenity, smiling, losing his shyness, he went up to her and in a strong German accent:

"Oh, I am glad! . . . At last! . . . I thought I should never . . . I was so surprised to receive no news down there . . . no telegrams. . . . And how is our dear Rudolf Kesselbach?"

The lady staggered back, as though she had been struck in the face, and at once fell into a chair and began to sob.

"What's the matter? . . . Why, what's the matter?" asked Steinweg.

M. Lenormand interposed:

"I see, sir, that you know nothing about certain events that have taken place recently. Have you been long travelling?"

"Yes, three months. . . . I had been up to the Rand. Then I went back to Capetown and wrote to Rudolf from there. But, on my way home by the East Coast route, I accepted some work at Port Said. Rudolf has had my letter, I suppose?"

"He is away. I will explain the reason of his absence. But, first, there is a point on which we should be glad of some information. It has to do with a person whom you knew and to whom you used to refer, in your intercourse with Mr. Kesselbach, by the name of Pierre Leduc."

"Pierre Leduc! What! Who told you?"

The old man was utterly taken aback.

He spluttered out again:

"Who told you? Who disclosed to you . . . ?"

"Mr. Kesselbach."

"Never! It was a secret which I confided to him and Rudolf keeps his secrets . . . especially this one . . ."

"Nevertheless, it is absolutely necessary that you should reply to our questions. We are at this moment engaged on an inquiry about Pierre Leduc which must come to a head without delay; and you alone can enlighten us, as Mr. Kesselbach is no longer here."

"Well, then," cried Steinweg, apparently making up his mind, "what do you want?"

"Do you know Pierre Leduc?"

"I have never seen him, but I have long been the possessor of a secret which concerns him. Through a number of incidents which I need not relate and thanks to a series of chances, I ended by acquiring the certainty that the man in whose discovery I was interested was leading a dissolute life in Paris and that he was calling himself Pierre Leduc, which is not his real name."

"But does he know his real name himself?"

"I presume so."

"And you?"

"Yes, I know it."

"Well, tell it to us."

He hesitated; then, vehemently:

"I can't," he said. "No, I can't."

"But why not?"

"I have no right to. The whole secret lies there. When I revealed the secret to Rudolf, he attached so much importance to it that he gave me a large sum of money to purchase my silence and he promised me a fortune, a real fortune, on the day when he should succeed, first, in finding Pierre Leduc and, next, in turning the secret to account." He smiled bitterly. "The large sum of money is already lost. I came to see how my fortune was getting on."

"Mr. Kesselbach is dead," said the chief detective.

Steinweg gave a bound:

"Dead! Is it possible? No, it's a trap. Mrs. Kesselbach, is it true?"

She bowed her head.

He seemed crushed by this unexpected revelation; and, at the same time, it must have been infinitely painful to him, for he began to cry:

"My poor Rudolf, I knew him when he was a little boy. . . . He used to come and play at my house at Augsburg. . . . I was very fond of him." And, calling Mrs. Kesselbach to witness, "And he of me, was he not, Mrs. Kesselbach? He must have told you. . . . His old Daddy Steinweg, he used to call me."

M. Lenormand went up to him and, in his clearest voice:

"Listen to me," he said. "Mr. Kesselbach died murdered. . . . Come, be calm . . . exclamations are of no use. . . . He died murdered, I say, and all the circumstances of the crime prove that the culprit knew about the scheme in question. Was there anything in the nature of that scheme that would enable you to guess . . . ?"

Steinweg stood dumfounded. He stammered:

"It was my fault. . . . If I had not suggested the thing to him . . ."

Mrs. Kesselbach went up to him, entreating him:

"Do you think . . . have you any idea? . . . Oh, Steinweg, I implore you! . . ."

"I have no idea. . . . I have not reflected," he muttered. "I must have time to reflect. . . ."

"Cast about in Mr. Kesselbach's surroundings," said M. Lenormand. "Did nobody take part in your interviews at that time? Was there nobody in whom he himself could have confided?"

"No."

"Think well."

Both the others, Dolores and M. Lenormand, leant toward him, anxiously awaiting his answer.

"No," he said, "I don't see. . . ."

"Think well," repeated the chief detective. "The murderer's Christian name and surname begin with an L and an M."

"An L," he echoed. "I don't see . . . an L . . . an M. . . ."

"Yes, the initials are in gold on the corner of a cigarette-case belonging to the murderer."

"A cigarette-case?" asked Steinweg, making an effort of memory.

"A gun-metal case . . . and one of the compartments is divided into two spaces, the smaller for cigarette-papers, the other for tobacco. . . ."

"Two spaces, two spaces," repeated Steinweg, whose thoughts seemed stimulated by that detail. "Couldn't you show it to me?"

"Here it is, or rather this is an exact reproduction," said M. Lenormand, giving him a cigarette-case.

"Eh! What!" said Steinweg, taking the case in his hands.

He looked at it with stupid eyes, examined it, turned it over in every direction and, suddenly, gave a cry, the cry of a man struck with a horrible idea. And he stood like that, livid, with trembling hands and wild, staring eyes.

"Speak, come, speak!" said M. Lenormand.

"Oh," he said, as though blinded with light, "now all is explained! . . ."

"Speak, speak!"

He walked across to the windows with a tottering step, then returned and, rushing up to the chief detective:

"Sir, sir . . . Rudolf's murderer . . . I'll tell you. . . . Well . . ."

He stopped short.

"Well?"

There was a moment's pause.... Was the name of the odious criminal about to echo through the great silence of the office, between those walls which had heard so many accusations, so many confessions? M. Lenormand felt as if he were on the brink of the unfathomable abyss and as if a voice were mounting, mounting up to him.... A few seconds more and he would know....

"No," muttered Steinweg, "no, I can't...."

"What's that you say?" cried the chief detective, furiously.

"I say that I can't."

"But you have no right to be silent. The law requires you to speak."

"To-morrow.... I will speak to-morrow... I must have time to reflect.... To-morrow, I will tell you all that I know about Pierre Leduc... all that I suppose about that cigarette-case.... To-morrow, I promise you...."

It was obvious that he possessed that sort of obstinacy against which the most energetic efforts are of no avail. M. Lenormand yielded:

"Very well. I give you until to-morrow, but I warn you that, if you do not speak to-morrow, I shall be obliged to go to the examining-magistrate."

He rang and, taking Inspector Dieuzy aside, said:

"Go with him to his hotel... and stay there.... I'll send you two men.... And mind you keep your eyes about you. Somebody may try to get hold of him."

The inspector went off with Steinweg; and M. Lenormand, returning to Mrs. Kesselbach, who had been violently affected by this scene, made his excuses.

"Pray accept all my regrets, madame.... I can understand how upset you must feel...."

He questioned her as to the period at which Mr. Kesselbach renewed his relations with old Steinweg and as to the length of time for which those relations lasted. But she was so much worn-out that he did not insist.

"Am I to come back to-morrow?" she asked.

"No, it's not necessary. I will let you know all that Steinweg says. May I see you down to your carriage? These three flights are rather steep...."

He opened the door and stood back to let her pass. At that moment shouts were heard in the passage and people came running up, inspectors on duty, office-messengers, clerks:

"Chief! Chief!"

"What's the matter?"

"Dieuzy!..."

"But he's just left here...."

"He's been found on the staircase...."

"Not dead?..."

"No, stunned, fainting...."

"But the man... the man who was with him... old Steinweg?"

"He's disappeared...."

"Damn it!"

He rushed along the passage and down the stairs, where he found Dieuzy lying on the first-floor landing, surrounded by people who were attending to him.

He saw Gourel coming up again:

"Oh, Gourel, have you been downstairs? Did you come across anybody?"

"No, chief...."

But Dieuzy was recovering consciousness and, almost before he had opened his eyes, mumbled:

"Here, on the landing, the little door...."

"Oh, hang it, the door of Court 7!"[13] shouted the chief detective. "Didn't I say that it was to be kept locked? . . . It was certain that, sooner or later . . ." He seized the door-handle. "Oh, of course! The door is bolted on the other side now!"

The door was partly glazed. He smashed a pane with the butt-end of his revolver, drew the bolt and said to Gourel:

"Run through this way to the exit on the Place Dauphine. . . ."

He went back to Dieuzy:

"Come, Dieuzy, tell me about it. How did you come to let yourself be put into this state?"

"A blow in the pit of the stomach, chief. . . ."

"A blow? From that old chap? . . . Why, he can hardly stand on his legs! . . ."

"Not the old man, chief, but another, who was walking up and down the passage while Steinweg was with you and who followed us as though he were going out, too. . . . When we got as far as this, he asked me for a light. . . . I looked for my matches . . . Then he caught me a punch in the stomach. . . . I fell down, and, as I fell, I thought I saw him open that door and drag the old man with him. . . ."

"Would you know him again?"

"Oh yes, chief . . . a powerful fellow, very dark-skinned . . . a southerner of sorts, that's certain. . . ."

"Ribeira," snarled M. Lenormand. "Always Ribeira! . . . Ribeira, *alias* Parbury. . . . Oh, the impudence of the scoundrel! He was afraid of what old Steinweg might say . . . and came to fetch him away under my very nose!" And, stamping his foot with anger, "But, dash it, how did he know that Steinweg was here, the blackguard! It's only four hours since I was chasing him in the Saint-Cucufa woods . . . and now he's here! . . . How did he know? . . . One would think he lived inside my skin! . . ."

He was seized with one of those fits of dreaming in which he seemed to hear nothing and see nothing. Mrs. Kesselbach, who passed at that moment, bowed without his replying.

But a sound of footsteps in the corridor roused him from his lethargy.

"At last, is that you, Gourel?"

"I've found out how it was, chief," said Gourel, panting for breath. "There were two of them. They went this way and out of the Place Dauphine. There was a motor-car waiting for them. There were two people inside: one was a man dressed in black, with a soft hat pulled over his eyes . . ."

"That's he," muttered M. Lenormand, "that's the murderer, the accomplice of Ribeira,—Parbury. And who was the other?"

"A woman, a woman without a hat, a servant-girl, it might be. . . . And good-looking, I'm told, with red hair."

"Eh, what! You say she had red hair?"

"Yes."

M. Lenormand turned round with a bound, ran down the stairs four steps at a time, hurried across the courtyard and came out on the Quai des Orfèvres:

"Stop!" he shouted.

A victoria and pair was driving off. It was Mrs. Kesselbach's carriage. The coachman heard and pulled up his horses. M. Lenormand sprang on the step:

"I beg a thousand pardons, madame, but I cannot do without your assistance. I will ask you to let me go with you. . . . But we must act swiftly. . . . Gourel, where's my taxi?"

"I've sent it away, chief."

"Well then, get another, quick!" . . .

The men all ran in different directions. But ten minutes elapsed before one of them returned with a motor-cab. M. Lenormand was boiling with impatience. Mrs. Kesselbach, standing on the pavement, swayed from side to side, with her smelling-salts in her hand.

---

[13] Since M. Lenormand left the detective service, two other criminals have escaped by the same door, after shaking off the officers in charge of them; the police kept both cases dark. Nevertheless, it would be very easy, if this communication is absolutely required, to remove the useless bolt on the other side of the door, which enables the fugitive to cut off all pursuit and to walk away quietly through the passage leading to Civil Court 7 and through the corridor of the Chief President's Court.

At last they were seated.

"Gourel, get up beside the driver and go straight to Garches."

"To my house?" asked Dolores, astounded.

He did not reply. He leant out of the window, waved his pass, explained who he was to the policeman regulating the traffic in the streets. At last, when they reached the Cours-la-Reine, he sat down again and said:

"I beseech you, madame, to give me plain answers to my questions. Did you see Mlle. Geneviève Ernemont just now, at about four o'clock?"

"Geneviève? . . . Yes. . . . I was dressing to go out."

"Did she tell you of the advertisement about Steinweg in the *Journal*?"

"She did."

"And it was that which made you come to see me?"

"Yes."

"Were you alone during Mlle. Ernemont's visit?"

"Upon my word, I can't say. . . . Why?"

"Recollect. Was one of your servants present?"

"Probably . . . as I was dressing. . . ."

"What are their names?"

"Suzanne and Gertrude."

"One of them has red hair, has she not?"

"Yes, Gertrude."

"Have you known her long?"

"Her sister has always been with me . . . and so has Gertrude, for years. . . . She is devotion and honesty personified. . . ."

"In short, you will answer for her?"

"Oh, absolutely!"

"Very well . . . very well."

It was half-past seven and the daylight was beginning to wane when the taxi-cab reached the House of Retreat. Without troubling about his companion, the chief detective rushed into the porter's lodge:

"Mrs. Kesselbach's maid has just come in, has she not?"

"Whom do you mean, the maid?"

"Why, Gertrude, one of the two sisters."

"But Gertrude can't have been out, sir. We haven't seen her go out."

"Still some one has just come in."

"No, sir, we haven't opened the door to anybody since—let me see—six o'clock this evening."

"Is there no other way out than this gate?"

"No. The walls surround the estate on every side and they are very high. . . ."

"Mrs. Kesselbach, we will go to your house, please."

They all three went. Mrs. Kesselbach, who had no key, rang. The door was answered by Suzanne, the other sister.

"Is Gertrude in?" asked Mrs. Kesselbach.

"Yes, ma'am, in her room."

"Send her down, please," said the chief detective.

After a moment, Gertrude came downstairs, looking very attractive and engaging in her white embroidered apron.

She had, in point of fact, a rather pretty face, crowned with red hair.

M. Lenormand looked at her for a long time without speaking, as though he were trying to read what lay behind those innocent eyes.

He asked her no questions. After a minute, he simply said:

"That will do, thank you. Come, Gourel."

He went out with the sergeant and, at once, as they followed the darkling paths of the garden, said:

"That's the one!"

"Do you think so, chief? She looked so placid!"

"Much too placid. Another would have been astonished, would have wanted to know why I sent for her. Not this one! Nothing but the concentrated effort of a face that is determined to smile at all costs. Only, I saw a drop of perspiration trickle from her temple along her ear."

"So that . . . ?

"So that everything becomes plain. Gertrude is in league with the two ruffians who are conspiring round the Kesselbach case, in order either to discover and carry out the famous scheme, or to capture the widow's millions. No doubt, the other sister is in the plot as well. At four o'clock, Gertrude, learning that I know of the advertisement in the *Journal*, takes advantage of her mistress's absence, hastens to Paris, finds Ribeira and the man in the soft hat and drags them off to the Palais, where Ribeira annexes Master Steinweg for his own purposes."

He reflected and concluded:

"All this proves, first, the importance which they attach to Steinweg and their fear of what he may reveal; secondly, that a regular plot is being hatched around Mrs. Kesselbach; thirdly, that I have no time to lose, for the plot is ripe."

"Very well," said Gourel, "but one thing remains unexplained. How was Gertrude able to leave the garden in which we now are and to enter it again, unknown to the porter and his wife?"

"Through a secret passage which the rogues must have contrived to make quite recently."

"And which would end, no doubt," said Gourel, "in Mrs. Kesselbach's house."

"Yes, perhaps," said M. Lenormand, "perhaps . . . But I have another idea."

They followed the circuit of the wall. It was a bright night; and, though their two forms were hardly distinguishable, they themselves could see enough to examine the stones of the walls and to convince themselves that no breach, however skilful, had been effected.

"A ladder, very likely?" suggested Gourel.

"No, because Gertrude is able to get out in broad daylight. A communication of the kind I mean can evidently not end out of doors. The entrance must be concealed by some building already in existence."

"There are only the four garden-houses," objected Gourel, "and they are all inhabited."

"I beg your pardon: the third, the Pavillon Hortense, is not inhabited."

"Who told you so?"

"The porter. Mrs. Kesselbach hired this house, which is near her own, for fear of the noise. Who knows but that, in so doing, she acted under Gertrude's influence?"

He walked round the house in question. The shutters were closed. He lifted the latch of the door, on the off-chance; the door opened.

"Ah, Gourel, I think we've struck it! Let's go in. Light your lantern. . . . Oh, the hall. . . . the drawing-room . . . the dining-room . . . that's no use. There must be a basement, as the kitchen is not on this floor."

"This way, chief . . . the kitchen-stairs are here."

They went down into a rather large kitchen, crammed full of wicker-work garden-chairs and flower-stands. Beside it was a wash-house, which also served as a cellar, and which presented the same untidy sight of objects piled one on the top of the other.

"What is that shiny thing down there, chief?"

Gourel stooped and picked up a brass pin with a head made of an imitation pearl.

"The pearl is quite bright still," said M. Lenormand, "which it would not be if it had been lying in this cellar long. Gertrude passed this way, Gourel."

Gourel began to demolish a great stack of empty wine-casks, writing desks and old rickety tables.

"You are wasting your time," said M. Lenormand. "If that is the way out, how would she have time first to move all those things and then to replace them behind her? Look, here is a shutter out of use, which has no valid reason for being fastened to the wall by that nail. Draw it back."

Gourel did so. Behind the shutter, the wall was hollowed out. By the light of the lantern they saw an underground passage running downwards.

"I was right," said M. Lenormand.. "The communication is of recent date. You see, it's a piece of work hurriedly done, and not intended to last for any length of time. . . . No masonry. . . . Two planks placed cross-wise at intervals, with a joist to serve as a roof; and that is all. It will hold up as best it may: well enough, in any case, for the object in view, that is to say . . ."

"That is to say what, chief?"

"Well, first to allow of the going backwards and forwards between Gertrude and her accomplices . . . and then, one day, one day soon, of the kidnapping, or rather the total, miraculous, incomprehensible disappearance of Mrs. Kesselbach."

They proceeded cautiously, so as not to knock against certain beams which did not look over-safe. It at once became evident that the tunnel was much longer than the fifty yards at most that separated the house from the boundary of the garden. It must, therefore, end at a fair distance from the walls and beyond the road that skirted the property.

"We are not going in the direction of Villeneuve and the lake are we?" asked Gourel.

"Not at all, the other way about," declared M. Lenormand.

The tunnel descended with a gentle slope. There was a step, then another; and they veered toward the right. They at once knocked up against a door which was fitted into a rubble frame, carefully cemented. M. Lenormand pushed it and it opened.

"One second, Gourel," he said, stopping. "Let us think. . . . It might perhaps be wiser to turn back."

"Why?"

"We must reflect that Ribeira will have foreseen the danger and presume that he has taken his precautions, in case the underground passage should be discovered. Now he knows that we are on his track. He knows that we are searching the garden. He no doubt saw us enter the house. How do I know that he is not at this moment laying a trap for us?"

"There are two of us, chief. . . ."

"And suppose there were twenty of them?"

He looked in front of him. The tunnel sloped upward again, closed by another door, which was at five or six yards' distance.

"Let us go so far," he said. "Then we shall see."

He passed through, followed by Gourel, whom he told to leave the first door open, and walked to the other door, resolving within himself to go no farther. But this second door was shut; and though the lock seemed to work, he could not succeed in opening it.

"The door is bolted," he said. "Let us make no noise and go back. The more so as, outside, by remembering the position of the tunnel, we can fix the line along which to look for the other outlet."

They therefore retraced their steps to the first door, when Gourel, who was walking ahead, gave an exclamation of surprise:

"Why, it's closed! . . ."

"How is that? When I told you to leave it open!"

"I did leave it open, chief, but the door must have fallen back of its own weight."

"Impossible! We should have heard the sound."

"Then? . . ."

"Then . . . then . . . I don't know . . ." He went up to the door. "Let's see, . . . there's a key . . . does it turn? . . . Yes, it turns. But there seems to be a bolt on the other side."

"Who can have fastened it?"

"They, of course! Behind our backs! . . . Perhaps they have another tunnel that runs above this one, alongside of it . . . or else they were waiting in that empty house. . . . In any case, we're caught in a trap. . . ."

He grew angry with the lock, thrust his knife into the chink of the door, tried every means and then, in a moment of weariness, said:

"There's nothing to be done!"

"What, chief, nothing to be done? In that case, we're diddled!"

"I dare say!" said M. Lenormand. . . .

They returned to the other door and came back again to the first. Both were solid, made of hard wood, strengthened with cross-beams . . . in short, indestructible.

"We should want a hatchet," said the chief of the detective-service, "or at the very least, a serious implement . . . a knife even, with which we might try to cut away the place where the bolt is most likely to be . . . and we have nothing. . . ."

He was seized with a sudden fit of rage and flung himself upon the obstacle, as though he hoped to do away with it. Then, powerless, beaten, he said to Gourel:

"Listen, we'll look into this in an hour or two. . . . I am tired out. . . . I am going to sleep. . . . Keep watch so long . . . and if they come and attack us . . ."

"Ah, if they come, we shall be saved, chief!" cried Gourel, who would have been relieved by a fight, however great the odds.

M. Lenormand lay down on the ground. In a minute, he was asleep.

When he woke up, he remained for some seconds undecided, not understanding; and he also asked himself what sort of pain it was that was tormenting him:

"Gourel!" he called. "Come! Gourel!"

Obtaining no reply, he pressed the spring of his lantern and saw Gourel lying beside him, sound asleep.

"What on earth can this pain be?" he thought. "Regular twitchings. . . . Oh, why, of course, I am hungry, that's all. . . . I'm starving! What can the time be?"

His watch marked twenty minutes past seven, but he remembered that he had not wound it up. Gourel's watch was not going either.

Gourel had awoke under the action of the same inward pangs, which made them think that the breakfast-hour must be long past and that they had already slept for a part of the day.

"My legs are quite numbed," said Gourel, "and my feet feel as if they were on ice. What a funny sensation!" He bent down to rub them and went on: "Why, it's not on ice that my feet were, but in water. . . . Look, chief . . . there's a regular pool near the first door. . . ."

"Soaked through," M. Lenormand replied. "We'll go back to the second door; you can dry yourself . . ."

"But what are you doing, chief?"

"Do you think I am going to allow myself to be buried alive in this vault? . . . Not if I know it; I haven't reached the age! . . . As the two doors are closed, let us try to pass through the walls."

One by one he loosened the stones that stood out at the height of his hand, in the hope of contriving another gallery that would slope upwards to the level of the soil. But the work was long and painful, for in this part of the tunnel, as he perceived the stones were cemented.

"Chief . . . chief," stammered Gourel, in a stifled voice. . . .

"Well?"

"You are standing with your feet in the water."

"Nonsense! . . . Why, so I am! . . . Well, it can't be helped. . . . I'll dry them in the sun. . . ."

"But don't you see?"

"What?"

"Why, it's rising, chief, it's rising! . . ."

"What's rising?"

"The water! . . ."

M. Lenormand felt a shudder pass over his skin. He suddenly understood. It was not a casual trickling through, as he had thought, but a carefully-prepared flood, mechanically, irresistibly produced by some infernal system.

"Oh, the scoundrel!" he snarled. "If ever I lay hands on him . . . !"

"Yes, yes, chief, but we must first get out of this. . . . And, as far as I can see . . ."

Gourel seemed completely prostrated, incapable of having an idea, of proposing a plan.

M. Lenormand knelt down on the ground and measured the rate at which the water was rising. A quarter, or thereabouts, of the first door was covered; and the water was half-way toward the second door.

"The progress is slow, but uninterrupted," he said "In a few hours it will be over our heads."

"But this is terrible, chief, it's horrible!" moaned Gourel.

"Oh, look here, don't come boring me with your lamentations, do you understand? Cry, if it amuses you, but don't let me hear you!"

"It's the hunger that weakens me, chief; my brain's going round."

"Bite your fist!"

As Gourel said, the position was terrible; and, if M. Lenormand had had less energy, he would have abandoned the vain struggle. What was to be done? It was no use hoping that Ribeira would have the charity to let them out. It was no use either hoping that the brothers Doudeville would rescue them, for the inspectors did not know of the existence of the tunnel. So no hope remained . . . no hope but that of an impossible miracle. . . .

"Come, come," said M. Lenormand, "this is too silly. We're not going to kick the bucket here! Hang it all, there must be something! . . . Show me a light, Gourel."

Flattening himself against the second door, he examined it from top to bottom, in every corner. There was an enormous bolt on that side, just as there probably was on the other. He unfastened the screws with the blade of his knife; and the bolt came off in his hand.

"And what next?" asked Gourel.

"What next?" he echoed. "Well, this bolt is made of iron, pretty long and very nearly pointed. Certainly, it's not as good as a pick-axe, but it's better than nothing and . . ."

Without finishing his sentence, he drove the implement into the side-wall of the tunnel, a little in front of the pillar of masonry that supported the hinges of the door. As he expected, once he had passed the first layer of cement and stones, he found soft earth:

"To work!" he cried.

"Certainly, chief, but would you explain . . . ?"

"It's quite simple. I want to dig round this pillar a passage, three or four yards long, which will join the tunnel on the other side of the door and allow us to escape."

"But it will take us hours; and meanwhile, the water is rising."

"Show me a light, Gourel."

"In twenty minutes, or half an hour at most, it will have reached our feet."

"Show me a light, Gourel."

M. Lenormand's idea was correct and, with some little exertion, by pulling the earth, which he first loosened with his implement, towards him and making it fall into the tunnel, he was not long in digging a hole large enough to slip into.

"It's my turn, chief!" said Gourel.

"Aha, you're returning to life, I see! Well, fire away! . . . You have only to follow the shape of the pillar."

At that moment, the water was up to their ankles. Would they have time to complete the work begun?

It became more difficult as they went on, for the earth which they disturbed was in their way; and, lying flat on their stomachs in the passage, they were obliged at every instant to remove the rubbish that obstructed them.

After two hours, the work was perhaps three-quarters through, but the water now covered their legs. Another hour and it would reach the opening of the hole which they were digging. And that would mean the end!

Gourel, who was exhausted by the want of food and who was too stout to move with any freedom in that ever-narrower passage, had had to give up. He no longer stirred, trembling with anguish at feeling that icy water which was gradually swallowing him up.

As for M. Lenormand, he worked on with indefatigable ardor. It was a terrible job, this ants' work performed in the stifling darkness. His hands were bleeding. He was fainting with hunger. The insufficiency of the air hampered his breathing; and, from time to time, Gourel's sighs reminded him of the awful danger that threatened him at the bottom of his hole.

But nothing could discourage him, for now he again found opposite him those cemented stones which formed the side-wall of the gallery. It was the most difficult part, but the end was at hand.

"It's rising," cried Gourel, in a choking voice, "it's rising!"

M. Lenormand redoubled his efforts. Suddenly the stem of the bolt which he was using leapt out into space. The passage was dug. He had now only to widen it, which became much easier once he was able to shoot the materials in front of him.

Gourel, mad with terror, was howling like a dying beast. M. Lenormand paid no attention to him. Safety was at hand.

Nevertheless, he had a few seconds of anxiety when he perceived, by the sound of the materials falling, that this part of the tunnel was also under water, which was natural, as the door did not form a sufficiently tight-fitting barrier. But what did it matter! The outlet was free. One last effort . . . he passed through.

"Come, Gourel," he cried, returning to fetch his companion.

He dragged him, half dead, by the wrists:

"Come along, booby, pull yourself together! We are saved."

"Do you really think so, chief? . . . The water's up to our chests. . . ."

"Never mind, as long as it's not over our mouths. . . . Where's your lantern?"

"It's not working."

"No matter." He gave an exclamation of delight. "One step . . . two steps! . . . A staircase. . . . At last!"

They emerged from the water, that accursed water which had almost swallowed them up; and it was a delicious sensation, a release that sent up their spirits.

"Stop!" said M. Lenormand.

His head had knocked against something. With arms outstretched, he pushed against the obstacle, which yielded at once. It was the flap of a trap-door; and, when this trap-door was opened, he found himself in a cellar into which the light of a fine night filtered through an air-hole.

He threw back the flap and climbed the last treads.

Then a veil fell over his eyes. Arms seized upon him. He felt himself as it were wrapped in a sheet, in a sort of sack, and then fastened with cords.

"Now for the other one!" said a voice.

The same operation must have been performed on Gourel; and the same voice said:

"If they call out, kill them at once. Have you your dagger?"

"Yes."

"Come along. You two, take this one . . . you two, that one. . . . No light . . . and no noise either. . . . It would be a serious matter. They've been searching the garden next door since this morning . . . there are ten or fifteen of them knocking about. . . . Go back to the house, Gertrude, and, if the least thing happens, telephone to me in Paris."

M. Lenormand felt that he was being lifted up and carried and, a moment after, that he was in the open air.

"Bring the cart nearer," said a voice.

M. Lenormand heard the sound of a horse and cart.

He was laid out on some boards. Gourel was hoisted up beside him. The horse started at a trot.

The drive lasted about half an hour.

"Halt!" commanded the voice. "Lift them out. Here, driver, turn the cart so that the tail touches the parapet of the bridge. . . . Good. . . . No boats on the river? Sure? Then let's waste no time. . . . Oh, have you fastened some stones to them?"

"Yes, paving-stones."

"Right away, then! Commend your soul to God, M. Lenormand, and pray for me, Parbury-Ribeira, better known by the name of Baron Altenheim. Are you ready? All right? Well, here's wishing you a pleasant journey, M. Lenormand!"

M. Lenormand was placed on the parapet. Someone gave him a push. He felt himself falling into space and he still heard the voice chuckling:

"A pleasant journey!"

Ten seconds later it was Sergeant Gourel's turn.

VII. PARBURY-RIBEIRA-ALTENHEIM

The girls were playing in the garden, under the supervision of Mlle. Charlotte, Geneviève's new assistant. Mme. Ernemont came out, distributed some cakes among them and then went back to the room which served as a drawing-room and parlor in one, sat down before a writing-desk and began to arrange her papers and account-books.

Suddenly, she felt the presence of a stranger in the room. She turned round in alarm:

"You!" she cried. "Where have you come from? How did you get in?"

"Hush!" said Prince Sernine. "Listen to me and do not let us waste a minute: Geneviève?"

"Calling on Mrs. Kesselbach."

"When will she be here?"

"Not before an hour."

"Then I will let the brothers Doudeville come. I have an appointment with them. How is Geneviève?"

"Very well."

"How often has she seen Pierre Leduc since I went away, ten days ago?"

"Three times; and she is to meet him to-day at Mrs. Kesselbach's, to whom she introduced him, as you said she must. Only, I may as well tell you that I don't think much of this Pierre Leduc of yours. Geneviève would do better to find some good fellow in her own class of life. For instance, there's the schoolmaster."

"You're mad! Geneviève marry a schoolmaster!"

"Oh, if you considered Geneviève's happiness first...."

"Shut up, Victoire. You're boring me with your cackle. I have no time to waste on sentiment. I'm playing a game of chess; and I move my men without troubling about what they think. When I have won the game, I will go into the question whether the knight, Pierre Leduc, and the queen, Geneviève, have a heart or not."

She interrupted him:

"Did you hear? A whistle...."

"It's the two Doudevilles. Go and bring them in; and then leave us."

As soon as the two brothers were in the room, he questioned them with his usual precision:

"I know what the newspapers have said about the disappearance of Lenormand and Gourel. Do you know any more?"

"No. The deputy-chief, M. Weber, has taken the case in hand. We have been searching the garden of the House of Retreat for the past week; and nobody is able to explain how they can have disappeared. The whole force is in a flutter.... No one has ever seen the like ... a chief of the detective-service disappearing, without leaving a trace behind him!"

"The two maids?"

"Gertrude has gone. She is being looked for."

"Her sister Suzanne?"

"M. Weber and M. Formerie have questioned her. There is nothing against her."

"Is that all you have to tell me?"

"Oh, no, there are other things, all the things which we did not tell the papers."

They then described the incidents that had marked M. Lenormand's last two days: the night visit of the two ruffians to Pierre Leduc's villa; next day, Ribeira's attempt to kidnap Geneviève and the chase through the Saint-Cucufa woods; old Steinweg's arrival, his examination at the detective-office in Mrs. Kesselbach's presence, his escape from the Palais...

"And no one knows these details except yourselves?"

"Dieuzy knows about the Steinweg incident: he told us of it."

"And they still trust you at the Prefecture of Police?"

"So much so that they employ us openly. M. Weber swears by us."

"Come," said the prince, "all is not lost. If M. Lenormand has committed an imprudence that has cost him his life, as I suppose he did, at any rate he performed some good work first; and we have only to continue it. The enemy has the start of us, but we will catch him up."

"It won't be an easy job, governor."

"Why not? It is only a matter of finding old Steinweg again, for the answer to the riddle is in his hands."

"Yes, but where has Ribeira got old Steinweg tucked away?"

"At his own place, of course."

"Then we should have to know where Ribeira hangs out."

"Well, of course!"

He dismissed them and went to the House of Retreat. Motor-cars were awaiting outside the door and two men were walking up and down, as though mounting guard.

In the garden, near Mrs. Kesselbach's house, he saw Geneviève sitting on a bench with Pierre Leduc and a thick-set gentleman wearing a single eye-glass. The three were talking and none of them saw him. But several people came out of the house: M. Formerie, M. Weber, a magistrate's clerk, and two inspectors. Geneviève went indoors and the gentleman with the eye-glass went up and spoke to the examining-magistrate and the deputy-chief of the detective-service and walked away with them slowly.

Sernine came beside the bench where Pierre Leduc was sitting and whispered:

"Don't move, Pierre Leduc; it's I."

"You! . . . you! . . ."

It was the third time that the young man saw Sernine since the awful night at Versailles; and each time it upset him.

"Tell me . . . who is the fellow with the eye-glass?"

Pierre Leduc turned pale and jabbered. Sernine pinched his arm:

"Answer me, confound it! Who is he?"

"Baron Altenheim."

"Where does he come from?"

"He was a friend of Mr. Kesselbach's. He arrived from Austria, six days ago, and placed himself at Mrs. Kesselbach's disposal."

The police authorities had, meanwhile, gone out of the garden; Baron Altenheim also.

The prince rose and, turning towards the Pavillon de l'Impératrice, continued:

"Has the baron asked you many questions?"

"Yes, a great many. He is interested in my case. He wants to help me find my family. He appealed to my childhood memories."

"And what did you say?"

"Nothing, because I know nothing. What memories have I? You put me in another's place and I don't even know who that other is."

"No more do I!" chuckled the prince. "And that's just what makes your case so quaint."

"Oh, it's all very well for you to laugh . . . you're always laughing! . . . But I'm beginning to have enough of it. . . . I'm mixed up in a heap of nasty matters . . . to say nothing of the danger which I run in pretending to be somebody that I am not."

"What do you mean . . . that you are not? You're quite as much a duke as I am a prince . . . perhaps even more so. . . . Besides, if you're not a duke, hurry up and become one, hang it all! Geneviève can't marry any one but a duke! Look at her: isn't she worth selling your soul for?"

He did not even look at Leduc, not caring what he thought. They had reached the house by this time; and Geneviève appeared at the foot of the steps, comely and smiling:

"So you have returned?" she said to the prince. "Ah, that's a good thing! I am so glad. . . . Do you want to see Dolores?"

After a moment, she showed him into Mrs. Kesselbach's room. The prince was taken aback. Dolores was paler still and thinner than on the day when he saw her last. Lying on a sofa, wrapped up in white stuffs, she looked like one of those sick people who have ceased to struggle against death. As for her, she had ceased to struggle against life, against the fate that was overwhelming her with its blows.

Sernine gazed at her with deep pity and with an emotion which he did not strive to conceal. She thanked him for the sympathy which he showed her. She also spoke of Baron Altenheim, in friendly terms.

"Did you know him before?" he asked.

"Yes, by name, and through his intimacy with my husband."

"I have met an Altenheim who lives in the Rue de Rivoli. Do you think it's the same?"

"Oh, no, this one lives in . . . As a matter of fact, I don't quite know; he gave me his address, but I can't say that I remember it. . . ."

After a few minutes' conversation, Sernine took his leave. Geneviève was waiting for him in the hall:

"I want to speak to you," she said eagerly, "on a serious matter. . . . Did you see him?"

"Whom?"

"Baron Altenheim. . . . But that's not his name . . . or, at least, he has another. . . . I recognized him . . . he does not know it."

She dragged him out of doors and walked on in great excitement.

"Calm yourself, Geneviève. . . ."

"He's the man who tried to carry me off. . . . But for that poor M. Lenormand, I should have been done for. . . . Come, you must know, for you know everything. . . ."

"Then his real name is . . ."

"Ribeira."

"Are you sure?"

"It was no use his changing his appearance, his accent, his manner: I knew him at once, by the horror with which he inspires me. But I said nothing . . . until you returned."

"You said nothing to Mrs. Kesselbach either?"

"No. She seemed so happy at meeting a friend of her husband's. But you will speak to her about it, will you not? You will protect her. . . . I don't know what he is preparing against her, against myself. . . . Now that M. Lenormand is no longer there, he has nothing to fear, he does as he pleases. Who can unmask him?"

"I can. I will be responsible for everything. But not a word to anybody."

They had reached the porter's lodge. The gate was opened. The prince said:

"Good-bye, Geneviève, and be quite easy in your mind. I am there."

He shut the gate, turned round and gave a slight start. Opposite him stood the man with the eye-glass, Baron Altenheim, with his head held well up, his broad shoulders, his powerful frame.

They looked at each other for two or three seconds, in silence. The baron smiled.

Then the baron said:

"I was waiting for you, Lupin."

For all his self-mastery, Sernine felt a thrill pass over him. He had come to unmask his adversary; and his adversary had unmasked him at the first onset. And, at the same time, the adversary was accepting the contest boldly, brazenly, as though he felt sure of victory. It was a swaggering thing to do and gave evidence of no small amount of pluck.

The two men, violently hostile one to the other, took each other's measure with their eyes.

"And what then?" asked Sernine.

"What then? Don't you think we have occasion for a meeting?"

"Why?"

"I want to talk to you."

"What day will suit you?"

"To-morrow. Let us lunch together at a restaurant."

"Why not at your place?"

"You don't know my address."

"Yes, I do."

With a swift movement, the prince pulled out a newspaper protruding from Altenheim's pocket, a paper still in its addressed wrapper, and said:

"No. 29, Villa Dupont."

"Well played!" said the other. "Then we'll say, to-morrow, at my place."

"To-morrow, at your place. At what time?"

"One o'clock."

"I shall be there. Good-bye."

They were about to walk away. Altenheim stopped:

"Oh, one word more, prince. Bring a weapon with you."

"Why?"

"I keep four men-servants and you will be alone."

"I have my fists," said Sernine. "We shall be on even terms."

He turned his back on him and then, calling him back:

"Oh, one word more, baron. Engage four more servants."

"Why?"

"I have thought it over. I shall bring my whip."

At one o'clock the next day, precisely, a horseman rode through the gate of the so-called Villa Dupont, a peaceful, countrified private road, the only entrance to which is in the Rue Pergolèse, close to the Avenue du Bois.

It is lined with gardens and handsome private houses; and, right at the end, it is closed by a sort of little park containing a large old house, behind which runs the Paris circular railway. It was here, at No. 29, that Baron Altenheim lived.

Sernine flung the reins of his horse to a groom whom he had sent on ahead and said:

"Bring him back at half-past two."

He rang the bell. The garden-gate opened and he walked to the front-door steps, where he was awaited by two tall men in livery who ushered him into an immense, cold, stone hall, devoid of any ornament. The door closed behind him with a heavy thud; and, great and indomitable as his courage was, he nevertheless underwent an unpleasant sensation at feeling himself alone, surrounded by enemies, in that isolated prison.

"Say Prince Sernine."

The drawing-room was near and he was shown straight in.

"Ah, there you are, my dear prince!" said the baron, coming toward him. "Well, will you believe—Dominique, lunch in twenty minutes. Until then, don't let us be interrupted—will you believe, my dear prince, that I hardly expected to see you?"

"Oh, really? Why?"

"Well, your declaration of war, this morning, is so plain that an interview becomes superfluous."

"My declaration of war?"

The baron unfolded a copy of the *Grand Journal* and pointed to a paragraph which ran as follows:

"We are authoritatively informed that M. Lenormand's disappearance has roused Arsène Lupin into taking action. After a brief enquiry and following on his proposal to clear up the Kesselbach case, Arsène Lupin has decided that he will find M. Lenormand, alive or dead, and that he will deliver the author or authors of that heinous series of crimes to justice."

"This authoritative pronouncement comes from you, my dear prince, of course?"

"Yes, it comes from me."

"Therefore, I was right: it means war."

"Yes."

Altenheim gave Sernine a chair, sat down himself and said, in a conciliatory tone:

"Well, no, I cannot allow that. It is impossible that two men like ourselves should fight and injure each other. We have only to come to an explanation, to seek the means: you and I were made to understand each other."

"I think, on the contrary, that two men like ourselves are not made to understand each other."

The baron suppressed a movement of impatience and continued:

"Listen to me, Lupin. . . . By the way, do you mind my calling you Lupin?"

"What shall I call you? Altenheim, Ribeira, or Parbury?"

"Oho! I see that you are even better posted than I thought! . . . Hang it all, but you're jolly smart! . . . All the more reason why we should agree." And, bending toward him, "Listen, Lupin, and ponder my words well; I have weighed them carefully, every one. Look here. . . . We two are evenly matched. . . . Does that make you smile? You are wrong: it may be that you possess resources which I do not; but I have others of which you know nothing. Moreover, as you are aware, I have few scruples, some skill and a capacity for changing my personality which an expert like yourself ought to appreciate. In short, the two adversaries are each as good as the other. But one question remains unanswered: why are we adversaries? We are pursuing the same object, you will say? And what then? Do you know what will come of our rivalry? Each of us will paralyze the efforts and destroy the work of the other; and we shall both miss our aim! And for whose benefit? Some Lenormand or other, a third rogue! . . . It's really too silly."

"It's really too silly, as you say," Sernine admitted. "But there is a remedy."

"What is that?"

"For you to withdraw."

"Don't chaff. I am serious. The proposal which I am going to make is not one to be rejected without examination. Here it is, in two words: let's be partners!"

"I say!"

"Of course, each of us will continue free where his own affairs are concerned. But, for the business in question, let us combine our efforts. Does that suit you? Hand in hand and share alike."

"What do you bring?"

"I?"

"Yes, you know what I'm worth; I've delivered my proofs. In the alliance which you are proposing, you know the figure, so to speak of my marriage-portion. What's yours?"

"Steinweg."

"That's not much."

"It's immense. Through Steinweg, we learn the truth about Pierre Leduc. Through Steinweg, we get to know what the famous Kesselbach plan is all about."

Sernine burst out laughing:

"And you need me for that?"

"I don't understand."

"Come, old chap, your offer is childish. You have Steinweg in your hands. If you wish for my collaboration, it is because you have not succeeded in making him speak. But for that fact, you would do without my services."

"Well, what of it?"

"I refuse."

The two men stood up to each other once more, violent and implacable.

"I refuse," said Sernine. "Lupin requires nobody, in order to act. I am one of those who walk alone. If you were my equal, as you pretend, the idea of a partnership would never have entered your head. The man who has the stature of a leader commands. Union implies obedience. I do not obey."

"You refuse? You refuse?" repeated Altenheim, turning pale under the insult.

"All that I can do for you, old chap, is to offer you a place in my band. You'll be a private soldier, to begin with. Under my orders, you shall see how a general wins a battle . . . and how he pockets the booty, by himself and for himself. Does that suit you . . . Tommy?"

Altenheim was beside himself with fury. He gnashed his teeth:

"You are making a mistake, Lupin," he mumbled, "you are making a mistake. . . . I don't want anybody either; and this business gives me no more difficulty than plenty of others which I have pulled off. . . . What I said was said in order to effect our object more quickly and without inconveniencing each other."

"You're not inconveniencing me," said Lupin, scornfully.

"Look here! If we don't combine, only one of us will succeed."

"That's good enough for me."

"And he will only succeed by passing over the other's body. Are you prepared for that sort of duel, Lupin? A duel to the death, do you understand? . . . The knife is a method which you despise; but suppose you received one, Lupin, right in the throat?"

"Aha! So, when all is said, that's what you propose?"

"No, I am not very fond of shedding blood. . . . Look at my fists: I strike . . . and my man falls. . . . I have special blows of my own. . . . But *the other one* kills . . . remember . . . the little wound in the throat. . . . Ah, Lupin, beware of him, beware of that one! . . . He is terrible, he is implacable. . . . Nothing stops him."

He spoke these words in a low voice and with such excitement that Sernine shuddered at the hideous thought of the unknown murderer:

"Baron," he sneered, "one would think you were afraid of your accomplice!"

"I am afraid for the others, for those who bar our road, for you, Lupin. Accept, or you are lost. I shall act myself, if necessary. The goal is too near . . . I have my hand on it. . . . Get out of my way, Lupin!"

He was all energy and exasperated will. He spoke forcibly and so brutally that he seemed ready to strike his enemy then and there.

Sernine shrugged his shoulders:

"Lord, how hungry I am!" he said, yawning. "What a time to lunch at!"

The door opened.

"Lunch is served, sir," said the butler.

"Ah, that's good hearing!"

In the doorway, Altenheim caught Sernine by the arm and, disregarding the servant's presence:

"If you take my advice . . . accept. This is a serious moment in your life . . . and you will do better, I swear to you, you will do better . . . to accept. . . ."

"Caviare!" cried Sernine. "Now, that's too sweet of you. . . . You remembered that you were entertaining a Russian prince!"

They sat down facing each other, with the baron's greyhound, a large animal with long, silver hair, between them.

"Let me introduce Sirius, my most faithful friend."

"A fellow-countryman," said Sernine. "I shall never forget the one which the Tsar was good enough to give me when I had the honor to save his life."

"Ah, you had that honor . . . a terrorist conspiracy, no doubt?"

"Yes, a conspiracy got up by myself. You must know, this dog—its name, by the way, was Sebastopol. . . ."

The lunch continued merrily. Altenheim had recovered his good humor and the two men vied with each other in wit and politeness. Sernine told anecdotes which the baron capped with others; and it was a succession of stories of hunting, sport and travel, in which the oldest names in Europe were constantly cropping up: Spanish grandees, English lords, Hungarian magyars, Austrian archdukes.

"Ah," said Sernine, "what a fine profession is ours! It brings us into touch with all the best people. Here, Sirius, a bit of this truffled chicken!"

The dog did not take his eyes off him, and snapped at everything that Sernine gave it.

"A glass of Chambertin, prince?"

"With pleasure, baron."

"I can recommend it. It comes from King Leopold's cellar."

"A present?"

"Yes, a present I made myself."

"It's delicious. . . . What a bouquet! . . . With this *pâté de foie gras*, it's simply wonderful! . . . I must congratulate you, baron; you have a first-rate chef."

"My chef is a woman-cook, prince. I bribed her with untold gold to leave Levraud, the socialist deputy. I say, try this hot chocolate-ice; and let me call your special attention to the little dry cakes that go with it. They're an invention of genius, those cakes."

"The shape is charming, in any case," said Sernine, helping himself. "If they taste as good as they look. . . . Here, Sirius, you're sure to like this. Locusta herself could not have done better."

He took one of the cakes and gave it to the dog. Sirius swallowed it at a gulp, stood motionless for two or three seconds, as though dazed, then turned in a circle and fell to the floor dead.

Sernine started back from his chair, lest one of the footmen should fall upon him unawares. Then he burst out laughing:

"Look here, baron, next time you want to poison one of your friends, try to steady your voice and to keep your hands from shaking. . . . Otherwise, people suspect you. . . . But I thought you disliked murder?"

"With the knife, yes," said Altenheim, quite unperturbed. "But I have always had a wish to poison some one. I wanted to see what it was like."

"By Jove, old chap, you choose your subjects well! A Russian prince!"

He walked up to Altenheim and, in a confidential tone, said:

"Do you know what would have happened if you had succeeded, that is to say, if my friends had not seen me return at three o'clock at the latest? Well, at half-past three the prefect of police would have known exactly all that there was to know about the so-called Baron Altenheim; and the said baron would have been copped before the day was out and clapped into jail."

"Pooh!" said Altenheim. "Prison one escapes from . . . whereas one does not come back from the kingdom where I was sending you."

"True, but you would have to send me there first; and that's not so easy."

"I only wanted a mouthful of one of those cakes."

"Are you quite sure?"

"Try."

"One thing's certain, my lad: you haven't the stuff yet which great adventurers are made of; and I doubt if you'll ever have it, considering the sort of traps you lay for me. A man who thinks himself worthy of leading the life which you and I have the honor to lead must also be fit to lead it, and, for that, must be prepared for every eventuality: he must even be prepared not to die if some ragamuffin or other tries to poison him. . . . An undaunted soul in an unassailable body: that is the ideal which he must set before himself . . . and attain. Try away, old chap. As for me, I am undaunted and unassailable. Remember King Mithridates!"

He went back to his chair:

"Let's finish our lunch. But as I like proving the virtues to which I lay claim, and as, on the other hand, I don't want to hurt your cook's feelings, just pass me that plate of cakes."

He took one of them, broke it in two and held out one half to the baron:

"Eat that!"

The other gave a movement of recoil.

"Funk!" said Sernine.

And, before the wondering eyes of the baron and his satellites, he began to eat the first and then the second half of the cake, quietly, conscientiously, as a man eats a dainty of which he would hate to miss the smallest morsel.

They met again.

That same evening, Prince Sernine invited Baron Altenheim to dinner at the Cabaret Vatel, with a party consisting of a poet, a musician, a financier and two pretty actresses, members of the Théâtre Français.

The next day, they lunched together in the Bois and, at night, they met at the Opéra.

They saw each other every day for a week. One would have thought that they could not do without each other and that they were united by a great friendship, built up of mutual confidence, sympathy and esteem.

They had a capital time, drinking good wine, smoking excellent cigars, and laughing like two madmen.

In reality, they were watching each other fiercely. Mortal enemies, separated by a merciless hatred, each feeling sure of winning and longing for victory with an unbridled will, they waited for the propitious moment: Altenheim to do away with Sernine; and Sernine to hurl Altenheim into the pit which he was digging for him.

Each knew that the catastrophe could not be long delayed. One or other of them must meet with his doom; and it was a question of hours, or, at most, of days.

It was an exciting tragedy, and one of which a man like Sernine was bound to relish the strange and powerful zest. To know your adversary and to live by his side; to feel that death is waiting for you at the least false step, at the least act of thoughtlessness: what a joy, what a delight!

One evening, they were alone together in the garden of the Rue Cambon Club, to which Altenheim also belonged. It was the hour before dusk, in the month of June, at which men begin to dine before the members come in for the evening's card-play. They were strolling round a little lawn, along which ran a wall lined with shrubs. Beyond the shrubs was a small door. Suddenly, while Altenheim was speaking, Sernine received the impression that his voice became less steady, that it was almost trembling. He watched him out of the corner of his eye. Altenheim had his hand in the pocket of his jacket; and Sernine *saw* that hand, through the cloth, clutch the handle of a dagger, hesitating, wavering, resolute and weak by turns.

O exquisite moment! Was he going to strike? Which would gain the day: the timid instinct that dare not, or the conscious will, intense upon the act of killing?

His chest flung out, his arms behind his back, Sernine waited, with alternate thrills of pleasure and of pain. The baron had ceased talking; and they now walked on in silence, side by side.

"Well, why don't you strike?" cried the prince, impatiently. He had stopped and, turning to his companion: "Strike!" he said. "This is the time or never. There is no one to see you. You can slip out through that little door; the key happens to be hanging on the wall; and good-bye, baron . . . unseen and unknown! . . . But, of course, all this was arranged . . . you brought me here. . . . And you're hesitating! Why on earth don't you strike?"

He looked him straight in the eyes. The other was livid, quivering with impotent strength.

"You milksop!" Sernine sneered. "I shall never make anything of you. Shall I tell you the truth? Well, you're afraid of me. Yes, old chap, you never feel quite sure what may happen to you when you're face to face with me. You want to act, whereas it's my acts, my possible acts that govern the situation. No, it's quite clear that you're not the man yet to put out my star!"

He had not finished speaking when he felt himself seized round the throat and dragged backward. Some one hiding in the shrubbery, near the little door, had caught him by the head. He saw a hand raised, armed with a knife with a gleaming blade. The hand fell; the point of the knife caught him right in the throat.

At the same moment Altenheim sprang upon him to finish him off; and they rolled over into the flower-borders. It was a matter of twenty or thirty seconds at most. Powerful and experienced wrestler as he was, Altenheim yielded almost immediately, uttering a cry of pain. Sernine rose and ran to the little door, which had just closed upon a dark form. It was too late. He heard the key turn in the lock. He was unable to open it.

"Ah, you scoundrel!" he said. "The day on which I catch you will be the day on which I shed my first blood! That I swear to God! . . ."

He went back, stooped and picked up the pieces of the knife, which had broken as it struck him.

Altenheim was beginning to move. Sernine asked:

"Well, baron, feeling better? You didn't know that blow, eh? It's what I call the direct blow in the solar plexus; that is to say, it snuffs out your vital sun like a candle. It's clean, quick, painless . . . and infallible. Whereas a blow with a dagger . . . ? Pooh! A man has only to wear a little steel-wove gorget, as I do, and he can set the whole world at defiance, especially your little pal in black, seeing that he always strikes at the throat, the silly monster! . . . Here, look at his favorite plaything . . . smashed to atoms!"

He offered him his hand:

"Come, get up, baron. You shall dine with me. And do please remember the secret of my superiority: an undaunted soul in an unassailable body."

He went back to the club rooms, reserved a table for two, sat down on a sofa, and while waiting for dinner, soliloquized, under his breath:

"It's certainly an amusing game, but it's becoming dangerous. I must get it over . . . otherwise those beggars will send me to Paradise earlier than I want to go. The nuisance is that I can't do anything before I find old Steinweg, for, when all is said, old Steinweg is the only interesting factor in the whole business; and my one reason for sticking to the baron is that I keep on hoping to pick up some clue or other. What the devil have they done with him? Altenheim is in daily communication with him: that is beyond a doubt; it is equally beyond a doubt that he is doing his utmost to drag out of him what he knows about the Kesselbach scheme. But where does he see him? Where has he got him shut up? With friends? In his own house, at 29, Villa Dupont?"

He reflected for some time, then lit a cigarette, took three puffs at it and threw it away. This was evidently a signal, for two young men came and sat down beside him. He did not seem to know them, but he conversed with them by stealth. It was the brothers Doudeville, got up that day like men of fashion.

"What is it, governor?"

"Take six of our men, go to 29, Villa Dupont and make your way in."

"The devil! How?"

"In the name of the law. Are you not detective-inspectors? A search..."

"But we haven't the right. . . ."

"Take it."

"And the servants? If they resist?"

"There are only four of them."

"If they call out?"

"They won't call out."

"If Altenheim returns?"

"He won't return before ten o'clock. I'll see to it. That gives you two hours and a half, which is more than you require to explore the house from top to bottom. If you find old Steinweg, come and tell me."

Baron Altenheim came up. Sernine went to meet him:

"Let's have some dinner, shall we? That little incident in the garden has made me feel hungry. By the way, my dear baron, I have a few bits of advice to give you. . . ."

They sat down to table.

After dinner, Sernine suggested a game of billiards. Altenheim accepted. When the game was over, they went to the baccarat-room. The croupier was just shouting:

"There are fifty louis in the bank. Any bids?"

"A hundred louis," said Altenheim.

Sernine looked at his watch. Ten o'clock. The Doudevilles had not returned. The search, therefore, had been fruitless.

"Banco," he said.

Altenheim sat down and dealt the cards:

"I give."

"No."

"Seven."

"Six. I lose," said Sernine. "Shall I double the stakes?"

"Very well," said the baron.

He dealt out the cards.

"Eight," said Sernine.

"Nine," said the baron, laying his cards down.

Sernine turned on his heels, muttering:

"That costs me three hundred louis, but I don't mind; it fixes him here."

Ten minutes later his motor set him down in front of 29, Villa Dupont; and he found the Doudevilles and their men collected in the hall:

"Have you hunted out the old boy?"

"No."

"Dash it! But he must be somewhere or other. Where are the four servants?"

"Over there, in the pantry, tied up, with the cook as well."

"Good. I would as soon they did not see me. Go all you others. Jean, stay outside and keep watch: Jacques, show me over the house."

He quickly ran through the cellar, the ground floor, the first and second floors and the attic. He practically stopped nowhere, knowing that he would not discover in a few minutes what his men had not been able to discover in three hours. But he carefully noted the shape and the arrangement of the rooms, and looked for some little detail which would put him on the scent.

When he had finished, he returned to a bedroom which Doudeville had told him was Altenheim's, and examined it attentively:

"This will do," he said, raising a curtain that concealed a dark closet, full of clothes. "From here I can see the whole of the room."

"But if the baron searches the house?"

"Why should he?"

"He will know that we have been here, through his servants."

"Yes, but he will never dream that one of us is putting up here for the night. He will think that the attempt failed, that is all, so I shall stay."

"And how will you get out?"

"Oh, that's asking me more than I can tell you! The great thing was to get in. Here I am, and here I stay. Go, Doudeville, and shut the doors as you go."

He sat down on a little box at the back of the cupboard. Four rows of hanging clothes protected him. Except in the case of a close investigation, he was evidently quite safe.

Two hours passed. He heard the dull sound of a horse's hoofs and the tinkling of a collar-bell. A carriage stopped, the front door slammed and almost immediately he heard voices, exclamations, a regular outcry that increased, probably, as each of the prisoners was released from his gag.

"They are explaining the thing to him," he thought. "The baron must be in a tearing rage. He now understands the reason for my conduct at the club to-night and sees that I have dished him nicely. . . . Dished? That depends. . . . After all, I haven't got Steinweg yet. . . . That is the first thing that he will want to know: did they get Steinweg? To find this out, he will go straight to the hiding-place. If he goes up, it means that the hiding-place is upstairs. If he goes down, then it is in the basement."

He listened. The sound of voices continued in the rooms on the ground floor, but it did not seem as if any one were moving. Altenheim must be cross-examining his confederates. It was half an hour before Sernine heard steps mounting the staircase.

"Then it must be upstairs," he said to himself. "But why did they wait so long?"

"Go to bed, all of you," said Altenheim's voice.

The baron entered his room with one of his men and shut the door:

"And I am going to bed, too, Dominique. We should be no further if we sat arguing all night."

"My opinion is," said the other, "that he came to fetch Steinweg."

"That is my opinion, too; and that's why I'm really enjoying myself, seeing that Steinweg isn't here."

"But where is he, after all? What have you done with him?"

"That's my secret; and you know I keep my secrets to myself. All that I can tell you is that he is in safe keeping, and that he won't get out before he has spoken."

"So the prince is sold?"

"Sold is the word. And he has had to fork out to attain this fine result! Oh, I've had a good time to-night! . . . Poor prince!"

"For all that," said the other, "we shall have to get rid of him."

"Make your mind easy, old man; that won't take long. Before a week's out you shall have a present of a pocket-book made out of Lupin-skin. But let me go to bed now. I'm dropping with sleep."

There was a sound of the door closing. Then Sernine heard the baron push the bolt, empty his pockets, wind up his watch and undress. He seemed in a gay mood, whistling and singing, and even talking aloud:

"Yes, a Lupin-skin pocket-book . . . in less than a week . . . in less than four days! . . . Otherwise he'll eat us up, the bully! . . . No matter, he missed his shot to-night. . . . His calculation was right enough, though . . . Steinweg was bound to be here. . . . Only, there you are! . . ."

He got into bed and at once switched off the light.

Sernine had come forward as far as the dividing curtain, which he now lifted slightly, and he saw the vague light of the night filtering through the windows, leaving the bed in profound darkness.

He hesitated. Should he leap out upon the baron, take him by the throat and obtain from him by force and threats what he had not been able to obtain by craft? Absurd? Altenheim would never allow himself to be intimidated.

"I say, he's snoring now," muttered Sernine. "Well, I'm off. At the worst, I shall have wasted a night."

He did not go. He felt that it would be impossible for him to go, that he must wait, that chance might yet serve his turn.

With infinite precautions, he took four or five coats and great-coats from their hooks, laid them on the floor, made himself comfortable and, with his back to the wall, went peacefully to sleep.

The baron was not an early riser. A clock outside was striking nine when he got out of bed and rang for his servant.

He read the letters which his man brought him, splashed about in his tub, dressed without saying a word and sat down to his table to write, while Dominique was carefully hanging up the clothes of the previous day in the cupboard and Sernine asking himself, with his fists ready to strike:

"I wonder if I shall have to stave in this fellow's solar plexus?"

At ten o'clock the baron was ready:

"Leave me," said he to the servant.

"There's just this waistcoat. . . ."

"Leave me, I say. Come back when I ring . . . not before."

He shut the door himself, like a man who does not trust others, went to a table on which a telephone was standing and took down the receiver:

"Hullo! . . . Put me on to Garches, please, mademoiselle. . . . Very well, I'll wait till you ring me up. . . ."

He sat down to the instrument.

The telephone-bell rang.

"Hullo!" said Altenheim. "Is that Garches? . . . Yes, that's right. . . . Give me number 38, please, mademoiselle. . . ."

A few seconds later, in a lower voice, as low and as distinct as he could make it, he began:

"Are you 38? . . . It's I speaking; no useless words. . . . Yesterday? . . . Yes, you missed him in the garden. . . . Another time, of course; but the thing's becoming urgent. . . . He had the house searched last night. . . . I'll tell you about it. . . . Found nothing, of course. . . . What? . . . Hullo! . . . No, old Steinweg refuses to speak. . . . Threats, promises, nothing's any good. . . . Hullo! . . . Yes, of course, he sees that we can do nothing. . . . We know just a part of the Kesselbach scheme and of the story of Pierre Leduc. . . . He's the only one who has the answer to the riddle. . . . Oh, he'll speak all right; that I'll answer for . . . this very night, too . . . If not . . . What? . . . Well, what can we do? Anything rather than let him escape! Do you want the prince to bag him from us? As for the prince, we shall have to cook his goose in three days from now. . . . You have an idea? . . . Yes, that's a good idea. . . . Oh, oh, excellent! I'll see to it. . . . When shall we meet? Will Tuesday do? Right you are. I'll come on Tuesday . . . at two o'clock. . . . Good-bye."

He replaced the receiver and went out.

A few hours later, while the servants were at lunch, Prince Sernine strolled quietly out of the Villa Dupont, feeling rather faint in the head and weak in the knees, and, while making for the nearest restaurant, he thus summed up the situation:

"So, on Tuesday next, Altenheim and the Palace Hotel murderer have an appointment at Garches, in a house with the telephone number 38. On Tuesday, therefore, I shall hand over the two criminals to the police and set M. Lenormand at liberty. In the evening, it will be old Steinweg's turn; and I shall learn, at last, whether Pierre Leduc is the son of a pork-butcher or not and whether he will make a suitable husband for Geneviève. So be it!"

At eleven o'clock on Tuesday morning Valenglay, the prime minister, sent for the prefect of police and M. Weber, the deputy-chief of the detective-service, and showed them an express letter which he had just received:

"Monsieur le Président du Conseil,

"Knowing the interest which you take in M. Lenormand, I am writing to inform you of certain facts which chance has revealed to me.

"M. Lenormand is locked up in the cellars of the Villa des Glycines at Garches, near the House of Retreat.

"The ruffians of the Palace Hotel have resolved to murder him at two o'clock to-day.

"If the police require my assistance, they will find me at half-past one in the garden of the House of Retreat, or at the garden-house occupied by Mrs. Kesselbach, whose friend I have the honor to be.

"I am, Monsieur le Président du Conseil,

"Your obedient servant,

"Prince Sernine."

"This is an exceedingly grave matter, my dear M. Weber," said Valenglay. "I may add that we can have every confidence in the accuracy of Prince Sernine's statements. I have often met him at dinner. He is a serious, intelligent man...."

"Will you allow me, Monsieur le Président," asked the deputy-chief detective, "to show you another letter which I also received this morning?"

"About the same case?"

"Yes."

"Let me see it."

He took the letter and read:

"Sir,

This is to inform you that Prince Paul Sernine, who calls himself Mrs. Kesselbach's friend, is really Arsène Lupin.

"One proof will be sufficient: *Paul Sernine* is the anagram of *Arsène Lupin*. Not a letter more, not a letter less. L. M."

And M. Weber added, while Valenglay stood amazed:

"This time, our friend Lupin has found an adversary who is a match for him. While he denounces the other, the other betrays him to us. And the fox is caught in the trap."

"What do you propose to do?"

"Monsieur le Président, I shall take two hundred men with me!"

VIII. THE OLIVE-GREEN FROCK-COAT

A quarter past twelve, in a restaurant near the Madeleine. The prince is at lunch. Two young men sit down at the next table. He bows to them and begins to speak to them, as to friends whom he has met by chance.

"Are you going on the expedition, eh?"

"Yes."

"How many men altogether?"

"Six, I think. Each goes down by himself. We're to meet M. Weber at a quarter to two, near the House of Retreat."

"Very well, I shall be there."

"What?"

"Am I not leading the expedition? And isn't it my business to find M. Lenormand, seeing that I've announced it publicly?"

"Then you believe that M. Lenormand is not dead, governor?"

"I'm sure of it."

"Do you know anything?"

"Yes, since yesterday I know for certain that Altenheim and his gang took M. Lenormand and Gourel to the bridge at Bougival and heaved them overboard. Gourel sank, but M. Lenormand managed to save himself. I shall furnish all the necessary proofs when the time comes."

"But, then, if he's alive, why doesn't he show himself?"

"Because he's not free."

"Is what you said true, then? Is he in the cellars of the Villa des Glycines?"

"I have every reason to think so."

"But how do you know? . . . What clue? . . ."

"That's my secret. I can tell you one thing: the revelation will be—what shall I say—sensational. Have you finished?"

"Yes."

"My car is behind the Madeleine. Join me there."

At Garches, Sernine sent the motor away, and they walked to the path that led to Geneviève's school. There he stopped:

"Listen to me, lads. This is of the highest importance. You will ring at the House of Retreat. As inspectors, you have your right of entry, have you not? You will then go to the Pavillon Hortense, the empty one. There you will run down to the basement and you will find an old shutter, which you have only to lift to see the opening of a tunnel which I discovered lately and which forms a direct communication with the Villa des Glycines. It was by means of this that Gertrude and Baron Altenheim used to meet. And it was this way that M. Lenormand passed, only to end by falling into the hands of his enemies."

"You think so, governor?"

"Yes, I think so. And now the point is this: you must go and make sure that the tunnel is exactly in the condition in which I left it last night; that the two doors which bar it are open; and that there is still, in a hole near the second door, a parcel wrapped in a piece of black cloth which I put there myself."

"Are we to undo the parcel?"

"No, that's not necessary. It's a change of clothes. Go; and don't let yourselves be seen more than you can help. I will wait for you."

Ten minutes later, they were back:

"The two doors are open," said one of the Doudevilles.

"And the black cloth parcel?"

"In its place near the second door."

"Capital! It is twenty-five past one. Weber will be arriving with his champions. They are to watch the villa. They will surround it as soon as Altenheim is inside. I have arranged with Weber that I shall ring the bell; the door will be opened; and I shall have my foot inside the citadel. Once there, I have my plan. Come, I've an idea that we shall see some fun."

And Sernine, after dismissing them, walked down the path to the school, soliloquizing as he went:

"All bodes well. The battle will be fought on the ground chosen by myself. I am bound to win. I shall get rid of my two adversaries and I shall find myself alone engaged in the Kesselbach case . . . alone, with two whacking trump-cards: Pierre Leduc and Steinweg. . . . Besides the king . . . that is to say, Bibi. Only, there's one thing: what is Altenheim up to? Obviously, he has a plan of attack of his own. On which side does he mean to attack me? And how does it come that he has not attacked me yet? It's rather startling. Can he have denounced me to the police?"

He went along the little playground of the school. The pupils were at their lessons. He knocked at the door.

"Ah, is that you?" said Mme. Ernemont, opening the door. "So you have left Geneviève in Paris?"

"For me to do that, Geneviève would have to be in Paris," he replied.

"So she has been, seeing that you sent for her."

"What's that?" he exclaimed catching hold of her arm.

"Why, you know better than I!"

"I know nothing. . . . I know nothing. . . . Speak! . . ."

"Didn't you write to Geneviève to meet you at the Gare Saint-Lazare?"

"And did she go?"

"Why, of course. . . . You were to lunch together at the Hôtel Ritz."

"The letter. . . . Show me the letter."

She went to fetch it and gave it to him.

"But, wretched woman, couldn't you see that it was a forgery? The handwriting is a good imitation . . . but it's a forgery. . . . Any one can see that." He pressed his clenched hands to his temples with rage. "That's the move I was wondering about. Oh, the dirty scoundrel! He's attacking me through her. . . . But how does he know? No, he does not know. . . . He's tried it on twice now . . . and it's because of Geneviève, because he's taken a fancy to her. . . . Oh, not that! Never! Listen, Victoire, are you sure that she doesn't love him? . . . Oh, I'm losing my head! . . . Wait . . . wait! . . . I must think . . . this isn't the moment. . . ."

He looked at his watch:

"Twenty-five minutes to two. . . . I have time. . . . Idiot that I am! Time to do what? How do I know where she is?"

He walked up and down like a madman; and his old nurse seemed astounded at seeing him so excited, with so little control of himself:

"After all," she said, "there is nothing to prove that she did not suspect the trap at the last moment. . . ."

"Where could she be?"

"I don't know . . . perhaps at Mrs. Kesselbach's."

"That's true . . . that's true. . . . You're right," he cried, filled with sudden hope.

And he set out at a run for the House of Retreat.

On the way, near the gate, he met the brothers Doudeville, who were entering the porter's lodge. The lodge looked out on the road; and this enabled them to watch the approaches to the Villa des Glycines. Without stopping, he went straight to the Pavillon de l'Impératrice, called Suzanne and told her to take him to Mrs. Kesselbach.

"Geneviève?" he asked.

"Geneviève?"

"Yes; hasn't she been here?"

"No, not for several days. . . ."

"But she is to come, is she not?"

"Do you think so?"

"Why, I'm certain of it. Where do you think she is? Can you remember? . . ."

"It's no use my trying. I assure you that Geneviève and I had made no arrangement to see each other." And, suddenly alarmed: "But you're not anxious, are you? Has anything happened to Geneviève?"

"No, nothing."

He had already left the room. An idea had occurred to him. Suppose Altenheim were not at the Villa des Glycines? Suppose the hour of the meeting had been changed!

"I must see him," he said to himself. "I must, at all costs."

And he ran along with a disordered air, indifferent to everything. But, in front of the lodge, he at once recovered his composure: he had caught sight of the deputy-chief of the detective-service talking to the brothers Doudeville in the garden.

Had he commanded his usual acute discernment, he would have perceived the little start which M. Weber gave as he approached; but he saw nothing:

"M. Weber, I believe?" he asked.

"Yes. . . . To whom have I the honor . . . ?"

"Prince Sernine."

"Ah, very good! Monsieur le Préfet de Police has told me of the great service which you are doing us, monsieur."

"That service will not be complete until I have handed the ruffians over to you."

"That won't take long. I believe that one of those ruffians has just gone in; a powerful-looking man, with a swarthy complexion. . . ."

"Yes, that's Baron Altenheim. Are your men here, M. Weber?"

"Yes, concealed along the road, at two hundred yards from this."

"Well, M. Weber, it seems to me that you might collect them and bring them to this lodge. From here we will go to the villa. As Baron Altenheim knows me, I presume they will open the door to me and I will go in . . . with you."

"It is an excellent plan," said M. Weber. "I shall come back at once."

He left the garden and walked down the road, in the opposite direction to the Villa des Glycines.

Sernine quickly took one of the brothers Doudeville by the arm:

"Run after him, Jacques . . . keep him engaged . . . long enough for me to get inside the Glycines. . . . And then delay the attack as long as you can. . . . Invent pretexts. . . . I shall want ten minutes. . . . Let the villa be surrounded . . . but not entered. And you, Jean, go and post yourself in the Pavillon Hortense, at the entrance to the underground passage. If the baron tries to go out that way, break his head."

The Doudevilles moved away, as ordered. The prince slipped out and ran to a tall gate, barred with iron, which was the entrance to the Glycines.

Should he ring? . . .

There was no one in sight. With one bound, he leapt upon the gate, placing his foot on the lock; and, hanging on to the bars, getting a purchase with his knees and hoisting himself up with his wrists, he managed, at the risk of falling on the sharp points of the bars, to climb over the gate and jump down.

He found a paved courtyard, which he crossed briskly, and mounted the steps of a pillared peristyle, on which the windows looked out. These were all closed to the very top, with full shutters. As he stood thinking how he should make his way into the house, the door was half opened, with a noise of iron that reminded him of the door in the Villa Dupont, and Altenheim appeared:

"I say, prince, is that the way you trespass on private property? I shall be forced to call in the gendarmes, my dear fellow!"

Sernine caught him by the throat and, throwing him down on a bench:

"Geneviève? . . . Where is Geneviève? If you don't tell me what you've done with her, you villain. . . ."

"Please observe," stammered the baron, "that you are making it impossible for me to speak."

Sernine released his hold of him:

"To the point! . . . And look sharp! . . . Answer. . . . Geneviève?"

"There is one thing," replied the baron, "which is much more urgent, especially where fellows like you and me are concerned, and that is to feel one's self at home. . . ."

And he carefully closed the front door, which he barricaded with bolts. Then, leading Sernine to the adjoining drawing-room, a room without furniture or curtains, he said:

"Now I'm your man. What can I do for you, prince?"

"Geneviève?"

"She is in perfect health."

"Ah, so you confess . . . ?"

"Of course! I may even tell you that your imprudence in this respect surprised me. Why didn't you take a few precautions? It was inevitable. . . ."

"Enough! Where is she?"

"You are not very polite."

"Where is she?"

"Between four walls, free. . . ."

"Free?"

"Yes, free to go from one wall to another."

"Where? Where?"

"Come, prince, do you think I should be fool enough to tell you the secret by which I hold you? You love the little girl . . ."

"Hold your tongue!" shouted Sernine, beside himself. "I forbid you. . . ."

"What next? Is there anything to be ashamed of? I love her myself and I have risked . . ."

He did not complete his sentence, frightened by the terrific anger of Sernine, a restrained, dumb anger that distorted the prince's features.

They looked at each other for a long time, each of them seeking for the adversary's weak point. At last, Sernine stepped forward and, speaking very distinctly, like a man who is threatening rather than proposing a compact:

"Listen to me," he said. "You remember the offer of partnership which you made me? The Kesselbach business for the two of us . . . we were to act together . . . we were to share the profits. . . . I refused. . . . To-day, I accept. . . ."

"Too late."

"Wait! I accept more than that: I give the whole business up. . . . I shall take no further part in it. . . . You shall have it all. . . . If necessary, I'll help you."

"What is the condition?"

"Tell me where Geneviève is."

The baron shrugged his shoulders:

"You're driveling, Lupin. I'm sorry for you . . . at your age. . . ."

There was a fresh silence between the two enemies, a terrible silence. Then the baron sneered:

"All the same, it's a holy joy to see you like that, sniveling and begging. I say, it seems to me that the private soldier is giving his general a sound beating!"

"You ass!" muttered Sernine.

"Prince, I shall send you my seconds this evening . . . if you are still in this world."

"You ass!" repeated Sernine, with infinite contempt.

"You would rather settle the matter here and now? As you please, prince: your last hour has struck. You can commend your soul to God. You smile! That's a mistake. I have one immense advantage over you! I kill . . . when it's necessary. . . ."

"You ass!" said Sernine once more. He took out his watch. "It is two o'clock, baron. You have only a few minutes left. At five past two, ten past at the very latest, M. Weber and half-a-dozen sturdy men, without a scruple amongst them, will lay hands on you. . . . Don't you smile, either. The outlet on which you're reckoning is discovered; I know it: it is guarded. So you are thoroughly caught. It means the scaffold, old chap."

Altenheim turned livid. He stammered:

"You did this? . . . You have had the infamy . . ."

"The house is surrounded. The assault is at hand. Speak . . . and I will save you."

"How?"

"The men watching the outlet in the Pavillon Hortense belong to me. I have only to give you a word for them and you are saved. Speak!"

Altenheim reflected for a few seconds and seemed to hesitate; but, suddenly, resolutely, declared:

"This is all bluff. You would never have been simple enough to rush into the lion's mouth."

"You're forgetting Geneviève. But for her, do you think I should be here? Speak!"

"No."

"Very well. Let us wait," said Sernine. "A cigarette?"

"Thank you."

A few seconds passed.

"Do you hear?" asked Sernine.

"Yes . . . yes . . ." said Altenheim, rising.

Blows rang against the gate. Sernine observed:

"Not even the usual summons . . . no preliminaries. . . . Your mind is still made up?"

"More so than ever."

"You know that, with the tools they carry, they won't take long?"

"If they were inside this room I should still refuse."

The gate yielded. They heard it creak on its hinges.

"To allow one's self to get nabbed," said Sernine, "is admissible. But to hold out one's own hands to the handcuffs is too silly. Come, don't be obstinate. Speak . . . and bolt!"

"And you?"

"I shall remain. What have I to be afraid of?"

"Look!"

The baron pointed to a chink between the shutters. Sernine put his eye to it and jumped back with a start:

"Oh, you scoundrel, so you have denounced me, too! It's not ten men that Weber's bringing, but fifty men, a hundred, two hundred. . . ."

The baron laughed open-heartedly:

"And, if there are so many of them, it's because they're after Lupin; that's obvious! Half-a-dozen would have been enough for me."

"You informed the police?"

"Yes."

"What proof did you give?"

"Your name: *Paul Sernine*, that is to say, *Arsène Lupin*."

"And you found that out all by yourself, did you? . . . A thing which nobody else thought of? . . . Nonsense! It was the other one. Admit it!"

He looked out through the chink. Swarms of policemen were spreading round the villa; and the blows were now sounding on the door. He must, however, think of one of two things: either his escape, or else the execution of the plan which he had contrived. But to go away, even for a moment, meant leaving Altenheim; and who could guarantee that the baron had not another outlet at his disposal to escape by? This thought paralyzed Sernine. The baron free! The baron at liberty to go back to Geneviève and torture her and make her subservient to his odious love!

Thwarted in his designs, obliged to improvise a new plan on the very second, while subordinating everything to the danger which Geneviève was running, Sernine passed through a moment of cruel indecision. With his eyes fixed on the baron's eyes, he would have liked to tear his secret from him and to go away; and he no longer even tried to convince him, so useless did all words seem to him. And, while pursuing his own thoughts, he asked himself what the baron's thoughts could be, what his weapons, what his hope of safety?

The hall-door, though strongly bolted, though sheeted with iron, was beginning to give way.

The two men stood behind that door, motionless. The sound of voices, the sense of words reached them.

"You seem very sure of yourself," said Sernine.

"I should think so!" cried the other, suddenly tripping him to the floor and running away.

Sernine sprang up at once, dived through a little door under the staircase, through which Altenheim had disappeared, and ran down the stone steps to the basement. . . .

A passage led to a large, low, almost pitch-dark room, where he found the baron on his knees, lifting the flap of a trap-door.

"Idiot!" shouted Sernine, flinging himself upon him. "You know that you will find my men at the end of this tunnel and that they have orders to kill you like a dog. . . . Unless . . . unless you have an outlet that joins on to this. . . . Ah, there, of course, I've guessed it! . . . And you imagine . . ."

The fight was a desperate one. Altenheim, a real colossus, endowed with exceptional muscular force, had caught his adversary round the arms and body and was pressing him against his own chest, numbing his arms and trying to smother him.

"Of course . . . of course," Sernine panted, with difficulty, "of course . . . that's well thought out. . . . As long as I can't use my arms to break some part of you, you will have the advantage . . . Only . . . can you . . . ?"

He gave a shudder. The trap-door, which had closed again and on the flap of which they were bearing down with all their weight, the trap-door seemed to move beneath them. He felt the efforts that were being made to raise it; and the baron must have felt them too, for he desperately tried to shift the ground of the contest so that the trap-door might open.

"It's 'the other one'!" thought Sernine, with the sort of unreasoning terror which that mysterious being caused him. "It's the other one. . . . If he gets through, I'm done for."

By dint of imperceptible movements, Altenheim had succeeded in shifting his own position; and he tried to drag his adversary after him. But Sernine clung with his legs to the baron's legs and, at the same time, very gradually, tried to release one of his hands.

Above their heads great blows resounded, like the blows of a battering-ram. . . .

"I have five minutes," thought Sernine. "In one minute this fellow will have to . . ." Then, speaking aloud, "Look out, old chap. Stand tight!"

He brought his two knees together with incredible force. The baron yelled, with a twisted thigh. Then Sernine, taking advantage of his adversary's pain, made an effort, freed his right arm and seized him by the throat:

"That's capital! . . . We shall be more comfortable like this. . . . No, it's not worth while getting out your knife. . . . If you do, I'll wring your neck like a chicken's. You see, I'm polite and considerate. . . . I'm not pressing too hard . . . just enough to keep you from even wanting to kick about."

While speaking he took from his pocket a very thin cord and, with one hand, with extreme skill, fastened his wrists. For that matter, the baron, now at his last gasp, offered not the least resistance. With a few accurate movements, Sernine tied him up firmly:

"How well you're behaving! What a good thing! I should hardly know you. Here, in case you were thinking of escaping, I have a roll of wire that will finish off my little work. . . . The wrists first. . . . Now the ankles. . . . That's it! . . . By Jove, how nice you look!"

The baron had gradually come to himself again. He spluttered:

"If you give me up, Geneviève will die."

"Really? . . . And how? . . . Explain yourself."

"She is locked up. No one knows where she is. If I'm put away, she will die of starvation."

Sernine shuddered. He retorted:

"Yes, but you will speak."

"Never!"

"Yes, you will speak. Not now; it's too late. But to-night." He bent down over him and, whispering in his ear, said, "Listen, Altenheim, and understand what I say. You'll be caught presently. To-night, you'll sleep at the Dépôt. That is fatal, irrevocable. I myself can do nothing to prevent it now. And, to-morrow, they will take you to the Santé; and later, you know where. . . . Well, I'm giving you one more chance of safety. To-night, you understand, I shall come to your cell, at the Dépôt, and you shall tell me where Geneviève is. Two hours later, if you have told the truth, you shall be free. If not . . . it means that you don't attach much value to your head."

The other made no reply. Sernine stood up and listened. There was a great crash overhead. The entrance-door yielded. Footsteps beat the flags of the hall and the floor of the drawing room. M. Weber and his men were searching.

"Good-bye, baron. Think it over until this evening. The prison-cell is a good counsellor."

He pushed his prisoner aside, so as to uncover the trap-door, and lifted it. As he expected, there was no longer any one below on the steps of the staircase.

He went down, taking care to leave the trap-door open behind him, as though he meant to come back.

There were twenty steps, at the bottom of which began the passage through which M. Lenormand and Gourel had come in the opposite direction. He entered it and gave an exclamation. He thought he felt somebody's presence there.

He lit his pocket-lantern. The passage was empty.

Then he cocked his revolver and said aloud:

"All right. . . . I'm going to fire."

No reply. Not a sound.

"It's an illusion, no doubt," he thought. "That creature is becoming an obsession. . . . Come, if I want to pull off my stroke and win the game, I must hurry. . . . The hole in which I hid the parcel of clothes is not far off. I shall take the parcel . . . and the trick is done. . . . And what a trick! One of Lupin's best! . . ."

He came to a door that stood open and at once stopped. To the right was an excavation, the one which M. Lenormand had made to escape from the rising water. He stooped and threw his light into the opening:

"Oh!" he said, with a start. "No, it's not possible . . . Doudeville must have pushed the parcel farther along."

But, search and pry into the darkness as he might, the parcel was gone; and he had no doubt but that it was once more the mysterious being who had taken it.

"What a pity! The thing was so neatly arranged! The adventure would have resumed its natural course, and I should have achieved my aim with greater certainty. . . . As it is, I must push along as fast as I can. . . . Doudeville is at the Pavillon Hortense. . . . My retreat is insured. . . . No more nonsense. . . . I must hurry and set things straight again, if I can. . . . And we'll attend to 'him' afterward. . . . Oh, he'd better keep clear of my claws, that one!"

But an exclamation of stupor escaped his lips; he had come to the other door; and this door, the last before the garden-house, was shut. He flung himself upon it. What was the good? What could he do?

"This time," he muttered, "I'm badly done!"

And, seized with a sort of lassitude, he sat down. He had a sense of his weakness in the face of the mysterious being. Altenheim hardly counted. But the other, that person of darkness and silence, the other loomed up before him, upset all his plans and exhausted him with his cunning and infernal attacks.

He was beaten.

Weber would find him there, like an animal run to earth, at the bottom of his cave.

"Ah, no!" he cried, springing up with a bound. "No! If there were only myself, well and good! . . . But there is Geneviève, Geneviève, who must be saved to-night. . . . After all, the game is not yet lost. . . . If the other one vanished just now, it proves that there is a second outlet somewhere near. . . . Come, come, Weber and his merry men haven't got me yet. . . ."

He had already begun to explore the tunnel and, lantern in hand, was examining the bricks of which the horrible walls were formed, when a yell reached his ears, a dreadful yell that made his flesh creep with anguish.

It came from the direction of the trap-door. And he suddenly remembered that he had left the trap-door open, at the time when he intended to return to the Villa des Glycines.

He hurried back and passed through the first door. His lantern went out on the road; and he felt something, or rather somebody, brush past his knees, somebody crawl along the wall. And, at that same moment, he had a feeling that this being was disappearing, vanishing, he knew not which way.

Just then his foot knocked against a step.

"This is the outlet," he thought, "the second outlet through which 'he' passes."

Overhead, the cry sounded again, less loud, followed by moans, by a hoarse gurgling. . . .

He ran up the stairs, came out in the basement room, and rushed to the baron.

Altenheim lay dying, with the blood streaming from his throat! His bonds were cut, but the wire that fastened his wrists and ankles was intact. *His accomplice, being unable to release him, had cut his throat.*

Sernine gazed upon the sight with horror. An icy perspiration covered his whole body. He thought of Geneviève, imprisoned, helpless, abandoned to the most awful of deaths, because the baron alone knew where she was hidden.

He distinctly heard the policemen open the little back door in the hall. He distinctly heard them come down the kitchen stairs.

There was nothing between him and them save one door, that of the basement room in which he was. He bolted the door at the very moment when the aggressors were laying hold of the handle.

The trap-door was open beside him; it meant possible safety, because there remained the second outlet.

"No," he said to himself, "Geneviève first. Afterward, if I have time, I will think of myself."

He knelt down and put his hand on the baron's breast. The heart was still beating.

He stooped lower still:

"You can hear me, can't you?"

The eyelids flickered feebly.

The dying man was just breathing. Was there anything to be obtained from this faint semblance of life?

The policemen were attacking the door, the last rampart.

Sernine whispered.

"I will save you. . . . I have infallible remedies. . . . One word only . . . Geneviève? . . ."

It was as though this word of hope revived the man's strength. Altenheim tried to utter articulate sounds.

"Answer," said Sernine, persisting. "Answer, and I will save you. . . . Answer. . . . It means your life to-day . . . your liberty to-morrow. . . . Answer! . . ."

The door shook under the blows that rained upon it.

The baron gasped out unintelligible syllables. Leaning over him, affrighted, straining all his energy, all his will to the utmost, Sernine panted with anguish. He no longer gave a thought to the policemen, his inevitable capture, prison. . . . But Geneviève. . . . Geneviève dying of hunger, whom one word from that villain could set free! . . .

"Answer! . . . You must! . . ."

He ordered and entreated by turns. Altenheim stammered, as though hypnotized and defeated by that indomitable imperiousness:

"Ri . . . Rivoli. . . ."

"Rue de Rivoli, is that it? You have locked her up in a house in that street . . . eh? Which number?"

A loud din . . . followed by shouts of triumph. . . . The door was down.

"Jump on him, lads!" cried M. Weber. "Seize him . . . seize both of them!"

And Sernine, on his knees:

"The number . . . answer. . . . If you love her, answer. . . . Why keep silence now?"

"Twenty . . . twenty-seven," whispered the baron.

Hands were laid on Sernine. Ten revolvers were pointed at him.

He rose and faced the policemen, who fell back with instinctive dread.

"If you stir, Lupin," cried M. Weber, with his revolver leveled at him, "I'll blow out your brains."

"Don't shoot." said Sernine, solemnly. "It's not necessary. I surrender."

"Humbug! This is another of your tricks!"

"No," replied Sernine, "the battle is lost. You have no right to shoot. I am not defending myself."

He took out two revolvers and threw them on the floor.

"Humbug!" M. Weber repeated, implacably. "Aim straight at his heart, lads! At the least movement, fire! At the least word, fire!"

There were ten men there. He placed five more in position. He pointed their fifteen right arms at the mark. And, raging, shaking with joy and fear, he snarled:

"At his heart! At his head! And no pity! If he stirs, if he speaks . . . shoot him where he stands!"

Sernine smiled, impassively, with his hands in his pockets. Death was there, waiting for him, at two inches from his chest, at two inches from his temples. Fifteen fingers were curled round the triggers.

"Ah," chuckled M. Weber, "this is nice, this is very nice! . . . And I think that this time we've scored . . . and it's a nasty look-out for you, Master Lupin! . . ."

He made one of his men draw back the shutters of a large air-hole, which admitted a sudden burst of daylight, and he turned toward Altenheim. But, to his great amazement, the baron, whom he thought dead, opened his eyes, glazed, awful eyes, already filled with all the signs of the coming dissolution. He stared at M. Weber. Then he seemed to look for somebody and, catching sight of Sernine, had a convulsion of anger. He seemed to be waking from his torpor; and his suddenly reviving hatred restored a part of his strength.

He raised himself on his two wrists and tried to speak.

"You know him, eh?" asked M. Weber.

"Yes."

"It's Lupin, isn't it?"

"Yes. . . . Lupin. . . ."

Sernine, still smiling, listened:

"Heavens, how I'm amusing myself!" he declared.

"Have you anything more to say?" asked M. Weber, who saw the baron's lips making desperate attempts to move.

"Yes."

"About M. Lenormand, perhaps?"

"Yes."

"Have you shut him up? Where? Answer! . . ."

With all his heaving body, with all his tense glance, Altenheim pointed to a cupboard in the corner of the room.

"There . . . there . . ." he said.

"Ah, we're burning!" chuckled Lupin.

M. Weber opened the cupboard. On one of the shelves was a parcel wrapped in black cloth. He opened it and found a hat, a little box, some clothes. . . . He gave a start. He had recognized M. Lenormand's olive-green frock-coat.

"Oh, the villains!" he cried. "They have murdered him!"

"No," said Altenheim, shaking his head.

"Then . . . ?"

"It's he . . . he . . ."

"What do you mean by 'he'? . . . Did Lupin kill the chief?"

"No. . . ."

Altenheim was clinging to existence with fierce obstinacy, eager to speak and to accuse. . . . The secret which he wished to reveal was at the tip of his tongue and he was not able, did not know how to translate it into words.

"Come," the deputy-chief insisted. "M. Lenormand is dead, surely?"

"No."

"He's alive?"

"Yes."

"I don't understand. . . . Look here, these clothes? This frock-coat? . . ."

Altenheim turned his eyes toward Sernine. An idea struck M. Weber:

"Ah, I see! Lupin stole M. Lenormand's clothes and reckoned upon using them to escape with. . . ."

"Yes . . . yes. . . ."

"Not bad," cried the deputy-chief. "It's quite a trick in his style. In this room, we should have found Lupin disguised as M. Lenormand, chained up, no doubt. It would have meant his safety; only he hadn't time. That's it, isn't it?"

"Yes . . . yes . . ."

But, by the appearance of the dying man's eyes, M. Weber felt that there was more, and that the secret was not exactly that. What was it, then? What was the strange and unintelligible puzzle which Altenheim wanted to explain before dying?

He questioned him again:

"And where is M. Lenormand himself?"

"There. . . ."

"What do you mean? Here?"

"Yes."

"But there are only ourselves here!"

"There's . . . there's . . ."

"Oh, speak!"

"There's . . . Ser . . . Sernine."

"Sernine! . . . Eh, what?"

"Sernine . . . Lenormand. . . ."

M. Weber gave a jump. A sudden light flashed across him.

"No, no, it's not possible," he muttered. "This is madness."

He gave a side-glance at his prisoner. Sernine seemed to be greatly diverted and to be watching the scene with the air of a playgoer who is thoroughly amused and very anxious to know how the piece is going to end.

Altenheim, exhausted by his efforts, had fallen back at full length. Would he die before revealing the solution of the riddle which his strange words had propounded? M. Weber, shaken by an absurd, incredible surmise, which he did not wish to entertain and which persisted in his mind in spite of him, made a fresh, determined attempt:

"Explain the thing to us. . . . What's at the bottom of it? What mystery?"

The other seemed not to hear and lay lifeless, with staring eyes.

M. Weber lay down beside him, with his body touching him, and, putting great stress upon his words, so that each syllable should sink down to the very depths of that brain already merged in darkness, said:

"Listen. . . . I have understood you correctly, have I not? Lupin and M. Lenormand. . . ."

He needed an effort to continue, so monstrous did the words appear to him. Nevertheless, the baron's dimmed eyes seemed to contemplate him with anguish. He finished the sentence, shaking with excitement, as though he were speaking blasphemy:

"That's it, isn't it? You're sure? The two are one and the same? . . ."

The eyes did not move. A little blood trickled from one corner of the man's mouth. . . . He gave two or three sobs. . . . A last spasm; and all was over . . .

A long silence reigned in that basement room filled with people.

Almost all the policemen guarding Sernine had turned round and, stupefied, not understanding or not willing to understand, they still listened to the incredible accusation which the dying scoundrel had been unable to put into words.

M. Weber took the little box which was in the parcel and opened it. It contained a gray wig, a pair of spectacles, a maroon-colored neckerchief and, in a false bottom, a pot or two of make-up and a case containing some tiny tufts of gray hair: in short, all that was needed to complete a perfect disguise in the character of M. Lenormand.

He went up to Sernine and, looking at him for a few seconds without speaking, thoughtfully reconstructing all the phases of the adventure, he muttered:

"So it's true?"

Sernine, who had retained his smiling calmness, replied:

"The suggestion is a pretty one and a bold one. But, before I answer, tell your men to stop worrying me with those toys of theirs."

"Very well," said M. Weber, making a sign to his men. "And now answer."

"What?"

"Are you M. Lenormand?"

"Yes."

Exclamations arose. Jean Doudeville, who was there, while his brother was watching the secret outlet, Jean Doudeville, Sernine's own accomplice, looked at him in dismay. M. Weber stood undecided.

"That takes your breath away, eh?" said Sernine. "I admit that it's rather droll. . . . Lord, how you used to make me laugh sometimes, when we were working together, you and I, the chief and the deputy-chief! . . . And the funniest thing is that you thought our worthy M. Lenormand dead . . . as well as poor Gourel. But no, no, old chap: there's life in the old dog yet!" He pointed to Altenheim's corpse. "There, it was that scoundrel who pitched me into the water, in a sack, with a paving-stone round my waist. Only, he forgot to take away my knife. And with a knife one rips open sacks and cuts ropes. So you see, you unfortunate Altenheim: if you had thought of that, you wouldn't be where you are! . . . But enough said. . . . Peace to your ashes!"

M. Weber listened, not knowing what to think. At last, he made a gesture of despair, as though he gave up the idea of forming a reasonable opinion.

"The handcuffs," he said, suddenly alarmed.

"If it amuses you," said Sernine.

And, picking out Doudeville in the front row of his assailants, he put out his wrists:

"There, my friend, you shall have the honour . . . and don't trouble to exert yourself. . . . I'm playing square . . . as it's no use doing anything else. . . ."

He said this in a tone that gave Doudeville to understand that the struggle was finished for the moment and that there was nothing to do but submit.

Doudeville fastened the handcuffs.

Without moving his lips or contracting a muscle of his face, Sernine whispered:

"27, Rue de Rivoli . . . Geneviève. . . ."

M. Weber could not suppress a movement of satisfaction at the sight:

"Come along!" he said. "To the detective-office!"

"That's it, to the detective-office!" cried Sernine. "M. Lenormand will enter Arsène Lupin in the jail-book; and Arsène Lupin will enter Prince Sernine."

"You're too clever, Lupin."

"That's true, Weber; we shall never get on, you and I."

During the drive in the motor-car, escorted by three other cars filled with policemen, he did not utter a word.

They did not stay long at the detective office. M. Weber, remembering the escapes effected by Lupin, sent him up at once to the finger-print department and then took him to the Dépôt, whence he was sent on to the Santé Prison.

The governor had been warned by telephone and was waiting for him. The formalities of the entry of commitment and of the searching were soon got over; and, at seven o'clock in the evening, Prince Paul Sernine crossed the threshold of cell 14 in the second division:

"Not half bad, your rooms," he declared, "not bad at all! . . . Electric light, central heating, every requisite . . . capital! Mr. Governor, I'll take this room."

He flung himself on the bed:

"Oh, Mr. Governor, I have one little favor to ask of you!"

"What is that?"

"Tell them not to bring me my chocolate before ten o'clock in the morning. . . . I'm awfully sleepy."

He turned his face to the wall. Five minutes later he was sound asleep.

IX. "SANTÉ PALACE"

There was one wild burst of laughter over the whole face of the world.

True, the capture of Arsène Lupin made a big sensation; and the public did not grudge the police the praise which they deserved for this revenge so long hoped-for and now so fully obtained. The great adventurer was caught. That extraordinary, genial, invisible hero was shivering, like any ordinary criminal, between the four walls of a prison cell, crushed in his turn by that formidable power which is called the law and which, sooner or later, by inevitable necessity shatters the obstacles opposed to it and destroys the work of its adversaries.

All this was said, printed, repeated and discussed *ad nauseam*. The prefect of police was created a commander, M. Weber an officer of the Legion of Honor. The skill and courage of their humblest coadjutors were extolled to the skies. Cheers were raised and pæans of victory struck up. Articles were written and speeches made.

Very well. But one thing, nevertheless, rose above the wonderful concert of praise, these noisy demonstrations of satisfaction; and that was an immense, spontaneous, inextinguishable and tumultuous roar of laughter.

Arsène Lupin had been chief of the detective-service for four years!!!

He had been chief detective for four years and, really, legally, he was chief detective still, with all the rights which the title confers, enjoying the esteem of his chiefs, the favor of the government and the admiration of the public.

For four years, the public peace and the defence of property had been entrusted to Arsène Lupin. He saw that the law was carried out. He protected the innocent and pursued the guilty.

And what services he had rendered! Never was order less disturbed, never was crime discovered with greater certainty and rapidity. The reader need but take back his mind to the Denizou case, the robbery at the Crédit Lyonnais, the attack on the Orléans express, the murder of Baron Dorf, forming a series of unforeseen and overwhelming triumphs, of magnificent feats of prowess fit to compare with the most famous victories of the most renowned detectives.[14]

Not so very long before, in a speech delivered at the time of the fire at the Louvre and the capture of the incendiaries, Valenglay, the prime minister, had said, speaking in defence of the somewhat arbitrary manner in which M. Lenormand had acted on that occasion:

"With his great powers of discernment, his energy, his qualities of decision and execution, his unexpected methods, his inexhaustible resources, M. Lenormand reminds us of the only man who, if he were still alive, could hope to hold his own against him: I mean Arsène Lupin. M. Lenormand is an Arsène Lupin in the service of society."

And, lo and behold, M. Lenormand was none other than Arsène Lupin!

That he was a Russian prince, who cared! Lupin was an old hand at such changes of personality as that. But chief detective! What a delicious irony! What a whimsical humor in the conduct of that extraordinary life!

M. Lenormand! . . . Arsène Lupin! . . .

People were now able to explain to themselves the apparently miraculous feats of intelligence which had quite recently bewildered the crowd and baffled the police. They understood how his accomplice had been juggled away in the middle of the Palais de Justice itself, in broad daylight and on the appointed day. Had he himself not said:

"My process is so ingenious and so simple. . . . How surprised people will be on the day when I am free to speak! 'Is that all?' I shall be asked. That is all; but it had to be thought of."

It was, indeed, childishly simple: all you had to do was to be chief of the detective-service.

---

[14] The murder of Baron Dorf, that mysterious and disconcerting affair, will one day be the subject of a story which will give an idea of Arsène Lupin's astonishing qualities as a detective.

Well, Lupin was chief of the detective-service; and every police-officer obeying his orders had made himself the involuntary and unconscious accomplice of Arsène Lupin.

What a comedy! What admirable bluff! It was the monumental and consoling farce of these drab times of ours. Lupin in prison, Lupin irretrievably conquered was, in spite of himself, the great conqueror. From his cell he shone over Paris. He was more than ever the idol, more than ever the master.

When Arsène Lupin awoke next morning, in his room at the "Santé Palace," as he at once nicknamed it, he had a very clear vision of the enormous sensation which would be produced by his arrest under the double name of Sernine and Lenormand and the double title of prince and chief of the detective-service.

He rubbed his hands and gave vent to his thoughts:

"A man can have no better companion in his loneliness than the approval of his contemporaries. O fame! The sun of all living men! . . ."

Seen by daylight, his cell pleased him even better than at night. The window, placed high up in the wall, afforded a glimpse of the branches of a tree, through which peeped the blue of the sky above. The walls were white. There was only one table and one chair, both fastened to the floor. But everything was quite nice and clean.

"Come," he said, "a little rest-cure here will be rather charming. . . . But let us see to our toilet. . . . Have I all I want? . . . No. . . . In that case, ring twice for the chambermaid."

He pressed the button of an apparatus beside the door, which released a signaling-disc in the corridor.

After a moment, bolts and bars were drawn outside, a key turned in the lock and a warder appeared.

"Hot water, please," said Lupin.

The other looked at him with an air of mingled amazement and rage.

"Oh," said Lupin, "and a bath-towel! By Jove, there's no bath-towel!"

The man growled:

"You're getting at me, aren't you? You'd better be careful!"

He was going away, when Lupin caught him roughly by the arm:

"Here! A hundred francs if you'll post a letter for me."

He took out a hundred-franc note, which he had concealed during the search, and offered it to him.

"Where's the letter?" said the warder, taking the money.

"Just give me a moment to write it."

He sat down at the table, scribbled a few words in pencil on a sheet of paper, put it in an envelope and addressed the letter:

"To Monsieur S. B. 42,

"Poste Restante,

"PARIS."

The warder took the letter and walked away.

"That letter," said Lupin to himself, "will reach destination as safely as if I delivered it myself. I shall have the reply in an hour at latest: just the time I want to take a good look into my position."

He sat down on his chair and, in an undertone, summed up the situation as follows:

"When all is said and done, I have two adversaries to fight at the present moment. There is, first, society, which holds me and which I can afford to laugh at. Secondly, there is a person unknown, who does not hold me, but whom I am not inclined to laugh at in the very least. It is he who told the police that I was Sernine. It was he who guessed that I was M. Lenormand. It was he who locked the door of the underground passage and it was he who had me clapped into prison."

Arsène Lupin reflected for a second and then continued:

"So, at long last, the struggle lies between him and me. And, to keep up that struggle, that is to say, to discover and get to the bottom of the Kesselbach case, here am I, a prisoner, while he is free, unknown, and inaccessible, and holds the two trump-cards which I considered mine: Pierre Leduc and old Steinweg. . . . In short, he is near the goal, after finally pushing me back."

A fresh contemplative pause, followed by a fresh soliloquy:

"The position is far from brilliant. On the one side, everything; on the other, nothing. Opposite me, a man of my own strength, or stronger, because he has not the same scruples that hamper me. And I am without weapons to attack him with."

He repeated the last sentence several times, in a mechanical voice, and then stopped and, taking his forehead between his hands, sat for a long time wrapped in thought.

"Come in, Mr. Governor," he said, seeing the door open.

"Were you expecting me?"

"Why, I wrote to you, Mr. Governor, asking you to come! I felt certain that the warder would give you my letter. I was so certain of it that I put your initials, S. B., and your age, forty-two, on the envelope!"

The governor's name, in point of fact, was Stanislas Borély, and he was forty-two years of age. He was a pleasant-looking man, with a very gentle character, who treated the prisoners with all the indulgence possible.

He said to Lupin:

"Your opinion of my subordinate's integrity was quite correct. Here is your money. It shall be handed to you at your release. . . . You will now go through the searching-room again."

Lupin went with M. Borély to the little room reserved for this purpose, undressed and, while his clothes were inspected with justifiable suspicion, himself underwent a most fastidious examination.

He was then taken back to his cell and M. Borély said:

"I feel easier. That's done."

"And very well done, Mr. Governor. Your men perform this sort of duty with a delicacy for which I should like to thank them by giving them a small token of my satisfaction."

He handed a hundred-franc note to M. Borély, who jumped as though he had been shot:

"Oh! . . . But . . . where does that come from?"

"No need to rack your brains, Mr. Governor. A man like myself, leading the life that I do, is always prepared for any eventuality: and no mishap, however painful—not even imprisonment—can take him unawares."

Seizing the middle finger of his left hand between the thumb and forefinger of the right, he pulled it off smartly and presented it calmly to M. Borély:

"Don't start like that, Mr. Governor. This is not my finger, but just a tube, made of gold-beater's skin and cleverly colored, which fits exactly over my middle finger and gives the illusion of a real finger." And he added, with a laugh, "In such a way, of course, as to conceal a third hundred-franc note. . . . What is a poor man to do? He must carry the best purse he can . . . and must needs make use of it on occasions. . . ."

He stopped at the sight of M. Borély's startled face:

"Please don't think, Mr. Governor, that I wish to dazzle you with my little parlor-tricks. I only wanted to show you that you have to do with a . . . client of a rather . . . special nature and to tell you that you must not be surprised if I venture, now and again, to break the ordinary rules and regulations of your establishment."

The governor had recovered himself. He said plainly:

"I prefer to think that you will conform to the rules and not compel me to resort to harsh measures. . . ."

"Which you would regret to have to enforce: isn't that it, Mr. Governor? That's just what I should like to spare you, by proving to you in advance that they would not prevent me from doing as I please: from corresponding with my friends, from defending the grave interests confided to me outside these walls, from writing to the newspapers that accept my inspiration, from pursuing the fulfilment of my plans and, lastly, from preparing my escape."

"Your escape!"

Lupin began to laugh heartily:

"But think, Mr. Governor, my only excuse for being in prison is . . . to leave it!"

The argument did not appear to satisfy M. Borély. He made an effort to laugh in his turn:

"Forewarned is forearmed," he said.

"That's what I wanted," Lupin replied. "Take all your precautions, Mr. Governor, neglect nothing, so that later they may have nothing to reproach you with. On the other hand, I shall arrange things in such a way that, whatever annoyance you may have to bear in consequence of my escape, your career, at least, shall not suffer. That is all I had to say to you, Mr. Governor. You can go."

And, while M. Borély walked away, greatly perturbed by his singular charge and very anxious about the events in preparation, the prisoner threw himself on his bed, muttering:

"What cheek, Lupin, old fellow, what cheek! Really, any one would think that you had some idea as to how you were going to get out of this!"

The Santé prison is built on the star plan. In the centre of the main portion is a round hall, upon which all the corridors converge, so that no prisoner is able to leave his cell without being at once perceived by the overseers posted in the glass box which occupies the middle of that central hall.

The thing that most surprises the visitor who goes over the prison is that, at every moment, he will meet prisoners without a guard of any kind, who seem to move about as though they were absolutely free. In reality, in order to go from one point to another—for instance, from their cell to the van waiting in the yard to take them to the Palais de Justice for the magistrate's examination—they pass along straight lines each of which ends in a door that is opened to them by a warder. The sole duty of the warder is to open and shut this door and to watch the two straight lines which it commands. And thus the prisoners, while apparently at liberty to come and go as they please, are sent from door to door, from eye to eye, like so many parcels passed from hand to hand.

Outside, municipal guards receive the object and pack it into one of the compartments of the "salad-basket."[* The French slang expression for its prison-van or "black Maria."—*Translator's Note*]

This is the ordinary routine.

In Lupin's case it was disregarded entirely. The police were afraid of that walk along the corridors. They were afraid of the prison-van. They were afraid of everything.

M. Weber came in person, accompanied by twelve constables—the best he had, picked men, armed to the teeth—fetched the formidable prisoner at the door of his cell and took him in a cab, the driver of which was one of his own men, with mounted municipal guards trotting on each side, in front and behind.

"Bravo!" cried Lupin. "I am quite touched by the compliment paid me. A guard of honor. By Jove, Weber, you have the proper hierarchical instinct! You don't forget what is due to your immediate chief." And, tapping him on the shoulder: "Weber, I intend to send in my resignation. I shall name you as my successor."

"It's almost done," said Weber.

"That's good news! I was a little anxious about my escape. Now I am easy in my mind. From the moment when Weber is chief of the detective-service . . . !"

M. Weber did not reply to the gibe. At heart, he had a queer, complex feeling in the presence of his adversary, a feeling made up of the fear with which Lupin inspired him, the deference which he entertained for Prince Sernine and the respectful admiration which he had always shown to M. Lenormand. All this was mingled with spite, envy and satisfied hatred.

They arrived at the Palais de Justice. At the foot of the "mouse-trap," a number of detectives were waiting, among whom M. Weber rejoiced to see his best two lieutenants, the brothers Doudeville.

"Has M. Formerie come?" he asked.

"Yes, chief, Monsieur le Juge d'Instruction is in his room."

M. Weber went up the stairs, followed by Lupin, who had the Doudevilles on either side of him.

"Geneviève?" whispered the prisoner.

"Saved. . . ."

"Where is she?"

"With her grandmother."

"Mrs. Kesselbach?"

"In Paris, at the Bristol."

"Suzanne?"

"Disappeared."

"Steinweg?"

"Released."

"What has he told you?"

"Nothing. Won't make any revelations except to you."

"Why?"

"We told him he owed his release to you."

"Newspapers good this morning?"

"Excellent."

"Good. If you want to write to me, here are my instructions."

They had reached the inner corridor on the first floor and Lupin slipped a pellet of paper into the hand of one of the brothers.

M. Formerie uttered a delicious phrase when Lupin entered his room accompanied by the deputy-chief:

"Ah, there you are! I knew we should lay hands on you some day or other!"

"So did I, Monsieur le Juge d'Instruction," said Lupin, "and I am glad that you have been marked out by fate to do justice to the honest man that I am."

"He's getting at me," thought M. Formerie. And, in the same ironical and serious tone as Lupin, he retorted, "The honest man that you are, sir, will be asked what he has to say about three hundred and forty-four separate cases of larceny, burglary, swindling and forgery, blackmail, receiving and so on. Three hundred and forty-four!"

"What! Is that all?" cried Lupin. "I really feel quite ashamed."

"Don't distress yourself! I shall discover more. But let us proceed in order. Arsène Lupin, in spite of all our inquiries, we have no definite information as to your real name."

"How odd! No more have I!"

"We are not even in a position to declare that you are the same Arsène Lupin who was confined in the Santé a few years back, and from there made his first escape."

"'His first escape' is good, and does you credit."

"It so happens, in fact," continued M. Formerie, "that the Arsène Lupin card in the measuring department gives a description of Arsène Lupin which differs at all points from your real description."

"How more and more odd!"

"Different marks, different measurements, different finger-prints. . . . The two photographs even are quite unlike. I will therefore ask you to satisfy us as to your exact identity."

"That's just what I was going to ask you. I have lived under so many distinct names that I have ended by forgetting my own. I don't know where I am."

"So I must enter a refusal to answer?"

"An inability."

"Is this a thought-out plan? Am I to expect the same silence in reply to all my questions?"

"Very nearly."

"And why?"

Lupin struck a solemn attitude and said:

"M. le Juge d'Instruction, my life belongs to history. You have only to turn over the annals of the past fifteen years and your curiosity will be satisfied. So much for my part. As to the rest, it does not concern me: it is an affair between you and the murderers at the Palace Hotel."

"Arsène Lupin, the honest man that you are will have to-day to explain the murder of Master Altenheim."

"Hullo, this is new! Is the idea yours, Monsieur le Juge d'Instruction?"

"Exactly."

"Very clever! Upon my word, M. Formerie, you're getting on!"

"The position in which you were captured leaves no doubt."

"None at all; only, I will venture to ask you this: what sort of wound did Altenheim die of?"

"Of a wound in the throat caused by a knife."

"And where is the knife?"

"It has not been found."

"How could it not have been found, if I had been the assassin, considering that I was captured beside the very man whom I am supposed to have killed?"

"Who killed him, according to you?"

"The same man that killed Mr. Kesselbach, Chapman, and Beudot. The nature of the wound is a sufficient proof."

"How did he get away?"

"Through a trap-door, which you will discover in the room where the tragedy took place."

M. Formerie assumed an air of slyness:

"And how was it that you did not follow that useful example?"

"I tried to follow it. But the outlet was blocked by a door which I could not open. It was during this attempt that 'the other one' came back to the room and killed his accomplice for fear of the revelations which he would have been sure to make. At the same time, he hid in a cupboard, where it was subsequently found, the parcel of clothes which I had prepared."

"What were those clothes for?"

"To disguise myself. When I went to the Glycines my plan was this: to hand Altenheim over to the police, to suppress my own identity as Prince Sernine and to reappear under the features. . . ."

"Of M. Lenormand, I suppose?"

"Exactly."

"No."

"What!"

M. Formerie gave a knowing smile and wagged his forefinger from left to right and right to left:

"No," he repeated.

"What do you mean by 'no'?"

"That story about M. Lenormand. . . ."

"Well?"

"Will do for the public, my friend. But you won't make M. Formerie swallow that Lupin and Lenormand were one and the same man." He burst out laughing. "Lupin, chief of the detective-service! No, anything you like, but not that! . . . There are limits. . . . I am an easy-going fellow. . . . I'll believe anything . . . but still. . . . Come, between ourselves, what was the reason of this fresh hoax? . . . I confess I can't see . . ."

Lupin looked at him in astonishment. In spite of all that he knew of M. Formerie, he could not conceive such a degree of infatuation and blindness. There was at that moment only one person in the world who refused to believe in Prince Sernine's double personality; and that was M. Formerie! . . .

Lupin turned to the deputy-chief, who stood listening open-mouthed:

"My dear Weber, I fear your promotion is not so certain as I thought. For, you see, if M. Lenormand is not myself, then he exists . . . and, if he exists, I have no doubt that M. Formerie, with all his acumen, will end by discovering him . . . in which case . . ."

"We shall discover him all right, M. Lupin," cried the examining-magistrate. "I'll undertake that, and I tell you that, when you and he are confronted, we shall see some fun." He chuckled and drummed with his fingers on the table. "How amusing! Oh, one's never bored when you're there, that I'll say for you! So you're M. Lenormand, and it's you who arrested your accomplice Marco!"

"Just so! Wasn't it my duty to please the prime minister and save the cabinet? The fact is historical."

M. Formerie held his sides:

"Oh, I shall die of laughing, I know I shall! Lord, what a joke! That answer will travel round the world. So, according to your theory, it was with you that I made the first enquiries at the Palace Hotel after the murder of Mr. Kesselbach? . . ."

"Surely it was with me that you investigated the case of the stolen coronet when I was Duc de Chamerace," retorted Lupin, in a sarcastic voice.

M. Formerie gave a start. All his merriment was dispelled by that odious recollection. Turning suddenly grave, he asked:

"So you persist in that absurd theory?"

"I must, because it is the truth. It would be easy for you to take a steamer to Cochin-China and to find at Saigon the proofs of the death of the real M. Lenormand, the worthy man whom I replaced and whose death-certificate I can show you."

"Humbug!"

"Upon my word, Monsieur le Juge d'Instruction, I don't care one way or the other. If it annoys you that I should be M. Lenormand, don't let's talk about it. We won't talk about myself; we won't talk about anything at all, if you prefer. Besides, of what use can it be to you? The Kesselbach case is such a tangled affair that I myself don't know where I stand. There's only one man who might help you. I have not succeeded in discovering him. And I don't think that you . . ."

"What's the man's name?"

"He's an old man, a German called Steinweg. . . . But, of course, you've heard about him, Weber, and the way in which he was carried off in the middle of the Palais de Justice?"

M. Formerie threw an inquiring glance at the deputy-chief. M. Weber said:

"I undertake to bring that person to you, Monsieur le Juge d'Instruction."

"So that's done," said M. Formerie, rising from his chair. "As you see, Lupin, this was merely a formal examination to bring the two duelists together. Now that we have crossed swords, all that we need is the necessary witness of our fencing-match, your counsel."

"Tut! Is it indispensable?"

"Indispensable."

"Employ counsel in view of such an unlikely trial?"

"You must."

"In that case, I'll choose Maître Quimbel."

"The president of the corporation of the bar. You are wise, you will be well defended."

The first sitting was over. M. Weber led the prisoner away.

As he went down the stairs of the "mouse-trap," between the two Doudevilles, Lupin said, in short, imperative sentences:

"Watch Steinweg. . . . Don't let him speak to anybody. . . . Be there to-morrow. . . . I'll give you some letters . . . one for you . . . important."

Downstairs, he walked up to the municipal guards surrounding the taxi-cab:

"Home, boys," he exclaimed, "and quick about it! I have an appointment with myself for two o'clock precisely."

There were no incidents during the drive. On returning to his cell, Lupin wrote a long letter, full of detailed instructions, to the brothers Doudeville and, two other letters.

One was for Geneviève:

"Geneviève, you now know who I am and you will understand why I concealed from you the name of him who twice carried you away in his arms when you were a little girl.

"Geneviève, I was your mother's friend, a distant friend, of whose double life she knew nothing, but upon whom she thought that she could rely. And that is why, before dying, she wrote me a few lines asking me to watch over you.

"Unworthy as I am of your esteem, Geneviève, I shall continue faithful to that trust. Do not drive me from your heart entirely.

"Arsène Lupin."

The other letter was addressed to Dolores Kesselbach:

"Prince Sernine was led to seek Mrs. Kesselbach's acquaintance by motives of self-interest alone. But a great longing to devote himself to her was the cause of his continuing it.

"Now that Prince Sernine has become merely Arsène Lupin, he begs Mrs. Kesselbach not to deprive him of the right of protecting her, at a distance and as a man protects one whom he will never see again."

There were some envelopes on the table. He took up one and took up a second; then, when he took up the third, he noticed a sheet of white paper, the presence of which surprised him and which had words stuck upon it, evidently cut out of a newspaper. He read:

"You have failed in your fight with the baron. Give up interesting yourself in the case, and I will not oppose your escape.

"L. M."

Once more, Lupin had that sense of repulsion and terror with which this nameless and fabulous being always inspired him, a sense of disgust which one feels at touching a venomous animal, a reptile:

"He again," he said. "Even here!"

That also scared him, the sudden vision which he at times received of this hostile power, a power as great as his own and disposing of formidable means, the extent of which he himself was unable to realize.

He at once suspected his warder. But how had it been possible to corrupt that hard-featured, stern-eyed man?

"Well, so much the better, after all!" he cried. "I have never had to do except with dullards. . . . In order to fight myself, I had to chuck myself into the command of the detective-service. . . . This time, I have some one to deal with! . . . Here's a man who puts me in his pocket . . . by sleight of hand, one might say. . . . If I succeed, from my prison cell, in avoiding his blows and smashing him, in seeing old Steinweg and dragging his confession from him, in setting the Kesselbach case on its legs and turning the whole of it into cash, in defending Mrs. Kesselbach and winning fortune and happiness for Geneviève . . . well, then Lupin will be Lupin still! . . ."

Eleven days passed. On the twelfth day, Lupin woke very early and exclaimed:

"Let me see, if my calculations are correct and if the gods are on my side, there will be some news to-day. I have had four interviews with Formerie. The fellow must be worked up to the right point now. And the Doudevilles, on their side, must have been busy. . . . We shall have some fun!"

He flung out his fists to right and left, brought them back to his chest, then flung them out again and brought them back again.

This movement, which executed thirty times in succession, was followed by a bending of his body backwards and forwards. Next came an alternate lifting of the legs and then an alternate swinging of the arms.

The whole performance occupied a quarter of an hour, the quarter of an hour which he devoted every morning to Swedish exercises to keep his muscles in condition.

Then he sat down to his table, took up some sheets of white paper, which were arranged in numbered packets, and, folding one of them, made it into an envelope, a work which he continued to do with a series of successive sheets. It was the task which he had accepted and which he forced himself to do daily, the prisoners having the right to choose the labor which they preferred: sticking envelopes, making paper fans, metal purses, and so on. . . .

And, in this way, while occupying his hands with an automatic exercise and keeping his muscles supple with mechanical bendings, Lupin was able to have his thoughts constantly fixed on his affairs. . . .

And his affairs were complicated enough, in all conscience!

There was one, for instance, which surpassed all the others in importance, and for which he had to employ all the resources of his genius. How was he to have a long, quiet conversation with old Steinweg? The necessity was immediate. In a few days, Steinweg would have recovered from his imprisonment, would receive interviews, might blab . . . to say nothing of the inevitable interference of the enemy, 'the other one.' And it was essential that Steinweg's secret, Pierre Leduc's secret, should be revealed to no one but Lupin. Once published, the secret lost all its value. . . .

The bolts grated, the key turned noisily in the lock.

"Ah, it's you, most excellent of jailers! Has the moment come for the last toilet? The hair-cut that precedes the great final cut of all?"

"Magistrate's examination," said the man, laconically.

Lupin walked through the corridors of the prison and was received by the municipal guards, who locked him into the prison-van.

He reached the Palais de Justice twenty minutes later. One of the Doudevilles was waiting near the stairs. As they went up, he said to Lupin:

"You'll be confronted to-day."

"Everything settled?"

"Yes."

"Weber?"

"Busy elsewhere."

Lupin walked into M. Formerie's room and at once recognized old Steinweg, sitting on a chair, looking ill and wretched. A municipal guard was standing behind him.

M. Formerie scrutinized the prisoner attentively, as though he hoped to draw important conclusions from his contemplation of him, and said:

"You know who this gentleman is?"

"Why, Steinweg, of course! . . ."

"Yes, thanks to the active inquiries of M. Weber and of his two officers, the brothers Doudeville, we have found Mr. Steinweg, who, according to you, knows the ins and outs of the Kesselbach case, the name of the murderer and all the rest of it."

"I congratulate you, Monsieur le Juge d'Instruction. Your examination will go swimmingly."

"I think so. There is only one 'but': Mr. Steinweg refuses to reveal anything, except in your presence."

"Well, I never! How odd of him! Does Arsène Lupin inspire him with so much affection and esteem?"

"Not Arsène Lupin, but Prince Sernine, who, he says, saved his life, and M. Lenormand, with whom, he says, he began a conversation. . . ."

"At the time when I was chief of the detective-service," Lupin broke in. "So you consent to admit."

"Mr. Steinweg," said the magistrate, "do you recognize M. Lenormand?"

"No, but I know that Arsène Lupin and he are one."

"So you consent to speak?"

"Yes . . . but . . . we are not alone."

"How do you mean? There is only my clerk here . . . and the guard . . ."

"Monsieur le Juge d'Instruction, the secret which I am about to reveal is so important that you yourself would be sorry . . ."

"Guard, go outside, please," said M. Formerie. "Come back at once, if I call. Do you object to my clerk, Steinweg?"

"No, no . . . it might be better . . . but, however . . ."

"Then speak. For that matter, nothing that you reveal will be put down in black on white. One word more, though: I ask you for the last time, is it indispensable that the prisoner should be present at this interview?"

"Quite indispensable. You will see the reason for yourself."

He drew the chair up to the magistrate's desk, Lupin remained standing, near the clerk. And the old man, speaking in a loud voice, said:

"It is now ten years since a series of circumstances, which I need not enter into, made me acquainted with an extraordinary story in which two persons are concerned."

"Their names, please."

"I will give the names presently. For the moment, let me say that one of these persons occupies an exceptional position in France, and that the other, an Italian, or rather a Spaniard . . . yes, a Spaniard . . ."

A bound across the room, followed by two formidable blows of the fist. . . . Lupin's two arms had darted out to right and left, as though impelled by springs and his two fists, hard as cannon balls, caught the magistrate and his clerk on the jaw, just below the ear.

The magistrate and the clerk collapsed over their tables, in two lumps, without a moan.

"Well hit!" said Lupin. "That was a neat bit of work."

He went to the door and locked it softly. Then returning:

"Steinweg, have you the chloroform?"

"Are you quite sure that they have fainted?" asks the old man, trembling with fear.

"What do you think! But it will only last for three or four minutes. . . . And that is not long enough."

The German produced from his pocket a bottle and two pads of cotton-wool, ready prepared.

Lupin uncorked the bottle, poured a few drops of the chloroform on the two pads and held them to the noses of the magistrate and his clerk.

"Capital! We have ten minutes of peace and quiet before us. That will do, but let's make haste, all the same; and not a word too much, old man, do you hear?" He took him by the arm. "You see what I am able to do. Here we are, alone in the very heart of the Palais de Justice, because I wished it."

"Yes," said the old man.

"So you are going to tell me your secret?"

"Yes, I told it to Kesselbach, because he was rich and could turn it to better account than anybody I knew; but, prisoner and absolutely powerless though you are, I consider you a hundred times as strong as Kesselbach with his hundred millions."

"In that case, speak; and let us take things in their proper order. The name of the murderer?"

"That's impossible."

"How do you mean, impossible? I thought you knew it and were going to tell me everything!"

"Everything, but not that."

"But . . ."

"Later on."

"You're mad! Why?"

"I have no proofs. Later, when you are free, we will hunt together. Besides, what's the good? And then, really, I can't tell you."

"You're afraid of him?"

"Yes."

"Very well," said Lupin. "After all, that's not the most urgent matter. As to the rest, you've made up your mind to speak?"

"Without reserve."

"Well, then, answer. Who is Pierre Leduc?"

"Hermann IV., Grand Duke of Zweibrucken-Veldenz, Prince of Berncastel, Count of Fistingen, Lord of Wiesbaden and other places."

Lupin felt a thrill of joy at learning that his *protégé* was definitely not the son of a pork-butcher!

"The devil!" he muttered. "So we have a handle to our name! . . . As far as I remember, the Grand-duchy of Zweibrucken-Veldenz is in Prussia?"

"Yes, on the Moselle. The house of Veldenz is a branch of the Palatine house of Zweibrucken. The grand-duchy was occupied by the French after the peace of Luneville and formed part of the department of Mont-Tonnerre. In 1814, it was restored in favor of Hermann I., the great grandfather of Pierre Leduc. His son, Hermann II., spent a riotous youth, ruined himself, squandered the finances of his country and made himself impossible to his subjects, who ended by partly burning the old castle at Veldenz and driving their sovereign out of his dominions. The grand-duchy was then administered and governed by three regents, in the name of Hermann II., who, by a curious anomaly, did not abdicate, but retained his title as reigning grand-duke. He lived, rather short of cash, in Berlin; later, he fought in the French war, by the side of Bismarck, of whom he was a friend. He was killed by a shell at the siege of Paris and, in dying, entrusted Bismarck with the charge of his son Hermann, that is, Hermann III."

"The father, therefore, of our Leduc," said Lupin.

"Yes. The chancellor took a liking to Hermann III., and used often to employ him as a secret envoy to persons of distinction abroad. At the fall of his patron Hermann III., left Berlin, travelled about and returned and settled in Dresden. When Bismarck died, Hermann III., was there. He himself died two years later. These are public facts, known to everybody in Germany; and that is the story of the three Hermanns, Grand-dukes of Zweibrucken-Veldenz in the nineteenth century."

"But the fourth, Hermann IV., the one in whom we are interested?"

"We will speak of him presently. Let us now pass on to unknown facts."

"Facts known to you alone," said Lupin.

"To me alone and to a few others."

"How do you mean, a few others? Hasn't the secret been kept?"

"Yes, yes, the secret has been well kept by all who know it. Have no fear; it is very much to their interest, I assure you, not to divulge it."

"Then how do you know it?"

"Through an old servant and private secretary of the Grand-duke Hermann, the last of the name. This servant, who died in my arms in South Africa, began by confiding to me that his master was secretly married and had left a son behind him. Then he told me the great secret."

"The one which you afterwards revealed to Kesselbach."

"Yes."

"One second . . . Will you excuse me? . . ."

Lupin bent over M. Formerie, satisfied himself that all was well and the heart beating normally, and said:

"Go on."

Steinweg resumed:

"On the evening of the day on which Bismarck died, the Grand-duke Hermann III. and his faithful manservant—my South African friend—took a train which brought them to Munich in time to catch the express for Vienna. From Vienna, they went to Constantinople, then to Cairo, then to Naples, then to Tunis, then to Spain, then to Paris, then to London, to St. Petersburg, to Warsaw . . . and in none of these towns did they stop. They took a cab, had their two bags put on the top, rushed through the streets, hurried to another station or to the landing-stage, and once more took the train or the steamer."

"In short, they were being followed and were trying to put their pursuers off the scent," Arsène Lupin concluded.

"One evening, they left the city of Treves, dressed in workmen's caps and linen jackets, each with a bundle slung over his shoulder at the end of a stick. They covered on foot the twenty-two miles to Veldenz, where the old Castle of Zweibrucken stands, or rather the ruins of the old castle."

"No descriptions, please."

"All day long, they remained hidden in a neighboring forest. At night, they went up to the old walls. Hermann ordered his servant to wait for him and himself scaled the wall at a breach known as the Wolf's Gap. He returned in an hour's time. In the following week, after more peregrinations, he went back home to Dresden. The expedition was over."

"And what was the object of the expedition?"

"The grand-duke never breathed a word about it to his servant. But certain particulars and the coincidence of facts that ensued enabled the man to build up the truth, at least, in part."

"Quick, Steinweg, time is running short now: and I am eager to know."

"A fortnight after the expedition, Count von Waldemar, an officer in the Emperor's body-guard and one of his personal friends, called on the grand-duke, accompanied by six men. He was there all day, locked up with the grand-duke in his study. There were repeated sounds of altercations, of violent disputes. One phrase even was overheard by the servant, who was passing through the garden, under the windows: 'Those papers were handed to you; His imperial Majesty is sure of it. If you refuse to give them to me of your own free will . . .' The rest of the sentence, the meaning of the threat and, for that matter, the whole scene can be easily guessed by what followed; Hermann's house was ransacked from top to bottom."

"But that is against the law."

"It would have been against the law if the grand-duke had objected; but he himself accompanied the count in his search."

"And what were they looking for? The chancellor's memoirs?"

"Something better than that. They were looking for a parcel of secret documents which were known to exist, owing to indiscretions that had been committed, and which were known for certain to have been entrusted to the Grand-duke Hermann's keeping."

Lupin muttered, excitedly:

"Secret documents . . . and very important ones, no doubt?"

"Of the highest importance. The publication of those papers would lead to results which it would be impossible to foresee, not only from the point of view of home politics, but also from that of Germany's relations with the foreign powers."

"Oh!" said Lupin, throbbing with emotion. "Oh, can it be possible? What proof have you?"

"What proof? The evidence of the grand-duke's wife, the confidences which she made to the servant after her husband's death."

"Yes . . . yes . . ." stammered Lupin. "We have the evidence of the grand-duke himself."

"Better still," said Steinweg.

"What?"

"A document, a document written in his own hand, signed by him and containing . . ."

"Containing what?"

"A list of the secret papers confided to his charge."

"Tell me, in two words. . . ."

"In two words? That can't be done. The document is a very long one, scattered all over with annotations and remarks which are sometimes impossible to understand. Let me mention just two titles which obviously refer to two bundles of secret papers: *Original letters of the Crown Prince to Bismarck* is one. The dates show that these letters were written during the three months of the reign of Frederick III. To picture what the letters may contain, you have only to think of the Emperor Frederick's illness, his quarrels with his son . . ."

"Yes, yes, I know. . . . And the other title?"

"*Photographs of the letters of Frederick III., and the Empress Victoria to the Queen of England.*"

"Do you mean to say that that's there?" asked Lupin, in a choking voice.

"Listen to the grand-duke's notes: *Text of the treaty with Great Britain and France*. And these rather obscure words: 'Alsace-Lorraine. . . . Colonies. . . . Limitation of naval armaments. . . .'"

"It says that?" blurted Lupin. "And you call that obscure? . . . Why, the words are dazzling with light! . . . Oh, can it be possible? . . . And what next, what next?"

As he spoke there was a noise at the door. Some one was knocking.

"You can't come in," said Lupin. "I am busy. . . . Go on, Steinweg."

"But . . ." said the old man, in a great state of alarm.

The door was shaken violently and Lupin recognized Weber's voice. He shouted:

"A little patience, Weber. I shall have done in five minutes."

He gripped the old man's arm and, in a tone of command:

"Be easy and go on with your story. So, according to you, the expedition of the grand duke and his servant to Veldenz Castle had no other object than to hide those papers?"

"There can be no question about that."

"Very well. But the grand-duke may have taken them away since."

"No, he did not leave Dresden until his death."

"But the grand-duke's enemies, the men who had everything to gain by recovering them and destroying them: can't they have tried to find out where the papers were?"

"They have tried."

"How do you know?"

"You can understand that I did not remain inactive and that my first care, after receiving those revelations, was to go to Veldenz and make inquiries for myself in the neighboring villages. Well, I learnt that, on two separate occasions, the castle was invaded by a dozen men, who came from Berlin furnished with credentials to the regents."

"Well?"

"Well, they found nothing, for, since that time, the castle has been found closed to the public."

"But what prevents anybody from getting in?"

"A garrison of fifty soldiers, who keep watch day and night."

"Soldiers of the grand-duchy?"

"No, soldiers drafted from the Emperor's own body-guard."

The din in the passage increased:

"Open the door!" a voice cried. "I order you to open the door!"

"I can't, Weber, old chap; the lock has stuck. If you take my advice, you had better cut the door all round the lock."

"Open the door!"

"And what about the fate of Europe, which we are discussing?"

He turned to the old man:

"So you were not able to enter the castle?"

"No."

"But you are persuaded that the papers in question are hidden there?"

"Look here, haven't I given you proofs enough? Aren't you convinced?"

"Yes, yes," muttered Lupin, "that's where they are hidden . . . there's no doubt about it . . . that's where they are hidden. . . ."

He seemed to see the castle. He seemed to conjure up the mysterious hiding-place. And the vision of an inexhaustible treasure, the dream of chests filled with riches and precious stones could not have excited him more than the idea of those few scraps of paper watched over by the Kaiser's guards. What a wonderful conquest to embark upon! And how worthy of his powers! And what a proof of perspicacity and intuition he had once more given by throwing himself at a venture upon that unknown track!

Outside, the men were "working" at the lock.

Lupin asked of old Steinweg:

"What did the grand-duke die of?"

"An attack of pleurisy, which carried him off in a few days. He hardly recovered consciousness before the end; and the horrible thing appears to have been that he was seen to make violent efforts, between his fits of delirium, to collect his thoughts and utter connected words. From time to time, he called his wife, looked at her in a desperate way and vainly moved his lips."

"In a word, he spoke?" said Lupin, cutting him short, for the "working" at the lock was beginning to make him anxious.

"No, he did not speak. But, in a comparatively lucid moment, he summoned up the energy to make some marks on a piece of paper which his wife gave him."

"Well, those marks . . . ?"

"They were illegible, for the most part."

"For the most part? But the others?" asked Lupin, greedily. "The others?"

"There were, first, three perfectly distinct figures: an 8, a 1, and a 3. . . ."

"Yes, 813, I know . . . and next?"

"And next, there were some letters . . . several letters, of which all that can be made out for certain are a group of three followed, immediately after, by a group of two letters."

"'APO ON,' is that it?"

"Oh, so you know! . . ."

The lock was yielding; almost all the screws had been taken out. Lupin, suddenly alarmed at the thought of being interrupted, asked:

"So that this incomplete word 'APO ON' and the number 813 are the formulas which the grand-duke bequeathed to his wife and son to enable them to find the secret papers?"

"Yes."

"What became of the grand-duke's wife?"

"She died soon after her husband, of grief, one might say."

"And was the child looked after by the family?"

"What family? The grand-duke had no brothers or sisters. Moreover, he was only morganatically and secretly married. No, the child was taken away by Hermann's old man-servant, who brought him up under the name of Pierre Leduc. He was a bad type of boy, self-willed, capricious and troublesome. One day, he went off and was never seen again."

"Did he know the secret of his birth?"

"Yes; and he was shown the sheet of paper on which Hermann III. had written the letters and figures."

"And after that this revelation was made to no one but yourself?"

"That's all."

"And you confided only in Mr. Kesselbach?"

"Yes. But, out of prudence, while showing him the sheet of letters and figures and the list of which I spoke to you, I kept both those documents in my own possession. Events have proved that I was right."

Lupin was now clinging to the door with both hands:

"Weber," he roared, "you're very indiscreet! I shall report you! . . . Steinweg, have you those documents?"

"Yes."

"Are they in a safe place?"

"Absolutely."

"In Paris?"

"No."

"So much the better. Don't forget that your life is in danger and that you have people after you."

"I know. The least false step and I am done for."

"Exactly. So take your precautions, throw the enemy off the scent, go and fetch your papers and await my instructions. The thing is cut and dried. In a month, at latest, we will go to Veldenz Castle together."

"Suppose I'm in prison?"

"I will take you out."

"Can you?"

"The very day after I come out myself. No, I'm wrong: the same evening . . . an hour later."

"You have the means?"

"Since the last ten minutes, an infallible means. You have nothing more to say to me?"

"No."

"Then I'll open the door."

He pulled back the door, and bowing to M. Weber:

"My poor old Weber, I don't know what excuse to make . . ."

He did not finish his sentence. The sudden inrush of the deputy-chief and three policeman left him no time.

M. Weber was white with rage and indignation. The sight of the two men lying outstretched quite unsettled him.

"Dead!" he exclaimed.

"Not a bit of it, not a bit of it," chuckled Lupin, "only asleep! Formerie was tired out . . . so I allowed him a few moments' rest."

"Enough of this humbug!" shouted M. Weber. And, turning to the policemen, "Take him back to the Santé. And keep your eyes open, damn it! As for this visitor . . ."

Lupin learnt nothing more as to Weber's intentions with regard to old Steinweg. A crowd of municipal guards and police constables hustled him down to the prison-van.

On the stairs Doudeville whispered:

"Weber had a line to warn him. It told him to mind the confrontation and to be on his guard with Steinweg. The note was signed 'L. M.'"

But Lupin hardly bothered his head about all this. What did he care for the murderer's hatred or old Steinweg's fate? He possessed Rudolf Kesselbach's secret!

X. LUPIN'S GREAT SCHEME

Contrary to his expectations, Lupin had no sort of annoyance to undergo in consequence of his assault on M. Formerie.

The examining-magistrate came to the Santé in person, two days later, and told him, with some embarrassment and with an affectation of kindness, that he did not intend to pursue the matter further.

"Nor I, either," retorted Lupin.

"What do you mean?"

"Well, I mean that I shall send no communication to the press about this particular matter nor do anything that might expose you to ridicule, Monsieur le Juge d'Instruction. The scandal shall not be made public, I promise. That is what you want, is it not?"

M. Formerie blushed and, without replying, continued:

"Only, henceforth, your examinations will take place here."

"It's quite right that the law should put itself out for Lupin!" said that gentleman.

The announcement of this decision, which interrupted his almost daily meetings with the Doudevilles, did not disturb Lupin. He had taken his precautions from the first day, by giving the Doudevilles all the necessary instructions and, now that the preparations were nearly completed, reckoned upon being able to turn old Steinweg's confidences to the best account without delay and to obtain his liberty by one of the most extraordinary and ingenious schemes that had ever entered his brain.

His method of correspondence was a simple one; and he had devised it at once. Every morning he was supplied with sheets of paper in numbered packets. He made these into envelopes; and, every evening, the envelopes, duly folded and gummed, were fetched away. Now Lupin, noticing that his packet always bore the same number, had drawn the inference that the distribution of the numbered packets was always affected in the same order among the prisoners who had chosen that particular kind of work. Experience showed that he was right.

It only remained for the Doudevilles to bribe one of the employees of the private firm entrusted with the supply and dispatch of the envelopes. This was easily done; and, thenceforward, Lupin, sure of success, had only to wait quietly until the sign agreed upon between him and his friends appeared upon the top sheet of the packet.

On the sixth day, he gave an exclamation of delight:

"At last!" he said.

He took a tiny bottle from a hiding-place, uncorked it, moistened the tip of his forefinger with the liquid which it contained and passed his finger over the third sheet in the packet.

In a moment, strokes appeared, then letters, then words and sentences.

He read:

"All well. Steinweg free. Hiding in country. Geneviève Ernemont good health. Often goes Hôtel Bristol to see Mrs. Kesselbach, who is ill. Meets Pierre Leduc there every time. Answer by same means. No danger."

So communications were established with the outside. Once more, Lupin's efforts were crowned with success. All that he had to do now was to execute his plan and lead the press campaign which he had prepared in the peaceful solitude of his prison.

Three days later, these few lines appeared in the *Grand Journal*:

"Quite apart from Prince Bismarck's *Memoirs*, which, according to well-informed people, contain merely the official history of the events in which the great chancellor was concerned, there exists a series of confidential letters of no little interest.

"These letters have been recently discovered. We hear, on good authority, that they will be published almost immediately."

My readers will remember the noise which these mysterious sentences made throughout the civilized world, the comments in which people indulged, the suggestions put forward and, in particular, the controversy that followed in the German press. Who had inspired those lines? What were the letters in question? Who had written them to the chancellor or who had received them from him? Was it an act of posthumous revenge? Or was it an indiscretion committed by one of Bismarck's correspondents?

A second note settled public opinion as to certain points, but, at the same time, worked it up to a strange pitch of excitement. It ran as follows:

"*To the Editor of the* Grand Journal,

"SANTÉ PALACE,

"Cell 14, Second Division.

"SIR,

"You inserted in your issue of Tuesday last a paragraph based upon a few words which I let fall, the other evening, in the course of a lecture, which I was delivering at the Santé on foreign politics. Your correspondent's paragraph, although accurate in all essential particulars, requires a slight correction. The letters exist, as stated, and it is impossible to deny their exceptional importance, seeing that, for ten years, they have been the object of an uninterrupted search on the part of the government interested. But nobody knows where they are hidden and nobody knows a single word of what they contain.

"The public, I am convinced, will bear me no ill-will if I keep it waiting for some time before satisfying its legitimate curiosity. Apart from the fact that I am not in possession of all the elements necessary for the pursuit of the truth, my present occupation does not allow me to devote so much time as I could wish to this matter.

"All that I can say for the moment is that the letters were entrusted by the dying statesman to one of his most faithful friends and that this friend had eventually to suffer the serious consequences of his loyalty. Constant spying, domiciliary visits, nothing was spared him.

"I have given orders to two of the best agents of my secret police to take up this scent from the start in a position to get to the bottom of this exciting mystery.

"I have the honor to be Sir,

"Your obedient servant,

"ARSÈNE LUPIN."

So it was Arsène Lupin who was conducting the case! It was he who, from his prison cell, was stage-managing the comedy or the tragedy announced in the first note. What luck! Everybody was delighted. With an artist like Lupin, the spectacle could not fail to be both picturesque and startling.

Three days later the *Grand Journal* contained the following letter from Arsène Lupin:

"The name of the devoted friend to whom I referred has been imparted to me. It was the Grand-Duke Hermann III., reigning (although dispossessed) sovereign of the Grand-duchy of Zweibrucken-Veldenz and a confidant of Prince Bismarck, whose entire friendship he enjoyed.

"A thorough search was made of his house by Count von W——, at the head of twelve men. The result of this search was purely negative, but the grand-duke was nevertheless proved to be in possession of the papers.

"Where had he hidden them? This was a problem which probably nobody in the world would be able to solve at the present moment.

"I must ask for twenty-four hours in which to solve it.

"ARSÈNE LUPIN."

And, twenty-four hours later, the promised note appeared:

"The famous letters are hidden in the feudal castle of Veldenz, the capital of the Grand-duchy of Zweibrucken. The castle was partly destroyed in the course of the nineteenth century.

"Where exactly are they hidden? And what are the letters precisely? These are the two problems which I am now engaged in unravelling; and I shall publish the solution in four days' time.

"ARSÈNE LUPIN."

On the day stated, men scrambled to obtain copies of the *Grand Journal*. To the general disappointment, the promised information was not given. The same silence followed on the next day and the day after.

What had happened?

It leaked out through an indiscretion at the Prefecture of Police. The governor of the Santé, it appeared, had been warned that Lupin was communicating with his accomplices by means of the packets of envelopes which he made. Nothing had been discovered; but it was thought best, in any case, to forbid all work to the insufferable prisoner.

To this the insufferable prisoner replied:

"As I have nothing to do now, I may as well attend to my trial. Please let my counsel, Maître Quimbel, know."

It was true. Lupin, who, hitherto, had refused to hold any intercourse with Maître Quimbel, now consented to see him and to prepare his defence.

On the next day Maître Quimbel, in cheery tones, asked for Lupin to be brought to the barristers' room. He was an elderly man, wearing a pair of very powerful spectacles, which made his eyes seem enormous. He put his hat on the table, spread out his brief-case and at once began to put a series of questions which he had carefully prepared.

Lupin replied with extreme readiness and even volunteered a host of particulars, which Maître Quimbel took down, as he spoke, on slips pinned one to the other.

"And so you say," continued the barrister, with his head over his papers, "that, at that time . . ."

"I say that, at that time . . ." Lupin answered.

Little by little, with a series of natural and hardly perceptible movements, he leant elbows on the table. He gradually lowered his arms, slipped his hand under Maître Quimbel's hat, put his finger into the leather band and took out one of those strips of paper, folded lengthwise, which the hatter inserts between the leather and the lining when the hat is a trifle too large.

He unfolded the paper. It was a message from Doudeville, written in a cipher agreed upon beforehand:

"I am engaged as indoor servant at Maître Quimbel's. You can answer by the same means without fear.

"It was L. M., the murderer, who gave away the envelope trick. A good thing that you foresaw this move!"

Hereupon followed a minute report of all the facts and comments caused by Lupin's revelations.

Lupin took from his pocket a similar strip of paper containing his instructions, quietly substituted it in the place of the other and drew his hand back again. The trick was played.

And Lupin's correspondence with the *Grand Journal* was resumed without further delay.

"I apologize to the public for not keeping my promise. The postal arrangements at the Santé Palace are woefully inadequate.

"However, we are near the end. I have in hand all the documents that establish the truth upon an indisputable basis. I shall not publish them for the moment. Nevertheless, I will say this: among the letters are some that were addressed to the chancellor by one who, at that time, declared himself his disciple and his admirer and who was destined, several years after, to rid himself of that irksome tutor and to govern alone.

"I trust that I make myself sufficiently clear."

And, on the next day:

"The letters were written during the late Emperor's illness. I need hardly add more to prove their importance."

Four days of silence, and then this final note, which caused a stir that has not yet been forgotten:

"My investigation is finished. I now know everything.

"By dint of reflection, I have guessed the secret of the hiding-place.

"My friends are going to Veldenz and, in spite of every obstacle, will enter the castle by a way which I am pointing out to them.

"The newspapers will then publish photographs of the letters, of which I already know the tenor; but I prefer to reproduce the whole text.

"This certain, inevitable publication will take place in a fortnight from to-day precisely, on the 22nd of August next.

"Between this and then I will keep silence . . . and wait."

The communications to the *Grand Journal* did, in fact, stop for a time, but Lupin never ceased corresponding with his friends, "*via* the hat," as they said among themselves. It was so simple! There was no danger. Who could ever suspect that Maître Quimbel's hat served Lupin as a letter-box?

Every two or three mornings, whenever he called, in fact, the celebrated advocate faithfully brought his client's letters: letters from Paris, letters from the country, letters from Germany; all reduced and condensed by Doudeville into a brief form and cipher language. And, an hour later, Maître Quimbel solemnly walked away, carrying Lupin's orders.

Now, one day, the governor of the Santé received a telephone message, signed, "L. M.," informing him that Maître Quimbel was, in all probability, serving Lupin as his unwitting postman and that it would be advisable to keep an eye upon the worthy man's visits. The governor told Maître Quimbel, who thereupon resolved to bring his junior with him.

So, once again, in spite of all Lupin's efforts, in spite of his fertile powers of invention, in spite of the marvels of ingenuity which he renewed after each defeat, once again Lupin found himself cut off from communication with the outside world by the infernal genius of his formidable adversary. And he found himself thus cut off at the most critical moment, at the solemn minute when, from his cell, he was playing his last trump-card against the coalesced forces that were overwhelming him so terribly.

On the 13th of August, as he sat facing the two counsels, his attention was attracted by a newspaper in which some of Maître Quimbel's papers were wrapped up.

He saw a heading in very large type

"813"

The sub-headings were:

"A FRESH MURDER

"THE EXCITEMENT IN GERMANY

"HAS THE SECRET OF THE 'APOON' BEEN DISCOVERED?"

Lupin turned pale with anguish. Below he read the words:

"Two sensational telegrams reach us at the moment of going to press.

"The body of an old man has been found near Augsburg, with his throat cut with a knife. The police have succeeded in identifying the victim: it is Steinweg, the man mentioned in the Kesselbach case.

"On the other hand, a correspondent telegraphs that the famous English detective, Holmlock Shears, has been hurriedly summoned to Cologne. He will there meet the Emperor; and they will both proceed to Veldenz Castle.

"Holmlock Shears is said to have undertaken to discover the secret of the 'APOON.'

"If he succeeds, it will mean the pitiful failure of the incomprehensible campaign which Arsène Lupin has been conducting for the past month in so strange a fashion."

Perhaps public curiosity was never so much stirred as by the duel announced to take place between Shears and Lupin, an invisible duel in the circumstances, an anonymous duel, one might say, in which everything would happen in the dark, in which people would be able to judge only by the final results, and yet an impressive duel, because of all the scandal that circled around the adventure and because of the stakes in dispute between the two irreconcilable enemies, now once more opposed to each other.

And it was a question not of small private interests, of insignificant burglaries, of trumpery individual passions, but of a matter of really world-wide importance, involving the politics of the three great western nations and capable of disturbing the peace of the world.

People waited anxiously; and no one knew exactly what he was waiting for. For, after all, if the detective came out victorious in the duel, if he found the letters, who would ever know? What proof would any one have of his triumph?

In the main, all hopes were centred on Lupin, on his well-known habit of calling the public to witness his acts. What was he going to do? How could he avert the frightful danger that threatened him? Was he even aware of it?

Those were the questions which men asked themselves.

Between the four walls of his cell, prisoner 14 asked himself pretty nearly the same questions; and he for his part, was not stimulated by idle curiosity, but by real uneasiness, by constant anxiety. He felt himself irrevocably alone, with impotent hands, an impotent will, an impotent brain. It availed him nothing that he was able, ingenious, fearless, heroic. The struggle was being carried on without him. His part was now finished. He had joined all the pieces and set all the springs of the great machine that was to produce, that was, in a manner of speaking, automatically to manufacture his liberty; and it was impossible for him to make a single movement to improve and supervise his handiwork.

At the date fixed, the machine would start working. Between now and then, a thousand adverse incidents might spring up, a thousand obstacles arise, without his having the means to combat those incidents or remove those obstacles.

Lupin spent the unhappiest hours of his life at that time. He doubted himself. He wondered whether his existence would be buried for good in the horror of a jail. Had he not made a mistake in his calculations? Was it not childish to believe that the event that was to set him free would happen on the appointed date?

"Madness!" he cried. "My argument is false. . . . How can I expect such a concurrence of circumstances? There will be some little fact that will destroy all . . . the inevitable grain of sand. . . ."

Steinweg's death and the disappearance of the documents which the old man was to make over to him did not trouble him greatly. The documents he could have done without in case of need; and, with the few words which Steinweg had told him, he was able, by dint of guess-work and his native genius, to reconstruct what the Emperor's letters contained and to draw up the plan of battle that would lead to victory. But he thought of Holmlock Shears, who was over there now, in the very centre of the battlefield, and who was seeking and who would find the letters, thus demolishing the edifice so patiently built up.

And he thought of "the other one," the implacable enemy, lurking round the prison, hidden in the prison, perhaps, who guessed his most secret plans even before they were hatched in the mystery of his thought.

The 17th of August! . . . The 18th of August! . . . The 19th! . . . Two more days. . . . Two centuries rather! Oh, the interminable minutes! . . .

Lupin, usually so calm, so entirely master of himself, so ingenious at providing matter for his own amusement, was feverish, exultant and depressed by turns, powerless against the enemy, mistrusting everything and everybody, morose.

The 20th of August! . . . .

He would have wished to act and he could not. Whatever he did, it was impossible for him to hasten the hour of the catastrophe. This catastrophe would take place or would not take place; but Lupin would not know for certain until the last hour of the last day was spent to the last minute. Then—and then alone—he would know of the definite failure of his scheme.

"The inevitable failure," he kept on repeating to himself. "Success depends upon circumstances far too subtle and can be obtained only by methods far too psychological. . . . There is no doubt that I am deceiving myself as to the value and the range of my weapons. . . . And yet . . ."

Hope returned to him. He weighed his chances. They suddenly seemed to him real and formidable. The fact was going to happen as he had foreseen it happening and for the very reasons which he had expected. It was inevitable. . . .

Yes, inevitable. Unless, indeed, Shears discovered the hiding-place. . . .

And again he thought of Shears; and again an immense sense of discouragement overwhelmed him.

The last day. . . .

He woke late, after a night of bad dreams.

He saw nobody that day, neither the examining magistrate nor his counsel.

The afternoon dragged along slowly and dismally, and the evening came, the murky evening of the cells. . . . He was in a fever. His heart beat in his chest like the clapper of a bell.

And the minutes passed, irretrievably. . . .

At nine o'clock, nothing. At ten o'clock, nothing.

With all his nerves tense as the string of a bow, he listened to the vague prison sounds, tried to catch through those inexorable walls all that might trickle in from the life outside.

Oh, how he would have liked to stay the march of time and to give destiny a little more leisure!

But what was the good? Was everything not finished? . . .

"Oh," he cried, "I am going mad! If all this were only over . . . that would be better. I can begin again, differently. . . . I shall try something else . . . but I can't go on like this, I can't go on. . . ."

He held his head in his hands, pressing it with all his might, locking himself within himself and concentrating his whole mind upon one subject, as though he wished to provoke, as though he wished to create the formidable, stupefying, inadmissible event to which he had attached his independence and his fortune:

"It must happen," he muttered, "it must; and it must, not because I wish it, but because it is logical. And it shall happen . . . it shall happen. . . ."

He beat his skull with his fists; and delirious words rose to his lips. . . .

The key grated in the lock. In his frenzy, he had not heard the sound of footsteps in the corridor; and now, suddenly, a ray of light penetrated into his cell and the door opened.

Three men entered.

Lupin had not a moment of surprise.

The unheard-of miracle was being worked; and this at once seemed to him natural and normal, in perfect agreement with truth and justice.

But a rush of pride flooded his whole being. At this minute he really received a clear sensation of his own strength and intelligence. . . .

"Shall I switch on the light?" asked one of the three men, in whom Lupin recognized the governor of the prison.

"No," replied the taller of his companions, speaking in a foreign accent. "This lantern will do."

"Shall I go?"

"Act according to your duty, sir," said the same individual.

"My instructions from the prefect of police are to comply entirely with your wishes."

"In that case, sir, it would be preferable that you should withdraw."

M. Borély went away, leaving the door half open, and remained outside, within call.

The visitor exchanged a few words with the one who had not yet spoken; and Lupin vainly tried to distinguish his features in the shade. He saw only two dark forms, clad in wide motoring-cloaks and wearing caps with the flaps lowered.

"Are you Arsène Lupin?" asked the man, turning the light of the lantern full on his face.

He smiled:

"Yes, I am the person known as Arsène Lupin, at present a prisoner in the Santé, cell 14, second division."

"Was it you," continued the visitor, "who published in the *Grand Journal* a series of more or less fanciful notes, in which there is a question of a so-called collection of letters . . . ?"

Lupin interrupted him.

"I beg your pardon, sir, but, before pursuing this conversation, the object of which, between ourselves, is none too clear to me, I should be much obliged if you would tell me to whom I have the honour of speaking."

"Absolutely unnecessary," replied the stranger.

"Absolutely essential," declared Lupin.

"Why?"

"For reasons of politeness, sir. You know my name and I do not know yours; this implies a disregard of good form which I cannot suffer."

The stranger lost patience:

"The mere fact that the governor of the prison brought us here shows . . ."

"That M. Borély does not know his manners," said Lupin. "M. Borély should have introduced us to each other. We are equals here, sir: it is no case of a superior and an inferior, of a prisoner and a visitor who condescends to come and see him. There are two men here; and one of those two men has a hat on his head, which he ought not to have."

"Now look here . . ."

"Take the lesson as you please, sir," said Lupin.

The stranger came closer to him and tried to speak.

"The hat first," said Lupin, "the hat. . . ."

"You shall listen to me!"

"No."

"Yes."

"No."

Matters were becoming virulent, stupidly. The second stranger, the one who had kept silent, placed his hand on his companion's shoulder and said, in German:

"Leave him to me."

"Why, it was understood . . ."

"Hush . . . and go away!"

"Leaving you alone?"

"Yes."

"But the door?"

"Shut it and walk away."

"But this man . . . you know who he is. . . . Arsène Lupin. . . ."

"Go away!"

The other went out, cursing under his breath.

"Pull the door!" cried the second visitor. "Harder than that. . . . Altogether! . . . That's right. . . ."

Then he turned, took the lantern and raised it slowly:

"Shall I tell you who I am?" he asked.

"No," replied Lupin.

"And why?"

"Because I know."

"Ah!"

"You are the visitor I was expecting."

"I?"

"Yes, Sire."

XI. CHARLEMAGNE

"Silence!" said the stranger, sharply. "Don't use that word."

"Then what shall I call Your . . ."

"Call me nothing."

They were both silent; and this moment of respite was not one of those which go before the struggle of two adversaries ready for the fray. The stranger strode to and fro with the air of a master accustomed to command and to be obeyed. Lupin stood motionless. He had abandoned his usual provocative attitude and his sarcastic smile. He waited, gravely and deferentially. But, down in the depths of his being, he revelled, eagerly, madly, in the marvellous situation in which he found himself placed: here, in his cell, he, a prisoner; he, the adventurer; he, the swindler, the burglar; he, Arsène Lupin . . . face to face with that demi-god of the modern world, that formidable entity, the heir of Cæsar and of Charlemagne.

He was intoxicated for a moment with the sense of his own power. The tears came to his eyes when he thought of his triumph. . . .

The stranger stood still.

And at once, with the very first sentence, they came to the immediate point:

"To-morrow is the 22nd of August. The letters are to be published to-morrow, are they not?"

"To-night, in two hours from now, my friends are to hand in to the *Grand Journal*, not the letters themselves, but an exact list of the letters, with the Grand-duke Hermann's annotations."

"That list shall not be handed in."

"It shall not be."

"You will give it to me."

"It shall be placed in the hands of Your . . . in your hands."

"Likewise, all the letters?"

"Likewise, all the letters."

"Without any of them being photographed?"

"Without any of them being photographed."

The stranger spoke in a very calm voice, containing not the least accent of entreaty nor the least inflection of authority. He neither ordered nor requested; he stated the inevitable actions of Arsène Lupin. Things would happen as he said. And they would happen, whatever Arsène Lupin's demands should be, at whatever price he might value the performance of those actions. The conditions were accepted beforehand.

"By Jove," said Lupin to himself, "that's jolly clever of him! If he leaves it to my generosity, I am a ruined man!"

The very way in which the conversation opened, the frankness of the words employed, the charm of voice and manner all pleased him infinitely.

He pulled himself together, lest he should relent and abandon all the advantages which he had conquered so fiercely.

And the stranger continued:

"Have you read the letters?"

"No."

"But some one you know has read them?"

"No."

"In that case . . ."

"I have the grand-duke's list and his notes. Moreover, I know the hiding-place where he put all his papers."

"Why did you not take them before this?"

"I did not know the secret of the hiding-place until I came here. My friends are on the way there now."

"The castle is guarded. It is occupied by two hundred of my most trusty men."

"Ten thousand would not be sufficient."

After a minute's reflection, the visitor asked:

"How do you know the secret?"

"I guessed it."

"But you had other elements of information which the papers did not publish?"

"No, none at all."

"And yet I had the castle searched for four days."

"Holmlock Shears looked in the wrong place."

"Ah!" said the stranger to himself. "It's an odd thing, an odd thing! . . ." And, to Lupin, "You are sure that your supposition is correct?"

"It is not a supposition: it is a certainty."

"So much the better," muttered the visitor. "There will be no rest until those papers cease to exist."

And, placing himself in front of Arsène Lupin:

"How much?"

"What?" said Lupin, taken aback.

"How much for the papers? How much do you ask to reveal the secret?"

He waited for Lupin to name a figure. He suggested one himself:

"Fifty thousand? . . . A hundred thousand?"

And, when Lupin did not reply, he said, with a little hesitation:

"More? Two hundred thousand? Very well! I agree."

Lupin smiled and, in a low voice, said:

"It is a handsome figure. But is it not likely that some sovereign, let us say, the King of England, would give as much as a million? In all sincerity?"

"I believe so."

"And that those letters are priceless to the Emperor, that they are worth two million quite as easily as two hundred thousand francs . . . three million as easily as two?"

"I think so."

"And, if necessary, the Emperor would give that three million francs?"

"Yes."

"Then it will not be difficult to come to an arrangement."

"On that basis?" cried the stranger, not without some alarm.

Lupin smiled again:

"On that basis, no. . . . I am not looking for money. I want something else, something that is worth more to me than any number of millions."

"What is that?"

"My liberty."

"What! Your liberty. . . . But I can do nothing. . . . That concerns your country . . . the law. . . . I have no power."

Lupin went up to him and, lowering his voice still more:

"You have every power, Sire. . . . My liberty is not such an exceptional event that they are likely to refuse you."

"Then I should have to ask for it?"

"Yes."

"Of whom?"

"Of Valenglay, the prime minister."

"But M. Valenglay himself can do no more than I."

"He can open the doors of this prison for me."

"It would cause a public outcry."

"When I say, open . . . half-open would be enough . . . We should counterfeit an escape. . . . The public so thoroughly expects it that it would not so much as ask for an explanation."

"Very well . . . but M. Valenglay will never consent. . . ."

"He will consent."

"Why?"

"Because you will express the wish."

"My wishes are not commands . . . to him!"

"No . . . but an opportunity of making himself agreeable to the Emperor by fulfilling them. And Valenglay is too shrewd a politician. . . ."

"Nonsense! Do you imagine that the French government will commit so illegal an act for the sole pleasure of making itself agreeable to me?"

"That pleasure will not be the sole one."

"What will be the other?"

"The pleasure of serving France by accepting the proposal which will accompany the request for my release."

"I am to make a proposal? I?"

"Yes, Sire."

"What proposal?"

"I do not know, but it seems to me that there is always a favorable ground on which to come to an understanding . . . there are possibilities of agreement. . . ."

The stranger looked at him, without grasping his meaning. Lupin leant forward and, as though seeking his words, as though putting an imaginary case, said:

"Let me suppose that two great countries are divided by some insignificant question . . . that they have different points of view on a matter of secondary importance . . . a colonial matter, for instance, in which their self-esteem is at stake rather than their interest. . . . Is it inconceivable that the ruler of one of those countries might come of his own accord to treat this matter in a new spirit of conciliation . . . and give the necessary instructions . . . so that . . ."

"So that I might leave Morocco to France?" said the stranger, with a burst of laughter.

The idea which Lupin was suggesting struck him as the most comical thing that he had ever heard; and he laughed heartily. The disparity was so great between the object aimed at and the means proposed!

"Of course, of course!" he resumed, with a vain attempt to recover his seriousness. "Of course, it's a very original idea: the whole of modern politics upset so that Arsène Lupin may be free! . . . The plans of the Empire destroyed so that Arsène Lupin may continue his exploits! . . . Why not ask me for Alsace and Lorraine at once?"

"I did think of it, Sire," replied Lupin, calmly. The stranger's merriment increased:

"Splendid! And you let me off?"

"This time, yes."

Lupin had crossed his arms. He, too, was amusing himself by exaggerating the part which he was playing; and he continued, with affected seriousness:

"A series of circumstances might one day arise which would put in my hands the power of *demanding* and *obtaining* that restitution. When that day comes, I shall certainly not fail to do so. For the moment, the weapons at my disposal oblige me to be more modest. Peace in Morocco will satisfy me."

"Just that?"

"Just that."

"Morocco against your liberty!"

"Nothing more . . . or, rather—for we must not lose sight entirely of the main object of this conversation—or, rather, a little good will on the part of one of the countries in question . . . and, in exchange, the surrender of the letters which are in my power."

"Those letters, those letters!" muttered the stranger irritably. "After all, perhaps they are not so valuable. . . ."

"There are some in your own hand, Sire; and you considered them valuable enough to come to this cell. . . ."

"Well, what does it matter?"

"But there are others of which you do not know the authorship and about which I can give you a few particulars."

"Oh, indeed!" said the stranger, rather anxiously.

Lupin hesitated.

"Speak, speak plainly," said the stranger. "Say what you have in your mind."

In the profound silence of the cell, Lupin declared, with a certain solemnity:

"Twenty years ago a draft treaty was prepared between Germany, Great Britain, and France."

"That's not true! It's impossible! Who could have done such a thing?"

"The Emperor's father and the Queen of England, his grandmother, both acting under the influence of the Empress Frederick."

"Impossible! I repeat, it is impossible!"

"The correspondence is in the hiding-place at Veldenz Castle; and I alone know the secret of the hiding-place."

The stranger walked up and down with an agitated step. Then he stopped short:

"Is the text of the treaty included in that correspondence?"

"Yes, Sire. It is in your father's own hand."

"And what does it say?"

"By that treaty, France and Great Britain granted and promised Germany an immense colonial empire, the empire which she does not at present possess and which has become a necessity to her, in these times, to ensure her greatness."

"And what did England demand as a set-off against that empire?"

"The limitation of the German fleet."

"And France?"

"Alsace and Lorraine."

The Emperor leant against the table in silent thought. Lupin continued:

"Everything was ready. The cabinets of Paris and London had been sounded and had consented. The thing was practically done. The great treaty of alliance was on the point of being concluded. It would have laid the foundations of a definite and universal peace. The death of your father destroyed that sublime dream. But I ask Your Imperial Majesty, what will your people think, what will the world think, when it knows that Frederick III., one of the heroes of 1870, a German, a pure and loyal German, respected by all, generally admired for his nobility of character, agreed to the restitution of Alsace-Lorraine and therefore considered that restitution just?"

He was silent for an instant leaving the problem to fix itself in its precise terms before the Emperor's conscience, before his conscience as a man, a son and a sovereign. Then he concluded:

"Your Imperial Majesty yourself must know whether you wish or do not wish history to record the existence of that treaty. As for me, Sire, you can see that my humble personality counts for very little in the discussion."

A long pause followed upon Lupin's words. He waited, with his soul torn with anguish. His whole destiny was at stake, in this minute which he had conceived and, in a manner, produced with such effort and such stubbornness, an historic minute, born of his brain, in which "his humble personality," for all that he might say, weighed heavily upon the fate of empires and the peace of the world.

Opposite him, in the shadow, Cæsar stood meditating.

What answer would he make? What solution would he give to the problem?

He walked across the cell for a few moments, which to Lupin seemed interminable. Then he stopped and asked:

"Are there any other conditions?"

"Yes, Sire, but they are insignificant."

"Name them."

"I have found the son of the Grand-duke of Zweibrucken-Veldenz. The grand-duchy must be restored to him."

"Anything else?"

"He loves a young girl, who loves him in her turn. She is the fairest and the most virtuous of her sex. He must marry her."

"Anything else?"

"That is all."

"There is nothing more?"

"Nothing. Your majesty need only have this letter delivered to the editor of the *Grand Journal*, who will then destroy, unread, the article which he may now receive at any moment."

Lupin held out the letter, with a heavy heart and a trembling hand. If the Emperor took it, that would be a sign of his acceptance.

The Emperor hesitated and then, with an abrupt movement, took the letter, put on his hat, wrapped his cloak round him and walked out without a word.

Lupin remained for a few seconds, staggering, as though dazed. . . .

Then, suddenly, he fell into his chair, shouting with joy and pride. . . .

"Monsieur le Juge d'Instruction, I am sorry to say good-bye to you to-day."

"Why, M. Lupin, are you thinking of leaving us?"

"With the greatest reluctance, I assure you, Monsieur le Juge d'Instruction. Our relations have been so very pleasant and cordial! But all good things must come to an end. My cure at the Santé Palace is finished. Other duties call me. I have resolved to make my escape to-night."

"Then I wish you good luck, M. Lupin."

"A thousand thanks, M. le Juge d'Instruction."

Arsène Lupin waited patiently for the hour of his escape, not without asking himself how it would be contrived and by what means France and Germany, uniting for the joint performance of this deserving work, would succeed in effecting it without creating too great a scandal.

Late in the afternoon, the warder told him to go to the entrance-yard. He hurried out and was met by the governor, who handed him ever to M. Weber. M. Weber made him step into a motor-car in which somebody was already seated.

Lupin had a violent fit of laughter:

"What, you, my poor old Weber! Have they let you in for this tiresome job? Are you to be responsible for my escape? Upon my word, you are an unlucky beggar! Oh, my poor old chap, what hard lines! First made famous through my arrest, you are now to become immortal through my escape!"

He looked at the other man:

"Well, well, Monsieur le Préfet de Police, so you are in the business too! That's a nasty thing for you, what? If you take my advice, you'll stay in the background and leave the honor and glory to Weber! It's his by right! . . . And he can stand a lot, the rascal!"

The car travelled at a fast pace, along the Seine and through Boulogne. At Saint-Cloud, they crossed the river.

"Splendid!" cried Lupin. "We're going to Garches! You want me there, in order to reënact the death of Altenheim. We shall go down into the underground passage, I shall disappear and people will say that I got through another outlet, known to myself alone! Lord, how idiotic!"

He seemed quite unhappy about it:

"Idiotic! Idiotic in the highest degree! I blush for shame! . . . And those are the people who govern us! . . . What an age to live in! . . . But, you poor devils, why didn't you come to me? I'd have invented a beautiful little escape for you, something of a miraculous nature. I had it all ready pigeon-holed in my mind! The public would have yelled with wonder and danced with delight. Instead of which . . . However, it's quite true that you were given rather short notice . . . but all the same . . ."

The programme was exactly as Lupin had foreseen. They walked through the grounds of the House of Retreat to the Pavillon Hortense. Lupin and his two companions went down the stairs and along the underground passage. At the end of the tunnel, the deputy-chief said:

"You are free."

"And there you are!" said Lupin. "Is that all? Well, my dear Weber, thank you very much and sorry to have given you so much trouble. Good-bye, Monsieur le Préfet; kind regards to the missus!"

He climbed the stairs that led to the Villa des Glycines, raised the trap-door and sprang into the room.

A hand fell on his shoulder.

Opposite him stood his first visitor of the day before, the one who had accompanied the Emperor. There were four men with him, two on either side.

"Look here," said Lupin, "what's the meaning of this joke? I thought I was free!"

"Yes, yes," growled the German, in his rough voice, "you are free . . . free to travel with the five of us . . . if that suits you."

Lupin looked at him, for a second, with a mad longing to hit him on the nose, just to teach him. But the five men looked devilish determined. Their leader did not betray any exaggerated fondness for him; and it seemed to him that the fellow would be only too pleased to resort to extreme measures. Besides, after all, what did he care?

He chuckled:

"If it suits me? Why, it's the dream of my life!"

A powerful covered car was waiting in the paved yard outside the villa. Two men got into the driver's seat, two others inside, with their backs to the motor. Lupin and the stranger sat down on the front seat.

"*Vorwarts!*" cried Lupin, in German. "*Vorwarts nach Veldenz!*"

The stranger said:

"Silence! Those men must know nothing. Speak French. They don't know French. But why speak at all?"

"Quite right," said Lupin to himself. "Why speak at all?"

The car travelled all the evening and all night, without any incident. Twice they stopped to take in petrol at some sleepy little town.

The Germans took it in turns to watch their prisoner, who did not open his eyes until the early morning.

They stopped for breakfast at an inn on a hillside, near which stood a sign-post. Lupin saw that they were at an equal distance from Metz and Luxemburg. From there, they took a road that slanted north-east, in the direction of Treves.

Lupin said to his travelling-companion:

"Am I right in believing that I have the honor of speaking to Count von Waldemar, the Emperor's confidential friend, the one who searched Hermann III.'s house in Dresden?"

The stranger remained silent.

"You're the sort of chap I can't stand at any price," muttered Lupin. "I'll have some fun with you, one of these days. You're ugly, you're fat, you're heavy; in short, I don't like you." And he added, aloud, "You are wrong not to answer me, Monsieur le Comte. I was speaking in your own interest: just as we were stepping in, I saw a motor come into sight, behind us, on the horizon. Did you see it?"

"No, why?"

"Nothing."

"Still. . . ."

"No, nothing at all . . . a mere remark. . . . Besides, we are ten minutes ahead . . . and our car is at least a forty-horse-power."

"It's a sixty," said the German, looking at him uneasily from the corner of his eye.

"Oh, then we're all right!"

They were climbing a little slope. When they reached the top, the count leant out of the window:

"Damn it all!" he swore.

"What's the matter?" asked Lupin.

The count turned to him and, in a threatening voice:

"Take care! If anything happens, it will be so much the worse for you."

"Oho! It seems the other's gaining on us! . . . But what are you afraid of, my dear count? It's no doubt a traveller . . . perhaps even some one they are sending to help us."

"I don't want any help," growled the German.

He leant out again. The car was only two or three hundred yards behind.

He said to his men, pointing to Lupin.

"Bind him. If he resists. . . ."

He drew his revolver.

"Why should I resist, O gentle Teuton?" chuckled Lupin. And he added, while they were fastening his hands, "It is really curious to see how people take precautions when they need not and don't when they ought to. What the devil do you care about that motor? Accomplices of mine? What an idea!"

Without replying, the German gave orders to the driver:

"To the right! . . . Slow down! . . . Let them pass. . . . If they slow down also, stop!"

But, to his great surprise, the motor seemed, on the contrary, to increase its speed. It passed in front of the car like a whirlwind, in a cloud of dust. Standing up at the back, leaning over the hood, which was lowered, was a man dressed in black.

He raised his arm.

Two shots rang out.

The count, who was blocking the whole of the left window, fell back into the car.

Before even attending to him, the two men leapt upon Lupin and finished securing him.

"Jackasses! Blockheads!" shouted Lupin, shaking with rage. "Let me go, on the contrary! There now, we're stopping! But go after him, you silly fools, catch him up! . . . It's the man in black, I tell you, the murderer! . . . Oh, the idiots! . . ."

They gagged him. Then they attended to the count. The wound did not appear to be serious and was soon dressed. But the patient, who was in a very excited state, had an attack of fever and became delirious.

It was eight o'clock in the morning. They were in the open country, far from any village. The men had no information as to the exact object of the journey. Where were they to go? Whom were they to send to?

They drew up the motor beside a wood and waited. The whole day went by in this way. It was evening before a squad of cavalry arrived, dispatched from Treves in search of the motor-car.

Two hours later, Lupin stepped out of the car, and still escorted by his two Germans, by the light of a lantern climbed the steps of a staircase that led to a small room with iron-barred windows.

Here he spent the night.

The next morning, an officer led him, through a courtyard filled with soldiers, to the centre of a long row of buildings that ran round the foot of a mound covered with monumental ruins.

He was shown into a large, hastily-furnished room. His visitor of two days back was sitting at a writing-table, reading newspapers and reports, which he marked with great strokes of red pencil:

"Leave us," he said to the officer.

And, going up to Lupin:

"The papers."

The tone was no longer the same. It was now the harsh and imperious tone of the master who is at home and addressing an inferior . . . and such an inferior! A rogue, an adventurer of the worst type, before whom he had been obliged to humiliate himself!

"The papers," he repeated.

Lupin was not put out of countenance. He said, quite calmly:

"They are in Veldenz Castle."

"We are in the out-buildings of the castle. Those are the ruins of Veldenz, over there."

"The papers are in the ruins."

"Let us go to them. Show me the way."

Lupin did not budge.

"Well?"

"Well, Sire, it is not as simple as you think. It takes some time to bring into play the elements which are needed to open that hiding-place."

"How long do you want?"

"Twenty-four hours."

An angry movement, quickly suppressed:

"Oh, there was no question of that between us!"

"Nothing was specified, neither that nor the little trip which Your Imperial Majesty made me take in the charge of half a dozen of your body-guard. I am to hand over the papers, that is all."

"And I am not to give you your liberty until you do hand over those papers."

"It is a question of confidence, Sire. I should have considered myself quite as much bound to produce the papers if I had been free on leaving prison; and Your Imperial Majesty may be sure that I should not have walked off with them. The only difference is that they would now be in your possession. For we have lost a day, Sire. And a day, in this business . . . is a day too much. . . . Only, there it is, you should have had confidence."

The Emperor gazed with a certain amazement at that outcast, that vagabond, who seemed vexed that any one should doubt his word.

He did not reply, but rang the bell:

"The officer on duty," he commanded.

Count von Waldemar appeared, looking very white.

"Ah, it's you, Waldemar? So you're all right again?"

"At your service, Sire."

"Take five men with you . . . the same men, as you're sure of them. Don't leave this . . . gentleman until to-morrow morning." He looked at his watch. "Until to-morrow morning at ten o'clock. No, I will give him till twelve. You will go wherever he thinks fit to go, you will do whatever he tells you to do. In short, you are at his disposal. At twelve o'clock, I will join you. If, at the last stroke of twelve, he has not handed me the bundle of letters, you will put him back in your car and, without losing a second, take him straight to the Santé Prison."

"If he tries to escape. . . ."

"Take your own course."

He went out.

Lupin helped himself to a cigar from the table and threw himself into an easy chair:

"Good! I just love that way of going to work. It is frank and explicit."

The count had brought in his men. He said to Lupin:

"March!"

Lupin lit his cigar and did not move.

"Bind his hands," said the count.

And, when the order was executed, he repeated:

"Now then, march!"

"No."

"What do you mean by no?"

"I'm wondering."

"What about?"

"Where on earth that hiding-place can be!"

The count gave a start and Lupin chuckled:

"For the best part of the story is that I have not the remotest idea where that famous hiding-place is nor how to set about discovering it. What do you say to that, my dear Waldemar, eh? Funny, isn't it? . . . Not the very remotest idea! . . ."

XII. THE EMPEROR'S LETTERS

The ruins of Veldenz are well known to all who visit the banks of the Rhine and the Moselle. They comprise the remains of the old feudal castle, built in 1377 by the Archbishop of Fistingen, an enormous dungeon-keep, gutted by Turenne's troops, and the walls, left standing in their entirety, of a large Renascence palace, in which the grand-dukes of Zweibrucken lived for three centuries.

It was this palace that was sacked by Hermann II.'s rebellious subjects. The empty windows display two hundred yawning cavities on the four frontages. All the wainscoting, the hangings and most of the furniture were burnt. You walk on the scorched girders of the floors; and the sky can be seen at intervals through the ruined ceilings.

Lupin, accompanied by his escort, went over the whole building in two hours' time:

"I am very pleased with you, my dear count. I don't think I ever came across a guide so well posted in his subject, nor—which is rare—so silent. And now, if you don't mind, we will go to lunch."

As a matter of fact, Lupin knew no more than at the first moment and his perplexity did nothing but increase. To obtain his release from prison and to strike the imagination of his visitor, he had bluffed, pretending to know everything; and he was still seeking for the best place at which to begin to seek.

"Things look bad," he said to himself, from time to time. "Things are looking about as bad as they can look."

His brain, moreover, was not as clear as usual. He was obsessed by an idea, the idea of "the other one," the murderer, the assassin, whom he knew to be still clinging to his footsteps.

How did that mysterious personality come to be on his tracks? How had he heard of Lupin's leaving prison and of his rush to Luxemburg and Germany? Was it a miraculous intuition? Or was it the outcome of definite information? But, if so, at what price, by means of what promises or threats was he able to obtain it?

All these questions haunted Lupin's mind.

At about four o'clock, however, after a fresh walk through the ruins, in the course of which he had examined the stones, measured the thickness of the walls, investigated the shape and appearance of things, all to no purpose, he asked the count:

"Is there no one left who was in the service of the last grand-duke who lived in the castle?"

"All the servants of that time went different ways. Only one of them continued to live in the district."

"Well?"

"He died two years ago."

"Any children?"

"He had a son, who married and who was dismissed, with his wife, for disgraceful conduct. They left their youngest child behind, a little girl, Isilda."

"Where does she live?"

"She lives here, at the end of these buildings. The old grandfather used to act as a guide to visitors, in the days when the castle was still open to the public. Little Isilda has lived in the ruins ever since. She was allowed to remain out of pity. She is a poor innocent, who is hardly able to talk and does not know what she says."

"Was she always like that?"

"It seems not. Her reason went gradually, when she was about ten years old."

"In consequence of a sorrow, of a fright?"

"No, for no direct cause, I am told. The father was a drunkard and the mother committed suicide in a fit of madness."

Lupin reflected and said:

"I should like to see her."

The count gave a rather curious smile:

"You can see her, by all means."

She happened to be in one of the rooms which had been set apart for her. Lupin was surprised to find an attractive little creature, too thin, too pale, but almost pretty, with her fair hair and her delicate face. Her sea-green eyes had the vague, dreamy look of the eyes of blind people.

He put a few questions to which Isilda gave no answer and others to which she replied with incoherent sentences, as though she understood neither the meaning of the words addressed to her nor those which she herself uttered.

He persisted, taking her very gently by the hand and asking her in an affectionate tone about the time when she still had her reason, about her grandfather, about the memories which might be called up by her life as a child playing freely among the majestic ruins of the castle.

She stood silent, with staring eyes; impassive, any emotion which she might have felt was not enough to rouse her slumbering intelligence.

Lupin asked for a pencil and paper and wrote down the number 813.

The count smiled again.

"Look here, what are you laughing at?" cried Lupin, irritably.

"Nothing . . . nothing. . . . I'm very much interested, that's all. . . ."

Isilda looked at the sheet of paper, when he showed it to her, and turned away her head, with a vacant air.

"No bite!" said the count, satirically.

Lupin wrote the letters "APOON."

Isilda paid no more attention than before.

He did not give up the experiment, but kept on writing the same letters, each time watching the girl's face.

She did not stir, but kept her eyes fixed on the paper with an indifference which nothing seemed to disturb. Then, all at once, she seized the pencil, snatched the last sheet out of Lupin's hands and, as though acting under a sudden inspiration, wrote two "L's" in the middle of a space left open by Lupin.

He felt a thrill.

A word had been formed: "APOLLON."

Meanwhile, Isilda clung to both pencil and paper and, with clutching fingers and a strained face, was struggling to make her hand submit to the hesitating orders of her poor little brain.

Lupin waited, feverishly.

She rapidly wrote another word, the word "DIANE."

"Another word! . . . Another word!" shouted Lupin.

She twisted her fingers round the pencil, broke the lead, made a big "J" with the stump and, now utterly exhausted, dropped the pencil.

"Another word! I must have another word!" said Lupin, in a tone of command, catching her by the arm.

But he saw by her eyes, which had once more become indifferent, that that fleeting gleam of intelligence could not shine out again.

"Let us go," he said.

He was walking away, when she ran after him and stood in his path. He stopped:

"What is it?"

She held out the palm of her hand.

"What? Money? . . . Is she in the habit of begging?" he asked the count.

"No," said Waldemar, "and I can't understand."

Isilda took two gold coins from her pocket and chinked them together, gleefully.

Lupin looked at them. They were French coins, quite new, bearing the date of that year.

"Where did you get these?" asked Lupin, excitedly.

"French money! . . . Who gave it you? . . . And when? . . . Was it to-day? Speak! . . . Answer! . . ." He shrugged his shoulders. "Fool that I am! As though she could answer! . . . My dear count, would you mind lending me forty marks? . . . Thanks . . . Here, Isilda, that's for you."

She took the two coins, jingled them with the others in the palm of her hand and then, putting out her arm, pointed to the ruins of the Renascence palace, with a gesture that seemed to call attention more particularly to the left wing and to the top of that wing.

Was it a mechanical movement? Or must it be looked upon as a grateful acknowledgment for the two gold coins?

He glanced at the count. Waldemar was smiling again.

"What makes the brute keep on grinning like that?" said Lupin to himself. "Any one would think that he was having a game with me."

He went to the palace on the off-chance, attended by his escort.

The ground-floor consisted of a number of large reception-rooms, running one into the other and containing the few pieces of furniture that had escaped the fire.

On the first floor, on the north side, was a long gallery, out of which twelve handsome rooms opened all exactly alike.

There was a similar gallery on the second floor, but with twenty-four smaller rooms, also resembling one another. All these apartments were empty, dilapidated, wretched to look at.

Above, there was nothing. The attics had been burnt down.

For an hour, Lupin walked, ran, rushed about indefatigably, with his eyes on the look-out.

When it began to grow dusk, he hurried to one of his twelve rooms on the first floor, as if he were selecting it for special reasons known to himself alone. He was rather surprised to find the Emperor there, smoking and seated in an arm-chair which he had sent for.

Taking no notice of his presence, Lupin began an inspection of the room, according to the methods which he was accustomed to employ in such cases, dividing the room into sections, each of which he examined in turn.

After twenty minutes of this work, he said:

"I must beg you, Sire, to be good enough to move. There is a fireplace here. . . ."

The Emperor tossed his head:

"Is it really necessary for me to move?"

"Yes, Sire, this fireplace . . ."

"The fireplace is just the same as the others and the room is no different from its fellows."

Lupin looked at the Emperor without understanding. The Emperor rose and said, with a laugh:

"I think, M. Lupin, that you have been making just a little fun of me."

"How do you mean, Sire?"

"Oh, it's hardly worth mentioning! You obtained your release on the condition of handing me certain papers in which I am interested and you have not the smallest notion as to where they are. I have been thoroughly—what do you call it, in French?—*roulé* 'done'!"

"Do you think so, Sire?"

"Why, what a man knows he doesn't have to hunt for! And you have been hunting for ten good hours! Doesn't it strike you as a case for an immediate return to prison?"

Lupin seemed thunderstruck:

"Did not Your Imperial Majesty fix twelve o'clock to-morrow as the last limit?"

"Why wait?"

"Why? Well, to allow me to complete my work!"

"Your work? But it's not even begun, M. Lupin."

"There Your Imperial Majesty is mistaken."

"Prove it . . . and I will wait until to-morrow."

Lupin reflected and, speaking in a serious tone:

"Since Your Imperial Majesty requires proofs in order to have confidence in me, I will furnish them. The twelve rooms leading out of this gallery each bear a different name, which is inscribed in French—obviously by a French decorative artist—over the various doors. One of the inscriptions, less damaged by the fire than the others, caught my eye as I was passing along the gallery. I examined the other doors: all of them bore hardly legible traces of names caned over the pediments. Thus I found a 'D' and an 'E' the first and last letters of 'Diane.' I found an 'A' and 'LON' which pointed to 'Apollon.' These are the French equivalents of Diana and Apollo, both of them mythological deities. The other inscriptions presented similar characteristics. I discovered traces of such names as Jupiter, Venus, Mercury, Saturn and so on. This part of the problem was solved: each of the twelve rooms bears the name of an Olympian god or goddess; and the letters APOON, completed by Isilda, point to the Apollo Room or Salle d'Apollon. So it is here, in the room in which we now are, that the letters are hidden. A few minutes, perhaps, will suffice in which to discover them."

"A few minutes or a few years . . . or even longer!" said the Emperor, laughing.

He seemed greatly amused; and the count also displayed a coarse merriment.

Lupin asked:

"Would Your Imperial Majesty be good enough to explain?"

"M. Lupin, the exciting investigation which you have conducted to-day and of which you are telling us the brilliant results has already been made by me . . . yes, a fortnight ago, in the company of your friend Holmlock Shears. Together we questioned little Isilda; together, we employed the same method in dealing with her that you did; and together we observed the names in the gallery and got as far as this room, the Apollo Room."

Lupin turned livid. He spluttered:

"Oh, did Shears get . . . as far as . . . this?"

"Yes, after four days' searching. True, it did not help us, for we found nothing. All the same, I know that the letters are not here."

Trembling with rage, wounded in his innermost pride, Lupin fired up under the gibe, as though he had been lashed with a whip. He had never felt humiliated to such a degree as this. In this fury, he could have strangled the fat Waldemar, whose laughter incensed him. Containing himself with an effort, he said:

"It took Shears four days, Sire, and me only four hours. And I should have required even less, if I had not been thwarted in my search."

"And by whom, bless my soul? By my faithful count? I hope he did not dare . . . !"

"No, Sire, but by the most terrible and powerful of my enemies, by that infernal being who killed his own accomplice Altenheim."

"Is he here? Do you think so?" exclaimed the Emperor, with an agitation which showed that he was familiar with every detail of the dramatic story.

"He is wherever I am. He threatens me with his constant hatred. It was he who guessed that I was M. Lenormand, the chief of the detective-service; it was he who had me put in prison; it was he, again, who pursued me, on the day when I came out. Yesterday, aiming at me in the motor, he wounded Count von Waldemar."

"But how do you know, how can you be sure that he is at Veldenz?"

"Isilda has received two gold coins, two French coins!"

"And what is he here for? With what object?"

"I don't know, Sire, but he is the very spirit of evil. Your Imperial Majesty must be on your guard: he is capable of anything and everything."

"It is impossible! I have two hundred men in the ruins. He cannot have entered. He would have been seen."

"Some one has seen him, beyond a doubt."

"Who?"

"Isilda."

"Let her be questioned! Waldemar, take your prisoner to where the girl is."

Lupin showed his bound hands:

"It will be a tough battle. Can I fight like this?"

The Emperor said to the count:

"Unfasten him. . . . And keep me informed."

In this way, by a sudden effort, bringing the hateful vision of the murder into the discussion, boldly, without evidence, Arsène Lupin gained time and resumed the direction of the search:

"Sixteen hours still," he said to himself, "it's more than I want."

He reached the premises occupied by Isilda, at the end of the old out-buildings. These buildings served as barracks for the two hundred soldiers guarding the ruins; and the whole of this, the left wing, was reserved for the officers.

Isilda was not there. The count sent two of his men to look for her. They came back. No one had seen the girl.

Nevertheless, she could not have left the precincts of the ruins. As for the Renascence palace, it was, so to speak, invested by one-half of the troops; and no one was able to obtain admittance.

At last, the wife of a subaltern who lived in the next house declared that she had been sitting at her window all day and that the girl had not been out.

"If she hadn't gone out," said Waldemar, "she would be here now: and she is not here."

Lupin observed:

"Is there a floor above?"

"Yes, but from this room to the upper floor there is no staircase."

"Yes, there is."

He pointed to a little door opening on a dark recess. In the shadow, he saw the first treads of a staircase as steep as a ladder.

"Please, my dear count," he said to Waldemar, who wanted to go up, "let me have the honor."

"Why?"

"There's danger."

He ran up and at once sprang into a low and narrow loft. A cry escaped him:

"Oh!"

"What is it?" asked the count, emerging in his turn.

"Here . . . on the floor. . . . Isilda. . . ."

He knelt down beside the girl, but, at the first glance, saw that she was simply stunned and that she bore no trace of a wound, except a few scratches on the wrists and hands. A handkerchief was stuffed into her mouth by way of a gag.

"That's it," he said. "The murderer was here with her. When we came, he struck her a blow with his fist and gagged her so that we should not hear her moans."

"But how did he get away?"

"Through here . . . look . . . there is a passage connecting all the attics on the first floor."

"And from there?"

"From there, he went down the stairs of one of the other dwellings."

"But he would have been seen!"

"Pooh, who knows? The creature's invisible. Never mind! Send your men to look. Tell them to search all the attics and all the ground-floor lodgings."

He hesitated. Should he also go in pursuit of the murderer?

But a sound brought him back to the girl's side. She had got up from the floor and a dozen pieces of gold money had dropped from her hands. He examined them. They were all French.

"Ah," he said, "I was right! Only, why so much gold? In reward for what?"

Suddenly, he caught sight of a book on the floor and stooped to pick it up. But the girl darted forward with a quicker movement, seized the book and pressed it to her bosom with a fierce energy, as though prepared to defend it against any attempt to take hold of it.

"That's it," he said. "The money was offered her for the book, but she refused to part with it. Hence the scratches on the hands. The interesting thing would be to know why the murderer wished to possess the book. Was he able to look through it first?"

He said to Waldemar:

"My dear count, please give the order."

Waldemar made a sign to his men. Three of them threw themselves on the girl and, after a hard tussle, in which the poor thing stamped, writhed and screamed with rage, they took the volume from her.

"Gently, child," said Lupin, "be calm. . . . It's all in a good cause. . . . Keep an eye on her, will you? Meanwhile, I will have a look at the object in dispute."

It was an odd volume of Montesquieu's *Voyage au temple de Guide*, in a binding at least a century old. But Lupin had hardly opened it before he exclaimed:

"I say, I say, this is queer! There is a sheet of parchment stuck on each right hand page; and those sheets are covered with a very close, small handwriting."

He read, at the beginning:

"*Diary of the Chevalier* GILLES DE MALRÊCHE, *French servant to His Royal Highness the Prince of* ZWEIBRUCKENVELDENZ, *begun in the Year of Our Lord* 1794."

"What! Does it say that?" asked the count.

"What surprises you?"

"Isilda's grandfather, the old man who died two years ago, was called Malreich, which is the German form of the same name."

"Capital! Isilda's grandfather must have been the son or the grandson of the French servant who wrote his diary in an odd volume of Montesquieu's works. And that is how the diary came into Isilda's hands."

He turned the pages at random:

"15 *September,* 1796. His Royal Highness went hunting.

"20 *September,* 1796. His Royal Highness went out riding. He was mounted on Cupidon."

"By Jove!" muttered Lupin. "So far, it's not very exciting."

He turned over a number of pages and read:

"12 *March,* 1803. I have remitted ten crowns to Hermann. He is giving music-lessons in London."

Lupin gave a laugh:

"Oho! Hermann is dethroned and our respect comes down with a rush!"

"Yes," observed Waldemar, "the reigning grand-duke was driven from his dominions by the French troops."

Lupin continued:

"1809. *Tuesday.* Napoleon slept at Veldenz last night. I made His Majesty's bed and this morning I emptied his slops."

"Oh, did Napoleon stop at Veldenz?"

"Yes, yes, on his way back to the army, at the time of the Austrian campaign, which ended with the battle of Wagram. It was an honor of which the grand-ducal family were very proud afterwards."

Lupin went on reading:

"28 *October,* 1814. His Royal Highness returned to his dominions.

"29 *October,* 1814. I accompanied His Royal Highness to the hiding-place last night and was happy to be able to show him that no one had guessed its existence. For that matter, who would have suspected that a hiding-place could be contrived in . . ."

Lupin stopped, with a shout. Isilda had suddenly escaped from the men guarding her, made a grab at him and taken to flight, carrying the book with her.

"Oh, the little mischief! Quick, you! . . . Go round by the stairs below. I'll run after her by the passage."

But she had slammed the door behind her and bolted it. He had to go down and run along the buildings with the others, looking for a staircase which would take them to the first floor.

The fourth house was the only one open. He went upstairs. But the passage was empty and he had to knock at doors, force locks and make his way into unoccupied rooms, while Waldemar, showing as much ardor in the pursuit as himself, pricked the curtains and hangings with the point of his sword.

A voice called out from the ground-floor, towards the right wing. They rushed in that direction. It was one of the officers' wives, who beckoned to them at the end of a passage and told them that the girl must be in her lodging.

"How do you know?" asked Lupin.

"I wanted to go to my room. The door was shut and I could not get in."

Lupin tried and found the door locked:

"The window!" he cried. "There must be a window!"

He went outside, took the count's sword and smashed the panes. Then, helped up by two men, he hung on to the wall, passed his arm through the broken glass, turned the latch and stumbled into the room.

He saw Isilda huddled before the fireplace, almost in the midst of the flames:

"The little beast!" he said. "She has thrown it into the fire!"

He pushed her back savagely, tried to take the book and burnt his hands in the attempt. Then, with the tongs, he pulled it out of the grate and threw the table cloth over it to stifle the blaze.

But it was too late. The pages of the old manuscript, all burnt up, were falling into ashes.

Lupin gazed at her in silence. The count said:

"One would think that she knew what she was doing."

"No, she does not know. Only, her grandfather must have entrusted her with that book as a sort of treasure, a treasure which no one was ever to set eyes on, and, with her stupid instinct, she preferred to throw it into the fire rather than part with it."

"Well then. . . ."

"Well then what?"

"You won't find the hiding-place."

"Aha, my dear count, so you did, for a moment, look upon my success as possible? And Lupin does not strike you as quite a charlatan? Make your mind easy, Waldemar: Lupin has more than one string to his bow. I shall succeed."

"Before twelve o'clock to-morrow?"

"Before twelve o'clock to-night. But, for the moment, I am starving with hunger. And, if your kindness would go so far. . . ."

He was taken to the sergeants' mess and a substantial meal prepared for him, while the count went to make his report to the Emperor.

Twenty minutes later, Waldemar returned and they sat down and dined together, opposite each other, silent and pensive.

"Waldemar, a good cigar would be a treat. . . . I thank you. . . . Ah, this one crackles as a self-respecting Havana should!"

He lit his cigar and, after a minute or two:

"You can smoke, count; I don't mind in the least; in fact, I rather like it."

An hour passed. Waldemar dozed and, from time to time, swallowed a glass of brandy to wake himself up.

Soldiers passed in and out, waiting on them.

"Coffee," asked Lupin.

They brought him some coffee.

"What bad stuff!" he grumbled. "If that's what Cæsar drinks! . . . Give me another cup all the same, Waldemar. We may have a long night before us. Oh, what vile coffee!"

He lit a second cigar and did not say another word. Ten minutes passed. He continued not to move or speak.

Suddenly, Waldemar sprang to his feet and said to Lupin, angrily:

"Hi! Stand up, there!"

Lupin was whistling a tune at the moment. He kept on whistling, peacefully.

"Stand up, I say!"

Lupin turned round. His Imperial Majesty had just entered. Lupin rose from his chair.

"How far are we?" asked the Emperor.

"I think, Sire, that I shall be able to satisfy Your Imperial Majesty soon."

"What? Do you know . . ."

"The hiding-place? Very nearly, Sire. . . . A few details still escape me . . . but everything will be cleared up, once we are on the spot: I have no doubt of it."

"Are we to stay here?"

"No, Sire, I will beg you to go with me to the Renascence palace. But we have plenty of time; and, if Your Imperial Majesty will permit me, I should like first to think over two or three points."

Without waiting for the reply, he sat down, to Waldemar's great indignation.

In a few minutes, the Emperor, who had walked away and was talking to the count, came up to him:

"Are you ready now, M. Lupin?"

Lupin kept silence. A fresh question. His head fell on his chest.

"But he's asleep; I really believe that he's asleep!"

Waldemar, beside himself with rage, shook him violently by the shoulder. Lupin fell from his chair, sank to the floor, gave two or three convulsive movements and then lay quite still.

"What's the matter with him?" exclaimed the Emperor. "He's not dead, I hope!"

He took a lamp and bent over him:

"How pale he is! A face like wax! . . . Look, Waldemar. . . . Feel his heart. . . . He's alive, is he not?"

"Yes, Sire," said the count, after a moment, "the heart is beating quite regularly."

"Then what is it? I don't understand. . . . What happened?"

"Shall I go and fetch the doctor?"

"Yes, run. . . ."

The doctor found Lupin in the same state, lying inert and quiet. He had him put on a bed, subjected him to a long examination and asked what he had had to eat.

"Do you suspect a case of poisoning, doctor?"

"No, Sire, there are no traces of poisoning. But I am thinking . . . what's on that tray and in that cup?"

"Coffee," said the count.

"For you?"

"No, for him. I did not have any."

The doctor poured out some coffee, tasted it and said:

"I was right. He has been put to sleep with a narcotic."

"But by whom?" cried the Emperor, angrily. "Look here, Waldemar; it's exasperating, the way things happen in this place!"

"Sire? . . ."

"Well, yes, I've had enough of it! . . . I am really beginning to believe that the man's right and that there is some one in the castle. . . . That French money, that narcotic. . . ."

"If any one had got into this enclosure, Sire, it would be known by this time. . . . We've been hunting in every direction for three hours."

"Still, I didn't make the coffee, I assure you. . . . And, unless you did. . . ."

"Oh, Sire!"

"Well, then, hunt about . . . search. . . . You have two hundred men at your disposal; and the out-houses are not so large as all that! For, after all, the ruffian is prowling round here, round these buildings . . . near the kitchen . . . somewhere or other! Go and bustle about!"

The fat Waldemar bustled about all night, conscientiously, because it was the master's order, but without conviction, because it was impossible for a stranger to hide among ruins which were so well-watched. And, as a matter of fact, the event proved that he was right: the investigations were fruitless; and no one was able to discover the mysterious hand that had prepared the narcotic drink.

Lupin spent the night lifeless on his bed. In the morning, the doctor, who had not left his side, told a messenger of the Emperor's that he was still asleep.

At nine o'clock, however, he made his first movement, a sort of effort to wake up.

Later on, he stammered:

"What time is it?"

"Twenty-five to ten."

He made a fresh effort; and it was evident that, in the midst of his torpor, his whole being was intent upon returning to life.

A clock struck ten.

He started and said:

"Let them carry me; let them carry me to the palace."

With the doctor's approval, Waldemar called his men and sent word to the Emperor. They laid Lupin on a stretcher and set out for the palace.

"The first floor," he muttered.

They carried him up.

"At the end of the corridor," he said. "The last room on the left."

They carried him to the last room, which was the twelfth, and gave him a chair, on which he sat down, exhausted.

The Emperor arrived: Lupin did not stir, sat looking, unconscious, with no expression in his eyes.

Then, in a few minutes, he seemed to wake, looked round him, at the walls, the ceilings, the people, and said:

"A narcotic, I suppose?"

"Yes," said the doctor.

"Have they found . . . the man?"

"No."

He seemed to be meditating and several times jerked his head with a thoughtful air: but they soon saw that he was asleep.

The Emperor went up to Waldemar:

"Order your car round."

"Oh? . . . But then, Sire . . . ?"

"Well, what? I am beginning to think that he is taking us in and that all this is merely play-acting, to gain time."

"Possibly . . . yes . . ." said Waldemar, agreeing.

"It's quite obvious! He is making the most of certain curious coincidences, but he knows nothing; and his story about gold coins and his narcotic are so many inventions! If we lend ourselves to his little game any longer, he'll slip out of your fingers. Your car, Waldemar."

The count gave his orders and returned. Lupin had not woke up. The Emperor, who was looking round the room, said to Waldemar:

"This is the Minerva room, is it not?"

"Yes, Sire."

"But then why is there an 'N' in two places?"

There were, in fact, two "N's," one over the chimneypiece, the other over an old dilapidated clock fitted into the wall and displaying a complicated set of works, with weights hanging lifeless at the end of their cords.

"The two 'N's' . . ." said Waldemar.

The Emperor did not listen to the answer. Lupin had moved again, opening his eyes and uttering indistinct syllables. He stood up, walked across the room and fell down from sheer weakness.

Then came the struggle, the desperate struggle of his brain, his nerves, his will against that hideous, paralyzing torpor, the struggle of a dying man against death, the struggle of life against extinction. And the sight was one of infinite sadness.

"He is suffering," muttered Waldemar.

"Or at least, he is pretending to suffer," declared the Emperor, "and pretending very cleverly at that. What an actor!"

Lupin stammered:

"An injection, doctor, an injection of caffeine . . . at once. . . ."

"May I, Sire?" asked the doctor.

"Certainly. . . . Until twelve o'clock, do all that he asks. He has my promise."

"How many minutes . . . before twelve o'clock?" asked Lupin.

"Forty," said somebody.

"Forty? . . . I shall do it. . . . I am sure to do it. . . . I've got to do it. . . ." He took his head in his two hands. "Oh, if I had my brain, the real brain, the brain that thinks! It would be a matter of a second! There is only one dark spot left . . . but I cannot . . . my thoughts escape me. . . . I can't grasp it . . . it's awful."

His shoulders shook. Was he crying?

They heard him repeating:

"813 . . . 813. . . ." And, in a lower voice, "813 . . . an '8' . . . a '1' . . . a '3' . . . yes, of course. . . . But why? . . . That's not enough. . . ."

The Emperor muttered:

"He impresses me. I find it difficult to believe that a man can play a part like that. . . ."

Half-past eleven struck . . . a quarter to twelve. . . .

Lupin remained motionless, with his fists glued to his temples.

The Emperor waited, with his eyes fixed on a chronometer which Waldemar held in his hand.

Ten minutes more . . . five minutes more . . .

"Is the car there, Waldemar? . . . Are your men ready?"

"Yes, Sire."

"Is that watch of yours a repeater, Waldemar?"

"Yes, Sire."

"At the last stroke of twelve, then. . . ."

"But . . ."

"At the last stroke of twelve, Waldemar."

There was really something tragic about the scene, that sort of grandeur and solemnity which the hours assume at the approach of a possible miracle, when it seems as though the voice of fate itself were about to find utterance.

The Emperor did not conceal his anguish. This fantastic adventurer who was called Arsène Lupin and whose amazing life he knew, this man troubled him . . . and, although he was resolved to make an end of all this dubious story, he could not help waiting . . . and hoping.

Two minutes more . . . one minute more . . .

Then they counted by seconds.

Lupin seemed asleep.

"Come, get ready," said the Emperor to the count.

The count went up to Lupin and placed his hand on his shoulder.

The silvery chime of the repeater quivered and struck . . . one, two, three, four, five . . .

"Waldemar, old chap, pull the weights of the old clock."

A moment of stupefaction. It was Lupin's voice, speaking very calmly.

Waldemar, annoyed at the familiarity of the address, shrugged his shoulders.

"Do as he says, Waldemar," said the Emperor.

"Yes, do as I say, my dear count," echoed Lupin, recovering his powers of chaff. "You know the ropes so well . . . all you have to do is to pull those of the clock . . . in turns . . . one, two . . . capital! . . . That's how they used to wind it up in the old days."

The pendulum, in fact, was started; and they heard its regular ticking.

"Now the hands," said Lupin. "Set them at a little before twelve . . . Don't move . . . Let me . . ."

He rose and walked to the face of the clock, standing two feet away, at most, with his eyes fixed, with every nerve attentive.

The twelve strokes sounded, twelve heavy, deep strokes.

A long silence. Nothing happened. Nevertheless, the Emperor waited, as though he were sure that something was going to happen. And Waldemar did not move, stood with wide-open eyes.

Lupin, who had stooped over the clock-face, now drew himself up, muttering:

"That's it . . . I have it. . . ."

He went back to his chair and commanded:

"Waldemar, set the hands at two minutes to twelve again. Oh, no, old chap, not backwards! The way the hands go! . . . Yes, I know, it will take rather long . . . but it can't be helped."

All the hours struck and the half hours, up to half-past eleven.

"Listen, Waldemar," said Lupin.

And he spoke seriously, without jesting, as though himself excited and anxious:

"Listen, Waldemar. Do you see on the face of the clock a little round dot marking the first hour? That dot is loose, isn't it? Put the fore-finger of your left hand on it and press. Good. Do the same with your thumb on the dot marking the third hour. Good. With your right hand, push in the dot at the eighth hour. Good. Thank you. Go and sit down, my dear fellow."

The minute-hand shifted, moved to the twelfth dot and the clock struck again.

Lupin was silent and very white. The twelve strokes rang out in the silence.

At the twelfth stroke, there was a sound as of a spring being set free. The clock stopped dead. The pendulum ceased swinging.

And suddenly, the bronze ornament representing a ram's head, which crowned the dial, fell forwards, uncovering a sort of little recess cut out of the stone wall.

In this recess was a chased silver casket.

Lupin took it and carried it to the Emperor:

"Would Your Imperial Majesty be so good as to open it yourself? The letters which you instructed me to look for are inside."

The Emperor raised the lid and seemed greatly astonished.

The casket was empty.

The casket was empty.

It was an enormous, unforeseen sensation. After the success of the calculation made by Lupin, after the ingenious discovery of the secret of the clock, the Emperor, who had no doubt left as to the ultimate success, appeared utterly confounded.

Opposite him was Lupin, pallid and wan, with drawn jaws and bloodshot eyes, gnashing his teeth with rage and impotent hate.

He wiped the perspiration from his forehead, then snatched up the casket, turned it over, examined it, as though he hoped to find a false bottom. At last, for greater certainty, in a fit of fury, he crushed it, with an irresistible grip.

That relieved him. He breathed more easily.

The Emperor said:

"Who has done this?"

"Still the same man, Sire, the one who is following the same road as I and pursuing the same aim: Mr. Kesselbach's murderer."

"When?"

"Last night. Ah, Sire, why did you not leave me free when I came out of prison! Had I been free, I should have come here without losing an hour. I should have arrived before him! I should have given Isilda money before he did! I should have read Malreich, the old French servant's diary, before he did!"

"So you think that it was through the revelations in the diary . . . ?"

"Why, yes, Sire! He had time to read them. And, lurking I don't know where, kept informed of all our movements by I don't know whom, he put me to sleep last night, in order to get rid of me."

"But the palace was guarded."

"Guarded by your soldiers, Sire. Does that count with a man like him? Besides, I have no doubt that Waldemar concentrated his search upon the out-buildings, thus thinning the posts in the palace."

"But the sound of the clock! Those twelve strokes in the night!"

"It was mere child's play, Sire, mere child's play, to him, to prevent the clock from striking!"

"All this seems very impossible to my mind."

"It all seems monstrous clear to mine, Sire! If it were possible to feel in every one of your soldiers' pockets here and now, or to know how much money they will each of them spend during the next twelve months, we should be sure to find two or three who are, at this moment, in possession of a few bank-notes: French bank-notes, of course."

"Oh!" protested Waldemar.

"But yes, my dear count, it is a question of price; and that makes no difference to 'him.' If 'he' wished, I am sure that you yourself . . ."

The Emperor, wrapped up in his own thoughts, was not listening. He walked across the room from left to right and right to left, then beckoned to one of the officers standing in the gallery:

"My car. . . . And tell them to get ready. . . . We're starting."

He stopped, watched Lupin for a moment and, going up to the count:

"You too, Waldemar, be off . . . Straight to Paris, without a break . . ."

Lupin pricked up his ears. He heard Waldemar reply:

"I should like to have a dozen additional guards. . . . With that devil of a man. . . ."

"Take them. And look sharp. You must get there to-night."

Lupin stamped his foot violently on the floor:

"Well, no, Sire! No, no, no! It shan't be, I swear it shan't! No, no never!"

"What do you mean?"

"And the letters, Sire? The stolen letters?"

"Upon my word! . . ."

"So!" cried Lupin, indignantly folding his arms. "So your Imperial Majesty gives up the struggle? You look upon the defeat as irretrievable? You declare yourself beaten? Well, I do not, Sire. I have begun and I mean to finish."

The Emperor smiled at this display of mettle:

"I do not give up, but my police will set to work."

Lupin burst out laughing:

"Excuse me, Sire! It is so funny! Your police! Your Imperial Majesty's police! Why, they're worth just about as much as any other police, that is to say, nothing, nothing at all! No, Sire, I will not return to the Santé! Prison I can afford to laugh at. But time enough has been wasted as it is. I need my freedom against that man and I mean to keep it."

The Emperor shrugged his shoulders:

"You don't even know who the man is."

"I shall know, Sire. And I alone can know. And he knows that I am the only one who can know. I am his only enemy. I am the only one whom he attacks. It was I whom he meant to hit, the other day, when he fired his revolver. He considered it enough to put me and me only to sleep, last night, to be free to do as he pleased. The fight lies between him and me. The outside world has nothing to say to it. No one can help me and no one can help him. There are two of us; and that is all. So far, chance has favored him. But, in the long run, it is inevitable, it is doomed that I should gain the day."

"Why?"

"Because I am the better man."

"Suppose he kills you?"

"He will not kill me. I shall draw his claws, I shall make him perfectly harmless. And you shall have the letters, Sire. They are yours. There is no power on earth than can prevent me from restoring them to you."

He spoke with a violent conviction and a tone of certainty that gave to the things which he foretold the real appearance of things already accomplished.

The Emperor could not help undergoing a vague, inexplicable feeling in which there was a sort of admiration combined with a good deal of that confidence which Lupin was demanding in so masterful a manner. In reality, he was hesitating only because of his scruples against employing this man and making him, so to speak, his ally. And, anxiously, not knowing what decision to take, he walked from the gallery to the windows without saying a word.

At last, he asked:

"And who says that the letters were stolen last night?"

"The theft is dated, Sire."

"What do you say?"

"Look at the inner side of the pediment which concealed the hiding-place. The date is written in white chalk: 'Midnight, 24 August.' . . ."

"So it is," muttered the Emperor, nonplussed. "How was it that I did not see?" And he added, betraying his curiosity, "Just as with those two 'N's' painted on the wall. . . . I can't understand. This is the Minerva Room."

"This is the room in which Napoleon, the Emperor of the French slept," said Lupin.

"How do you know?"

"Ask Waldemar, Sire. As for myself, when I was turning over the old servants' diary, it came upon me as a flash of light. I understood that Shears and I had been on the wrong scent. APOON, the imperfect word written by the Grand-duke Hermann on his death-bed, is a contraction not of Apollon, but of Napoleon."

"That's true . . . you are right," said the Emperor. "The same letters occur in both words and in the same order. The grand-duke evidently meant to write 'Napoleon.' But that figure 813? . . ."

"Ah, that was the point that gave me most trouble. I always had an idea that we must add up the three figures 8, 1 and 3; and the number 12, thus obtained, seemed to me at once to apply to this room, which is the twelfth leading out of the gallery. But that was not enough for me. There must be something else, something which my enfeebled brain could not succeed in translating into words. The sight of that clock, situated precisely in the Napoleon Room, was a revelation to me. The number 12 evidently meant twelve o'clock. The hour of noon! The hour of midnight! Is this not the solemn moment which a man most readily selects? But why those three figures 8, 1 and 3, rather than any others which would have given the same total? . . . It was then that I thought of making the clock strike for the first time, by way of experiment. And it was while making it strike that I saw the dots of the first, third and eighth hour were movable and that they alone were movable. I therefore obtained three figures, 1, 3 and 8, which, placed in a more prophetic order, gave the number 813. Waldemar pushed the three dots, the spring was released and Your Imperial Majesty knows the result. . . . This, Sire, is the explanation of that mysterious word and of those three figures 8, 1, 3 which the grand-duke wrote with his dying hand and by the aid of which he hoped that his son would one day recover the secret of Veldenz and become the possessor of the famous letters which he had hidden there."

The Emperor listened with eager attention, more and more surprised at the ingenuity, perspicacity, shrewdness and intelligent will which he observed in the man.

"Waldemar," he said, when Lupin had finished.

"Sire?"

But, just as he was about to speak, shouts were heard in the gallery outside.

Waldemar left the room and returned:

"It's the mad girl, Sire. They won't let her pass."

"Let her come in." cried Lupin, eagerly. "She must come in, Sire."

At a sign from the Emperor, Waldemar went out to fetch Isilda.

Her entrance caused a general stupefaction. Her pale face was covered with dark blotches. Her distorted features bore signs of the keenest suffering. She panted for breath, with her two hands clutched against her breast.

"Oh!" cried Lupin, struck with horror.

"What is it?" asked the Emperor.

"Your doctor, Sire. There is not a moment to lose."

He went up to her:

"Speak, Isilda. . . . Have you seen anything? Have you anything to say?"

The girl had stopped; her eyes were less vacant, as though lighted up by the pain. She uttered sounds. . . . but not a word.

"Listen," said Lupin. "Answer yes or no . . . make a movement of the head . . . Have you seen him? Do you know where he is? . . . You know who he is. . . . Listen! if you don't answer. . . ."

He suppressed a gesture of anger. But, suddenly, remembering the experiment of the day before and that she seemed rather to have retained a certain optical memory of the time when she enjoyed her full reason, he wrote on the white wall a capital "L" and "M."

She stretched out her arm toward the letters and nodded her head as though in assent.

"And then?" said Lupin. "What then? . . . Write something yourself."

But she gave a fearful scream and flung herself to the ground, yelling.

Then, suddenly, came silence, immobility. One last convulsive spasm. And she moved no more.

"Dead?" asked the Emperor.

"Poisoned, Sire."

"Oh, the poor thing! . . . And by whom?"

"By 'him,' Sire. She knew him, no doubt. He must have been afraid of what she might tell."

The doctor arrived. The Emperor pointed to the girl. Then, addressing Waldemar:

"All your men to turn out . . . Make them go through the houses . . . telegraph to the stations on the frontier. . . ."

He went up to Lupin:

"How long do you want to recover the letters?"

"A month, Sire . . . two months at most."

"Very well. Waldemar will wait for you here. He shall have my orders and full powers to grant you anything you wish."

"What I should like, Sire, is my freedom."

"You are free."

Lupin watched him walk away and said, between his teeth:

"My freedom first. . . . And afterward, when I have given you back the letters, O Majesty, one little shake of the hand! Then we shall be quits! . . ."

XIII. THE SEVEN SCOUNDRELS

"Will you see this gentleman, ma'am?"

Dolores Kesselbach took the card from the footman and read:

"André Beauny. . . . No," she said, "I don't know him."

"The gentleman seems very anxious to see you, ma'am. He says that you are expecting him."

"Oh . . . possibly. . . . Yes, bring him here."

Since the events which had upset her life and pursued her with relentless animosity, Dolores, after staying at the Hôtel Bristol had taken up her abode in a quiet house in the Rue des Vignes, down at Passy. A pretty garden lay at the back of the house and was surrounded by other leafy gardens. On days when attacks more painful than usual did not keep her from morning till night behind the closed shutters of her bedroom, she made her servants carry her under the trees, where she lay stretched at full length, a victim to melancholy, incapable of fighting against her hard fate.

Footsteps sounded on the gravel-path and the footman returned, followed by a young man, smart in appearance and very simply dressed, in the rather out-of-date fashion adopted by some of our painters, with a turn-down collar and a flowing necktie of white spots on a blue ground.

The footman withdrew.

"Your name is André Beauny, I believe?" said Dolores.

"Yes, madame."

"I have not the honor . . ."

"I beg your pardon, madame. Knowing that I was a friend of Mme. Ernemont, Geneviève's grandmother, you wrote to her, at Garches, saying that you wished to speak to me. I have come."

Dolores rose in her seat, very excitedly:

"Oh, you are . . ."

"Yes."

She stammered:

"Really? . . . Is it you? . . . I do not recognize you."

"You don't recognize Prince Paul Sernine?"

"No . . . everything is different . . . the forehead . . . the eyes. . . . And that is not how the . . ."

"How the newspapers represented the prisoner at the Santé?" he said, with a smile. "And yet it is I, really."

A long silence followed, during which they remained embarrassed and ill at ease.

At last, he asked:

"May I know the reason . . . ?"

"Did not Geneviève tell you? . . ."

"I have not seen her . . . but her grandmother seemed to think that you required my services . . ."

"That's right . . . that's right. . . ."

"And in what way . . . ? I am so pleased . . ."

She hesitated a second and then whispered:

"I am afraid."

"Afraid?" he cried.

"Yes," she said, speaking in a low voice, "I am afraid, afraid of everything, afraid of to-day and of to-morrow . . . and of the day after . . . afraid of life. I have suffered so much. . . . I can bear no more."

He looked at her with great pity in his eyes. The vague feeling that had always drawn him to this woman took a more precise character now that she was asking for his protection. He felt an eager need to devote himself to her, wholly, without hope of reward.

She continued:

"I am alone now, quite alone, with servants whom I have picked up on chance, and I am afraid. . . . I feel that people are moving about me."

"But with what object?"

"I do not know. But the enemy is hovering around and coming closer."

"Have you seen him? Have you noticed anything?"

"Yes, the other day two men passed several times in the street and stopped in front of the house."

"Can you describe them?"

"I saw one of them better than the other. He was tall and powerful, clean-shaven and wore a little black cloth jacket, cut quite short."

"A waiter at a café, perhaps?"

"Yes, a head-waiter. I had him followed by one of my servants. He went down the Rue de la Pompe and entered a common-looking house. The ground-floor is occupied by a wine-shop: it is the first house in the street, on the left. Then, a night or two ago, I saw a shadow in the garden from my bedroom window."

"Is that all?"

"Yes."

He thought and then made a suggestion:

"Would you allow two of my men to sleep downstairs, in one of the ground-floor rooms?"

"Two of your men? . . ."

"Oh, you need not be afraid! They are decent men, old Charolais and his son, and they don't look in the least like what they are. . . . You will be quite safe with them. . . . As for me . . ."

He hesitated. He was waiting for her to ask him to come again. As she was silent, he said:

"As for me, it is better that I should not be seen here. . . . Yes, it is better . . . for your sake. My men will let me know how things go on. . . ."

He would have liked to say more and to remain and to sit down beside her and comfort her. But he had a feeling that they had said all that they had to say and that a single word more, on his side, would be an insult.

Then he made her a very low bow and went away.

He went up the garden, walking quickly, in his haste to be outside and master his emotion. The footman was waiting for him at the hall-door. As he passed out into the street, somebody rang, a young woman.

He gave a start:

"Geneviève!"

She fixed a pair of astonished eyes upon him and at once recognized him, although bewildered by the extreme youthfulness of his appearance; and this gave her such a shock that she staggered and had to lean against the door for support. He had taken off his hat and was looking at her without daring to put out his hand. Would she put out hers? He was no longer Prince Sernine: he was Arsène Lupin. And she knew that he was Arsène Lupin and that he had just come out of prison.

It was raining outside. She gave her umbrella to the footman and said:

"Please open it and put it somewhere to dry."

Then she walked straight in.

"My poor old chap!" said Lupin to himself, as he walked away. "What a series of blows for a sensitive and highly-strung creature like yourself! You must keep a watch on your heart or . . . Ah, what next? Here are my eyes beginning to water now! That's a bad sign. M. Lupin: you're growing old!"

He gave a tap on the shoulder to a young man who was crossing the Chaussee de la Muette and going toward the Rue des Vignes. The young man stopped, stared at him and said:

"I beg your pardon, monsieur, but I don't think I have the honor . . ."

"Think again, my dear M. Leduc. Or has your memory quite gone? Don't you remember Versailles? And the little room at the Hôtel des Trois-Empereurs?"

The young man bounded backwards:

"You!"

"Why, yes, I! Prince Sernine, or rather Lupin, since you know my real name! Did you think that Lupin had departed this life? . . . Oh, yes, I see, prison. . . . You were hoping . . . Get out, you baby!" He patted him gently on the shoulder. "There, there, young fellow, don't be frightened: you have still a few nice quiet days left to write your poems in. The time has not yet come. Write your verses . . . poet!"

Then he gripped Leduc's arm violently and, looking him full in the face, said:

"But the time is drawing near . . . poet! Don't forget that you belong to me, body and soul. And prepare to play your part. It will be a hard and magnificent part. And, as I live, I believe you're the man to play it!"

He burst out laughing, turned on one foot and left young Leduc astounded.

A little further, at the corner of the Rue de la Pompe, stood the wine-shop of which Mrs. Kesselbach had spoken to him. He went in and had a long talk with the proprietor.

Then he took a taxi and drove to the Grand Hotel, where he was staying under the name of André Beauny, and found the brothers Doudeville waiting for him.

Lupin, though used to that sort of pleasure, nevertheless enjoyed the marks of admiration and devotion with which his friends overwhelmed him:

"But, governor, tell us . . . what happened? We're accustomed to all sorts of wonders with you; but still, there are limits. . . . So you are free? And here you are, in the heart of Paris, scarcely disguised. . . . !"

"Have a cigar," said Lupin.

"Thank you, no."

"You're wrong, Doudeville. These are worth smoking. I have them from a great connoisseur, who is good enough to call himself my friend."

"Oh, may one ask . . . ?"

"The Kaiser! Come, don't look so flabbergasted, the two of you! And tell me things: I haven't seen the papers. What effect did my escape have on the public?"

"Tremendous, governor!"

"What was the police version?"

"Your flight took place at Garches, during an attempt to reënact the murder of Altenheim. Unfortunately, the journalists have proved that it was impossible."

"After that?"

"After that, a general fluster. People wondering, laughing and enjoying themselves like mad."

"Weber?"

"Weber is badly let in."

"Apart from that, no news at the detective-office? Nothing discovered about the murderer? No clue to help us to establish Altenheim's identity?"

"No."

"What fools they are! And to think that we pay millions a year to keep those people. If this sort of thing goes on, I shall refuse to pay my rates. Take a seat and a pen. I will dictate a letter which you must hand in to the *Grand Journal* this evening. The world has been waiting for news of me long enough. It must be gasping with impatience. Write."

He dictated:

"To the Editor of the *Grand Journal:*

"SIR,

"I must apologize to your readers for disappointing their legitimate impatience.

"I have escaped from prison and I cannot possibly reveal how I escaped. In the same way, since my escape, I have discovered the famous secret and I cannot possibly disclose what the secret is nor how I discovered it.

"All this will, some day or other, form the subject of a rather original story which my biographer-in-ordinary will publish from my notes. It will form a page of the history of France which our grandchildren will read with interest.

"For the moment, I have more important matters to attend to. Disgusted at seeing into what hands the functions which I once exercised have fallen, tired of finding the Kesselbach-Altenheim case still dragging along, I am discharging M. Weber and resuming the post of honor which I occupied with such distinction and to the general satisfaction under the name of M. Lenormand.

"I am, Sir,

"Your obedient servant.

"ARSÈNE LUPIN,

"*Chief of the Detective-service.*"

At eight o'clock in the evening, Arsène Lupin and Jean Doudeville walked into Caillard's, the fashionable restaurant, Lupin in evening-clothes, but dressed like an artist, with rather wide trousers and a rather loose tie, and Doudeville in a frock-coat, with the serious air and appearance of a magistrate.

They sat down in that part of the restaurant which is set back and divided from the big room by two columns.

A head-waiter, perfectly dressed and supercilious in manner, came to take their orders, note-book in hand. Lupin selected the dinner with the nice thought of an accomplished epicure:

"Certainly," he said, "the prison ordinary was quite acceptable; but, all the same, it is nice to have a carefully-ordered meal."

He ate with a good appetite and silently, contenting himself with uttering, from time to time, a short sentence that marked his train of thought:

"Of course, I shall manage . . . but it will be a hard job. . . . Such an adversary! . . . What staggers me is that, after six months' fighting, I don't even know what he wants! . . . His chief accomplice is dead, we are near the end of the battle and yet, even now, I can't understand his game. . . . What is the wretch after? . . . My own plan is quite clear: to lay hands on the grand-duchy, to shove a grand-duke of my own making on the throne, to give him Geneviève for a wife . . . and to reign. That is what I call lucid, honest and fair. But he, the low fellow, the ghost in the dark: what is he aiming at?"

He called:

"Waiter!"

The head-waiter came up:

"Yes, sir?"

"Cigars."

The head-waiter stalked away, returned and opened a number of boxes.

"Which do you recommend?"

"These Upmanns are very good, sir."

Lupin gave Doudeville an Upmann, took one for himself and cut it. The head-waiter struck a match and held if for him. With a sudden movement, Lupin caught him by the wrist:

"Not a word. . . . I know you. . . . Your real name is Dominique Lecas!"

The man, who was big and strong, tried to struggle away. He stifled a cry of pain: Lupin had twisted his wrist.

"Your name is Dominique . . . you live in the Rue de la Pompe, on the fourth floor, where you retired with a small fortune acquired in the service—listen to me, you fool, will you, or I'll break every bone in your body!—acquired in the service of Baron Altenheim, at whose house you were butler."

The other stood motionless, his face pallid with fear. Around them, the small room was empty. In the restaurant beside it, three gentlemen sat smoking and two couples were chatting over their liquors.

"You see, we are quiet . . . we can talk."

"Who are you? Who are you?"

"Don't you recollect me? Why, think of that famous luncheon in the Villa Dupont! . . . You yourself, you old flunkey, handed me the plate of cakes . . . and such cakes!"

"Prince. . . . Prince. . . ." stammered the other.

"Yes, yes, Prince Arsène, Prince Lupin in person. . . . Aha, you breathe again! . . . You're saying to yourself that you have nothing to fear from Lupin, isn't that it? Well, you're wrong, old chap, you have everything to fear." He took a card from his pocket and showed it to him. "There, look, I belong to the police now. Can't be helped: that's what we all come to in the end, all of us robber-kings and emperors of crime."

"Well?" said the head-waiter, still greatly alarmed.

"Well, go to that customer over there, who's calling you, get him what he wants and come back to me. And no nonsense, mind you: don't go trying to get away. I have ten men outside, with orders to keep their eyes on you. Be off."

The head-waiter obeyed. Five minutes after, he returned and, standing in front of the table, with his back to the restaurant, as though discussing the quality of the cigars with his customers, he said:

"Well? What is it?"

Lupin laid a number of hundred-franc notes in a row on the table:

"One note for each definite answer to my questions."

"Done!"

"Now then. How many of you were there with Baron Altenheim?"

"Seven, without counting myself."

"No more?"

"No. Once only, we picked up some workmen in Italy to make the underground passage from the Villa des Glycines, at Garches."

"Were there two underground passages?"

"Yes, one led to the Pavillon Hortense and the other branched off from the first and ran under Mrs. Kesselbach's house."

"What was the object?"

"To carry off Mrs. Kesselbach."

"Were the two maids, Suzanne and Gertrude, accomplices?"

"Yes."

"Where are they?"

"Abroad."

"And your seven pals, those of the Altenheim gang?"

"I have left them. They are still going on."

"Where can I find them?"

Dominique hesitated. Lupin unfolded two notes of a thousand francs each and said:

"Your scruples do you honor, Dominique. There's nothing for it but to swallow them like a man and answer."

Dominique replied:

"You will find them at No. 3, Route de la Revolte, Neuilly. One of them is called the Broker."

"Capital. And now the name, the real name of Altenheim. Do you know it?"

"Yes, Ribeira."

"Dominique, Dominique, you're asking for trouble. Ribeira was only an assumed name. I asked you the real name."

"Parbury."

"That's another assumed name."

The head-waiter hesitated. Lupin unfolded three hundred franc notes.

"Pshaw, what do I care!" said the man. "After all, he's dead, isn't he? Quite dead."

"His name," said Lupin.

"His name? The Chevalier de Malreich."

Lupin gave a jump in his chair:

"What? What do you say? The Chevalier—say it again—the Chevalier . . . ?"

"Raoul de Malreich."

A long pause. Lupin, with his eyes fixed before him, thought of the mad girl at Veldenz, who had died by poison: Isilda bore the same name, Malreich. And it was the name borne by the small French noble who came to the court of Veldenz in the eighteenth century.

He resumed his questions:

"What country did this Malreich belong to?"

"He was of French origin, but born in Germany . . . I saw some papers once . . . that was how I came to know his name. . . . Oh, if he had found it out, he would have wrung my neck, I believe!"

Lupin reflected and said:

"Did he command the lot of you?"

"Yes."

"But he had an accomplice, a partner?"

"Oh hush . . . hush . . . !"

The head-waiter's face suddenly expressed the most intense alarm. Lupin noticed the same sort of terror and repulsion which he himself felt when he thought of the murderer.

"Who is he? Have you seen him?"

"Oh, don't let us talk of that one . . . it doesn't do to talk of him."

"Who is he, I'm asking you."

"He is the master . . . the chief. . . . Nobody knows him."

"But you've seen him, you. Answer me. Have you seen him?"

"Sometimes, in the dark . . . at night. Never by daylight. His orders come on little scraps of paper . . . or by telephone."

"His name?"

"I don't know it. We never used to speak of him. It was unlucky."

"He dresses in black, doesn't he?"

"Yes, in black. He is short and slender . . . with fair hair. . . ."

"And he kills, doesn't he?"

"Yes, he kills . . . he kills where another might steal a bit of bread."

His voice shook. He entreated:

"Let us stop this . . . it won't do to talk of him. . . . I tell you . . . it's unlucky."

Lupin was silent, impressed, in spite of himself, by the man's anguish. He sat long thinking and then rose and said to the head-waiter:

"Here, here's your money; but, if you want to live in peace, you will do well not to breathe a word of our conversation to anybody."

He left the restaurant with Doudeville and walked to the Porte Saint-Denis without speaking, absorbed in all that he had heard. At last, he seized his companion's arm and said:

"Listen to me, Doudeville, carefully. Go to the Gare du Nord. You will get there in time to catch the Luxemburg express. Go to Veldenz, the capital of the grand-duchy of Zweibrucken-Veldenz. At the town-hall, you will easily obtain the birth-certificate of the Chevalier de Malreich and further information about the family. You will be back on the day after to-morrow: that will be Saturday."

"Am I to let them know at the detective-office?"

"I'll see to that. I shall telephone that you are ill. Oh, one word more: on Saturday, meet me at twelve o'clock in a little café on the Route de la Revolte, called the Restaurant Buffalo. Come dressed as a workman."

The next day, Lupin, wearing a short smock and a cap, went down to Neuilly and began his investigations at No. 3, Route de la Revolte. A gateway opened into an outer yard; and here he found a huge block of workmen's dwellings, a whole series of passages and workshops, with a swarming population of artisans, women and brats. In a few minutes, he had won the good-will of the portress, with whom he chatted for an hour on the most varied topics. During this hour, he saw three men pass, one after the other, whose manner struck him:

"That's game," he thought, "and gamy game at that! . . . They follow one another by scent! . . . Look quite respectable, of course, but with the eye of the hunted deer which knows that the enemy is all around and that every tuft, every blade of grass may conceal an ambush."

That afternoon and on the Saturday morning, he pursued his inquiries and made certain that Altenheim's seven accomplices all lived on the premises. Four of them openly followed the trade of second-hand clothes-dealers. Two of the others sold newspapers; and the third described himself as a broker and was nicknamed accordingly.

They went in and out, one after the other, without appearing to know one another. But, in the evening, Lupin discovered that they met in a sort of coach-house situated right at the back of the last of the yards, a place in which the Broker kept his wares piled up: old iron, broken kitchen-ranges, rusty stove-pipes . . . and also, no doubt, the best part of the stolen goods.

"Come," he said, "the work is shaping nicely. I asked my cousin of Germany for a month and I believe a fortnight will be enough for my purpose. And what I like about it is that I shall start operations with the scoundrels who made me take a header in the Seine. My poor old Gourel, I shall revenge you at last. And high time too!"

At twelve o'clock on Saturday, he went to the Restaurant Buffalo, a little low-ceilinged room to which brick-layers and cab-drivers resorted for their mid-day meal. Some one came and sat down beside him:

"It's done, governor."

"Ah, is it you, Doudeville? That's right! I'm dying to know. Have you the particulars? The birth-certificate? Quick, tell me."

"Well, it's like this: Altenheim's father and mother died abroad."

"Never mind about them."

"They left three children."

"Three?"

"Yes. The eldest would have been thirty years old by now. His name was Raoul de Malreich."

"That's our man, Altenheim. Next?"

"The youngest of the children was a girl, Isilda. The register has an entry, in fresh ink, 'Deceased.'"

"Isilda. . . . Isilda," repeated Lupin. "That's just what I thought: Isilda was Altenheim's sister. . . . I saw a look in her face which I seemed to recognize. . . . So that was the link between them. . . . But the other, the third child, or rather the second?"

"A son. He would be twenty-six by now."

"His name?"

"Louis de Malreich."

Lupin gave a little start:

"That's it! Louis de Malreich.... The initials L. M.... The awful and terrifying signature!... The murderer's name is Louis de Malreich.... He was the brother of Altenheim and the brother of Isilda and he killed both of them for fear of what they might reveal."

Lupin sat long, silent and gloomy, under the obsession, no doubt, of the mysterious being.

Doudeville objected:

"What had he to fear from his sister Isilda? She was mad, they told me."

"Mad, yes, but capable of remembering certain details of her childhood. She must have recognized the brother with whom she grew up . . . and that recollection cost her her life." And he added, "Mad! But all those people were mad.... The mother was mad.... The father a dipsomaniac.... Altenheim a regular brute beast.... Isilda, a poor innocent.... As for the other, the murderer, he is the monster, the crazy lunatic...."

"Crazy? Do you think so, governor?"

"Yes, crazy! With flashes of genius, of devilish cunning and intuition, but a crack-brained fool, a madman, like all that Malreich family. Only madmen kill and especially madmen of his stamp. For, after all . . ."

He interrupted himself; and his face underwent so great a change that Doudeville was struck by it:

"What's the matter, governor?"

"Look."

A man had entered and hung his hat—a soft, black felt hat—on a peg. He sat down at a little table, examined the bill of fare which a waiter brought him, gave his order and waited motionless, with his body stiff and erect and his two arms crossed over the table-cloth.

And Lupin saw him full-face.

He had a lean, hard visage, absolutely smooth and pierced with two sockets in the depths of which appeared a pair of steel-gray eyes. The skin seemed stretched from bone to bone, like a sheet of parchment, so stiff and so thick that not a hair could have penetrated through it.

And the face was dismal and dull. No expression enlivened it. No thought seemed to abide under that ivory forehead; and the eye-lids, entirely devoid of lashes, never flickered, which gave the eyes the fixed look of the eyes in a statue.

Lupin beckoned to one of the waiters:

"Who is that gentleman?"

"The one eating his lunch over there?"

"Yes."

"He is a customer. He comes here two or three times a week."

"Can you tell me his name?"

"Why, yes . . . Leon Massier."

"Oh!" blurted Lupin, very excitedly. "L. M. . . . the same two letters . . . could it be Louis de Malreich?"

He watched him eagerly. Indeed, the man's appearance agreed with Lupin's conjectures, with what he knew of him and of his hideous mode of existence. But what puzzled him was that look of death about him: where he anticipated life and fire, where he would have expected to find the torment, the disorder, the violent facial distortion of the great accursed, he beheld sheer impassiveness.

He asked the waiter:

"What does he do?"

"I really can't say. He's a rum cove . . . He's always quite alone.... He never talks to anybody . . . We here don't even know the sound of his voice.... He points his finger at the dishes on the bill of fare which he wants.... He has finished in twenty minutes; then he pays and goes...."

"And he comes back again?"

"Every three or four days. He's not regular."

"It's he, it cannot be any one else," said Lupin to himself. "It's Malreich. There he is . . . breathing . . . at four steps from me. There are the hands that kill. There is the brain that gloats upon the smell of blood. There is the monster, the vampire! . . ."

And, yet, was it possible? Lupin had ended by looking upon Malreich as so fantastic a being that he was disconcerted at seeing him in the flesh, coming, going, moving. He could not explain to himself how the man could eat bread and meat like other men, drink beer like any one else: this man whom he had pictured as a foul beast, feeding on live flesh and sucking the blood of his victims.

"Come away, Doudeville."

"What's the matter with you, governor? You look quite white!"

"I want air. Come out."

Outside, he drew a deep breath, wiped the perspiration from his forehead and muttered:

"That's better. I was stifling." And, mastering himself, he added, "Now we must play our game cautiously and not lose sight of his tracks."

"Hadn't we better separate, governor? Our man saw us together. He will take less notice of us singly."

"Did he see us?" said Lupin, pensively. "He seems to me to see nothing, to hear nothing and to look at nothing. What a bewildering specimen!"

And, in fact, ten minutes later, Leon Massier appeared and walked away, without even looking to see if he was followed. He had lit a cigarette and smoked, with one of his hands behind his back, strolling along like a saunterer enjoying the sunshine and the fresh air and never suspecting that his movements could possibly be watched.

He passed through the toll-gates, skirted the fortifications, went out again through the Porte Champerret and retraced his steps along the Route de la Revolte.

Would he enter the buildings at No. 3? Lupin eagerly hoped that he would, for that would have been a certain proof of his complicity with the Altenheim gang; but the man turned round and made for the Rue Delaizement, which he followed until he passed the Velodrome Buffalo.

On the left, opposite the cycling-track, between the public tennis-court and the booths that line the Rue Delaizement, stood a small detached villa, surrounded by a scanty garden. Leon Massier stopped, took out his keys, opened first the gate of the garden and then the door of the house and disappeared.

Lupin crept forward cautiously. He at once noticed that the block in the Route de la Revolte stretched back as far as the garden-wall. Coming still nearer, he saw that the wall was very high and that a coach-house rested against it at the bottom of the garden. The position of the buildings was such as to give him the certainty that his coach-house stood back to back with the coach-house in the inner yard of No. 3, which served as a lumber-room for the Broker.

Leon Massier, therefore, occupied a house adjoining the place in which the seven members of the Altenheim gang held their meetings. Consequently, Leon Massier was, in point of fact, the supreme leader who commanded that gang; and there was evidently a passage between the two coach-houses through which he communicated with his followers.

"I was right," said Lupin. "Leon Massier and Louis de Malreich are one and the same man. The situation is much simpler than it was."

"There is no doubt about that," said Doudeville, "and everything will be settled in a few days."

"That is to say, I shall have been stabbed in the throat."

"What are you saying, governor? There's an idea!"

"Pooh, who knows? I have always had a presentiment that that monster would bring me ill-luck."

Thenceforth it became a matter of watching Malreich's life in such a way that none of his movements went unobserved. This life was of the oddest, if one could believe the people of the neighborhood whom Doudeville questioned. "The bloke from the villa," as they called him, had been living there for a few months only. He saw and received nobody. He was not known to keep a servant of any kind. And the windows, though they were left wide open, even at night, always remained dark and were never lit with the glow of a lamp or candle.

Moreover, Leon Massier most often went out at the close of day and did not come in again until very late . . . at dawn, said people who had come upon him at sunrise.

"And does any one know what he does?" asked Lupin of his companion, when they next met.

"No, he leads an absolutely irregular existence. He sometimes disappears for several days together . . . or, rather, he remains indoors. When all is said, nobody knows anything."

"Well, we shall know; and that soon."

He was wrong. After a week of continuous efforts and investigations, he had learnt no more than before about that strange individual. The extraordinary thing that constantly happened was this, that, suddenly, while Lupin was following him, the man, who was ambling with short steps along the streets, without ever turning round or ever stopping, the man would vanish as if by a miracle. True, he sometimes went through houses with two entrances. But, at other times, he seemed to fade away in the midst of the crowd, like a ghost. And Lupin was left behind, petrified, astounded, filled with rage and confusion.

He at once hurried to the Rue Delaizement and stood on guard outside the villa. Minutes followed upon minutes, half-hour upon half-hour. A part of the night slipped away. Then, suddenly, the mysterious man hove in sight. What could he have been doing?

"An express message for you, governor," said Doudeville, at eight o'clock one evening, as he joined him in the Rue Delaizement.

Lupin opened the envelope. Mrs. Kesselbach implored him to come to her aid. It appeared that two men had taken up their stand under her windows, at night, and one of them had said:

"What luck, we've dazzled them completely this time! So it's understood; we shall strike the blow to-night."

Mrs. Kesselbach thereupon went downstairs and discovered that the shutter in the pantry did not fasten, or, at least, that it could be opened from the outside.

"At last," said Lupin, "it's the enemy himself who offers to give battle. That's a good thing! I am tired of marching up and down under Malreich's windows."

"Is he there at this moment?"

"No, he played me one of his tricks again in Paris, just as I was about to play him one of mine. But, first of all, listen to me, Doudeville. Go and collect ten of our men and bring them to the Rue des Vignes. Look here, bring Marco and Jérôme, the messenger. I have given them a holiday since the business at the Palace Hotel: let them come this time. Daddy Charolais and his son ought to be mounting guard by now. Make your arrangements with them, and at half-past eleven, come and join me at the corner of the Rue des Vignes and the Rue Raynouard. From there we will watch the house."

Doudeville went away. Lupin waited for an hour longer, until that quiet thoroughfare, the Rue Delaizement, was quite deserted, and then, seeing that Leon Massier did not return, he made up his mind and went up to the villa.

There was no one in sight. . . . He took a run and jumped on the stone ledge that supported the railings of the garden. A few minutes later, he was inside.

His plan was to force the door of the house and search the rooms in order to find the Emperor's letters which Malreich had stolen from Veldenz. But he thought a visit to the coach-house of more immediate importance.

He was much surprised to see that it was open and, next, to find, by the light of his electric lantern, that it was absolutely empty and that there was no door in the back wall. He hunted about for a long time, but met with no more success. Outside, however, he saw a ladder standing against the coach-house and obviously serving as a means of reaching a sort of loft contrived under the slate roof.

The loft was blocked with old packing-cases, trusses of straw and gardener's frames, or rather it seemed to be blocked, for he very soon discovered a gangway that took him to the wall. Here, he knocked up against a cucumber-frame, which he tried to move. Failing to effect his purpose, he examined the frame more closely and found, first, that it was fixed to the wall and, secondly, that one of the panes was missing. He passed his arm through and encountered space. He cast the bright light of the lantern through the aperture and saw a big shed, a coach-house larger than that of the villa and filled with old iron-work and objects of every kind.

"That's it," said Lupin to himself. "This window has been contrived in the Broker's lumber-room, right up at the top, and from here Louis de Malreich sees, hears and watches his accomplices, without being seen or heard by them. I now understand how it is that they do not know their leader."

Having found out what he wanted, he put out his light and was on the point of leaving, when a door opened opposite him, down below. Some one came in and lit a lamp. He recognized the Broker. He thereupon resolved to stay where he was, since the expedition, after all, could not be done so long as that man was there.

The Broker took two revolvers from his pocket. He tested the triggers and changed the cartridges, whistling a music-hall tune as he did so.

An hour elapsed in this way. Lupin was beginning to grow restless, without, however, making up his mind to go.

More minutes passed, half an hour, an hour. . . .

At last, the man said aloud:

"Come in."

One of the scoundrels slipped into the shed; and, one after the other, a third arrived and a fourth. . . .

"We are all here," said the Broker. "Dieudonne and Chubby will meet us down there. Come, we've no time to lose. . . . Are you armed?"

"To the teeth."

"That's all right. It'll be hot work."

"How do you know, Broker?"

"I've seen the chief. . . . When I say that I've seen him, no . . . but he spoke to me. . . ."

"Yes," said one of the men, "in the dark, at a street-corner, as usual. Ah, Altenheim's ways were better than that. At least, one knew what one was doing."

"And don't you know?" retorted the Broker. "We're breaking in at the Kesselbach woman's."

"And what about the two watchers? The two coves whom Lupin posted there?"

"That's their look-out: there's seven of us. They had better give us as little trouble as possible."

"What about the Kesselbach?"

"Gag her first, then bind her and bring her here. . . . There, on that old sofa. . . . And then wait for orders."

"Is the job well paid?"

"The Kesselbach's jewels to begin with."

"Yes, if it comes off . . . but I'm speaking of the certainty."

"Three hundred-franc notes apiece, beforehand, and twice as much again afterwards."

"Have you the money?"

"Yes."

"That's all right. You can say what you like, but, as far as paying goes, there's no one to equal that bloke." And, in a voice so low that Lupin could hardly hear, "I say, Broker, if we're obliged to use the knife, is there a reward?"

"The same as usual, two thousand."

"If it's Lupin?"

"Three thousand."

"Oh, if we could only get him!"

One after the other, they left the lumber-room. Lupin heard the Broker's parting words:

"This is the plan of attack. We divide into three lots. A whistle; and every one runs forward. . . ."

Lupin hurriedly left his hiding-place, went down the ladder, ran round the house, without going in, and climbed back over the railings:

"The Broker's right; it'll be hot work. . . . Ah, it's my skin they're after! A reward for Lupin! The rascals!"

He passed through the toll-gate and jumped into a taxi:

"Rue Raynouard."

He stopped the cab at two hundred yards from the Rue des Vignes and walked to the corner of the two streets. To his great surprise, Doudeville was not there.

"That's funny," said Lupin. "It's past twelve. . . . This business looks suspicious to me."

He waited ten minutes, twenty minutes. At half-past twelve, nobody had arrived. Further delay was dangerous. After all, if Doudeville and his men were prevented from coming, Charolais, his son and he, Lupin, himself were enough to repel the attack, without counting the assistance of the servants.

He therefore went ahead. But he caught sight of two men who tried to hide in the shadow of a corner wall.

"Hang it!" he said. "That's the vanguard of the gang, Dieudonne and Chubby. I've allowed myself to be out-distanced, like a fool."

Here he lost more time. Should he go straight up to them, disable them and then climb into the house through the pantry-window, which he knew to be unlocked? That would be the most prudent course and would enable him, moreover, to take Mrs. Kesselbach away at once and to remove her to a place of safety.

Yes, but it also meant the failure of his plan; it meant missing this glorious opportunity of trapping the whole gang, including Louis de Malreich himself, without doubt.

Suddenly a whistle sounded from somewhere on the other side of the house. Was it the rest of the gang, so soon? And was an offensive movement to be made from the garden?

But, at the preconcerted signal, the two men climbed through the window and disappeared from view.

Lupin scaled the balcony at a bound and jumped into the pantry. By the sound of their footsteps, he judged that the assailants had gone into the garden; and the sound was so distinct that he felt easy in his mind: Charolais and his son could not fail to hear the noise.

He therefore went upstairs. Mrs. Kesselbach's bedroom was on the first landing. He walked in without knocking.

A night-light was burning in the room; and he saw Dolores, on a sofa, fainting. He ran up to her, lifted her and, in a voice of command, forcing her to answer:

"Listen. . . . Charolais? His son . . . Where are they?"

She stammered:

"Why, what do you mean? . . . They're gone, of course! . . ."

"What, gone?"

"You sent me word . . . an hour ago . . . a telephone-message. . . ."

He picked up a piece of blue paper lying beside her and read:

"Send the two watchers away at once . . . and all my men. . . . Tell them to meet me at the Grand Hotel. Have no fear."

"Thunder! And you believed it? . . . But your servants?"

"Gone."

He went up to the window. Outside, three men were coming from the other end of the garden.

From the window in the next room, which looked out on the street, he saw two others, on the pavement.

And he thought of Dieudonne, of Chubby, of Louis de Malreich, above all, who must now be prowling around, invisible and formidable.

"Hang it!" he muttered. "I half believe they've done me this time!"

XIV. THE MAN IN BLACK

At that moment, Arsène Lupin felt the impression, the certainty, that he had been drawn into an ambush, by means which he had not the time to perceive, but of which he guessed the prodigious skill and address. Everything had been calculated, everything ordained; the dismissal of his men, the disappearance or treachery of the servants, his own presence in Mrs. Kesselbach's house.

Clearly, the whole thing had succeeded, exactly as the enemy wished, thanks to circumstances almost miraculously fortunate; for, after all, he might have arrived before the false message had sent his friends away. But then there would have been a battle between his own gang and the Altenheim gang. And Lupin, remembering Malreich's conduct, the murder of Altenheim, the poisoning of the mad girl at Veldenz, Lupin asked himself whether the ambush was aimed at him alone or whether Malreich had not contemplated the possibility of a general scuffle, involving the killing of accomplices who had by this time become irksome to him.

It was an intuition, rather, a fleeting idea, that just passed through his mind. The hour was one for action. He must defend Dolores, the abduction of whom was, in all likelihood, the first and foremost reason of the attack.

He half-opened the casement window on the street and levelled his revolver. A shot, rousing and alarming the neighborhood, and the scoundrels would take to their heels.

"Well, no," he muttered, "no! It shall not be said that I shirked the fight. The opportunity is too good. . . . And, then, who says that they would run away! . . . There are too many of them to care about the neighbors."

He returned to Dolores' room. There was a noise downstairs. He listened and, finding that it came from the staircase, he locked the door.

Dolores was crying and throwing herself about the sofa.

He implored her:

"Are you strong enough? We are on the first floor. I could help you down. We can lower the sheets from the window. . . ."

"No, no, don't leave me. . . . I am frightened. . . . I haven't the strength . . . they will kill me. . . . Oh, protect me!"

He took her in his arms and carried her to the next room. And, bending over her:

"Don't move; and keep calm. I swear to you that not one of those men shall touch you, as long as I am alive."

The door of the first room was tried. Dolores, clinging to him with all her might, cried:

"Oh, there they are! There they are! . . . They will kill you . . . you are alone! . . ."

Eagerly, he said:

"No, I am not alone. . . . You are here. . . . You are here beside me. . . ."

He tried to release himself. She took his head in her two hands, looked him deep in the eyes and whispered:

"Where are you going? What are you going to do? No . . . you must not die. . . . I won't have it . . . you must live . . . you must."

She stammered words which he did not catch and which she seemed to stifle between her lips lest he should hear them; and, having spent all her energy, exhausted, she fell back unconscious.

He leant over her and gazed at her for a moment. Softly, lightly, he pressed a kiss upon her hair.

Then he went back to the first room, carefully closed the door between the two and switched on the electric light.

"One second, my lads!" he cried. "You seem in a great hurry to get yourselves smashed to pieces! . . . Don't you know that Lupin's here? I'll make you dance!"

While speaking, he unfolded a screen in such a way as to hide the sofa on which Mrs. Kesselbach had been lying; and he now spread dresses and coverings over it. The door was on the point of giving way under the blows of the men outside.

"Here I am! Coming! Are you ready? Now, gentlemen, one at a time! . . ."

He briskly turned the key and drew the bolt.

Shouts, threats, a roar of infuriated animals came through the open doorway.

Yet none of them dared come forward. Before rushing at Lupin, they hesitated, seized with alarm, with fear....

This was what he had reckoned on.

Standing in the middle of the room, full in the light, with outstretched arm, he held between his fingers a sheaf of bank-notes, which he divided, counting them one by one, into seven equal shares. And he calmly said:

"Three thousand francs' reward for each of you, if Lupin is sent to his last account? That's what you were promised, isn't it? Here's double the money!"

He laid the bundles on the table, within reach of the scoundrels.

The Broker roared:

"Humbug! He's trying to gain time. Shoot him down!"

He raised his arm. His companions held him back.

And Lupin continued:

"Of course, this need not affect your plan of campaign. You came here, first, to kidnap Mrs. Kesselbach and, secondly, to lay hands on her jewels. Far be it from me to interfere with your laudable intentions!"

"Look here, what are you driving at?" growled the Broker, listening in spite of himself.

"Aha, Broker, I'm beginning to interest you, am I? . . . Come in, old chap. . . . Come in, all of you. . . . There's a draught at the top of those stairs . . . and such pretty fellows as you mustn't run the risk of catching cold. . . . What, are we afraid? Why, I'm all by myself! . . . Come, pull yourselves together, my lambs!"

They entered the room, puzzled and suspicious.

"Shut the door, Broker . . . we shall be more comfortable. Thanks, old man. Oh, by the way, I see the notes are gone. Therefore we're agreed. How easy it is for honest men to come to terms!"

"Well . . . and next?"

"Next? Well, as we're partners . . ."

"Partners?"

"Why, haven't you accepted my money? We're working together, old man, and we will carry off the young woman together first and carry off the jewels after."

The Broker grinned:

"Don't want you for that."

"Yes, you do, old man."

"Why?"

"Because you don't know where the jewels are hidden and I do."

"We'll find out."

"To-morrow. Not to-night."

"Well, let's hear. What do you want?"

"My share of the jewels."

"Why didn't you take the lot, as you know where they are?"

"Can't get at them by myself. There's a way of doing it, but I don't know it. You're here, so I'm making use of you."

The Broker hesitated:

"Share the jewels. . . . Share the jewels. . . . A few bits of glass and brass, most likely. . . ."

"You fool! . . . There's more than a million's worth."

The men quivered under the impression made upon them.

"Very well," said the Broker. "But suppose the Kesselbach gets away? She's in the next room, isn't she?"

"No, she's in here."

Lupin for a moment pulled back one of the leaves of the screen, revealing the heap of dresses and bed-clothes which he had laid out on the sofa:

"She's here, fainting. But I shan't give her up till we've divided."

"Still . . ."

"You can take it or leave it. I don't care if I am alone. You know what I'm good for. So please yourselves. . . ."

The men consulted with one another and the Broker said:

"Where is the hiding-place you're talking of?"

"Under the fireplace. But, when you don't know the secret, you must first lift up the whole chimneypiece, looking-glass, marble and all in a lump, it seems. It's no easy job."

"Pooh, we're a smart lot, we are! Just you wait and see. In five minutes . . ."

He gave his orders and his pals at once set to work with admirable vigor and discipline. Two of them, standing on chairs, tried to lift the mirror. The four others attacked the fireplace itself. The Broker, on his knees, kept his eyes on the hearth and gave the word of command:

"Cheerily, lads! . . . Altogether, if you please! . . . Look out! . . . One, two . . . ah, there, it's moving! . . ."

Standing behind them, with his hands in his pockets, Lupin watched them affectionately and, at the same time, revelled with all his pride, as an artist and master, in this striking proof of his authority, of his might, of the incredible sway which he wielded over others. How could those scoundrels for a second accept that improbable story and lose all sense of things, to the point of relinquishing every chance of the fight in his favor?

He took from his pockets two great massive and formidable revolvers and, calmly, choosing the first two men whom he would bring down and the two who would fall next, he aimed as he might have aimed at a pair of targets in a rifle-gallery.

Two shots together and two more. . . .

Loud yells of pain. . . . Four men came tumbling down, one after the other, like dolls at a cockshy.

"Four from seven leaves three," said Lupin. "Shall I go on?"

His arms remained outstretched, levelled at the Broker and his two pals.

"You swine!" growled the Broker, feeling for a weapon.

"Hands up," cried Lupin, "or I fire! . . . That's it. . . . Now, you two, take away his toys. . . . If not . . . !"

The two scoundrels, shaking with fear, caught hold of their leader and compelled him to submit.

"Bind him! . . . Bind him, confound it! . . . What difference does it make to you? . . . Once I'm gone, you're all free. . . . Come along, have you finished? The wrists first . . . with your belts. . . . And the ankles. . . . Hurry up! . . ."

The Broker, beaten and disabled, made no further resistance. While his pals were binding him, Lupin stooped over them and dealt them two terrific blows on the head with the butt-end of his revolver. They sank down in a heap.

"That's a good piece of work," he said, taking breath. "Pity there are not another fifty of them. I was just in the mood. . . . And all so easily done . . . with a smile on one's face. . . . What do you think of it, Broker?"

The scoundrel lay cursing. Lupin said:

"Cheer up, old man! Console yourself with the thought that you are helping in a good action, the rescue of Mrs. Kesselbach. She will thank you in person for your gallantry."

He went to the door of the second room and opened it:

"What's this?" he said, stopping on the threshold, taken aback, dumfounded.

The room was empty.

He went to the window, saw a ladder leaning against the balcony, a telescopic steel ladder, and muttered:

"Kidnapped . . . kidnapped . . . Louis de Malreich. . . . Oh, the villain! . . ."

He reflected for a minute, trying to master his anguish of mind, and said to himself that, after all, as Mrs. Kesselbach seemed to be in no immediate danger, there was no cause for alarm.

But he was seized with a sudden fit of rage and flew at the seven scoundrels, gave a kick or two to those of the wounded who stirred, felt for his bank-notes and put them back in his pocket, then gagged the men's mouths and tied their hands with anything that he could find—blind-cords, curtain-loops, blankets and sheets reduced to strips—and, lastly, laid in a row on the carpet, in front of the sofa, seven bundles of humanity, packed tight together and tied up like so many parcels:

"Mummies on toast!" he chuckled. "A dainty dish for those who like that sort of thing! . . . You pack of fools, how does this suit you, eh? There you are, like corpses at the Morgue. . . . Serves you right for attacking Lupin, Lupin the protector of the widow and orphan! . . . Are you trembling? Quite unnecessary, my lambs! Lupin never hurt a fly yet! . . . Only, Lupin is a decent man, he can't stand vermin; and the Lupin knows his duty. I ask you, is life possible with a lot of scamps like you about? Think of it: no respect for other people's lives; no respect for property, for laws, for society; no conscience; no anything! What are we coming to? Lord, what are we coming to?"

Without even taking the trouble to lock them in, he left the room, went down the street and walked until he came to his taxi. He sent the driver in search of another and brought both cabs back to Mrs. Kesselbach's house.

A good tip, paid in advance, avoided all tedious explanations. With the help of the two men, he carried the seven prisoners down and plumped them anyhow, on one another's knees, into the cabs. The wounded men yelled and moaned. He shut the doors, shouting:

"Mind your hands!"

He got up beside the driver of the front cab.

"Where to?" asked the man.

"36, Quai des Orfevers: the detective-office."

The motors throbbed, the drivers started the gear and the strange procession went scooting down the slopes of the Trocadero.

In the streets, they passed a few vegetable-carts. Men carrying long poles were turning out the street-lamps.

There were stars in the sky. A cool breeze was wafted through the air.

Lupin sang aloud:

The Place de la Concorde, the Louvre. . . . In the distance, the dark bulk of Notre Dame. . . .

He turned round and half opened the door:

"Having a good time, mates? So am I, thank you. It's a grand night for a drive and the air's delicious! . . ."

They were now bumping over the ill-paved quays. And soon they arrived at the Palais de Justice and the door of the detective-office.

"Wait here," said Lupin to the two drivers, "and be sure you look after your seven fares."

He crossed the outer yard and went down the passage on the right leading to the rooms of the central office. He found the night inspectors on duty.

"A bag, gentlemen," he said, as he entered, "a fine bag too. Is M. Weber here? I am the new commissary of police for Auteuil."

"M. Weber is in his flat. Do you want him sent for?"

"Just one second. I'm in a hurry. I'll leave a line for him."

He sat down at a table and wrote:

"MY DEAR WEBER,

"I am bringing you the seven scoundrels composing Altenheim's gang, the men who killed Gourel (and plenty of others) and who killed me as well, under the name of M. Lenormand.

"That only leaves their leader unaccounted for. I am going to effect his arrest this minute. Come and join me. He lives in the Rue Delaizement, at Neuilly and goes by the name of Leon Massier.

"Kind regards.

"Yours,

"ARSÈNE LUPIN,

"*Chief of the Detective-service.*"

He sealed the letter:

"Give that to M. Weber. It's urgent. Now I want seven men to receive the goods. I left them on the quay."

On going back to the taxis, he was met by a chief inspector:

"Ah, it's you M. Lebœuf!" he said. "I've made a fine haul. . . . The whole of Altenheim's gang. . . . They're there in the taxi-cabs."

"Where did you find them?"

"Hard at work kidnapping Mrs. Kesselbach and robbing her house. But I'll tell you all about it when the time comes."

The chief inspector took him aside and, with the air of surprise:

"I beg your pardon, monsieur, but I was sent for to see the commissary of police for Auteuil. And I don't seem to . . . Whom have I the honor of addressing?"

"Somebody who is making you a handsome present of seven hooligans of the finest quality."

"Still, I should like to know. . . ."

"My name?"

"Yes."

"Arsène Lupin."

He nimbly tripped the chief inspector up, ran to the Rue de Rivoli, jumped into a passing taxi-cab and drove to the Porte des Ternes.

The Route de la Revolte was close by. He went to No. 3.

For all his coolness and self-command, Arsène Lupin was unable to control his excitement. Would he find Dolores Kesselbach? Had Louis de Malreich taken her either to his own place or to the Broker's shed?

Lupin had taken the key of the shed from the Broker, so that it was easy for him, after ringing and walking across the different yards, to open the door and enter the lumber-shop.

He switched on his lantern and took his bearings. A little to the right was the free space in which he had seen the accomplices hold their last confabulation. On the sofa mentioned by the Broker he saw a black figure, Dolores lay wrapped in blankets and gagged.

He helped her up.

"Ah, it's you, it's you!" she stammered. "They haven't touched you!"

And, rising and pointing to the back of the shop:

"There . . . he went out that side . . . I heard him. . . . I am sure. . . . You must go . . . please!"

"I must get you away first," he said.

"No, never mind me . . . go after him. . . . I entreat you. . . . Strike him!"

Fear, this time, instead of dejecting her, seemed to be giving her unwonted strength; and she repeated, with an immense longing to place her terrible enemy in his power:

"Go after him first. . . . I can't go on living like this. . . . You must save me from him. . . . I can't go on living. . . ."

He unfastened her bonds, laid her carefully on the sofa and said:

"You are right. . . . Besides, you have nothing to fear here. . . . Wait for me, I shall come back."

As he was going away, she caught hold of his hand:

"But you yourself?"

"Well?"

"If that man . . ."

It was as though she dreaded for Lupin the great, final contest to which she was exposing him and as though, at the last moment, she would have been glad to hold him back.

He said:

"Thank you, have no fear. What have I to be afraid of? He is alone."

And, leaving her, he went to the back of the shed. As he expected, he found a ladder standing against the wall which brought him to the level of the little window through which he had watched the scoundrels hold their meeting. It was the way by which Malreich had returned to his house in the Rue Delaizement.

He, therefore, took the same road, just as he had done a few hours earlier, climbed into the loft of the other coach-house and down into the garden. He found himself at the back of the villa occupied by Malreich.

Strange to say, he did not doubt, for a moment that Malreich was there. He would meet him inevitably; the formidable battle which they were waging against each other was nearing its end. A few minutes more and, one way or another, all would be over.

He was amazed, on grasping the handle of a door, to find that the handle turned and the door opened under his pressure. The villa was not even locked.

He passed through a kitchen, a hall and up a staircase; and he walked deliberately, without seeking to deaden the sound of his footsteps.

On the landing, he stopped. The perspiration streamed from his forehead; and his temples throbbed under the rush of his blood. Nevertheless, he remained calm, master of himself and conscious of his least thoughts. He laid two revolvers on a stair:

"No weapons," he said to himself. "My hands only, just the effort of my two hands. . . . That's quite enough. . . . That will be better. . . ."

Opposite him were three doors. He chose the middle one, turned the handle and encountered no obstacle. He went in. There was no light in the room, but the rays of the night entered through the wide-open window and, amid the darkness, he saw the sheets and the white curtains of the bed.

And somebody was standing beside it.

He savagely cast the gleam of his lantern upon that form.

Malreich!

The pallid face of Malreich, his dim eyes, his cadaverous cheek-bones, his scraggy neck. . . .

And all this stood motionless, opposite him, at five steps' distance; and he could not have said whether that dull face, that death-face, expressed the least terror or even a grain of anxiety.

Lupin took a step forward . . . and a second . . . and a third. . . .

The man did not move.

Did he see? Did he understand? It was as though the man's eyes were gazing into space and that he thought himself possessed by an hallucination, rather than looking upon a real image.

One more step. . . .

"He will defend himself," thought Lupin, "he is bound to defend himself."

And Lupin thrust out his arms.

The man did not make a movement. He did not retreat; his eyelids did not blink.

The contact took place.

And it was Lupin, scared and bewildered, who lost his head. He knocked the man back upon his bed, stretched him at full length, rolled him in the sheets, bound him in the blankets and held him under his knee, like a prey . . . whereas the man had not made the slightest movement of resistance.

"Ah!" shouted Lupin, drunk with delight and satisfied hatred. "At last I have crushed you, you odious brute! At last I am the master!"

He heard a noise outside, in the Rue Delaizement; men knocking at the gate. He ran to the window and cried:

"Is that you, Weber? Already? Well done! You are a model servant! Break down the gate, old chap, and come up here; delighted to see you!"

In a few minutes, he searched his prisoner's clothes, got hold of his pocket-book, cleared the papers out of the drawers of the desk and the davenport, flung them on the table and went through them.

He gave a shout of joy: the bundle of letters was there, the famous bundle of letters which he had promised to restore to the Emperor.

He put back the papers in their place and went to the window:

"It's all finished, Weber! You can come in! You will find Mr. Kesselbach's murderer in his bed, all ready tied up.... Good-bye, Weber!"

And Lupin, tearing down the stairs, ran to the coach-house and went back to Dolores Kesselbach, while Weber was breaking into the villa.

Single-handed, he had arrested Altenheim's seven companions!

And he had delivered to justice the mysterious leader of the gang, the infamous monster, Louis de Malreich!

A young man sat writing at a table on a wide wooden balcony.

From time to time, he raised his head and cast a vague glance toward the horizon of hills, where the trees, stripped by the autumn, were shedding their last leaves over the red roofs of the villas and the lawns of the gardens. Then he went on writing.

Presently he took up his paper and read aloud:

Nos jours s'en vont à la dérive,

Comme emportés par un courant

Qui les pousse vers une rive

Où l'on n'aborde qu'en mourant.

(*Our days go by, adrift, adrift, Borne along by current swift That urges them toward the strand Where not until we die, we land).

"Not so bad," said a voice behind him. "Mme. Amable Tastu might have written that, or Mrs. Felicia Hemans. However, we can't all be Byrons or Lamartines!"

"You!... You!..." stammered the young man, in dismay.

"Yes, I, poet, I myself, Arsène Lupin come to see his dear friend Pierre Leduc."

Pierre Leduc began to shake, as though shivering with fever. He asked, in a low voice:

"Has the hour come?"

"Yes, my dear Pierre Leduc: the hour has come for you to give up, or rather to interrupt the slack poet's life which you have been leading for months at the feet of Geneviève Ernemont and Mrs. Kesselbach and to perform the part which I have allotted to you in my play ... oh, a fine play, I assure you, thoroughly well-constructed, according to all the canons of art, with top notes, comic relief and gnashing of teeth galore! We have reached the fifth act; the grand finale is at hand; and you, Pierre Leduc, are the hero. There's fame for you!"

The young man rose from his seat:

"And suppose I refuse?"

"Idiot!"

"Yes, suppose I refuse? After all, what obliges me to submit to your will? What obliges me to accept a part which I do not know, but which I loathe in advance and feel ashamed of?"

"Idiot!" repeated Lupin.

And forcing Pierre Leduc back into his chair, he sat down beside him and, in the gentlest of voices:

"You quite forget, my dear young man, that you are not Pierre Leduc, but Gérard Baupré. That you bear the beautiful name of Pierre Leduc is due to the fact that you, Gérard Baupré, killed Pierre Leduc and robbed him of his individuality."

The young man bounded with indignation:

"You are mad! You know as well as I do that you conceived the whole plot...."

"Yes, I know that, of course; but the law doesn't know it; and what will the law say when I come forward with proof that the real Pierre Leduc died a violent death and that you have taken his place?"

The young man, overwhelmed with consternation, stammered:

"No one will believe you.... Why should I have done that? With what object?"

"Idiot! The object is so self-evident that Weber himself could have perceived it. You lie when you say that you will not accept a part which you do not know. You know your part quite well. It is the part which Pierre Leduc would have played were he not dead."

"But Pierre Leduc, to me, to everybody, was only a name. Who was he? Who am I?"

"What difference can that make to you?"

"I want to know. I want to know what I am doing!"

"And, if you know, will you go straight ahead?"

"Yes, if the object of which you speak is worth it."

"If it were not, do you think I would take all this trouble?"

"Who am I? Whatever my destiny, you may be sure that I shall prove worthy of it. But I want to know. Who am I?"

Arsène Lupin took off his hat, bowed and said: "Hermann IV., Grand-duke of Zweibrucken-Veldenz, Prince of Berncastel, Elector of Treves and lord of all sorts of places."

Three days later, Arsène Lupin took Mrs. Kesselbach away in a motor-car in the direction of the frontier. The journey was accomplished in silence, Lupin remembered with emotion Dolores's terrified conduct and the words which she spoke in the house in the Rue des Vignes, when he was about to defend her against Altenheim's accomplices. And she must have remembered also, for she remained embarrassed and evidently perturbed in his presence.

In the evening they reached a small castle, all covered with creepers and flowers, roofed with an enormous slate cap and standing in a large garden full of ancestral trees.

Here Mrs. Kesselbach found Geneviève already installed, after a visit to the neighboring town, where she had engaged a staff of servants from among the country-people.

"This will be your residence, madame," said Lupin. "You are at Bruggen Castle. You will be quite safe here, while waiting the outcome of these events. I have written to Pierre Leduc and he will be your guest from to-morrow."

He started off again at once, drove to Veldenz and handed over to Count von Waldemar the famous letters which he had recaptured:

"You know my conditions, my dear Waldemar," said Lupin. "The first and most important thing is to restore the House of Zweibrucken-Veldenz and to reinstate the Grand-duke Hermann IV., in the grand-duchy."

"I shall open negotiations with the Council of Regency to-day. According to my information, it will not be a difficult matter. But this Grand-duke Hermann. . . ."

"His Royal Highness is at present staying at Bruggen Castle, under the name of Pierre Leduc. I will supply all the necessary proofs of his identity."

That same evening, Lupin took the road back to Paris, with the intention of actively hurrying on the trial of Malreich and the seven scoundrels.

It would be wearisome to recapitulate the story of the case: the facts, down to the smallest details, are in the memory of one and all. It was one of those sensational events which still form a subject of conversation and discussion among the weather-beaten laborers in the remotest villages.

But what I wish to recall is the enormous part played by Lupin in the conduct of the case and in the incidents appertaining to the preliminary inquiry. As a matter of fact, it was he who managed the inquiry. From the very start, he took the place of the authorities, ordering police-searches, directing the measures to be taken, prescribing the questions to be put to the prisoners, assuming the responsibility for everything.

We can all remember the universal amazement when, morning after morning, we read in the papers those letters, so irresistible in their masterly logic, signed, by turns:

"ARSÈNE LUPIN, *Examining-magistrate*."

"ARSÈNE LUPIN, *Public Prosecutor*."

"ARSÈNE LUPIN, *Minister of Justice*."

"ARSÈNE LUPIN, *Copper*."

He flung himself into the business with a spirit, an ardor, a violence, even, that was astonishing in one usually so full of light-hearted chaff and, when all was said, so naturally disposed by temperament to display a certain professional indulgence.

No, this time he was prompted by hatred.

He hated Louis de Malreich, that bloodthirsty scoundrel, that foul brute, of whom he had always been afraid and who, even beaten, even in prison, still gave him that sensation of dread and repugnance which one feels at the sight of a reptile.

Besides, had not Malreich had the audacity to persecute Dolores?

"He has played and lost," said Lupin. "He shall pay for it with his head."

That was what he wanted for his terrible enemy: the scaffold, the bleak, dull morning when the blade of the guillotine slides down and kills. . . .

It was a strange prisoner whom the examining-magistrate questioned for months on end between the four walls of his room, a strange figure, that bony man, with the skeleton face and the lifeless eyes!

He seemed quite out of himself. His thoughts were not there, but elsewhere. And he cared so little about answering!

"My name is Leon Massier."

That was the one sentence to which he confined himself.

And Lupin retorted.

"You lie. Leon Massier, born at Perigueux, left fatherless at the age of ten, died seven years ago. You took his papers. But you forgot his death-certificate. Here it is."

And Lupin sent a copy of the document to the public prosecutor.

"I am Leon Massier," declared the prisoner, once again.

"You lie," replied Lupin. "You are Louis de Malreich, the last surviving descendant of a small French noble who settled in Germany in the eighteenth century. You had a brother who called himself Parbury, Ribeira and Altenheim, by turns: you killed your brother. You had a sister, Isilda de Malreich: you killed your sister."

"I am Leon Massier."

"You lie. You are Malreich. Here is your birth-certificate. Here are your brother's and your sister's."

And Lupin sent the three certificates.

Apart from the question of his identity, Malreich, crushed, no doubt, by the accumulation of proofs brought up against him, did not defend himself. What could he say? They had forty notes written in his own hand—a comparison of the handwritings established the fact—written in his own hand to the gang of his accomplices, forty notes which he had omitted to tear up after taking them back. And all these notes were orders relating to the Kesselbach case, the capture of M. Lenormand and Gourel, the pursuit of old Steinweg, the construction of the underground passages at Garches and so on. What possibility was there of a denial?

One rather odd thing baffled the law officers. The seven scoundrels, when confronted with their leader, all declared that they did not know him, because they had never seen him. They received his instructions either by telephone, or else in the dark, by means of those same little notes which Malreich slipped into their hands without a word.

But, for the rest, was not the existence of the communication between the villa in the Rue Delaizement and the Broker's shed an ample proof of complicity? From that spot, Malreich saw and heard. From that spot, the leader watched his men.

Discrepancies? Apparently irreconcilable facts? Lupin explained them all away. In a celebrated article, published on the morning of the trial, he took up the case from the start, revealed what lay beneath it, unravelled its web, showed Malreich, unknown to all, living in the room of his brother, the sham Major Parbury, passing unseen along the passages of the Palace Hotel and murdering Mr. Kesselbach, murdering Beudot the floor-waiter, murdering Chapman the secretary.

The trial lingers in the memory. It was both terrifying and gloomy: terrifying because of the atmosphere of anguish that hung over the crowd of onlookers and the recollection of crime and blood that obsessed their minds: gloomy, heavy, darksome, stifling because of the tremendous silence observed by the prisoner.

Not a protest, not a movement, not a word. A face of wax that neither saw nor heard. An awful vision of impassive calmness! The people in court shuddered. Their distraught imaginations conjured up a sort of supernatural being rather than a man, a sort of genie out of the Arabian Nights, one of those Hindu gods who symbolize all that is ferocious, cruel, sanguinary and pernicious.

As for the other scoundrels, the people did not even look at them, treated them as insignificant supers overshadowed by that stupendous leader.

The most sensational evidence was that given by Mrs. Kesselbach. To the general astonishment and to Lupin's own surprise, Dolores, who had answered none of the magistrate's summonses and who had retired to an unknown spot, Dolores appeared, a sorrow-stricken widow, to give damning evidence against her husband's murderer.

She gazed at him for many seconds and then said, simply:

"That is the man who entered my house in the Rue des Vignes, who carried me off and who locked me up in the Broker's shed. I recognize him."

"On your oath?"

"I swear it before God and man."

Two days later, Louis de Malreich, *alias* Leon Massier was sentenced to death. And his overpowering personality may be said to have absorbed that of his accomplices to such an extent that they received the benefit of extenuating circumstances.

"Louis de Malreich have you nothing to say?" asked the presiding judge.

He made no reply.

One question alone remained undecided in Lupin's eyes: why had Malreich committed all those crimes? What did he want? What was his object?

Lupin was soon to understand; and the day was not far off when, gasping with horror, struck, mortally smitten with despair, he would know the awful truth.

For the moment, although the thought of it constantly hovered over his mind, he ceased to occupy himself with the Malreich case. Resolved to get a new skin, as he put it; reassured, on the other hand, as to the fate of Mrs. Kesselbach and Geneviève, over whose peaceful existence he watched from afar; and, lastly, kept informed by Jean Doudeville, whom he had sent to Veldenz, of all the negotiations that were being pursued between the court of Berlin and the regent of Zweibrucken-Veldenz, he employed all his time in winding up the past and preparing for the future.

The thought of the different life which he wished to lead under the eyes of Mrs. Kesselbach filled him with new ambitions and unexpected sentiments, in which the image of Dolores played a part, without his being able to tell exactly how or why.

In a few weeks, he got rid of all the proofs that could have compromised him sooner or later, all the traces that could have led to his ruin. He gave each of his old companions a sum of money sufficient to keep them from want for the rest of their lives and said good-bye to them, saying that he was going to South America.

One morning, after a night of careful thought and a deep study of the situation, he cried:

"It's done. There's nothing to fear now. The old Lupin is dead. Make way for the young one."

His man brought him a telegram from Germany. It contained the news for which he had been waiting. The Council of Regency, greatly influenced by the Court of Berlin, had referred the question to the electors; and the electors, greatly influenced by the Council of Regency, had declared their unshaken attachment to the old dynasty of the Veldenz. Count von Waldemar was deputed, together with three delegates selected from the nobility, the army and the law, to go to Bruggen Castle, carefully to establish the identity of the Grand-duke Hermann IV. and to make all the arrangements with His Royal Highness for his triumphal entry into the principality of his fathers, which was to take place in the course of the following month.

"This time, I've pulled it off," said Lupin to himself. "Mr. Kesselbach's great scheme is being realized. All that remains for me to do is to make Waldemar swallow Pierre Leduc; and that is child's play. The banns between Geneviève and Pierre shall be published to-morrow. And it shall be the grand-duke's affianced bride that will be presented to Waldemar."

Full of glee, he started in his motor for Bruggen Castle.

He sang in the car, he whistled, he chatted to his chauffeur:

"Octave, do you know whom you have the honor of driving? The master of the world! . . . Yes, old man, that staggers you, eh? Just so, but it's the truth. I am the master of the world."

He rubbed his hands and went on soliloquizing:

"All the same, it was a long job. It's a year since the fight began. True, it was the most formidable fight I ever stood to win or lose. . . . By Jupiter, what a war of giants!" And he repeated, "But this time, I've pulled it off! The enemies are in the water. There are no obstacles left between the goal and me. The site is free: let us build upon it! I have the materials at hand, I have the workmen: let us build, Lupin! And let the palace be worthy of you!"

He stopped the car at a few hundred yards from the castle, so that his arrival might create as little fuss as possible, and said to Octave:

"Wait here for twenty minutes, until four o'clock, and then drive in. Take my bags to the little chalet at the end of the park. That's where I shall sleep."

At the first turn of the road, the castle appeared in sight, standing at the end of a dark avenue of lime trees. From the distance, he saw Geneviève passing on the terrace.

His heart was softly stirred:

"Geneviève, Geneviève," he said, fondly. "Geneviève . . . the vow which I made to the dying mother is being fulfilled as well. . . . Geneviève a grand-duchess! . . . And I, in the shade, watching over her happiness . . . and pursuing the great schemes of Arsène Lupin!"

He burst out laughing, sprang behind a cluster of trees that stood to the left of the avenue and slipped along the thick shrubberies. In this way, he reached the castle without the possibility of his being seen from the windows of the drawing-room or the principal bedrooms.

He wanted to see Dolores before she saw him and pronounced her name several times, as he had pronounced Geneviève's, but with an emotion that surprised himself:

"Dolores. . . . Dolores. . . ."

He stole along the passages and reached the dining-room. From this room, through a glass panel, he could see half the drawing-room.

He drew nearer. Dolores was lying on a couch; and Pierre Leduc, on his knees before her, was gazing at her with eyes of ecstasy. . . .

XV. THE MAP OF EUROPE

Pierre Leduc loved Dolores!

Lupin felt a keen, penetrating pain in the depths of his being, as though he had been wounded in the very source of life; a pain so great that, for the first time, he had a clear perception of what Dolores had gradually, unknown to himself, become to him.

Pierre Leduc loved Dolores! And he was looking at her as a man looks at the woman he loves.

Lupin felt a murderous instinct rise up within him, blindly and furiously. That look, that look of love cast upon Dolores, maddened him. He received an impression of the great silence that enveloped Dolores and Pierre Leduc; and in silence, in the stillness of their attitude there was nothing living but that look of love, that dumb and sensuous hymn in which the eyes told all the passion, all the desire, all the transport, all the yearning that one being can feel for another.

And he saw Mrs. Kesselbach also. Dolores' eyes were invisible under their lowered lids, the silky eyelids with the long black lashes. But how she seemed to feel that look of love which sought for hers! How she quivered under that impalpable caress!

"She loves him . . . she loves him," thought Lupin, burning with jealousy.

And, when Pierre made a movement:

"Oh, the villain! If he dares to touch her, I will kill him!"

Then, realizing the disorder of his reason and striving to combat it, he said to himself:

"What a fool I am! What, you, Lupin, letting your self go like this! . . . Look here, it's only natural that she should love him. . . . Yes, of course, you expected her to show a certain emotion at your arrival . . . a certain agitation. . . . You silly idiot, you're only a thief, a robber . . . whereas he is a prince and young. . . ."

Pierre had not stirred further. But his lips moved and it seemed as though Dolores were waking. Softly, slowly, she raised her lids, turned her head a little and her eyes met the young man's eyes with the look that offers itself and surrenders itself and is more intense than the most intense of kisses.

What followed came suddenly and unexpectedly, like a thunder-clap. In three bounds, Lupin rushed into the drawing-room, sprang upon the young man, flung him to the ground and, with one hand on his rival's chest, beside himself with anger, turning to Mrs. Kesselbach, he cried:

"But don't you know? Hasn't he told you, the cheat? . . . And you love him, you love that! Does he look like a grand-duke? Oh, what a joke!"

He grinned and chuckled like a madman, while Dolores gazed at him in stupefaction:

"He, a grand-duke! Hermann IV., Grand-duke of Zweibrucken-Veldenz! A reigning sovereign! Elector of Treves! But it's enough to make one die of laughing! He! Why, his name is Baupré, Gérard Baupré, the lowest of ragamuffins . . . a beggar, whom I picked up in the gutter! . . . A grand-duke? But it's I who made him a grand-duke! Ha, ha, ha, what a joke! . . . If you had seen him cut his little finger . . . he fainted three times . . . the milksop! . . . Ah, you allow yourself to lift your eyes to ladies . . . and to rebel against the master! . . . Wait a bit, Grand-duke of Zweibrucken-Veldenz, I'll show you!"

He took him in his arms, like a bundle, swung him to and fro for a moment and pitched him through the open window:

"Mind the rose trees, grand-duke! There are thorns!"

When he turned round, Dolores was close to him and looking at him with eyes which he had never seen in her before, the eyes of a woman who hates and who is incensed with rage. Could this possibly be Dolores, the weak, ailing Dolores?

She stammered:

"What are you doing? . . . How dare you? . . . And he. . . . Then it's true? . . . lied to me? . . ."

"Lied to you?" cried Lupin, grasping the humiliation which she had suffered as a woman. "Lied to you? He, a grand-duke! A puppet, that's all, a puppet of which I pulled the string . . . an instrument which I tuned, to play upon as I chose! Oh, the fool, the fool!"

Overcome with renewed rage, he stamped his foot and shook his fist at the open window. And he began to walk up and down the room, flinging out phrases in which all the pent-up violence of his secret thought burst forth:

"The fool! Then he didn't see what I expected of him? He did not suspect the greatness of the part he was to play? Oh, I shall have to drive it into his noddle by force, I see! Lift up your head, you idiot! You shall be grand-duke by the grace of Lupin! And a reigning sovereign! With a civil list! And subjects to fleece! And a palace which Charlemagne shall rebuild for you! And a master that shall be I, Lupin! Do you understand, you numskull? Lift up your head, dash it! Higher than that! Look up at the sky, remember that a Zweibrucken was hanged for cattle-lifting before the Hohenzollerns were ever heard of. And you are a Zweibrucken, by Jove, no less; and I am here, I, I, Lupin! And you shall be grand-duke, I tell you! A paste-board grand-duke? Very well! But a grand-duke all the same, quickened with my breath and glowing with my ardor. A puppet? Very well. But a puppet that shall speak *my* words and make *my* movements and perform *my* wishes and realize *my* dreams . . . yes . . . my dreams."

He stood motionless, as though dazzled by the glory of his conception. Then he went up to Dolores and, sinking his voice, with a sort of mystic exaltation, he said:

"On my left, Alsace-Lorraine. . . . On my right, Baden, Wurtemburg, Bavaria. . . . South Germany . . . all those disconnected, discontented states, crushed under the heel of the Prussian Charlemagne, but restless and ready to throw off the yoke at any moment. . . . Do you understand all that a man like myself can do in the midst of that, all the aspirations that he can kindle, all the hatred that he can produce, all the angry rebellion that he can inspire?"

In a still lower voice, he repeated:

"And, on my left, Alsace-Lorraine! . . . Do you fully understand? . . . Dreams? Not at all! It is the reality of the day after to-morrow, of to-morrow! . . . Yes. . . . I wish it. . . . I wish it. . . . Oh, all that I wish and all that I mean to do is unprecedented! . . . Only think, at two steps from the Alsatian frontier! In the heart of German territory! Close to the old Rhine! . . . A little intrigue, a little genius will be enough to change the surface of the earth. Genius I have . . . and to spare. . . . And I shall be the master! I shall be the man who directs. The other, the puppet can have the title and the honors. . . . I shall have the power! . . . I shall remain in the background. No office: I will not be a minister, nor even a chamberlain. Nothing. I shall be one of the servants in the palace, the gardener perhaps. . . . Yes, the gardener. . . . Oh, what a tremendous life! To grow flowers and alter the map of Europe!"

She looked at him greedily, dominated, swayed by the strength of that man. And her eyes expressed an admiration which she did not seek to conceal.

He put his hands on Dolores' shoulders and said:

"That is my dream. Great as it is, it will be surpassed by the facts: that I swear to you. The Kaiser has already seen what I am good for. One day, he will find me installed in front of him, face to face. I hold all the trumps. Valenglay will act at my bidding. . . . England also. . . . The game is played and won. . . . That is my dream. . . . There is another one. . . ."

He stopped suddenly. Dolores did not take her eyes from him; and an infinite emotion changed every feature of her face.

A vast joy penetrated him as he once more felt, and clearly felt, that woman's confusion in his presence. He no longer had the sense of being to her . . . what he was, a thief, a robber; he was a man, a man who loved and whose love roused unspoken feelings in the depths of a friendly soul.

Then he said no more, but he lavished upon her, unuttered, every known word of love and admiration; and he thought of the life which he might lead somewhere, not far from Veldenz, unknown and all-powerful. . . .

A long silence united them. Then she rose and said, softly:

"Go away, I entreat you to go. . . . Pierre shall marry Geneviève, I promise you that, but it is better that you should go . . . that you should not be here. . . . Go. Pierre shall marry Geneviève."

He waited for a moment. Perhaps he would rather have had more definite words, but he dared not ask for anything. And he withdrew, dazed, intoxicated and happy to obey, to subject his destiny to hers!

On his way to the door, he came upon a low chair, which he had to move. But his foot knocked against something. He looked down. It was a little pocket-mirror, in ebony, with a gold monogram.

Suddenly, he started and snatched up the mirror. The monogram consisted of two letters interlaced, an "L" and an "M."

An "L" and an "M!"

"Louis de Malreich," he said to himself, with a shudder.

He turned to Dolores:

"Where does this mirror come from? Whose is it? It is important that I should . . ."

She took it from him and looked at it:

"I don't know. . . . I never saw it before . . . a servant, perhaps. . . ."

"A servant, no doubt," he said, "but it is very odd . . . it is one of those coincidences. . . ."

At that moment, Geneviève entered by the other door, and without seeing Lupin, who was hidden by a screen, at once exclaimed:

"Why, there's your glass, Dolores! . . . So you have found it, after making me hunt for it all this time! . . . Where was it?" And the girl went away saying, "Oh, well, I'm very glad it's found! . . . How upset you were! . . . I will go and tell them at once to stop looking for it. . . ."

Lupin had not moved. He was confused, and tried in vain to understand. Why had Dolores not spoken the truth? Why had she not at once said whose the mirror was?

An idea flashed across his mind; and he asked, more or less at random:

"Do you know Louis de Malreich?"

"Yes," she said, watching him, as though striving to guess the thoughts that beset him.

He rushed toward her, in a state of intense excitement:

"You know him? Who was he? Who is he? Who is he? And why did you not tell me? Where have you known him? Speak . . . answer. . . . I implore you. . . ."

"No," she said.

"But you must, you must. . . . Think! Louis de Malreich! The murderer! The monster! . . . Why did you not tell me?"

She, in turn, placed her hands on Lupin's shoulders and, in a firm voice, declared:

"Listen, you must never ask me, because I shall never tell. . . . It is a secret which I shall take with me to the grave. . . . Come what may, no one will ever know, no one in the wide world, I swear it!"

He stood before her for some minutes, anxiously, with a confused brain.

He remembered Steinweg's silence and the old man's terror when Lupin asked him to reveal the terrible secret. Dolores also knew and she also refused to speak.

He went out without a word.

The open air, the sense of space, did him good. He passed out through the park-wall and wandered long over the country. And he soliloquized aloud:

"What does it mean? What is happening? For months and months, fighting hard and acting, I have been pulling the strings of all the characters that are to help me in the execution of my plans; and, during this time, I have completely forgotten to stoop over them and see what is going on in their hearts and brains. I do not know Pierre Leduc, I do not know Geneviève, I do not know Dolores. . . . And I have treated them as so many jumping-jacks, whereas they are live persons. And to-day I am stumbling over obstacles."

He stamped his foot and cried:

"Over obstacles that do not exist! What do I care for the psychological state of Geneviève, of Pierre? . . . I will study that later, at Veldenz, when I have secured their happiness. But Dolores . . . she knew Malreich and said nothing! . . . Why? What relation united them? Was she afraid of him? Is she afraid that he will escape from prison and come to revenge himself for an indiscretion on her part?"

At night, he went to the chalet which he had allotted to his own use at the end of the park and dined in a very bad temper, storming at Octave, who waited on him and who was always either too slow or too fast:

"I'm sick of it, leave me alone. . . . You're doing everything wrong to-day. . . . And this coffee. . . . It's not fit to drink."

He pushed back his cup half-full and, for two hours, walked about the park, sifting the same ideas over and over again. At last, one suggestion took definite shape within his mind:

"Malreich has escaped from prison. He is terrifying Mrs. Kesselbach. By this time, he already knows the story of the mirror from her. . . ."

Lupin shrugged his shoulders:

"And to-night he's coming to pull my leg, I suppose! I'm talking nonsense. The best thing I can do is to go to bed."

He went to his room, undressed and got into bed. He fell asleep at once, with a heavy sleep disturbed by nightmares. Twice he woke and tried to light his candle and twice fell back, as though stunned by a blow.

Nevertheless, he heard the hours strike on the village clock, or rather he thought that he heard them strike, for he was plunged in a sort of torpor in which he seemed to retain all his wits.

And he was haunted by dreams, dreams of anguish and terror. He plainly heard the sound of his window opening. He plainly, through his closed eyelids, through the thick darkness, *saw* a form come toward the bed.

And the form bent over him.

He made the incredible effort needed to raise his eyelids and look . . . or, at least, he imagined that he did. Was he dreaming? Was he awake? He asked himself the question in despair.

A further sound. . . .

He took up the box of matches by his bedside:

"Let's have a light on it," he said, with a great sense of elation.

He struck a match and lit the candle.

Lupin felt the perspiration stream over his skin, from head to foot, while his heart ceased beating, stopped with terror. *The man was there.*

Was it possible? No, no . . . and yet he *saw*. . . . Oh, the fearsome sight! . . . The man, the monster, was there. . . .

"He shall not . . . he shall not," stammered Lupin madly.

The man, the monster was there, dressed in black, with a mask on his face and with his felt hat pulled down over his fair hair.

"Oh, I am dreaming. . . . I am dreaming!" said Lupin, laughing. "It's a nightmare! . . ."

Exerting all his strength and all his will-power, he tried to make a movement, one movement, to drive away the vision.

He could not.

And, suddenly, he remembered: the coffee! The taste of it . . . similar to the taste of the coffee which he had drunk at Veldenz!

He gave a cry, made a last effort and fell back exhausted. But, in his delirium, he felt that the man was unfastening the top button of his pajama-jacket and baring his neck, felt that the man was raising his arm, saw that the hand was clutching the handle of a dagger, a little steel dagger similar to that which had struck Kesselbach, Chapman, Altenheim and so many others. . . .

A few hours later, Lupin woke up, shattered with fatigue, with a scorched palate.

He lay for several minutes collecting his thoughts and, suddenly, remembering, made an instinctive defensive movement, as though he were being attacked:

"Fool that I am!" he cried, jumping out of bed. "It was a nightmare, an hallucination. It only needs a little reflection. Had it been 'he,' had it really been a man, in flesh and blood, who lifted his hand against me last night, he would have cut my throat like a rabbit's. 'He' doesn't hesitate. Let's be logical. Why should he spare me? For the sake of my good looks? No, I have been dreaming, that's all. . . ."

He began to whistle and dressed himself, assuming the greatest calmness, but his brain never ceased working and his eyes sought about. . . .

On the floor, on the window-ledge, not a trace. As his room was on the ground-floor and as he slept with his window open, it was evident that his assailant would have entered that way.

Well, he discovered nothing; and nothing either at the foot of the wall outside, or on the gravel of the path that ran round the chalet.

"Still . . . still . . ." he repeated, between his teeth. . . .

He called Octave:

"Where did you make the coffee which you gave me last night?"

"At the castle, governor, like the rest of the things. There is no range here."

"Did you drink any of it?"

"No."

"Did you throw away what was left in the coffee-pot?"

"Why, yes, governor. You said it was so bad. You only took a few mouthfuls."

"Very well. Get the motor ready. We're leaving."

Lupin was not the man to remain in doubt. He wanted to have a decisive explanation with Dolores. But, for this, he must first clear up certain points that seemed to him obscure and see Jean Doudeville who had sent him some rather curious information from Veldenz.

He drove, without stopping, to the grand-duchy, which he reached at two o'clock. He had an interview with Count de Waldemar, whom he asked, upon some pretext, to delay the journey of the delegates of the Regency to Bruggen. Then he went in search of Doudeville, in a tavern at Veldenz.

Doudeville took him to another tavern, where he introduced him to a shabbily-dressed little gentleman, Herr Stockli, a clerk in the department of births, deaths and marriages. They had a long conversation. They went out together and all three passed stealthily through the offices of the town-hall. At seven o'clock, Lupin dined and set out again. At ten o'clock he arrived at Bruggen Castle and asked for Geneviève, so that she might take him to Mrs. Kesselbach's room.

He was told that Mlle. Ernemont had been summoned back to Paris by a telegram from her grandmother.

"Ah!" he said. "Could I see Mrs. Kesselbach?"

"Mrs. Kesselbach went straight to bed after dinner. She is sure to be asleep."

"No, I saw a light in her boudoir. She will see me."

He did not even wait for Mrs. Kesselbach to send out an answer. He walked into the boudoir almost upon the maid's heels, dismissed her and said to Dolores:

"I have to speak to you, madame, on an urgent matter. . . . Forgive me . . . I confess that my behavior must seem importunate. . . . But you will understand, I am sure. . . ."

He was greatly excited and did not seem much disposed to put off the explanation, especially as, before entering the room, he thought he heard a sound.

Yet Dolores was alone and lying down. And she said, in her tired voice:

"Perhaps we might . . . to-morrow. . . ."

He did not answer, suddenly struck by a smell that surprised him in that boudoir, a smell of tobacco. And, at once, he had the intuition, the certainty, that there was a man there, at the moment when he himself arrived, and that perhaps the man was there still, hidden somewhere....

Pierre Leduc? No, Pierre Leduc did not smoke. Then who?

Dolores murmured:

"Be quick, please."

"Yes, yes, but first . . . would it be possible for you to tell me . . . ?"

He interrupted himself. What was the use of asking her? If there were really a man in hiding, would she be likely to tell?

Then he made up his mind and, trying to overcome the sort of timid constraint that oppressed him at the sense of a strange presence, he said, in a very low voice, so that Dolores alone should hear:

"Listen, I have learnt something . . . which I do not understand . . . and which perplexes me greatly. You will answer me, will you not, Dolores?"

He spoke her name with great gentleness and as though he were trying to master her by the note of love and affection in his voice.

"What have you learnt?" she asked.

"The register of births at Veldenz contains three names which are those of the last descendants of the family of Malreich, which settled in Germany...."

"Yes, you have told me all that...."

"You remember, the first name is Raoul de Malreich, better known under his *alias* of Altenheim, the scoundrel, the swell hooligan, now dead . . . murdered."

"Yes."

"Next comes Louis de Malreich, the monster, this one, the terrible murderer who will be beheaded in a few days from now."

"Yes."

"Then, lastly, Isilda, the mad daughter...."

"Yes."

"So all that is quite positive, is it not?"

"Yes."

"Well," said Lupin, leaning over her more closely than before, "I have just made an investigation which showed to me that the second of the three Christian names, or rather a part of the line on which it is written, has at some time or other, been subjected to erasure. The line is written over, in a new hand, with much fresher ink; but the writing below is not quite effaced, so that...."

"So that . . . ?" asked Mrs. Kesselbach, in a low voice.

"So that, with a good lens and particularly with the special methods which I have at my disposal, I was able to revive some of the obliterated syllables and, without any possibility of a mistake, in all certainty, to reconstruct the old writing. I then found not Louis de Malreich, but..."

"Oh, don't, don't!..."

Suddenly shattered by the strain of her prolonged effort of resistance, she lay bent in two and, with her head in her hands, her shoulders shaken with convulsive sobs, she wept.

Lupin looked for long seconds at this weak and listless creature, so pitifully helpless. And he would have liked to stop, to cease the torturing questions which he was inflicting upon her. But was it not to save her that he was acting as he did? And, to save her, was it not necessary that he should know the truth, however painful?

He resumed:

"Why that forgery?"

"It was my husband," she stammered, "it was my husband who did it. With his fortune, he could do everything; and he bribed a junior clerk to have the Christian name of the second child altered for him on the register."

"The Christian name and the sex," said Lupin.

"Yes," she said.

"Then," he continued, "I am not mistaken: the original Christian name, the real one, was Dolores?"

"Yes."

"But why did your husband . . . ?"

She whispered in a shame-faced manner, while the tears streamed down her cheeks.

"Don't you understand?"

"No."

"But think," she said, shuddering, "I was the sister of Isilda, the mad woman, the sister of Altenheim, the ruffian. My husband—or rather my affianced husband—would not have me remain that. He loved me. I loved him too, and I consented. He suppressed Dolores de Malreich on the register, he bought me other papers, another personality, another birth-certificate; and I was married in Holland under another maiden name, as Dolores Amonti."

Lupin reflected for a moment and said, thoughtfully:

"Yes . . . yes . . . I understand. . . . But then Louis de Malreich does not exist; and the murderer of your husband, the murderer of your brother and sister, does not bear that name. . . . His name. . . ."

She sprang to a sitting posture and, eagerly:

"His name! Yes, that is his name . . . yes, it is his name nevertheless. . . . Louis de Malreich. . . . L. M. . . . Remember. . . . Oh, do not try to find out . . . it is the terrible secret. . . . Besides, what does it matter? . . . They have the criminal. . . . He is the criminal. . . . I tell you he is. Did he defend himself when I accused him, face to face? Could he defend himself, under that name or any other? It is he . . . it is he . . . He committed the murders. . . . He struck the blows. . . . The dagger. . . . The steel dagger. . . . Oh, if I could only tell all I know! . . . Louis de Malreich. . . . If I could only . . ."

She fell back on the sofa in a fit of hysterical sobbing; and her hand clutched Lupin's and he heard her stammering, amid inarticulate words:

"Protect me . . . protect me. . . . You alone, perhaps. . . . Oh, do not forsake me. . . . I am so unhappy! . . . Oh, what torture . . . what torture! . . . It is hell! . . ."

With his free hand, he stroked her hair and forehead with infinite gentleness; and, under his caress, she gradually relaxed her tense nerves and became calmer and quieter.

Then he looked at her again and long, long asked himself what there could be behind that fair, white brow, what secret was ravaging that mysterious soul. She also was afraid. But of whom? Against whom was she imploring him to protect her?

Once again, he was obsessed by the image of the man in black, by that Louis de Malreich, the sinister and incomprehensible enemy, whose attacks he had to ward off without knowing whence they came or even if they were taking place.

He was in prison, watched day and night. Tush! Did Lupin not know by his own experience that there are beings for whom prison does not exist and who throw off their chains at the given moment? And Louis de Malreich was one of those.

Yes, there was some one in the Santé prison, in the condemned man's cell. But it might be an accomplice or some victim of Malreich . . . while Malreich himself prowled around Bruggen Castle, slipped in under cover of the darkness, like an invisible spectre, made his way into the chalet in the park and, at night, raised his dagger against Lupin asleep and helpless.

And it was Louis de Malreich who terrorized Dolores, who drove her mad with his threats, who held her by some dreadful secret and forced her into silence and submission.

And Lupin imagined the enemy's plan: to throw Dolores, scared and trembling, into Pierre Leduc's arms, to make away with him, Lupin, and to reign in his place, over there, with the grand-duke's power and Dolores's millions.

It was a likely supposition, a certain supposition, which fitted in with the facts and provided a solution of all the problems.

"Of all?" thought Lupin. "Yes. . . . But then, why did he not kill me, last night, in the chalet? He had but to wish . . . *and he did not wish*. One movement and I was dead. He did not make that movement. Why?"

Dolores opened her eyes, saw him and smiled, with a pale smile:

"Leave me," she said:

He rose, with some hesitation. Should he go and see if the enemy was behind the curtain or hidden behind the dresses in a cupboard?

She repeated, gently:

"Go . . . I am so sleepy. . . ."

He went away.

But, outside, he stopped behind some trees that formed a dark cluster in front of the castle. He saw a light in Dolores' boudoir. Then the light passed into the bedroom. In a few minutes, all was darkness.

He waited. If the enemy was there, perhaps he would come out of the castle. . . .

An hour elapsed. . . . Two hours. . . . Not a sound. . . .

"There's nothing to be done," thought Lupin. "Either he is burrowing in some corner of the castle . . . or else he has gone out by a door which I cannot see from here. Unless the whole thing is the most ridiculous supposition on my part. . . ."

He lit a cigarette and walked back to the chalet.

As he approached it, he saw, at some distance from him, a shadow that appeared to be moving away.

He did not stir, for fear of giving the alarm.

The shadow crossed a path. By the light of the moon, he seemed to recognize the black figure of Malreich.

He rushed forward.

The shadow fled and vanished from sight.

"Come," he said, "it shall be for to-morrow. And, this time. . . ."

Lupin went to Octave's, his chauffeur's, room, woke him and said:

"Take the motor and go to Paris. You will be there by six o'clock in the morning. See Jacques Doudeville and tell him two things: first, to give me news of the man under sentence of death; and secondly, as soon as the post-offices open, to send me a telegram which I will write down for you now. . . ."

He worded the telegram on a scrap of paper and added:

"The moment you have done that, come back, but this way, along the wall of the park. Go now. No one must suspect your absence."

Lupin went to his own room, pressed the spring of his lantern and began to make a minute inspection. "It's as I thought," he said presently. "Some one came here to-night, while I was watching beneath the window. And, if he came, I know what he came for. . . . I was certainly right: things are getting warm. . . . The first time, I was spared. This time, I may be sure of my little stab."

For prudence's sake, he took a blanket, chose a lonely spot in the park and spent the night under the stars.

Octave was back by ten o'clock in the morning:

"It's all right, governor. The telegram has been sent."

"Good. And is Louis de Malreich still in prison?"

"Yes. Doudeville passed his cell at the Santé last night as the warder was coming out. They talked together. Malreich is just the same, it appears: silent as the grave. He is waiting."

"Waiting for what?"

"The fatal hour of course. They are saying, at headquarters, that the execution will take place on the day after to-morrow."

"That's all right, that's all right," said Lupin. "And one thing is quite plain: he has not escaped."

He ceased to understand or even to look for the explanation of the riddle, so clearly did he feel that the whole truth would soon be revealed to him. He had only to prepare his plan, for the enemy to fall into the trap.

"Or for me to fall into it myself," he thought, laughing.

He felt very gay, very free from care; and no fight had ever looked more promising to him.

A footman came from the castle with the telegram which he had told Doudeville to send him and which the postman had just brought. He opened it and put it in his pocket.

A little before twelve o'clock, he met Pierre Leduc in one of the avenues and said, off-hand:

"I am looking for you . . . things are serious. . . . You must answer me frankly. Since you have been at the castle, have you ever seen a man there, besides the two German servants whom I sent in?"

"No."

"Think carefully. I'm not referring to a casual visitor. I mean a man who hides himself, a man whose presence you might have discovered or, less than that, whose presence you might have suspected from some clue or even by some intuition?"

"No. . . . Have you . . . ?"

"Yes. Some one is hiding here . . . some one is prowling about. . . . Where? And who is it? And what is his object? I don't know . . . but I shall know. I already have a suspicion. Do you, on your side, keep your eyes open and watch. And, above all, not a word to Mrs. Kesselbach. . . . It is no use alarming her. . . ."

He went away.

Pierre Leduc, taken aback and upset, went back to the castle. On his way, he saw a piece of blue paper on the edge of the lawn. He picked it up. It was a telegram, not crumpled, like a piece of paper that had been thrown away, but carefully folded: obviously lost.

It was addressed to "Beauny," the name by which Lupin was known at Bruggen. And it contained these words:

"We know the whole truth. Revelations impossible by letter. Will take train to-night. Meet me eight o'clock to-morrow morning Bruggen station."

"Excellent!" said Lupin, who was watching Pierre Leduc's movements from a neighboring coppice. "Excellent! In two minutes from now, the young idiot will have shown Dolores the telegram and told her all my fears. They will talk about it all day. And 'the other one' will hear, 'the other one' will know, because he knows everything, because he lives in Dolores' own shadow and because Dolores is like a fascinated prey in his hands. . . . And, to-night. . . ."

He walked away humming to himself:

"To-night . . . to-night . . . we shall dance. . . . Such a waltz, my boys! The waltz of blood, to the tune of the little nickel-plated dagger! . . . We shall have some fun, at last! . . ."

He reached the chalet, called to Octave, went to his room, flung himself on his bed, and said to the chauffeur:

"Sit down in that chair, Octave, and keep awake. Your master is going to take forty winks. Watch over him, you faithful servant."

He had a good sleep.

"Like Napoleon on the morning of Austerlitz," he said, when he woke up.

It was dinner-time. He made a hearty meal and then, while he smoked a cigarette, inspected his weapons and renewed the charges of his two revolvers:

"Keep your powder dry and your sword sharpened, as my chum the Kaiser says. Octave!"

Octave appeared.

"Go and have your dinner at the castle, with the servants. Tell them you are going to Paris to-night, in the motor."

"With you, governor?"

"No, alone. And, as soon as dinner is over, make a start, ostensibly."

"But I am not to go to Paris. . . ."

"No, remain outside the park, half a mile down the road, until I come. You will have a long wait."

He smoked another cigarette, went for a stroll, passed in front of the castle, saw a light in Dolores' rooms and then returned to the chalet.

There he took up a book. It was *The Lives of Illustrious Men*.

"There is one missing: the most illustrious of all. But the future will put that right; and I shall have my Plutarch some day or other."

He read the life of Cæsar and jotted down a few reflections in the margin.

At half-past eleven, he went to his bedroom.

Through the open window, he gazed into the immense, cool night, all astir with indistinct sounds. Memories rose to his lips, memories of fond phrases which he had read or uttered; and he repeatedly whispered Dolores's name, with the fervor of a stripling who hardly dares confide to the silence the name of his beloved.

He left the window half open, pushed aside a table that blocked the way, and put his revolvers under his pillow. Then, peacefully, without evincing the least excitement, he got into bed, fully dressed as he was, and blew out the candle.

And his fear began.

It was immediate. No sooner did he feel the darkness around him than his fear began!

"Damn it all!" he cried.

He jumped out of bed, took his weapons and threw them into the passage:

"My hands, my hands alone! Nothing comes up to the grip of my hands!"

He went to bed again. Darkness and silence, once more. And, once more, his fear....

The village clock struck twelve....

Lupin thought of the foul monster who, outside, at a hundred yards, at fifty yards from where he lay, was trying the sharp point of his dagger:

"Let him come, let him come?" whispered Lupin, shuddering. "Then the ghosts will vanish...."

One o'clock, in the village....

And minutes passed, endless minutes, minutes of fever and anguish.... Beads of perspiration stood at the roots of his hair and trickled down his forehead; and he felt as though his whole frame were bathed in a sweat of blood....

Two o'clock....

And now, somewhere, quite close, a hardly perceptible sound stirred, a sound of leaves moving ... but different from the sound of leaves moving in the night breeze....

As Lupin had foreseen, he was at once pervaded by an immense calm. All his adventurous being quivered with delight. The struggle was at hand, at last!

Another sound grated under the window, more plainly this time, but still so faint that it needed Lupin's trained ear to distinguish it.

Minutes, terrifying minutes.... The darkness was impenetrable. No light of star or moon relieved it.

And, suddenly, without hearing anything, he *knew* that the man was in the room.

And the man walked toward the bed. He walked as a ghost walks, without displacing the air of the room, without shaking the objects which he touched.

But, with all his instinct, with all his nervous force, Lupin saw the movements of the enemy and guessed the very sequence of his ideas.

He himself did not budge, but remained propped against the wall, almost on his knees, ready to spring.

He felt that the figure was touching, feeling the bed-clothes, to find the spot at which it must strike. Lupin heard its breath. He even thought that he heard the beating of its heart. And he noticed with pride that his own heart beat no louder than before ... whereas the heart of the other ... oh, yes, he could hear it now, that disordered, mad heart, knocking, like a clapper of a bell, against the cavity of the chest!

The hand of the other rose....

A second, two seconds....

Was he hesitating? Was he once more going to spare his adversary?

And Lupin, in the great silence, said:

"But strike! Why don't you strike?"

A yell of rage.... The arm fell as though moved by a spring.

Then came a moan.

Lupin had caught the arm in mid-air at the level of the wrist. . . . And, leaping out of bed, tremendous, irresistible, he clutched the man by the throat and threw him.

That was all. There was no struggle. There was no possibility even of a struggle. The man lay on the floor, nailed, pinned by two steel rivets, which were Lupin's hands. And there was not a man in the world strong enough to release himself from that grip.

And not a word. Lupin uttered none of those phrases in which his mocking humor usually delighted. He had no inclination to speak. The moment was too solemn.

He felt no vain glee, no victorious exaltation. In reality, he had but one longing, to know who was there: Louis de Malreich, the man sentenced to death, or another? Which was it?

At the risk of strangling the man, he squeezed the throat a little more . . . and a little more . . . and a little more still. . . .

And he felt that all the enemy's strength, all the strength that remained to him, was leaving him. The muscles of the arm relaxed and became lifeless. The hand opened and dropped the dagger.

Then, free to move as he pleased, with his adversary's life hanging in the terrible clutch of his fingers, he took his pocket-lantern with one hand, laid his finger on the spring, without pressing, and brought it close to the man's face.

He had only to press the spring to wish to know and he would know.

For a second, he enjoyed his power. A flood of emotion upheaved him. The vision, of his triumph dazzled him. Once again, superbly, heroically, he was the master.

He switched on the light. The face of the monster came into view.

Lupin gave a shriek of terror.

Dolores Kesselbach!

XVI. ARSÈNE LUPIN'S THREE MURDERS

A cyclone passed through Lupin's brain, a hurricane in which roars of thunder, gusts of wind, squalls of all the distraught elements were tumultuously unchained in the chaotic night.

And great flashes of lightning shot through the darkness. And, by the dazzling gleam of those lightning-flashes, Lupin, scared, shaken with thrills, convulsed with horror, saw and tried to understand.

He did not move, clinging to the enemy's throat, as if his stiffened fingers were no longer able to release their grip. Besides, although he now *knew*, he had not, so to speak, the exact feeling that it was Dolores. It was still the man in black, Louis de Malreich, the foul brute of the darkness; and that brute he held and did not mean to let go.

But the truth rushed upon the attack of his mind and of his consciousness; and, conquered, tortured with anguish, he muttered:

"Oh, Dolores! . . . Dolores! . . ."

He at once saw the excuse: it was madness. She was mad. The sister of Altenheim and Isilda, the daughter of the last of the Malreichs, of the demented mother, of the drunken father, was herself mad. A strange madwoman, mad with every appearance of sanity, but mad nevertheless, unbalanced, brain-sick, unnatural, truly monstrous.

That he most certainly understood! It was homicidal madness. Under the obsession of an object toward which she was drawn automatically, she killed, thirsting for blood, unconsciously, infernally.

She killed because she wanted something, she killed in self-defence, she killed because she had killed before. But she killed also and especially for the sake of killing. Murder satisfied sudden and irresistible appetites that arose in her. At certain seconds in her life, in certain circumstances, face to face with this or that being who had suddenly become the foe, her arm had to strike.

And she struck, drunk with rage, ferociously, frenziedly.

A strange madwoman, not answerable for her murders, and yet so lucid in her blindness, so logical in her mental derangement, so intelligent in her absurdity! What skill, what perseverance, what cunning contrivances, at once abominable and admirable!

And Lupin, in a rapid view, with prodigious keenness of outlook, saw the long array of bloodthirsty adventures and guessed the mysterious paths which Dolores had pursued.

He saw her obsessed and possessed by her husband's scheme, a scheme which she evidently understood only in part. He saw her, on her side, looking for that same Pierre Leduc whom her husband was seeking, looking for him in order to marry him and to return, as queen, to that little realm of Veldenz from which her parents had been ignominiously driven.

And he saw her at the Palace Hotel, in the room of her brother, Altenheim, at the time when she was supposed to be at Monte Carlo. He saw her, for days together, spying upon her husband, creeping along the walls, one with the darkness, undistinguishable and unseen in her shadowy disguise.

And, one night, she found Mr. Kesselbach fastened up . . . and she stabbed him.

And, in the morning, when on the point of being denounced by the floor-waiter . . . she stabbed him.

And, an hour later, when on the point of being denounced by Chapman, she dragged him to her brother's room . . . and stabbed him.

All this pitilessly, savagely, with diabolical skill.

And, with the same skill, she communicated by telephone with her two maids, Gertrude and Suzanne, both of whom had arrived from Monte Carlo, where one of them had enacted the part of her mistress. And Dolores, resuming her feminine attire, discarding the fair wig that altered her appearance beyond recognition, went down to the ground-floor, joined Gertrude at the moment when the maid entered the hotel and pretended herself to have just arrived, all ignorant of the tragedy that awaited her.

An incomparable actress, she played the part of the wife whose life is shattered. Every one pitied her. Every one wept for her. Who could have suspected her?

And then came the war with him, Lupin, that barbarous contest, that unparalleled contest which she waged, by turns, against M. Lenormand and Prince Sernine, spending her days stretched on her sofa, ill and fainting, but her nights on foot, scouring the roads indefatigable and terrible.

And the diabolical contrivances: Gertrude and Suzanne, frightened and subdued accomplices, both of them serving her as emissaries, disguising themselves to represent her, perhaps, as on the day when old Steinweg was carried off by Baron Altenheim, in the middle of the Palais de Justice.

And the series of murders: Gourel drowned; Altenheim, her brother, stabbed. Oh, the implacable struggle in the underground passages of the Villa des Glycines, the invisible work performed by the monster in the dark: how clear it all appeared to-day!

And it was she who tore off his mask as Prince Sernine, she who betrayed him to the police, she who sent him to prison, she who thwarted all his plans, spending her millions to win the battle.

And then events followed faster: Suzanne and Gertrude disappeared, dead, no doubt! Steinweg, assassinated! Isilda, the sister, assassinated!

"Oh, the ignominy, the horror of it!" stammered Lupin, with a start of revulsion and hatred.

He execrated her, the abominable creature. He would have liked to crush her, to destroy her. And it was a stupefying sight, those two beings, clinging to each other, lying motionless in the pale dawn that began to mingle with the shades of the night.

"Dolores. . . . Dolores. . . ." he muttered, in despair.

He leapt back, terror-stricken, wild-eyed. What was it? What was that? What was that hideous feeling of cold which froze his hands?

"Octave! Octave?" he shouted, forgetting that the chauffeur was not there.

Help, he needed help, some one to reassure him and assist him. He shivered with fright. Oh, that coldness, that coldness of death which he had felt! Was it possible? . . . Then, during those few tragic minutes, with his clenched fingers, he had. . . .

Violently, he forced himself to look. Dolores did not stir.

He flung himself on his knees and drew her to him.

She was dead.

He remained for some seconds a prey to a sort of numbness in which his grief seemed to be swallowed up. He no longer suffered. He no longer felt rage nor hatred nor emotion of any kind . . . nothing but a stupid prostration, the sensation of a man who has received a blow with a club and who does not know if he is still alive, if he is thinking, or if he is the sport of a nightmare.

Nevertheless, it seemed to him that an act of justice had taken place, and it did not for a second occur to him that it was he who had taken life. No, it was not he. It was outside him and his will. It was destiny, inexorable destiny that had accomplished the work of equity by slaying the noxious beast.

Outside, the birds were singing. Life was recommencing under the old trees, which the spring was preparing to bring into bud. And Lupin, waking from his torpor, felt gradually welling up within him an indefinable and ridiculous compassion for the wretched woman, odious, certainly, abject and twenty times criminal, but so young still and now . . . dead.

And he thought of the tortures which she must have undergone in her lucid moments, when reason returned to the unspeakable madwoman and brought the sinister vision of her deeds.

"Protect me. . . . I am so unhappy!" she used to beg.

It was against herself that she asked to be protected, against her wild-beast instincts, against the monster that dwelt within her and forced her to kill, always to kill.

"Always?" Lupin asked himself.

And he remembered the night, two days since, when, standing over him, with her dagger raised against the enemy who had been harassing her for months, against the indefatigable enemy who had run her to earth after each of her crimes, he remembered that, on that night, she had not killed. And yet it would have been easy: the enemy lay lifeless and powerless. One blow and the implacable struggle was over. No, she had not killed, she too had given way to feelings stronger than her own cruelty, to mysterious feelings of pity, of sympathy, of admiration for the man who had so often mastered her.

No, she had not killed, that time. And now, by a really terrifying vicissitude of fate, it was he who had killed her.

"I have taken life!" he thought, shuddering from head to foot. "These hands have killed a living being; and that creature is Dolores! . . . Dolores! . . . Dolores! . . ."

He never ceased repeating her name, her name of sorrow, and he never ceased staring at her, a sad, lifeless thing, harmless now, a poor hunk of flesh, with no more consciousness than a little heap of withered leaves or a little dead bird by the roadside.

Oh! how could he do other than quiver with compassion, seeing that of those two, face to face, he was the murderer, and she, who was no more, the victim?

"Dolores! . . . Dolores! . . . Dolores! . . ."

The daylight found Lupin seated beside the dead woman, remembering and thinking, while his lips, from time to time, uttered the disconsolate syllables:

"Dolores! . . . Dolores! . . ."

He had to act, however, and, in the disorder of his ideas, he did not know how to act nor with what act to begin:

"I must close her eyes first," he said.

The eyes, all empty, filled only with death, those beautiful gold-spangled eyes, had still the melancholy softness that gave them their charm. Was it possible that those eyes were the eyes of a monster? In spite of himself and in the face of the implacable reality, Lupin was not yet able to blend into one single being those two creatures whose images remained so distinct at the back of his brain.

He stooped swiftly, lowered the long, silky eyelids, and covered the poor distorted face with a veil.

Then it seemed to him that Dolores was farther away and that the man in black was really there, this time, in his dark clothes, in his murderer's disguise.

He now ventured to touch her, to feel in her clothes. In an inside pocket were two pocket-books. He took one of them and opened it. He found first a letter signed by Steinweg, the old German. It contained the following lines:

"Should I die before being able to reveal the terrible secret, let it be known that the murderer of my friend Kesselbach is his wife, whose real name is Dolores de Malreich, sister to Altenheim and sister to Isilda.

"The initials L. and M. relate to her. Kesselbach never, in their private life, called his wife Dolores, which is the name of sorrow, but Letitia, which denotes joy. L. M.—Letitia de Malreich—were the initials inscribed on all the presents which he used to give her, for instance, on the cigarette-case which was found at the Palace Hotel and which belonged to Mrs. Kesselbach. She had contracted the smoking-habit on her travels.

"Letitia! She was indeed the joy of his life for four years, four years of lies and hypocrisy, in which she prepared the death of the man who loved her so well and who trusted her so whole-heartedly.

"Perhaps I ought to have spoken at once. I had not the courage, in memory of my old friend Kesselbach, whose name she bore.

"And then I was afraid. . . . On the day when I unmasked her, at the Palais de Justice, I read my doom in her eyes.

"Will my weakness save me?"

"Him also," thought Lupin, "him also she killed! . . . Why, of course, he knew too much! . . . The initials . . . that name, Letitia . . . the secret habit of smoking!"

And he remembered the previous night, that smell of tobacco in her room.

He continued his inspection of the first pocket-book. There were scraps of letters, in cipher, no doubt handed to Dolores by her accomplices, in the course of their nocturnal meetings. There were also addresses on bits of paper, addresses of milliners and dressmakers, but addresses also of low haunts, of common hotels. . . . And names . . . twenty, thirty names . . . queer names: Hector the Butcher, Armand of Grenelle, the Sick Man . . .

But a photograph caught Lupin's eye. He looked at it. And, at once, as though shot from a spring, dropping the pocket-book, he bolted out of the room, out of the chalet and rushed into the park.

He had recognized the portrait of Louis de Malreich, the prisoner at the Santé!

Not till then, not till that exact moment did he remember: the execution was to take place next day.

And, as the man in black, as the murderer was none other than Dolores Kesselbach, Louis de Malreich's name was really and truly Leon Massier and he was innocent!

Innocent? But the evidence found in his house, the Emperor's letters, all, all the things that accused him beyond hope of denial, all those incontrovertible proofs?

Lupin stopped for a second, with his brain on fire:

"Oh," he cried, "I shall go mad, I, too! Come, though, I must act . . . the sentence is to be executed . . . to-morrow . . . to-morrow at break of day."

He looked at his watch:

"Ten o'clock. . . . How long will it take me to reach Paris? Well . . . I shall be there presently . . . yes, presently, I must. . . . And this very evening I shall take measures to prevent. . . . But what measures? How can I prove his innocence? . . . How prevent the execution? Oh, never mind! Once I am there, I shall find a way. My name is not Lupin for nothing! . . . Come on! . . ."

He set off again at a run, entered the castle and called out:

"Pierre! Pierre! . . . Has any one seen M. Pierre Leduc? . . . Oh, there you are! . . . Listen. . . ."

He took him on one side and jerked out, in imperious tones:

"Listen, Dolores is not here. . . . Yes, she was called away on urgent business . . . she left last night in my motor. . . . I am going too. . . . Don't interrupt, not a word! . . . A second lost means irreparable harm. . . . You, send away all the servants, without any explanation. Here is money. In half an hour from now, the castle must be empty. And let no one enter it until I return. . . . Not you either, do you understand? . . . I forbid you to enter the castle. . . . I'll explain later . . . serious reasons. Here, take the key with you. . . . Wait for me in the village. . . ."

And once more, he darted away.

Five minutes later, he was with Octave. He jumped into the car:

"Paris!"

The journey was a real race for life or death. Lupin, thinking that Octave was not driving fast enough, took the steering-wheel himself and drove at a furious, break-neck speed. On the road, through the villages, along the crowded streets of the towns they rushed at sixty miles an hour. People whom they nearly upset roared and yelled with rage: the meteor was far away, was out of sight.

"G—governor," stammered Octave, livid with dismay, "we shall be stuck!"

"You, perhaps, the motor, perhaps; but I shall arrive!" said Lupin.

He had a feeling as though it were not the car that was carrying him, but he carrying the car and as though he were cleaving space by dint of his own strength, his own will-power. Then what miracle could prevent his arriving, seeing that his strength was inexhaustible, his will-power unbounded?

"I shall arrive because I have got to arrive," he repeated.

And he thought of the man who would die, if he did not arrive in time to save him, of the mysterious Louis de Malreich, so disconcerting with his stubborn silence and his expressionless face.

And amid the roar of the road, under the trees whose branches made a noise as of furious waves, amid the buzzing of his thoughts, Lupin, all the same, strove to set up an hypothesis. And this hypothesis became gradually more defined, logical, probable, certain, he said to himself, now that he knew the hideous truth about Dolores and saw all the resources and all the odious designs of that crazy mind:

"Yes, it was she who contrived that most terrible plot against Malreich. What was it she wanted? To marry Pierre Leduc, whom she had bewitched, and to become the sovereign of the little principality from which she had been banished. The object was attainable, within reach of her hand. There was one sole obstacle. . . . I, Lupin, who, for weeks and weeks, persistently barred her road; I, whom she encountered after every murder; I, whose perspicacity she dreaded; I, who would never lay down my arms before I had discovered the culprit and found the letters stolen from the Emperor. . . . Well, the culprit should be Louis de Malreich, or rather, Leon Massier. Who was this Leon Massier? Did she know him before her marriage? Had she been in love with him? It is probable; but this, no doubt, we shall never know. One thing is certain, that she was struck by the resemblance to Leon Massier in figure and stature which she might attain by dressing up like him, in black clothes, and putting on a fair wig. She must have noticed the eccentric life led by that lonely man, his nocturnal expeditions, his manner of walking in the streets and of throwing any who might follow him off the scent. And it was in consequence of these observations and in anticipation of possible eventualities that she advised Mr. Kesselbach to erase the name of Dolores from the register of births and to replace it by the name of Louis, so that the initials might correspond with those of Leon Massier. . . . The moment arrived at which she must act; and thereupon she concocted her plot and proceeded to put it into execution. Leon lived in the Rue Delaizement. She ordered her accomplices to take up their quarters in the street that backed on to it. And she herself told me the address of Dominique the head-waiter, and put me on the track of the seven scoundrels, knowing perfectly well that, once on the track, I was bound to follow it to the end, that is to say, beyond the seven scoundrels, till I came up with their leader, the man who watched them and who commanded them, the man in black, Leon Massier, Louis de Malreich. . . . As a matter of fact, I came up with the seven scoundrels first. Then what would happen? Either I should be beaten or we should all destroy one another, as she must have hoped, that night in the Rue des Vignes. In either case Dolores would have been rid of me. But what really happened was this: I captured the seven scoundrels. Dolores fled from the Rue des Vignes. I found her in the Broker's shed. She sent me after Leon Massier, that is to say, Louis de Malreich. I found in his house the Emperor's letters, *which she herself had placed there*, and I delivered him to justice and I revealed the secret communication, *which she herself had caused to be made*, between the two coach-houses, and I produced all the evidence *which she herself had prepared*, and I proved, by means of documents *which she herself had forged*, that Leon Massier had stolen the social status of Leon Massier and that his real name was Louis de Malreich. . . . And Louis de Malreich was sentenced to death. . . . And Dolores de Malreich, victorious at last, safe from all suspicion once the culprit was discovered, released from her infamous and criminal past, her husband dead, her brother dead, her sister dead, her two maids dead, Steinweg dead, delivered by me from her accomplices, whom I handed over to Weber all packed up, delivered, lastly, from herself by me, who was sending the innocent man whom she had substituted for herself to the scaffold, Dolores de Malreich, triumphant, rich with the wealth of her millions and loved by Pierre Leduc, Dolores de Malreich would sit upon the throne of her native grand-duchy. . . . Ah," cried Lupin, beside himself with excitement, "that man shall not die! I swear it as I live: he shall not die!"

"Look out, governor," said Octave, scared, "we are near the town now. . . . the outskirts . . . the suburbs. . . ."

"What shall I care?"

"But we shall topple over. . . . And the pavement is greasy . . . we are skidding. . . ."

"Never mind."

"Take care. . . . Look ahead. . . ."

"What?"

"A tram-car, at the turn. . . ."

"Let it stop!"

"Do slow down, governor!"

"Never!"

"But we have no room to pass!"

"We shall get through."

"We can't get through."

"Yes, we can."

"Oh, Lord!"

A crash . . . outcries. . . . The motor had run into the tram-car, cannoned against a fence, torn down ten yards of planking and, lastly, smashed itself against the corner of a slope.

"Driver, are you disengaged?"

Lupin, lying flat on the grass of the slope, had hailed a taxi-cab.

He scrambled to his feet, gave a glance at his shattered car and the people crowding round to Octave's assistance and jumped into the cab:

"Go to the Ministry of the Interior, on the Place Beauvau . . . Twenty francs for yourself. . . ."

He settled himself in the taxi and continued:

"No, no, he shall not die! No, a thousand times no, I will not have that on my conscience! It is bad enough to have been tricked by a woman and to have fallen into the snare like a schoolboy. . . . That will do! No more blunders for me! I have had that poor wretch arrested. . . . I have had him sentenced to death. . . . I have brought him to the foot of the scaffold . . . but he shall not mount it! . . . Anything but that! If he mounts the scaffold, there will be nothing left for me but to put a bullet through my head."

They were approaching the toll-house. He leant out:

"Twenty francs more, driver, if you don't stop."

And he shouted to the officials:

"Detective-service!"

They passed through.

"But don't slow down, don't slow down, hang it!" roared Lupin. "Faster! . . . Faster still! Are you afraid of running over the old ladies? Never mind about them! I'll pay the damage!"

In a few minutes, they were at the Ministry of the Interior. Lupin hurried across the courtyard and ran up the main staircase. The waiting-room was full of people. He scribbled on a sheet of paper, "Prince Sernine," and, hustling a messenger into a corner, said:

"You know me, don't you? I'm Lupin. I procured you this berth; a snug retreat for your old age, eh? Only, you've got to show me in at once. There, take my name through. That's all I ask of you. The premier will thank you, you may be sure of that . . . and so I will. . . . But, hurry you fool! Valenglay is expecting me. . . ."

Ten seconds later, Valenglay himself put his head through the door of his room and said:

"Show the prince in."

Lupin rushed into the room, slammed the door and, interrupting the premier, said:

"No, no set phrases, you can't arrest me. . . . It would mean ruining yourself and compromising the Emperor. . . . No, it's not a question of that. Look here. Malreich is innocent. . . . I have discovered the real criminal. . . . It's Dolores Kesselbach. She is dead. Her body is down there. I have undeniable proofs. There is no doubt possible. It was she. . . ."

He stopped. Valenglay seemed not to understand.

"But, look here, Monsieur le President, we must save Malreich. . . . Only think . . . a judicial error! . . . An innocent man guillotined! . . . Give your orders . . . say you have fresh information . . . anything you please . . . but, quick, there is no time to lose. . . ."

Valenglay looked at him attentively, then went to a table, took up a newspaper and handed it to him, pointing his finger at an article as he did so.

Lupin cast his eye at the head-line and read:

"EXECUTION OF THE MONSTER"

"Louis de Malreich underwent the death-penalty this morning. . . ."

He read no more. Thunderstruck, crushed, he fell into the premier's chair with a moan of despair. . . .

How long he remained like that he could not say. When he was outside again, he remembered a great silence and then Valenglay bending over him and sprinkling water on his forehead. He remembered, above all, the premier's hushed voice whispering:

"Listen . . . you won't say anything about this will you? Innocent, perhaps, I don't say not. . . . But what is the use of revelations, of a scandal? A judicial error can have serious consequences. Is it worth while? . . . A rehabilitation? For what purpose? He was not even sentenced under his own name. It is the name of Malreich which is held up to public execration . . . the name of the real criminal, as it happens. . . . So . . ."

And, pushing Lupin gradually toward the door, he said:

"So go. . . . Go back there. . . . Get rid of the corpse. . . . And let not a trace remain, eh? Not the slightest trace of all this business. . . . I can rely on you, can I not?"

And Lupin went back. He went back like a machine, because he had been told to do so and because he had no will left of his own.

He waited for hours at the railway-station. Mechanically, he ate his dinner, took a ticket and settled down in a compartment.

He slept badly. His brain was on fire between nightmares and half-waking intervals in which he tried to make out why Malreich had not defended himself:

"He was a madman . . . surely . . . half a madman. . . . He must have known her formerly . . . and she poisoned his life . . . she drove him crazy. . . . So he felt he might as well die. . . . Why defend himself?"

The explanation only half satisfied him, and he promised himself sooner or later to clear up the riddle and to discover the exact part which Massier had played in Dolores' life. But what did it matter for the moment? One fact alone stood out clearly, which was Massier's madness, and he repeated, persistently:

"He was a madman . . . Massier was undoubtedly mad. Besides, all those Massiers . . . a family of madmen. . . ."

He raved, mixing up names in his enfeebled brain.

But, on alighting at Bruggen Station, in the cool, moist air of the morning, his consciousness revived. Things suddenly assumed a different aspect. And he exclaimed:

"Well, after all, it was his own look-out! He had only to protest. . . . I accept no responsibility. . . . It was he who committed suicide. . . . He was only a dumb actor in the play. . . . He has gone under. . . . I am sorry. . . . But it can't be helped!"

The necessity for action stimulated him afresh. Wounded, tortured by that crime of which he knew himself to be the author for all that he might say, he nevertheless looked to the future:

"Those are the accidents of war," he said. "Don't let us think about it. Nothing is lost. On the contrary! Dolores was the stumbling-block, since Pierre Leduc loved her. Dolores is dead. Therefore Pierre Leduc belongs to me. And he shall marry Geneviève, as I have arranged! And he shall reign! And I shall be the master! And Europe, Europe is mine!"

He worked himself up, reassured, full of sudden confidence, and made feverish gestures as he walked along the road, whirling an imaginary sword, the sword of the leader whose will is law, who commands and triumphs:

"Lupin, you shall be king! You shall be king, Arsène Lupin!"

He inquired in the village of Bruggen and heard that Pierre Leduc had lunched yesterday at the inn. Since then, he had not been seen.

"Oh?" asked Lupin. "Didn't he sleep here?"

"No."

"But where did he go after his lunch?"

"He took the road to the castle."

Lupin walked away in some surprise. After all, he had told the young man to lock the doors and not to return after the servants had gone.

He at once received a proof that Pierre had disobeyed him: the park gates were open.

He went in, hunted all over the castle, called out. No reply.

Suddenly, he thought of the chalet. Who could tell? Perhaps Pierre Leduc, worrying about the woman he loved and driven by an intuition, had gone to look for her in that direction. And Dolores' corpse was there!

Greatly alarmed, Lupin began to run.

At first sight, there seemed to be no one in the chalet.

"Pierre! Pierre!" he cried.

Hearing no sound, he entered the front passage and the room which he had occupied.

He stopped short, rooted to the threshold.

Above Dolores' corpse, hung Pierre Leduc, with a rope round his neck, dead.

Lupin impatiently pulled himself together from head to foot. He refused to yield to a single gesture of despair. He refused to utter a single violent word. After the cruel blows which fate had dealt him, after Dolores' crimes and death, after Massier's execution, after all those disturbances and catastrophes, he felt the absolute necessity of retaining all his self-command. If not, his brain would undoubtedly give way. . . .

"Idiot!" he said, shaking his fist at Pierre Leduc. "You great idiot, couldn't you wait? In ten years we should have had Alsace-Lorraine again!"

To relieve his mind, he sought for words to say, for attitudes; but his ideas escaped him and his head seemed on the point of bursting.

"Oh, no, no!" he cried. "None of that, thank you! Lupin mad too! No, old chap! Put a bullet through your head, if you like; and, when all is said, I don't see any other way out. But Lupin drivelling, wheeled about in a bath-chair . . . no! Style, old fellow, finish in style!"

He walked up and down, stamping his feet and lifting his knees very high, as certain actors do when feigning madness. And he said:

"Swagger, my lad, swagger! The eyes of the gods are upon you! Lift up your head! Pull in your stomach, hang it! Throw out your chest! . . . Everything is breaking up around you. What do you care? . . . It's the final disaster, I've played my last card, a kingdom in the gutter, I've lost Europe, the whole world ends in smoke. . . . Well . . . and what of it? Laugh, laugh! Be Lupin, or you're in the soup. . . . Come, laugh! Louder than that, louder, louder! That's right! . . . Lord, how funny it all is! Dolores, old girl, a cigarette!"

He bent down with a grin, touched the dead woman's face, tottered for a second and fell to the ground unconscious.

After lying for an hour, he came to himself and stood up. The fit of madness was over; and, master of himself, with relaxed nerves, serious and silent, he considered the position.

He felt that the time had come for the irrevocable decisions that involve a whole existence. His had been utterly shattered, in a few days, under the assault of unforeseen catastrophes, rushing up, one after the other, at the very moment when he thought his triumph assured. What should he do? Begin again? Build up everything again? He had not the courage for it. What then?

The whole morning, he roamed tragically about the park and gradually realized his position in all its slightest details. Little by little, the thought of death enforced itself upon him with inflexible rigor.

But, whether he decided to kill himself or to live, there was first of all a series of definite acts which he was obliged to perform. And these acts stood out clearly in his brain, which had suddenly become quite cool.

The mid-day Angelus rang from the church-steeple.

"To work!" he said, firmly.

He returned to the chalet in a very calm frame of mind, went to his room, climbed on a stool, and cut the rope by which Pierre Leduc was hanging:

"You poor devil!" he said. "You were doomed to end like that, with a hempen tie around your neck. Alas, you were not made for greatness: I ought to have foreseen that and not hooked my fortune to a rhymester!"

He felt in the young man's clothes and found nothing. But, remembering Dolores' second pocket-book, he took it from the pocket where he had left it.

He gave a start of surprise. The pocket-book contained a bundle of letters whose appearance was familiar to him; and he at once recognized the different writings.

"The Emperor's letters!" he muttered, slowly. "The old chancellor's letters! The whole bundle which I myself found at Leon Massier's and which I handed to Count von Waldemar! . . . How did it happen? . . . Did she take them in her turn from that blockhead of a Waldemar?" And, suddenly, slapping his forehead, "Why, no, the blockhead is myself. These are the real letters! She kept them to blackmail the Emperor when the time came. And the others, the ones which I handed over, are copies, forged by herself, of course, or by an accomplice, and placed where she knew that I should find them. . . . And I played her game for her, like a mug! By Jove, when women begin to interfere . . . !"

There was only a piece of pasteboard left in the pocket-book, a photograph. He looked at it. It was his own.

"Two photographs . . . Massier and I . . . the two she loved best, no doubt . . . For she loved me. . . . A strange love, built up of admiration for the adventurer that I am, for the man who, by himself, put away the seven scoundrels whom she had paid to break my head! A strange love! I felt it throbbing in her the other day, when I told her my great dream of omnipotence. Then, really, she had the idea of sacrificing Pierre Leduc and subjecting her dream to mine. If the incident of the mirror had not taken place, she would have been subdued. But she was afraid. I had my hand upon the truth. My death was necessary for her salvation and she decided upon it." He repeated several times, pensively, "And yet she loved me. . . . Yes, she loved me, as others have loved me . . . others to whom I have brought ill-luck also. . . . Alas, all those who love me die! . . . And this one died too, strangled by my hand. . . . What is the use of living? . . . What is the use of living?" he asked again, in a low voice. "Is it not better to join them, all those women who have loved me . . . and who have died of their love . . . Sonia, Raymonde, Clotilde, Destange, Miss Clarke? . . ."

He laid the two corpses beside each other, covered them with the same sheet, sat down at a table and wrote:

"I have triumphed over everything and I am beaten. I have reached the goal and I have fallen. Fate is too strong for me. . . . And she whom I loved is no more. I shall die also."

And he signed his name:

"Arsène Lupin."

He sealed the letter and slipped it into a bottle which he flung through the window, on the soft ground of a flower-border.

Next, he made a great pile on the floor with old newspapers, straw and shavings, which he went to fetch in the kitchen. On the top of it he emptied a gallon of petrol. Then he lit a candle and threw it among the shavings.

A flame at once arose and other flames leapt forth, quick, glowing, crackling.

"Let's clear out," said Lupin. "The chalet is built of wood, it will all flare up like a match. And, by the time they come from the village, break down the gates and run to this end of the park, it will be too late. They will find ashes, the remains of two charred corpses and, close at hand, my farewell letter in a bottle. . . . Good-bye, Lupin! Bury me simply, good people, without superfluous state . . . a poor man's funeral . . . No flowers, no wreaths. . . . Just a humble cross and a plain epitaph; 'Here lies Arsène Lupin, adventurer.'"

He made for the park wall, climbed over it, and turning round, saw the flames soaring up to the sky. . . .

He wandered back toward Paris on foot, bowed down by destiny, with despair in his heart. And the peasants were amazed at the sight of this traveller who paid with bank-notes for his fifteen-penny meals.

Three foot-pads attacked him one evening in the forest. He defended himself with his stick and left them lying for dead. . . .

He spent a week at an inn. He did not know where to go. . . . What was he to do? What was there for him to cling to? He was tired of life. He did not want to live. . . .

"Is that you?"

Mme. Ernemont stood in her little sitting-room in the villa at Garches, trembling, scared and livid, staring at the apparition that faced her.

Lupin! . . . It was Lupin.

"You!" she said. "You! . . . But the papers said . . ."

He smiled sadly:

"Yes, I am dead."

"Well, then . . . well, then . . ." she said, naïvely.

"You mean that, if I am dead, I have no business here. Believe me, I have serious reasons, Victoire."

"How you have changed!" she said, in a voice full of pity.

"A few little disappointments. . . . However, that's over. . . . Tell me, is Geneviève in?"

She flew at him, in a sudden rage:

"You leave her alone, do you hear? Geneviève? You want to see Geneviève, to take her back? Ah, this time I shall not let her out of my sight! She came back tired, white as a sheet, nervous; and the color has hardly yet returned to her cheeks. You shall leave her alone, I swear you shall."

He pressed his hand hard on the old woman's shoulder:

"I *will*—do you understand?—I *will* speak to her."

"No."

"I mean to speak to her."

"No."

He pushed her about. She drew herself up and, crossing her arms:

"You shall pass over my dead body first, do you hear? The child's happiness lies in this house and nowhere else. . . . With all your ideas of money and rank, you would only make her miserable. Who is this Pierre Leduc of yours? And that Veldenz of yours? Geneviève a grand-duchess! You are mad. That's no life for her! . . . You see, after all, you have thought only of yourself in this matter. It was your power, your fortune you wanted. The child you don't care a rap about. Have you so much as asked yourself if she loved your rascally grand-duke? Have you asked yourself if she loved anybody? No, you just pursued your object, that is all, at the risk of hurting Geneviève and making her unhappy for the rest of her life. . . . Well, I won't have it! What she wants is a simple, honest existence, led in the broad light of day; and that is what you can't give her. Then what are you here for?"

He seemed to waver, but, nevertheless, he murmured in a low voice and very sadly:

"It is impossible that I should never see her again, it is impossible that I should not speak to her. . . ."

"She believes you dead."

"That is exactly what I do not want! I want her to know the truth. It is a torture to me to think that she looks upon me as one who is no more. Bring her to me, Victoire."

He spoke in a voice so gentle and so distressed that she was utterly moved, and said:

"Listen. . . . First of all, I want to know. . . . It depends upon what you intend to say to her. . . . Be frank, my boy. . . . What do you want with Geneviève?"

He said, gravely:

"I want to say this: 'Geneviève, I promised your mother to give you wealth, power, a fairy-like existence. And, on the day when I had attained my aim, I would have asked you for a little place, not very far from you. Rich and happy, you would have forgotten—yes, I am sure of it—you would have forgotten who I am, or rather who I was. Unfortunately, fate has been too strong for me. I bring you neither wealth nor power. And it is I, on the contrary, who have need of you. Geneviève, will you help me?'"

"To do what?" asked the old woman, anxiously.

"To live. . . ."

"Oh!" she said. "Has it come to that, my poor boy? . . ."

"Yes," he answered, simply, without any affectation of sorrow, "yes, it has come to that. Three human beings are just dead, killed by me, killed by my hands. The burden of the memory is more than I can bear. I am alone. For the first time in my life, I need help. I have the right to ask that help of Geneviève. And her duty is to give it to me. . . . If not . . ."

"If not . . . ?"

"Then all is over."

The old woman was silent, pale and quivering with emotion. She once more felt all her affection for him whom she had fed at her breast and who still and in spite of all remained "her boy." She asked:

"What do you intend to do with her?"

"We shall go abroad. We will take you with us, if you like to come. . . ."

"But you forget . . . you forget. . . ."

"What?"

"Your past. . . ."

"She will forget it too. She will understand that I am no longer the man I was, that I do not wish to be."

"Then, really, what you wish is that she should share your life, the life of Lupin?"

"The life of the man that I shall be, of the man who will work so that she may be happy, so that she may marry according to her inclination. We will settle down in some nook or other. We will struggle together, side by side. And you know what I am capable of. . . ."

She repeated, slowly, with her eyes fixed on his:

"Then, really, you wish her to share Lupin's life?"

He hesitated a second, hardly a second, and declared, plainly:

"Yes, yes, I wish it, I have the right."

"You wish her to abandon all the children to whom she has devoted herself, all this life of work which she loves and which is essential to her happiness?"

"Yes, I wish it, it is her duty."

The old woman opened the window and said:

"In that case, call her."

Geneviève was in the garden, sitting on a bench. Four little girls were crowding round her. Others were playing and running about.

He saw her full-face. He saw her grave, smiling eyes. She held a flower in her hand and plucked the petals one by one and gave explanations to the attentive and eager children. Then she asked them questions. And each answer was rewarded with a kiss to the pupil.

Lupin looked at her long, with infinite emotion and anguish. A whole leaven of unknown feelings fermented within him. He had a longing to press that pretty girl to his breast, to kiss her and tell her how he respected and loved her. He remembered the mother, who died in the little village of Aspremont, who died of grief.

"Call her," said Victoire. "Why don't you call her?"

He sank into a chair and stammered:

"I can't. . . . I can't do it. . . . I have not the right. . . . It is impossible. . . . Let her believe me dead. . . . That is better. . . ."

He wept, his shoulders shaking with sobs, his whole being overwhelmed with despair, swollen with an affection that arose in him, like those backward flowers which die on the very day of their blossoming.

The old woman knelt down beside him and, in a trembling voice, asked:

"She is your daughter, is she not?"

"Yes, she is my daughter."

"Oh, my poor boy!" she said, bursting into tears. "My poor boy! . . ."

EPILOGUE: THE SUICIDE

"To horse!" said the Emperor.

He corrected himself, on seeing the magnificent ass which they brought him:

"To donkey, rather! Waldemar, are you sure this animal is quiet to ride and drive?"

"I will answer for him as I would for myself, Sire," declared the count.

"In that case, I feel safe," said the Emperor, laughing. And, turning to the officers with him, "Gentlemen, to horse!"

The market-place of the village of Capri was crowded with sight-seers, kept back by a line of Italian carabiniers, and, in the middle, all the donkeys of the place, which had been requisitioned to enable the Emperor to go over that island of wonders.

"Waldemar," said the Emperor, taking the head of the cavalcade, "what do we begin with?"

"With Tiberius's Villa, Sire."

They rode under a gateway and then followed a roughly-paved path, rising gradually to the eastern promontory of the island.

The Emperor laughed and enjoyed himself and good-humoredly chaffed the colossal Count von Waldemar, whose feet touched the ground on either side of the unfortunate donkey borne down under his weight.

In three-quarters of an hour, they arrived first at Tiberius's Leap, an enormous rock, a thousand feet high, from which the tyrant caused his victims to be hurled into the sea. . . .

The Emperor dismounted, walked up to the hand-rail and took a glance at the abyss. Then he went on foot to the ruins of Tiberius's Villa, where he strolled about among the crumbling halls and passages.

He stopped for a moment.

There was a glorious view of the point of Sorrento and over the whole island of Capri. The glowing blue of the sea outlined the beautiful curve of the bay; and cool perfumes mingled with the scent of the citron-trees.

"The view is finer still, Sire," said Waldemar, "from the hermit's little chapel, at the summit."

"Let us go to it."

But the hermit himself descended by a steep path. He was an old man, with a hesitating gait and a bent back. He carried the book in which travellers usually write down their impressions.

He placed the book on a stone seat.

"What am I write?" asked the Emperor.

"Your name, Sire, and the date of your visit . . . and anything you please."

The Emperor took the pen which the hermit handed him and bent down to write.

"Take care, Sire, take care!"

Shouts of alarm . . . a great crash from the direction of the chapel. . . . The Emperor turned round. He saw a huge rock come rolling down upon him like a whirlwind.

At the same moment, he was seized round the body by the hermit and flung to a distance of ten yards away.

The rock struck against the stone seat where the Emperor had been standing a quarter of a second before and smashed the seat into fragments. But for the hermit, the Emperor would have been killed.

He gave him his hand and said, simply:

"Thank you."

The officers flocked round him.

"It's nothing, gentlemen. . . . We have escaped with a fright . . . though it was a fine fright, I confess. . . . All the same, but for the intervention of this worthy man . . ."

And, going up to the hermit:

"What is your name, my friend?"

The hermit had kept his head concealed in his hood. He pushed it back an inch or so and, in a very low voice, so as to be heard by none but the Emperor, he said:

"The name of a man, Sire, who is very pleased that you have shaken him by the hand."

The Emperor gave a start and stepped back. Then, at once controlling himself:

"Gentlemen," he said to the officers, "I will ask you to go up to the chapel. More rocks can break loose; and it would perhaps be wise to warn the authorities of the island. You will join me later. I want to thank this good man."

He walked away, accompanied by the hermit. When they were alone, he said:

"You! Why?"

"I had to speak to you, Sire. If I had asked for an audience . . . would you have granted my request? I preferred to act directly and I intended to make myself known while Your Imperial Majesty was signing the book, when that stupid accident . . ."

"Well?" said the Emperor.

"The letters which I gave Waldemar to hand to you, Sire, are forgeries."

The Emperor made a gesture of keen annoyance:

"Forgeries? Are you sure?"

"Absolutely sure, Sire."

"Yet that Malreich . . ."

"Malreich was not the culprit."

"Then who was?"

"I must beg Your Imperial Majesty to treat my answer as secret and confidential. The real culprit was Mrs. Kesselbach."

"Kesselbach's own wife?"

"Yes, Sire. She is dead now. It was she who made or caused to be made the copies which are in your possession. She kept the real letters."

"But where are they?" exclaimed the Emperor. "That is the important thing! They must be recovered at all costs! I attach the greatest value to those letters. . . ."

"Here they are, Sire."

The Emperor had a moment of stupefaction. He looked at Lupin, looked at the letters, then at Lupin again and pocketed the bundle without examining it.

Clearly, this man was puzzling him once more. Where did this scoundrel spring from who, possessing so terrible a weapon, handed it over like that, generously, unconditionally? It would have been so easy for him to keep the letters and to make such use of them as he pleased! No, he had given his promise and he was keeping his word.

And the Emperor thought of all the astounding things which that man had done.

"The papers said that you were dead," he said.

"Yes, Sire. In reality, I am dead. And the police of my country, glad to be rid of me, have buried the charred and unrecognizable remains of my body."

"Then you are free?"

"As I always have been."

"And nothing attaches you to anything?"

"Nothing, Sire."

"In that case . . ."

The Emperor hesitated and then, explicitly:

"In that case, enter my service. I offer you the command of my private police. You shall be the absolute master. You shall have full power, even over the other police."

"No, Sire."

"Why not?"

"I am a Frenchman."

There was a pause. The Emperor was evidently pleased with the answer. He said:

"Still, as you say that no link attaches you . . ."

"That is, one, Sire, which nothing can sever." And he added, laughing, "I am dead as a man, but alive as a Frenchman. I am sure that Your Imperial Majesty will understand."

The Emperor took a few steps up and down. Then he said:

"I should like to pay my debt, however. I heard that the negotiations for the grand-duchy of Veldenz were broken off...."

"Yes, Sire, Pierre Leduc was an imposter. He is dead."

"What can I do for you? You have given me back those letters.... You have saved my life.... What can I do?"

"Nothing, Sire."

"You insist upon my remaining your debtor?"

"Yes, Sire."

The Emperor gave a last glance at that strange man who set himself up in his presence as his equal. Then he bowed his head slightly and walked away without another word.

"Aha, Majesty, I've caught you this time!" said Lupin, following him with his eyes. And, philosophically, "No doubt it's a poor revenge ... and would rather have recovered Alsace-Lorraine.... But still..."

He interrupted himself and stamped his foot on the ground:

"You confounded Lupin! Will you never change, will you always remain hateful and cynical to the last moment of your existence? Be serious, hang it all! The time has come, now or never, to be serious!"

He climbed the path that leads to the chapel and stopped at the place where the rock had broken loose. He burst out laughing:

"It was a good piece of work and His Imperial Majesty's officers did not know what to make of it. But how could they guess that I myself loosened that rock, that, at the last moment, I gave the decisive blow of the pick-axe and that the aforesaid rock rolled down the path which I had made between it and ... an emperor whose life I was bent on saving?"

He sighed:

"Ah, Lupin, what a complex mind you have! All that trouble because you had sworn that this particular Majesty should shake you by the hand! A lot of good it has done you! 'An Emperor's hand five fingers has, no more,' as Victor Hugo might have said."

He entered the chapel and, with a special key, opened the low door of a little sacristy. On a heap of straw, lay a man, with his hands and legs bound and a gag in his mouth.

"Well, my friend, the hermit," said Lupin, "it wasn't so very long, was it? Twenty-four hours at the most. ... But I have worked jolly hard on your behalf! Just think, you have saved the Emperor's life! Yes, old chap. You are the man who saved the Emperor's life. I have made your fortune, that's what I've done. They'll build a cathedral for you and put up a statue to you when you're dead and gone. Here, take your things."

The hermit, nearly dead with hunger, staggered to his feet. Lupin quickly put on his own clothes and said:

"Farewell, O worthy and venerable man. Forgive me for this little upset. And pray for me. I shall need it. Eternity is opening its gate wide to me. Farewell."

He stood for a few moments on the threshold of the chapel. It was the solemn moment at which one hesitates, in spite of everything, before the terrible end of all things. But his resolution was irrevocable and, without further reflection, he darted out, ran down the slope, crossed the level ground of Tiberius's Leap and put one leg over the hand-rail:

"Lupin, I give you three minutes for play-acting. 'What's the good?' you will say. 'There is nobody here.' Well ... and what about you? Can't you act your last farce for yourself? By Jove, the performance is worth it. ... *Arsène Lupin*, heroic comedy in eighty scenes.... The curtain rises on the death-scene ... and the principal part is played by Lupin in person.... 'Bravo, Lupin!' ... Feel my heart, ladies and gentlemen ... seventy beats to the minute.... And a smile on my lips.... 'Bravo, Lupin! Oh, the rogue, what cheek he has!' ... Well, jump, my lord.... Are you ready? It's the last adventure, old fellow. No regrets? Regrets? What for, heavens above? My life was splendid. Ah, Dolores, Dolores, if you had not come into it, abominable monster that you were!...... And you, Malreich, why did you not speak? ... And you, Pierre Leduc.... Here I am! ... My three dead friends, I am about to join you.... Oh, Geneviève, my dear Geneviève! ... Here, have you done, you old play-actor? ... Right you are! Right you are! I'm coming...."

He pulled his other leg over, looked down the abyss at the dark and motionless sea and, raising his head:

"Farewell, immortal and thrice-blessed nature! *Moriturus te salutat!* Farewell, all that is beautiful on earth! Farewell, splendor of things. Farewell, life!"

He flung kisses to space, to the sky, to the sun. . . . Then, folding his arms, he took the leap.

Sidi-bel-Abbes. The barracks of the Foreign Legion. An adjutant sat smoking and reading his newspaper in a small, low-ceilinged room.

Near him, close to the window opening on the yard, two great devils of non-commissioned officers were jabbering in guttural French, mixed with Teutonic phrases.

The door opened. Some one entered. It was a slightly-built man, of medium height, smartly-dressed.

The adjutant rose, glared angrily at the intruder and growled:

"I say, what on earth is the orderly up to? . . . And you, sir, what do you want?"

"Service."

This was said frankly, imperiously. The two non-coms burst into a silly laugh. The man looked at them askance.

"In other words, you wish to enlist in the Legion?" asked the adjutant.

"Yes, but on one condition."

"Conditions, by Jove! What conditions?"

"That I am not left mouldering here. There is a company leaving for Morocco. I'll join that."

One of the non-coms gave a fresh chuckle and was heard to say:

"The Moors are in for a bad time. The gentleman's enlisting."

"Silence!" cried the man, "I don't stand being laughed at."

His voice sounded harsh and masterful.

The non-com, a brutal-looking giant, retorted:

"Here, recruity, you'd better be careful how you talk to me, or . . ."

"Or what?"

"You'll get something you won't like, that's all!"

The man went up to him, took him round the waist, swung him over the ledge of the window and pitched him into the yard.

Then he said to the other: "Go away."

The other went away.

The man at once returned to the adjutant and said:

"Lieutenant, pray be so good as to tell the major that Don Luis Perenna, a Spanish grandee and a Frenchman at heart, wishes to take service in the Foreign Legion. Go, my friend."

The flabbergasted adjutant did not move.

"Go, my friend, and go at once. I have no time to waste."

The adjutant rose, looked at his astounding visitor with a bewildered eye and went out in the tamest fashion.

Then Lupin lit a cigarette and, sitting down in the adjutant's chair, said, aloud:

"As the sea refused to have anything to say to me, or rather as I, at the last moment, refused to have anything to say to the sea, we'll go and see if the bullets of the Moors are more compassionate. And, in any case, it will be a smarter finish... Face the enemy, Lupin, and all for France!..."

THE END

BOOK FIVE.
THE CRYSTAL STOPPER

I. THE ARRESTS

The two boats fastened to the little pier that jutted out from the garden lay rocking in its shadow. Here and there lighted windows showed through the thick mist on the margins of the lake. The Enghien Casino opposite blazed with light, though it was late in the season, the end of September. A few stars appeared through the clouds. A light breeze ruffled the surface of the water.

Arsene Lupin left the summer-house where he was smoking a cigar and, bending forward at the end of the pier:

"Growler?" he asked. "Masher?... Are you there?"

A man rose from each of the boats, and one of them answered:

"Yes, governor."

"Get ready. I hear the car coming with Gilbert and Vaucheray."

He crossed the garden, walked round a house in process of construction, the scaffolding of which loomed overhead, and cautiously opened the door on the Avenue de Ceinture. He was not mistaken: a bright light flashed round the bend and a large, open motor-car drew up, whence sprang two men in great-coats, with the collars turned up, and caps.

It was Gilbert and Vaucheray: Gilbert, a young fellow of twenty or twenty-two, with an attractive cast of features and a supple and sinewy frame; Vaucheray, older, shorter, with grizzled hair and a pale, sickly face.

"Well," asked Lupin, "did you see him, the deputy?"

"Yes, governor," said Gilbert, "we saw him take the 7.40 tram for Paris, as we knew he would."

"Then we are free to act?"

"Absolutely. The Villa Marie-Therese is ours to do as we please with."

The chauffeur had kept his seat. Lupin gave him his orders:

"Don't wait here. It might attract attention. Be back at half-past nine exactly, in time to load the car unless the whole business falls through."

"Why should it fall through?" observed Gilbert.

The motor drove away; and Lupin, taking the road to the lake with his two companions, replied:

"Why? Because I didn't prepare the plan; and, when I don't do a thing myself, I am only half-confident."

"Nonsense, governor! I've been working with you for three years now... I'm beginning to know the ropes!"

"Yes, my lad, you're beginning," said Lupin, "and that's just why I'm afraid of blunders... Here, get in with me... And you, Vaucheray, take the other boat... That's it... And now push off, boys... and make as little noise as you can."

Growler and Masher, the two oarsmen, made straight for the opposite bank, a little to the left of the casino.

They met a boat containing a couple locked in each other's arms, floating at random, and another in which a number of people were singing at the top of their voices. And that was all.

Lupin shifted closer to his companion and said, under his breath:

"Tell me, Gilbert, did you think of this job, or was it Vaucheray's idea?"

"Upon my word, I couldn't tell you: we've both of us been discussing it for weeks."

"The thing is, I don't trust Vaucheray: he's a low ruffian when one gets to know him... I can't make out why I don't get rid of him..."

"Oh, governor!"

"Yes, yes, I mean what I say: he's a dangerous fellow, to say nothing of the fact that he has some rather serious peccadilloes on his conscience."

He sat silent for a moment and continued:

"So you're quite sure that you saw Daubrecq the deputy?"

"Saw him with my own eyes, governor."

"And you know that he has an appointment in Paris?"

"He's going to the theatre."

"Very well; but his servants have remained behind at the Enghien villa...."

"The cook has been sent away. As for the valet, Leonard, who is Daubrecq's confidential man, he'll wait for his master in Paris. They can't get back from town before one o'clock in the morning. But..."

"But what?"

"We must reckon with a possible freak of fancy on Daubrecq's part, a change of mind, an unexpected return, and so arrange to have everything finished and done with in an hour."

"And when did you get these details?"

"This morning. Vaucheray and I at once thought that it was a favourable moment. I selected the garden of the unfinished house which we have just left as the best place to start from; for the house is not watched at night. I sent for two mates to row the boats; and I telephoned to you. That's the whole story."

"Have you the keys?"

"The keys of the front-door."

"Is that the villa which I see from here, standing in its own grounds?"

"Yes, the Villa Marie-Therese; and as the two others, with the gardens touching it on either side, have been unoccupied since this day week, we shall be able to remove what we please at our leisure; and I swear to you, governor, it's well worth while."

"The job's much too simple," mumbled Lupin. "No charm about it!"

They landed in a little creek whence rose a few stone steps, under cover of a mouldering roof. Lupin reflected that shipping the furniture would be easy work. But, suddenly, he said:

"There are people at the villa. Look... a light."

"It's a gas-jet, governor. The light's not moving."

The Growler stayed by the boats, with instructions to keep watch, while the Masher, the other rower, went to the gate on the Avenue de Ceinture, and Lupin and his two companions crept in the shadow to the foot of the steps.

Gilbert went up first. Groping in the dark, he inserted first the big door-key and then the latch-key. Both turned easily in their locks, the door opened and the three men walked in.

A gas-jet was flaring in the hall.

"You see, governor..." said Gilbert.

"Yes, yes," said Lupin, in a low voice, "but it seems to me that the light which I saw shining did not come from here..."

"Where did it come from then?"

"I can't say... Is this the drawing-room?"

"No," replied Gilbert, who was not afraid to speak pretty loudly, "no. By way of precaution, he keeps everything on the first floor, in his bedroom and in the two rooms on either side of it."

"And where is the staircase?"

"On the right, behind the curtain."

Lupin moved to the curtain and was drawing the hanging aside when, suddenly, at four steps on the left, a door opened and a head appeared, a pallid man's head, with terrified eyes.

"Help! Murder!" shouted the man.

And he rushed back into the room.

"It's Leonard, the valet!" cried Gilbert.

"If he makes a fuss, I'll out him," growled Vaucheray.

"You'll jolly well do nothing of the sort, do you hear, Vaucheray?" said Lupin, peremptorily. And he darted off in pursuit of the servant. He first went through a dining-room, where he saw a lamp still lit, with plates and a bottle around it, and he found Leonard at the further end of a pantry, making vain efforts to open the window:

"Don't move, sportie! No kid! Ah, the brute!"

He had thrown himself flat on the floor, on seeing Leonard raise his arm at him. Three shots were fired in the dusk of the pantry; and then the valet came tumbling to the ground, seized by the legs by Lupin, who snatched his weapon from him and gripped him by the throat:

"Get out, you dirty brute!" he growled. "He very nearly did for me... Here, Vaucheray, secure this gentleman!"

He threw the light of his pocket-lantern on the servant's face and chuckled:

"He's not a pretty gentleman either... You can't have a very clear conscience, Leonard; besides, to play flunkey to Daubrecq the deputy...! Have you finished, Vaucheray? I don't want to hang about here for ever!"

"There's no danger, governor," said Gilbert.

"Oh, really?... So you think that shots can't be heard?..."

"Quite impossible."

"No matter, we must look sharp. Vaucheray, take the lamp and let's go upstairs."

He took Gilbert by the arm and, as he dragged him to the first floor:

"You ass," he said, "is that the way you make inquiries? Wasn't I right to have my doubts?"

"Look here, governor, I couldn't know that he would change his mind and come back to dinner."

"One's got to know everything when one has the honour of breaking into people's houses. You numskull! I'll remember you and Vaucheray... a nice pair of gossoons!..."

The sight of the furniture on the first floor pacified Lupin and he started on his inventory with the satisfied air of a collector who has looked in to treat himself to a few works of art:

"By Jingo! There's not much of it, but what there is is pucka! There's nothing the matter with this representative of the people in the question of taste. Four Aubusson chairs... A bureau signed 'Percier-Fontaine,' for a wager... Two inlays by Gouttieres... A genuine Fragonard and a sham Nattier which any American millionaire will swallow for the asking: in short, a fortune... And there are curmudgeons who pretend that there's nothing but faked stuff left. Dash it all, why don't they do as I do? They should look about!"

Gilbert and Vaucheray, following Lupin's orders and instructions, at once proceeded methodically to remove the bulkier pieces. The first boat was filled in half an hour; and it was decided that the Growler and the Masher should go on ahead and begin to load the motor-car.

Lupin went to see them start. On returning to the house, it struck him, as he passed through the hall, that he heard a voice in the pantry. He went there and found Leonard lying flat on his stomach, quite alone, with his hands tied behind his back:

"So it's you growling, my confidential flunkey? Don't get excited: it's almost finished. Only, if you make too much noise, you'll oblige us to take severer measures... Do you like pears? We might give you one, you know: a choke-pear!..."

As he went upstairs, he again heard the same sound and, stopping to listen, he caught these words, uttered in a hoarse, groaning voice, which came, beyond a doubt, from the pantry:

"Help!... Murder!... Help!... I shall be killed!... Inform the commissary!"

"The fellow's clean off his chump!" muttered Lupin. "By Jove!... To disturb the police at nine o'clock in the evening: there's a notion for you!"

He set to work again. It took longer than he expected, for they discovered in the cupboards all sorts of valuable knick-knacks which it would have been very wrong to disdain and, on the other hand, Vaucheray and Gilbert were going about their investigations with signs of laboured concentration that nonplussed him.

At long last, he lost his patience:

"That will do!" he said. "We're not going to spoil the whole job and keep the motor waiting for the sake of the few odd bits that remain. I'm taking the boat."

They were now by the waterside and Lupin went down the steps. Gilbert held him back:

"I say, governor, we want one more look round five minutes, no longer."

"But what for, dash it all?"

"Well, it's like this: we were told of an old reliquary, something stunning..."

"Well?"

"We can't lay our hands on it. And I was thinking... There's a cupboard with a big lock to it in the pantry... You see, we can't very well..." He was already on his way to the villa. Vaucheray ran back too.

"I'll give you ten minutes, not a second longer!" cried Lupin. "In ten minutes, I'm off."

But the ten minutes passed and he was still waiting.

He looked at his watch:

"A quarter-past nine," he said to himself. "This is madness."

And he also remembered that Gilbert and Vaucheray had behaved rather queerly throughout the removal of the things, keeping close together and apparently watching each other. What could be happening?

Lupin mechanically returned to the house, urged by a feeling of anxiety which he was unable to explain; and, at the same time, he listened to a dull sound which rose in the distance, from the direction of Enghien, and which seemed to be coming nearer... People strolling about, no doubt...

He gave a sharp whistle and then went to the main gate, to take a glance down the avenue. But, suddenly, as he was opening the gate, a shot rang out, followed by a yell of pain. He returned at a run, went round the house, leapt up the steps and rushed to the dining-room:

"Blast it all, what are you doing there, you two?"

Gilbert and Vaucheray, locked in a furious embrace, were rolling on the floor, uttering cries of rage. Their clothes were dripping with blood. Lupin flew at them to separate them. But already Gilbert had got his adversary down and was wrenching out of his hand something which Lupin had no time to see. And Vaucheray, who was losing blood through a wound in the shoulder, fainted.

"Who hurt him? You, Gilbert?" asked Lupin, furiously.

"No, Leonard."

"Leonard? Why, he was tied up!"

"He undid his fastenings and got hold of his revolver."

"The scoundrel! Where is he?"

Lupin took the lamp and went into the pantry.

The man-servant was lying on his back, with his arms outstretched, a dagger stuck in his throat and a livid face. A red stream trickled from his mouth.

"Ah," gasped Lupin, after examining him, "he's dead!"

"Do you think so?... Do you think so?" stammered Gilbert, in a trembling voice.

"He's dead, I tell you."

"It was Vaucheray... it was Vaucheray who did it..."

Pale with anger, Lupin caught hold of him:

"It was Vaucheray, was it?... And you too, you blackguard, since you were there and didn't stop him! Blood! Blood! You know I won't have it... Well, it's a bad lookout for you, my fine fellows... You'll have to pay the damage! And you won't get off cheaply either... Mind the guillotine!" And, shaking him violently, "What was it? Why did he kill him?"

"He wanted to go through his pockets and take the key of the cupboard from him. When he stooped over him, he saw that the man unloosed his arms. He got frightened... and he stabbed him..."

"But the revolver-shot?"

"It was Leonard... he had his revolver in his hand... he just had strength to take aim before he died..."

"And the key of the cupboard?"

"Vaucheray took it...."

"Did he open it?"

"Yes."

"And did he find what he was after?"

"Yes."

"And you wanted to take the thing from him. What sort of thing was it? The reliquary? No, it was too small for that.... Then what was it? Answer me, will you?..."

Lupin gathered from Gilbert's silence and the determined expression on his face that he would not obtain a reply. With a threatening gesture, "I'll make you talk, my man. Sure as my name's Lupin, you shall come out with it. But, for the moment, we must see about decamping. Here, help me. We must get Vaucheray into the boat..."

They had returned to the dining-room and Gilbert was bending over the wounded man, when Lupin stopped him:

"Listen."

They exchanged one look of alarm... Some one was speaking in the pantry ... a very low, strange, very distant voice... Nevertheless, as they at once made certain, there was no one in the room, no one except the dead man, whose dark outline lay stretched upon the floor.

And the voice spake anew, by turns shrill, stifled, bleating, stammering, yelling, fearsome. It uttered indistinct words, broken syllables.

Lupin felt the top of his head covering with perspiration. What was this incoherent voice, mysterious as a voice from beyond the grave?

He had knelt down by the man-servant's side. The voice was silent and then began again:

"Give us a better light," he said to Gilbert.

He was trembling a little, shaken with a nervous dread which he was unable to master, for there was no doubt possible: when Gilbert had removed the shade from the lamp, Lupin realized that the voice issued from the corpse itself, without a movement of the lifeless mass, without a quiver of the bleeding mouth.

"Governor, I've got the shivers," stammered Gilbert.

Again the same voice, the same snuffling whisper.

Suddenly, Lupin burst out laughing, seized the corpse and pulled it aside:

"Exactly!" he said, catching sight of an object made of polished metal. "Exactly! That's it!... Well, upon my word, it took me long enough!"

On the spot on the floor which he had uncovered lay the receiver of a telephone, the cord of which ran up to the apparatus fixed on the wall, at the usual height.

Lupin put the receiver to his ear. The noise began again at once, but it was a mixed noise, made up of different calls, exclamations, confused cries, the noise produced by a number of persons questioning one another at the same time.

"Are you there?... He won't answer. It's awful... They must have killed him. What is it?... Keep up your courage. There's help on the way... police... soldiers..."

"Dash it!" said Lupin, dropping the receiver.

The truth appeared to him in a terrifying vision. Quite at the beginning, while the things upstairs were being moved, Leonard, whose bonds were not securely fastened, had contrived to scramble to his feet, to unhook the receiver, probably with his teeth, to drop it and to appeal for assistance to the Enghien telephone-exchange.

And those were the words which Lupin had overheard, after the first boat started:

"Help!... Murder!... I shall be killed!"

And this was the reply of the exchange. The police were hurrying to the spot. And Lupin remembered the sounds which he had heard from the garden, four or five minutes earlier, at most:

"The police! Take to your heels!" he shouted, darting across the dining room.

"What about Vaucheray?" asked Gilbert.

"Sorry, can't be helped!"

But Vaucheray, waking from his torpor, entreated him as he passed:

"Governor, you wouldn't leave me like this!"

Lupin stopped, in spite of the danger, and was lifting the wounded man, with Gilbert's assistance, when a loud din arose outside:

"Too late!" he said.

At that moment, blows shook the hall-door at the back of the house. He ran to the front steps: a number of men had already turned the corner of the house at a rush. He might have managed to keep ahead of them, with Gilbert, and reach the waterside. But what chance was there of embarking and escaping under the enemy's fire?

He locked and bolted the door.

"We are surrounded... and done for," spluttered Gilbert.

"Hold your tongue," said Lupin.

"But they've seen us, governor. There, they're knocking."

"Hold your tongue," Lupin repeated. "Not a word. Not a movement."

He himself remained unperturbed, with an utterly calm face and the pensive attitude of one who has all the time that he needs to examine a delicate situation from every point of view. He had reached one of those minutes which he called the "superior moments of existence," those which alone give a value and a price to life. On such occasions, however threatening the danger, he always began by counting to himself, slowly— "One... Two... Three... Four.... Five... Six"—until the beating of his heart became normal and regular. Then and not till then, he reflected, but with what intensity, with what perspicacity, with what a profound intuition of possibilities! All the factors of the problem were present in his mind. He foresaw everything. He admitted everything. And he took his resolution in all logic and in all certainty.

After thirty or forty seconds, while the men outside were banging at the doors and picking the locks, he said to his companion:

"Follow me."

Returning to the dining-room, he softly opened the sash and drew the Venetian blinds of a window in the side-wall. People were coming and going, rendering flight out of the question.

Thereupon he began to shout with all his might, in a breathless voice:

"This way!... Help!... I've got them!... This way!"

He pointed his revolver and fired two shots into the tree-tops. Then he went back to Vaucheray, bent over him and smeared his face and hands with the wounded man's blood. Lastly, turning upon Gilbert, he took him violently by the shoulders and threw him to the floor.

"What do you want, governor? There's a nice thing to do!"

"Let me do as I please," said Lupin, laying an imperative stress on every syllable. "I'll answer for everything... I'll answer for the two of you... Let me do as I like with you... I'll get you both out of prison ... But I can only do that if I'm free."

Excited cries rose through the open window.

"This way!" he shouted. "I've got them! Help!"

And, quietly, in a whisper:

"Just think for a moment... Have you anything to say to me?... Something that can be of use to us?"

Gilbert was too much taken aback to understand Lupin's plan and he struggled furiously. Vaucheray showed more intelligence; moreover, he had given up all hope of escape, because of his wound; and he snarled:

"Let the governor have his way, you ass!... As long as he gets off, isn't that the great thing?"

Suddenly, Lupin remembered the article which Gilbert had put in his pocket, after capturing it from Vaucheray. He now tried to take it in his turn.

"No, not that! Not if I know it!" growled Gilbert, managing to release himself.

Lupin floored him once more. But two men suddenly appeared at the window; and Gilbert yielded and, handing the thing to Lupin, who pocketed it without looking at it, whispered:

"Here you are, governor... I'll explain. You can be sure that..."

He did not have time to finish... Two policemen and others after them and soldiers who entered through every door and window came to Lupin's assistance.

Gilbert was at once seized and firmly bound. Lupin withdrew:

"I'm glad you've come," he said. "The beggar's given me a lot of trouble. I wounded the other; but this one..."

The commissary of police asked him, hurriedly:

"Have you seen the man-servant? Have they killed him?"

"I don't know," he answered.

"You don't know?..."

"Why, I came with you from Enghien, on hearing of the murder! Only, while you were going round the left of the house, I went round the right. There was a window open. I climbed up just as these two ruffians were about to jump down. I fired at this one," pointing to Vaucheray, "and seized hold of his pal."

How could he have been suspected? He was covered with blood. He had handed over the valet's murderers. Half a score of people had witnessed the end of the heroic combat which he had delivered. Besides, the uproar was too great for any one to take the trouble to argue or to waste time in entertaining doubts. In the height of the first confusion, the people of the neighbourhood invaded the villa. One and all lost their heads. They ran to every side, upstairs, downstairs, to the very cellar. They asked one another questions, yelled and shouted; and no one dreamt of checking Lupin's statements, which sounded so plausible.

However, the discovery of the body in the pantry restored the commissary to a sense of his responsibility. He issued orders, had the house cleared and placed policemen at the gate to prevent any one from passing in or out. Then, without further delay, he examined the spot and began his inquiry. Vaucheray gave his name; Gilbert refused to give his, on the plea that he would only speak in the presence of a lawyer. But, when he was accused of the murder, he informed against Vaucheray, who defended himself by denouncing the other; and the two of them vociferated at the same time, with the evident wish to monopolize the commissary's attention. When the commissary turned to Lupin, to request his evidence, he perceived that the stranger was no longer there.

Without the least suspicion, he said to one of the policemen:

"Go and tell that gentleman that I should like to ask him a few questions."

They looked about for the gentleman. Some one had seen him standing on the steps, lighting a cigarette. The next news was that he had given cigarettes to a group of soldiers and strolled toward the lake, saying that they were to call him if he was wanted.

They called him. No one replied.

But a soldier came running up. The gentleman had just got into a boat and was rowing away for all he was worth. The commissary looked at Gilbert and realized that he had been tricked:

"Stop him!" he shouted. "Fire on him! He's an accomplice!..."

He himself rushed out, followed by two policemen, while the others remained with the prisoners. On reaching the bank, he saw the gentleman, a hundred yards away, taking off his hat to him in the dusk.

One of the policemen discharged his revolver, without thinking.

The wind carried the sound of words across the water. The gentleman was singing as he rowed:

> *"Go, little bark,*
>
> *Float in the dark..."*

But the commissary saw a skiff fastened to the landing-stage of the adjoining property. He scrambled over the hedge separating the two gardens and, after ordering the soldiers to watch the banks of the lake and to seize the fugitive if he tried to put ashore, the commissary and two of his men pulled off in pursuit of Lupin.

It was not a difficult matter, for they were able to follow his movements by the intermittent light of the moon and to see that he was trying to cross the lakes while bearing toward the right—that is to say, toward the village of Saint-Gratien. Moreover, the commissary soon perceived that, with the aid of his men and thanks perhaps to the comparative lightness of his craft, he was rapidly gaining on the other. In ten minutes he had decreased the interval between them by one half.

"That's it!" he cried. "We shan't even need the soldiers to keep him from landing. I very much want to make the fellow's acquaintance. He's a cool hand and no mistake!"

The funny thing was that the distance was now diminishing at an abnormal rate, as though the fugitive had lost heart at realizing the futility of the struggle. The policemen redoubled their efforts. The boat shot across the water with the swiftness of a swallow. Another hundred yards at most and they would reach the man.

"Halt!" cried the commissary.

The enemy, whose huddled shape they could make out in the boat, no longer moved. The sculls drifted with the stream. And this absence of all motion had something alarming about it. A ruffian of that stamp might easily lie in wait for his aggressors, sell his life dearly and even shoot them dead before they had a chance of attacking him.

"Surrender!" shouted the commissary.

The sky, at that moment, was dark. The three men lay flat at the bottom of their skiff, for they thought they perceived a threatening gesture.

The boat, carried by its own impetus, was approaching the other.

The commissary growled:

"We won't let ourselves be sniped. Let's fire at him. Are you ready?" And he roared, once more, "Surrender... if not...!"

No reply.

The enemy did not budge.

"Surrender!... Hands up!... You refuse?... So much the worse for you... I'm counting... One... Two..."

The policemen did not wait for the word of command. They fired and, at once, bending over their oars, gave the boat so powerful an impulse that it reached the goal in a few strokes.

The commissary watched, revolver in hand, ready for the least movement. He raised his arm:

"If you stir, I'll blow out your brains!"

But the enemy did not stir for a moment; and, when the boat was bumped and the two men, letting go their oars, prepared for the formidable assault, the commissary understood the reason of this passive attitude: there was no one in the boat. The enemy had escaped by swimming, leaving in the hands of the victor a certain number of the stolen articles, which, heaped up and surmounted by a jacket and a bowler hat, might be taken, at a pinch, in the semi-darkness, vaguely to represent the figure of a man.

They struck matches and examined the enemy's cast clothes. There were no initials in the hat. The jacket contained neither papers nor pocketbook. Nevertheless, they made a discovery which was destined to give the case no little celebrity and which had a terrible influence on the fate of Gilbert and Vaucheray: in one of the pockets was a visiting-card which the fugitive had left behind... the card of Arsene Lupin.

At almost the same moment, while the police, towing the captured skiff behind them, continued their empty search and while the soldiers stood drawn up on the bank, straining their eyes to try and follow the fortunes of the naval combat, the aforesaid Arsene Lupin was quietly landing at the very spot which he had left two hours earlier.

He was there met by his two other accomplices, the Growler and the Masher, flung them a few sentences by way of explanation, jumped into the motor-car, among Daubrecq the deputy's armchairs and other valuables, wrapped himself in his furs and drove, by deserted roads, to his repository at Neuilly, where he left the chauffeur. A taxicab brought him back to Paris and put him down by the church of Saint-Philippe-du-Roule, not far from which, in the Rue Matignon, he had a flat, on the entresol-floor, of which none of his gang, excepting Gilbert, knew, a flat with a private entrance. He was glad to take off his clothes and rub himself down; for, in spite of his strong constitution, he felt chilled to the bone. On retiring to bed, he emptied the contents of his pockets, as usual, on the mantelpiece. It was not till then that he noticed, near his pocketbook and his keys, the object which Gilbert had put into his hand at the last moment.

And he was very much surprised. It was a decanter-stopper, a little crystal stopper, like those used for the bottles in a liqueur-stand. And this crystal stopper had nothing particular about it. The most that Lupin observed was that the knob, with its many facets, was gilded right down to the indent. But, to tell the truth, this detail did not seem to him of a nature to attract special notice.

"And it was this bit of glass to which Gilbert and Vaucheray attached such stubborn importance!" he said to himself. "It was for this that they killed the valet, fought each other, wasted their time, risked prison... trial... the scaffold!..."

Too tired to linger further upon this matter, exciting though it appeared to him, he replaced the stopper on the chimney-piece and got into bed.

He had bad dreams. Gilbert and Vaucheray were kneeling on the flags of their cells, wildly stretching out their hands to him and yelling with fright:

"Help!... Help!" they cried.

But, notwithstanding all his efforts, he was unable to move. He himself was fastened by invisible bonds. And, trembling, obsessed by a monstrous vision, he watched the dismal preparations, the cutting of the condemned men's hair and shirt-collars, the squalid tragedy.

"By Jove!" he said, when he woke after a series of nightmares. "There's a lot of bad omens! Fortunately, we don't err on the side of superstition. Otherwise...!" And he added, "For that matter, we have a talisman which, to judge by Gilbert and Vaucheray's behaviour, should be enough, with Lupin's help, to frustrate bad luck and secure the triumph of the good cause. Let's have a look at that crystal stopper!"

He sprang out of bed to take the thing and examine it more closely. An exclamation escaped him. The crystal stopper had disappeared...

II. EIGHT FROM NINE LEAVES ONE

Notwithstanding my friendly relations with Lupin and the many flattering proofs of his confidence which he has given me, there is one thing which I have never been quite able to fathom, and that is the organization of his gang.

The existence of the gang is an undoubted fact. Certain adventures can be explained only by countless acts of devotion, invincible efforts of energy and powerful cases of complicity, representing so many forces which all obey one mighty will. But how is this will exerted? Through what intermediaries, through what subordinates? That is what I do not know. Lupin keeps his secret; and the secrets which Lupin chooses to keep are, so to speak, impenetrable.

The only supposition which I can allow myself to make is that this gang, which, in my opinion, is very limited in numbers and therefore all the more formidable, is completed and extended indefinitely by the addition of independent units, provisional associates, picked up in every class of society and in every country of the world, who are the executive agents of an authority with which, in many cases, they are not even acquainted. The companions, the initiates, the faithful adherents—men who play the leading parts under the direct command of Lupin—move to and fro between these secondary agents and the master.

Gilbert and Vaucheray evidently belonged to the main gang. And that is why the law showed itself so implacable in their regard. For the first time, it held accomplices of Lupin in its clutches—declared, undisputed accomplices—and those accomplices had committed a murder. If the murder was premeditated, if the accusation of deliberate homicide could be supported by substantial proofs, it meant the scaffold. Now there was, at the very least, one self-evident proof, the cry for assistance which Leonard had sent over the telephone a few minutes before his death:

"Help!... Murder!... I shall be killed!..."

The desperate appeal had been heard by two men, the operator on duty and one of his fellow-clerks, who swore to it positively. And it was in consequence of this appeal that the commissary of police, who was at once informed, had proceeded to the Villa Marie-Therese, escorted by his men and a number of soldiers off duty.

Lupin had a very clear notion of the danger from the first. The fierce struggle in which he had engaged against society was entering upon a new and terrible phase. His luck was turning. It was no longer a matter of attacking others, but of defending himself and saving the heads of his two companions.

A little memorandum, which I have copied from one of the note-books in which he often jots down a summary of the situations that perplex him, will show us the workings of his brain:

"One definite fact, to begin with, is that Gilbert and Vaucheray humbugged me. The Enghien expedition, undertaken ostensibly with the object of robbing the Villa Marie-Therese, had a secret purpose. This purpose obsessed their minds throughout the operations; and what they were looking for, under the furniture and in the cupboards, was one thing and one thing alone: the crystal stopper. Therefore, if I want to see clear ahead, I must first of all know what this means. It is certain that, for some hidden reason, that mysterious piece of glass possesses an incalculable value in their eyes. And not only in theirs, for, last night, some one was bold enough and clever enough to enter my flat and steal the object in question from me."

This theft of which he was the victim puzzled Lupin curiously.

Two problems, both equally difficult of solution, presented themselves to his mind. First, who was the mysterious visitor? Gilbert, who enjoyed his entire confidence and acted as his private secretary, was the only one who knew of the retreat in the Rue Matignon. Now Gilbert was in prison. Was Lupin to suppose that

Gilbert had betrayed him and put the police on his tracks? In that case, why were they content with taking the crystal stopper, instead of arresting him, Lupin?

But there was something much stranger still. Admitting that they had been able to force the doors of his flat—and this he was compelled to admit, though there was no mark to show it—how had they succeeded in entering the bedroom? He turned the key and pushed the bolt as he did every evening, in accordance with a habit from which he never departed. And, nevertheless—the fact was undeniable—the crystal stopper had disappeared without the lock or the bolt having been touched. And, although Lupin flattered himself that he had sharp ears, even when asleep, not a sound had waked him!

He took no great pains to probe the mystery. He knew those problems too well to hope that this one could be solved other than in the course of events. But, feeling very much put out and exceedingly uneasy, he then and there locked up his entresol flat in the Rue Matignon and swore that he would never set foot in it again.

And he applied himself forthwith to the question of corresponding with Vaucheray or Gilbert.

Here a fresh disappointment awaited him. It was so clearly understood, both at the Sante Prison and at the Law Courts, that all communication between Lupin and the prisoners must be absolutely prevented, that a multitude of minute precautions were ordered by the prefect of police and minutely observed by the lowest subordinates. Tried policemen, always the same men, watched Gilbert and Vaucheray, day and night, and never let them out of their sight.

Lupin, at this time, had not yet promoted himself to the crowning honour of his career, the post of chief of the detective-service, [*See Book 813] and, consequently, was not able to take steps at the Law Courts to insure the execution of his plans. After a fortnight of fruitless endeavours, he was obliged to bow.

He did so with a raging heart and a growing sense of anxiety.

"The difficult part of a business," he often says, "is not the finish, but the start."

Where was he to start in the present circumstances? What road was he to follow?

His thoughts recurred to Daubrecq the deputy, the original owner of the crystal stopper, who probably knew its importance. On the other hand, how was Gilbert aware of the doings and mode of life of Daubrecq the deputy? What means had he employed to keep him under observation? Who had told him of the place where Daubrecq spent the evening of that day? These were all interesting questions to solve.

Daubrecq had moved to his winter quarters in Paris immediately after the burglary at the Villa Marie-Therese and was now living in his own house, on the left-hand side of the little Square Lamartine that opens out at the end of the Avenue Victor-Hugo.

First disguising himself as an old gentleman of private means, strolling about, cane in hand, Lupin spent his time in the neighbourhood, on the benches of the square and the avenue. He made a discovery on the first day. Two men, dressed as workmen, but behaving in a manner that left no doubt as to their aims, were watching the deputy's house. When Daubrecq went out, they set off in pursuit of him; and they were immediately behind him when he came home again. At night, as soon as the lights were out, they went away.

Lupin shadowed them in his turn. They were detective-officers.

"Hullo, hullo!" he said to himself. "This is hardly what I expected. So the Daubrecq bird is under suspicion?"

But, on the fourth day, at nightfall, the two men were joined by six others, who conversed with them in the darkest part of the Square Lamartine. And, among these new arrivals, Lupin was vastly astonished to recognize, by his figure and bearing, the famous Prasville, the erstwhile barrister, sportsman and explorer, now favourite at the Elysee, who, for some mysterious reason, had been pitchforked into the headquarters of police as secretary-general, with the reversion of the prefecture.

And, suddenly, Lupin remembered: two years ago, Prasville and Daubrecq the deputy had had a personal encounter on the Place du Palais-Bourbon. The incident made a great stir at the time. No one knew the cause of it. Prasville had sent his seconds to Daubrecq on the same day; but Daubrecq refused to fight.

A little while later, Prasville was appointed secretary-general.

"Very odd, very odd," said Lupin, who remained plunged in thought, while continuing to observe Prasville's movements.

At seven o'clock Prasville's group of men moved away a few yards, in the direction of the Avenue Henri-Martin. The door of a small garden on the right of the house opened and Daubrecq appeared. The two detectives followed close behind him and, when he took the Rue-Taitbout train, jumped on after him.

Prasville at once walked across the square and rang the bell. The garden-gate was between the house and the porter's lodge. The portress came and opened it. There was a brief conversation, after which Prasville and his companions were admitted.

"A domiciliary visit," said Lupin. "Secret and illegal. By the strict rules of politeness, I ought to be invited. My presence is indispensable."

Without the least hesitation he went up to the house, the door of which had not been closed, and, passing in front of the portress, who was casting her eyes outside, he asked, in the hurried tones of a person who is late for an appointment:

"Have the gentlemen come?"

"Yes, you will find them in the study."

His plan was quite simple: if any one met him, he would pretend to be a tradesman. But there was no need for this subterfuge. He was able, after crossing an empty hall, to enter a dining-room which also had no one in it, but which, through the panes of a glass partition that separated the dining-room from the study, afforded him a view of Prasville and his five companions.

Prasville opened all the drawers with the aid of false keys. Next, he examined all the papers, while his companions took down the books from the shelves, shook the pages of each separately and felt inside the bindings.

"Of course, it's a paper they're looking for," said Lupin. "Bank-notes, perhaps..."

Prasville exclaimed:

"What rot! We shan't find a thing!"

Yet he obviously did not abandon all hope of discovering what he wanted, for he suddenly seized the four bottles in a liqueur-stand, took out the four stoppers and inspected them.

"Hullo!" thought Lupin. "Now he's going for decanter-stoppers! Then it's not a question of a paper? Well, I give it up."

Prasville next lifted and examined different objects; and he asked:

"How often have you been here?"

"Six times last winter," was the reply.

"And you have searched the house thoroughly?"

"Every one of the rooms, for days at a time, while he was visiting his constituency."

"Still... still..." And he added, "Has he no servant at present?"

"No, he is looking for one. He has his meals out and the portress keeps the house as best she can. The woman is devoted to us..."

Prasville persisted in his investigations for nearly an hour and a half, shifting and fingering all the knick-knacks, but taking care to put everything back exactly where he found it. At nine o'clock, however, the two detectives who had followed Daubrecq burst into the study:

"He's coming back!"

"On foot?"

"Yes."

"Have we time?"

"Oh, dear, yes!"

Prasville and the men from the police-office withdrew, without undue haste, after taking a last glance round the room to make sure that there was nothing to betray their visit.

The position was becoming critical for Lupin. He ran the risk of knocking up against Daubrecq, if he went away, or of not being able to get out, if he remained. But, on ascertaining that the dining-room windows afforded a direct means of exit to the square, he resolved to stay. Besides, the opportunity of obtaining a close view of Daubrecq was too good to refuse; and, as Daubrecq had been out to dinner, there was not much chance of his entering the dining-room.

Lupin, therefore, waited, holding himself ready to hide behind a velvet curtain that could be drawn across the glazed partition in case of need.

He heard the sound of doors opening and shutting. Some one walked into the study and switched on the light. He recognized Daubrecq.

The deputy was a stout, thickset, bull-necked man, very nearly bald, with a fringe of gray whiskers round his chin and wearing a pair of black eye-glasses under his spectacles, for his eyes were weak and strained. Lupin noticed the powerful features, the square chin, the prominent cheek-bones. The hands were brawny and covered with hair, the legs bowed; and he walked with a stoop, bearing first on one hip and then on the other, which gave him something of the gait of a gorilla. But the face was topped by an enormous, lined forehead, indented with hollows and dotted with bumps.

There was something bestial, something savage, something repulsive about the man's whole personality. Lupin remembered that, in the Chamber of Deputies, Daubrecq was nicknamed "The Wild Man of the Woods" and that he was so labelled not only because he stood aloof and hardly ever mixed with his fellow-members, but also because of his appearance, his behaviour, his peculiar gait and his remarkable muscular development.

He sat down to his desk, took a meerschaum pipe from his pocket, selected a packet of caporal among several packets of tobacco which lay drying in a bowl, tore open the wrapper, filled his pipe and lit it. Then he began to write letters.

Presently he ceased his work and sat thinking, with his attention fixed on a spot on his desk.

He lifted a little stamp-box and examined it. Next, he verified the position of different articles which Prasville had touched and replaced; and he searched them with his eyes, felt them with his hands, bending over them as though certain signs, known to himself alone, were able to tell him what he wished to know.

Lastly, he grasped the knob on an electric bell-push and rang. The portress appeared a minute later.

He asked:

"They've been, haven't they?"

And, when the woman hesitated about replying, he insisted:

"Come, come, Clemence, did you open this stampbox?"

"No, sir."

"Well, I fastened the lid down with a little strip of gummed paper. The strip has been broken."

"But I assure you,..." the woman began.

"Why tell lies," he said, "considering that I myself instructed you to lend yourself to those visits?"

"The fact is..."

"The fact is that you want to keep on good terms with both sides... Very well!" He handed her a fifty-franc note and repeated, "Have they been?"

"Yes."

"The same men as in the spring?"

"Yes, all five of them... with another one, who ordered them about."

"A tall, dark man?"

"Yes."

Lupin saw Daubrecq's mouth hardening; and Daubrecq continued:

"Is that all?"

"There was one more, who came after they did and joined them... and then, just now, two more, the pair who usually keep watch outside the house."

"Did they remain in the study?"

"Yes, sir."

"And they went away when I came back? A few minutes before, perhaps?"

"Yes, sir."

"That will do."

The woman left the room. Daubrecq returned to his letter-writing. Then, stretching out his arm, he made some marks on a white writing-tablet, at the end of his desk, and rested it against the desk, as though he wished to keep it in sight. The marks were figures; and Lupin was able to read the following subtraction-sum:

"9 - 8 = 1"

And Daubrecq, speaking between his teeth, thoughtfully uttered the syllables:

"Eight from nine leaves one... There's not a doubt about that," he added, aloud. He wrote one more letter, a very short one, and addressed the envelope with an inscription which Lupin was able to decipher when the letter was placed beside the writing-tablet:

"To Monsieur Prasville, Secretary-general of the Prefecture of Police."

Then he rang the bell again:

"Clemence," he said, to the portress, "did you go to school as a child?"

"Yes, sir, of course I did."

"And were you taught arithmetic?"

"Why, sir..."

"Well, you're not very good at subtraction."

"What makes you say that?"

"Because you don't know that nine minus eight equals one. And that, you see, is a fact of the highest importance. Life becomes impossible if you are ignorant of that fundamental truth."

He rose, as he spoke, and walked round the room, with his hands behind his back, swaying upon his hips. He did so once more. Then, stopping at the dining-room, he opened the door:

"For that matter, there's another way of putting the problem. Take eight from nine; and one remains. And the one who remains is here, eh? Correct! And monsieur supplies us with a striking proof, does he not?"

He patted the velvet curtain in which Lupin had hurriedly wrapped himself:

"Upon my word, sir, you must be stifling under this! Not to say that I might have amused myself by sticking a dagger through the curtain. Remember Hamlet's madness and Polonius' death: 'How now! A rat? Dead, for a ducat, dead!' Come along, Mr. Polonius, come out of your hole."

It was one of those positions to which Lupin was not accustomed and which he loathed. To catch others in a trap and pull their leg was all very well; but it was a very different thing to have people teasing him and roaring with laughter at his expense. Yet what could he answer back?

"You look a little pale, Mr. Polonius... Hullo! Why, it's the respectable old gentleman who has been hanging about the square for some days! So you belong to the police too, Mr. Polonius? There, there, pull yourself together, I sha'n't hurt you!... But you see, Clemence, how right my calculation was. You told me that nine spies had been to the house. I counted a troop of eight, as I came along, eight of them in the distance, down the avenue. Take eight from nine and one remains: the one who evidently remained behind to see what he could see. Ecce homo!"

"Well? And then?" said Lupin, who felt a mad craving to fly at the fellow and reduce him to silence.

"And then? Nothing at all, my good man... What more do you want? The farce is over. I will only ask you to take this little note to Master Prasville, your employer. Clemence, please show Mr. Polonius out. And, if ever he calls again, fling open the doors wide to him. Pray look upon this as your home, Mr. Polonius. Your servant, sir!..."

Lupin hesitated. He would have liked to talk big and to come out with a farewell phrase, a parting speech, like an actor making a showy exit from the stage, and at least to disappear with the honours of war. But his defeat was so pitiable that he could think of nothing better than to bang his hat on his head and stamp his feet as he followed the portress down the hall. It was a poor revenge.

"You rascally beggar!" he shouted, once he was outside the door, shaking his fist at Daubrecq's windows. "Wretch, scum of the earth, deputy, you shall pay for this!... Oh, he allows himself...! Oh, he has the cheek to...! Well, I swear to you, my fine fellow, that, one of these days..."

He was foaming with rage, all the more as, in his innermost heart, he recognized the strength of his new enemy and could not deny the masterly fashion in which he had managed this business. Daubrecq's coolness, the assurance with which he hoaxed the police-officials, the contempt with which he lent himself to their visits at his house and, above all, his wonderful self-possession, his easy bearing and the impertinence of his conduct in the presence of the ninth person who was spying on him: all this denoted a man of character, a strong man, with a well-balanced mind, lucid, bold, sure of himself and of the cards in his hand.

But what were those cards? What game was he playing? Who held the stakes? And how did the players stand on either side? Lupin could not tell. Knowing nothing, he flung himself headlong into the thick of the fray, between adversaries desperately involved, though he himself was in total ignorance of their positions, their weapons, their resources and their secret plans. For, when all was said, he could not admit that the object of all those efforts was to obtain possession of a crystal stopper!

One thing alone pleased him: Daubrecq had not penetrated his disguise. Daubrecq believed him to be in the employ of the police. Neither Daubrecq nor the police, therefore, suspected the intrusion of a third thief in the business. This was his one and only trump, a trump that gave him a liberty of action to which he attached the greatest importance.

Without further delay, he opened the letter which Daubrecq had handed him for the secretary-general of police. It contained these few lines:

"Within reach of your hand, my dear Prasville, within reach of your hand! You touched it! A little more and the trick was done... But you're too big a fool.

And to think that they couldn't hit upon any one better than you to make me bite the dust. Poor old France!

"*Good-bye, Prasville. But, if I catch you in the act, it will be a bad lookout for you: my maxim is to shoot at sight.*

"*DAUBRECQ*"

"Within reach of your hand," repeated Lupin, after reading the note. "And to think that the rogue may be writing the truth! The most elementary hiding-places are the safest. We must look into this, all the same. And, also, we must find out why Daubrecq is the object of such strict supervision and obtain a few particulars about the fellow generally."

The information supplied to Lupin by a private inquiry-office consisted of the following details:

"*ALEXIS DAUBRECQ, deputy of the Bouches-du-Rhone for the past two years; sits among the independent members. Political opinions not very clearly defined, but electoral position exceedingly strong, because of the enormous sums which he spends in nursing his constituency. No private income. Nevertheless, has a house in Paris, a villa at Enghien and another at Nice and loses heavily at play, though no one knows where the money comes from. Has great influence and obtains all he wants without making up to ministers or, apparently, having either friends or connections in political circles.*" "

That's a trade docket," said Lupin to himself. "What I want is a domestic docket, a police docket, which will tell me about the gentleman's private life and enable me to work more easily in this darkness and to know if I'm not getting myself into a tangle by bothering about the Daubrecq bird. And time's getting short, hang it!"

One of the residences which Lupin occupied at that period and which he used oftener than any of the others was in the Rue Chateaubriand, near the Arc de l'Etoile. He was known there by the name of Michel Beaumont. He had a snug flat here and was looked after by a manservant, Achille, who was utterly devoted to his interests and whose chief duty was to receive and repeat the telephone-messages addressed to Lupin by his followers.

Lupin, on returning home, learnt, with great astonishment, that a woman had been waiting to see him for over an hour:

"What! Why, no one ever comes to see me here! Is she young?"

"No... I don't think so."

"You don't think so!"

"She's wearing a lace shawl over her head, instead of a hat, and you can't see her face... She's more like a clerk... or a woman employed in a shop. She's not well-dressed..."

"Whom did she ask for?"

"M. Michel Beaumont," replied the servant.

"Queer. And why has she called?"

"All she said was that it was about the Enghien business... So I thought that..."

"What! The Enghien business! Then she knows that I am mixed up in that business... She knows that, by applying here..."

"I could not get anything out of her, but I thought, all the same, that I had better let her in."

"Quite right. Where is she?"

"In the drawing-room. I've put on the lights."

Lupin walked briskly across the hall and opened the door of the drawing-room:

"What are you talking about?" he said, to his man. "There's no one here."

"No one here?" said Achille, running up.

And the room, in fact, was empty.

"Well, on my word, this takes the cake!" cried the servant. "It wasn't twenty minutes ago that I came and had a look, to make sure. She was sitting over there. And there's nothing wrong with my eyesight, you know."

"Look here, look here," said Lupin, irritably. "Where were you while the woman was waiting?"

"In the hall, governor! I never left the hall for a second! I should have seen her go out, blow it!"

"Still, she's not here now..."

"So I see," moaned the man, quite flabbergasted.

"She must have got tired of waiting and gone away. But, dash it all, I should like to know how she got out!"

"How she got out?" said Lupin. "It doesn't take a wizard to tell that."

"What do you mean?"

"She got out through the window. Look, it's still ajar. We are on the ground-floor... The street is almost always deserted, in the evenings. There's no doubt about it."

He had looked around him and satisfied himself that nothing had been taken away or moved. The room, for that matter, contained no knick-knack of any value, no important paper that might have explained the woman's visit, followed by her sudden disappearance. And yet why that inexplicable flight?

"Has any one telephoned?" he asked.

"No."

"Any letters?"

"Yes, one letter by the last post."

"Where is it?"

"I put it on your mantel-piece, governor, as usual."

Lupin's bedroom was next to the drawing-room, but Lupin had permanently bolted the door between the two. He, therefore, had to go through the hall again.

Lupin switched on the electric light and, the next moment, said:

"I don't see it..."

"Yes... I put it next to the flower-bowl."

"There's nothing here at all."

"You must be looking in the wrong place, governor."

But Achille moved the bowl, lifted the clock, bent down to the grate, in vain: the letter was not there.

"Oh blast it, blast it!" he muttered. "She's done it... she's taken it... And then, when she had the letter, she cleared out... Oh, the slut!..."

Lupin said:

"You're mad! There's no way through between the two rooms."

"Then who did take it, governor?"

They were both of them silent. Lupin strove to control his anger and collect his ideas. He asked:

"Did you look at the envelope?"

"Yes."

"Anything particular about it?"

"Yes, it looked as if it had been written in a hurry, or scribbled, rather."

"How was the address worded?... Do you remember?" asked Lupin, in a voice strained with anxiety.

"Yes, I remembered it, because it struck me as funny..."

"But speak, will you? Speak!"

"It said, 'Monsieur de Beaumont, Michel.'"

Lupin took his servant by the shoulders and shook him:

"It said 'de' Beaumont? Are you sure? And 'Michel' after 'Beaumont'?"

"Quite certain."

"Ah!" muttered Lupin, with a choking throat. "It was a letter from Gilbert!"

He stood motionless, a little pale, with drawn features. There was no doubt about it: the letter was from Gilbert. It was the form of address which, by Lupin's orders, Gilbert had used for years in corresponding with him. Gilbert had at last—after long waiting and by dint of endless artifices—found a means of getting a letter posted from his prison and had hastily written to him. And now the letter was intercepted! What did it say? What instructions had the unhappy prisoner given? What help was he praying for? What stratagem did he suggest?

Lupin looked round the room, which, contrary to the drawing-room, contained important papers. But none of the locks had been forced; and he was compelled to admit that the woman had no other object than to get hold of Gilbert's letter.

Constraining himself to keep his temper, he asked:

"Did the letter come while the woman was here?"

"At the same time. The porter rang at the same moment."

"Could she see the envelope?"

"Yes."

The conclusion was evident. It remained to discover how the visitor had been able to effect her theft. By slipping from one window to the other, outside the flat? Impossible: Lupin found the window of his room shut. By opening the communicating door? Impossible: Lupin found it locked and barred with its two inner bolts.

Nevertheless, a person cannot pass through a wall by a mere operation of will. To go in or out of a room requires a passage; and, as the act was accomplished in the space of a few minutes, it was necessary, in the circumstances, that the passage should be previously in existence, that it should already have been contrived in the wall and, of course, known to the woman. This hypothesis simplified the search by concentrating it upon the door; for the wall was quite bare, without a cupboard, chimney-piece or hangings of any kind, and unable to conceal the least outlet.

Lupin went back to the drawing-room and prepared to make a study of the door. But he at once gave a start. He perceived, at the first glance, that the left lower panel of the six small panels contained within the cross-bars of the door no longer occupied its normal position and that the light did not fall straight upon it. On leaning forward, he saw two little tin tacks sticking out on either side and holding the panel in place, similar to a wooden board behind a picture-frame. He had only to shift these. The panel at once came out.

Achille gave a cry of amazement. But Lupin objected:

"Well? And what then? We are no better off than before. Here is an empty oblong, eight or nine inches wide by sixteen inches high. You're not going to pretend that a woman can slip through an opening which would not admit the thinnest child of ten years old!"

"No, but she can have put her arm through and drawn the bolts."

"The bottom bolt, yes," said Lupin. "But the top bolt, no: the distance is far too great. Try for yourself and see."

Achille tried and had to give up the attempt.

Lupin did not reply. He stood thinking for a long time. Then, suddenly, he said:

"Give me my hat... my coat..."

He hurried off, urged by an imperative idea. And, the moment he reached the street, he sprang into a taxi:

"Rue Matignon, quick!..."

As soon as they came to the house where he had been robbed of the crystal stopper, he jumped out of the cab, opened his private entrance, went upstairs, ran to the drawing-room, turned on the light and crouched at the foot of the door leading to his bedroom.

He had guessed right. One of the little panels was loosened in the same manner.

And, just as in his other flat in the Rue Chateaubriand, the opening was large enough to admit a man's arm and shoulder, but not to allow him to draw the upper bolt.

"Hang!" he shouted, unable any longer to master the rage that had been seething within him for the last two hours. "Blast! Shall I never have finished with this confounded business?"

In fact, an incredible ill-luck seemed to dog his footsteps, compelling him to grope about at random, without permitting him to use the elements of success which his own persistency or the very force of things placed within his grasp. Gilbert gave him the crystal stopper. Gilbert sent him a letter. And both had disappeared at that very moment.

And it was not, as he had until then believed, a series of fortuitous and independent circumstances. No, it was manifestly the effect of an adverse will pursuing a definite object with prodigious ability and incredible boldness, attacking him, Lupin, in the recesses of his safest retreats and baffling him with blows so severe and so unexpected that he did not even know against whom he had to defend himself. Never, in the course of his adventures, had he encountered such obstacles as now.

And, little by little, deep down within himself, there grew a haunting dread of the future. A date loomed before his eyes, the terrible date which he unconsciously assigned to the law to perform its work of vengeance, the date upon which, in the light of a wan April morning, two men would mount the scaffold, two men who had stood by him, two comrades whom he had been unable to save from paying the awful penalty...

III. THE HOME LIFE OF ALEXIS DAUBRECQ

When Daubrecq the deputy came in from lunch on the day after the police had searched his house he was stopped by Clemence, his portress, who told him that she had found a cook who could be thoroughly relied on.

The cook arrived a few minutes later and produced first-rate characters, signed by people with whom it was easy to take up her references. She was a very active woman, although of a certain age, and agreed to do the work of the house by herself, without the help of a man-servant, this being a condition upon which Daubrecq insisted.

Her last place was with a member of the Chamber of Deputies, Comte Saulevat, to whom Daubrecq at once telephoned. The count's steward gave her a perfect character, and she was engaged.

As soon as she had fetched her trunk, she set to work and cleaned and scrubbed until it was time to cook the dinner.

Daubrecq dined and went out.

At eleven o'clock, after the portress had gone to bed, the cook cautiously opened the garden-gate. A man came up.

"Is that you?" she asked.

"Yes, it's I, Lupin."

She took him to her bedroom on the third floor, overlooking the garden, and at once burst into lamentations:

"More of your tricks and nothing but tricks! Why can't you leave me alone, instead of sending me to do your dirty work?"

"How can I help it, you dear old Victoire? [*See Hollow Needle] When I want a person of respectable appearance and incorruptible morals, I think of you. You ought to be flattered."

"That's all you care about me!" she cried. "You run me into danger once more; and you think it's funny!"

"What are you risking?"

"How do you mean, what am I risking? All my characters are false."

"Characters are always false."

"And suppose M. Daubrecq finds out? Suppose he makes inquiries?"

"He has made inquiries."

"Eh? What's that?"

"He has telephoned to the steward of Comte Saulevat, in whose service you say that you have had the honour of being."

"There, you see, I'm done for!"

"The count's steward could not say enough in your praise."

"He does not know me."

"But I know him. I got him his situation with Comte Saulevat. So you understand..."

Victoire seemed to calm down a little:

"Well," she said, "God's will be done... or rather yours. And what do you expect me to do in all this?"

"First, to put me up. You were my wet-nurse once. You can very well give me half your room now. I'll sleep in the armchair."

"And next?"

"Next? To supply me with such food as I want."

"And next?"

"Next? To undertake, with me and under my direction, a regular series of searches with a view..."

"To what?"

"To discovering the precious object of which I spoke to you."

"What's that?"

"A crystal stopper."

"A crystal stopper... Saints above! A nice business! And, if we don't find your confounded stopper, what then?"

Lupin took her gently by the arm and, in a serious voice:

"If we don't find it, Gilbert, young Gilbert whom you know and love, will stand every chance of losing his head; and so will Vaucheray."

"Vaucheray I don't mind... a dirty rascal like him! But Gilbert..."

"Have you seen the papers this evening? Things are looking worse than ever. Vaucheray, as might be expected, accuses Gilbert of stabbing the valet; and it so happens that the knife which Vaucheray used belonged to Gilbert. That came out this morning. Whereupon Gilbert, who is intelligent in his way, but easily frightened, blithered and launched forth into stories and lies which will end in his undoing. That's how the matter stands. Will you help me?"

Thenceforth, for several days, Lupin moulded his existence upon Daubrecq's, beginning his investigations the moment the deputy left the house. He pursued them methodically, dividing each room into sections which he did not abandon until he had been through the tiniest nooks and corners and, so to speak, exhausted every possible device.

Victoire searched also. And nothing was forgotten. Table-legs, chair-rungs, floor-boards, mouldings, mirror- and picture-frames, clocks, plinths, curtain-borders, telephone-holders and electric fittings: everything that an ingenious imagination could have selected as a hiding-place was overhauled.

And they also watched the deputy's least actions, his most unconscious movements, the expression of his face, the books which he read and the letters which he wrote.

It was easy enough. He seemed to live his life in the light of day. No door was ever shut. He received no visits. And his existence worked with mechanical regularity. He went to the Chamber in the afternoon, to the club in the evening.

"Still," said Lupin, "there must be something that's not orthodox behind all this."

"There's nothing of the sort," moaned Victoire. "You're wasting your time and we shall be bowled out."

The presence of the detectives and their habit of walking up and down outside the windows drove her mad. She refused to admit that they were there for any other purpose than to trap her, Victoire. And, each time that she went shopping, she was quite surprised that one of those men did not lay his hand upon her shoulder.

One day she returned all upset. Her basket of provisions was shaking on her arm.

"What's the matter, my dear Victoire?" said Lupin. "You're looking green."

"Green? I dare say I do. So would you look green..."

She had to sit down and it was only after making repeated efforts that she succeeded in stuttering:

"A man... a man spoke to me... at the fruiterer's."

"By jingo! Did he want you to run away with him?"

"No, he gave me a letter..."

"Then what are you complaining about? It was a love-letter, of course!"

"No. 'It's for your governor,' said he. 'My governor?' I said. 'Yes,' he said, 'for the gentleman who's staying in your room.'"

"What's that?"

This time, Lupin had started:

"Give it here," he said, snatching the letter from her. The envelope bore no address. But there was another, inside it, on which he read:

"Monsieur Arsene Lupin,
c/o Victoire."

"The devil!" he said. "This is a bit thick!" He tore open the second envelope. It contained a sheet of paper with the following words, written in large capitals:

"Everything you are doing is useless and dangerous... Give it up."

Victoire uttered one moan and fainted. As for Lupin, he felt himself blush up to his eyes, as though he had been grossly insulted. He experienced all the humiliation which a duellist would undergo if he heard the most secret advice which he had received from his seconds repeated aloud by a mocking adversary.

However, he held his tongue. Victoire went back to her work. As for him, he remained in his room all day, thinking.

That night he did not sleep.

And he kept saying to himself:

"What is the good of thinking? I am up against one of those problems which are not solved by any amount of thought. It is certain that I am not alone in the matter and that, between Daubrecq and the police, there is, in addition to the third thief that I am, a fourth thief who is working on his own account, who knows me and who reads my game clearly. But who is this fourth thief? And am I mistaken, by any chance? And... oh, rot!... Let's get to sleep!..."

But he could not sleep; and a good part of the night went in this way.

At four o'clock in the morning he seemed to hear a noise in the house. He jumped up quickly and, from the top of the staircase, saw Daubrecq go down the first flight and turn toward the garden.

A minute later, after opening the gate, the deputy returned with a man whose head was buried in an enormous fur collar and showed him into his study.

Lupin had taken his precautions in view of any such contingency. As the windows of the study and those of his bedroom, both of which were at the back of the house, overlooked the garden, he fastened a rope-ladder to his balcony, unrolled it softly and let himself down by it until it was level with the top of the study windows.

These windows were closed by shutters; but, as they were bowed, there remained a semi-circular space at the top; and Lupin, though he could not hear, was able to see all that went on inside.

He then realized that the person whom he had taken for a man was a woman: a woman who was still young, though her dark hair was mingled with gray; a tall woman, elegantly but quite unobtrusively dressed, whose handsome features bore the expression of weariness and melancholy which long suffering gives.

"Where the deuce have I seen her before?" Lupin asked himself. "For I certainly know that face, that look, that expression."

She stood leaning against the table, listening impassively to Daubrecq, who was also standing and who was talking very excitedly. He had his back turned to Lupin; but Lupin, leaning forward, caught sight of a glass in which the deputy's image was reflected. And he was startled to see the strange look in his eyes, the air of fierce and brutal desire with which Daubrecq was staring at his visitor.

It seemed to embarrass her too, for she sat down with lowered lids. Then Daubrecq leant over her and it appeared as though he were ready to fling his long arms, with their huge hands, around her. And, suddenly, Lupin perceived great tears rolling down the woman's sad face.

Whether or not it was the sight of those tears that made Daubrecq lose his head, with a brusque movement he clutched the woman and drew her to him. She repelled him, with a violence full of hatred. And, after a brief struggle, during which Lupin caught a glimpse of the man's bestial and contorted features, the two of them stood face to face, railing at each other like mortal enemies.

Then they stopped. Daubrecq sat down. There was mischief in his face, and sarcasm as well. And he began to talk again, with sharp taps on the table, as though he were dictating terms.

She no longer stirred. She sat haughtily in her chair and towered over him, absent-minded, with roaming eyes. Lupin, captivated by that powerful and sorrowful countenance, continued to watch her; and he was vainly seeking to remember of what or of whom she reminded him, when he noticed that she had turned her head slightly and that she was imperceptibly moving her arm.

And her arm strayed farther and farther and her hand crept along the table and Lupin saw that, at the end of the table, there stood a water-bottle with a gold-topped stopper. The hand reached the water-bottle, felt it, rose gently and seized the stopper. A quick movement of the head, a glance, and the stopper was put back in its place. Obviously, it was not what the woman hoped to find.

"Dash it!" said Lupin. "She's after the crystal stopper too! The matter is becoming more complicated daily; there's no doubt about it."

But, on renewing his observation of the visitor, he was astounded to note the sudden and unexpected expression of her countenance, a terrible, implacable, ferocious expression. And he saw that her hand was continuing its stealthy progress round the table and that, with an uninterrupted and crafty sliding movement, it was pushing back books and, slowly and surely, approaching a dagger whose blade gleamed among the scattered papers.

It gripped the handle.

Daubrecq went on talking. Behind his back, the hand rose steadily, little by little; and Lupin saw the woman's desperate and furious eyes fixed upon the spot in the neck where she intended to plant the knife:

"You're doing a very silly thing, fair lady," thought Lupin.

And he already began to turn over in his mind the best means of escaping and of taking Victoire with him.

She hesitated, however, with uplifted arm. But it was only a momentary weakness. She clenched her teeth. Her whole face, contracted with hatred, became yet further convulsed. And she made the dread movement.

At the same instant Daubrecq crouched and, springing from his seat, turned and seized the woman's frail wrist in mid-air.

Oddly enough, he addressed no reproach to her, as though the deed which she had attempted surprised him no more than any ordinary, very natural and simple act. He shrugged his shoulders, like a man accustomed to that sort of danger, and strode up and down in silence.

She had dropped the weapon and was now crying, holding her head between her hands, with sobs that shook her whole frame.

He next came up to her and said a few words, once more tapping the table as he spoke.

She made a sign in the negative and, when he insisted, she, in her turn, stamped her foot on the floor and exclaimed, loud enough for Lupin to hear:

"Never!... Never!..."

Thereupon, without another word, Daubrecq fetched the fur cloak which she had brought with her and hung it over the woman's shoulders, while she shrouded her face in a lace wrap.

And he showed her out.

Two minutes later, the garden-gate was locked again. "Pity I can't run after that strange person," thought Lupin, "and have a chat with her about the Daubrecq bird. Seems to me that we two could do a good stroke of business together."

In any case, there was one point to be cleared up: Daubrecq the deputy, whose life was so orderly, so apparently respectable, was in the habit of receiving visits at night, when his house was no longer watched by the police.

He sent Victoire to arrange with two members of his gang to keep watch for several days. And he himself remained awake next night.

As on the previous morning, he heard a noise at four o'clock. As on the previous morning, the deputy let some one in.

Lupin ran down his ladder and, when he came to the free space above the shutters, saw a man crawling at Daubrecq's feet, flinging his arms round Daubrecq's knees in frenzied despair and weeping, weeping convulsively.

Daubrecq, laughing, pushed him away repeatedly, but the man clung to him. He behaved almost like one out of his mind and, at last, in a genuine fit of madness, half rose to his feet, took the deputy by the throat and flung him back in a chair. Daubrecq struggled, powerless at first, while his veins swelled in his temples. But soon, with a strength far beyond the ordinary, he regained the mastery and deprived his adversary of all power of movement. Then, holding him with one hand, with the other he gave him two great smacks in the face.

The man got up, slowly. He was livid and could hardly stand on his legs. He waited for a moment, as though to recover his self-possession. Then, with a terrifying calmness, he drew a revolver from his pocket and levelled it at Daubrecq.

Daubrecq did not flinch. He even smiled, with a defiant air and without displaying more excitement than if he had been aimed at with a toy pistol.

The man stood for perhaps fifteen or twenty seconds, facing his enemy, with outstretched arm. Then, with the same deliberate slowness, revealing a self-control which was all the more impressive because it followed upon a fit of extreme excitement, he put up his revolver and, from another pocket, produced his note-case.

Daubrecq took a step forward.

The man opened the pocketbook. A sheaf of banknotes appeared in sight.

Daubrecq seized and counted them. They were thousand-franc notes, and there were thirty of them.

The man looked on, without a movement of revolt, without a protest. He obviously understood the futility of words. Daubrecq was one of those who do not relent. Why should his visitor waste time in beseeching him or even in revenging himself upon him by uttering vain threats and insults? He had no hope of striking that unassailable enemy. Even Daubrecq's death would not deliver him from Daubrecq.

He took his hat and went away.

At eleven o'clock in the morning Victoire, on returning from her shopping, handed Lupin a note from his accomplices.

He opened it and read:

"The man who came to see Daubrecq last night is Langeroux the deputy, leader of the independent left. A poor man, with a large family."

"Come," said Lupin, "Daubrecq is nothing more nor less than a blackmailer; but, by Jupiter, he has jolly effective ways of going to work!"

Events tended to confirm Lupin's supposition. Three days later he saw another visitor hand Daubrecq an important sum of money. And, two days after that, one came and left a pearl necklace behind him.

The first was called Dachaumont, a senator and ex-cabinet-minister. The second was the Marquis d'Albufex, a Bonapartist deputy, formerly chief political agent in France of Prince Napoleon.

The scene, in each of these cases, was very similar to Langeroux the deputy's interview, a violent tragic scene, ending in Daubrecq's victory.

"And so on and so forth," thought Lupin, when he received these particulars. "I have been present at four visits. I shall know no more if there are ten, or twenty, or thirty... It is enough for me to learn the names of the visitors from my friends on sentry-go outside. Shall I go and call on them?... What for? They have no reason to confide in me... On the other hand, am I to stay on here, delayed by investigations which lead to nothing and which Victoire can continue just as well without me?"

He was very much perplexed. The news of the inquiry into the case of Gilbert and Vaucheray was becoming worse and worse, the days were slipping by, and not an hour passed without his asking himself, in anguish, whether all his efforts—granting that he succeeded—would not end in farcical results, absolutely foreign to the aim which he was pursuing.

For, after all, supposing that he did fathom Daubrecq's underhand dealings, would that give him the means of rescuing Gilbert and Vaucheray?

That day an incident occurred which put an end to his indecision. After lunch Victoire heard snatches of a conversation which Daubrecq held with some one on the telephone. Lupin gathered, from what Victoire reported, that the deputy had an appointment with a lady for half-past eight and that he was going to take her to a theatre:

"I shall get a pit-tier box, like the one we had six weeks ago," Daubrecq had said. And he added, with a laugh, "I hope that I shall not have the burglars in during that time."

There was not a doubt in Lupin's mind. Daubrecq was about to spend his evening in the same manner in which he had spent the evening six weeks ago, while they were breaking into his villa at Enghien. To know the person whom he was to meet and perhaps thus to discover how Gilbert and Vaucheray had learnt that Daubrecq would be away from eight o'clock in the evening until one o'clock in the morning: these were matters of the utmost importance.

Lupin left the house in the afternoon, with Victoire's assistance. He knew through her that Daubrecq was coming home for dinner earlier than usual.

He went to his flat in the Rue Chateaubriand, telephoned for three of his friends, dressed and made himself up in his favourite character of a Russian prince, with fair hair and moustache and short-cut whiskers.

The accomplices arrived in a motor-car.

At that moment, Achille, his man, brought him a telegram, addressed to M. Michel Beaumont, Rue Chateaubriand, which ran:

"Do not come to theatre this evening. Danger of your intervention spoiling everything."

There was a flower-vase on the chimney-piece beside him. Lupin took it and smashed it to pieces.

"That's it, that's it," he snarled. "They are playing with me as I usually play with others. Same behaviour. Same tricks. Only there's this difference..."

What difference? He hardly knew. The truth was that he too was baffled and disconcerted to the inmost recesses of his being and that he was continuing to act only from obstinacy, from a sense of duty, so to speak, and without putting his ordinary good humour and high spirits into the work.

"Come along," he said to his accomplices.

By his instructions, the chauffeur set them down near the Square Lamartine, but kept the motor going. Lupin foresaw that Daubrecq, in order to escape the detectives watching the house, would jump into the first taxi; and he did not intend to be outdistanced.

He had not allowed for Daubrecq's cleverness.

At half-past seven both leaves of the garden-gate were flung open, a bright light flashed and a motor-cycle darted across the road, skirted the square, turned in front of the motor-car and shot away toward the Bois at a speed so great that they would have been mad to go in pursuit of it.

"Good-bye, Daisy!" said Lupin, trying to jest, but really overcome with rage.

He eyed his accomplices in the hope that one of them would venture to give a mocking smile. How pleased he would have been to vent his nerves on them!

"Let's go home," he said to his companions.

He gave them some dinner; then he smoked a cigar and they set off again in the car and went the round of the theatres, beginning with those which were giving light operas and musical comedies, for which he presumed that Daubrecq and his lady would have a preference. He took a stall, inspected the lower-tier boxes and went away again.

He next drove to the more serious theatres: the Renaissance, the Gymnase.

At last, at ten o'clock in the evening, he saw a pit-tier box at the Vaudeville almost entirely protected from inspection by its two screens; and, on tipping the boxkeeper, was told that it contained a short, stout, elderly gentleman and a lady who was wearing a thick lace veil.

The next box was free. He took it, went back to his friends to give them their instructions and sat down near the couple.

During the entr'acte, when the lights went up, he perceived Daubrecq's profile. The lady remained at the back of the box, invisible. The two were speaking in a low voice; and, when the curtain rose again, they went on speaking, but in such a way that Lupin could not distinguish a word.

Ten minutes passed. Some one tapped at their door. It was one of the men from the box-office.

"Are you M. le Depute Daubrecq, sir?" he asked.

"Yes," said Daubrecq, in a voice of surprise. "But how do you know my name?"

"There's a gentleman asking for you on the telephone. He told me to go to Box 22."

"But who is it?"

"M. le Marquis d'Albufex."

"Eh?"

"What am I to say, sir?"

"I'm coming... I'm coming..."

Daubrecq rose hurriedly from his seat and followed the clerk to the box-office.

He was not yet out of sight when Lupin sprang from his box, worked the lock of the next door and sat down beside the lady.

She gave a stifled cry.

"Hush!" he said. "I have to speak to you. It is most important."

"Ah!" she said, between her teeth. "Arsene Lupin!" He was dumbfounded. For a moment he sat quiet, open-mouthed. The woman knew him! And not only did she know him, but she had recognized him through his disguise! Accustomed though he was to the most extraordinary and unusual events, this disconcerted him.

He did not even dream of protesting and stammered:

"So you know?... So you know?..."

He snatched at the lady's veil and pulled it aside before she had time to defend herself:

"What!" he muttered, with increased amazement. "Is it possible?"

It was the woman whom he had seen at Daubrecq's a few days earlier, the woman who had raised her dagger against Daubrecq and who had intended to stab him with all the strength of her hatred.

It was her turn to be taken aback:

"What! Have you seen me before?..."

"Yes, the other night, at his house... I saw what you tried to do..."

She made a movement to escape. He held her back and, speaking with great eagerness:

"I must know who you are," he said. "That was why I had Daubrecq telephoned for."

She looked aghast:

"Do you mean to say it was not the Marquis d'Albufex?"

"No, it was one of my assistants."

"Then Daubrecq will come back?..."

"Yes, but we have time... Listen to me... We must meet again... He is your enemy... I will save you from him..."

"Why should you? What is your object?"

"Do not distrust me... it is quite certain that our interests are identical... Where can I see you? To-morrow, surely? At what time? And where?"

"Well..."

She looked at him with obvious hesitation, not knowing what to do, on the point of speaking and yet full of uneasiness and doubt.

He pressed her:

"Oh, I entreat you... answer me just one word... and at once... It would be a pity for him to find me here... I entreat you..."

She answered sharply:

"My name doesn't matter... We will see each other first and you shall explain to me... Yes, we will meet... Listen, to-morrow, at three o'clock, at the corner of the Boulevard..."

At that exact moment, the door of the box opened, so to speak, with a bang, and Daubrecq appeared.

"Rats!" Lupin mumbled, under his breath, furious at being caught before obtaining what he wanted.

Daubrecq gave a chuckle:

"So that's it... I thought something was up... Ah, the telephone-trick: a little out of date, sir! I had not gone half-way when I turned back."

He pushed Lupin to the front of the box and, sitting down beside the lady, said:

"And, now my lord, who are we? A servant at the police-office, probably? There's a professional look about that mug of yours."

He stared hard at Lupin, who did not move a muscle, and tried to put a name to the face, but failed to recognize the man whom he had called Polonius.

Lupin, without taking his eyes from Daubrecq either, reflected. He would not for anything in the world have thrown up the game at that point or neglected this favourable opportunity of coming to an understanding with his mortal enemy.

The woman sat in her corner, motionless, and watched them both.

Lupin said:

"Let us go outside, sir. That will make our interview easier."

"No, my lord, here," grinned the deputy. "It will take place here, presently, during the entr'acte. Then we shall not be disturbing anybody."

"But..."

"Save your breath, my man; you sha'n't budge."

And he took Lupin by the coat-collar, with the obvious intention of not letting go of him before the interval.

A rash move! Was it likely that Lupin would consent to remain in such an attitude, especially before a woman, a woman to whom he had offered his alliance, a woman—and he now thought of it for the first time—who was distinctly good-looking and whose grave beauty attracted him. His whole pride as a man rose at the thought.

However, he said nothing. He accepted the heavy weight of the hand on his shoulder and even sat bent in two, as though beaten, powerless, almost frightened.

"Eh, clever!" said the deputy, scoffingly. "We don't seem to be swaggering quite so much."

The stage was full of actors who were arguing and making a noise.

Daubrecq had loosened his grasp slightly and Lupin felt that the moment had come. With the edge of his hand, he gave him a violent blow in the hollow of the arm, as he might have done with a hatchet.

The pain took Daubrecq off his guard. Lupin now released himself entirely and sprang at the other to clutch him by the throat. But Daubrecq had at once put himself on the defensive and stepped back and their four hands seized one another.

They gripped with superhuman energy, the whole force of the two adversaries concentrating in those hands. Daubrecq's were of monstrous size; and Lupin, caught in that iron vise, felt as though he were fighting not with a man, but with some terrible beast, a huge gorilla.

They held each other against the door, bending low, like a pair of wrestlers groping and trying to lay hold of each other. Their bones creaked. Whichever gave way first was bound to be caught by the throat and strangled. And all this happened amid a sudden silence, for the actors on the stage were now listening to one of their number, who was speaking in a low voice.

The woman stood back flat against the partition, looking at them in terror. Had she taken sides with either of them, with a single movement, the victory would at once have been decided in that one's favour. But which of them should she assist? What could Lupin represent in her eyes? A friend? An enemy?

She briskly made for the front of the box, forced back the screen and, leaning forward, seemed to give a signal. Then she returned and tried to slip to the door.

Lupin, as though wishing to help her, said:

"Why don't you move the chair?"

He was speaking of a heavy chair which had fallen down between him and Daubrecq and across which they were struggling.

The woman stooped and pulled away the chair. That was what Lupin was waiting for. Once rid of the obstacle, he caught Daubrecq a smart kick on the shin with the tip of his patent-leather boot. The result was the same as with the blow which he had given him on the arm. The pain caused a second's apprehension and distraction, of which he at once took advantage to beat down Daubrecq's outstretched hands and to dig his ten fingers into his adversary's throat and neck.

Daubrecq struggled. Daubrecq tried to pull away the hands that were throttling him; but he was beginning to choke and felt his strength decreasing.

"Aha, you old monkey!" growled Lupin, forcing him to the floor. "Why don't you shout for help? How frightened you must be of a scandal!"

At the sound of the fall there came a knocking at the partition, on the other side.

"Knock away, knock away," said Lupin, under his breath. "The play is on the stage. This is my business and, until I've mastered this gorilla..."

It did not take him long. The deputy was choking. Lupin stunned him with a blow on the jaw; and all that remained for him to do was to take the woman away and make his escape with her before the alarm was given.

But, when he turned round, he saw that the woman was gone.

She could not be far. Darting from the box, he set off at a run, regardless of the programme-sellers and check-takers.

On reaching the entrance-lobby, he saw her through an open door, crossing the pavement of the Chaussee d'Antin.

She was stepping into a motor-car when he came up with her.

The door closed behind her.

He seized the handle and tried to pull at it.

But a man jumped up inside and sent his fist flying into Lupin's face, with less skill but no less force than Lupin had sent his into Daubrecq's face.

Stunned though he was by the blow, he nevertheless had ample time to recognize the man, in a sudden, startled vision, and also to recognize, under his chauffeur's disguise, the man who was driving the car. It was the Growler and the Masher, the two men in charge of the boats on the Enghien night, two friends of Gilbert and Vaucheray: in short, two of Lupin's own accomplices.

When he reached his rooms in the Rue Chateaubriand, Lupin, after washing the blood from his face, sat for over an hour in a chair, as though overwhelmed. For the first time in his life he was experiencing the pain of treachery. For the first time his comrades in the fight were turning against their chief.

Mechanically, to divert his thoughts, he turned to his correspondence and tore the wrapper from an evening paper. Among the late news he found the following paragraphs:

"THE VILLA MARIE-THERESE CASE"

"The real identity of Vaucheray, one of the alleged murderers of Leonard the valet, has at last been ascertained. He is a miscreant of the worst type, a hardened criminal who has already twice been sentenced for murder, in default, under another name. "No doubt, the police will end by also discovering the real name of his accomplice, Gilbert. In any event, the examining-magistrate is determined to commit the prisoners for trial as soon as possible. "The public will have no reason to complain of the delays of the law."

In between other newspapers and prospectuses lay a letter.

Lupin jumped when he saw it. It was addressed:

"Monsieur de Beaumont, Michel."

"Oh," he gasped, "a letter from Gilbert!"

It contained these few words:

"Help, governor!... I am frightened. I am frightened..."

Once again, Lupin spent a night alternating between sleeplessness and nightmares. Once again, he was tormented by atrocious and terrifying visions.

IV. THE CHIEF OF THE ENEMIES

"Poor boy!" murmured Lupin, when his eyes fell on Gilbert's letter next morning. "How he must feel it!"

On the very first day when he saw him, he had taken a liking to that well-set-up youngster, so careless, gay and fond of life. Gilbert was devoted to him, would have accepted death at a sign from his master. And Lupin also loved his frankness, his good humour, his simplicity, his bright, open face.

"Gilbert," he often used to say, "you are an honest man. Do you know, if I were you, I should chuck the business and become an honest man for good."

"After you, governor," Gilbert would reply, with a laugh.

"Won't you, though?"

"No, governor. An honest man is a chap who works and grinds. It's a taste which I may have had as a nipper; but they've made me lose it since."

"Who's they?"

Gilbert was silent. He was always silent when questioned about his early life; and all that Lupin knew was that he had been an orphan since childhood and that he had lived all over the place, changing his name and taking up the queerest jobs. The whole thing was a mystery which no one had been able to fathom; and it did not look as though the police would make much of it either.

Nor, on the other hand, did it look as though the police would consider that mystery a reason for delaying proceedings. They would send Vaucheray's accomplice for trial—under his name of Gilbert or any other name—and visit him with the same inevitable punishment.

"Poor boy!" repeated Lupin. "They're persecuting him like this only because of me. They are afraid of his escaping and they are in a hurry to finish the business: the verdict first and then... the execution.

"Oh, the butchers!... A lad of twenty, who has committed no murder, who is not even an accomplice in the murder..."

Alas, Lupin well knew that this was a thing impossible to prove and that he must concentrate his efforts upon another point. But upon which? Was he to abandon the trail of the crystal stopper?

He could not make up his mind to that. His one and only diversion from the search was to go to Enghien, where the Growler and the Masher lived, and make sure that nothing had been seen of them since the murder at the Villa Marie-Therese. Apart from this, he applied himself to the question of Daubrecq and nothing else.

He refused even to trouble his head about the problems set before him: the treachery of the Growler and the Masher; their connection with the gray-haired lady; the spying of which he himself was the object.

"Steady, Lupin," he said. "One only argues falsely in a fever. So hold your tongue. No inferences, above all things! Nothing is more foolish than to infer one fact from another before finding a certain starting-point. That's where you get up a tree. Listen to your instinct. Act according to your instinct. And as you are persuaded, outside all argument, outside all logic, one might say, that this business turns upon that confounded stopper, go for it boldly. Have at Daubrecq and his bit of crystal!"

Lupin did not wait to arrive at these conclusions before settling his actions accordingly. At the moment when he was stating them in his mind, three days after the scene at the Vaudeville, he was sitting, dressed like a retired tradesman, in an old overcoat, with a muffler round his neck, on a bench in the Avenue Victor-Hugo, at some distance from the Square Lamartine. Victoire had his instructions to pass by that bench at the same hour every morning.

"Yes," he repeated to himself, "the crystal stopper: everything turns on that... Once I get hold of it..."

Victoire arrived, with her shopping-basket on her arm. He at once noticed her extraordinary agitation and pallor:

"What's the matter?" asked Lupin, walking beside his old nurse.

She went into a big grocer's, which was crowded with people, and, turning to him:

"Here," she said, in a voice torn with excitement. "Here's what you've been hunting for."

And, taking something from her basket, she gave it to him.

Lupin stood astounded: in his hand lay the crystal stopper.

"Can it be true? Can it be true?" he muttered, as though the ease of the solution had thrown him off his balance.

But the fact remained, visible and palpable. He recognized by its shape, by its size, by the worn gilding of its facets, recognized beyond any possible doubt the crystal stopper which he had seen before. He even remarked a tiny, hardly noticeable little scratch on the stem which he remembered perfectly.

However, while the thing presented all the same characteristics, it possessed no other that seemed out of the way. It was a crystal stopper, that was all. There was no really special mark to distinguish it from other stoppers. There was no sign upon it, no stamp; and, being cut from a single piece, it contained no foreign object.

"What then?"

And Lupin received a quick insight into the depth of his mistake. What good could the possession of that crystal stopper do him so long as he was ignorant of its value? That bit of glass had no existence in itself; it counted only through the meaning that attached to it. Before taking it, the thing was to be certain. And how could he tell that, in taking it, in robbing Daubrecq of it, he was not committing an act of folly?

It was a question which was impossible of solution, but which forced itself upon him with singular directness.

"No blunders!" he said to himself, as he pocketed the stopper. "In this confounded business, blunders are fatal."

He had not taken his eyes off Victoire. Accompanied by a shopman, she went from counter to counter, among the throng of customers. She next stood for some little while at the pay-desk and passed in front of Lupin.

He whispered her instructions:

"Meet me behind the Lycee Janson."

She joined him in an unfrequented street:

"And suppose I'm followed?" she said.

"No," he declared. "I looked carefully. Listen to me. Where did you find the stopper?"

"In the drawer of the table by his bed."

"But we had felt there already."

"Yes; and I did so again this morning. I expect he put it there last night."

"And I expect he'll want to take it from there again," said Lupin.

"Very likely."

"And suppose he finds it gone?"

Victoire looked frightened.

"Answer me," said Lupin. "If he finds it gone, he'll accuse you of taking it, won't he?"

"Certainly."

"Then go and put it back, as fast as you can."

"Oh dear, oh dear!" she moaned. "I hope he won't have had time to find out. Give it to me, quick."

"Here you are," said Lupin.

He felt in the pocket of his overcoat.

"Well?" said Victoire, holding out her hand.

"Well," he said, after a moment, "it's gone."

"What!"

"Yes, upon my word, it's gone... somebody's taken it from me."

He burst into a peal of laughter, a laughter which, this time, was free from all bitterness.

Victoire flew out at him:

"Laugh away!... Putting me in such a predicament!..."

"How can I help laughing? You must confess that it's funny. It's no longer a tragedy that we're acting, but a fairy-tale, as much a fairy-tale as Puss in Boots or Jack and the Beanstalk. I must write it when I get a few weeks to myself: The Magic Stopper; or, The Mishaps of Poor Arsene."

"Well... who has taken it from you?"

"What are you talking about?... It has flown away... vanished from my pocket: hey presto, begone!"

He gave the old servant a gentle push and, in a more serious tone:

"Go home, Victoire, and don't upset yourself. Of course, some one saw you give me the stopper and took advantage of the crowd in the shop to pick my pocket of it. That only shows that we are watched more closely than I thought and by adversaries of the first rank. But, once more, be easy. Honest men always come by their own... Have you anything else to tell me?"

"Yes. Some one came yesterday evening, while M. Daubrecq was out. I saw lights reflected upon the trees in the garden."

"The portress' bedroom?"

"The portress was up."

"Then it was some of those detective-fellows; they are still hunting. I'll see you later, Victoire. You must let me in again."

"What! You want to..."

"What do I risk? Your room is on the third floor. Daubrecq suspects nothing."

"But the others!"

"The others? If it was to their interest to play me a trick, they'd have tried before now. I'm in their way, that's all. They're not afraid of me. So till later, Victoire, at five o'clock exactly."

One further surprise awaited Lupin. In the evening his old nurse told him that, having opened the drawer of the bedside table from curiosity, she had found the crystal stopper there again.

Lupin was no longer to be excited by these miraculous incidents. He simply said to himself:

"So it's been brought back. And the person who brought it back and who enters this house by some unexplained means considered, as I did, that the stopper ought not to disappear. And yet Daubrecq, who knows that he is being spied upon to his very bedroom, has once more left the stopper in a drawer, as though he attached no importance to it at all! Now what is one to make of that?"

Though Lupin did not make anything of it, nevertheless he could not escape certain arguments, certain associations of ideas that gave him the same vague foretaste of light which one receives on approaching the outlet of a tunnel.

"It is inevitable, as the case stands," he thought, "that there must soon be an encounter between myself and the others. From that moment I shall be master of the situation."

Five days passed, during which Lupin did not glean the slightest particular. On the sixth day Daubrecq received a visit, in the small hours, from a gentleman, Laybach the deputy, who, like his colleagues, dragged himself at his feet in despair and, when all was done, handed him twenty thousand francs.

Two more days; and then, one night, posted on the landing of the second floor, Lupin heard the creaking of a door, the front-door, as he perceived, which led from the hall into the garden. In the darkness he distinguished, or rather divined, the presence of two persons, who climbed the stairs and stopped on the first floor, outside Daubrecq's bedroom.

What were they doing there? It was not possible to enter the room, because Daubrecq bolted his door every night. Then what were they hoping?

Manifestly, a handiwork of some kind was being performed, as Lupin discovered from the dull sounds of rubbing against the door. Then words, uttered almost beneath a whisper, reached him:

"Is it all right?"

"Yes, quite, but, all the same, we'd better put it off till to-morrow, because..."

Lupin did not hear the end of the sentence. The men were already groping their way downstairs. The hall-door was closed, very gently, and then the gate.

"It's curious, say what one likes," thought Lupin. "Here is a house in which Daubrecq carefully conceals his rascalities and is on his guard, not without good reason, against spies; and everybody walks in and out as in a booth at a fair. Victoire lets me in, the portress admits the emissaries of the police: that's well and good; but who is playing false in these people's favour? Are we to suppose that they are acting alone? But what fearlessness! And how well they know their way about!"

In the afternoon, during Daubrecq's absence, he examined the door of the first-floor bedroom. And, at the first glance, he understood: one of the lower panels had been skilfully cut out and was only held in place by invisible tacks. The people, therefore, who had done this work were the same who had acted at his two places, in the Rue Matignon and the Rue Chateaubriand.

He also found that the work dated back to an earlier period and that, as in his case, the opening had been prepared beforehand, in anticipation of favourable circumstances or of some immediate need.

The day did not seem long to Lupin. Knowledge was at hand. Not only would he discover the manner in which his adversaries employed those little openings, which were apparently unemployable, since they did not allow a person to reach the upper bolts, but he would learn who the ingenious and energetic adversaries were with whom he repeatedly and inevitably found himself confronted.

One incident annoyed him. In the evening Daubrecq, who had complained of feeling tired at dinner, came home at ten o'clock and, contrary to his usual custom, pushed the bolts of the hall-door. In that case, how would the others be able to carry out their plan and go to Daubrecq's room? Lupin waited for an hour after Daubrecq put out his light. Then he went down to the deputy's study, opened one of the windows ajar and returned to the third floor and fixed his rope-ladder so that, in case of need, he could reach the study without passing though the house. Lastly, he resumed his post on the second-floor landing.

He did not have to wait long. An hour earlier than on the previous night some one tried to open the hall-door. When the attempt failed, a few minutes of absolute silence followed. And Lupin was beginning to think that the men had abandoned the idea, when he gave a sudden start. Some one had passed, without the least sound to interrupt the silence. He would not have known it, so utterly were the thing's steps deadened by the stair-carpet, if the baluster-rail, which he himself held in his hand, had not shaken slightly. Some one was coming upstairs.

And, as the ascent continued, Lupin became aware of the uncanny feeling that he heard nothing more than before. He knew, because of the rail, that a thing was coming and he could count the number of steps climbed by noting each vibration of the rail; but no other indication gave him that dim sensation of presence which we feel in distinguishing movements which we do not see, in perceiving sounds which we do not hear. And yet a blacker darkness ought to have taken shape within the darkness and something ought, at least, to modify the quality of the silence. No, he might well have believed that there was no one there.

And Lupin, in spite of himself and against the evidence of his reason, ended by believing it, for the rail no longer moved and he thought that he might have been the sport of an illusion.

And this lasted a long time. He hesitated, not knowing what to do, not knowing what to suppose. But an odd circumstance impressed him. A clock struck two. He recognized the chime of Daubrecq's clock. And the chime was that of a clock from which one is not separated by the obstacle of a door.

Lupin slipped down the stairs and went to the door. It was closed, but there was a space on the left, at the bottom, a space left by the removal of the little panel.

He listened. Daubrecq, at that moment, turned in his bed; and his breathing was resumed, evenly and a little stertorously. And Lupin plainly heard the sound of rumpling garments. Beyond a doubt, the thing was there, fumbling and feeling through the clothes which Daubrecq had laid beside his bed.

"Now," thought Lupin, "we shall learn something. But how the deuce did the beggar get in? Has he managed to draw the bolts and open the door? But, if so, why did he make the mistake of shutting it again?"

Not for a second—a curious anomaly in a man like Lupin, an anomaly to be explained only by the uncanny feeling which the whole adventure produced in him—not for a second did he suspect the very simple truth which was about to be revealed to him. Continuing his way down, he crouched on one of the bottom steps of the staircase, thus placing himself between the door of the bedroom and the hall-door, on the road which Daubrecq's enemy must inevitably take in order to join his accomplices.

He questioned the darkness with an unspeakable anguish. He was on the point of unmasking that enemy of Daubrecq's, who was also his own adversary. He would thwart his plans. And the booty captured from Daubrecq he would capture in his turn, while Daubrecq slept and while the accomplices lurking behind the hall-door or outside the garden-gate vainly awaited their leader's return.

And that return took place. Lupin knew it by the renewed vibration of the balusters. And, once more, with every sense strained and every nerve on edge, he strove to discern the mysterious thing that was coming toward him. He suddenly realized it when only a few yards away. He himself, hidden in a still darker recess, could not be seen. And what he saw—in the very vaguest manner—was approaching stair by stair, with infinite precautions, holding on to each separate baluster.

"Whom the devil have I to do with?" said Lupin to himself, while his heart thumped inside his chest.

The catastrophe was hastened. A careless movement on Lupin's part was observed by the stranger, who stopped short. Lupin was afraid lest the other should turn back and take to flight. He sprang at the adversary and was stupefied at encountering nothing but space and knocking against the stair-rail without seizing the form which he saw. But he at once rushed forward, crossed the best part of the hall and caught up his antagonist just as he was reaching the door opening on the garden.

There was a cry of fright, answered by other cries on the further side of the door.

"Oh, hang it, what's this?" muttered Lupin, whose arms had closed, in the dark, round a little, tiny, trembling, whimpering thing.

Suddenly understanding, he stood for a moment motionless and dismayed, at a loss what to do with his conquered prey. But the others were shouting and stamping outside the door. Thereupon, dreading lest Daubrecq should wake up, he slipped the little thing under his jacket, against his chest, stopped the crying with his handkerchief rolled into a ball and hurried up the three flights of stairs.

"Here," he said to Victoire, who woke with a start. "I've brought you the indomitable chief of our enemies, the Hercules of the gang. Have you a feeding-bottle about you?"

He put down in the easy-chair a child of six or seven years of age, the tiniest little fellow in a gray jersey and a knitted woollen cap, whose pale and exquisitely pretty features were streaked with the tears that streamed from the terrified eyes.

"Where did you pick that up?" asked Victoire, aghast.

"At the foot of the stairs, as it was coming out of Daubrecq's bedroom," replied Lupin, feeling the jersey in the hope that the child had brought a booty of some kind from that room.

Victoire was stirred to pity:

"Poor little dear! Look, he's trying not to cry!... Oh, saints above, his hands are like ice! Don't be afraid, sonnie, we sha'n't hurt you: the gentleman's all right."

"Yes," said Lupin, "the gentleman's quite all right, but there's another very wicked gentleman who'll wake up if they go on making such a rumpus outside the hall-door. Do you hear them, Victoire?"

"Who is it?"

"The satellites of our young Hercules, the indomitable leader's gang."

"Well...?" stammered Victoire, utterly unnerved.

"Well, as I don't want to be caught in the trap, I shall start by clearing out. Are you coming, Hercules?"

He rolled the child in a blanket, so that only its head remained outside, gagged its mouth as gently as possible and made Victoire fasten it to his shoulders:

"See, Hercules? We're having a game. You never thought you'd find gentlemen to play pick-a-back with you at three o'clock in the morning! Come, whoosh, let's fly away! You don't get giddy, I hope?"

He stepped across the window-ledge and set foot on one of the rungs of the ladder. He was in the garden in a minute.

He had never ceased hearing and now heard more plainly still the blows that were being struck upon the front-door. He was astounded that Daubrecq was not awakened by so violent a din:

"If I don't put a stop to this, they'll spoil everything," he said to himself.

He stood in an angle of the house, invisible in the darkness, and measured the distance between himself and the gate. The gate was open. To his right, he saw the steps, on the top of which the people were flinging themselves about; to his left, the building occupied by the portress.

The woman had come out of her lodge and was standing near the people, entreating them:

"Oh, do be quiet, do be quiet! He'll come!"

"Capital!" said Lupin. "The good woman is an accomplice of these as well. By Jingo, what a pluralist!"

He rushed across to her and, taking her by the scruff of the neck, hissed:

"Go and tell them I've got the child... They can come and fetch it at my place, Rue Chateaubriand."

A little way off, in the avenue, stood a taxi which Lupin presumed to be engaged by the gang. Speaking authoritatively, as though he were one of the accomplices, he stepped into the cab and told the man to drive him home.

"Well," he said to the child, "that wasn't much of a shake-up, was it?... What do you say to going to bye-bye on the gentleman's bed?"

As his servant, Achille, was asleep, Lupin made the little chap comfortable and stroked his hair for him. The child seemed numbed. His poor face was as though petrified into a stiff expression made up, at one and the same time, of fear and the wish not to show fear, of the longing to scream and a pitiful effort not to scream.

"Cry, my pet, cry," said Lupin. "It'll do you good to cry."

The child did not cry, but the voice was so gentle and so kind that he relaxed his tense muscles; and, now that his eyes were calmer and his mouth less contorted, Lupin, who was examining him closely, found something that he recognized, an undoubted resemblance.

This again confirmed certain facts which he suspected and which he had for some time been linking in his mind. Indeed, unless he was mistaken, the position was becoming very different and he would soon assume the direction of events. After that...

A ring at the bell followed, at once, by two others, sharp ones.

"Hullo!" said Lupin to the child. "Here's mummy come to fetch you. Don't move."

He ran and opened the door.

A woman entered, wildly:

"My son!" she screamed. "My son! Where is he?"

"In my room," said Lupin.

Without asking more, thus proving that she knew the way, she rushed to the bedroom.

"As I thought," muttered Lupin. "The youngish woman with the gray hair: Daubrecq's friend and enemy."

He walked to the window and looked through the curtains. Two men were striding up and down the opposite pavement: the Growler and the Masher.

"And they're not even hiding themselves," he said to himself. "That's a good sign. They consider that they can't do without me any longer and that they've got to obey the governor. There remains the pretty lady with the gray hair. That will be more difficult. It's you and I now, mummy."

He found the mother and the boy clasped in each other's arms; and the mother, in a great state of alarm, her eyes moist with tears, was saying:

"You're not hurt? You're sure? Oh, how frightened you must have been, my poor little Jacques!"

"A fine little fellow," said Lupin.

She did not reply. She was feeling the child's jersey, as Lupin had done, no doubt to see if he had succeeded in his nocturnal mission; and she questioned him in a whisper.

"No, mummy," said the child. "No, really."

She kissed him fondly and petted him, until, in a little while, the child, worn out with fatigue and excitement, fell asleep. She remained leaning over him for a long time. She herself seemed very much worn out and in need of rest.

Lupin did not disturb her contemplation. He looked at her anxiously, with an attention which she did not perceive, and he noticed the wider rings round her eyes and the deeper marks of wrinkles. Yet he considered her handsomer than he had thought, with that touching beauty which habitual suffering gives to certain faces that are more human, more sensitive than others.

She wore so sad an expression that, in a burst of instinctive sympathy, he went up to her and said: "I do not know what your plans are, but, whatever they may be, you stand in need of help. You cannot succeed alone."

"I am not alone."

"The two men outside? I know them. They're no good. I beseech you, make use of me. You remember the other evening, at the theatre, in the private box? You were on the point of speaking. Do not hesitate to-day."

She turned her eyes on him, looked at him long and fixedly and, as though unable to escape that opposing will, she said:

"What do you know exactly? What do you know about me?"

"There are many things that I do not know. I do not know your name. But I know..."

She interrupted him with a gesture; and, resolutely, in her turn, dominating the man who was compelling her to speak:

"It doesn't matter," she exclaimed. "What you know, after all, is not much and is of no importance. But what are your plans? You offer me your help: with what view? For what work? You have flung yourself headlong into this business; I have been unable to undertake anything without meeting you on my path: you must be contemplating some aim... What aim?"

"What aim? Upon my word, it seems to me that my conduct..."

"No, no," she said, emphatically, "no phrases! What you and I want is certainties; and, to achieve them, absolute frankness. I will set you the example. M. Daubrecq possesses a thing of unparalleled value, not in itself, but for what it represents. That thing you know. You have twice held it in your hands. I have twice taken it from you. Well, I am entitled to believe that, when you tried to obtain possession of it, you meant to use the power which you attribute to it and to use it to your own advantage..."

"What makes you say that?"

"Yes, you meant to use it to forward your schemes, in the interest of your own affairs, in accordance with your habits as a..."

"As a burglar and a swindler," said Lupin, completing the sentence for her.

She did not protest. He tried to read her secret thoughts in the depths of her eyes. What did she want with him? What was she afraid of? If she mistrusted him, had he not also reasons to mistrust that woman who had twice taken the crystal stopper from him to restore it to Daubrecq? Mortal enemy of Daubrecq's though she were, up to what point did she remain subject to that man's will? By surrendering himself to her, did he not risk surrendering himself to Daubrecq? And yet he had never looked upon graver eyes nor a more honest face.

Without further hesitation, he stated:

"My object is simple enough. It is the release of my friends Gilbert and Vaucheray."

"Is that true? Is that true?" she exclaimed, quivering all over and questioning him with an anxious glance.

"If you knew me..."

"I do know you... I know who you are. For months, I have taken part in your life, without your suspecting it... and yet, for certain reasons, I still doubt..."

He said, in a more decisive tone:

"You do not know me. If you knew me, you would know that there can be no peace for me before my two companions have escaped the awful fate that awaits them."

She rushed at him, took him by the shoulders and positively distraught, said:

"What? What did you say? The awful fate?... Then you believe... you believe..."

"I really believe," said Lupin, who felt how greatly this threat upset her, "I really believe that, if I am not in time, Gilbert and Vaucheray are done for."

"Be quiet!... Be quiet!" she cried, clutching him fiercely. "Be quiet!... You mustn't say that... There is no reason... It's just you who suppose..."

"It's not only I, it's Gilbert as well..."

"What? Gilbert? How do you know?"

"From himself?"

"From him?"

"Yes, from Gilbert, who has no hope left but in me; from Gilbert, who knows that only one man in the world can save him and who, a few days ago, sent me a despairing appeal from prison. Here is his letter."

She snatched the paper greedily and read in stammering accents:

"Help, governor!... I am frightened!... I am frightened!..."

She dropped the letter. Her hands fluttered in space. It was as though her staring eyes beheld the sinister vision which had already so often terrified Lupin. She gave a scream of horror, tried to rise and fainted.

V. THE TWENTY-SEVEN

The child was sleeping peacefully on the bed. The mother did not move from the sofa on which Lupin had laid her; but her easier breathing and the blood which was now returning to her face announced her impending recovery from her swoon.

He observed that she wore a wedding-ring. Seeing a locket hanging from her bodice, he stooped and, turning it, found a miniature photograph representing a man of about forty and a lad—a stripling rather—in a schoolboy's uniform. He studied the fresh, young face set in curly hair:

"It's as I thought," he said. "Ah, poor woman!"

The hand which he took between his grew warmer by degrees. The eyes opened, then closed again. She murmured:

"Jacques..."

"Do not distress yourself... it's all right he's asleep."

She recovered consciousness entirely. But, as she did not speak, Lupin put questions to her, to make her feel a gradual need of unbosoming herself. And he said, pointing to the locket:

"The schoolboy is Gilbert, isn't he?"

"Yes," she said.

"And Gilbert is your son?"

She gave a shiver and whispered:

"Yes, Gilbert is my son, my eldest son."

So she was the mother of Gilbert, of Gilbert the prisoner at the Sante, relentlessly pursued by the authorities and now awaiting his trial for murder!

Lupin continued:

"And the other portrait?"

"My husband."

"Your husband?"

"Yes, he died three years ago."

She was now sitting up. Life quivered in her veins once more, together with the horror of living and the horror of all the ghastly things that threatened her. Lupin went on to ask:

"What was your husband's name?"

She hesitated a moment and answered:

"Mergy."

He exclaimed:

"Victorien Mergy the deputy?"

"Yes."

There was a long pause. Lupin remembered the incident and the stir which it had caused. Three years ago, Mergy the deputy had blown out his brains in the lobby of the Chamber, without leaving a word of explanation behind him; and no one had ever discovered the slightest reason for that suicide.

"Do you know the reason?" asked Lupin, completing his thought aloud.

"Yes, I know it."

"Gilbert, perhaps?"

"No, Gilbert had disappeared for some years, turned out of doors and cursed by my husband. It was a very great sorrow, but there was another motive."

"What was that?" asked Lupin.

But it was not necessary for Lupin to put further questions. Madame Mergy could keep silent no longer and, slowly at first, with all the anguish of that past which had to be called up, she told her story:

"Twenty-five years ago, when my name was Clarisse Darcel and my parents living, I knew three young men at Nice. Their names will at once give you an insight into the present tragedy: they were Alexis Daubrecq, Victorien Mergy and Louis Prasville. The three were old acquaintances, had gone to college in the same year and served in the same regiment. Prasville, at that time, was in love with a singer at the opera-house at Nice. The two others, Mergy and Daubrecq, were in love with me. I shall be brief as regards all this and, for the rest, as regards the whole story, for the facts tell their own tale. I fell in love with Victorien Mergy from the first. Perhaps I was wrong not to declare myself at once. But true love is always timid, hesitating and shy; and I did not announce my choice until I felt quite certain and quite free. Unfortunately, that period of waiting, so delightful for those who cherish a secret passion, had permitted Daubrecq to hope. His anger was something horrible."

Clarisse Mergy stopped for a few seconds and resumed, in a stifled voice:

"I shall never forget it... The three of us were in the drawing-room. Oh, I can hear even now the terrible words of threat and hatred which he uttered! Victorien was absolutely astounded. He had never seen his friend like this, with that repugnant face, that bestial expression: yes, the expression of a wild beast... Daubrecq ground his teeth. He stamped his feet. His bloodshot eyes—he did not wear spectacles in those days—rolled in their sockets; and he kept on saying, 'I shall be revenged ... I shall be revenged... Oh, you don't know what I am capable of!... I shall wait ten years, twenty years, if necessary... But it will come like a thunderbolt... Ah, you don't know!... To be revenged... To do harm... for harm's sake... what joy! I was born to do harm... And you will both beseech my mercy on your knees, on your knees, yes, on your knees...' At that moment, my father entered the room; and, with his assistance and the footman's, Victorien Mergy flung the loathsome creature out of doors. Six weeks later, I married Victorien."

"And Daubrecq?" asked Lupin, interrupting her. "Did he not try..."

"No, but on our wedding-day, Louis Prasville, who acted as my husband's best man in defiance of Danbrecq's opposition, went home to find the girl he loved, the opera-singer, dead, strangled..."

"What!" said Lupin, with a start. "Had Daubrecq..."

"It was known that Daubrecq had been persecuting her with his attentions for some days; but nothing more was known. It was impossible to discover who had gone in or out during Prasville's absence. There was not a trace found of any kind: nothing, absolutely nothing."

"But Prasville..."

"There was no doubt of the truth in Prasville's mind or ours. Daubrecq had tried to run away with the girl, perhaps tried to force her, to hustle her and, in the course of the struggle, maddened, losing his head, caught her by the throat and killed her, perhaps without knowing what he was doing. But there was no evidence of all this; and Daubrecq was not even molested."

"And what became of him next?"

"For some years we heard nothing of him. We knew only that he had lost all his money gambling and that he was travelling in America. And, in spite of myself, I forgot his anger and his threats and was only too ready to believe that he had ceased to love me and no longer harboured his schemes of revenge. Besides, I was so happy that I did not care to think of anything but my happiness, my love, my husband's political career, the health of my son Antoine."

"Antoine?"

"Yes, Antoine is Gilbert's real name. The unhappy boy has at least succeeded in concealing his identity."

Lupin asked, with some hesitation:

"At what period did... Gilbert... begin?"

"I cannot tell you exactly. Gilbert—I prefer to call him that and not to pronounce his real name—Gilbert, as a child, was what he is to-day: lovable, liked by everybody, charming, but lazy and unruly. When he was fifteen, we put him to a boarding-school in one of the suburbs, with the deliberate object of not having him too much at home. After two years' time he was expelled from school and sent back to us."

"Why?"

"Because of his conduct. The masters had discovered that he used to slip out at night and also that he would disappear for weeks at a time, while pretending to be at home with us."

"What used he to do?"

"Amuse himself backing horses, spending his time in cafes and public dancing-rooms."

"Then he had money?"

"Yes."

"Who gave it him?"

"His evil genius, the man who, secretly, unknown to his parents, enticed him away from school, the man who led him astray, who corrupted him, who took him from us, who taught him to lie, to waste his substance and to steal."

"Daubrecq?"

"Daubrecq."

Clarisse Mergy put her hands together to hide the blushes on her forehead. She continued, in her tired voice:

"Daubrecq had taken his revenge. On the day after my husband turned our unhappy child out of the house, Daubrecq sent us a most cynical letter in which he revealed the odious part which he had played and the machinations by which he had succeeded in depraving our son. And he went on to say, 'The reformatory, one of these days... Later on, the assize-court ... And then, let us hope and trust, the scaffold!'"

Lupin exclaimed:

"What! Did Daubrecq plot the present business?"

"No, no, that is only an accident. The hateful prophecy was just a wish which he expressed. But oh, how it terrified me! I was ailing at the time; my other son, my little Jacques, had just been born. And every day we heard of some fresh misdeed of Gilbert's—forgeries, swindles—so much so that we spread the news, in our immediate surroundings, of his departure for abroad, followed by his death. Life was a misery; and it became still more so when the political storm burst in which my husband was to meet his death."

"What do you mean?"

"A word will be enough: my husband's name was on the list of the Twenty-seven."

"Ah!"

The veil was suddenly lifted from Lupin's eyes and he saw, as in a flash of lightning, a whole legion of things which, until then, had been hidden in the darkness.

Clarisse Mergy continued, in a firmer voice:

"Yes, his name was on it, but by mistake, by a piece of incredible ill-luck of which he was the victim. It is true that Victorien Mergy was a member of the committee appointed to consider the question of the Two-Seas Canal. It is true that he voted with the members who were in favour of the company's scheme. He was even paid—yes, I tell you so plainly and I will mention the sum—he was paid fifteen thousand francs. But he was paid on behalf of another, of one of his political friends, a man in whom he had absolute confidence and of whom he was the blind, unconscious tool. He thought he was showing his friend a kindness; and it proved his own undoing. It was not until the day after the suicide of the chairman of the company and the disappearance of the secretary, the day on which the affair of the canal was published in the papers, with its whole series of swindles and abominations, that my husband knew that a number of his fellow-members had been bribed and learnt that the mysterious list, of which people suddenly began to speak, mentioned his name with theirs and with the names of other deputies, leaders of parties and influential politicians. Oh, what awful days those were! Would the list be published? Would his name come out? The torture of it! You remember the mad excitement in the Chamber, the atmosphere of terror and denunciation that prevailed. Who owned the list? Nobody could say. It was known to be in existence and that was all. Two names were sacrificed to public odium. Two men were swept away by the storm. And it remained unknown where the denunciation came from and in whose hands the incriminating documents were."

"Daubrecq," suggested Lupin.

"No, no!" cried Madame Mergy. "Daubrecq was nothing at that time: he had not yet appeared upon the scene. No, don't you remember, the truth came out suddenly through the very man who was keeping it back: Germineaux, the ex-minister of justice, a cousin of the chairman of the Canal Company. As he lay dying of consumption, he wrote from his sick-bed to the prefect of police, bequeathing him that list of names, which, he said, would be found, after his death, in an iron chest in the corner of his room. The house was surrounded by police and the prefect took up his quarters by the sick man's bedside. Germineaux died. The chest was opened and found to be empty."

"Daubrecq, this time," Lupin declared.

"Yes, Daubrecq," said Madame Mergy, whose excitement was momentarily increasing. "Alexis Daubrecq, who, for six months, disguised beyond recognition, had acted as Germineaux's secretary. It does not matter how he discovered that Germineaux was the possessor of the paper in question. The fact remains that he broke open the chest on the night before the death. So much was proved at the inquiry; and Daubrecq's identity was established."

"But he was not arrested?"

"What would have been the use? They knew well enough that he must have deposited the list in a place of safety. His arrest would have involved a scandal, the reopening of the whole case..."

"So..."

"So they made terms."

Lupin laughed:

"That's funny, making terms with Daubrecq!"

"Yes, very funny," said Madame Mergy, bitterly. "During this time he acted and without delay, shamelessly, making straight for the goal. A week after the theft, he went to the Chamber of Deputies, asked for my husband and bluntly demanded thirty thousand francs of him, to be paid within twenty-four hours. If not, he threatened him with exposure and disgrace. My husband knew the man he was dealing with, knew him to be implacable and filled with relentless hatred. He lost his head and shot himself."

"How absurd!" Lupin could not help saying. "How absurd! Daubrecq possesses a list of twenty-seven names. To give up any one of those names he is obliged, if he would have his accusation believed, to publish the list itself—that is to say, to part with the document, or at least a photograph of it. Well, in so doing, he creates a scandal, it is true, but he deprives himself, at the same time, of all further means of levying blackmail."

"Yes and no," she said.

"How do you know?"

"Through Daubrecq himself. The villain came to see me and cynically told me of his interview with my husband and the words that had passed between them. Well, there is more than that list, more than that famous bit of paper on which the secretary put down the names and the amounts paid and to which, you will remember, the chairman of the company, before dying, affixed his signature in letters of blood. There is more than that. There are certain less positive proofs, which the people interested do not know of: the correspondence between the chairman and the secretary, between the chairman and his counsel, and so on. Of course, the list scribbled on the bit of paper is the only evidence that counts; it is the one incontestable proof which it would be no good copying or even photographing, for its genuineness can be tested most absolutely. But, all the same, the other proofs are dangerous. They have already been enough to do away with two deputies. And Daubrecq is marvelously clever at turning this fact to account. He selects his victim, frightens him out of his senses, points out to him the inevitable scandal; and the victim pays the required sum. Or else he kills himself, as my husband did. Do you understand now?"

"Yes," said Lupin.

And, in the silence that followed, he drew a mental picture of Daubrecq's life. He saw him the owner of that list, using his power, gradually emerging from the shadow, lavishly squandering the money which he extorted from his victims, securing his election as a district-councillor and deputy, holding sway by dint of threats and terror, unpunished, invulnerable, unattackable, feared by the government, which would rather submit to his orders than declare war upon him, respected by the judicial authorities: so powerful, in a word, that Prasville had been appointed secretary-general of police, over the heads of all who had prior claims, for the sole reason that he hated Daubrecq with a personal hatred.

"And you saw him again?" he asked.

"I saw him again. I had to. My husband was dead, but his honour remained untouched. Nobody suspected the truth. In order at least to defend the name which he left me, I accepted my first interview with Daubrecq."

"Your first, yes, for there have been others."

"Many others," she said, in a strained voice, "yes, many others... at the theatre... or in the evening, at Enghien... or else in Paris, at night ... for I was ashamed to meet that man and I did not want people to know it... But it was necessary... A duty more imperative than any other commanded it: the duty of avenging my husband..."

She bent over Lupin and, eagerly:

"Yes, revenge has been the motive of my conduct and the sole preoccupation of my life. To avenge my husband, to avenge my ruined son, to avenge myself for all the harm that he has done me: I had no other dream, no other object in life. That is what I wanted: to see that man crushed, reduced to poverty, to tears—as though he still knew how to cry!—sobbing in the throes of despair..."

"You wanted his death," said Lupin, remembering the scene between them in Daubrecq's study.

"No, not his death. I have often thought of it, I have even raised my arm to strike him, but what would have been the good? He must have taken his precautions. The paper would remain. And then there is no revenge in killing a man... My hatred went further than that... It demanded his ruin, his downfall; and, to achieve that, there was but one way: to cut his claws. Daubrecq, deprived of the document that gives him his immense power, ceases to exist. It means immediate bankruptcy and disaster... under the most wretched conditions. That is what I have sought."

"But Daubrecq must have been aware of your intentions?"

"Certainly. And, I assure you, those were strange meetings of ours: I watching him closely, trying to guess his secret behind his actions and his words, and he... he..."

"And he," said Lupin, finishing Clarisse's thought, "lying in wait for the prey which he desires... for the woman whom he has never ceased to love... whom he loves... and whom he covets with all his might and with all his furious passion..."

She lowered her head and said, simply:

"Yes."

A strange duel indeed was that which brought face to face those two beings separated by so many implacable things! How unbridled must Daubrecq's passion be for him to risk that perpetual threat of death and to introduce to the privacy of his house this woman whose life he had shattered! But also how absolutely safe he must feel himself!

"And your search ended... how?" asked Lupin.

"My search," she replied, "long remained without fruit. You know the methods of investigation which you have followed and which the police have followed on their side. Well, I myself employed them, years before either of you did, and in vain. I was beginning to despair. Then, one day, when I had gone to see Daubrecq in his villa at Enghien, I picked up under his writing-table a letter which he had begun to write, crumpled up and thrown into the waste-paper-basket. It consisted of a few lines in bad English; and I was able to read this: 'Empty the crystal within, so as to leave a void which it is impossible to suspect.' Perhaps I should not have attached to this sentence all the importance which it deserved, if Daubrecq, who was out in the garden, had not come running in and begun to turn out the waste-paper-basket, with an eagerness which was very significant. He gave me a suspicious look: 'There was a letter there,' he said. I pretended not to understand. He did not insist, but his agitation did not escape me; and I continued my quest in this direction. A month later, I discovered, among the ashes in the drawing-room fireplace, the torn half of an English invoice. I gathered that a Stourbridge glass-blower, of the name of John Howard, had supplied Daubrecq with a crystal bottle made after a model. The word 'crystal' struck me at once. I went to Stourbridge, got round the foreman of the glass-works and learnt that the stopper of this bottle had been hollowed out inside, in accordance with the instruction in the order, so as to leave a cavity, the existence of which would escape observation."

Lupin nodded his head:

"The thing tallies beyond a doubt. Nevertheless, it did not seem to me, that, even under the gilt layer... And then the hiding-place would be very tiny!"

"Tiny, but large enough," she said. "On my return from England, I went to the police-office to see Prasville, whose friendship for me had remained unchanged. I did not hesitate to tell him, first, the reasons which had driven my husband to suicide and, secondly, the object of revenge which I was pursuing. When I informed him of my discoveries, he jumped for joy; and I felt that his hatred for Daubrecq was as strong as ever. I learnt from him that the list was written on a slip of exceedingly thin foreign-post-paper, which, when rolled up into a sort of pellet, would easily fit into an exceedingly limited space. Neither he nor I had the least hesitation. We knew the hiding-place. We agreed to act independently of each other, while continuing to correspond in secret. I put him in touch with Clemence, the portress in the Square Lamartine, who was entirely devoted to me..."

"But less so to Prasville," said Lupin, "for I can prove that she betrays him."

"Now perhaps, but not at the start; and the police searches were numerous. It was at that time, ten months ago, that Gilbert came into my life again. A mother never loses her love for her son, whatever he may do, whatever he may have done. And then Gilbert has such a way with him... well, you know him. He cried, kissed my little Jacques, his brother and I forgave him."

She stopped and, weary-voiced, with her eyes fixed on the floor, continued:

"Would to Heaven that I had not forgiven him! Ah, if that hour could but return, how readily I should find the horrible courage to turn him away! My poor child... it was I who ruined him!..." And, pensively, "I should have had that or any sort of courage, if he had been as I pictured him to myself and as he himself told me that he had long been: bearing the marks of vice and dissipation, coarse, deteriorated.

"But, though he was utterly changed in appearance, so much so that I could hardly recognize him, there was, from the point of view of—how shall I put it?—from the moral point of view, an undoubted improvement. You had helped him, lifted him; and, though his mode of life was hateful to me, nevertheless he retained a certain self-respect... a sort of underlying decency that showed itself on the surface once more... He was gay, careless, happy... And he used to talk of you with such affection!"

She picked her words, betraying her embarrassment, not daring, in Lupin's presence, to condemn the line of life which Gilbert had selected and yet unable to speak in favour of it.

"What happened next?" asked Lupin.

"I saw him very often. He would come to me by stealth, or else I went to him and we would go for walks in the country. In this way, I was gradually induced to tell him our story, of his father's suicide and the object which I was pursuing. He at once took fire. He too wanted to avenge his father and, by stealing the crystal stopper, to avenge himself on Daubrecq for the harm which he had done him. His first idea—from which, I am bound to tell you, he never swerved—was to arrange with you."

"Well, then," cried Lupin, "he ought to have...!"

"Yes, I know... and I was of the same opinion. Unfortunately, my poor Gilbert—you know how weak he is!—was under the influence of one of his comrades."

"Vaucheray?"

"Yes, Vaucheray, a saturnine spirit, full of bitterness and envy, an ambitious, unscrupulous, gloomy, crafty man, who had acquired a great empire over my son. Gilbert made the mistake of confiding in him and asking his advice. That was the origin of all the mischief. Vaucheray convinced him and convinced me as well that it would be better if we acted by ourselves. He studied the business, took the lead and finally organized the Enghien expedition and, under your direction, the burglary at the Villa Marie-Therese, which Prasville and his detectives had been unable to search thoroughly, because of the active watch maintained by Leonard the valet. It was a mad scheme. We ought either to have trusted in your experience entirely, or else to have left you out altogether, taking the risk of fatal mistakes and dangerous hesitations. But we could not help ourselves. Vaucheray ruled us. I agreed to meet Daubrecq at the theatre. During this time the thing took place. When I came home, at twelve o'clock at night, I heard the terrible result: Leonard murdered, my son arrested. I at once received an intuition of the future. Daubrecq's appalling prophecy was being realized: it meant trial and sentence. And this through my fault, through the fault of me, the mother, who had driven my son toward the abyss from which nothing could extricate him now."

Clarisse wrung her hands and shivered from head to foot. What suffering can compare with that of a mother trembling for the head of her son? Stirred with pity, Lupin said: "We shall save him. Of that there is not the shadow of a doubt. But, it is necessary that I should know all the details. Finish your story, please. How did you know, on the same night, what had happened at Enghien?"

She mastered herself and, with a face wrung with fevered anguish, replied:

"Through two of your accomplices, or rather two accomplices of Vaucheray, to whom they were wholly devoted and who had chosen them to row the boats."

"The two men outside: the Growler and the Masher?"

"Yes. On your return from the villa, when you landed after being pursued on the lake by the commissary of police, you said a few words to them, by way of explanation, as you went to your car. Mad with fright, they rushed to my place, where they had been before, and told me the hideous news. Gilbert was in prison! Oh, what an awful night! What was I to do? Look for you? Certainly; and implore your assistance. But where was I to find you?... It was then that the two whom you call the Growler and the Masher, driven into a corner by circumstances, decided to tell me of the part played by Vaucheray, his ambitions, his plan, which had long been ripening..."

"To get rid of me, I suppose?" said Lupin, with a grin.

"Yes. As Gilbert possessed your complete confidence, Vaucheray watched him and, in this way, got to know all the places which you live at. A few days more and, owning the crystal stopper, holding the list of the Twenty-seven, inheriting all Daubrecq's power, he would have delivered you to the police, without compromising a single member of your gang, which he looked upon as thenceforth his."

"The ass!" muttered Lupin. "A muddler like that!" And he added, "So the panels of the doors..."

"Were cut out by his instructions, in anticipation of the contest on which he was embarking against you and against Daubrecq, at whose house he did the same thing. He had under his orders a sort of acrobat, an extraordinarily thin dwarf, who was able to wriggle through those apertures and who thus detected all your correspondence and all your secrets. That is what his two friends revealed to me. I at once conceived the idea of saving my elder son by making use of his brother, my little Jacques, who is himself so slight and so intelligent, so plucky, as you have seen. We set out that night. Acting on the information of my companions, I went to Gilbert's rooms and found the keys of your flat in the Rue Matignon, where it appeared that you were to sleep. Unfortunately, I changed my mind on the way and thought much less of asking for your help than of recovering the crystal stopper, which, if it had been discovered at Enghien, must obviously be at your flat. I was right in my calculations. In a few minutes, my little Jacques, who had slipped into your bedroom, brought it to me. I went away quivering with hope. Mistress in my turn of the talisman, keeping it to myself, without telling Prasville, I had absolute power over Daubrecq. I could make him do all that I wanted; he would become the slave of my will and, instructed by me, would take every step in Gilbert's favour and obtain that he should be given the means of escape or else that he should not be sentenced. It meant my boy's safety."

"Well?"

Clarisse rose from her seat, with a passionate movement of her whole being, leant over Lupin and said, in a hollow voice:

"There was nothing in that piece of crystal, nothing, do you understand? No paper, no hiding-place! The whole expedition to Enghien was futile! The murder of Leonard was useless! The arrest of my son was useless! All my efforts were useless!"

"But why? Why?"

"Why? Because what you stole from Daubrecq was not the stopper made by his instructions, but the stopper which was sent to John Howard, the Stourbridge glassworker, to serve as a model."

If Lupin had not been in the presence of so deep a grief, he could not have refrained from one of those satirical outbursts with which the mischievous tricks of fate are wont to inspire him. As it was, he muttered between his teeth:

"How stupid! And still more stupid as Daubrecq had been given the warning."

"No," she said. "I went to Enghien on the same day. In all that business Daubrecq saw and sees nothing but an ordinary burglary, an annexation of his treasures. The fact that you took part in it put him off the scent."

"Still, the disappearance of the stopper..."

"To begin with, the thing can have had but a secondary importance for him, as it is only the model."

"How do you know?"

"There is a scratch at the bottom of the stem; and I have made inquiries in England since."

"Very well; but why did the key of the cupboard from which it was stolen never leave the man-servant's possession? And why, in the second place, was it found afterward in the drawer of a table in Daubrecq's house in Paris?"

"Of course, Daubrecq takes care of it and clings to it in the way in which one clings to the model of any valuable thing. And that is why I replaced the stopper in the cupboard before its absence was noticed. And that also is why, on the second occasion, I made my little Jacques take the stopper from your overcoat-pocket and told the portress to put it back in the drawer."

"Then he suspects nothing?"

"Nothing. He knows that the list is being looked for, but he does not know that Prasville and I are aware of the thing in which he hides it."

Lupin had risen from his seat and was walking up and down the room, thinking. Then he stood still beside Clarisse and asked:

"When all is said, since the Enghien incident, you have not advanced a single step?"

"Not one. I have acted from day to day, led by those two men or leading them, without any definite plan."

"Or, at least," he said, "without any other plan than that of getting the list of the Twenty-seven from Daubrecq."

"Yes, but how? Besides, your tactics made things more difficult for me. It did not take us long to recognize your old servant Victoire in Daubrecq's new cook and to discover, from what the portress told us, that Victoire was putting you up in her room; and I was afraid of your schemes."

"It was you, was it not, who wrote to me to retire from the contest?"

"Yes."

"You also asked me not to go to the theatre on the Vaudeville night?"

"Yes, the portress caught Victoire listening to Daubrecq's conversation with me on the telephone; and the Masher, who was watching the house, saw you go out. I suspected, therefore, that you would follow Daubrecq that evening."

"And the woman who came here, late one afternoon..."

"Was myself. I felt disheartened and wanted to see you."

"And you intercepted Gilbert's letter?"

"Yes, I recognized his writing on the envelope."

"But your little Jacques was not with you?"

"No, he was outside, in a motor-car, with the Masher, who lifted him up to me through the drawing-room window; and he slipped into your bedroom through the opening in the panel."

"What was in the letter?"

"As ill-luck would have it, reproaches. Gilbert accused you of forsaking him, of taking over the business on your own account. In short, it confirmed me in my distrust; and I ran away."

Lupin shrugged his shoulders with irritation:

"What a shocking waste of time! And what a fatality that we were not able to come to an understanding earlier! You and I have been playing at hide-and-seek, laying absurd traps for each other, while the days were passing, precious days beyond repair."

"You see, you see," she said, shivering, "you too are afraid of the future!"

"No, I am not afraid," cried Lupin. "But I am thinking of all the useful work that we could have done by this time, if we had united our efforts. I am thinking of all the mistakes and all the acts of imprudence which we should have been saved, if we had been working together. I am thinking that your attempt to-night to search the clothes which Daubrecq was wearing was as vain as the others and that, at this moment, thanks to our foolish duel, thanks to the din which we raised in his house, Daubrecq is warned and will be more on his guard than ever."

Clarisse Mergy shook her head:

"No, no, I don't think that; the noise will not have roused him, for we postponed the attempt for twenty-four hours so that the portress might put a narcotic in his wine." And she added, slowly, "And then, you see, nothing can make Daubrecq be more on his guard than he is already. His life is nothing but one mass of precautions against danger. He leaves nothing to chance... Besides, has he not all the trumps in his hand?"

Lupin went up to her and asked:

"What do you mean to convey? According to you, is there nothing to hope for on that side? Is there not a single means of attaining our end?"

"Yes," she murmured, "there is one, one only..."

He noticed her pallor before she had time to hide her face between her hands again. And again a feverish shiver shook her frame.

He seemed to understand the reason of her dismay; and, bending toward her, touched by her grief:

"Please," he said, "please answer me openly and frankly. It's for Gilbert's sake, is it not? Though the police, fortunately, have not been able to solve the riddle of his past, though the real name of Vaucheray's accomplice has not leaked out, there is one man, at least, who knows it: isn't that so? Daubrecq has recognized your son Antoine, through the alias of Gilbert, has he not?"

"Yes, yes..."

"And he promises to save him, doesn't he? He offers you his freedom, his release, his escape, his life: that was what he offered you, was it not, on the night in his study, when you tried to stab him?"

"Yes... yes... that was it..."

"And he makes one condition, does he not? An abominable condition, such as would suggest itself to a wretch like that? I am right, am I not?"

Clarisse did not reply. She seemed exhausted by her protracted struggle with a man who was gaining ground daily and against whom it was impossible for her to fight. Lupin saw in her the prey conquered in advance, delivered to the victor's whim. Clarisse Mergy, the loving wife of that Mergy whom Daubrecq had really murdered, the terrified mother of that Gilbert whom Daubrecq had led astray, Clarisse Mergy, to save her son from the scaffold, must, come what may and however ignominious the position, yield to Daubrecq's wishes. She would be the mistress, the wife, the obedient slave of Daubrecq, of that monster with the appearance and the ways of a wild beast, that unspeakable person of whom Lupin could not think without revulsion and disgust.

Sitting down beside her, gently, with gestures of pity, he made her lift her head and, with his eyes on hers, said:

"Listen to me. I swear that I will save your son: I swear it... Your son shall not die, do you understand?... There is not a power on earth that can allow your son's head to be touched as long as I am alive."

"I believe you... I trust your word."

"Do. It is the word of a man who does not know defeat. I shall succeed. Only, I entreat you to make me an irrevocable promise."

"What is that?"

"You must not see Daubrecq again."

"I swear it."

"You must put from your mind any idea, any fear, however obscure, of an understanding between yourself and him... of any sort of bargain..."

"I swear it."

She looked at him with an expression of absolute security and reliance; and he, under her gaze, felt the joy of devotion and an ardent longing to restore that woman's happiness, or, at least, to give her the peace and oblivion that heal the worst wounds:

"Come," he said, in a cheerful tone, rising from his chair, "all will yet be well. We have two months, three months before us. It is more than I need... on condition, of course, that I am unhampered in my movements. And, for that, you will have to withdraw from the contest, you know."

"How do you mean?"

"Yes, you must disappear for a time; go and live in the country. Have you no pity for your little Jacques? This sort of thing would end by shattering the poor little man's nerves... And he has certainly earned his rest, haven't you, Hercules?"

The next day Clarisse Mergy, who was nearly breaking down under the strain of events and who herself needed repose, lest she should fall seriously ill, went, with her son, to board with a friend who had a house on the skirt of the Forest of Saint-Germain. She felt very weak, her brain was haunted by visions and her nerves were upset by troubles which the least excitement aggravated. She lived there for some days in a state of physical and mental inertia, thinking of nothing and forbidden to see the papers.

One afternoon, while Lupin, changing his tactics, was working out a scheme for kidnapping and confining Daubrecq; while the Growler and the Masher, whom he had promised to forgive if he succeeded, were watching the enemy's movements; while the newspapers were announcing the forthcoming trial for murder of Arsene Lupin's two accomplices, one afternoon, at four o'clock, the telephone-bell rang suddenly in the flat in the Rue Chateaubriand.

Lupin took down the receiver:

"Hullo!"

A woman's voice, a breathless voice, said:

"M. Michel Beaumont?"

"You are speaking to him, madame. To whom have I the honour..."

"Quick, monsieur, come at once; Madame Mergy has taken poison."

Lupin did not wait to hear details. He rushed out, sprang into his motor-car and drove to Saint-Germain.

Clarisse's friend was waiting for him at the door of the bedroom.

"Dead?" he asked.

"No," she replied, "she did not take sufficient. The doctor has just gone. He says she will get over it."

"And why did she make the attempt?"

"Her son Jacques has disappeared."

"Carried off?"

"Yes, he was playing just inside the forest. A motor-car was seen pulling up. Then there were screams. Clarisse tried to run, but her strength failed and she fell to the ground, moaning, 'It's he... it's that man... all is lost!' She looked like a madwoman."

"Suddenly, she put a little bottle to her lips and swallowed the contents."

"What happened next?"

"My husband and I carried her to her room. She was in great pain."

"How did you know my address, my name?"

"From herself, while the doctor was attending to her. Then I telephoned to you."

"Has any one else been told?"

"No, nobody. I know that Clarisse has had terrible things to bear... and that she prefers not to be talked about."

"Can I see her?"

"She is asleep just now. And the doctor has forbidden all excitement."

"Is the doctor anxious about her?"

"He is afraid of a fit of fever, any nervous strain, an attack of some kind which might cause her to make a fresh attempt on her life. And that would be..."

"What is needed to avoid it?"

"A week or a fortnight of absolute quiet, which is impossible as long as her little Jacques..."

Lupin interrupted her: "You think that, if she got her son back..."

"Oh, certainly, there would be nothing more to fear!"

"You're sure? You're sure?... Yes, of course you are!... Well, when Madame Mergy wakes, tell her from me that I will bring her back her son this evening, before midnight. This evening, before midnight: it's a solemn promise."

With these words, Lupin hurried out of the house and, stepping into his car, shouted to the driver:

"Go to Paris, Square Lamartine, Daubrecq the deputy's!"

VI. THE DEATH-SENTENCE

Lupin's motor-car was not only an office, a writing-room furnished with books, stationery, pens and ink, but also a regular actor's dressing-room, containing a complete make-up box, a trunk filled with every variety of wearing-apparel, another crammed with "properties"—umbrellas, walking-sticks, scarves, eye-glasses and so on—in short, a complete set of paraphernalia which enabled him to alter his appearance from top to toe in the course of a drive.

The man who rang at Daubrecq the deputy's gate, at six o-clock that evening, was a stout, elderly gentleman, in a black frock-coat, a bowler hat, spectacles and whiskers.

The portress took him to the front-door of the house and rang the bell. Victoire appeared.

Lupin asked:

"Can M. Daubrecq see Dr. Vernes?"

"M. Daubrecq is in his bedroom; and it is rather late..."

"Give him my card, please."

He wrote the words, "From Mme. Mergy," in the margin and added:

"There, he is sure to see me."

"But..." Victoire began.

"Oh, drop your buts, old dear, do as I say, and don't make such a fuss about it!"

She was utterly taken aback and stammered:

"You!... is it you?"

"No, it's Louis XIV!" And, pushing her into a corner of the hall, "Listen... The moment I'm done with him, go up to your room, put your things together anyhow and clear out."

"What!"

"Do as I tell you. You'll find my car waiting down the avenue. Come, stir your stumps! Announce me. I'll wait in the study."

"But it's dark in there."

"Turn on the light."

She switched on the electric light and left Lupin alone.

"It's here," he reflected, as he took a seat, "it's here that the crystal stopper?byes?... Unless Daubrecq always keeps it by him... But no, when people have a good hiding-place, they make use of it. And this is a capital one; for none of us... so far..."

Concentrating all his attention, he examined the objects in the room; and he remembered the note which Daubrecq wrote to Prasville:

> *"Within reach of your hand, my dear Prasville!...*
> *You touched it! A little more and the trick was done..."*

Nothing seemed to have moved since that day. The same things were lying about on the desk: books, account-books, a bottle of ink, a stamp-box, pipes, tobacco, things that had been searched and probed over and over again.

"The bounder!" thought Lupin. "He's organized his business jolly cleverly. It's all dove-tailed like a well-made play."

In his heart of hearts, though he knew exactly what he had come to do and how he meant to act, Lupin was thoroughly aware of the danger and uncertainty attending his visit to so powerful an adversary. It was quite within the bounds of possibility that Daubrecq, armed as he was, would remain master of the field and that the conversation would take an absolutely different turn from that which Lupin anticipated.

And this prospect angered him somewhat.

He drew himself up, as he heard a sound of footsteps approaching.

Daubrecq entered.

He entered without a word, made a sign to Lupin, who had risen from his chair, to resume his seat and himself sat down at the writing-desk. Glancing at the card which he held in his hand:

"Dr. Vernes?"

"Yes, monsieur le depute, Dr. Vernes, of Saint-Germain."

"And I see that you come from Mme. Mergy. A patient of yours?"

"A recent patient. I did not know her until I was called in to see her, the other day, in particularly tragic circumstances."

"Is she ill?"

"Mme. Mergy has taken poison."

"What!"

Daubrecq gave a start and he continued, without concealing his distress:

"What's that you say? Poison! Is she dead?"

"No, the dose was not large enough. If no complications ensue, I consider that Mme. Mergy's life is saved."

Daubrecq said nothing and sat silent, with his head turned to Lupin.

"Is he looking at me? Are his eyes open or shut?" Lupin asked himself.

It worried Lupin terribly not to see his adversary's eyes, those eyes hidden by the double obstacle of spectacles and black glasses: weak, bloodshot eyes, Mme. Mergy had told him. How could he follow the secret train of the man's thought without seeing the expression of his face? It was almost like fighting an enemy who wielded an invisible sword.

Presently, Daubrecq spoke:

"So Mme. Mergy's life is saved... And she has sent you to me... I don't quite understand... I hardly know the lady."

"Now for the ticklish moment," thought Lupin. "Have at him!"

And, in a genial, good-natured and rather shy tone, he said:

"No, monsieur le depute, there are cases in which a doctor's duty becomes very complex... very puzzling... And you may think that, in taking this step... However, to cut a long story short, while I was attending Mme. Mergy, she made a second attempt to poison herself... Yes; the bottle, unfortunately, had been left within her reach. I snatched it from her. We had a struggle. And, railing in her fever, she said to me, in broken words, 'He's the man... He's the man... Daubrecq the deputy... Make him give me back my son. Tell him to... or else I would rather die... Yes, now, to-night... I would rather die.' That's what she said, monsieur le depute... So I thought that I ought to let you know. It is quite certain that, in the lady's highly nervous state of mind... Of course, I don't know the exact meaning of her words... I asked no questions of anybody... obeyed a spontaneous impulse and came straight to you."

Daubrecq reflected for a little while and said:

"It amounts to this, doctor, that you have come to ask me if I know the whereabouts of this child whom I presume to have disappeared. Is that it?"

"Yes."

"And, if I did happen to know, you would take him back to his mother?"

There was a longer pause. Lupin asked himself:

"Can he by chance have swallowed the story? Is the threat of that death enough? Oh, nonsense it's out of the question!... And yet... and yet... he seems to be hesitating."

"Will you excuse me?" asked Daubrecq, drawing the telephone, on his writing-desk, toward him. "I have an urgent message."

"Certainly, monsieur le depute."

Daubrecq called out:

"Hullo!... 822.19, please, 822.19."

Having repeated the number, he sat without moving.

Lupin smiled:

"The headquarters of police, isn't it? The secretary-general's office..."

"Yes, doctor... How do you know?"

"Oh, as a divisional surgeon, I sometimes have to ring them up."

And, within himself, Lupin asked:

"What the devil does all this mean? The secretary-general is Prasville... Then, what?..."

Daubrecq put both receivers to his ears and said:

"Are you 822.19? I want to speak to M. Prasville, the secretary-general ... Do you say he's not there?... Yes, yes, he is: he's always in his office at this time... Tell him it's M. Daubrecq... M. Daubrecq the deputy... a most important communication."

"Perhaps I'm in the way?" Lupin suggested.

"Not at all, doctor, not at all," said Daubrecq. "Besides, what I have to say has a certain bearing on your errand." And, into the telephone, "Hullo! M. Prasville?... Ah, it's you, Prasville, old cock!... Why, you seem quite staggered! Yes, you're right, it's an age since you and I met. But, after all, we've never been far away in thought... And I've had plenty of visits from you and your henchmen... In my absence, it's true. Hullo!... What?... Oh, you're in a hurry? I beg your pardon!... So am I, for that matter... Well, to come to the point, there's a little service I want to do you... Wait, can't you, you brute?... You won't regret it... It concerns your renown... Hullo!... Are you listening?... Well, take half-a-dozen men with you... plain-clothes detectives, by preference: you'll find them at the night-office... Jump into a taxi, two taxis, and come along here as fast as you can... I've got a rare quarry for you, old chap. One of the upper ten... a lord, a marquis Napoleon himself... in a word, Arsene Lupin!"

Lupin sprang to his feet. He was prepared for everything but this. Yet something within him stronger than astonishment, an impulse of his whole nature, made him say, with a laugh:

"Oh, well done, well done!"

Daubrecq bowed his head, by way of thanks, and muttered:

"I haven't quite finished... A little patience, if you don't mind." And he continued, "Hullo! Prasville!... No, no, old chap, I'm not humbugging... You'll find Lupin here, with me, in my study... Lupin, who's worrying me like the rest of you... Oh, one more or less makes no difference to me! But, all the same, this one's a bit too pushing. And I am appealing to your sense of kindness. Rid me of the fellow, do... Half-a-dozen of your satellites and the two who are pacing up and down outside my house will be enough... Oh, while you're about it, go up to the third floor and rope in my cook as well... She's the famous Victoire: you know, Master Lupin's old nurse... And, look here, one more tip, to show you how I love you: send a squad of men to the Rue Chateaubriand, at the corner of the Rue Balzac... That's where our national hero lives, under the name of Michel Beaumont... Do you twig, old cockalorum? And now to business. Hustle!"

When Daubrecq turned his head, Lupin was standing up, with clenched fists. His burst of admiration had not survived the rest of the speech and the revelations which Daubrecq had made about Victoire and the flat in the Rue Chateaubriand. The humiliation was too great; and Lupin no longer bothered to play the part of the small general practitioner. He had but one idea in his head: not to give way to the tremendous fit of rage that was urging him to rush at Daubrecq like a bull.

Daubrecq gave the sort of little cluck which, with him, did duty for a laugh. He came waddling up, with his hands in his trouser-pockets, and said, incisively:

"Don't you think that this is all for the best? I've cleared the ground, relieved the situation... At least, we now know where we stand. Lupin versus Daubrecq; and that's all about it. Besides, think of the time saved! Dr. Vernes, the divisional surgeon, would have taken two hours to spin his yarn! Whereas, like this, Master Lupin will be compelled to get his little story told in thirty minutes... unless he wants to get himself collared and his accomplices nabbed. What a shock! What a bolt from the blue! Thirty minutes and not a minute more. In thirty minutes from now, you'll have to clear out, scud away like a hare and beat a disordered retreat. Ha, ha, ha, what fun! I say, Polonius, you really are unlucky, each time you come up against Bibi Daubrecq! For it was you who were hiding behind that curtain, wasn't it, my ill-starred Polonius?"

Lupin did not stir a muscle. The one and only solution that would have calmed his feelings, that is to say, for him to throttle his adversary then and there, was so absurd that he preferred to accept Daubrecq's gibes without attempting to retort, though each of them cut him like the lash of a whip. It was the second time, in the same room and in similar circumstances, that he had to bow before that Daubrecq of misfortune and maintain the most ridiculous attitude in silence. And he felt convinced in his innermost being that, if he opened his mouth, it would be to spit words of anger and insult in his victor's face. What was the good? Was it not essential that he should keep cool and do the things which the new situation called for?

"Well, M. Lupin, well?" resumed the deputy. "You look as if your nose were out of joint. Come, console yourself and admit that one sometimes comes across a joker who's not quite such a mug as his fellows. So you thought that, because I wear spectacles and eye-glasses, I was blind? Bless my soul, I don't say that I at once suspected Lupin behind Polonius and Polonius behind the gentleman who came and bored me in the box at the Vaudeville. No, no! But, all the same, it worried me. I could see that, between the police and Mme. Mergy, there was a third bounder trying to get a finger in the pie. And, gradually, what with the words let fall by the portress, what with watching the movements of my cook and making inquiries about her in the proper quarter, I began to understand. Then, the other night, came the lightning-flash. I heard the row in the house, in spite of my being asleep. I managed to reconstruct the incident, to follow up Mme. Mergy's traces, first, to the Rue Chateaubriand and, afterward, to Saint-Germain... And then... what then? I put different facts together: the Enghien burglary... Gilbert's arrest... the inevitable treaty of alliance between the weeping mother and the leader of the gang... the old nurse installed as cook... all these people entering my house through the doors or through the windows... And I knew what I had to do. Master Lupin was sniffing at the secret. The scent of the Twenty-seven attracted him. I had only to wait for his visit. The hour has arrived. Good-evening, Master Lupin."

Daubrecq paused. He had delivered his speech with the evident satisfaction of a man entitled to claim the appreciation of the most captious critics.

As Lupin did not speak, he took out his watch: "I say! Only twenty-three minutes! How time flies! At this rate, we sha'n't have time to come to an explanation." And, stepping still closer to Lupin, "I'm bound to say, I'm disappointed. I thought that Lupin was a different sort of gentleman. So, the moment he meets a more or less serious adversary, the colossus falls to pieces? Poor young man! Have a glass of water, to bring you round!" Lupin did not utter a word, did not betray a gesture of irritation. With absolute composure, with a precision of movement that showed his perfect self-control and the clear plan of conduct which he had adopted, he gently pushed Daubrecq aside, went to the table and, in his turn, took down the receiver of the telephone:

"I want 565.34, please," he said.

He waited until he was through; and then, speaking in a slow voice and picking out every syllable, he said:

"Hullo!... Rue Chateaubriand?... Is that you, Achille?... Yes, it's the governor. Listen to me carefully, Achille... You must leave the flat! Hullo!... Yes, at once. The police are coming in a few minutes. No, no, don't lose your head... You've got time. Only, do what I tell you. Is your bag still packed?... Good. And is one of the sides empty, as I told you?... Good. Well, go to my bedroom and stand with your face to the chimney-piece. Press with your left hand on the little carved rosette in front of the marble slab, in the middle, and with your right hand on the top of the mantel-shelf. You'll see a sort of drawer, with two little boxes in it. Be careful. One of them contains all our papers; the other, bank-notes and jewellery. Put them both in the empty compartment of the bag. Take the bag in your hand and go as fast as you can, on foot, to the corner of the Avenue Victor-Hugo and the Avenue de Montespan. You'll find the car waiting, with Victoire. I'll join you there... What?... My clothes? My knickknacks?... Never mind about all that... You be off. See you presently."

Lupin quietly pushed away the telephone. Then, taking Daubrecq by the arm, he made him sit in a chair by his side and said:

"And now listen to me, Daubrecq."

"Oho!" grinned the deputy. "Calling each other by our surnames, are we?"

"Yes," said Lupin, "I allowed you to." And, when Daubrecq released his arm with a certain misgiving, he said, "No, don't be afraid. We sha'n't come to blows. Neither of us has anything to gain by doing away with the other. A stab with a knife? What's the good? No, sir! Words, nothing but words. Words that strike home, though. Here are mine: they are plain and to the point. Answer me in the same way, without reflecting: that's far better. The boy?"

"I have him."

"Give him back."

"No."

"Mme. Mergy will kill herself."

"No, she won't."

"I tell you she will."

"And I tell you she will not."

"But she's tried to, once."

"That's just the reason why she won't try again."

"Well, then..."

"No."

Lupin, after a moment, went on:

"I expected that. Also, I thought, on my way here, that you would hardly tumble to the story of Dr. Vernes and that I should have to use other methods."

"Lupin's methods."

"As you say. I had made up my mind to throw off the mask. You pulled it off for me. Well done you! But that doesn't change my plans."

"Speak."

Lupin took from a pocketbook a double sheet of foolscap paper, unfolded it and handed it to Daubrecq, saying:

"Here is an exact, detailed inventory, with consecutive numbers, of the things removed by my friends and myself from your Villa Marie-Therese on the Lac d'Enghien. As you see, there are one hundred and thirteen items. Of those one hundred and thirteen items, sixty-eight, which have a red cross against them, have been sold and sent to America. The remainder, numbering forty-five, are in my possession... until further orders. They happen to be the pick of the bunch. I offer you them in return for the immediate surrender of the child."

Daubrecq could not suppress a movement of surprise:

"Oho!" he said. "You seem very much bent upon it."

"Infinitely," said Lupin, "for I am persuaded that a longer separation from her son will mean death to Mme. Mergy."

"And that upsets you, does it... Lothario?"

"What!"

Lupin planted himself in front of the other and repeated:

"What! What do you mean?"

"Nothing... Nothing... Something that crossed my mind... Clarisse Mergy is a young woman still and a pretty woman at that."

Lupin shrugged his shoulders:

"You brute!" he mumbled. "You imagine that everybody is like yourself, heartless and pitiless. It takes your breath away, what, to think that a shark like me can waste his time playing the Don Quixote? And you wonder what dirty motive I can have? Don't try to find out: it's beyond your powers of perception. Answer me, instead: do you accept?"

"So you're serious?" asked Daubrecq, who seemed but little disturbed by Lupin's contemptuous tone.

"Absolutely. The forty-five pieces are in a shed, of which I will give you the address, and they will be handed over to you, if you call there, at nine o'clock this evening, with the child."

There was no doubt about Daubrecq's reply. To him, the kidnapping of little Jacques had represented only a means of working upon Clarisse Mergy's feelings and perhaps also a warning for her to cease the contest upon which she had engaged. But the threat of a suicide must needs show Daubrecq that he was on the wrong track. That being so, why refuse the favourable bargain which Arsene Lupin was now offering him?

"I accept," he said.

"Here's the address of my shed: 99, Rue Charles-Lafitte, Neuilly. You have only to ring the bell."

"And suppose I send Prasville, the secretary-general, instead?"

"If you send Prasville," Lupin declared, "the place is so arranged that I shall see him coming and that I shall have time to escape, after setting fire to the trusses of hay and straw which surround and conceal your credence-tables, clocks and Gothic virgins."

"But your shed will be burnt down..."

"I don't mind that: the police have their eye on it already. I am leaving it in any case."

"And how am I to know that this is not a trap?"

"Begin by receiving the goods and don't give up the child till afterward. I trust you, you see."

"Good," said Daubrecq; "you've foreseen everything. Very well, you shall have the nipper; the fair Clarisse shall live; and we will all be happy. And now, if I may give you a word of advice, it is to pack off as fast as you can."

"Not yet."

"Eh?"

"I said, not yet."

"But you're mad! Prasville's on his way!"

"He can wait. I've not done."

"Why, what more do you want? Clarisse shall have her brat. Isn't that enough for you?"

"No."

"Why not?"

"There is another son."

"Gilbert."

"Yes."

"Well?"

"I want you to save Gilbert."

"What are you saying? I save Gilbert!"

"You can, if you like; it only means taking a little trouble." Until that moment Daubrecq had remained quite calm. He now suddenly blazed out and, striking the table with his fist:

"No," he cried, "not that! Never! Don't reckon on me!... No, that would be too idiotic!"

He walked up and down, in a state of intense excitement, with that queer step of his, which swayed him from right to left on each of his legs, like a wild beast, a heavy, clumsy bear. And, with a hoarse voice and distorted features, he shouted:

"Let her come here! Let her come and beg for her son's pardon! But let her come unarmed, not with criminal intentions, like last time! Let her come as a supplicant, as a tamed woman, as a submissive woman, who understands and accepts the situation... Gilbert? Gilbert's sentence? The scaffold? Why, that is where my strength lies! What! For more than twenty years have I awaited my hour; and, when that hour strikes, when fortune brings me this unhoped-for chance, when I am at last about to know the joy of a full revenge—and such a revenge!—you think that I will give it up, give up the thing which I have been pursuing for twenty years? I save Gilbert? I? For nothing? For love? I, Daubrecq?... No, no, you can't have studied my features!"

He laughed, with a fierce and hateful laugh. Visibly, he saw before him, within reach of his hand, the prey which he had been hunting down so long. And Lupin also summoned up the vision of Clarisse, as he had seen her several days before, fainting, already beaten, fatally conquered, because all the hostile powers were in league against her.

He contained himself and said:

"Listen to me."

And, when Daubrecq moved away impatiently, he took him by the two shoulders, with that superhuman strength which Daubrecq knew, from having felt it in the box at the Vaudeville, and, holding him motionless in his grip, he said:

"One last word."

"You're wasting your breath," growled the deputy.

"One last word. Listen, Daubrecq: forget Mme. Mergy, give up all the nonsensical and imprudent acts which your pride and your passions are making you commit; put all that on one side and think only of your interest..."

"My interest," said Daubrecq, jestingly, "always coincides with my pride and with what you call my passions."

"Up to the present, perhaps. But not now, not now that I have taken a hand in the business. That constitutes a new factor, which you choose to ignore. You are wrong. Gilbert is my pal. Gilbert is my chum. Gilbert has to be saved from the scaffold. Use your influence to that end, and I swear to you, do you hear, I swear that we will leave you in peace. Gilbert's safety, that's all I ask. You will have no more battles to wage with Mme. Mergy, with me; there will be no more traps laid for you. You will be the master, free to act as you please. Gilbert's safety, Daubrecq! If you refuse..."

"What then?"

"If you refuse, it will be war, relentless war; in other words, a certain defeat for you."

"Meaning thereby..."

"Meaning thereby that I shall take the list of the Twenty-seven from you."

"Rot! You think so, do you?"

"I swear it."

"What Prasville and all his men, what Clarisse Mergy, what nobody has been able to do, you think that you will do!"

"I shall!"

"And why? By favour of what saint will you succeed where everybody else has failed? There must be a reason?"

"There is."

"What is it?"

"My name is Arsene Lupin."

He had let go of Daubrecq, but held him for a time under the dominion of his authoritative glance and will. At last, Daubrecq drew himself up, gave him a couple of sharp taps on the shoulder and, with the same calm, the same intense obstinacy, said:

"And my name's Daubrecq. My whole life has been one desperate battle, one long series of catastrophes and routs in which I spent all my energies until victory came: complete, decisive, crushing, irrevocable victory. I have against me the police, the government, France, the world. What difference do you expect it to make to me if I have M. Arsene Lupin against me into the bargain? I will go further: the more numerous and skilful my enemies, the more cautiously I am obliged to play. And that is why, my dear sir, instead of having you arrested, as I might have done—yes, as I might have done and very easily—I let you remain at large and beg charitably to remind you that you must quit in less than three minutes."

"Then the answer is no?"

"The answer is no."

"You won't do anything for Gilbert?"

"Yes, I shall continue to do what I have been doing since his arrest—that is to say, to exercise indirect influence with the minister of justice, so that the trial may be hurried on and end in the way in which I want to see it end."

"What!" cried Lupin, beside himself with indignation. "It's because of you, it's for you..."

"Yes, it's for me, Daubrecq; yes, by Jove! I have a trump card, the son's head, and I am playing it. When I have procured a nice little death-sentence for Gilbert, when the days go by and Gilbert's petition for a reprieve is rejected by my good offices, you shall see, M. Lupin, that his mummy will drop all her objections to calling herself Mme. Alexis Daubrecq and giving me an unexceptionable pledge of her good-will. That fortunate issue is inevitable, whether you like it or not. It is foredoomed. All I can do for you is to invite you to the wedding and the breakfast. Does that suit you? No? You persist in your sinister designs? Well, good luck, lay your traps, spread your nets, rub up your weapons and grind away at the Complete Foreign-post-paper Burglar's Handbook. You'll need it. And now, good-night. The rules of open-handed and disinterested hospitality demand that I should turn you out of doors. Hop it!"

Lupin remained silent for some time. With his eyes fixed on Daubrecq, he seemed to be taking his adversary's size, gauging his weight, estimating his physical strength, discussing, in fine, in which exact part to attack him. Daubrecq clenched his fists and worked out his plan of defence to meet the attack when it came.

Half a minute passed. Lupin put his hand to his hip-pocket. Daubrecq did the same and grasped the handle of his revolver.

A few seconds more. Coolly, Lupin produced a little gold box of the kind that ladies use for holding sweets, opened it and handed it to Daubrecq:

"A lozenge?"

"What's that?" asked the other, in surprise.

"Cough-drops."

"What for?"

"For the draught you're going to feel!"

And, taking advantage of the momentary fluster into which Daubrecq was thrown by his sally, he quickly took his hat and slipped away.

"Of course," he said, as he crossed the hall, "I am knocked into fits. But all the same, that bit of commercial-traveller's waggery was rather novel, in the circumstances. To expect a pill and receive a cough-drop is by way of being a sort of disappointment. It left the old chimpanzee quite flummoxed."

As he closed the gate, a motor-car drove up and a man sprang out briskly, followed by several others.

Lupin recognized Prasville:

"Monsieur le secretaire-general," he muttered, "your humble servant. I have an idea that, some day, fate will bring us face to face: and I am sorry, for your sake; for you do not inspire me with any particular esteem and you have a bad time before you, on that day. Meanwhile, if I were not in such a hurry, I should wait till you leave and I should follow Daubrecq to find out in whose charge he has placed the child whom he is going to hand back to me. But I am in a hurry. Besides, I can't tell that Daubrecq won't act by telephone. So let us not waste ourselves in vain efforts, but rather join Victoire, Achille and our precious bag."

Two hours later, Lupin, after taking all his measures, was on the lookout in his shed at Neuilly and saw Daubrecq turn out of an adjoining street and walk along with a distrustful air.

Lupin himself opened the double doors:

"Your things are in here, monsieur le depute," he said. "You can go round and look. There is a job-master's yard next door: you have only to ask for a van and a few men. Where is the child?"

Daubrecq first inspected the articles and then took Lupin to the Avenue de Neuilly, where two closely veiled old ladies stood waiting with little Jacques.

Lupin carried the child to his car, where Victoire was waiting for him.

All this was done swiftly, without useless words and as though the parts had been got by heart and the various movements settled in advance, like so many stage entrances and exits.

At ten o'clock in the evening Lupin kept his promise and handed little Jacques to his mother. But the doctor had to be hurriedly called in, for the child, upset by all those happenings, showed great signs of excitement and terror. It was more than a fortnight before he was sufficiently recovered to bear the strain of the removal which Lupin considered necessary. Mme. Mergy herself was only just fit to travel when the time came. The journey took place at night, with every possible precaution and under Lupin's escort.

He took the mother and son to a little seaside place in Brittany and entrusted them to Victoire's care and vigilance.

"At last," he reflected, when he had seen them settled, "there is no one between the Daubrecq bird and me. He can do nothing more to Mme. Mergy and the kid; and she no longer runs the risk of diverting the struggle through her intervention. By Jingo, we have made blunders enough! First, I have had to disclose myself to Daubrecq. Secondly, I have had to surrender my share of the Enghien movables. True, I shall get those back, sooner or later; of that there is not the least doubt. But, all the same, we are not getting on; and, in a week from now, Gilbert and Vaucheray will be up for trial."

What Lupin felt most in the whole business was Daubrecq's revelation of the whereabouts of the flat. The police had entered his place in the Rue Chateaubriand. The identity of Lupin and Michel Beaumont had been recognized and certain papers discovered; and Lupin, while pursuing his aim, while, at the same time, managing various enterprises on which he had embarked, while avoiding the searches of the police, which were becoming more zealous and persistent than ever, had to set to work and reorganize his affairs throughout on a fresh basis.

His rage with Daubrecq, therefore, increased in proportion to the worry which the deputy caused him. He had but one longing, to pocket him, as he put it, to have him at his bidding by fair means or foul, to extract his secret from him. He dreamt of tortures fit to unloose the tongue of the most silent of men. The boot, the rack, red-hot pincers, nailed planks: no form of suffering, he thought, was more than the enemy deserved; and the end to be attained justified every means.

"Oh," he said to himself, "oh, for a decent bench of inquisitors and a couple of bold executioners!... What a time we should have!"

Every afternoon the Growler and the Masher watched the road which Daubrecq took between the Square Lamartine, the Chamber of Deputies and his club. Their instructions were to choose the most deserted street and the most favourable moment and, one evening, to hustle him into a motor-car.

Lupin, on his side, got ready an old building, standing in the middle of a large garden, not far from Paris, which presented all the necessary conditions of safety and isolation and which he called the Monkey's Cage.

Unfortunately, Daubrecq must have suspected something, for every time, so to speak, he changed his route, or took the underground or a tram; and the cage remained unoccupied.

Lupin devised another plan. He sent to Marseilles for one of his associates, an elderly retired grocer called Brindebois, who happened to live in Daubrecq's electoral district and interested himself in politics. Old Brindebois wrote to Daubrecq from Marseilles, announcing his visit. Daubrecq gave this important constituent a hearty welcome, and a dinner was arranged for the following week.

The elector suggested a little restaurant on the left bank of the Seine, where the food, he said, was something wonderful. Daubrecq accepted.

This was what Lupin wanted. The proprietor of the restaurant was one of his friends. The attempt, which was to take place on the following Thursday, was this time bound to succeed.

Meanwhile, on the Monday of the same week, the trial of Gilbert and Vaucheray opened.

The reader will remember—and the case took place too recently for me to recapitulate its details—the really incomprehensible partiality which the presiding judge showed in his cross-examination of Gilbert. The thing was noticed and severely criticised at the time. Lupin recognized Daubrecq's hateful influence.

The attitude observed by the two prisoners differed greatly. Vaucheray was gloomy, silent, hard-faced. He cynically, in curt, sneering, almost defiant phrases, admitted the crimes of which he had formerly been guilty. But, with an inconsistency which puzzled everybody except Lupin, he denied any participation in the murder of Leonard the valet and violently accused Gilbert. His object, in thus linking his fate with Gilbert's, was to force Lupin to take identical measures for the rescue of both his accomplices.

Gilbert, on the other hand, whose frank countenance and dreamy, melancholy eyes won every sympathy, was unable to protect himself against the traps laid for him by the judge or to counteract Vaucheray's lies. He burst into tears, talked too much, or else did not talk when he should have talked. Moreover, his counsel, one of the Leaders of the bar, was taken ill at the last moment—and here again Lupin saw the hand of Daubrecq—and he was replaced by a junior who spoke badly, muddied the whole case, set the jury against him and failed to wipe out the impression produced by the speeches of the advocate-general and of Vaucheray's counsel.

Lupin, who had the inconceivable audacity to be present on the last day of the trial, the Thursday, had no doubt as to the result. A verdict of guilty was certain in both cases.

It was certain because all the efforts of the prosecution, thus supporting Vaucheray's tactics, had tended to link the two prisoners closely together. It was certain, also and above all, because it concerned two of Lupin's accomplices. From the opening of the inquiry before the magistrate until the delivery of the verdict, all the proceedings had been directed against Lupin; and this in spite of the fact that the prosecution, for want of sufficient evidence and also in order not to scatter its efforts over too wide an area, had decided not to include Lupin in the indictment. He was the adversary aimed at, the leader who must be punished in the person of his friends, the famous and popular scoundrel whose fascination in the eyes of the crowd must be destroyed for good and all. With Gilbert and Vaucheray executed, Lupin's halo would fade away and the legend would be exploded.

Lupin... Lupin... Arsene Lupin: it was the one name heard throughout the four days. The advocate-general, the presiding judge, the jury, the counsel, the witnesses had no other words on their lips. Every moment, Lupin was mentioned and cursed at, scoffed at, insulted and held responsible for all the crimes committed. It was as though Gilbert and Vaucheray figured only as supernumeraries, while the real criminal undergoing trial was he, Lupin, Master Lupin, Lupin the burglar, the leader of a gang of thieves, the forger, the incendiary, the hardened offender, the ex-convict, Lupin the murderer, Lupin stained with the blood of his victim, Lupin lurking in the shade, like a coward, after sending his friends to the foot of the scaffold.

"Oh, the rascals know what they're about!" he muttered. "It's my debt which they are making my poor old Gilbert pay."

And the terrible tragedy went on.

At seven o'clock in the evening, after a long deliberation, the jury returned to court and the foreman read out the answers to the questions put from the bench. The answer was "Yes" to every count of the indictment, a verdict of guilty without extenuating circumstances.

The prisoners were brought in. Standing up, but staggering and white-faced, they received their sentence of death.

And, amid the great, solemn silence, in which the anxiety of the onlookers was mingled with pity, the assize-president asked:

"Have you anything more to say, Vaucheray?"

"Nothing, monsieur le president. Now that my mate is sentenced as well as myself, I am easy... We are both on the same footing... The governor must find a way to save the two of us."

"The governor?"

"Yes, Arsene Lupin."

There was a laugh among the crowd.

The president asked:

"And you, Gilbert?"

Tears streamed down the poor lad's cheeks and he stammered a few inarticulate sentences. But, when the judge repeated his question, he succeeded in mastering himself and replied, in a trembling voice:

"I wish to say, monsieur le president, that I am guilty of many things, that's true... I have done a lot of harm... But, all the same, not this. No, I have not committed murder... I have never committed murder... And I don't want to die... it would be too horrible..."

He swayed from side to side, supported by the warders, and he was heard to cry, like a child calling for help:

"Governor... save me!... Save me!... I don't want to die!"

Then, in the crowd, amid the general excitement, a voice rose above the surrounding clamour:

"Don't be afraid, little 'un!... The governor's here!"

A tumult and hustling followed. The municipal guards and the policemen rushed into court and laid hold of a big, red-faced man, who was stated by his neighbours to be the author of that outburst and who struggled hand and foot.

Questioned without delay, he gave his name, Philippe Bonel, an undertaker's man, and declared that some one sitting beside him had offered him a hundred-franc note if he would consent, at the proper moment, to shout a few words which his neighbour scribbled on a bit of paper. How could he refuse?

In proof of his statements, he produced the hundred-franc note and the scrap of paper.

Philippe Bonel was let go.

Meanwhile, Lupin, who of course had assisted energetically in the individual's arrest and handed him over to the guards, left the law-courts, his heart heavy with anguish. His car was waiting for him on the quay. He flung himself into it, in despair, seized with so great a sorrow that he had to make an effort to restrain his tears. Gilbert's cry, his voice wrung with affliction, his distorted features, his tottering frame: all this haunted his brain; and he felt as if he would never, for a single second, forget those impressions.

He drove home to the new place which he had selected among his different residences and which occupied a corner of the Place de Clichy. He expected to find the Growler and the Masher, with whom he was to kidnap Daubrecq that evening. But he had hardly opened the door of his flat, when a cry escaped him: Clarisse stood before him; Clarisse, who had returned from Brittany at the moment of the verdict.

He at once gathered from her attitude and her pallor that she knew. And, at once, recovering his courage in her presence, without giving her time to speak, he exclaimed:

"Yes, yes, yes... but it doesn't matter. We foresaw that. We couldn't prevent it. What we have to do is to stop the mischief. And to-night, you understand, to-night, the thing will be done."

Motionless and tragic in her sorrow, she stammered:

"To-night?"

"Yes. I have prepared everything. In two hours, Daubrecq will be in my hands. To-night, whatever means I have to employ, he shall speak."

"Do you mean that?" she asked, faintly, while a ray of hope began to light up her face.

"He shall speak. I shall have his secret. I shall tear the list of the Twenty-seven from him. And that list will set your son free."

"Too late," Clarisse murmured.

"Too late? Why? Do you think that, in exchange for such a document, I shall not obtain Gilbert's pretended escape?... Why, Gilbert will be at liberty in three days! In three days..."

He was interrupted by a ring at the bell:

"Listen, here are our friends. Trust me. Remember that I keep my promises. I gave you back your little Jacques. I shall give you back Gilbert."

He went to let the Growler and the Masher in and said:

"Is everything ready? Is old Brindebois at the restaurant? Quick, let us be off!"

"It's no use, governor," replied the Masher.

"No use? What do you mean?"

"There's news."

"What news? Speak, man!"

"Daubrecq has disappeared."

"Eh? What's that? Daubrecq disappeared?"

"Yes, carried off from his house, in broad daylight."

"The devil! By whom?"

"Nobody knows... four men... there were pistols fired... The police are on the spot. Prasville is directing the investigations."

Lupin did not move a limb. He looked at Clarisse Mergy, who lay huddled in a chair.

He himself had to bow his head. Daubrecq carried off meant one more chance of success lost...

VII. THE PROFILE OF NAPOLEON

Soon as the prefect of police, the chief of the criminal-investigation department and the examining-magistrates had left Daubrecq's house, after a preliminary and entirely fruitless inquiry, Prasville resumed his personal search.

He was examining the study and the traces of the struggle which had taken place there, when the portress brought him a visiting-card, with a few words in pencil scribbled upon it.

"Show the lady in," he said.

"The lady has some one with her," said the portress.

"Oh? Well, show the other person in as well."

Clarisse Mergy entered at once and introduced the gentleman with her, a gentleman in a black frock-coat, which was too tight for him and which looked as though it had not been brushed for ages. He was shy in his manner and seemed greatly embarrassed how to dispose of his old, rusty top-hat, his gingham umbrella, his one and only glove and his body generally.

"M. Nicole," said Clarisse, "a private teacher, who is acting as tutor to my little Jacques. M. Nicole has been of the greatest help to me with his advice during the past year. He worked out the whole story of the crystal stopper. I should like him, as well as myself—if you see no objection to telling me—to know the details of this kidnapping business, which alarms me and upsets my plans; yours too, I expect?"

Prasville had every confidence in Clarisse Mergy. He knew her relentless hatred of Daubrecq and appreciated the assistance which she had rendered in the case. He therefore made no difficulties about telling her what he knew, thanks to certain clues and especially to the evidence of the portress.

For that matter, the thing was exceedingly simple. Daubrecq, who had attended the trial of Gilbert and Vaucheray as a witness and who was seen in court during the speeches, returned home at six o'clock. The portress affirmed that he came in alone and that there was nobody in the house at the time. Nevertheless, a few minutes later, she heard shouts, followed by the sound of a struggle and two pistol-shots; and from her lodge she saw four masked men scuttle down the front steps, carrying Daubrecq the deputy, and hurry toward the gate. They opened the gate. At the same moment, a motor-car arrived outside the house. The four men bundled themselves into it; and the motor-car, which had hardly had time to stop, set off at full speed.

"Were there not always two policemen on duty?" asked Clarisse.

"They were there," said Prasville, "but at a hundred and fifty yards' distance; and Daubrecq was carried off so quickly that they were unable to interfere, although they hastened up as fast as they could."

"And did they discover nothing, find nothing?"

"Nothing, or hardly anything... Merely this."

"What is that?"

"A little piece of ivory, which they picked up on the ground. There was a fifth party in the car; and the portress saw him get down while the others were hoisting Daubrecq in. As he was stepping back into the car, he dropped something and picked it up again at once. But the thing, whatever it was, must have been broken on the pavement; for this is the bit of ivory which my men found."

"But how did the four men manage to enter the house?" asked Clarisse.

"By means of false keys, evidently, while the portress was doing her shopping, in the course of the afternoon; and they had no difficulty in secreting themselves, as Daubrecq keeps no other servants. I have every reason to believe that they hid in the room next door, which is the dining-room, and afterward attacked Daubrecq here, in the study. The disturbance of the furniture and other articles proves how violent the struggle was. We found a large-bore revolver, belonging to Daubrecq, on the carpet. One of the bullets had smashed the glass over the mantel-piece, as you see."

Clarisse turned to her companion for him to express an opinion. But M. Nicole, with his eyes obstinately lowered, had not budged from his chair and sat fumbling at the rim of his hat, as though he had not yet found a proper place for it.

Prasville gave a smile. It was evident that he did not look upon Clarisse's adviser as a man of first-rate intelligence:

"The case is somewhat puzzling, monsieur," he said, "is it not?"

"Yes... yes," M. Nicole confessed, "most puzzling."

"Then you have no little theory of your own upon the matter?"

"Well, monsieur le secretaire-general, I'm thinking that Daubrecq has many enemies."

"Ah, capital!"

"And that several of those enemies, who are interested in his disappearance, must have banded themselves against him."

"Capital, capital!" said Prasville, with satirical approval. "Capital! Everything is becoming clear as daylight. It only remains for you to furnish us with a little suggestion that will enable us to turn our search in the right direction."

"Don't you think, monsieur le secretaire-general, that this broken bit of ivory which was picked up on the ground..."

"No, M. Nicole, no. That bit of ivory belongs to something which we do not know and which its owner will at once make it his business to conceal. In order to trace the owner, we should at least be able to define the nature of the thing itself."

M. Nicole reflected and then began:

"Monsieur le secretaire-general, when Napoleon I fell from power..."

"Oh, M. Nicole, oh, a lesson in French history!"

"Only a sentence, monsieur le secretaire-general, just one sentence which I will ask your leave to complete. When Napoleon I fell from power, the Restoration placed a certain number of officers on half-pay. These officers were suspected by the authorities and kept under observation by the police. They remained faithful to the emperor's memory; and they contrived to reproduce the features of their idol on all sorts of objects of everyday use; snuff-boxes, rings, breast-pins, pen-knives and so on."

"Well?"

"Well, this bit comes from a walking-stick, or rather a sort of loaded cane, or life-preserver, the knob of which is formed of a piece of carved ivory. When you look at the knob in a certain way, you end by seeing that the outline represents the profile of the Little Corporal. What you have in your hand, monsieur le secretaire-general, is a bit of the ivory knob at the top of a half-pay officer's life-preserver."

"Yes," said Prasville, examining the exhibit, "yes, I can make out a profile... but I don't see the inference..."

"The inference is very simple. Among Daubrecq's victims, among those whose names are inscribed on the famous list, is the descendant of a Corsican family in Napoleon's service, which derived its wealth and title from the emperor and was afterward ruined under the Restoration. It is ten to one that this descendant, who was the leader of the Bonapartist party a few years ago, was the fifth person hiding in the motor-car. Need I state his name?"

"The Marquis d'Albufex?" said Prasville.

"The Marquis d'Albufex," said M. Nicole.

M. Nicole, who no longer seemed in the least worried with his hat, his glove and his umbrella, rose and said to Prasville:

"Monsieur le secretaire-general, I might have kept my discovery to myself, and not told you of it until after the final victory, that is, after bringing you the list of the Twenty-seven. But matters are urgent. Daubrecq's disappearance, contrary to what his kidnappers expect, may hasten on the catastrophe which you wish to avert. We must therefore act with all speed. Monsieur le secretaire-general, I ask for your immediate and practical assistance."

"In what way can I help you?" asked Prasville, who was beginning to be impressed by his quaint visitor.

"By giving me, to-morrow, those particulars about the Marquis d'Albufex which it would take me personally several days to collect."

Prasville seemed to hesitate and turned his head toward Mme. Mergy. Clarisse said:

"I beg of you to accept M. Nicole's services. He is an invaluable and devoted ally. I will answer for him as I would for myself."

"What particulars do you require, monsieur?" asked Prasville.

"Everything that concerns the Marquis d'Albufex: the position of his family, the way in which he spends his time, his family connections, the properties which he owns in Paris and in the country."

Prasville objected:

"After all, whether it's the marquis or another, Daubrecq's kidnapper is working on our behalf, seeing that, by capturing the list, he disarms Daubrecq."

"And who says, monsieur le secretaire-general, that he is not working on his own behalf?"

"That is not possible, as his name is on the list."

"And suppose he erases it? Suppose you then find yourself dealing with a second blackmailer, even more grasping and more powerful than the first and one who, as a political adversary, is in a better position than Daubrecq to maintain the contest?"

The secretary-general was struck by the argument. After a moment's thought, he said:

"Come and see me in my office at four o'clock tomorrow. I will give you the particulars. What is your address, in case I should want you?"

"M. Nicole, 25, Place de Clichy. I am staying at a friend's flat, which he has lent me during his absence."

The interview was at an end. M. Nicole thanked the secretary-general, with a very low bow, and walked out, accompanied by Mme. Mergy:

"That's an excellent piece of work," he said, outside, rubbing his hands. "I can march into the police-office whenever I like, and set the whole lot to work."

Mme. Mergy, who was less hopefully inclined, said:

"Alas, will you be in time? What terrifies me is the thought that the list may be destroyed."

"Goodness gracious me, by whom? By Daubrecq?"

"No, but by the marquis, when he gets hold of it."

"He hasn't got it yet! Daubrecq will resist long enough, at any rate, for us to reach him. Just think! Prasville is at my orders!"

"Suppose he discovers who you are? The least inquiry will prove that there is no such person as M. Nicole."

"But it will not prove that M. Nicole is the same person as Arsene Lupin. Besides, make yourself easy. Prasville is not only beneath contempt as a detective: he has but one aim in life, which is to destroy his old enemy, Daubrecq. To achieve that aim, all means are equally good; and he will not waste time in verifying the identity of a M. Nicole who promises him Daubrecq. Not to mention that I was brought by you and that, when all is said, my little gifts did dazzle him to some extent. So let us go ahead boldly."

Clarisse always recovered confidence in Lupin's presence. The future seemed less appalling to her; and she admitted, she forced herself to admit, that the chances of saving Gilbert were not lessened by that hideous death-sentence. But he could not prevail upon her to return to Brittany. She wanted to fight by his side. She wanted to be there and share all his hopes and all his disappointments.

The next day the inquiries of the police confirmed what Prasville and Lupin already knew. The Marquis d'Albufex had been very deeply involved in the business of the canal, so deeply that Prince Napoleon was obliged to remove him from the management of his political campaign in France; and he kept up his very extravagant style of living only by dint of constant loans and makeshifts. On the other hand, in so far as concerned the kidnapping of Daubrecq, it was ascertained that, contrary to his usual custom, the marquis had not appeared in his club between six and seven that evening and had not dined at home. He did not come back until midnight; and then he came on foot.

M. Nicole's accusation, therefore, was receiving an early proof. Unfortunately—and Lupin was no more successful in his own attempts—it was impossible to obtain the least clue as to the motor-car, the chauffeur and the four people who had entered Daubrecq's house. Were they associates of the marquis, compromised in the canal affair like himself? Were they men in his pay? Nobody knew.

The whole search, consequently, had to be concentrated upon the marquis and the country-seats and houses which he might possess at a certain distance from Paris, a distance which, allowing for the average speed of a motor-car and the inevitable stoppages, could be put at sixty to ninety miles.

Now d'Albufex, having sold everything that he ever had, possessed neither country-houses nor landed estates.

They turned their attention to the marquis' relations and intimate friends. Was he able on this side to dispose of some safe retreat in which to imprison Daubrecq?

The result was equally fruitless.

And the days passed. And what days for Clarisse Mergy! Each of them brought Gilbert nearer to the terrible day of reckoning. Each of them meant twenty-four hours less from the date which Clarisse had instinctively fixed in her mind. And she said to Lupin, who was racked with the same anxiety:

"Fifty-five days more... Fifty days more... What can one do in so few days?... Oh, I beg of you... I beg of you..."

What could they do indeed? Lupin, who would not leave the task of watching the marquis to any one but himself, practically lived without sleeping. But the marquis had resumed his regular life; and, doubtless suspecting something, did not risk going away.

Once alone, he went down to the Duc de Montmaur's, in the daytime. The duke kept a pack of boar-hounds, with which he hunted the Forest of Durlaine. D'Albufex maintained no relations with him outside the hunt.

"It is hardly likely," said Prasville, "that the Duc de Montmaur, an exceedingly wealthy man, who is interested only in his estates and his hunting and takes no part in politics, should lend himself to the illegal detention of Daubrecq the deputy in his chateau."

Lupin agreed; but, as he did not wish to leave anything to chance, the next week, seeing d'Albufex go out one morning in riding-dress, he followed him to the Gare du Nord and took the same train.

He got out at Aumale, where d'Albufex found a carriage at the station which took him to the Chateau de Montmaur.

Lupin lunched quietly, hired a bicycle and came in view of the house at the moment when the guests were going into the park, in motor-cars or mounted. The Marquis d'Albufex was one of the horsemen.

Thrice, in the course of the day, Lupin saw him cantering along. And he found him, in the evening, at the station, where d'Albufex rode up, followed by a huntsman.

The proof, therefore, was conclusive; and there was nothing suspicious on that side. Why did Lupin, nevertheless, resolve not to be satisfied with appearances? And why, next day, did he send the Masher to find out things in the neighbourhood of Montmaur? It was an additional precaution, based upon no logical reason, but agreeing with his methodical and careful manner of acting.

Two days later he received from the Masher, among other information of less importance, a list of the house-party at Montmaur and of all the servants and keepers.

One name struck him, among those of the huntsmen. He at once wired:

"Inquire about huntsman Sebastiani."

The Masher's answer was received the next day:

"Sebastiani, a Corsican, was recommended to the Duc de Montmaur by the Marquis d'Albufex. He lives at two or three miles from the house, in a hunting-lodge built among the ruins of the feudal stronghold which was the cradle of the Montmaur family."

"That's it," said Lupin to Clarisse Mergy, showing her the Masher's letter. "That name, Sebastiani, at once reminded me that d'Albufex is of Corsican descent. There was a connection..."

"Then what do you intend to do?"

"If Daubrecq is imprisoned in those ruins, I intend to enter into communication with him."

"He will distrust you."

"No. Lately, acting on the information of the police, I ended by discovering the two old ladies who carried off your little Jacques at Saint-Germain and who brought him, the same evening, to Neuilly. They are two old maids, cousins of Daubrecq, who makes them a small monthly allowance. I have been to call on those Demoiselles Rousselot; remember the name and the address: 134 bis, Rue du Bac. I inspired them with confidence, promised them to find their cousin and benefactor; and the elder sister, Euphrasie Rousselot, gave me a letter in which she begs Daubrecq to trust M. Nicole entirely. So you see, I have taken every precaution. I shall leave to-night."

"We, you mean," said Clarisse.

"You!"

"Can I go on living like this, in feverish inaction?" And she whispered, "I am no longer counting the days, the thirty-eight or forty days that remain to us: I am counting the hours."

Lupin felt that her resolution was too strong for him to try to combat it. They both started at five o'clock in the morning, by motor-car. The Growler went with them.

So as not to arouse suspicion, Lupin chose a large town as his headquarters. At Amiens, where he installed Clarisse, he was only eighteen miles from Montmaur.

At eight o'clock he met the Masher not far from the old fortress, which was known in the neighbourhood by the name of Mortepierre, and he examined the locality under his guidance.

On the confines of the forest, the little river Ligier, which has dug itself a deep valley at this spot, forms a loop which is overhung by the enormous cliff of Mortepierre.

"Nothing to be done on this side," said Lupin. "The cliff is steep, over two hundred feet high, and the river hugs it all round."

Not far away they found a bridge that led to the foot of a path which wound, through the oaks and pines, up to a little esplanade, where stood a massive, iron-bound gate, studded with nails and flanked on either side by a large tower.

"Is this where Sebastiani the huntsman lives?" asked Lupin.

"Yes," said the Masher, "with his wife, in a lodge standing in the midst of the ruins. I also learnt that he has three tall sons and that all the four were supposed to be away for a holiday on the day when Daubrecq was carried off."

"Oho!" said Lupin. "The coincidence is worth remembering. It seems likely enough that the business was done by those chaps and their father."

Toward the end of the afternoon Lupin availed himself of a breach to the right of the towers to scale the curtain. From there he was able to see the huntsman's lodge and the few remains of the old fortress: here, a bit of wall, suggesting the mantel of a chimney; further away, a water-tank; on this side, the arches of a chapel; on the other, a heap of fallen stones.

A patrol-path edged the cliff in front; and, at one of the ends of this patrol-path, there were the remains of a formidable donjon-keep razed almost level with the ground.

Lupin returned to Clarisse Mergy in the evening. And from that time he went backward and forward between Amiens and Mortepierre, leaving the Growler and the Masher permanently on the watch.

And six days passed. Sebastiani's habits seemed to be subject solely to the duties of his post. He used to go up to the Chateau de Montmaur, walk about in the forest, note the tracks of the game and go his rounds at night.

But, on the seventh day, learning that there was to be a meet and that a carriage had been sent to Aumale Station in the morning, Lupin took up his post in a cluster of box and laurels which surrounded the little esplanade in front of the gate.

At two o'clock he heard the pack give tongue. They approached, accompanied by hunting-cries, and then drew farther away. He heard them again, about the middle of the afternoon, not quite so distinctly; and that was all. But suddenly, amid the silence, the sound of galloping horses reached his ears; and, a few minutes later, he saw two riders climbing the river-path.

He recognized the Marquis d'Albufex and Sebastiani. On reaching the esplanade, they both alighted; and a woman—the huntsman's wife, no doubt—opened the gate. Sebastiani fastened the horses' bridles to rings fixed on a post at a few yards from Lupin and ran to join the marquis. The gate closed behind them.

Lupin did not hesitate; and, though it was still broad daylight, relying upon the solitude of the place, he hoisted himself to the hollow of the breach. Passing his head through cautiously, he saw the two men and Sebastiani's wife hurrying toward the ruins of the keep.

The huntsman drew aside a hanging screen of ivy and revealed the entrance to a stairway, which he went down, as did d'Albufex, leaving his wife on guard on the terrace.

There was no question of going in after them; and Lupin returned to his hiding-place. He did not wait long before the gate opened again.

The Marquis d'Albufex seemed in a great rage. He was striking the leg of his boot with his whip and mumbling angry words which Lupin was able to distinguish when the distance became less great:

"Ah, the hound!... I'll make him speak... I'll come back to-night... to-night, at ten o'clock, do you hear, Sebastiani?... And we shall do what's necessary... Oh, the brute!"

Sebastiani unfastened the horses. D'Albufex turned to the woman:

"See that your sons keep a good watch... If any one attempts to deliver him, so much the worse for him. The trapdoor is there. Can I rely upon them?"

"As thoroughly as on myself, monsieur le marquis," declared the huntsman. "They know what monsieur le marquis has done for me and what he means to do for them. They will shrink at nothing."

"Let us mount and get back to the hounds," said d'Albufex.

So things were going as Lupin had supposed. During these runs, d'Albufex, taking a line of his own, would push off to Mortepierre, without anybody's suspecting his trick. Sebastiani, who was devoted to him body and soul, for reasons connected with the past into which it was not worth while to inquire, accompanied him; and together they went to see the captive, who was closely watched by the huntsman's wife and his three sons.

"That's where we stand," said Lupin to Clarisse Mergy, when he joined her at a neighbouring inn. "This evening the marquis will put Daubrecq to the question—a little brutally, but indispensably—as I intended to do myself."

"And Daubrecq will give up his secret," said Clarisse, already quite upset.

"I'm afraid so."

"Then..."

"I am hesitating between two plans," said Lupin, who seemed very calm. "Either to prevent the interview..."

"How?"

"By forestalling d'Albufex. At nine o'clock, the Growler, the Masher and I climb the ramparts, burst into the fortress, attack the keep, disarm the garrison... and the thing's done: Daubrecq is ours."

"Unless Sebastiani's sons fling him through the trapdoor to which the marquis alluded..."

"For that reason," said Lupin, "I intend to risk that violent measure only as a last resort and in case my other plan should not be practicable."

"What is the other plan?"

"To witness the interview. If Daubrecq does not speak, it will give us the time to prepare to carry him off under more favourable conditions. If he speaks, if they compel him to reveal the place where the list of the Twenty-seven is hidden, I shall know the truth at the same time as d'Albufex, and I swear to God that I shall turn it to account before he does."

"Yes, yes," said Clarisse. "But how do you propose to be present?"

"I don't know yet," Lupin confessed. "It depends on certain particulars which the Masher is to bring me and on some which I shall find out for myself."

He left the inn and did not return until an hour later as night was falling. The Masher joined him.

"Have you the little book?" asked Lupin.

"Yes, governor. It was what I saw at the Aumale newspaper-shop. I got it for ten sous."

"Give it me."

The Masher handed him an old, soiled, torn pamphlet, entitled, on the cover, A Visit to Mortepierre, 1824, with plans and illustrations.

Lupin at once looked for the plan of the donjon-keep.

"That's it," he said. "Above the ground were three stories, which have been razed, and below the ground, dug out of the rock, two stories, one of which was blocked up by the rubbish, while the other... There, that's where our friend Daubrecq lies. The name is significant: the torture-chamber... Poor, dear friend!... Between the staircase and the torture-chamber, two doors. Between those two doors, a recess in which the three brothers obviously sit, gun in hand."

"So it is impossible for you to get in that way without being seen."

"Impossible... unless I come from above, by the story that has fallen in, and look for a means of entrance through the ceiling... But that is very risky..."

He continued to turn the pages of the book. Clarisse asked:

"Is there no window to the room?"

"Yes," he said. "From below, from the river—I have just been there—you can see a little opening, which is also marked on the plan. But it is fifty yards up, sheer; and even then the rock overhangs the water. So that again is out of the question."

He glanced through a few pages of the book. The title of one chapter struck him: The Lovers' Towers. He read the opening lines:

"In the old days, the donjon was known to the people of the neighbourhood as the Lovers' Tower, in memory of a fatal tragedy that marked it in the Middle Ages. The Comte de Mortepierre, having received proofs of his wife's faithlessness, imprisoned her in the torture-chamber, where she spent twenty years. One night, her lover, the Sire de Tancarville, with reckless courage, set up a ladder in the river and then clambered up the face of the cliff till he came to the window of the room. After filing the bars, he succeeded in releasing the woman he loved and bringing her down with him by means of a rope. They both reached the top of the ladder, which was watched by his friends, when a shot was fired from the patrol-path and hit the man in the shoulder. The two lovers were hurled into space...."

There was a pause, after he had read this, a long pause during which each of them drew a mental picture of the tragic escape. So, three or four centuries earlier, a man, risking his life, had attempted that surprising feat and would have succeeded but for the vigilance of some sentry who heard the noise. A man had ventured! A man had dared! A man done it!

Lupin raised his eyes to Clarisse. She was looking at him... with such a desperate, such a beseeching look! The look of a mother who demanded the impossible and who would have sacrificed anything to save her son.

"Masher," he said, "get a strong rope, but very slender, so that I can roll it round my waist, and very long: fifty or sixty yards. You, Growler, go and look for three or four ladders and fasten them end to end."

"Why, what are you thinking of, governor?" cried the two accomplices. "What, you mean to... But it's madness!"

"Madness? Why? What another has done I can do."

"But it's a hundred chances to one that you break your neck."

"Well, you see, Masher, there's one chance that I don't."

"But, governor..."

"That's enough, my friends. Meet me in an hour on the river-bank."

The preparations took long in the making. It was difficult to find the material for a fifty-foot ladder that would reach the first ledge of the cliff; and it required an endless effort and care to join the different sections.

At last, a little after nine o'clock, it was set up in the middle of the river and held in position by a boat, the bows of which were wedged between two of the rungs, while the stern was rammed into the bank.

The road through the river-valley was little used, and nobody came to interrupt the work. The night was dark, the sky heavy with moveless clouds.

Lupin gave the Masher and the Growler their final instructions and said, with a laugh:

"I can't tell you how amused I am at the thought of seeing Daubrecq's face when they proceed to take his scalp or slice his skin into ribbons. Upon my word, it's worth the journey."

Clarisse also had taken a seat in the boat. He said to her:

"Until we meet again. And, above all, don't stir. Whatever happens, not a movement, not a cry."

"Can anything happen?" she asked.

"Why, remember the Sire de Tancarville! It was at the very moment when he was achieving his object, with his true love in his arms, that an accident betrayed him. But be easy: I shall be all right."

She made no reply. She seized his hand and grasped it warmly between her own.

He put his foot on the ladder and made sure that it did not sway too much. Then he went up.

He soon reached the top rung.

This was where the dangerous ascent began, a difficult ascent at the start, because of the excessive steepness, and developing, mid-way, into an absolute escalade.

Fortunately, here and there were little hollows, in which his feet found a resting-place, and projecting stones, to which his hands clung. But twice those stones gave way and he slipped; and twice he firmly believed that all was lost. Finding a deeper hollow, he took a rest. He was worn out, felt quite ready to throw up the enterprise, asked himself if it was really worth while for him to expose himself to such danger:

"I say!" he thought. "Seems to me you're showing the white feather, Lupin, old boy. Throw up the enterprise? Then Daubrecq will babble his secret, the marquis will possess himself of the list, Lupin will return empty-handed, and Gilbert..."

The long rope which he had fastened round his waist caused him needless inconvenience and fatigue. He fixed one of the ends to the strap of his trousers and let the rope uncoil all the way down the ascent, so that he could use it, on returning, as a hand-rail.

Then he once more clutched at the rough surface of the cliff and continued the climb, with bruised nails and bleeding fingers. At every moment he expected the inevitable fall. And what discouraged him most was to hear the murmur of voices rising from the boat, murmur so distinct that it seemed as though he were not increasing the distance between his companions and himself.

And he remembered the Sire de Tancarville, alone, he too, amid the darkness, who must have shivered at the noise of the stones which he loosened and sent bounding down the cliff. How the least sound reverberated through the silence! If one of Daubrecq's guards was peering into the gloom from the Lovers' Tower, it meant a shot... and death.

And he climbed... he climbed... He had climbed so long that he ended by imagining that the goal was passed. Beyond a doubt, he had slanted unawares to the right or left and he would finish at the patrol-path. What a stupid upshot! And what other upshot could there be to an attempt which the swift force of events had not allowed him to study and prepare?

Madly, he redoubled his efforts, raised himself by a number of yards, slipped, recovered the lost ground, clutched a bunch of roots that came loose in his hand, slipped once more and was abandoning the game in despair when, suddenly, stiffening himself and contracting his whole frame, his muscles and his will, he stopped still: a sound of voices seemed to issue from the very rock which he was grasping.

He listened. It came from the right. Turning his head, he thought that he saw a ray of light penetrating the darkness of space. By what effort of energy, by what imperceptible movements he succeeded in dragging himself to the spot he was never able exactly to realize. But suddenly he found himself on the ledge of a fairly wide opening, at least three yards deep, which dug into the wall of the cliff like a passage, while its other end, much narrower, was closed by three bars.

Lupin crawled along. His head reached the bars. And he saw...

VIII. THE LOVERS' TOWER

The torture-chamber showed beneath him. It was a large, irregular room, divided into unequal portions by the four wide, massive pillars that supported its arched roof. A smell of damp and mildew came from its walls and from its flags moistened by the water that trickled from without. Its appearance at any time must have been gruesome. But, at that moment, with the tall figures of Sebastiani and his sons, with the slanting gleams of light that fell between the pillars, with the vision of the captive chained down upon the truckle-bed, it assumed a sinister and barbarous aspect.

Daubrecq was in the front part of the room, four or five yards down from the window at which Lupin lurked. In addition to the ancient chains that had been used to fasten him to his bed and to fasten the bed to an iron hook in the wall, his wrists and ankles were girt with leather thongs; and an ingenious arrangement caused his least movement to set in motion a bell hung to the nearest pillar.

A lamp placed on a stool lit him full in the face.

The Marquis d'Albufex was standing beside him. Lupin could see his pale features, his grizzled moustache, his long, lean form as he looked at his prisoner with an expression of content and of gratified hatred.

A few minutes passed in profound silence. Then the marquis gave an order:

"Light those three candles, Sebastiani, so that I can see him better."

And, when the three candles were lit and he had taken a long look at Daubrecq, he stooped over him and said, almost gently:

"I can't say what will be the end of you and me. But at any rate I shall have had some deuced happy moments in this room. You have done me so much harm, Daubrecq! The tears you have made me shed! Yes, real tears, real sobs of despair... The money you have robbed me of! A fortune!... And my terror at the thought that you might give me away! You had but to utter my name to complete my ruin and bring about my disgrace!... Oh, you villain!..."

Daubrecq did not budge. He had been deprived of his black glasses, but still kept his spectacles, which reflected the light from the candles. He had lost a good deal of flesh; and the bones stood out above his sunken cheeks.

"Come along," said d'Albufex. "The time has come to act. It seems that there are rogues prowling about the neighbourhood. Heaven forbid that they are here on your account and try to release you; for that would mean your immediate death, as you know... Is the trapdoor still in working order, Sebastiani?"

Sebastiani came nearer, knelt on one knee and lifted and turned a ring, at the foot of the bed, which Lupin had not noticed. One of the flagstones moved on a pivot, disclosing a black hole.

"You see," the marquis continued, "everything is provided for; and I have all that I want at hand, including dungeons: bottomless dungeons, says the legend of the castle. So there is nothing to hope for, no help of any kind. Will you speak?"

Daubrecq did not reply; and he went on:

"This is the fourth time that I am questioning you, Daubrecq. It is the fourth time that I have troubled to ask you for the document which you possess, in order that I may escape your blackmailing proceedings. It is the fourth time and the last. Will you speak?"

The same silence as before. D'Albufex made a sign to Sebastiani. The huntsman stepped forward, followed by two of his sons. One of them held a stick in his hand.

"Go ahead," said d'Albufex, after waiting a few seconds.

Sebastiani slackened the thongs that bound Daubrecq's wrists and inserted and fixed the stick between the thongs.

"Shall I turn, monsieur le marquis?"

A further silence. The marquis waited. Seeing that Daubrecq did not flinch, he whispered:

"Can't you speak? Why expose yourself to physical suffering?"

No reply.

"Turn away, Sebastiani."

Sebastiani made the stick turn a complete circle. The thongs stretched and tightened. Daubrecq gave a groan.

"You won't speak? Still, you know that I won't give way, that I can't give way, that I hold you and that, if necessary, I shall torture you till you die of it. You won't speak? You won't?... Sebastiani, once more."

The huntsman obeyed. Daubrecq gave a violent start of pain and fell back on his bed with a rattle in his throat.

"You fool!" cried the marquis, shaking with rage. "Why don't you speak? What, haven't you had enough of that list? Surely it's somebody else's turn! Come, speak... Where is it? One word. One word only... and we will leave you in peace... And, to-morrow, when I have the list, you shall be free. Free, do you understand? But, in Heaven's name, speak!... Oh, the brute! Sebastiani, one more turn."

Sebastiani made a fresh effort. The bones cracked.

"Help! Help!" cried Daubrecq, in a hoarse voice, vainly struggling to release himself. And, in a spluttering whisper, "Mercy... mercy."

It was a dreadful sight... The faces of the three sons were horror-struck. Lupin shuddered, sick at heart, and realized that he himself could never have accomplished that abominable thing. He listened for the words that were bound to come. He must learn the truth. Daubrecq's secret was about to be expressed in syllables, in words wrung from him by pain. And Lupin began to think of his retreat, of the car which was waiting for him, of the wild rush to Paris, of the victory at hand.

"Speak," whispered d'Albufex. "Speak and it will be over."

"Yes... yes..." gasped Daubrecq.

"Well...?"

"Later... to-morrow..."

"Oh, you're mad!... What are you talking about: to-morrow?... Sebastiani, another turn!"

"No, no!" yelled Daubrecq. "Stop!"

"Speak!"

"Well, then... the paper... I have hidden the paper..."

But his pain was too great. He raised his head with a last effort, uttered incoherent words, succeeded in twice saying, "Marie... Marie..." and fell back, exhausted and lifeless.

"Let go at once!" said d'Albufex to Sebastiani. "Hang it all, can we have overdone it?"

But a rapid examination showed him that Daubrecq had only fainted. Thereupon, he himself, worn out with the excitement, dropped on the foot of the bed and, wiping the beads of perspiration from his forehead, stammered:

"Oh, what a dirty business!"

"Perhaps that's enough for to-day," said the huntsman, whose rough face betrayed a certain emotion. "We might try again to-morrow or the next day..."

The marquis was silent. One of the sons handed him a flask of brandy. He poured out half a glass and drank it down at a draught:

"To-morrow?" he said. "No. Here and now. One little effort more. At the stage which he has reached, it won't be difficult." And, taking the huntsman aside, "Did you hear what he said? What did he mean by that word, 'Marie'? He repeated it twice."

"Yes, twice," said the huntsman. "Perhaps he entrusted the document to a person called Marie."

"Not he!" protested d'Albufex. "He never entrusts anything to anybody. It means something different."

"But what, monsieur le marquis?"

"We'll soon find out, I'll answer for it."

At that moment, Daubrecq drew a long breath and stirred on his couch.

D'Albufex, who had now recovered all his composure and who did not take his eyes off the enemy, went up to him and said:

"You see, Daubrecq, it's madness to resist... Once you're beaten, there's nothing for it but to submit to your conqueror, instead of allowing yourself to be tortured like an idiot... Come, be sensible."

He turned to Sebastiani:

"Tighten the rope... let him feel it a little that will wake him up... He's shamming death..." Sebastiani took hold of the stick again and turned until the cord touched the swollen flesh. Daubrecq gave a start.

"That'll do, Sebastiani," said the marquis. "Our friend seems favourably disposed and understands the need for coming to terms. That's so, Daubrecq, is it not? You prefer to have done with it? And you're quite right!"

The two men were leaning over the sufferer, Sebastiani with his hand on the stick, d'Albufex holding the lamp so as to throw the light on Daubrecq's face: "His lips are moving... he's going to speak. Loosen the rope a little, Sebastiani: I don't want our friend to be hurt... No, tighten it: I believe our friend is hesitating... One turn more... stop! ... That's done it! Oh, my dear Daubrecq, if you can't speak plainer than that, it's no use! What? What did you say?"

Arsene Lupin muttered an oath. Daubrecq was speaking and he, Lupin, could not hear a word of what he said! In vain, he pricked up his ears, suppressed the beating of his heart and the throbbing of his temples: not a sound reached him.

"Confound it!" he thought. "I never expected this. What am I to do?"

He was within an ace of covering Daubrecq with his revolver and putting a bullet into him which would cut short any explanation. But he reflected that he himself would then be none the wiser and that it was better to trust to events in the hope of making the most of them.

Meanwhile the confession continued beneath him, indistinctly, interrupted by silences and mingled with moans. D'Albufex clung to his prey:

"Go on!... Finish, can't you?..."

And he punctuated the sentences with exclamations of approval:

"Good!... Capital!... Oh, how funny!... And no one suspected?... Not even Prasville?... What an ass!... Loosen a bit, Sebastiani: don't you see that our friend is out of breath?... Keep calm, Daubrecq... don't tire yourself... And so, my dear fellow, you were saying..."

That was the last. There was a long whispering to which d'Albufex listened without further interruption and of which Arsene Lupin could not catch the least syllable. Then the marquis drew himself up and exclaimed, joyfully:

"That's it!... Thank you, Daubrecq. And, believe me, I shall never forget what you have just done. If ever you're in need, you have only to knock at my door and there will always be a crust of bread for you in the kitchen and a glass of water from the filter. Sebastiani, look after monsieur le depute as if he were one of your sons. And, first of all, release him from his bonds. It's a heartless thing to truss one's fellow-man like that, like a chicken on the spit!"

"Shall we give him something to drink?" suggested the huntsman.

"Yes, that's it, give him a drink."

Sebastiani and his sons undid the leather straps, rubbed the bruised wrists, dressed them with an ointment and bandaged them. Then Daubrecq swallowed a few drops of brandy.

"Feeling better?" said the marquis. "Pooh, it's nothing much! In a few hours, it won't show; and you'll be able to boast of having been tortured, as in the good old days of the Inquisition. You lucky dog!"

He took out his watch. "Enough said! Sebastiani, let your sons watch him in turns. You, take me to the station for the last train."

"Then are we to leave him like that, monsieur le marquis, free to move as he pleases?"

"Why not? You don't imagine that we are going to keep him here to the day of his death? No, Daubrecq, sleep quietly. I shall go to your place tomorrow afternoon; and, if the document is where you told me, a telegram shall be sent off at once and you shall be set free. You haven't told me a lie, I suppose?"

He went back to Daubrecq and, stooping over him again:

"No humbug, eh? That would be very silly of you. I should lose a day, that's all. Whereas you would lose all the days that remain to you to live. But no, the hiding-place is too good. A fellow doesn't invent a thing like that for fun. Come on, Sebastiani. You shall have the telegram to-morrow."

"And suppose they don't let you into the house, monsieur le marquis?"

"Why shouldn't they?"

"The house in the Square Lamartine is occupied by Prasville's men."

"Don't worry, Sebastiani. I shall get in. If they don't open the door, there's always the window. And, if the window won't open, I shall arrange with one of Prasville's men. It's a question of money, that's all. And, thank goodness, I shan't be short of that, henceforth! Good-night, Daubrecq."

He went out, accompanied by Sebastiani, and the heavy door closed after them.

Lupin at once effected his retreat, in accordance with a plan which he had worked out during this scene.

The plan was simple enough: to scramble, by means of his rope, to the bottom of the cliff, take his friends with him, jump into the motor-car and attack d'Albufex and Sebastiani on the deserted road that leads to Aumale Station. There could be no doubt about the issue of the contest. With d'Albufex and Sebastiani prisoners; it would be an easy matter to make one of them speak. D'Albufex had shown him how to set about it; and Clarisse Mergy would be inflexible where it was a question of saving her son.

He took the rope with which he had provided himself and groped about to find a jagged piece of rock round which to pass it, so as to leave two equal lengths hanging, by which he could let himself down. But, when he found what he wanted, instead of acting swiftly—for the business was urgent—he stood motionless, thinking. His scheme failed to satisfy him at the last moment.

"It's absurd, what I'm proposing," he said to himself. "Absurd and illogical. How can I tell that d'Albufex and Sebastiani will not escape me? How can I even tell that, once they are in my power, they will speak? No, I shall stay. There are better things to try... much better things. It's not those two I must be at, but Daubrecq. He's done for; he has not a kick left in him. If he has told the marquis his secret, there is no reason why he shouldn't tell it to Clarisse and me, when we employ the same methods. That's settled! We'll kidnap the Daubrecq bird." And he continued, "Besides, what do I risk? If the scheme miscarries, Clarisse and I will rush off to Paris and, together with Prasville, organize a careful watch in the Square Lamartine to prevent d'Albufex from benefiting by Daubrecq's revelations. The great thing is for Prasville to be warned of the danger. He shall be."

The church-clock in a neighbouring village struck twelve. That gave Lupin six or seven hours to put his new plan into execution. He set to work forthwith.

When moving away from the embrasure which had the window at the bottom of it, he had come upon a clump of small shrubs in one of the hollows of the cliff. He cut away a dozen of these, with his knife, and whittled them all down to the same size. Then he cut off two equal lengths from his rope. These were the uprights of the ladder. He fastened the twelve little sticks between the uprights and thus contrived a rope-ladder about six yards long.

When he returned to this post, there was only one of the three sons beside Daubrecq's bed in the torture-chamber. He was smoking his pipe by the lamp. Daubrecq was asleep.

"Hang it!" thought Lupin. "Is the fellow going to sit there all night? In that case, there's nothing for me to do but to slip off..."

The idea that d'Albufex was in possession of the secret vexed him mightily. The interview at which he had assisted had left the clear impression in his mind that the marquis was working "on his own" and that, in securing the list, he intended not only to escape Daubrecq's activity, but also to gain Daubrecq's power and build up his fortune anew by the identical means which Daubrecq had employed.

That would have meant, for Lupin, a fresh battle to wage against a fresh enemy. The rapid march of events did not allow of the contemplation of such a possibility. He must at all costs spike the Marquis d'Albufex' guns by warning Prasville.

However, Lupin remained held back by the stubborn hope of some incident that would give him the opportunity of acting.

The clock struck half-past twelve.

It struck one.

The waiting became terrible, all the more so as an icy mist rose from the valley and Lupin felt the cold penetrate to his very marrow.

He heard the trot of a horse in the distance:

"Sebastiani returning from the station," he thought.

But the son who was watching in the torture-chamber, having finished his packet of tobacco, opened the door and asked his brothers if they had a pipeful for him. They made some reply; and he went out to go to the lodge.

And Lupin was astounded. No sooner was the door closed than Daubrecq, who had been so sound asleep, sat up on his couch, listened, put one foot to the ground, followed by the other, and, standing up, tottering a little, but firmer on his legs than one would have expected, tried his strength.

"Well" said Lupin, "the beggar doesn't take long recovering. He can very well help in his own escape. There's just one point that ruffles me: will he allow himself to be convinced? Will he consent to go with me? Will he not think that this miraculous assistance which comes to him straight from heaven is a trap laid by the marquis?"

But suddenly Lupin remembered the letter which he had made Daubrecq's old cousins write, the letter of recommendation, so to speak, which the elder of the two sisters Rousselot had signed with her Christian name, Euphrasie.

It was in his pocket. He took it and listened. Not a sound, except the faint noise of Daubrecq's footsteps on the flagstones. Lupin considered that the moment had come. He thrust his arm through the bars and threw the letter in.

Daubrecq seemed thunderstruck.

The letter had fluttered through the room and lay on the floor, at three steps from him. Where did it come from? He raised his head toward the window and tried to pierce the darkness that hid all the upper part of the room from his eyes. Then he looked at the envelope, without yet daring to touch it, as though he dreaded a snare. Then, suddenly, after a glance at the door, he stooped briskly, seized the envelope and opened it.

"Ah," he said, with a sigh of delight, when he saw the signature.

He read the letter half-aloud:

"Rely implicitly on the bearer of this note. He has succeeded in discovering the marquis' secret, with the money which we gave him, and has contrived a plan of escape. Everything is prepared for your flight. EUPHRASIE ROUSSELOT"

He read the letter again, repeated, "Euphrasie... Euphrasie..." and raised his head once more.

Lupin whispered:

"It will take me two or three hours to file through one of the bars. Are Sebastiani and his sons coming back?"

"Yes, they are sure to," replied Daubrecq, in the same low voice, "but I expect they will leave me to myself."

"But they sleep next door?"

"Yes."

"Won't they hear?"

"No, the door is too thick."

"Very well. In that case, it will soon be done. I have a rope-ladder. Will you be able to climb up alone, without my assistance?"

"I think so... I'll try... It's my wrists that they've broken... Oh, the brutes! I can hardly move my hands... and I have very little strength left. But I'll try all the same... needs must..."

He stopped, listened and, with his finger to his mouth, whispered:

"Hush!"

When Sebastiani and his sons entered the room, Daubrecq, who had hidden the letter and lain down on his bed, pretended to wake with a start.

The huntsman brought him a bottle of wine, a glass and some food:

"How goes it, monsieur le depute?" he cried. "Well, perhaps we did squeeze a little hard... It's very painful, that thumbscrewing. Seems they often did it at the time of the Great Revolution and Bonaparte... in the days of the chauffeurs.[15] A pretty invention! Nice and clean... no bloodshed... And it didn't last long either! In twenty minutes, you came out with the missing word!" Sebastiani burst out laughing. "By the way, monsieur le depute, my congratulations! A capital hiding-place. Who would ever suspect it?... You see, what put us off, monsieur le marquis and me, was that name of Marie which you let out at first. You weren't telling a lie; but there you are, you know: the word was only half-finished. We had to know the rest. Say what you like, it's amusing! Just think, on your study-table! Upon my word, what a joke!"

The huntsman rose and walked up and down the room, rubbing his hands:

"Monsieur le marquis is jolly well pleased, so pleased, in fact, that he himself is coming to-morrow evening to let you out. Yes, he has thought it over; there will be a few formalities: you may have to sign a cheque or two, stump up, what, and make good monsieur le marquis' expense and trouble. But what's that to you? A trifle! Not to mention that, from now on, there will be no more chains, no more straps round your wrists; in short, you will be treated like a king! And I've even been told—look here!—to allow you a good bottle of old wine and a flask of brandy."

Sebastiani let fly a few more jests, then took the lamp, made a last examination of the room and said to his sons:

"Let's leave him to sleep. You also, take a rest, all three of you. But sleep with one eye open. One never can tell..." They withdrew.

Lupin waited a little longer and asked, in a low voice:

"Can I begin?"

"Yes, but be careful. It's not impossible that they may go on a round in an hour or two."

Lupin set to work. He had a very powerful file; and the iron of the bars, rusted and gnawed away by time, was, in places, almost reduced to dust. Twice Lupin stopped to listen, with ears pricked up. But it was only the patter of a rat over the rubbish in the upper story, or the flight of some night-bird; and he continued his task, encouraged by Daubrecq, who stood by the door, ready to warn him at the least alarm.

"Oof!" he said, giving a last stroke of the file. "I'm glad that's over, for, on my word, I've been a bit cramped in this cursed tunnel... to say nothing of the cold..."

He bore with all his strength upon the bar, which he had sawn from below, and succeeded in forcing it down sufficiently for a man's body to slip between the two remaining bars. Next, he had to go back to the end of the embrasure, the wider part, where he had left the rope-ladder. After fixing it to the bars, he called Daubrecq:

"Psst!... It's all right... Are you ready?"

"Yes... coming... One more second, while I listen... All right... They're asleep... give me the ladder."

Lupin lowered it and asked:

"Must I come down?"

"No... I feel a little weak... but I shall manage."

Indeed, he reached the window of the embrasure pretty quickly and crept along the passage in the wake of his rescuer. The open air, however, seemed to make him giddy. Also, to give himself strength, he had drunk half the bottle of wine; and he had a fainting-fit that kept him lying on the stones of the embrasure for half an hour. Lupin, losing patience, was fastening him to one end of the rope, of which the other end was knotted round the bars and was preparing to let him down like a bale of goods, when Daubrecq woke up, in better condition:

"That's over," he said. "I feel fit now. Will it take long?"

"Pretty long. We are a hundred and fifty yards up."

"How was it that d'Albufex did not foresee that it was possible to escape this way?"

"The cliff is perpendicular."

"And you were able to..."

---

[15] *The name given to the brigands in the Vendee, who tortured their victims with fire to make them confess where their money was hidden.—Translator's Note.*

"Well, your cousins insisted... And then one has to live, you know, and they were free with their money."

"The dear, good souls!" said Daubrecq. "Where are they?"

"Down below, in a boat."

"Is there a river, then?"

"Yes, but we won't talk, if you don't mind. It's dangerous."

"One word more. Had you been there long when you threw me the letter?"

"No, no. A quarter of an hour or so. I'll tell you all about it... Meanwhile, we must hurry."

Lupin went first, after recommending Daubrecq to hold tight to the rope and to come down backward. He would give him a hand at the difficult places.

It took them over forty minutes to reach the platform of the ledge formed by the cliff; and Lupin had several times to help his companion, whose wrists, still bruised from the torture, had lost all their strength and suppleness.

Over and over again, he groaned:

"Oh, the swine, they've done for me!... The swine!... Ah, d'Albufex, I'll make you pay dear for this!..."

"Ssh!" said Lupin.

"What's the matter?"

"A noise... up above..."

Standing motionless on the platform, they listened. Lupin thought of the Sire de Tancarville and the sentry who had killed him with a shot from his harquebus. He shivered, feeling all the anguish of the silence and the darkness.

"No," he said, "I was mistaken... Besides, it's absurd... They can't hit us here."

"Who would hit us?"

"No one... no one... it was a silly notion..."

He groped about till he found the uprights of the ladder; then he said:

"There, here's the ladder. It is fixed in the bed of the river. A friend of mine is looking after it, as well as your cousins."

He whistled:

"Here I am," he said, in a low voice. "Hold the ladder fast." And, to Daubrecq, "I'll go first."

Daubrecq objected:

"Perhaps it would be better for me to go down first."

"Why?"

"I am very tired. You can tie your rope round my waist and hold me... Otherwise, there is a danger that I might..."

"Yes, you are right," said Lupin. "Come nearer."

Daubrecq came nearer and knelt down on the rock. Lupin fastened the rope to him and then, stooping over, grasped one of the uprights in both hands to keep the ladder from shaking:

"Off you go," he said.

At the same moment, he felt a violent pain in the shoulder:

"Blast it!" he said, sinking to the ground.

Daubrecq had stabbed him with a knife below the nape of the neck, a little to the right.

"You blackguard! You blackguard!"

He half-saw Daubrecq, in the dark, ridding himself of his rope, and heard him whisper:

"You're a bit of a fool, you know!... You bring me a letter from my Rousselot cousins, in which I recognize the writing of the elder, Adelaide, but which that sly puss of an Adelaide, suspecting something and meaning to put me on my guard, if necessary, took care to sign with the name of the younger sister, Euphrasie Rousselot. You see, I tumbled to it! So, with a little reflection... you are Master Arsene Lupin, are you not? Clarisse's protector, Gilbert's saviour... Poor Lupin, I fear you're in a bad way... I don't use the knife often; but, when I do, I use it with a vengeance."

He bent over the wounded man and felt in his pockets:

"Give me your revolver, can't you? You see, your friends will know at once that it is not their governor; and they will try to secure me... And, as I have not much strength left, a bullet or two... Good-bye, Lupin. We shall meet in the next world, eh? Book me a nice flat, with all the latest conveniences.

"Good-bye, Lupin. And my best thanks. For really I don't know what I should have done without you. By Jove, d'Albufex was hitting me hard! It'll be a joke to meet the beggar again!"

Daubrecq had completed his preparations. He whistled once more. A reply came from the boat.

"Here I am," he said.

With a last effort, Lupin put out his arm to stop him. But his hand touched nothing but space. He tried to call out, to warn his accomplices: his voice choked in his throat.

He felt a terrible numbness creep over his whole being. His temples buzzed.

Suddenly, shouts below. Then a shot. Then another, followed by a triumphant chuckle. And a woman's wail and moans. And, soon after, two more shots.

Lupin thought of Clarisse, wounded, dead perhaps; of Daubrecq, fleeing victoriously; of d'Albufex; of the crystal stopper, which one or other of the two adversaries would recover unresisted. Then a sudden vision showed him the Sire de Tancarville falling with the woman he loved. Then he murmured, time after time:

"Clarisse... Clarisse... Gilbert..." A great silence overcame him; an infinite peace entered into him; and, without the least revolt, he received the impression that his exhausted body, with nothing now to hold it back, was rolling to the very edge of the rock, toward the abyss.

IX. IN THE DARK

An hotel bedroom at Amiens.

Lupin was recovering a little consciousness for the first time. Clarisse and the Masher were seated by his bedside.

Both were talking; and Lupin listened to them, without opening his eyes. He learned that they had feared for his life, but that all danger was now removed. Next, in the course of the conversation, he caught certain words that revealed to him what had happened in the tragic night at Mortepierre: Daubrecq's descent; the dismay of the accomplices, when they saw that it was not the governor; then the short struggle: Clarisse flinging herself on Daubrecq and receiving a wound in the shoulder; Daubrecq leaping to the bank; the Growler firing two revolver-shots and darting off in pursuit of him; the Masher clambering up the ladder and finding the governor in a swoon:

"True as I live," said the Masher, "I can't make out even now how he did not roll over. There was a sort of hollow at that place, but it was a sloping hollow; and, half dead as he was, he must have hung on with his ten fingers. Crikey, it was time I came!"

Lupin listened, listened in despair. He collected his strength to grasp and understand the words. But suddenly a terrible sentence was uttered: Clarisse, weeping, spoke of the eighteen days that had elapsed, eighteen more days lost to Gilbert's safety.

Eighteen days! The figure terrified Lupin. He felt that all was over, that he would never be able to recover his strength and resume the struggle and that Gilbert and Vaucheray were doomed... His brain slipped away from him. The fever returned and the delirium.

And more days came and went. It was perhaps the time of his life of which Lupin speaks with the greatest horror. He retained just enough consciousness and had sufficiently lucid moments to realize the position exactly. But he was not able to coordinate his ideas, to follow a line of argument nor to instruct or forbid his friends to adopt this or that line of conduct.

Often, when he emerged from his torpor, he found his hand in Clarisse's and, in that half-slumbering condition in which a fever keeps you, he would address strange words to her, words of love and passion, imploring her and thanking her and blessing her for all the light and joy which she had brought into his darkness.

Then, growing calmer and not fully understanding what he had said, he tried to jest:

"I have been delirious, have I not? What a heap of nonsense I must have talked!"

But Lupin felt by Clarisse's silence that he could safely talk as much nonsense as ever his fever suggested to him. She did not hear. The care and attention which she lavished on the patient, her devotion, her vigilance, her alarm at the least relapse: all this was meant not for him, but for the possible saviour of Gilbert. She anxiously watched the progress of his convalescence. How soon would he be fit to resume the campaign? Was it not madness to linger by his side, when every day carried away a little hope?

Lupin never ceased repeating to himself, with the inward belief that, by so doing, he could influence the course of his illness:

"I will get well... I will get well..."

And he lay for days on end without moving, so as not to disturb the dressing of his wound nor increase the excitement of his nerves in the smallest degree.

He also strove not to think of Daubrecq. But the image of his dire adversary haunted him; and he reconstituted the various phases of the escape, the descent of the cliff.... One day, struck by a terrible memory, he exclaimed:

"The list! The list of the Twenty-seven! Daubrecq must have it by now... or else d'Albufex. It was on the table!"

Clarisse reassured him:

"No one can have taken it," she declared. "The Growler was in Paris that same day, with a note from me for Prasville, entreating him to redouble his watch in the Square Lamartine, so that no one should enter, especially d'Albufex..."

"But Daubrecq?"

"He is wounded. He cannot have gone home."

"Ah, well," he said, "that's all right!... But you too were wounded..."

"A mere scratch on the shoulder."

Lupin was easier in his mind after these revelations. Nevertheless, he was pursued by stubborn notions which he was unable either to drive from his brain or to put into words. Above all, he thought incessantly of that name of "Marie" which Daubrecq's sufferings had drawn from him. What did the name refer to? Was it the title of one of the books on the shelves, or a part of the title? Would the book in question supply the key to the mystery? Or was it the combination word of a safe? Was it a series of letters written somewhere: on a wall, on a paper, on a wooden panel, on the mount of a drawing, on an invoice?

These questions, to which he was unable to find a reply, obsessed and exhausted him.

One morning Arsene Lupin woke feeling a great deal better. The wound was closed, the temperature almost normal. The doctor, a personal friend, who came every day from Paris, promised that he might get up two days later. And, on that day, in the absence of his accomplices and of Mme. Mergy, all three of whom had left two days before, in quest of information, he had himself moved to the open window.

He felt life return to him with the sunlight, with the balmy air that announced the approach of spring. He recovered the concatenation of his ideas; and facts once more took their place in his brain in their logical sequence and in accordance with their relations one to the other.

In the evening he received a telegram from Clarisse to say that things were going badly and that she, the Growler and the Masher were all staying in Paris. He was much disturbed by this wire and had a less quiet night. What could the news be that had given rise to Clarisse's telegram?

But, the next day, she arrived in his room looking very pale, her eyes red with weeping, and, utterly worn out, dropped into a chair:

"The appeal has been rejected," she stammered.

He mastered his emotion and asked, in a voice of surprise:

"Were you relying on that?"

"No, no," she said, "but, all the same... one hopes in spite of one's self."

"Was it rejected yesterday?"

"A week ago. The Masher kept it from me; and I have not dared to read the papers lately."

"There is always the commutation of sentence," he suggested.

"The commutation? Do you imagine that they will commute the sentence of Arsene Lupin's accomplices?"

She ejaculated the words with a violence and a bitterness which he pretended not to notice; and he said:

"Vaucheray perhaps not... But they will take pity on Gilbert, on his youth..."

"They will do nothing of the sort."

"How do you know?"

"I have seen his counsel."

"You have seen his counsel! And you told him..."

"I told him that I was Gilbert's mother and I asked him whether, by proclaiming my son's identity, we could not influence the result... or at least delay it."

"You would do that?" he whispered. "You would admit..."

"Gilbert's life comes before everything. What do I care about my name! What do I care about my husband's name!"

"And your little Jacques?" he objected. "Have you the right to ruin Jacques, to make him the brother of a man condemned to death?"

She hung her head. And he resumed:

"What did the counsel say?"

"He said that an act of that sort would not help Gilbert in the remotest degree. And, in spite of all his protests, I could see that, as far as he was concerned, he had no illusions left and that the pardoning commission are bound to find in favour of the execution."

"The commission, I grant you; but what of the president of the Republic?"

"The president always goes by the advice of the commission."

"He will not do so this time."

"And why not?"

"Because we shall bring influence to bear upon him."

"How?"

"By the conditional surrender of the list of the Twenty-seven!"

"Have you it?"

"No, but I shall have it."

His certainty had not wavered. He made the statement with equal calmness and faith in the infinite power of his will.

She had lost some part of her confidence in him and she shrugged her shoulders lightly:

"If d'Albufex has not purloined the list, one man alone can exercise any influence; one man alone: Daubrecq."

She spoke these words in a low and absent voice that made him shudder. Was she still thinking, as he had often seemed to feel, of going back to Daubrecq and paying him for Gilbert's life?

"You have sworn an oath to me," he said. "I'm reminding you of it. It was agreed that the struggle with Daubrecq should be directed by me and that there would never be a possibility of any arrangement between you and him."

She retorted:

"I don't even know where he is. If I knew, wouldn't you know?"

It was an evasive answer. But he did not insist, resolving to watch her at the opportune time; and he asked her, for he had not yet been told all the details:

"Then it's not known what became of Daubrecq?"

"No. Of course, one of the Growler's bullets struck him. For, next day, we picked up, in a coppice, a handkerchief covered with blood. Also, it seems that a man was seen at Aumale Station, looking very tired and walking with great difficulty. He took a ticket for Paris, stepped into the first train and that is all..."

"He must be seriously wounded," said Lupin, "and he is nursing himself in some safe retreat. Perhaps, also, he considers it wise to lie low for a few weeks and avoid any traps on the part of the police, d'Albufex, you, myself and all his other enemies."

He stopped to think and continued:

"What has happened at Mortepierre since Daubrecq's escape? Has there been no talk in the neighbourhood?"

"No, the rope was removed before daybreak, which proves that Sebastiani or his sons discovered Daubrecq's flight on the same night. Sebastiani was away the whole of the next day."

"Yes, he will have informed the marquis. And where is the marquis himself?"

"At home. And, from what the Growler has heard, there is nothing suspicious there either."

"Are they certain that he has not been inside Daubrecq's house?"

"As certain as they can be."

"Nor Daubrecq?"

"Nor Daubrecq."

"Have you seen Prasville?"

"Prasville is away on leave. But Chief-inspector Blanchon, who has charge of the case, and the detectives who are guarding the house declare that, in accordance with Prasville's instructions, their watch is not relaxed for a moment, even at night; that one of them, turn and turn about, is always on duty in the study; and that no one, therefore, can have gone in."

"So, on principle," Arsene Lupin concluded, "the crystal stopper must still be in Daubrecq's study?"

"If it was there before Daubrecq's disappearance, it should be there now."

"And on the study-table."

"On the study-table? Why do you say that?"

"Because I know," said Lupin, who had not forgotten Sebastiani's words.

"But you don't know the article in which the stopper is hidden?"

"No. But a study-table, a writing-desk, is a limited space. One can explore it in twenty minutes. One can demolish it, if necessary, in ten."

The conversation had tired Arsene Lupin a little. As he did not wish to commit the least imprudence, he said to Clarisse:

"Listen. I will ask you to give me two or three days more. This is Monday, the 4th of March. On Wednesday or Thursday, at latest, I shall be up and about. And you can be sure that we shall succeed."

"And, in the meantime..."

"In the meantime, go back to Paris. Take rooms, with the Growler and the Masher, in the Hotel Franklin, near the Trocadero, and keep a watch on Daubrecq's house. You are free to go in and out as you please. Stimulate the zeal of the detectives on duty."

"Suppose Daubrecq returns?"

"If he returns, that will be so much the better: we shall have him."

"And, if he only passes?"

"In that case, the Growler and the Masher must follow him."

"And if they lose sight of him?"

Lupin did not reply. No one felt more than he how fatal it was to remain inactive in a hotel bedroom and how useful his presence would have been on the battlefield! Perhaps even this vague idea had already prolonged his illness beyond the ordinary limits.

He murmured:

"Go now, please."

There was a constraint between them which increased as the awful day drew nigh. In her injustice, forgetting or wishing to forget that it was she who had forced her son into the Enghien enterprise, Mme. Mergy did not forget that the law was pursuing Gilbert with such rigour not so much because he was a criminal as because he was an accomplice of Arsene Lupin's. And then, notwithstanding all his efforts, notwithstanding his prodigious expenditure of energy, what result had Lupin achieved, when all was said? How far had his intervention benefited Gilbert?

After a pause, she rose and left him alone.

The next day he was feeling rather low. But on the day after, the Wednesday, when his doctor wanted him to keep quiet until the end of the week, he said:

"If not, what have I to fear?"

"A return of the fever."

"Nothing worse?"

"No. The wound is pretty well healed."

"Then I don't care. I'll go back with you in your car. We shall be in Paris by mid-day."

What decided Lupin to start at once was, first, a letter in which Clarisse told him that she had found Daubrecq's traces, and, also, a telegram, published in the Amiens papers, which stated that the Marquis d'Albufex had been arrested for his complicity in the affair of the canal.

Daubrecq was taking his revenge.

Now the fact that Daubrecq was taking his revenge proved that the marquis had not been able to prevent that revenge by seizing the document which was on the writing-desk in the study. It proved that Chief-inspector Blanchon and the detectives had kept a good watch. It proved that the crystal stopper was still in the Square Lamartine.

It was still there; and this showed either that Daubrecq had not ventured to go home, or else that his state of health hindered him from doing so, or else again that he had sufficient confidence in the hiding-place not to trouble to put himself out.

In any case, there was no doubt as to the course to be pursued: Lupin must act and he must act smartly. He must forestall Daubrecq and get hold of the crystal stopper.

When they had crossed the Bois de Boulogne and were nearing the Square Lamartine, Lupin took leave of the doctor and stopped the car. The Growler and the Masher, to whom he had wired, met him.

"Where's Mme. Mergy?" he asked.

"She has not been back since yesterday; she sent us an express message to say that she saw Daubrecq leaving his cousins' place and getting into a cab. She knows the number of the cab and will keep us informed."

"Nothing further?"

"Nothing further."

"No other news?"

"Yes, the Paris-Midi says that d'Albufex opened his veins last night, with a piece of broken glass, in his cell at the Sante. He seems to have left a long letter behind him, confessing his fault, but accusing Daubrecq of his death and exposing the part played by Daubrecq in the canal affair."

"Is that all?"

"No. The same paper stated that it has reason to believe that the pardoning commission, after examining the record, has rejected Vaucheray and Gilbert's petition and that their counsel will probably be received in audience by the president on Friday."

Lupin gave a shudder.

"They're losing no time," he said. "I can see that Daubrecq, on the very first day, put the screw on the old judicial machine. One short week more... and the knife falls. My poor Gilbert! If, on Friday next, the papers which your counsel submits to the president of the Republic do not contain the conditional offer of the list of the Twenty-seven, then, my poor Gilbert, you are done for!"

"Come, come, governor, are you losing courage?"

"I? Rot! I shall have the crystal stopper in an hour. In two hours, I shall see Gilbert's counsel. And the nightmare will be over."

"Well done, governor! That's like your old self. Shall we wait for you here?"

"No, go back to your hotel. I'll join you later."

They parted. Lupin walked straight to the house and rang the bell.

A detective opened the door and recognized him:

"M. Nicole, I believe?"

"Yes," he said. "Is Chief-inspector Blanchon here?"

"He is."

"Can I speak to him?"

The man took him to the study, where Chief-inspector Blanchon welcomed him with obvious pleasure.

"Well, chief-inspector, one would say there was something new?"

"M. Nicole, my orders are to place myself entirely at your disposal; and I may say that I am very glad to see you to-day."

"Why so?"

"Because there is something new."

"Something serious?"

"Something very serious."

"Quick, speak."

"Daubrecq has returned."

"Eh, what!" exclaimed Lupin, with a start. "Daubrecq returned? Is he here?"

"No, he has gone."

"And did he come in here, in the study?"

"Yes."

"This morning."

"And you did not prevent him?"

"What right had I?"

"And you left him alone?"

"By his positive orders, yes, we left him alone."

Lupin felt himself turn pale. Daubrecq had come back to fetch the crystal stopper!

He was silent for some time and repeated to himself:

"He came back to fetch it... He was afraid that it would be found and he has taken it... Of course, it was inevitable... with d'Albufex arrested, with d'Albufex accused and accusing him, Daubrecq was bound to defend himself. It's a difficult game for him. After months and months of mystery, the public is at last learning that the infernal being who contrived the whole tragedy of the Twenty-Seven and who ruins and kills his adversaries is he, Daubrecq. What would become of him if, by a miracle, his talisman did not protect him? He has taken it back."

And, trying to make his voice sound firm, he asked:

"Did he stay long?"

"Twenty seconds, perhaps."

"What! Twenty seconds? No longer?"

"No longer."

"What time was it?"

"Ten o'clock."

"Could he have known of the Marquis d'Albufex' suicide by then?"

"Yes. I saw the special edition of the Paris-Midi in his pocket."

"That's it, that's it," said Lupin. And he asked, "Did M. Prasville give you no special instructions in case Daubrecq should return?"

"No. So, in M. Prasville's absence, I telephoned to the police-office and I am waiting. The disappearance of Daubrecq the deputy caused a great stir, as you know, and our presence here has a reason, in the eyes of the public, as long as that disappearance continues. But, now that Daubrecq has returned, now that we have proofs that he is neither under restraint nor dead, how can we stay in the house?"

"It doesn't matter," said Lupin, absently. "It doesn't matter whether the house is guarded or not. Daubrecq has been; therefore the crystal stopper is no longer here."

He had not finished the sentence, when a question quite naturally forced itself upon his mind. If the crystal stopper was no longer there, would this not be obvious from some material sign? Had the removal of that object, doubtless contained within another object, left no trace, no void?

It was easy to ascertain. Lupin had simply to examine the writing-desk, for he knew, from Sebastiani's chaff, that this was the spot of the hiding-place. And the hiding-place could not be a complicated one, seeing that Daubrecq had not remained in the study for more than twenty seconds, just long enough, so to speak, to walk in and walk out again.

Lupin looked. And the result was immediate. His memory had so faithfully recorded the picture of the desk, with all the articles lying on it, that the absence of one of them struck him instantaneously, as though that article and that alone were the characteristic sign which distinguished this particular writing-table from every other table in the world.

"Oh," he thought, quivering with delight, "everything fits in! Everything! ... Down to that half-word which the torture drew from Daubrecq in the tower at Mortepierre! The riddle is solved. There need be no more hesitation, no more groping in the dark. The end is in sight."

And, without answering the inspector's questions, he thought of the simplicity of the hiding-place and remembered Edgar Allan Poe's wonderful story in which the stolen letter, so eagerly sought for, is, in a manner of speaking, displayed to all eyes. People do not suspect what does not appear to be hidden.

"Well, well," said Lupin, as he went out, greatly excited by his discovery, "I seem doomed, in this confounded adventure, to knock up against disappointments to the finish. Everything that I build crumbles to pieces at once. Every victory ends in disaster."

Nevertheless, he did not allow himself to be cast down. On the one hand, he now knew where Daubrecq the deputy hid the crystal stopper. On the other hand, he would soon learn from Clarisse Mergy where Daubrecq himself was lurking. The rest, to him, would be child's play.

The Growler and the Masher were waiting for him in the drawing-room of the Hotel Franklin, a small family-hotel near the Trocadero. Mme. Mergy had not yet written to him.

"Oh," he said, "I can trust her! She will hang on to Daubrecq until she is certain."

However, toward the end of the afternoon, he began to grow impatient and anxious. He was fighting one of those battles—the last, he hoped—in which the least delay might jeopardize everything. If Daubrecq threw Mme. Mergy off the scent, how was he to be caught again? They no longer had weeks or days, but only a few hours, a terribly limited number of hours, in which to repair any mistakes that they might commit.

He saw the proprietor of the hotel and asked him:

"Are you sure that there is no express letter for my two friends?"

"Quite sure, sir."

"Nor for me, M. Nicole?"

"No, sir."

"That's curious," said Lupin. "We were certain that we should hear from Mme. Audran."

Audran was the name under which Clarisse was staying at the hotel.

"But the lady has been," said the proprietor.

"What's that?"

"She came some time ago and, as the gentlemen were not there, left a letter in her room. Didn't the porter tell you?"

Lupin and his friends hurried upstairs. There was a letter on the table.

"Hullo!" said Lupin. "It's been opened! How is that? And why has it been cut about with scissors?"

The letter contained the following lines:

"Daubrecq has spent the week at the Hotel Central. This morning he had his luggage taken to the Gare de —- and telephoned to reserve a berth in the sleeping-car —- for —-

"I do not know when the train starts. But I shall be at the station all the afternoon. Come as soon as you can, all three of you. We will arrange to kidnap him."

"What next?" said the Masher. "At which station? And where's the sleeping-car for? She has cut out just the words we wanted!"

"Yes," said the Growler. "Two snips with the scissors in each place; and the words which we most want are gone. Who ever saw such a thing? Has Mme. Mergy lost her head?"

Lupin did not move. A rush of blood was beating at his temples with such violence that he glued his fists to them and pressed with all his might. His fever returned, burning and riotous, and his will, incensed to the verge of physical suffering, concentrated itself upon that stealthy enemy, which must be controlled then and there, if he himself did not wish to be irretrievably beaten.

He muttered, very calmly:

"Daubrecq has been here."

"Daubrecq!"

"We can't suppose that Mme. Mergy has been amusing herself by cutting out those two words. Daubrecq has been here. Mme. Mergy thought that she was watching him. He was watching her instead."

"How?"

"Doubtless through that hall-porter who did not tell us that Mme. Mergy had been to the hotel, but who must have told Daubrecq. He came. He read the letter. And, by way of getting at us, he contented himself with cutting out the essential words."

"We can find out... we can ask..."

"What's the good? What's the use of finding out how he came, when we know that he did come?"

He examined the letter for some time, turned it over and over, then stood up and said:

"Come along."

"Where to?"

"Gare de Lyon."

"Are you sure?"

"I am sure of nothing with Daubrecq. But, as we have to choose, according to the contents of the letter, between the Gare de l'Est and the Gare de Lyon, [16]I am presuming that his business, his pleasure and his health are more likely to take Daubrecq in the direction of Marseilles and the Riviera than to the Gare de l'Est."

It was past seven when Lupin and his companions left the Hotel Franklin. A motor-car took them across Paris at full speed, but they soon saw that Clarisse Mergy was not outside the station, nor in the waiting-rooms, nor on any of the platforms.

"Still," muttered Lupin, whose agitation grew as the obstacles increased, "still, if Daubrecq booked a berth in a sleeping-car, it can only have been in an evening train. And it is barely half-past seven!"

A train was starting, the night express. They had time to rush along the corridor. Nobody... neither Mme. Mergy nor Daubrecq...

But, as they were all three going, a porter accosted them near the refreshment-room:

"Is one of you gentlemen looking for a lady?"

"Yes, yes,... I am," said Lupin. "Quick, what is it?"

"Oh, it's you, sir! The lady told me there might be three of you or two of you.... And I didn't know..."

"But, in heaven's name, speak, man! What lady?"

"The lady who spent the whole day on the pavement, with the luggage, waiting."

"Well, out with it! Has she taken a train?"

"Yes, the train-de-luxe, at six-thirty: she made up her mind at the last moment, she told me to say. And I was also to say that the gentleman was in the same train and that they were going to Monte Carlo."

"Damn it!" muttered Lupin. "We ought to have taken the express just now! There's nothing left but the evening trains, and they crawl! We've lost over three hours."

The wait seemed interminable. They booked their seats. They telephoned to the proprietor of the Hotel Franklin to send on their letters to Monte Carlo. They dined. They read the papers. At last, at half-past nine, the train started.

And so, by a really tragic series of circumstances, at the most critical moment of the contest, Lupin was turning his back on the battlefield and going away, at haphazard, to seek, he knew not where, and beat, he knew not how, the most formidable and elusive enemy that he had ever fought.

And this was happening four days, five days at most, before the inevitable execution of Gilbert and Vaucheray.

It was a bad and painful night for Lupin. The more he studied the situation the more terrible it appeared to him. On every side he was faced with uncertainty, darkness, confusion, helplessness.

---

[16] *These are the only two main-line stations in Paris with the word* de *in their name. The others have* du, *as the Gare du Nord or the Gare du Luxembourg,* d' *as the Gare d'Orleans, or no participle at all, as the Gare Saint-Lazare or the Gare Montparnasse.—Translator's Note.*

True, he knew the secret of the crystal stopper. But how was he to know that Daubrecq would not change or had not already changed his tactics? How was he to know that the list of the Twenty-seven was still inside that crystal stopper or that the crystal stopper was still inside the object where Daubrecq had first hidden it?

And there was a further serious reason for alarm in the fact that Clarisse Mergy thought that she was shadowing and watching Daubrecq at a time when, on the contrary, Daubrecq was watching her, having her shadowed and dragging her, with diabolical cleverness, toward the places selected by himself, far from all help or hope of help.

Oh, Daubrecq's game was clear as daylight! Did not Lupin know the unhappy woman's hesitations? Did he not know—and the Growler and the Masher confirmed it most positively—that Clarisse looked upon the infamous bargain planned by Daubrecq in the light of a possible, an acceptable thing? In that case, how could he, Lupin, succeed? The logic of events, so powerfully moulded by Daubrecq, led to a fatal result: the mother must sacrifice herself and, to save her son, throw her scruples, her repugnance, her very honour, to the winds!

"Oh, you scoundrel!" snarled Lupin, in a fit of rage. "If I get hold of you, I'll make you dance to a pretty tune! I wouldn't be in your shoes for a great deal, when that happens."

They reached Monte Carlo at three o'clock in the afternoon. Lupin was at once disappointed not to see Clarisse on the platform at the station.

He waited. No messenger came up to him.

He asked the porters and ticket-collectors if they had noticed, among the crowd, two travellers answering to the description of Daubrecq and Clarisse. They had not.

He had, therefore, to set to work and hunt through all the hotels and lodging-houses in the principality. Oh, the time wasted!

By the following evening, Lupin knew, beyond a doubt, that Daubrecq and Clarisse were not at Monte Carlo, nor at Monaco, nor at the Cap d'Ail, nor at La Turbie, nor at Cap Martin.

"Where can they be then?" he wondered, trembling with rage.

At last, on the Saturday, he received, at the poste restante, a telegram which had been readdressed from the Hotel Franklin and which said:

"He got out at Cannes and is going on to San Remo, Hotel Palace des Ambassadeurs. "CLARISSE."

The telegram was dated the day before.

"Hang it!" exclaimed Lupin. "They passed through Monte Carlo. One of us ought to have remained at the station. I did think of it; but, in the midst of all that bustle..."

Lupin and his friends took the first train for Italy.

They crossed the frontier at twelve o'clock. The train entered the station at San Remo at twelve-forty.

They at once saw an hotel-porter, with "Ambassadeurs-Palace" on his braided cap, who seemed to be looking for some one among the arrivals.

Lupin went up to him:

"Are you looking for M. Nicole?"

"Yes, M. Nicole and two gentlemen."

"From a lady?"

"Yes, Mme. Mergy."

"Is she staying at your hotel?"

"No. She did not get out. She beckoned to me, described you three gentlemen and told me to say that she was going on to Genoa, to the Hotel Continental."

"Was she by herself?"

"Yes."

Lupin tipped the man, dismissed him and turned to his friends:

"This is Saturday. If the execution takes place on Monday, there's nothing to be done. But Monday is not a likely day... What I have to do is to lay hands on Daubrecq to-night and to be in Paris on Monday, with the document. It's our last chance. Let's take it."

The Growler went to the booking-office and returned with three tickets for Genoa.

The engine whistled.

Lupin had a last hesitation: "No, really, it's too childish! What are we doing? We ought to be in Paris, not here!... Just think!..."

He was on the point of opening the door and jumping out on the permanent way. But his companions held him back. The train started. He sat down again. And they continued their mad pursuit, travelling at random, toward the unknown...

And this happened two days before the inevitable execution of Gilbert and Vaucheray.

X. EXTRA-DRY?

On one of the hills that girdle Nice with the finest scenery in the world, between the Vallon de Saint-Silvestre and the Vallon de La Mantega, stands a huge hotel which overlooks the town and the wonderful Baie des Anges. A crowd flocks to it from all parts, forming a medley of every class and nation.

On the evening of the same Saturday when Lupin, the Growler and the Masher were plunging into Italy, Clarisse Mergy entered this hotel, asked for a bedroom facing south and selected No. 130, on the second floor, a room which had been vacant since that morning.

The room was separated from No. 129 by two partition-doors. As soon as she was alone, Clarisse pulled back the curtain that concealed the first door, noiselessly drew the bolt and put her ear to the second door:

"He is here," she thought. "He is dressing to go to the club... as he did yesterday."

When her neighbour had gone, she went into the passage and, availing herself of a moment when there was no one in sight, walked up to the door of No. 129. The door was locked.

She waited all the evening for her neighbour's return and did not go to bed until two o'clock. On Sunday morning, she resumed her watch.

The neighbour went out at eleven. This time he left the key in the door.

Hurriedly turning the key, Clarisse entered boldly, went to the partition-door, raised the curtain, drew the bolt and found herself in her own room.

In a few minutes, she heard two chambermaids doing the room in No. 129.

She waited until they were gone. Then, feeling sure that she would not be disturbed, she once more slipped into the other room.

Her excitement made her lean against a chair. After days and nights of stubborn pursuit, after alternate hopes and disappointments, she had at last succeeded in entering a room occupied by Daubrecq. She could look about at her ease; and, if she did not discover the crystal stopper, she could at least hide in the space between the partition-doors, behind the hanging, see Daubrecq, spy upon his movements and surprise his secret.

She looked around her. A travelling-bag at once caught her attention. She managed to open it; but her search was useless.

She ransacked the trays of a trunk and the compartments of a portmanteau. She searched the wardrobe, the writing-table, the chest of drawers, the bathroom, all the tables, all the furniture. She found nothing.

She gave a start when she saw a scrap of paper on the balcony, lying as though flung there by accident:

"Can it be a trick of Daubrecq's?" she thought, out loud. "Can that scrap of paper contain..."

"No," said a voice behind her, as she put her hand on the latch.

She turned and saw Daubrecq.

She felt neither astonishment nor alarm, nor even any embarrassment at finding herself face to face with him. She had suffered too deeply for months to trouble about what Daubrecq could think of her or say, at catching her in the act of spying.

She sat down wearily.

He grinned:

"No, you're out of it, dear friend. As the children say, you're not 'burning' at all. Oh, not a bit of it! And it's so easy! Shall I help you? It's next to you, dear friend, on that little table... And yet, by Jove, there's not much on that little table! Something to read, something to write with, something to smoke, something to eat... and that's all... Will you have one of these candied fruits?... Or perhaps you would rather wait for the more substantial meal which I have ordered?"

Clarisse made no reply. She did not even seem to listen to what he was saying, as though she expected other words, more serious words, which he could not fail to utter.

He cleared the table of all the things that lay upon it and put them on the mantel-piece. Then he rang the bell.

A head-waiter appeared. Daubrecq asked:

"Is the lunch which I ordered ready?"

"Yes, sir."

"It's for two, isn't it?"

"Yes, sir."

"And the champagne?"

"Yes, sir."

"Extra-dry?"

"Yes, sir."

Another waiter brought a tray and laid two covers on the table: a cold lunch, some fruit and a bottle of champagne in an ice-pail.

Then the two waiters withdrew.

"Sit down, dear lady. As you see, I was thinking of you and your cover is laid."

And, without seeming to observe that Clarisse was not at all prepared to do honour to his invitation, he sat down, began to eat and continued:

"Yes, upon my word, I hoped that you would end by consenting to this little private meeting. During the past week, while you were keeping so assiduous a watch upon me, I did nothing but say to myself, 'I wonder which she prefers: sweet champagne, dry champagne, or extra-dry?' I was really puzzled. Especially after our departure from Paris. I had lost your tracks, that is to say, I feared that you had lost mine and abandoned the pursuit which was so gratifying to me. When I went for a walk, I missed your beautiful dark eyes, gleaming with hatred under your hair just touched with gray. But, this morning, I understood: the room next to mine was empty at last; and my friend Clarisse was able to take up her quarters, so to speak, by my bedside. From that moment I was reassured. I felt certain that, on coming back—instead of lunching in the restaurant as usual—I should find you arranging my things to your convenience and suiting your own taste. That was why I ordered two covers: one for your humble servant, the other for his fair friend."

She was listening to him now and in the greatest terror. So Daubrecq knew that he was spied upon! For a whole week he had seen through her and all her schemes!

In a low voice, anxious-eyed, she asked:

"You did it on purpose, did you not? You only went away to drag me with you?"

"Yes," he said.

"But why? Why?"

"Do you mean to say that you don't know?" retorted Daubrecq, laughing with a little cluck of delight.

She half-rose from her chair and, bending toward him, thought, as she thought each time, of the murder which she could commit, of the murder which she would commit. One revolver-shot and the odious brute was done for.

Slowly her hand glided to the weapon concealed in her bodice.

Daubrecq said:

"One second, dear friend... You can shoot presently; but I beg you first to read this wire which I have just received."

She hesitated, not knowing what trap he was laying for her; but he went on, as he produced a telegram:

"It's about your son."

"Gilbert?" she asked, greatly concerned.

"Yes, Gilbert... Here, read it."

She gave a yell of dismay. She had read:

"Execution on Tuesday morning."

And she at once flung herself on Daubrecq, crying:

"It's not true!... It's a lie... to madden me... Oh, I know you: you are capable of anything! Confess! It won't be on Tuesday, will it? In two days! No, no... I tell you, we have four days yet, five days, in which to save him... Confess it, confess it!"

She had no strength left, exhausted by this fit of rebellion; and her voice uttered none but inarticulate sounds.

He looked at her for a moment, then poured himself out a glass of champagne and drank it down at a gulp. He took a few steps up and down the room, came back to her and said:

"Listen to me, darling..."

The insult made her quiver with an unexpected energy. She drew herself up and, panting with indignation, said:

"I forbid you... I forbid you to speak to me like that. I will not accept such an outrage. You wretch!..."

He shrugged his shoulders and resumed:

"Pah, I see you're not quite alive to the position. That comes, of course, because you still hope for assistance in some quarter. Prasville, perhaps? The excellent Prasville, whose right hand you are... My dear friend, a forlorn hope... You must know that Prasville is mixed up in the Canal affair! Not directly: that is to say, his name is not on the list of the Twenty-seven; but it is there under the name of one of his friends, an ex-deputy called Vorenglade, Stanislas Vorenglade, his man of straw, apparently: a penniless individual whom I left alone and rightly. I knew nothing of all that until this morning, when, lo and behold, I received a letter informing me of the existence of a bundle of documents which prove the complicity of our one and only Prasville! And who is my informant? Vorenglade himself! Vorenglade, who, tired of living in poverty, wants to extort money from Prasville, at the risk of being arrested, and who will be delighted to come to terms with me. And Prasville will get the sack. Oh, what a lark! I swear to you that he will get the sack, the villain! By Jove, but he's annoyed me long enough! Prasville, old boy, you've deserved it..."

He rubbed his hands together, revelling in his coming revenge. And he continued:

"You see, my dear Clarisse... there's nothing to be done in that direction. What then? What straw will you cling to? Why, I was forgetting: M. Arsene Lupin! Mr. Growler! Mr. Masher!... Pah, you'll admit that those gentlemen have not shone and that all their feats of prowess have not prevented me from going my own little way. It was bound to be. Those fellows imagine that there's no one to equal them. When they meet an adversary like myself, one who is not to be bounced, it upsets them and they make blunder after blunder, while still believing that they are hoodwinking him like mad. Schoolboys, that's what they are! However, as you seem to have some illusions left about the aforesaid Lupin, as you are counting on that poor devil to crush me and to work a miracle in favour of your innocent Gilbert, come, let's dispel that illusion. Oh! Lupin! Lord above, she believes in Lupin! She places her last hopes in Lupin! Lupin! Just wait till I prick you, my illustrious windbag!"

He took up the receiver of the telephone which communicated with the hall of the hotel and said:

"I'm No. 129, mademoiselle. Would you kindly ask the person sitting opposite your office to come up to me?... Huh!... Yes, mademoiselle, the gentleman in a gray felt hat. He knows. Thank you, mademoiselle."

Hanging up the receiver, he turned to Clarisse:

"Don't be afraid. The man is discretion itself. Besides, it's the motto of his trade: 'Discretion and dispatch.' As a retired detective, he has done me a number of services, including that of following you while you were following me. Since our arrival in the south, he has been less busy with you; but that was because he was more busy elsewhere. Come in, Jacob."

He himself opened the door, and a short, thin man, with a red moustache, entered the room.

"Please tell this lady, Jacob, in a few brief words, what you have done since Wednesday evening, when, after letting her get into the train-de-luxe which was taking me from the Gare de Lyon to the south, you yourself remained on the platform at the station. Of course, I am not asking how you spent your time, except in so far as concerns the lady and the business with which I entrusted you."

Jacob dived into the inside-pocket of his jacket and produced a little note-book of which he turned over the pages and read them aloud in the voice of a man reading a report:

"Wednesday evening, 8.15. Gare de Lyon. Wait for two gents, Growler and Masher. They come with another whom I don't know yet, but who can only be M. Nicole. Give a porter ten francs for the loan of his cap and blouse. Accost the gents and tell them, from a lady, 'that they were gone to Monte Carlo.' Next, telephone to the porter at the Hotel Franklin. All telegrams sent to his boss and dispatched by said boss will be read by said hotel-porter and, if necessary, intercepted.

"Thursday. Monte Carlo. The three gents search the hotels.

"Friday. Flying visits to La Turbie, the Cap d'Ail, Cap Martin. M. Daubrecq rings me up. Thinks it wiser to send the gents to Italy. Make the porter of the Hotel Franklin send them a telegram appointing a meeting at San Remo.

"Saturday. San Remo. Station platform. Give the porter of the Ambassadeurs-Palace ten francs for the loan of his cap. The three gents arrive. They speak to me. Explain to them that a lady traveller, Mme. Mergy, is going on to Genoa, to the Hotel Continental. The gents hesitate. M. Nicole wants to get out. The others hold him back. The train starts. Good luck, gents! An hour later, I take the train for France and get out at Nice, to await fresh orders."

Jacob closed his note-book and concluded:

"That's all. To-day's doings will be entered this evening."

"You can enter them now, M. Jacob. '12 noon. M. Daubrecq sends me to the Wagon-Lits Co. I book two berths in the Paris sleeping-car, by the 2.48 train, and send them to M. Daubrecq by express messenger. Then I take the 12.58 train for Vintimille, the frontier-station, where I spend the day on the platform watching all the travellers who come to France. Should Messrs. Nicole, Growler and Masher take it into their heads to leave Italy and return to Paris by way of Nice, my instructions are to telegraph to the headquarters of police that Master Arsene Lupin and two of his accomplices are in train number so-and-so."

While speaking, Daubrecq led Jacob to the door. He closed it after him, turned the key, pushed the bolt and, going up to Clarisse, said:

"And now, darling, listen to me."

This time, she uttered no protest. What could she do against such an enemy, so powerful, so resourceful, who provided for everything, down to the minutest details, and who toyed with his adversaries in such an airy fashion? Even if she had hoped till then for Lupin's interference, how could she do so now, when he was wandering through Italy in pursuit of a shadow?

She understood at last why three telegrams which she had sent to the Hotel Franklin had remained unanswered. Daubrecq was there, lurking in the dark, watching, establishing a void around her, separating her from her comrades in the fight, bringing her gradually, a beaten prisoner, within the four walls of that room.

She felt her weakness. She was at the monster's mercy. She must be silent and resigned.

He repeated, with an evil delight:

"Listen to me, darling. Listen to the irrevocable words which I am about to speak. Listen to them well. It is now 12 o'clock. The last train starts at 2.48: you understand, the last train that can bring me to Paris to-morrow, Monday, in time to save your son. The evening-trains would arrive too late. The trains-de-luxe are full up. Therefore I shall have to start at 2.48. Am I to start?"

"Yes."

"Our berths are booked. Will you come with me?"

"Yes."

"You know my conditions for interfering?"

"Yes."

"Do you accept them?"

"Yes."

"You will marry me?"

"Yes."

Oh, those horrible answers! The unhappy woman gave them in a sort of awful torpor, refusing even to understand what she was promising. Let him start first, let him snatch Gilbert from the engine of death whose vision haunted her day and night... And then... and then... let what must come come...

He burst out laughing:

"Oh, you rogue, it's easily said!... You're ready to pledge yourself to anything, eh? The great thing is to save Gilbert, isn't it? Afterward, when that noodle of a Daubrecq comes with his engagement-ring, not a bit of it! Nothing doing! We'll laugh in his face!... No, no, enough of empty words. I don't want promises that won't be kept: I want facts, immediate facts."

He came and sat close beside her and stated, plainly:

"This is what I propose... what must be... what shall be... I will ask, or rather I will demand, not Gilbert's pardon, to begin with, but a reprieve, a postponement of the execution, a postponement of three or four weeks. They will invent a pretext of some sort: that's not my affair. And, when Mme. Mergy has become Mme. Daubrecq, then and not till then will I ask for his pardon, that is to say, the commutation of his sentence. And make yourself quite easy: they'll grant it."

"I accept... I accept," she stammered.

He laughed once more:

"Yes, you accept, because that will happen in a month's time... and meanwhile you reckon on finding some trick, an assistance of some kind or another... M. Arsene Lupin..."

"I swear it on the head of my son."

"The head of your son!... Why, my poor pet, you would sell yourself to the devil to save it from falling!..."

"Oh, yes," she whispered, shuddering. "I would gladly sell my soul!"

He sidled up against her and, in a low voice:

"Clarisse, it's not your soul I ask for... It's something else... For more than twenty years my life has spun around that longing. You are the only woman I have ever loved... Loathe me, hate me—I don't care—but do not spurn me... Am I to wait? To wait another month?... No, Clarisse, I have waited too many years already..."

He ventured to touch her hand. Clarisse shrank back with such disgust that he was seized with fury and cried:

"Oh, I swear to heaven, my beauty, the executioner won't stand on such ceremony when he catches hold of your son!... And you give yourself airs! Why, think, it'll happen in forty hours! Forty hours, no more, and you hesitate... and you have scruples, when your son's life is at stake! Come, come, no whimpering, no silly sentimentality... Look things in the face. By your own oath, you are my wife, you are my bride from this moment... Clarisse, Clarisse, give me your lips..."

Half-fainting, she had hardly the strength to put out her arm and push him away; and, with a cynicism in which all his abominable nature stood revealed, Daubrecq, mingling words of cruelty and words of passion, continued:

"Save your son!... Think of the last morning: the preparations for the scaffold, when they snip away his shirt and cut his hair... Clarisse, Clarisse, I will save him... Be sure of it... All my life shall be yours ... Clarisse..."

She no longer resisted. It was over. The loathsome brute's lips were about to touch hers; and it had to be, and nothing could prevent it. It was her duty to obey the decree of fate. She had long known it. She understood it; and, closing her eyes, so as not to see the foul face that was slowly raised to hers, she repeated to herself:

"My son... my poor son."

A few seconds passed: ten, twenty perhaps. Daubrecq did not move. Daubrecq did not speak. And she was astounded at that great silence and that sudden quiet. Did the monster, at the last moment, feel a scruple of remorse?

She raised her eyelids.

The sight which she beheld struck her with stupefaction. Instead of the grinning features which she expected to see, she saw a motionless, unrecognizable face, contorted by an expression of unspeakable terror: and the eyes, invisible under the double impediment of the spectacles, seemed to be staring above her head, above the chair in which she lay prostrate.

Clarisse turned her face. Two revolver-barrels, pointed at Daubrecq, showed on the right, a little above the chair. She saw only that: those two huge, formidable revolvers, gripped in two clenched hands. She saw only that and also Daubrecq's face, which fear was discolouring little by little, until it turned livid. And, almost at the same time, some one slipped behind Daubrecq, sprang up fiercely, flung one of his arms round Daubrecq's neck, threw him to the ground with incredible violence and applied a pad of cotton-wool to his face. A sudden smell of chloroform filled the room.

Clarisse had recognized M. Nicole.

"Come along, Growler!" he cried. "Come along, Masher! Drop your shooters: I've got him! He's a limp rag... Tie him up."

Daubrecq, in fact, was bending in two and falling on his knees like a disjointed doll. Under the action of the chloroform, the fearsome brute sank into impotence, became harmless and grotesque.

The Growler and the Masher rolled him in one of the blankets of the bed and tied him up securely.

"That's it! That's it!" shouted Lupin, leaping to his feet.

And, in a sudden reaction of mad delight, he began to dance a wild jig in the middle of the room, a jig mingled with bits of can-can and the contortions of the cakewalk and the whirls of a dancing dervish and the acrobatic movements of a clown and the lurching steps of a drunken man. And he announced, as though they were the numbers in a music-hall performance:

"The prisoner's dance!... The captive's hornpipe!... A fantasia on the corpse of a representative of the people!... The chloroform polka!... The two-step of the conquered goggles! Olle! Olle! The blackmailer's fandango! Hoot! Hoot! The McDaubrecq's fling!... The turkey trot!... And the bunny hug!... And the grizzly bear!... The Tyrolean dance: tra-la-liety!... Allons, enfants de la partie!... Zing, boum, boum! Zing, boum, boum!..."

All his street-arab nature, all his instincts of gaiety, so long suppressed by his constant anxiety and disappointment, came out and betrayed themselves in roars of laughter, bursts of animal spirits and a picturesque need of childlike exuberance and riot.

He gave a last high kick, turned a series of cartwheels round the room and ended by standing with his hands on his hips and one foot on Daubrecq's lifeless body.

"An allegorical tableau!" he announced. "The angel of virtue destroying the hydra of vice!"

And the humour of the scene was twice as great because Lupin was appearing under the aspect of M. Nicole, in the clothes and figure of that wizened, awkward, nervous private tutor.

A sad smile flickered across Mme. Mergy's face, her first smile for many a long month. But, at once returning to the reality of things, she besought him:

"Please, please... think of Gilbert!"

He ran up to her, caught her in his arms and, obeying a spontaneous impulse, so frank that she could but laugh at it, gave her a resounding kiss on either cheek:

"There, lady, that's the kiss of a decent man! Instead of Daubrecq, it's I kissing you... Another word and I'll do it again... and I'll call you darling next... Be angry with me, if you dare. Oh, how happy I am!"

He knelt before her on one knee. And, respectfully:

"I beg your pardon, madame. The fit is over."

And, getting up again, resuming his whimsical manner, he continued, while Clarisse wondered what he was driving at:

"What's the next article, madame? Your son's pardon, perhaps? Certainly! Madame, I have the honour to grant you the pardon of your son, the commutation of his sentence to penal servitude for life and, to wind up with, his early escape. It's settled, eh, Growler? Settled, Masher, what? You'll both go with the boy to New Caledonia and arrange for everything. Oh, my dear Daubrecq, we owe you a great debt! But I'm not forgetting you, believe me! What would you like? A last pipe? Coming, coming!"

He took one of the pipes from the mantel-piece, stooped over the prisoner, shifted his pad and thrust the amber mouth-piece between his teeth:

"Draw, old chap, draw. Lord, how funny you look, with your plug over your nose and your cutty in your mouth. Come, puff away. By Jove, I forgot to fill your pipe! Where's your tobacco, your favourite Maryland? ... Oh, here we are!..."

He took from the chimney an unopened yellow packet and tore off the government band:

"His lordship's tobacco! Ladies and gentlemen, keep your eyes on me! This is a great moment. I am about to fill his lordship's pipe: by Jupiter, what an honour! Observe my movements! You see, I have nothing in my hands, nothing up my sleeves!..."

He turned back his cuffs and stuck out his elbows. Then he opened the packet and inserted his thumb and fore-finger, slowly, gingerly, like a conjurer performing a sleight-of-hand trick before a puzzled audience, and, beaming all over his face, extracted from the tobacco a glittering object which he held out before the spectators.

Clarisse uttered a cry.

It was the crystal stopper.

She rushed at Lupin and snatched it from him:

"That's it; that's the one!" she exclaimed, feverishly. "There's no scratch on the stem! And look at this line running down the middle, where the gilt finishes... That's it; it unscrews!... Oh, dear, my strength's going!..." She trembled so violently that Lupin took back the stopper and unscrewed it himself.

The inside of the knob was hollow; and in the hollow space was a piece of paper rolled into a tiny pellet.

"The foreign-post-paper," he whispered, himself greatly excited, with quivering hands.

There was a long silence. All four felt as if their hearts were ready to burst from their bodies; and they were afraid of what was coming.

"Please, please..." stammered Clarisse.

Lupin unfolded the paper.

There was a set of names written one below the other, twenty-seven of them, the twenty-seven names of the famous list: Langeroux, Dechaumont, Vorenglade, d'Albufex, Victorien Mergy and the rest.

And, at the foot, the signature of the chairman of the Two-Seas Canal Company, the signature written in letters of blood.

Lupin looked at his watch:

"A quarter to one," he said. "We have twenty minutes to spare. Let's have some lunch."

"But," said Clarisse, who was already beginning to lose her head, "don't forget..."

He simply said:

"All I know is that I'm dying of hunger."

He sat down at the table, cut himself a large slice of cold pie and said to his accomplices:

"Growler? A bite? You, Masher?"

"I could do with a mouthful, governor."

"Then hurry up, lads. And a glass of champage to wash it down with: it's the chloroform-patient's treat. Your health, Daubrecq! Sweet champagne? Dry champagne? Extra-dry?"

XI. THE CROSS OF LORRAINE

The moment Lupin had finished lunch, he at once and, so to speak, without transition, recovered all his mastery and authority. The time for joking was past; and he must no longer yield to his love of astonishing people with claptrap and conjuring tricks. Now that he had discovered the crystal stopper in the hiding-place which he had guessed with absolute certainty, now that he possessed the list of the Twenty-seven, it became a question of playing off the last game of the rubber without delay.

It was child's play, no doubt, and what remained to be done presented no difficulty. Nevertheless, it was essential that he should perform these final actions with promptness, decision and infallible perspicacity. The smallest blunder was irretrievable. Lupin knew this; but his strangely lucid brain had allowed for every contingency. And the movements and words which he was now about to make and utter were all fully prepared and matured:

"Growler, the commissionaire is waiting on the Boulevard Gambetta with his barrow and the trunk which we bought. Bring him here and have the trunk carried up. If the people of the hotel ask any questions, say it's for the lady in No. 130."

Then, addressing his other companion:

"Masher, go back to the station and take over the limousine. The price is arranged: ten thousand francs. Buy a chauffeur's cap and overcoat and bring the car to the hotel."

"The money, governor."

Lupin opened a pocketbook which had been removed from Daubrecq's jacket and produced a huge bundle of bank-notes. He separated ten of them:

"Here you are. Our friend appears to have been doing well at the club. Off with you, Masher!"

The two men went out through Clarisse's room. Lupin availed himself of a moment when Clarisse Mergy was not looking to stow away the pocketbook with the greatest satisfaction:

"I shall have done a fair stroke of business," he said to himself. "When all the expenses are paid, I shall still be well to the good; and it's not over yet."

Then turning to Clarisse Mergy, he asked:

"Have you a bag?"

"Yes, I bought one when I reached Nice, with some linen and a few necessaries; for I left Paris unprepared."

"Get all that ready. Then go down to the office. Say that you are expecting a trunk which a commissionaire is bringing from the station cloakroom and that you will want to unpack and pack it again in your room; and tell them that you are leaving."

When alone, Lupin examined Daubrecq carefully, felt in all his pockets and appropriated everything that seemed to present any sort of interest.

The Growler was the first to return. The trunk, a large wicker hamper covered with black moleskin, was taken into Clarisse's room. Assisted by Clarisse and the Growler, Lupin moved Daubrecq and put him in the trunk, in a sitting posture, but with his head bent so as to allow of the lid being fastened:

"I don't say that it's as comfortable as your berth in a sleeping-car, my dear deputy," Lupin observed. "But, all the same, it's better than a coffin. At least, you can breathe. Three little holes in each side. You have nothing to complain of!"

Then, unstopping a flask:

"A drop more chloroform? You seem to love it!..."

He soaked the pad once more, while, by his orders, Clarisse and the Growler propped up the deputy with linen, rugs and pillows, which they had taken the precaution to heap in the trunk.

"Capital!" said Lupin. "That trunk is fit to go round the world. Lock it and strap it."

The Masher arrived, in a chauffeur's livery:

"The car's below, governor."

"Good," he said. "Take the trunk down between you. It would be dangerous to give it to the hotel-servants."

"But if any one meets us?"

"Well, what then, Masher? Aren't you a chauffeur? You're carrying the trunk of your employer here present, the lady in No. 130, who will also go down, step into her motor... and wait for me two hundred yards farther on. Growler, you help to hoist the trunk up. Oh, first lock the partition-door!"

Lupin went to the next room, closed the other door, shot the bolt, walked out, locked the door behind him and went down in the lift.

In the office, he said:

"M. Daubrecq has suddenly been called away to Monte Carlo. He asked me to say that he would not be back until Tuesday and that you were to keep his room for him. His things are all there. Here is the key."

He walked away quietly and went after the car, where he found Clarisse lamenting:

"We shall never be in Paris to-morrow! It's madness! The least breakdown..."

"That's why you and I are going to take the train. It's safer..."

He put her into a cab and gave his parting instructions to the two men:

"Thirty miles an hour, on the average, do you understand? You're to drive and rest, turn and turn about. At that rate, you ought to be in Paris between six and seven to-morrow evening. But don't force the pace. I'm keeping Daubrecq, not because I want him for my plans, but as a hostage... and then by way of precaution... I like to feel that I can lay my hands on him during the next few days. So look after the dear fellow... Give him a few drops of chloroform every three or four hours: it's his one weakness... Off with you, Masher... And you, Daubrecq, don't get excited up there. The roof'll bear you all right... If you feel at all sick, don't mind... Off you go, Masher!"

He watched the car move into the distance and then told the cabman to drive to a post-office, where he dispatched a telegram in these words:

"M. Prasville, Prefecture de Police, Paris:

"Person found. Will bring you document eleven o'clock to-morrow morning. Urgent communication. "CLARISSE."

Clarisse and Lupin reached the station by half-past two.

"If only there's room!" said Clarisse, who was alarmed at the least thing.

"Room? Why, our berths are booked!"

"By whom?"

"By Jacob... by Daubrecq."

"How?"

"Why, at the office of the hotel they gave me a letter which had come for Daubrecq by express. It was the two berths which Jacob had sent him. Also, I have his deputy's pass. So we shall travel under the name of M. and Mme. Daubrecq and we shall receive all the attention due to our rank and station. You see, my dear madam, that everything's arranged."

The journey, this time, seemed short to Lupin. Clarisse told him what she had done during the past few days. He himself explained the miracle of his sudden appearance in Daubrecq's bedroom at the moment when his adversary believed him in Italy:

"A miracle, no," he said. "But still a remarkable phenomenon took place in me when I left San Remo, a sort of mysterious intuition which prompted me first to try and jump out of the train—and the Masher prevented me—and next to rush to the window, let down the glass and follow the porter of the Ambassadeurs-Palace, who had given me your message, with my eyes. Well, at that very minute, the porter aforesaid was rubbing his hands with an air of such satisfaction that, for no other reason, suddenly, I understood everything: I had been diddled, taken in by Daubrecq, as you yourself were. Heaps of little details flashed across my mind. My adversary's scheme became clear to me from start to finish. Another minute... and the disaster would have been beyond remedy. I had, I confess, a few moments of real despair, at the thought that I should not be able to repair all the mistakes that had been made. It depended simply on the time-table of the trains, which would either allow me or would not allow me to find Daubrecq's emissary on the railway-platform at San Remo. This time, at last, chance favoured me. We had hardly alighted at the first station when a train passed, for France. When we arrived at San Remo, the man was there. I had guessed right. He no longer wore his hotel-porter's cap and frock-coat, but a jacket and bowler. He stepped into a second-class compartment. From that moment, victory was assured."

"But... how...?" asked Clarisse, who, in spite of the thoughts that obsessed her, was interested in Lupin's story.

"How did I find you? Lord, simply by not losing sight of Master Jacob, while leaving him free to move about as he pleased, knowing that he was bound to account for his actions to Daubrecq. In point of fact, this morning, after spending the night in a small hotel at Nice, he met Daubrecq on the Promenade des Anglais. They talked for some time. I followed them. Daubrecq went back to the hotel, planted Jacob in one of the passages on the ground-floor, opposite the telephone-office, and went up in the lift. Ten minutes later I knew the number of his room and knew that a lady had been occupying the next room, No. 130, since the day before. 'I believe we've done it,' I said to the Growler and the Masher. I tapped lightly at your door. No answer. And the door was locked."

"Well?" asked Clarisse.

"Well, we opened it. Do you think there's only one key in the world that will work a lock? So I walked in. Nobody in your room. But the partition-door was ajar. I slipped through it. Thenceforth, a mere hanging separated me from you, from Daubrecq and from the packet of tobacco which I saw on the chimney-slab."

"Then you knew the hiding-place?"

"A look round Daubrecq's study in Paris showed me that that packet of tobacco had disappeared. Besides..."

"What?"

"I knew, from certain confessions wrung from Daubrecq in the Lovers' Tower, that the word Marie held the key to the riddle. Since then I had certainly thought of this word, but with the preconceived notion that it was spelt M A R I E. Well, it was really the first two syllables of another word, which I guessed, so to speak, only at the moment when I was struck by the absence of the packet of tobacco."

"What word do you mean?"

"Maryland, Maryland tobacco, the only tobacco that Daubrecq smokes."

And Lupin began to laugh:

"Wasn't it silly? And, at the same time, wasn't it clever of Daubrecq? We looked everywhere, we ransacked everything. Didn't I unscrew the brass sockets of the electric lights to see if they contained a crystal stopper? But how could I have thought, how could any one, however great his perspicacity, have thought of tearing off the paper band of a packet of Maryland, a band put on, gummed, sealed, stamped and dated by the State, under the control of the Inland Revenue Office? Only think! The State the accomplice of such an act of infamy! The Inland R-r-r-revenue Awfice lending itself to such a trick! No, a thousand times no! The Regie[17] is not perfect. It makes matches that won't light and cigarettes filled with hay. But there's all the difference in the world between recognizing that fact and believing the Inland Revenue to be in league with Daubrecq with the object of hiding the list of the Twenty-seven from the legitimate curiosity of the government and the enterprising efforts of Arsene Lupin! Observe that all Daubrecq had to do, in order to introduce the crystal stopper, was to bear upon the band a little, loosen it, draw it back, unfold the yellow paper, remove the tobacco and fasten it up again. Observe also that all we had to do, in Paris, was to take the packet in our hands and examine it, in order to discover the hiding-place. No matter! The packet itself, the plug of Maryland made up and passed by the State and by the Inland Revenue Office, was a sacred, intangible thing, a thing above suspicion! And nobody opened it. That was how that demon of a Daubrecq allowed that untouched packet of tobacco to lie about for months on his table, among his pipes and among other unopened packets of tobacco. And no power on earth could have given any one even the vaguest notion of looking into that harmless little cube. I would have you observe, besides..." Lupin went on pursuing his remarks relative to the packet of Maryland and the crystal stopper. His adversary's ingenuity and shrewdness interested him all the more inasmuch as Lupin had ended by getting the better of him. But to Clarisse these topics mattered much less than did her anxiety as to the acts which must be performed to save her son; and she sat wrapped in her own thoughts and hardly listened to him.

"Are you sure," she kept on repeating, "that you will succeed?"

"Absolutely sure."

"But Prasville is not in Paris."

"If he's not there, he's at the Havre. I saw it in the paper yesterday. In any case, a telegram will bring him to Paris at once."

"And do you think that he has enough influence?"

"To obtain the pardon of Vaucheray and Gilbert personally. No. If he had, we should have set him to work before now. But he is intelligent enough to understand the value of what we are bringing him and to act without a moment's delay."

"But, to be accurate, are you not deceived as to that value?"

"Was Daubrecq deceived? Was Daubrecq not in a better position than any of us to know the full power of that paper? Did he not have twenty proofs of it, each more convincing than the last? Think of all that he was able to do, for the sole reason that people knew him to possess the list. They knew it; and that was all. He did not use the list, but he had it. And, having it, he killed your husband. He built up his fortune on the ruin and the disgrace of the Twenty-seven. Only last week, one of the gamest of the lot, d'Albufex, cut his throat in a prison. No, take it from me, as the price of handing over that list, we could ask for anything we pleased. And we are asking for what? Almost nothing ... less than nothing... the pardon of a child of twenty. In other words, they will take us for idiots. What! We have in our hands..."

He stopped. Clarisse, exhausted by so much excitement, sat fast asleep in front of him.

They reached Paris at eight o'clock in the morning.

Lupin found two telegrams awaiting him at his flat in the Place de Clichy.

One was from the Masher, dispatched from Avignon on the previous day and stating that all was going well and that they hoped to keep their appointment punctually that evening. The other was from Prasville, dated from the Havre and addressed to Clarisse:

"Impossible return to-morrow Monday morning. Come to my office five o'clock. Reckon on you absolutely."

"Five o'clock!" said Clarisse. "How late!"

"It's a first-rate hour," declared Lupin.

"Still, if..."

---

[17] *The department of the French excise which holds the monopoly for the manufacture and sale of tobacco, cigars, cigarettes and matches—Translator's Note.*

"If the execution is to take place to-morrow morning: is that what you mean to say?... Don't be afraid to speak out, for the execution will not take place."

"The newspapers..."

"You haven't read the newspapers and you are not to read them. Nothing that they can say matters in the least. One thing alone matters: our interview with Prasville. Besides..."

He took a little bottle from a cupboard and, putting his hand on Clarisse's shoulder, said:

"Lie down here, on the sofa, and take a few drops of this mixture."

"What's it for?"

"It will make you sleep for a few hours... and forget. That's always so much gained."

"No, no," protested Clarisse, "I don't want to. Gilbert is not asleep. He is not forgetting."

"Drink it," said Lupin, with gentle insistence. She yielded all of a sudden, from cowardice, from excessive suffering, and did as she was told and lay on the sofa and closed her eyes. In a few minutes she was asleep.

Lupin rang for his servant:

"The newspapers... quick!... Have you bought them?"

"Here they are, governor."

Lupin opened one of them and at once read the following lines:

"ARSENE LUPIN'S ACCOMPLICES"

"We know from a positive source that Arsene Lupin's accomplices, Gilbert and Vaucheray, will be executed to-morrow, Tuesday, morning. M. Deibler has inspected the scaffold. Everything is ready."

He raised his head with a defiant look.

"Arsene Lupin's accomplices! The execution of Arsene Lupin's accomplices! What a fine spectacle! And what a crowd there will be to witness it! Sorry, gentlemen, but the curtain will not rise. Theatre closed by order of the authorities. And the authorities are myself!"

He struck his chest violently, with an arrogant gesture:

"The authorities are myself!"

At twelve o'clock Lupin received a telegram which the Masher had sent from Lyons:

"All well. Goods will arrive without damage."

At three o'clock Clarisse woke. Her first words were:

"Is it to be to-morrow?"

He did not answer. But she saw him look so calm and smiling that she felt herself permeated with an immense sense of peace and received the impression that everything was finished, disentangled, settled according to her companion's will.

They left the house at ten minutes past four. Prasville's secretary, who had received his chief's instructions by telephone, showed them into the office and asked them to wait. It was a quarter to five.

Prasville came running in at five o'clock exactly and, at once, cried:

"Have you the list?"

"Yes."

"Give it me."

He put out his hand. Clarisse, who had risen from her chair, did not stir.

Prasville looked at her for a moment, hesitated and sat down. He understood. In pursuing Daubrecq, Clarisse Mergy had not acted only from hatred and the desire for revenge. Another motive prompted her. The paper would not be handed over except upon conditions.

"Sit down, please," he said, thus showing that he accepted the discussion.

Clarisse resumed her seat and, when she remained silent, Prasville said:

"Speak, my friend, and speak quite frankly. I do not scruple to say that we wish to have that paper."

"If it is only a wish," remarked Clarisse, whom Lupin had coached in her part down to the least detail, "if it is only a wish, I fear that we shall not be able to come to an arrangement."

Prasville smiled:

"The wish, obviously, would lead us to make certain sacrifices."

"Every sacrifice," said Mme. Mergy, correcting him.

"Every sacrifice, provided, of course, that we keep within the bounds of acceptable requirements."

"And even if we go beyond those bounds," said Clarisse, inflexibly.

Prasville began to lose patience:

"Come, what is it all about? Explain yourself."

"Forgive me, my friend, but I wanted above all to mark the great importance which you attach to that paper and, in view of the immediate transaction which we are about to conclude, to specify—what shall I say?—the value of my share in it. That value, which has no limits, must, I repeat, be exchanged for an unlimited value."

"Agreed," said Prasville, querulously.

"I presume, therefore, that it is unnecessary for me to trace the whole story of the business or to enumerate, on the one hand, the disasters which the possession of that paper would have allowed you to avert and, on the other hand, the incalculable advantages which you will be able to derive from its possession?"

Prasville had to make an effort to contain himself and to answer in a tone that was civil, or nearly so:

"I admit everything. Is that enough?"

"I beg your pardon, but we cannot explain ourselves too plainly. And there is one point that remains to be cleared up. Are you in a position to treat, personally?"

"How do you mean?"

"I want to know not, of course, if you are empowered to settle this business here and now, but if, in dealing with me, you represent the views of those who know the business and who are qualified to settle it."

"Yes," declared Prasville, forcibly.

"So that I can have your answer within an hour after I have told you my conditions?"

"Yes."

"Will the answer be that of the government?"

"Yes."

Clarisse bent forward and, sinking her voice:

"Will the answer be that of the Elysee?"

Prasville appeared surprised. He reflected for a moment and then said:

"Yes."

"It only remains for me to ask you to give me your word of honour that, however incomprehensible my conditions may appear to you, you will not insist on my revealing the reason. They are what they are. Your answer must be yes or no."

"I give you my word of honour," said Prasville, formally.

Clarisse underwent a momentary agitation that made her turn paler still. Then, mastering herself, with her eyes fixed on Prasville's eyes, she said:

"You shall have the list of the Twenty-seven in exchange for the pardon of Gilbert and Vaucheray."

"Eh? What?"

Prasville leapt from his chair, looking absolutely dumbfounded:

"The pardon of Gilbert and Vaucheray? Of Arsene Lupin's accomplices?"

"Yes," she said.

"The murderers of the Villa Marie-Therese? The two who are due to die to-morrow?"

"Yes, those two," she said, in a loud voice. "I ask? I demand their pardon."

"But this is madness! Why? Why should you?"

"I must remind you, Prasville, that you gave me your word..."

"Yes... yes... I know... But the thing is so unexpected..."

"Why?"

"Why? For all sorts of reasons!"

"What reasons?"

"Well... well, but... think! Gilbert and Vaucheray have been sentenced to death!"

"Send them to penal servitude: that's all you have to do."

"Impossible! The case has created an enormous sensation. They are Arsene Lupin's accomplices. The whole world knows about the verdict."

"Well?"

"Well, we cannot, no, we cannot go against the decrees of justice."

"You are not asked to do that. You are asked for a commutation of punishment as an act of mercy. Mercy is a legal thing."

"The pardoning-commission has given its finding..."

"True, but there remains the president of the Republic."

"He has refused."

"He can reconsider his refusal."

"Impossible!"

"Why?"

"There's no excuse for it."

"He needs no excuse. The right of mercy is absolute. It is exercised without control, without reason, without excuse or explanation. It is a royal prerogative; the president of the Republic can wield it according to his good pleasure, or rather according to his conscience, in the best interests of the State."

"But it is too late! Everything is ready. The execution is to take place in a few hours."

"One hour is long enough to obtain your answer; you have just told us so."

"But this is confounded madness! There are insuperable obstacles to your conditions. I tell you again, it's impossible, physically impossible."

"Then the answer is no?"

"No! No! A thousand times no!"

"In that case, there is nothing left for us to do but to go."

She moved toward the door. M. Nicole followed her. Prasville bounded across the room and barred their way:

"Where are you going?"

"Well, my friend, it seems to me that our conversation is at an end. As you appear to think, as, in fact, you are certain that the president of the Republic will not consider the famous list of the Twenty-seven to be worth..."

"Stay where you are," said Prasville.

He turned the key in the door and began to pace the room, with his hands behind his back and his eyes fixed on the floor.

And Lupin, who had not breathed a word during the whole of this scene and who had prudently contented himself with playing a colourless part, said to himself:

"What a fuss! What a lot of affectation to arrive at the inevitable result! As though Prasville, who is not a genius, but not an absolute blockhead either, would be likely to lose the chance of revenging himself on his mortal enemy! There, what did I say? The idea of hurling Daubrecq into the bottomless pit appeals to him. Come, we've won the rubber."

Prasville was opening a small inner door which led to the office of his private secretary.

He gave an order aloud:

"M. Lartigue, telephone to the Elysee and say that I request the favour of an audience for a communication of the utmost importance."

He closed the door, came back to Clarisse and said:

"In any case, my intervention is limited to submitting your proposal."

"Once you submit it, it will be accepted."

A long silence followed. Clarisse's features expressed so profound a delight that Prasville was struck by it and looked at her with attentive curiosity. For what mysterious reason did Clarisse wish to save Gilbert and Vaucheray? What was the incomprehensible link that bound her to those two men? What tragedy connected those three lives and, no doubt, Daubrecq's in addition?

"Go ahead, old boy," thought Lupin, "cudgel your brains: you'll never spot it! Ah, if we had asked for Gilbert's pardon only, as Clarisse wished, you might have twigged the secret! But Vaucheray, that brute of a Vaucheray, there really could not be the least bond between Mme. Mergy and him.... Aha, by Jingo, it's my turn now!... He's watching me ... The inward soliloquy is turning upon myself... 'I wonder who that M. Nicole can be? Why has that little provincial usher devoted himself body and soul to Clarisse Mergy? Who is that old bore, if the truth were known? I made a mistake in not inquiring... I must look into this.... I must rip off the beggar's mask. For, after all, it's not natural that a man should take so much trouble about a matter in which he is not directly interested. Why should he also wish to save Gilbert and Vaucheray? Why? Why should he?...'" Lupin turned his head away. "Look out!... Look out!... There's a notion passing through that red-tape-merchant's skull: a confused notion which he can't put into words. Hang it all, he mustn't suspect M. Lupin under M. Nicole! The thing's complicated enough as it is, in all conscience!..."

But there was a welcome interruption. Prasville's secretary came to say that the audience would take place in an hour's time.

"Very well. Thank you," said Prasville. "That will do."

And, resuming the interview, with no further circumlocution, speaking like a man who means to put a thing through, he declared:

"I think that we shall be able to manage it. But, first of all, so that I may do what I have undertaken to do, I want more precise information, fuller details. Where was the paper?"

"In the crystal stopper, as we thought," said Mme. Mergy.

"And where was the crystal stopper?"

"In an object which Daubrecq came and fetched, a few days ago, from the writing-desk in his study in the Square Lamartine, an object which I took from him yesterday."

"What sort of object?"

"Simply a packet of tobacco, Maryland tobacco, which used to lie about on the desk."

Prasville was petrified. He muttered, guilelessly:

"Oh, if I had only known! I've had my hand on that packet of Maryland a dozen times! How stupid of me!"

"What does it matter?" said Clarisse. "The great thing is that the discovery is made."

Prasville pulled a face which implied that the discovery would have been much pleasanter if he himself had made it. Then he asked:

"So you have the list?"

"Yes."

"Show it to me."

And, when Clarisse hesitated, he added:

"Oh, please, don't be afraid! The list belongs to you, and I will give it back to you. But you must understand that I cannot take the step in question without making certain."

Clarisse consulted M. Nicole with a glance which did not escape Prasville. Then she said:

"Here it is."

He seized the scrap of paper with a certain excitement, examined it and almost immediately said:

"Yes, yes... the secretary's writing: I recognize it.... And the signature of the chairman of the company: the signature in red.... Besides, I have other proofs.... For instance, the torn piece which completes the left-hand top corner of this sheet..."

He opened his safe and, from a special cash-box, produced a tiny piece of paper which he put against the top left corner:

"That's right. The torn edges fit exactly. The proof is undeniable. All that remains is to verify the make of this foreign-post-paper."

Clarisse was radiant with delight. No one would have believed that the most terrible torture had racked her for weeks and weeks and that she was still bleeding and quivering from its effects.

While Prasville was holding the paper against a window-pane, she said to Lupin:

"I insist upon having Gilbert informed this evening. He must be so awfully unhappy!"

"Yes," said Lupin. "Besides, you can go to his lawyer and tell him."

She continued:

"And then I must see Gilbert to-morrow. Prasville can think what he likes."

"Of course. But he must first gain his cause at the Elysee."

"There can't be any difficulty, can there?"

"No. You saw that he gave way at once."

Prasville continued his examination with the aid of a magnifying-glass and compared the sheet with the scrap of torn paper. Next, he took from the cash-box some other sheets of letter-paper and examined one of these by holding it up to the light:

"That's done," he said. "My mind is made up. Forgive me, dear friend: it was a very difficult piece of work.... I passed through various stages. When all is said, I had my suspicions... and not without cause..."

"What do you mean?" asked Clarisse.

"One second.... I must give an order first."

He called his secretary:

"Please telephone at once to the Elysee, make my apologies and say that I shall not require the audience, for reasons which I will explain later."

He closed the door and returned to his desk. Clarisse and Lupin stood choking, looking at him in stupefaction, failing to understand this sudden change. Was he mad? Was it a trick on his part? A breach of faith? And was he refusing to keep his promise, now that he possessed the list?

He held it out to Clarisse:

"You can have it back."

"Have it back?"

"And return it to Daubrecq."

"To Daubrecq?"

"Unless you prefer to burn it."

"What do you say?"

"I say that, if I were in your place, I would burn it."

"Why do you say that? It's ridiculous!"

"On the contrary, it is very sensible."

"But why? Why?"

"Why? I will tell you. The list of the Twenty-seven, as we know for absolutely certain, was written on a sheet of letter-paper belonging to the chairman of the Canal Company, of which there are a few samples in this cash-box. Now all these samples have as a water-mark a little cross of Lorraine which is almost invisible, but which can just be seen in the thickness of the paper when you hold it up to the light. The sheet which you have brought me does not contain that little cross of Lorraine."[18]

Lupin felt a nervous trembling shake him from head to foot and he dared not turn his eyes on Clarisse, realizing what a terrible blow this was to her. He heard her stammer:

"Then are we to suppose... that Daubrecq was taken in?"

"Not a bit of it!" exclaimed Prasville. "It is you who have been taken in, my poor friend. Daubrecq has the real list, the list which he stole from the dying man's safe."

"But this one..."

"This one is a forgery."

"A forgery?"

---

[18] *The Cross of Lorraine is a cross with two horizontal lines or bars across the upper half of the perpendicular beam*

"An undoubted forgery. It was an admirable piece of cunning on Daubrecq's part. Dazzled by the crystal stopper which he flashed before your eyes, you did nothing but look for that stopper in which he had stowed away no matter what, the first bit of paper that came to hand, while he quietly kept..."

Prasville interrupted himself. Clarisse was walking up to him with short, stiff steps, like an automaton. She said:

"Then..."

"Then what, dear friend?"

"You refuse?"

"Certainly, I am obliged to; I have no choice."

"You refuse to take that step?"

"Look here, how can I do what you ask? It's not possible, on the strength of a valueless document..."

"You won't do it?... You won't do it?... And, to-morrow morning... in a few hours... Gilbert..."

She was frightfully pale, her face sunk, like the face of one dying. Her eyes opened wider and wider and her teeth chattered...

Lupin, fearing the useless and dangerous words which she was about to utter, seized her by the shoulders and tried to drag her away. But she thrust him back with indomitable strength, took two or three more steps, staggered, as though on the point of falling, and, suddenly, in a burst of energy and despair, laid hold of Prasville and screamed:

"You shall go to the Elysee!... You shall go at once!... You must!... You must save Gilbert!"

"Please, please, my dear friend, calm yourself..."

She gave a strident laugh:

"Calm myself!... When, to-morrow morning, Gilbert... Ah, no, no, I am terrified... it's appalling.... Oh, run, you wretch, run! Obtain his pardon!... Don't you understand? Gilbert... Gilbert is my son! My son! My son!"

Prasville gave a cry. The blade of a knife flashed in Clarisse's hand and she raised her arm to strike herself. But the movement was not completed. M. Nicole caught her arm in its descent and, taking the knife from Clarisse, reducing her to helplessness, he said, in a voice that rang through the room like steel:

"What you are doing is madness!... When I gave you my oath that I would save him! You must... live for him... Gilbert shall not die.... How can he die, when... I gave you my oath?..."

"Gilbert... my son..." moaned Clarisse.

He clasped her fiercely, drew her against himself and put his hand over her mouth:

"Enough! Be quiet!... I entreat you to be quiet.... Gilbert shall not die..."

With irresistible authority, he dragged her away like a subdued child that suddenly becomes obedient; but, at the moment of opening the door, he turned to Prasville:

"Wait for me here, monsieur," he commanded, in an imperative tone. "If you care about that list of the Twenty-seven, the real list, wait for me. I shall be back in an hour, in two hours, at most; and then we will talk business."

And abruptly, to Clarisse:

"And you, madame, a little courage yet. I command you to show courage, in Gilbert's name."

He went away, through the passages, down the stairs, with a jerky step, holding Clarisse under the arm, as he might have held a lay-figure, supporting her, carrying her almost. A court-yard, another court-yard, then the street.

Meanwhile, Prasville, surprised at first, bewildered by the course of events, was gradually recovering his composure and thinking. He thought of that M. Nicole, a mere supernumerary at first, who played beside Clarisse the part of one of those advisers to whom we cling in the serious crises of our lives and who suddenly, shaking off his torpor, appeared in the full light of day, resolute, masterful, mettlesome, brimming over with daring, ready to overthrow all the obstacles that fate placed on his path.

Who was there that was capable of acting thus?

Prasville started. The question had no sooner occurred to his mind than the answer flashed on him, with absolute certainty. All the proofs rose up, each more exact, each more convincing than the last.

Hurriedly he rang. Hurriedly he sent for the chief detective-inspector on duty. And, feverishly:

"Were you in the waiting-room, chief-inspector?"

"Yes, monsieur le secretaire-general."

"Did you see a gentleman and a lady go out?"

"Yes."

"Would you know the man again?"

"Yes."

"Then don't lose a moment, chief-inspector. Take six inspectors with you. Go to the Place de Clichy. Make inquiries about a man called Nicole and watch the house. The Nicole man is on his way back there."

"And if he comes out, monsieur le secretaire-general?"

"Arrest him. Here's a warrant."

He sat down to his desk and wrote a name on a form:

"Here you are, chief-inspector. I will let the chief-detective know."

The chief-inspector seemed staggered:

"But you spoke to me of a man called Nicole, monsieur le secretaire-general."

"Well?"

"The warrant is in the name of Arsene Lupin."

"Arsene Lupin and the Nicole man are one and the same individual."

XII. THE SCAFFOLD

"I will save him, I will save him," Lupin repeated, without ceasing, in the taxicab in which he and Clarisse drove away. "I swear that I will save him."

Clarisse did not listen, sat as though numbed, as though possessed by some great nightmare of death, which left her ignorant of all that was happening outside her. And Lupin set forth his plans, perhaps more to reassure himself than to convince Clarisse. "No, no, the game is not lost yet. There is one trump left, a huge trump, in the shape of the letters and documents which Vorenglade, the ex-deputy, is offering to sell to Daubrecq and of which Daubrecq spoke to you yesterday at Nice. I shall buy those letters and documents of Stanislas Vorenglade at whatever price he chooses to name. Then we shall go back to the police-office and I shall say to Prasville, 'Go to the Elysee at once ... Use the list as though it were genuine, save Gilbert from death and be content to acknowledge to-morrow, when Gilbert is saved, that the list is forged.

"'Be off, quickly!... If you refuse, well, if you refuse, the Vorenglade letters and documents shall be reproduced to-morrow, Tuesday, morning in one of the leading newspapers.' Vorenglade will be arrested. And M. Prasville will find himself in prison before night."

Lupin rubbed his hands:

"He'll do as he's told!... He'll do as he's told!... I felt that at once, when I was with him. The thing appeared to me as a dead certainty. And I found Vorenglade's address in Daubrecq's pocket-books, so... driver, Boulevard Raspail!"

They went to the address given. Lupin sprang from the cab, ran up three flights of stairs.

The servant said that M. Vorenglade was away and would not be back until dinner-time next evening.

"And don't you know where he is?"

"M. Vorenglade is in London, sir."

Lupin did not utter a word on returning to the cab. Clarisse, on her side, did not even ask him any questions, so indifferent had she become to everything, so absolutely did she look upon her son's death as an accomplished fact.

They drove to the Place de Cichy. As Lupin entered the house he passed two men who were just leaving the porter's box. He was too much engrossed to notice them. They were Prasville's inspectors.

"No telegram?" he asked his servant.

"No, governor," replied Achille.

"No news of the Masher and the Growler?"

"No, governor, none."

"That's all right," he said to Clarisse, in a casual tone. "It's only seven o'clock and we mustn't reckon on seeing them before eight or nine. Prasville will have to wait, that's all. I will telephone to him to wait."

He did so and was hanging up the receiver, when he heard a moan behind him. Clarisse was standing by the table, reading an evening-paper. She put her hand to her heart, staggered and fell.

"Achille, Achille!" cried Lupin, calling his man. "Help me put her on my bed... And then go to the cupboard and get me the medicine-bottle marked number four, the bottle with the sleeping-draught."

He forced open her teeth with the point of a knife and compelled her to swallow half the bottle:

"Good," he said. "Now the poor thing won't wake till to-morrow... after."

He glanced through the paper, which was still clutched in Clarisse' hand, and read the following lines:

"The strictest measures have been taken to keep order at the execution of Gilbert and Vaucheray, lest Arsene Lupin should make an attempt to rescue his accomplices from the last penalty. At twelve o'clock to-night a cordon of troops will be drawn across all the approaches to the Sante Prison. As already stated, the execution will take place outside the prison-walls, in the square formed by the Boulevard Arago and the Rue de la Sante.

"We have succeeded in obtaining some details of the attitude of the two condemned men. Vaucheray observes a stolid sullenness and is awaiting the fatal event with no little courage:

"'Crikey,' he says, 'I can't say I'm delighted; but I've got to go through it and I shall keep my end up.' And he adds, 'Death I don't care a hang about! What worries me is the thought that they're going to cut my head off. Ah, if the governor could only hit on some trick to send me straight off to the next world before I had time to say knife! A drop of Prussic acid, governor, if you please!'

"Gilbert's calmness is even more impressive, especially when we remember how he broke down at the trial. He retains an unshaken confidence in the omnipotence of Arsene Lupin:

"'The governor shouted to me before everybody not to be afraid, that he was there, that he answered for everything. Well, I'm not afraid. I shall rely on him until the last day, until the last minute, at the very foot of the scaffold. I know the governor! There's no danger with him. He has promised and he will keep his word. If my head were off, he'd come and clap it on my shoulders and firmly! Arsene Lupin allow his chum Gilbert to die? Not he! Excuse my humour!'

"There is a certain touching frankness in all this enthusiasm which is not without a dignity of its own. We shall see if Arsene Lupin deserves the confidence so blindly placed in him."

Lupin was hardly able to finish reading the article for the tears that dimmed his eyes: tears of affection, tears of pity, tears of distress.

No, he did not deserve the confidence of his chum Gilbert. Certainly, he had performed impossibilities; but there are circumstances in which we must perform more than impossibilities, in which we must show ourselves stronger than fate; and, this time, fate had been stronger than he. Ever since the first day and throughout this lamentable adventure, events had gone contrary to his anticipations, contrary to logic itself. Clarisse and he, though pursuing an identical aim, had wasted weeks in fighting each other. Then, at the moment when they were uniting their efforts, a series of ghastly disasters had come one after the other: the kidnapping of little Jacques, Daubrecq's disappearance, his imprisonment in the Lovers' Tower, Lupin's wound, his enforced inactivity, followed by the cunning manoeuvres that dragged Clarisse—and Lupin after her—to the south, to Italy. And then, as a crowning catastrophe, when, after prodigies of will-power, after miracles of perseverance, they were entitled to think that the Golden Fleece was won, it all came to nothing. The list of the Twenty-seven had no more value than the most insignificant scrap of paper.

"The game's up!" said Lupin. "It's an absolute defeat. What if I do revenge myself on Daubrecq, ruin him and destroy him? He is the real victor, once Gilbert is going to die."

He wept anew, not with spite or rage, but with despair. Gilbert was going to die! The lad whom he called his chum, the best of his pals would be gone for ever, in a few hours. He could not save him. He was at the end of his tether. He did not even look round for a last expedient. What was the use?

And his persuasion of his own helplessness was so deep, so definite that he felt no shock of any kind on receiving a telegram from the Masher that said:

"Motor accident. Essential part broken. Long repair.

Arrive to-morrow morning."

It was a last proof to show that fate had uttered its decree. He no longer thought of rebelling against the decision.

He looked at Clarisse. She was peacefully sleeping; and this total oblivion, this absence of all consciousness, seemed to him so enviable that, suddenly yielding to a fit of cowardice, he seized the bottle, still half-filled with the sleeping-draught, and drank it down.

Then he stretched himself on a couch and rang for his man:

"Go to bed, Achille, and don't wake me on any pretence whatever."

"Then there's nothing to be done for Gilbert and Vaucheray, governor?" said Achille.

"Nothing."

"Are they going through it?"

"They are going through it."

Twenty minutes later Lupin fell into a heavy sleep. It was ten o'clock in the evening.

The night was full of incident and noise around the prison. At one o'clock in the morning the Rue de la Sante, the Boulevard Arago and all the streets abutting on the gaol were guarded by police, who allowed no one to pass without a regular cross-examination.

For that matter, it was raining in torrents; and it seemed as though the lovers of this sort of show would not be very numerous. The public-houses were all closed by special order. At four o'clock three companies of infantry came and took up their positions along the pavements, while a battalion occupied the Boulevard Arago in case of a surprise. Municipal guards cantered up and down between the lines; a whole staff of police-magistrates, officers and functionaries, brought together for the occasion, moved about among the troops.

The guillotine was set up in silence, in the middle of the square formed by the boulevard and the street; and the sinister sound of hammering was heard.

But, at five o'clock, the crowd gathered, notwithstanding the rain, and people began to sing. They shouted for the footlights, called for the curtain to rise, were exasperated to see that, at the distance at which the barriers had been fixed, they could hardly distinguish the uprights of the guillotine.

Several carriages drove up, bringing official persons dressed in black. There were cheers and hoots, whereupon a troop of mounted municipal guards scattered the groups and cleared the space to a distance of three hundred yards from the square. Two fresh companies of soldiers lined up.

And suddenly there was a great silence. A vague white light fell from the dark sky. The rain ceased abruptly.

Inside the prison, at the end of the passage containing the condemned cells, the men in black were conversing in low voices. Prasville was talking to the public prosecutor, who expressed his fears:

"No, no," declared Prasville, "I assure you, it will pass without an incident of any kind."

"Do your reports mention nothing at all suspicious, monsieur le secretaire-general?"

"Nothing. And they can't mention anything, for the simple reason that we have Lupin."

"Do you mean that?"

"Yes, we know his hiding-place. The house where he lives, on the Place de Clichy, and where he went at seven o'clock last night, is surrounded. Moreover, I know the scheme which he had contrived to save his two accomplices. The scheme miscarried at the last moment. We have nothing to fear, therefore. The law will take its course."

Meanwhile, the hour had struck.

They took Vaucheray first; and the governor of the prison ordered the door of his cell to be opened. Vaucheray leapt out of bed and cast eyes dilated with terror upon the men who entered.

"Vaucheray, we have come to tell you..."

"Stow that, stow that," he muttered. "No words. I know all about it. Get on with the business."

One would have thought that he was in a hurry for it to be over as fast as possible, so readily did he submit to the usual preparations. But he would not allow any of them to speak to him:

"No words," he repeated. "What? Confess to the priest? Not worth while. I have shed blood. The law sheds my blood. It's the good old rule. We're quits."

Nevertheless, he stopped short for a moment:

"I say, is my mate going through it too?"

And, when he heard that Gilbert would go to the scaffold at the same time as himself, he had two or three seconds of hesitation, glanced at the bystanders, seemed about to speak, was silent and, at last, muttered:

"It's better so.... They'll pull us through together... we'll clink glasses together."

Gilbert was not asleep either, when the men entered his cell.

Sitting on his bed, he listened to the terrible words, tried to stand up, began to tremble frightfully, from head to foot, like a skeleton when shaken, and then fell back, sobbing:

"Oh, my poor mummy, poor mummy!" he stammered.

They tried to question him about that mother, of whom he had never spoken; but his tears were interrupted by a sudden fit of rebellion and he cried:

"I have done no murder... I won't die. I have done no murder..."

"Gilbert," they said, "show yourself a man."

"Yes, yes... but I have done no murder... Why should I die?"

His teeth chattered so loudly that words which he uttered became unintelligible. He let the men do their work, made his confession, heard mass and then, growing calmer and almost docile, with the voice of a little child resigning itself, murmured:

"Tell my mother that I beg her forgiveness."

"Your mother?"

"Yes... Put what I say in the papers... She will understand... And then..."

"What, Gilbert?"

"Well, I want the governor to know that I have not lost confidence."

He gazed at the bystanders, one after the other, as though he entertained the mad hope that "the governor" was one of them, disguised beyond recognition and ready to carry him off in his arms:

"Yes," he said, gently and with a sort of religious piety, "yes, I still have confidence, even at this moment... Be sure and let him know, won't you?... I am positive that he will not let me die. I am certain of it..."

They guessed, from the fixed look in his eyes, that he saw Lupin, that he felt Lupin's shadow prowling around and seeking an inlet through which to get to him. And never was anything more touching than the sight of that stripling—clad in the strait-jacket, with his arms and legs bound, guarded by thousands of men—whom the executioner already held in his inexorable hand and who, nevertheless, hoped on.

Anguish wrung the hearts of all the beholders. Their eyes were dimmed with tears:

"Poor little chap!" stammered some one.

Prasville, touched like the rest and thinking of Clarisse, repeated, in a whisper:

"Poor little chap!"

But the hour struck, the preparations were finished. They set out.

The two processions met in the passage. Vaurheray, on seeing Gilbert, snapped out:

"I say, kiddie, the governor's chucked us!"

And he added a sentence which nobody, save Prasville, was able to understand:

"Expect he prefers to pocket the proceeds of the crystal stopper."

They went down the staircases. They crossed the prison-yards. An endless, horrible distance.

And, suddenly, in the frame of the great doorway, the wan light of day, the rain, the street, the outlines of houses, while far-off sounds came through the awful silence.

They walked along the wall, to the corner of the boulevard.

A few steps farther Vaucheray started back: he had seen!

Gilbert crept along, with lowered head, supported by an executioner's assistant and by the chaplain, who made him kiss the crucifix as he went.

There stood the guillotine.

"No, no," shouted Gilbert, "I won't... I won't... Help! Help!"

A last appeal, lost in space.

The executioner gave a signal. Vaucheray was laid hold of, lifted, dragged along, almost at a run.

And then came this staggering thing: a shot, a shot fired from the other side, from one of the houses opposite.

The assistants stopped short.

The burden which they were dragging had collapsed in their arms.

"What is it? What's happened?" asked everybody.

"He's wounded..."

Blood spurted from Vaucheray's forehead and covered his face.

He spluttered:

"That's done it... one in a thousand! Thank you, governor, thank you."

"Finish him off! Carry him there!" said a voice, amid the general confusion.

"But he's dead!"

"Get on with it... finish him off!"

Tumult was at its height, in the little group of magistrates, officials and policemen. Every one was giving orders:

"Execute him!... The law must take its course!... We have no right to delay! It would be cowardice!... Execute him!"

"But the man's dead!"

"That makes no difference!... The law must be obeyed!... Execute him!"

The chaplain protested, while two warders and Prasville kept their eyes on Gilbert. In the meantime, the assistants had taken up the corpse again and were carrying it to the guillotine.

"Hurry up!" cried the executioner, scared and hoarse-voiced. "Hurry up! ... And the other one to follow... Waste no time..."

He had not finished speaking, when a second report rang out. He spun round on his heels and fell, groaning:

"It's nothing... a wound in the shoulder... Go on... The next one's turn!"

But his assistants were running away, yelling with terror. The space around the guillotine was cleared. And the prefect of police, rallying his men, drove everybody back to the prison, helter-skelter, like a disordered rabble: the magistrates, the officials, the condemned man, the chaplain, all who had passed through the archway two or three minutes before.

In the meanwhile, a squad of policemen, detectives and soldiers were rushing upon the house, a little old-fashioned, three-storied house, with a ground-floor occupied by two shops which happened to be empty. Immediately after the first shot, they had seen, vaguely, at one of the windows on the second floor, a man holding a rifle in his hand and surrounded with a cloud of smoke.

Revolver-shots were fired at him, but missed him. He, standing calmly on a table, took aim a second time, fired from the shoulder; and the crack of the second report was heard. Then he withdrew into the room.

Down below, as nobody answered the peal at the bell, the assailants demolished the door, which gave way almost immediately. They made for the staircase, but their onrush was at once stopped, on the first floor, by an accumulation of beds, chairs and other furniture, forming a regular barricade and so close-entangled that it took the aggressors four or five minutes to clear themselves a passage.

Those four or five minutes lost were enough to render all pursuit hopeless. When they reached the second floor they heard a voice shouting from above:

"This way, friends! Eighteen stairs more. A thousand apologies for giving you so much trouble!"

They ran up those eighteen stairs and nimbly at that! But, at the top, above the third story, was the garret, which was reached by a ladder and a trapdoor. And the fugitive had taken away the ladder and bolted the trapdoor.

The reader will not have forgotten the sensation created by this amazing action, the editions of the papers issued in quick succession, the newsboys tearing and shouting through the streets, the whole metropolis on edge with indignation and, we may say, with anxious curiosity.

But it was at the headquarters of police that the excitement developed into a paroxysm. Men flung themselves about on every side. Messages, telegrams, telephone calls followed one upon the other.

At last, at eleven o'clock in the morning, there was a meeting in the office of the prefect of police, and Prasville was there. The chief-detective read a report of his inquiry, the results of which amounted to this: shortly before midnight yesterday some one had rung at the house on the Boulevard Arago. The portress, who slept in a small room on the ground-floor, behind one of the shops pulled the rope. A man came and tapped at her door. He said that he had come from the police on an urgent matter concerning to-morrow's execution. The portress opened the door and was at once attacked, gagged and bound.

Ten minutes later a lady and gentleman who lived on the first floor and who had just come home were also reduced to helplessness by the same individual and locked up, each in one of the two empty shops. The third-floor tenant underwent a similar fate, but in his own flat and his own bedroom, which the man was able to enter without being heard. The second floor was unoccupied, and the man took up his quarters there. He was now master of the house.

"And there we are!" said the prefect of police, beginning to laugh, with a certain bitterness. "There we are! It's as simple as shelling peas. Only, what surprises me is that he was able to get away so easily."

"I will ask you to observe, monsieur le prefet, that, being absolute master of the house from one o'clock in the morning, he had until five o'clock to prepare his flight."

"And that flight took place...?"

"Over the roofs. At that spot the houses in the next street, the Rue de la Glaciere, are quite near and there is only one break in the roofs, about three yards wide, with a drop of one yard in height."

"Well?"

"Well, our man had taken away the ladder leading to the garret and used it as a foot-bridge. After crossing to the next block of buildings, all he had to do was to look through the windows until he found an empty attic, enter one of the houses in the Rue de la Glaciere and walk out quietly with his hands in his pockets. In this way his flight, duly prepared beforehand, was effected very simply and without the least obstacle."

"But you had taken the necessary measures."

"Those which you ordered, monsieur le prefet. My men spent three hours last evening visiting all the houses, so as to make sure that there was no stranger hiding there. At the moment when they were leaving the last house I had the street barred. Our man must have slipped through during that few minutes' interval."

"Capital! Capital! And there is no doubt in your minds, of course: it's Arsene Lupin?"

"Not a doubt. In the first place, it was all a question of his accomplices. And then... and then... no one but Arsene Lupin was capable of contriving such a master-stroke and carrying it out with that inconceivable boldness."

"But, in that case," muttered the prefect of police—and, turning to Prasville, he continued—"but, in that case, my dear Prasville, the fellow of whom you spoke to me, the fellow whom you and the chief-detective have had watched since yesterday evening, in his flat in the Place de Clichy, that fellow is not Arsene Lupin?"

"Yes, he is, monsieur le prefet. There is no doubt about that either."

"Then why wasn't he arrested when he went out last night?"

"He did not go out."

"I say, this is getting complicated!"

"It's quite simple, monsieur le prefet. Like all the houses in which traces of Arsene Lupin are to be found, the house in the Place de Cichy has two outlets."

"And you didn't know it?"

"I didn't know it. I only discovered it this morning, on inspecting the flat."

"Was there no one in the flat?"

"No. The servant, a man called Achille, went away this morning, taking with him a lady who was staying with Lupin."

"What was the lady's name?"

"I don't know," replied Prasville, after an imperceptible hesitation.

"But you know the name under which Arsene Lupin passed?"

"Yes. M. Nicole, a private tutor, master of arts and so on. Here is his card."

As Prasville finished speaking, an office-messenger came to tell the prefect of police that he was wanted immediately at the Elysee. The prime minister was there already.

"I'm coming," he said. And he added, between his teeth, "It's to decide upon Gilbert's fate."

Prasville ventured:

"Do you think they will pardon him, monsieur le prefet?"

"Never! After last night's affair, it would make a most deplorable impression. Gilbert must pay his debt to-morrow morning."

The messenger had, at the same time, handed Prasville a visiting-card. Prasville now looked at it, gave a start and muttered:

"Well, I'm hanged! What a nerve!"

"What's the matter?" asked the prefect of police.

"Nothing, nothing, monsieur le prefet," declared Prasville, who did not wish to share with another the honour of seeing this business through. "Nothing... an unexpected visit... I hope soon to have the pleasure of telling you the result."

And he walked away, mumbling, with an air of amazement:

"Well, upon my word! What a nerve the beggar has! What a nerve!"

The visiting-card which he held in his hand bore these words:

M. Nicole,

Master of Arts, Private Tutor.

XIII. THE LAST BATTLE

When Prasville returned to his office he saw M. Nicole sitting on a bench in the waiting-room, with his bent back, his ailing air, his gingham umbrella, his rusty hat and his single glove:

"It's he all right," said Prasville, who had feared for a moment that Lupin might have sent another M. Nicole to see him. "And the fact that he has come in person proves that he does not suspect that I have seen through him." And, for the third time, he said, "All the same, what a nerve!"

He shut the door of his office and called his secretary:

"M. Lartigue, I am having a rather dangerous person shown in here. The chances are that he will have to leave my office with the bracelets on. As soon as he is in my room, make all the necessary arrangements: send for a dozen inspectors and have them posted in the waiting-room and in your office. And take this as a definite instruction: the moment I ring, you are all to come in, revolvers in hand, and surround the fellow. Do you quite understand?"

"Yes, monsieur le secretaire-general."

"Above all, no hesitation. A sudden entrance, in a body, revolvers in hand. Send M. Nicole in, please."

As soon as he was alone, Prasville covered the push of an electric bell on his desk with some papers and placed two revolvers of respectable dimensions behind a rampart of books.

"And now," he said to himself, "to sit tight. If he has the list, let's collar it. If he hasn't, let's collar him. And, if possible, let's collar both. Lupin and the list of the Twenty-seven, on the same day, especially after the scandal of this morning, would be a scoop in a thousand."

There was a knock at the door.

"Come in!" said Prasville.

And, rising from his seat:

"Come in, M. Nicole, come in."

M. Nicole crept timidly into the room, sat down on the extreme edge of the chair to which Prasville pointed and said:

"I have come...to resume... our conversation of yesterday... Please excuse the delay, monsieur."

"One second," said Prasville. "Will you allow me?"

He stepped briskly to the outer room and, seeing his secretary:

"I was forgetting, M. Lartigue. Have the staircases and passages searched... in case of accomplices."

He returned, settled himself comfortably, as though for a long and interesting conversation, and began:

"You were saying, M. Nicole?"

"I was saying, monsieur le secretaire-general, that I must apologize for keeping you waiting yesterday evening. I was detained by different matters. First of all, Mme. Mergy...."

"Yes, you had to see Mme. Mergy home."

"Just so, and to look after her. You can understand the poor thing's despair... Her son Gilbert so near death... And such a death!... At that time we could only hope for a miracle... an impossible miracle. I myself was resigned to the inevitable... You know as well as I do, when fate shows itself implacable, one ends by despairing."

"But I thought," observed Prasville, "that your intention, on leaving me, was to drag Daubrecq's secret from him at all costs."

"Certainly. But Daubrecq was not in Paris."

"Oh?"

"No. He was on his way to Paris in a motor-car."

"Have you a motor-car, M. Nicole?"

"Yes, when I need it: an out-of-date concern, an old tin kettle of sorts. Well, he was on his way to Paris in a motor-car, or rather on the roof of a motor-car, inside a trunk in which I packed him. But, unfortunately, the motor was unable to reach Paris until after the execution. Thereupon..."

Prasville stared at M. Nicole with an air of stupefaction. If he had retained the least doubt of the individual's real identity, this manner of dealing with Daubrecq would have removed it. By Jingo! To pack a man in a trunk and pitch him on the top of a motorcar!... No one but Lupin would indulge in such a freak, no one but Lupin would confess it with that ingenuous coolness!

"Thereupon," echoed Prasville, "you decided what?"

"I cast about for another method."

"What method?"

"Why, surely, monsieur le secretaire-general, you know as well as I do!"

"How do you mean?"

"Why, weren't you at the execution?"

"I was."

"In that case, you saw both Vaucheray and the executioner hit, one mortally, the other with a slight wound. And you can't fail to see..."

"Oh," exclaimed Prasville, dumbfounded, "you confess it? It was you who fired the shots, this morning?"

"Come, monsieur le secretaire-general, think! What choice had I? The list of the Twenty-seven which you examined was a forgery. Daubrecq, who possessed the genuine one, would not arrive until a few hours after the execution. There was therefore but one way for me to save Gilbert and obtain his pardon; and that was to delay the execution by a few hours."

"Obviously."

"Well, of course. By killing that infamous brute, that hardened criminal, Vaucheray, and wounding the executioner, I spread disorder and panic; I made Gilbert's execution physically and morally impossible; and I thus gained the few hours which were indispensable for my purpose."

"Obviously," repeated Prasville.

"Well, of course," repeated Lupin, "it gives us all—the government, the president and myself—time to reflect and to see the question in a clearer light. What do you think of it, monsieur le secretaire-general?"

Prasville thought a number of things, especially that this Nicole was giving proof, to use a vulgar phrase, of the most infernal cheek, of a cheek so great that Prasville felt inclined to ask himself if he was really right in identifying Nicole with Lupin and Lupin with Nicole.

"I think, M. Nicole, that a man has to be a jolly good shot to kill a person whom he wants to kill, at a distance of a hundred yards, and to wound another person whom he only wants to wound."

"I have had some little practice," said M. Nicole, with modest air.

"And I also think that your plan can only be the fruit of a long preparation."

"Not at all! That's where you're wrong! It was absolutely spontaneous! If my servant, or rather the servant of the friend who lent me his flat in the Place de Clichy, had not shaken me out of my sleep, to tell me that he had once served as a shopman in that little house on the Boulevard Arago, that it did not hold many tenants and that there might be something to be done there, our poor Gilbert would have had his head cut off by now... and Mme. Mergy would most likely be dead."

"Oh, you think so?"

"I am sure of it. And that was why I jumped at that faithful retainer's suggestion. Only, you interfered with my plans, monsieur le secretaire-general."

"I did?"

"Yes. You must needs go and take the three-cornered precaution of posting twelve men at the door of my house. I had to climb five flights of back stairs and go out through the servants' corridor and the next house. Such useless fatigue!"

"I am very sorry, M. Nicole. Another time..."

"It was the same thing at eight o'clock this morning, when I was waiting for the motor which was bringing Daubrecq to me in his trunk: I had to march up and down the Place de Clichy, so as to prevent the car from stopping outside the door of my place and your men from interfering in my private affairs. Otherwise, once again, Gilbert and Clarisse Mergy would have been lost."

"But," said Prasville, "those painful events, it seems to me, are only delayed for a day, two days, three days at most. To avert them for good and all we should want..."

"The real list, I suppose?"

"Exactly. And I daresay you haven't got it."

"Yes, I have."

"The genuine list?"

"The genuine, the undoubtedly genuine list."

"With the cross of Lorraine?"

"With the cross of Lorraine."

Prasville was silent. He was labouring under violent emotion, now that the duel was commencing with that adversary of whose terrifying superiority he was well aware; and he shuddered at the idea that Arsene Lupin, the formidable Arsene Lupin, was there, in front of him, calm and placid, pursuing his aims with as much coolness as though he had all the weapons in his hands and were face to face with a disarmed enemy.

Not yet daring to deliver a frontal attack, feeling almost intimidated, Prasville said:

"So Daubrecq gave it up to you?"

"Daubrecq gives nothing up. I took it."

"By main force, therefore?"

"Oh, dear, no!" said M. Nicole, laughing. "Of course, I was ready to go to all lengths; and, when that worthy Daubrecq was dug out of the basket in which he had been travelling express, with an occasional dose of chloroform to keep his strength up, I had prepared things so that the fun might begin at once. Oh, no useless tortures... no vain sufferings! No... Death, simply... You press the point of a long needle on the chest, where the heart is, and insert it gradually, softly and gently. That's all but the point would have been driven by Mme. Mergy. You understand: a mother is pitiless, a mother whose son is about to die!... 'Speak, Daubrecq, or I'll go deeper.... You won't speak?... Then I'll push another quarter of an inch... and another still.' And the patient's heart stops beating, the heart that feels the needle coming... And another quarter of an inch... and one more... I swear before Heaven that the villain would have spoken!... We leant over him and waited for him to wake, trembling with impatience, so urgent was our hurry... Can't you picture the scene, monsieur le secretaire-general? The scoundrel lying on a sofa, well bound, bare-chested, making efforts to throw off the fumes of chloroform that dazed him. He breathes quicker... He gasps... He recovers consciousness...his lips move.... Already, Clarisse Mergy whispers, 'It's I... it's I, Clarisse... Will you answer, you wretch?' She has put her finger on Daubrecq's chest, at the spot where the heart stirs like a little animal hidden under the skin. But she says to me, 'His eyes... his eyes... I can't see them under the spectacles... I want to see them...' And I also want to see those eyes which I do not know, I want to see their anguish and I want to read in them, before I hear a word, the secret which is about to burst from the inmost recesses of the terrified body. I want to see. I long to see. The action which I am about to accomplish excites me beyond measure. It seems to me that, when I have seen the eyes, the veil will be rent asunder. I shall know things. It is a presentiment. It is the profound intuition of the truth that keeps me on tenterhooks. The eye-glasses are gone. But the thick opaque spectacles are there still. And I snatch them off, suddenly. And, suddenly, startled by a disconcerting vision, dazzled by the quick light that breaks in upon me and laughing, oh, but laughing fit to break my jaws, with my thumb—do you understand? with my thumb—hop, I force out the left eye!"

M. Nicole was really laughing, as he said, fit to break his jaws. And he was no longer the timid little unctuous and obsequious provincial usher, but a well-set-up fellow, who, after reciting and mimicking the whole scene with impressive ardour, was now laughing with a shrill laughter the sound of which made Prasville's flesh creep:

"Hop! Jump, Marquis! Out of your kennel, Towzer! What's the use of two eyes? It's one more than you want. Hop! I say, Clarisse, look at it rolling over the carpet! Mind Daubrecq's eye! Be careful with the grate!"

M. Nicole, who had risen and pretended to be hunting after something across the room, now sat down again, took from his pocket a thing shaped like a marble, rolled it in the hollow of his hand, chucked it in the air, like a ball, put it back in his fob and said, coolly:

"Daubrecq's left eye."

Prasville was utterly bewildered. What was his strange visitor driving at? What did all this story mean? Pale with excitement, he said:

"Explain yourself."

"But it's all explained, it seems to me. And it fits in so well with things as they were, fits in with all the conjectures which I had been making in spite of myself and which would inevitably have led to my solving the mystery, if that damned Daubrecq had not so cleverly sent me astray! Yes, think, follow the trend of my suppositions: 'As the list is not to be discovered away from Daubrecq,' I said to myself, 'it cannot exist away from Daubrecq. And, as it is not to be discovered in the clothes he wears, it must be hidden deeper still, in himself, to speak plainly, in his flesh, under his skin...'"

"In his eye, perhaps?" suggested Prasville, by way of a joke...

"In his eye? Monsieur le secretaire-general, you have said the word."

"What?"

"I repeat, in his eye. And it is a truth that ought to have occurred to my mind logically, instead of being revealed to me by accident. And I will tell you why. Daubrecq knew that Clarisse had seen a letter from him instructing an English manufacturer to 'empty the crystal within, so as to leave a void which it was unpossible to suspect.' Daubrecq was bound, in prudence, to divert any attempt at search. And it was for this reason that he had a crystal stopper made, 'emptied within,' after a model supplied by himself. And it is this crystal stopper which you and I have been after for months; and it is this crystal stopper which I dug out of a packet of tobacco. Whereas all I had to do..."

"Was what?" asked Prasville, greatly puzzled.

M. Nicole burst into a fresh fit of laughter:

"Was simply to go for Daubrecq's eye, that eye 'emptied within so as to leave a void which it is impossible to suspect,' the eye which you see before you."

And M. Nicole once more took the thing from his pocket and rapped the table with it, producing the sound of a hard body with each rap.

Prasville whispered, in astonishment:

"A glass eye!"

"Why, of course!" cried M. Nicole, laughing gaily. "A glass eye! A common or garden decanter-stopper, which the rascal stuck into his eyesocket in the place of an eye which he had lost—a decanter-stopper, or, if you prefer, a crystal stopper, but the real one, this time, which he faked, which he hid behind the double bulwark of his spectacles and eye-glasses, which contained and still contains the talisman that enabled Daubrecq to work as he pleased in safety."

Prasville lowered his head and put his hand to his forehead to hide his flushed face: he was almost possessing the list of the Twenty-seven. It lay before him, on the table.

Mastering his emotion, he said, in a casual tone:

"So it is there still?"

"At least, I suppose so," declared M. Nicole.

"What! You suppose so?"

"I have not opened the hiding-place. I thought, monsieur le secretaire-general, I would reserve that honour for you."

Prasville put out his hand, took the thing up and inspected it. It was a block of crystal, imitating nature to perfection, with all the details of the eyeball, the iris, the pupil, the cornea.

He at once saw a movable part at the back, which slid in a groove. He pushed it. The eye was hollow.

There was a tiny ball of paper inside. He unfolded it, smoothed it out and, quickly, without delaying to make a preliminary examination of the names, the hand-writing or the signatures, he raised his arms and turned the paper to the light from the windows.

"Is the cross of Lorraine there?" asked M. Nicole.

"Yes, it is there," replied Prasville. "This is the genuine list."

He hesitated a few seconds and remained with his arms raised, while reflecting what he would do. Then he folded up the paper again, replaced it in its little crystal sheath and put the whole thing in his pocket. M. Nicole, who was looking at him, asked:

"Are you convinced?"

"Absolutely."

"Then we are agreed?"

"We are agreed."

There was a pause, during which the two men watched each other without appearing to. M. Nicole seemed to be waiting for the conversation to be resumed. Prasville, sheltered behind the piles of books on the table, sat with one hand grasping his revolver and the other touching the push of the electric bell. He felt the whole strength of his position with a keen zest. He held the list. He held Lupin:

"If he moves," he thought, "I cover him with my revolver and I ring. If he attacks me, I shoot."

And the situation appeared to him so pleasant that he prolonged it, with the exquisite relish of an epicure.

In the end, M. Nicole took up the threads:

"As we are agreed, monsieur le secretaire-general, I think there is nothing left for you to do but to hurry. Is the execution to take place to-morrow?"

"Yes, to-morrow."

"In that case, I shall wait here."

"Wait for what?"

"The answer from the Elysee."

"Oh, is some one to bring you an answer?"

"Yes."

"You, monsieur le secretaire-general."

Prasville shook his head:

"You must not count on me, M. Nicole."

"Really?" said M. Nicole, with an air of surprise. "May I ask the reason?"

"I have changed my mind."

"Is that all?"

"That's all. I have come to the conclusion that, as things stand, after this last scandal, it is impossible to try to do anything in Gilbert's favour. Besides, an attempt in this direction at the Elysee, under present conditions, would constitute a regular case of blackmail, to which I absolutely decline to lend myself."

"You are free to do as you please, monsieur. Your scruples do you honour, though they come rather late, for they did not trouble you yesterday. But, in that case, monsieur le secretaire-general, as the compact between us is destroyed, give me back the list of the Twenty-seven."

"What for?"

"So that I may apply to another spokesman."

"What's the good? Gilbert is lost."

"Not at all, not at all. On the contrary, I consider that, now that his accomplice is dead, it will be much easier to grant him a pardon which everybody will look upon as fair and humane. Give me back the list."

"Upon my word, monsieur, you have a short memory and none too nice a conscience. Have you forgotten your promise of yesterday?"

"Yesterday, I made a promise to a M. Nicole."

"Well?"

"You are not M. Nicole."

"Indeed! Then, pray, who am I?"

"Need I tell you?"

M. Nicole made no reply, but began to laugh softly, as though pleased at the curious turn which the conversation was taking; and Prasville felt a vague misgiving at observing that fit of merriment. He grasped the butt-end of his revolver and wondered whether he ought not to ring for help.

M. Nicole drew his chair close to the desk, put his two elbows on the table, looked Prasville straight in the face and jeered:

"So, M. Prasville, you know who I am and you have the assurance to play this game with me?"

"I have that assurance," said Prasville, accepting the sneer without flinching.

"Which proves that you consider me, Arsene Lupin—we may as well use the name: yes, Arsene Lupin—which proves that you consider me fool enough, dolt enough to deliver myself like this, bound hand and foot into your hands."

"Upon my word," said Prasville, airily, patting the waistcoat-pocket in which he had secreted the crystal ball, "I don't quite see what you can do, M. Nicole, now that Daubrecq's eye is here, with the list of the Twenty-seven inside it."

"What I can do?" echoed M. Nicole, ironically.

"Yes! The talisman no longer protects you; and you are now no better off than any other man who might venture into the very heart of the police-office, among some dozens of stalwart fellows posted behind each of those doors and some hundreds of others who will hasten up at the first signal."

M. Nicole shrugged his shoulders and gave Prasville a look of great commiseration:

"Shall I tell you what is happening, monsieur le secretaire-general? Well, you too are having your head turned by all this business. Now that you possess the list, your state of mind has suddenly sunk to that of a Daubrecq or a d'Albufex. There is no longer even a question, in your thoughts, of taking it to your superiors, so that this ferment of disgrace and discord may be ended. No, no; a sodden temptation has seized upon you and intoxicated you; and, losing your head, you say to yourself, 'It is here, in my pocket. With its aid, I am omnipotent. It means wealth, absolute, unbounded power. Why not benefit by it? Why not let Gilbert and Clarisse Mergy die? Why not lock up that idiot of a Lupin? Why not seize this unparalleled piece of fortune by the forelock?'"

He bent toward Prasville and, very softly, in a friendly and confidential tone, said:

"Don't do that, my dear sir, don't do it."

"And why not?"

"It is not to your interest, believe me."

"Really!"

"No. Or, if you absolutely insist on doing it, have the kindness first to consult the twenty-seven names on the list of which you have just robbed me and reflect, for a moment, on the name of the third person on it."

"Oh? And what is the name of that third person?"

"It is the name of a friend of yours."

"What friend?"

"Stanislas Vorenglade, the ex-deputy."

"And then?" said Prasville, who seemed to be losing some of his self-confidence.

"Then? Ask yourself if an inquiry, however summary, would not end by discovering, behind that Stanislas Vorenglade, the name of one who shared certain little profits with him."

"And whose name is?"

"Louis Prasville."

M. Nicole banged the table with his fist.

"Enough of this humbug, monsieur! For twenty minutes, you and I have been beating about the bush. That will do. Let us understand each other. And, to begin with, drop your pistols. You can't imagine that I am frightened of those playthings! Stand up, sir, stand up, as I am doing, and finish the business: I am in a hurry."

He put his hand on Prasville's shoulder and, speaking with great deliberation, said:

"If, within an hour from now, you are not back from the Elysee, bringing with you a line to say that the decree of pardon has been signed; if, within one hour and ten minutes, I, Arsene Lupin, do not walk out of this building safe and sound and absolutely free, this evening four Paris newspapers will receive four letters selected from the correspondence exchanged between Stanislas Vorenglade and yourself, the correspondence which Stanislas Vorenglade sold me this morning. Here's your hat, here's your overcoat, here's your stick. Be off. I will wait for you."

Then happened this extraordinary and yet easily understood thing, that Prasville did not raise the slightest protest nor make the least show of fight. He received the sudden, far-reaching, utter conviction of what the personality known as Arsene Lupin meant, in all its breadth and fulness. He did not so much as think of carping, of pretending—as he had until then believed—that the letters had been destroyed by Vorenglade the deputy or, at any rate, that Vorenglade would not dare to hand them over, because, in so doing, Vorenglade was also working his own destruction. No, Prasville did not speak a word. He felt himself caught in a vise of which no human strength could force the jaws asunder. There was nothing to do but yield. He yielded.

"Here, in an hour," repeated M. Nicole.

"In an hour," said Prasville, tamely. Nevertheless, in order to know exactly where he stood, he added, "The letters, of course, will be restored to me against Gilbert's pardon?"

"No."

"How do you mean, no? In that case, there is no object in..."

"They will be restored to you, intact, two months after the day when my friends and I have brought about Gilbert's escape... thanks to the very slack watch which will be kept upon him, in accordance with your orders."

"Is that all?"

"No, there are two further conditions: first, the immediate payment of a cheque for forty thousand francs."

"Forty thousand francs?"

"The sum for which Stanislas Vorenglade sold me the letters. It is only fair..."

"And next?"

"Secondly, your resignation, within six months, of your present position."

"My resignation? But why?"

M. Nicole made a very dignified gesture:

"Because it is against public morals that one of the highest positions in the police-service should be occupied by a man whose hands are not absolutely clean. Make them send you to parliament or appoint you a minister, a councillor of State, an ambassador, in short, any post which your success in the Daubrecq case entitles you to demand. But not secretary-general of police; anything but that! The very thought of it disgusts me."

Prasville reflected for a moment. He would have rejoiced in the sudden destruction of his adversary and he racked his brain for the means to effect it. But he was helpless.

He went to the door and called:

"M. Lartigue." And, sinking his voice, but not very low, for he wished M. Nicole to hear, "M. Lartigue, dismiss your men. It's a mistake. And let no one come into my office while I am gone. This gentleman will wait for me here."

He came back, took the hat, stick and overcoat which M. Nicole handed him and went out.

"Well done, sir," said Lupin, between his teeth, when the door was closed. "You have behaved like a sportsman and a gentleman... So did I, for that matter... perhaps with too obvious a touch of contempt... and a little too bluntly. But, tush, this sort of business has to be carried through with a high hand! The enemy's got to be staggered! Besides, when one's own conscience is clear, one can't take up too bullying a tone with that sort of individual. Lift your head, Lupin. You have been the champion of outraged morality. Be proud of your work. And now take a chair, stretch out your legs and have a rest. You've deserved it."

When Prasville returned, he found Lupin sound asleep and had to tap him on the shoulder to wake him.

"Is it done?" asked Lupin.

"It's done. The pardon will be signed presently. Here is the written promise."

"The forty thousand francs?"

"Here's your cheque."

"Good. It but remains for me to thank you, monsieur."

"So the correspondence..."

"The Stanislas Vorenglade correspondence will be handed to you on the conditions stated. However, I am glad to be able to give you, here and now, as a sign of my gratitude, the four letters which I meant to send to the papers this evening."

"Oh, so you had them on you?" said Prasville.

"I felt so certain, monsieur le secretaire-general, that we should end by coming to an understanding."

He took from his hat a fat envelope, sealed with five red seals, which was pinned inside the lining, and handed it to Prasville, who thrust it into his pocket. Then he said:

"Monsieur le secretaire-general, I don't know when I shall have the pleasure of seeing you again. If you have the least communication to make to me, one line in the agony column of the Journal will be sufficient. Just head it, 'M. Nicole.' Good-day to you."

And he withdrew.

Prasville, when he was alone, felt as if he were waking from a nightmare during which he had performed incoherent actions over which his conscious mind had no control. He was almost thinking of ringing and causing a stir in the passages; but, just then, there was a tap at the door and one of the office-messengers came hurrying in.

"What's the matter?" asked Prasville.

"Monsieur le secretaire-general, it's Monsieur le Depute Daubrecq asking to see you... on a matter of the highest importance."

"Daubrecq!" exclaimed Prasville, in bewilderment. "Daubrecq here! Show him in."

Daubrecq had not waited for the order. He ran up to Prasville, out of breath, with his clothes in disorder, a bandage over his left eye, no tie, no collar, looking like an escaped lunatic; and the door was not closed before he caught hold of Prasville with his two enormous hands:

"Have you the list?"

"Yes."

"Have you bought it?"

"Yes."

"At the price of Gilbert's pardon?"

"Yes."

"Is it signed?"

"Yes."

Daubrecq made a furious gesture:

"You fool! You fool! You've been trapped! For hatred of me, I expect? And now you're going to take your revenge?"

"With a certain satisfaction, Daubrecq. Remember my little friend, the opera-dancer, at Nice... It's your turn now to dance."

"So it means prison?"

"I should think so," said Prasville. "Besides, it doesn't matter. You're done for, anyhow. Deprived of the list, without defence of any kind, you're bound to fall to pieces of your own weight. And I shall be present at the break-up. That's my revenge."

"And you believe that!" yelled Daubrecq, furiously. "You believe that they will wring my neck like a chicken's and that I shall not know how to defend myself and that I have no claws left and no teeth to bite with! Well, my boy, if I do come to grief, there's always one who will fall with me and that is Master Prasville, the partner of Stanislas Vorenglade, who is going to hand me every proof in existence against him, so that I may get him sent to gaol without delay. Aha, I've got you fixed, old chap! With those letters, you'll go as I please, hang it all, and there will be fine days yet for Daubrecq the deputy! What! You're laughing, are you? Perhaps those letters don't exist?"

Prasville shrugged his shoulders:

"Yes, they exist. But Vorenglade no longer has them in his possession."

"Since when?"

"Since this morning. Vorenglade sold them, two hours ago, for the sum of forty thousand francs; and I have bought them back at the same price."

Daubrecq burst into a great roar of laughter:

"Lord, how funny! Forty thousand francs! You've paid forty thousand francs! To M. Nicole, I suppose, who sold you the list of the Twenty-seven? Well, would you like me to tell you the real name of M. Nicole? It's Arsene Lupin!"

"I know that."

"Very likely. But what you don't know, you silly ass, is that I have come straight from Stanislas Vorenglade's and that Stanislas Vorenglade left Paris four days ago! Oh, what a joke! They've sold you waste paper! And your forty thousand francs! What an ass! What an ass!"

He walked out of the room, screaming with laughter and leaving Prasville absolutely dumbfounded.

So Arsene Lupin possessed no proof at all; and, when he was threatening and commanding and treating Prasville with that airy insolence, it was all a farce, all bluff!

"No, no, it's impossible," thought the secretary-general. "I have the sealed envelope.... It's here.... I have only to open it."

He dared not open it. He handled it, weighed it, examined it... And doubt made its way so swiftly into his mind that he was not in the least surprised, when he did open it, to find that it contained four blank sheets of note-paper.

"Well, well," he said, "I am no match for those rascals. But all is not over yet."

And, in point of fact, all was not over. If Lupin had acted so daringly, it showed that the letters existed and that he relied upon buying them from Stanislas Vorenglade. But, as, on the other hand, Vorenglade was not in Paris, Prasville's business was simply to forestall Lupin's steps with regard to Vorenglade and obtain the restitution of those dangerous letters from Vorenglade at all costs. The first to arrive would be the victor.

Prasville once more took his hat, coat and stick, went downstairs, stepped into a taxi and drove to Vorenglade's flat.

Here he was told that the ex-deputy was expected home from London at six o'clock that evening.

It was two o'clock in the afternoon. Prasville therefore had plenty of time to prepare his plan.

He arrived at the Gare du Nord at five o'clock and posted all around, in the waiting-rooms and in the railway-offices, the three or four dozen detectives whom he had brought with him.

This made him feel easy. If M. Nicole tried to speak to Vorenglade, they would arrest Lupin. And, to make assurance doubly sure, they would arrest whosoever could be suspected of being either Lupin or one of Lupin's emissaries.

Moreover, Prasville made a close inspection of the whole station. He discovered nothing suspicious. But, at ten minutes to six, Chief-inspector Blanchon, who was with him, said:

"Look, there's Daubrecq."

Daubrecq it was; and the sight of his enemy exasperated the secretary-general to such a pitch that he was on the verge of having him arrested. But he reflected that he had no excuse, no right, no warrant for the arrest.

Besides, Daubrecq's presence proved, with still greater force, that everything now depended on Stanislas Vorenglade. Vorenglade possessed the letters: who would end by having them? Daubrecq? Lupin? Or he, Prasville?

Lupin was not there and could not be there. Daubrecq was not in a position to fight. There could be no doubt, therefore, about the result: Prasville would reenter into possession of his letters and, through this very fact, would escape Daubrecq's threats and Lupin's threats and recover all his freedom of action against them.

The train arrived.

In accordance with orders, the stationmaster had issued instructions that no one was to be admitted to the platform. Prasville, therefore, walked on alone, in front of a number of his men, with Chief-inspector Blanchon at their head.

The train drew up.

Prasville almost at once saw Stanislas Vorenglade at the window of a first-class compartment, in the middle of the train.

The ex-deputy alighted and then held out his hand to assist an old gentleman who was travelling with him.

Prasville ran up to him and said, eagerly:

"Vorenglade... I want to speak to you..."

At the same moment, Daubrecq, who had managed to pass the barrier, appeared and exclaimed:

"M. Vorenglade, I have had your letter. I am at your disposal."

Vorenglade looked at the two men, recognized Prasville, recognized Daubrecq, and smiled:

"Oho, it seems that my return was awaited with some impatience! What's it all about? Certain letters, I expect?"

"Yes... yes..." replied the two men, fussing around him.

"You're too late," he declared.

"Eh? What? What do you mean?"

"I mean that the letters are sold."

"Sold! To whom?"

"To this gentleman," said Vorenglade, pointing to his travelling-companion, "to this gentleman, who thought that the business was worth going out of his way for and who came to Amiens to meet me."

The old gentleman, a very old man wrapped in furs and leaning on his stick, took off his hat and bowed.

"It's Lupin," thought Prasville, "it's Lupin, beyond a doubt."

And he glanced toward the detectives, was nearly calling them, but the old gentleman explained:

"Yes, I thought the letters were good enough to warrant a few hours' railway journey and the cost of two return tickets."

"Two tickets?"

"One for me and the other for one of my friends."

"One of your friends?"

"Yes, he left us a few minutes ago and reached the front part of the train through the corridor. He was in a great hurry."

Prasville understood: Lupin had taken the precaution to bring an accomplice, and the accomplice was carrying off the letters. The game was lost, to a certainty. Lupin had a firm grip on his victim. There was nothing to do but submit and accept the conqueror's conditions.

"Very well, sir," said Prasville. "We shall see each other when the time comes. Good-bye for the present, Daubrecq: you shall hear from me." And, drawing Vorenglade aside, "As for you, Vorenglade, you are playing a dangerous game."

"Dear me!" said the ex-deputy. "And why?"

The two men moved away.

Daubrecq had not uttered a word and stood motionless, as though rooted to the ground.

The old gentleman went up to him and whispered:

"I say, Daubrecq, wake up, old chap... It's the chloroform, I expect..."

Daubrecq clenched his fists and gave a muttered growl.

"Ah, I see you know me!" said the old gentleman. "Then you will remember our interview, some months ago, when I came to see you in the Square Lamartine and asked you to intercede in Gilbert's favour. I said to you that day, 'Lay down your arms, save Gilbert and I will leave you in peace. If not, I shall take the list of the Twenty-seven from you; and then you're done for.' Well, I have a strong suspicion that done for is what you are. That comes of not making terms with kind M. Lupin. Sooner or later, you're bound to lose your boots by it. However, let it be a lesson to you.

"By the way, here's your pocketbook which I forgot to give you. Excuse me if you find it lightened of its contents. There were not only a decent number of bank-notes in it, but also the receipt from the warehouse where you stored the Enghien things which you took back from me. I thought I might as well save you the trouble of taking them out yourself. It ought to be done by now. No, don't thank me: it's not worth mentioning. Good-bye, Daubrecq. And, if you should want a louis or two, to buy yourself a new decanter-stopper, drop me a line. Good-bye, Daubrecq."

He walked away. He had not gone fifty steps when he heard the sound of a shot. He turned round. Daubrecq had blown his brains out.

"De profundis," murmured Lupin, taking off his hat.

Two months later, Gilbert, whose sentence had been commuted to one of penal servitude for life, made his escape from the Ile de Re, on the day before that on which he was to have been transported to New Caledonia.

It was a strange escape. Its least details remained difficult to understand; and, like the two shots on the Boulevard Arago, it greatly enhanced Arsene Lupin's prestige.

"Taken all round," said Lupin to me, one day, after telling me the different episodes of the story, "taken all around, no enterprise has ever given me more trouble or cost me greater exertions than that confounded adventure which, if you don't mind, we will call, The Crystal Stopper; or, Never Say Die. In twelve hours, between six o'clock in the morning and six o'clock in the evening, I made up for six months of bad luck, blunders, gropings in the dark and reverses. I certainly count those twelve hours among the finest and the most glorious of my life."

"And Gilbert?" I asked. "What became of him?"

"He is farming his own land, way down in Algeria, under his real name, his only name of Antoine Mergy. He is married to an Englishwoman, and they have a son whom he insisted on calling Arsene. I often receive a bright, chatty, warm-hearted letter from him."

"And Mme. Mergy?"

"She and her little Jacques are living with them."

"Did you see her again?"

"I did not."

"Really!"

Lupin hesitated for a few moments and then said with a smile:

"My dear fellow, I will let you into a secret that will make me seem ridiculous in your eyes. But you know that I have always been as sentimental as a schoolboy and as silly as a goose. Well, on the evening when I went back to Clarisse Mergy and told her the news of the day—part of which, for that matter, she already knew—I felt two things very thoroughly. One was that I entertained for her a much deeper feeling than I thought; the other that she, on the contrary, entertained for me a feeling which was not without contempt, not without a rankling grudge nor even a certain aversion."

"Nonsense! Why?"

"Why? Because Clarisse Mergy is an exceedingly honest woman and because I am... just Arsene Lupin."

"Oh!"

"Dear me, yes, an attractive bandit, a romantic and chivalrous cracksman, anything you please. For all that, in the eyes of a really honest woman, with an upright nature and a well-balanced mind, I am only the merest riff-raff."

I saw that the wound was sharper than he was willing to admit, and I said:

"So you really loved her?"

"I even believe," he said, in a jesting tone, "that I asked her to marry me. After all, I had saved her son, had I not?... So... I thought. What a rebuff!... It produced a coolness between us... Since then..."

"You have forgotten her?"

"Oh, certainly! But it required the consolations of one Italian, two Americans, three Russians, a German grand-duchess and a Chinawoman to do it!"

"And, after that...?"

"After that, so as to place an insuperable barrier between myself and her, I got married."

"Nonsense! You got married, you, Arsene Lupin?"

"Married, wedded, spliced, in the most lawful fashion. One of the greatest names in France. An only daughter. A colossal fortune... What! You don't know the story? Well, it's worth hearing."

And, straightway, Lupin, who was in a confidential vein, began to tell me the story of his marriage to Angelique de Sarzeau-Vendome, Princesse de Bourbon-Conde, to-day Sister Marie-Auguste, a humble nun in the Visitation Convent... (*See The Confessions of Arsene Lupin)

But, after the first few words, he stopped, as though his narrative had suddenly ceased to interest him, and he remained pensive.

"What's the matter, Lupin?"

"The matter? Nothing."

"Yes, yes... There... now you're smiling... Is it Daubrecq's secret receptacle, his glass eye, that's making you laugh?"

"Not at all."

"What then?"

"Nothing, I tell you... only a memory."

"A pleasant memory?"

"Yes!... Yes, a delightful memory even. It was at night, off the Ile de Re, on the fishing-smack in which Clarisse and I were taking Gilbert away.... We were alone, the two of us, in the stern of the boat... And I remember ... I talked... I spoke words and more words... I said all that I had on my heart... And then... then came silence, a perturbing and disarming silence."

"Well?"

"Well, I swear to you that the woman whom I took in my arms that night and kissed on the lips—oh, not for long: a few seconds only, but no matter!—I swear before heaven that she was something more than a grateful mother, something more than a friend yielding to a moment of susceptibility, that she was a woman also, a woman quivering with emotion ..." And he continued, with a bitter laugh, "Who ran away next day, never to see me again."

He was silent once more. Then he whispered: "Clarisse... Clarisse... On the day when I am tired and disappointed and weary of life, I will come to you down there, in your little Arab house ... in that little white house, Clarisse, where you are waiting for me..." THE END.

Made in the USA
Monee, IL
17 February 2021